WILBUR SMITH

A FALCON FLIES

THE DARK OF THE SUN

THE SUNBIRD

WILBUR SMITH

Heinemann/Octopus

A Falcon Flies first published in Great Britain
in 1980 by William Heinemann Ltd
The Dark of the Sun first published in Great Britain
in 1965 by William Heinemann Ltd
The Sunbird first published in Great Britain
in 1972 by William Heinemann Ltd

This edition first published in Great Britain in 1983
jointly by

William Heinemann Limited   Martin Secker & Warburg Limited
10 Upper Grosvenor Street   54 Poland Street
London W1   London W1

and

Octopus Books Limited
59 Grosvenor Street
London W1

ISBN 0 905712 68 4

Second impression, reprinted 1984

Printed and Bound in Great Britain by Collins, Glasgow

WILBUR SMITH

A FALCON FLIES

A Falcon Flies

*Once again this book is for my wife
Danielle Antoinette*

1860

Africa crouched low on the horizon, like a lion in ambush, tawny and gold in the early sunlight, seared by the cold of the Benguela Current.

Robyn Ballantyne stood by the ship's rail and stared towards it. She had been standing like that since an hour before dawn, long before the land could be seen. She had known it was there, sensed its vast enigmatic presence in the darkness, detected its breath, warm and spicy dry, over the clammy cold exhalations of the current on which the great ship rode.

It was her cry, not that of the masthead, which brought Captain Mungo St. John charging up the companionway from his stern quarters, and the rest of the ship's company crowding to the ship's side to stare and jabber. For seconds only, Mungo St. John gripped the teak rail, staring at the land, before whirling to call his orders in the low but piercing tone which seemed to carry to every corner of the ship.

'Stand by to go about!'

Tippoo the mate scattered the crew to their duties with knotted rope-end and clubbed fists. For two weeks, furious winds and low, sullen skies had denied them a glimpse of sun or moon, or of any other heavenly body on which to establish a position. On dead reckoning the tall clipper should have been one hundred nautical miles further west, well clear of this treacherous coast with its uncharted hazards and wild deserted shores.

The Captain was freshly awakened, the thick dark mane of his hair tangled, rippling now in the wind, his cheeks lightly flushed with sleep, and also with anger and alarm beneath the smooth darkly tanned skin. Yet his eyes were clear, the whites contrasting starkly against the golden-flecked yellow of the iris. Once again, even in this moment of distraction and confusion, Robyn wondered at the sheer physical presence of the man – a dangerous, disturbing quality that at the same time both repelled and attracted her intensely.

His white linen shirt had been stuffed hastily into his breeches, and the front was unfastened. The skin of his chest was dark and smooth also, as if it had been oiled, and the hair upon it was crisp and black, tight whorls of it that made her blush, reminding her too clearly of that morning early in the voyage – the first morning that they had run into the warm blue waters of the Atlantic Ocean below latitude 35° north, the morning which for her had been the subject of much torment and troubled prayer since.

That morning, she had heard the splash and drum of water on the deck above her, and the clank of the ship's pump. She had left the makeshift desk in her tiny cabin on which she was working at her journal, slipped a shawl over her shoulders and gone up on to the maindeck, stepping unsuspectingly into the bright white sunlight and then stopping aghast.

There were two seamen working the pump lustily, and the clear sea water hissed from its throat in a solid jet. Naked, Mungo St. John stood beneath it, lifting his face and his arms towards it, the water sleeking his black hair down over his face and neck, flattening his body hair over his chest and the muscled plane of his belly. She had stood and stared, completely frozen, unable to tear her eyes away. The two seamen had turned their heads and grinned lewdly at her while they kept the handles pumping the hissing water.

Of course she had seen a man's naked body before, laid out on the dissection table, soft white flesh collapsing over bone, and with belly pouch slit open and the internal organs spilling out of it like butchers' offal, or between the grubby blankets of the fever hospital, sweating and stinking and racked with the convulsions of onrushing death – but never like this, not healthy and vital and overwhelming like this.

This was a marvellous symmetry and balance of trunk to long powerful legs, of broad shoulders to narrow waist. There was a lustre to the skin, even where the sun had not gilded it. This was not an untidy tangle of masculine organs, half-hidden by a bush of coarse hair, shameful and vaguely revolting. This was vibrant manhood, and she had been struck with sudden insight as to the original sin of Eve, the serpent and the apples, here offered again, and she had gasped aloud. He had heard her and stepped from under the thundering jet of water, and flicked the hair from his eyes. He saw her standing near, unable to move or tear her eyes away, and he smiled that lazy, taunting smile, making no move to cover himself, the water still streaming down his body, and sparkling like diamond chips on his skin.

'Good morning, Doctor Ballantyne,' he had murmured. 'Perhaps I am to be the subject of one of your scientific studies?'

Only then had she been able to break the spell, to whirl and rush back to her smelly little cabin. She expected to be greatly disturbed, as she threw herself on the narrow planks of her bunk, waiting to be overwhelmed by a sense of sin and shame, but it did not come. Instead, she was confused by a contraction of her chest and lungs that left her breathless, and a remarkable warmth of her cheeks and the skin of her throat, a prickling of the fine dark hairs at the nape of her neck, and the same warmth of other parts of her body which had so alarmed her that she flung herself hurriedly off the bunk and on to her knees to plead for a proper sense of her own unworthiness and a true understanding of her essential baseness and irretrievable wickedness. It was an exercise she had undertaken a thousand times in her twenty-three years, but seldom with so little success.

For the thirty-eight days of the voyage since then, she had tried to avoid those flecked yellow eyes and that lazy taunting smile, and had taken to eating most of her meals in her cabin, even in the daunting heat of the equator, when the taint of the bucket behind the canvas screen in the corner of the cabin had done little to pique her appetite. Only when she knew that heavy weather would keep him on deck did she join her brother and the others in the ship's small saloon.

Watching him now as he conned his ship off the hostile coast, she felt that disturbing prickle once again, and she turned away quickly to the land that was now swinging across the bows. The tackle roared through the blocks and the yards creaked and crackled, the canvas flogged and then filled again with a crash like cannon.

At the sight of the land she almost overcame those earlier memories and was instead filled with such a sense of awe, that she wondered if it were possible that the land of birth could call so clearly and so undeniably to the blood of its children.

It did not seem possible that nineteen years had passed since as a four-year-old waif, clinging to her mother's long skirts she had last seen that great flat-topped mountain that guarded the southernmost tip of the continent sink slowly beneath the horizon. It was one of the only clear memories of this land that she retained. She could still almost feel the coarse cheap stuff that a missionary's wife must wear and hear the sobs that her mother tried to stifle and feel them shake her mother's legs beneath the skirts, as she clung closer. Vividly she recalled the fear and confusion of the little girl at her mother's distress, understanding with childlike intuition that their lives were in upheaval, but knowing only that the tall figure that had been up to that time the centre of her small existence was now missing.

'Don't cry, baby,' her mother had whispered. 'We will see Papa again soon. Don't cry, my little one.' But those words had made her doubt that she would ever see her father again, and she had pushed her face into the coarse skirt, too proud even at that age to let the others hear her wail.

As always it had been her brother Morris who had comforted her, three years her senior, a man of seven years, born like her in Africa, on the banks of a far wild river with a strange exotic name, Zouga, which had given him his middle name. Morris Zouga Ballantyne – she liked the Zouga best and always used it, it reminded her of Africa.

She turned her head back towards the quarterdeck, and there he was now, tall but not as tall as Mungo St. John, to whom he was speaking excitedly, pointing at the lion-coloured land, his face animated. The features he had inherited from their father were heavy but strong, the nose bony and beaked and the line of the mouth determined, harsh perhaps.

He lifted the glass to his eye again and studied the low coastline, scanning it with the care that he took with any project from the smallest to the greatest, before lowering it and turning back to Mungo St. John. They spoke together quietly. An unlikely relationship had developed between the two men, a mutual, though guarded respect each for the other's strengths and accomplishments. But if the truth be told, it was Zouga who pursued the relationship most assiduously. Always one to profit by any opportunity, he had milked Mungo St. John of his knowledge and experience. He had done it with an exercise of charm, but since leaving Bristol harbour he had drawn from the Captain most of what he had learned in many years of trading and voyaging along the coasts of this vast savage continent, and Zouga had written all of it down in one of his calf-bound ledgers, storing knowledge against the day.

In addition to this, the Captain had genially undertaken to instruct Zouga in the mystery and art of astronomical navigation. Each day local apparent noon would find the two of them huddled on the sunny side of the quarterdeck with brass sextants poised, waiting for a glimpse of the fiery orb through the layers of cloud, or, when the sky was clear, eagerly sighting it, swaying to the ship's motion, to hold the sun in the field of the lens as they brought it down to the horizon.

At other times they cut the monotony of a long tack with a contest of arms, taking turns at an empty corked brandy bottle thrown over the stern by a crewman, using a magnificent pair of percussion duelling pistols that Mungo St. John brought up from his cabin still in their velvet-lined case, and loaded with care on the chart table.

They shouted with laughter, and congratulated each other as the bottles burst in mid-air in an explosion of shards bright as diamond chips in the sunlight.

At other times Zouga brought up the new Sharps breechloading rifle, a gift from one of the sponsors of the expedition, 'the Ballantyne Africa Expedition', as the *Standard*, that great daily newspaper, had named it.

The Sharps was a magnificent weapon, accurate up to the incredible range of 800 yards, with the power to knock down a bull bison at a thousand. The men who were wiping out the great herds of buffalo from the American prairie at this very time had earned the title 'Sharpshooters' with this weapon.

Mungo St. John towed a barrel at the end of an 800-yard length of cable to act as a target, and they shot for a wager of a shilling a bout. Zouga was an accomplished marksman, the best in his regiment, but he had already lost over five guineas to Mungo St. John.

Not only were the Americans manufacturing the finest firearms in the world (already John Browning had patented a breechloading repeating rifle that Winchester was evolving into the most formidable weapon known to man), but the Americans were also far and away the finest marksmen. This pointed up the difference between the tradition of the frontiersman with his long rifle, and that of massed British infantry firing smooth-bore muskets in strictly commanded volleys. Mungo St. John, an American, handled both the long-barrelled duelling pistol and the Sharps rifle as though they were an extension of his own body.

Now Robyn turned away from the two men, looked back at the land and felt a small dismay to see it already sinking lower into the cold green sea.

She yearned towards it with a quiet desperation, as she had ever since that day of departure so long ago. Her whole life in the intervening years seemed to have been a long preparation for this moment, so many obstacles overcome, obstacles made mountainous by the fact she was a woman; there had been so much struggle against temptation to give in to despair, a struggle that others had read as wilfulness and vaunting pride, as stubbornness and immodesty.

Her education had been gleaned with such toil from the library of her uncle William, despite his active discouragement. 'Too much book learning will only plague you, my dear. It is not a woman's place to trouble herself with certain things. You would do better to assist your mother in the kitchen and learn to sew and knit.'

'I can do both already, Uncle William.'

Later, his reluctant and grumbling assistance changed only slowly into active support when he at last assessed the depth of her intelligence and determination.

Uncle William was her mother's eldest brother, and he had taken in the family when the three of them had returned almost destitute from that far savage land. They had only the father's stipend from the London Missionary Society, a mere £50 per annum, and William Moffat was not a wealthy man, a physician at Kings Lynn with a small practice, hardly sufficient for the ready-made family with which he found himself saddled.

Of course, later – many years later – there had been money, a great deal of money, some said as much as three thousand pounds, the royalties from Robyn's father's books, but it had been Uncle William who had shielded and sustained them through the lean times.

William had somehow found the money to purchase Zouga's commission in his regiment, even selling his two prized hunters and making that humiliating journey to Cheapside and the moneylenders to do so.

With what William could raise, it was perforce not a fashionable regiment, and not even the regular army, but the 13th Regiment of Madras Native Infantry, a line regiment of the East India Company.

It was Uncle William who had instructed Robyn until she was as advanced in formal education as he was himself, and who had then aided and abetted her in the great deception of which she could never bring herself to be ashamed. In 1854 no hospital medical school in all of England would enrol a woman amongst their student body.

With her uncle's help, and active connivance, she had enrolled, using his sponsorship and the assertion that she was his nephew, at St. Matthew's Hospital in the east end of London.

It helped that her name needed only changing from Robyn to Robin, that she was tall and small-breasted, that her voice had a depth and huskiness that she could exaggerate. She had kept her thick, dark hair cropped short, and learned to wear trousers with such panache that ever since, the tangle of petticoats and crinolines around her legs had irritated her.

The hospital governors had only discovered the fact that she was a woman after she had obtained her medical qualification from the Royal College of Surgeons at the age of twenty-one. They had immediately petitioned the Royal College to withdraw the honour, and the ensuing scandal had swept the length and breadth of England, made more fascinating by the fact that she was the daughter of Doctor Fuller Ballantyne, the famous African explorer, traveller, medical missionary and author. In the end, the governors of St. Matthew's had been forced to retreat, for Robyn Ballantyne and her Uncle William had found a champion in the small, rotund person of Oliver Wicks, editor of the *Standard*.

With a true journalist's eye, Wicks had recognized good copy, and in a scathing editorial had called upon the British tradition of fair play, ridiculed the dark hints of sexual orgies in the operating rooms and pointed up the considerable achievement of this bright and sensitive young girl against almost unsurmountable odds. Yet even when her qualification had been confirmed, it was for her only a short step along the road back to Africa, on which she had determined so long ago.

The venerable directors of the London Missionary Society had been considerably alarmed by the offer of the services of a woman. Missionary wives were one thing, were indeed highly desirable to shield the missionaries themselves against physical blandishments and temptations amongst the unclothed heathen, but a lady missionary was another thing entirely.

There was a further complication which weighed heavily against Doctor Robyn Ballantyne's application. Her father was Fuller Ballantyne, who had resigned from the Society six years previously before disappearing once again into the African hinterland; in their eyes he had completely discredited himself. It was clear to them that the father was more interested in exploration and personal aggrandizement than in leading the benighted heathen into the bosom of Jesus Christ. In fact, so far as they were aware, Fuller Ballantyne had made only one convert in all his thousands of miles of African travel, his personal gunbearer.

He seemed to have made himself a crusader against the African slave trade, rather than an emissary of Christ. He had swiftly changed his first missionary station in Africa into a sanctuary for runaway slaves. The station at Koloberg had been on the southern edge of the great Kalahari Desert, a little oasis in the wilderness where a clear, strong spring of water gushed from the ground, and it had been founded with an enormous expenditure of the Society's funds.

Once Fuller had made it a slave refuge, the inevitable had happened. The Trek Boers from the little independent republics which ringed the mission station to the south were the original owners of the slaves to whom Fuller Ballantyne gave sanctuary. They called 'Commando', the medium through which the Trek Boers dispensed frontier justice. They came riding into Koloberg an hour before dawn, dark swift horsemen, a hundred of them, dressed in coarse homespun, bearded and burned by the sun to the colour of Africa's dark earth. The bright flashes of their muzzle-loaders lit the dawn, and then the burning thatch of the buildings of Fuller Ballantyne's mission station made it bright day.

They roped the recaptured slaves together with the station servants and freedmen into long lines, and drove them away southwards, leaving Fuller Ballantyne standing with his family huddled about him, a few pathetic possessions which they had managed to save from the flames scattered at their feet, and the smoke from the smouldering, roofless buildings drifting in eddies about them.

It had confirmed in Fuller Ballantyne his hatred of the institution of slavery, and it had given him the excuse for which he had unwittingly been searching, the excuse to rid himself of the encumbrances which had until then prevented him from answering the call of the vast, empty land to the north.

His wife and two small children were packed off back to England for their own good, and with them went a letter to the directors of the London Missionary Society. God had made his will clear to Fuller Ballantyne. He was bidden to journey to the north, to carry God's word across Africa, a missionary at large, no longer tied to one small station, but with the whole of Africa as his parish.

The directors were greatly troubled by the loss of their station, but they were further dismayed by the prospect of having to mount what seemed to be a costly expedition of exploration into an area which all the world knew was merely a vast desert, unpeopled and unwatered except around the littoral, a burning sand desert which stretched to the Mediterranean Sea four thousand miles northward.

They wrote hurriedly to Fuller Ballantyne, uncertain where exactly the letter should be addressed, but feeling the need to deny all responsibility and to express their deep concern; they ended by stating strongly that no further funds other than his stipend of £50 per annum could be voted for Fuller Ballantyne's highly irregular activities. They need not have expended their energy and emotions, for Fuller Ballantyne had departed. With a handful of porters, his Christian gunbearer, a Colt revolver, a percussion rifle, two boxes of medicines, his journals and navigational instruments, Fuller Ballantyne had disappeared.

He emerged eight years later, down the Zambezi river, appearing at the Portuguese settlement near the mouth of that river, to the great chagrin of the settlers there who, after 200 years of occupation, had pushed no further than 100 miles upstream.

Fuller Ballantyne returned to England and his book *A Missionary in Darkest Africa* created a tremendous sensation. Here was a man who had made the 'Transversa', the overland passage of Africa from west to east coast, who had seen, where there should be desert, great rivers and lakes, cool pleasant grassy uplands, great herds of game and strange peoples – but most of all he had seen the terrible depredations of the slave-raiders upon the continent, and his revelations rekindled the anti-slavery zeal of Wilberforce in the hearts of the British people.

The London Missionary Society was embarrassed by the instant fame of their prodigal, and they hurried to make amends. Fuller Ballantyne had chosen the sites for future missionary stations in the interior, and at the cost of many thousands of pounds they gathered together groups of devoted men and women and sent them out to the selected sites.

The British Government, prevailed upon by Fuller Ballantyne's description of the Zambezi river as a wide roadway to the rich interior of Africa, nominated Fuller Ballantyne Her Majesty's Consul, and financed an elaborate expedition to open this artery of trade and civilization to the interior.

Fuller had returned to England to write his book, but during this period of reunion with his family, they saw almost as little of the great man as when he was in the depths of Africa. When he was not locked in Uncle William's study writing the epic of his travels, he was in London hounding the Foreign Office or the directors of the L.M.S. And when he had gained from these sources all that he needed for his return to Africa, then he was travelling about England lecturing in Oxford or preaching the sermon from the pulpit of Canterbury cathedral.

Then abruptly he was gone again, taking their mother with him. Robyn would always remember the feel of his spiky whiskers as he stooped to kiss his daughter farewell for the second time. In her mind her father and God were somehow the same person, all-powerful, all-righteous, and her duty to them was blind, accepting adoration.

Years later, when the missionary sites chosen by Fuller Ballantyne had proved to be death-traps, when the surviving missionaries had stumbled back to civilization, their fellows and spouses dead of fever and famine, killed by wild animals and by the wilder men whom they had gone out to save, then Fuller Ballantyne's star had begun to fade.

The Foreign Office expedition to the Zambezi river, led by Ballantyne, had faltered and failed upon the terrible rapids and deep falls of the Kaborra–Bassa gorge through which the Zambezi crashed and roared, dropping a thousand feet in twenty miles. Men wondered how Ballantyne, who had claimed to have followed the Zambezi down from its source to the sea, could have not known of such a formidable obstacle to his dreams. They began to question his other claims, while the British Foreign Office, parsimonious as ever, was considerably miffed by the waste of funds on the abortive expedition and withdrew the title of Consul.

The London Missionary Society wrote another of their lengthy letters to Fuller Ballantyne, requesting him in future to confine his activities to the conversion of the heathen and the propagation of God's word.

Fuller Ballantyne had replied by posting them his resignation, thereby saving the society £50 per annum. At the same time he had penned a letter of encouragement to his two children urging them to show fortitude and faith, and sent the manuscript, in which he vindicated his conduct of the expedition, to his publisher. Then he had taken the few guineas that remained from the huge royalties that his other books had earned and had disappeared once more into the interior of Africa. That was eight years previously and no one had heard from him since.

Now here was this man's daughter, already nearly as notorious as the father, demanding admission to the Society as a working missionary.

Once again, Uncle William had come to Robyn's aid, dear mild bumbling Uncle William with his thick pebble spectacles and wild grey bush of untamable hair. With her he had gone before the board of directors and reminded them that Robyn's grandfather, Robert Moffat, was one of the most successful of all African missionaries, with tens of thousands of conversions to his credit. Indeed the old man was still working at Kuruman and had only recently published his dictionary of the Sechuana language. Robyn herself was dedicated and devout, with medical training and a good knowledge of African languages taught her by her now deceased mother, daughter of the same Robert Moffat, and by virtue of the reverence with which the said Robert Moffat was regarded by even the most war-like African king, Mzilikazi of the Ndebele, or as some people called them, the Matabele, the granddaughter would find immediate acceptance amongst the tribes.

The directors had listened stonily.

Then Uncle William had gone on to suggest that Oliver Wicks, the editor of the *Standard* who had championed the girl against the attempt by the governors of St. Matthew's Hospital to deprive her of her medical qualification, would be interested in their reasons for refusing her application to the Society.

The directors sat up and listened with great attention, conferred quietly and accepted Robyn's application. They had then seconded her to another missionary movement who in turn sent her to the industrial slums of northern England.

It was her brother Zouga who had found the way back to Africa for both of them.

He had returned from India on leave, a man of considerable achievement, already a major in the Indian army, promotion that he had won in the field, with the reputation of being a soldier and military administrator of great promise for one so young.

Despite this, Zouga was every bit as dissatisfied with his lot as was Robyn. Like their father, they were both lone wolves, responding badly to authority and regimentation. In spite of the promising start to his military career, Zouga recognized the fact that he had already made powerful enemies in India, and he had begun to doubt that his future lay on that continent. Like Robyn, he was still a searcher, and they had greeted each other after the parting of years with a warmth that they had seldom displayed during their childhood.

Zouga took her to dinner at the Golden Boar. It was such a change from Robyn's daily surroundings that she accepted a second glass of claret and became gay and sparkling.

'By God, Sissy, you really are a pretty thing, you know,' he had told her at last. He had taken to swearing now, and though it had shocked her at first, she had grown accustomed to it quickly enough. She had heard a lot worse in the slums where she worked. 'You are too good to spend your life amongst those ghastly crones.'

It changed the mood between them instantly, and she was able at last to lean close to her brother and pour out all her frustrations. He listened sympathetically, reaching across the table to squeeze her hand so that she went on quietly but with utter determination.

'Zouga, I have to get back to Africa. I'll die if I don't. I just know it. I will shrivel up and die.'

'Good Lord, Sissy, why Africa?'

'Because I was born there, because my destiny is there – and because Papa is there, somewhere.'

'I was born there also.' Zouga smiled, and when he did so it softened the harsh line of his mouth. 'But I don't know about my destiny. I wouldn't mind going back for the hunting, of course, but as for Father – don't you often think that Papa's main concern was always Fuller Ballantyne? I cannot imagine that you still harbour any great filial love for him.'

'He is different from other men, Zouga, you cannot judge him by the usual yardstick.'

'There are many who might agree with that,' Zouga murmured drily. 'At the L.M.S. and at the Foreign Office – but as a father?'

'I love him!' she said defiantly. 'After God, I love him best.'

'He killed mother, you know.' Zouga's mouth hardened into its usual grim line. 'He took her out to the Zambezi in fever season and he killed her as certainly as if he'd put a pistol to her head.'

Robyn conceded after a short, regretful silence, 'He was never a father nor a husband – but as a visionary, a blazer of trails, as a torchbearer . . .'

Zouga laughed and squeezed her hand.

'Really, Sissy!'

'I have read his books, all his letters, every one he ever wrote to mother or to us, and I know that my place is there. In Africa, with Papa.'

Zouga lifted his hand from hers and carefully stroked his thick side whiskers. 'You always had a way of making me feel excited—' Then, seemingly going off at a tangent, 'Did you hear that they have found diamonds on the Orange river?' He lifted his glass and examined the lees in the bottom of it attentively. 'We are so very different, you and I, and yet in some ways so much alike.' He poured fresh wine into his glass and went on casually. 'I am in debt, Sissy.'

The word chilled her. Since her childhood she had been taught a dread of it.

'How much?' she asked at last quietly.

'Two hundred pounds.' He shrugged.

'So much!' she breathed, and then, 'You haven't been gambling, Zouga?'

That was one of the other dread words in Robyn's vocabulary.

'Not gambling?' she repeated.

'As a matter of fact, I have,' Zouga laughed. 'And thank God for that. Without it I would be a thousand guineas under.'

'You mean you gamble – and actually win?' Her horror faded a little, became tinged with fascination.

'Not always, but most of the time.'

She studied him carefully, perhaps for the first time. He was only twenty-six years old, but he had the presence and aplomb of a man ten years older. He was already a hard, professional soldier, tempered in the skirmishes on the border of Afghanistan where his regiment had spent four years. She knew they had been cruel encounters against fierce hill tribes, and that Zouga had distinguished himself. His rapid promotion was proof of that.

'Then how are you in debt, Zouga?' she asked.

'Most of my brother officers, even my juniors, have private fortunes. I am a major now, I have to keep some style. We hunt, we shoot, mess bills, polo ponies—' He shrugged again.

'Will you ever be able to repay it?'

'I could marry a rich wife,' he smiled, 'or find diamonds.'

Zouga sipped his wine, slumped down in his chair, not looking at her, and went on quietly.

'I was reading Cornwallis Harris's book the other day – do you remember the big game we saw when we lived at Koloberg?'

She shook her head.

'No, you were only a baby. But I do. I remember the herds of springbok and wildebeest on the trek down to the Cape. One night there was a lion, I saw it clearly in the light of the campfire. Harris's book described his hunting expeditions up as far as the Limpopo – nobody has been further than that, except Papa, of course. A damned sight better than potting pheasant or black buck. Did you know that Harris made nearly five thousand pounds from his book?'

Zouga pushed his glass away, straightened up in his seat and selected a cigar from his silver case. While he prepared and lit it, he was frowning thoughtfully.

'You want to go to Africa for spiritual reasons. I probably need to go to

Africa, for much better reasons, for blood and for money. I make you a proposal. The Ballantyne Expedition!' He lifted his glass to her.

She laughed then, uncertainly, thinking he was joking, but lifted her own glass which was still almost full. 'My word on it. But how? Zouga, how do we get there?'

'What was the name of that newspaper fellow?' Zouga demanded.

'Wicks,' she said, 'Oliver Wicks. But why should he help us?'

'I'll find a good reason why he should.' And Robyn remembered how, even as a child, he had been an eloquent and persuasive pleader of causes.

'You know I rather think you might.'

They drank then, and when she lowered her glass, she had been as happy as she could ever remember being in all her life.

It was another six weeks before she saw Zouga again, striding towards her through the bustle of London Bridge Station as she clambered down from the carriage. He stood tall above the crowd, with the high beaver top hat on his head and the three-quarter length paletot cloak flaring from his shoulders.

'Sissy!' he called, laughing at her, as he lifted her from her feet. 'We are going – we really are going.'

He had a cab waiting for them, and the driver whipped up the horses the moment they were aboard.

'The London Missionary Society were no use at all,' he told her, still with his arm around her shoulders as the cab clattered and lurched over the cobbles. 'I had them down on my list for five hundred iron men, and they nearly had apoplexy. I had the feeling they would rather Papa stayed lost in darkest Africa, and they would pay five hundred to keep him there.'

'You went to the directors?' she demanded.

'Played my losing tricks first,' Zouga smiled. 'The next was Whitehall – actually managed to see the First Secretary. He was damned civil, took me to lunch at the Travellers', and was truly very sorry that they were not able to give financial assistance. They remembered Papa's Zambezi fiasco too clearly, but he did give me letters. A dozen letters, to every conceivable person – to the Governor at the Cape, to Kemp the Admiral at Cape Town, and all the others.'

'Letters won't get us far.'

'Then I went to see your newspaper friend. Extraordinary little man. Smart as a whip. I told him we were going to Africa to find Papa – and he jumped up and clapped his hands like a child at a Punch and Judy show.' Zouga hugged Robyn tighter. 'To tell the truth, I used your name shamelessly – and it did the trick. He will have all the story rights to our diaries and journals, and the publishing rights to both books.'

'Both books?' Robyn pulled away from him and looked into his face.

'Both.' He grinned at her. 'Yours and mine.'

'I am to write a book?'

'You certainly are. A woman's account of the expedition. I have already signed the contract on your behalf.'

She laughed then, but breathlessly. 'You're going too far, much too fast.'

'Little Wicks was in for five hundred, and the next on the list was the Society for the Extinction of the Slave Trade – they were easy. His Royal Highness is the Society's patron, and he had read Papa's books. We are to report on the state of the trade in the interior of the continent north of the Tropic of Capricorn, and they came up with another 500 guineas.'

'Oh Zouga, you are a magician.'

'Then there was the Worshipful Company of London Merchants Trading into Africa. For the last hundred years they have based all their activities on the west coast, I convinced them that they needed a survey of the east coast. I have been appointed the Worshipful Company's Agent, with instructions to examine the market in palm oil, gum-copal, copper and ivory – and they have come up with the third and last 500 guineas – and a presentation Sharps rifle.'

'One thousand five hundred guineas,' Robyn breathed, and Zouga nodded.

'We are going back home in style.'

'When?'

'I have booked passage on an American trading clipper. We sail from Bristol in six weeks, for Good Hope and Quelimane in Mozambique. I have written asking leave from my regiment for two years – you will have to do the same with the L.M.S.'

It had all happened with dreamlike rapidity after that. The directors of the L.M.S., perhaps relieved that they were not to pay for her passage nor the expense of relocating Robyn in the African interior, in a flush of extravagance decided to continue her stipend during the period she was away, and made a guarded promise to review the position at the end of that time. If she proved herself capable – then there would be a permanent post in Africa thereafter. It was more than she had ever expected, and she had thrown herself wholeheartedly into assisting Zouga with the preparations for departure.

There was so much to do that six weeks was barely sufficient, and it seemed only days had passed before the mountain of the expedition's equipment was being swayed down into the holds of the big graceful Baltimore clipper.

The *Huron* proved as swift as she looked, another wise choice by Zouga Ballantyne, and under Mungo St. John's skilful navigation she made good her westings before attempting to cross the belt of the doldrums at their narrowest point. They were becalmed not a single day and sped across the line at 29° west and immediately Mungo St. John put her on the port tack to stand down across the south east trades. *Huron* clawed her way southwards with the flying fish sailing ahead of her, close on the wind until she broke from their grip at last with Ilha da Trindade on the horizon. The north-wester came howling at them and *Huron* fled before it, under low, sullen, scudding skies day after day that denied them sight of sun or moon or stars, until she almost hurled herself ashore 200 miles up the west coast of Africa from her destination at the Cape of Good Hope.

'Mr. Mate!' Mungo St. John called in his clear carrying voice as *Huron* settled down to reach across the wind, pulling swiftly away from the land.

'Captain!' Tippoo bellowed back from the foot of the mainmast, a great blurt of sound from the bull chest.

'Take the name of the masthead watch.'

Tippoo ducked his cannon-ball head on its thick neck like a bare-knuckle fighter taking a punch, and looked up the mast, slitting his eyes in the heavy folds of flesh.

'Twenty minutes more and he would have had us on the beach.' St. John's voice was cold, deadly. 'I'll have him on the grating before this day is out, and we will get a peep of his backbone.'

Tippoo licked his thick lips involuntarily, and Robyn, standing near him, felt her stomach heave. There had been three floggings already on this voyage and she knew what to expect. Tippoo was half-Arab, half-African, a honey-coloured giant of a man with a shaven head that was covered with a mesh of tiny pale scars from a thousand violent encounters. He wore a loose embroidered, high-necked tunic over his huge frame, but the forearms that protruded from the wide sleeves were thick as a woman's thighs.

Robyn turned quickly to Zouga as he came down the deck towards her.

'We had a good look at the land, Sissy. Our first definite fix since Ilha da Trindade. If this wind holds we will be in Table Bay in another five days.'

'Zouga, can't you intercede with the Captain?' she demanded, and Zouga looked startled.

'He is going to flog that poor devil.'

'Damn right too,' Zouga growled 'The man nearly had us on the rocks.'

'Can't you stop him?'

'I wouldn't dream of interfering with his running of this ship – and nor will I allow you to.'

'Do you have no humanity at all?' she demanded of her brother coldly, but there were bright hot spots of anger on her cheeks, and her eyes snapped clear angry green. 'You call yourself a Christian.'

'When I do, I speak softly though, my dear.' Zouga made the reply he knew would annoy her most. 'And I don't flaunt it at every turn in the conversation.'

Their arguments were always sudden as summer thunderstorms on the African veld, and as spectacular.

Mungo St. John sauntered forward to lean his elbow on the railing of his quarterdeck, a long Havana cheroot of coarse black tobacco held between white teeth. He mocked her silently with those flecked yellow eyes, infuriating her further, until she heard her own voice going shrill and she turned from Zouga, and rounded on him.

'The man you had flogged last week could be crippled for life,' she shouted at him.

'Doctor Ballantyne – how would you like Tippoo to carry you down and lock you in your cabin?' Mungo St. John asked. 'Until you regain your temper and your manners.'

'You cannot do that,' she flared at him.

'I can, I assure you – that and much more.'

'He's right,' Zouga assured her softly. 'On this ship he can do virtually anything he wants.' He laid his hand on her upper arm. 'Steady now, Sissy. The fellow will be lucky to get away with the loss of a little skin.'

Robyn found she was panting with anger and a sense of helplessness.

'If you are squeamish, Doctor, I will excuse you from witnessing punishment,' Mungo St. John mocked her still. 'We must make allowance for the fact that you are a woman.'

'I have never asked for consideration on that score, not once in all my life.' She tried to get her anger back under control, and she shook off her brother's hand and turned away from them.

She walked with stiff back and squared shoulders up into the bows, trying to maintain an aloof dignity, but the ship's motion was awkward and her damned skirts fluttered around her legs. She realized she had thought the word, and she would ask forgiveness later – but not now, and suddenly she said it aloud.

'Damn you, Captain Mungo St. John, damn you to hell!'

She stood in the bows, and the wind pulled her hair out of the neat chignon at the nape of her neck and flicked it in her face. It was her mother's thick silken dark hair, shot with tones of russet and chestnut, and as a pale ray of greenish sunlight at last broke through the cloud cover, it turned to a glowing halo around her small neat head.

She stared ahead angrily, hardly noticing the hellish beauty of the scene about her. The cold, green waters, smoked with mist banks, opened and closed about the ship like pearly curtains. Wisps of mist trailed from the sails and yards as though she was on fire.

In patches, the surface of the sea simmered and darkened, for these waters were rich in microscopic sea life, which supported vast shoals of sardine that rose to the surface to feed, to be fed on in turn by flocks of shrieking seabirds that plunged upon them from high above, hitting the water in little cotton puffs of spray.

A thicker bank of mist took the tall ship in its damp cold grip so that when Robyn glanced back she could only just make out the ghostly figures of the Captain and her brother on the quarterdeck.

Then just as suddenly they plunged out again into open sea, and sunny skies. The clouds which had covered them for all these weeks rolled away towards the south while the wind itself increased in strength and veered swiftly into the east, whipping the tops from the waves in graceful ostrich plumes of curling spray.

At the same moment Robyn saw the other ship. It was startlingly close, and she opened her mouth to shout – but a dozen other voices forestalled her.

'Sail oh!'

'Sail fine on the port quarter.'

She was close enough to make out the thin, tall smoke stack between the main and mizzenmasts. Her hull was painted black with a red line below her gunports; five guns each side.

The black hull had a sinister air to it, and the pile of her canvas was not shimmering white as that of *Huron*, but was sullied dirty grey by the belchings from her smoke stack.

Mungo St. John played the field of his telescope swiftly over her. Her boilers were unlit, there was not even a tremble of heat from the mouth of her stack. She was under easy canvas only.

'Tippoo!' he called softly, and it seemed that the mate's bulk appeared beside him with the magical speed of a genie.

'Have you seen her before?'

Tippoo grunted and turned his head to spit over the lee rail.

'Lime-juicer,' he said. 'I seen her last in Table Bay eight years back. She called *Black Joke*.'

'Cape Squadron?'

Tippoo grunted, and at that moment the gunboat bore up sharply and at the same time her colours broke out at the masthead. The crisp white and bright scarlet of her ensign shrieked a challenge, a challenge that all the world had learned to heed, and heed swiftly. Only the ships of one nation on earth need not heave to the instant that challenge was flown. The *Huron* was immune, she had only to hoist the Stars and Stripes, and even this importunate representative of the Royal Navy would be forced to respect it.

But Mungo St. John was thinking swiftly. Six days before he sailed from Baltimore Harbour, in May, 1860, Abraham Lincoln had been nominated presidential candidate for the United States of America. If elected, as seemed highly likely, he would be invested early in the New Year, and then one of his first actions would surely be to grant to Great Britain the privileges agreed by the Treaty of Brussels, including the right of search of American ships upon the high seas which previous American presidents had so steadfastly denied.

Soon, perhaps sooner than he expected, Mungo St. John might have to run his clipper in deadly earnest against one of these ships of the Cape Squadron. It was a heaven-sent opportunity to match his ship, and to observe the capabilities of the other.

He swept one last glance about him, that took in the sea, the wind-driven lines of foam upon it, the piled white pyramids of canvas above him and the evil black hull to leeward – and then his decision was made easier. On the wind came the thud of a gun and a long feather of gunsmoke spurted from one of the gunboat's bow-chasers, demanding instant obedience.

Mungo St. John smiled. 'The insolent bastard!' To Tippoo he said, 'We'll try him on a few points of sailing,' to the helmsman beside him, softly, 'Put the helm down.' And as *Huron* paid off swiftly before the wind, beginning to point directly away from the threatening black ship, 'Shake out all reefs, Mr. Mate. Set fore and maintop, hoist studding sails and skysails, crack on the main royal – yes, and flying jib too. By God, we'll show that grubby little coal-guzzling lime-juicer how they build them down Baltimore way!'

Even in her anger, Robyn was thrilled by the manner in which the American worked his ship. With his crew swarming out across the yards to the reefing points, the mainsails swelled out to their full extent, dazzling white in the sunshine, and then high above, seemingly at the very base of the aching blue heaven itself, new unfamiliar-shaped sails popped open like over-ripe cotton pods and the long, graceful hull reacted instantly to the pressures thrust upon her.

'By God, she sails like a witch,' Zouga shouted, laughing with excitement, as she knifed into the crests of the Atlantic rollers and he hustled his sister back from the bows before the first green sheets of water came aboard and swept *Huron*'s decks.

More and still more canvas burst open, and the thick trees of her masts began to arch like drawn longbows under the unbearable pressures of thousands of square feet of spread sails. Now *Huron* seemed to fly, taking off from the crest of each roller and smashing into the face of the next with a crash that shocked her timbers and jarred the teeth of her crew in their skulls.

'A cast of the log, Mr. Mate,' Mungo St. John called, and when Tippoo bellowed back, 'A touch better than sixteen knots, Cap'n!' the Captain laughed aloud, and strode to the stern rail.

The gunboat was falling astern as though she was standing still, although every inch of her grey canvas was spread. Already she was at extreme cannon range.

Again powder-smoke bloomed briefly on her black bows, and this time it seemed that it was more than merely a warning, for Mungo St. John saw the fall of shot. It struck the crest of a roller two cable lengths astern and skipped across the green torn waters, before plunging beneath the surface almost alongside *Huron*'s tall side.

'Captain, you are endangering the lives of your crew and passengers.' The voice arrested him and St. John turned to the tall young woman who stood beside him, and he raised one thick black eyebrow in polite enquiry.

'That is a British man-of-war, sir, and we are acting like criminals. They are firing live shot now. You have only to heave to, or at the very least show your colours.'

'I think my sister is right, Captain St. John.' Zouga stood beside her. 'I do not understand your behaviour either.'

Huron staggered violently to a larger crest, driven wild by the mountainous press of sail, Robyn lost her balance and fell against the Captain's chest, but instantly pulled away, colouring fiercely at the contact.

'This is the coast of Africa, Major Ballantyne. Nothing is what it appears to be. Here only a fool would accept a strange armed vessel at its face value. Now if you and the good doctor will excuse me, I must attend to my duties.'

He strode forward to gaze down at the maindeck, judging the mood of his crew and the wild abandon of his ship. He unhooked the keyring from his belt and tossed it to Tippoo. 'The arms chest, Mr. Mate, a pair of pistols to you and the second mate. Shoot any hand who attempts to interfere with the setting of the sails.' He had recognized the fear which gripped the crew. Most of them had never seen a ship driven like this, there might easily be an attempt to shorten sail rather than have her run herself under.

At that moment *Huron* put her shoulder into the Atlantic and took it aboard in a solid roaring green wall. One of the topmast men was not quick enough on to the rat-lines. The water plucked him up and flung him down the length of the deck, until he crashed into the side, and lay huddled against the bulwark like a clump of uprooted kelp on a storm-driven beach.

Two of his fellows tried to reach him, but the next wave drove them back as it came pouring aboard waist-deep and then cascading in a roaring white torrent over the side, and when it was gone the fallen topmast man was gone with it and the deck was empty.

'Mr. Tippoo, look you to those skysails, they are not drawing as they should.'

Mungo St. John turned back to the stern rail, ignoring Robyn Ballantyne's horrified and accusing glare.

Already the British gunboat was hull down and her sails were barely discernible among the grey beards of the breaking Atlantic rollers, but suddenly Mungo St. John saw something change, and he reached quickly for the telescope in its slot under the chart table. There was a fine black line, as though drawn in Indian ink, extending from the tiny cone of the Englishman's sails for a short way across the bumpy horizon.

'Smoke! She has her boiler fired at last,' he grunted, as Tippoo appeared at his shoulder, with the pistols thrust into his belt.

'One screw. She no catch us.' Tippoo nodded his round shaven head.

'No, not downwind in a full gale,' Mungo St. John agreed. 'But I'd like to try her on the wind. We'll harden up now, Mr. Mate, on the port tack again. I want to see if I can run up to windward of her and pass her out of cannon shot.'

The unexpected manoeuvre caught the gunboat commander completely off-guard, and he was a few minutes slow in altering course to cut the shorter leg of the triangle and prevent the *Huron* wresting the weather gage from him.

Huron went streaming past him at extreme cannon-shot hard on the wind, her yards sheeted around as close-hauled as she would sail. He tried a shot across her dipping, plunging bows with no visible fall of shot, and then he came around to follow her into the wind, and immediately the flaws in the design and construction of his ship were pointed up as clearly as they had been while both ships were running before the wind.

In order to accommodate the heavy boiler and machinery to drive the big bronze screw under her counter, serious compromise had been made with the design of her masts and the amount of canvas she could carry.

Within five miles it became clear that with all sail set and the boilers belching a solid greasy slug of coal smoke over the stern the *Black Joke* could not point as high into the wind as the beautiful tall ship ahead of her. She was drifting steadily away to leeward, and although the difference in their speeds was not as dramatic as when running before the wind, yet *Huron* was headreaching on her steadily.

The gunboat's commander pointed her higher and higher, trying desperately to hold the bigger ship directly over his bows, but all his sails were shaking and luffing before he could do so.

In a fury of frustration, he took in all his canvas, stripping his poles bare and relying only on the drive of his steam boiler pointed up directly into the very eye of the wind, much much higher than *Huron* could sail. But the gunboat's speed bled away when her screw received no help from her sails. Even though her mast and rigging were bare, the storm whistled and howled head-on through them, acting as a great drogue that slowed her further and *Huron* forged ahead more swiftly.

'A bastard contraption.' Mungo St. John watched her battle with all his attention, judging her performance at every point of the wind. 'We are toying with her. As long as there is a breath of wind we'll romp away from her.'

Astern, the gunboat's commander had abandoned his attempt to run the clipper down with steam power alone, and had come back on to a fine reach with all his canvas set, plugging along stubbornly in *Huron*'s streaming wake – until abruptly, with no warning at all, *Huron* sailed into a deep hole in the wind.

The line of the gale was drawn clearly across the surface of the sea. On one side, the water was darkened and furrowed by the talons of the wind, on the other, the humped backs of the rollers in the calm had a polished velvety gloss to them.

As *Huron* crossed that line of demarcation, the clamour of the wind which for week after week had battered their ears, fell to an eerie unnatural silence, and the ship's motion changed from the vital charge of a living, straining sea creature, to the patternless rolling and wallowing of a dead log.

Overhead her canvas volleyed and flapped in the directionless eddies created by her own rolling and pitching, and her tackle crashed and clattered so that it seemed that she might roll her masts clean out of her hull.

Far astern, the black-painted gunboat scrambled on eagerly, swiftly beginning to narrow the distance between them, the black column of coal smoke now rising straight up into the stillness of air, giving her a jubilant and menacing air.

Mungo St. John ran to the forward rail of the quarterdeck, and stared over his bows. He could see the wind two or three miles ahead clawing at the sea and ruffling it to a sombre shade of indigo, but between them was the oily undulating surface of the calm.

He swung back and the gunboat was closer, sending her smoke spurting high against the bright windswept blue of the sky, so certain of herself now that her gunports were swinging open and the stubby barrels of her 32-pounder cannon protruding from the black sides of her hull, the churning wash of her screw tumbling out from under her counter and sparkling whitely in the sunlight.

With no way upon *Huron*, the helmsman could not hold any course, and the clipper drifted around broadside to the on-rushing man-of-war putting her bows directly into the rollers.

They could make out the individual figures of the three officers on the gunboat's bridge now. Again the bow-chaser fired, and the shell lifted a tall column of water so high and close under the *Huron*'s bows that it collapsed upon the deck and streamed out through the scuppers.

Mungo St. John took one last despairing sweep of the horizon, hoping even now for a resurgence of the wind, and then he capitulated.

'Hoist the colours, Mr. Tippoo,' he called, and as the gaudy scrap of cloth drooped from the mainyard in the windless air, he watched through the lens of his telescope the consternation it caused upon the gunboat's bridge. That was the last flag they had hoped to see.

They were now close enough to discern the individual expressions of chagrin and alarm and indecision of the naval officers.

'There'll be no prize money for you – not this time around,' Mungo St. John murmured with grim satisfaction, and snapped the telescope shut.

The gunboat came on and then rounded up to *Huron*, within easy hail, showing her full broadside, the long 32-pounder cannon gaping menacingly.

The tallest officer on her bridge seemed also the oldest, for his hair was white in the sunlight. He came to the gunboat's near rail and lifted the voice trumpet to his mouth.

'What ship?'

'*Huron*, out of Baltimore and Bristol,' Mungo St. John hailed back. 'With a cargo of trade goods for Good Hope and Quelimane.'

'Why did you not answer my challenge, sir?'

'Because, sir, I do not acknowledge your right to challenge ships of the United States of America on the high seas.'

Both captains knew just what a thorny and controversial question that reply posed, but the Englishman hesitated only a second.

'Do you, sir, accede to my right to satisfy myself as to your nationality and your ship's port of registry?'

'As soon as you run in your guns you may come aboard for that purpose, Captain. But do not send one of your junior officers.'

Mungo St. John was making a fine point of humiliating the commander of the *Black Joke*. But inwardly he was still seething at the fluke of wind and weather which had allowed the gunboat to come up with him.

The *Black Joke* launched a longboat on the heavy swell with an immaculate show of seamanship, and it pulled swiftly to *Huron*'s side. While the Captain scrambled up the rope ladder, the boat's crew backed off and rested on their oars.

The naval officer came in through the entry port, so lithe and agile that Mungo St. John realized his error in thinking him an elderly man. It was the white-blond hair that had misled him – he was evidently less than thirty years of age. He did not wear a uniform coat, for his ship had been cleared for action, and he was dressed in a plain white linen shirt, breeches and soft boots. There were a pair of pistols in his belt and a naval cutlass in its scabbard on his hip.

'Captain Codrington of Her Majesty's auxiliary cruiser *Black Joke*,' he introduced himself stiffly. His hair was bleached in silver white splashes from the salt and the sun, with darker streaks beneath and it was tied with a leather thong in a short queue at the nape of his neck. His face was weathered to honey-golden brown by the same sun, so that the faded blue of his eyes was in pale contrast.

'Captain St. John, owner and master of this vessel.'

Neither man made any move to shake hands, and they seemed to bristle like two dog wolves meeting for the first time.

'I hope you do not intend to detain me longer than is necessary. You can assure yourself that my government will be fully appraised of this incident.'

'May I inspect your papers, Captain?' The young naval officer ignored the threat, and followed St. John on to the quarterdeck. There he hesitated for the first time when he caught sight of Robyn and her brother standing together at the far rail, but he recovered immediately, bowed slightly and then turned his full attention to the packet of documents that Mungo St. John had ready for his inspection on the chart table.

He stooped over the table, working swiftly through the pile until with a shock of discovery he straightened.

'Damn me – Mungo St. John – your reputation precedes you, sir.' The Englishman's expression was strained with strong emotion. 'And what a noble one it is, too.' There was a bitter sting in his voice. 'The first trader ever to carry more than three thousand souls across the middle passage in a single, twelve-month period – small wonder you can afford such a magnificent vessel.'

'You are on dangerous ground, sir,' Mungo St. John warned him with that lazy, taunting grin. 'I am fully aware of the lengths to which the officers of your service will go for a few guineas of prize money.'

'Where are you going to pick up your next cargo of human misery, Captain St. John?' the Englishman cut in brusquely. 'On such a fine ship you should be able to pack in two thousand.' He had gone pale with unfeigned anger, actually trembling slightly with the force of it.

'If you have finished your investigation—' St. John's smile did not slip, but the naval officer went on speaking.

'We have made the west coast a little too hot for you now, have we? Even when you hide behind that pretty piece of silk,' the naval officer glanced up at the flag on the mainyard, 'so you are going to work the east coast now, are you, sir? They tell me you can get a prime slave for two dollars – two for a 10-shilling musket.'

'I must ask you to leave now.' St. John took the document from his hand, and when their fingers touched, the Englishman wiped his hand on his own thigh as though to cleanse it of the contact.

'I'd give five years' pay to have the hatches off your holds,' he said bitterly, leaning forward to stare at Mungo St. John with those pale fierce eyes.

'Captain Codrington!' Zouga Ballantyne stepped towards the group. 'I am a British subject and an officer in Her Majesty's army. I can assure you that there are no slaves aboard this vessel.' He spoke sharply.

'If you are an Englishman, then you should be ashamed to travel in such company.' Codrington glanced beyond Zouga. 'And that applies equally to you, madam!'

'You overreach yourself, sir,' Zouga told him grimly. 'I have already given you my assurance.'

Codrington's gaze had flicked back to Robyn Ballantyne's face. Her distress was evident, unfeigned. The accusation had shattered her, that she, the daughter of Fuller Ballantyne, the great champion of freedom and sworn adversary of slavery – she, the accredited agent of the Society for the Extinction of the Slave Trade should be travelling aboard a notorious slaver.

She was pale, the green eyes huge and liquid with the shock of it.

'Captain Codrington,' her voice was husky and low, 'my brother is right – I also assure you that there are no slaves aboard this ship.'

The Englishman's expression softened, she was not a beautiful woman, but there was a freshness and wholesomeness about her which was difficult to resist.

'I will accept your word, madam.' He inclined his head. 'Indeed, only a madman would carry black ivory towards Africa, but,' and his voice hardened again, 'if only I were able to enter her holds, I'd find enough down there to run her into Table Bay under a prize crew and have her condemned out of hand at the next session of the Court of Mixed Commission.'

Codrington swung on his heel to face Mungo St. John again.

'Oh yes, I know that your slave decks will be struck to make way for your trade cargo, but the spare planks are aboard and it won't take you a day to set them up again,' Codrington almost snarled, 'and I'll wager there are open gratings under those hatch covers,' he pointed down at the maindeck, but without taking his eyes from Mungo St. John's face, 'that there are shackles in the lower decks to take the chains and leg irons—'

'Captain Codrington, I find your company wearying,' Mungo St. John drawled softly. 'You have sixty seconds to leave this ship, before I have my mate assist you over the side.'

Tippoo stepped forward, hairless as an enormous toad, and stood a foot behind Codrington's left shoulder.

With a visible effort, the English captain retained his temper, as he inclined his head towards Mungo St. John.

'May God grant we meet again, sir.' He turned back to Robyn and saluted her briefly.

'May I wish you a pleasant continuation of your voyage, madam.'

'Captain Codrington, I think you are mistaken,' she almost pleaded with him. He did not reply but stared at her for a moment longer, the pale eyes were direct and disturbing – the eyes of a prophet or a fanatic – then he turned and went with a gangling boyish stride to *Huron*'s entry port.

Tippoo had stripped off the high-necked tunic and oiled his upper body so it gleamed in the sunlight with the metallic lustre of the skin of some exotic reptile.

He stood stolidly on flat bare feet, balancing effortlessly to the *Huron*'s roll, his thick arms hanging at his side and the lash of the whip coiled on the deck at his feet.

There was a grating fixed at the ship's side and the sailor who had been at the masthead lookout when they had raised the African coast, was spread-eagled upon it like a stranded starfish on a rock exposed at low tide. He twisted his head awkwardly to look back over his shoulder at the mate, and his face was white with terror.

'You were excused witnessing punishment, Doctor Ballantyne,' Mungo St. John told her quietly.

'I feel it my duty to suffer this barbaric—'

'As you wish,' he cut her short with a nod, and turned away. 'Twenty, Mr. Tippoo.'

'Twenty it is, Cap'n.'

With no expression at all Tippoo stepped up behind the man, hooked his finger into the back of his collar and ripped the shirt down to the belt. The man's back was pale as suet pudding, but studded with fat purple carbuncles, the sailor's affliction, caused by salty, wet clothing and the unhealthy diet.

Tippoo stepped back and flicked out the lash so that it extended to its full length along the seamed oak planking.

'Ship's company!' Mungo St. John called. 'The charge is inattention to duty, and endangering the ship's safety.' They shuffled their bare feet, but not one of them looked up at him. 'The sentence is twenty lashes.'

On the grating the man turned his face away and closed his eyes tightly, hunching his shoulders.

'Lay on, Mr. Tippoo,' Mungo St. John said, and Tippoo squinted carefully at the bare, white skin, through which the knuckles of the spine showed clearly. He reared back, one thickly muscled arm thrown high above his head, and the lash snaked higher, hissing like an angry cobra, then he stepped forward into the stroke, pivoting the full weight and force of his shoulders into it.

The man on the grating shrieked, and his body convulsed in a spasm that smeared the skin from his wrists against the coarse hemp bonds.

The white skin opened in a thin bright scarlet line, from one side of his ribs to the other, and one of the angry purple carbuncles between his shoulder blades erupted in a spurt of yellow matter that ran down the pale skin and soaked into the waistband of his breeches.

'One,' said Mungo St. John, and the man on the grating began to sob quietly.

Tippoo stepped back, shook out the lash carefully, squinted at the bloody line across the white shuddering flesh, reared back and grunted as he stepped forward into the next stroke.

'Two,' said Mungo St. John. Robyn felt her gorge rise to choke her. She fought it down, and forced herself to watch. She could not allow him to see her weakness.

On the tenth stroke the body on the grating relaxed suddenly, the head lolled sideways and the fists unclenched slowly so that she could see the little bloody half-moon wounds where the nails had been driven into the palms. There was no further sign of life during the rest of the leisurely ritual of punishment.

At the twentieth stroke, she almost flung herself down the ladder to the maindeck and was feeling for the pulse before they could cut the body down from the grating.

'Praise be to God,' she whispered as she felt it fluttering under her fingers, and then to the seamen who were lifting the man down, 'Gently now!' She saw that Mungo St. John had got his wish, for the white porcelain crests of the spinal column were jutting up through the sliced meat of the back muscles.

She had a cotton dressing ready and she placed it across the ruined back as they laid him on to an oak plank and hustled him towards the forecastle.

In the narrow, crowded forecastle, thick with the fumes of cheap pipe tobacco and the almost solid reek of bilges and wet clothing, of unwashed men and mouldering food, they laid the man on the mess table and she worked as best she could in the guttering light of the oil-lamp in its gimbals overhead. She stitched back the flaps and ribbons of mushy, torn flesh with horsehair sutures and then bound up the whole in weak phenol solution, treatment which Joseph Lister had recently pioneered with much success against mortification.

The man was conscious again and whimpering with pain. She gave him five drops of laudanum, and promised to visit him the following day to change the bindings.

As she packed away her instruments and closed her black valise, one of the crew, a little pockmarked bosun, named Nathaniel, picked it up and when she nodded her thanks, he muttered with embarrassment, 'We are beholden, missus.'

It had taken all of them time to accept her ministrations. First it had been only the lancing of carbuncles and sea-boils, calomel for the flux and the grippe, but later, after a dozen successful treatments, which included a fractured humerus, an ulcerated and ruptured eardrum and the banishing of a venereal chancre with mercury, she had become a firm favourite amongst the crew, and her sick-call a regular feature of shipboard life.

The bosun climbed the companionway behind her, carrying the valise, but before they reached the deck, an idea struck her and she stooped to him, placing a hand on his shoulder.

'Nathaniel,' she asked urgently, but in a low voice, 'is there a way of entering the ship's hold without lifting the maindeck hatches?'

The man looked startled, and she shook his shoulder roughly. 'Is there?' she demanded.

'Aye, ma'am, there is.'

'Where? How?'

'Through the lazaretto, below the officers' saloon – there is a hatchway through the forward bulkhead.'

'Is it locked?'

'Aye, ma'am, it is – and Captain St. John keeps the keys on his belt.'

'Tell nobody that I asked,' she ordered him, and hastened up on the maindeck.

At the foot of the mainmast, Tippoo was washing down the lash in a bucket of seawater that was already tinged pale pink; he looked up at her, still stripping the water off the leather between thick hairless fingers – and he grinned at Robyn as she passed, squatting down on thick, brown haunches with his loin cloth drawn up into his crotch, swinging his round bald head on its bull neck to follow her.

She found herself panting a little with fear and revulsion, and she swept her skirts aside as she passed him. At the door of her cabin she took the valise from Nathaniel with a word of thanks, and then slumped down upon her bunk.

Her thoughts and her emotions were in uproar, for she had still not recovered from the sudden avalanche of events that had interrupted the leisurely pattern of the voyage.

The boarding by Captain Codrington of the Royal Navy overshadowed even her anger at the flogging or her joy at her first view of Africa in nearly two decades – and now his accusations rankled and disturbed her.

After a few minutes' rest she lifted the lid of her travelling-chest that filled most of the clear space in the tiny cabin, and had to unpack much of it before she found the pamphlets from the anti-slavery society with which she had been armed in London before departure.

She sat down to study them once again, a history of the struggle against the trade up to the present time. As she read, her anger and frustration reawakened at the tale of unenforceable international agreements, all with built-in escape clauses: laws that made it an act of piracy to indulge in the trade north of the equator, but allowed it to flourish unchecked in the southern hemisphere; treaties and agreements signed by all nations, except those most actively engaged in the trade, Portugal, Brazil, Spain. Other great nations – France – using the trade to goad their traditional enemy, Great Britain, shamelessly exploiting Britain's commitment to its extinction, trading political advantage for vague promises of support.

Then there was America, a signatory to the Treaty of Brussels which Britain had engineered, agreeing to the abolition of the trade, but not to the abolition of the institution of slavery itself. America agreed that the transport of human souls into captivity was tantamount to active piracy, and that vessels so engaged were liable to seizure under prize and condemnation by courts of Admiralty or Mixed Commission, agreed also to the equipment clause, that ships equipped for transport of slaves, although not actually with a cargo of slaves on board at the time of seizure, could be taken as prize.

There was America agreeing to all of this – and then denying to the warships of the Royal Navy the right of search. The most America would allow was that British officers could assure themselves of the legality of the claim to American ownership, and if that was proven, they could not search, not even though the stink of slaves rose from her holds to offend the very heavens, or the clank of chains and the half-human cries from her 'tween decks came near to deafening them – still they could not search.

Robyn dropped one pamphlet back into her chest, and selected another publication from the society.

ITEM, in the previous year, 1859, estimated 169,000 slaves had been transported from the coasts of Africa to the mines of Brazil, and the plantations of Cuba, and to those of the Southern States of America.

ITEM, the trade in slaves by the Omani Arabs of Zanzibar could not be estimated except by observation of the numbers passing through the markets of that island. Despite the British Treaty with the Sultan as early as 1822, the British Consul at Zanzibar had counted almost 200,000 slaves landed during the previous twelve-month period. The corpses were not landed, nor were the sick and dying, for the Zanzibar customs dues were payable to the Sultan per capita, live or dead.

The dead and those so enfeebled or diseased as to have little hope of survival were thrown overboard, at the edge of the deep water beyond the coral reef. Here a permanent colony of huge man-eating sharks cruised the area by day and by night. Within minutes of the first body, dead or still living, striking the water, the surface around the dhow was torn into a seething white boil by the great fish. The British Consul estimated a forty-per-cent mortality rate amongst slaves making the short passage from the mainland to the island.

Robyn dropped that pamphlet and before picking up the next, she reflected a moment on the sheer multitudes involved in the whole grisly business.

'Five million since the turn of the century,' she whispered, 'five million souls. No wonder that they call it the greatest crime against humanity in the history of the world.'

She opened the next pamphlet and skimmed quickly over an examination of the profits that accrued to a successful trader.

In the interior of Africa, up near the lake country where few white men had ever reached, Fuller Ballantyne had discovered – her father's name in print gave her a prickle of pride and of melancholy – Fuller had discovered that a prime slave changed hands for a cupful of porcelain beads, two slaves for an obsolete Tower musket that cost thirteen shillings in London, or a Brown Bess musket that cost two dollars in New York.

At the coast the same slave cost ten dollars, while on the slave market in Brazil he would sell for five hundred dollars. But once he was taken north of the equator, the risks to the trader increased and the price rose dramatically – a thousand dollars in Cuba, fifteen hundred in Louisiana.

Robyn lowered the text, and thought swiftly. The English Captain had challenged that *Huron* could carry 2,000 slaves at a time. Landed in America, they would be worth an unbelievable three million dollars, an amount which would buy fifteen ships like *Huron*. A single voyage would make a man rich beyond mundane dreams of greed, all risks were acceptable to the traders to win such vast wealth.

But had Captain Codrington been justified in his accusations? Robyn knew the counter-accusations that were made against the officers of the Royal Navy, that their zeal arose from the promise of prize money rather than a hatred of the trade and a love of humanity. That every sail they raised was considered a slaver, and that they were swift to apply the Equipment Clause in the widest possible interpretation.

Robyn was searching for the pamphlet that dealt in detail with this Equipment Clause and she found it next on the pile before her.

To enable a ship to be seized as a slaver under the clause, she need only satisfy one of the stipulated conditions. She could be taken if her hatches were equipped with open gratings to ventilate her holds; if there were dividing bulkheads in her holds to facilitate the installation of slave decks; if there were spare planks aboard for laying as slave decks; if she carried shackles and bolts, or leg irons and cuffs; if she carried too many water casks for the number of her crew and passengers; if she had disproportionally large numbers of mess tubs, or her rice boilers were too big, or if she carried unreasonable quantities of rice or farina.

Even if she carried native matting that might be used as bedding for slaves, she could be seized and run in under a prize crew. These were wide powers given to men who could profit financially by seizure.

Was Captain Codrington one of these, were those pale fanatical eyes merely a mask for avarice and a desire for personal gain?

Robyn found herself hoping they were, or at least that in the case of *Huron* he had been mistaken. But then why had Captain St. John put down his helm, and run for it the moment he sighted the British cruiser?

Robyn was confused and miserable, haunted with guilt. She needed comfort and she slipped a lace Stuart cap over her head and shoulders before venturing out on to the deck again, for the wind had risen to an icy gale and *Huron* was always a tender ship, she heeled heavily as she beat southwards, flinging spray high into the falling night.

Zouga was in his cabin, dressed in shirt-sleeves and smoking a cigar as he worked over the lists of the expedition's equipment that would still have to be obtained once they reached Good Hope.

He called to her to enter when she knocked, and rose to greet her with a smile.

'Sissy, are you well? It was a most unpleasant business, even though unavoidable. I hope it has not unsettled you.'

'The man will recover,' she said, and Zouga changed the subject as he settled her on his bunk, the only other seating in the cabin.

'I sometimes think we would have been better off with less money to spend on this expedition. There is always such a temptation to accumulate too much equipment. Papa made the Transversa with only five porter loads, while we will need a hundred porters at the least, each carrying eighty pounds.'

'Zouga, I must speak to you. This is the first opportunity I have had.'

An expression of distaste flickered across the strong, harsh features as though he sensed what she was about to say. But before he could deny her she blurted out, 'Is this ship a slaver, Zouga?'

Zouga removed the cigar from his mouth and inspected the tip minutely before he replied.

'Sissy, a slaver stinks so you can smell it for fifty leagues downwind, and even after the slaves are removed there is no amount of lye that will get rid of the smell. *Huron* does not have the stench of a slaver.'

'This ship is on her first voyage under this ownership,' Robyn reminded him quietly. 'Codrington accused Captain St. John of using his profits from previous voyages to purchase her. She is still clean.'

'Mungo St. John is a gentleman.' Zouga's tone had an edge of impatience to it now. 'I am convinced of that.'

'The plantation owners of Cuba and Louisiana are amongst the most elegant gentlemen that you could find outside the court of St. James,' she reminded him.

'I am prepared to accept his word as a gentleman,' Zouga snapped.

'Are you not a little eager, Zouga?' she asked with a deceptive sweetness, but his tone had kindled sparks in her eyes like the green lights in an emerald. 'Would it not seriously impede your plans to find ourselves shipped on board a slaver?'

'Damn me, woman, I have his word.' Zouga was getting truly angry now. 'St. John is engaged in legitimate trade. He hopes for a cargo of ivory and palm oil.'

'Have you asked to inspect the ship's hold?'

'He has given his word.'

'Will you ask him to open the holds?'

Zouga hesitated, his gaze wavered a moment, and then he made his decision.

'No, I will not,' he said flatly. 'That would be an insult to him and quite rightly, he would resent it.'

'And if we found what you are afraid to find, it would discredit the purpose of our expedition,' she agreed.

'As the leader of this mission, I have made the decision—'

'Papa would never let anything stand in his way either, not even Mama or the family—'

'Sissy, if you still feel that way when we reach the Cape, I will arrange for passage on another vessel to Quelimane. Will that satisfy you?'

She did not reply but continued to stare at him with a flat accusing gaze.

'If we did find evidence,' he waved his hands with agitation, 'what could we do about it?'

'We could make a sworn deposition to the Admiralty at Cape Town.'

'Sissy,' he sighed wearily at her intransigence, 'don't you understand? If I were to challenge St. John, we could gain nothing. If the accusation is unwarranted we would place ourselves in a damned awkward position, and if in the very unlikely event that this ship is equipped for the trade, we would then be in considerable danger. Do not underestimate that danger, Robyn. St. John is a determined man.' He stopped and shook his head decisively, the fashionable curls dangling over his ears. 'I am not going to endanger you, myself – or the whole expedition. That is my decision, and I will insist that you abide by it.'

After a long pause, Robyn slowly dropped her gaze to her hands, and inter-meshed her fingers.

'Very well, Zouga.'

His relief was obvious. 'I am grateful for your compliance, my dear.' He stooped over her and kissed her forehead. 'Let me escort you to dinner.'

She was about to refuse, to tell him she was tired and that, once again, she would dine alone in her cabin, and then an idea struck her, and she nodded.

'Thank you, Zouga,' she told him, and then looked up with one of those sudden smiles so brilliant, so warm and so rare as to disarm him completely. 'I am fortunate to have such a handsome dinner companion.'

She sat between Mungo St. John and her brother, and had her brother not known better, he might have suspected her of flirting outrageously with the

Captain. She was all smiles and sparkles, leaning forward attentively to listen whenever he spoke, recharging his glass whenever it was less than half filled with wine and laughing delightedly at his dry sallies.

Zouga was amazed and a little alarmed by the transformation, while St. John had never seen her like this. He had covered his original surprise with an amused half-smile. However, in this mood Robyn Ballantyne was an attractive companion. Her stubborn, rather sharp face softened to the edge of prettiness, while her best features, her hair, her perfect skin, her eyes and fine white teeth, gleamed and flashed in the lamplight. Mungo St. John's own mood became expansive, he laughed more readily and his interest was clearly piqued. With Robyn plying his glass, he drank more than on any other night of the voyage, and when his steward served a good plum duff he called for a bottle of brandy to wash it down.

Zouga had also been infected by the strangely festive air of the dinner, and he protested as vigorously as St. John when suddenly Robyn declared herself to be exhausted and stood up from the board, but she was adamant.

In her cabin she could still hear the occasional shouts of laughter from the saloon, as she went quietly about her preparations. She slid the locking bar into place to assure her privacy. Then she knelt beside her chest and wormed her way down to the bottom layers, from which she retrieved a pair of man's moleskin breeches, a flannel shirt and cravat, with a high-buttoned monkey jacket to go over them, and well-worn half boots.

This had been her uniform and her disguise as a medical student at St. Matthew's Hospital. Now she stripped herself naked, and for a moment enjoyed the wicked freedom of the feeling, even indulging herself to the extent of gazing down at her nudity. She was not too certain if it was a sin to enjoy one's own body, but she suspected that it was. Nevertheless she persisted.

Her legs were straight and strong, her hips flared with a graceful curve and then narrowed abruptly into her waist, her belly was almost flat with just an interesting little bulge below the navel. Now here was definitely sinful ground – of this there was no doubt. But still she could not deny the temptation to let her gaze linger a moment. She understood fully the technical purpose and the physical workings of all her body's highly complicated machinery, both visible and concealed. It was only the feelings and emotions which sprang from this source which both confused and worried her, for they had taught her none of this at St. Matthew's. She passed on hurriedly to safer ground, lifting her arms to pile the tresses of her hair on to the top of her head and hold them in place with a soft cloth cap.

Her breasts were round and neat as ripening apples, so firm as hardly to change their shape as she moved her arms. Their resemblance to fruit pleased her and she spent a few moments longer than was necessary in adjusting the cloth cap upon her head looking down at them. But there was a limit to self-indulgence, and she swept the flannel shirt over her head, pulled the tails down around her waist, stepped into the breeches – how good they felt again after so long in those hobbling skirts – and then, sitting upon the bunk, she pulled on the half-boots and buckled the ankle straps of the breeches under the arch of her foot, before standing to clinch the belt at her waist.

She opened her black valise, took out the roll of surgical instruments and selected one of the sturdier scalpels, folded out the blade and tested it with her thumb. It was stingingly sharp. She closed the blade and slipped it into her hip pocket. It was the only weapon available to her.

She was ready now, and she closed the shutter on the bull's eye lantern, darkening the cabin completely before climbing, fully dressed, into her bunk, pulling the rough woollen blanket to her chin and settling down to wait. The laughter from the saloon became more abandoned, and she imagined that the brandy bottle was being cruelly punished by the men. A long while later she heard her brother's heavy, uneven footsteps on the companion way past her cabin and then there was only the creak and pop of the ship's timbers as she heeded to the wind, and far away the regular tapping of some loose piece of equipment.

She was so keyed, with both fear and anticipation, that there was never any danger of her falling asleep. However, the time passed with wearying slowness. Each time that she opened the shutter of the lantern to check her pocket-watch, the hands seemed hardly to have moved. Then, somehow, it was two o'clock in the morning, the hour when the human body and spirit are at their lowest ebb.

She rose quietly from her bunk, picked up the darkened lantern and went to the door of her cabin. The locking bolt clattered like a volley of musketry, but then it was open and she slipped through.

In the saloon a single oil-lamp still burned smokily, throwing agitated shadows against the wooden bulkheads, while the empty brandy bottle had fallen to the deck, and rolled back and forth with the ship's motion. Robyn squatted to pull off her boots and, leaving them at the entrance, she went forward on bare feet, crossed the saloon and stepped into the passageway that led to the stern quarters.

Her breath was short, as though she had run far, and she paused to lift the shutter of the bull's-eye lantern and flash a narrow beam of light into the darkness ahead. The door to Mungo St. John's cabin was closed.

She crept towards it, guiding herself with one hand on the bulkhead and at last her fingers closed over the doorhandle.

'Please God,' she whispered, and achingly slowly twisted the handle. It turned easily, and then the door slid open an inch along its track, enough for her to peep through into the cabin beyond.

There was just light to see, for the deck above was pierced for a repeating compass so that even while in his bunk the master could at a glance tell his ship's heading. The compass was lit by the dull yellow glow of the helmsman's lantern and the reflection allowed Robyn to make out the cabin's central features.

The bunk was screened off by a dark curtain and the rest of the furnishings were simple. The locked doors of the arms chest to the left, with a row of hooks beyond from which hung a boat cloak and the clothing that St. John had been wearing at dinner. Facing the door was a solid teak desk with racks to hold the brass navigational instruments, sextant, straight edge, dividers, and on the bulkhead above it were affixed the barometer and the ship's chronometer.

The Captain had evidently emptied his pockets on to the desk top before undressing. Scattered amongst the charts and ship's papers were a clasp knife, a silver cigar case, a tiny gold inlaid pocket pistol of the type favoured by professional gamblers, a pair of chunky ivory dice – Zouga and St. John must have fallen to gaming again after she left them – and then most important, what she had hoped to find, the bunch of ship's keys, that St. John usually wore on a chain from his belt, lay in the centre of the desk.

An inch at a time Robyn slid the door further open, watching the dark alcove to the right of the cabin. The curtains billowed slightly with each roll of the ship, and she screwed her nerves tighter as she imagined the movement to be that of a man about to leap out at her.

When the door was open enough to allow her to pass through, it required a huge effort of will to take the first step.

Half-way across the cabin she froze; now she was only inches from the bunk. She peered into the narrow gap in the curtaining and saw the gleam of naked flesh, and heard the deep regular breathing of the sleeping man. It reassured her and she went on swiftly to the desk.

She had no way of learning which keys fitted the lazaretto and the hatch to the main hold. She had to take the whole heavy bunch, and realized that it would mean returning to the cabin later. She did not know if she would have the courage to do that, and as she lifted the bunch her hand shook so it jangled sharply. Startled, she clutched it to her bosom and stared fearfully at the alcove. There was no movement beyond the curtains, and she glided back towards the door on silent bare feet.

It was only when the door closed again that the curtains of the alcove were jerked open, and Mungo St. John lifted himself on one elbow. He paused only a moment and then swung his legs out of the bunk and stood up. He reached the desk in two quick strides and checked the top.

'The keys!' he hissed, and reached out for his breeches hanging on the rack beside him, pulling them on swiftly and then stooping to open one of the drawers in his desk.

He lifted the lid of the rosewood case and took out the pair of long-barrelled duelling pistols, thrust them into his waistband, and started for the door of the cabin.

Robyn found the correct key to the lazaretto on the third attempt and the door gave reluctantly, dragging on the hinge with a squeal that sounded to her like a bugle call commanding a charge of heavy cavalry.

She locked the door behind her again, feeling a rush of relief to know that nobody could follow her now and she opened the shutter of the lantern and looked about her swiftly.

The lazaretto was no more than a large cupboard used as a pantry for the officers' personal stores. Sides of smoked ham and dried polonies hung from hooks on the deck above, there were fat rounds of cheese in the racks, boxes of tinned goods, racks of black bottles with waxed stoppers, bags of flour and rice, and, facing Robyn, another hatch with the locking bar chained in place by a padlock the size of her doubled fists.

The key, when she found it, was equally massive, as thick as her middle finger, and the hatch so heavy that it took all of her strength to drag it aside. Then she had to double over to get through the low opening.

Behind her, Mungo St. John heard the scrape of wood on wood and dropped silently down the steps to the door of the lazaretto. With a cocked pistol in one hand, he laid his ear to the oak planking to listen for a moment before trying the handle.

'God's breath!' he muttered angrily as he found it locked, and then turned away and raced on bare feet up the companionway to the cabin of his first mate.

At the first touch on his thickly muscled shoulder, Tippoo was fully awake, his eyes glistening in the gloom like those of a wild animal.

'Someone has broken into the hold,' St. John hissed at him, and Tippoo reared up out of his bunk, a huge dark figure.

'We find him,' he grunted, as he bound the loin cloth around his waist. 'Then we feed fish with him.'

The main hold seemed vast as a cathedral. The beam of the lantern could not reach into its deepest recesses, and a great mass of cargo was piled high, in some places as high as the maindeck fifteen feet above her.

She saw at once that the cargo had been loaded in such a way that it could be unloaded piecemeal, that any single item could be identified and swung up through the hatches without the necessity of unloading the whole. This, of course, must be essential in a ship trading from port to port. She saw also that the goods were carefully packaged and clearly labelled. Flashing the lantern around her she saw that the cases of equipment for their own expedition were packed here, 'Ballantyne Africa Expedition' stencilled in black on the raw, white wood.

She clambered up the rampart of cases and bales and balanced on the peak, turning the lantern upwards towards the square opening of the hatch, trying to see if there was an open grating, and immediately she was frustrated for the white canvas cover had been stretched around the lower surface also. She stood at full stretch to try and touch the hatch, to feel for the shape of a grating under the canvas, but her fingertips were inches short of the hatch and a sudden wild plunge of the ship under her sent her flying backwards into the deep aisle between the piles of cargo. She managed to keep her grip on the lantern, but hot oil from its reservoir splashed over her hand, threatening to blister the skin.

Once again she crawled up and over the mountains of cargo, searching for the evidence that she hoped not to find. There was no dividing bulkhead in the hold, but the main mast pierced the deck above and came through the hold to rest its foot on the keel, and there were stepped wedges fixed to the thick column of Norwegian pine.

Perhaps they were there to hold the slave decks. Robyn knelt beside the mast and sighted across the hold to the outward curved side of the ship. In line with the wedges on the mast were heavy wooden ledges, like shallow shelves, and she thought that these might be supports for the outer edges of the slave decks. She guessed that they were between two and a half and three feet apart, which she had read was the average height of the between decks in a slaver.

She tried to imagine what this hold might look like with those decks in place, tiers of low galleries just high enough for a man to crawl into doubled over. She counted the shelves and there were five of them – five piles of decks, each with its layer of naked black humanity laid out sardine fashion, each one in physical contact with his neighbour on either side, lying there in his own filth and that of the slaves above him which leaked through the seams of the deck. She tried to imagine the heat of the middle passage when the ship lay becalmed in the baking doldrums, she tried to imagine 2,000 of them vomiting and purging with seasickness as the ship reared and plunged in the wild seas where the Mozambique current scoured the Agulhas bank. She tried to imagine an epidemic of cholera or smallpox taking hold of that mass of misery, but her imagination could not rise to the task, and she pushed the hideous images aside and crawled on over the heaving cargo, flashing her lantern into each corner, searching for more solid evidence than the narrow ledges.

If there was planking on board it would be laid flat upon the deck, below this cargo, and there was no way in which Robyn could reach it.

Ahead of her she saw a dozen huge casks bolted to the forward bulkhead. They could be water barrels, or they could be filled with trade rum, or the rum could be replaced with water when the slaves were taken on board. There was no means of checking the contents, but she knocked on the oak with the hilt of her scalpel and the dull tone assured her that the casks contained something.

She squatted down on one of the bales and slit the stitching with the scalpel, thrusting her hand into the opening she grasped a handful and pulled it out to examine it in the lamp light.

Trade beads, ropes of them strung on cotton threads, a *bitil* of beads was as long as the interval between fingertip and wrist, four *bitil* made a *khete*. These beads were made of scarlet porcelain, they were the most valued variety called *sam sam*. An African of the more primitive tribes would sell his sister for a *khete* of these, his brother for two *khete*.

Robyn crawled on, examining crates and bales – bolts of cotton cloth from the mills of Salem, called *merkani* in Africa, a corruption of the word 'American' and the chequered cloth from Manchester known as *kaniki*. Then there were long wooden crates marked simply 'Five Pieces', and she could guess that they contained muskets. However, firearms were common trade goods to the coast, and no proof of the intention to buy slaves – they could just as readily be used to purchase ivory or gum-copal.

She was tired now with the effort of climbing and blundering around over the heaving slopes and peaks of cargo, and with the nervous tension of the search.

She paused to rest a moment, leaning back against one of the bales of *merkani* cloth, and as she did so something dug painfully into her back, forcing her to change her position. Then she realized that cloth should not have hard lumps in it. She shuffled around and once again slit the sacking cover of the bale.

Protruding from between the folded layers of cloth, there was something black and cold to the touch. She pulled it out and it was heavy iron, looped and linked, and she recognized it instantly. In Africa they were called 'the bracelets of death'. Here, at last, was proof, positive and irrefutable, for these sleeve slave cuffs with the light marching chains were the unmistakable stigmata of the trade.

Robyn tore the bale wider open, there were hundreds of the iron cuffs concealed between layers of cloth. Even if it had been possible, a perfunctory search by a naval boarding party was highly unlikely to have uncovered this sinister hoard.

She selected one set of cuffs with which to confront her brother and she started aft towards the lazaretto, filled suddenly with desire to be out of this dark cavern with its menacing shadows, and back once more in the safety of her own cabin.

She had almost reached the entrance to the lazaretto when suddenly there was a loud scraping sound from the deck above, and she froze with alarm. When the sound was repeated, she had enough of her wits still about her to douse the snuffer of her lantern, and then immediately regretted having done so for the darkness seemed to crush down upon her with a suffocating weight and she felt panic rising up to take possession of her.

With a crash like a cannon shot the main hatch flew open, and as she swung back towards it she saw the white pin-pricks of the stars outlined by the square opening. Then a huge, dark shape dropped through, landing lightly on the piled bales beneath, and at almost the same instant the hatch thudded closed again, blotting out the starlight.

Now Robyn's terror came bubbling to the surface. There was somebody locked in the hold with her, and the knowledge held her riveted for long, precious seconds, before she plunged back towards the lazaretto hatch, suppressing the scream that choked up into her throat.

The shape she had glimpsed for a moment was unmistakable. She knew that it was Tippoo in the hold with her, and it spurred her terror. She could imagine the great hairless toadlike figure, moving towards her in the darkness, with repulsive reptilian swiftness, could almost see the pink tongue flickering out over thick cruel lips, and her haste became uncontrolled. She lost her footing in the darkness and fell heavily, tumbling backwards into one of the deep gullies between banks of cargo, cracking the back of her skull on a wooden case, half-stunning herself so that she lost her grip on the extinguished lantern and could not find it when she groped for it. When she scrambled to her knees again, she had lost all sense of direction in the total blackness of the hold.

She knew that her best defence was to remain still and silent until she could place the man who was hunting her, and she crouched down in a crack between two crates. Her pulse beat in her ears like a drum, deafening her – and her heart seemed to have crammed up into her throat so that she must fight for each breath.

It took many minutes and all her determination to bring herself under control, to be able to think again.

She tried to decide in which direction lay the lazaretto hatch, her only means of escape, but she knew that the only way she would be able to find it would be to grope her way to the ship's wooden side and follow it around. The prospect of doing this, with that grotesque creature hunting her in the darkness, was appalling. She shrank down as far as she could into the narrow space and listened.

The hold was filled with small sounds that she had not noticed before, the heave and creak of the ship's timbers, the shifts of the cargo against its retaining ropes and netting – but then she heard the movement of a living thing close behind her and she caught the shriek of terror before it reached her lips, as she lifted her arm to protect her head. Frozen like that, she waited for a blow which never came.

Instead she heard another movement pass behind her turned shoulder, a whisper of sound, yet so chilling that she felt all power of movement drained from her legs. He was here, very close in the blackness, toying with her, cruel as a cat. He had smelt her out. With some sort of animal sense, Tippoo had found her unerringly in the darkness, and now he crouched over her ready to strike and she could only wait.

Something touched her shoulder, and before she could jerk away it swarmed up over her neck, brushed her face. She flung herself backwards and screamed, striking out wildly with the steel chain and handcuffs which she still held in her right hand.

The thing was furry and quick, and it squealed sharply, like an angry piglet as she struck again and again. Then it was gone, and she heard the scamper of small feet across the rough wood of the crate and she realized that it had been one of the ship's rats, big as a tom cat.

Robyn shuddered, revolted, but with a lift of relief that was shortlived.

There was a flash of light, so unexpected that it almost blinded her, and a lantern beam was thrown in a single swift sweep about the hold, and then extinguished, so that the darkness seemed even more crushing than before.

The hunter had heard her scream, and had flashed his lantern in her direction, had probably seen her, for she had clambered out of her niche between the crates. Now at least she knew in which direction to move, the brief flash of light had orientated her once again, she knew where to find the hatch.

She threw herself over a pile of soft bales, clawing herself towards the hatch, then checking her flight to think a moment. Tippoo must have known how she had entered the hold and would know that she would try to escape in the same direction. She must move with care, with stealth, ready for the moment when he flashed the lantern again, taking care not to rush headlong into the trap he was certainly setting for her.

She changed her grip on the iron chain, only then realizing its potential as a weapon, much more effective than the short-bladed scalpel in her pocket. A weapon! For the first time she was thinking of defending herself, not merely crouching like a chicken before the stoop of the hawk. 'Robbie was always the plucky one.' She could almost hear her mother's voice, troubled but touched with pride, when she had defended herself effectively against the village ruffians, or joined her brother on some of his more hair-raising escapades, and she realized she needed all of that pluck now.

With the chain gripped in her right hand, she started stealthily back towards the hatch, crawling, slithering forward on her belly, pausing to listen every few seconds. It seemed like a complete round of eternity before her outreaching fingers touched the solid planking of the after bulkhead. She was within feet of the hatch now, and that was where he would be waiting for her.

She crouched down, with her back firmly against the planking and waited for the flutter of her heart to abate enough to allow her to hear, but any noise her hunter made was covered by the creak and pop and groan of the working wooden hull, and the thud and hiss of the sea as *Huron* beat up hard to the wind.

Then she wrinkled her nose at a new smell that overlaid the pervading reek of the bilges. It was the hot oil smell of a shuttered lantern burning very close by, and now when she listened for it, she thought she could hear the pinkle and tick of the heated metal of the lantern. He must be close, very close, guarding the hatchway, ready to flash the lantern at the moment he could place her whereabouts accurately.

With the slowness of spreading oil she rose to face into the darkness where he was, she slipped the scalpel into the palm of her left hand, and she drew back her right arm with the chain and iron cuff dangling from her fist, ready to strike.

Then she pitched the scalpel with a short underhanded throw, judging the distance to drop it close enough to force him to move again, but far enough to make him move away from her.

The tiny missile struck something soft, the sound muted, almost lost in other small sounds, but then it slithered softly along the deck, like a hesitant footfall and instantly light flooded the hold.

Tippoo's monstrous shape sprang out of the darkness, huge, menacing, unbelievably close. He held the unhooded lantern high in his left hand, and the yellow light glistened on the bare round dome of his yellow skull, and on the broad plain of his back, the muscle rippling and tensing into valleys and ridges as he swung back the heavy club in his right hand, his head hunched down on the thick corded neck. He was facing away from her, but only for an instant. As he realized that there was nobody in front of him, he reacted with animal swiftness, ducking the great round head on to his chest, beginning to swing away.

She moved entirely by instinct. She swung the heavy iron manacle on the length of chain. It hummed in a glittering circle in the lamplight, and it caught Tippoo high on the temple with a crack like a branch breaking in a high wind, and the thin layer of yellow scalp opened like the mouth of a purse with a crimson velvet lining. Tippoo swayed drunkenly on straddled legs that started to buckle under him. She pulled back the chain and swung again with all the weight of her body and the strength of her fear behind the stroke. Again a deep red wound bloomed on the polished yellow dome of his skull and he went down slowly on to his knees, an attitude she had seen him adopt so often as he prayed on the quarterdeck, making the Moslem obeisance towards Mecca. Now again, his forehead touched the deck, but this time with his blood dribbling into a puddle under it.

The lantern clattered on to the deck, still burning, and in its light Tippoo rolled heavily on to his side with his breath snoring in his throat and his eyes rolled up into his head, glaring ghastly white and unseeing, his thick legs kicking out convulsively.

Robyn stared at the prostrate giant, aghast at the damage she had done, already feeling the need to administer to any hurt or crippled being – but it lasted for only seconds, as Tippoo's eyes rolled back into their deep sockets, and she saw the pupils beginning to focus. The yellow gleaming body heaved, the movement of limbs was no long spasmodic but more co-ordinated and determined, the head lifted, still lolling, but swinging questingly from side to side.

Unbelievably, the man was no longer crippled by those two cutting blows, had been stunned for seconds only, in seconds more he would be fully conscious and in his fury more dangerous than ever. With a sob Robyn flew at the open hatch of the lazaretto. As she passed him, cruel fingers hooked at her ankle, pulling her off balance so she almost fell before she could kick herself free and dive through the opening.

Tippoo was on hands and knees in the light of the fallen lantern, creeping towards her as she threw all her weight against the hatch. As it thudded into its jamb, she dropped the locking bar into its seating, and at that moment Tippoo's shoulder crashed into the far side of the hatch with a force that shook it in its frame.

Her frantic fingers were so clumsy that it took three attempts to secure the padlock and chain, and only then could she sink to the deck and sob away her fear until her relief came to buoy her up and give her renewed strength.

When she dragged herself to her feet, she was light-headed, intoxicated with the strange fierce jubilation that she had never felt before. She knew it sprang from having fought herself out of danger, from the unfamiliar experience of inflicting punishment on a hated adversary – and she knew she would feel guilt for it later, but not now.

The keys were still in the door between the lazaretto and saloon where she had left them. She pushed the door open quickly and paused in the opening an instant, feeling the quick flare of alarm overtake her feeling of elation.

She had only an instant of time to realize that somebody had trimmed the saloon lamp, and then fingers seized her wrist from behind and swung her off balance, bearing her down heavily to the deck and holding her there with one arm twisted up between her shoulderblades.

'Keep still, damn you – or I'll twist your head off your shoulders.' Mungo St. John's voice was low and fierce in her ear.

Her arm holding the chain was trapped under her, and now her captor shifted his weight over her, placing his knee in the small of her back and bearing down so painfully that she wanted to cry out with the agony that flared up her curved spine.

'Tippoo flushed you out quickly enough,' St. John murmured with grim satisfaction. 'Now let's have a look at you – before we stretch you out on the grating.'

He reached forward and pulled off the cloth cap that covered her head, and she heard his little grunt of surprise as her hair tumbled loose in a slippery shining mass in the lamplight. His grasp slackened and the pressure of his knee into the base of her spine eased. Roughly he grasped her shoulder to turn her on to her back so he could see her face.

She rolled easily towards him and then as her trapped arm came free, she hurled the chain at his face. He threw up both hands to catch the blow. As slippery as an eel she wormed out from under him and flew at the door to the saloon.

He was quick, quicker than she was, and his fingers were steely, they caught in the thin worn flannel of her shirt and it ripped from collar to hem. She turned and lashed at him with the chain again, but now he was ready for her, and he caught her wrist, trapping it.

She kicked wildly at his shins, and succeeded in hooking an ankle behind his heel and they went down together in a tangle on to the wooden deck, and Robyn found herself carried along by a fierce uncaring madness. She was hissing and snarling like a cat as she raked at his eyes with her nails, raising a bloody line down his neck. The tatters of her shirt flapped around her waist and the coarse dark hair of his chest rasped against the tender points of her naked breasts so that dimly in her madness she realized that he wore only breeches, and the man smell of his body filled her nostrils as he tried to smother her wild struggles with his body.

She reached up towards him with her open mouth, trying to sink her teeth into that flushed handsome face, but he caught a handful of her hair at the back of her head and twisted it. The pain seemed to flow down through her body and explode at the base of her belly in a warm soft spasm that took her breath and crammed it down into her lungs.

He held her helplessly and she felt the strength going out of her, to be replaced by spreading languor, and she stared up into his face with a kind of wonder as though she had never seen it before. She saw his teeth were very white, his lips drawn back into a rictus of emotion, and fierce yellow eyes unfocused and smoky with a kind of madness that matched her own.

She made one last feeble effort to repel him, driving her knee upwards, aimed at the fork of his lower body, but he trapped it between his thighs and then holding her thus he reared up over her and looked down at her bared bosom.

'Sweet Mother of God!' he croaked, and she saw the cords strain tight in his throat, saw the hot yellow fire in his eyes and she could not move, not even when he freed his hooked fingers from the twisted tresses of her hair and ran them slowly down her body, cupping first one tight small breast and then the other in the palm of his hand.

She felt his touch had gone, though the memory lingered on her skin like butterflies' wings. Then his fingers were back, tugging demandingly at the fastenings of her breeches. She closed her eyes and refused to let her mind consider what was about to happen. She knew that there was nothing she could do to escape, and cried out softly with the strange elation of the martyr.

But her cry seemed to touch something deep in him, the smoky yellow eyes focused for a moment, the predatory expression of the face became uncertain and then tinged with horror as he looked down at her spread white body. Swiftly he rolled away from her.

'Cover yourself!' he said harshly, and she was overwhelmed with a cold avalanche of loss, followed immediately by as great a rush of shame and of guilt.

She scrambled to her knees, clutching her clothing around her, suddenly shivering, but not with cold.

'You should not have struggled,' he said and though he was obviously fighting to control it his voice shook as hers did.

'I hate you,' she whispered foolishly, and then it became true. She hated him for what he had aroused in her, for the sickness and the guilt that followed it, and for the sense of loss and bereavement with which he had left her.

'I should kill you,' he muttered, not looking at her. 'I should have Tippoo do it.'

She felt no fear at the threat. She had rearranged her clothing as best she could, but still she knelt opposite him.

'Go!' he almost shouted at her. 'Get back to your cabin.'

She rose slowly, hesitated a moment and then turned to the companionway.

'Doctor Ballantyne!' he stopped her, and she turned back. He had risen and now he stood beside the door to the lazaretto, the keys in his one hand, the slave cuff and chain in the other. 'It would be best not to tell your brother of what you discovered tonight.' His voice was controlled now, cold and low. 'I would not have the same scruples with him. We will be at Cape Town in four days,' he went on. 'After that you may do as you will. Until then you will not provoke me again. One chance is already too many.'

She stared at him mutely, feeling small and helpless.

'Goodnight, Doctor Ballantyne.'

She hardly had time to pack her breeches and torn shirt away in the bottom of her chest, inspect and run a salve on her bruises, pull on her nightdress and climb into her narrow bunk before someone pounded on the cabin door.

'Who is it?' she called huskily and breathless, not yet fully recovered from the night's stresses.

'Sissy, it's me.' Zouga's voice. 'Someone has beaten Tippoo's skull in. He's bleeding all over the deck – can you come?'

Robyn glowed with a fierce spark of pagan glee, which she tried immediately to suppress with less than complete success.

'I'm coming.'

There were three men in the saloon, Zouga, the second mate and Tippoo. Mungo St. John was not there. Tippoo sat stolidly on a stool under the oil lamp, naked except for his cotton loin cloth, and his neck and shoulders ran with sheets of dark slick blood.

The second mate held a wad of grubby cotton to his skull and when Robyn lifted it away the wounds began spurting merrily..

'Brandy,' she demanded, and rinsed her hands and her instruments in the spirit – she was an admirer and believer in the teachings of Jenner and Lister – before she probed the points of her forceps into the open wound. She gripped the vessels and twisted them closed. Tippoo made no move, his expression never changed – and she was still carried along on the pagan mood, in direct defiance to the oath of Hippocrates which she had sworn.

'I must clean the wounds,' she told him, and quickly, before her conscience could prevent it, she tipped the raw brandy into the wounds and swabbed them out.

Tippoo sat still as a temple carving of a Hindu devil, making no acknowledgement of the harsh spirit burning open tissue.

Robyn tied off the vessels with silk thread, leaving an end hanging from the wounds, and then she sutured the lips closed, laying precise neat stitches and pulling them up tightly so that the smooth bald scalp came up in a sharp little peak of flesh with each tug.

'I will pull the thread when the vessels mortify,' she told him. 'The stitches will be ready to come out in a week.' She would not deplete her stock of laudanum, she decided, the man obviously was impervious to pain, and she was still in the throes of unchristian spite.

Tippoo lifted the round head. 'You good doctor,' he told her solemnly, and she learned then a lesson that would last her throughout her life – the stronger the purge, the more astringent or foultasting the medicine, and the more radical the surgery, then the more impressed with the surgeon's skill was the African patient.

'Yes,' Tippoo nodded gravely, 'you one bloody fine doctor.' And he opened one huge paw. In his palm lay the scalpel that Robyn had lost in *Huron*'s hold. Without expression he placed it in Robyn's own unresisting hand, and with that eerie swiftness was gone from the saloon, leaving her staring after him.

Huron flew southwards, meeting the long South Atlantic rollers and spurning them carelessly, brushing them aside with her shoulder and letting them cream over her rail and then tumble away astern in a long smooth wake.

There were seabirds in company with them now, beautiful gannets with yellow throats and black diamonds painted around their eyes, coming in from the east and soaring above their wake, shrieking and diving for the galley scraps when they were thrown overboard. There were seals too, lifting their whiskered heads high above the surface to stare curiously after the towering clipper as she burst the sea open with her sharp bows in her flight into the south.

Smeared across the brilliant blue water were long serpentine trails of seabamboo, torn from the rocky shoreline by the gales and storms of this uneasy and troubled sea.

All these were indications of the land which was always just below the eastern horizon, and Robyn spent many hours of each day alone at the port rail staring towards it, longing for another glimpse of it, smelling the dryness and the spiced aroma of its grass and herbs on the wind, seeing its blown dust in the marvellous reds and glowing gold of the sunsets, but denied sight of it by the offing that St. John was making before coming back on to the starboard tack for the final run into Table Bay.

However, as soon as Mungo St. John appeared on his quarterdeck Robyn would hurry below without another glance in his direction and she locked herself in her cabin, brooding there alone so that even her brother sensed that something troubled her. He tried a dozen times to draw her out. She sent him away each time, refusing to open the cabin to him.

'I'm all right, Zouga. I just want to be alone.'

And when he tried to join her in her solitary vigils at the ship's rail, she was short and unbending, exasperating him so that he stamped away and let her be.

She was afraid to talk to him, afraid that she would blurt out her discovery of slaving equipment in *Huron*'s hold and put him in deadly danger. She knew her brother well enough not to trust his temper and not to doubt his courage. Neither did she doubt Mungo St. John's warning. He would kill Zouga to protect himself – he could do it himself, she had seen him handle a pistol, or he could send Tippoo to do the work in the night. She had to protect Zouga, until they reached Cape Town, or until she did what she had to do.

'Vengeance is mine, saith the Lord.' She had found the passage in her Bible and studied it carefully, and then she had prayed for guidance which had not been given – and she had ended more confused and troubled than she had begun.

She prayed again kneeling on the bare deck beside her bunk until her knees ached, and slowly her duty became clear to her.

Three thousand souls sold into slavery in a single year – that was what the Royal Naval Captain had accused him of. How many thousands before that, how many thousands more in the years to come if *Huron* and her captain were allowed to continue their depredations, if nobody could prevent them ravaging the east coast of Africa, her land, her people, those peoples whom she was sworn to protect and minister to and to lead into the fold of the Saviour.

Her father, Fuller Ballantyne, was one of the great champions of freedom, the unrelenting adversary of this abominable trade. He had called it 'the running sore on the conscience of the civilized world that must be rooted out with all the means at our disposal.' She was her father's daughter, had made her oath in the sight of God.

This man, this monster, epitomized the sickening evil and monstrous cruelty of the whole filthy business.

'Please show me my duty, oh Lord,' she prayed, and always there was her own guilt and shame. Shame that his eyes had probed her half-naked body, that his hands had touched and fondled her, shame that he had debased her further, by stripping bare his own body. Hastily she thrust the image aside, it was too clear, too overpowering. 'Help me to be strong,' she prayed quickly.

There was shame and there was guilt, a terrible corrosive guilt in the fact that his gaze, his touch, his body, had not revolted and disgusted her, but had filled her instead with a sinful delight. He had tempted her to sin. For the first time in all her twenty-three years she had encountered real sin, and she had not been strong enough. She hated him for that.

'Show me my duty, oh Lord,' she prayed aloud and rose stiffly from her knees to sit on the edge of the bunk. She held her well-worn leather-bound Bible in her lap and whispered again.

'Please give unto your faithful servant guidance.' And she let the book fall open, and with her eyes closed placed her forefinger on the text. When she opened her eyes again she gave a start of surprise, guidance obtained by this little ritual of hers was usually not so unequivocal, for she had chosen Numbers 35. 19. 'The revenger of blood himself shall slay the murderer: when he meeteth him, he shall slay him.'

Robyn had no illusions as to the difficulty she would have in performing the heavy duty placed upon her by God's direct injunction, or how easily roles might be reversed and she become herself the victim rather than the avenger.

The man was as dangerous as he was wicked and time was against her. The accurate observation of the sun that Zouga had made at noon that day placed the ship within a hundred and fifty miles of Table Bay, and the wind stood fair and boisterous. Dawn the next day would reveal that great flat-topped mountain rising out of the sea. She had no time for elaborate planning. Whatever she did must be direct and swift.

There were half a dozen bottles in her medicine chest whose contents would serve – but no, poison was the most disgusting of deaths to inflict. She had seen a man die of strychnine poison when she was at St. Matthew's. She would never forget the arching spine as his back muscles convulsed until the man stood on the top of his head and on his heels like a drawn bow.

It must be some other means, there was the big naval Colt revolver which Zouga kept in his cabin. He had instructed her in its loading and discharge, or there was the Sharps rifle, but both of those belonged to her brother. She did not want to see him swinging from the gallows on the parade ground below the castle at Cape Town. The more uncomplicated and direct the plan, the greater was its chance of success, she realized, and at the thought she knew just how it must be done.

There was a polite knock on her cabin door, and she started.

'Who is it?'

'Jackson, Doctor.' He was the Captain's steward. 'Dinner is served in the saloon.'

She had not realized how late it had grown.

'I will not be dining tonight.'

'You must keep your strength up, ma'am,' Jackson entreated through the closed door.

'Are you the doctor, then?' she asked tartly, and he went shuffling off down the companionway.

She had not eaten since breakfast but she was not hungry, her stomach muscles were rigid with tension. She lay a while on her bunk, gathering her resolve and then she stood up, selected one of her oldest dresses, in a dark heavy wool. It would be the least loss to her wardrobe, and the dark colour would make it less conspicuous in the shadows.

She left her cabin and went quietly up to the maindeck. There was no one but the helmsman on the quarterdeck, his weathered brown face lit faintly by the binnacle lamp.

She moved quietly across to the skylight of the saloon and looked down.

Mungo St. John sat at the head of the table, with a joint of steaming salt beef in front of him. He was carving thin slices of meat, laughing across the board at one of Zouga's sallies. One quick glance was enough. Unless there was a call from the lookout or a need to change sail, Mungo St. John would not move for another half hour at the least.

Robyn went back down the ladder, passed her own cabin and down the companionway to the after quarters. She reached Mungo St. John's quarters and tried the door. Once again it slid open easily, she stepped through and closed it behind her again.

It took her only a few minutes to find the case of pistols in the drawer of the teak desk. She opened it on the desk top and took out one of the beautiful weapons. The mottled Damascus steel barrels were inlaid with bright gold, a hunting scene with horses and hounds and huntsmen.

Robyn sat down on the edge of the bunk, held the weapon muzzle-up between her knees while she unscrewed the silver powder flask and measured the fine powder into the cup. It was a familiar chore, for Zouga had spent hours in her instruction. She rammed the charge down into the long, elegant barrel under the felt wad, and then selected a perfect sphere of lead from the ball compartment of the case, wrapped that in an oiled patch of felt to give it a close fit in the rifled barrel and then rammed it down on top of the powder charge.

Then she reversed the pistol, pointing it down at the deck while she fitted one of the copper percussion caps over the nipple of the breech, drew back the hammer until it clicked at full cock, and laid it on the bunk beside her. She did the same with the other pistol, and when they were both loaded and cocked, she placed them on the edge of the desk, butts towards her, ready for immediate use.

Then she stood and, in the centre of the cabin, lifted her skirts around her waist and loosened the draw string of her drawers. She let them fall to the deck, and the air was cool on her naked buttocks so that she felt the little goose pimples rise on her skin. She dropped her skirts and picked up the cotton under-garment. Holding it across her chest she tore it half through and threw it across the cabin, then she took the fastenings of her bodice in both hands and ripped them down almost to her waist, the hooks and eyes hung on the torn threads of cotton.

She looked at herself in the polished metal mirror on the bulkhead beside the door. There was a lustre in her green eyes and her cheeks were flushed.

For the first time in her life, she thought her image beautiful – not beautiful, she corrected herself, but proud and wild and strong as an avenger should be. She was glad he would see her like this before he died, and she lifted her hand and rearranged one of the thick tresses of hair that had broken free of its retaining ribbon.

She sat back on the bunk and picked up a loaded pistol in each hand, she aimed first the one and then the other at the brass handle of the door, and then laid them in her lap and settled down to wait.

She had left her watch in her own cabin so she could not tell how long she waited. The voices and laughter from the officers' saloon were completely muffled by the closed door, but every time a plank creaked or some part of the ship's gear clattered, her nerves sprang tight and she lifted the pistols to cover the doorway.

Then suddenly she heard his footsteps, there was no mistaking them for any other man aboard. They reminded her somehow of a caged leopard packing its bars, quick, light and alert. He was on the deck above her, but the footsteps were so close that it seemed he was in the cabin with her. She looked up at the deck, swinging her head slightly to follow his turns from one side of the quarterdeck to the other.

She knew what he was doing, she had watched him on a dozen other nights. First he would talk quietly with the helmsman, checking the slate on which the ship's course was chalked before going back to inspect the log trailing astern. Then he would light one of his thin black Havana cigars and begin pacing the deck, with his hands clasped in the small of his back as he walked, darting quick glances up at the trim of his sails, studying the stars and the clouds for signs of change in the weather, pausing to feel the scent of the sea and the run of the ship under him before pacing on again.

Suddenly the footsteps stopped and Robyn froze, the moment had come. He had paused to flip the stub of his cigar over the rail and watch it fizzle into darkness as it hit the surface of the sea.

There was still time for her to escape, and she felt her resolve weaken. She half rose. She could still reach her own cabin if she moved now, but her legs would not carry her across the cabin. Then she heard his footsteps cross the deck above her with a different tread. He was coming down. It was too late.

Almost choking on her own breath, she sank back on to the bunk and lifted both pistols. They wavered uncertainly and she realized that her hands were shaking. With a tremendous effort she stilled them. The door slammed open and Mungo St. John stooped into the cabin, and then stopped as he saw the dark figure and the twin barrels that menaced him.

'They are loaded and cocked,' she said huskily. 'And I will not hesitate.'

'I see.' He straightened slowly, so the dark head just brushed the deck overhead.

'Close the door,' she said, and he pushed it closed with his foot, his arms folded on his chest, and that mocking half-smile on his lips. It made her forget her carefully rehearsed speech, and she stuttered slightly, and was immediately furious with herself.

'You are a slaver,' she blurted, and he inclined his head, still smiling. 'And I have to stop you.'

'How do you propose doing that?' he asked with polite interest.

'I am going to kill you.'

'That should do it,' he admitted, and now he smiled, a flash of white teeth in the gloom. 'Unfortunately they would probably hang you for it, if my crew didn't tear you to pieces before that.'

'You assaulted me,' she said. She glanced at her torn drawers lying near his feet and then with the butt of one pistol touched her torn bodice.

'A rape, by God!' Now he chuckled aloud, and she felt herself blushing vividly at the word.

'It's no laughing matter, Captain St. John. You have sold thousands of human souls into the most vile bondage.'

He took one slow pace towards her and she half rose, panic in her voice.

'Don't move! I warn you.'

He took another pace and she thrust both pistols towards him at the full stretch of her arms.

'I shall fire.'

The smile never wavered on his lips and the yellow flecked eyes held hers steadily as he took another lazy pace closer.

'You have the most beautiful green eyes I have ever seen,' he said, and the pistols shook in her hands.

'Here,' he said gently. 'Give them to me.'

He took the two gold-worked barrels in one hand and turned their muzzles upwards, pointing them at the deck above them. With the other hand he gently began to open her fingers, untangling them from trigger and butt.

'This is not why you came here,' he said, and her fingers went slack. He took the pistols out of her hands and uncocked them before laying them back in their velvet-lined nests within the rosewood case.

His smile was no longer mocking, and his voice was soft, almost tender as he lifted her to her feet.

'I am glad you came.'

She tried to turn her face away, but he took her chin between his fingers and lifted it. As he brought his mouth down to hers, she saw his lips opening, and the warm wet touch was a physical shock.

His mouth tasted slightly salty, perfumed with cigar smoke. She tried to keep her lips closed, but the pressure of his own lips forced them gently open and then his tongue was invading her. His fingers were still on her face, stroking her cheek, smoothing her hair back from her temples, touching lightly her closed eyelids – and she lifted her face higher to his touch.

Even when he slowly unfastened the last hooks of her bodice and eased it down off her shoulders, her only response was to feel the strength go out of her thighs so she had to lean against his hard chest for support.

Then he lifted his mouth from hers, leaving it empty, cooling after the warmth and she opened her eyes. With a sense of disbelief, she saw that his head was bowing to her breast, and she was looking down on the thick dark curls that covered the back of his neck. She knew it must stop now, before he did what she could hardly believe he was about to do.

When she tried to protest, it was only a whimper in her throat. When she tried to seize his head and thrust it away from her, her fingers merely curled into the springing crisp curls the way a cat claws a velvet cushion, and instead of thrusting him away, she drew his head down and arched her back slightly so that her breasts rose to meet him.

Yet she was unprepared for the feel of his mouth. It seemed as though he were about to suck her very soul out through the swollen, aching tips. It was too strong, she tried not to cry out, remembering that the last time she had done so, it had broken the spell – but it was too strong.

It was a sobbing choked-up little cry, and now her legs gave way under her. Still holding his head she sagged backwards on to the low bunk, and he knelt beside the bunk without lifting his mouth from her body. She arched her back and raised her buttocks off the bunk at his touch and allowed him to draw out her billowing skirts from under her and drop them to the deck.

Suddenly, he pulled abruptly away and she almost screamed to him not to go away again – but he had crossed to the door and locked it. Then, as he came back to where she lay, his own clothing seemed to fall away from his body like morning mist from mountain peak, and she came up on one elbow to stare at him openly. She had never seen anything so beautiful, she thought.

'The devil is beautiful also.' A tiny inner voice tried to warn her, but it was far away and so small that she could ignore it. Besides it was too late, far too late to listen to warnings now – for already he was coming over her.

She expected pain, but not the deep splitting incursion that racked her. Her head was flung back and her eyes flooded with the tears of it. Yet even in the stinging agony of it there was never a thought to reject this stretching, tearing invasion and she clung to him with both her arms about his neck. It seemed that he suffered with her, for except for that single swift deep stroke, he had not moved, trying to alleviate her agony by his utter stillness, his body was rigid as hers, she could feel the muscles taut to the point of tearing, and he cradled her in his arms.

Then suddenly she could breathe again, and she took in air with a great rushing sob, and immediately the pain began to change its shape, becoming something she could not describe to herself. It started as a spark of heat, deep within her, and flared slowly so she was forced to meet it with a slow voluptuous movement of her hips. She seemed to break free of earth and rise up through flames, that flickered redly through her clenched eyelids. There was only one reality – and that was the hard body that rocked and plunged above her. The heat seemed to fill her until she could not bear it any longer. Then at the last moment when she thought she might die of it, it burst within her – and she felt herself falling, like a tumbling leaf, down, down, at last, to the hard narrow bunk in a half-dark cabin in a tall ship on a wind-driven sea.

When next she could open her eyes his face was very close to hers. He was staring at her with a thoughtful, solemn expression.

She tried to smile, it was a shaky unconvincing effort.

'Please don't look at me like that.' Her voice was even deeper, more husky than it usually was.

'I don't think I ever saw you before,' he whispered and traced the line of her lips with his fingertip. 'You are so different.'

'Different from what?'

'Different from other women.' His reply gave her a pang.

He made the first movement of withdrawing from her, but she tightened her grip on him panic-stricken at the thought of losing him yet.

'We will only have this one night,' she told him, and he did not reply. He lifted one eyebrow, and waited for her to speak again.

'You don't dispute it,' she challenged. There was that mocking little smile beginning to curl his lip again, and it annoyed her.

'No, I was wrong, you are like all other women,' he smiled. 'You have to talk, always you have to talk.'

She let him go, as punishment for those words, but as he slithered free of her she felt a terrible emptiness and she regretted his going fiercely, beginning to hate him for it.

'You have no God,' she accused him.

'Isn't it strange,' he chided her gently, 'that most of the worst crimes in history have been committed by men with God's name upon their lips.'

The truth of it deflated her momentarily, and she struggled into a sitting position.

'You are a slaver.'

'I don't really want to argue with you, you know.' But she would not accept that.

'You buy and sell human beings.'

'What are you trying to prove to me?' He chuckled now, further angering her.

'I'm telling you that there is a void between us that can never be bridged.'

'We have just done so, convincingly,' and she flushed bright scarlet down her neck on to her bosom.

'I have sworn to devote my life to destroy all you stand for,' she said fiercely, pushing her face close to his.

'Woman, you talk too much,' he told her lazily, and covered her mouth with his own, holding her like that while she struggled, gagging her with his lips so her protests were muffled and incomprehensible. Then when her struggles had subsided he pushed her easily backwards on to the bunk and came over her again.

In the morning when she woke, he was gone, but the bolster beside her was indented by his head. She pressed her face into it and the smell of his hair and of his skin still lingered, though the heat of his blood had dissipated and the linen was cool against her cheeks.

The ship was in the grip of intense excitement. She could hear the voices from the deck above as she scurried down the empty passageway to her own cabin, dreading meeting a member of the crew, or more especially meeting her brother. What excuse could she have for being abroad in the dawn, with her cabin unslept in and her clothing torn and rumpled?

Her escape was a matter of seconds only, for as she locked and leaned thankfully against the door of her cabin, Zouga beat upon it with his fist from the far side.

'Robyn, wake up! Get dressed. Land is in sight. Come and see!'

Swiftly she bathed her body with a square of flannel dipped into the enamelled jug of cold sea water. She was tender, swollen and sensitive and there was a trace of blood on the cloth.

'The trace of shame,' she told herself severely, but it was difficult to sustain the emotion. Instead she felt a soaring sense of physical well-being – and a hearty appetite for her breakfast.

Her step was light, almost skipping as she went up on to the maindeck and the wind tugged playfully at her skirts.

Her first concern was for the man. He stood at the weather rail, in shirt-sleeves only, and immediately a storm of conflicting feelings and thoughts assailed her, the chief of which was that he was so lean and dark and devil-may-care that he should be kept behind bars as a menace to all womenkind.

Then he lowered the telescope, turned and saw her by the companionway and bowed slightly, and she inclined her head an inch in reply, very cool and very dignified. Then Zouga hurried to meet her, laughing and excited, and took her arm as he led her to the rail.

The mountain towered out of the steely green Atlantic, a great grey buttress of solid rock, riven and rent by deep ravines and gullies choked with dark green growth. She had not remembered it so huge, seeming to fill the whole eastern horizon and reaching up into the heavens, for its summit was covered in a thick shimmering white mattress of cloud. The cloud rolled endlessly over the edge of the mountain like a froth of boiling milk pouring over the rim of the pot, but as it sank so it was sucked into nothingness, disappearing miraculously to leave the lower slopes of the mountain clear and close, each detail of the rock-face finely etched and the tiny buildings at its foot as startling white as the wing feathers of the gulls that milled the air about the clipper.

'We'll dine tonight in Cape Town,' Zouga shouted over the wind, and the thought of food flooded Robyn's mouth with saliva.

Jackson, the steward, had the hands spread a tarpaulin to break the wind and they breakfasted under its lee, in the sunshine. It was a festive meal, for Mungo St. John called for champagne and they toasted the successful voyage and the good landfall in the bubbling yellow wine.

Then Mungo St. John ended it. 'The wind comes through there, funnelled down that break in the mountain.' He pointed ahead, and they saw the surface at the mouth of the bay seething with the rush of it. 'Many a ship has been dismasted by that treacherous blast. We'll be shortening sail in a few minutes.' And he signalled to Jackson to clear away the trestles that carried the remains of their breakfast, excused himself with a bow and went back to his quarterdeck.

Robyn watched him strip the canvas off the upper yards, taking in two reefs in the main and setting a storm jib so that *Huron* met the freak wind readily and ran in for Table Bay, giving Robben Island a good berth to port. When the ship had settled on to its new heading, Robyn went up on to the quarterdeck.

'I must speak with you,' she told him, and St. John cocked his eyebrow at her.

'You could not have chosen a better time—' and with the eloquent spread of his hands indicated wind and current and the dangerous shore close under their bows.

'This will be the last opportunity,' she told him quickly. 'My brother and I will be leaving this ship immediately you drop anchor in Table Bay.'

The mocking grin slid slowly from his lips.

'If you are determined, then it seems that we have nothing more to say to each other.'

'I want you to know why.'

'I know why,' he said, 'but I doubt that you do.'

She stared at him, but he turned away to call a change of heading to the helmsman and then to the figure at the foot of the mainmast.

'Mr. Tippoo, I'll have another reef on her, if you please.'

He came back to her side, but not looking at her, his head tilted back to watch the miniature figures of his crew on the mainyards high above them.

'Have you ever seen sixteen thousand acres of cotton with the pods ready for plucking?' he asked quietly. 'Have you ever seen the bales going down river on the barges to the mills?'

She did not answer, and he went on without waiting. 'I have seen both, Doctor Ballantyne, and no man dare tell me that the men who work my fields are treated like cattle.'

'You are a cotton-planter?'

'I am, and after this voyage I will have a sugar plantation on the island of Cuba – half my cargo to pay for the land and half of it to work the cane.'

'You are worse than I thought,' she whispered. 'I thought you were merely one of the devil's minions. Now I know you are the devil himself.'

'You are going into the interior.' St. John looked down at her now. 'When you get there, if you ever do, you will see true human misery. You will see cruelties that no American slave-owner would dream of. You will see the slaughter of human beings by war and disease and wild beast that will baulk your belief in heaven. Besides this savagery, the barracoons and the slave quarters are an earthly paradise.'

'Do you dare suggest that by catching and chaining these poor creatures you do them favour?' Robyn demanded, aghast at his effrontery.

'Have you ever visited a Louisiana plantation, Doctor?' Then answering his own question, 'No, of course, you have not. I invite you to do so. Come down to Bannerfield as my guest one day – and then compare the state of my slaves to the savage blacks you will see in Africa, or even to those damned souls that inhabit the slums and workhouses of your own lovely little green island.'

She remembered those raddled and hopeless human creatures with whom she had worked in the mission hospital. She was speechless. Then suddenly his grin was wicked again. 'Think of it only as forced enlightenment of the heathen. I lead them out of the darkness into the ways of God and civilization – just as you are determined to do – but my methods are more effective.'

'You are incorrigible sir.'

'No, ma'am. I am a sea-captain and a planter. I am also a trader in, and an owner of, slaves – and I will fight to the death to defend my right to be all of those things.'

'What *right* is that you speak of?' she demanded.

'The right of the cat over the mouse, of the strong over the weak, Doctor Ballantyne. The natural law of existence.'

'Then I can only repeat, Captain St. John, that I will leave this ship at the very first opportunity.'

'I am sorry that is your decision.' The hard fierce look in the yellow eyes softened a little. 'I wish it were otherwise.'

'I shall devote my life to fighting you and men like you.'

'And what a waste that will be of a lovely woman.' He shook his head regretfully. 'But then your resolve may give us reason to meet again – I must hope that that is so.'

'One final word Captain St. John – I shall never forgive last night.'

'And I, Doctor Ballantyne, will never forget it.'

Zouga Ballantyne checked his horse at the side of the road, just before it crossed the narrow neck between the crags of Table Mountain and Signal Hill, one of its satellite promontories.

He swung down out of the saddle to rest his mount, for it had been a hard pull up the steep slope from the town, and he tossed the reins to the Hottentot groom who accompanied him on the second horse. Zouga was sweating lightly and there was a residual pulse of dullness behind his eyes from the wine he had drunk the night before, the magnificent rich sweet wine of Constantia, one of the most highly prized vintages in the world, but capable of delivering as thick a head as any of the cheap and common grogs they sold in the waterfront bars.

In the five days since they had disembarked, the friendliness of the Cape Colony citizens had almost overwhelmed them. They had slept only the first night at a public inn in Buitengracht Street, then Zouga had called upon one of the Cape Colony's more prominent merchants, a Mr. Cartwright. He had presented his letters of introduction from the directors of the Worshipful Company of London Merchants Trading into Africa, and Cartwright had immediately placed at their disposal the guest bungalow set in the gardens of his large and gracious home on the mountain slope above the old East India Company's gardens.

Every evening since then had been a gay whirl of dinners and dances. Had Robyn and Zouga not insisted otherwise, the days would have been filled with equivalent frivolity – picnics, sailing and fishing expeditions, riding in the forest, long leisurely lunches on the lawns under spreading oak trees that reminded him so vividly of England.

However, Zouga had avoided these diversions and had managed to accomplish much of the work of the expedition. Firstly there had been the supervising of the unloading of equipment from *Huron* – in itself a major undertaking as the crates had to be swayed up from the hold and lowered into lighters alongside before making the perilous return through the surf to land on the beach at Rogger Bay.

Then he had to arrange temporary warehousing for the cargo. Here again Mr. Cartwright had been of assistance. Still Zouga found himself fiercely resenting his sister's insistence that had made all this heavy work necessary.

'Damn me, Sissy, even Papa used to travel in the company of Arab slave-traders when he had to. If this fellow St. John *is* a trader, we would do well to learn all we can from him – his methods and sources of supply. No one could give us better information for our report to the society.'

None of his arguments had prevailed, and only when Robyn had threatened to write home to the Society's directors in London, and to follow that up with a frank talk to the editor to the *Cape Times*, had Zouga acceded, with the worst grace possible, to her demands.

Now he looked down longingly at *Huron*, lying well out from the beach, snubbing around on her anchor cable to point into the rumbustious south-easterly wind. Even under bare poles she seemed on the point of flight.

Zouga guessed that St. John would be sailing within days, leaving them to await the next ship that might be bound for the Arab and Portuguese coasts.

Zouga had already presented his letter of introduction from the Foreign Secretary to the Admiral of the Cape Squadron of the Royal Navy, and been promised all consideration. Nevertheless, he spent many hours of each morning visiting the shipping agents and owners in the port in hope of an earlier passage.

'Damn the silly wench,' he muttered aloud, thinking bitterly of his sister and her foibles. 'She could cost us weeks, even months.'

Time was, of course, of the very essence. They had to be clear of the fever-ridden coast before the monsoon struck and risk of malaria became suicidal.

At that moment there was the crack of cannon shot from the slopes of the hill above him, and as he glanced up he saw the feather of gunsmoke drifting away from the lookout station on Signal Hill.

The gunshot was to alert the townsfolk that a ship was entering Table Bay, and Zouga shaded his eyes with his cap as the vessel came into view beyond the point of land. He was not a seaman but he recognized instantly the ugly silhouette and single smoke stack of the Royal Naval gunboat that had pursued *Huron* so doggedly. Was it really two weeks ago, he wondered, the days had passed so swifly. *Black Joke,* the gunboat, had her boilers fired and a thin banner of dark smoke drifted away downwind as she rounded up into the bay, her yards training around as she pointed through the wind and she passed within half a mile of where *Huron* was already at anchor. The proximity of the two ships raised interesting possibilities of the feud between the two captains being revived, Zouga realized, but his immediate feeling was of intense disappointment. He had hoped that the vessel might have been a trader that could have offered the expedition further passage up the east coast – and he turned away abruptly, took the reins from the groom and swung up easily into the saddle.

'Which way?' he asked the servant, and the little yellow-skinned lad in Cartwright's plum-coloured livery indicated the left branch of the road that forked over the neck and dropped down across the dragon's-back of the Cape peninsula to the ocean shore on the far side.

It was another two hours' ride, the last twenty minutes along a rutted cart track, before they reached the sprawling thatched building hidden away in one of the ravines of the mountain slope behind a grove of milkwood trees. The slopes behind the building were thick with protea bushes in full flower and the long-tailed sugar-birds haggled noisily over the blazing blooms. To one side a waterfall smoked with spray as it fell from the sheer rock face and then formed a deep green pool on which a flotilla of ducks cruised.

The building had a dilapidated air to it, the walls needed whitewashing and the thatch hung in untidy clumps from the eaves. Under the milkwood trees were scattered items of ancient equipment, a wagon with one wheel missing and the woodwork almost entirely eaten away by worm, a rusty hand forge in which a red hen was sitting upon a clutch of eggs, and mouldering saddlery and ropes hung from the branches of the trees.

As Zouga swung down from the saddle, a pack of half a dozen dogs came storming out of the front porch, snarling and barking around Zouga's legs so that he lashed out at them with his riding whip and with his boots, changing the snarls to startled yelps and howls.

'Who the hell are you and what do you want?' A voice carried through the uproar, and Zouga took one more cut at a great shaggy Boerhound with a ridge of coarse hair fully erect between his shoulders, catching him fairly on the snout and forcing him to circle out of range, with fangs still bared and murderous growls rumbling up his throat.

Then he looked up at the man on the stoep of the building. He carried a double-barrelled shotgun in the crook of his arm, and both hammers were at full cock. He was so tall that he had to stoop beneath the angle of the roof, but he was thin as a blue-gum tree, as though the flesh and fat had been burned off his bones by ten thousand tropical suns.

'Do I have the honour of addressing Mr. Thomas Harkness?' Zouga called over the clamour of the dog pack.

'I ask the questions here,' the lean giant bellowed back. His beard was as white as the thunderhead clouds of a summer's day on the highveld and it hung to his belt buckle. Hair of the same silver covered his head and flowed down to the collar of his leather jerkin.

His face and his arms were burned to the colour of plug tobacco, and were speckled by the raised blemishes like little moles and freckles, where years of the fierce African sun had destroyed the upper layers of his skin. The pupils of his eyes were black and bright as drops of fresh tar, but the whites were smoky yellow, the colour of the malarial fevers and the pestilences of Africa.

'What is your name, boy?' His voice was strong and deep. Without the beard he might have been fifty years of age, but Zouga knew with certainty that he was seventy-three. He carried his one shoulder higher than the other and the arm on that side hung at an awkward angle to the joint. Zouga knew that a lion had chewed through the shoulder and through the bone of the upper arm, before Harkness had been able to reach his hunting knife on his belt with the other hand and stab it between the forelegs, up into the heart. That had been forty years before and the injury had become the Harkness hallmark.

'Ballantyne, sir.' Zouga shouted to make himself heard above the dogs. 'Morris Zouga Ballantyne.'

The old man whistled once, a fluting double note that stilled the dogs and brought them back around his legs. He had not lowered the shotgun and a frown puckered his sharp features.

'Fuller Ballantyne's pup, is it?'

'That's right, sir.'

'By God, any son of Fuller Ballantyne's is good enough for a charge of my buckshot in the rump. Don't cock your butt when you get back on that horse, boy, for I'm a man who tempts very easily.'

'I've ridden a long way to see you, Mr. Harkness.' Zouga smiled that frank and winning smile of his, standing his ground. 'I'm one of your greatest admirers. I've read everything that has ever been written about you and everything you have written yourself.'

'I doubt that,' Harkness growled, 'they burned most of mine. Too strong for their lily livers.' But the hostile glint in his eyes turned to a twinkle and he cocked his head as he studied the young man before him.

'I have no doubt that you're as ignorant and arrogant as your Daddy, but you've got a fairer turn of speech.' And he stared again at the toes of Zouga's boots, and let his gaze move up slowly.

'Priest,' he asked, 'like your Daddy?'

'No, sir, soldier.'

'Regiment?'

'13th Madras Foot.'

'Rank?'

'Major.'

Harkness' expression eased with each reply until his gaze once more locked with Zouga's.

'Teetotal? Like your Daddy?'

'Perish the thought!' Zouga assured him vehemently and Harkness smiled for the first time as he let the muzzles of the shotgun droop until they pointed at the ground. He tugged at the long spikes of his beard for a moment, then reached a decision.

'Come.' He jerked his head and led the way into the house. There was one huge central room, the high ceiling of dried reed stems kept it cool and the narrow windows kept it gloomy. The floor was of peach-pip shells set into a plaster of mud and cow-dung and the walls were three-foot thick.

Zouga paused in the threshold and blinked with surprise at the collection of strange articles that covered the walls, were piled on every table and chair, and packed to the rafters in the dark corners.

There were books, thousands of books, cloth and leatherbound books, pamphlets and journals, atlases and encyclopaedias. There were weapons, assegai of Zulu, shield of Matabele, bow of Bushman with its quiver of poisoned arrows and, of course, guns – dozens of them in racks or merely propped against the walls. There were hunting trophies, the beautiful zigzag-striped hide of zebra, the dark bush of the lion's mane, the elegant curved horn of harris-buck, teeth of hippopotamus and warthog, and then the long, yellow arcs of ivory thicker than a woman's thigh and taller than a man's head. There were rocks, piles of rocks that glittered and sparkled, crystal rocks of purple and green, metallic nodules, native copper redder than gold, hairy strands of raw asbestos – all of it covered with a fine layer of dust and piled untidily wherever it had fallen.

The room smelled of skins and dogs and damp, of stale brandy and fresh turpentine, and there were stacks of new canvases already stretched in their wooden frames, while other canvases stood on their easels with the subjects sketched in charcoal outline, or partly blocked in with bright oil paint. On the walls were hung some finished pictures.

Zouga crossed to examine one of them while the old man blew into a pair of glass tumblers and polished them on his shirt-tail.

'What do you think of my lions?' he asked, as Zouga studied a huge canvas entitled 'Lion Hunt on the Gariep River. Feb. 1846'.

Zouga made an appreciative sound in the back of his throat. Zouga was himself a dauber and scribbler, but he considered that the meticulous reproduction of the subject was the painter's duty, while these paintings had a guileless, almost childlike joy in every primitive line. The colours also were gay and made no pretence to imitate nature, while the perspectives were wildly improbable. The mounted figure with the flowing beard in the background dominated the pride of lions in the foreground. Yet Zouga knew that these strange creations had remarkable value. Cartwright had paid ten guineas for a fanciful landscape. Zouga could only believe it was a fad amongst the colony's fashionable set.

'They say my lions look like English sheepdogs.' Harkness glowered at them. 'What do you think, Ballantyne?'

'Perhaps,' Zouga started, then saw the old man's expression change. 'But tremendously ferocious sheep dogs!' he added swiftly, and Harkness laughed out loud for the first time.

'By God, you'll do!' He shook his head as he half-filled the tumblers with the dark brown local brandy, the fearsome 'Cape Smoke', and brought one glass to Zouga.

'I like a man who speaks his mind. Rot all hypocrites.' He raised his own glass in a toast. 'Especially hypocritical preachers who don't give a damn for God, for truth or for their fellow men.'

Zouga fancied that he recognized the description, but raised his glass. 'Rot them!' he agreed, and managed to suppress a gasp as the liquor exploded in his throat and sizzled behind his eyes.

'Good,' he said hoarsely, and Harkness wiped his silver moustache, left and right, with his thumb before he demanded,

'Why have you come?'

'I want to find my father, and I think you may be able to tell me where to search.'

'Find him?' fulminated the old man. 'We should all be extremely grateful he is lost, and pray each day that he remains that way.'

'I understand how you feel, sir,' Zouga nodded. 'I read the book that was published after the Zambezi expedition.'

Harkness had accompanied Fuller Ballantyne on that ill-fated venture, acting as second-in-command, expedition manager and recording artist. He had been caught up in the squabbling and blame-fixing that had marred the enterprise from the beginning. Fuller Ballantyne had dismissed him, accusing him of theft of the expedition stores, trading on his own account, artistic incompetence, neglecting his duties to hunt for ivory, and total ignorance of the countryside and its trails, of the tribes and their customs and had included these accusations in his account of the expedition, implying that the blame for the expedition's failure could be laid on Thomas Harkness' uneven shoulders.

Now even mention of that book brought the colour to the sun-raddled face and made the white whiskers twitch.

'I crossed the Limpopo for the first time in the year that Fuller Ballantyne was born. I drew the map that he used to reach Lake Ngami.' Harkness stopped and made a dismissive gesture. 'I might as well try and reason with the baboons barking from the tops of the kopjes.' Then he peered more closely at Zouga.

'What do you know about Fuller? Since he sent you home to the old country, how often have you seen him? How much time have you spent in his company?'

'He came home once.'

'How much time did he spend with you and your mother?'

'Some months – but he was always in Uncle William's study writing, or he was up at London, Oxford or Birmingham to lecture.'

'But you, nevertheless, conceived a burning filial love and duty for the sainted and celebrated father?'

Zouga shook his head. 'I hated him,' he said quietly. 'I could hardly bear the days until he went away again.'

Harkness tilted his head on one side, surprised, speechless for a moment, and Zouga drank the last few drops of liquor in the glass.

'I never told anybody that before.' He seemed puzzled himself. 'I hardly even admitted it to myself. I hated him for what he did to us, to me and my sister, but especially to my mother.'

Harkness took the empty tumbler from his fingers, refilled it and handed it back. He spoke quietly.

'I also will tell you something that I have never told another man. I met your mother at Kuruman, my God, so long ago. She was sixteen or seventeen and I was nearly forty. She was so pretty, so shy and yet so filled with a special quality of joy. I asked her to marry me. The only woman I ever asked.' Harkness stopped himself, turned away to his painting, and peered at it. 'Damned sheep dogs!' he snapped, and then without turning back to face Zouga, 'So why do you want to find your father? Why have you come out to Africa?'

'Two reasons,' Zouga told him. 'Both good. To make my own reputation and my own fortune.'

Harkness swivelled to face him. 'Damn me, but you can be direct.' There was a tinge of respect in his expression now. 'How do you plan to achieve those very desirable ends?'

Zouga explained swiftly – the newspaper sponsorship, that of the Society for the Extinction of the Slave Trade.

'You'll find much grist for your mill,' Harkness interjected. 'The coast is still rife with the trade, despite what you'll hear in London town.'

'I am also an agent for the Worshipful Company of London Merchants Trading into Africa, but I have my own goods to trade, and 5,000 cartridges for my Sharps rifle.'

Harkness wandered across the dim room and stopped before one of the gigantic elephant tusks propped against the far wall. It was so old and heavy that there was very little taper from root to tip, the point worn blunt and rounded. One third of its length was smooth and a clear lovely butter yellow colour, where it had been buried in the jaw of the beast, the rest of it was stained dark with vegetable juices and scarred from the battles and foragings of sixty years.

'This one weighs one hundred and sixty pounds – its value in London is six shillings a pound.' He slapped it with his open palm. 'There are still bulls like that out there, thousands of them. But take a tip from an old dog – forget your fancy Sharps, and use one of the ten-bore elephant guns. They throw a ball that weighs a quarter of a pound, and though they kick like the devil himself, they drive better than any of these new-fangled rifles.' There was a lightness in the worn old features, a sparkle in the dark eyes. 'Another tip – get in close. Forty paces at the outside, and go for the heart. Forget what you'll hear about the brain shot, go for the heart—' He broke off suddenly and waggled his head, grinning ruefully. 'By God, but it's enough to make a man want to be young again!'

He came back and studied Zouga directly, and a thought occurred to him with a suddenness that struck him like a physical blow, taking him so by surprise that he almost spoke it aloud.

'If Helen had given me a different answer, you could be my son.' But he held back the words, and asked instead:

'How can I help you, then?'

'You can tell me where I can start to search for Fuller Ballantyne.'

Harkness threw up his hands, palms uppermost. 'It's a vast land – so big that you could travel across it for a lifetime.'

'That's why I have come to you.'

Harkness went to the long table of yellow Cape deal that ran nearly the full length of the room and with the twisted arm swept a clear space amongst the books and papers and paint pots.

'Bring a chair,' he instructed, and when they sat facing each other across the cleared space, he recharged both their glasses and placed what remained in the bottle between them.

'Where did Fuller Ballantyne go?' Harkness asked, and took a silver tress from the thick beard and began to twist it around his forefinger. The finger was long and bony and covered with the thick ridges of ancient scar tissue where the recoil of overheated or overcharged firearms had driven the trigger guard to the bone.

'Where did Fuller Ballantyne go?' he repeated, but Zouga realized the question was rhetorical, and he said nothing.

'After the Zambezi expedition, his fortune was exhausted, his reputation all but destroyed – and to a man like Fuller Ballantyne that was unbearable. His entire life had been an endless hunt for glory. No risk, no sacrifice was too great, his own or others. He would steal and lie – aye, even kill for it.'

Zouga looked up sharply, challenging.

'Kill,' Harkness nodded. 'Anybody who stood in his way. I have seen him, but that is another tale. Now we want to know where he went.'

Harkness stretched out and selected a roll of parchment from the cluttered table-top, checked it quickly and grunted with approval, as he spread it between them.

It was a map of Central Africa, east to west coast, south to the Limpopo, north to the lakes, drawn in India ink and the borders were illuminated by Harkness' characteristic figures and animals.

Instantly Zouga coveted it with his very soul. All that Harkness had accused his father of he felt in his own heart. He had to have this, even if it was necessary to steal – or, by God, kill. He had to have it.

The map was huge – at least five feet square – hand-drawn on the finest-quality linen-backed paper. It was unique, the detail enormous; the notations were profuse but succinct, the observations first hand, the details precise, written in a tiny elegant script that needed a reading glass to be deciphered with ease.

'Here heavy concentrations of elephant herds during June to September.'

'Here I sampled gold reef in ancient workings at two ounces to the ton.'

'Here rich copper is worked by Gutus people.'

'Here slave convoys depart for the coast in June.'

There was literally hundreds of these notations, each in a neatly numbered box, that corresponded to the exact location on the map.

Harkness watched Zouga's face, with a sly half-smile on his face, and then handed him a reading-glass to continue his examination.

It took Zouga a few minutes to realize that the pink shaded areas indicated the 'fly corridors' of the high African plateau. The safe areas through which domestic animals could be moved to avoid the tsetse fly belts. The terrible Ngana disease which the fly carried could decimate the herds. Knowledge of these corridors had been gathered by the African tribes over hundreds of years, and here it was faithfully recorded by Thomas Harkness. The value of this knowledge was incalculable.

'Here Mzilikazi's border impis kill all travellers.'

'Here there is no water between May and October.'

'Here dangerous malarial vapours during October to December.'

The areas of greatest hazard were signposted, while the known routes to the interior were clearly marked, though there were few enough of these.

The cities of the African kings were marked, as was the location of their military kraals, the areas of influence of each were defined and the names of the subservient chiefs noted.

'Here concession to hunt elephant must be obtained from Chief Mafa. He is treacherous.'

Harkness watched the young man eagerly poring over the priceless document. His expression was almost fond, and he nodded his head once as a memory passed like a shadow behind his eyes. He spoke at last.

'Your father would be trying to restore his reputation at a single stroke,' Harkness mused. 'He would have to feed that monstrous ego. There are two areas that come immediately to mind. Here!'

He placed his open hand across an enormous area to the north and west of the defined shape of Lake Marawi. In this area the copious and authoritative notations were replaced by meagre, hesitant observations obtained from hearsay or native legend, and by speculation followed by a question mark.

'Sheikh Assab of the Omani Arabs reports River Lualaba runs north and west. Possible flow into Lake Tanganyika.' The dotted outlines of rivers, instead of crisp detail. 'Pemba, the Chief of the Marakan, reports huge lake shaped like butterfly twenty-five days march from Khoto Khota. Called Lomani. Possible source of Luapula and of Herodotus fountain.' The lake was sketched in. 'Question. Is Lake Tanganyika connected to Lake Albert? Question. Is Lake Tanganyika connected to Lake Lomani. If so, Lomani is ultimate source of Nile river?'

Harkness touched the two question marks with his gnarled and bony finger.

'Here,' said Harkness. 'The big question marks. The Nile river. That would attract Fuller. He spoke of it often.' Harkness chuckled. 'Always with

the same introductory words, *"of course, the fame matters not at all to me".'*
The old man shook his silver head. 'It mattered not less than the air he
breathed. Yes, the source of the Nile river and the fame that it would bring
its discoverer – that would fascinate him.'

Harkness stared for a long time at the empty spaces, dreaming perhaps,
visions awakening behind the bright black eyes. He aroused himself at last,
shaking his shaggy head as if to clear it.

'There would be only one other feat that would attract as much attention,
would be greeted with as much acclaim.' Harkness ran his spread hand
southwards down the parchment to cover another vast void in the web of
mountains and rivers. 'Here,' he said softly. 'The forbidden kingdom of the
Monomatapas.'

The name itself had an eerie quality. *Monomatapa.* The sound of it raised
the fine hair on the back of Zouga's neck.

'You have heard of it?' Harkness asked.

'Yes,' Zouga nodded. 'They say it is the Ophir of the Bible, where Sheba
mined her gold. Have you travelled there?'

Harkness shook his head. 'Twice I started out,' he shrugged. 'No white
man has travelled there. Even Mzilikazi's impis have not raided that far east.
The Portuguese made one attempt to reach the Emperor Monomatapa. That
was in 1569. The party was wiped out, and there were no survivors.'
Harkness made a sound of disgust. 'As you could expect of the Ports, they
abandoned any further attempt to reach Monomatapa. For the 200 years
since then they have been content to sit in their seraglios at Tete and
Quelimane, breeding half-castes, and picking up the slaves and ivory that
filter down out of the interior.'

'But still there are the legends of the Monomatapa. I heard them from my
father. Gold and great walled cities.'

Harkness stood up from the table with the grace of a man half his age and
crossed to an iron-bound chest against the wall behind his chair. The chest
was not locked but the lid required both the old man's skinny arms to lift it.

He came back with a draw-string bag made of softly tanned leather. It was
obviously weighty for he carried it in both hands. He pulled the mouth open,
and upended the contents on to the linen map.

There was no mistaking the lovely yellow metal, it had the deep glowing
lustre which has bewitched mankind for thousands of years. Zouga could not
resist the urge to reach out and touch it. It had a marvellous soapy feeling
against his fingertips. The precious metal had been beaten into heavy round
beads, each the size of the top joint of Zouga's little finger and the beads had
been strung on to animal sinew to form a necklace.

'Fifty-eight ounces,' Harkness told him, 'and the metal is of unusual purity,
I have had it assayed.'

The old man lifted the necklace over his own head and let it lie against the
snowy fall of his beard. It was only then that Zouga realized that there was
a pendant on the string of golden beads.

It was in the shape of a bird, a stylized falcon-like shape with folded wings.
It was seated upon a rounded plinth that was decorated with a triangular
design, like a row of sharks' teeth. The figure was the size of a man's thumb.
The gold metal was polished by the touch of human skin over the ages so that
some of the detail had been lost. The eyes of the bird were glassy green chips.

'It was a gift from Mzilikazi. He has no use for gold, nor for emeralds –
yes, the stones are emeralds,' Harkness nodded. 'One of Mzilikazi's warriors
killed an old woman in the Burnt Land. They found the leather pouch on her
body.'

'Where is the Burnt Land?' Zouga asked.

'I'm sorry.' Harkness fiddled with the little golden bird. 'I should have explained. King Mzilikazi's impis have laid waste to the land along his borders, in some places to a depth of a hundred miles and more. They have killed all who lived there and they maintain it as a buffer strip against any hostile force. The Boer commandos from the south particularly, but from any other hostile invader also. Mzilikazi calls it the Burnt Land, and it was here, to the east of his kingdom, that his border guards killed this solitary old woman. They described her as a very strange old woman, not of any known tribe, speaking a language they did not understand.'

Harkness lifted the necklace from his neck and dropped it carelessly back into the bag, and Zouga felt bereft. He would have liked to feel the full weight and the texture of the metal in his hands for a little longer. Harkness went on quietly:

'Of course you have heard the talk of gold and walled cities, like everybody else. But that is the closest I have ever come to corroboration.'

'Did my father know about the necklace?' Zouga asked, and Harkness nodded. 'Fuller wanted to purchase it, he offered me almost twice its gold value.'

They were both silent for a long while, each brooding on his own thoughts until Zouga stirred.

'How would a man like my father try to reach the Monomatapa?'

'Not from the south nor from the west. Mzilikazi, the Matabele king, will let no man pass through the Burnt Land. I feel that Mzilikazi has some deep superstition attached to the land beyond his eastern border. He does not venture there himself, nor does he allow others to do so.' Harkness shook his head. 'No, Fuller would have to try from the east, from the Portuguese coast, from one of their settlements.' Harkness began to trace out the possible approach marches on the linen chart. 'Here there are high mountains. I have seen them at a distance and they seemed a formidable barrier.' Outside, night had already fallen, and Harkness interrupted himself to order Zouga, 'Tell your groom to off-saddle the horses and take them to the stables. It is too late to return. You will have to stay overnight.'

When Zouga returned a Malay servant had drawn the curtains, lit the lanterns and laid a meal of yellow rice and chicken cooked in a fiery curry – and Harkness had opened another bottle of the Cape brandy. He went on talking as though there had been no interruption. They ate the meal and pushed the enamelled tin plates away to return to the map, and the hours passed unnoticed by either of them.

In the intimate lantern light, the sense of drama and excitement that gripped them both was heightened by the brandy they drank. Once in a while Harkness would rise to fetch some souvenir of his travels to reinforce a point, a sample of quartz rock in which the seams of native gold were clearly visible in the lamplight.

'If there is visible gold, it's rich,' Harkness told Zouga.

'Why did you never mine the reefs you found?'

'I could never stay long enough in one place,' Harkness grinned ruefully. 'There was always another river to cross, a range of mountains or a lake that I had to reach – or I was following a herd of elephant. There was never time to sink a shaft, or build a house, or raise a herd.'

When the dawn was rising, peeping into the huge gloomy room around the curtains, Zouga exclaimed suddenly, 'Come with me. Come with me to find Monomatapa!' And Harkness laughed.

'I thought it was your father you were intent on finding.'

'You know better!' Zouga laughed with him. Somehow he felt at home with the old man, as if he had known him all his life. 'But can you imagine my father's face when you come to rescue him?'

'It would be worth it,' Harkness admitted, and then the laughter faded, and gave way to an expression of such deep regret, of such consuming sorrow that Zouga felt a compulsion to reach out across the table and touch the misshapen shoulder.

Harkness pulled away from his touch. He had lived alone too long. He would never again be able to take comfort from a fellow man.

'Come with me,' Zouga repeated, letting his hand drop to the table-top between them.

'I have made my last journey into the interior,' Harkness said tonelessly. 'Now all I have are my paint pots and my memories.'

He lifted his eyes to the ranks of framed canvas with their brilliant joyous images.

'You are still strong, vital,' Zouga insisted. 'Your mind is so clear.'

'Enough!' Harkness' voice was harsh, bitter. 'I am tired now. You must go. Now, immediately.'

Zouga felt his anger rise hotly to his cheeks at the abrupt rejection, this sudden change of mood, and he stood quickly. For a few seconds he stood looking down at the old man.

'Go!' said Harkness again.

Zouga nodded abruptly. 'Very well.' His eyes slid down to the map. He knew he must have it at any price, though he sensed that there was no price that Harkness would accept. He must plan and scheme for it, but he would have it.

He turned and strode to the front door, and the dogs that had slept around their feet rose and followed him.

'Garniet!' Zouga shouted angrily. 'Bring the horses.' And he stood in the doorway rocking impatiently on his toes and heels, hands clasped behind his back, his shoulders stiff, not looking around at the thin stooped figure who still sat at the table in the lamp-light.

The groom brought the horses at last, and still without turning Zouga called roughly, 'Good day to you, Mr. Harkness.'

The reply was in a frail old man's quaver that he hardly recognized.

'Come again. We have more to discuss. Come back – in two days.'

The stiffness went out of Zouga's stance. He started to turn back, but the old man waved him away with a brusque gesture and Zouga stamped down the front steps, vaulted into the saddle and whipped his mount into a gallop along the narrow rutted track.

Harkness sat at the table until long after the hoof beats had faded. Strange that the pain had receded to the very back of his consciousness during the hours that he had sat with the youngster. He had felt young and strong, as though he had suckled upon the vigour and the youth of the other.

Then it had come back with a savage rush at Zouga Ballantyne's invitation, almost as if to remind him that his life was no longer his, that it was already forfeit to the hyena that lived deep in his belly, each day growing stronger, bigger, as it fed upon his vitals. When he closed his eyes he could imagine it, the way that he had seen it so often in the light of a thousand camp fires – up there in the wonderful land that he would never visit again. The thing within him had the same furtive slinking presence and he could taste the fetid breath of it in his throat. Now he gasped as the full strength of the pain returned, as the beast buried its fangs deeper into his gut.

He knocked over the chair in his haste to reach the precious bottle in the back of the cabinet and he gulped a mouthful of the clear pungent liquid without measuring it into the spoon. It was too much, he knew that, but each day he needed more to keep the hyena at bay, and each day the relief took longer to come.

He clung to the corner of the cabinet and waited for it. 'Please,' he whispered, 'please let it end soon.'

There were half a dozen messages and invitations awaiting Zouga on his return to the Cartwright estate that morning, but the one which gave him most excitement was on official Admiralty paper, a polite request to call upon the Hon. Ernest Kemp, Rear-Admiral of the Blue, Officer Commanding the Cape Squadron.

Zouga shaved and changed his clothing, selecting his best jacket for the occasion although it was a long dusty ride to Admiralty House. Despite missing a night's sleep, he felt vital and alert.

The Admiral's secretary kept him waiting only a few minutes before showing him through, and Admiral Kemp came around from behind his desk to greet Zouga amiably, for the young man came highly recommended and Fuller Ballantyne's name still commanded respect in Africa.

'I have some news which I hope will please you, Major Ballantyne. But first, a glass of Madeira?'

Zouga had to curb his impatience while the Admiral poured the syrupy wine. The Admiral's study was decorated richly, with velvet furnishings and a fashionable profusion of ornaments, small statues, bric-a-brac, stuffed birds in glass showcases, family portraits in ornate frames and pretty ceramics, potted plants and the kind of paintings which Zouga admired.

The Admiral was tall but stooped, as though to accommodate his long frame to the limited headroom between the decks of one of Her Majesty's ships. He seemed old for the responsible appointment he held, guarding the Empire's lifeline to India and the East, but the ageing may have been caused by ill-health rather than years. There were dark-toned pouches of skin below his eyes and other marks of sickness carved around his mouth and evident in the distended blue veins on the back of his hands as he handed a glass of Madeira to Zouga.

'Your good health, Major Ballantyne.' And then after he had tasted his own wine, 'I think I have a berth for you. A ship of my squadron anchored in Table Bay yesterday, and as soon as she has replenished her coal bunkers and revictualled I shall detach her for independent duty in the Mozambique channel.'

Zouga knew from his meetings with the directors of the Society for the Extinction of the Slave Trade, that one part of the Admiral's standing orders read:

'You are requested and required to dispose the ships of your squadron in such manner as most expediently to prevent vessels of whatever Christian nation from engaging in the slave trade on the coast of the African continent south of the equator.'

Clearly Kemp intended a sweep of the eastern seaboard with elements of his squadron, and Zouga felt awakening delight as the Admiral went on genially, 'It will not need much of a diversion for my ship to call at Quelimane, and to land you and your party.'

'I cannot thank you sufficient, Admiral.' His pleasure was transparent, and Admiral Kemp smiled in sympathy. He had put himself out more than his usual wont, for the youngster was attractive and likeable, deserving of encouragement, but now there were other matters awaiting his attention and as he pulled out his gold hunter and consulted it pointedly he went on,

'You should be ready to sail in five days' time.' He returned the watch to the fob of his uniform coat. 'I hope we will see you on Friday? My Secretary did send you an invitation, did he not? Your sister will be with you, I hope.'

'Indeed, sir.' Zouga stood in obedience to his dismissal. 'And my sister and I are honoured.'

In fact Robyn had said, 'I do not waste my evenings, Zouga, and I have no intention of enduring the company of a fleet of tipsy sailors nor of suffering the wagging tongues of their wives.'

The Cape wives were agog with the presence in their midst of the notorious Robyn Ballantyne who had impersonated a man and invaded, successfully, an exclusive masculine preserve. Half of them were deliciously scandalized, and the rest were awed and admiring. However, Zouga was certain that she would pay this price for their passage to Quelimane.

'Very well then.' Admiral Kemp nodded. 'Thank you for calling on me.' And then, as Zouga started for the door, 'Oh, by the way, Ballantyne. The ship is the *Black Joke*, Captain Codrington commanding. My Secretary will give you a letter for him, and I suggest you call upon him to introduce yourself and to learn the date of sailing.'

The name came as a shock, and Zouga checked his stride as he thought quickly of the complication which the choice of ship might bring.

Zouga was sensitive to any threat to the expedition, and Codrington had struck him as being a hot-headed, almost fanatical character. He could not afford any slur to his leadership, and Codrington had seen him sailing in company with a suspected slaver. He could not be sure what Codrington would do.

It was a delicate decision: accept the berth and risk Codrington's denunciation, or refuse the offer of passage and perhaps wait for months in Cape Town before another vessel offered them another.

If they were delayed that long, it would mean missing the cooler and dryer period between the monsoons, they would have to cross the pestilential and fever-ridden coastal lowlands in the most dangerous season.

Zouga made his decision. 'Thank you, Admiral Kemp. I will call on Captain Codrington as soon as possible.'

Thomas Harkness had asked Zouga to return on the second day, and the map was more important even than swift passage to Quelimane.

Zouga sent Garniet, the Cartwrights' groom, down to the beach with a sealed letter addressed to Captain Codrington and with instructions to take one of the water boats out to *Black Joke* and deliver it personally to Codrington. It was a warning, couched in the most polite terms, that Zouga and Robyn would call on the Captain the following morning. Zouga had become aware that his sister had an effect on men quite out of proportion to her physical appearance – even Admiral Kemp had asked for her personally – and he had no compunction in using her to take the edge off Codrington's temper. He would have to warn her to exert her charm, but now there was more important business.

He had mounted on Cartwright's big bay gelding and ridden halfway down the gravelled drive between the oaks, when a thought struck him and he swung the horse's head and cantered back to the guest bungalow again. The Naval Colt revolver was on the top layer of his chest, already fully loaded and with caps on the nipples. He carried it under the tail of his coat while he went back out to the tethered gelding, and then slipped the revolver surreptitiously into the saddlebag as he swung up into the saddle.

He knew he had to have the Harkness map at any price, but he deliberately refused to think what that price might be.

He pushed his mount hard up the steep road to the neck between the peaks, and gave him only a few minutes to blow before starting down the far slope.

The air of dilapidation which hung over the thatched building in the milkwood grove seemed to have deepened. It seemed totally deserted, silent and desolate. He dismounted and threw his reins over a milkwood branch and stooped to ease the girth. Then he quietly unfastened the buckle of the saddlebag and slipped the Colt into his waistband and pulled his coat over it.

As he started towards the stoep, the big ridge-backed Boerhound rose from where it had lain in the shadows and came to meet him. In contrast to its previous ferocity, the animal was subdued, its tail and ears drooping and it whined softly when it recognized Zouga.

He went up on to the stoep and hammered on the front door with his fist, and heard the blows reverberate through the room beyond. Beside him, the Boerhound cocked its head and watched him expectantly, but silence settled again over the old building.

Twice more Zouga beat upon the door, before he tried the handle. It was locked. He rattled the brass lock and put his shoulder to the door; but it was heavy teak in a solid frame. Zouga jumped down off the stoep and circled the house, squinting his eyes at the fierce reflected sunlight from the white-washed walls. The windows were shuttered.

Beyond the farmyard stood the old slave quarters, now used by Harkness' servant, and Zouga called loudly for him, but his room was deserted and the ashes cold in the cooking place. Zouga went back to the main house and stood by the locked kitchen door.

He knew that he should go back to his horse and ride away, but he needed the map, even if just for long enough to make a copy. Harkness was not here, and in three days, perhaps less, he would be sailing out of Table Bay.

There was a pile of broken rusted garden tools in the corner of the stoep. Zouga selected a hand scythe, and carefully probed the metal point of the blade into the crack between jamb and door. The lock was old and worn, the tongue slipped back easily under the blade and he jerked the door open with his free hand.

It was still not too late. He paused in the doorway for many seconds, and then he took a deep breath and stepped quietly into the gloom of the interior.

There was a long passage leading past closed doors towards the front room. Zouga went down it, opening doors quietly as he passed. In one room was a huge four-poster bedstead with the curtains opened and the bed clothes in disorder.

Quickly Zouga passed on to the main room. It was in semi-darkness and he stopped to let his eyes adjust, and immediately was aware of a low sound. The hive-murmur of insects seemed to fill the high room. It was a disturbing, almost menacing sound, and Zouga felt the skin prickle on his forearms.

'Mr. Harkness!' he called hoarsely, and the hum rose to a loud buzzing. Something alighted on his cheek and crawled across his skin. He struck it away with a shudder of revulsion and stumbled across to the nearest window. His fingers were clumsy on the fastening of the shutters. A shaft of white sunlight burned into the room as the shutter swung open.

Thomas Harkness sat in one of the carved wingback chairs across the cluttered table, and stared at Zouga impassively.

The flies crawled over him, big metallic blue and green flies that glittered in the sunlight. They swarmed with evident glee upon the deep dark wound in the centre of his chest. The snowy beard was black with clotted blood, and blood had formed a congealed pool beneath his chair.

Zouga was rooted by the shock for many seconds, and then reluctantly he took a step forward. The old man had propped one of his big-bored elephant guns against the table leg, reversing the weapon so the muzzle pressed into his own chest and his hands were still locked around the barrel.

'What did you do that for?' Zouga demanded stupidly, speaking aloud, and Harkness stared back at him.

Harkness had removed the boot from his right foot, and depressed the trigger with his bare toe. The massive impact of the heavy lead ball had driven the chair and the man in back against the wall, but he had retained his death grip on the barrel.

'That was a stupid thing to do.' Zouga took a cheroot from his case and lit it with a Swan Vesta. The smell of death was in the room, coating the back of his throat and the roof of his mouth. Zouga drew deeply on the tobacco smoke.

There was no reason at all to feel grief. He had known the old man for a single day and night. He had come here for one reason only – to get the map the best way he was able. It was ridiculous now to have the deep ache of sorrow turning his legs leaden and stinging the backs of his eyes. Was he mourning the passing of an era perhaps, rather than the man himself? Harkness and the legends of Africa were interwoven. The man had been history itself.

Slowly Zouga approached the figure in the chair, and then reaching out drew his palm slowly down over the old face, ruined by the elements and by pain, closing the lids down over the staring black eyes.

The old man looked more peaceful that way.

Zouga hooked one leg over the corner of the cluttered table, and smoked the cheroot slowly, in almost companionable silence with Thomas Harkness. Then he dropped the stub in the big copper spittoon beside the chair and went through to the bedroom.

He took one of the blankets off the bed and brought it back.

He brushed the flies away into an angry buzzing circle, and threw the blanket over the seated figure. As he drew it up over the head, he murmured softly, 'Get in close, old man, and go for the heart,' the advice that Harkness had given him as a farewell. Then he turned away briskly to the laden table, and began shuffling through the jumbled pieces of canvas and paper, and slowly his impatience turned to alarm – and then to panic as he hunted through pile after pile without finding the map.

He was panting when at last he straightened up and glared at the blanket-covered figure.

'You knew I was coming for it, didn't you!'

He left the table and went to the chest, lifted the lid against groaning hinges and the leather bag with its golden contents was gone also. He ransacked the chest down to its floorboards, but it was not there. Then he started to search in earnest, going carefully through any possible hiding-place in the crowded room. An hour later he went back and perched on the edge of the table once more.

'Damn you, for a cunning old bastard,' he said quietly. He took one more slow look about the room, making certain that he overlooked nothing. The painting of the lion hunt was no longer on the easel, he noticed.

Suddenly the humour of the situation struck him, and his scowl lightened, he began to chuckle ruefully to himself.

'You had the last joke on the Ballantynes, didn't you? By God, but you always did things your way, Tom Harkness, I'll grant you that.'

He stood up slowly, and placed his hand on the blanket-covered shoulder. 'You win, old man. Take your secrets with you then.' He could feel the twisted old bones through the cloth and he shook him gently and then he went out quickly to his horse for there was much to do. It took him the rest of the day to cross the neck again and reach the magistrate's court, then to get back with the coroner and his assistants.

They buried Thomas Harkness that evening, wrapped in the blanket, under the milkwood grove, for the heat was oppressive in the valley and they could not wait for a coffin to be carted out from the city.

Zouga left the coroner to take charge of the estate, to list the equipment and livestock in the yard and put his seals on the doors of the old house until the contents could be taken in.

Zouga rode home in the golden Cape dusk, his boots dusty and his shirt sticky with sweat. He was exhausted from the day's exertions, and low in spirits, still oppressed by grief for the old man, and angry with him for the last trick he had played.

The groom took his horse in front of the bungalow.

'Did you deliver the letter to Captain Codrington?' Zouga demanded, and hardly waited for the reply as he went up into the house. He needed a drink now, and while he poured whisky into a cut crystal glass, his sister came into the room, and reached up casually to kiss his cheek, wrinkling her nose at the tickle of his whiskers and the smell of his sweat.

'You had best change. We are dining with the Cartwrights tonight,' Robyn told him. 'I could not avoid it.' And then as an afterthought, 'Oh, Zouga, a coloured servant delivered something for you this morning, just after you had left. I had it put in the study.'

'Who is it from?'

Robyn shrugged. 'The servant spoke only kitchen Dutch and he seemed terrified. He fled before I could find someone to question him.'

With the whisky glass in his hand Zouga crossed to the door of the study, and stopped there abruptly. His expression changed, and he strode through the doorway.

Minutes later Robyn heard his shout of triumphant laughter, and curiously she crossed to the open door. Zouga stood beside the heavy carved stinkwood desk.

On the desk-top lay a draw-string bag of tanned and stained leather from which spilled a heavy necklace of gleaming gold; beside the bag was spread a magnificently illustrated map on a backing of linen parchment, and Zouga stood with his back to her. He held at arm's length a flamboyant picture in oils in a large frame, a figure on horseback with a band of ferocious wild animals in the foreground, and as she watched, Zouga reversed the picture. There was a message freshly carved into the wood of the frame.

For Zouga Ballantyne. May you find the road to all your Monomatapas – would only that I could have gone with you.

                                              Tom Harkness.

Zouga was laughing still, but there was a strange quality to the laughter and when he turned towards her she realized with a shock that her brother's eyes were bright with tears.

Zouga brushed the crumbs from his lips with the damask table napkin and chuckled as he picked up the sheet of newsprint and shook it open again at the second page.

'Damn me, Sissy, I should have known better than to leave you alone.' He read further and laughed outright. 'Did you really say that to him? Did you really?'

'I cannot remember my exact words,' Robyn told him primly, 'you must remember it was in the heat of battle.'

They sat on the terrace of the bungalow under the pergola of vines, through which the early sun flicked golden coins of light upon the breakfast table.

The previous day the editor of the *Cape Times*, with a speculator's eye to making a profit on Dr. Robyn Ballantyne's notoriety, had invited her on a tour of the military hospital at Observatory, and in innocence, Robyn had believed that the visit was at the invitation of the Colony's administration and she had welcomed the opportunity to widen her professional experience.

The visit had succeeded beyond the editor's most extravagant expectations, for the surgeon-general of the Colony had scheduled a tour for the same day and he had walked into the hospital's main operating room, followed by his staff, at the moment that Robyn was expressing herself on the subject of sponges to the hospital matron.

The surgeon's sponges were kept in pails of water, clean water from the galvanized rainwater tanks at the rear of the building. The pails were under the operating table, where the surgeon could reach them readily, and after swabbing away blood and pus and other matter the sponge was dropped into a collection tray, later to be washed out and returned to the original pail of fresh water.

'I assure you, doctor, that my nurses wash the swabs out most thoroughly.' The matron was a formidable figure with the flattened features of a bulldog bitch and the same aggressive thrust to her jaw. She stopped, plunged her hand into the pail, and selected one of the sponges and proffered it to Robyn.

'You can see for yourself how soft and white they are.'

''Just like the soft white germs that swarm in them.' Robyn was angry, with red spots of colour in her cheeks. 'Have none of you here ever heard of Joseph Lister?'

The surgeon-general answered her question from the doorway.

'The answer to that question, Doctor Ballantyne, is NO we have never heard of that person, whoever he may be. We do not have time to concern ourselves with the opinions of every crank or, for that matter, with male impersonators.'

The surgeon-general had a very good idea of the identity of the young woman before him. He had followed the gossip which was the Colony's main recreation, and he did not approve of Robyn.

On the other hand, Robyn had no idea as to the identity of the elderly gentleman with the bushy grey whiskers and beetling brows, though by the dried blood stains on the front of his frock coat she guessed that he was a surgeon of the old school, one who operated in his street clothes and let the stains advertise his profession. Here was a much more worthy adversary than the hospital matron, and she rounded on him with the battle light bright in her eyes.

'Then, sir, I am amazed that you admit so readily your ignorance and your bigotry.'

The surgeon-general spluttered for breath and a ready answer.

'By God, madam, you do not truly expect me to look for dangerous poisons in each speck of dust, in each drop of water, on my own hands even.' He held them up for her inspection, shaking them in Robyn's face. There were dark rinds of dried blood under the nails, for he had operated that morning. He pushed his face close to hers, and she drew back a little as his spittle flew angrily.

'Yes, sir,' she told him loudly. 'Look for them there, and on each breath you exhale, on those filthy clothes.'

The editor scribbled delightedly in his shorthand notebook, as the exchanges became more violent, more loaded with personal insult. He had not bargained for anything so spectacular, but the climax came when Robyn had goaded her adversary until he used an oath as potent as his rage.

'Your choice of words is as foul as these lowly little white sponges of yours,' she told him, and let him have the sponge full in the face, hurling it with all her strength so that water flew and dripped from his whiskers on to the front of his frock coat as Robyn marched from the operating room.

'You hit him?' Zouga lowered the newspaper, and stared across the table at his sister. 'Really, Sissy, sometimes you are no lady.'

'True,' Robyn agreed unrepentantly. 'But that is not the first time you have made that observation. Besides, I had no idea that he was the surgeon-general.'

Zouga shook his head in mock disapproval and read to her. 'His considered opinion of you, as expressed to the editor, is that you are a fledgling doctor of dubious qualification very recently obtained from an obscure school of medicine, by even more dubious means.'

'Oh, rich!' Robyn clapped her hands. 'He's a better orator than a surgeon.'

'He goes on to say that he is considering going to law to obtain redress.'

'For assault with a sponge.' Robyn laughed lightly as she stood up from the breakfast table. 'A fig for him, but we must hurry if we are to keep our appointment with Captain Codrington.'

Her mood was still gay as she stood beside Zouga in the stern of the water lighter when they came longside the steel side of the gunboat.

The south-east wind had raked the surface of Table Bay into a cottonfield of white caps, and had spread a thick white table-cloth of cloud upon the flat-topped mountain. The people of the Colony called this wind 'The Cape Doctor', for without it the summers would have been oppressive and enervating. However, it provided a constant hazard to shipping and the bottom of the bay was littered with wrecks. *Black Joke* had two men on her anchor watch as she lunged and fretted against her cable.

As the lighter came alongside, the thick canvas hoses were passed down and a dozen men on the pumps began to transfer the cargo into the gunboat's boiler room tanks, before any attempt was made to take visitors aboard.

As Robyn came up through the entry port to the maindeck she looked immediately to the quarterdeck. Codrington was in shirt-sleeves, he was a head taller than the group of warrant officers around him, and his sun-bleached blond hair shone in the sunlight like a beacon.

The group was giving its attention to the coal lighter which was secured against the port side of the ship.

'Have the hands secure a tarpaulin over the buckets.' Codrington shouted down to his boatswain in the lighter. 'Else you'll have us looking like a party of chimneysweeps.'

The deck was alive with the purposeful pandemonium of revictualling, bunkering and watering, and with Zouga beside her, Robyn picked her way through the litter. Codrington turned away from the rail and saw them.

He seemed younger than Robyn remembered, for his expression was relaxed and his manner easy. He had an almost boyish air when contrasted to the grizzled and weatherbeaten sailors about him, but the illusion was dispelled the moment he recognized his visitors. Suddenly his features were stern and the line of his mouth altered, the eyes chilled to the hardness of pale sapphires.

'Captain Codrington,' Zouga greeted him with his most studied charm. 'I am Major Ballantyne.'

'We have met before, sir,' Codrington acknowledged, making no effort to return the smile.

Zouga went on unruffled, 'May I present my sister, Doctor Ballantyne?'

Codrington glanced back at Robyn. 'Your servant, ma'am.' It was more a nod than a bow. 'I have read something of your further exploits since our last meeting in this morning's news-sheet.' For a moment the stern expression cracked, and there was a mischievous spark in the blue eyes. 'You have strong views, ma'am, and an even stronger right hand.'

Then he turned back to Zouga. 'I have orders from Admiral Kemp to convey you and your party to Quelimane. No doubt you will find our company dull, after your previous travelling companions.' Deliberately Codrington turned and looked across a half mile of wind creamed green water to where *Huron* still lay at her anchor, and for the first time Zouga fidgeted uncomfortably as he followed the direction of the Captain's eyes. Codrington went on. 'Be that as it may, I would be grateful if you could present yourselves aboard this ship before noon on the day after tomorrow when I expect a fair tide to leave the bay. Now you must excuse me. I must attend to the management of my ship.' With a nod, not offering to shake hands or make any other civility, Codrington turned away to his waiting warrant officers, and Zouga's charm deserted him. His face darkened and seemed to swell with anger at the abrupt dismissal.

'The fellow has a damnable cheek,' he growled fiercely to Robyn. For a moment he hesitated and then with a curt, 'Come, let us leave,' he turned, crossed the deck, and clambered down into the water lighter, but Robyn made no move.

She waited quietly until Codrington had finished the discussion with his boatswain, and looked up again, feigning surprise to see her still there.

'Captain Codrington, we left *Huron* on my insistence. That is why we are now seeking other passage.' She spoke in a low husky voice, but her manner was so intense that his expression wavered.

'You were correct. That ship is a slaver and St. John is a slave-master. I proved it.'

'How?' he demanded, his manner altering instantly.

'I cannot speak now. My brother—' She glanced back at the entry port, expecting her brother to reappear at any moment. He had given her strict instructions as to how he expected her to act towards Codrington.

'I will be at the landing-place at Rogger Bay this afternoon,' she went on quickly.

'What time?'

'Three o'clock,' she said, and turned away, lifted her skirts above her ankles and hurried to the ship's side.

Admiral Kemp sat impatiently in the immense carved abbot's chair which his junior officers referred to as the 'throne'. The size of it emphasized the thinness of the old man's body. It seemed his shoulders were too narrow to support the mass of gold lace which decorated his blue uniform. He clasped the arms of the chair to keep from fidgeting, for this young officer always made him uneasy.

Clinton Codrington leaned forward towards him and spoke quickly, persuasively, using the finely shaped hands to emphasize each point. The Admiral found this much energy and enthusiasm wearying. He preferred men with less mercurial temperament, who could be relied on to carry out orders to the letter without introducing startling improvisations.

Officers with a reputation for brilliance he viewed with deep suspicion. He had never had that reputation as a young man, in fact his nickname had been 'Slogger' Kemp, and he believed that the word brilliance was a pseudonym for instability.

The nature of duty on this station made it necessary for young men like Codrington to be detached for months at a time on independent service, instead of being kept with the battle fleet under the strict eye of a senior officer, ready with a signal of rebuke to check any hot-headedness.

Kemp had an uneasy conviction that he was going to be seriously embarrassed by this particular officer before his appointment of Commander to the Cape Squadron terminated, and allowed him to collect his knighthood and retire to the peace and beloved seclusion of his Surrey home. That his future plans had not already been prejudiced by young Codrington was only a matter of the utmost good fortune, and Kemp had difficulty keeping his expression neutral when he remembered the Calabash affair.

Codrington had run down on the slave barracoons at Calabash on a clear June morning so that the five Argentinian slave ships had spotted his topsails while he was thirty miles out, and had immediately begun frantically re-landing their cargoes of slaves on the beach.

By the time *Black Joke* reached them, the five captains were grinning smugly, their holds empty, and nearly two thousand miserable slaves in clear view squatting in long lines on the shore. To add to the slavers' complacency they were a good twenty nautical miles south of the equator, and therefore at that time beyond the jurisdiction of the Royal Navy. The barracoons had been sited at Calabash to take full advantage of this provision in the international agreements.

The slavers' complacency turned to indignation when the *Black Joke* ran out her guns, and under their menace sent boats with armed seamen on board them.

The Spanish masters, under their Argentinian flags of convenience, protested vigorously and volubly the presence of armed boarding parties.

'We are not a boarding party,' Codrington explained reasonably to the senior captain. 'We are armed advisors, and our advice is that you begin taking aboard your cargo again – and swiftly.'

The Spaniard continued his protests until the crack of a gun from the *Black Joke* drew his attention to the five nooses already dangling from the gunboat's yardarm. The Spaniard was certain that the nooses could not be put to the use for which they were very obviously intended – then he looked once more into the chilled sapphire eyes of the very young silver-haired English officer and decided not to make any bets on it.

Once the slaves were re-embarked the Englishman, their self-appointed armed advisor, gave them his next piece of unsolicited advice. That was that the slave fleet up-anchor and set a course which five hours later intercepted the equatorial line.

Here Captain Codrington made a very precise observation of the sun's altitude, consulted his almanac and invited the Spanish captain to check his workings and confirm his finding that they were now in 0°05' North latitude. Then the Englishman immediately arrested him and seized the five vessels; the armed advisors changing their status, without visible pain or discomfort, to that of prize crews.

When Codrington sailed his five prizes into Table Bay, Admiral Kemp listened aghast to the Spaniard's account of his capture, and then immediately retired to his bed with bowel spasms and migraine headache. From his darkened bedroom he dictated first the order confining Codrington to his ship and the ship to its anchorage, and then his horrified report to the First Lord of the Admiralty.

This episode, which might so easily have ended with Codrington court-martialled and beached for life and with the abrupt termination of Admiral Kemp's dogged advance towards his knighthood and retirement, had in fact brought both men riches and advancement.

The sloop carrying Kemp's despatch to the First Lord passed another southbound in mid-ocean, which in its turn bore despatches for the Admiral Commanding the Cape Squadron from not only the First Lord but the Foreign Secretary as well.

Kemp was requested and required in the future to apply the 'equipment clause' to the ships of all Christian nations – with the glaring exception of the United States of America – in all latitudes, both north *and* south of the equatorial line.

The despatches were dated four days previous to Codrington's raid upon the Calabash barracoons, making his actions not only legal but highly meritous.

From the very brink of professional disaster, Admiral Kemp had been snatched back, with his knighthood assured and a large sum of prize money paid into his account at Messrs. Coutts of the Strand. The five Spaniards were condemned at the next session of the Court of Mixed Commission at Cape Town. Kemp's own share of the prize money had amounted to several thousand pounds, that of his junior captain to nearly twice that amount, and both officers had received personal letters of commendation from the First Lord.

None of this had done anything to increase Kemp's trust or liking for his junior, and now he listened with mounting horror to the suggestion that he sanction the boarding and search of the American trading clipper, which was at present enjoying the hospitality of the port.

For some sickening moments Kemp contemplated his place in history as the officer who had precipitated the second war with the former American colonies. There was nothing equivocal about the view of the American Government as to the sanctity of their shipping, and there were specific sections of Kemp's Admiralty orders covering the subject.

'Admiral Kemp,' Codrington was clearly burning with enthusiasm for the enterprise, 'it is absolutely beyond question that the *Huron* is a slaver, and is equipped for the trade in terms of the act. She is no longer upon the high seas, but lying at anchor within British territorial waters. I can be aboard her within two hours, with impartial witnesses, a Supreme Court judge even.'

Kemp cleared his throat noisily. He had in fact tried to speak, but so appalled was he that the words had not reached his lips. Codrington seemed to take the sound as encouragement.

'This man, St. John, is one of the most infamous slavers of modern times. His name is a legend on the coast. They say he carried over 3,000 slaves one year across the middle passage. It's a golden opportunity for us.'

Kemp found his voice at last. 'I dined at Government House on Wednesday. Mr. St. John was in the company as his Excellency's personal guest. I considered Mr. St. John to be a gentleman, and I know he is a man of considerable substance and influence in his own country,' he said flatly, no trace of emotion in his voice. His self-control surprised even himself.

'He is a slaver.' Robyn Ballantyne spoke for the first time since she had seated herself at the window of the Admiral's study. The two men had forgotten her existence, but now they both turned to her.

'I have been inside the *Huron*'s main hold and she is fully equipped for the trade,' she said, her voice low but clear, and Kemp felt a sour feeling rising within him. He wondered that he had thought this young woman enchanting at their first meeting. Kemp liked young females and he had personally instructed his secretary to send the invitations to the Ballantynes, brother and sister, but now he regretted it. He could see, of course, that what he had mistaken for spirit was in fact the mischievousness of the born troublemaker, and that far from being pretty she was in fact downright plain, with a large nose and heavy jaw. He had found her a refreshing change from the simpering and giggling young ladies of the Colony – and realized now that the preference had been unwise. He wondered if he could have his secretary withdraw the invitation.

'I would think, Admiral Kemp, that it was your duty to send a search party aboard the *Huron*,' Robyn told him – and Kemp leaned back in the big chair and breathed heavily through his mouth. As an Admiral of the Blue it had been some years since anybody had dared point out his duty for him. His grip on his self-control slackened.

He stared at the young person. Did he detect a peculiar venom in her voice? He wondered. She had been a passenger on *Huron*. She had left the ship the instant it reached Table Bay. There was no doubt the woman was 'fast' and that Captain St. John was a handsome man.

There was a fine story here, Kemp concluded, as he asked drily, 'Is it true, Miss Ballantyne, that you assaulted the surgeon-general in a fit of ungovernable rage?'

Robyn gaped at him for a moment, the change of direction taking her completely off-balance, and before she could reply he went on,

'You are clearly a highly emotional young lady. I would have to consider very carefully committing a hostile act against an important citizen of a friendly nation on your unsupported testimony.'

He pulled the gold watch from his fob pocket, and consulted it with his full attention.

'Thank you for calling on me, Miss Ballantyne.' Once again he did not use her professional title. 'We look forward to seeing you tomorrow evening. Perhaps you would allow me a private word with Captain Codrington.'

Robyn felt her cheeks burning as she rose from the window seat.

'Thank you, Admiral, you have been very kind and patient,' she said tightly, and swept from the room.

Kemp was not so mild with Codrington. While the young Captain stood to attention before him, he leaned forward in the throne and the veins stood out like twisted blue ropes in the back of his hands as he gripped the arms of the chair.

'You were misguided in bringing that young person here to discuss navy business,' he snapped.

'Sir, I needed to convince you.'

'That's enough, Codrington. I have heard all you have to say. Now you listen to me.'

'Aye, aye, sir.'

'You are naive not to take into account the changed circumstances in the American administration. Are you not aware that Mr. Lincoln is likely to be elected to the presidency?'

'I am, sir.'

'Then even you may be dimly aware that very delicate considerations are in the balance. The Foreign Office is confident that the new administration will have a markedly changed attitude to the trade.'

'Sir!' Codrington agreed stiffly.

'Can you imagine what it will mean to us to have full right of search of American shipping on the high seas?'

'Sir.'

'We will have that – once Mr. Lincoln takes the oath, and if no junior officers of this service take independent action to prejudice the attitude of the Americans.'

'Sir.' Codrington stood rigid, staring over the Admiral's head at a painting of a lightly veiled Venus on the panelled wall behind him.

'Codrington,' Kemp spoke now with cold menace, 'you have had one very close shave at Calabash. I swear to you, if you let your wild nature get the better of you once more, I will have you hounded from the service.'

'Sir.'

'You are now under the strictest injunction not to approach closer than a cable's length to the trade clipper *Huron*, and if you should encounter her again at sea, you will pay her passing honours and give her a wide berth. Do I make myself sufficiently clear?'

'Sir.' Only Codrington's lips moved, and the Admiral took two long controlled breaths before going on.

'When will you sail for the Mozambique channel?' he asked, his voice more reasonable.

'I have your orders to take the flood on Saturday, sir.'

'Can you advance that sailing?'

'Yes, sir, but it would mean leaving without fully charged magazines – we expect the powder barge alongside at dawn on Saturday.'

Kemp shook his head, and sighed. 'I would feel better with you at sea,' he muttered. 'But, very well then, I will look to see you flying the Blue Peter at first light on Saturday morning.'

Robyn Ballantyne was waiting for him in the borrowed Cartwright carriage, under the portico of Admiralty House.

Codrington came down the steps, with his cocked hat under his arm and climbed stiffly into the buttoned leather seat beside her.

The Hottentot coachman flicked his whip at the shiny rumps, and they swayed in unison as the carriage jerked away down the tree-lined driveway.

Neither of them spoke until they had left the Admiralty grounds, and were whirling down the hill towards the Liesbeeck bridge with the coachman holding them on a light brake.

'What do we do now?' Robyn asked.

'Nothing,' said Clinton Codrington.

Twenty minutes later as they came around the shoulder of the mountain and looked down at the bay where *Huron* rode at anchor, Robyn spoke again.

'Can't you think of anything to stop this monster?'

'Can you?' he asked sharply, and neither of them spoke again until they reached the landing-place.

The fishing-boats were in and beached already, their catch laid out on the sand, a glittering silver and ruby-red pile around which the housewives and their servants bartered and bargained with the brown barelegged fishermen, while the fish horns blared to summon more customers down from the town. The two in the parked carriage watched the commotion with unnatural attention, avoiding each other's eyes.

'You will be at the Admiralty ball tomorrow night? I heard Slogger Kemp say so.'

'No,' Robyn shook her heard fiercely. 'I cannot abide the frivolous chatter and silly behaviour of these occasions, and I particularly do not want to be again the guest of that man.'

Codrington turned to her for the first time since they had reached the landing. She was a fine-looking woman, he thought, with that clear lustre to her skin and the thoughtful dark-green eyes under their dark curved brows. He liked a tall strong woman, and he had learned enough of her spirit to accord her respect, a respect that could easily become fascination, he realized.

'Could I prevail upon you to change your mind?' he asked quietly, and she glanced at him, startled. 'I would undertake to provide sober conversation and a dignified dancing partner.'

'I do not dance, Captain.'

'That is a great relief,' he admitted. 'For neither do I, when I have a choice.' He smiled. She could not remember seeing him smile before. It changed him completely. The coldness went from the pale blue eyes and they darkened with merriment while two deep laughter lines formed at the corner of his mouth and arched up to touch the thin straight nose.

'Slogger Kemp keeps a wonderful chef.' He was wheedling now. 'Fine food and serious conversation.'

His teeth were porcelain white and very regular against the deep-water tan. She felt the corners of her own mouth tugging upwards, and he saw the change in her and pressed his advantage.

'I may have further news, some further plan for *Huron* to discuss with you.'

'That makes it irresistible.' She laughed outright at last, with surprisingly unforced gaiety that made some of the nearest bystanders glance around at her and smile in sympathy.

'I will call for you. Where? When?' He had not realized how attractive she truly was until she laughed.

'No.' She laid her hand on his forearm. 'My brother will accompany me, but if you are there I look forward to our momentous conversation.' She felt the devil in her again, and squeezed his arm, finding pleasure in his immediate response, the way the muscles in his forearm corded under her finger-tips.

'Wait,' she told the coachman and watched the slim tall figure go down the beach to where *Black Joke*'s whaler waited for him.

He was wearing his dress uniform for the visit to his commanding Admiral. The gold lace epaulettes emphasized the breadth of his shoulders and his sword belt nipped his waist. Abruptly, she wondered whether his body hair was as blond as the queue that was twisted up at the nape of his neck – and then instantly was shocked and agitated at herself. She would never have harboured a thought like that before. Before what? she asked herself and the answer was clear; before that night on *Huron*. Mungo St. John had much to answer for. Comfortably placing blame where it belonged, she pulled her eyes away from the lithe figure of Clinton Codrington and leaned forward to tell the coachman,

'Home, please.'

She would not attend the Admiral's ball, she decided, and then she began to recite silently to herself the Christian articles of faith.

However, Zouga prevailed over her good intentions. The two of them shared the open carriage with the eldest, unmarried Cartwright daughter, for it was one of the balmy nights of a Cape autumn.

Cartwright and his wife followed in the closed carriage, in serious discussion for the entire journey.

'I am sure he is quite taken with Aletta,' Mrs. Cartwright had stated.

'My dear, the fellow has no fortune whatsoever.'

'Expectations,' Mrs. Cartwright told him benignly. 'I understand he will make thousands from this expedition. He is one of those young men who will get on in life, I am certain of that.'

'I prefer money in the bank, my dear.'

'He has created quite a stir, I assure you – such a serious and sensible young man, and so very attractive. It would be quite a feather in Aletta's cap, and you could make a place for him in the firm.'

Every lamp in Admiralty House was lit and a blaze of golden light welcomed the guests. There were coloured lanterns hung in the trees to illuminate the garden.

The marine band in scarlet and gold had converted the open gazebo into a bandstand, and already there were dancers on the open-air dance floor whirling furiously through the opening waltz, waving and calling greetings to the late-comers in the carriages as they trotted up the curved driveway and took their turn to alight under the portico of the main entrance.

Bewigged footmen in household uniform with silken hose and buckled shoes placed the steps and handed down the ladies on to the welcoming red carpet. At the head of the stairs the major domo announced each group in a low throaty bellow.

'Major and Doctor Ballantyne. Miss Cartwright.'

Robyn had not grown altogether accustomed to the scandalized ripple of feminine interest that followed her entrance to any public gathering here in the Colony. The quick exchange of glances, the nods and murmurs behind covering fans. It still left her with a heightened pulse and a feeling of bitter disdain for all of them.

'Did you bring your sponge, Sissy? They expect you to hit somebody with it,' Zouga murmured, and she shook his arm to silence him, but he went on: 'or to drop your skirts and run up the staircase in your breeches.'

'You are wicked.' She felt the tension go out of her, and she smiled her thanks at him and they were into the throng of uniforms, gold lace on navy blue or dress scarlet, with, here and there, the dead black of evening dress relieved by the high stock and white lace ruffles of silk shirts.

The women's skirts were taffeta and flounced silk over pyramids of petticoats. However, they were at least two years behind the London fashions, for only the most daring ladies had bared their shoulders and powdered them dead white.

Robyn's own dress made no concession to fashion, for it was years old, the only one that she possessed even vaguely suitable for the occasion. The cloth was wool, the skirt narrow, the bodice adorned with neither seed pearls nor sequins. There were neither ostrich feathers nor diamantines to sparkle in her hair. She should have been dowdy, but instead she was strikingly different.

When she had told Codrington that she did not dance it was because she had never had the occasion, and she regretted it now as she watched Zouga lead Aletta Cartwright on to the floor and swirl away in the graceful dip and turn of the waltz.

She knew that nobody would invite her to dance, and that if they did she would be awkward and untutored. She turned away quickly – seeking a familiar or friendly face. She did not want to be left standing alone in the crowd. She began bitterly to regret that she had not stood by her resolution to stay away.

Her relief came with such a rush that she could have thrown her arms around his neck and embraced him. Instead she said evenly, 'Ah, Captain Codrington. Good evening.'

He really was one of the better-looking men in the room, she thought. She could sense the resentment of some of the younger women, so quite deliberately she took his arm as he offered it, but was surprised that he led her immediately through into the garden.

'He's here!' he said quietly, as soon as they were out of earshot of the others.

She did not have to ask who, and she felt the little jolt of shock that kept her silent for a moment.

'You've seen him?'

'He arrived five minutes before you did – in the Governor's carriage.'

'Where is he now?'

'He went into Slogger's study – with the Governor.' Clinton's face was set and hard. 'The fellow flaunts himself.'

A servant approached them with a silver tray of champagne flutes. Robyn shook her head distractedly but Clinton took a glass and drank it in two gulps.

'The devil of it is that nobody can touch him,' he fumed.

When the evening turned chill, the Marine band moved on to the orchestral balcony above the ballroom floor and punched out the dance tunes with a bouncing martial air that set the dancers spinning and prancing.

One dancer stood out above the others, not merely because of his physical height. When the others hopped and strained with gasping breath and flushed faces, Mungo St. John seemed to turn and dip and glide with measured, unhurried grace although he completed a circuit of the ballroom floor more swiftly than any other dancer. Always there was one of the prettiest women in the room swinging in the circle of his arms, laughing up at him, cheeks flushed with excitement, and a dozen others watching him with covert envy over the shoulders of their own partners.

Clinton and Robyn watched him also, from the raised and colonnaded balcony that surrounded the dance floor. They stood in a small circle of Clinton's brother officers and their ladies, making no serious effort to contribute to the light chatter around them.

Robyn found herself hoping that St. John would look up at her, would catch her eye so that she could flash her hatred at him; but he never glanced once in her direction.

She even thought of suggesting to Clinton Codrington that they should dance, despite her earlier protestations, but quickly decided against it. She knew that as a dancer, the naval captain would not be able to stand comparison with the elegant American.

When she went in to dinner on Clinton's arm, she saw St. John ahead of them. He had a blond woman on his arm, notoriously the Colony's prettiest, richest and most voracious widow. Her coiffure was an elaborate creation of diamanté and ostrich feathers, her shoulders were bared and she showed more of her bosom than she concealed beneath a brocaded bodice stiff with seed pearls.

Mungo St. John wore simple black and white evening dress with more panache than any of the most elaborate military uniforms around him.

Robyn watched the woman tap his shoulder with her fan to attract his attention and then reach up on tiptoe to whisper in his ear, while St. John stooped gravely to listen.

'The woman's a brazen whore,' Robyn hissed, and beside her Clinton covered his shock at the word, and then nodded.

'And he's the very devil himself.'

It was as though St. John heard them, for he glanced up and saw them watching him across the room. He bowed and smiled at Robyn.

It was such an intimate, completely knowing smile that she felt as though he had stripped her naked again, the way he had in the stern cabin of *Huron*, and immediately she felt the same feeling of helplessness overwhelm her.

With a huge effort she managed to turn away, but Clinton had been watching her. She could not meet his eyes, she felt he would be able to read it all if she did.

Two hours after midnight the Marine band was playing the less strenuous airs for the lovers and romantics who still circled the ballroom floor, but most of the company had gone up to the cardrooms on the first floor, if not to play themselves, then to crowd around the tables and watch with hushed attention and the occasional bursts of applause at a particularly audacious or successful coup.

In the largest room the game was whist and the players were Slogger Kemp and the older guests. In the second room the younger set were at the light-hearted chemin-de-fer and Zouga smiled at Robyn as she passed. He and Aletta Cartwright were playing a single hand between them, and the girl squealed with glee as she won a handful of silver shillings.

Robyn and Clinton passed on into the third and smallest salon. Here it was the game that had once been popular only in America. Recently, however, it had come into sudden vogue at court when the Queen had found it fascinating, and in consequence it was all the rage around the empire despite the odd name – poker.

In spite of Her Majesty's interest in it, it was still not considered a game for ladies to play in mixed company. Only men sat at the green baize, although the ladies fluttered around them like bright butterflies.

Mungo St. John sat facing the doorway so that Robyn saw him the instant she stepped into the room. He lazed in his chair, the waves of his dark hair unruffled and sleeked down as if carved from polished ebony, holding a tight fan of cards low against the snowy lace front of his shirt. There was a long black unlit cheroot between his teeth, and as Robyn watched the blond widow leaned across his shoulder displaying the creamy cleavage between her breasts and held a Vesta to the cheroot.

St. John sucked flame into the tip of the cheroot, blew a long feather of blue smoke and thanked her with a slant of his eyes before he made his next bid.

He was an obvious winner, a careless pile of gold spilled across the table in front of him, each coin embossed with the Grecian style head of Queen

Victoria looking much younger than her forty-one years – and as they watched, he won again.

Excitement seemed to exude from the man like a tangible substance, infecting the women about the table so they exclaimed at every wager he made, and sighed with disappointment if he folded his cards and declined to play a hand. The same excitement spread to the five other men at the table. It was obvious in the glitter of the eyes, in the white knuckles of the fingers that held their cards, in the rash calls and the imprudent urge that made them remain in play long after chance and the odds were evidently against them. It was clear that all of them saw St. John as the main adversary, and the tension went out of each hand if he was not in play.

Robyn felt herself held by the same fascination, and unconsciously tightened her grip on Clinton's arm as the suspense mounted in each hand and the gold coins tinkled in the centre of the table, and she heard herself gasp with chagrin or relief at the show of cards that ended each hand.

Unconsciously, she had moved closer to the table drawing Clinton with her, so that when one of the players exclaimed with disgust, 'Fifty guineas is enough for one night. Will you excuse me, gentlemen?' gathered his few remaining coins from the table and pushed back his chair, they had to stand back to allow him to leave.

With surprise Robyn felt Clinton disengage her fingers from his arm, and then he slipped quietly into the vacant chair.

'May I join you, gentlemen?'

There were preoccupied grunts of acknowledgement but only St. John looked up and asked civilly,

'Are you aware of the stakes, Captain?'

Clinton did not reply but took a roll of five-pound notes from an inside pocket and placed them beside him. The amount surprised Robyn, it could not have been less than one hundred pounds. Then she remembered that Clinton Codrington had been for many years one of the most successful blockade commanders on the slave coasts. Her brother had repeated to her the rumour that during that period he had won prize money in excess of ten thousand pounds, yet somehow she had never thought of him as a rich man.

Then with sudden intuition Robyn realized that by that gesture Clinton had laid down a silent challenge, and with a little smile Mungo St. John had accepted it.

Robyn felt a flare of alarm. She was certain that Clinton Codrington had chosen an opponent too experienced and skilled. She remembered that Zouga who relied on gambling to eke out his regimental pay, had been no match for the man, even with moderate stakes, and in his frustration Clinton had been drinking steadily during the evening. She was sure his judgement would be faulty even if he had any knowledge of the game.

Almost immediately St. John subtly altered the style of his play, doubling the stakes before the draw, crowding the game, dominating it, playing from the strength and confidence of his already considerable winnings, and Clinton seemed immediately uncertain of himself, hesitant in accepting the doubled stakes, discarding rather than going at risk for more than a few guineas, lacking the nerve to meet St. John head on.

Robyn moved slightly to a position from which she could watch both men. Clinton was pale under the deep-water tan, the rims of his nostril bloodless and his lips compressed into a thin line, and she remembered that he had drunk a dozen glasses of champagne during the evening.

He was nervous, indecisive, every watcher could sense it, and their disappointment was evident. They had hoped for a dramatic confrontation when Clinton had made the flamboyant gesture of placing a hundred pounds on the table, but when the amount was slowly whittled away by unexciting over-cautious play, their interest was transferred to a lively exchange between Mungo St. John and one of the Cloete sons, the family that owned half the Constantia valley with its fabled vineyards.

They laughed at the light banter with which the two men made their bets, and admired the grace of the loser and the easy manner of the winner. The other players at the table were almost forgotten, picking up an uncontested ante or falling before the aggression of the leading pair.

Robyn could only pity Clinton, nervous and pale – when he fumbled his cards to expose prematurely one of his few winning hands and suffer the chuckles of the spectators as he picked up odd guineas instead of the fifty that might have been his if he had played it correctly.

Robyn tried to catch his eye, to make him leave before he was further humiliated, but Clinton played on doggedly refusing to look up at her.

Cloete won a hand with four of a kind and as was his right called for a pot to celebrate his good fortune.

'Three of a kind to open the pot and guinea sweeteners,' he announced and grinned across the table at St. John. 'To your liking, sir?'

'Very much so,' St. John smiled back, and the other players tried to cover their discomfiture. It was a dangerous game – requiring one of the players to be dealt an initial three of a kind to commence the game, but for every unsuccessful deal each player had to contribute a guinea to the pot, and when a lucky player achieved the minimum requirement, he could advance the stakes by as much again as was in the centre of the table. It could amount swiftly to a huge sum, and there was no option of withdrawal – a very dangerous game.

Ten times the deal failed to produce an opening hand, and then with the pot at seventy guineas Mungo St. John announced quietly,

'She is open, gentlemen, as wide open as my mother-in-law's mouth.'

Play had stopped at the other tables in the room as St. John went on,

'It will cost you another seventy iron men to stay in the game.' He had doubled the pot, and the watchers applauded the bet and then looked eagerly to the other players.

'I am your man,' said Cloete, but at last there was a breathlessness to his voice. He counted out the notes and gold coins and spilled them into the considerable pile in the centre.

Three other players withdrew, dropping their cards with alacrity, clearly relieved to have got out of danger for a mere ten guineas, but Clinton Codrington hunched miserably over his cards and St. John had to prod him gently for his decision.

'Please don't hurry, Captain. We have all evening.'

And Clinton looked up at him and nodded jerkily, not trusting his voice, then pushed a sheath of notes into the centre of the table.

'Three players,' St. John said, and swiftly counted the money in the pot. 'Two hundred and ten guineas!'

The next bid could double that amount, and the one after could redouble it. The room was silent now, the players at the other tables in the room had left their seats to watch as the dealer gave two cards to Mungo St. John to replace those he tossed into the centre of the table. He was buying honestly, trying to add to the triplets with which he had opened the pot, neither faking a flush nor a full house. Cloete bought three cards, evidently looking for a third to a high pair – and then it was Clinton's turn to request cards.

'One,' he mumbled, and held up a single finger. The finger quivered slightly. The dealer slid the card across to him and he covered it with his hand unable to bring himself to look at it yet. It was all too obvious that he was attempting to find the missing card to a flush or straight.

'The opener to bet,' said the dealer. 'Mr. St. John.'

There was a pause as St. John fanned open his cards, and then he said evenly without a change of expression.

'The bet is doubled.'

'Four hundred and twenty guineas,' said somebody loudly, and this time nobody applauded but every eye swivelled to Cloete as he consulted his cards. Then shook his head abruptly, and let them drop. He had not found another king to go with the original pair.

Now everybody looked to the remaining player. A transformation had come over Clinton Codrington, it was hard to define it exactly. There was just a touch of colour under the tanned cheeks, his lips were slightly parted and for the first time he was looking directly at St. John – but somehow confidence and a barely suppressed eagerness shone from him. There was no mistaking it. The man positively glowed.

'Double again,' he said loudly. 'Eight hundred and forty guineas.' He could hardly contain himself, and every man in the room knew he had found the card he needed to transform his hand from worthlessness to a certain winner.

St. John did not have to deliberate more than a few seconds.

'Congratulations,' he smiled. 'You found what you were looking for, I must concede this one to you.'

He dropped his cards and pushed them away from him.

'May we see the cards you required to open the pot?' Clinton asked diffidently.

'I beg your pardon.' St. John's tone was lightly ironical, and he flipped his hand, face upwards. There were three sevens and two odd cards.

'Thank you,' said Clinton. His manner had changed again. The trembling eagerness, the nervous indecision, both had disappeared. He was calm, almost icy as he began to gather in the piles of scattered gold and bank notes.

'What cards did he have?' demanded one of the women petulantly.

'He does not have to show them,' her partner explained. 'He beat the others out without a showdown.'

'Oh, I'd die to see them,' she squeaked.

Clinton paused in gathering his winnings and looked up at her.

'I beg of you, madam, not to do so,' Clinton smiled. 'I would not wish to have your life on my conscience.'

He turned his cards face upwards on the green baize, and it took the company many seconds to realize what they were looking at. There were cards of every suit, and not one of them matched another.

There were delighted exclamations, for the hand was utterly worthless. It could have been beaten by a single pair of sevens, to say nothing of the triple sevens which St. John had discarded.

With this valueless hand the young naval captain had beaten the American, out-smarting him for almost 900 guineas. It was a spectacular coup. The company gradually realized how carefully it had been engineered, how Clinton had lured his adversary, how he had made a pretence at fumbling uncertainly until exactly the right moment, the moment when he had struck boldly and decisively. They burst into spontaneous applause, the ladies oohing with admiration and the men calling congratulation.

'Oh jolly good play, sir!'

St. John held the smile, but his lips drew tighter with the effort, and there was a savage glitter in his eyes as he stared at the cards and realized how he had been duped.

The applause subsided, some of the spectators were beginning to turn away still discussing the hand, and St. John began gathering the cards to shuffle when Clinton Codrington spoke. His voice was low but clear, so that nobody about the tables could miss a word of it.

'Even a black-birder's luck can run out at last,' he said. 'I must admit, I would rather have caught you at your dirty slaver's game than beaten you out of a few guineas tonight.'

The company froze, gaping at Clinton with expressions of horror and comical amazement. The silence in the room seemed impenetrable, the only sound was the ripple and click of the cards as Mungo St. John began to shuffle them, splitting the pack with a click and then running them into each other under his thumbs in a blur of movement.

He did not look down at his hands as he rippled the cards. He never removed his gaze from Clinton's face, and his smile had still not slipped – only there was a flush of colour under the dark suntouched skin.

'You like to live dangerously?' St. John smiled the question.

'Oh, no.' Clinton shook his head. 'I am in no danger. In my experience, slavers are all cowards.'

Mungo St. John's smile disappeared, extinguished instantly, and his expression was coldly murderous, but his fingers never broke the rhythm of cut and ripple, and the cards flowed under his fingers as Clinton went on evenly, 'I was led to believe that so-called Louisiana gentlemen had some exalted code of honour,' he shrugged. 'I suggest, sir, that you are a living contradiction of that notion.'

Every listener was stunned. Not one of them could doubt what they were hearing; the accusation of slave-dealing. To an Englishman, there could be no worse insult.

The last English duels had been fought in 1840 when Lord Cardigan shot Captain Tuckett, and in 1843 when Munro shot his brother-in-law Colonel Fawcett. In consequence of these encounters, the Queen had made her desire for reform known, and the articles of war were amended in the following year, making duelling an offence. Of course, gentlemen still went abroad, mostly to France, to settle affairs of honour with pistol or sword. But this was Cape Colony, one of the jewels of the Empire and the Naval Captain was one of Her Majesty's commissioned officers. The evening had proved diverting beyond any expectations, and now there was the promise of blood and violent death charging the gaming-room.

'Gentlemen,' an urgent persuasive voice interrupted them. The Admiral's flag-captain had come through from the whist room at the Admiral's orders. 'There has been some misunderstanding.'

But neither of the two men as much as glanced in his direction.

'I don't think there has been any misunderstanding at all,' Mungo St. John said coldly, his gaze still locked with Clinton's. 'Captain Codrington's insults cannot possibly be misinterpreted.'

'Mr. St. John, may I remind you that you are on British soil, subject to Her Majesty's laws.' The flag-captain was becoming desperate.

'Oh, Mr. St. John sets little store by laws. He sails his slave ship, fully equipped, into a British harbour.' Clinton stared at the American with cold blue eyes. He would have gone on, but St. John interrupted him harshly, speaking to the flag-captain but addressing the words to Clinton Codrington. 'I would not dream of abusing Her Majesty's hospitality. In any event I will sail with the tide before noon this day, and in four days I shall be far beyond

Her Majesty's territory, in latitude 31° 38′ south. There is a wide river mouth there, between tall bluffs of stone – a good landing and a wide beach. It is unmistakable.' St. John stood up. He had recovered his urbane air, and now he adjusted the ruffles of his shirt front and gave the lovely widow his arm. He paused for a moment to look down at Clinton. 'Who knows but that you and I may meet again, when we must certainly discuss the question of honour once more. Until then I give you good morrow, sir.'

He turned away and the spectators fell back ahead of him and seemed to form a guard of honour as St. John and his lady sauntered casually from the room.

The flag-captain flung one furious glare at Clinton.

'The Admiral wishes to speak with you, sir,' and then he hurried after the departing couple, followed them down the curve of the staircase and caught up with them at the double doors of carved teak.

'Mr. St. John, Admiral Kemp asked me to convey his compliments. He sets no store by the rash accusations of one of his junior captains. If he did, he would be obliged to send a party aboard your ship.'

'None of us would like that,' St. John nodded. 'Nor the consequences.'

'Indeed,' the flag-captain assured him. 'Nevertheless the Admiral feels that, in the circumstances, you should take advantage of the next fair wind and tide to proceed on your passage.'

'Please return my compliments to the Admiral – and convey my assurance that I will clear the Bay before noon.'

At that moment the widow's coach came up, and St. John nodded distantly to the flag-captain and handed the lady up the steps.

From the deck of *Black Joke* they watched the clipper raise her anchor, her master skilfully backing and filling his topsails to run up on her cable, and break the anchor flukes out of the mud and sand of the bottom of the bay. As soon as it was free, he piled on his canvas, sail after sail bursting out in quick successive explosions of brilliant white, and *Huron* tore eagerly out of Table Bay on the south-east wind.

She would be out of sight beyond the lighthouse at Mouille Point for almost four hours before *Black Joke* was ready to follow her out of the bay. The Admiralty powder barge was alongside, and all the elaborate precautions for taking on explosives were in force. The red swallow-tail warning flag at the masthead, the boiler fires in the engine room extinguished, the crew barefooted, the decks kept wet with a constant stream from the hoses to prevent a chance spark, and each powder barrel carefully inspected for leakage as it came aboard.

While the engineer refired his boilers the last members of the Ballantyne expedition came aboard. Once again, Zouga's letters of introduction had proved invaluable, and together with his persuasive manner had provided him with the most valuable addition so far to his expedition.

Old Tom Harkness had warned him during the long night discussion, 'Don't try to cross the Chimanimani Mountains without a force of trained men. Beyond the narrow coastal belt there is only one law and it is promulgated from the muzzle of a gun.'

On the strength of the letters, the commander of the Cape Town garrison had allowed Zouga to ask for volunteers from his regiment of Hottentot Infantry. 'They are the only natives of Africa who understand the working of a firearm,' Harkness had told him. 'They are the devil with drink and women, but they can fight and march, and most of them are hardened to fever and famine. Pick them carefully and watch them every moment, night as well as day.'

Zouga's request for volunteers had been most enthusiastically received. By reputation the Hottentots could scent plunder or a willing lady from fifty miles, and the pay and rations that Zouga offered were almost thrice that of the British army. They had volunteered to a man and Zouga's difficulty had been in selecting ten of them.

Zouga had taken an instant liking to these wiry little men, with their almost oriental features, slanted eyes and high cheekbones. Despite appearances, they were more African than almost any other breed. They were the original inhabitants that the first navigators had found on the beach at Table Bay – and they had taken readily to the white man's ways, and more than readily to his vices.

Zouga had solved his problem by making one selection only. This was a man with an ageless face, it might have been forty years or eighty, for the skin was the colour and texture of a papyrus parchment, each wrinkle seemed to have been eroded into it by wind and driven dust, but the little peppercorns of hair that covered his skull were untinged with silver.

'I taught Captain Harris to hunt elephant,' he boasted.

'Where was that?' Zouga demanded, for Cornwallis Harris was one of the most famous of the old African hunters. His book *The Wild Sports of Africa* was the great classic of the African chase.

'I took him to the Cashan mountains.' Harris's expedition to the Cashan mountains, which the Boers now called Magaliesberg, was in 1829, thirty-one years previously. That would make the little Hottentot somewhere between fifty and sixty years old, if he were telling the truth.

'Harris did not mention your name,' he said. 'I have read his account carefully.'

'Jan Bloom – that was my name then.' Zouga nodded. Bloom had been one of Harris's most intrepid hunter-retainers.

'Why is your name Jan Cheroot now?' Zouga asked and the dark eyes had twinkled with pixie merriment.

'Sometimes a man gets tired of a name, like he does of a woman, and for his health or his life he changes both.'

The long military-issue Enfield rifle was as tall as Jan Cheroot, but it seemed an extension of his wizened little body.

'Pick nine other men. The best,' Zouga told him, and Sergeant Cheroot brought them aboard while the gunboat was working up a head of steam in her boilers.

Each man carried his Enfield over his shoulder, his worldly possessions in the haversack on his back and fifty rounds in the pouches on his belt.

It needed only the 'Rogue's March' to welcome them, Zouga thought wryly, as he watched them come in through the entry port, each one bestowing upon him a beatific grin and a salute so vigorous that it nearly swung the donor off his feet.

Sergeant Cheroot lined them up at the rail. Their original scarlet uniform jackets had suffered strange mutations to ten different shades, ranging from sun-faded pink to dusty puce, and each peppercorn head wore its brimless infantry cap cocked at a different angle from all the others. Thin shanks were bound up with grubby puttees, and brown bare feet slapped the oak planking of the deck in unison as Cheroot brought them to attention, Enfields at the slope and happy grins on each puckish face.

'Very well, Sergeant.' Zouga acknowledged the salute. 'Now let's have the packs open, and the bottles over the side.'

The grins wilted, and they exchanged crestfallen glances – the Major had looked so young and gullible.

'You hear the Major, *julle klomp dom skaape.*' Gleefully Jan Cheroot likened them to 'a herd of stupid sheep' in the kitchen Dutch of the Cape, and as he turned back to Zouga there was for the first time a gleam of respect in the dark eyes.

There are two passages from which a ship may chose when sailing the south-eastern coast of Africa. The master may stay outside the 100-fathom line which marks the edge of the continental shelf, for here the opposing forces of the Mozambique current and the prevailing winds can generate a sea which seamen call with awe the '100 year wave', a wave over 200 foot from crest to trough, which will overwhelm even the sturdiest vessel as though it were a drifting autumn leaf. The alternative and only slightly less hazardous passage lies close inshore, in the shallows where the rocky reefs await a careless navigator.

For the sake of speed Clinton Codrington chose the inshore passage, so that always the land was in sight as they bustled northwards. Day after day the shimmering white beaches and dark rocky headlands unreeled ahead of *Black Joke*'s bows, sometimes almost lost in the smoky blue sea-fret, and at other times brutally clear under the African sun.

Clinton kept steam in his boilers and the single bronze screw spinning under his counter with every sail set and trained around to glean the smallest puff of the wind, as he drove *Black Joke* on to the rendezvous that Mungo St. John had set. His haste was symptom of a compulsion that Robyn Ballantyne only began fully to understand during those days and nights that they drove east and north, for Clinton Codrington sought her company constantly and she spent many hours of each day with him, or all of it that could be spared from the management of the vessel – beginning with the assembly of the ship's company for morning prayers.

Most naval captains went through the motions of divine service once a week, but Captain Codrington held prayers every morning and it did not take Robyn long to realize that his faith and sense of Christian duty was, if anything, greater than her own. He did not seem to experience the terrible doubts and temptations to which she was always such a prey, and if it had not been unchristian to do so she would have felt envy for his sense and secure faith.

'I wanted to go into the church, like my father and my elder brother, Ralph, before me,' he told her.

'Why did you not?'

'The Almightly led me into the path He had chosen for me,' Clinton said simply, and it did not seem pretentious when he said it. 'I know now He meant me to be a shepherd for His flock, here in this land,' and he pointed at the silver beaches and blue mountains. 'I did not realize it at the time, but His ways are wonderful. This is the work He has chosen for me.'

Suddenly she realized how deep was his commitment to the war he was waging against the trade, it was almost a personal crusade. His whole being directed at its destruction, for he truly believed that he was the instrument of God's will.

Yet, like many deeply religious men, he kept his belief closely guarded, never flaunting it in sanctimonious posturing or biblical quotation. The only time he spoke of his God was during the daily prayers and when he was alone with her on his quarterdeck. Quite naturally, he assumed that her belief matched, if not outstripped, his own. She did nothing to disillusion him, for she enjoyed his patent admiration, his deference to the fact that she had been appointed as a missionary, and when she was truthful to herself, which was more and more often these days, she liked the way he looked, the sound of his voice, and even the smell of him. It was a man's smell, like tanned leather or the pelt of an otter she had once had as a pet at King's Lynn.

He was good to be near, a man, as the pale missionary initiates and medical students she had known, had not been men. He was the Christian warrior. She found a comfort in his presence, not like the wicked excitement of Mungo St. John, but something deeper and more satisfying. She looked upon him as her champion, as though the deadly assignation to which he was hurrying was on her behalf, to wipe out the knowledge of sin and to atone for her disgrace.

On the third day they passed the settlement on the shore of Algoa Bay, where the 5,000 British settlers brought out by Governor Somerset forty years before in 1820 had landed and still eked a hard existence from the unforgiving African earth. The white flecks of painted walls looked pitifully insignificant in that wilderness of water and sky and land, and at last Robyn started to come to some small understanding of the vastness of this continent and how puny were the scratches that man had made upon it. For the first time she felt a small cold dread at her own temerity that had brought her so far, so young and so inexperienced, to venture she was not sure what. She hugged her shawl about her shoulders and shivered in the cutting wind that poured in off the green sea. The Africa she had dreamed of so often seemed harsh and unwelcoming now.

As *Black Joke* closed swiftly with the rendezvous that St. John had appointed, Clinton Codrington became quieter, and was more often alone in his cabin. He understood clearly the ordeal that faced him. Zouga Ballantyne had discussed it with him on almost every occasion that presented itself. Zouga was unwavering in his opposition to the meeting.

'You have chosen a formidable opponent, sir,' he told Clinton bluntly. 'And I mean no offence when I say I doubt you are a match for him with either pistol or sword – but he'll choose pistols, you can wager on that.'

'He challenged,' Clinton said quietly. 'My weapon is the naval cutlass. We will fight with those.'

'I cannot support you there.' Zouga shook his head. 'If there was a challenge, and I could make a case against that – but if there was one, it came from you, sir. If you fight, it will be with pistols.'

Day after day he tried to persuade Clinton to miss the rendezvous.

'Damn it, man. Nobody fights duels any more, especially against a man who can split the cheroot in your mouth with either hand, at twenty paces.' Or again, 'There was no challenge, Captain Codrington, I was there, and I would stake my honour on it.' At another time, 'You will lose your commission, sir. You have Admiral Kemp's direct order to avoid the meeting, and it is obvious that Kemp is waiting for an opportunity to haul you before a court martial.' Then again, 'By God, sir, you will serve no one – least of all yourself – by being shot to death on some deserted and Godforsaken shore. If St. John is a slaver, then your chance to take him at more favourable odds will come later.'

When Zouga's best arguments made no dent on Clinton's resolve Zouga went to Robyn in her cabin.

'You seem to have some influence on the fellow. Can you not persuade him, Sissy?'

'Zouga, why are you so determined to prevent Captain Codrington defending his honour?'

'He's a likable enough chap, and I do not wish to see him pipped.'

'And if he were, you might find it difficult to reach Quelimane. Is that not so?' Robyn asked sweetly. 'Your concern is most Christian.'

'St. John can choose which of his eyes he will put a ball into. You have seen him shoot.' Zouga ignored the accusation.

'I believe it is Captain Codrington's duty to destroy that monster. God protects the righteous.'

'In my experience he protects only those who shoot fastest and straightest,' Zouga growled with frustration.

'That is blasphemy,' Robyn told him.

'You deserve to hear some real blasphemy for your stubbornness,' Zouga told her curtly and strode out of the cabin. He had learned through long experience when he was wasting his time.

They passed the mouth of the Kei river – the frontier of British influence and beyond it was the wilderness, unclaimed and untamed, peopled by the tribes which had been driven back inexorably by the white advance, and by scattered bands of renegades and bastards, wandering hunters and hardy travellers and traders.

Even the trekking Boers had by-passed this land, going on into the interior, circling out beyond the mountain massif that divided the littoral from the highland plateau.

Far to the north they had turned back and crossed the mountains again and reached the coast, fighting and shattering the impis of the Zulu nation, beginning to settle the fertile coastal strip until the British ships had sailed into Port Natal, following them up from the Cape Colony, from whence they had trekked so long and so hard to avoid British rule. The Boers had loaded their waggons once more, and driving their herds before them, climbed back over the range that they called the Dragon mountains and abandoned the land they had wrested from the Zulu king Dingaan with the flame and smoke of their muskets.

However, this coast along which *Black Joke* now steamed lay between the English colonies of Cape and Natal, claimed by none, except the wild tribesmen who watched the black-hulled vessel pass almost within arrow shot.

Clinton Codrington had marked the point where latitude 31° 38' south intersected the coast, and the estuary was shown on the chart with the notation 'St. John's river', named, probably, by one of the early Portuguese navigators, but it was ironic that it should bear the same name as the man they were hastening to meet. When *Black Joke* steamed around the last headland the description that St. John had given of his namesake was instantly recognizable.

Steep, heavily wooded hills rose almost sheer about a wide lagoon. The forest was very dense dark green, with tall galleries of trees, festooned with lianas. Through the telescope could be made out the troops of little grey vervet monkeys and the brilliant plumage of exotic birds that sported and fluttered through the top branches.

The river came down a deep rocky gorge torn through the barrier of hills, filling the reed-lined lagoon and then flowing out over the bar between the curved white pillows of a sandy beach.

To dispel any doubt that this was the rendezvous, *Huron* lay at anchor a cable's length beyond the first line of breakers, in the deep, where the shoal water turned from pale green to blue.

Clinton Codrington examined her carefully through his telescope, then without a word passed the instrument to Zouga. While he in turn glassed the big Clipper, Clinton asked softly, 'Will you act for me?'

Zouga lowered the glass with surprise. 'I expected one of your own officers.'

'I could not ask them.' Clinton shook his head. 'Slogger Kemp would mark their service records if he ever heard of it.'

'You do not have the same qualms about my career,' Zouga pointed out.

'You are on extended absence from your regiment, and you have not been expressly ordered, as I and my officers have been.'

Zouga thought quickly, duelling was not so seriously considered in the army as it was in the Royal Navy, in fact the army manuals still contained no express prohibitions, and a chance to meet with St. John was also a last chance to avert this ridiculous affair that so seriously threatened the continuance of his expedition.

'I accept, then,' Zouga said shortly.

'I am extremely grateful to you, sir,' said Clinton as shortly.

'Let us hope you are as grateful after the business is over,' Zouga told him drily. 'I had best go across to *Huron* right away. It will be dark in an hour.'

Tippoo caught the line as it was thrown from the gunboat's whaler, and held it while Zouga gathered his cloak and jumped the gap of surging green water to the boarding ladder, clambering up before the next swell could soak his boats.

Mungo St. John waited for him at the foot of the mainmast. He held himself unsmiling and aloof, until Zouga hurried to him and offered his right hand, then he relaxed and returned the smile.

'Damn it, Mungo, cannot we make an end to this nonsense?'

'Certainly, Zouga,' Mungo St. John agreed. 'An apology from your man would settle it.'

'The man is a fool,' Zouga shook his head. 'Why take the risk?'

'I don't consider there is any risk, but let me remind you he called me a coward.'

'There is no chance then?' The two of them had become good friends during the weeks they had spent together and Zouga felt he could press further. 'I admit the fellow is a prig, but if you kill him, you'll make it damned awkward for me, don't you know?'

Mungo St. John threw back his head and laughed delightedly. 'You and I could work together, do you know that, Zouga? You are a pragmatist, like I am. I make a prophecy – you'll go a long way in this world.'

'Not very far, if you kill the man who is taking me.' And Mungo St. John chuckled again and clapped a friendly hand upon his shoulder.

'I'm sorry, my friend. Not this time,' and Zouga sighed with resignation.

'You have a choice of weapons.'

'Pistols,' said Mungo St. John.

'Of course,' Zouga nodded. 'Dawn tomorrow on the beach there.' He pointed to the land with his chin. 'Will that suit you?'

'Admirably. Tippoo here will act for me.'

'Does he understand the conventions?' Zouga asked doubtfully, as he glanced at the half-naked figure that waited near at hand.

'He understands enough to blow Codrington's head off at the shoulders if he levels his pistol a moment before the signal.' Mungo St. John flashed that cruel white smile. 'And that's all he needs to know, as far as I am concerned.'

Robyn Ballantyne slept not a minute during the night and it still lacked

two hours of dawn when she bathed and dressed. On an impulse she chose
her old moleskin breeches and man's woollen jacket. There would be the need
to disembark through the surf from the ship's boat and skirts would hamper
her, added to which the morning was damp and chill and her jacket was of
good thick Scottish tweed.

She laid out her black leather bag, and checked its contents, making certain
she had everything she needed to cleanse and staunch a bullet wound, to bind
up torn flesh or hold together shattered bone, and to reduce the agony of
either man.

All of them had taken it without question that Robyn would be on the
beach that morning. The gunboat did not rate a surgeon, and neither did
Huron. She was ready with an hour to wait, and she opened her journal and
began making the previous day's entry, when there was a light tap on her
door.

When she opened it, Clinton Codrington stood in the opening, his face pale
and strained in the smoky lamplight and she knew intuitively that he had
slept as little as she had. He recovered swiftly from the first shock of seeing
her in breeches, dragging his eyes up to her face again.

'I hoped I might speak with you,' he muttered shyly. 'It will be the last
opportunity before . . .'

She took his arm and drew him into the cabin. 'You have not breakfasted?'
she asked sternly.

'No, ma'am.' He shook his head and his eyes dropped to her trousered legs,
and then jerked up guiltily to her face again.

'The medicine worked?' she asked.

He nodded, too embarrassed to reply. She had administered a purge the
evening before, for as a surgeon she could dread the effects of a pistol ball
through a full bowel or through a belly loaded with breakfast.

She touched his forehead. 'You are warm, you have not taken a chill?' She
felt protective towards him, like a mother almost, for he seemed once again so
young and untried.

'I wondered if we might pray together.' His voice was so low that she
barely caught the words, and she felt a warm, almost suffocating rush of
affection for him.

'Come,' she whispered, and she took his hand.

They knelt together on the bare deck of the tiny cabin, still holding hands,
and she spoke for both of them, and he made the responses in a soft but firm
voice.

When they rose stiffly at last, he kept her hand in his for a while longer.

'Miss Ballantyne – I mean, Doctor Ballantyne – I cannot tell you now
what a profound effect meeting you has had on my life.'

She felt herself blushing and tried feebly to disengage her hand, but he
clung to it.

'I would like to have your permission to talk to you again in this vein
after,' he paused, 'if this morning goes as we hope it will.'

'Oh, it will,' she said fiercely. 'It will – I know it will.' Hardly knowing
what she was doing she pressed herself swiftly to him and reaching up kissed
him full on the mouth. For a moment he froze, and then clumsily he crushed
her to him so that the brass buttons of his coat dug into her bosom and his
teeth crushed her lips until she felt them bruising.

'My darling,' he whispered. 'Oh, my darling.'

The strength of his reaction startled her, but almost immediately she found
she was enjoying the strength of his embrace, and she tried to free her arms
to return it – but he misunderstood her movements and released her hurriedly.

'Forgive me,' he blurted out. 'I don't know what came over me.'

Her disappointment was sharp enough to turn instantly to annoyance at his timidity. Buttons and teeth notwithstanding, it had felt very pleasant indeed.

Both boats left the two ships at the same time, and they converged through the thin pearly morning mist as their crews pulled for the low lines of breaking surf and the pale outline of the beach in the dawn.

They landed within a hundred yards of each other, surfing in on the crest of the same low, green wave and the oarsmen leapt out waist-deep to run the boats high up the white sand.

Both parties moved separately over the crest of the sand bar and then down to the edge of the lagoon, screened from the boat crews by the intervening dunes and the stands of tall fluffy-headed reeds.

Mungo St. John and Tippoo halted at one end, and Mungo lit a cheroot and stood with both hands on his hips staring out at the crests of the hills, ignoring the activity about him. He was dressed in black tight-fitting breeches and a white silk shirt with full sleeves, open at the throat to reveal the dark curls of his body hair. The white shirt would give his opponent a fair aiming point, he was observing the conventions scrupulously.

Robyn watched him covertly as she stood beside Clinton Codrington at the further end of the clearing. She tried to capture the hatred she felt for St. John, to hold on to her outrage at the way he had abused her, but it was a difficult emotion to sustain. Rather, she was excited and with a strange sense of elation, the satanic presence of this man heightened the feeling. She caught herself staring openly and dragged her eyes off him.

Beside her Clinton stood very erect. He wore his blue uniform jacket with the gold lace of his rank gleaming even in the soft pink light of early dawn. He had scraped the sun-bleached hair back from his forehead and temples and bound it at the nape of his neck, leaving clean the purposeful line of his jaw.

Zouga went forward to meet Tippoo who carried under his arm the rosewood case of pistols. When they met in the centre of the level ground, he opened the case and proffered it, standing straddle-legged and attentive, while Zouga took each weapon from its velvet nest and loaded it with a carefully measured charge of black powder before ramming home the dark-blue leaden ball and setting the cap on the nipple.

The sight of the long-barrelled weapons reminded Robyn forecefully of that night aboard *Huron*, and she bit her lip and shifted uncomfortably.

'Do not fret yourself, Miss Ballantyne.' Clinton mistook her emotion, and whispered soothingly to comfort her while he unbuttoned his jacket and shrugged out of it. Beneath it he also wore a plain white shirt to give St. John a fair aim. He handed her the jacket and would have spoken again but Zouga called.

'Will the principals come forward.'

And Clinton gave her another tightly strained smile before he strode out, his heels leaving deep prints in the damp yellow sand.

He faced Mungo St. John, holding his gaze steadily, both of them completely expressionless.

'Gentlemen, I appeal to both of you to settle this affair without bloodshed.' Zouga went through the ritual attempt at reconciliation. 'Captain Codrington, as challenger, will you tender an apology?'

Clinton shook his head once, curtly.

'Mr. St. John, is there any other way in which we can avoid bloodshed?'

'I think not, sir,' St. John drawled as he carefully tapped half an inch of grey ash from his cheroot.

'Very well,' Zouga nodded and went on immediately to set the conditions of the meeting. 'At the command "Proceed" each of you gentlemen will take ten paces, which I will count aloud. Immediately after the count of ten I will give the command "Fire" upon which you will be at liberty to turn and discharge your weapon.'

Zouga paused and glanced at Tippoo, there was a long-barrelled muzzle-loading pistol thrust into the waistband of his baggy breeches.

'Both seconds are armed.' Zouga laid his right hand on the butt of the Colt pistol in his own belt. 'If either principal attempts to fire before the command to do so, then he will immediately be shot down by the seconds.'

He paused again looking from one to the other. 'Is that clearly understood, gentlemen?' They both nodded. 'Do either of you have a question?' Zouga waited in silence for a few seconds then went on. 'Very well, we will proceed. Mr. St. John you have first choice of weapon.'   Mungo St. John dropped the cheroot and ground it into the sand with his heel, before stepping forward. Tippoo offered him the rosewood case and after a momentary hesitation St. John lifted out one of the beautifully inlaid weapons. He pointed at the sky and cocked the hammer with a sweep of his free hand.

Clinton took the remaining pistol and weighed it experimentally in his hand, settling the butt deeply into the vee formed by thumb and forefinger, turning half away and lifting the pistol at full stretch of his arm to aim it at one of the black and bright yellow bishop birds that chattered in the reeds nearby.

With relief Robyn watched the familiar ease with which her champion handled the weapon, and she felt completely certain of the outcome now. Good must triumph, and she started to pray again, silently, only her lips moving as she recited the twenty-third psalm.

'Though I walk through the valley of the shadow of death.'

'Take your positions, gentlemen.' Zouga stepped back and gestured to Robyn. Still praying, she hurried to where Zouga stood, and fell in a few paces behind him, well out on the flank from the lines of fire of the two principals.

Beside Zouga, Tippoo drew the long, clumsy-looking pistol from the sash around his waist and cocked the big ornate hammer, the bore of the barrel gaped like a cannon as he lifted it into the 'present' position. Zouga drew his own Colt revolver and stood quietly while the two principals walked the last few paces towards each other and then turned back to back.

Beyond them the early sun was gilding the hilltops with bright gold, but leaving the lagoon still in shadow so the still dark waters steamed with wisps of mist. In the silence a ghostly grey heron croaked hoarsely and then launched into flight from the edge of the reedbank with slow wingbeats, its neck drawn back into a snakelike 'S' to balance the long beak.

'Proceed!' called Zouga, so loudly that Robyn started violently.

The two men stepped out, away from each other, with deliberate strides, heeling heavily in the yielding sand, pacing to the count that Zouga called.

'Five.' Mungo St. John was smiling softly, as though at some secret joke, and his white silk sleeve fluttered like a moth's wing around the uplifted arm that held the slim steel-blue barrel pointed at the dawn sky.

'Six.' Clinton leaned forward, stepping out with long legs clad in white uniform breeches. His face was set, pale as a mask, his lips drawn into a thin determined line.

'Seven.' Robyn felt the beat of her heart crescendo, thumping painfully against the cage of her ribs so that she could not breathe.

'Eight.' She noticed for the first time the patches of sweat that had soaked through the armpits of Clinton's white shirt, despite the chill of the dawn air.

'Nine.' Suddenly she was deadly afraid for him, all her faith dissolved in a sudden premonition of disaster rushing down upon her.

'Ten!' She wanted to scream to them to stop. She wanted to rush forward and throw herself into the space between the two men. She didn't want them to die, either of them. She tried to fill her lungs but her throat was closed and dry, she tried to drive her legs forward but they were locked rigidly under her, beyond her control.

'Fire!' shouted Zouga, his voice cracking with the tension that gripped all the watchers and out on the damp dark-yellow sand both men turned, like a pair of dancers in a meticulously rehearsed ballet of death.

Their right arms out-flung towards each other in a gesture like that of parted lovers, the left hand on the hip to balance, the classic stance of the expert marksman.

Time seemed suspended, the movements of the two men graceful but measured, without the urgency of onrushing death.

The silence was complete, there was no wind to rustle the reeds, no bird nor animal called from the looming forest across the lagoon, the footfalls of the two men were deadened by the yielding sand – the world seemed to hold its breath.

And then the crash of pistol fire awoke the echoes and sent them bounding and booming across the gorge, leaping from cliff to cliff, startling the birds into raucous flight.

The two shots were within one hundredth of a second of each other, so that they blended into a single blurt of sound. From the levelling blue barrels the dead white powder smoke spurted, and then the barrels were flung upwards in unison with the shock of discharge.

Both men reeled backwards, keeping their feet, but Robyn had seen the smoke fly from the muzzle of Mungo St. John's pistol a fraction of a second earlier, and then an instant later Mungo's big dark head flinched as though he had been struck with an open hand across the cheek.

After that one staggered pace backwards, he steadied, drawing himself to his full height, the pistol still smoking in his raised hand, staring at his adversary, and Robyn felt a rush of relief. Mungo St. John was unscathed. She wanted to run to him, and then suddenly the joy withered, a dark red snake of blood slithered from the thick hair at his temple down the smoothly shaven olive skin of his cheek and dripped with slow sullen drops on to the white silk of his shirt.

She lifted her hand to her mouth to cover the cry that rose within her, and then her attention was distracted by another movement in the corner of her vision and she swung her head with a jerky movement towards Clinton Codrington.

He also had been standing erect, with almost military bearing, but now he began to bow slowly forward at the waist. The right hand holding the pistol hung at his side and now his fingers opened and the ornate weapon dropped into the sand at his feet.

He lifted the empty hand and placed it across his chest with fingers outspread in a gesture that seemed reverential and slowly his body bent forward and now his legs gave way under him and he dropped to his knees, as though in prayer. Kneeling, he lifted his hand away from his chest and examined with an expression of mild surprise the small smear of blood that coated his fingers and then he pitched forward face down on to the sand.

At last Robyn could move. She raced forward and dropped to her knees beside Clinton's fallen body, and with strength of panic rolled him on to his back. The front of the white linen shirt was damp with a little blood around the neat puncture in the cloth six inches to the left of the line of mother of pearl buttons.

He had been half-turned to fire and the ball had taken him low and left, at the level of the lungs, she saw instantly. The lungs! She felt despair overwhelm her. It would mean death, no less certain because it was slow and agonizing. She would have to watch this man drown inexorably in his own blood.

Sand crunched beside her and she looked up.

Mungo St. John stood over her, his shirt a mess of wet blood. He was holding a silk kerchief to his temple to staunch the copious flow where the pistol ball had stripped a long ribbon of scalp off his skull above the ear.

His eyes were bleak, his expression forbidding and his voice cold and distant as he told her quietly.

'I trust you will be satisfied at last, madam.' Then he turned abruptly up the white dune towards the beach. She wanted to run after him, to restrain him, to explain – to explain she knew not what, but her duty was here, with the man more gravely stricken. Her fingers shook as she unbuttoned the front of Clinton's shirt and saw the dark blue hole punched into the pale flesh from which a little thick slow blood oozed. So little blood at the mouth of the wound – it was the worst indication – the bleeding would be inside, deep inside the chest cavity.

Zouga, my bag,' she called sharply.

Zouga came to her, carrying the bag and went down on one knee beside her.

'I am but lightly struck,' murmured Clinton. 'I have no pain. Just a feeling of numbness here.'

Zouga did not reply. He had seen a multitude of gunshot wounds in India, pain was no indication of the severity. A ball through the hand or foot was unbearable agony, another through both lungs was only mildly discomforting.

Only one thing puzzled him and that was why Mungo St. John's shot had been so wide. At twenty paces he would surely have taken the head shot, aiming between the eyes with an expectation of the ball deviating less than an inch from the point of aim, yet the shot had taken Clinton low in the chest.

While Robyn pressed a dressing over the wicked little blue mouth of the wound, Zouga picked the pistol out of the sand. The barrel was still warm and there was the peppery whiff of burned powder as he examined it and saw instantly why Mungo's shot had struck wide.

There was a bluish smear of bright new lead on the steel trigger guard.

Mungo St. John had indeed aimed at the head, but Clinton had lifted the pistol to his eye at the same instant directly in the line of sight. St. John's ball had struck the metal guard and been deflected downwards.

That would account for the fact that Clinton's own ball had been high, for as a less expert marksman he would surely have aimed for St. John's chest. The strike of the ball had thrown his weapon upwards at the moment of discharge.

Zouga looked up and handed the pistol to Tippoo who waited impassively close at hand. Without a word, Tippoo took the weapon, turned away and followed his master over the dunes.

By the time four seamen from the gunboat could carry Clinton Codrington down the beach using his boat cloak as a hammock, St. John was climbing up from the *Huron*'s whaler on to his maindeck, and before they could rig a block and tackle to lift the prostrate form of her captain into *Black Joke* – *Huron* had broken out her anchor and was spreading sail before the south-westerly breeze and bearing away with the sunrise transforming her into a vessel etched in golden fire.

For twenty-four hours Clinton Codrington surprised Robyn with the strength of his recovery. She looked to see blood on his lips, and she expected him to experience the agony of breathing as the damaged lung collapsed. Every few hours she listened with her sounding trumpet to his chest, stooping over the bunk in his cabin to catch the hiss and saw of his breathing, listening for the bubbling sound of blood, or for the dry rubbing of the lung against the rib cage, and was puzzled when none of these symptoms occurred.

Indeed Clinton was unaccountably resilient for a patient with ball through the chest cavity. He complained only of stiffness reaching up into his left armpit and semi-paralysis of that arm – and he was vociferous in his advice to his surgeon.

'You will bleed me, of course?' he asked.

'I will not,' Robyn told him shortly as she cleaned the area around the wound and then lifted him into a sitting position to bandage his chest.

'You should take at least a pint,' Clinton insisted.

'Have you not bled enough?' Robyn asked witheringly, but he was undaunted.

'There is black rotten blood that must be taken off.' Clinton indicated the massive bruise that was spreading around his chest like some dark parasitic plant around the smooth pale trunk.

'You must bleed me,' Clinton insisted, for all his adult life he had been exposed to the ministrations of naval surgeons. 'If you don't, fever is sure to follow.'

He offered Robyn the inner curve of his elbow where the thin white scars over the blue blood vessels marked where he had been bled before.

'We no longer live in the dark ages,' Robyn told him tartly. 'This is 1860,' and she pushed him down on the bolster and covered him with a grey ship's blanket against the shivering and chilling nausea which she knew must soon accompany such a wound. It did not come, and for the next twenty hours he continued to manage the ship from his bunk, and he chafed at the restraint she placed on him. However, Robyn knew the pistol ball was still in there and that there must be drastic consequences. She wished that there was some technique that could enable a surgeon to locate the whereabouts of a foreign body accurately, and then allow him to enter the rib cage and remove it.

That evening she fell asleep in the rope chair beside his bunk, awakening once to hold the enamel cup of water to his lips when he complained of thirst and noting the dryness and heat of his skin, and in the morning all her fears were confirmed.

He was only semi-conscious, and the pain was fierce. He moaned and cried out at the smallest movement. His eyes were sunken into plum-coloured cavities, his tongue was thickly coated with white and his lips were dried and cracked. He pleaded for drink and his skin was hot, the heat increasing every hour until it seemed to be burning out the core of his being, and he was restless and flushed, tossing in the narrow bunk, fighting off the blankets with which she tried to keep him covered, and whimpering in his delirium at the agony of movement. His breath was sawing painfully in his swollen and bruised chest, his eyes were glittering bright, and when Robyn unwound the bandage to sponge his body with cool water there was only a little pale fluid staining the dressing, but her nostrils flared as she smelled it. It was so horribly familiar, she always thought of that stench as the fetid breath of death itself.

The wound had shrunk, but the crust that had formed over it was so thin that it cracked at one of Clinton's restless movements and through it rose a thick droplet of custard-coloured matter. Immediately the smell was stronger. This was not the benign pus of healing, but the malignant pus that she so dreaded to see in a wound.

She swabbed it away carefully, and then with cold seawater sponged his chest and the hard hot swollen flesh below his armpit. The bruising was extensive and it had changed colour, dark blue as storm clouds, tinged with the yellow of sulphur and the virulent rose of some flower from the gardens of Hell itself.

There was one area just below the point of his shoulder blade particularly sensitive for he screamed when she touched it, and a sparse prickle of sweat broke out across his forehead and amongst the fine golden bristles of his unshaven cheeks.

She replaced the bandage with a fresh dressing and then forced between his dry lips four grams of laudanum mixed with a warm draught of calomel. She watched while he fell into a restless drug-induced sleep.

'Another twenty-four hours,' she whispered aloud, watching him toss and mutter. She had seen it so often. Soon the pus would suffuse his whole body, building up steadily around the ball deep in his chest. She was helpless. No surgeon could enter the rib cage, it had never been done before.

She looked up as Zouga stooped into the cabin. He was grave and quiet, standing beside her chair for a moment and placing a hand on her shoulder comfortingly.

'He improves?' he asked softly.

She shook her head, and he nodded as though he had expected the response.

'You must eat.' He offered her the pannikin. 'I brought you some pea soup. It has bacon in it, it's very good.'

She had not realized how hungry she was and she ate gratefully, breaking the hard ship's bread into the broth and Zouga went on quietly.

'I loaded the pistols with less than a full charge, as little as I dared.' He shook his head irritably. 'Damned bad luck. After Mungo's ball hit the trigger guard, I'd not have expected it to have entered the chest – it must have lost most of its power.'

She looked up quickly. 'It struck the trigger guard – you did not tell me.'

He shrugged. 'It's not important now. But the ball was deflected.'

She sat very still in her chair for ten minutes after he was gone, and then purposefully she stood over the bunk and stripped back the blanket, unwound the bandage and examined the wound again.

Very carefully she began to sound the ribs beneath it, pressing in with thumb gently to feel for the give of shattered bone. The ribs were all firm, yet that was no proof that the ball had not driven between two of them.

She pressed her thumb into the swelling towards the outside of his chest, and although he thrashed around weakly, she thought she felt the rasp of bone against bone – as though the rib had been chipped or even as if a long splinter had been cracked off it.

She felt a little flutter of excitement, and extended her examination gradually backwards, guided by his delirious cries of pain, until once again she reached the lower point of his shoulder and he came upright in the bunk with another wild yell of agony, breaking out once more into the burning sweat of high fever. But with the tip of her finger she thought she had felt something, something that was neither bone nor knotted muscle.

The excitement quickened her breathing. From the angle at which Clinton had stood, half-turned away from Mungo St. John, she now believed that it was possible that the ball had followed a different path from that which she had assumed.

If the pistol had been undercharged with powder, and if the ball had struck the trigger guard, it was just possible that it had not had the velocity to penetrate the rib cage, it had been turned by the bone and ploughed along under the skin, skidding along the groove between two ribs following the track that she had just probed, and lodging at last in the thick bed of the *latissimus dorsi* and *tenes major* muscle.

She stood back from the bunk. She could be very wrong, she realized, but if she was he would die anyway, and that very soon.

'I will cut for it,' she decided, the decision direct and swift. She glanced up at the skylight in the roof of the cabin. There was only an hour or two of good daylight left.

'Zouga!' she called as she raced from the cabin. 'Zouga! Come quickly!'

Robyn administered another five grams of laudanum before they moved Clinton. It was as large a dose as she dared, for he had taken nearly fifteen grams in the preceding thirty-six hours. She waited as long as she could in the failing light for the drug to begin taking effect. Then she passed the word to Lieutenant Denham to shorten sail, reduce engine revolutions and make the ship's motion as easy as possible.

Zouga had chosen two seamen to assist them. One was the boatswain, a burly and greying sailor, the other was the officers' steward who had impressed Robyn with his quiet, controlled manner.

Now as the three of them half-lifted Clinton and rolled him on to his side, the steward spread a sheet of fresh white canvas on the bunk under him to receive the spilled blood, then Zouga swiftly knotted the lengths of soft cotton rope around Clinton's wrists and ankles. He had chosen cotton in preference to the coarse hemp which would tear the skin, and he made the bowline knots that would not slip under pressure.

The boatswain helped him to tie down the ends at the head and foot of the bunk, stretching out the almost naked white body so that for an instant it reminded Robyn of the painting of the crucifixion that stood in Uncle William's study at King's Lynn – the Roman legionaries spreadeagling Christ upon the cross before driving home the nails. She shook her head irritably, driving the memory from her mind, concentrating all her attention on the task ahead.

'Wash your hands!' she ordered Zouga, indicating the bucket of almost boiling water and yellow lye soap the steward had provided.

'Why?'

'Do it,' she snapped, in no mood to argue. Her own hands were pink with the heat of the water and tingled with the harsh soap, as she wiped her instruments with the cloth dipped in a mug of the pungent ship's rum, laying them out on the shelf above the bunk, and then with the same cloth swabbed the hot discoloured flesh at the base of Clinton's shoulder blade. He jerked against his bonds and muttered an incoherent protest, but she ignored it and nodded to the boatswain.

He seized Clinton's head, drawing it back slightly, and thrust a thick pad of felt, a piece of wadding for the maindeck cannon, between his teeth, holding it in place.

'Zouga!'

He took Clinton's shoulders and locked them in his powerful fingers, preventing Clinton from rolling on to his belly.

'Good.'

Robyn took one of the razor-sharp scalpels from the shelf, and then with the forefinger of her other hand probed brutally down to where she had felt that hard foreign body.

Clinton's back arched and he let out a shattering cry that was muffled by the wadding, but Robyn felt it clearly this time, hard and unyielding in the swollen flesh.

She cut swiftly, without hesitation, opening the skin cleanly, following the direction of the muscle fibre beneath, dissecting down through layer after layer of muscle, separating the bluish membrane capsules that covered each of the muscles with the hilt of the scalpel, probing deeper and deeper with her fingers towards that elusive lump in the flesh.

Clinton writhed and heaved at his bonds, his breathing rasping in the back of his throat, his teeth locked into the felt wadding in a fierce rictus so that cords of muscle stood out along his jawline and white spittle frothed upon his lips.

His wild lunges made her task that much more difficult, and her fingers were slippery with blood in his hot flesh, but she found the rubbery pulsing snake of the lateral thoracic artery and worked past it gently, pinching off the smaller spurting blood vessels with the forceps, and tying them with a loop of catgut, torn between the need for speed and the danger of doing greater damage.

Finally she had to use the blade again, and she reversed the scalpel and paused a moment to locate the lump with the tip of her forefinger.

She could feel the sweat sliding down her cheek, and she was aware of the strained tense faces of the men who held Clinton as they watched her work.

She guided the scalpel down into the open wound, and then cut down firmly and a sudden bright yellow fountain spouted up through her fingers, and the cloying stomach-twisting stench of corruption that filled the hot little cabin made her gasp.

That sharp rush of pus lasted only a second, and then there was something black and sodden blocking the wound. She picked it out with the forceps, releasing another lesser welling up of the thick custardy matter.

'The wad,' Zouga grunted with the effort of holding down the struggling naked body. They all stared at the soft rotten object in the teeth of her forceps.

The patch of cloth had been carried deeply into the flesh by the passage of the ball, and Robyn felt a surging lift of relief – she had been right.

Quickly she went back to work, running her finger into the tunnel cut by the ball until she felt it with her fingertip.

'There it is!' She spoke for the first time since she had cut, but the metal pellet was slippery and heavy, she could not prise it loose and she had to cut again and then lock the teeth of the pair of bone forceps over it. It came out with reluctant suck of clinging tissue, and she dropped it impatiently on the shelf. It made a heavy clunk against the wood. There was a temptation to come out immediately, to sew up and bind up – but she resisted it and took an extra ten seconds to probe the wound thoroughly. She was almost immediately justified, there was another rotting and stinking tatter of cloth in the wound track.

'A piece of the shirt.' She identified the white shreds, and Zouga's face mirrored his disgust. 'Now we can come out,' Robyn went on complacently.

She left a bristle in the wound to allow the remaining pus to drain off. It stuck out stiffly between the stitches with which she closed up.

When she stood back at last she was smugly satisfied with her work. There had been nobody at St. Matthew's who could lay down stitches so neatly and regularly, not even the senior surgeons could match her.

Clinton had collapsed with the shock of deep surgery. His body was wet and slick with his sweat, and the skin at his wrists and ankles had been smeared away where he had fought against his bonds.

'Let him loose,' she said softly. She felt a vast pride, almost of ownership, in him now, as though he were her special creation, for she had dragged him back almost bodily from the abyss. Pride was sin, she knew, but it did not make the sensation any the less agreeable, and in the circumstances, she decided, she had earned the pleasure of a little sin.

Clinton's recovery was almost miraculous. By the next morning he was fully conscious, and the fever had abated to leave him pale and shaky, with just enough strength to argue bitterly when she had him carried up into the sunshine and laid behind the canvas wind shelter that the carpenter had rigged under the poop.

'Cold air is bad for gunshot wounds, everybody knows that.'

'And I suppose I should bleed you before closing you up in that hot little hell hole you call a cabin,' Robyn asked tartly.

'A navy surgeon would do so,' he muttered.

'Then thank your Maker that I am not one.'

On the second day he was sitting up unaided and eating voraciously, by the third he was managing the ship from his litter, and on the fourth day he was on his quarterdeck once more, although his arm was in a sling and he was still pale and gaunt where the fever had wasted away the flesh from his face, but strong enough to keep on his feet for an hour at a time before resorting to the rope chair the carpenter had rigged at the rail. That day Robyn withdrew the bristle from the wound and was relieved at the tiny quantity of benign pus that followed it out. They watched the little town of Port Natal come up ahead of them, the primitive buildings huddled under the whale-backed mountain they called the Bluff like chickens under the wing of the hen. *Black Joke* did not call, even though this was the furthest outpost of the British Empire on this coast, but steamed on briskly into the north, each day becoming perceptibly warmer with the sun standing higher at noon and the sea changing to the darker azure of the tropics beneath *Black Joke*'s bows, and once again the flying fish sported ahead of them on filmy silver wings.

The evening before they reached the Portuguese settlement of Lourenço Marques on the deep bight of Delagoa Bay, Robyn dressed the stitches in Clinton's side, making small cooing and clucking sounds of satisfaction and approval as she saw how cleanly they were healing.

When she helped him into his shirt and then buttoned it for him, like a mother dressing her child, he told her gravely,

'I am aware you have saved my life.'

'Even though you do not approve of my methods?' she asked with a twinkle of a smile.

'I ask your forgiveness for my impertinence.' He dropped his eyes. 'You have proved yourself to be a brilliant physician.'

She made a modest murmur of denial, but when he insisted, 'No, I truly mean that. I think you are gifted,' Robyn protested no further, but moved slightly to make it easier for him to reach her with his good arm, but his declaration of faith in her skills seemed to have exhausted his courage for the moment.

That evening she vented some of her frustration by confiding to her journal that, 'Captain Codrington is clearly a man that can be trusted by a woman, in any circumstances – though a little more boldness would make him a great deal more attractive.'

She was about to close the journal and lock it away in her chest, when another thought occurred to her, and she thumbed back through the preceding pages each crammed with her small neat script, until she reached the single sheet that had become a milestone in her life. The entry for the day before *Huron* reached Cape Town she had left blank. What words were there to describe it? Each moment of it would be engraved forever on her memory. She stared for many minutes at the empty sheet, and then she made a silent calculation, subtracting one date from another. When she had the answer she felt a chill of foreboding, and went over the calculation again, reaching the same answer.

She closed the journal slowly and stared at the lantern flame.

She had missed her lunar courses by almost a week, and with a prickle of dread lifting the fine hair at the nape of her neck she laid her hand upon her own belly as if there was something to feel there – like the pistol ball in Clinton's flesh.

Black Joke called at Lourenço Marques for coal bunkers, despite the town's notoriety as a fever port. The swamps and mangroves that half-circled the town to the southwards spread the miasmic airs across the port.

Although Robyn had only very limited first-hand experience of the peculiar fevers of Africa, she had made a close study of all the writings on the subject – the most notable of these being probably those of her own father. Fuller Ballantyne had written a long paper for the British Medical Association, in which he recognized four distinct types of African fever – the recurrent fevers with a definite cycle, he divided into three categories – quotidian, tertian and quartan – by the length of the cycle. These he called the malarial fevers. The fourth type was the black vomit, or the yellow jack.

In his own unmistakable style, Fuller Ballantyne had shown that these diseases were neither contagious nor infectious. He had done so by a horrifying but courageous demonstration to a group of sceptical brother physicians at the military hospital at Algoa Bay.

While the other physicians watched, he had collected a wine glass of fresh vomit from a victim of the yellow jack. Fuller had toasted them with the awful draught and then drunk it down at a single swallow. His colleagues had waited, with a certain keen anticipation for his demise and had some difficulty in hiding their disappointment when he showed no ill effects and set off a week later to walk across Africa. Fuller Ballantyne was a man it was easier to admire than to like. The episode had become part of the legend that surrounded him.

In his writings her father insisted that the disease could only be contracted by breathing the night air of tropical areas, particularly those airs released by swamps or other large bodies of stagnant water. However, some individuals most certainly had a natural resistance to the disease, and this resistance was probably hereditary. He cited the African tribes who lived in known malarial areas, and his own family and that of his wife who had lived and worked in Africa for sixty years with only mild afflictions.

Fuller wrote of the 'seasoning fever' – the first dose of which either killed or gave partial immunity to the subject. He used the example of the high mortality rate amongst newly-arrived Europeans in Africa.

He quoted the case of Nathaniel Isaacs who in 1832 left Port Natal in a party with twenty-one newly arrived white men to hunt hippopotamus in the estuary and swamps of St. Lucia river. Within four weeks nineteen had perished – while Isaacs and the other survivor were so wracked with the disease that they were invalids for almost a year thereafter.

These losses were unnecessary, Fuller Ballantyne pointed out. There was a preventative and a cure that had been known for hundreds of years though under various names, Peruvian bark, or Chinchona bark, more recently called essence of quinine when manufactured in powder form by the Quaker brothers Luke and John Howard. Taken at the dosage of five grains daily it was a highly effective preventative, for even if the disease was subsequently contracted, it was in such mild form as to be no more dangerous than a common cold and responded immediately to a more massive dose of twenty-five grains of quinine.

Of course, Robyn had heard the accusation that her father played down the dangers of the disease to further his grand design. Fuller Ballantyne had a vision of Africa settled by colonists of British stock, bringing to the savage continent the true God, and all the benefits of British justice and ingenuity. His catastrophic expedition to the Zambezi had been in pursuit of this vision, for the great river was to have been his highway to the high and healthy plateau of the interior where his Englishmen would settle, driving out the slavers, bringing the warring and godless tribes to order, and taming and cultivating the savage earth.

Part of his vision had died upon the terrible torrents and rapids of the Kaborra-Bassa gorge.

With a sneaking sensation of disloyalty Robyn admitted to herself that there was probably some shred of justification in the accusation, for she had as a child seen her father in the grip of a malarial fever brought out by the cold of an English winter. It had not seemed as mild as a common cold then. Despite this, there was no one in the medical profession who doubted that Fuller Ballantyne was probably one of the world's leading authorities on the disease and that he had a real talent in diagnosing and treating it. So she followed his dictates faithfully, administering the daily five grains of quinine to herself, to Zouga and under protest to Captain Codrington. She had no success with Zouga's Hottentot musketeers, however. At the first dose Jan Cheroot had begun staggering in circles, clutching his throat and rolling his eyes horribly, crying to all his Hottentot gods that he had been poisoned. Only a tot of ship's rum saved him, but none of the other Hottentots would touch the white powder after that. Not even the thought of a tot of rum would tempt them, which was a measure of their opposition to the cure. Robyn could only hope that they possessed the resistance to the fever that her father spoke of.

Her store of quinine was meant to last for the duration of the expedition, possibly as long as two years, so she had reluctantly to refrain from pressing any of it on *Black Joke*'s seamen. She stilled her conscience with the fact that none of them would be spending a night ashore, therefore they would not be exposed to the dangerous airs. She prevailed upon Clinton Codrington to anchor in the outer roads where the onshore breeze kept the air sweet and, as an added attraction, the distance offshore prevented the swarms of mosquitoes and other flying insects from coming on board during the night.

The first night at anchor, the sound of music, of drunken laughter and the shrill cries of women at play and at work carried across the still waters to the nine Hottentot musketeers in their corner of the forecastle, and the lights of the bordels and bars along the waterfront were as irresistible to the nine as a candle to a hawk moth. Temptation was made unbearable by the weight and heat of the golden sovereign that each of them carried in some secret place upon his person, the princely advance that Major Ballantyne had made against their salaries.

Sergeant Cheroot woke Zouga a little before midnight, his features a mask of outrage.

'They are gone.' He was shaking with anger.

'Where?' Zouga was still more asleep than awake.

'They swim like rats,' stormed Cheroot. 'They all go drinking and awhoring.' The thought of it was insupportable. 'We must catch them. They will burn their brains out on smoke and pox themselves—' His rage was mixed with an equal portion of raw envy, and once they were ashore his enthusiasm for the chase was almost a frenzy. Cheroot had an unerring instinct that led him directly to the lowest dives on the waterfront.

'You go in, Master,' he told Zouga. 'I'll wait around the back,' and he twitched the short oaken club in his hand with gleeful anticipation.

The tobacco smoke and the fumes of cheap rum and gin were like a solid wall, but the musketeers saw Zouga the moment he stooped through the doorway into the yellow lantern light. There were four of them. They overturned two tables and smashed a dozen bottles in their eagerness to depart, jamming in a solid knot in the doorway to the rear alley before bursting out into the night beyond.

It took Zouga half a minute to push and wrestle his way through the crowd. The women of a dozen rich shades between gold and ebony reached out to pluck shamelessly at the more private areas of his anatomy as he passed, forcing him to defend himself, and the men deliberately blocked his path until he drew the Colt revolver from under his coat tails – only then they sullenly opened a way for him to pass. When he reached the back door Sergeant Cheroot had the four Hottentots laid out in a row in the filth and dust of the alley.

'You haven't killed them?' Zouga asked anxiously.

'*Nee wat!* They got heads of solid bone.' Cheroot tucked the club back in his belt, and stooped to pick up one of the bodies. The strength of his wiry little body was out of all proportion to its size. He carried them down to the beach one at a time as though they were bags of straw, and dumped them head first into the waiting whaler.

'Now we find the others.'

They ferreted them out, singly and in pairs, from the fan-tan parlours and the gin hells, tracking down the ninth and last to the embrace of an enormous naked Somali lady in one of the shacks of mud walls and corrugated iron roofs behind the waterfront.

It was almost dawn when Zouga climbed wearily out of the whaler on to *Black Joke*'s deck and booted the ninth Hottentot down the forecastle ladder. He started for his own cabin, red-eyed and irritable, aching with fatigue when it occurred to him that he had not noticed Sergeant Cheroot amongst the dark figures in the whaler, and his penetrating voice and biting sarcasm had been silent on the return from the beach.

Zouga's mood was murderous as he landed once again, and picked his way through the narrow filth-choked alleys to the mud and iron shack. The woman made up four of Jan Cheroot. She was a mountain of polished dark flesh, gleaming with oil, each of her widespread thighs thicker than his waist, her great mammaries each as large as his head, and Jan Cheroot's head was buried between them as though he was drowning himself in exotic and abundant flesh so that his ecstatic cries were almost smothered.

The woman looked down at him fondly, chuckling to herself as she watched Sergeant Cheroot's upended buttocks. They were skinny and a delicate shade of buttercup yellow, but they seemed to blur with the speed of movement, and the shock waves they created were transferred into the mountain of flesh beneath him, creating ripples and waves that undulated through the woman's belly and elephantine haunches, travelling up to agitate the pendulous folds that hung from her upper arms, and at last breaking in a wobbling heaving surf of gleaming black flesh around Sergeant Cheroot's head.

On the final return to the gunboat, Sergeant Cheroot sat, a small dejected figure, in the bows of the whaler. His post-coital tristesse considerably enhanced by the buzzing in his ears and the ache in his head. Only Englishmen had the alarming habit of bunching up a hand suddenly, and then hitting with more effect than a man wielding a club or hurling a brick. Sergeant Cheroot found his respect for his new master increasing daily.

'You should be an example to the men,' Zouga growled at him as he hoisted him up the ladder by the collar of his uniform jacket.

'I know that, Master,' Cheroot agreed miserably. 'But I was in love.'

'Are you still in love?' Zouga demanded harshly.

'No, Master, with me love don't last too long,' Cheroot assured him hurriedly.

'I am a modestly wealthy man,' Clinton Codrington told Robyn seriously. 'Since my days as a midshipman I have saved as much of my pay as I did not need to live by, and of recent years I have been fortunate in the matter of prize money. This, together with the legacy of my mother, would enable me to care very comfortably for a wife.'

They had lunched with the Portuguese Governor at his invitation and the *vinho verde* that had accompanied the meal of succulent seafood and tasteless stringy beef had given Clinton a flush of courage.

Rather than returning immediately to the ship after the meal, he had suggested a tour of the principal city of the Portuguese possessions on the east coast of the African continent.

The Governor's dilapidated carriage rumbled over the rutted roads and splashed through the puddles formed by the overflow from the open sewers. A raucous flock of ragged child-beggars followed them, dancing in their dirty rags to keep pace with the bony, sway-backed mule that drew the carriage, and holding up their tiny pink-palmed hands for alms. The sun was fierce but not as fierce as the smells.

It was not the appropriate setting for what Clinton Codrington had in mind, and with relief he handed Robyn down from the carriage, scattered the beggars by hurling a handful of copper coins down the dusty street, and hurried Robyn into the cool gloom of the Roman Catholic cathedral. The cathedral was the most magnificent building in the city, its towers and spires rising high above the hovels and shacks that surrounded it.

However, Robyn had difficulty in concentrating on Clinton's declaration in these popish surroundings, amongst the gaudy idols, saints and virgins in scarlet and gold leaf. The reek of incense and the flickering of the massed banks of candles distracted her, even though what he was saying was what she wanted to hear, she wished he had chosen some other place to say it.

That very morning she had been taken by a sudden spell of vomiting, and a mild nausea persisted even now. As a physician she knew exactly what that heralded.

Before the courtesy visit to the Portuguese Governor's mouldering palace, she had tentatively decided that she would have to take the initiative. That attack of vapours had convinced her of the urgency of the situation, and she had pondered how she could induce Clinton Codrington to stake some sort of claim to the burden she was convinced she was carrying.

When Zouga had still lived at King's Lynn with Uncle William, she had discovered a cheaply printed novel of a most disreputable type concealed amongst the military texts on Zouga's desk. From a furtive study of this publication she had learned that it was possible for a woman to seduce a man, as well as the other way around. Unfortunately, the author had not provided a detailed description of the procedures. She had not even been certain if it were possible in a carriage, or whether anything should be said during the process, but now Clinton was obviating the necessity for experiment by a straight-forward declaration. Her relief was tinged with shades of disappointment, after having been forced into the decision to carry out his seduction, she had found herself looking forward to the experience.

Now, however, she forced herself to assume an attentive expression and, when he hesitated, to encourage him with a nod or a gesture.

'Even though I am without powerful friends in the service, yet my record is such that I would never expect half-pay appointment, and although it might sound immodest I would confidently look forward to hoisting my own broad pennant before I am fifty years of age.'

It was typical of him that he was already thinking twenty-five years ahead. It required an effort to prevent her irritation showing, for Robyn preferred to live in the present, or at least the immediately foreseeable future.

'I should point out that an Admiral's wife enjoys a great deal of social prestige,' he went on comfortably, and her irritation flared higher. Prestige was something she had always intended to win at first hand – crusader against the slave trade, celebrated pioneer in tropical medicine, writer of admired books on African travel.

She could not contain it longer, but her voice was sweet and demure. 'A woman can have a career as well as being a wife.'

Clinton drew himself up stiffly. 'A wife's place is in the home,' he intoned, and she opened her mouth, then slowly closed it again. She knew she was bargaining from weakness, and when she was silent Clinton was encouraged. 'To begin with a comfortable little house, near the harbour in Portsmouth. Of course, once there are children one would have to seek larger premises—'

'You would want many children?' she asked still sweetly, but with colour mounting in her cheeks.

'Oh yes, indeed. One a year,' and Robyn recalled those pale drabs with whom she had worked, women with brats hanging from both breasts and every limb, with another one always in the belly. She shuddered, and he was immediately concerned.

'Are you cold?'

'No. No, please go on.' She felt trapped, and not for the first time resented the role that her sex had forced upon her.

'Miss Ballantyne – Doctor Ballantyne – what I have been trying to say to you – is that I would be greatly honoured if you could find it in yourself to consent to become my wife.'

Now when it came she was not really ready for it, and her confusion was genuine.

'Captain Codrington, this comes as such a surprise—'

'I do not see why. My admiration for you must be apparent, and the other day you led me to believe—' He hesitated, and then with a rush, 'you even allowed me to embrace you.'

Suddenly she was overcome with the urge to burst out laughing, if only he had known her further intentions towards him – but she skittered away from the subject, her expression as solemn as his.

'When would we be able to marry?' she asked instead.

'Well, on my return to—'

'There is a British consul at Zanzibar, and you are bound there, are you not?' she interrupted quickly. 'He could perform the ceremony.'

Clinton's face lit with slow, deep joy. 'Oh Miss Ballantyne, does that mean – can I take it that—' He took a pace towards her, and she had a vivid image of a tiny house in Portsmouth bursting at the seams with little blond replicas of himself, and she took a quick pace backwards and went on hurriedly.

'I need time to think.'

He stopped, joy faded and he said heavily, 'Of course.'

'It means such a change in my life, I would have to abandon all my plans. The expedition – it's such a big decision.'

'I could wait – a year, longer if necessary. Until after the expedition, as long as you wished,' he told her earnestly, and she felt a flutter of panic deep in her belly.

'No, I mean I need a few days, that is all,' and she laid her hand on his forearm. 'I will give you an answer before we reach Quelimane. I promise you that.'

Sheikh Yussuf was a worried man. For eight days the big dhow-rigged vessel had lain within sight of land, the single, huge lateen sail drooped from the long yard, the sea about her was velvet smooth during the day and afire with phosphorus during the long moonless, windless nights.

So deep and utter was the calm that not the slightest swell moved the surface. The dhow lay so still that she might have been hard aground.

The Sheikh was a master mariner who owned a fleet of trading vessels and who for forty years had threaded the seaways of the Indian Ocean. He knew intimately each island, each headland and the tricks of the tides that swirled about them. He knew the great roads that the currents cut across the waters the way a post coachman knows each turn and dip of the road between his stages, and he could run them without compass or sextant, steering only by the heavenly bodies a thousand miles and more across open water, making his unerring landfalls on the great horn of Africa, on the coast of India and back again on the island of Zanzibar.

In forty years he had never known the monsoon wind to fail for eight successive days at this season of the year. All his calculations had been based on the wind standing steady out of the south-east, day and night, hour after hour, day after day.

He had taken on his cargo with that expectation, calculating that he could discharge again on Zanzibar Island within six days of loading. Naturally, a man expected losses, they were an integral part of his calculations. Ten per cent losses was the very least, twenty was more likely, thirty was acceptable, forty was always possible and even losses of fifty per cent would still leave the voyage in profit.

But not this. He looked up at the stubby foremast from which drooped the fifteen-foot-long scarlet banner of the Sultan of Zanzibar, beloved of Allah, ruler of all the Omani Arabs and overlord of vast tracts of eastern Africa. The banner was faded and soiled as the lateen sail, both of them veterans of fifty such voyages, of calms and hurricanes, of baking sun and the driving torrential rains of the high monsoon. The golden Arabic script that covered the banner was barely legible now, and he had lost count of the number of times it had been taken down from the masthead and carried at the head of his column of armed men deep into the interior of that brooding land on the horizon.

How many times had that banner wafted out proudly, long and sinuous as a serpent on the breeze, as he brought his vessel up under the fort at Zanzibar Island. Sheikh Yussuf caught himself dreaming again. It was an old man's failing. He straightened up on the pile of cushions and precious rugs of silk and gold thread, and looked down from his command position on the poop deck. His crew lay like dead men in the shade of the sail, their grubby robes folded up over their heads against the heat. Let them lie, he decided, there was nothing mortal man could do now, except wait. It was in the hands of Allah now. 'There is one God,' he murmured. 'And Mohammed is his prophet.' It did not occur to him to question his fate, to rail or pray against it. It was God's will, and God is great.

Yet he could not help feeling regret. It was thirty years since he had taken such a fine cargo as this, and at prices that compared with those of thirty years before.

Three hundred and thirty black pearls, each one perfectly formed, young, by Allah, not one of them over sixteen years of age. They were of a people he had never encountered before, for he had never before traded so far south. It was only in this last season that he had heard of the new source of black pearl from beyond the Djinn Mountains, that forbidden land from which no man returned.

A new people, well favoured and beautifully formed, strong and tall, sturdy limbs, not those stickline legs of the people from beyond the lakes; these had full-moon faces and good strong white teeth. Sheikh Yussuf nodded over his pipe, the water bubbled softly in the bowl of the hookah at each inhalation and he let the smoke trickle out softly between his lips. It had stained his white beard pale yellow at the corners of his mouth, and at each lungful he felt the delightful lethargy steal through his old veins, and take the edge off the cold frost of age which seemed always now to chill his blood.

There was suddenly a higher pitched shriek, that rose above the low hubbub which enveloped the dhow. The sound was part of the ship, day and night it came up from the slave hold below the dhow's maindeck.

Sheikh Yussuf removed the mouthpiece from his lips and cocked his head to listen, combing his fingers through his scraggling white beard – but the shriek was not repeated. It was perhaps the final cry from one of his fine black pearls.

Sheikh Yussuf sighed, the din from below decks had slowly decreased in volume while the dhow lay becalmed, and he was able to judge with great accuracy how high his losses were by that volume. He knew he had already lost half of them. Another quarter at the very least would perish before he could reach Zanzibar, many more would go even after they were landed, only the very hardiest would be fit for the market, and then only after careful convalescence.

Another indication of his losses, though not as accurate, was the smell.

Some of them must have gone on the very first day of the calm and without the wind the heat had been blinding. It would be even worse in the holds, the corpses would be swollen to twice life-size. The smell was bad, he could not recall a worse stench in all his forty years. It was a pity that there was no way in which to remove the bodies, but this could only be done in port.

Sheikh Yussuf dealt only in young females. They were smaller and much hardier than males of the same age, and could be loaded more densely. He had been able to reduce the clearance between each deck by six inches, which meant an entire extra deck could be built into the hold.

Females had a remarkable ability to go without water for longer periods than the males, like the camel of the desert they seemed able to exist on the accumulated fat in their thighs, buttocks and bosoms, and to make the Mozambique passage even in the fairest conditions of wind and tide required five days without water.

Another consideration was the loss of males destined for China and the Far East by the necessary surgery. The Chinese buyers insisted that all male slaves be castrated before they would purchase. It was a logical precaution to prevent breeding with local populations, but one that entailed additional losses to the trader who must perform the operation.

The final reason that Sheikh Yussuf dealt only in comely young females was that they commanded a price almost twice that of a young male slave in the Zanzibar market.

Before Sheikh Yussuf loaded his wares, he allowed them to fatten for at least a week in his barracoons, with as much to eat and drink as they could force down their throats. Then they were stripped naked, except for light chains, and at low tide taken out to the dhow where it lay high and dry on the shoaling beach.

The first girls aboard were made to lie on the bare boards of the hull in the bottom of the hold, each on her left side with her knees raised slightly so that the knees of the girl behind her could fit against the back of her legs, the front of her pelvis against buttocks, belly against back, like a row of spoons in a rack.

At intervals the chains were snapped into the ring bolts already set into the deck. This was not only for security but also to prevent the layer of human bodies sliding about in rough weather, piling up in heaps and crushing those beneath.

Once the bottom of the hold was covered with a layer of humanity, the next deck was placed in position over them, so close that they could not attempt to sit upright nor roll over. The next layer of girls was laid over them, and the next deck over them again.

To reach the lower decks meant laboriously unchaining and unloading each layer of humanity, and lifting the intervening decks. It could not even be attempted at sea. However, with the trade wind standing fair, it was a straight run down the channel, and the wind blowing in through the canvas scoops and ports, kept the air below decks breathable, and the heat bearable.

Sheikh Yussuf sighed again and lifted his rheumy eyes to the unbroken blue line of the eastern horizon.

'This will be my last voyage,' he decided, whispering aloud in the way of old men. 'Allah has been good and I am a rich man with many strong sons. Perhaps this is his sign to me. This will indeed be my last voyage.'

It was almost as though he had been overheard, for the scarlet banner moved lazily, like an adder emerging from long hibernation, then slowly reared its head, and Sheikh Yussuf felt the wind on his seared and wrinkled cheek.

He stood up suddenly, quick and supple as a man half his age, and stamped his bare foot on the deck.

'Up,' he cried. 'Up, my children. Here is the wind at last.' And while his crew scrambled to their feet, he took the long tiller under his arm and threw back his head to watch the sail bulge outwards, and the thick clumsy pole of the mainmast heel slowly across a horizon suddenly dark with the scurry of the trade wind.

Clinton Codrington caught the first whiff of it during the night. It woke him from a nightmare that he had lived through on many other nights, but when he lay sweating in his narrow wooden bunk the smell persisted and he threw a boat cloak over his bare shoulders and hurried up on deck.

It came in gusts out of the darkness, for minutes at a time the warm sweet rush of the trade wind brought only the iodine and salt smell of the sea, then suddenly there was another curdled whiff of it. It was a smell that Clinton would never forget, like the smell of a cage full of carnivorous beasts that had never been cleaned, the stench of excrement and rotten flesh, and his nightmare came rushing back upon him in full strength.

Ten years before, when Clinton had been a very junior midshipman aboard the old *Widgeon*, one of the very first gunboats of the anti-slavery squadron, they had taken a slaver in northern latitudes. She was a schooner of 300 tons burden, out of Lisbon, but flying a Brazilian flag of convenience, with the unlikely name of *Hirondelle Blanche*, the *White Swallow*. Clinton had been ordered into her as prize-master with orders to run her into the nearest Portuguese port and deliver her to the Courts of Mixed Commission to be condemned as a prize.

They had made the capture a hundred nautical miles off the Brazilian coast, after the *Hirondelle Blanche* and her five hundred black slaves had almost completed the dreaded middle passage. Under orders, Clinton had turned the schooner and sailed her back to the Cape Verde Islands, crossing the equator to do so and lying three days becalmed in the doldrums before breaking from their suffocating grip.

In the harbour of Praia, on the principal island of São Tiago, Clinton had been refused permission to land any of his slaves, and they had lain sixteen days waiting for the Portuguese president of the Court of Mixed Commission to reach a decision. Finally, the President had decided, after strenuous representation by the owners of the *Hirondelle Blanche* that he had no jurisdiction in the case, and ordered Clinton to sail her back to Brazil and submit the vessel to the Brazilian courts.

However, Clinton knew very well what a Brazilian court would decide, and instead set a course for the British naval station on St. Helena Island, once more crossing the equator with his burden of human misery.

By the time he dropped anchor in Jamestown roads, the surviving slaves aboard had made three consecutive crossings of the terrible middle passage. There were only twenty-six of them still alive, and the smell of a slaver had become part of the nightmares which still plagued Clinton ten years later.

Now he stood on the darkened deck and flared his nostrils, the same smell coming to him out of the tropical night, horrible and unmistakable. He had to drag himself away with a physical effort to give the orders to fire *Black Joke*'s furnace and work up a head of steam in her boilers, ready for the dawn.

Sheikh Yussuf recognized the dark shape with a sense of utter disbelief, and the dismay of one finally deserted by Allah.

She was still five miles distant, indistinct in the dusty pink light of the dawn, but coming up swiftly, a thick column of black smoke smearing away on her beam, carried low over the green waters of the inshore channel by the boisterous trade wind. The same wind spread out her ensign to full view from the poop of the dhow, and in the field of Sheikh Yussuf's ancient brass and leatherbound telescope it snapped and flickered, the snowy white field crossed by bold bright scarlet.

How he hated that flag, the symbol of an arrogant, bullying people, tyrants of the oceans, captors of continents. He had seen gunboats like this one in Aden and Calcutta, he had seen that same flag flying in every far corner of every sea he had ever sailed. Very clearly he knew what it all meant.

He put up the helm, in that gesture acknowledging the final end to a disastrous voyage, the dhow came around reluctantly, creaking in every timber, the great sail flogging before it could be trimmed to take the wind over the stern.

There had seemed to be so little risk, he thought with weary resignation. Of course, the treaty that the Sultan had made with the Zanzibar consul of these dangerous infidels allowed his subjects to trade in the black pearls, between any of the Sultan's possessions, with the proviso that only Omani Arabs loyal to the Sultan could indulge in the lucrative traffic. No person of Christian European extraction, not even a converted Moslem, could sail under the Sultan's flag, and not even an Omani Arab might trade beyond the borders of the Sultan's possessions.

The Sultan's African possessions had been very carefully defined in the treaty, and here was he, Sheikh Yussuf, with a cargo of three hundred and thirty living, dying and dead slaves at least one hundred and fifty miles south of the furthest of the Sultan's borders, with a British gunboat bearing down upon him. Truly the ways of Allah were wonderful, passing the comprehension of man, Sheikh Yussuf thought with only the slightest taste of bitterness in his throat, as he hung grimly on to the tiller and made his run for the land.

A gun thumped from the gunboat's bows, powder smoke flew bright as a seabird's wing in the first rays of the low sun, and Sheikh Yussuf spat passionately over the lee bulwark and said aloud.

'El Sheetan, the Devil,' using for the first time the name with which, in time, Captain Clinton Codrington would be known throughout the length of the Mozambique channel, and as far north as the great Horn of Africa.

The bronze screw under *Black Joke*'s counter thrashed out a long wide wake behind her. She still had main and jib set, but Codrington would shorten to 'fighting sail' just as soon as he had made the adjustment to counter the dhow's turn away towards the land.

Zouga and Robyn were on the quarterdeck to watch the chase, infected by the restrained businesslike excitement which gripped the vessel so that Zouga laughed aloud and called, 'Gone away! Tally-ho!' as the dhow turned, and Clinton glanced at him with a conspiratory grin.

'She's a slaver. Apart from the stink, that turn-away proves it beyond doubt.'

Robyn strained forward to watch the filthy little vessel, with its discoloured and patched sail, the unpainted timbers of the hull striped with zebra stripes of human excrement and other wastes. It was her first view of a slaver actually carrying on its grisly trade, and she felt herself filled with a new purpose; she had come so far for this moment, and she tried to capture every detail of it all for her journal.

'Mr. Denham, give him a gun, if you please' ordered Clinton.

The bow-chaser thudded, but the dhow held to her new course.

'Be ready to round up and send the boat away on the instant.' Clinton's excitement had given way to obvious anxiety. He turned to look across at his boarding-party. They had been issued with cutlass and pistol, and waited now in the waist under the command of a young ensign.

Clinton would dearly have liked to command the boarding-party himself, but his arm was still in its sling and the stitches still in the wound. To go aboard a dhow in a rough sea, and fight its crew required both hands and the agility which his wound denied him. Reluctantly he had put Ferris in charge of the boarders.

Now he looked back at the dhow, and his expression was grim.

'He is going to beach.'

They were all silent now, staring ahead, watching the slaver run in towards the land.

'But there is a coral reef.' Robyn spoke for them all, pointing to the black points that broke the surface a quarter of a mile short of the land itself, they looked like a necklace of sharks teeth, and the surf broke and swirled about them as it was driven in upon the trade wind.

'Yes,' Clinton agreed. 'They will run it up on the coral and escape across the lagoon.'

'But, what about the slaves?' Robyn asked, horrified, and nobody answered her.

Black Joke rushed on purposefully, but with the wind almost dead astern the dhow trained her long boom around to go on to her best point of sailing. The boom was longer than the hull itself, and the huge triangular mainsail bulged far out, almost touching the surface of the water as she hurled down upon the reef.

'We may just cut her off,' Zouga said loudly, but he did not have the seaman's eye for bearing and speed, and Clinton Codrington shook his head angrily.

'Not this time.'

But it was very finely run. Clinton held his course up until the very last moment, and the dhow passed a mere two hundred yards ahead of his bows. So close that they could clearly make out the features of the helmsman on the vessel's poopdeck, a skinny old Arab in long, flowing robe and with the tasselled fez on his head that declared that he had made the pilgrimage to Mecca. On his belt glittered the gold filigree hilt of the short curved dagger of a sheikh, and his long scraggling white beard fluttered in the wind as he leaned on the long tiller and turned his head to watch the high black hull bearing down on him.

'I could put a bullet through the bastard,' Zouga growled.

'It's too late for that,' Clinton told him, for the dhow had passed beneath their bows and the gunboat was as close to the menacing fangs of coral as she dared go. Clinton called to his quartermaster at the gunboat's wheel, 'Heave to! And bring her head to wind.' Then, spinning on his heel, 'Away, the boarding-party!'

There was a squeal of davits as the crowded whaler dropped out of sight towards the choppy green sea alongside, but already the dhow was pitching wildly in the lines of seething white surf that guarded the reef.

It was two days since that dead flat calm had broken, and since then the trades had worked up a goodly swell. It came sweeping in across the inshore channel, in low green humps with dark wind-scarred backs, but as soon as they felt the tilt of the land, they peaked up eagerly, the crests turning opaque as green jelly, shivering and wobbling, and then collapsing on themselves and surging in tumultuous white water up on to the black fangs of the reef.

The dhow caught one of the taller swells, threw up her stern and went racing down upon it like a surf boat, with the skinny old Arab at the tiller prancing like a trained monkey on the stick of the tiller to hold her in the wave, but the dhow was not built for this work, and she dug her shoulder rebelliously into the sliding, roaring chute of green water, breaching so fiercely to the wave that the water poured aboard her in a green wall and she wallowed broadside, half swamped before she took the reef with a force that snapped off her single mast at deck level and sent yard and sail and rigging crashing over the side.

In an instant she was transformed into a broken hulk, and clearly the watchers on *Black Joke*'s deck could hear the crackle and rending of her bottom timbers.

'There they go!' Clinton muttered angrily, as the dhow's crew began to abandon her, leaping over the side and using the swells to carry them over the reef into the quieter waters of the lagoon, thrashing and kicking until the beach shelved up beneath them.

They saw the old Arab steersman amongst the survivors. He waded ashore, beard and robe plastered against his body with seawater, and then lifted his robes to his waist, exposing skinny legs and shrunken buttocks as he scampered up the white beach with the agility of a goat and disappeared amongst the palm groves.

Black Joke's whaler pulled swiftly into the first line of breakers, the Ensign in the stern peering over his shoulder to judge the surf, and then catching his wave taking her in with a rush, swinging sharply into the lee of the dhow's stranded hull where there was calmer water.

They watched the Ensign and four of his men go up over the side, pistols and cutlasses drawn, but by this time the last of the Arab crew were staggering up the beach and into the sanctuary of the palm grove a quarter of a mile away across the lagoon.

The Ensign led his men below decks, and they waited on *Black Joke*'s quarterdeck, watching the abandoned dhow through the telescope. A minute passed before the Ensign appeared on deck again. He crossed quickly to the dhow's rail and leaned against it to vomit over the side, then straightened up and wiped his mouth on the back of his sleeve, before shouting an order down to the oarsmen in the whaler.

Immediately the whaler shot out from the lee of the hull, and pulled lustily back through the surf towards *Black Joke*.

The boatswain came in through the entry port, and knuckled his forehead to his captain.

'Mr. Ferris's compliments, sir, and he needs a carpenter to get the slave decks open, and two good men with bolt cutters for the chains.' He had gabbled this out on a single breath, and he paused to refill his lungs. 'Mr. Ferris says as how it's fierce bad below decks, and some of them is trapped – and he needs the doctor—'

'I'm ready to go,' Robyn cut in.

'Wait,' Clinton snapped, but Robyn had gathered her skirts and run.

'If my sister goes, I'm going too.'

'Very well, then, Ballantyne, I'm obliged for your assistance,' Clinton nodded. 'Tell Ferris we have an incoming tide, full moon tonight, so it will make springs. There is a twenty-two foot tidal fall on this coast. He will have less than an hour in which to work.'

Robyn appeared on deck again, lugging her black leather valise, and she had exchanged skirts for breeches once more. The seamen on deck gawked at her legs curiously, but she ignored them and hurried to the ship's side. The boatswain gave her a hand and she scrambled down into the whaler with Zouga carrying her valise behind her.

The ride in through the surf was terrifying and exhilarating at the same time; the whaler tilted forward at an alarming angle, the water hissing and creaming alongside, with a belly-swooping rush that ended alongside the dhow's heavily canted side.

The deck was running with water and listed so steeply that Robyn had to crawl up it on her hands and knees, and each time a wave struck the hull, it quivered and shook and more water came streaming down over the deck.

The Ensign and his boarding-party had ripped the hatches off the main hold, and as she reached them, Robyn gagged and choked with the solid stench that came out of that square opening. She had believed herself hardened to the smell of death and corruption, but never had she experienced anything like this.

'Did you bring the bolt-cutters?' the Ensign demanded, white-faced with nausea and horror.

The bolt-cutters were heavy-duty shears, used for cutting the shrouds and halyards from a dismasted vessel. Two men wielded them now, as they lifted a bunch of small black bodies through the hatch, all of them fastened together at wrist and ankle by the clanking black steel links. It reminded Robyn of the cut-out paper dolls she had amused herself with as a child, fashioning with scissors a single figure from the folded sheet, and then pulling out a chain of identical dolls. The cutters crunched through the light chain and the limp little bodies fell apart.

'They are children,' she cried out aloud, and the men around her worked in grim silence, dragging them out of the hatch, cutting them free and dropping them on to the tilted wet deck.

Robyn seized the first of them, a skeletal stick figure, crusted and streaked with dried filth, vomit and faeces, head lolling as she lifted it into her lap.

'No.' There was no life. The eyeballs had dried already. She let the head drop and a seaman dragged it away.

'No,' and 'No,' and 'No again.' Some of them were already in an advanced state of putrification; at a word from the Ensign, the seamen began dropping the wasted corpses over the side, to make room for those still coming up from below.

Robyn found her first live one, there was feeble pulse and fluttering breath, but it did not need a physician's instinct to tell that the hold on life was tenuous. She worked swiftly, apportioning her time to where the chance of life seemed greater.

Another taller wave struck the dhow, and it tilted sharply, the timbers crackled and snapped deep inside her.

'Tides flooding. Work faster,' shouted the Ensign. They were into the hull now. Robyn could hear the thud of sledge hammers and the rip of irons as they began to tear the slave decks out of her.

Zouga was in there, stripped to the waist, leading the attack on the wooden barricades. He was an officer, with the easy way of command and his natural leadership was swiftly acknowledged by the seamen around him.

The hubbub reminded Robyn of a rookery at sundown, the shrieks of the returning birds and the answering cries from the chicks in the nests. The mass of black girls were aroused from the lethargy of approaching death by the dhow's wild antics, the crash of breaking timbers and the flood of cold salt water into the hold.

Some of those lying in the bilges were already drowning as the hold flooded, and some of them realized that there was a rescue team aboard, and cried aloud with the last strength of waning hope.

Alongside the slaver, the whaler was moored, and she was almost filled with the wasted bodies in which some life still burned, while on the surface of the lagoon bobbed a hundred or more corpses with gas-swollen bellies like the corks on a fishing-net.

'Take them to the ship,' the Ensign shouted down to his oarsmen in the whaler, 'and come back for more.' As he spoke, another white-crested wave struck the dhow solidly and she heeled, but she was pinned down by the spikes of coral driven through her bottom timbers, otherwise she would have turned turtle.

'Robyn!' Zouga shouted at her from the hatch. 'We need you!'

For a moment she did not even glance at him, but shook her head at the sailor beside her.

'No, she's gone.' Expressionlessly the sailor picked up the frail body and dumped it over the side.

Then Robyn scrambled up to the hatch and dropped through it.

It was a descent into the pit, dark after the brilliant noon tide, so that she paused for a moment to let her vision adjust.

The tilting deck beneath her feet was slippery with human waste, so that she had to cling for a handhold.

The air was so thick that for a minute she nearly panicked, as though she were being smothered by a stinking damp pillow. She almost fought her way back into the sweet sunlight, but then she forced herself to take a gulp of it, and though her guts heaved and she tasted the bitter flooding into the back of her throat, she kept it down.

Then her own discomfort was forgotten as she made out the chaos about her.

'That last wave,' Zouga grunted as he steadied her with an arm about her shoulder, 'the decks have collapsed.'

Like a house of cards they had folded in upon each other, raw splinters of timber thrusting up out of the gloom, baulks crossed like the blades of a scissors, with small dark bodies trapped in the jaws, others crushed by the fallen beams, squashed so that they were no longer recognizable as human, others dangling head down on their ankle-chains, suspended in space, writhing weakly as crippled insects, or hanging quietly, swinging to the dhow's movements.

'Oh, sweet Mother of God, where to begin,' Robyn whispered. She let go her handhold, starting forward and her feet shot out from under her on the slick-coated deck, and she went plunging down into the hold.

She struck heavily and pain flared in her back and lower body, but she dragged herself on to her knees. Her own pain seemed insignificant in this terrible prison.

'Are you all right?' Zouga asked anxiously, but she shrugged his hands away.

There was one girl screaming. Robyn crawled to her. Her legs were crushed below the knees, trapped under a baulk of hand-hewn timber.

'Can you move that?' she asked Zouga.

'No, she's done for. Come, there are others—'

'No.' Robyn crawled back to where her bag had fallen. The pain was bad, but she forced it below the surface of her consciousness.

She had only seen a leg amputation performed once before. When she started the girl threw off the seamen who held her and attacked Robyn like a tortured wild cat. Her nails raked skin from Robyn's cheek, but by the time Robyn had freed the first leg below the knee, the child was silent and limp. She died before Robyn had reached the bone of the second leg, and Robyn was weeping chokingly to herself as she left the body still hanging in the grip of the timber baulk.

She scrubbed her hands together, they were bloodied to the elbows, her palms sticky against each other. She felt consumed by guilt at her failure, without the strength to move. Dully, she stared about her now.

The hold was more than half flooded, the tide pounded remorselessly at the ship's hull.

'We have to get out,' Zouga called to her urgently, and when she did not turn her head, he seized her shoulder and shook her roughly. 'There's nothing more we can do. It will capsize at any moment.'

Robyn was staring down into the stinking black waters which sloshed from one end of the hold to the other, a single hand broke through the surface directly below her, a child's hand with soft pink palm and pretty tapered fingers spread in a gesture of appeal. The iron cuff seemed too large for the narrow wrist, and weighted it down so the hand sank gently disappearing from her sight. She stared after it with infinite regret, then Zouga hauled her roughly to her feet.

'Come on, damn it!' His face was savage, haunted with the horrors he had experienced in this fetid, half-flooded hull.

The next wave hit the swamped hull, and this time it broke the grip of the coral. Timber squealed as it twisted and tore, and the dhow began to roll, the filthy waters rose up out of the darkness into a steep black wave and burst about them, shoulder deep.

The damaged slave decks broke free, sliding down over each other, tumultuous and lethal, releasing a fresh layer of tightly packed black bodies to tumble loosely into the flooded depths.

'Robyn! We'll be trapped.' He dragged her up towards the square of brilliant sunlight, clambering over timbers and bodies.

'We can't leave them,' Robyn resisted.

'They're finished, damn it. The whole thing is going. We have to get out.'

She pulled her arm free, stumbled, collapsed backwards, hit something so that pain flared through her lower body again and she cried out with the strength of it. She was lying on her side, couched on a pile of linked bodies, and there was a face a foot from hers. It was alive, she had never seen such eyes, cat fierce, falcon bright, the colour of boiling honey.

'This one is strong enough!' Robyn thought, and then she shouted. 'Help me Zouga.'

'For God's sake, Robyn.'

She crawled forward and reached the black child, and the deck tilted viciously under her, fresh cold water bursting into the hull.

'Leave her,' shouted Zouga.

The fresh flood swirled up around Robyn's head, and the chained girl disappeared below it.

Robyn lunged for her, groping blindly below the surface, feeling panic rise in her when she could not find the child.

Ducking her head under, choking as the pain in her belly made her gasp and she swallowed water, she at last got a grip on the girl's shoulder, feeling her struggling as desperately as she.

Together they came out above the surface, coughing and gasping weakly, Robyn holding the girl's mouth just clear of the surface, but when she tried to lift her further the chain anchored them both and she screamed.

'Zouga, help me!'

Another surge of water, smelling like raw sewage, filled her mouth and both of them went under once more.

She thought she would never come up again, but stubbornly she held on, sliding one arm under the girl's armpit, and with the other hand gripping her chin, forcing it up so that when they broke out again the girl's face was lifted to take another precious breath of the stinking air, and Zouga was with them.

He took a double turn of the chain around his wrists and threw all his weight on to it. In the gloom of the hull he towered over them, the light from the hatch highlighting the bulging wet muscles in his arms and shoulders as he strained at the chain, his mouth opened in a silent scream of effort, sinewy cords standing out of his throat.

Another wave hissed over them, and this time Robyn was not ready for it, she felt the burn of it in her lungs and knew she was drowning. She need only release her hold on the girl's head and shoulders and she would be free to breathe, but she held on stubbornly, determined suddenly that she would never let this little soul go. She had seen it in the girl's eyes, the fierce will to live. This one she could save, this one out of three hundred or more was the only one she could be certain of saving. She had to have her.

The wave receded and Zouga was still there, his hair streaming with water, slicked down over his face and into his eyes, and now he shifted slightly, jamming his legs against one of the heavy timbers, and he reared back once more against the chain, and a low bellow broke from his throat in the agony of effort.

The ring bolt that held the loop of chain to the deck ripped out cleanly, and Zouga dragged both women clear of the water, the chain slithering after them for ten feet or more before coming up hard against the next ring bolt.

Robyn had never suspected Zouga capable of such strength, she had never seen his naked upper body – not since he was a child – had not realized that he had the lean hard muscle of a prizefighter. But even so, he could not repeat the effort, and the girl was still chained. They had won only a temporary respite. Zouga was bellowing now, and the young naval Ensign scrambled down through the open hatch. To re-enter the doomed hull was an act of courage in itself, Robyn realized, as she saw that the Ensign carried the cutting shears, lugging the heavy tool with him as he floundered towards the struggling group in the bottom of the hold.

The hull rolled through another five degrees, the water swirling higher towards them hungrily, it sucked at their bodies. Had not Zouga given them the extra few feet of chain they would be far below the surface now.

Zouga stooped over her and helped her hold the black girl's head above the water, while the Ensign groped for the chain links and fed them into the jaws of the shears. But the blades had been blunted and chipped by the heavy work they had already done, and the Ensign was still only a lad. Zouga pushed him aside.

Again muscle bunched in his shoulders and upper arms and the chain parted with a metallic clunk. Zouga cut twice at ankle and at wrist, then he dropped the shears, picked the frail naked body up against his chest and climbed frantically up towards the hatch.

Robyn tried to follow him, but something tore deep in her belly, she felt it go, tearing like brittle parchment, and the pain was a lance that transfixed her. She doubled over it, clutching herself, unable to move, and the wave hit her, knocking her down, swirling her over the broken timbers into the dark waters, and the darkness began to fill her head. There was temptation to let go now, to let the water and darkness take her, it would be so easy, but she gathered her anger and her obstinacy to her and went on fighting. She was still fighting when Zouga reached her, and dragged her up towards the light.

As they crawled out through the hatch into the sunlight, so the dhow rolled all the way, flinging them as though from a catapult over the side into the shocking cold of the green waters.

As the dhow capsized so the last faint cries from within her were extinguished, and the hull began to break up under the remorseless hammer of the sea. When Robyn and Zouga surfaced, still clinging together, the whaler was hovering over them, the Ensign risking all to come in over the reef for the pick-up.

Strong hands reached down, and the overladen boat heeled dangerously as they were pulled aboard. Then the Ensign swung the bows to meet the next boiling line of surf and they climbed its steep side and crashed over the top, the seamen pulling frantically to hold her bows on.

Robyn crawled to where the black girl lay on a heap of other bodies in the bottom of the boat, her relief at finding her aboard and still alive outweighing the pain of her sodden lungs and the deep ache in her belly.

Robyn rolled the girl on to her back, and lifted her lolling head to cushion it from the pounding of the whaler's hull over the steep swells that threatened to crack her skull against the floorboards.

She saw immediately that the girl was older than she had imagined, although the body was desiccated, dried out and wasted. Yet her pelvis had the breadth of maturity. She would be sixteen years old at least, Robyn thought, and pulled a corner of the tarpaulin over her body to screen her from the men's gaze.

The girl opened her eyes again, and stared at Robyn solemnly. Those eyes were still the colour of dark honey, but the ferocity had dimmed to some other emotion as she looked up into Robyn's face.

'*Ngi ya bonga*,' the girl whispered, and with a shock Robyn realized that she understood the words. She was transported in an instant to another land and another woman, her mother, Helen Ballantyne, teaching her those same words, repeating them to her until Robyn had them perfected.

'*Ngi ya bonga*, I praise you!'

Robyn tried to find a reply, but her mind was as battered as her body, and it had been so long ago that she had learned the language, the circumstances so different that the words came only haltingly.

'*Velapi wena*, who are you and from where do you come?'

The black girl's eyes flew wide with shock.

'You!' she whispered. 'You speak the language of the people.'

They had taken on board twenty-eight living black girls. By the time *Black Joke* got under way again and turned from the land, towards the open sea, the dhow's hull had burst open and the planking and timbers swung and pitched end over end as they sawed across the exposed reef.

A squawking raucous flock of seabirds squabbled over the reef, hovering above the gruesome remnants that were mixed in the floating debris of the wreck, dropping to seize a tidbit and rise again on delicate fans of pearly wings.

In the deeper water along the seaward side of the reef, the shark packs were gathering, lashing themselves into a frenzy, the stubby rounded triangle of their dorsal fins crisscrossing the green sweep of the current, while every few seconds a long torpedo-shaped body would break clear of the surface in an ecstasy of greed, falling back heavily with a boom like distant cannon as it struck the surface.

Twenty-eight from three hundred and more was no great haul, Robyn thought, as she hobbled along the line of barely living bodies, her own bruised limbs protesting every step, and her despair deepened as she realized how far gone they were. It was easy to see which of them had already lost the will to resist. She had read her father's treatise on the sick African, and she knew how important this will to resist was in treating a primitive people. A perfectly healthy man could will himself to die, and once he did so there was nothing that could save him.

That night, despite Robyn's constant attention, twenty-two of the girls died and were carried aft to be dropped over *Black Joke*'s stern. By morning, all the others were sinking into the coma and fever of renal failure, their kidneys, shrivelled and atrophied by lack of fluid, were no longer filtering the urinal wastes from the bodies' systems. There was only one treatment and that was to force the patient to drink.

The little Nguni girl resisted strongly. Robyn knew that she belonged to the Nguni group of peoples, although she was uncertain of which tribe, for many of them spoke variations of the original Zulu, and the girl's accent and pronunciation had been strange to Robyn's ear.

Robyn had tried to keep her talking, keep her conscious and keep the will to resist burning in her. She had conceived an almost maternal possessiveness for the child, and though she tried to spread her attention fairly amongst the other survivors, she always returned to where the girl lay under a strip of tarpaulin and held the pannikin of weak sugar solution to her lips.

They shared only a few hundred words in which to converse, as the girl rested between each painful sip of fluid.

'I am called Juba,' the child whispered, in answer to Robyn's question. Even the sound of it brought back to Robyn the memory of the cooing of the plump blue-grey ring-necked doves in the wild fig trees that grew above the mission cottage in which she had been born.

'Little Dove. It is a pretty name.' And the girl smiled shyly, and went on in that dry tortured whisper. Much of it Robyn could not follow, but she listened and nodded, realizing with a pang that the sense of it was going, Juba was sinking into delirium, that she was talking to phantoms from her past. Now she tried to resist when Robyn forced her to drink, muttering and crying out in fear or anger, gagging on the tiny mouthfuls of liquid.

'You must rest yourself,' Zouga told Robyn brusquely. 'You have been with her for almost two days without sleeping. You're killing yourself.'

'I am quite well, thank you,' Robyn told him, but her face was gaunt and white with fatigue and pain.

'At least let me take you down to your cabin.'

By this time Juba was the only black girl still alive, all the other had gone over the stern to feed the following shark pack.

'Very well,' Robyn agreed, and Zouga carried the child down from the makeshift shelter on the aft deck which Robyn had used as a surgery.

The steward brought a canvas pallet filled with straw and laid it on the deck of Robyn's tiny cabin. There was only just room for it, and Zouga laid the naked body upon it.

Robyn was tempted to stretch out on her own narrow bunk to rest for a while, but she knew that if she let go now, even for a moment, she would fall into a death-like sleep, and her patient would die of such neglect.

Alone in the cabin, she sat cross-legged on the straw pallet, wedged her back against the sea-chest, and lifted Juba into her lap. Doggedly she went on with the task of forcing liquid between the girl's lips, drop by drop, hour after hour.

Through the single port, the light turned to a ruby glow at the short tropical sunset and then it swiftly faded. It was almost completely dark in the cabin when suddenly Robyn felt a copious warm flood soak through her skirts into her lap, and she smelt the strong ammoniacal taint of the girl's urine.

'Thank you, God,' she whispered. 'Oh, thank you, God!' The girl's kidneys were functioning again, she was safe. Robyn rocked the girl in her lap, feeling no revulsion from her soaked skirts, welcoming them as the promise of life.

'You did it,' she whispered. 'You did, with sheer pluck, my little dove.'

She had just enough strength left herself to wipe down the child's body with a cloth soaked in sea water, then she stepped out of her soiled dress and collapsed face down on her hard narrow bunk.

Robyn slept for ten hours, and then the cramps woke her groaning. Her knees were drawn up against her chest by the severity of the pain, and her belly muscles were hard as stone and it felt as though she had been clubbed across the back, a deep bruised sensation that alarmed her seriously.

For many minutes after waking she believed herself seriously stricken, and then with a rush of relief and joy that was far stronger than the pain she realized what was happening to her. She dragged herself across the cabin, doubled over with the pain, and bathed in the bucket of cold sea water. Then she knelt beside Juba on the pallet.

The girl's fever had abated. The skin felt cooler to the touch. Her continued recovery added to Robyn's sense of deep pleasure and relief. Now she would have to find the right moment to tell Clinton Codrington that she would not marry him, and the vision of the little house above the Portsmouth harbour receded. Despite the pain, she felt free, light of body, like a bird poised on the point of flight.

She filled the pannikin with water and lifted Juba's head.

'We will be all right now,' she told the girl, and Juba opened her eyes.

'We'll both be all right now,' she repeated, watching the girl drink thirstily, smiling happily to herself.

Juba's recovery was swift. Soon she ate with a robust appetite. Her body filled almost before Robyn's eyes, her skin took on the lustre of health and youth again, her eyes regained the sparkle of high spirits – and Robyn realized with proprietorial approval that she was a pretty girl, no, more than that, she had natural grace and poise, the voluptuous curve of bosom and buttock which ladies of high fashion tried to achieve with bustle and padded bodice. She possessed also a sweet moon-face, the big wide-set eyes and full sculptured lips that were exotic and strangely beautiful.

Juba could not understand Robyn's concern with having her cover her breasts and legs, but Robyn had seen the seamen's eyes when the girl followed her up on to the deck with only a scrap of canvas covering the most vital point of her anatomy and showing no concern at all when the wind lifted the canvas and fluttered it like a beckoning flag. Robyn commandeered one of Zouga's oldest shirts. It hung to Juba's knees and she belted it at the waist with a bright ribbon that had the child cooing with the eternal feminine delight in pretty things.

She followed Robyn about like a puppy, and Robyn's ear tuned to the Nguni language. Her vocabulary expanded swiftly, and the two of them chatted late every night, sitting side by side on the straw pallet.

Clinton Codrington began showing acute signs of jealousy. He had become used to having more of her company, and Robyn was using the girl as an excuse to taper off their relationship, preparing him for the news that she must deliver before they reached Quelimane.

Zouga also disapproved of her growing intimacy with the girl.

'Sissy, you must remember that she is a native. It never pays to let them get too familiar,' Zouga told her gravely. 'I've seen that happen too often in India. One has to keep one's reserve. After all, you are an English woman.'

'And she is a Matabele of Zanzi blood, which makes her an aristocrat, for her family came up with Mzilikazi from the south. Her father was a famous general and she can trace her bloodline back to Senzangakhona, the King of the Zulu, and the father of Chaka himself. We, on the other hand, can trace our family as far as great grandfather, who was a cattle herd.'

Zouga's expression stiffened. He did not enjoy discussing the family origins.

'We are English. The greatest and most civilized people in the world's history.'

'Grandfather Moffat knows Mzilikazi,' Robyn pointed out, 'and thinks him a great gentleman.'

'You are being foolish,' Zouga snapped. 'How can you compare the English race to these blood-thirsty savages.' But he stooped out of the cabin for he did not wish to continue the discussion. As usual, Robyn had her facts correct and her logic was infuriating.

His own grandfather, Robert Moffat, had first met Mzilikazi back in '29 and over the years the two men had become firm and trusted friends. The King relied on Moffat, whom he called Tshedi, for counsel in his dealings with the world beyond his borders and for medical treatment for the gout which plagued him as he grew older.

The route northwards to the land of the Matabele always passed through Robert Moffat's mission station at Kuruman. A prudent traveller would ask for a safe conduct from the old missionary, and the Matabele impis guarding the Burnt Land along the border would honour that safe conduct.

Indeed, the ease with which Fuller Ballantyne had moved through the wild, untamed tribes along the Zambezi river as far west as Lake Ngami, unmolested and unharmed, was in great part due to his relationship with Robert 'Tshedi' Moffat. The mantle of protection which the Matabele King spread over his old friend extended to his immediate family, and was recognized by all the tribes within range of the Matabele long arm, an arm that wielded the assegai, the terrible stabbing spear which King Chaka of the Zulu had first conceived, and with which he had conquered his known world.

In his pique at Robyn's comparison of the ancestry of his family and that of the pretty half-naked black girl, Zouga at first missed the significance of what she had told him. When it struck him, he hurried back to Robyn's cabin.

'Sissy,' he burst out excitedly. 'If she comes from Mzilikazi country – why! that's almost a thousand miles due west of Quelimane. She must have passed through the land of Monomatapa to reach this coast. Get her to tell us about it.'

He regretted his childhood inattention to the language when his mother had taught them. He concentrated savagely now as the two girls chatted animatedly, and began recognizing some of the words, but it needed Robyn to translate the full sense for him.

Juba's father was a famous Induna, a great warrior who had fought the Boers at Mosega, and a hundred other battles since then, his shield had been thick with the tassels of cow tails, black and white, each of which signified a heroic deed.

He had been granted the headring of the Induna when he was still a young man of less than thirty summers, and had become one of the highest elders in the council of the nation. He had fifty wives, many of them of pure Zanzi blood like his own, a hundred and twelve sons and uncounted daughters. Although all the cattle of the nation belonged to the King, yet over five thousand were put in the charge of Juba's father, a mark of the King's high favour.

He was a great man – perhaps too great for his own safety. Somebody whispered the word 'treason' in the King's ear, and the King's executioners had surrounded the kraal in the dawn, and called out Juba's father.

He had stooped out through the low entrance of his thatched beehive hut, naked from the embrace of his favourite wife.

'Who calls?' he cried into the dawn, and then he saw the ring of black figures, tall in their feather headdresses, but standing motionless, silent and menacing.

'In the King's name,' a voice answered him, and out of the ranks stepped a figure he recognized immediately. It was one of the King's Indunas also, a man named Bopa, a short powerful man, with a deep-muscled bare chest and a head so heavy that the broad features seemed to have been carved out of a chunk of granite from the kopjes across the Nyati River.

There was no appeal, no escape, not that either consideration even passed briefly through the old Induna's mind.

'In the King's name.' That was sufficient. Slowly he drew himself to his full height. Despite the grey cap of his hair, he was still a finely built warrior with broad rangy shoulders and the ridged battle scars crawled across his chest and flanks like live serpents.

'The Black Elephant,' he began to recite the praise names of his King. 'Bayete! The Thunder of the Heavens. The Shaker of the Earth. Bayete!'

Still calling the King's names he went down on one knee, and the King's executioner stepped up behind him.

The wives and elder children had crawled from their huts now, and huddled together in dread, watching from the shadows, their voices blending in a single cry of horror and sorrow as the executioner drove his short thick-bladed assegai between the Induna's shoulder blades, and two hands' breadth out of his chest. As he withdrew the blade, there was the crude sucking sound of steel leaving flesh and the old Induna's life blood spurted head high as he fell forward on to his face.

With his smeared red blade the King's executioner commanded his warriors forward, for the sentence of death included the old man's wives, every one of their sons and daughers, the household slaves, and their children, every inhabitant of the large village, three hundred or more souls.

The executioners worked swiftly, but there was a change in the ancient ritual of death. The old women, the grey-headed slaves died swiftly, not honoured with the blade but clubbed to death with the heavy knob-kerries that each warrior carried. The infants, and unweaned toddlers were snatched up by the ankles, and their brains were dashed from their skulls against the trunk of a tree, against the heavy poles of the cattle enclosure or against a convenient rock. It was very swift, for the warriors were highly trained and disciplined troops and this was something they had done many times before.

Yet this time there was a difference, the younger women, the adolescent children, even those on the verge of puberty, were hustled forward and the King's executioner glanced at them appraisingly, and with a gesture of the bloody spear sent them left or right.

On the left hand was swift death, while those who were sent right were forced into a trot and led away towards the east, towards the sunrise as the girl Juba explained it to Robyn.

'Many days we travelled,' her voice sinking, the horror of it still in the dark brown eyes. 'I do not know how long it was. Those who fell were left where they lay, and we went on.'

'Ask her what she remembers of the country,' Zouga demanded.

'There were rivers,' the girl replied. 'Many rivers and great mountains.' Her memories were confused, she could make no estimates of distance, they had encountered no other people, no villages nor towns, they had seen no cattle nor standing crops. Juba shook her head to each of Zouga's questions, and when he showed her the Harkness map in a forlorn hope that she might be able to point out features upon it, the child giggled in confusion. Drawn symbols on parchment were beyond her comprehension, she could not begin to relate them to features of landscape.

'Tell her to go on,' he ordered Robyn impatiently.

'At the end we passed through deep gorges in high mountains where the slopes were covered with tall trees, and the rivers fell with white spray, until at last we came to where the *bunu* – the white men – waited.'

'The white men?' Robyn demanded.

'Men of your people,' the girl nodded. 'With a pale skin and pale eyes. There were many men, some white and others brown or black men, but dressed as the white men were dressed, and armed with the *isibamu*, with guns.' The Matabele people knew well the power and effect of firearms, they had encountered enemies armed with them at least thirty years before. Even some of the Matabele Indunas carried muskets, although they always handed these to a servant to carry when there was serious fighting in the offing.

'These people had built kraals, such as we build for our cattle, but these were filled with people, a great multitude of people and with them we were bound with the *insimbi*, the links of iron.' She rubbed her wrists instinctively at the memory, and the callouses raised by the slave cuffs still blemished the skin of her forearms.

'Each day that we stayed at this place in the mountains, more people came. Sometimes only as many as the fingers on both your hands, on other days there were great numbers so we could hear their lamentations at a distance. And always there were warriors guarding them.

'Then before the sun one morning, at the time of the horns,' Robyn recalled the expression for the time of dawning when the horns of the cattle first show against the morning sky, 'they led us from the kraals, wearing the *insimbi*, and we formed a great snake of people so long that the head was out of sight ahead of me in the forest while the tail was still up in the clouds of the mountains when we came down the Hyena Road.'

'The Hyena Road, *Ndlele umfisi*.' It was the first time that Robyn had heard the name spoken. It conjured up an image of a dark trail through the forests, beaten by tens of thousands of bare feet, with the loathsome eaters of dead flesh slinking along beside it, chuckling and shrieking their inane chorus.

'Those that died, and those that fell and could not rise again were released from their chains and dragged to one side. The *fisi* have grown so bold along the road, that they rushed out of the bushes and devoured the bodies while we passed in full sight. It was worst when the body still lived.'

Juba broke off and stared unseeingly at the bulkhead across the cabin. Slowly her eyes filled with tears, and Robyn took her hand and held it in her lap.

'I know not how long we followed the Hyena Road,' Juba went on, 'for each day became as the one before it, and as the one that followed it, until at last we came to the sea.'

Afterwards Zouga and Robyn discussed the girl's story.

'She must have gone through the kingdom of Monomatapa, and yet she says there were no towns nor signs of occupation.'

'The slavers might have avoided contact with Monomatapa's people.'

'I wish she had seen and remembered more.'

'She was in a slave caravan,' Robyn pointed out. 'Survival was her only concern.'

'If only these damned people could even read a map.'

'It's a different culture, Zouga,' and he saw the spark in her eye, and sensed the drift of the conversation and turned it aside swiftly.

'Perhaps the legend of Monomatapa is only a myth, perhaps there are no gold mines.'

'The important thing about Juba's story is that the Matabele are dealing in slaves, they have never done so before.'

'Nonsense!' grunted Zouga. 'They are the greatest predators since Genghis Khan! They and all the Zulu splinter tribes – the Shangaan, the Angoni and the Matabele. War is their way of life, and plunder is their main crop. Their whole nation was built on a system of slave-taking.'

'But they have never sold them before,' said Robyn mildly. 'At least as far as we know from all that grandfather and Harris and the others have written.'

'The Matabele never found a market before,' Zouga replied reasonably. 'Now they have at last made contact with the slave-masters, and found an opening to the coast. That was all it lacked before.'

'We must witness this, Zouga,' Robyn spoke with quiet determination. 'We have to bear witness to this terrible crime against humanity and carry word back to London.'

'If only the child had seen evidence of the Monomatapa, or the gold mines,' muttered Zouga. 'You must ask her if there were elephant.' He pored over the Harkness map, lamenting the blank spaces. 'I cannot believe that it does not exist. There is too much evidence.' Zouga looked up at his sister. 'One other thing – I seem to have forgotten almost every word of the language that mother taught us, except some of the nursery rhymes and lullabies. '*Munya, mabili zinthatu, Yolala umdade-wethu,*'* he recited, and then chuckled and shook his head. 'I shall have to study it again, you and Juba will have to help me.'

The Zambezi comes to the sea through a delta of vast swampland, and a hundred confused shallow channels spread out for thirty miles down the low featureless coastline.

Floating islands of papyrus grass break free from the main pastures which blanket the waters of the delta and are carried out to sea on the dirty brown

* 'One, two, three,
  Go to sleep my little sister.'

water. Some of these islands are many acres in extent and the roots of the plants so entangled that they can support the weight of a heavy animal. On occasions small herds of buffalo are trapped and carried twenty miles out to sea before the action of the waves smashes up the islands and plunges the great bovine animals into the water, prey for the big sharks which cruise the tainted estuary waters for just such a prize.

The muddy smell of the swamps carries far from the land when the wind is right, and the same wind carries strange insects with it. There is a tiny spider no bigger than the head of a wax Vesta which lives in the papyrus banks of the delta. It spins a gossamer web on which it launches itself into the breeze in such numbers that the gossamer fills the sky in clouds, like the smoke from a raging bush-fire, rising many hundreds of feet and eddying and swirling in misty columns that are touched by the sunset into shades of pink and lovely pale mauve.

The river pours a muddy brown effluent into the sea, silt enriched with the bodies of drowned animals and birds, and the huge Zambezi crocodiles join the shark packs at the feast.

Black Joke found the first of these hideous creatures ten miles from land, wallowing in the low swells like a log, the rough scales glittering wetly in the sunlight until the gunboat approached too closely and the reptile dived with a lash and swirl of its powerful ridged tail.

Black Joke steamed obliquely across the multiple mouths of the river, none of which offered passage for a vessel of her size. She was headed further north for the Congone channel which was the only passage upriver to the town of Quelimane.

Clinton Codrington planned to enter it the following morning, after having lain hove-to during the night off the mouth. Robyn knew that she must remove the stitches from the wound under his armpit, though she would have liked to leave them a few days longer. They must come out before she left the gunboat at Quelimane.

She decided to use the same opportunity to give him the answer for which he had waited so patiently. She knew it was going to be painful for him to hear that she would not marry him, and she felt guilty that she had so encouraged him. It was alien to her nature to inflict suffering on another, and she would try to tell him as gently as possible.

She ordered him to her cabin for the removal of the horsehair stitches, seating him on the narrow bunk naked to the waist, with his arm raised. She was delighted with the way the wound had healed, and proud of the neatness of her work. She cooed over each knot as she snipped it with the pointed scissors, then seized it with the forceps and gently tugged and worried it free of his flesh. The stitches left twin punctures, one on each side of the raised purple welt of the scar and they were clean and dry. Only one of them leaked a single drop of blood which she swabbed away gently.

Robyn was training Juba as her assistant, teaching her to hold the tray of instruments, and receive the discarded and soiled dressings or instruments. Now she stood back and appraised the healed wound, without looking at Juba.

'You may go now,' she said quietly. 'I will call you when I need you.'

Juba smiled like a conspirator, and murmured, 'He is truly beautiful, so white and smooth,' and Robyn blushed pinkly, for that was exactly what she had been thinking. Clinton's body, unlike that of Mungo St. John, was hairless as a girl's but finely muscled, and the skin had an almost marble sheen to it.

'His eyes are like two moons when he looks at you, Nomusa,' Juba went on with relish, and Robyn tried to frown at her but her lips kept puckering into a smile.

'Go swiftly,' she snapped, and Juba giggled.

'There is a time to be alone,' and she rolled her eyes lewdly. 'I shall guard the door, and hardly listen at all, Nomusa,' Robyn found it impossible to be angry when the child used that name, for it meant 'the daughter of mercy', and Robyn found it highly acceptable. She would have had difficulty picking a better name for herself, and she was smiling as she hurried Juba from the cabin with a gentle slap and a push.

Clinton must have had some idea of the exchange, for he was buttoning his shirt as she turned back to him, and looking embarrassed.

She drew a deep breath folded her arms and began.

'Captain Codrington, I have thought unceasingly of the great honour you have done me by inviting me to be your wife.'

'However,' Clinton forestalled her, and she faltered, the prepared speech forgotten, for her next word would indeed have been, 'However'.

'Miss Ballantyne, I mean Doctor Ballantyne, I would rather you did not say the rest of it.' His face was pale and intense, he really was beautiful now, she thought, with a pang. 'That way I can still cherish hope.'

She shook her head vehemently, but he lifted a hand.

'I have come to realize that you have a duty, to your father and the poor unhappy people of this land. I understand and deeply admire that.'

Robyn felt her heart go out to him, he was so good and so perceptive to have understood that about her.

'However, I feel sure that one day, you and I shall . . .'

She wanted to spare him pain.

'Captain,' she began, shaking her head again.

'No,' he said. 'Nothing you say will ever make me abandon hope. I am a very patient man, and I realize that now is not the time. But I know in the depths of my soul that our destiny binds us together, even if I must wait ten or fifty years.'

A time-span of that magnitude no longer frightened Robyn. She relaxed visibly.

'I love you, my dear Doctor Ballantyne, nothing will ever alter that, and in the meantime I ask only your good opinion, and friendship.'

'You have both,' she said, with truth and relief. It had been a great deal easier than she had expected, yet strange that a shadow of regret lingered.

There was no further opportunity to speak privately, for Clinton was fully occupied with bringing *Black Joke* into the treacherous channel, with its shifting banks and uncharted shoals guarding the mouth. The channel meandered twenty miles through the mangrove forests to the port of Quelimane on the northern bank.

The heat in the delta was rendered scarcely bearable by the humid effluxion of mud and rotting vegetation that rose from the mangrove forests. The weird shapes of the mangroves fascinated Robyn, and she stood by the rail and watched them slide past. Each tree stood clear of the slick chocolate-coloured mud on its pyramid of roots, like the multiple legs of a grotesque insect reaching up to join the thick pulpy stem which in turn extended upwards to the roof of poisonous green foliage. Amongst the roots skittered the purple and yellow fiddler crabs, each of them holding aloft a single disproportionally huge claw, and waving it in menace or ponderous greeting at the passing vessel.

Black Joke's wake spread across the channel, flopping wavelets on the mud banks and startling the small green and purple night herons into laborious flight.

Around a bend in the channel the decaying buildings of Quelimane came into view, dominated by the square towers of the stucco church. The plaster was falling away in unsightly chunks and the whitewash was streaked and splotched with grey and green mould, like a ripening cheese.

This port had once been one of the most busy slave ports on the entire African coast. The Zambezi river had acted as a highway to the interior for the slave-masters, and the Shire river, its major tributary, led directly to Lake Marawi and the highlands which had been the mother lode from which hundreds and thousands of black slaves had poured.

When the Portuguese, under British pressure, had signed the Brussels Agreement, the barracoons at Quelimane and Lourenço Marques and Mozambique Island had been closed down. However, the slaving dhow that *Black Joke* had intercepted proved that the abominable trade still flourished covertly along the Portuguese coast. That was typical of these people, Clinton Codrington thought.

Clinton curled his lip with distaste. In the many hundred years since their great navigators had opened up this coast, the Portuguese had clung to the narrow unhealthy strip of the littoral, making only one half-hearted effort to penetrate the interior and since then, lying here like their disintegrating buildings and crumbling empire, content with the bribes and extortions of petty officialdom and their seraglios of women, tolerant of any crimes or evil as long as there was a little dash or profit in it.

As he worked *Black Joke* in towards the quay, he could see them gathering already, gaudy vultures, in their fool's motley of uniform, tarnished gold braid and ornate swords sported by even the lowliest customs officer.

There would be endless forms and declarations, unless he was firm, and always the open palm and the leering wink. Well, this time there would be none of that. This was a ship of the Queen's Navy.

'Mr. Denham,' Clinton called sharply, 'issue pistols and cutlasses to the anchor watch, and nobody comes aboard without the express permission of the officer of the watch.'

He turned away to shake hands briefly with Zouga; they had found little in common during the voyage and the parting was cool.

'Never thank you enough, sir,' said Zouga briskly.

'Only my duty, Major.' But already Zouga's eyes were following Sergeant Cheroot as he assembled his men on the foredeck. They were in full marching order, eager to be ashore after the tedious voyage.

'I must see to my men, Captain,' Zouga excused himself and hurried forward.

Clinton turned to Robyn and looked steadily into her green eyes.

'I beg a small token of remembrance,' he said quietly.

In response to his request she reached up and took one of the cheap paste earrings from her lobe. As they shook hands, she slipped the little ornament into his palm, and he touched it briefly to his lips before slipping it into his pocket.

'I will wait,' he repated, 'ten or even fifty years.'

Black Joke had come up-channel on the flood, unloaded the mountainous stores of the Ballantyne Africa Expedition on to the stone quay during slack water, and two hours later thrown off her mooring ropes and swung sharply across the ebb, pointing her high bows down the channel.

From his position on the quarterdeck, Clinton Codrington stared across the widening gap at the slim, tall figure in long skirts standing on the very edge of the quay. Beyond her, her brother did not look up from his lists as he checked the stores and equipment. Sergeant Cheroot stood armed guard with his little pug-featured Hottentots, and the idlers and watchers kept well clear.

The Portuguese officials had treated the red wax seals and ribbons which decorated Zouga's letters of authority from the Portuguese ambassador in London with great respect. However, even more important was the fact that Zouga was an officer of Queen Victoria's army, that he had arrived in a Royal Navy gunboat, and lastly that there was every reason to believe that the same gunboat would remain in the area for the foreseeable future.

The Governor of Portuguese East Africa himself would not have commanded greater respect. Already minor officials were scampering about the squalid little town arranging the best accommodation, securing warehousing for the stores, commandeering river transport for the next leg of the journey up-river to Tete, the last outpost of Portuguese empire on the Zambezi, drafting orders to have bearers and guides meet the expedition at Tete, and doing everything else that the young British officer casually demanded as though it was his God-given right.

In this turmoil of activity Robyn Ballantyne stood alone, staring after the blue-clad figure on *Black Joke's* quarterdeck. How tall he was, and his hair caught the sunlight in a flash of white gold as he lifted his hand in farewell. She waved until *Black Joke* disappeared behind a palisade of mangrove, though her masts and fuming smoke-stack stayed in view for a long time after. She watched until they, too, dwindled to nothingness, and only the smear of black smoke lay low over the tops of the green mangrove.

Clinton Codrington stood on his deck, hands clasped loosely at the small of his back, and an expression of near rapture in the pale blue eyes. In this temper the knight-errant of old must have ridden out at chance, Clinton thought.

He did not find the notion at all melodramatic. He felt truly ennobled by his love, sensing somehow that he must earn something so precious, and that the opportunity to do so lay ahead of him. The earring that Robyn had given him was suspended by a thread around his neck, lying under his shirt against his skin. He touched it now, peering impatiently ahead down the channel. It seemed to him that for the first time he had a steady direction in his life, constant as the pole star to the navigator.

This gallant mood was still strong five days later when *Black Joke* rounded the headland of Ras Elat and steamed into the anchorage. There were eight large dhows keeled over on the exposed sand bar at low tide. The tidal fall on this coast at full springs was twenty-two feet. These craft were designed to take the ground readily, and it facilitated loading. The long ranks of chained slaves were being goaded out to the stranded vessels, slipping and splashing through the shallow tidal pools, to await patiently their turn to climb the ladder up the side of the dhow.

Black Joke's unannounced arrival caused pandemonium, and the beach was alive with running, stumbling figures, the screams and shrieks of the slaves, the pop of the kurbash whips, and the frantic cries of the slave-masters carried clearly to *Black Joke's* deck as she dropped her anchor just beyond the reef and rounded up to the wind.

Clinton Codrington stared longingly at the heeled vessels and the concourse of panicky humanity, the way a slum-child stares at the display in the window of a food shop.

His orders were clear, had been spelled out by Admiral Kemp with painful attention to detail. The Admiral remembered with lingering horror his young

Captain's capture of the slaving fleet at Calabash after forcing the masters to load their cargoes and sail north of the equator. He wanted no repetition of this type of risky action on this patrol.

Black Joke's commander was strictly adjured to respect the territorial integrity of the Sultan of the Omani Arabs, and the exact letter of the treaty that the British Consul had negotiated at Zanzibar.

Clinton Codrington was strictly forbidden to interfere with any subject of the Sultan who was engaged in trade between any of the Sultan's dominions. He was denied even the right of search of any vessel flying the red-and-gold flag of Omani on any of the Sultan's recognized trade routes, and these were carefully defined for Captain Codrington's benefit.

He was to confine his patrol to intercepting only vessels that did not belong to the Sultan, particularly vessels of the European powers. Naturally no American vessel might be searched on the high seas. Within these limits, Captain Codrington had powers of independent action.

Far from being allowed to seize or search the Sultan's vessels, Clinton was ordered to use the first opportunity to make a courtesy call on the port of Zanzibar. There he would take counsel from the British Consul as how best to use his influence to reinforce the existing treaties, and especially to remind the Sultan of his own obligations under those treaties.

So now Clinton paced his deck like a caged lion at feeding time, and glowered helplessly, through the pass in the coral reef, at the slaving fleet of Omani engaged in legitimate trade, for the Gulf of Elat was very much part of the Sultan's possessions, and had so been recognized by Her Majesty's Government.

After the first wild panic ashore, the beach and dhows were now deserted, but Clinton was aware of the thousands of watchful eyes upon him from the mud-walled town and the shadows of the coconut groves.

The thought of hauling his anchor and sailing away filled him with bitter chagrin, and he stood bare-headed and stared with cold hungry blue eyes at the prize spread before him.

The palace of the Sheikh of Elat, Mohamed Bin Salim, was an unpainted mud-walled building in the centre of the town. The only opening in the parapeted wall was the gate, closed by thick, brass-studded double doors in carved teak, which led through to the dusty central courtyard.

In this courtyard, under the spreading branches of an ancient takamaka tree the Sheikh was in earnest conclave with his senior advisors and the emissaries of his supreme sovereign – the Sultan of Zanzibar. They were discussing a matter, literally, of life or death.

Sheikh Mohamed Bin Salim had the plump smooth body of the *bon vivant,* the bright red lips of the sensualist, and the hooded eyes of a falcon.

He was a very worried man, for his ambition had led him into dire danger. His ambition had been quite simply to accumulate the sum of one million gold rupees in his treasury, and he had very nearly satisfied that reasonable goal, when his overlord, the omnipotent Sultan of Zanzibar, had sent his emissaries to call the Sheikh to account.

Sheikh Mohamed had begun to satisfy his ambition ten years previously by very gently mulching the Sultan's tithe, and each year since then he had increased his depredations. Like all greedy men, one successful coup was the signal for the next. The Sultan had known this, for though he was old, he was also exceedingly cunning. He knew that the missing tithes were safely stored for him in the Sheikh's treasure house, to be collected whenever he felt inclined. He need only benignly feign ignorance of the Sheikh's manipulations, until he was so deeply in the trap than no squirming or squealing would get him out again. After ten years that moment had arrived. The Sultan would collect not only his due but the Sheikh's own accumulations.

Further retribution would be a lengthy business. It would begin with a beating on the soles of the Sheikh's bare feet, until all those delicate little bones were cracked or fractured, making it extremely painful for the Sheikh to be marched into the Sultan's presence. There, the final judgement would be read, and it would end with the knotted strip of buffalo hide wound up tighter and tighter around the forehead, until first the Sheikh's falcon eyes popped from their sockets and then his skull collapsed like a bursting melon. The Sultan truly enjoyed these spectacles – and had been looking forward to this particular one for ten years.

Both men knew the ritual, and it had begun with the polite visit of the Sultan's emissaries who even now were sitting opposite the Sheikh under the takamaka, sipping thick black coffee from the brass thimbles, munching the yellow and pink coconut sweetmeats, and smiling at the Sheikh with cold passionless eyes.

It was into this chilling atmosphere that the messengers from the harbour came running to fling themselves prostrate and gabble out the news of the British warship, whose great guns threatened the harbour and the town.

The Sheikh listened quietly and then dismissed the messengers, before turning back to his distinguished guests.

'This is a serious business,' he began, relieved to be able to change the subject under discussion. 'It would be wise to view this strange vessel.'

'The Ferengi have a treaty with our master,' pronounced one greybeard, 'and they set great store by these pieces of paper.'

They all nodded, none of them showing the agitation which filled all of their breasts. Although this coast had only received passing attention from these brash northern people, still it had been enough to engender fear and apprehension.

The Sheikh deliberated for a few minutes, stroking his thick curly beard, hooding his eyes as the ideas began to flow. His mind had been almost paralysed with the extent of the disaster which had overtaken him, but now it began to work again.

'I must go out to this warship,' he announced. There was an immediate hubbub of protest, but he held up his hand to silence them. He was still the Sheikh of Elat, and they had, perforce, to hear him out.

'It is my duty to ascertain the intentions of the commander and to send word immediately to our master.'

Clinton Codrington had almost resigned himself to give the order to weigh anchor. There had been no sign of life on the beach for many hours, and there was nothing he could accomplish here. His hope that he might catch a European slaver, actually taking on slaves in the anchorage, had proved forlorn. He should have sailed hours ago, the sun was half-way down the sky already and he did not want to run the dangers of the inshore channel in darkness, but some instinct had kept him here.

He kept returning to the starboard rail, and glassing the flat-roofed mud buildings that just showed amongst the palm trees. Each time his junior officers stiffened expectantly, then relaxed as he turned away without a word or change of expression.

This time Clinton saw movement, the flash of white robes in the deserted, single street of the town, and as he watched through the telescope he felt a prickle of excitement and a lift of self-congratulation. A small deputation was emerging from the grove and coming down the beach.

'Pass the word to my steward to lay out my number ones and sword,' he ordered without lowering his glass. The party on the beach was led by a portly figure in blindingly white robes and a full head-dress that gleamed with gold. Behind him a bearer carried the long floating banner, scarlet and gold, of the Sultan.

'We'll treat him as a Governor,' Clinton decided. 'And give him four guns.' With that he turned on his heel and went to his cabin to change his uniform.

The Arab climbed out of the little felucca and came in through the entry port puffing for breath, assisted by two house-slaves. As his foot touched the deck, the first gun of the salute crashed out unexpectedly, and the Sheikh let out a whinny like a wild stallion and leapt two feet straight up in the air, the high colour flying from his cheeks leaving them ashen and trembling.

Clinton stepped forward, resplendent in cocked hat, blue and gold jacket, white breeches and sword, and took the Sheikh's arm to steady him through the rest of the salute, and to prevent him stampeding back into the crazily rocking felucca where the oarsmen were in equal terror.

'Will you step this way, Your Excellency,' Clinton murmured, and without releasing his iron grip on the Sheikh's pudgy arm, marched him briskly down to his cabin.

Translation was a problem, but one of the Sheikh's entourage had a smattering of French and some English. It was almost dark before Clinton was able to see through the flowery verbiage and the atrocious rendering of his mother tongue. When it came it was like a great light filling the cabin, and Clinton found himself buoyed up with a savage, warlike glee.

The fat Sheikh, Governor of Elat, with his soft, red lips, was asking for the protection of her Britannic Majesty against the injustices and tyrannies of the Sultan of Zanzibar.

'*Dites lui je ne peux pas* – oh, damn it, tell him I can only protect him if he declares Elat free of the Sultan's dominions, *comprenez-vous?*'

'*Je m'excuse, je ne comprends pas.*'

It was tedious, especially in view of Clinton's eagerness to remove the province of Elat from under the sway of Zanzibar.

The Foreign Office had provided all commanders of the Atlantic anti-slavery squadrons with blank treaty forms, drawn up with deference to protocol and in correct legal terminology. These were for signature of any indigenous chiefs, warlords, petty princes and native kings who could be induced to place their mark upon them.

These documents started with a declaration of mutual recognition between Her Majesty's government and the signatory, went on in vague terms to promise protection and free trade, and ended in very specific terms with a round condemnation of the slave trade and the granting of rights to Her Majesty's government to search, seize and destroy all ships engaged in such trade within the signatory's territorial waters. Further it granted rights to Her Majesty's Navy to land troops, destroy barracoons, free slaves, arrest slave-masters and do any such other act as should be deemed necessary to the extinction of the trade in all the signatory's lands and possessions.

Admiral Kemp in Cape Town had overlooked the fact that Captain Codrington had a good supply of these documents in his possession. They had been intended for use entirely on the West African coast north of the equator. The good Admiral would have been a very worried man indeed if he had realized that he had detached his most brilliant but mercurial junior on independent patrol armed with anything so explosive.

'He must sign here,' Clinton explained briskly, 'and I will give him an order on the British treasury for a hundred guineas.' The treaty made provision for annual tribute to be paid to the signatory. Clinton considered a hundred guineas sufficient. He was not sure of what authority he had to write treasury orders, but Sheikh Mohamed was delighted. He had negotiated for life alone, and received not only the protection of this fine warship but the promise of good gold as well. He was smiling happily, pursing his red lips as he signed his long signature under his new title 'Prince and Supreme Ruler of the sovereign possessions of Elat and Ras Telfa.'

'Good,' said Clinton briskly, rolling his copy of the treaty and slipping the retaining ribbon over it as he hurried to the door of his cabin.

'Mr. Denham,' he bellowed up the companionway, 'I want a landing-party, muskets, pistols, cutlasses and carrying combustibles, forty men ready to go ashore at first light tomorrow!' He was grinning as he turned back and told the Sheikh's translator, 'It would be best if His Excellency remained on board tonight. We will see him safely installed at noon tomorrow.' And for the first time the Sheikh felt a thrill of apprehension. This Ferengi had the cold blue merciless eyes of a devil. 'El Sheetan,' he thought, 'the very devil.' And made the sign against the evil eye.

'Sir, may I speak?' Mr. Denham, *Black Joke*'s First Lieutenant, looked puzzled in the light of the binnacle. It was an hour short of sunrise and he glanced down at the ranks of armed seamen squatting on the foredeck.

'Speak your heart,' Clinton invited him magnanimously. Lieutenant Denham was not accustomed to this jovial mood from his captain, and he expressed himself cautiously. In essence Lieutenant Denham's view came very close to those of the Admiral in Cape Town.

'If you would like to make a protest against my orders, Lieutenant,' Clinton interrupted him cheerfully, 'I will be pleased to enter it in the ship's log.'

Thus absolved of responsibility for having been party to an act of war on the territory of a foreign ruler, Lieutenant Denham was so relieved that when Clinton told him, 'I am taking command of the landing party. You will command the ship in my absence,' he shook Clinton's hand impulsively.

'Good luck, sir,' he blurted.

They went ashore in two boats, the whaler leading through the pass in the reef and the gig following two lengths astern. The moment the keel touched, Clinton sprang knee-deep into the blood-warm water and the rush of armed men followed him ashore. He drew his cutlass and his shoes squelched as he led his team of five men to the nearest dhow at a dead run.

As he jumped down from the ladder on to the dhow's heavily canted deck, an Arab watchman ducked out of the stern cabin and aimed a long jezail at Clinton's head, the range was point blank and Clinton struck out instinctively in an underhand parry, just as the gun's lock clicked and smoke and spark shot from the pan under the steel and flint.

His blade clashed against the steel barrel, deflecting it upwards as the jezail roared an instant after the snap of the lock, and a blinding billow of smoke and burning powder struck his face and singed his eyebrows, but the chunk of beaten potleg howled inches over his head. When his vision cleared the watchman had thrown his empty weapon aside, leaped over the side of the dhow and was hopping and hobbling across the sand towards the grove of palms.

'Search her, and then put fire into her,' Clinton ordered brusquely.

It was the first chance he had had to look across at the other dhows of the fleet. One of them was already on fire, the flames bright in the early light, rising straight up with little smoke. The furled mainsail was blackening like a dried leaf, and he could hear the crackle of the tinder-dry timbers of the hull and stern cabin. His seamen were spilling out of her and straggling across to the next vessel.

'She's aflame, sir,' his boatswain panted, and a hot gust of air struck Clinton's cheek at that moment and a quiver of heat hung over the main hatch.

'We'd best be getting on,' he said mildly, and scrambled down the ladder on to the packed damp sand. Behind him the flames roared like a cageful of wild animals.

The biggest dhow, a two-hundred tonner, lay ahead of them and Clinton reached it fifty paces ahead of his men.

'Make sure there is nobody below,' he ordered, and one of the seamen came back on deck carrying a rolled silk prayer rug under his arm.

'Belay that!' snapped Clinton. 'There'll be no looting.'

Reluctantly the seaman dropped the precious burden back into the hatchway, and the flames sucked up in a hot breath to accept it as though it was an offering to Baal.

By the time they reached the tree-line, all eight of the stranded vessels were burning fiercely, the stubby masts collapsing as they burned through at the base, the furled sails disappearing in bright explosions of flame. In one of the burning hulls a keg of powder went up with a thunderous crash of sound, and a tall column of dark smoke hovered over the beach for a few seconds, shaped like a gigantic grey octopus before it drifted slowly out across the reef, leaving the dhow shattered, its timbers scattered across the sand, the flames extinguished by the shock wave of the explosion.

'Was there anybody aboard her?' Clinton demanded quietly.

'No, sir.' His boatswain was panting beside him, red-faced with excitement, and with a bared cutlass in his hand. 'All accounted for.'

Clinton hid his relief behind a cool nod, and spent a few precious minutes drawing his men into an orderly formation, giving them time to regain their breath, and getting them well in hand again.

'Check your muskets,' he ordered, and there was the click of the locks. 'Fix bayonets.' Metal rattled on metal as the long blades were fitted to the barrels of the Enfield rifles. 'If there is resistance we'll find it in the town, I fancy,' and he ran an eye down the uneven ranks. They were neither marines nor lobster-backs, he thought with quick affection. They might not be perfect in drill, but they were men with spirit and initiative, not parade-ground automatons.

'Come along then.' He waved them forward into the dusty street between the mud-brown flat-roofed buildings. The town smelled of wood smoke and raw sewage, of rice cooked with saffron and of ghee, clarified butter.

'Shall we burn 'em?' His boatswain jerked a thumb at the buildings that flanked the deserted street.

'No, we are here to protect them,' Clinton told him stiffly. 'They belong to our new ally, the Sheikh.'

'I see, sir,' the boatswain grunted, looking mildly perplexed, and Clinton took pity on him.

'We are after the barracoons,' he explained, as they trotted up the street in compact formation. They halted where the road branched left and right.

The heat was oppressive and the silence menacing. There was no wind and the coconut groves had stilled the eternal clatter of their fronds. From the beach far behind them, came the faint popping of burning timbers, and overhead the ubiquitous pied crows of Africa circled and cawed raucously, but the buildings and dense coconut groves were deserted.

'I don't like this,' one of the men croaked behind Clinton. He could understand the man's point of view. A seaman always felt awkward when parted from his ship, and there were a mere forty of them, out of sight of the beach and surrounded by thousands of unseen but none the less savage warriors. Clinton knew he must keep the momentum of surprise rolling through the town, yet he hesitated a moment longer until he realized that the amorphous sacklike shape lying on the edge of the right hand street was a human body, naked and black and very dead. One of the slaves trampled in the previous day's panic and left where he had fallen.

That way must lie the barracoons, he decided. 'Quiet!' he cautioned his men, and cocking his head, listened with all his attention to the faint sussuration on the still air. It might have been the wind except there was no wind, or the flames, except that the flames were behind them. It was the distant sound of human voices, he decided, many voices, thousands of voices.

'This way. Follow me.' They went forward at a full run, taking the right fork and running immediately into the ambush which had been so carefully prepared for them.

The volley of musket fire crashed out from both sides of the narrowing track, and powder smoke rolled out towards them and hung like a thick, pearly curtain amonst the palm boles and the cashew nut trees.

Through the smoke danced the ethereal robed figures of the attackers, brandishing the long-barrelled jezails or swinging the half-moon-bladed scimitars, with wild shrieks of 'Allah Akbar, Allah is great!'

They rushed down on the little band of seamen, caught in enfilade on the narrow track. There were at least a hundred of them, Clinton judged instantly, and they were pressing in determinedly. Those scimitars were glittering bright – bare steel has a particularly chilling effect.

'Close up,' Clinton shouted. 'We'll give them a volley then take the bayonet to them, through the smoke.'

The first rank of racing Arabs were almost on top of the levelled Enfields. Incongruously, Clinton noticed that many of them had tucked up the skirts of their robes, leaving their legs bared to the thighs. Their skins varied from the colour of ivory to tobacco, and there were wrinkled grey beards in the front rank, screaming and howling with rage and battle-lust. They had just seen their livelihood burned to heaps of ash upon the beach. All that remained to them of their wealth was the contents of the barracoons set back amongst the groves of cashew nut and coconut trees.

'Fire!' roared Clinton, and the solid blast of sound deafened him for a moment. The gun-smoke wiped out all vision ahead of him and then hung on the windless morning in an impenetrable fog bank.

'Forward!' howled Clinton and led the charge into the smoke. He stumbled over the body of an Arab. The man's turban had unwound and come down over his eyes, soaked with blood like the sultan's scarlet banner which Clinton could see waving ahead of him above the smoke.

A figure loomed ahead of him, and he heard the fluting whistle of a scimitar blade, like wild goose wings overhead. He ducked. The sharp breeze puffed a loose strand of hair into his eyes, as the blade passed an inch from his forehead, and Clinton straightened from the knees and put his whole body into the counter-lunge.

The point of his blade went in with a dead, soggy feel, sliding grudgingly through flesh until the point grated on bone. The Arab dropped his scimitar and clutched the cutlass blade with bare hands. Clinton leaned back and jerked the cutlass free of flesh. As the blade slid through the Arab's nerveless fingers the tendons parted with a faint popping sound, and the man went down on his knees, holding his mutilated hands up in front of his eyes with a look of amazement on his face.

Clinton ran on to catch up with his seamen, and found them scattered in little groups amongst the grove, laughing and shouting with excitement.

'They've run like steeplechasers, sir,' the boatswain called. 'Grand National, ten to one the field!' He snatched up the fallen banner of the Sultan and waved it furiously over his head, completely overtaken by excitement.

'Did we lose anybody?' Clinton demanded. He also felt the dizzy euphoria of battle. The killing of the Arab, far from sickening him, had elated him. In that moment he was quite capable of turning back and taking the man's scalp. However, the question sobered them.

'Jedrow caught one in the belly, but he can walk. Wilson got a sword cut in the arm.'

'Send them back to the beach. They can escort each other. The rest of you, come on!'

They found the barracoons a quarter of a mile further on. The guards had fled.

The slave-pens stretched out for a half mile along both banks of a small stream that provided both drinking water and sewage disposal for the inmates.

They were unlike the barracoons that Clinton had captured and sacked on the west coast, for those had been built by European traders with the white man's orderly eye. There was no resemblance in these sprawling compounds built of rough, unbarked forest poles, bound together with rope made from plaited palm fronds. Behind the outer barricades were open godowns with thatched roofs in which the chained slaves could find some shelter from sun and rain. The only thing the same was the smell. An epidemic of tropical dysentery had swept through the barracoons and most of the sheds contained the decomposing bodies of the victims. The crows and buzzards and vultures were waiting patiently in the palms and cashew trees, misshapen, dark silhouettes against the hard bright blue of the morning sky.

Clinton met the new ruler of the state of Elat, Sheikh Mohamed, at the water's edge and escorted him up the beach. The incoming tide was dousing the pile of smouldering ash that marked the last resting-places of eight fine dhows, and the Sheikh tottered uncertainly, like a man in deep shock, relying for support on the sturdy shoulder of one of his house-slaves, looking about him with lugubrious disbelief at the carnage that had overtaken him. The Sheikh owned one third shares in every one of those smoking piles of ash.

He had to rest when they reached the tree-line above the beach. A slave placed a carved wooden stool in the shade, and another waved a fan of plaited palm fronds over his head to keep off the flies and to cool his heated brow that was dewed with the heavy sweat of despair.

His misery was completed by the lecture in broken French and pidgin English which 'El Sheetan', the mad British sea Captain with the devil's eyes, was relaying to him through the shocked and incredulous interpreter. Such things could only be repeated in a hoarse whisper, and the Sheikh greeted each new revelation with a soft cry of 'Waai!' and the upturning of his eyes to heaven.

He learned that the village blacksmiths had been dragged out of the bushes and were already knocking the fetters off long rows of perplexed slaves.

'Waai!' wailed the Sheikh. 'Does the devil not realize that those slaves have already been purchased and that the tax has been collected.'

Comfortably Clinton explained that once the slaves were freed, they would be marched back into the interior, and the Sheikh would send guards with them to see them safely home, and to warn any slave caravans that they encountered on the down-route that all the ports of Elat were now closed to the trade.

'Waai!' This time the Sheikh's eyes actually brimmed with tears. 'He will beggar me. My wives and children will starve.'

'El Sheetan counsels you to enlarge the trade in gum copal and copra,' explained the interpreter in a sepulchral voice. 'And as your closest ally, he promises to call upon your regularly with his great ship of many guns, to make certain that you heed this advice.'

'Waai!' The Sheikh plucked at his beard, so that long curly hairs came out between his fingers. 'This ally makes one long for ordinary enemies.'

Twenty-four hours later *Black Joke* sailed into Telfa bay, forty miles further up the coast. Nobody had thought to warn the slaving fleet that was anchored there of the new policies of the state of Elat to which the territory now belonged.

The five dhows in the outer anchorage managed to cut their anchor cables and slip away into the maze of shallow coral channels and shoals to the north of the bay, where *Black Joke* could not follow.

However, there were another six smaller vessels on the beach and four magnificent double-decked ocean-going dhows lying in the inner anchorage. Clinton Codrington burned two of them and seized the four newest and biggest vessels, put prize crews into them and sent them south to the nearest British base at Port Natal.

Two days later, off the beach at Kilwa, Clinton Codrington exercised his ship at gunnery practice. Running out his thirty-two pounders, and firing them in broadsides which set the surface of the lagoon seething and dancing with foam and white fountains of spray. The thunder of gunfire burst against the far hills and rumbled back across the sky like cannon balls rolled across a wooden deck.

The Sultan's local governor was reduced to a quivering jelly of terror by this display of might, and had to be carried bodily into *Black Joke*'s whaler to be rowed out to a conclave with the gunboat's Captain. Clinton had the treaty forms already filled out and ready for signature when they carried the Governor aboard to learn that he was heir to a kingdom to which he had never aspired, and a title which he knew was too grandiose not to bring with it certain retribution from somebody whose name he did not dare to breathe aloud.

Admiral Kemp, sitting in his study in the magnificent mansion of Admiralty House, overlooking the wide smoky-blue haze of the Cape flats to the far mountains of the Hottentots Holland, hopefully dismissed the first reports as the wild imaginings of some crazed subordinate who had served too long in the godforsaken outpost of Port Natal, and who was suffering from the bush madness of 'El Cafard' that sometimes affects a person so isolated.

Then the details began to arrive with every despatch from the north, and they were too graphic to be lightly dismissed. An armada of captured prizes was arriving in the bay of Port Natal, twenty-six sizeable dhows to date, some of them loaded with slaves.

The Lieutenant-Governor of Port Natal was desperate for the Admiral's advice as to what should be done with the dhows. The slaves had been taken ashore, released and immediately been contracted as indentured labourers to the hardy and hopeful gentlemen who were attempting to raise cotton and sugarcane in the wilderness of the Umgeni valley. The shortage of labour was critical, the local Zulu tribesmen much preferred cattle raiding and beer drinking to agricultural labour, so the Governor would be delighted to receive as many freed slaves as the Royal Navy wished to send him. (The Admiral was not entirely certain of the difference between indentured labourers and slaves.) However, what was the Lieutenant-Governor to do with twenty-six – no, the latest figure was thirty-two captured dhows. A further flotilla of six vessels had arrived as the Governor was dictating his report.

Two weeks later, one of the captured dhows, which had been purchased into the Colonial Service by the Lieutenant-Governor, arrived in Table Bay bearing a further batch of despatches.

One of these was from Sir John Bannerman, H.M. Consul on the island of Zanzibar. Another was from the Sultan of Omani in person, with copies to the Foreign Secretary in London and, quite remarkably, to the Governor-General in Calcutta. The Sultan evidently believed that as the representative of the Queen of England the Governor-General would have some jurisdiction in the Indian Ocean, which was virtually his front garden.

Admiral Kemp split the seals on both packets with a queasy feeling of impending doom.

'Good God!' he groaned, as he began reading, and then, 'Oh sweet merciful Jesus, no!' And later, 'It's too much, it's like some sort of nightmare!'

Captain Codrington, one of the most junior post-captains on the Admiralty list, seemed to have taken powers unto himself which would have made a Wellington or a Bonaparte pause.

He had annexed to the British Crown vast African territories, which hitherto had formed part of the Sultan's dominions. With a high hand he had negotiated with various local chiefs and dignitaries of dubious title and authority, pledging recognition and good British gold. 'Good God!' the admiral cried again in real anguish, 'What will that blighter Palmerston have to say.' As a staunch Tory, Kemp had no great opinion of the new Whig prime minister.

Since the troubles in India, the sepoy risings of a few years previously, the British government was very wary of accepting further responsibility for overseas territory and backward peoples. Their orders were specific, and Captain Codrington's recent activity went far from the essence of those orders.

The scramble for Africa was still in the future, and the spirit of the Little Englanders motivated British foreign policy – of this Admiral Kemp was very painfully aware. Daunting as this was, yet it was far from the entire story, Kemp realized, as he read on into the Consul's despatch, his breath rasping hoarsely, his colour rising steadily, and his eyes behind the gold-wire framed reading-glasses swimming with tears of rage and frustration.

'When I get my hands on that puppy—' he promised himself.

Captain Codrington seemed to have declared single-handed war upon the Sultan. Yet even in his outrage the Admiral felt a prickle of professional appreciation for the scope of his subordinate's operations.

There was a formidable list of over thirty separate incidents recited by H.M. Consul. The puppy had stormed fortified castles, raided ashore to burn and destroy barracoons, released tens of thousands of slaves, seized slaving vessels on the high seas, burned others at their moorings, and wreaked the kind of chaos worthy of a marauding Nelson himself.

The Admiral's reluctant admiration for Codrington's technical conduct of the campaign in no way lessened his determination to exact vengeance for the disruption of his life and career that those actions presaged.

'Nothing can save him this time. Nothing!' the Admiral rumbled, as he turned to study the Sultan's protest. This was obviously the work of a professional letter-writer, and every paragraph began and ended with incongruous and flowery enquiries after Kemp's health, between which were sandwiched cries of anguish, screams of outrage, and bitter protest against the broken promises and treaties of Her Majesty's government.

At the very end the letter-writer had not been able to resist adding a prayer for the Admiral and the Queen's prosperity and health in this life, and happiness in the one to follow. This detracted a little from the tone of injury in which the protests and demands had been couched.

The Sultan assessed his losses at over fourteen lakhs of rupees, almost a million of sterling, in plundered shipping and released slaves, and that did not take into account the irreplaceable damage to his prestige, nor the break-down of the entire trade along the coast. The confusion was such that some ports might never again be opened to the trade. The system of gathering slaves in the interior of the continent and the network of routes to the coastal ports had been so sadly disrupted that they might take years to re-open, to say nothing of the gross shortage of shipping resulting from the depredations of 'El Sheetan'. Those ports still open to the trade were swamped with patient slaves, waiting for the dhows which were already scattered wrecks upon the reefs and beaches of the Mozambique channel, or sailing southwards under prize crews.

'Nothing can save him,' repeated Admiral Kemp, and then paused. His own career was finished also. He realized that, and he felt the deep injustice of it. For forty years he had put not a single foot wrong, and his retirement was so close, so very close. He shook off the lethargy of despair, and began to draft his orders.

The first was to all ships of his squadron, to detach immediately and to steam in search of *Black Joke*. In despair he realized that it might take as much as six weeks for his orders to reach his commanders, for they were scattered across two oceans. It might also take as long again for them to search out the errant gunboat in the maze of islands and bays along the Mozambique channel.

However, when they did so, Captain Codrington was to be relieved of his command with immediate effect. Lieutenant Denham was to take over as temporary commander, with orders to bring *Black Joke* into Table Bay as soon as possible.

Admiral Kemp was confident that he could assemble sufficient senior officers on the Cape Station to convene an immediate court-martial. It might help his own position a little if he could report to the First Lord that a savage sentence had already been handed down to Codrington.

Then there was a despatch to H.M. Consul in Zanzibar, suggesting he keep the Sultan reassured and quiescent until the situation could once more be brought under control – and until instructions could be forwarded from the Foreign Office in London regarding possible redress and compensation, although naturally at this stage, no promises or commitments were to be given the Sultan, beyond expressions of good faith and commiseration.

Then there was the onerous task of making his report to the Admiralty. There were no words to soften the actions of his subordinate, and his own responsibility. Besides he had been a serving officer too long to make any such attempt. Yet when the bare facts were stated, even in the beloved unemotional jargon of the navy, they seemed so magnified that Admiral Kemp was himself utterly appalled, all over again. The packet-boat was delayed five hours while the Admiral completed, sealed and addressed this missive. It would be in London in less than a month.

His last despatch was addressed to the officer commanding Her Majesty's ship *Black Joke* in person. And in it Admiral Kemp allowed himself to give expression to some of his own bitterness, taking a sour sadistic pleasure in weighing the relative effectiveness of such words as 'corsair' and 'pirate' – or 'malicious' and 'irresponsible'. He had his little masterpiece of venom written out in five copies to be disseminated in every direction and by every available means that might most speedily bring the puppy to heel. Yet when they were sent, all he could do was wait – and that was the worst part of the affair. Uncertainty and inaction seemed to corrode his very soul.

He dreaded each new arrival in Table Bay, and whenever the signal gun on the hill above the town boomed its brief feather of gunsmoke, his spirit quailed and that sour ache of dread stabbed him in his guts.

Each new despatch lengthened the toll of destruction and depredation, until at last there was a report from the culprit himself, sewn up in a package of canvas and addressed to Admiral Kemp, delivered by the prize crew of a particularly valuable dhow over eighty feet long and of a hundred-ton burden.

The tone in which Captain Codrington listed his achievements infuriated the Admiral as much as the deeds themselves. In an almost casual opening paragraph, Captain Codrington recorded the addition of some million square miles of Africa to the Empire.

He had the grace to admit that his action may have exceeded his orders, and he explained away the discrepancy winningly. 'It had been my firm intention to avoid scrupulously, whilst on this service, every act of a political nature. However, I was forced to accept the cession of the kingdoms of Elat and Telfa by the entreaties of the Sheikh and the Imam – together with that of their people, who seek refuge from the inimical and savage acts of the Sultan of Zanzibar.'

This was hard fare to serve their Lordships, especially the First Lord, Lord Somerset, who had always grudged the use of his men and ships to fight against slavery. However, much worse was to follow. Captain Codrington went on to lecture the Admiral and to deliver a few homilies for their Lordships' instruction.

'By God's providence, an Englishman with no other force than the character of his noble nation has brought to these poor people salvation. Their Lordships must pardon me for using an unfashionable argument,' a sneer at the Little Englanders, 'however, it is as clear to me as the African sun that God has prepared this continent for the only nation on earth that has the public virtue sufficient to govern it for its own benefit, and for the only people who take the revealed word for their moral law.'

Admiral Kemp gulped as he read it, swallowed the wrong way, and was prostrated with a coughing fit from which he recovered some minutes later to read on.

'In all the foregoing I have been influenced by no personal motive or interest, by no desire of vainglory, but my endeavours have solely been to use the powers granted me to the honour of my God, my Queen and to the benefit of my country and all mankind.'

The Admiral removed his reading glasses and stared at the glass case of stuffed songbirds on the wall opposite him.

'To write that, he is either the world's greatest fool – or a brave man or both,' he decided at last.

Admiral Kemp was wrong in his estimate. In fact, Clinton Codrington was having an attack of cockiness and self-importance occasioned by the sense of limitless power which this command had given him. He had been wielding this power for many months, and his judgement and good sense had warped. Yet he still truly believed that he was fulfilling, in this order, the will of God, his patriotic duty and the spirit of his orders from the Lords of the Admiralty.

He was also fully aware that he had demonstrated superior professional ability in carrying out a series of land and sea actions, nearly always against superior numbers, without a single reverse and with the loss of only three men killed in action and less than a dozen wounded. There was only one area in which Clinton had any reservations regarding the success of the patrol up to this time.

Huron was still on the coast, he had intelligence of her from a dozen sources. Mungo St. John was trading, paying top prices for only the best merchandise, hand-picked by either himself or his mate, the bald yellow giant, Tippoo. They were taking only healthy, mature men and women fit to withstand the long voyage back around Good Hope and across the middle passage, and there was a shortage of this type of merchandise.

For Clinton every dawn brought the hope that *Black Joke* would once again raise that towering pyramid of beautiful white sails, but each day the hope faded slowly with the passage of the fierce tropical sun across the heavens, to be extinguished each night as the huge red orb plunged into the sea, and to be resurrected again with the next dawn.

Once they missed the big American clipper by a single day. She had slipped out of the bay at Lindi twenty-four hours before *Black Joke*'s arrival, after taking on fifty prime slaves. The watchers from the beach could not be certain if she had turned north or south, for she had made her offing below the horizon, and had been lost to sight from the shore before coming around on to her intended course.

Clinton guessed *Huron* would go south, and had steamed in pursuit for three days, over an empty sea, down a seemingly deserted coast with barren anchorages before admitting that St. John had sailed away from him again, and he was forced to abandon the hunt.

At the very least he knew that if *Huron* had turned north, St. John was still trading, and there was always a chance of another encounter. He prayed for it every evening. It was all that he needed to make this patrol a clean sweep, so that he could fly a broom from his masthead when he sailed into Table Bay again.

This time he had the sworn and witnessed depositions of the men who had sold St. John his slaves as proof positive that *Huron* was trading. He did not have to rely on the equipment clause, or the dubious rights of search. He had his proof and somehow he knew his chance would come.

The tide was running at full flow for Clinton. He was imbued with a new sense of worthiness, a new, iron-clad confidence in himself and his own good fortune. He carried himself differently, chin higher, shoulders squarer, and if his gait was not yet a swagger, it was at least an assured stride. He smiled more often and when he did there was a wicked curl to his upper lip and a devilish twinkle in the pale blue eyes. He had even grown a full moustache, golden and curling that gave him a piratical air, and his crew, who had always respected his cold precise management of the ship, but felt little affection for him, now cheered him when he came back on board from one of his forays ashore.

'Good old Tongs!' It was his new nickname from 'Hammer and Tongs'. They had never had a pet name for him before, but now they were a proud ship, proud of themselves, and proud of their twenty-seven-year-old 'Old Man'.

'Give 'em hell, Tongs!' they cheered behind him as he led them, naked cutlass in hand, over the outer stockade of a barracoon with musket smoke swirling around his lanky figure.

'At 'em, the Jokers!' they cheered themselves, as they leaped the gap between *Black Joke*'s rail and the deck of a slaving dhow, swinging their cutlasses, pistols popping as they drove the slavers down into their own holds and battened the hatches down on them, or chased them over the side where the sharks were cruising.

They knew they were creating a legend. Tongs and his Jokers sweeping the slavers from the Mozambique channel, a hell of a story to tell the nippers back home, and a good slice of prize money to prove the tale.

It was in this mood that *Black Joke* sailed into Zanzibar harbour, the stronghold of the Omani sultan, little Daniel into the lion's den. The gunners on the parapets of the fort, though they stood with the slow match burning in their hands, could not bring themselves to touch them to the huge bronze cannon as the ugly little gunboat came fussing up the Zanzibar roads.

Black Joke had her yards manned with neatly uniformed seamen. A spectacular display, geometrical white ranks of men against the backdrop of tropical anvil-headed thunder-clouds.

Her officers were in cocked hats and full ceremonial dress, uniform, swords, white gloves and white breeches, and as she made her turn into the inner harbour, *Black Joke* began firing her courtesy salute – which was a signal for most of the population to head for the hills, jamming the narrow alleyways of the old city with a lamenting torrent of refugees.

The Sultan himself fled his palace, and with most of his court took refuge in the British consulate, overlooking the harbour.

'I am not a coward,' the Sultan explained bitterly to Sir John Bannerman, 'but the Captain of that ship is a madman. Allah himself does not know what he will do next.'

Sir John was a large man, of large appetite. He possessed a noble belly like the glacis of a mediaeval castle and full mutton-chop whiskers around a florid face, but the clear intelligent eyes, and the wide friendly mouth of a man of humanity and humour. He was a noted oriental scholar, and had written books of travel and of religious and political appraisal of the East, as well as a dozen translations of minor Arabic poets.

He was also a confirmed opponent of the slave trade, for the Zanzibar markets were held in the square below the windows of his residence and from his bedroom terrace he could watch on any morning the slaving dhows unloading their pitiful cargoes on the stone wharf they called, with cruel humour, the 'Pearl Gate'.

For seven years he had patiently negotiated a series of treaties with the Sultan, each one nipping a few more twigs off the flourishing growth which he detested, but found almost impossible to prune effectively, let alone root out entirely.

In all the Sultan's territories Sir John had absolute jurisdiction only over the community of Hindu traders on the island, for they were British subjects, and Sir John published a bulletin requiring them to free all their slaves forthwith, against a penalty of £100 for non-compliance.

His bulletin made no mention of compensation, so the most influential of the merchants sent Sir John a defiance which was the Pushtu equivalent of 'The hell with you and your bulletins'.

Sir John, with his one good foot, personally kicked in the merchant's door, dragged him out from under his charpoy bed, dropped him to his knees with a full-blooded round-house punch, chained him around the neck and marched him through the city streets to the consulate and locked him in the wine cellar until the fine was paid and the slaves' manumission papers signed. There had been no further defiance and no takers for the Hindu merchant's subsequent, privately circulated offer to pay another £100 to anybody who would stick a knife between Sir John's ribs during one of his evening promenades through the old city. Thus it was that Sir John was still bluff and hale as he stood on his terrace puffing a cigar – his only indisposition was the gouty foot thrust into a carpet slipper. He watched the little black-hulled gunboat coming up the channel.

'She behaves like a flagship,' he smiled indulgently, and beside him, Said the Sultan of Zanzibar, hissed like a faulty steam valve.

'El Sheetan!' His wrinkled turkey neck turned bright red with impotent anger, his bony nose beaked like that of an unhappy parrot. 'He sails here, into my harbour, and my gunners stand by their cannons like dead men. He who has beggared me, who has plunged my empire into ruins – what does he dare here?'

The answer that Clinton 'Tongs' Codrington would have given him was quite simple. He was carrying out to the letter the orders given him in Cape Town many months previously by Admiral Kemp, the Commander of the South Atlantic and Indian Ocean Squadron.

'You are further requested and required to take advantage of the first opportunity to call into the harbour of Zanzibar, where you will accord to his Royal Highness the Sultan of Omani full honours, while taking the advice of Her Majesty's Consul, Sir John Bannerman, as to reinforcing existing treaties between His Royal Highness and Her Britannic Majesty's Government.'

Which, being translated, was an instruction to show the Union Jack against a background of thirty-two pounder cannons, and by doing so remind the Sultan of his commitments under the various treaties.

'To teach the naughty old beggar to mind his P's and Q's,' as Clinton explained cheerfully to Lieutenant Denham with a twirl of his new golden moustache.

'I would have thought, sir, that the lesson had already been given,' Denham answered darkly.

'Not at all,' Clinton demurred. 'The treaties with the new sultans on the mainland no longer affect the Zanzibar fellow. We still have to ginger this old boy up a little.'

Sir John Bannerman limped up on to *Black Joke*'s deck, favouring his gouty foot and cocked a lively eye at the young naval officer who stepped forward to greet him.

'Well, sir, you have been busy indeed,' he murmured. My God, the fellow was little more than a boy, a fresh-faced youngster, despite the cocked hat and moustache. It was difficult to believe that he had created such havoc with this tiny ship.

They shook hands, and Bannerman found himself liking the boy, despite the turmoil that he brought into the Consul's normally tranquil existence.

'A glass of madeira, sir?' Clinton suggested.

'Damned decent of you, I must say.'

In the small cabin, Bannerman mopped his streaming face, and came directly to business.

'By God, you've put the cat amongst the pigeons,' he wagged his big head.

'I don't see . . .'

'Now, listen to me,' Bannerman snapped, 'and I'll explain to you the facts of life as they apply to eastern Africa in general, and Zanzibar in particular.'

Half an hour later, Clinton had lost much of his new-found bumptiousness.

'What should we do?' he asked.

'Do?' Bannerman asked. 'What we do is take full advantage of the situation which you have precipitated, before these idiots in Whitehall come stumbling in. Thanks to you the Sultan is at last in a mood to sign the treaty I have been after for five years. I'll trade a handful of these utterly illegal, untenable treaties that you have made with non-existent states and mythical princes for one that will truss the old goat up the way I've wanted him for years.'

'Excuse me, Sir John,' Clinton looked slightly perplexed, 'from what you said earlier, I understood that you heartily disapproved of my recent actions.'

'On the contrary,' Sir John grinned at him expansively, 'you have stirred my blood, and made me proud to be an Englishman again. I say, do you have a little more of the madeira?'

He raised the glass to Clinton. 'My hearty congratulations, Captain Codrington. I only wish that I could do something to save you from the fate that so certainly awaits you, once the Admiralty and Lord Palmerston catch up with you.' Sir John drank half the glass, smacked his lips, 'Jolly good stuff,' he nodded, set the glass aside and went on briskly, 'Now, we have to work fast and get the Sultan to sign an iron-clad treaty – before Whitehall rushes in with apologies and protestations of good faith which will put to naught all the fine work you have done to date. Something tells me that won't be very long,' he added lugubriously, and then more brightly, 'You could have your ship's guns run out whilst we are ashore. Do wear your sword. Oh, and one other thing, don't take your eyes off the old goat while I do the talking. There is already talk about your eyes – that extraordinary colour of blue, don't you know – and the Sultan has heard about them already. As you probably know, they now call you "El Sheetan" on this coast, and the Sultan is a man who sets great store by djinns and the occult.'

Sir John's predictions as to the imminent arrival of tidings from higher sources was almost clairvoyant, for as he spoke H.M. sloop *Penguin*, with urgent despatches on board for Sir John Bannerman, for the Sultan, and for Captain Codrington, was on a fair wind, which, if it held, would bring her into Zanzibar harbour within the next two days. Time was shorter than even Sir John believed.

With some trepidation, the Sultan had moved back into his palace. He had only half believed Sir John's assurances, but, on the other hand, the palace was half a mile from the harbour where that evil black ship was displaying its formidable broadside of carronades, while the consulate was on the harbour front – or the front line of fire, depending on how one looked at it.

On Sir John's advice Clinton had come ashore with a bodyguard of a dozen picked seamen, who could be trusted to resist the temptations of the old city's red-light area, the grog and the women that seamen dream of. It was dusk when the party plunged into the labyrinth of narrow alleys, where the balconies almost met overhead, led by Sir John who despite his game leg set a good pace, picking his way around heaps of noisome garbage and avoiding the puddles in the uneven paving that looked like a cold minestrone soup and smelled a great deal higher.

He chatted affably with Clinton, pointing out the various sites and buildings of interest, relating the island's history and giving a quick perceptive character-sketch of the Sultan and the more important men in his empire, including those unfortunate new princes who had signed Clinton's blank treaty forms.

'That's one thing, Sir John. I wouldn't want anything to happen to them,' Clinton cut in for the first time. 'I hope they won't be victimized for having, well, how can one say, for having seceded from the Sultan's empire—'

'Forlorn hope.' Sir John waggled his head. 'Not one of them will be alive by Ramadan. The old goat has a nasty streak.'

'Couldn't we put a clause in the new treaty to protect them?'

'We could, but it would be a waste of paper and ink.' Sir John clapped his shoulder. 'Your concern is misplaced. The finest collection of ruffians, rogues and assassins south of the equator, or north of it, for that matter. One of the side benefits of the whole business, getting rid of that lot. Old goat will have a lovely time, compensate him for the loss of face when he straps their heads or hands them the cup of datura tea. Ghastly death, datura poisoning. Oh, by the way, you must look at these gates.' They had reached the front of the palace. 'One of the most magnificent examples of craftsmanship on the island.'

The massive teak doors were fifteen feet high, intricately carved, but in accordance with Moslem law the carvings depicted neither human nor animal figures. They were the only impressive feature of the drab square building with its blank walls relieved by the wooden balconies high above street level, shuttered against the night air and the gaze of the curious.

The gates swung open at their approach, and the palace guards armed with ancient jezails were the first living beings they had seen since leaving the harbour. The city was still deserted, and cowering under the menace of *Black Joke*'s guns.

Clinton noticed, since Sir John had mentioned it, that the guards averted their gaze as he passed, one of them actually covering his face with the loose tail of his turban. So the business of the eyes was true. He was not sure whether to feel insulted or amused.

'You must see these.' Sir John stopped him in the cavernous ante-chamber lit with guttering oil lamps suspended in heavy brass chandeliers from a ceiling lost in the gloom. 'The heaviest recorded specimens in the world, one of them over three-hundred-pounds weight.'

They were a pair of African elephant tusks, suspended on the stone wall with retaining bands of copper, two incredible curves of ancient ivory, as thick as a girl's waist, taller than a man could reach, with hardly any taper from hilt to blunt tip, gleaming with the lustre of precious porcelain.

'You have not hunted these beasts?'

Clinton shook his head, he had never even seen one of them, but the huge teeth impressed him none the less.

'Before my foot, I shot them in India and in Africa. No other sport to beat that, incredible animals.' He patted one of the tusks. 'The Sultan killed this one when he was a young man, with a jezail! But there aren't any monsters like that around any more, more's the pity. Come along, mustn't keep the old goat waiting.'

They went on through half a dozen chambers, each of them Aladdin's caves of rare treasures, carved jade, beautifully worked ivory carvings, a plam tree and suspended moon, the symbol of Mohamed, in solid gold, carpets of silk and thread of gold and silver, a collection of fifty priceless Korans in silver and golden containers set with precious and semi-precious stones.

'Look at that shiner.' Sir John stopped again, and pointed out a native cut diamond in the hilt of an Arabian scimitar. The diamond was cushion-shaped and a little out of true, but burning with a weird blue and icy fire even in the semi-dark. 'Legend says the sword was Saladin's, I doubt it, but the stone is one hundred and fifty-five carats. I weighed it myself.' And then as he took Clinton's arm and stumped off again, 'Old goat is rich as Croesus. He has been milking rupees out of the mainland for forty years, and his father for fifty years before that. Ten rupees for every slave, ten for every kilo of ivory. God knows how much for copra and gum-copal concessions.'

Clinton saw instantly why Sir John called him the old goat. The resemblance was startling, from the white, pointed beard and square yellow teeth to the mournful Roman nose and elongated ears.

He took one look at Clinton, catching his eye for a split part of a second, before he looked away hurriedly, blanching visibly, as he waved his two visitors to the piles of velvet and silk cushions.

'Keep the old beady eye on him,' Sir John counselled aside, 'and don't eat anything.' He indicated the display of sweetmeats and sugared cakes on the bronze trays. 'If they aren't poisoned, they'll probably turn your stomach anyway. It's going to be a long night.'

The prediction was accurate, the talk went on hour after tedious hour, in flowing Arabic hyperbole and flowery diplomacy, that concealed the hard bargaining. Clinton understood not a word. He forced himself not to fidget, though his buttocks and legs soon lost all feeling from the unusual position on the cushions, yet he maintained a stern expression and kept his gaze fixed on the Sultan's wrinkled and whiskered visage. Sir John assured him later that it had helped greatly to shorten the negotiations, yet it seemed a full round of eternity before Sir John and the Sultan were exchanging polite fixed smiles and deep bows of agreement.

There was a triumphant gleam in Sir John's eye, as he strode out of the palace, and he took Clinton's arm affectionately.

'Whatever happens to you, my dear fellow, generations unborn will have reason to bless your name. We have done it, you and I. The old goat has agreed. The trade will wither and die out within the next few years now.'

On the walk back through the narrow streets, Sir John was as lively and cheerful as a man returning from a convivial party rather than the bargaining table. His servants were still waiting his coming, and all the lamps in the consulate were burning.

Clinton would have liked immediately to go back aboard his ship, but Sir John restrained him with an arm about his shoulder, as he called for his Hindu butler to bring champagne. On the silver tray with the green bottle and crystal glasses was a small package in stitched and sealed canvas. While the uniformed butler poured the champagne, Sir John handed Clinton the package.

'This came in earlier on a trading dhow. I did not have the opportunity to deliver it to you before we left for the palace.'

Clinton accepted it warily, and read the address:- 'Captain Clinton Codrington, Officer Cammanding Her Majesty's Ship *Black Joke*. Please forward to H.M. Consul at Zanzibar to await collection.

The address was repeated in French, and Clinton felt a quick thrill kindle his blood as he recognized the bold round script in which the package was addressed. It took an effort to restrain himself from ripping the package open immediately.

However, Sir John was handing him a glass of wine, and Clinton suffered through the toasts, the loyal toast to the Queen, and that ironical one to the Sultan and the new treaty, before he blurted out, 'Excuse me, Sir John, I believe this to be a communication of importance,' and the Consul waved him into his study and closed the door after him to give Clinton privacy.

On the leather top of the marquetry desk, Clinton slit the seals and stitching of the package with a silver knife from the Consul's desk set. From it fell a thick sheath of closely written notepaper, and a woman's earring of paste and silver, the twin to the one that Clinton wore under his shirt against his chest.

Black Joke groped her way out through the dark, unbuoyed channel an hour before the first flush of dawn in the eastern sky. Turning southwards she set all canvas and worked up swiftly to her best speed.

She was making eleven knots when she passed the sloop *Penguin* a little before midnight the following night. *Penguin* bearing her urgent dispatches was hull down on the eastern horizon and her running lights were obscured by a heavy tropical deluge, the first fanfare of the coming monsoon that passed between the two vessels hiding them from each other's lookouts.

By dawn the two ships were fifty nautical miles apart, and rapidly widening the gap, while Clinton Codrington paced his quarterdeck impatiently, stopping at every turn to peer impatiently into the south.

He was hurrying to answer the most poignant appeal, the most pressing duty of a dutiful man, the call for succour from the woman he loved, a woman in terrible and pressing jeopardy.

The flow of the Zambezi had a majesty that Zouga Ballantyne had seen on no other great river, neither the Thames, nor the Rhine, nor the Ganges.

The water was the almost iridescent green of molten slag pouring down the side of a steel-yard dump, and it formed powerful, slowly turning vortices in the angles of the broad bends, while in the shallows it seemed to roil upon itself as though the leviathan of all the world sported below its dark mysterious surface. Here the main channel was more than a mile across, though there were other lesser channels, and other narrower mouths beyond the waving banks of papyrus and cotton-headed reeds.

The small flotilla of boats hardly seemed to move against the current. In the lead was the steam launch *Helen*, named after Zouga's mother.

Fuller Ballantyne had designed the vessel and had it manufactured in Scotland for the disastrous Zambezi expedition which had penetrated only as far as the Kaborra-Bassa gorge. The launch was almost ten years old now, and for most of that time had been the victim of the engineering prowess of the Portuguese trader who had purchased her from Fuller Ballantyne when the expedition was abandoned.

The launch's steam engine creaked and thudded, leaked steam from every pipe and joint, and sprayed sparks and thick black smoke from her wood-burning furnace, exerting herself far beyond the dictates of her age and maker's specifications as she towed the three deeply laden barges against the flow of the mighty river. They were making good a mere fifteen miles a day, and it was more than two hundred up river from Quelimane to Tete.

Zouga had chartered the launch and her barges to carry the expedition upstream to the jump-off point at Tete. He and Robyn rode in the first barge, together with the most valuable and delicate equipment: the medical stores, the navigational equipment, sextants, barometers and chronometers, the ammunition and firearms, and the personal camping gear.

In the third and last barge, under the bright and restless eye of Sergeant Cheroot, were the few porters that had been recruited at Quelimane. Zouga was assured that the additional hundred porters that he needed could be procured at Tete, but it had seemed prudent to sign on these healthy and vigorous men, as they became available. So far there had been no desertions, which was something unusual for the beginning of a long safari, when the proximity of home and hearth could be expected to exert sudden irresistible attractions on the weaker souls.

In the middle barge, on the tow-line directly behind Zouga, were the bulkier stores. In the main these were trade goods, cloth and beads, knives and axes, some cheap muskets and lead bars for ball, bags of black powder and flints. These were essential commodities with which to buy fresh provisions, to bribe local headmen for right to passage, to purchase concessions to hunt and prospect, and generally sustain the expedition's objects.

In charge of this middle barge was Zouga's newest and most dubious acquisition, who had been hired as guide, translator and camp manager. His slight admixture of blood showed in his skin, a smooth dark olive and his hair, thick and lustrous as a woman's. His teeth were very white and he flashed them in a perpetually ready smile. Yet, even when he smiled, his eyes were cold and black as those of an angry mamba.

The Governor in Quelimane had assured Zouga that this man was the most famous elephant hunter and traveller in all the Portuguese territories. He had ventured further into the interior than any other living Portuguese, and he spoke a dozen of the local dialects and understood the customs of the local tribes.

'You cannot travel without him,' the Governor assured Zouga. 'It would be madness to do so. Even your own father, the famous Dr. Fuller Ballantyne, made use of his services. It was he who showed your sainted father the way to reach Lake Marawi.'

Zouga had raised an eyebrow. 'My father was the first man to reach Lake Marawi.'

'The first *white* man,' the Governor corrected him delicately, and Zouga smiled as he realized that it was one of the subtle distinctions which Fuller Ballantyne used to protect the value of his discoveries and explorations. Of course, there had been men living on the shores of the lake for at least two thousand years, and the Arabs and Mulattos had traded there for two hundred years, but they were not *white* men. That made an enormous difference.

Zouga had at last acceded to the Governor's suggestions when he had realized that this paragon was also the Governor's nephew, and that the further course of the expedition would be much smoothed by employing somebody so well connected.

He had reason to reconsider this opinion within the first few days. The man was a braggart and a bore. He had an endless fund of tales, of which he was always the hero, and the evident disregard for the truth that these demonstrated made all his facts and information suspect.

Zouga was uncertain just how well the man spoke the tribal dialects. He seemed to prefer to communicate with the toe of his boot or the *sjambok* of cured hippopotamus hide which he always carried. As for his hunting prowess, he certainly expended a great deal of powder and shot.

Zouga was sprawled on the barge's afterdeck, in the shade of the canvas awning, and he was sketching on the board he held on his knees. It was a pastime he had taken up in India, and though he knew that he had no great talent, yet it filled the idle hours of camp life and served as a useful record of places and persons, of events and animals. Zouga intended incorporating some of the sketches and water colours in the book describing the expedition. The book which would make his fortune and reputation.

He was trying to capture on paper the river's immensity, and the tallness of that aching blue sky set with the afternoon's building thunderheads, when there was the sharp crack of a rifle shot, and he looked up frowning with annoyance.

'He is at it again.' Robyn dropped her book into her lap and glanced back at the second barge.

Camacho Nuño Alvares Pereira sat high on the barge's cargo, reloading the rifle, ramrodding the charge down the long barrel. The high beaver hat sat on his head like a chimney stack and the bunch of white ostrich feathers plumed out above the crown like smoke from the furnace. Zouga could not see what he had fired at, but he guessed what would be his next target, for the steamer was being pushed out by the current to the outside of a broad bend in the river, and it was forced to steer between two low sandbanks.

The sand shone in the sunlight with the peculiar brilliance of an alpine snowfield, contrasting with the dark shapes upon it that looked like rounded granite boulders.

As the steamer slowly closed the gap, the shapes resolved into a troop of sprawling somnolent hippopotami. There were a dozen of them, one a huge scarred bull, lying on his side and exposing the expanse of his belly.

Zouga glanced back from the huge sleeping animals to the figure of Camacho Pereira on the second barge. Camacho lifted the plumed beaver and waved it in jovial salute. His teeth flashing like a semaphore even at that distance.

'You chose him,' said Robyn sweetly, following the direction of his gaze.

'That's a great comfort.' Zouga glanced at his sister. 'They told me he was the greatest sportsman and guide on the east coast.'

They both watched Camacho finish loading the rifle and setting the cap on its nipple.

The sleeping hippopotami suddenly became aware of the approaching vessels.

They scrambled upright with amazing alacrity for such clumsy-looking animals, and galloped over the white sand, scattering clouds of it under their huge feet and then entered the water in a high crashing cascade of thrown spray, disappearing swiftly, and leaving the water churned and flecked with foam. Standing in the bows of the first barge, Zouga could clearly see the dark shapes below the surface of the water, galloping in comical slow motion, their movements inhibited by the water. They were silhouetted against the lighter-coloured sandbanks, and as he watched them, the ungainly creatures evoked his sympathy and amusement. He remembered a nursery rhyme that his Uncle William had recited to him as a child that began: 'A hippo – what – amus?'

Zouga was still smiling as the bull hippo surfaced fifty paces from the barge's side. The bulky grey head broke clear, the flaps of flesh that sealed the nostrils flared open as he breathed and the small round ears fluttered like the wings of a bird as he cleared them of water.

For a moment he stared at the strange vessels through pinkly inflamed, piggy blue eyes. Then he opened the full gape of his jaws, a cavern the colour and the texture of a pink rose. The tusks were yellow and curved to murderous cutting edges, quite capable of biting a bullock cleanly in half, and he no longer seemed fat and comical. Instead he looked exactly what he was, the most dangerous of all African big game.

Zouga knew that the hippopotamus had killed more human beings than all the elephant and lion and buffalo together. With ease they could crunch in the fragile hull of a dugout canoe, the ubiquitous *makoro* of Africa, and then cut in half the terrified swimmers. They would readily leave the water to chase and kill any human who they believed threatened a calf, and in areas where they had been hunted they would attack without provocation. However, the steel hulls of the barges were invulnerable even to the jaws and tusks of the massive creature, and Zouga could afford to watch with complete objectivity.

From the bull's gaping pink jaws came a challenging series of bellows, each mounting in volume and menace as he moved closer to drive off the intruders who threatened his females and their young. Camacho put his hand up behind his head, and tilted the beaver hat at a jaunty angle over one eye. As always, he was smiling as he swung up the rifle and fired.

Zouga saw the strike of the bullet deep in the animal's throat, it severed an artery and instantly bright crimson blood gushed against the roof of the open mouth, discolouring the gleaming tusks, and pouring in a quick flood over the rubbery, bewhiskered lips. The bull's bellow rose into a piercing scream of agony, and he lunged half clear of the surface in a burst of white water.

'I keel heem!' roared Camacho, and his shout of laughter filled the sudden void of silence as the bull dived below the surface, leaving his blood to swirl away down the current.

Robyn had jumped up and was clinging to the barge's rail, a flush overlaying her sunbronzed cheeks and throat.

'That was callous butchery,' she said quietly.

'No point in it,' Zouga agreed. 'The animal will die below the surface and be washed out to sea.'

But he was wrong, for the bull surfaced again, closer to the barge. His jaws still gaping and streaming gouts of blood, he thrashed and lunged in maddened circles, his bellows distorted by blood and water, as his death frenzy rose to a crescendo. Perhaps the bullet had damaged his brain, making it impossible for him to close his jaws or to control his limbs.

'I keel heem!' roared Camacho, dancing with excitement on the foredeck of the second barge, pouring shot after shot into the immense grey body, grabbing a rifle from his black gunbearer or from his second loader as soon as it was primed.

His two black servants worked with the expertise of long practice, so that it seemed that Camacho always had a loaded rifle ready to snatch and waiting hands ready to take the smoking weapon from him the moment he had fired.

Slowly the string of barges drew away upstream, leaving the stricken animal wallowing with increasing feebleness in its own expanding circle of blood-tinged waters, until at last it rolled belly upwards, all four stubby legs sticking up towards the sky for a moment before it sank at last and the blood was diluted and swept away downstream.

'That was sickening,' whispered Robyn.

'Yes, but he has trained those gunbearers of his damned well,' said Zouga thoughtfully. 'If one is going to hunt elephant, that is the way to do it.'

Two hours before sunset the *Helen* edged in towards the south bank. For the first time since leaving Quelimane there was some feature on the shore, beyond the endless reed swamps and sandbanks.

The bank was steeper here, rising ten feet above the river, and game paths had been cut into the grey earth by thousands of sharp hooves, and polished to shiny clay by the sliding wet bellies of the long lizardlike shapes of the big crocodiles that came tobogganing down the almost vertical slope when they were disturbed by *Helen*'s churning propeller. The heavily armoured reptiles with the staring yellow eyes set on a hard horny scale atop the long saurian head repulsed Robyn, the first African animal to do so.

There were trees on the bank now, not just waving stands of papyrus. Chief of these were the graceful palms with stems sculptured like a claret bottle.

'Ivory palms,' Zouga told her. 'The fruit has a kernel like a ball of ivory.'

Then far beyond the palms, low against the ruddy evening sky, they could make out the first silhouette of hills and kopjes. They were leaving the delta at last, and that night the company would camp on firm ground, instead of soft white sand, and burn heavy logs on the camp fires rather than the pulpy papyrus stems.

Zouga checked the sentries that Sergeant Cheroot had placed over the irreplaceable cargoes in the barges on which the whole expedition depended, then he supervised the siting of the tents before taking the Sharps rifle and starting out into the open forest and grassland beyond the camp site.

'I come weeth you,' offered Camacho. 'We keel something.'

'Your job is to make camp,' Zouga told him coolly, and the Portuguese flashed his smile and shrugged.

'I make one damn fine camp – you see.'

But as Zouga disappeared amongst the trees, the smile slid off his face, and he hawked in his throat and spat in the dust. Then he turned back into the turmoil of men raising canvas on poles, or dragging in branches of freshly cut thorns to build the *scherm* against marauding lions or scavenging hyena.

Camacho lashed out at a bare black back. 'Hurry, you one mother, twenty-seven fathers.' The man cried out at the pain of the cured hippo-hide whip, redoubling his efforts as a purple welt, thick as a man's little finger, rose across his sweat-oiled muscles.

Camacho strode on towards the small grove of trees which Zouga had picked as the site for the tents of his sister and himself, and he saw that the tents had already been erected and that the woman was busy with the evening muster when she treated the ailments of the camp.

She had been seated at the collapsible camp table, but as Camacho approached, she rose and stooped to examine the foot of one of the bearers whose axe had slipped and almost severed a toe.

The Portuguese stopped abruptly, and his throat dried out as he watched her. As soon as they had left Quelimane, the woman had taken to wearing men's breeches. Camacho found them more provocative than naked flesh itself. It was the first time he had ever seen a white woman dressed like this, and he found it hard to take his eyes off her. Whenever she was in sight, he would watch her surreptitiously, waiting hungrily for the moment when she stooped or leaned forward and the moleskin stretched over her buttocks, as it was now. It lasted too short a time, for the woman straightened up and began speaking to the little black girl who seemed more of a companion to her than a servant.

Still Camacho leaned against the bole of one of the tall umsivu trees and watched her with those black eyes gone velvet and swimming with desire. He was carefully weighing the consequences of what he had dreamed about every night since they had left Quelimane. He had imagined every detail, every expression, every word, each movement and each sigh or cry.

It was not as improbable as it seemed at first. She was an English woman, of course, daughter of a famous man of God, both facts should have been prohibitive to his intentions. However, Camacho had a canny instinct when it came to women, there was a sensuality about her eye and in the full soft lips, and she moved with animal awareness of her body. Camacho stirred restlessly and thrust his hands into his pockets, kneading and tugging gently at himself.

He was fully aware that he was a magnificent specimen of masculinity – those thick tresses of black hair, the gypsy feyness of eyes, the blazing smile, and powerful and well-proportioned body. He was attractive, perhaps irresistibly so, for more than once he had intercepted a quizzical appraising look from the woman. Often the admixture of his blood was attractive to white women, it was an exoticism, the attraction of the forbidden and dangerous, and he sensed in this woman a rebellious disregard for the rules of society. It was possible, no more than possible, Camacho decided, and there was unlikely to be a better opportunity than now. The cold stiff English brother was out of camp, would be so for another hour or more, and the woman had finished attending the little group of sick bearers. A servant had brought a kettle of boiling water to her tent, and she was closing the fly.

Camacho had watched this little ritual every evening. Once the oil lamp had cast her shadow upon the canvas, and he had watched her silhouette lowering those tantalizing breeches, and then using the sponge to – he shuddered deliciously at the memory, and pushed himself away from the tree trunk.

Robyn mixed the hot water from the kettle into the enamel basin. It was still scalding hot, but she liked it so that it reddened the skin and left her feeling glowing with cleanliness. She began to unbutton the flannel shirt, sighing with pleasant weariness, when something scratched on the fly of the tent.

'Who is it?' she called sharply, and felt a faint stir of alarm as she recognized the low voice. 'What do you want?'

'I want talk you, missus.' Camacho's tone was conspiratorial.

'Not now, I am busy.' The man repelled her, and yet in a contrary manner, fascinated her as well. She had found herself staring at him more than once – as she would at a beautiful but poisonous insect. She was annoyed that he had noticed and was vaguely aware that it was unwise to show even the vaguest interest in a man like that.

'Come back tomorrow.' It suddenly occurred to her that Zouga was not in the camp, and she had sent little Juba on an errand.

'I cannot wait. I am sick.'

That was one appeal she could not deny.

'Oh very well. Wait,' she called, and buttoned her shirt, and then as an excuse perhaps to delay the moment turned her attention to her instruments still spread on the table that had been carried into the tent. It reassured her to touch them, and rearrange the bottles and pots of medicines.

'Enter,' she called at last, and faced the entrance of the tent.

Camacho stooped through the entrance, and for the first time she realized how tall he was. His presence in the small tent was almost overpowering, and his smile seemed to light up the interior. His teeth were startlingly white and perfect, she found herself staring again, like a chicken at the dancing cobra perhaps. He was beautiful in a decadent, overblown way, he was bare-headed, all dark dancing hair and scalding eyes.

'What is the trouble?' she asked, trying to sound brisk and businesslike.

'I show you.'

'Very well,' she nodded, and he unbuttoned his shirt. His skin had the sheen of wet marble, but was deep olive in colour, and his body hair grew in crisply springing whorls. His belly was moulded like that of a greyhound and his waist narrow as a girl's. She ran her eyes down his body, quite certain that her gaze was level and professional, but there was no denying the fact that he was an extraordinary animal.

'Where is it?' she asked, and with a single movement he had unclinched and lowered the light duck trousers that were all he wore on his lower body.

'Where?' she asked, and realized that her voice croaked, and she could not go on with the question, for suddenly it dawned upon her that she had been the victim of a carefully planned ruse, and she was in a potentially dangerous position.

'Is that where it hurts?' she found her voice was still a husky whisper.

'Yes,' his voice was a whisper also, and he made a slow stroking movement. 'You can fix, maybe.' He took a step towards her.

'I can fix, certainly,' she said softly, and her hand dropped on to the array of surgical instruments. She actually experienced a twinge of real regret, for it was a superior example of nature's art, and afterwards she was relieved that she had selected a needle probe – and not one of the razorlike scalpels that she had reached for.

The instant before she stabbed, he realized what was about to happen and an expression of utter terror blanched his swarthy, handsome face. He tried frantically to return it to whence it had come, but fear had slowed his hand.

He screamed like a teenage girl as the probe plunged into him, and kept on screaming as he spun around on the same spot as though one foot had been nailed to the ground. Now he was using both hands to hold himself, and once again, with cool professional interest, Robyn noticed the quite miraculous change that had taken place.

She advanced the probe once more into the ready position, and Camacho could no longer stand his ground. He snatched up his trousers, and with a last terrified howl, launched himself head-first into the tent pole. The collision checked him only a moment, and then he was gone, and Robyn found herself trembling violently and yet she was strangely elated. It had been an unusual and instructive experience. However, she would have to use her own personal code when describing it in her journal.

From that evening onwards the Portuguese kept well away from Robyn, and she was relieved not to have those hot dark eyes caressing her wherever she turned. She thought of telling Zouga of the incident, but decided that the embarrassment to both of them and the difficulty of finding the correct words was not worth it. Then there would be the extreme reaction which Zouga would almost certainly have, or that she expected he would have. She had learned never to expect the obvious reaction from her brother, behind the cool and reserved exterior she suspected there existed mysterious passions and dark emotions. After all, they were full-blooded brother and sister, and if she was so afflicted, why should he not be also?

On the other hand, she suspected that, like a cornered wild animal, the Portuguese could be a grave danger even to an experienced soldier and man of action like Zouga. She had a horror of forcing her brother into a position which might lead, if not to his death, then at least to serious injury. Besides which, she had effectively taken care of the man herself. He would be no further trouble, she decided comfortably, and she dismissed Camacho from her mind, and concentrated instead on the pleasure of the last few leisurely days of the voyage up-stream.

The river had narrowed, and the flow was swifter, so that the rate of the convoy's advance slowed even further. The banks provided an ever-changing panorama. Sitting under the awning, with Zouga sketching or writing beside her, she was able to call his attention to the new birds and trees and animals and to have the benefit of his knowledge, gathered to be sure mostly from books, but still wide-reaching and interesting.

The hills of the escarpment rose in a series of cockscombs, so two-dimensional that they seemed to be cut out from thin sheets of some opaque material that allowed the colours of the sunrise to glow through with a weird luminosity. As the sun rose higher, the colours washed out to ethereal eggshell blues, and finally faded altogether in the heat haze of midday, to reappear in the late afternoon in a new suit of totally different colours – pale pinks and ash of roses, ripe plum and delicate apricot.

The hills formed a backdrop to the forests that now ran in a narrow belt along the river banks. Tall galleries of trees, with spreading upper branches in which the troops of vervet monkeys frolicked. The trunks of these trees were daubed with multi-coloured lichens, sulphurous yellows, burnt oranges and the blues and greens of a summer sea. The tangled ropes of lianas, which as a child Robyn had called 'monkey ropes', dangled down from the upper branches to touch the surface of the river or cascade into the dense dark greens of the undergrowth.

Beyond this narrow strip of vegetation, there were occasional glimpses of a different forest on the higher, drier ground, and Robyn saw again with a sharp nostalgic pang the ugly and bloated baobab tree with its crubby bare little branches topping the huge swollen stem. The African legends that her mother had repeated to her so often, explained how Nkulu-kulu, the great great one, had planted the baobab upside down, with its roots in the air.

Nearly every baobab had a nest of one of the big birds of prey in its bare branches, each a shaggy mass of dried twigs and small branches looking like a small, air-borne haystack. Often the birds were at the nest site, sitting on a look-out branch, with that typical raptorial stillness, or soaring above in wide circles, with only an occasional lazy flap of the spread wings, and the stiff tip-feathers feeling the air currents like the fingers of a concert pianist upon the ivory keys.

There was very little game along this part of the river, and the rare antelope rushed back into cover at the first distant approach – a pale blur of movement, with a mere fleeting glimpse of the tall corkscrew horns of a greater kudu, or the flirt of the white, powder-puff underside of a reedbuck's tail.

The game close to the river had been heavily hunted, if not by the Portuguese themselves then by their armed servants, for nearly two hundred years.

When Zouga asked Camacho, 'Do you ever find elephant on this part of the river?' the Portuguese had flashed his smile and declared, 'If I find heem, I keel heem.'

A sentiment that was probably shared by nearly every traveller along this busy waterway, and which accounted for the timidity and scarcity of game in the area.

Camacho was reduced to firing at the roosting fish eagles on their fishing-perches overhanging the water. These handsome birds had the same snowy white head, breast and shoulders of the famous American bald eagle, and a body of lovely dark russet and glistening black. When a shout of Camacho's laughter signalled a hit, a bird would tumble untidily over its disproportionately large wings as it fell into the green water, reduced from imperial dignity to awkward and ungainly death by the strike of the lead bullet.

Within a few days Camacho had recovered from the peculiar, bow-legged and deliberate gait, with which he favoured the injury that Robyn had inflicted on him, and his laughter regained its ringing timbre. But there were other injuries that did not heal so readily, those to his pride and his masculinity. His lust had been changed on the instant to burning hatred, and the more he brooded upon it the more corrosive it became and the deeper his craving for vengeance.

However, his personal considerations would have to wait. There was still much important work for him to do. His uncle, the Governor of Quelimane, had placed great trust in him by assigning him to this task – and his uncle would be unforgiving of any failure. The family fortune was involved, and to a lesser extent the family honour, although this last was a commodity that through constant attrition had lost much of its lustre. However, the family fortunes had suffered considerably since Portugal had been forced to heed the Brussels Treaty. What was left to the family had to be protected. Gold before honour, and honour only when it does not affect the profits – this might have been the family motto.

His uncle had been perceptive, as always, in recognizing in this English expedition a further threat to their interests. It was, after all, headed by the son of a notorious trouble-maker who could be expected to aggravate the enormous damage done by the father. Furthermore, nobody could be sure of the real objects of the expedition.

Major Ballantyne's assertion that it was an expedition to find his missing father was, of course, utterly absurd. That explanation was much too simple and direct, and the English were never simple or direct. This elaborate expedition must have cost many thousands of English pounds, a huge sum of money, far beyond the means of a junior army officer, or the family of a missionary whose futile effort to navigate the Zambezi had ended in disgrace and ridicule, a sick old man who must have perished years ago in the uncharted wilderness.

No, there was another motive for all this activity – and the Governor wanted to know what it was.

It was, of course, possible that this was a clandestine reconnaissance by an officer of the British army ordered by his overbearing government. Who knew what outrageous designs they had upon the sovereign territory of the glorious Portuguese empire? The avarice of this impudent race of shopkeepers and tradesmen was scarcely to be believed. The Governor did not trust them, despite their traditional alliance with Portugal.

On the other hand, it might indeed be a private expedition, but the Governor never lost sight of the fact that it was led by the son of that notorious old busy-body who had possessed the scavenging eye of a vulture. Who knew what the old devil had stumbled upon out their in the unknown land, a mountain of gold or silver, the fabled lost city of Monomatapa with all its treasures intact: anything was possible. Of course, the old missionary would have sent news of the discovery to his own son. If there was a mountain of gold out there, then the Governor would be very pleased to know about it.

Even if there were no new treasures to discover, there were certainly old ones to protect. It would be Camacho Pereira's duty to steer the expedition away from certain areas, to prevent it stumbling on secrets known not even to the Governor's masters in Lisbon.

Camacho's orders were clear: distract the Englishman by accounts of the insurmountable difficulty of travel in certain directions, the swamps, the mountain ranges, the disease, the savage animals and even more savage men, and contrast that with the friendly people in pleasant lands, rich with ivory, that lay in other directions.

If this was unsuccessful – and Major Ballantyne had all the earmarks of arrogance and intractability peculiar to his nation – then Camacho was to use what other means of persuasion came to hand. This was an euphemism perfectly understood by both the Governor and his nephew.

Camacho had almost convinced himself that this was really the only sensible course of action. Beyond Tete there was no law, except that of the knife, and Camacho had always lived by that law. Now he savoured the thought. He had found the Englishman's unconcealed contempt as galling as the woman's rejection had been painful.

He had convinced himself that the reason for the attitude towards him of both brother and sister was his Mulatto blood. This was a sensitive area of Camacho's self-esteem, for even in Portuguese territories where miscegenation was almost universal practice, mixed blood still carried a stigma. He would enjoy the work ahead, for not only would it wipe out the insults he had suffered, but it would bring rich pickings, and even after they had been shared out with his uncle, and others, there would still be much profit in it for himself.

The equipment that the expedition carried represented, in Camacho's view, a vast fortune. There were barge-loads of excellent trade goods. Camacho had taken the first opportunity to check secretly the contents of the packs. There were firearms, and valuable instruments, chronometers and sextants, and there was a forged-steel field-safe that the Englishman kept locked and guarded. The merciful God alone knew how many golden English sovereigns it contained, and if He did not know – then his good uncle the Governor knew less. It would make the division of spoils more in Camacho's favour. The more he brooded upon it, the more he looked forward to the arrival at Tete, and the jump-off into the unexplored territory beyond.

To Robyn the tiny town of Tete marked her real arrival in Africa, and her return to the world for which she had trained so assiduously and yearned for so deeply.

She was secretly glad that Zouga had used the unloading of the barges as an excuse not to accompany her.

'You find the place, Sissy, and we'll go there together tomorrow.'

She had changed back into skirts, for small and isolated as it was, Tete was still a backwater of civilized behaviour and there was no point in giving offence to the local inhabitants. Though she found the heavy folds about her legs annoying, she soon forgot them as she walked the single, dusty street of the village where her father and mother must have walked together for the last time, and peered at the mud-walled trading stores built haphazardly along a rough line with the bank of the river.

She stopped at one of these little *duka*'s and found that the storekeeper could understand a mixture of her basic Swahili, English and Nguni language, enough anyway to direct her on to where the village street petered out in a mere footpath that meandered off into the acacia forest.

The forest was hushed in the heat of the noon, even the birds were silent and the mood weighed on Robyn, depressing her and awakening the memories of long-ago mourning.

She saw a flash of white amongst the trees ahead, and stopped, reluctant to go on to what she knew she would find. For a moment she was transported to girlhood again, to a grey November day standing beside her Uncle William waving upwards at the passenger decks of the departing ship, her eyes so dimmed with tears that she could not make out at the crowded rail the beloved face for which she searched, while the distance between ship and quay opened like the gulf between life and death.

Robyn shook the memory away and went on. There were six graves amongst the trees, she had not expected that, but then she recalled that there had been heavy mortality amongst the members of her father's Kaborra-Bassa expedition, four of disease, one drowned and a suicide.

The grave for which she searched stood a little apart from the others. It was demarcated by a square of whitewashed river stones and at the head was a cross built of mortar. It also had been whitewashed. Unlike the other graves, it had been kept cleaned of grass and weed, and the cross and stones freshly painted. There was even a small bunch of wilted wild flowers standing in a cheap blue china vase. They were not more than a few days old. That surprised Robyn.

Standing at the foot of the grave she read the still fully legible lettering on the plaster cross:

In loving memory of
Helen
beloved wife of Fuller Morris Ballantyne.
Born August 4th 1814. Died of fever December 16th 1852.
God's will be done.

Robyn closed her eyes and waited for the tears to come up from deep inside, but there were no tears, they had been shed long ago. Instead there were only the memories.

Little fragments of memory played over and over in her mind – the smell of strawberries as they gathered them together in Uncle William's garden, standing on tiptoe to place one of the lush red fruit between her mother's white teeth and then eating the half that was left especially for her; lying cuddled under her bed-clothes as she listened drowsily to her mother's voice reading aloud to her in the candlelight; the lessons at the kitchen table in winter, under the elm trees in summer and her own eagerness to learn and to please; her first pony ride, her mother's hands holding her in the saddle, her legs too short for the stirrups; the feel of the soapy sponge down her back as her mother stooped over the iron hipbath; the sound of her mother's laughter, and then at night the sound of her weeping beyond the thin partition beside her cot; then the final memory of the smell of violets and lavender as she pressed her face to her mother's bodice.

'Why must you go, Mama?'

'Because your father needs me. Because your father has sent for me, at last.'

And Robyn's own terrible consuming jealousy at the words, mingled with the sense of impending loss.

Robyn knelt in the soft cushion of dust beside the grave, and began to pray, and as she whispered, the memories came crowding back, happy ones and sad ones together, and she had not felt so close to her mother in all the intervening years.

She did not know how long she had knelt there, it seemed an eternity, when a shadow fell across the earth in front of her and she looked up, jerked back to the present with a little gasp of surprise and alarm.

A woman and child stood near her, a black woman, with a pleasant, even pretty, face. Not young, in her middle thirties possibly, though it was always difficult to guess an African's age. She wore European-style clothing, cast-offs probably, for they were so faded that the original pattern was hardly visible, but starched and fastidiously clean. Robyn sensed that they had been donned for the occasion.

Although the child wore the brief leather kilt of the local Shangaan tribe, he was clearly not a full-blooded African. He could not have been more than seven or eight years of age, a sturdy boy, with a head of dusty-coloured curls and oddly pale-coloured eyes. There was something vaguely familiar about him that made Robyn stare.

He carried a small bunch of the yellow acacia flowers in his hands, and smiled shyly at Robyn before hanging his head and shuffling his feet in the dust. The woman said something to him and tugged at his hand, and he came hesitantly to Robyn and handed her the flowers.

'Thank you,' she said automatically, and raised the bouquet to her nose. They were faintly, but sweetly perfumed.

The woman hiked her skirts and squatted beside the grave, removed the wilted flowers and then handed the little blue china vase to the boy. He scampered away towards the river-bank.

While he was gone the woman plucked out the first green sprouts of weeds from the mound of the grave and then rearranged the whitewashed stones carefully. The familiar manner in which she performed the chore left no doubt in Robyn's mind that she was responsible for the upkeep of her mother's grave.

Both women maintained a friendly, comfortable silence, but when their eyes met they smiled and Robyn nodded her thanks. The child came trotting back, muddy to the knees and slopping water from the vase, but puffed up with self-importance. He had clearly performed this task before.

The woman took the vase from him and set it carefully on the grave, then both of them looked expectantly towards Robyn and watched her while she arranged the acacia flowers in the vase.

'Your mother?' said the woman softly, and Robyn was startled to hear her speak English.

'Yes,' she tried to hide her surprise. 'My mother.'

'Good lady.'

'You knew her?'

'Please?'

After the valiant opening, the woman had very little English, and their communication was halting, until Robyn, out of the habit of talking to little Juba, said something in Matabele. The woman's face lit with pleasure and she answered swiftly in a language which was obviously one of the Nguni group, and whose inflection and vocabulary differed very little from that to which Robyn was accustomed.

'You are Matabele?' Robyn demanded.

'I am Angoni,' the woman put in hastily, for there was rivalry and hostility between even the closely related tribes of the Nguni.

Her tribe, the Angoni, had swept northwards from their origins in the grassy hills of Zululand, and crossed the Zambezi river thirty years before, she explained in her lilting musical dialect. They had conquered the land along the northern shore of Lake Marawi. It was from there that the woman had been sold to one of the Omani slave-masters, and had come down the Shire river in chains.

Unable to keep up with the slave caravan, reduced by starvation, and the fevers and hardships of the long journey, she had been freed of her chains and left for the hyenas beside the slave road. It was there that Fuller Ballantyne had found her and taken her into his own small camp.

She had responded to his rough nursing and when she was recovered, Fuller had baptized her with the Christian name of Sarah.

'So my father's detractors are mistaken,' Robyn laughed, and spoke in English. 'He made more than one convert.'

Sarah did not understand but laughed in sympathy. By now it was almost dusk and the two women, followed by the half-naked child, left the little cemetery and started back along the footpath, with Sarah still telling how when Robyn's mother, summoned at last by Fuller Ballantyne, arrived in Tete with other members of the Kaborra-Bassa expedition, Sarah had been presented to her by Fuller as a personal servant.

By now they had stopped at a fork in the path, and after a moment of hesitation Sarah invited Robyn to her village which was only a short way off the path. Robyn glanced up at the sun and shook her head, it would be dark in an hour and Zouga would be certain to turn out the camp to search for her if she had not returned by then.

She had enjoyed the hours spent with the young woman and the bright sweet child, and when she saw Sarah's obvious disappointment, she said quickly, 'Although I must go – I will return tomorrow at the same time. I wish to hear all you can tell me of my mother and my father.'

Sarah sent the little boy with her as far as the buildings of the village, and after the first few yards Robyn quite naturally took the boy's hand, and he skipped along beside her, chattering gay childish nonsense, which helped to lift her sombre mood until Robyn laughed and chattered with him.

Before they reached the outskirts of Tete, Robyn's fears were confirmed. They met Zouga and Sergeant Cheroot. Zouga was armed with the Sharps rifle and angry with relief the moment he saw her.

'Damn me, Sissy, but you have had us all beside ourselves. You've been missing for five hours.'

The child stared at Zouga with wide eyes. He had never seen anything like this tall lordly man with the imperious manner and sharp commanding voice. He must be a great chief, and he slipped his hand out of Robyn's, retreated two paces, then turned and darted away like a sparrow from the circling hawk.

Some of Zouga's anger left him as he watched the child go, and a small smile touched his lips.

'For a moment I thought you'd picked up another stray.'

'Zouga, I found Mama's grave.' Robyn hurried to him and took his arm. 'It's only a mile or so.'

Zouga's expression changed again and he glanced up at the sun that was already on the tops of the acacia trees and turning deep smouldering red.

'We'll come back tomorrow,' he said. 'I don't like to leave the camp after dark, there are too many jackals lurking about – two legged jackals.' Firmly, he led her back towards the village, continuing his explanation as they walked.

'We are still having a great deal of difficulty obtaining porters, despite the fact that the Governor in Quelimane assured me they would be readily available, and the good Lord knows there are any amount of able-bodied men hereabouts. Yet that strutting poppinjay Pereira finds obstacles at every turn.' The frown made him look much older than his years as did the full beard which he had allowed to grow since disembarking from *Black Joke*. 'He says that the porters refuse to contract until they know the direction and duration of the safari.'

'That seems logical,' Robyn agreed. 'I know I wouldn't carry one of those huge packs, unless I knew where I was going.'

'I don't think at all that it's the porters – there is no reason why the destination should worry them. I am offering top wages, and not a single man has come forward.'

'What is it, then?'

'Pereira has been trying to wheedle our intentions out of me, ever since we left the coast. I think this is a form of blackmail, no porters until I tell him.'

'Then why don't you tell him?' Robyn asked, and Zouga shrugged.

'Because he is too damned insistent. It's not a casual interest, and instinct warns me not to trust him with any information which it is not essential for him to know.'

They walked on in silence until they reached the perimeter of the camp. Zouga had laid it out on the lines of a military base, with an outer stockade of acacia thorn branches, a Hottentot guard at the gate and the *boma* for the porters separated from the stores depot by the tent lines.

'It looks like home already,' Robyn congratulated him, and would have left him for her own tent when Camacho Pereira hurried forward.

'Ah! Major, I wait for you with good news.'

'That's a pleasant change,' Zouga murmured drily.

'I find man who has seen your father, not eight months ago.'

Robyn turned back instantly, her excitement matching that of the flamboyant Portuguese and she spoke directly to him for the first time since the incident in her tent.

'Where is he? Oh, this is wonderful news.'

'If it's true,' qualified Zouga, with considerably less enthusiasm.

'I bring the man, damned quick – you see!' Camacho promised, and hurried away towards the porters' *boma*, shouting as he went.

Within ten minutes he returned dragging with him a skinny old man dressed in greasy tatters of animal skins, and with his eyes rolling up into his head with terror.

As soon as Camacho released him, the old man prostrated himself before Zouga who sat in one of the canvas camp chairs under the awning of the dining tent, and gabbled replies to the queries that Camacho shouted at him in hectoring tones.

'What dialect is that he speaks?' Zouga interrupted within the first few seconds.

'Chichewa,' Camacho replied. 'He no speak other.'

Zouga glanced at Robyn, but she shook her head. They had to rely entirely on Camacho's rendition of the old man's replies.

It seemed that the old man had seen 'Manali', the man with the red shirt, at Zimi on the Lualaba river. Manali had been camped there with a dozen porters, and the old man had seen him with his own eyes.

'How does he know it was my father?' Zouga asked.

Everybody knew 'Manali', the old man explained, he was a living legend from the coast to 'Chona langa', the land where the sun sets.

'When did he see Manali?'

One moon before the coming of the last rains, which made it in October of the previous year, as Camacho had said, about eight months' previously.

Zouga sat lost in thought, but his gaze fixed with such ferocity on the unfortunate who grovelled before him that the old man suddenly burst out on a plaintive note that made Camacho's handsome face darken with anger and he touched the skeletal ribs with the toe of his boot, a threatening gesture that quieted the old man instantly.

'What did he say?' Robyn demanded.

'He swears he speak the truth only,' Camacho assured her, resurrecting his smile with an effort.

'What else does he know of Manali?' Zouga asked.

'He speak with the porters of Manali, they say they go follow the Lualaba river.'

It made some sense, Zouga thought. If Fuller Ballantyne was indeed seeking the source of the Nile river to recover his lost reputation, then that is where he would have gone. The Lualaba, which was reputed to run directly northward, was one of obvious choices for the source river.

Camacho questioned the old man for another ten minutes, and would have taken the hippo-hide whip to jog his memory, but Zouga stopped him with a gesture of annoyance. It was obvious that there was nothing further to learn from him.

'Give him a bolt of *merkani* cloth and a *kete* of beads – and let him go,' Zouga ordered and the old man's gratitude was pathetic to watch.

Zouga and Robyn sat later than usual beside the camp fire, while it collapsed slowly upon itself in spasmodic torrents of rising sparks and the murmur of sleepy voices from the porters' *boma* died into silence.

'If we go north,' Robyn mused, watching her brother's face, 'we will be going into the stronghold of the slave trade, from Lake Marawi northwards. From that area into which no white man, not even Pater, has ever ventured must come all the slaves for the markets of Zanzibar and the Omani Arabs—'

'What about the evidence of the trade to the south,' Zouga glanced across the clearing at the silent figure of Juba, waiting patiently by the entrance to Robyn's tent. 'That girl is the living proof that a new trade is flourishing south of the Zambezi.'

'Yes, but it seems to be nothing compared to the activity north of here.'

'The northern trade has been fully documented. Father reached Marawi and followed the slave caravans down to the coast fifteen years ago, and Bannerman at Zanzibar has written a dozen reports on the Zanzibar market,' Zouga pointed out, nursing a precious tumbler of his fast-dwindling supply of whisky, and staring into the ashes of the fire. 'Whereas nobody knows anything about the trade with the Monomatapa and the Matabele south of here.'

'Yes, I acknowledge that,' Robyn admitted reluctantly. 'However, in his *Missionary Travels* father wrote that the Lualaba was the source of the Nile and he would one day prove it by following it from its headwaters. Besides which, he has been seen in the north.'

'Has he, though?' Zouga asked mildly.

'That old man . . .'

'. . . Was lying. Somebody put him up to it, and I don't need more than one guess,' Zouga finished.

'How do you know he was lying?' Robyn demanded.

'If you live long enough in India you develop an instinct for the lie,' Zouga smiled at her. 'Besides why would father wait eight years *after* he disappeared to explore the Lualaba river. He would have gone there directly – if he had gone north.'

'My dear brother,' Robyn's voice was stinging, 'it would not be the legend of Monomatapa that makes you so stubbornly determined to go south of the river, would it? Is that gleam in your eye the gleam of gold?'

'That is a mean thought,' Zouga smiled again. 'But what does intrigue me is the determination of that great guide and explorer, Camacho Pereira, to discourage any journey to the south, and instead to lead us northwards.'

Long after Robyn had disappeared into her tent and the lantern within was extinguished Zouga sat on beside the fire, nursing the whisky in the tumbler and staring into the fading coals. When he reached his decision he drained the last drop of precious golden brown spirit in the glass and stood up abruptly. He strode down the lines to where Camacho Pereira's tent stood at the furthest end of the camp.

There was a lantern burning within even at this late hour, and when Zouga called out, a squeak of alarm in feminine tones was quickly hushed with a man's low growl and a few minutes later Camacho Pereira pulled the fly aside and peered out at Zouga warily.

He had thrown a blanket over his shoulders to cover his nudity, but in one hand he carried a pistol and relaxed only slightly as he recognized Zouga.

'I have decided,' Zouga told him brusquely, 'that we'll go north, up the Shire river to Lake Marawi – and then on to the Lualaba river.'

Camacho's face shone like the full moon as he smiled.

'That is very good. Very good – much ivory, we find your father – you see, we find him damn soon.'

Before noon the following day Camacho, with a great deal of shouting and swishing of the kurbash, marched a hundred strong healthy men into the camp. 'I find you porters,' he announced. 'Plenty porters – damn good, hey?'

The Christian girl Sarah was waiting beside the grave again when Robyn came down through the acacia forest the following afternoon.

The child saw her first and ran to greet her, he was laughing with pleasure, and Robyn was struck once again by the familiarity of his face. It was something about his mouth and his eyes. The resemblance to somebody she had known was so forcible that she stopped dead and stared at him, but could not recapture the memory before the boy took her hand and led her to where his mother waited.

They went through the little ritual of changing the flowers on the grave and then settled side by side on a fallen acacia branch. It was cooler in the shade and in the branches above their heads a pair of shrikes hunted little green caterpillars. The birds were black and white across the back and wings, but their breasts were a striking shade of crimson that glowed like the blood of a dying gladiator, and Robyn watched them with rare pleasure while she and Sarah talked quietly.

Sarah was telling her about her mother, how brave and uncomplaining she had been in the terrible heat of the Kaborra-Bassa where the black ironstone cliffs turned the gorge into a furnace.

'It was the bad season,' Sarah explained. 'The hot season before the rains break.' Robyn recalled her father's written account of the expedition in which he had laid the blame for the delays upon his subordinates, old Harkness and Commander Stone, so that they had missed the cool season, and entered the gorge in the suicide month of November.

'Then when the rains came, the fever came with it,' Sarah went on. 'It was very bad. The white men and your mother became sick very quickly.' Perhaps her mother had lost much of her immunity to malaria during the years in England while she waited for her husband's summons. 'Even Manali himself became sick. It was the first time I had seen him sick of the fever. He was filled with the devils for many days,' the expression described vividly the delirium of malarial fever, Robyn thought. 'So he did not know when your mother died.'

They were silent again. The child, bored by the interminable talk of the two women, threw a stone at the birds in the acacia branches above their heads, and with a flash of their marvellous crimson breasts the two shrikes winged away towards the river, and again the child engaged Robyn's attention. It was as if she had known that face all her life.

'My mother?' Robyn asked, still watching the child.

'Her water turned black,' said Sarah simply. The blackwater fever – Robyn felt her skin prickle. When malaria changed its course, attacking the kidneys and transforming them into thin-walled sacks of clotted black blood, that could rupture at the patient's smallest movement. The blackwater fever, when the urine changed to dark mulberry-coloured blood, and few, very few victims, ever recovered.

'She was strong,' Sarah went on quietly. 'She was the last of them to go.' She turned her head towards the other neglected graves. The curly pods of the acacia were scattered thickly over the unadorned mounds. 'We buried her here, while Manali was still with his devils. But later, when he could walk he came with the book and said the words for her. He build the cross with his own hands.'

'Then he went away again?' Robyn asked.

'No, he was very sick, and new devils came to him. He wept for your mother.' The thought of her father weeping was something so completely alien that Robyn could not imagine it. 'He spoke often of the river that had destroyed him.'

Through the acacia trees there were glimpses of the wide green river, and both their heads turned towards it naturally.

'He came to hate that river as though it was a living enemy that had denied him a road to his dreams. He was like a man demented, for the fever came and went. At times he would battle with his devils, shouting his defiance the way a warrior *giyas* at the enemy host.' The *giya* was a challenge dance with which the Nguni warrior baits his adversary. 'At other times he would speak wildly of machines that would tame his enemy, of walls that he would build across the waters to carry men and ships up above the gorge.' Sarah broke off, her lovely dark moon face stricken with the memory, and the child sensed her distress and came to her, kneeling on the earth and laying his dusty little head in her lap. She stroked the tight cap of curls with an absentminded caress.

With a sudden little chill of shock Robyn recognised the child. Her expression changed so drastically that Sarah followed the direction of her gaze, looking down with all her attention at the head in her lap, then up again to meet Robyn's eyes. It did not really need words to pass, the question was posed and answered with silent exchange of feminine understanding, and Sarah drew the child towards her with a protective gesture.

'It was only after your mother . . .' Sarah began to explain and then fell silent, and Robyn went on staring at the little boy. It was Zouga at the same age, a dusky miniature Zouga. It was only the colour of his skin which had prevented her from seeing it immediately.

Robyn felt as though the earth had lurched beneath her feet, then it steadied again and she felt a strange sense of release. Fuller Ballantyne was no longer the godlike figure hewn from unforgiving, unbending granite that had overshadowed her entire life.

She held out both her hands to the child and he went to her unhesitatingly, trustingly. Robyn embraced him, and his skin was smooth and warm and she kissed him. He wriggled against her like a puppy, and she felt a deep glow of affection and of gratitude to the child.

'He was very sick,' said Sarah softly, 'and alone. They had all gone or died, and he was sad, so that I feared for his life.'

Robyn nodded understanding. 'And you loved him?'

'There was no sin in it, for he was a God,' said Sarah simply.

'No,' thought Robyn with intense relief. 'He was a man, and I, his daughter, am a woman.'

In that moment she knew that she never need again feel shame and guilt for her body and the demands and desires which sprang from it. She hugged the child who was proof of her father's humanity, and Sarah smiled with relief.

For the first time in her life Robyn was able to face the fact that she loved her father, and she understood part of the compulsion that over the years had grown stronger rather than dwindling.

The longing she had felt for the father had been submerged completely by the awe and majesty of the legend. Now she knew why she was here, on the banks of this majestic river, on the very frontier of the known world. She had come not to find Fuller Ballantyne, but to discover rather the father and the self that she had never known before.

'Where is he, Sarah, where is my father? Which way did he go?' she demanded eagerly, but the woman dropped her eyes.

'I do not know,' she whispered. 'I woke one morning and he was gone. I do not know where he is, but I will wait for him, until he returns to me and his son.' She looked up quickly. 'He will come back?' she asked pathetically. 'If not to me then for the child?'

'Yes,' Robyn answered with certainty that she did not feel. 'Of course he will come back.'

The selection of porters was a lengthy business, and after Zouga had signalled his choice with a slap on the shoulder, the men were sent to Robyn's tent to be examined for signs of disease or infirmity that might prevent them performing their duties.

Then came the allocation of packs.

Although Zouga had already made up and weighed each pack, making sure that not one of them exceeded the stipulated eighty pounds weight, the newly engaged porters had to watch the loads reweighed publicly, and then there was interminable haggling over the size and balance of the burden that each of them would carry for months, perhaps even years ahead.

Although Zouga brusquely forbade Pereira to hasten the selection process with his kurbash, and entered good-naturedly into the spirit of banter and bargain, he was, in fact, using the occasion to assess the spirit of his men, to pick out the malcontents who would sour that spirit in the hardships ahead, and also to select the natural leaders to whom the others turned instinctively for decision.

The following day when planning the order of march, Zouga used the knowledge he had gained in this way. To begin with, seven of the more obvious trouble-makers were given a *khete* of beads each and ordered out of the camp without explanation or apology. Then Zouga called out five of the brightest and best and made them captains of divisions of twenty porters each.

They would be responsible for maintaining the pace of the march, for preventing pilfering of the loads, making and breaking camp, distributing rations, and acting as the spokesmen of each division, presenting complaints to and transmitting orders from Zouga.

When the roll was complete there were one hundred and twenty-six names upon it, including Sergeant Cheroot's Hottentots, the porters who had come up from Quelimane, Comacho Pereira and the two principals – Robyn and Zouga himself.

It would be a slow and unwieldy caravan unless properly organized, that was bad enough – but on the march it would also be very vulnerable. Zouga gave much thought to defence of the column, and he and Sergeant Cheroot shared the last quarter bottle of whisky as they pooled their experience and planned the order of march.

Zouga, with a small party of local guides and personal bearers, planned to travel independently of the main caravan, reconnoitering the terrain ahead of the march, and making himself free to prospect and hunt as the opportunity arose. He would return most nights to rejoin the caravan, but would be equipped to spend many days out of contact.

Camacho Pereira with five of the Hottentot musketeers would lead the van of the main column, and even when Robyn chaffed him lightly, Zouga saw nothing ludicrous in Camacho marching under the Union Jack.

'It's an English expedition, and we will carry the flag,' Zouga replied stiffly.

'Rule, Britannia,' Robyn laughed irreverently, and Zouga ignored her and went on describing the order of march.

The divisions of porters would remain separate but closed up, and Sergeant Cheroot with the remainder of his musketeers would form the rearguard of the column.

There was a simple system of signals to control the movements of the column, a pre-arranged series of blasts on the kudu-horn trumpets would sound the 'march' or 'halt', the 'close up' or 'form square'.

For four days Zouga exercised the column in these evolutions and though proficiency would only come much later, at last he felt that they were ready to make a start, and he told Robyn so.

'But how are we to cross the river?' she asked looking across at the north bank.

The river was half a mile wide, and the heavy rainfalls over millions of square miles had drained into it. The flow was swift and powerful. If they were going northwards to the Shire river and Lake Marawi they would need a flotilla of dugout canoes and many days to make the crossing to the north bank.

The steam launch *Helen* had long ago departed on the flood of the river, making good at least twenty knots with the current pushing her, so she would already be back in Quelimane.

'All the arrangements have been made,' Zouga told her, and she had to be satisfied with that.

On the last day Robyn allowed Juba to accompany her to the cemetery for the first time, and both of them were laden with gifts. Bolts of trade cloth and a thirty-five-pound bag of ceramic beads, the most sought-after scarlet *sam-sam* variety.

It was as much as she dare ask for from the expedition's stores without arousing Zouga's ire and interest.

She had thought of telling Zouga of Sarah and the child, but had wisely decided against it.

Zouga's reaction to finding a half-brother of mixed blood was too terrible to contemplate. Zouga had acquired his opinions on caste and colour in the hard school of the Indian army, and to find that his own father had trespassed against these iron rules would be too much of a shock. Instead, Robyn had mentioned that she had met one of her father's former servants, who tended their mother's grave over the years. The gift would have to be in proportion to these services.

Sarah and her child were waiting by the grave, and she accepted the gifts with a gracious little curtsy and her palms held together at the level of her eyes.

'We leave tomorrow,' Robyn explained, and saw the immediate regret in Sarah's eyes, followed by acceptance.

'It is God's will,' and Robyn could almost hear her father saying it.

Juba and the child soon became involved in collecting the pods from a kaffir boom tree nearby and stringing together the pretty scarlet lucky beans, each with its little black eye at the end to make necklaces and bracelets. The two of them, girl and boy, made a delightfully uninhibited pair, their laughter and shrill happy voices a pleasant background to the talk under the acacia tree.

Robyn and Sarah had become friends in the short time they had known each other. Her father had written in his *Missionary Travels* that he preferred the company of black people to white, and certainly all the evidence seemed to point that way. It seemed that Fuller Ballantyne had done nothing but squabble with his own kind. Contact with other white men seemed to bring out in him all the pettiness, suspicion and jealousy of his complex nature; while he had spent the greater part of his life with black men, and received from them trust and honour and lasting friendships. His relationship with Sarah was only a natural extension of those feelings, Robyn realized. She contrasted these feelings with those of her brother, and knew that he could never cross the dividing line. A black man could possible earn Zouga's liking and even his respect, but the gulf was too wide. For Zouga they would always be 'those people', and she guessed that he could never change in that. If he lived on in Africa for another fifty years, he would never learn to understand them, while she, within weeks, had made real friendships. She wondered if, like her father, she would come one day to prefer them to her own kind. It didn't seem possible now, but she recognized in herself the capacity for adjustment and change.

Beside her, Sarah was speaking, so softly, so shyly that Robyn had to make an effort to tear herself away from her own thoughts and ask:

'What was that you said?'

'Your father, Manali, will you tell him about the boy when you find him?'

'He did not know?' Robyn was stunned, and Sarah shook her head.

'Why did you not go with him then?' Robyn demanded.

'He did not wish it. He said the journey would be too hard, but in reality, he is like an old bull elephant who does not like to stay too long with his cows but always must follow the wind.'

Camacho Pereira towered above the wiry little tribesmen, checking off their names against the camp register. This evening he wore a jerkin of kudu skin that was decorated with fancy stitching and trade beads, and unfastened down the front to expose bulging hairy chest and the flat belly with its ridged muscles like the patterns in the sand of a windswept beach.

'We feed them too much,' he told Zouga. 'Fat nigger is lazy nigger.' He chuckled when he saw Zouga's expression, for that word had already been the cause of dissension. Zouga had forbidden him to use it, particularly in front of the expedition's black servants, for some of them it was the only word of English they understood. 'Feed small, kick heavy and they work hard,' Camacho went on with relish.

Zouga ignored these gems of philosophy. He had heard them before, many times. Instead he turned to the captains of divisions, and watched them finish the rationing.

Two of them, their arms floury to the elbows, dipped into the bags of meal and doled it out to the shrinking line of porters. Each man had his calabash or chipped enamel basin to receive the scoop of stone-ground red-brown grain. Then one of the other captains slapped a split and smoked river fish on top of the pile. The fish looked like Scotch kippers, but their odour punched like a prize-fighter. Weevils, maggots and all, they were a delicacy that the porters would miss once they left the river.

Pereira suddenly hauled a man out of the line and hit him a lusty clout across the back of the head with the stock of his kurbash.

'He come twice, try for double,' he explained cheerfully, and took a playful kick at the man as he ran. If it had landed it would have knocked him off his feet, but all the porters had come to anticipate Camacho's flying boots.

Zouga waited until the last porter had been rationed, then he called to the captains.

'*Indaba!* Tell the men, *indaba.*'

It was the call to council, to discuss affairs of consequence, and the whole camp left the cooking fires and came hurrying, agog with excitement.

Zouga paced up and down before the ranks of intent squatting black men, drawing out the moment, for he had come quickly to realize the African love of the theatrical. Most of them could understand the basic Nguni which Zouga now spoke with some fluency, for many of them were Shangaans or Angoni.

Now he spread his arms to his audience, paused for a second and then announced portentously,

'*Kusasa isufari*, tomorrow the march begins!'

There was a hive murmur of comment and excitement, and then one of the captains rose from the front rank.

'*Phi? Phi?* Where? Which way?'

Zouga lowered his arms, and let the suspense build up for a few moments, and then he stabbed out towards the far blue southern hills with a bunched fist.

'*Laphaya!* That way!'

They roared with approval, just as they would have done if Zouga had pointed north or west for that matter. They were ready to go now. The direction was not important. The captains of divisions, the indunas, were shouting out the translation to those who had not understood and the first roar of the crowd settled to a boisterous rumble of comment and speculation, but it died away suddenly, and Zouga turned quickly.

Camacho Pereira had stepped beside Zouga, and his face was swollen and dark with rage. This was the first time he had heard Zouga's intention to go southwards so that when he started to speak, it was so forcefully that droplets of spittle flew from his lips. He was using one of the local dialects, and speaking so swiftly that Zouga understood only a word here and there. The sense was unmistakable, however, and he saw the shock on the faces of the men who squatted before them.

Camacho was warming them of the dangers beyond the southern hills. Zouga heard the word 'Monomatapa' and knew that he was speaking of the terrible armies of the legendary empire, merciless legions whose favourite sport was to cut off a man's genitals and force him to eat them himself. The shock of the listening black faces was changing swiftly to terror and Camacho had been speaking for only a few seconds, a minute more and nothing would induce the caravan to march, two minutes more and most of his porters would have deserted by morning.

There was nothing to be gained by arguing with the Portuguese except an unseemly shouting match, which would be watched with interest by the entire assembled camp. One thing that Zouga had learned was that the African, like the Asians he had come to know well in India, were immensely respectful of a victor and impressed by success. He could demonstrate neither qualities by becoming embroiled in an undignified wrangle in a language that none of the spectators could understand.

'Pereira!' he snapped, in a tone that cut through the Portuguese's torrent of words, and for an instant stilled them. Zouga had the Englishman's peculiar sense of fair play which made him warn an enemy before an attack. As the Portuguese turned to face him, Zouga swung in towards him with two light steps and he flicked his left hand at Camacho's eyes, forcing him to throw up both hands to protect his face. As he did so, Zouga slammed his fist into his belly, just under the ribs, with a force that doubled him in the middle, his breath whooshing out of his gaping mouth in an agonized explosion of sound and his hand dropping to cover his injured belly, leaving his face open for the next blow.

It was a short chopping left-handed shot that took Camacho cleanly under the right ear, on the hinge of the jaw. The plumed beaver hat spun off his head. His eyes rolled up into his skull, leaving the whites glaring madly, and Camacho's knees gave way under him. He pitched forward, making no effort to cushion his fall and dropped face down on to the grey sandy soil.

The silence lasted only a second, and then a shout went up from the watchers. Most of them had felt Camacho's boots or his kurbash, and they hugged one another happily. The trepidation that Camacho's little speech had raised was completely lost in wonder at the swiftness and the effect of those two blows. Most of them had never seen a man strike with a bunched hand, and the novelty of this form of combat impressed and delighted them.

Casually, Zouga turned his back on the prone figure. Not a trace of anger showed on his face, in fact he was smiling slightly as he strolled down the front rank of men and lifted one hand to quieten them.

'There are soldiers who travel with us,' he told them, in a low voice that yet reached clearly to every one of them, 'and you have seen them shoot.' He had made sure they had, and that news of the prowess in weapons of Sergeant Cheroot's men would travel ahead of them.

'You see that flag?' He flung one hand dramatically at the red and white and blue jack floating above the main tent on its improvised flag pole. 'No man, no chief nor warrior dare. . . .'

'Zouga!' shrieked Robyn. To the terrible urgency of her tone Zouga reacted instantly, spinning aside with two dancing paces, and the crowd exploded with a single word, a deep drawn-out 'Jee!'

It is a blood-chilling sound, for it is the cry with which an African warrior encourages himself or another in the fatal moments of a battle to the death.

Camacho's stroke had been aimed at the small of Zouga's back. He was a man who had fought with the knife many times before, and he had not taken the more tempting target between the shoulder blades, where the point could turn against the ribs. He had gone for the soft area above the kidneys, and even with Robyn's warning Zouga was not quite quick enough. The point raked his hip, slitting the cloth of his breeches in a six-inch rent, beneath which skin and flesh opened cleanly and the bright blood spread swiftly to the knee.

'Jee!' The deep sonorous chant of the watchers as Camacho reversed the stroke of his extended right hand, cutting sideways at Zouga's belly. The blade twinkled and hissed like an angry cobra, ten inches of tempered steel, and Zouga threw up his hands and sucked in his belly muscles as he jumped back. There was a sharp tug as the point caught in his shirt, but it did not touch the skin.

'Jee!' again as Camacho lunged. His face was bloated and mottled with purple and white, the eyes squinting with rage and the after-effects of the blow to his jaw. Zouga felt the sting of the wound on his hip pulling open as he swayed back out of the path of the blade, and the stronger flood of warm blood down his leg.

He paused out of range of the knife for Zouga had heard the snap of a weapon being cocked and from the corner of his eye he saw Sergeant Cheroot levelling the Enfield, waiting for a clear shot at the Portuguese.

'No! Don't shoot!' Zouga called urgently. He did not relish a bullet in his own belly, for he and Camacho were dancing close together, with the weaving point of the knife seeming to bind them to each other.

'Don't shoot, Sergeant!' There was another reason why he could afford no interference. There were a hundred men judging him now, men with whom he would march and work in the months and years ahead. He needed their respect.

'Jee!' sang the watchers, and Camacho was panting with rage. Again the blade in his right hand whispered like the wing of a swallow in flight, and this time Zouga over-reacted, blundering back half a dozen paces, and then losing his balance for a moment he dropped on one knee and put a hand to the ground to steady himself. But as Camacho charged again, he rebounded to his feet and arched his hips aside, the way a matador swings out of the line of the bull's run. In the hand that had touched the ground, Zouga held a handful of the coarse grey sand.

His eyes were locked to those of the Portuguese, it was the eyes not the knife hand that would signal Camacho's intentions. They flickered left, while the hand feigned the other way, and Zouga moved in past the blade, and was ready again when Camacho rounded.

They faced each other, shuffling in a slow circle that stirred wisps of pale dust around their feet. Camacho kept the knife low, and stirred it gently as though he was conducting a slow passage of music, but Zouga studying his eyes saw the first small nervous flickers of uncertainty.

He jumped in, launching himself off the right foot.

'Jee!' roared the watchers, and for the first time Camacho broke ground, falling back and then turning hurriedly as Zouga checked and feinted to his open side.

Twice more Zouga drove him back with threats, until it needed only a feint with his upper body to make Camacho scramble away. The watchers were laughing now, mocking shouts of glee every time he gave ground, and the rage that had flushed Camacho's face had given way to fear, the angry purple mottling had chilled to white. Zouga was still watching his eyes, as they darted from side to side seeking an escape – but the knife kept weaving between them, bright and razor sharp, broad as three fingers and grooved along its length to break the suction of clinging wet flesh once it was buried.

Camacho's eyes flickered away once more and Zouga moved, pulling the knife hand around as he crossed the man's front, holding out his empty hand for the eyes to follow, keeping the other low and moving in as close to the knife as he dared, then at the moment that Camacho lunged, using the momentum of his avoiding turn, he hurled the handful of coarse sand into Camacho's eyes – blinding him, and still in the same movement reversing his direction, and going straight in on the knife, chancing it all on locking the wrist before the man could see again.

'Jee!' the crowd roared as Camacho's wrist slapped into Zouga's palm, and he locked it down with all his strength.

Tears were already streaming from Camacho's eyes, and his lids fluttered, grinding the sharp grains across the unseeing eyeballs. He could not judge nor meet Zouga's weight as, still locked grimly to the wrist, he threw him off-balance. As Camacho went over, Zouga reared back, resisting with all his strength, holding the knife arm against the fall. Something went with a loud rubbery popping sound in Camacho's shoulder and he screamed, as he sprawled again, face down, with the arm twisted up behind him.

Once again Zouga jerked viciously, and this time Camacho screeched like a girl and the knife dropped from his fingers. He made a feeble effort to snatch it with the other hand, but Zouga trod down on the blade with a booted foot, then scooped it up, released the damaged arm and stepped back holding the heavy weapon in his right hand.

'*Bulala!*' chanted the watchers. '*Bulala!* Kill him! Kill him!' They wanted to see the blood, for that was the fitting end and they hungered for it.

Zouga stabbed the blade deeply into the trunk of the acacia tree and then wrenched against the steel. It snapped at the hilt with a crack like a pistol shot, and he dropped the hilt contemptuously.

'Sergeant Cheroot,' he said, 'get him out of this camp.'

'I should shoot him,' the little Hottentot told him as he came up, and thrust the muzzle of the Enfield rifle into the fallen man's belly.

'If he tries to enter the camp again, you can shoot him. But now just get him out.'

'Big mistake.' Sergeant Cheroot's pug face took on a theatrically mournful expression. 'Always stamp on the scorpion – before he stings.'

'You are hurt.' Robyn was running towards him.

'It's a scratch.' Zouga unwound the bandanna from around his throat and pressed it to the wound in his hip as he strode away towards his tent, forcing himself not to favour it with a limp. He had to get away quickly for the reaction was on him, he felt dizzy and nauseated, the wound stung abominably, and he did not want anybody to see that his hands were trembling.

'I reset the shoulder,' Robyn told Zouga as she bound up his hip wound. 'I don't think there is anything broken, and it went in again very neatly – but you,' she shook her head, 'you won't be able to march with that. Every step will pull against the stitches.'

She was right, it was four days before the march could begin, and Camacho Pereira put that time to good use. He had left an hour after Robyn reset his dislocated shoulder, four paddlers taking a dugout canoe down the Zambezi with the current. When they would have pulled into the bank to make camp, Camacho snarled at them from the bows where he crouched, hugging the injured arm, that even after being set and strapped into a sling, still ached so fiercely that it lit little white sparks of agony behind his closed eyelids every time he tried to doze.

He also would have liked to rest, but his hatred drove him onwards, and the dugout canoe arrowed down-current under a fat yellow moon that paled slowly at the coming of the new day.

Camacho went ashore on the south bank of Zambezi at noon at the small native village at Chamba, a hundred miles below Tete. He paid off the crew of the dugout and he hired two bearers to carry his rifle and blanket roll. Then he set off again immediately along the network of narrow foot paths that crisscross the entire African continent like the blood vessels of a living body, laid down by wandering men and migrating animals over the centuries.

Two days later he reached the Hyena Road that runs from the mountains of Dismay, Inyangaza, to the sea. The Hyena Road was a secret track. Although it paralleled the old road from the coast to Vila Manica, it kept forty miles north of it, following the course of the Pungwe river so that there would be water for the multitudes who unwillingly used the road on their long, last journey from their homeland to other lands, other continents.

Vila Manica was the last outpost of the Portuguese administration in East Africa. A decree by the Governor in council forbade any man, black or white, Portuguese or foreigner, to journey beyond that clay-walled fort towards the haunting range of mountains with the chilling name. It was for this reason that the Hyena Road had been secretly opened by enterprising men, and pushed up through the dense forests of the lower slopes to the bleak and open grasslands atop the mountains.

The march from Chamba to the Pungwe river was a hundred and fifty miles. To make it in three days with the agony of a healing shoulder was good going, and once they reached it, the temptation to rest was almost irresistible. But Camacho kicked his two bearers to their feet and drove them with stinging words and lash along the deserted road towards the mountains.

The road was twice as wide as any of the other footpaths they had followed to reach it, wide enough for a double column rather than the Indian file that was the usual order of African travel. Although the surface had been beaten hard by the passage of thousands of bare feet, it was a source of satisfaction to Camacho that the road had clearly not been used for many months, except by the occasional herd of antelope, and once, perhaps a week before, by an old bull elephant, whose huge piles of dung had long dried out.

'The caravan has not passed yet,' Camacho muttered, as he scanned the trees ahead for the shapes of the vultures and searched without success for the sly skulking shapes of hyena in the undergrowth beside the road.

True there were human bones scattered along the route, here and there the thick knuckle of the thigh bone that had defied even the iron jaws of the scavengers, or other splintered fragments that they had overlooked, but even these were dried out and bleached white. They were the debris of the previous caravan that had passed this way three months before.

He had reached the road in time, and now he hurried along it, pausing now and then to listen or to send one of the bearers up a tree to search ahead.

However, it was two days later that they heard the first faint sound of many voices, and this time Camacho himself climbed to the highest fork of one of the umsisa trees beside the track, and peering ahead he saw the vultures circling, a wide slow wheel of tiny black specks turning against the silver and blue ranges of cloud, as though caught in a hidden vortex of the high heavens.

He sat in the fork thirty feet above the ground, while the sound of voices grew stronger, became the sound of singing. This was no sound of joy, but a terrible mourning dirge, slow and heart-breaking, rising and fading as flukes of the breeze and folds of the ground blanketed the sound, but each time it came back a little stronger, until Camacho could make out far away the head of the column, like the head of a maimed serpent writhing out of the forest into an open glade a mile ahead.

He slid down the trunk of the umsisa, and hurried forward. There was an armed party ahead of the main column, five blacks dressed in the tatters of cast-off European-style clothing and carrying muskets, but at their head was a white man, a little man with a face like a vicious gnome, wrinkled and burned darkly by the sun. The thick dropping black moustache was laced with grey, but he stepped out with a bouncing elastic stride and he recognized Camacho from two hundred paces and snatched his hat off his head and waved it.

He shouted 'Camacho!' and the two men ran to embrace, and then hold each other at arm's length, laughing with pleasure. It was Camacho who sobered first, the laughter changing to a scowl as he said,

'Alphonse, my beloved brother, I have bad tidings – the worst possible.'

'The Englishman?' Alphonse was still smiling, he had a tooth missing from the front of his upper jaw, which made the cold humourless smile seem less dangerous than it really was.

'Yes, the Englishman,' Camacho nodded. 'You know of him?'

'My father sent a message. I know.' Alphonse was the Governor of Quelimane's eldest surviving son, full-blooded Portuguese by the lawfully wedded bride who had come out forty years previously from Lisbon, a pale sickly mail-order bride, who had borne three sons in swift succession, the first two of which had succumbed to malaria and infantile dysentery even before the appearance of the little wizened yellowed mite whom they had named Alphonse Jose Vila y Pereira, and expected to bury with his brothers before the end of the rains.

However, it was the mother they had buried in the end, and the child had flourished at the breast of a black wet nurse.

'He did not go north, then?' Alphonse demanded, and Camacho dropped his eyes guiltily, for he was speaking to the eldest, full-blooded and legitimate son.

Camacho himself was a bastard and a half-breed, son of one of the Governor's once beautiful Mulatto concubines, now fat and faded and forgotten in one of the back rooms of the seraglio. He was not even recognized as a son, but had to bear the ignominious title of nephew. This in itself was enough for him to show respect for the other, but added to this Alphonse was as determined as their father had been at the same age, though even crueller and harder. Camacho had seen him sing a plaintive fado as he flogged a man to death, accompanying the traditional love song with the flute and percussion of the lash.

'He did not go north,' Camacho agreed uneasily.

'You were told to see that he did.'

'I could not stop him. He is English,' Camacho's voice croaked a little, 'he is stubborn.'

'We will speak again of that,' Alphonse promised coldly. 'Now, swiftly tell me where he is and what he plans to do.'

Camacho recited the explanation he had prepared, skirting delicately around the most offensive parts of the story, and dwelling on subjects such as the wealth that the Ballantyne expedition carried with it rather than his own brutal beating at the Englishman's hands.

Alphonse had thrown himself down in the shade of a tree beside the track and listened broodingly, chewing at the straggling ends of his moustache, filling in for himself the conspicuous gaps in his half-brother's recital, and speaking again only at the end.

'When will he leave the valley of the Zambezi?'

'Soon,' Camacho hedged, for the unpredictable Englishman might already be half-way to the escarpment. 'Although I cut him deeply, it may be he has had himself carried in a *mushila* (litter).'

'He must not be allowed to enter the Monomatapa,' Alphonse said flatly, and came to his feet with a single lithe movement. 'The best place to do the business would be in the bad ground below the rim of the valley.'

He glanced back along the winding road. The head of the column was a mile away still, across a glade of open golden grass. The shuffling double rank of bowed creatures, yoked at the neck, did not seem human, though the singing was sad and beautiful.

'I can spare fifteen men.'

'It will not be enough,' Camacho cut in swiftly.

'It will be,' said his brother coldly, 'if you do the business in the night.'

'Twenty men,' Camacho pleaded. 'He has soldiers with him, trained soldiers and he is a soldier himself.'

Alphonse was silent, weighing risk and advantage – but the worst part of the Hyena Road already lay behind the column, and each mile nearer the coast, the land was tamer, the risk diminished and the need for guards less pressing.

'Twenty!' he agreed abruptly, and turned to Camacho. 'But not one of the foreigners must escape.' Looking into his brother's cold black eyes, Camacho felt his skin crawl. 'Leave no sign, bury them deep, so the jackal and hyena do not dig them out. Use the porters to carry the expedition's equipment to the place in the hills, and when they have done so, kill them also. We will bring it down with the next caravan to the coast.'

'Si. Si. I understand.'

'Do not fail us again, my beloved cousin-brother.' Alphonse made the endearment a threat, and Camacho swallowed with a nervous little gulp.

'I will leave as soon as I have rested.'

'No,' Alphonse shook his head. 'You will leave immediately. Once that Englishman enters the land beyond the mountains, there will soon be no more slaves. It is bad enough that there has been no gold for twenty years and more, but if the river of slaves were to dry up, both my father and I would be displeased – very displeased.'

At Zouga's order the long mournful blast of the kudu-horn trumpet shattered the silence of the utterly dark hour before the dawn.

The Indunas took up the cry 'Safari! We march!' and they prodded the sleeping porters off their reed sleeping-mats. The camp fires had burned down to dim red mounds of coals smothered in the soft grey powder of their own ash. As fresh logs were thrown upon them they flared up in a false dawn that lit the underside of the umbrella-shaped acacia trees with wavering yellow light.

The smell of roasting *ropoko* cakes rose on tendrils of pale smoke straight into the windless dark sky. The muted voices became louder, more cheerful as the flames drove away the chills and the nightmares.

'Safari!' The cry was taken up, and the divisions assembled, ghostly figures in the gloom, emerging more clearly as the growing dawn light paled the sky and snuffed out the stars.

'Safari!' And the mass of men and equipment resolved itself and order grew out of chaos.

Like those long columns of big shiny black serowe ants that endlessly cross and re-cross the African earth, the stream of porters moved steadily away into the still gloomy forest.

As each of them passed Zouga and Robyn standing together at the gate of the thorn *scherm*, they shouted a greeting and executed a few prancing steps to demonstrate their loyalty and enthusiasm – while Robyn laughed with them and Zouga called encouragement.

'We no longer have a guide, and we don't know where we are going.' She took Zouga's arm. 'What is to become of us?'

'If we knew, it would take all the fun out of it.'

'At least a guide.'

'While you thought I was hunting I went out as far as the escarpment which is further than that swaggering Portuguese ever went, further than any white man, except of course Pater, has ever been. Follow me, Sissy, I am your guide.'

She looked up at him now in the strengthening light of coming dawn.

'I knew you were not hunting,' she told him.

'The escarpment is rugged and very broken, but I have examined two passes through the telescope that I think will go—'

'And beyond that?'

He laughed, 'We will find out.' Then he squeezed her around the waist. 'That is the whole fun of the thing.'

She studied his face with full attention for a few moments. The new full beard emphasized the strong, almost stubborn, lines of his jaw. There was a piratical devil-may-care lift to the corner of his lips, and Robyn realized that no man of conventional mind would have proposed and engineered this expedition. She knew he possessed courage, his exploits in India had proved that beyond doubt, and yet when she looked at his sketches and water colours and read the rough notes he was making for the book, she discovered a sensitivity and an imagination she had never before suspected. He was a difficult person to know and understand.

Perhaps she could have told him about Sarah and the child or even about

Mungo St. John, and that night in the main cabin of *Huron*, for when he laughed like this, the stern features softened with humour and humanity, and green lights sparkled in his eyes.

'That's what we are here for, Sissy, the fun of it all.'

'And the gold,' she teased, 'and the ivory.'

'Yes, by God, the gold and ivory as well. Come on, Sissy, this is where it truly begins,' and he limped after the column as its tail disappeared into the acacia forest, favouring his injured leg and using a freshly cut staff to move across the sandy earth. For a moment Robyn hesitated and then she shrugged aside her doubts and ran to catch up with her brother.

That first day the porters were rested and eager, the valley floor flat and the going easy, so Zouga ordered *tirikeza*, the double march, so that even at their slow pace the column left many miles of dusty grey earth behind them that day.

They marched until the heat came up in the middle of the morning and the merciless sun dried the sweat the moment it burst through their pores and left tiny salt crystals on the skin, that sparkled like diamond chips. Then they found shade and lay like dead men through the heat of noon, stirring again only when the lowering sun gave the illusion of cooling the air and the blast of the kudu-horn trumpet forced them to their feet again.

The second stage of the *tirikeza* lasted until sunset when it became too dark to see the ground under their feet.

The fires were dying and the voices of the porters in their thorn bush *scherms* had slowly descended through the occasional mutter and soft murmur to ultimate silence before Zouga left his tent and limped silently as a night creature out of the camp.

He carried the Sharps rifle slung over his shoulder, the staff in one hand and a bull's eye lantern in the other, while the Colt revolver hung in its holster upon his belt. Once clear of the camp, he stepped out as briskly as his leg would allow two miles along the freshly beaten footpath that the column had made that afternoon until he reached the fallen tree trunk that was the agreed rendezvous.

He stopped and whistled softly, and a smaller figure stepped out from the undergrowth into the moonlight, carrying a rifle at high-port. The jaunty step and alert set of head on narrow shoulders was unmistakable.

'All is well, Sergeant.'

'We are ready, Major.'

Zouga inspected the ambush positions that Sergeant Cheroot had chosen for his men astride the path. The little Hottentot had a good eye for ground and Zouga found his trust and liking for him increasing with every such display of competence.

'A pull?' Jan Cheroot asked now, with the clay pipe already in his mouth.

'No smoking,' Zouga shook his head. 'They will smell it.' And Jan Cheroot reluctantly buttoned the pipe into his hip pocket.

Zouga had chosen a position in the centre of the line, where he could make himself comfortable against the trunk of the fallen tree. He settled down with a sigh, his leg thrust out stiffly ahead of him – after the *tirikeza* it was going to be a long wearying night.

The moon was a few days short of full, and it was almost light enough to read the headlines of a newspaper. The bush was alive with the scurry and rustle of small animals, and it kept their nerves tightened and their ears strained to catch the other sounds for which they waited.

Zouga was the first to hear the click of a pebble striking against another. He whistled softly and Jan Cheroot snapped his fingers, imitating the sound of a black scarab beetle to show that he was alert. The moon had dropped low upon the hills, and its light through the forest trees laid silver and black tiger stripes upon the earth and played tricks with the eye.

Something moved in the forest, and then was gone, but Zouga picked up the whisper of bare feet scuffling the sandy disturbed earth of the path, and then suddenly they were there, and very close, man shapes in file, hurrying, silent, furtive. Zouga counted them, eight – no nine. Each of them straight-backed under the bulky burden he carried balanced upon his head. Zouga's anger simmered to the surface and yet at the same time he felt a grim sense of satisfaction that he had not wasted the night.

As the leading figure in the file came level with the fallen tree trunk, Zouga pointed the muzzle of the Sharps rifle straight into the air and pressed the trigger. The crash of the shot broke the night into a hundred echoes that bounced and rebounded through the forest, and the silence magnified it until it seemed like the thunder of all the heaven.

The echoes had not dispersed, and the nine dark figures were still frozen with shock when Jan Cheroot's Hottentots fell upon them from every direction in a shrieking pack.

The sound of their cries was so shrill, so inhuman, that it even startled Zouga, while the effect on the victims was miraculous. They let fall the burdens they carried, and dropped to earth in a paralysis of superstitious awe, adding their wails and screams to the pandemonium. Then the thud and clatter of cudgels against skull and cringing flesh mingled with it all, and the screams and howls rose to a new pitch.

Jan Cheroot's men had spent much time and care on selecting and cutting their clubs and now they wielded them with a lusty glee, making up for a night of discomfort and boredom. Sergeant Cheroot himself was in the thick of it, and in his excitement he had almost lost his voice. He was yipping squeakily like a demented fox terrier with a cat up a tree.

Zouga knew he would have to stop it soon, before they killed or seriously maimed somebody, but the punishment was richly earned, and he gave it a minute more. He even joined in himself when one of the prostrate figures scrambled to its feet and tried to dart away into the undergrowth. Zouga swung his staff and brought him down again with a blow to the back of his knees, and when he sprang up again as though he were on springs, Zouga dropped him in the dust with a short right-handed punch to the side of the head.

Then, stepping back out of the fray, Zouga took one of his few remaining cheroots from his top pocket, and lit it from the chimney of the lantern, inhaling with deep satisfaction, while around him the enthusiasm of his Hottentots flagged a little as they tired and Jan Cheroot regained his voice and became coherent for the first time.

'*Slat hulle, kerels!* Hit them, boys!'

It was time to stop it, Zouga decided and opened the shutter of the lantern. 'That's enough, Sergeant,' he ordered, and the thuds of blows became intermittent and then ceased while the Hottentots rested on the cudgels, panting and streaming with the honest sweat of their exertions.

The deserting porters lay moaning and whimpering in pitiful heaps, with their loot scattered about them. Some of the packs had burst open, and trade cloth and beads, flasks of gunpowder, knives, mirrors and glass jewellery were strewn about and trodden into the dirt. Zouga's fury returned at full strength when he recognized the tin box which contained his dress uniform and hat. He delivered a last kick at the nearest figure and then growled at Sergeant Cheroot,

'Get them on their feet and clean it up.'

The nine deserters were marched into camp, roped together and bearing not only the heavy burdens which they had stolen – but also an impressive set of contusions, cuts and bruises. Lips were swollen and split, some teeth were missing, a good many eyes were puffed closed and most of their heads were as lumpy as newly-picked Jerusalem artichokes.

More painful than their injuries, however, was the ridicule of the entire camp which turned out to a man to jeer and mock them with laughter.

Zouga lined up the captives, with their booty piled in front of them, and in the presence of their peers made a speech in limping but expressive Swahili in which he likened them to sneaking jackals and lurking hyena and fined them each a month's wages.

The audience was delighted with the show, and hooted at every insult while the culprits tried physically to shrink themselves into insignificance. There was not one of the watching porters who would not have done the same thing. In fact, had the escape succeeded, most of them would have followed the next night, but now that it had been foiled, they could enjoy the vicarious pleasure of having escaped punishment, and the discomfort of their companions who had committed the sin of being caught.

During the noon rest that divided the two stages of the next day's *tirikeza*, the clusters of porters chatting in the shade of the mopani groves agreed that they had found a strong master to follow, one whom it would not be easy to cheat, and it gave them all confidence for the future of the safari. Coming directly after his defeat of the Portuguese, the recapture of the deserting porters added immeasurably to Zouga's standing.

The four indunas of the divisions agreed that it was fitting that such a man have a praise-name. They conferred at length, and after considering many suggestions, finally decided on 'Bakela'.

'Bakela' means 'the one-who-strikes-with-the-fist', for this was still the one of Zouga's many accomplishments which impressed them most.

Where Bakela led, they were now prepared to follow, and though Zouga spread a dragnet of his faithful Hottentots behind the column each of the following nights, no more fish swam into it.

'How many?' Zouga whispered, and Jan Cheroot rocked on his heels, sucking softly on the empty clay pipe and squinting his oriental eyes thoughtfully, before he shrugged,

'Too many to count. Two hundred, three hundred, perhaps even four.'

The ground had been ploughed up into soft fluffy dust by the multitude of huge cloven hooves, and the dark pats of dung were round and shaped in little concentric circles, completely indistinguishable from those of domestic cattle, and the rank smell of cattle was heavy on the heated air of the Zambezi valley.

For an hour they had followed a small herd through the open mopani forest, stooping under the low branches with the thick shiny double leaves, each of them shaped like the cloven spoor that they followed, and now where the spoor emerged from the forest it had been joined by another much larger herd.

'How close?' Zouga asked again, and Jan Cheroot slapped his own neck where one of the buffalo flies had settled. It was the size of a honey bee, but dull black and the long needle of its proboscis stung as though it was white hot.

'We are so close that the flies that follow the herd still linger,' and he pushed his forefinger into the nearest pat of wet dung, 'and the body heat is still in the dung, but,' Jan Cheroot went on as he wiped his finger on a handful of dry grass, 'but they have gone into bad ground—' and he pointed ahead with his chin.

A week before they had reached the escarpment of the valley, but each of the possible passes that Zouga had examined through the telescope had proved on closer inspection to be dead-ends, the gorges pinching out into abrupt rock faces, or falling off into some terrifying abyss.

They had turned westwards, following the edge of the escarpment, Zouga ranging ahead with his small scouting party. Yet day after day those impassable heights loomed at their left hand, rising sheer into the unknown. Even below the main escarpment, the ground was tortured and riven by deep forges and ravines, by cliffs of dark rock and hills of enormous tumbled boulders. The ravines were choked with the drab grey stands of thorn, so densely interwoven that a man would have to crawl in on hands and knees, and his vision would be limited to a few feet ahead, yet the herd of many hundreds of buffalo that they were following had disappeared into one of these narrow gorges, their thick hides impervious to the cruel red-tipped thorn.

Zouga took the telescope from his haversack carried by his bearer, and carefully scanned the ground ahead. It had a wild and menacing beauty and for the hundredth time in the last few days he wondered if there was a way through this maze to the empire of Monomatapa.

'Did you hear that?' Zouga demanded, lowering the glass suddenly. It had sounded like the distant lowing of the milk herd as it returned to the farmyard.

'Ja!' Sergeant Cheroot nodded, as again the mournful sound echoed against the black ironstone cliffs, and was answered by the bleat of a calf. 'They are lying up in the jessie bush. They won't move again until sunset.'

Zouga glanced up at the sun. It was four hours or so from its zenith. He had over a hundred mouths to feed, and they had rationed out the last of the dried fish two days before.

'We will have to go in after them,' he said, and Jan Cheroot removed the stem of the pipe from between yellow teeth and spat reflectively in the dust.

'I am a very happy man,' he said. 'Why would I want to die now?'

Zouga lifted the glass again, and while he scanned the ridges of higher ground about the choked valley, he imagined what it would be like in there. When the first shot was fired, the jessie bush would be filled with huge, furiously charging black animals.

The fluky breeze coming down the steep narrow valley brought with it another powerful whiff of the herd smell before it faded.

'The wind is down the valley,' he said.

'They have not smelled us,' Cheroot agreed, but that was not what Zouga had meant. Again he examined the nearest ridge of high ground. A man could work his way along the edge of it, up towards the head of the narrow valley.

'Sergeant, we are going to flush them out,' he smiled, 'like spring pheasant.'

Zouga had found the native names of his personal bearers hard to pronounce, and tiresome to remember. There were four of them, he had selected them with care, rejecting half a dozen others in the process, and he had rechristened them Matthew, Mark, Luke and John. They had earned enormous prestige by being so honoured, and had proved keen and willing to learn their duties. In a few days they were already proficient at reloading, though not yet of the same standard as Camacho Pereira's gunbearers – but that would come.

Zouga carried the Sharps rifle, but each of the four bearers had one of the heavy four-to-the-pound elephant guns that Harkness had recommended to Zouga. At any time he had only to reach back over his shoulder and a loaded and primed weapon would be thrust into his hand.

Apart from the elephant guns, his bearers carried his blanket roll, water bottle, canvas food bag, spare ball and powder, and the little clay fire pot from which a smouldering ball of moss and wood pulp could be blown into flame in a few seconds. It was wise to conserve the amenities of civilization, such as Swan Vestas, for the months and years ahead.

Zouga relieved Luke, the quickest and most wiry of the four, of all his equipment except the fire pot, pointed out the path along the cliff, and explained carefully to him what he was to do.

All of them listened with approval, even Sergeant Cheroot nodded sagely at the end. 'My old mother tells me, before she throws me out, "Jan", she says, "remember it's brains what counts." '

In the mouth of the valley, where it debouched out into the mopani forest, was a low outcrop of rock, the black ironstone boulders had been split into strange shapes by sun and erosion, and they formed a natural redoubt, with chest-high walls behind which a man could crouch. A hundred paces directly ahead, the dense palisade of iron-grey thorn blocked the valley, but the ground between was fairly open, with a few stunted second-growth mopani bushes and clumps of coarse dried razor grass as high as a man's shoulder.

Zouga moved his party into the lee of the rocks, and himself scrambled onto the highest point to follow through his glass the progress of the almost naked bearer as he picked his way cautiously along the rim of the cliff. Within half an hour he had worked so far up the escarpment that he had disappeared from Zouga's view.

It was another hour before, from the head of the valley, a thin tendril of pure white smoke rose gently into the heated air, and then bent into the elegant shape of an ostrich plume before the gentle breath of the breeze.

With miraculous suddenness the rising column of white smoke was surrounded by another living cloud, hundreds of tiny black specks that weaved and darted about and around it. The faint but excited bird cries carried down to where Zouga waited, and through the glass he could make out the rainbow, turquoise and sapphire plumage of the blue jay as they rolled and dived for the insects put to flight by the flames. Competing with them for the feast, were the iridescent black drongas with their long, forked tails catching the sunlight with metallic glitter as they swirled above the spreading smoke clouds.

Luke was doing his job well. Zouga grunted with satisfaction, as new columns of smoke rose at intervals, sealing off the valley from side to side as they spread to meet each other. Now there was a solid wall of smoke from one cliff to the other, and as the smoke turned dirty black, billowing upwards, spinning upon itself, carrying flaming fragments of leaves and twigs within it, it began to roll ponderously down the valley.

It reminded Zouga of a snow avalanche he had watched in the high Himalayas, the slow majestic progress gathering weight and momentum, building up its own wind storm as it sucked the valley of air.

He could see the tops of the flames now, leaping above the thorn, and hear the sound of them, like the whispering waters of a distant river. The alarm bellow of a bull buffalo rang like the blast of a war trumpet from the ironstone cliffs, and the whisper of flames rose swiftly to a dull crackling roar.

The smoke clouds rose across the sun, plunging them into an unnatural gloom, and Zouga felt a sharp drop in his spirits at the extinction of the bright morning sun, that infernal swirling pall of dun smoke seemed to hold a world of menace.

From the edge of the jessie bush broke a herd of kudu, led by a magnificent bull with his corkscrew horns laid flat along his back. He saw Zouga standing on the pinnacle of rock, and snorted with alarm, swinging away out of easy shot with his cows flying big-eared and scary behind him, their fluffy white tails flickered away amongst the mopani groves.

Zouga scrambled down from his too obvious position, and propped himself comfortably against the rock, checked the nipple on the cap of the Sharps and then cocked the big hammer.

Ahead of the flames, a pale white dust cloud was rising over the tops of the jessie bush, and another sound was added to the roar of flames. It was a low thunder that made the earth tremble under their feet.

'They are coming,' Jan Cheroot muttered to himself, and his little eyes sparkled.

A single buffalo burst from the palisade of thorn. He was an old bull, almost bald across the shoulders and rump, the dusty grey skin criss-crossed by a thousand ancient scars and scabby with the bites of bush ticks. The big bell-shaped ears were torn and tattered, and one thickly curved horn was broken off at the tip. He came out at a crabbing gallop, dust exploding at each hoof beat like miniature mortar bursts.

He was on a line to pass the rocky redoubt at twenty paces, and Zouga let him come on to twice that distance before he threw up the Sharps rifle.

He aimed for the fold of thick skin under the throat that marked the frontal aiming point for the heart and its complex of arteries and blood vessels. He hardly noticed the recoil nor the blurt of the shot as he watched for the strike of the lead bullet. There was a little spurt of dust off the grey hide precisely on his aiming point, and the sound of the hit was exactly like his headmaster swinging the malacca cane against his own schoolboy backside, sharp and meaty.

The bull took the bullet without a stumble or lurch, instead it swung towards them, and seemed immediately to double in size as it lifted its nose into the high attitude of the charge.

Zouga reached for his second gun, but he groped in vain. Mark, his number two, showed the whites of his eyes in a flash of terror, let out a squawk, hurled the elephant gun aside, and went bounding away towards the mopani grove.

The bull saw him and swerved again, thundering ten feet past Zouga as it went after the fleeing bearer. Waving the empty Sharps, Zouga shouted desperately for another rifle, but the bull was past him in a grey blur and it caught Mark as he reached the tree line.

The great bossed head dropped until the snout almost touched the earth, and then flew up again in a powerful tossing motion that bunched the muscle in the thick black neck. Mark was looking back over his shoulder, his eyes wide and glaring white in the black face, rivulets of sweat pouring down his naked back, his mouth a pink gape as he screamed.

Then he was in the air. Legs and arms tumbling wildly, he went up like a rag doll thrown by a petulant child and disappeared into the thick green canopy of mopani foliage overhead. Without missing a stride, the bull drove on into the forest, but that was all that Zouga saw, for a cry from Sergeant Cheroot made him turn again.

'*Hier kom hulle!* Here they come!'

Across their whole front, the earth seemed to move, as though racked by the convulsions of an earthquake. Shoulder to shoulder, nose to rump, the main herd broke from cover, flattening the thorn bush under the great wave of bodies, filling the valley from side to side.

They lifted behind them a dense curtain of pale dust, from which the front ranks seemed endlessly to emerge, their great bossed heads nodding in unison as they pounded on, long silver strings of saliva dangling from open jaws as they bellowed in alarm and anger, and the roar of their hooves drowned the sound of the flames.

Matthew and John, Zouga's two remaining bearers, had stood their ground, and one of them snatched away the empty Sharps and thrust the thick stock of an elephant gun into Zouga's hand.

The weapon seemed heavy and unbalanced after the Sharps, and the sights were crudely fashioned, a blunt cone for the foresight, and a deep vee for the backsight.

The solid wall of bodies was bearing down upon them with frightening speed. The cows were a dark chocolate colour, and their horns were more delicately curved. The calves that raced at their flanks were sleek russet with crowns of reddish curls between the rudimentary little horn spikes. The herd was so tightly packed that it seemed impossible that they could split open to pass the rock. There was a tall rangy cow in the leading rank, coming straight on to Zouga.

He held half a bead aiming into the centre of her chest, and squeezed off the shot. The firing cap popped with a tiny puff of white smoke, and a heartbeat later the elephant gun vomited a deafening gust of powder smoke and bright flame, the burning patches went spinning away over the heads of the charging buffalo, and Zouga felt as though one of them had kicked in his shoulder. He staggered backwards, the barrel thrown high by the recoil, but the big red cow seemed to run into an invisible barrier. A quarter of a pound of mercury-hardened lead drove into her chest, and brought her down in a rolling sliding tangle of hooves and horns.

'Tom Harkness! That one was yours!' Zouga shouted, offering the kill to the memory of the old white bearded hunter, and he grabbed the next loaded rifle.

There was a prime bull, big and black, a ton of enraged bovine flesh. It had seen Zouga, and was coming in over the rocks in a long scrambling leap – hunting him out, so close that Zouga seemed to touch it with the gaping muzzle of the four-to-the-pound. Again the great clanging burst of sound and flame and smoke, and half the bull's head flew away in a gust of bone chips and bloody fragments. It reared up on its hind legs, striking out with fore hooves, and then crashed over in a cloud of dust.

Impossibly, the herd split, galloping down each side of their rocky hide, a heaving, grunting, forked river of striving muscle and bone. Jan Cheroot was yipping shrilly with the fever of the chase, ducking down behind the rock to reload, biting open the paper cartridge with powder dribbling down his chin, spitting the ball into the muzzle and then plying the ramrod in a frenzy, before bobbing up again to fire into the solid heaving press of gigantic bodies.

It lasted for two minutes, which seemed to take a round of eternity, and then they were left choking and gasping in the swirling clouds of dust, surrounded by half a dozen huge black carcasses, with the drum-beats of the herd fading away into the mopani forest, and a louder more urgent din roaring down on them from in front.

The first tongue of heat licked across then, and Zouga heard the lock of sunbleached hair that hung on his forehead frizzle sharply and smelt the stink of it. At the same instant, the dust cloud fell abruptly aside, and for seconds they stared at a spectacle which deprived them of power of movement.

The jessie bush was not burning, it was exploding into sheets of flame.

'Run!' shouted Zouga. 'Get out of here!'

The sleeve of his shirt charred, and the air he breathed scorched his lungs painfully. As they reached the edge of the mopani forest, the shiny green leaves about their heads shrivelled and yellowed, curling their edges in the heat, and Zouga felt his eyeballs drying out as the dark smoke clouds rolled over them. He knew that they were experiencing only the heat and smoke carried on the wind, but if the flames were able to jump the gap, then they were all doomed. Ahead of him, the Hottentots and the other bearers were shadowy wraiths, staggering forward but weakening and losing direction.

Then, as suddenly as they had been engulfed by them, the billowing smoke clouds lifted. The flames had not been able to jump the open ground, and the heat came only in gusts. A ray of sunshine pierced the thick gloom overhead, and a puff of sweet fresh air came through. They sucked at it gratefully, and huddled in awed silence, beating at their clothing which still smouldered in patches. Zouga's face was blackened and blistered, and his lungs still convulsed in spasms of coughing. As he caught his breath, he grunted hoarsely,

'Well the meat is cooked already,' and he pointed back at the buffalo carcasses.

At that moment something fell limply out of the dense top branches of a mopani tree, and then picked itself up and limped painfully towards them. Zouga let out a husky growl of laughter.

'Oh, thou swift of foot,' he greeted Mark, the bearer, and the others took up the mockery.

'When you fly, the eagles are put to shame,' Jan Cheroot hooted.

'Your true home is in the treetops,' Matthew added with relish, 'with your hairy brethren.'

By evening they had hacked the buffalo carcasses into wet red chunks, and spread these on the smoking racks. The racks were waist high, cross-poles set in forked branches, with a slow smoking fire of wet mopani wood smouldering under it.

Here was meat for the caravan that would last them many weeks.

Camacho Pereira had no doubts that by simply following the line of the escarpment, keeping just below the bad broken ground, he must at last cut the spoor of the caravan. A hundred men, in column, would blaze a track that even a blind man would trip over.

His certainty dwindled with each day's march through the quivering, breathless heat that seemed to rebound from black kopjes and the ironstone cliffs which glittered in the aching sunlight like the scales of some monstrous reptile.

Of the men that his half-brother, Alphonse, had given him, he had already lost two. One had stepped on something that looked like a pile of dried leaves, but which had transformed itself instantly into six feet of infuriated gaboon adder, thick as a man's calf, with a repulsively beautiful diamond-patterned back, and a head the size of a man's fist. The gaping mouth was a lovely shade of salmon pink, and the curved fangs three inches long. It had plunged them into the man's thigh and squirted half a cupful of the most toxic venom in Africa into his bloodstream.

After blowing the serpent to shreds with volleys of rifle fire, Camacho and his companions had wagered all their expectations of loot on exactly how long it would take the victim to die. Camacho, the only one who owned a watch, was elected timekeeper, and they gathered around where the dying man lay, either urging him to give up the useless struggle or pleading with him raucously to hang on a little longer.

When he went into back-arching convulsions, with his eyes rolled up into his skull, his jaws locked into a grinning rictus and he lost control of his sphincter muscle, Camacho knelt beside him, holding a bunch of smouldering tambooti leaves under his nostrils to shock him out of it, and crooning, 'Ten minutes more – hang on for just ten minutes more for your old friend Machito!'

The last convulsion ended with a dreadful gangling expulsion of breath, and when the heart beat faded completely, Camacho stood and kicked the corpse with disgust.

'He always was a dung-eating jackal.'

When they began to strip the corpse of all items of any possible value, five coins, heavy golden mohurs of the East India Company, fell out of the folds of his turban.

There was not one man in all that company who would not have willingly sold his mother into slavery for a single gold mohur, let alone five.

At the first gleam of gold, all their knives came out with a sardonic metallic snickering, and the first man to snatch for the treasure reeled away, trying to push his intestines back into the long clean slice through his stomach wall.

'Leave them lie,' Camacho shouted. 'Don't touch them until the lots are drawn!'

Not one of them trusted another, and the knives stayed out while the lots were cast, and grudgingly the winners were allowed one at a time to claim their prize.

The man with the belly wound could not march without his stomach falling out, and because he could not march, he was as good as dead. The dead, as everybody knows, have no need of personal possessions. The logic was apparent to all. They left him his shirt and breeches, both torn and badly stained anyway, but stripped him of all else as they had stripped the first corpse. Then, with a few ribald pleasantries, they propped him against the base of a marula tree, with the naked corpse of the snake-bite victim beside him for company, and they marched away along the line of the escarpment.

They had gone a hundred yards when Camacho was overcome by a rush of compassion. He and the dying man had fought and marched and whored together for many years. He turned back.

The man gave him a haggard grin, his dry crusted lips cracking with the effort. Camacho answered him with that marvellous flashing smile as he dropped the man's loaded pistol in his lap.

'It would be better to use it *before* the hyena find you tonight,' he told him.

'The thirst is terrible,' the man croaked, a tiny bead of blood appeared on his deeply cracked lower lip, bright as an emperor's ruby in the sunlight. He eyed the two-gallon water bottle on Camacho's hip.

Camacho resettled the water bottle on its strap so it was out of sight behind his back. The contents sloshed seductively.

'Try not to think about it,' he counselled.

There was a point where compassion ended and stupidity began. Who knew where and when they would find the next water? In this God-blasted desolation, water was an item not to be wasted on a man who was already as good as dead.

He patted the man's shoulder comfortingly, gave him a last lovely smile and then swaggered away amongst the grey ironthorn scrub, whistling softly under his breath with the plumed beaver cocked over one eye.

'Camachito went back to make sure we had forgotten nothing.' The one-eyed Abyssinian greeted him as he caught up with the column, and they shouted with laughter. Their spirits were still high, the water-bottles more than half filled and the prospects of immense loot danced like a will-o-the-wisp down the valley ahead of them.

That had been ten days ago, the last three of which without water, for you could not count the cupful of mud and elephant piss they had from the last puddled water-hole. Apart from the lack of water, the going had become appalling. Camacho had never marched through such broken and harsh terrain, toiling up one rocky slope and then battling down through tearing thorn to the next dry river course, and then up again.

Also, it now seemed highly probable that either the Englishman had changed his mind and gone north of the Zambezi river after all, in which case they had lost him, or else, and Camacho's skin crawled at the thought, or else they had crossed the spoor of the caravan in the early dawn or late evening when the light was too bad to make it out clearly. It was an easy mistake to make, they had crossed hundreds of game tracks each day, and the spoor could have been wiped by a herd of game, or one of the fierce short-lived little whirlwinds, the dust devils which ravaged the valley at this season of the year.

To cap all Camacho's tribulations, his band of noble warriors was on the point of mutiny. They were talking quite openly about turning back. There never had been an Englishman and a caravan of riches, even if there had, he was now far from here and getting further every day. They were exhausted by these switchback ridges and valleys and the water bottles were nearly all of them dry, which made it hard to maintain enthusiasm for the venture. The ringleaders were reminding the others that in their absence, their share of the profits of the slave caravan were blowing in the wind. Fifty slaves, for certain, were worth a hundred mythical Englishmen. They had many excellent reasons for turning back.

Camacho, on the other hand, had nothing to return for, apart from his half-brother's ire. He also had a score to settle, two scores. He still hoped that they might manage to take the Englishman and his sister alive, especially the woman. Even in the thirst and the heat, his groin swelled at the memory of her in men's breeches. He jerked himself back to reality, and he glanced over his shoulder at the straggling line of ruffians who followed him.

Soon it would be necessary to kill one of his men, he had decided hours ago. Dung-eaters all of them – it was the only language they truly understood. He must make an example to stiffen their backbones, and keep them slogging onwards.

He had already decided which one it would be. The one-eyed Abyssinian was the biggest talker, the most eloquent apostle of the return to the coast, and what made his choice even more attractive was that his left side was blind. The problem was that the job must be done properly. The others would be impressed by the knife but not the gun. However, the Abyssinian allowed no man into that blind spot. Without making it too obvious, Camacho had twice sidled up on his left, but each time the Abyssinian had swung his head with its frizzed-up halo of dense curly hair towards him, and given him a grin with a slow trickle of a tear running down his cheek from that obscenely empty eye-socket.

However, Camacho was a persistent man, and an inventive one, for he noticed that whenever he moved out of the Abyssinian's blind spot, the man relaxed, and immediately became more verbose and arrogant. Twice more Camacho tried an approach from the left, and twice more was met with a single cold beady stare. He was establishing a pattern, teaching the victim that threat came only from the left, and when they halted in the middle of the morning, he ostentatiously squatted on the right. The Abyssinian grinned at him as he wiped the spout of his almost empty water bottle on his sleeve.

'This is the place. I go no further.' The one-eyed man announced in fluent Portuguese. 'I make the oath on Christ's sacred wounds.' And he touched the Coptic gold cross that hung around his neck. 'Not another step forward. I am going back.'

Fanning himself with the beaver hat, Camacho shrugged, and answered the cold grin with his own sunny smile. 'Let's drink to your going then.' With his free hand, he lifted his own water bottle, and shook it slightly. There was a cupful, no more. All their eyes went instinctively to the bottle. Here water was life, even the Abyssinian's single eye fastened on it.

Then Camacho let it slip from his fingers. It looked like an accident, the bottle rolled to the Abyssinian's feet with clear water glugging out on to the baked earth, and, with an exclamation, the man stooped for it with his right hand, his knife hand.

Nobody really saw Camacho move. He had been holding the knife in the lining of the beaver hat. Suddenly it seemed to reappear behind the Abyssinian's right ear, just the carved bone handle protruding, the blade completely buried. The Abyssinian lifted his hand with a mystified expression and touched the hilt of the knife, blinked his single eye rapidly, opened his mouth and then closed it firmly and fell forward on top of the water bottle.

Camacho was standing over them, a cocked pistol in each hand.

'Who else wishes to make an oath on Christ's sacred wounds?' he smiled at them, his teeth very big and white and square. 'Nobody? Very well then, I will make an oath. I make it on the long-lost maidenheads of your sisters which they sold a hundred times for an escudo the bunch.'

Even they were shocked by such blasphemy.

'I make it on your flaccid and puny manhoods which it will be my great pleasure to shoot off,' he was interrupted, and broke off in mid-sentence.

There was a faint popping sound on the hushed heated morning, so distant, so indistinct, that for a moment none of them recognized it as the sound of gunfire. Camacho recovered first, he thrust the pistols into his waistband. They were no longer needed – and he ran to the crest of the rocky kopje on which they sat.

There was a column of dun-coloured smoke rising into the washed-out blue sky far ahead. In this terrain, it lay a day's march away against the steep and fearsome edge of the escarpment.

Around him his men, once again loyal and filled with fire, were laughing and hugging each other with delight. It was a pity about the Abyssinian, Camacho conceded, like all his people he had been a good fighter, and now they had found the Englishman, he would be missed.

Camacho cupped the cheroot in both hands and inhaled deeply. Holding the smoke in his lungs, he squinted his eyes against the flat glare of rising noon. The sun had bleached all colour from the landscape, only the shadows were cut clearly, very sharp-edged and black below each tree and rock.

Across the narrow valley the long column of men he was watching moved at the pace of the slowest. Camacho doubted if they were making a single mile in an hour.

He removed the beaver hat from his head and blew the smoke into it gently, so that it dispersed into nothingness instead of standing in the still air to draw the eye of a watcher.

Camacho saw nothing odd in that the leading Hottentot musketeer in the column carried an English flag. Even in this barren, forsaken corner of the earth, although its gaudy folds were already dulled with dust and the ends shredded by grasping thorn, it was the promise of protection, a warning to those who might check their passage. All caravans in Africa went under a banner.

Camacho dragged on the black cheroot and considered once again how infallible was the advice of his brother Alphonse. The night was the only time to do the business. Here the column was spread out for more than a mile, there were wide gaps between each of the four divisions – and with himself he had eighteen men left. If he attacked in daylight, he would be forced to concentrate them on the detachments of Hottentot musketeers at the head and tail of the caravan. He imagined vividly what might happen at the first shot. One hundred porters would drop their packs and scatter away into the bush, and when the fighting was over he would have nobody to carry the loot.

It was necessary, furthermore, for him to wait until the Englishman rejoined the caravan. He guessed that Zouga Ballantyne was scouting or hunting, but that he would rejoin the column before nightfall.

The woman was there. He had another glimpse of her at that moment as she stepped up on to a log that lay across the path; for a moment she balanced there, long-legged, in those maddening breeches, and then jumped down off the log. Camacho passed a pleasant few minutes in erotic imaginings. He had been twenty days without a woman and it had put a razor edge to his appetite which even the hot hard trek had not dulled.

He sighed happily, and then squinted his eyes again as he concentrated on the immediate problems. Alphonse was right, they would have to wait until night. And tonight would be a good night for it, three days after the full moon, and yet the moon would rise very late, an hour or so after midnight.

He would let the Englishman come in, let the camp settle down, let the fires die, and let the Hottentot sentries drowse off. Then when the moon rose and the vitality of the camp was at its lowest ebb, he and his men would go in.

Every one of his men was good with the knife, the fact that they had lived so long showed that, Camacho smiled to himself, and they would have an opportunity to prove it again tonight. He personally would mark the position of the sentries while it was still light. They would start with them, Camacho did not expect more than three or four. After the sentries, then the Hottentot musketeers that were sleeping. They were the most dangerous, and after them there would be time for indulgence.

He would go to the woman's tent himself, he squirmed slightly at the thought and adjusted his dressing. It was just a terrible pity that he could not take care of the Englishman as well. He would send two of his best men to do that work. He had dreamed of driving a long wooden spike up between the Englishman's buttocks, and then taking wagers on how long he would take to die, amusing himself and the company while regaining some of his previous losses at the same time.

Then reluctantly, and prudently, he had decided not to chance such pleasures, not with a man like that. Best to cut his throat while he still slept. They could have their fun with the woman instead, Camacho decided firmly.

His single regret was that he would have only a short time with her, before the others demanded their turns, though a few minutes would probably be enough for him. Strange how months of craving could be satiated so swiftly, and after that brief out-pouring become indifference and even distaste. That was a very philosophical thought, Camacho realized. Once again he had astonished himself with his own wisdom and sensitivity to things of the mind. He had often thought that if he had ever learned to read and write he could have been a great man, like his father the Governor. After all, the blood in his veins was that of aristocrats and Dons, only slightly diluted.

He sighed, yes, five minutes would suffice and then the others could have her, and when they also had finished they could play the betting game with the long wooden stake – and, of course, there was a more amusing place to put it. He chuckled aloud at the thought and took a last draw on the cheroot, and the stub was so short that the ember scorched his fingers. He dropped it and crushed it under his heel. He moved like a panther, slipping quietly over the skyline and circling out stealthily to get ahead of the creeping caravan.

Zouga had left his bearers tending the smoking-racks, feeding the fire with chips of wet wood, and turning the hunks of red meat so they cured evenly. It was wearisome work, for the racks had to be guarded at all times from the hyena and jackals, the crows and kites which hung about the camp, while there was always wood to cut and the baskets of mopani bark to weave in which the smoked meat would be carried.

Jan Cheroot was happy to escape with Zouga as he marched back to find the main caravan and guide it to the buffalo camp. Even the tsetse fly could not repress his high spirits. They had been in 'fly-country' for a week or more now. Tom Harkness had called these importunate little insects 'the guardians of Africa' and certainly they made it impossible for man to move his domestic animals through vast tracts of country.

Here they were one of the many reasons why the Portuguese colonization had been confined to the low coastal littoral. Their cavalry had never been able to penetrate this deadly screen, nor had their draught animals been able to drag their war trains up from the coast.

They were the reason, also, why Zouga had not attempted to use waggons or beasts of burden to carry his stores. There was not even a dog with the caravan, for only man and wild game were immune to the dreadful consequences of the bite.

In some areas of the 'fly-belt' there were so few of the insects as to cause little annoyance, but in others they swarmed like hiving bees, plaguing and persecuting even during the moonlight periods of the night.

That day on the march back to rejoin the column, Zouga and Jan Cheroot suffered the worst infestation of fly they had yet met with in the valley of the Zambezi. They rose from the ground to sit thickly upon their legs, and clustered on the backs of their necks and between their shoulder blades, so that he and Jan Cheroot took turns to walk behind each other and brush them off with a freshly cut buffalo tail.

As suddenly as they had entered it, they found themselves out of the 'fly-belt' and with blessed relief from the torment they settled down to rest in the shade. Within half an hour they heard distant singing, and as they waited for the caravan to come up, they smoked and chatted in the desultory fashion of the good companions they had become.

During one of the long pauses in their talk Zouga thought he saw vague movement on the far side of the shallow valley in front of them. Probably a herd of kudu or a troop of baboon, both of which were plentiful in the valley, but apart from the buffalo herd the only game they had encountered since leaving Tete.

The approaching caravan would have alarmed whatever it was, Zouga thought, removing his cap and using it to drive away the persistent cloud of tiny black mopani bees which hovered around his head, attracted by the moisture of his eyes and lips and nostrils. The movement in the forest opposite was not repeated. Whatever it was had probably crossed the ridge. Zouga turned back to listen to Jan Cheroot.

'The rains only stopped six weeks ago,' Jan Cheroot was musing aloud. 'The water-holes and rivers up on the high ground will still be full, not here, of course – this ground drains too steeply.' He indicated the dry and rocky water course below them. 'So the herds spread out, and follow their old roads.' He was explaining the complete lack of elephant, or even recent evidence of elephant herds in the valley, and Zouga listened with attention, for here was an expert speaking. 'The old elephant roads, they used to run from the flat mountain of Good Hope to the swamps of the far Sud,' he pointed north. 'But each year they shrink as we, the *jagters* (hunters), and men like us, follow the herds and drive them deeper and deeper into the interior.'

Jan Cheroot was silent again, and his pipe gurgled noisily as he sucked on it.

'My father told me that he killed the last elephants south of the Olifants river – the river of elephants – when he was still a young man. He boasted that he killed twelve elephants that day, he alone with his old *roer* (muzzle-loader) that was too heavy to hold to the shoulder. He had to rest it on the crutch of a forked stick he carried for it. Twelve elephants in one day – by one man. That is a feat.' He gurgled his pipe again, and then spat a little yellow tobacco juice. 'But then my father was even more famous as a liar than he was as a hunter,' Jan Cheroot chuckled and shook his head fondly.

Zouga smiled, and then the smile vanished and his head jerked up. He narrowed his eyes, for a tiny dart of reflected sunlight had struck his eye coming from the same place across the valley. Whatever he had seen was still there, and it was neither kudu nor baboon. It had to be a man, for only metal or glass could have shot that reflection. Jan Cheroot had noticed nothing and he was musing on.

'When I rode with Cornwallis Harris, we found the first elephant on the Cashan mountains, that's a thousand miles further north of where my father killed his herd. There was nothing in between – it had all been hunted bare. Now there are no elephant in the Cashan mountains. My brother Stephan was there two years ago. He tells me that there are no elephant south of the Limpopo river. The Boers graze their herds where we hunted ivory – perhaps we will find no elephant even up there on the high ground, perhaps there are no elephant left in all the world.'

Zouga was not really listening any more. He was thinking about the man on the opposite side of the valley. It was probably somebody from the caravan, a party sent ahead to cut firewood for the night's bivouac, yet it was still early to think of making camp.

The singing of the bearers was louder now. There was a single voice carrying the marching song. Zouga recognized it. The man was a tall Angoni, with a fine tenor voice, and a poet who improvised his own verses, adding to them and altering them on the march. Zouga, cocking his head, could make out the words.

'Have you heard the Fish Eagle cry above Marawi?
Have you seen the setting sun turn the snows of Kilimanjaro to blood?'

And then the chorus coming in after him, those haunting African voices, so beautiful, so moving,

'Who will lead us to these wonders, my brother?
We will leave the women to weep,
We will let their sleeping mats grow cold,
If a strong man leads, we will follow him, my brother.'

Zouga smiled at the next verse, as he recognized his name.

'Bakela will lead us like a father leads his children,
Bakela will give you a *khete* of *sam sam* beads—
Bakela will feed you upon the fat of the hippopotamus and meat of the buffalo—'

Zouga closed his mind against the distraction, concentrating on the man across the valley. Here, a hundred miles from the nearest habitations of men, it must have been somebody from the caravan – woodcutter, honey-hunter, deserter, who knew?

Zouga stood up and stretched, and Jan Cheroot knocked out his pipe and stood with him. The head of the column appeared amongst the trees lower down the slope, the red, white and blue banner flapped lazily open and then drooped again dejectedly.

Zouga glanced once more at the opposite slope, it seemed deserted again. He was tired, the soles of his feet felt as though he had marched across burning embers, for they had been going hard since dawn, and the barely healed knife wound in his hip ached dully.

He should really go up that slope to check what he had seen, but it was steep and rocky. It would take another half an hour of scrambling to reach the crest and return. They went down to meet the caravan, and when Zouga saw Robyn striding along with that easy coltish grace of hers behind the standard bearer, he lifted his cap and waved it above his head.

She ran to meet him, laughing like a child with delight. He had been gone three days.

Below a polished face of smooth black rock, that when the river was in spate would be a roaring cascade, there was a bend in the dry water bed filled with pure white sand.

On the banks above it the wild mahogany stood tall and vigorous, its roots in water and the baboon had been scratching in the sand below the bank.

Robyn and Zouga sat together on the edge of the dry waterfall, watching the men that Zouga had set to digging for water.

'I pray there will be enough.' Robyn watched them with interest. 'I have not used my bath since we left Tete.' Her enamelled hip bath was the expedition's single bulkiest item of equipment.

'I'll be satisfied with enough for a pot of tea,' Zouga replied vaguely, but he was clearly distracted.

'Something is worrying you?' she asked.

'I was thinking of a valley in Kashmir.'

'Was it like this?'

'Not really – it is just that,' he shrugged. In that far away valley, when he had been a young ensign leading a patrol ahead of the battalion, he had seen something as he had today. Something of no account, a stray movement, a glint of light that might have been off a gunbarrel, or the horn of a wild goat. Then, as now, it had been too much trouble to check it. That night he had lost three men, killed while they fought their way out of the valley. The fight had earned praise from his Colonel, but the men remained dead.

He glanced up at the slanting sun, there was an hour of light left. He knew he should have climbed that slope. While Robyn watched him with a puzzled expression, he wavered a few seconds longer and then with an exclamation of exasperation stood up wearily. His feet still ached abominably and he rubbed his hip where the knife-wound throbbed. It was going to be a long walk back down the valley.

Zouga used a deep and narrow ravine to get out of the camp unobtrusively, and once clear he scrambled out and kept to the thicker bush just above the river-bed until he reached a tangled barrier of driftwood carried down during the recent rains which blocked the dry water-course from bank to bank.

He used this to cover his crossing, and started up the far slope. He went very carefully, dodging from one tree to another and watching and listening before each move.

On the crest there was a faint movement of cooler air, the evening breeze coming down the escarpment that cooled the sweat on his neck and almost made the hard climb worth-while. It seemed that was all the reward he would get. The stony ground was too hard to carry sign, and it was deserted of life, animal or human. However, Zouga was determined to make up for his previous sloth. He stayed too long. It would be fully dark before he reached the camp again, moonrise was late, and he risked a broken leg moving over this sort of terrain in the pitch dark.

He turned to go back, and he smelt it before he saw it, and the hair prickled along his forearms and he felt his belly muscles contract, yet it was such a commonplace smell. He stooped and picked up the small squashed brown object.

He had smoked the last of his own cheroots two days before, perhaps that was why his nose was so sensitive to the smell of tobacco.

The cigar had been smoked down to a thin rind, and crushed out so it resembled a scrap of dried bark. Without the smell to guide him, he would never have found it. Zouga shredded it between his fingers, and there was still a little residual dampness of saliva in the chewed end. He lifted his fingers and sniffed them. He knew where he had smelled that particular scented type of Portuguese tobacco before.

Camacho left fifteen of his men well back off the crest, in a tumble of rock that looked like a ruined castle, and whose caves and overhangs gave shade and concealment. They would sleep, he knew, and he grudged it to them. His own eyelids were drooping as he lay belly down in cover, on the other side of the ridge watching the caravan making camp.

He had only two of his men with him to help him mark the sentries and *scherms*, the watch fires and the tent sites. They would be able to lead the others in, even in the complete darkness before the moon, if that should become necessary. Camacho hoped not. In the dark mistakes could be made, and it needed only a shot or a single shout. No, they would wait for the moon, he decided.

The Englishman had come into camp earlier, just before the caravan halted. He had the Hottentot with him, and they both hobbled stiffly like men who had made long, hard marches. Good, he would sleep soundly, was probably doing so already, for Camacho had not seen him in the last hour. He must be in the tent beside the woman's. He had seen a servant carrying a steaming bucket of water to her.

They had watched the Hottentot Sergeant set only two sentries. The Englishman must be feeling very secure, two sentries merely to watch against lions. They would probably both be fast asleep by midnight. They would never wake again. He, personally, would cut one of them. He smiled in anticipation, and he would send a good knife to cut the other.

The remaining Hottentots had built their usual lean-to shelter and thatched it in a rudimentary fashion. There was no chance of rain, not at this season and not with that unblemished eggshell-blue sky. It was almost two hundred paces from the tents, a groan or a whimper would not carry that far. Good, Camacho nodded again. It was working out better than he had hoped.

As always, the two tents were set close together, almost touching. The gallant Englishman guarding the woman, Camacho smiled again, and felt his drowsiness lifting miraculously and his groin charged once more. He wished the night away, for he had already waited so long.

Night came with the dramatic suddenness of Africa, within minutes the valley was filled with shadows, the sunset made its last theatrical flare of apricot and old gold light and then it was dark.

For an hour more Camacho could see the occasional dark figure silhouetted by the flames of the camp fires. Once the sound of singing carried softly and sweetly to the ridge, and the other camp sounds, the clank of a bucket, the thud of a log thrown on the fire, the drowsy murmur of voices, showed that the routine was unaltered, and the camp completely unaware.

The noises faded and the fires died. The silence and the darkness was disturbed only by the piping lament of a jackal across the valley.

The star patterns turned slowly across the sky marking the passage of the hours, and then gradually paled out before the greater brilliance of the rising moon.

'Fetch the others,' Camacho told the man nearest him, and rose stiffly to his feet, stretching like a cat to relieve numbed muscles. They came silently, and gathered close about Camacho, to listen to his final whispered instructions.

When he finished whispering, he looked from one to the other in turn. Their faces in the bright moonlight had the pale greenish hues of freshly exhumed corpses, but they nodded their agreement to his words, and then followed him down the slope, dark silent shapes like a troop of wolves; they reached the dry water course in the gut of the valley, and split into their prearranged groups.

Camacho moved up the newly beaten path towards the camp. He carried his knife in his right hand and his musket in the other, and his feet made a barely audible brushing sound through the short dry grass. Ahead of him, beneath the outspread branches of a mukusi tree, he could make out the shape of the sentry, where he had been placed six hours before. The man was asleep, curled like a dog on the hard earth. Camacho nodded with satisfaction and crept closer. He saw the man had pulled a dark blanket over his head. The mosquitoes had bothered him also, Camacho grinned and knelt beside him.

With his free hand he felt softly for the man's head through the blanket, then the hand stilled. He gave a little grunt of surprise, and jerked the blanket aside. It had been arranged over the exposed roots of the mukusi tree to look like the shape of a sleeping man, and Camacho swore quietly but with great vehemence.

The sentry had chosen the wrong time to sneak away from his post. He was probably back in the lean-to shelter snoring happily on a mattress of dry grass. They would get him with the others, when they cleaned out the shelter. Camacho went on up the slope into the camp. In the moonlight the canvas of the tents shone ghostly silver, a beacon on which his lust could concentrate. Camacho slipped the sling of the musket over his shoulder as he hurried forward, towards the left-hand tent, and then checked as another dark figure emerged from the shadows, the knife in his right hand instinctively came up and then he recognized his own man, one of those whom he had sent to cut the Englishman's throat.

The man nodded jerkily, all was well so far and they went forward together, separating only as they approached the two tents. Camacho would not use the fly opening of the woman's tent – for he knew it would be laced closed, and if there were any surprises they would be at the entrance. He slipped around the side of the tent, and stooped to one of the hooded ventilator openings. He ran the point of blade into it and then drew it upwards in a single stroke. Although it was heavy canvas, the blade had been whetted expertly, and the side wall split with only a whisper of sound.

Camacho stepped through the opening, and while he waited for his eyesight to adjust to the deeper darkness of the interior, he fumbled with the fastening of his breeches, grinning happily to himself as he made out the narrow collapsible cot and the little white tent of the muslin mosquito net. He shuffled towards it slowly, careful not to trip over the cases of medical stores that were piled between him and the cot.

Standing over the cot, he ripped the muslin netting aside violently, and lunged full length on to the cot, groping for the woman's head to smother her cries, the loose ends of his belt flapping at his waist, and his breeches sagging around his hips.

For a moment he was paralysed with shock at the fact that the cot was empty. Then he groped frantically over every inch of it, before coming to his feet again and hoisting his breeches with his free hand. He was confused, disconnected, and wild ideas flashed through his mind. Perhaps the woman had left the cot to answer a call of nature, but then why was the fly carefully laced closed. She had heard him and was hiding behind the cases, armed with a scalpel, and he swung round panicking to lash out with the knife, but the tent was empty.

Then the coincidence of the missing sentry and the empty cot struck him with force, and he felt deep and urgent concern. Something was happening that he did not understand. He charged for the rent in the canvas, tripped and sprawled over one of the cases and rolled on to his feet again, nimble as a cat. He ran out, clinching his belt and looking about him wildly, unslinging his musket and only just preventing himself from calling aloud to his men.

He ran to the Englishman's tent, just as his man came running out of the long dark tear in the canvas side, brandishing his knife, his face pale and fearful in the moonlight. He saw Camacho, screamed and struck out at him wildly with the long silver blade.

'Silence, you fool,' Camacho snarled at him.

'He's gone,' the man panted, craning to stare about into the deep shadows that the moon cast under the trees. 'They've gone. They've all gone.'

'Come!' snapped Camacho, and led him at a run down towards the lean-to that the Hottentot musketeers had built.

Before they reached it they met their companions running towards them in a disorderly bunch.

'Machito?' somebody called nervously.

'Shut your mouth,' Camacho growled at them, but the man blurted on.

'The *scherm* is empty, they have gone.'

'The Devil has taken them.'

'There is nobody.'

There was an almost superstitious frenzy of awe on them all, the darkness and the silent empty camp turned them all into cowards. Camacho found himself, for once, without an order to give, uncertain of what to do. His men crowded around him helplessly, seeming to take comfort from each other's physical presence, cocking and fiddling with their muskets and peering nervously into the shadows.

'What do we do now?' A voice asked the question that Camacho had feared, and somebody else threw a log from the pile on to the smouldering watch fire in the centre of the camp.

'Don't do that,' Camacho ordered uncertainly, but instinctively they were all drawn to the warmth and comfort of the orange tongue of flame that soared up brightly, blowing like a dragon's breath.

They turned their backs towards it, forming a half circle and faced outwards into the dark which in contrast to the flames was suddenly impenetrably black.

It was out of this darkness that it came. There was no warning, just the sudden thunderous burst of sound and flame, the long line of spurting muzzle flashes, blooming briefly and murderously, and then the sound of the striking balls in their midst, like a handful of children's marbles hurled into a mud puddle, as the musket balls slogged into human flesh.

Immediately men were hurled lightly about by the heavy lead slugs, and the little band about the watch fire was thrown into struggling, shouting confusion.

One of them flew backwards, at a run, doubled in the middle where a ball had taken him low in the belly. He tripped over the burning log and fell full length into the blazing watch fire. His hair and beard flared like a torch of pine needles and his scream rang wildly through the tree tops.

Camacho himself threw up his musket, aiming blindly into the night from whence the Englishman's voice was chanting the ritual infantry orders for mass volley fire.

'Section One. Reload. Section Two. Three paces forward. One round volley fire.'

Camacho realized that the devastating blast of close range musketry that had just swept them, would be repeated within seconds. With mild derision Camacho

had watched on many a hot afternoon as the Englishman drilled his double line
of red-jacketed puppets, the front rank levelling and firing on command, then
the second rank taking three paces forward in unison, stepping through the gaps
in the first rank and in their turn levelling and firing. The same evolutions
which, when magnified ten thousand times, had broken the charge of French
cavalry up the slope at Quatre Bras, now filled Camacho with unutterable
terror, and he flung up his musket and fired it unsighted into the darkness, in
the direction of the cool, precise English voice. He fired at the same instant as
one of his own men who had been knocked down by the first volley scrambled
to his feet only lightly wounded, directly in front of Camacho's musket muzzle.
Camacho shot him cleanly between the shoulder blades at a range of two feet,
so close that the powder burn scorched the man's shirt. It smouldered in little
red sparks as he sprawled at full length on his face once more, until the glowing
sparks were quenched by the quick flow of the man's heart blood.

'Fool!' Camacho howled at the corpse, and turned to run.

Behind him the English voice called, 'Fire!'

Camacho threw himself down on to hard earth, howling again as his hands
and knees sank into the hot ash of the watch fire and he felt his breeches char
and his skin blister.

The second volley swept over his head, and around him more men were falling
and screaming, and Camacho rebounded to his feet at a dead run. He had lost
both his knife and musket.

'Section One, three paces forward, one round volley fire.'

The night was suddenly filled with running, shouting figures, as the porters
burst out of their encampment. There was no direction or purpose in their flight.
They ran like Camacho, driven by gunfire and their own terrible panic, scattering
away into the surrounding bush, singly and in small groups.

Before the command ordering the next volley of musket fire, Camacho ducked
behind the hillock of porters' packs, which had been piled close to the Englishman's tent and covered with waterproof tarpaulin.

Camacho was sobbing with the agony of his scorched hands and knees, and
with the humiliation of having walked so guilelessly into the Englishman's trap.

He found his terror giving way to bitter and spiteful hatred. As little groups
of terrified porters stumbled towards him out of the darkness, he drew one of
the pistols from his belt and shot the leader in the head and then leapt up
howling like a demented ghost – they ran and he knew they would not stop
until, miles away in the trackless wilderness, they dropped with exhaustion,
easy prey for lion or hyena. It gave him a moment's sour satisfaction, and he
looked around for some other damage he could wreak.

The pile of stores behind which he crouched and the dying fire in front of the
Englishman's deserted tent caught his attention. He snatched a brand from the
fire, blew it into flame and tossed it flaring brighly on to the high canvas-covered
pile of stores and equipment, then flinched as another volley crashed out of the
darkness, and he heard the Englishman's voice.

'As a line of skirmishers, take the bayonet to them now, men.'

Camacho jumped down into the dry river-bed, and blundered through the
crunching sugary sand to the far bank, where he scrambled thankfully into the
dense riverine bush.

At the re-assembly point on the ridge there were three of his men already
waiting, two of them had lost their muskets and all three were as shaken and
sweaty and breathless as Camacho himself.

Two more came in while they regained their breath and power of speech.
One was badly hit, his shoulders shattered by a musket ball.

'There won't be any others,' he gasped, 'those little yellow bastards caught them with bayonets as they were crossing the river.'

'They'll be here any minute.' Camacho dragged himself to his feet again, looking back down into the valley. He saw with grim satisfaction that the pile of stores was blazing brightly, despite the efforts of half a dozen tiny dark figures to beat out the flames. He had only moments to enjoy the spectacle, for lower down the slope came the thin, but warlike cries of the Hottentot musketeers and the thud and flash of their musket fire.

'Help me,' cried the man with the shattered shoulder. 'Don't leave me here, my friends, my comrades, give me an arm,' he pleaded, trying to struggle back on to his feet, but he was speaking to the empty night, and as the rush of footsteps down the far slope of the hill dwindled, his knees buckled under him and he sank back on to the rock earth sweating with pain and the terror which lasted only until one of the Hottentots drove the point of a bayonet into his chest and out between his shoulder blades.

Zouga strode angrily through the camp in the rising heat and bright sunlight of morning. His face and arms were blackened with soot, his eyes still red and smarting from the smoke of the fires, his beard was scorched and his eyelashes burned half away from fighting the flames. They had lost most of their stores and equipment for the fire had run away through the tents and thatched shelters. Zouga paused to glance at the charred and trodden scraps of canvas that were all that were left of the tents; they would miss them when the rains broke, but that was the very least of their losses.

He tried to make a mental list of the most grievous damage they had suffered. There were firstly only forty-six porters left out of more than one hundred. Of course, he could expect Jan Cheroot and his Hottentots to bring in a few more. They were at this moment scouring the valleys and hills around the camp for scattered survivors. He could still hear the kudu-horn trumpets calling in the stragglers. However, many would have risked the long and dangerous journey back to Tete rather than a recurrence of the night's attack, and they would have seized the opportunity to desert. Others would be lost after their midnight flight and panic. They would fall prey to wild animals or succumb to thirst. Half a dozen had been killed by random musketry fire and by the retreating brigands who had deliberately fired into the masses of unarmed porters. Four others were so badly wounded that they would die before nightfall.

That was the most serious loss, for without porters they were helpless. Without porters to carry them, what remained of the carefully selected equipment and trade goods were as useless to them as if they had left them in London or dumped them overboard from *Huron*'s deck.

Of the equipment itself, it would take them hours to count their losses, to find what had burned and what they could salvage from the stinking, smouldering mass of cloth and canvas, what they could pick out of the trodden and dusty mess scattered down the rock hillside. The scene reminded Zouga forcefully of so many other battlefields, the terrible destruction and waste affronted him, as it has done before.

The few remaining porters were already at work, picking over the field like a line of harvesters, retrieving anything of value from the ash and the dust. Little Juba was with them concentrating on the search for Robyn's medical stores, and books and instruments.

Robyn herself had set up an emergency clinic under the wide green branches of the mukusi tree in the centre of the camp, and when Zouga paused to look at the wounded men who still awaited her attention, and at the dead bodies laid out in a neat row and covered with a blanket or a scrap of charred and dirty canvas, he was angry with himself all over again.

Though what alternative had there been for him, he wondered.

If he had turned the camp into an armed fortress, it would have meant enduring a long drawn-out siege with Camacho's wolves skulking around the perimeter, sniping and harrying them until their opportunity came.

No, he had been right to set the trap and end it at a single stroke. At least now he could be certain that the Portuguese were still in full flight for the coast, but the price had been too high, and Zouga was still angry.

The expedition, so well conceived and lavishly equipped, had ended in disaster before it had achieved a single one of its objectives. The loss of equipment and life had been heavy, but that was not what burned so acidly in Zouga's stomach as he paused at the perimeter of the devastated camp and lifted his eyes longingly towards the high broken ground of the southern escarpment. It was the idea of having to give up, before he had begun, and when he was so close, so very close. Twenty, fifty, not more than a hundred miles ahead of him lay the frontier of the empire of Monomatapa. Behind him, one hundred miles to the north was the dirty little village of Tete, and the wide river which was the beginning of the long ignoble road back to England, back to obscurity, back to a commission in a third-rate regiment, back to conformity and the wearying discipline of the cantonments of the Indian army. Only now that he was doomed to return to that life did he realize how deeply he had hated and resented it, just how much the desire to escape it had brought him here to this wild untouched land. Like a long-term prisoner who has tasted one day of sweet freedom, so the prospect of return to his cage was that much more painful, now. The pain of it cramped his chest, and he had to breathe deeply to control it.

He turned away from the southern vista of ragged peaks and savage black rock cliffs, and he walked slowly to where his sister worked quietly in the shade of the mukusi. She was pale, with dark smudges of fatigue and strain under her green eyes. Her blouse was speckled with spots of her patients' blood, and her forehead appeared blistered with tiny beads of perspiration.

She had started work in the darkness, by the light of a bull's eye lantern and now it was mid-morning.

She looked up wearily as Zouga stood over her.

'We won't be able to go on,' he said quietly. She stared at him a moment without change of expression, and then dropped her eyes and went on smearing salve on the badly burned leg of one of the porters. She had treated the worst cases first, and was now finishing with the burns and abrasions.

'We've lost too much vital equipment,' Zouga explained. 'Stores that we need to survive,' Robyn did not look up this time, 'And we've not enough porters to carry what is left.'

Robyn began bandaging the leg with her full attention.

'Papa made the Transversa with four porters,' she observed mildly.

'Papa was a man,' Zouga pointed out reasonably, and Robyn's hands stilled ominously and her eyes narrowed, but Zouga had not noticed. 'A woman cannot travel or survive without the necessities of civilization,' he went on seriously. 'That is why I am sending you back to Tete. I'm sending Sergeant Cheroot and five of his Hottentots to escort you. You'll have no difficulty, once you reach Tete. I will send with you what remains in cash, a hundred pounds for the launch down river to Quelimane and a passage to Cape Town on a trader. There you can draw on the money I deposited in Cape Town to pay for a passage on the mailship.'

She looked up at him. 'And you?' she asked.

Until then he had not made the decision. 'The important thing is what happens to you,' he told her gravely, and then he knew what he was going to do. 'You will have to go back and I am going on alone.'

'It'll take more than Jan Cheroot and five of his damned Hottentots to carry me,' she told him, and the oath was a measure of her determination.

'Be reasonable, Sissy.'

'Why should I start now?' she asked sweetly.

Zouga opened his mouth to reply angrily, then closed it slowly and stared at her. There was a hard uncompromising line to her lips, and the prominent, almost masculine, jaw was clenched stubbornly.

'I don't want to argue,' he said.

'Good,' she nodded. 'That way you won't waste any more of your precious time.'

'Do you know what you are letting yourself in for?' he asked quietly.

'As well as you do,' she replied.

'We won't have trade goods to buy our way through the tribes.' She nodded. 'That means we'll have to fight our way through if anyone tries to stop us.'

He saw the shadow in her eyes at that, but there was no wavering of her determination.

'No tents for shelter, no canned food, no sugar or tea.' He knew what that meant to her. 'We will live straight off the land, and what we can't scavenge or kill or carry, we go without. We'll have nothing but powder and shot.'

'You'd be a fool to leave the quinine,' she told him quietly, and he hesitated.

'The bare minimum of medicines,' he agreed, 'and remember, it won't be for just a week or a month.'

'We'll probably go a great deal faster than we have so far,' she answered quietly, as she stood up and brushed off the seat of her breeches.

The choice of what to take and what to leave had been nicely balanced, Zouga thought, as he listed and weighed the new loads.

He had chosen paper and writing equipment in place of sugar and most of the tea. His navigational instruments in place of spare boots, for the boots they wore could be resoled with raw buffalo hide. Quinine and other medicines together with Robyn's instruments in place of the extra clothing and blankets. Powder and shot in place of trade beads and cloth.

The pile of abandoned equipment grew steadily, cases of potted jams, bags of sugar, canned foods, insect nets, folding camp chairs and cots, cooking pots, Robyn's enamel hip bath and her flowered chamber pot, trade goods, *merkani* cloth and beads, hand mirrors and cheap knives. When the pile was complete, Zouga put fire into it, a token of finality and of determination. Yet they watched it burn with trepidation.

There were two small concessions Zouga had made: a single case of Ceylon tea for, as Robyn pointed out, no Englishman could be expected to explore undiscovered territories without that sovereign brew, and the sealed tin which contained Zouga's dress uniform, for their very lives might depend on impressing a savage African potentate. Otherwise they had divested themselves of all but the very essentials.

Chief of these essentials was the ammunition, the sacks of first-grade Curtis and May black powder and the ingots of soft lead, the bullet moulds, the flask of quicksilver to harden the balls and the boxes of copper caps. Out of the remaining forty-six porters, thirty of them carried this powder and shot.

Jan Cheroot's musketeers were horrified when they were informed that their field packs would in future hold two hundred, and not fifty, rounds of Enfield ammunition.

'We are warriors, not porters,' his Corporal told him loftily. Jan Cheroot used the metal scabbard of his long bayonet to reason with him, and Robyn dressed the superficial wounds in the Corporal's scalp.

'They now understand the need for carrying extra ammunition, Major,' Jan Cheroot reported to Zouga cheerfully.

It truly was interesting to realize how much fat they could shed, Zouga mused, as he watched the shorter, more manageable column start out. It was less than a hundred and fifty yards from head to tail, and the pace of its march was almost doubled. The main body nearly matched the speed of Zouga's advance party – falling only a mile or so behind during the first day's march.

That first day they reached the scene of the buffalo hunt before noon, and found more than bark baskets of cured black buffalo meat awaiting there. Zouga's head gunbearer, Matthew, came running to meet him through the forest and he was so excited as to be almost incoherent.

'The father of all elephant,' he gibbered, shaking like a man in fever, 'the grandfather of the father of all elephants!'

Jan Cheroot squatted beside the spoor and grinned like a gnome in a successful piece of sorcery, his slant eyes almost disappearing in the web of wrinkles and folds of yellow skin.

'Our luck has come at last,' he exulted. 'This is indeed an elephant to sing about.'

He took a roll of twine out of the bulging pocket of his tunic and used it to measure the circumference of one of the huge pad marks. It was well over five feet, close to six feet around.

'Double that is how high he stands at the shoulder,' Jan Cheroot explained. 'What an elephant!'

Matthew had at last controlled his excitement enough to explain how he had awoken that dawn, when the light was grey and uncertain, and seen the herd passing close to the camp in deathly silence, three great grey ghostly shapes, moving out of the forest and entering the blackened and barren valley through which the fire had swept. They were gone so swiftly, that it had seemed that they had never existed, but their spoor was impressed so clearly into the soft layer of fire ash that every irregularity in the immense footprints, the whorls and wavy creases of the horny pads, were clearly visible.

'There was one of them, bigger and taller than the others, his teeth were long as a throwing spear and so heavy that he held his head low and moved like an old man, a very old man.'

Now Zouga also shivered with excitement, even in the stultifying heat of the burned-out valley, where it seemed the blackened earth had retained the heat of the flames. Jan Cheroot, mistaking the small movement, grinned wickedly around the stem of his clay pipe.

'My old father used to say that even a brave man is frightened three times when he hunts the elephant, once when he sees its spoor, twice when he hears its voice and the third time when he see the beast – big and black as an ironstone kopje.'

Zouga did not trouble to deny the accusation, he was following the run of the spoor with his eyes. The three huge animals had moved up the centre of the valley, heading directly into the bad ground of the escarpment rim.

'We will follow them,' he said quietly.

'Of course,' Jan Cheroot nodded, 'that is what we came for.'

The spoor led them over the cold grey ash, amongst the blackened and bared branches of the burned-out jessie bush and up the rising funnel of the narrow valley.

Jan Cheroot led. He had discarded his faded tunic for a sleeveless leather jerkin with loops for the Enfield cartridges across the chest. Zouga followed him closely, carrying the Sharps and fifty extra rounds, together with his two-gallon water bottle. His gunbearers, in strict order of seniority backed him, each with his burden of blankets and water bottles, food bag, powder flask and ball pouch, and of course the big smooth-bored elephant guns.

Zouga was anxious to see Jan Cheroot work. The man talked a very good elephant hunt, but Zouga wanted to know if he was as good on the spoor as he was at telling about it around the camp fire. The first test came swiftly when the valley pinched out against another low cliff of impassable rock, and it seemed as though the great beasts they followed had taken wing and soared away above the earth.

'Wait,' said Jan Cheroot and cast swiftly along the base of the cliff. A minute later he whistled softly and Zouga went forward.

There was a smudge of dark ash on a block of ironstone, and another above it, seeming to lead directly into sheer rock face.

Jan Cheroot scrambled up over the loose scree at the foot of the cliff, and disappeared abruptly. Zouga slung his rifle and followed him. The blocks of ironstone had fractured in the shape of a giant's staircase – each step as high as his waist so that he had to use a hand to climb.

Even the elephants would have extended themselves to make each step, rising on their back legs as he had seen them do at the circus, for an elephant is incapable of jumping. They must keep two feet on the earth before they can heave their ungainly bulks upwards.

Zouga reached the spot where Jan Cheroot had disappeared and stopped short in amazement at the threshold of the stone portals, invisible from below, which marked the beginning of the ancient elephant road.

The portals were symmetrically formed in fractured rock, and had eroded through the softer layers, leaving straight joints so they seemed to have been worked by a mason. The opening was so narrow that it seemed impossible that such a large animal could pass through, and looking above the level of his own head, Zouga saw how over the centuries their rough skin had worn the stone smooth as thousands upon thousands of elephant had squeezed through the gap. He reached up and plucked a coarse black bristle, almost as thick as a Swan Vesta, from a crack in the face. Beyond the natural gateway, the gap in the cliffs widened and rose at a more gentle pitch. Already Jan Cheroot was four hundred yards up the pathway.

'Come!' he called, and they followed him up.

The elephant road might have been surveyed and constructed by the corps of engineers, for never was the gradient steeper than thirty degrees and when there were natural steps they were never higher than a man or an elephant could comfortably negotiate, although it seemed there were always accidents, for within a quarter of a mile they found where one of the big animals had missed his footing and struck the tip of one tusk against the ironstone edge.

The tusk had snapped above the point, and twenty pounds of ivory lay in the path. The fragment was worn and stained, so thick around that Zouga could not span it with both hands, but where it had sheered the fresh ivory was a lovely finely grained porcelain white.

Jan Cheroot whistled again when he saw the girth of the fragment of tusk. 'I have never seen an elephant so big,' he whispered, and instinctively checked the priming of his musket.

They followed the road out of the rocky pass on to forested slopes, where the trees were different, more widely spaced, and here the three old bulls had paused to strip off long slabs of bark from the msasa trunks before moving on. A mile further along the road, they found the chewed balls of bark still wet and smelling of elephant saliva, a rank gamey smell. Zouga held one of the big stringy balls to his nostrils and inhaled the elephant smell. It was the most exciting odour he had ever known.

When they rounded a shoulder of the mountain, there was a terrifying drop of open blue space before them in which the tiny shapes of vultures soared. Zouga was sure that it was the end of the road.

'Come!' Jan Cheroot whistled and they stepped out on to the narrow secret ledge, with the deep drop close at hand and followed the road that had been smoothed for them by tens of thousands of roughly padded feet over the centuries.

Zouga at last was allowing himself to hope, for the road climbed always, and there seemed to be a definite purpose and direction to it – unlike the meandering game trails of the valley. This road was going somewhere, climbing and bearing determinedly southwards.

Zouga paused a moment and looked back. Far behind and below the sunken plain of the Zambezi shimmered in the blue and smoky haze of heat. The gigantic baobab trees seemed like children's miniatures, the terrible ground over which they had laboured for weeks seemed smooth and inviting, and far away just visible through the haze the serpentine belt of darker, denser vegetation marked the course of the great wide river itself.

Zouga turned his back upon it and followed Jan Cheroot up around the shoulder of the mountain, and a new and majestic vista opened around him as dramatically as though a theatre curtain had been drawn aside.

Another steep slope stretched away above the cliffs, and there were luxuriant forests of marvellously shaped trees, the colours of their foliage was pink and flaming scarlet and iridescent green. These lovely forests reached up to a rampart of rocky peaks that Zouga was certain must mark the highest point of the escarpment.

There was something different with this new scene, and it took Zouga some moments to realize what it was. Then suddenly he drew a deep breath of pleasure. The air fanning down from the crest was sweet and cool as that on a summer's evening on the South Downs, but carrying with it the scent of strange shrubs and flowers and the soft exotic perfume of that beautiful pink and red forest of msasa trees.

That was not all, Zouga realized suddenly. There was something more important still. They had left the tsetse 'fly-belt' behind them. It was many hours and a thousand feet of climbing since he had noticed the last of the deadly little insects. The land ahead of them now was clean, they were entering a land where man could live and rear his animals. They were leaving the killing heat of that harsh and forbidding valley for something softer and cleaner, something good, Zouga was certain of it, at last.

He stared about him with delight and wonder. Below him in the void a pair of vultures came planing in on wide-stretched pinions, so close that he could see every individual feather in their wingtips, and above the shaggy mound of their nest that clung precariously to a fissure in the sheer rock cliff they beat at the air, hovering, before settling upon the nest site. Clearly Zouga heard the impatient cries of the hungry nestlings.

On the rock shelf high above his head a family of hyrax, the plump rabbit-like rock dassie, sat in a row and stared down at him with patent astonishment, fluffy as children's toys, until at last they took fright and disappeared into their rocky warrens with the speed of a conjurer's illusion.

The sun, sinking through the last quadrant of its course, lit it all with richer and mellower light, and turned the cloud ranges to splendour, tall mushroom-shaped thunderheads of silver and brightest gold, touched with fleshy pink tongues and the tinge of wild roses.

Now at last Zouga could not doubt where the elephant road was leading him and he felt his spirits soaring, his body wearied from the climb was suddenly recharged with vigour, with vaulting expectations. For he knew that those rugged peaks above him were the threshold, the very frontiers of the fabled kingdom of Monomatapa.

He wanted to push past Jan Cheroot on the narrow track, and run ahead up the broad beautiful forested slope that led to the crest, but the little yellow Hottentot stopped him with a hand upon his shoulder.

'Look!' he hissed softly. 'There they are!'

Zouga followed his outflung arm and saw instantly. Far ahead amongst those magical red and pink groves something moved, vast and grey and slow, ethereal and insubstantial as a shadow. He stared at it, feeling his heartbeat quicken at this, his first glimpse of an African elephant in its savage habitat, but the slow grey movement was immediately screened by the dense foliage.

'My telescope.' He snapped his fingers urgently behind his back, never taking his eyes from the spot where the huge beast had disappeared, and Matthew thrust the thick cylinder of cool brass into his hand.

With fingers that shook slightly he pulled out the sections of the spy-glass, but before he could lift it to his eye the tree that had screened the elephant's body began to tremble and shake as though it had been struck by a whirlwind, and faintly they heard the rending crackle of tearing timber, the squealing protest of living wood, and slowly the tall tree leaned outwards and then toppled with a crack that echoed off the cliffs like a cannon shot.

Zouga lifted the telescope and rested it on Matthew's patient shoulder. He focused the eye-piece. Abruptly, in the rounded field of the glass, the elephant was very close. His head was framed by the foliage of the tree he had uprooted. The vast ears seemed wide as a clipper's mainsail as they flapped lazily and he could see the puffs of dust that their breeze raised from the massive grey withers.

Clearly he could see the dark wet tear-path from the little eye down the sered and wrinkled cheek, and when the animal raised its head, Zouga drew breath sharply at the unbelievable size of the double arches of stained yellow ivories. One tip was foreshortened, broken off cleanly, and the ivory was brilliant snowy white in the fresh break.

As Zouga watched, the bull used his trunk, with its rubbery fingers of flesh at the tip, to pluck a handful of the delicate new leaves from the fallen tree. He used his trunk with the finesse of an expert surgeon, and then drooped open his triangular lower lip and thrust the leaves far down his own throat, and his rheumy old eyes wept with slow contentment.

An urgent tap on his shoulder disturbed Zouga and irritably he lifted his eye from the telescope. Jan Cheroot was pointing further up the slope.

Two other elephants had drifted into view from out of the forest. Zouga refocused upon them and then gasped. He had thought the first elephant massive, and here was another bull just as big – yet it was the third elephant which daunted his belief.

Beside him Jan Cheroot was whispering with suppressed tension making his voice hoarse and his slanted black eyes shine.

'The younger bulls are his two askari, his indunas. They are his ears and his eyes. For in his great age he is probably almost deaf and more than half blind, but look at him. Is he not still a king?'

The oldest bull was tall and gaunt, taller by almost a head than his protégés, but the flesh seemed to have wasted off the ancient frame. His skin hung in baggy folds and creases from the massive framework of bones. He was thin in the way that some old men are thin; time had eroded him, seeming to leave only skin and stringy sinew and brittle bone. Matthew had been right in his description, the bull moved the way an old man moves, as though each joint protested with rheumatic pangs, and the weight of ivory he had carried for a hundred years was at last too much for him.

The ivory had once been the symbol of his majesty, and it was still perfect, flaring out from the lip and then turning in again so the points almost met. The gracious curves seemed perfectly matched, and the ivory was a lovely, butter yellow, unblemished despite the dominance battles he had fought with them, despite the forest trees that the bull had toppled with them and stripped of their bark or the desert roots he had dug from stony soil with them.

But now, at last, these great tusks were a burden to him, they wearied him and he carried his head low as they ached in his old jaws. It had been many years now since he had used them as fearsome weapons to keep control of the breeding herds. It had been as many years since he had sought the company of the young cows and their noisy squealing calves.

Now the long yellow ivories were a mortal danger to him, as well as a source of discomfort and pain. They made him attractive to man, his only enemy in nature. Always it seemed that the hunters were camped upon his spoor, and the man-smell was associated with the flash and thudding discharge of muzzle-loading firearms, or the rude stinging intrusion of sharpened steel into his tired old flesh.

There were pieces of beaten iron pot-leg and of round hardened lead ball deep in his body, the shot lying against the bone castle of his skull had become encysted with gristle and formed lumps as big as ripe apples beneath the skin, while the scars from arrows and stabbing spears, from the fire-hardened wood spikes of the dead-fall-trap had thickened into shiny grey scars and become part of the rough, folded and creased mantle of his bald grey hide.

Without his two askari he would long ago have fallen to the hunters. It was a strangely intimate relationship that knit the little herd of old bulls, and it had lasted for twenty years or more. Together they had trekked tens of thousands of miles, from the Cashan mountains in the far south, across the burning, waterless wastes of the Kalahari desert, along the dry river beds where they had knelt and with their tusks dug for water in the sand. They had wallowed together in the shallow lake of Ngami while the wings of the water fowl darkened the sky above them, and they had stripped the bark from the forests along Linyati and Chobe, and crossed those wide rivers, walking on the bottom with just the tips of their trunks raised above the surface to give them breath.

Over the seasons they had swung in a great circle through the wild land that lay north of the Zambezi, feasting on the fruits of different forests scattered over a thousand miles, timing their arrival as each crop of berries came into full ripening.

They had crossed lakes and rivers, had stayed long in the hot swamps of the Sud where the midday heat, reaching 120°, soothed the aches in the old bull's bones. But then the wanderlust had driven them on to complete the circle of their migration, south again over mountain ranges and across the low alluvial plains of the great rivers, following secret trails and ancient passes that their ancestors had forged and which they had first trodden as calves at their mother's flank.

In these last dozen seasons, however, there were men where there had never been men before. There were white-robed Arabs in the north around the lakes, with their long-barrelled jezails. There were big bearded men in the south, dressed in dark rough homespun and hunting from tough shaggy little ponies, while everywhere they met the tiny little bushmen with their wicked poisoned arrows, or the Nguni regiments hunting a thousand strong, driving the game into set positions where the plumed spearmen waited.

With each round of the seasons, the elephant ranges were shrinking, new terrors and new dangers waited in the ancient ancestral feeding grounds and the old bull was tired and his bones ached and the ivory in his jaws weighed him down. Still he moved on up the slope to the head of the pass with slow determination and dignity, driven on by his instincts, by the need for space about him, by the memory of the taste of the fruits he knew were already ripening in a distant forest on the shores of a far-away lake.

'We must hurry.' Jan Cheroot's voice roused Zouga, for he had been mesmerized by the sight of the regal old animal, filled with a strange feeling of *déjà-vu*, as though he had lived this moment before, as though this meeting was part of his destiny. The old bull filled him with awe, with a sense of timelessness and grandeur, so he was reluctant to return to the reality of the moment.

'The day dies fast,' Jan Cheroot insisted, and Zouga glanced over his shoulder to where the sun was setting like a mortally wounded warrior bleeding upon the clouds.

'Yes,' he acknowledged, and then frowned as he realized that Jan Cheroot was stripping off his puttees and breeches, folding them and stuffing them together with his blanket and food bag into a crevice in the rock face beside him.

'I run faster like this,' he answered Zouga's silent enquiry with a twinkling grin.

Zouga followed his example, leaving his own pack and pulling off the webbing belt from which hung knife and compass, stripping down to good running order, but he stopped short of removing his breeches. Jan Cheroot's skinny naked yellow buttocks were totally devoid of dignity and his dangling penis played hide-and-seek from under his shirt tails. There were some conventions that an officer of the Queen must observe, Zouga decided firmly, and one was to keep his breeches on in public. He followed Jan Cheroot along the narrow ledge, until they stepped off it on to the forested slope and immediately their forward vision was limited to a dozen yards by the lichen-covered tree trunks. From higher up the slope, however, they could hear the crackle and the ripping sound as the bull with the broken tusk fed on the uprooted tree.

Jan Cheroot worked out swiftly across the slope to avoid the askari, to circle around him and come at the lead bull. Twice he paused to check the wind. It held steadily down the slope into their faces and the colourful leaves above their heads quivered and sighed at its passing.

They had gone a hundred yards when the sounds of the feeding bull ceased abruptly; again Jan Cheroot paused and the little group of hunters froze with him, every man instinctively holding his breath as they listened, but there was only the sound of the wind and the singing whine of a cicada in the branches above.

'He has moved on to join the others,' Jan Cheroot whispered at last. Zouga was also certain that the bull could not yet have suspected their presence. The wind was steady, he could not have scented them. Zouga knew that the eyesight of the elephant was as weak as his hearing and sense of smell were acute, but they had made no sound.

Yet this was a clear demonstration of the benefits that the three old bulls derived from their association. It was always difficult for the hunter to place each of them accurately, especially in thick forest such as this, and the two askaris seemed always to take station on the lead bull to cover and protect him. To come at him, the hunter must penetrate the screen they threw around him.

Standing now, listening and waiting, Zouga wondered if a genuine affection existed between the three animals, whether they derived the pleasure of companionship from each other, and whether the askaris would mourn or pine when the old bull fell at last with the musket ball in his brain or his heart.

'Come!' Silently Jan Cheroot made the open-handed signal to advance and they went on up the slope, stooping under the low trailing branches, Zouga keeping four paces out on the Hottentot's flank to open his field of vision and fire, concentrating his whole being in his eyes and his ears. Far up the slope there was the snap of a breaking twig and it stopped them dead once more, breathing shallowly with the tension, but the sound fastened all their attention ahead so none of them saw the askari.

The elephant waited with the stillness of granite, his sered hide grey and rough as the lichen-covered tree trunks, the shadows thrown by the low sun barred him and broke up the shape of his great body so he blended into the forest, grey and unearthly as mist, and they tiptoed past him at twenty paces without seeing him.

He let the hunters pass him and get up above the wind and when the acrid stench of carnivorous man was borne thickly down to him through the forest, he took it in his trunk and lifted it to his mouth and sprayed the tainted air over the little olfactory organs under his upper lip, and his smell buds flared open like soft wet pink rose buds and the askari bull squealed.

It was a sound that seemed to bounce against the sky, and ring from the peaks above them, it was an expression of all the hatred and pain, the terrible memories of that acrid man-smell from a hundred other encounters, and the askari bull squealed again and launched his huge body up the slope to destroy the source of that evil odour.

Zouga spun to the piercing din, his shocked eardrums still buzzing with the sound, and the forest shook with the bull's charge. The dense shiny vegetation burst open, like a storm surf running on to rock, and the bull came through.

Zouga was not conscious of his own movements, he was aware only that he was looking at the bull over the open sights of the Sharps rifle, and the blast of shot seemed muted and far off after the ringing squeal that initiated the charge. He saw dust fly from the bull's forehead in a brief little puff, saw the grey skin ripple like that of a stallion stung by a bee, and he reached back and found the stubby wooden stock of one of the big elephant guns in his hand. Again, there was no awareness of conscious movement, but over the crude vee of the sight the elephant appeared much closer. Zouga seemed to be leaning back to look up at the gigantic head and the long shafts of yellow ivory reached out over him, blotting out the sky. Clearly he could see the bright white porcelain break in one point of the left-hand tusk.

He heard Jan Cheroot beside him, and heard his excited shrieks.

'*Skiet hom!* Shoot him!'

Then the heavy weapon leapt against his own shoulder, driving him back a pace, and he saw the tiny fountain of bright blood squirting out of the elephant's throat like a lovely scarlet flamingo feather. He reached back for the next loaded gun, although he knew there would be no time to fire again.

He was surprised that he felt no fear, although he knew he was a dead man. The elephant was on him, his life was forfeit, there could be no question, yet he went on with the motions of living, hefting the new gun, thumbing back the clumsy hammer as he swung the barrel up.

The shape of the huge animal above him had altered, it was no longer so close, and he realized with a thrill that the bull was turning, it had been unable to endure the fearful punishment of the heavy-bored guns.

He was turning, passing by them with blood streaming down his head and chest. As he passed, he exposed his neck and flank, and Zouga shot him a hand's span behind the joint of his shoulder on the line of the lungs and the ball slogged into his rib cage.

The bull was going, crashing away up the slope, and with the fourth gun Zouga hit him high in the back, aiming for the bony knuckles of the spine where they showed through the scabby grey hide of the sloping back and the bull whipped his thick tufted tail at the agony of the strike and disappeared into the forest, gone like a wraith in the failing light of the sunset.

Zouga and Jan Cheroot stared at each other speechlessly, each of them holding a smoking weapon at high port across his chest, and they listened to the run of the bull up the slope ahead of them.

Zouga found his voice first, he turned to his gunbearers.

'Load!' he hissed at them, for they also were paralysed by the close passage of violent, thundering death, but his command liberated them and they each snatched a handful of black powder from the bag slung at their sides and poured it into the still-hot muzzles of the guns.

'The lead bull and the other askari will run,' lamented Jan Cheroot, himself frantically busy with ramrod of his Enfield.

'We can still catch them before the summit,' Zouga told him, grabbing the first loaded gun. An elephant goes on a steep uphill at a very measured pace that a good runner can gain upon, but downhill he goes like a run-away locomotive, nothing can catch him, not even a good horse.

'We must catch them before the crest,' Zouga repeated, and launched himself at the slope. Weeks of hard going over bad terrain had toughened him, and the driving lust of the hunter was the spur. He flew at the slope.

Awareness of his own lack of experience that had resulted in such poor shooting, made Zouga more fiercely determined to close with the lead bull and vindicate himself. He guessed that as a complete novice he had failed to find the vitals with any of the balls he had fired, he had missed brain and heart and lungs by inches, inflicting pain and mutilation, instead of the quick kill for which the true huntsman strives. He wanted desperately to have another chance to end it cleanly, and he pelted up the slope.

Before he had gone two hundred yards, he had evidence that his shooting had not been as wide as he had at first believed. He checked at a spot where it looked as though someone had thrown a bucket of blood across the stony earth. The blood was a peculiarly bright scarlet, and it frothed with tiny bubbles, lung blood. There was no question, that last ball fired into the bull's back as he went away up the slope must have raked the lungs. It was a killing shot, but a slow killer. The old bull was drowning in his own bright arterial blood, desperately trying to rid himself of it by squirting it out through his trunk as it bubbled up into his throat.

He was dying, but it would take time still, and Zouga raced on after him.

He had not expected the bull to stand again. He expected him to run until he dropped, or until the hunters caught up with him. Zouga knew the folly of attributing human motives and loyalties to wild animals, even so it seemed that the stricken bull had determined to sacrifice himself in order to allow the lead bull and the second askari to escape across the pass at the crest of the mountains.

Up the slope, he was waiting for Zouga, listening for him with those vast grey ears spread wide, his chest with the girth of a Cognac cask of Limousine oak racked and strained to force air into his torn lung.

He charged as soon as he heard the man. His huge ears cocked back and rolled at the tips, trunk curled at his chest, shrilling and squealing, blowing a fine red mist of blood from his trunk, pounding through the forest so the earth trembled with each massive footfall and the branches crackled and broke like a discharge of musketry.

Panting, Zouga stood to meet the charge, ducking his head and weaving for a clean shot through the thick forest. At the last moment the bull broke off the charge, and swerved up the slope again. Each time the hunters began to move forward, he launched another thunderous mock-attack, forcing them to stand to meet him, and then breaking off again.

Minutes passed between each charge, and the hunters were pinned down in the thick forest, fretting with the knowledge that already the lead bull and his surviving protégé must have reached the crest and gone away in a rush like an avalanche down the far side.

Zouga was learning two hard lessons: the first, as old Tom Harkness had tried to teach him, was that only a novice or a fool undercuts an elephant. The light ball of the Sharps might be highly effective on American bison, but the African elephant had ten times the body weight and resistance. Standing in the msasa forests, listening to the squealing and crashing of the wounded monster, Zouga determined never again to use the light American rifle on heavy game.

The second lesson he was learning was that if the first ball does not kill, then it seems to numb and anaesthetize heavy game to further punishment. Kill cleanly, or the subsequent shots into heart and lungs seem to be without effect. It was not only anger and provocation which made a wounded animal so dangerous, it was also this shock-induced immortality.

After standing down half a dozen mock charges, Zouga abandoned caution and patience, and he ran forward shouting to meet the next charge.

'Whoa there!' he called. 'Come on then, old fellow!'

This time he got in close, and crashed another ball through the bull's rib cage as he turned away. He had controlled his first wild excitement, and the ball struck precisely at the point of aim. He knew it was a heart shot, but the bull came again squealing, and Zouga fired a last time before the angry trumpeting and shrilling turned to a long sad bellow, that echoed off the peaks and rang out into the blue void of sky beyond the cliffs.

They heard him go down, the impact of the heavy body against the earth made it shiver under their feet. Cautiously, the little group of hunters went forward through the forest and they found him kneeling, his forelegs folded neatly under his chest, his long, yellow ivories propping up the dusty wrinkled old head, still facing down the slope as though defiant even in death.

'Leave him,' shouted Jan Cheroot. 'Follow the others.' And they ran on past him.

Night caught them before they reached the crest of the slope, the sudden impenetrably black night of central Africa, so they lost the spoor and missed the pass.

'We will have to let them go,' Jan Cheroot lamented in the darkness, his yellow face a pale blob at Zouga's shoulder.

'Yes,' Zouga agreed. 'This time we must let them go.' But somehow he knew there would be another time. The feeling that the old bull was part of his destiny was still strongly with Zouga. Yes, there would be another time, of that he was certain.

That night for the first time Zouga ate the hunter's greatest delicacy: slices of elephant heart threaded on to a green stick with cubes of white fat cut out from the chest cavity, salted and peppered, and roasted over the slow coals of the camp fire, eaten with cold cakes of stone-ground corn and washed down with a mug of tea, steaming hot, bitter, strong and unsweetened. He could not remember a finer meal, and afterwards Zouga lay down on the hard earth, covered by a single blanket and protected from the chill of the wind by the huge carcass of the old bull, and slept as though he also had been struck down, without dreams, without rolling over even once in his sleep.

In the morning, by the time they had chopped out one of the tusks and laid it under the msasa trees, they could already hear the singing of the porters as the main body of the caravan filed along the narrow ledge, rounding the shoulder of the mountain and then came up on to the slope.

Robyn was a hundred paces ahead of the standard-bearer, and when she reached the carcass of the bull she stopped.

'We heard the gunfire last evening,' she said.

'He's a fine old bull,' Zouga told her, indicating the freshly chopped tusk. It was the unbroken right-hand ivory, taller than Zouga, but a third of its length had been buried in the skull. This portion was smooth, unblemished white, whereas the rest of it was stained by vegetable juices.

'It will weigh almost a hundred pounds,' he went on, touching the tusks with the toe of his boot. 'Yes, he's a fine old bull.'

'Not any more, he isn't,' Robyn told him quietly, watching Jan Cheroot and the gunbearers hacking away at the enormous mutilated head. Little chips of white bone flew in the early sunlight, as they whittled away the heavy skull to free the second tusk. Robyn watched the butchery for a few seconds only before going on up the slope towards the crest.

Zouga was irritated and angry with her, for she had detracted from his own vaulting pleasure in his first elephant hunt. So, an hour later when he heard Robyn calling to him from higher up the slope, he ignored her cries. However, she was persistent, as always, and at last with an exclamation of exasperation, he followed her up through the forest. She came running down to meet him, with the unrestrained infectious joy of a child shining on her face.

'Oh Zouga.' She seized his hand, and began to drag him impetuously up the slope. 'Come and see, you must come and see.'

The old elephant road crossed the saddle, through a deep pass, guarded on each hand by grey buttresses of rough grey rock and as they took the last few paces over the highest point a new and beautiful world opened below and ahead of them. Zouga gasped involuntarily, for he had not anticipated anything like this.

Low foothills fell away from beneath their feet, regular as the swells of the ocean, covered with stately trees whose trunks were tall and grey as the oaks of Windsor Park, and then beyond the hills the undulating lightly forested grass-lands, golden as fields of ripe wheat, spread to a tall blue horizon. There were streams of clear water meandering through the glades of pale grass, where herds of wild game drank or lazed upon the banks.

There were buffalo everywhere Zouga looked, black bovine shapes, standing shoulder to shoulder in dark masses under the umbrella branches of the acacia trees. Closer at hand a troop of sable antelope, that loveliest of all antelope, jet black above but with snowy bellies, their long symmetrical curve of horn extended backwards almost to touch the haunches, followed the herd bull in long file to the water, pausing unafraid to stare curiously at the interlopers, forming a frieze of stately, almost Grecian, design.

The endless stretch of land was dotted with hills like ruined natural castles of stone, seeming to have been built in past aeons by giants and ogres from mammoth blocks of stone, and tumbled now in fastastic shapes, some with fairy turrets and spires, others again flat topped, geometrically laid out as though by a meticulous architect with plumb-line and theodolite.

This lovely scene was lit by a peculiar pearly luminosity of the morning light, so that even the furthest hills, probably more than a hundred miles distant, were sharply silhouetted through the sweet clear air.

'It's beautiful,' Robyn murmured, still holding Zouga's hand.

'The kingdom of Monomatapa,' Zouga answered her, his own voice husky with emotion.

'No,' Robyn answered softly. 'There is no sign of man here, this is the new Eden.'

Zouga was silent, letting his eyes rove across the scene, searching for, but not finding, any evidence of man. It was a land untouched, unspoiled.

'A new land, there for the taking!' he said, still holding Robyn's hand. They were as close, in that moment, as they had ever been or would ever be again, and the land awaited them, wide, limitless, empty and beautiful.

At last, reluctantly, he left Robyn at the head of the pass and went back through the grey rock portals to bring on the caravan. He found the second tusk removed, and both of them bound up with bark rope on to the carrying-poles of newly cut msasa wood, but the porters had laid aside their packs and were indulging in an orgy of fresh meat, and that most sought-after of African spoils, thick white globs of elephant fat.

They had cut a trapdoor into the belly of the elephant carcass, and pulled out the entrails, and these glistened in the early sunlight, huge rubbery tubes of purple and yellow guts, already swelling and ballooning with the trapped gases they contained.

Half a dozen porters, stripped mother-naked, had crawled into the interior of the elephant's carcass, disappearing completely from view and wading almost waist-deep in the clotting, congealing bath of trapped blood. They crawled out, painted with it from head to foot, eyes and grinning teeth startlingly white in the grisly shining wet red visages, their arms filled with tidbits of liver and fat and spleen.

These delicacies were hacked into pieces with the blade of an assegai and thrown on the glowing coals of one of half a dozen fires, then snatched up again, black on the outside and more than half raw within to be wolfed down with every appearance of ecstatic pleasure.

There would be no moving them until they were satiated, Zouga realized. So he left instructions to Jan Cheroot, himself already pot-bellied with the meat he had gorged, to follow as soon as the carcass had been either eaten or packed up for carrying, and taking the Sharps rifle returned back up the slope to where he had left Robyn.

He called for her, fruitlessly, for almost half an hour, and was really becoming concerned for her safety when her reply echoed off the cliffs, and looking upwards he saw her standing on a ledge a hundred feet above him, waving him to come up to her.

Zouga climbed up swiftly to where she stood on the ledge, and checked the rebuke that he had ready for her when he saw her expression. She was pale, a sickly greyish colour, under the gilding of the sun, and her eyes were reddened and still swimming with tears.

'What is it, Sissy?' he asked with quick concern, but she seemed unable to reply, the words choking in her throat so she had to swallow thickly, and motion him to follow her.

The ledge on which they stood was narrow, but level – and was cut back under the cliff, forming a low long cavern. The cavern had been used before by other men, for the rocky roof was blackened with the sooty smoke of countless cooking-fires, and the back wall was decorated with the lyrically childlike paintings of the little yellow bushmen who over the centuries must have used this as a regular camp during their endless wanderings.

The paintings lacked both perspective and accurate form, but they captured the essential nature of all they recorded, from the graceful sweep of the giraffe's neck, to the bulky shoulders of the Cape buffalo with the mournful drooping horns framing the lifted nose.

The bushman artist saw himself and his tribe as frail, sticklike figures, with drawn bows, dancing and prancing about the quarry, and again, out of all proportion to the rest of the painting, each little man sported a massively erect penis. Even in the heat of the chase, such was the universal conceit of all male kind, Zouga thought.

Zouga was enchanted by the frozen cavalcade of man and beast which covered the walls of the cave, and he had already determined to camp here so that he could have more time to study and record this treasure house of primitive art, when Robyn was calling him again.

He followed her along the ledge until they reached the point where it ended abruptly, forming a balcony over the dreaming land ahead of them. Zouga's attention was torn between this fresh vista of forest and glade and the cave art at his shoulder, but Robyn summoned him again impatiently.

There were strata of multi-coloured rock running horizontally through the rock face of the cliff. The different layers of rock varied in hardness, and the erosion of a softer layer had formed the long low cavern beyond the ledge.

This layer of rock was a soapy green colour, where it had not been painted over by the bushmen artists or discoloured with the smoke of their fires, and here at the point overlooking the empire of Monomatapa someone had used a metal tool to scrape a smooth square plaque into the green soapstone. The freshly cut surface stood out rawly as though it had been done that very day, but the words gave the lie to that impression.

There was a simple Christian cross chiselled deeply into the stone, and below it the name and the date, the lettering very carefully cut and designed by an expert penman.

'FULLER MORRIS BALLANTYNE'

Zouga exclaimed aloud at seeing his father's name, so clearly rendered by his father's own hand.

Despite the apparent freshness of the cut, the date was seven years previously – 20th July, 1853. After that single exclamation they were both speechless, staring at the inscription, each of them gripped by differing emotion – Robyn by a resurgence of filial love and duty, by a crushing desire to be with her father again after so many years, the vast empty place in her life aching more excruciatingly at the prospect of being soon filled. Her eyes refilled with tears, and they broke from her eyelids and ran down her cheeks.

'Please, God,' she prayed silently, 'lead me to my father. Dear God, grant me that I am not too late.'

Zouga's emotions were as strong, but different. He felt a corroding resentment that any other man, father or not, should have preceded him through these rocky gates into the kingdom of Monomatapa. This was his land, and he did not want to share it with another. Especially, he did not want to share it with that monster of cruelty and conceit that was his father.

He stared coldly at the inscription that followed the name and date, but inwardly he seethed with anger and resentment.

'In God's Holy name.' The words were carved below his father's name.

It was typical of Fuller Ballantyne that he should carve his own name here with cross and credentials as the Lord's ambassador, as he had on trees and rocks at a hundred other places across the continent which he regarded as a personal gift from his God.

'You were right, Zouga dear. You are leading us to him, as you promised. I should never have doubted you.'

If he had been alone Zouga realized that he might have defaced that inscription, scraped the rock bare with his hunting knife, but as he had the thought, he realized how futile it would be, for such an action would not wipe out the ghostly presence of the man himself.

Zouga turned away from the rock wall and its taunting plaque. He stared out over the new land – but somehow his heady pleasure in it had been dimmed by the knowledge that another man had passed this way ahead of him. He sat down with his feet dangling over the sheer drop to wait for Robyn to tire of staring at her father's name.

However, the caravan of porters came before she did that. Zouga heard the singing from the forested slope behind the pass long before the head of the line crossed the saddle. The porters had voluntarily doubled their own loads, and they struggled up the slope under the enormous weight of elephant meat and fat and marrow bones, bound up in baskets of green msasa leaves and bark rope.

If Zouga had asked them to carry that weight of trade cloth or beads, or even gunpowder, he would have had an immediate mutiny to deal with, he thought grimly, but at least they were carrying the tusks. He could see them near the head of the line. Each tusk slung on a long pole, a man at either end, but even here they had hung extra baskets of meat on the same pole as the tusk. The total weight must have been well over three hundred pounds, and they struggled up the slope uncomplainingly, even cheerfully.

Slowly, the caravan wound out of the forest and entered the gut of the pass, beginning to move directly under where Zouga sat, the figures of the porters and of Jan Cheroot's Hottentot musketeers foreshortened by the angle. Zouga rose to his feet, he wanted to order Jan Cheroot to camp just beyond the point where the pass debouched on to the foothills. From where Zouga stood, he could see a patch of green grass against the foot of the cliffs far below him, and a pair of pale grey herons hunting frogs in this verdant marshy area. There was certainly a spring, and with the meat upon which they had gorged, his servants would be burning with thirst by nightfall.

The spring would be a good place to camp, and it would allow him the following morning to copy and record the Bushman paintings in the cavern. He cupped his hands to his mouth to hail Jan Cheroot – when a crash like the broadside from a ship-of-the-line filled the pass with thunder that echoed and bounced back and forth between the cliffs.

For many seconds Zouga could not understand what was happening – for the thunderous bursts of sound were repeated, almost drowning the thin screams of his porters. They were throwing down their burdens and scattering like a flight of doves under the stoop of the falcon.

Then another movement caught his attention, a large round shape went bounding down the scree slope below the cliffs, charging straight at his panic-stricken caravan. For a moment Zouga believed it was some sort of living predator that was attacking his servants, and, running along the lip of the ledge, he unslung the Sharps rifle, ready to fire down into the pass as soon as he could get a sight on one of the dark bounding shapes.

Then he realized that at each leap the thing struck sparks and fine grey smoke from the scree slope, and he could smell the faint smell, like burnt salt-petre that the sparks left in the air. He realized abruptly that they were giant rounded boulders rolling down upon his caravan, not one but a dozen or more, each weighing many tons, an onslaught which seemed to spring from the very air itself, and he looked wildly about for its source, goaded by the screams of his men and the sight of the rolling boulders smashing open packs of his precious irreplaceable provisions and scattering them across the rocky ground of the saddle.

Far below him, he heard the thudding report of an Enfield rifle, and glancing back he saw the tiny figure of Jan Cheroot aiming almost directly upwards at the sky, and following the direction of his rifle Zouga saw movement, just a flicker of movement on the edge of the cliff, outlined against the blue soaring vault of the heavens.

The deluge of huge boulders was coming from the very top of the cliff, and as Zouga stared, another and then another came raining down into the pass. Zouga squinted his eyes, head thrown back, as he studied the cliff rim. There was some animal up there. Zouga did not at first think of man, for he had already convinced himself that this new land was devoid of human presence.

He felt an almost superstitious chill of horror that some pack of giant apes was on top of the cliff, bombarding his men with huge rocks, then he shook himself free of the feeling, and looked quickly for some way to get higher up his side of the pass, to reach a position from where he could fire across the rocky gateway at the attackers on the opposite cliff and give some protection to his servants.

Almost immediately he discovered another ledge rising at a steep angle from the one on which he stood. Only a soldier's eye would have picked it out. The tiny feet of the little rock hyrax that used it had put a light sheen on the rock and it was this that had drawn Zouga's attention to the narrow pathway.

'Stay here!' he shouted at Robyn, but she stepped in front of him.

'Zouga, what are you going to do?' she demanded, and then before he could answer. 'Those are men up there! You cannot fire upon them!' Her cheeks were still smeared with tears, but her pale face was set and determined.

'Get out of the way,' he snapped at her.

'Zouga, it will be murder.'

'That's what they are trying to do to my men.'

'We must bargain with them.' Robyn caught at his arm as he pushed past her, but he shook her off and ran to the higher ledge.

'It will be murder!' Robyn's cry followed him, and as he climbed, Zouga was reminded of the words of old Tom Harkness. The accusation that his father would not stop at killing anybody who stood in his way. This was what he had meant, Zouga was suddenly sure of it. He wondered if his father had fought his way through this pass, just as Zouga himself was about to do.

'If the champion of the Almighty can do it, then what a fine example to follow,' he muttered to himself as he went up the steep ledge.

Below him the Enfield rifle thudded again, the sound muted by distance, almost lost in the roar of a new avalanche of murderous rock. Jan Cheroot could only hope to discourage his attackers with rifle fire from that angle; only if one of them actually leaned far out over the edge of the cliff would he be vulnerable to fire from the gut of the pass.

Zouga climbed in cold anger, stepping unhesitatingly over dangerous spots in the narrow ledge where small pieces of rock crumbled under his boots and went rattling down into the pass hundreds of feet below.

Abruptly he came out on to a broader ledge, formed by the strata of rock, which rose at a gentler pitch so that now Zouga could run along it without fear of losing his footing. He climbed swiftly, it was less than ten minutes since that first boulder had come crashing down into the pass; the attackers were continuing the bombardment, the hill reverberated with the crash and rumble of flying boulders.

Ahead of Zouga on the ledge, a pair of tiny grey klipspringer went bouncing up over broken rock, seeming to flit on the tips of their elongated hooves, terrified by the men and the rumble of falling rock. They reached the corner of the ledge and one after another they made what seemed suicidal leaps out into space, phenomenal leaps that carried them forty feet to the next sheer wall of rock, rock which seemed devoid of foothold, but they clung to it like flies and scrambled swiftly up out of sight over the top of the cliff.

Zouga envied them that birdlike agility as he toiled up the steep incline, sweat soaking his shirt and streaming stingingly into his eyes. He could not stop to rest, for far below him a thin wailing scream of agony told him that at least one of the flying boulders had struck down a porter.

He turned another steep corner in the goat track, scrambled over the rim, and was suddenly out upon the flat table-like summit, dotted with little clumps of broom-bush and sparse stiff yellow grass, like hedgehog quills.

Zouga threw himself down on the edge of the plateau, heaving and straining for breath and he struck the sweat from his eyes, peering across the deep void of the pass at the cliffs on the opposite side. He found himself on a level with the heights opposite. It was three or four hundred yards across, easy range for the Sharps – though one of the smooth-bore four-to-the-pounds would have been hopelessly inaccurate at that distance.

While he primed the rifle, he studied the ground opposite him and saw almost immediately why the attackers had chosen that side of the pass in preference to the one on which Zouga lay.

They were on a flat-topped pinnacle of sheer rock, with no visible access to it from any direction, what path there was would be secret and highly defensible. The attackers had an inexhaustible supply of missiles for the rounded boulders were scattered everywhere upon the heights, varying in size from that of a man's head to that of an elephant carcass, and as Zouga watched them they were using heavy raw timber baulks to lever one of these over the edge of the cliff.

Zouga's hands were shaking and he fought to bring them under control, but the Sharps rifle wavered as he tried to take a sight on the little group of men across the open void of space. There were not more than two dozen of them, all of them naked except for a brief kilt of leather, their dark skins polished with a sheen of sweat in the sunlight.

He was regaining his breath swiftly, and now he wriggled forward on his belly and propped the stock of the Sharps rifle on a rock in front of him. It was a dead rest, and as he levelled his gaze over the open sights the group of men succeeded in working the huge boulder over the edge of the cliff.

It went with a brief grating that carried clearly to Zouga, and then it fell with the soft rushing of eagle's wings until it struck again in the pass two hundred feet below – and once again the hills rang and rumbled to the force and weight of it.

The little group of black men had drawn back from the edge of the cliff, resting a moment before they selected another missile. Only one of them wore a headdress. It looked like a cap made from the mane of a male lion, long tawny hair tipped with black. It made the man taller than his companions, and he seemed to be giving orders to them, gesticulating and pushing those nearest to him.

'You'll do, my beauty!' Zouga whispered. He had regained his breath now, and the sweat was cooling his back and his neck. He pushed up the leaf of his backsight to its 300-yard adjustment and then settled down on his elbows to peer over it. The rifle was rock-steady on its rest, while he took a fine bead on the man with the lion headdress.

He touched off the shot, and while the crack of it still stung his eardrums he saw a tiny chip of rock fly from the lip of the cliff across the valley. 'Low, but very nicely on line,' he told himself, opened the breech of the Sharps and forced the paper cartridge into it.

The shot had startled the little group of men. They peered about them, mystified, not certain of what it was or from where it had come. The tall figure in the headdress moved cautiously forward to the edge of the cliff and stooped to examine the fresh chip on the ironstone rim, touching it with one finger.

Zouga set the cap, and thumbed back the hammer. He gave it a full bead, and aimed at the waving yellow headdress, set the hair-trigger and then with a lover's touch stroked the curved trigger.

The bullet told loudly, a meaty slap like a housewife beating a carpet, and the man in the lion headdress spun round sharply, his arms jerking out wide, his legs shuffling in a grotesque little dance, they collapsed under him and he flopped on the very edge of the cliff like a harpooned catfish.

His companions stood frozen, making no effort to help him as he slid towards the edge of the cliff, and a final spasmodic jerk of his legs tumbled him into the void. He fell for a long time, his outspread limbs spinning like the spokes of a wagon wheel, and there was another meaty thump as he landed at last on the broken scree slope far below.

Zouga fired again, into the tight knot of men, not attempting to single out one of them, and he hit two of them with a single bullet, for even at that range the Sharps could drive the hardened lead ball through a man's body with hardly any loss of velocity, and the group was bunched up.

As the ball whacked into them, they split into separate racing figures, their yells of fright carrying clearly to where Zouga lay, and before he could fire again, they had disappeared into a narrow rocky gulley with the miraculous speed of a troop of little furry hyrax.

The silence was sudden and startling after the uproar of falling boulders and heavy gun fire and it lasted for many minutes, broken at last by the shrill voice of Jan Cheroot calling up from the deep gut of the pass. Zouga stood up, and hanging on to the branch of a monkey orange tree, leaned out over the edge of the cliff.

'Take the caravan through, Sergeant.' He pitched his voice to carry, and the echoes mocked him with his own words. 'Sergeant – Sergeant – Sergeant –'

'I will cover you – cover you – cover you,' taunted the echoes.

Zouga called the little Matabele maiden from the fireside where she knelt beside Robyn, helping her treat one of the porters who had been struck by a flying splinter of rock during the attack, and whose shoulder had been laid open to the bone.

'Juba,' he told her, 'I want you to come with me.' And the girl glanced back at Robyn, hesitating to obey him. Zouga's irritation flared again. He and Robyn had not spoken again since Zouga had broken up the attack with rifle fire, and Jan Cheroot had reassembled the caravan and led it out of the deadly trap of the gorge to where it was camped now in the foothills beyond the pass.

'Come,' Zouga repeated, and the child dropped her eyes at his tone and followed him submissively as he started back towards the pass.

Zouga moved back cautiously, pausing every fifty paces or so to survey the clifftops suspiciously, although he was fairly certain that there would be no renewal of the boulder rolling. However, he kept in close under the sheer rock face so that any boulder would fall beyond them.

The going was difficult over the loose scree, and through the thick scrub that covered it. It took them nearly an hour to get back to the spot where Zouga had marked the fall of the body of the warrior in the lion headdress, and then they had to search for nearly as long again before they found the corpse.

He had fallen into a deep crevice between two rocks, and he lay at the bottom of it on his back. The body appeared unmarked except for the small black bullet hole low on the left side of his naked chest.

The eyes were still wide open, but he had lost his headdress.

After a moment Zouga turned to Juba enquiringly. 'Who is he? Of what tribe is he?' he asked, and the child showed no concern at the presence of violent death. She had seen very much worse in her short life.

'Mashona!' she told Zouga scornfully. Juba was Matabele of Zanzi blood, and there was no more noble breeding outside the kraal of King Mzilikazi himself. She felt nothing but contempt for all the other tribes of Africa, especially for these people.

'Mashona!' she repeated. 'Eaters of dirt.'

It was the ultimate term of denigration that the Matabele applied to all the tribes that they have taken into slavery, or driven to the very point of extinction.

'It is always the way these baboons fight.' She indicated the dead man with a toss of her pretty head. 'They stand on the hilltops and throw down stones.'

Her dark eyes sparkled. 'It becomes more difficult each year for our young men to blood their spears, and until they do so the King will not give them leave to marry.' She broke off, and Zouga smiled ironically. The child's resentment was clearly not so much at the Mashona's alleged lack of sportsmanship, but at the havoc that this wrought on the Matabele marriage markets.

Zouga scrambled down into the rocky crevice, and stooped over the dead warrior. Despite Juba's contempt, the man was well formed, with straight strong limbs, and handsome intelligent features. For the first time Zouga felt a twinge of regret at having fired the ball which had caused that innocuous-looking little wound. It was a good thing that the warrior lay upon his back for the exit would have been ghastly. A soldier should never examine the bodies of the men he kills in the heat of battle. Zouga had made that discovery long ago in India, for afterwards there was always this moment of guilt and remorse. He shrugged it away, for he had not come either to gloat over the kill or to torture himself with it, but to merely identify his enemy.

Why had these warriors attacked the caravan without warning, he wondered? Were they the border guards of the fabled Monomatapa? It seemed the most likely explanation, though, of course, they could be ordinary bandits, like the dacoits of India with whom he had made bitter acquaintance.

Zouga stared moodily down at the corpse. Who had he been? And how much danger did his tribe still present to Zouga's caravan? But there was nothing more to learn and Zouga began to straighten up again when he noticed the necklace around the corpse's throat. He knelt again to examine it.

It was made of cheap trade beads on a thong of gut, a gaudy little trifle except for the pendant that had hung on to his chest but had slipped back under the armpit, half concealed so that Zouga noticed it now for the first time.

He pulled it free, examined it a moment and then slipped the entire necklace off over the man's head. When he put his hand around the back of the dead man's head to lift it he felt the pieces of skull grate together deep in his head like shards of broken pottery under his fingers. He lowered the shattered head and stood up with the necklace twined about his fingers, examining the pendant.

It had been carved from ivory that had yellowed with age, and tiny black cracks formed a fine web across its polished surfaces. Zouga held it to catch the sunlight, and turned it between his fingers to study it from every angle.

He had seen another figurine that was almost a twin to this one, a golden figurine that was now in a bank vault in Cape Town where he had deposited it before they had sailed on board the gunboat *Black Joke.*

This was the same stylized bird-like shape, perched on a round plinth. The plinth was decorated with the same triangular shark's-teeth pattern, and the bird had the same swelling chest and short, sharply pointed wings folded across its back. It could have been a pigeon or a dove, except for one detail. The beak was the curved and hooked weapon of a raptor.

It was a falcon, he knew it beyond any doubt, and it was certain that the heraldic bird had some deep significance. The golden necklace that Tom Harkness had left him must have belonged to a king or a queen or a high priest. The choice of material, gold, was an indication of that. Now here was the same shape, worn by a man who seemed to be a chieftain, and once again the shape was faithfully copied in a precious material, ivory.

The falcon of Monomatapa, Zouga wondered, studying the ancient pendant, ancient it must be, for the ivory had acquired a deep patina and lustre.

Zouga looked up at the little Matabele girl, standing almost naked above him, and watching him with interest.

'Do you see this?' he asked.

'It is a bird.'

'Have you seen it before?'

Juba shook her head, and her fat little breasts joggled at the movement.

'It is a Mashona thing,' and she shrugged. What would a daughter of the sons of Senzangakhona and Chaka want with such a nonsense?

On an impulse, Zouga lifted the necklace and dropped it over his own head, letting the ivory falcon fall inside the vee of his flannel shirt, where it nested against the darkly springing curls of his body hair.

'Come!' he told Juba. 'There is nothing more for us here,' and he led the way back towards the camp beyond the pass.

The land into which the old bull had led them by the secret road through the pass was an elephant kingdom. Perhaps the pressure of the hunters moving up from the far southern tip of the continent had driven them into this unpeopled world. The herds were everywhere. Each day Zouga and Jan Cheroot hunting far ahead of the main caravan came up with the huge grey pachyderms, and they shot them down.

They shot and killed forty-eight elephant the first month and almost sixty the second, and Zouga meticulously recorded each kill in his journal, the circumstances of the hunt, the weight of each tusk, and the exact location of the cache in which they buried them.

His small band of porters could not carry even a small part of such a mass of ivory, and the distance and direction which they must still travel was uncertain. Zouga buried his treasure, always near a readily recognizable landmark, a distinctive tree, or an unusual rock, a hilltop or a confluence of rivers, to enable him to find it again.

He would return one day for it, and when he did, it would have dried off its excess moisture and be easier for the porters to carry.

In the meantime, he spent all his daylight hours in pursuit of the quarry, walking and running great distances until his body was hard and fit as that of a highly trained athlete, and his arms and face a deep mahogany brown, even his full beard and moustache gilded to shades of gold by the bright sunlight.

Every day he learned from Jan Cheroot the tricks of bush-lore, until he could run a difficult spoor over rocky ground without a check. He learned to anticipate the turns and the twists that the driven herds made to get below the wind and take his scent. He learned to anticipate the pattern of their movements so that by cutting across the circuitous spoor he could save many hours of dogged pursuit. He learned to judge the sex and size and age and ivory of a beast by the mark of its rounded pads in the earth.

He found that if the herd was allowed to settle into that swinging gait between a trot and a canter, then they could keep it up for a day and a night without pause – whereas if they were taken in the full heat of noon, he could run them hard for the first five miles, winding them, bringing the tiny calves to a standstill so the cows stopped with them – flapping their huge ears to fan themselves, thrusting their trunk down their own throat to suck the water out of their belly and spray it over their head and neck.

He learned to find the heart and the brain, the lungs and the spine hidden in that amorphous mountain of grey hide and flesh. He learned to break the shoulder when the beast stood broadside, dropping him as though he had been struck by lightning, or to take the hip-shot as he ran choking in the dust cloud behind the herd, shattering the hip joint and pinning the beast for an unhurried coup-de-grâce.

He hunted the herds on the hilltops where they had climbed to catch the soothing evening breeze. At dawn he hunted in the thick forests and the open glades, and at noon he hunted them in the old overgrown gardens of a vanished people. For the land that he had first believed devoid of human presence was not, and had never been so, for unnumbered thousands of years.

Beyond the abandoned gardens where once man had planted his crops, but where now the elephant herds had returned to reclaim their heritage, Zouga found the remains of huge native cities, the long deserted keystones of a once-flourishing civilization, though all that remained were the circular outlines of the thatch-and-daub huts on the bare earth, the blackened hearth stones, and the charred fence poles of the cattle enclosures which must once have penned great herds. Judging by the height of the secondary growth in the ancient gardens, no man had farmed here for many decades.

It seemed strange to find these great grey herds of elephant ranging slowly through the ruined towns and fields. Zouga was reminded of a line from that strange exotic poetry that had been published in London the previous year, and which he had read just before sailing.

> They say the Lion and the Lizard keep
> The Courts where Jamshyd gloried and drank deep:
> And Bahram, that great Hunter – the Wild Ass
> Stamps o'er his Head, and he lies fast asleep.

Zouga scratched amongst foundations of the huts and found the deep ash, which must once have been the wooden walls and thatched roofs. In one ancient village Zouga counted a thousand such dwellings, before giving up the count. A numerous people, but where had they gone?

He found a partial answer in an ancient battlefield on the open ground beyond the thousand huts. The bones were white as daisies in the sunlight, bleached and dried out, most of them half buried in the rich red soil or covered by the dense fields of waving fluffy-topped grass.

The human remains covered an area of many acres and they lay in clumps and chains like newly-cut wheat awaiting the reavers. Nearly every one of the skulls had been crushed in as if by a fierce blow with a club or mace.

Zouga realized that it was not so much a battlefield as a killing ground, for such slaughter could not be called warfare. If this toll had been repeated at each of the ruined towns he had stumbled upon, then the final total of the dead must have been in the tens or even hundreds of thousands. It was small wonder that what human presence remained was in tiny scattered groups, like the handful of warriors that had tried to prevent them crossing the pass of the elephant road. There were others. Occasionally, Zouga spied the smoke from a cooking fire rising from the highest point of one of the strangely-shaped rock hillocks that dotted the land in all directions. If these were the survivors of the vanished civilization, then they still lived in terror of the fate that had overtaken their forbears.

When Zouga and his hunting party approached any of these tiny elevated settlements, they found the crests were fortified with built up walls of rock, and they were greeted with a hail of boulders rolled down the slope upon them, that forced them to retreat hurriedly. Often there were small cultivated gardens on the level ground below the fortified hill tops.

In the gardens grew millet, ropoko and big sweet yams, but most important for Zouga, dark green native tobacco. The soil was rich, the ropoko grew twice the height of a man and the corn sprays were loaded with red grain.

The tobacco leaves were thick-stemmed, the size of an elephant's ear. Zouga rolled the tip leaves into powerful cigars that had a rich distinction of taste and as he smoked them, he pondered how the plant had reached this distant land from its far origins. There must once have been an avenue of trade between these people and the coast. The trade beads on the necklace he had taken from the body at the pass, and now these exotic plants proved that, as did the tamarind trees, native of India, which grew amongst the ruins of the ancient villages.

Zouga wondered what a colony of British settlers with their industry and sophisticated agricultural technique, plough and crop rotation, seed selection and fertilization, might make of this lush rich soil, as he moved on slowly through the sparsely populated, well-timbered land that abounded with game and game birds, and was fed by strong clear streams of water.

Whenever he returned to the main body of the caravan, he made his meticulous observations of the sun and worked with chronometer and almanac to compute his exact positions, to add them, and his own succinct descriptions, to the map that old Tom Harkness had bequeathed him. The map increased in value, as new rivers were marked in, new boundaries set to the fly-belts and the 'fly-corridors' extended, as Zouga's observations of the terrain, of soil and vegetation types began to cover the blank portions of the old parchment.

If he was not immersed in his map, then he worked as long as the light was good enough on his journal and the manuscript which was an adjunct to it – and while he did so, Jan Cheroot and the porters brought in the latest harvest of ivory, only just beginning to stink, and buried it.

Totalling the harvest from the lists in his journal, Zouga found that he had over twelve thousand pounds of tusks cached along his route. They were worth six shillings a pound in London, nearly four thousand pounds sterling. The trick was to get it to London. Zouga grinned to himself as he completed the calculation, a dozen waggons, or five hundred porters, and two thousand miles to carry it – that was all it required.

At each river-crossing Zouga took the flat black iron pan, which doubled as laundry tub and cooking pot, and for miles in each direction along the river bed he worked the gravel. He would fill the pan from a likely spot under the bank in the bend of the river, and then set the contents swirling awash, dipping and turning the pan, spilling a little of the lighter gravel at each turn, refilling with water and spinning it again until at last he was left with a smear of the finest and heaviest material lying around the bottom of the pan in a 'tail'. Always the tail was dark and uninteresting, without the golden sparkle for which he longed so ardently.

When he detailed all these activities in his journal, only one thing gave Zouga a pause – and that was what to call this new and beautiful land. So far there was no evidence at all that it was the empire of Monomatapa, or even that Monomatapa existed. The timid, scattered and demoralized people he had so far encountered were certainly not the warriors of a powerful emperor. One other consideration decided him not to use that name. If he did so, it was tacit acknowledgement that the land had already been claimed, and each day that he travelled through the empty wilderness the dreams of himself claiming it for a queen and a nation seemed less far-fetched. Zouga began to use the name 'Zambezia' – the land below the Zambezi river – and that was how he wrote it in his journal and in the thick bundle of pages of his manuscript.

With all this work to impede progress, the pace of the caravan was leisurely, or, as Robyn told Zouga furiously, 'You would make a snail look like a Derby-winner.' For although Zouga might cover two hundred miles in the sweeping circular patterns of the hunt, the caravan camped and waited for his return, and then waited another four or five days as Jan Cheroot and the porters ferried in the loads of wet ivory.

'For all you know, Morris Zouga, your own father might by dying out there somewhere for want of a handful of medicine, while you . . .'

'If he has survived eight years already, the old devil is unlikely to turn up his toes for another few days.' Zouga's light tone covered the irritation he felt. Since he had killed the Mashona at the pass on the elephant road, the feeling between brother and sister had been strained to the point where each of them found it difficult to maintain a civil tone of voice on the few occasions when they spoke together.

Zouga's long and frequent absences from the main body were not entirely on account of his dedication to the chase and exploration of the surrounding countryside. He found it less wearying on the nerves to be away from his sister. That ecstatic mood when they had stood like two children on Christmas morning, hand in hand, upon the heights of the escarpment, was months in the past.

Brooding beside his solitary camp fire, with the hyena giggling and shrieking over the freshly killed elephant carcasses in the nearby forest, Zouga thought how it was really a miracle that two such definite personalities as his and Robyn's, whose objects were so widely divergent, should have come this far without serious disagreement. It had been too good to last indefinitely, and now he wondered how it might end. He should have followed his instincts and sent Robyn back to Tete and Cape Town when he had the excuse to do so, for the collision course on which they were so clearly set could only end in disaster for the entire expedition.

When he rejoined the main body the following day he would have it out with her, one way or the other. She would have at last to accept that he was the leader of the expedition and as such, his decisions were final. If she did so, then he could make some concession to her wishes, though the hunt for Fuller Ballantyne was very low on Zouga's list of priorities. It would probably be best for all of them, Fuller Ballantyne not excluded, if he had long ago been laid by his faithful bearers in a hero's grave.

The thought gave Zouga a prick of guilt, and he knew he would never write it, not even in the most private pages of his journal, nor would he voice it to his sister. But the idea persisted, even while he rolled into his blanket, with a small fire at his feet and another at his head to break the thick crunching white frost which would cover the earth and grass at dawn, serenaded by Jan Cheroot's snores which took the basso profundo to the soprano of the hyena packs. Zouga fell asleep at last.

Having made the decision to assert his authority, Zouga rolled out of his blanket in the frosty dawn determined on a forced march that would take them back to where he had left Robyn and the caravan twelve days previously. He reckoned it was forty miles, perhaps a little less, to the main camp site and he set a cruel pace, not even taking the usual noon break, but pushing on remorselessly.

Zouga had deliberately left the main body encamped below a distinctively shaped kopje, whose rocky spires could be clearly seen from many miles around and which Zouga had named 'Mount Hampden' in memory of a childhood visit to that castle.

They were still far out when Zouga had his first misgivings. There was no smoke rising from the base of the hills, and there should have been. He had left almost a ton of elephant meat curing on the smoking-racks, and on the outward march he had been able to look back and see the rising column of smoke long after the crests of the hills had disappeared below the tops of the forest trees.

'There is no smoke!' he told Jan Cheroot, and the little Hottentot nodded.

'I did not want to be the first to say that.'

'Can Camacho have followed us this far?'

'There are other man-eating animals out here beside the Portuguese,' Jan Cheroot said, and cocked his head at an inquisitive birdlike angle as Zouga began swiftly to strip down to light running order. Then, still without another word, Jan Cheroot followed his example, and handed his breeches and other traps to the bearers.

'Follow as fast as you can!' Zouga told them, snatching a spare powder-bag from Matthew and turning away and breaking into a run.

Jan Cheroot fell in at his shoulder and they ran as they had run so often before, at the driving pace which could bring a breeding herd of elephant to a winded standstill within a few miles. All Zouga's feelings of antagonism towards his sister were swept away in the rush of deep concern for her safety. A series of horrific images flashed through his mind, of a sacked camp site, of mutilated bodies lying in the bloody trampled grass, shattered by the balls of the Portuguese muskets, or stabbed to death by the broad-bladed assegais of plumed and kilted warriors.

He found himself praying for her safety, repeating the formulas of his childhood which he had used so seldom since then, and unconsciously he increased the pace, until Jan Cheroot grunted a protest at his shoulder, and then slowly fell back, as Zouga forged powerfully ahead.

He reached the foot of the hill a mile ahead of Jan Cheroot, and turned to face the lowering red orb of the sun as he skirted the rocky base, crested a low rise and stopped there, hunting for breath, his chest swelling and subsiding and the sweat running down into his beard.

He stared down at the shaded dell, until the tall mukusi trees where he had left the caravan and his heart plunged. He felt physically nauseated with horror. The camp site was deserted, the fires were cold black ash and the thatched lean-to shelters had already acquired that dejected air of all deserted habitation. Still fighting for breath, Zouga plunged down the gentle slope into the abandoned camp, and looked about him wildly, for the bodies. There were none, and his first thought was of slavers. They would have taken them all, and he shuddered with horror at the thought of what Robyn must have suffered.

Zouga ran to her hut first. It was totally devoid of any trace of her. He ran to the next hut and the next – all of them were empty, but in the last hut he found a single body. It was curled on the sandy floor of the primitive shelter, and wrapped in a blanket. The blanket was drawn up over the head and wound tightly around the trunk.

Reluctant to discover his sister's horribly mutilated corpse, Zouga knelt beside it. Sweat half-blinded him as he reached out a hand that trembled with dread and exhaustion and gently drew back the fold of a grey blanket that covered the still head.

The corpse came to life with a howl of fright and leapt two feet into the air, gibbering wildly, trying to throw off the blanket and lashing out with feet and fists to defend itself.

'Hellhound!' Zouga had so christened the laziest of his porters, a skinny fellow with a vast appetite for meat and less enthusiasm for anything that involved physical exertion. 'What has happened? Where is Nomusa?'

Hellhound, once he had been quieted and had sufficiently recovered from shock, had a brief note to answer his questions. The single scrap of paper torn from Robyn's journal was double-folded and sealed with a splash of red wax, it read:

> Dear Zouga,
>   I am of the opinion that further delay will seriously prejudice the interests of the sponsors of this expedition.
>   Accordingly, I have decided to move on at a speed better suited to achieving our objects before the onset of the rainy season.
>   I leave Hellhound to await your eventual return. Do follow at your own speed.
>
>   Your affectionate sister,
>   Robyn.

The note was dated ten days previously, and it was all she had left him. There was not even a pouch of salt or a bag of tea leaves, both of which commodities Zouga had been without for days.

Zouga's numbing shock lasted until Jan Cheroot reached the deserted camp, but by the time his exhausted bearers came, black rage had begun to replace all other emotion. He would have made a night march of it in pursuit of the caravan, but though he kicked their ribs as they lay and cursed them coldly, his bearers were so exhausted that they could not rise from where they had thrown themselves down.

Robyn had great difficulty getting the bearers to break camp and take up their packs. Her first efforts to do so were greeted with amusement and light laughter, for none of them believed she was serious. Even Juba could not understand that Nomusa, a woman, was taking command of the caravan.

When all argument failed, Robyn took the hippo-hide kurbash whip to the little yellow Hottentot Corporal, whom Jan Cheroot had left in command of his musketeers. The Corporal shouted frantic orders to his men from the upper branches of the mukusi where Robyn had him treed.

They were on the march within the hour, but the light laughter had given way to scowls and sulks. They were all convinced that the safari was now doomed, for who had ever heard of a woman, a young woman – worst of all a young white woman – leading into the unknown. Within half a mile most of the porters were complaining of thorns in the feet or bad blood behind the eyes, afflictions common only to porters reluctant to advance.

Robyn got them to their feet again by firing a shot from the big naval Colt revolver over their heads, it almost sprained her wrist, but proved an amazingly effective cure for both feet and eyes, and finally they made a fair day's march of it, south and west, ten miles, as Robyn reckoned it as she marked her journal that night.

Despite the brave countenance she put on before the porters and musketeers, Robyn had her own doubts. She had watched closely as Zouga plotted a course with the prismatic compass, and she had mastered the technique of sighting a distant hill or other feature and marching upon it, before again sighting ahead on another feature. It was the only way to maintain a direct line of march in this rolling forested country.

She had studied, whenever she had the opportunity, the Harkness map, and had seen the wisdom of Zouga's choice of direction. He was aiming to traverse this wide unexplored land he had called Zambezia, and eventually to hit the road that their grandfather, Robert Moffat, had pioneered from his mission station at Kuruman to the town of the Matabele king, Mzilikazi, at Thabas Indunas.

However, Zouga's intention had been to cut south of the frontiers of the Matabele kingdom, avoiding the Burnt Land where, according to Tom Harkness, the rapacious border impis of Mzilikazi killed all travellers. Neither she nor Zouga could trust to their relationship to Moffat to protect them.

Once they gained the wagon road to Kuruman, they would be back in the known world, and the road would lead them to the series of waterholes that grandfather Moffat had marked. At Kuruman, after the family reunion, the road to Cape Town was long and wearying, but well travelled and in less than a year they could be back in London. The delicate part was to grope the way south of Matabele land, through the untold hazards still ahead and to reach the road.

Robyn did not truly anticipate that she would be called upon to perform this feat of navigation entirely on her own. It could only be a matter of days before Zouga reached Mount Hampden camp and then hurried to catch up with the main body. There would be an interesting clash of wills then. However, at the end of it, she was certain that Zouga would be convinced that their father's whereabouts and safety were more important than the slaughter of animals, whose teeth could probably never be retrieved from their burial mounds.

This was a gesture of defiance only, soon Zouga would be with her once more. In the meantime, however, she had an unpleasantly hollow and lonely sensation beneath her ribs as she strode along in her tight-fitting breeches, the Hottentot standard-bearer carrying the grubbied and tattered Union Jack a few paces behind her, and a sullen line of porters straggling along behind that again.

They camped the second night on the edge of a river that had been reduced to a string of still green pools in the sugary white sand of the river bed. On the steep bank stood a small grove of strangler figs, the smooth pale trunk and branches had crept up like thick and sinuous pythons to smother the host trees. The parasites were now taller and more robust than the rotting remains that supported them had ever been, and the clusters of ripening figs covered their branches. Fat green pigeons came to feed on the fruits, flicked their wings and whistled their shrill cry, unlike that of any other pigeon, that to Robyn sounded like 'Oh well, oh very well!' and they cocked their heads to peer down through the green leaves at the men camped below.

The porters had cut the *scherms* of thorn branches and lit the cooking fires when they all heard the lion roar. The sound checked the murmur of voices for only a few seconds, for it was very faint and distant, seeming to come from miles downstream, and it was a sound to which they had all long grown accustomed.

There had hardly been a night since they had crossed the pass on the elephant road that they had not heard the lions, and in the morning found the pug marks, sometimes almost the size of a soup plate, in the soft earth around the camp where the big inquisitive cats had circled them during the night.

However, Robyn had never seen one of them for they are almost entirely nocturnal, and her first tremors of trepidation had long turned to indifference. She felt quite secure behind the *scherm* of thornbush, and now at the distant muttering rumble she hardly bothered to look up from her journal in which she was exaggerating only slightly the competent manner in which she had directed the day's march.

'We are making as good a time as we ever did when Z was leading,' she wrote smugly, but did not go on to mention the mood of the porters.

The lion roared only once, and when it was not repeated, the sullen talk around the cooking fires was resumed and Robyn bowed her head once more over her journal.

A few hours after the setting of the sun the camp settled for the night, and lying under her hastily thatched shelter with Juba curled on the mattress of freshly cut grass beside her, Robyn listened to the melodious African voices of her porters fade gradually into silence. She sighed once, deeply, and fell instantly asleep – to wake with a confusion of sound and movement all around her.

She knew that it was late by the frostiness of the air, the utter darkness and her own sleep-drugged stupor. The night rang with the terrified shouts of men and the rush of their feet. Then there was the thudding report of a musket, the crash of heavy logs being thrown on the watch fires and then, heart-stoppingly, the screams of Juba close to her head.

'Nomusa! Nomusa!'

Still groggy with sleep, Robyn struggled up. She was not certain what she was dreaming and what was reality.

'What is it?'

'A devil!' shrieked Juba. 'Devils have come to kill us all.'

Robyn flung off her blanket, and ran out of the shelter bare-footed, dressed only in her flannel nightgown with ribbons in her hair.

At that moment the new logs blazed up on the watch fire, and she saw naked yellow and black bodies, and terrified faces, whites of rolling eyes and open shouting mouths.

The little Hottentot Corporal, stark naked, pranced beyond the fire, brandishing his musket, and as Robyn ran towards him he fired it blindly into the darkness.

Robyn caught his arm as he began to reload.

'What is it?' she shouted into his ear.

'*Leeuw!* Lion!' His eyes were glittering with fright and bubbles of spittle ran from the corners of his mouth.

'Where is it?'

'It has taken Sakkie! It pulled him out of his blankets.'

'Quiet!' Robyn shouted. 'Keep quiet all of you!'

Now, at last, they all turned instinctively to her for leadership.

'Quiet!' she repeated, and the gabble of fright and uncertainty died swiftly.

'Sakkie!' she called in the silence, and the missing Hottentot's voice answered her faintly from below the steep bank of the river-bed.

'*Die leeuw het my! The lion has me! Die duiwel gaan my dood maak,* the devil is going to kill me,' and he broke off with a shriek of agony.

Above the high-pitched shriek they all clearly heard the crunch of bone, and the muffled growl like that of a dog with food in its jaws. With a rush of horror that raised goose pimples along her arms, Robyn realized that she was listening to the sounds of a man being eaten alive not fifty yards from where she stood.

'*Hy vreet my bene,*' the voice out of the darkness rang with unbearable agony.

'He is eating my legs,' and the gruesome cracking, tearing sounds made Robyn's gorge rise to choke her. Without thinking, she snatched a burning brand from the fire and holding it aloft shouted at the Hottentot Corporal. 'Come on! We must save him!'

She ran forward to the lip of the bank before she realized she was alone, and unarmed.

She looked back. Not one of the men around the fire had followed her. They stood in a tight group, shoulder to shoulder, clutching muskets or axes or assegais, but rooted where they stood.

'He is finished.' The Corporal's voice shook with fright. 'Leave him. It's too late. Leave him.'

Robyn hurled the burning brand she held down into the river-bed below her feet, and before its flames faded and pinched out she thought she saw something big and dark and terrifying on the edge of the shadows.

Robyn ran back to the group and snatched a musket from one of the Hottentots. Thumbing back the hammer, she ran once more to the river bank and peered down into the dry bed. It was utterly dark, until suddenly there was somebody at her shoulder, holding high a burning branch from the fire.

'Juba! Go back!' Robyn snapped at the child. Juba was completely naked except for a single string of beads about her hips, and the firelight glinted on her sleek black body.

She could not answer Robyn, for tears were rolling down her plump cheeks and her throat was closed with terror, but she shook her head fiercely at the order to retreat.

Below them, outlined against the white sand of the dry river, was that grotesque dark shape, and the screams of the dying man blended with the grisly wet growls of the animal.

Robyn lifted the musket, but hesitated for fear of hitting the Hottentot. Disturbed by the light, the lion rose, becoming huge and black; swiftly it dragged the weakly wriggling body, dangling between its forelegs back into the darkness beyond the feeble circle of light from the flames.

Robyn drew a deep breath and the heavy musket shook in her hands, but she lifted her chin in a gesture of decision and holding up the skirts of her long nightdress in one hand, went down the path into the river-bed. Juba followed her like a faithful puppy, pressing so hard against her that they nearly lost their balance, but she kept the burning brand on high, though it shook, and the flames wavered smokily.

'Brave girl!' Robyn encouraged her. 'Good brave girl!'

They stumbled through the loose white sand that covered the ankles of their bare feet at each pace.

Ahead of them, at the extreme limit of their vision, moved the menacing black shadow, and the deep muttering growls seemed to fill the night around them.

'Leave it!' Robyn shouted, her voice quavering and breaking. 'Drop it – this instant!'

Unconsciously she was using the same commands as she had given her terrier as a child when it refused to deliver the rubber ball.

Ahead of her in the darkness Sakkie heard her, and bleated feebly. 'Help me – for God's love, help me.' But the lion pulled him away, leaving a long wet drag mark through the sand.

Robyn was tiring rapidly, her arms ached from the weight of the heavy weapon, each breath burned her throat as she panted, but she could not seem to get enough air, for an iron band of fear cramped her chest. She sensed that the lion would only retreat a certain distance before it lost patience with the shouting and harassment, and her instinct was right.

Suddenly she made out the full shape of the lion ahead of them. It had dropped the maimed body and stood over it now like a tomcat with its mouse, but it was as big as a Shetland pony, with the dark ruff of its mane fully erect, seeming to double its size.

In the light of the flames, its eyes glowed a bright ferocious gold, and it opened its jaws and roared. The very air dinned upon Robyn's eardrums, causing her actual physical pain as that great gust of sound struck her. It rose to an unbearable pitch, so that involuntarily she reeled backwards with Juba clinging to her. The child wailed with despair, losing control of her body so that in the light of the flames her urine shot in sharp little spurts down her legs, and as the lion launched into its charge she dropped the torch into the sand, plunging them all into complete darkness.

Robyn lifted the musket in front of her, as a defensive reflex rather than a planned act of aggression, and when the barrel was at waist-level she pulled the trigger with all her strength. The cap flashed, flaring brightly in the blackness and for an instant she saw the lion. It was so close that the long barrel of the musket seemed to touch its huge shaggy head. The mouth was wide open, still emitting those shattering gusts of sound, and the fangs that lined the deep, meat-red gape of jaws were long and white and cruel. The eyes burned yellow as living flames, and Robyn found that she was screaming, but the sound was lost completely in the roaring of the enraged animal.

Then an instant after the flash of the cap the musket fired, bucking so savagely in her hands that it almost tore itself from her grip, and the butt, not anchored against her shoulder, was driven back into her stomach with a force that expelled the air from her lungs, and sent her reeling in the loose white sand. Juba, clinging to her legs and wailing with despair, tripped her and she went over backwards, sprawling full length at the same moment that the full weight of the lion lunged into her.

If Robyn had not fallen, the charge would have stove in her ribs, and snapped her neck, for the lion was over four hundred pounds weight of driving bone and muscle. As it was, it knocked her out of her senses for she never knew how long, but she became conscious again, with the strong cat-reek of the lion in her nostrils, and an immense weight crushing her into the sand. She wriggled weakly, but the weight was suffocating her, and gouts of hot blood, so hot it seemed to scald her, were spurting over her head and neck.

'Nomusa!' Juba's voice, high with anguish and very close, but those shattering roars were silent. There was just the unbearable weight and the rank smell of lion.

Robyn's strength came back to her with a rush, and she struggled and kicked, and the weight above her rolled loosely aside, slithering off her, and she dragged herself free of it. Immediately Juba clung to her again, throwing her arms about Robyn's neck.

Robyn comforted her as though she were an infant, patting her and kissing her cheek that was wet and hot with tears.

'It's over! There, now. It's all over,' she mumbled, aware that her hair was sodden with the lion's blood, and that a dozen men, led cautiously by the Hottentot Corporal, had lined the high riverbank, each of them holding aloft a torch of burning grass.

In the dim yellow light the lion lay stretched out beside Robyn in the sand. The ball from the musket had struck him full in the nose, passed cleanly through the brain and lodged in the base of his neck, killing the great cat in mid-air, so the lifeless body had pinned Robyn to the sand.

'The lion is dead!' Robyn quavered as she called to the men, and they came down in a close bunch, timidly at first and then boldly when they saw the huge yellow carcass.

'It was the shot of a true huntress,' announced the Corporal grandly. 'An inch high and the ball would have bounced off the skull, an inch lower and it would have missed the brain.'

'Sakkie,' Robyn's voice still shook, 'where is Sakkie?'

He was still alive, and they carried him in his blanket up into the camp. His wounds were fearsome, and Robyn knew there was not the smallest chance of saving him. One arm from wrist to elbow had been chewed so that not a piece of bone bigger than the top joint of her finger remained. One foot was gone just above the ankle, bitten clean off and swallowed in one piece. He had been bitten through pelvis and spine, while through a tear in his diaphragm below the ribs the mottled pink of his lungs swelled out with each breath.

Robyn knew that to attempt to cut and sew that dreadfully torn flesh or to saw the splintered bone stumps would be inflicting futile agony on the little yellow man. She had him laid close to the fire, she plugged the worst holes gently, and then covered him with blankets and fur karosses. She administered a dose of laudanum so powerful as to be almost lethal in itself. Then she sat next to Sakkie and held his hand.

'A doctor must know when to let a man die with dignity,' her professor at St. Matthew's had once told her. And a little before dawn Sakkie opened his eyes, the pupils dilated widely by the massive dose of the drug and smiled at her just once before he died.

His brother Hottentots buried him in a small cave in one of the granite kopjes and they blocked the opening with boulders that the hyena could not roll aside.

When the Corporal and his Hottentots came down from the hill, they indulged in a brief ritual of mourning which consisted mainly of emitting loud theatrical cries of anguish and firing their muskets in the air to speed Sakkie's soul on its journey, after which they ate a hearty breakfast of smoked elephant meat, and the Corporal came to Robyn, dry eyed and grinning broadly.

'We are now ready to march, Nomusa!' he told her, and with a stamp of his right foot, which began with the knee lifted under his chin, he gave her one of those widely extravagant salutes, a mark of deep respect that up to that date had been reserved exclusively for Major Zouga Ballantyne.

During that day's march, the porters sang again for the first time since leaving Zouga's camp at Mount Hampden.

> 'She is your mother and your father too,
> She will dress your wounds
> She will stand over you while you sleep
> We, your children, greet you, Nomusa,
> The girl child of mercy.'

It was not only the caravan's rate of advance under Zouga that had irritated and annoyed Robyn. It was also their complete failure to make contact with any of the indigenous tribes, with any of the inhabitants of the scattered and fortified villages.

To her it seemed completely logical that the only way that they would be able to trace Fuller Ballantyne through this wilderness was by asking questions of those who must have seen him pass, and almost certainly had spoken and traded with him.

Robyn could not believe that her father would have adopted the same high-handed actions to force a passage past anybody or anything that stood in the way of the caravan as Zouga had done.

When she closed her eyes she could still see clearly in her mind's eye the tiny falling body of the black man in the tall headdress, shot down ruthlessly by her brother. She had rehearsed in her mind how she or her father would have passed through the elephant road without gunfire and slaughter. The tactful withdrawal, the offering of small gifts, the cautious parley and eventual agreement.

'It was plain bloody murder!' she repeated to herself for the hundreth time. 'And what we have done since then has been blatant robbery.'

Zouga had helped himself to the standing crops of the villages they had passed, to tobacco, millet and yams, not even bothering to leave a handful of salt or a few stick of dried elephant meat as token payment.

'We should try to communicate with these people, Zouga,' she had remonstrated.

'They are a sullen and dangerous people.'

'Because they expect you to rob and murder them – and, as God is my witness, you have not disappointed them, have you?'

The same argument had run its well-worn course many times, neither of them relenting, each holding stubbornly to their own view. Now at least she was free to attempt to establish contact with these people, Mashona, as Juba called them disparagingly, without her brother's impatience and arrogance to distract her and alarm the timid black people.

On the fourth day after leaving Zouga's camp, they came in sight of an extraordinary geological formation. It was as though a high dam wall had been constructed across the horizon, a great dyke of rock running almost exactly north and south to the very limit of the eye.

Almost directly in their line of march was the only breach in this rampart, and from the altered vegetation, the denser growth and deeper green, it was clear that a river flowed through the gap. Robyn ordered a small adjustment in their line of march and headed for the pass.

When they were still some miles distant Robyn was delighted to make out the first signs of human habitation that they had come across since leaving Mount Hampden.

There were fortified walls on the cliffs above the breach in the long low hill, high above the river bed, and as they drew closer, Robyn could see the gardens on the banks of the river, defended by high brush and thorn barriers with little thatched look-out huts standing high on stilts in the centre of the dark luscious green stands of young millet.

'We will fill our bellies tonight,' the Hottentot Corporal gloated. 'That corn is ripe enough to eat.'

'We will camp here, Corporal,' Robyn told him firmly.

'But we are still a mile . . .'

'Here!' Robyn repeated.

They were all puzzled and resentful when Robyn forbade entry to the tempting gardens, and confined them all to the perimeter of the camp, except for the water and wood parties. But resentment turned to genuine alarm when Robyn left the camp herself, accompanied only by Juba, and as far as they could see completely unarmed.

'These people are savages,' the Corporal tried to intercept her. 'They will kill you, and then Major Zouga will kill me.'

The two women entered the nearest garden, and carefully approached the look-out hut. On the earth below the rickety ladder that rose to the elevated platform a fire had burned down to ash, but flared again when Robyn knelt and fanned it. Robyn threw a few dry branches upon it and then sent Juba for an armful of green leaves. The column of smoke drew the attention of the watchers on the cliff above the gorge.

Robyn could see their distant figures on the skyline, standing very still and intent. It was an eerie feeling to know that so many eyes were upon them, but Robyn was not relying entirely on the fact that they were women, nor was she relying on their patently peaceful intentions, nor even upon the prayers which she had offered up so diligently to protect them. On the principle that the Almighty helps those who show willing, she had Zouga's big Colt pistol stuffed into the waistband of her breeches and covered by the tail of her flannel shirt.

Next to the smoking beacon fire, Robyn left a half pound of salt in a small calabash gourd, and a bundle of sticks of black smoked elephant meat which was the last of her stock.

Early the next morning Robyn and Juba again visited the garden and found the meat and salt had been taken, and that there were the fresh footprints of bare feet overlaying their own in the dust.

'Corporal,' Robyn told the Hottentot with a confidence she did not feel, 'we are going out to shoot meat.'

Corporal grinned beatifically. They had eaten the last of the smoked meat, weevils and all, the previous evening, and he flung her one of his more flamboyant salutes, his right arm quivering at the peak of his cap, his fingers spread stiffly, the stamp of his right foot raising dust, before he hurried away shouting orders to his men to prepare for the hunt.

Zouga had long ago declared the Sharps rifle to be too light for elephant, and left it in camp, favouring the big four-to-the-pound smooth bores to the more expensive breech-loading rifle. Robyn took it now and inspected it with trepidation. Previously she had only fired it at a target, and now in the privacy of her grass hut she rehearsed loading and cocking the weapon. She was not sure that she would be capable of cold-bloodedly aiming it at a living animal, and had to reassure herself of the absolute necessity of procuring food for the many mouths and stomachs that now depended upon her. The Corporal did not share her doubts, he had seen her shoot a charging lion between the eyes, and trusted her now implicitly. Within an hour's walk they found a herd of buffalo in the thick reed beds along the river. Robyn had listened to Zouga talking of the hunt with enough attention to know the necessity of keeping below the wind – and in the reeds with visibility down to a few feet and with the commotion created by two hundred cows and bleating calves they crept up to a range at which nobody could miss.

Her Hottentots blazed away with their muskets, while Robyn herself fired grimly into the galloping bellowing bodies that charged wildly past her after the first shot had startled them.

After the dust had settled and the thick bank of powder smoke had drifted away on the faint breeze, they found six of the big black animals lying dead in the reedbeds. Her entourage were delighted, hacking the bodies into manageable chunks which they slung on long poles and carried singing up to the camp. Their delight turned to amazement when Robyn ordered that an entire haunch of fresh buffalo be taken out and left next to the hut in the millet garden.

'These people are eaters of roots and dirt,' Juba explained patiently. 'Meat is too good for them.'

'To kill this meat we have risked our lives,' the Corporal began his protest, then caught the look in Robyn's eye, broke off and coughed and shuffled his feet. 'Nomusa, could we not give them a little less than a haunch? The hooves make a good stew, and these people are savages, they will eat anything,' he pleaded. 'A whole haunch . . .'

She sent him away muttering and shaking his head sorrowfully.

During the night, Juba woke her, and the two of them sat and listened to the faint throb of drums and the singing that carried down from the hilltop village, clearly the sounds of feasting and jubilation.

'They have probably not seen so much meat at one time in all their lives,' Juba murmured sulkily.

In the morning Robyn found, in place of the buffalo meat, a bark basket containing fifteen hen's eggs the size of pigeons eggs, and two large earthen pots of millet beer. The look of the bubbling thin grey gruel almost turned Robyn's stomach. She gave the beer to the Corporal to distribute, and her followers drank it with such obvious relish, smacking their lips and nodding over it like connoisseurs over an ancient bottle of claret, that Robyn controlled her heaving stomach and tasted some; it was tart and refreshing and strong enough to set the Hottentots chattering and laughing raucously.

With Juba following her, each of them carrying a bundle of half-dried buffalo meat, Robyn returned to the gardens, certain that the exchange of gifts had proved it possible to establish friendly contact. They sat under the shelter and waited. The hours passed without a sign of the Mashona appearing. The hushed heat of noon gave way to long, cool shadows of evening – and then, for the first time, Robyn noticed a gentle stir amongst the millet plants that was neither wind nor bird.

'Do not move,' she cautioned Juba.

Slowly a human shape showed itself, a frail bent figure dressed in tatters of a skin kilt. Robyn could not tell whether it was man or woman, and she didn't dare stare openly at it, for fear of frightening it away.

The figure emerged from the stand of millet, crouched down on its haunches, and it hopped hesitantly towards them, with long pauses between each tentative hop. It was so thin and wrinkled and dried out that it looked like one of the unbandaged mummies that Robyn had seen in the Egyptian section of the British Museum.

It was definitely a man, she realized at last, sneaking a glance in his direction, for with each hop his shrivelled and stringy genitals flapped out from under the short kilt.

Closer still, Robyn saw that his cap of woolly hair was pure white with age, and in the seamed and pouched sockets his eyes wept slow tears of fright, as though these were the last drops of liquid that his desiccated old body contained.

Neither Juba nor Robyn moved or looked directly at him until he squatted a dozen paces from them, then slowly Robyn turned her head towards him. The old man whimpered with fear.

It was clear to Robyn that he had been selected as an emissary because he was the least valuable member of the tribe, and Robyn wondered what threats had been made to force him to come down from the hilltop.

Moving very slowly and calmly, as though she were dealing with a timid wild creature, Robyn held out a stick of half-cured buffalo meat. The old man stared at it, fascinated. As Juba had told her, these people probably existed almost entirely on their meagre crops and such roots and wild fruit as they could glean in the forest. Meat was a rare treat, and such an unproductive member of the tribe would be given only a very little of what there was.

The way he stared at the piece in Robyn's hand made her believe that the old man had not had so much as a taste of the buffalo haunch. He was more than half starved. He rolled his tongue loosely around in his toothless mouth, gathering his courage, and then shuffled close enough to hold out the claws of his bony fingers, palms cupped upwards in the polite gesture of acceptance.

'There you are, dearie.' Robyn placed the stick in his hands and the man snatched it to his mouth, sucking noisily upon it, worrying it with his smooth gums, drooling silver strings of saliva as his mouth flooded, his eyes streaming again, this time with pleasure rather than fear.

Robyn laughed with delight, and the old man rapidly blinked his eyes and then cackled around the stick of meat, the sound so comical that Juba laughed also, the laughter of the two younger women rippling and tinkling without restraint. Almost immediately, the dense leaves of the millet garden stirred and rustled, as other dark, half-naked figures came slowly forward, their anxiety relieved by the sound of laughing women.

The hilltop settlement consisted of not more than a hundred individuals, men, women and children, and every one of them came out to stare and laugh and clap as Robyn and Juba climbed the steep twisting path. The old silver-headed man, almost unbearably proud of his achievement, led Robyn by the hand possessively, screeching out explanations to those around, pausing every now and then to perform a little shuffling dance of triumph.

Mothers held up their infants to look at this marvellous being, and the children ran forward to touch Robyn's legs and then squeal with their own courage, skipping away ahead of her up the path.

The pathway followed the contours of the hillside, and it passed between defensive gateways and under terraced walls. Above the path at every steep place were piled boulders, ready to be hurled down upon an enemy, but now Robyn's ascent was a triumphant progress, and she came out into the village surrounded by a welcoming throng of singing, dancing women.

The village was laid out in a circular pattern of thatched and windowless huts. The walls were of plastered clay with low doorways and beside each hut was a granary of the same materials but raised on poles to protect it from vermin. Apart from a few diminutive chickens, there were no domestic animals.

The space between the huts, and the central courtyard was swept, and the whole village had an air of order and cleanliness. The people themselves were handsome, though none of them carried any excess flesh or fat. Robyn was reminded by their slim, lithe bodies that they were almost exclusively vegetarian. They had alert and intelligent faces, and the laughter and singing with which they welcomed her was easy and unaffected.

'These are the people whom Zouga shot down like animals,' she thought, looking around her with pleasure.

They had set a low carved stool in the shade for her and Juba squatted beside her. As soon as Robyn was seated, the old man squealed importantly and a giggling young girl brought her a pot of the millet beer. Only when she had drunk a mouthful of the beer did the crowd fall silent, and draw aside to let a commanding figure come through.

On his head was a tall headdress of animal fur, similar to the one worn by the chieftain on the elephant road pass. He wore a cloak of leopard skin over his shoulders, the skins so worn that they must have been very old, probably the heredity symbol of his chieftainship. He sat down on another stool facing Robyn. He was a man of middle age, with a pleasant humorous face, and a lively imagination – for he followed Robyn's sign language with attention, and then acted out his own replies with facial expressions and gestures that Robyn understood readily.

This way he asked her from where she came and she showed him the north and made a circle of her hands towards the sun for each day's travel. He wanted to know who was her husband and how many children she had. That she was both unmarried and childless was a source of amazement to the whole village.

More beer was brought out in the clay pots and Robyn felt slightly light-headed, and her cheeks turned pink and her eyes shone. Juba was contemptuous of their hosts.

'They do not have even a goat!' she pointed out scornfully.

'Perhaps your brave young men have stolen them all,' Robyn answered tartly, and raised her beer pot in salute to the chief.

The chief clapped his hands, signalling his drummers to stoop to their instruments. The drums were hollowed tree trunks, beaten with a pair of short wooden clubs to a frantic rhythm that soon had the drummers running with rivulets of sweat and glassy-eyed with the mesmeric effects of the beat. The chieftain threw off his leopard-skin cloak and launched himself into the dance, swirling and leaping until his necklaces and bracelets jangled and rattled.

On his chest he wore a pendant of ivory, snowy-white polished ivory, and it caught the firelight, for by now the sun was long set. Robyn had not noticed the ornament before for it had been covered by the cloak, but now she felt her eye drawn repeatedly to the bouncing white disc.

The disc seemed too perfectly shaped, and as the chief came bounding up to her stool to perform a solo pass before her Robyn saw that it was decorated with a regular pattern around its border. The next moment her heart raced with excitement for the decoration was writing, she was not sure in what language, but it was Latin script, that was certain. Then the chief had gone, leaping away to prance in front of his drummers, exhorting them to greater efforts.

Robyn had to wait until the chief exhausted himself, and staggered panting back to his stool to quaff a pot of the thick grey beer, before she could lean forward and get her first close look at the ornament.

She had been mistaken. It was not ivory but porcelain, and its perfect shape and whiteness was immediately accounted for. It was an item of European manufacture, the lid of a small pot, the type in which tooth-powder or potted meats are sold. The writing was English, printed in neat capitals were the words:

'PATUM PEPERIUM – THE GENTLEMAN'S RELISH.'

She felt her skin go clammy with excitement. Clearly she remembered her father's rage when the pantry at King's Lynn had been bare of this delicacy. She remembered as a small girl running down the village street in the rain to the grocer to buy another pot.

'It is my one weakness, my only weakness,' she remembered her father's exact words while he spread the savoury paste on his toast, his anger mollified so that he came near to making a joke of it. 'Without my Gentleman's Relish, I doubt I would have had strength for the Transversa.'

When Robyn's mother left for Africa on that last ill-fated voyage, there had been a dozen cases of the relish in her luggage. There was only one possible way that the porcelain lid could have reached her.

Robyn stretched out a hand and touched it, but the chief's expression changed instantly and he jumped back, out of reach. The singing and drumming came to an abrupt halt, and the consternation of the entire village made Robyn realize that the porcelain lid was a charm of great personal magic, and that it was a disaster that another hand had touched it.

She made an attempt to mollify the chief, but swiftly he covered himself with his leopard cloak and stalked away to his hut at the end of the village. The festivities were clearly ended. The rest of the villagers were subdued and crept away after the chief, leaving only the silver-haired toothless ancient, possessive as ever, to lead Robyn to the hut which had earlier been set aside for her.

She lay awake most of the night on the plaited reed sleeping-mat, excited at the evidence that her father had passed this way, and worried that she had ruined her relationship with the Mashona chief and would learn no more of the ornament and, through it, of her father.

She did not have an early opportunity to meet the chief again, and make amends for her breach of manners. The villagers kept away from her, obviously hoping she would go, but she stayed on stubbornly in the hilltop village, attended only by the faithful old man. For Robyn was the most important thing that had ever happened in his long life, and he was not going to relinquish her for the chief or for anybody else.

In the end, there was nothing for it but to send the chief an extravagant gift. She used the last *khete* of *sam-sam* beads and one of the double-bladed axes.

The chief could not resist such princely bribes, and though his attitude was cooler and more reserved than at first, he listened attentively while Robyn asked her questions, acting out little charades, which the chief discussed seriously with his elders, before giving his answers.

The answer was southwards again, south for five circles of the sun, and the chief would send somebody to guide Robyn. He was obviously pleased to be rid of her at least, for, though her gifts were welcome, the chief was still deeply troubled by the ill-fortune that her sacrilegious action must bring upon the tribe.

For a guide the chief chose the silver-headed old man, ridding himself of a useless mouth and an unwelcome visitor at one stroke.

Robyn had doubted that her guide's thin legs could carry him either very fast or very far. However, the old man surprised her. He armed himself with a long throwing spear which looked as old and frail as he did himself and on his head he balanced a rolled sleeping-mat and a clay cooking pot – these clearly constituted his total worldly possessions. He girded up his tattered kilts and set off southwards at a pace that had Robyn's porters grumbling again. Robyn had to restrain him.

It took a little time to get the old man to understand that he was now her language tutor. As they marched she pointed at herself, and everything around them, naming them clearly in English, and then looking at him enquiringly. He returned the look with equal enquiry in his rheumy old eyes. However, she persevered, repeating her own name 'Nomusa' as she touched her chest, and suddenly he understood.

He slapped his own chest. 'Karanga,' he squeaked. 'Karanga!' Once again his enthusiasm for this new activity was such that she had to restrain him. Within a few days Robyn had dozens of verbs and hundreds of nouns which she could begin stringing together, much to old Karanga's delight.

However, it was four days before Robyn realized that there had been an initial misunderstanding. Karanga was not the old man's name, but the name of his tribe. It was too late to rectify, because by that time everybody in the caravan was calling him 'Karanga', and the old man answered to it readily. It was difficult to get him to leave Robyn's side. He followed her wherever she went, much to Juba's disgust and undisguised jealousy.

'He smells,' she told Robyn virtuously. 'He smells very bad.' Which was true, Robyn had to admit.

'But after a while you do not notice it, so much.' There was one thing, however, which could not be so readily overlooked, it appeared from under the old man's kilts whenever he squatted, which he did whenever at rest. Robyn solved this by giving old Karanga a pair of Zouga's woollen underwear and taking her chances with her brother's wrath later. The underwear filled old Karanga with almost unbearable pride. He preened and strutted like a peacock, as they flapped around his long thin legs.

Old Karanga led them cautiously wide of every occupied village along their route, although he assured Robyn they were also of the same tribe. There seemed to be no trade nor commerce between these settlements, each perched on its fortified hilltop in suspicious and hostile isolation.

By this time, Robyn could speak enough of the language to find out from Karanga more about the great wizard – from whom the chief had received the magical porcelain talisman, and the story filled her with excitement and anticipation.

Many rainy seasons ago, old Karanga was not sure how many, at his age every season blurred into the one before or the one after, anyway, at some not too far distant date an extraordinary man had come out of the forest, even as she had come, and like her he had been fair skinned. However, his hair and beard were the colour of flames (he showed her the camp fire), and he was without doubt a magician and prophet and rainmaker, for the day he arrived the long drought had broken with thunderous storms that filled the rivers for the first time in many years.

This pale wizard had performed other rare and wonderful feats, transforming himself first into a lion and then into an eagle, raising the dead from the grave, and directing the lightning with a wave of his hand. The tale had lost nothing in the retelling Robyn noted wryly.

'Did anybody speak to him?' Robyn asked.

'We were all too afraid,' Karanga admitted, shaking theatrically with terror, 'but I myself saw the wizard as an eagle fly over village and drop the talisman from the sky.' He flapped his skinny old arms in pantomime.

The strong anchovy smell would have attracted the bird to the discarded pot, Robyn reflected, but when it proved inedible the bird would have dropped it, by chance over Karanga's village.

'The wizard stayed a short time near our village and then went away to the south. We have heard that he travelled swiftly, obviously in his guise as a lion.

'We heard of his miracles, the word shouted from hilltop to hilltop or tapped out by the drums. How he cured others sick to death, how he challenged the ancestral spirits of the Karanga in their most sacred places shouting abuse at them so all who heard him trembled.

'We heard also how he slew the high priestess of the dead, an Umlimo of vast power in her own stronghold. This strange pale magician slew her and destroyed her sacred relics.'

In fact he had raged through the land like a man-eating lion, which of course he was, until finally he came to rest upon a dark hilltop far to the south, the mountain of iron, Thaba Simbi, where he stayed to perform diverse curses and miracles so that the people came to him from far and wide to buy his services with corn and other offerings.

'Is he still there?' Robyn demanded.

Old Karanga rolled his watery eyes and shrugged. 'It is always difficult and dangerous to predict the comings and goings of wizards and magicians,' that eloquent gesture seemed to say.

The journey was not so straightforward as Robyn had hoped, for the further he went from his own village the less certain old Karanga became of his direction, or of the exact location of the Iron Mountain, which he had told her of.

At the beginning of each day's march, he informed Robyn confidently that they would reach their destination that day, and as they went into camp each evening he told her apologetically that it would be the next day for certain.

Twice he pointed out rocky kopjes, 'That is indeed the Iron Mountain', but each time they were driven off with a hail of boulders and throwing spears from the heights.

'I was mistaken,' Karanga mumbled. 'there is a darkness in my eyes sometimes, even under the noonday sun.'

'Have you verily and truly seen this mountain?' Robyn demanded sternly, almost at the end of her patience, and Karanga hung his silver-wrinkled head and with great industry picked at his nostrils with a bony finger to hide his discomfiture.

'It is true that I have not personally seen this place, not with my own eyes, but I have been told by one who spoke with a man who himself . . .' he admitted, and Robyn was so angry that she shouted at him in English.

'You naughty old devil, why did you not say so before!'

Old Karanga understood the tone, if not the words, and his misery was so apparent that she could not sustain her anger for more than an hour, his gratitude when she once more allowed him to carry her water bottle and food bag was pathetic to see.

Robyn was now consumed with impatience. She had no way of knowing how far behind her was Zouga and his hunting-party. He might have returned to the camp at Mount Hampden and found her note the very day after her departure, or he might still be killing elephant a hundred miles away, completely unaware that she had marched without him.

Her disapproval of her brother, and her anger at his recent actions, had gradually evoked a sense of competition in her. She had come so far and accomplished so much on her own – from the contact with the Karanga village to following the traces of her father so far and so doggedly – that she fiercely resented the idea of his arrival when she was at the very point of making the prayed-for and long-delayed reunion with Fuller Ballantyne. She guessed how the tale would be told in Zouga's journal, and in the book that would follow it. She knew who would get all the credit for the arduous search, and its brilliantly successful conclusion.

Once she had thought that fame and praise meant little to her, she believed she would be content to leave that to her brother. She had believed that her own reward would be her father's embrace, and the deep personal knowledge that she had brought some comfort or some surcease to the suffering black peoples of her Africa.

'I still do not know myself all that well,' she admitted, as she called the third successive *tirikeza*, double-marching her porters relentlessly to keep ahead of Zouga wherever he might be.

'I want to find Pater, I want to find him alone, and I want the world to know I found him.'

'Pride is sinful, but then I have always been a sinner. Forgive me, Sweet Jesus, I will make it up in a thousand other ways. Only forgive this one small unimportant sin,' she prayed in her rude grass shelter, and as she did so she listened with one ear for the shouts of Zouga's bearers coming into camp, and her heart tripped at each sudden noise. She was tempted to break camp and call a night march towards the next distant hill they had seen on the horizon at sunset and which old Karanga had once again confidently declared to be the Iron Mountain. The moon was full and would rise in an hour, that one march might be all that was necessary to keep ahead of her brother.

However, her porters were exhausted, even Juba was complaining of thorns in her feet. It seemed that only she and old Karanga were able to maintain this pace for day after day. She must let them rest.

The next morning she had them away when the grass was still bent under the weight of dew drops, and before she had gone a mile her breeches were soaked to the thighs. During the last few days' march the character of the land had altered. The elevated plateau of rolling grassland and open forest across which they had marched so long now seemed to be dipping southwards, and the single peak which she had seen the night before slowly evolved into a whole

series of hills stretching across her horizon from west to east, and she felt her
spirits sag.

What chance would she ever have of finding one man's camp, one single
hilltop, amongst so many? But she slogged on doggedly, and she and Karanga
reached the first foothills before noon well ahead of the column. She checked
Zouga's barometer nestling in its velvet-lined wooden case, and found that the
altitude was still well over 1,200 feet, though they had dropped two hundred
feet in the last two days' march.

Then, followed closely by Karanga, and at a little distance by Juba, she
climbed the rocky shoulder of one of the foothills and from its height had a
clearer view ahead over the confused and broken ground. She could see that the
hills descended sharply into the south. Perhaps they had crossed the highlands
and before them lay the descent to one of the known rivers that Tom Harkness
had marked upon his map. She tried to remember the names, Shashi and Tati
and Macloutsi.

Suddenly she was starting to feel very lonely and uncertain again. The land
was so vast, she felt like a tiny insect pinned to an endless plain beneath the high
pitiless blue sky. She turned and looked back into the north, using the long,
brass-bound telescope to search for any signs of Zouga's party. She was not
certain if she was relieved or disappointed to find none.

'Karanga!' she called, and he scrambled to his feet readily and looked up at
her on the pinnacle of rock on which she stood. His expression was trusting as
that of a pet-dog.

'Which way now?' she demanded, and he dropped his eyes and stood on one
bird-thin leg, scratching his calf with the other foot as he pondered the question.
Then with an apologetic gesture he indicated the nearest half dozen promontories
along the skyline ahead with a hesitant all-embracing gesture, and Robyn felt
her heart sink further. She had to admit at last that she was lost.

She knew then that she would have to do one of two things. Either camp
where she was until Zouga came up, or turn back along her own spoor until she
met him. Neither alternative was attractive, and she put off the decision until
the morrow.

There was water in the river-bed below her, the usual shallow warm green
pools, foul with bird and animal droppings.

Suddenly she felt very tired. While the expectations of success had buoyed her
up she had not noticed it, but now she felt deflated and the marrow of her bones
ached with weariness.

'We will camp here,' she told the Corporal. 'Take two men and find meat.'

They had marched so hard and long since leaving Karanga's village that there
had been no time to hunt. By this time the last of the dried buffalo meat smelt
like badly cured hides and was full of bacon beetles. She could only eat it in a
strong curry and the curry powder was almost finished. They needed fresh meat
desperately, but she was too dispirited to lead the hunting party.

The porters had not finished thatching the low lean-to roof that would be her
home for the night when she heard a fusillade of musket fire close by in the
forest, and an hour later the Corporal came into camp. They had found a large
herd of the lovely sable antelope, Harris buck, as Zouga insisted on calling
them, and had succeeded in bringing down five fat chocolate-coloured cows. The
porters, chattering happily, left en masse to help bring in the meat, and Robyn
wandered listlessly down the river-bed, accompanied only by Juba, until she
found a secluded pool.

'I must smell as good as old Karanga,' she thought, scrubbing herself with
handfuls of white sand for she had weeks previously used the last of her soap.
She washed out her clothing and spread it to dry on the smooth, water-worn

rocks around the pool. Then, still naked, she sat in the sunlight and Juba knelt behind her and combed out her hair so that it could dry.

Juba was obviously pleased to have Robyn to herself again, without old Karanga hovering nearby. Even though Robyn was silent and dejected. Juba loved to play with her hair and delighted in the reddish lights that flared in the sunlight as the comb stroked through it.

She chatted merrily as she worked and gurgled with laughter at her own sallies, so that neither of them heard the footsteps in the sand, and it was only when the shadow fell at Robyn's feet that she realized that they were not alone. With a cry of alarm she rose, snatching up her still wet breeches and holding them to her breast to cover her nudity.

The woman who stood before her was unarmed, nervous as she was and shy. Not a young woman, though her skin was smooth and unlined and she had all her teeth still. She was almost certainly Mashona with the finer, more Egyptian features than the Nguni, and she wore the short kilt that left her upper body bare. Her naked breasts were large, out of proportion to the slim upright body, the nipples were raised and drawn-out as though she had recently been nursing an infant.

'I heard the guns,' she whispered shyly, and Robyn felt a lift of relief when he understood the language. It was Karanga. 'I came when I heard the guns. I came to lead you to Manali.'

Robyn felt the quick rush of tears scald her eyes at the name, and the leap of her heart made her gasp aloud.

Manali, the man who wears a red shirt – her father had always stoutly maintained that the colour red discouraged tsetse fly and other stinging insects, and that good thick flannel staved off the ague of fever.

Robyn jumped to her feet, completely oblivious now of her nudity and rushed to the woman, seizing her arm and shaking it.

'Manali!' she cried, and then in English. 'Where is he? Oh, take me to him this instant.'

It was more than mere chance, and old Karanga's faltering guidance, that had led her, Robyn decided exultantly as she followed her new guide along one of the narrow winding game paths. It was blood calling to blood. Instinctively, like a migrating swallow, she had flown straight to her father.

She felt like shouting aloud, singing her joy to the forest while the woman went swiftly ahead of Robyn, her narrow, smoothly muscled back and shoulders hardly moved above the gliding roll of her hips, that graceful walk of the African woman trained from childhood to carry a burden upon her head so smoothly that not a drop spills from a brimming pot.

She did not move swiftly enough for Robyn's expectations. Already Robyn could imagine the powerful figure of her father striding towards her, the great flaming bush of his beard, the deep compelling voice as he called her name, and swung her high as he had when she was a child, then the crushing embrace of his arms.

She imagined his joy matching hers, and after the first heady moments of reunion, then the serious hours of discussion, the recital of the long years between, the growing trust and intimacy between them that they had lacked before, so that finally they could march together to a common goal. In the long years ahead, he could hand the torch to her confident that his faith and work would go forward in loving and loyal hands.

What would be his first words when he saw and recognized her? How immense his surprise? She laughed aloud breathlessly, of course, he would be deeply touched and grateful that she had come so far, so determinedly to be with him, and she, Robyn, knew that she would not be able to hold back her own tears of joy, she could imagine her father tenderly wiping them away. The tone of his voice would betray the pent-up love of all the intervening years that had parted them, and which would be so sweet that she could hardly bear it.

Ahead of her, in the fading light of a dying day the Mashona woman led them on to a steep pathway, climbing at a traverse across the western slope of the highest hill. Robyn laughed again when she realized that it was the same hill that old Karanga had pointed out from twenty miles away. He had been right in the end, she must praise him lavishly for that. In her own happiness she wanted to give joy to all the world.

The path came out on a level shelf just below the crest, with a shallow cliff at the back of it and the slope of the hill falling away steeply towards the sunset, and a breathtaking view across the forest and savannah. The entire land turned pink and gold in the low sun and the stupendous flat-topped thunderheads of cloud rose along the dark blue horizon. The setting was right for this magical moment, but Robyn glanced at it only once and then her full attention fastened on what lay ahead of her.

In the face of the cliff was the mouth of a low cave, the slanting rays of the sun struck fully into it showing that it was not very deep, but had been occupied for a long time. The roof and walls were blackened with the soot of the cooking fire, the floor had been swept bare except for the fire at the entrance, with its circle of blackened hearth stones and a small clay pot standing upon them.

The clearing in front of the cave was bare also, trodden by feet over many years, and there was the offal of human occupation scattered about it, the bare bones of small animals, scraps of fur, chips of wood and shards of broken pottery. There was the odour of rotting food fragments, unwashed leather garments, woodsmoke and human excrement that confirmed the other evidence that men had lived here for a long time.

There was a single human figure crouched over the smoky little fire, an old crone, bowed by age, a mere bundle of filthy fur blankets, motheaten and ragged, looking more like an ancient ape than a human being. It did not stir, and Robyn barely glanced at it for something else held her attention.

In the back of the cave, lit by the last fleeting sunlight, stood a bed. It was made of rudely cut poles, and tied together with bark rope, yet it stood on four legs in European style, not the African sleeping-mat, and it was piled with a stained fur kaross that might have contained a human shape.

On a ledge directly above the bed stood a brass telescope, a teak box similar to the one that held Zouga's sextant and chronometer, but scarred and battered with age, and a small cheap tin chest. The chest was much battered also, most of the original paint chipped away so the bare metal showed.

Robyn remembered that box so vividly, open in Uncle William's study at Kings Lynn, the papers from it overflowing on to the desk top and her father bowed over them, steel-rimmed spectacles on the end of his beaked nose, tugging at his thick red beard as he worked.

Robyn gave a little choking cry, and ran forward passing the old crone sitting at the fire, crossing the cave, and flinging herself on her knees beside the crude bedstead.

'Pater!' Her voice husked over with emotion rasped her own throat. 'Pater! It's me – Robyn.'

There was no movement beneath the fur blanket and she put out a hand, then stopped before it touched.

'He is dead,' she thought miserably. 'I am too late!'

She forced her hand to move again, and touched the malodorous pile of old furs. They collapsed under her touch, and it took her seconds to realize that she had been mistaken. The bed was empty, the discarded blanket had fallen in the shape of a man, but the bed was empty.

Bewildered, Robyn rose to her feet and turned back towards the entrance of the cave. The Karanga woman stood by the fire, watching her expressionlessly, while little Juba hung back fearfully at the far side of the clearing.

'Where is he?' Robyn spread her hands to emphasize the question. 'Where is Manali?'

The Karanga woman dropped her eyes. For a moment Robyn did not understand, and then she too looked down at the grotesque figure that crouched by the fire at her feet.

She felt a cold steel band lock about her chest and squeeze her heart so that it took an effort of will to force her feet to move back across the swept floor of the cave.

The Mashona woman was watching Robyn expressionlessly. She had clearly not understood the English question, but she waited with the endless patience of Africa. Robyn was about to appeal to her again, when the skeletal figure across the smoky little fire started to rock from side to side agitatedly, and a querulous slurred old man's voice began to chant some strange litany, like a magical incantation.

It took Robyn some moments to realize that the accents were faintly Scots and the words, though blurred and jumbled, were a parody of the 23rd psalm.

'Yea! Though I walk through the valley of the shadow of death, I shall fear no evil.'

As suddenly as it had begun the chanting broke off, and the rocking ceased. The frail figure froze into stillness and silence again. Across the fire, the Mashona woman stooped and gently as a mother with a child, she drew back the kaross from the head and shoulder of the figure at her feet.

Fuller Ballantyne had shrivelled, his face lined and roughened like the bark of an old oak. It seemed as though the smoke of the fire had etched his skin, collecting in the creases, crusting it with soot.

His hair and beard had fallen out in clumps, as though from some disgusting disease, and what was left of it was pure white but stringed and darkened with dirt to a tobacco yellow at the corners of the mouth and at the nostrils.

Only his eyes still seemed to live, they rolled in their sockets, and it needed only one look at them for Robyn to realize that her father was mad. This was not Fuller Ballantyne, this was not the great explorer, the powerful evangelist and enemy of slavery. He had gone long ago, leaving a filthy shrivelled lunatic in his place.

'Pater,' she stared at him in disbelief, feeling the world spin and lurch beneath her. 'Pater,' she repeated, and across the fire the crouched figure gibbered with abrupt falsetto girlish laughter, and then began to rave incoherently, snatches of English giving way to a half-dozen dialects of Africa, the cries becoming more agitated, his thin pale arms thrown wildly in the air.

'I have sinned against thee, my God,' he screamed and clawed at his own beard, a tuft of the thin pale hair coming away in the hooked fingers. 'I am not worthy to be thy servant.' He tore at himself again, this time leaving a thin livid scratch down the pouched and wrinkled cheek, though it seemed that the wasted body had no blood left to shed.

The Mashona woman leaned over him and caught the bony wrist, restraining him. The action was so familiar that she must have performed it often. Then gently she stooped and lifted him. The body seemed to weigh no more than that of a child for she carried him without visible effort to the crude pole bed. One of his legs was bound up in a rudimentary splint and stuck straight out ahead of him.

Robyn stayed on beside the fire, hanging her head. She found that she was still shivering, until the woman came back to her, touching her arm.

'He is very sick.'

Only then could Robyn force back her revulsion and her horror. She stood, hesitated only a moment longer, and then went to her father. With Juba and the Mashona woman helping her, she began her examination, taking refuge behind her professional rituals and procedures while she regained control of her emotions. He was thinner than she had ever seen a living human body, thinner than the starved brats of gin-soaked slum sluts.

'There has been little food,' said the woman, 'and what there is, he will not eat. I have had to feed him like a small baby.' Robyn did not then understand what she meant, but she went on grimly with her examination.

The starved body was verminous, the bunches of little white nits hanging like grapes in the thin white pubic hair, and his whole body was crusted with filth and traces of his own incontinence.

Feeling under the staring rib cage her fingertips encountered the hard distended shape of liver and spleen, and Fuller Ballantyne screamed when she did so. The swelling and extreme tenderness were certain indications of massive malarial infection of long duration, and evidence of terrible neglect.

'Where is the medicine, the *umuthi*, of Manali?'

'It was long ago finished, together with the powder and shot for the gun. Everything was finished long ago,' the woman shook her head, 'long, long ago, and when it was finished, the people no longer came with gifts to feed us.' It was suicidal to remain in a malarial area without supplies of quinine. Fuller Ballantyne of all people knew that. The acknowledged world expert on malarial fever and its treatment – how could he have neglected his own often-repeated advice. She found the reasons almost immediately, as she opened his mouth, forcing open his lower jaw despite his feeble protests.

Most of his teeth had been rotted out by the disease, and his throat and palate were covered by the characteristic lesions. She released his jaw, allowing him to close the ruined mouth, and gently she touched the bridge of his nose, feeling the soggy collapsing bone and gristle. There could be no doubt at all, the disease was far advanced, had long ago begun its final assault upon the once magnificent brain. It was syphilis, in the terminal stages, the general paralysis of the insane. The disease of the lonely man that led inevitably to this lonely madman's death.

As Robyn worked, so her horror and revulsion gave way swiftly to the compassion of the healer, to the sympathy of one who had lived with human weakness and folly and had come far along the road of understanding. She knew now why her father had not turned back when his supplies of vital medicines ran perilously low, the half-destroyed brain had not recognized the dangers which he had previously described so clearly.

She found herself praying for him as she worked, praying silently but with the words coming more readily than they usually did.

'Judge him as he was, Oh Lord, judge him by his service in your name – not by his small sins, but by his great achievements. Look not upon this ruined pathetic thing, but on the strong and vital man who carried your work forward without flinching.'

As she prayed, she lifted the heavy kaross of his legs, and the smell of corruption made her blink and the frail figure began immediately to struggle with renewed strength, that needed both Juba and the Mashona woman to control.

Robyn stared at the legs, and realized the other reason why her father had never left this land. He had been physically unable to do so. The splints that held the leg had been whittled out of native timber. The leg had been fractured, probably at more than one place below the hip. Perhaps the hip joint itself had gone, that vulnerable neck of the femur. But what was certain was that the breaks had not mended cleanly. Perhaps the bindings of the splints had been too tight, for the deep suppurating ulcerations went down to the very bone, and the smell was a solid jarring thing.

Quickly she covered his lower body, there was nothing she could do until she had her medical chest and instruments, and now she was merely inflicting unnecessary pain and humiliation. Her father was still struggling and bleating like a petulant child, rolling his head from side to side, the toothless mouth darkly agape.

The Mashona woman leaned over him, and took one of her own dark tight breasts in her hand, squeezing out the nipple between her fingers, and then she paused and looked up shyly, imploringly at Robyn.

Only then did Robyn understand, and respecting the privacy of woman and the poor maimed thing that had been her father, she dropped her eyes and turned away towards the entrance of the cave.

'I must fetch my *umuthi*. I will return here later tonight.'

Behind her, the childlike bleats gave way abruptly to small snuffling sounds of comfort.

Robyn felt no shock or outrage as she went down the steep pathway in the moonlight. Instead she felt immense pity for Fuller Ballantyne who had made the full circle back to infancy. She felt also a deep gratitude to the woman, and a sense of wonder at her loyalty and dedication. How long had she stayed on with Fuller Ballantyne after all reason for staying was gone?

She remembered her own mother, and her devotion to the same man, she remembered Sarah and her child still waiting patiently beside a far-off river. And then there was Robyn herself, come so far and so determinedly. Fuller Ballantyne always had the power to attract as powerfully as he could repel.

Holding Juba's hand for her own comfort as well as that of the child, Robyn hurried along the moonlit path on the bank of the river, and with relief saw the glow of the camp fires in the forest ahead of her. On the return journey she would have bearers to carry her medical chest, and armed Hottentot musketeers as escort.

Her relief was short-lived, for as she answered the challenge of the Hottentot sentry and entered the circle of firelight, a familiar figure rose from beside the camp fire and came striding to meet her, tall and powerful, golden-bearded and handsome as a god from Greek mythology, and every bit as wrathful.

'Zouga!' she gasped. 'I didn't expect you.'

'No,' he agreed icily. 'I'm sure that you did not.'

'Why?' she thought desperately. 'Why must he come now? Why not a day later, when I have had time to clean and treat my father? Oh God, why now? Zouga will never understand – Never! Never! Never!'

Robyn and her escort could not hope to keep pace with Zouga. They fell swiftly behind him as he climbed the pathway in the night, months of hard hunting had toned him to the peak of physical condition and he ran at the hill.

She had not been able to warn him. What words were there to describe the creature in the cave on the hilltop. She had told him simply

'I have found Pater.'

It had deflected his anger instantly. The bitter accusations shrivelled on his tongue, and the realization dawned in his eyes.

They had found Fuller Ballantyne. They had accomplished one of the three major objectives of the expedition. She knew that Zouga was already seeing it in print, almost composing the paragraph that would describe the moment, imagining the newspaper urchins shouting the headlines in the streets of London.

For the first time in her life she came close to hating her brother, and her voice was crisp as hoar-frost as she told him, 'And don't you forget it was me. I was the one who made the march and broke trail, and I was the one who found him.'

She saw the shift in his green eyes in the firelight.

'Of course, Sissy.' He smiled at her thinly, an obvious effort. 'Who could ever forget that? Where is he?'

'First I must assemble what I need.'

He had stayed with her until they reached the foot of the hill, and then had been unable to restrain himself. He had gone at the slope at a pace that none of them had been able to equal. Robyn came out in the little clearing in front of the cave. Her heart was racing and her breathing ragged from the climb so that she had to pause and fight for breath, holding one hand to her breast.

The fire in front of the cave had been built up to a fair blaze, but it left the depths of the cave in discreet shadow. Zouga stood in front of the fire. His back to the cave.

As Robyn regained her breath, she went forward. She saw that Zouga's face was deathly pale, in the firelight his sun-bronzing had faded to a muddy tone. He stood erect, as though on the parade ground, and he stared directly ahead of him.

'Have you seen Pater?' Robyn asked. His distress and utter confusion gave her a sneaking and spiteful pleasure.

'There is a native woman with him,' Zouga whispered, 'in his bed.'

'Yes,' Robyn nodded. 'He is very sick. She is caring for him.'

'Why did you not warn me?'

'That he is sick?' she asked.

'That he had gone native.'

'He's dying, Zouga.'

'What are we going to tell the world?'

'The truth,' she suggested quietly. 'That he is sick and dying.'

'You must never mention the woman.' Zouga's voice, for the first time that she could remember, was uncertain, he seemed to be groping for words. 'We must protect the family.'

'Then what must we tell about his disease, the disease that is killing him?'

Zouga's eyes flickered to her face. 'Malaria?'

'The pox, Zouga. The French sickness, the Italian plague – or, if you prefer it, syphilis, Zouga. He is dying of syphilis.'

Zouga flinched, and then he whispered, 'It's not possible.'

'Why not, Zouga?' she asked. 'He was a man, a great man – but a man nevertheless.'

She stepped past him. 'And now I have work to do.'

An hour later when she looked for him again, Zouga had gone back down the hill to the camp beside the river pools. She remained to work over her father for the rest of that night and most of the following day.

By the time she had bathed and cleaned him, shaved off the infested body hair and trimmed the stringy beard and locks of yellowed hair, treated the ulcerations of his leg, she was exhausted both physically and emotionally. She had seen approaching death too many times not to recognize it now. She knew that all she could hope for was to give comfort and to smooth the lonely road that her father must travel.

When she had done all that was possible, she covered him with a clean blanket and then tenderly caressed the short soft hair which she had so lovingly trimmed. Fuller opened his eyes. They were a pale empty shade of blue, like an African summer sky. The last sunlight of the day was washing the cave, and as Robyn leaned over him, it sparkled in her hair in chips of ruby light.

She saw something move in the empty eyes, a shadow of the man who had once been there, and Fuller's lips parted. Twice he tried to speak and then he said one word, so husky and light that she missed it. Robyn leaned closer to him.

'What is it?' she asked.

'Helen!' This time clearer.

Robyn felt the tears choke up her throat at the sound of her mother's name.

'Helen.' Fuller said it for the last time, and then the flicker of comprehension in his eyes was gone.

She stayed on beside him, but there was nothing more. That name had been the last link with reality and now the link was broken.

As the last light of the day faded, Robyn lifted her eyes from her father's face and for the first time realized that the tin chest was missing from the ledge at the back of the cave.

Using the lid of his own writing-case as a desk, screened from the camp by the thin wall of thatch, Zouga worked swiftly through the contents of the chest.

His horror at the discovery of his father had long ago been submerged by the fascination of the treasures which the chest contained. The disgust, the shame, would return again when he had time to think about it, he knew that. He knew also that there would be hard decisions to make then, and that he would have to use all his force of personality and of brotherly superiority to control Robyn, and make her agree to a common version of the discovery of Fuller Ballantyne and a tactful description of the circumstances to which he had been reduced.

The tin chest contained four leather and canvasbound journals, each of five hundred pages, and the pages were covered on both sides either with writing or with hand drawn maps. There was also a bundle of loose sheets, two or three hundred of them tied together with plaited bark string, and a cheap wooden pen case with a partition for spare nibs, and cut-outs for two ink bottles. One bottle was dry, and the pen nibs had obviously been sharpened many times, for they were almost worn away. Zouga sniffed the ink in the remaining bottle. It seemed to be an evil-smelling mixture, of fat and soot and vegetable dyes that Fuller had concocted when his supplies of the manufactured item were exhausted.

The last journal and most of the loose pages were written with this mixture, and they had faded and smeared, making the handwriting that much more difficult to decipher, for by this stage Fuller Ballantyne's hand had deteriorated almost as much as his mind. Whereas the first two journals were written in the small, precise and familiar script, this slowly turned into a loose sloping scrawl as uncontrolled as some of the ideas expressed by it. The history of his father's madness was plotted therein with sickening fascination.

The pages of the leatherbound journals were not numbered, and there were many gaps between the dates of one entry and the next, which made Zouga's work easier. He read swiftly, an art he had developed when acting as regimental intelligence officer with huge amounts of reading, reports, orders and departmental manuals, to get through each day.

The first books of writing were ground that had been travelled before, meticulous observations of celestial position, of climate and altitude, backed up by shrewdly observed descriptions of terrain and population. Sandwiched between these were accusations and complaints about authority, whether it were the directors of the London Missionary Society, or 'The Imperial Factor' as Fuller Ballantyne referred to the Foreign Secretary and his department in Whitehall.

There were detailed explanations of his reasons for leaving Tete and travelling south with a minimally equipped expedition, and then, quite suddenly, two pages devoted to an account of a sexual liaison with an ex-slave girl, an Angoni girl whom Fuller had christened 'Sarah' and who he suspected was about to bear his child. His reasons for abandoning her at Tete were direct and without pretence. 'I know that a woman, even a hardy native, carrying a child would delay me. As I am on God's work, I can brook no such check.'

Although what Zouga had seen on the hilltop should have conditioned him for this sort of revelation, still he could not bring himself to terms with it. Using his hunting-knife, whetted to a razor edge, he slit the offending pages from the journal, and as he crumpled them and threw them in the camp fire he muttered, 'The old devil had no right to write this filth.'

Twice more he found sexual references which he removed from the journal, and by then the handwriting was showing the first deterioration, and passages of great lucidity were followed by wild ravings and the dreams and imaginings of a diseased mind.

More often Fuller referred to himself as the instrument of God's wrath, his blazing sword against the heathen and the ungodly. The weirdest and patently lunatic passages Zouga cut from the journal and burned. He knew he must work swiftly, before Robyn came down from the hilltop. He knew that what he was doing was right, for his father's memory and place in posterity and also for those who would have to live on after him, Robyn and Zouga himself, and their children and children's children.

It was a chilling experience to see his father's great love and compassion for the African people, and the very land itself changing and becoming a bitter unreasoning hatred. Against the Matabele people, whom he referred to as the Ndebele – or the Amandebele – he railed: 'These leonine peoples who acknowledge no God at all, whose diet consists of the devil's brew and half-cooked meat, both in vast quantities, and whose greatest delight is spearing to death defenceless women and children, are ruled over by the most merciless despot since Caligula, the most grossly blood-besotted monster since Attila himself.'

Of the other tribes he was at least as scornful. 'The Rozwis are a sly and secret people, the timid and treacherous descendants of the slave-trading and gold-mad kings they called the Mambos. Their dynasties destroyed by the marauding Ndebele and their monstrous Nguni brothers the Shangaans of Gungundha and the blood-smattered Angoni.'

The Karangas were 'cowards and devil-worshippers, lurking in their caves and hilltop fortresses, committing unspeakable sacrilege and offending in the face of the Almighty by their blasphemous ceremonies in the ruined cities where once their Monomatapa held sway.'

The reference to Monomatapa and ruined cities checked Zouga's eyes in the middle of the page. Then he read on eagerly, hoping for elaboration of the mention of ruined cities, but Fuller's mind had flown on to other ideas, the theme of suffering and sacrifice which has always been the spine of Christian belief.

'I thank God, my Almighty Father, that he has chosen me as his sword, and that as the mark of his love and condescension he has made his mark upon me. This dawn when I awoke there were the stigmata in my feet and hands, the wound in my side, and the bleeding scratches from the crown of thorns upon my forehead. I have felt the same sweet pain as Christ himself.'

The disease had reached that part of his brain that affected his eyes, and sense of feeling. His faith had become religious mania. Zouga cut out this and the following pages and consigned them to the flames of the camp fire.

Ranting madness was followed by cool sanity, as though the disease had tides which ebbed and flowed within his brain. The next entry in the journal was dated five days after that claiming the stigmata. It began with a celestial observation that placed him not far from where Zouga sat reading the words, always making allowances for the inaccuracy of a chronometer that had not been checked for almost two years. There was no further reference to the stigmata. They had healed as miraculously as they had bloomed. Instead there was a brisk and businesslike entry in the old neat script.

'The Karanga people practise a form of ancestor worship, which calls for sacrifice. It is extremely difficult to make any one of them discuss either this ceremony or even the basic precepts of this abominable religion. However, my command of the Karanga language is now sufficient to have earned the respect and trust of those members of the tribe with whom I have succeeded in making contact. The spiritual centre of their religion is in a place which they refer to as "the burial place of the kings," or in their language "Zimbabwe" or "Simbabwee" where the idols which represent their ancestors stand.

'It would seem that this place is situated to the south and east of my present position.

'The head of this foul belief is a priestess, referred to as the "Umlimo" who once dwelt in the "burial place of the kings" but fled from there at the coming of the Angoni marauders. She lives in another sacred place, and commands such sway that even the godless Ndebele, that sanguine tyrant Mzilikazi, send gifts for her oracle.

'So deeply ingrained is the power of this evil belief into the minds of all these people, that they are strongly resistant to the word of Christ which I bear.

'It has come to me in a revelation which can only be the voice of God Almighty himself that he has chosen me to march upon this citadel of evil, this "Simbabwee", and to throw down the images of the ungodly – even as Moses threw down and destroyed the golden calf on his descent from the mountain.

'God Almighty has further revealed to me that I have been chosen to seek out the High Priestess of evil in her secret place and to destroy her, and by so doing break the hold that she has over the minds of these people, that they might become receptive to the Holy Word of Christ which I bring them.'

Zouga raced on through the pages, it seemed as though they were being written by two different men, the rational being with the neat script and the raving religious maniac with the wild looping hand. In some passages the change came from one line to the next, in others the one character was maintained for page after page. Zouga could not afford to miss a word of it.

It was well after noon, and his eyes felt grainy and tender from continually scanning the cramped sheets, blurred and faded from the improvised ink which Fuller was now using.

'November 3rd. Position. 20° 05 S. 30° 50 E. Temperature 103° in the shade. Heat unbearable. Rain threatens each day and never comes. Have reached the lair of the Umlimo.'

The single laconic entry electrified Zouga. He almost missed it, for it was squeezed into the bottom of a page. He turned that page and on the next the madman had taken over again, writing in vaunting hyperbole and thunderous religious ecstasy.

'I praise God, my Maker. The one true and Almighty Saviour for whom all things are possible. Thy will be done!

'The Umlimo knew me as the instrument of God's wrath when I confronted her in that reeking charnel house, for she spoke in the voices of Belal and Beelzebub, the hideous voices of Azazel and Beliar, all Satan's myriad alter-egos.

'But I stood before her strong and proud in God's word, and when she saw she could not move me, she fell silent.

'So I slew her, and cut off her head and carried it out into the light. And God spoke to me in the night and said in his small still voice "Go on, my faithful and well-beloved servant. You cannot rest until the graven images of the godless are cast down."

'So I rose, and God's hand held me up and carried me onwards.'

How much of this was fact, and how much was the ranting of madness, fantasy of a diseased brain, Zouga could not know, but he read on furiously.

'And the Almighty guided me until I came at last alone to the foul city where the devil-worshippers commit their sacrilege. My bearers would not follow me, terrified of the devils. Even old Joseph who was always at my side could not force his legs to carry him through the gateway in the high stone wall. I left him cringing in the forest, and went in alone to walk between the high towers of stone.

'As God had revealed to me, I found the graven images of the heathen all decked with flowers and gold, the blood of the sacrifice not yet dried, and I broke them and cast them down and no man could oppose me for I was the sword of Zion, the finger of God's own hand.'

The entry broke off abruptly, as though the writer had been overwhelmed by the strength of his own religious fervour, and Zouga flipped through the next one hundred pages of the journal searching for further reference to the city and its gold-decked images, but there was none.

Like the miraculous blooming of the stigmata upon Fuller's hands and feet and body and brow, perhaps this was also the imaginings of a lunatic.

Zouga returned to the original entry, describing Fuller's meeting with the Umlimo, the sorceress whom he had slain. He wrote the latitude and longitude into his own journal, copied the rough sketch map and made cryptic notes of the text, pondering it for clues that might lead or guide him. Then, quite deliberately, he cut out the pages from Fuller's own journal and held them one at a time over the fire, letting them crinkle and brown, then catch and flare before he dropped them and watched them curl and blacken. He stirred the ashes to dust with a stick before he was satisfied.

The last of the four journals was only partially filled, and contained a detailed description of a caravan route running from 'the blood-soaked lands where Mzilikazi's evil impis hold sway' eastwards five hundred miles or more 'to where the reeking ships of the traders surely wait to welcome the poor souls who survive the hazards of this infamous road'.

'I have followed the road as far as the eastern rampart of mountains, and always the evidence of the passing of the caravans is there for all the world to see. That grisly evidence which I have come to know so well, the bleaching bones and the circling vultures. Is there not a corner of this savage continent which is free from the ravages of the traders?'

These revelations would interest Robyn more than they did him. Zouga glanced through them swiftly and then marked them for her attention. There was a great deal on slavery and the traders, a hundred pages or more – and then the penultimate entry.

'We have today come up with a caravan of slaves, winding through the hilly country towards the east. I have counted the miserable victims from afar, using the telescope and there are almost a hundred of them, mostly half-grown children and young women. They are yoked together in pairs with forked tree trunks about their necks in the usual manner.

'The slave-masters are black men, I have been unable to descry either Arabs or men of European extraction amongst them. Although they wear no tribal insignia, no plumes nor regalia, I have no doubt they are Amandebele, for their physique is distinctive, and they come from the direction of that tyrant Mzilikazi's kingdom. They are furthermore armed with the broad bladed stabbing spear and long ox-hide shields of that people, while two or three of them carry trade muskets.

'At this moment they are encamped not more than a league from where I lie, and in the dawn they will continue their fateful journey towards the east where the Arab and Portuguese slave-masters no doubt wait to purchase the miserable human cattle and load them like cargo for the cruel voyage half across the world.

'God has spoken to me, clearly I have heard his voice as he enjoined me to go down, and, like his sword, cut down the ungodly, free the slaves and minister to the meek and the innocent.

'Joseph is with me, that true and trusted companion of the years, and he will be well able to serve my second gun. His marksmanship is not of the best, but he has courage and God will be with us.'

The next entry was the last. Zouga had come to the end of the four journals.

'God's ways are wonderful and mysterious, passing all understanding. He lifteth up and he casteth down. With Joseph beside me I went down, as God had commanded, to the camp of the slavemasters. We fell upon them, even as the Israelites fell upon the Philistines. At first it seemed that we must prevail for the ungodly fled before us. Then God in all his knowing wisdom deserted us. One of the ungodly leapt upon Joseph while he was reloading, and though I put a ball through his chest he impaled poor Joseph from breast bone to spine with that terrible spear, before himself falling dead.

'Alone I carried on the fight, God's fight, and the slave-masters scattered into the forest before my wrath. Then one of them turned and at extreme range fired his musket in my direction. The ball struck me in the hip.

'I managed, I do not know how, to drag muself away before the slave-masters returned to slay me. They did not attempt to follow me, and I have regained the shelter which I left to make the attempt. However, I am sorely smitten and reduced to dire straits. I have managed to remove the musket ball from my own hip, but I fear the bone is cracked through and I am crippled.

'In addition I have lost both my firearms, Joseph's musket lies with him where he fell, and I was so badly hurt as to be unable to carry my weapon off the field. I sent the woman back to find them, but they have been carried away by the slave-traders.

'My remaining porters, seeing the state to which I have been reduced and knowing that I could not prevent it, have all deserted, but not before they had looted the camp and carried away almost everything of value, not excluding my medicine chest. Only the woman remains. I was angry at first when she attached herself to my party, but now I see God's hand in this – for although she is a heathen, yet she is loyal and true beyond all others, now that Joseph is dead.

'What is a man in this cruel land without a musket or quinine? Is there a lesson in this for me and posterity, a lesson that God has chosen me to teach? Can a white man live here? Will he not always be the alien, and will Africa tolerate him once he has lost his weapons and expended his medicines?'

Then a single poignant cry of agony.

'Oh God, has this all been in vain? I came to bring your Word and nobody has listened to my voice. I came to change the ways of the wicked and nothing is changed. I came to open a way for Christianity, and no Christian has followed me. Please, my God, give me a sign that I have not followed the wrong road to a false destination.'

Zouga leaned back and rubbed his eyes with the heels of both hands. He found himself deeply moved, his eyes stinging not only from fatigue.

Fuller Ballantyne was an easy man to hate, but a hard man to despise.

Robyn chose the place with care. The secluded pools on the river, away from the main camp, where nobody could overlook or overhear them. She chose the time, in the heat of midday – when most of the Hottentots and all the porters would be asleep in the shade. She had given Fuller five drops of the precious laudanum to quiet him, and left him with the Mashona girl and Juba to care for him while she went down the hill to Zouga.

They had barely exchanged a dozen words during the ten days since he had caught up with her. In all that time he had not returned to the cave on the hilltop, and she had seen him only once when she had gone down to the river camp for supplies.

When she had sent Juba down with a tersely worded note, demanding the return of Fuller's tin chest of papers, he had sent a porter with it immediately. In fact, with such alacrity that Robyn was immediately suspicious.

This distrust was a symptom of their rapidly deteriorating relationship. She knew that she and Zouga must talk, must discuss the future, before the opportunity to talk was past.

He was waiting for her beside the green river pools, as she had asked him to be, sitting in the mottled shade beneath a wild fig tree, quietly smoking a hand-rolled cheroot of native tobacco. He stood up courteously as soon as he saw her, but his expression was reserved and his eyes guarded.

'I do not have much time, Zouga dear.' Robyn tried to lessen the tension between them by using the small endearment, and Zouga nodded gravely. 'I must get back to Pater.' She hesitated. 'I did not want to ask you to come up the hill since you find it distasteful.' She saw the green sparks in his eyes kindle immediately, and went on quickly. 'We must decide what we should do now. Obviously we cannot stay on here indefinitely.'

'What do you suggest?'

'Pater is much stronger. I have subdued the malaria with quinine and the other disease,' she worded it tactfully, 'has responded to the mercury. It is only the leg that truly worries me now.'

'You told me he was dying,' Zouga reminded her levelly, and she could not help herself, despite her good intentions she flared at him.

'Well, I am sorry to disappoint you, then.'

Zouga's face stiffened into a handsome, bronzed mask. She could see the effort it took him to control his own temper, and his voice was thick with it as he answered.

'That's not worthy of you.'

'I'm sorry,' she agreed, and drew a deep breath. 'Zouga, he has rallied strongly. Food and medicine, care and his own natural strength have made an immense difference. I am even convinced that if we could get him to civilization to a skilled surgeon – we could cure the ulceration of his leg, and possibly even induce the bone to mend.'

Zouga was silent for a long time, and though his face was expressionless, she could see the play of emotion in his eyes.

He spoke at last. 'Father is mad.' She did not answer. 'Can you cure his mind?'

'No.' She shook her head. 'That will get worse, but with care and skilled attention in a good hospital, we can improve his body and he could live for many years still.'

'To what purpose?' Zouga insisted.

'He would be comfortable and perhaps happy.'

'And all the world would know that he was a syphilitic madman,' Zouga went on quietly for her. 'Would it not be kinder to let the legend stand untarnished? No, more than that, to add to it by our own account, rather than drag back this poor diseased and demented thing for all his enemies, his numerous enemies, to mock?'

'Is that why you tampered with his journals?' Robyn's voice was shrill, even in her own ears.

'That's a dangerous accusation.' He was losing his control also. 'Can you prove it?'

'I don't have to prove it; we both know it's so.'

'You cannot move him.' Zouga changed direction. 'He is crippled.'

'He could be carried on a litter. We have more than enough porters.'

'Which way would you take him?' Zouga demanded. 'He would never survive the route over which we have travelled – and the route southwards is uncharted.'

'Pater himself has charted the slave road in his journal. We will follow that. It will lead us directly to the coast.'

'With the major objectives of the expedition unfulfilled?' Zouga asked quickly.

'The major objectives were to find Fuller Ballantyne, and report on the slave trade, both of which we can accomplish if we march down the slave road to the sea.' Robyn broke off, and then made a show of dawning comprehension. 'Oh dear, how silly of me, you mean the gold and the ivory. Those were the major objectives all along, were they not, my dear brother?'

'We have a duty to our sponsors.'

'And none to that poor sick old man up there?' Robyn flung out one hand dramatically, and then spoiled the effect by stamping her foot. Angry with herself as well as with him, she yelled at him. 'I am taking Pater down to the coast, and quickly as I can.'

'I say you are not.'

'And I say the hell with you, Morris Zouga Ballantyne!' The oath gave her a dark pleasure, and she turned and strode away from him, long-legged in her tight-fitting breeches.

Two days later Robyn was ready to march. All exchanges between Zouga and herself since their final meeting at the river had been in the form of written notes, and Robyn realized that her brother would be keeping copies of all this correspondence to justify his actions later.

She had briefly repudiated his written command not to attempt a march with the sick man. Zouga had listed half a dozen reasons, each neatly enumerated, why she should remain. Once he had her written defiance, his next note sent up the hill in Juba's sweating little hand was magnanimous, written for future readers other than herself, Robyn decided sourly.

'If you insist on this folly,' he began, and he went on to offer her the protection of the entire force of Hottentot musketeers – with the exception of Sergeant Cheroot who had expressed a desire to remain with Zouga. Under the Corporal they would form an escort capable, as Zouga worded it 'of bringing you and your charge safely to the coast, and protecting you from any hazards upon the way.'

He insisted that she take most of the remaining porters. He would keep five porters to carry his essential stores, together with his four gunbearers, Matthew, Mark, Luke and John.

He also ordered her to take the Sharps rifle and all the remaining stores, 'leaving me only sufficient powder and shot, and the bare minimum of medicines to enable me to complete the further objectives of this expedition which I deem to be of prime importance.'

His final note reiterated all his reasons for keeping Fuller Ballantyne on the hilltop, and asked her once more to reconsider her decision. Robyn saved him the trouble of making fair copies by simply turning over the note and scribbling on it. 'My mind is made up. I will march at first light tomorrow for the coast.' Then she dated and signed it.

The next morning, before sun-up, Zouga sent a team of porters up the hill, carrying a litter of mopani poles. The poles had been peeled of their rough bark and bound together with raw-hide strips from the green hide of a freshly killed roan antelope, and the body of the litter was made from the same interwoven hide strips. Fuller Ballantyne had to be strapped into the litter to prevent him throwing himself out of it.

When Robyn brought them down again, walking beside the litter to try and calm the crazy old man on it, the Hottentot escort and the porters were ready to join her on the march. Zouga was waiting also, standing a little aside as though he had already dissociated himself, but Robyn went to him directly.

'At least we know each other now,' she said huskily. 'We may not be able to rub along together, Zouga. I doubt we ever could have, or ever will be able to, but that does not mean I do not respect you, and love you even more than I respect you.'

Zouga flushed and looked away. As she should have known, such a declaration could only embarrass him.

'I have made sure that you have a hundred pounds of gunpowder, that is more than you could ever need,' he said.

'Do you not wish to say farewell to Pater?'

Zouga nodded stiffly, and followed her to the litter, avoiding looking at the Mashona woman who stood beside it and spoke formally to Fuller Ballantyne.

'Good-bye, sir. I wish you a swift safe journey and a speedy return to good health.'

The wizened toothless face, revolved towards him upon its scrawny neck. The shaven head had a pale porcelain gloss in the grey dawn light, and the eyes were bird-bright, glittering with madness.

'God is my shepherd, I shall fear no evil,' Fuller cawed, mouthing the words so they were barely understandable.

'Quite right, sir,' Zouga nodded seriously. 'No doubt at all about that.' He touched his cap in a military salute and stepped back. He nodded to the porters and they lifted the litter and moved away towards the pale orange and yellow sunrise.

Brother and sister stood side by side for the last time watching the column of escort and porters file past, and when the last of them had gone and only little Juba remained beside her, Robyn reached up impulsively and threw her arms around Zouga's neck, embraced him almost fiercely.

'I try to understand you, won't you do the same for me?'

For a moment she thought he might unbend, she felt the hard erect body sway and soften, and then Zouga straightened again.

'This is not good-bye,' he said. 'Once I have done what is necessary, I shall follow you. We'll meet again.'

Robyn dropped her arms to her sides, and stood back.

'Until then,' she agreed wistfully, sad that he had not been able to make even a show of affection.

'Until then,' she repeated, and turned away. Juba followed her away into the forest, after the departing column.

Zouga waited until the singing of the porters dwindled, and the only sound was the sweet wild bird chorus that greets each dawn in Africa, and the distant melancholy whooping of a hyena slinking away to its earth.

There were many emotions warring in him. Guilt that he had let a woman, however well supported, attempt the journey to the coast; worry that once she reached it, her accounts would be the first to reach London; doubt as to the authenticity of the clues which Fuller Ballantyne had left for him to follow, but overlying it all a sense of relief and excitement that he was at last answerable only to himself, free to range as fast and far as hard legs and harder determination would take him.

He shook himself, a physical purging of guilt and doubt, leaving only the excitement and soaring sense of anticipation, and he turned to where Sergeant Cheroot waited at the perimeter of the forlorn and deserted camp.

'When you smile, your face makes the children cry,' Zouga told him, 'but when you frown . . . What troubles you now, oh mighty hunter of elephants?'

The little Hottentot lugubriously indicated the bulky tin box that contained Zouga's dress uniform and hat.

'Say not another word, Sergeant,' Zouga warned him.

'But the porters complain, they have carried it so far.'

'And they will carry it to the gates of hell itself, if I say so. Safari!' Zouga raised his voice, elated with the sense of excitement still strongly upon him. 'We march!'

Zouga was prepared for wide discrepancies in the positions that his father had fixed by celestial observation, and his own. A few seconds of error in the chronometers would put them many miles out.

So he treated with suspicion the terrain features which he saw ahead and which seemed to match with uncanny accuracy the sketch maps he had copied from Fuller's journals.

Yet as each day's march that he made opened up country that fitted his father's descriptions, he became more confident, more certain that the Umlimo and the ruined city were real and that they lay not many days' march ahead.

It was beautiful country they passed through, though the air was more sultry as they descended the sloping plateau towards the south and west. The long dry season, now drawing to its close, had seared the grasslands to the colour of fields of ripening wheat, and turned the foliage of the forests to a hundred shades of plum reds and soft apricots. Many of the trees were bare of all leaves, lifting arthritically contorted limbs to the sky as if beseeching it for the relief of rain.

Each day the thunderheads built up, tall silver ranges of cloud turning purple and sullen leaden blue, threatening rain, but never making good that threat, though the thunder muttered, and in the evenings the lightning flickered low on the horizon as though great armies were locked in battle far to the east.

The big game was concentrated on the remaining water, the deeper river pools and the strongest water-holes, so that each day's march was through a wonderland of wild animals.

In one herd Zouga counted thirty-two giraffe, from the old stink-bull almost black with age, his long neck taller than the trees on which he fed, to the pale beige splotched calves on their disproportionately long legs, galloping away in that slow rocking gait with their long tufted tails twisted up over their backs.

Every clearing had its family of rhinoceros, the cows with the distinctively long slender nose horn, running their calves ahead of them, guiding them with a touch of the horn on the flank. There were herds of Cape buffalo, a thousand strong, flowing in a black dense mass across the open glades, steaming with pale dust like the lava from an active volcano.

Then there were elephant. There was not one day they did not cut fresh spoor, veritable roads through the forest, tall trees pushed down or still standing but stripped of their bark so the trunks were naked and weeping with fresh sap, the earth beneath them strewn with chewed twigs and bunches of picked leaves only just beginning to wither, the huge piles of fibrous dung standing like monuments to the passing of the great grey beasts, and the baboon and the plump brown pheasant scratching and foraging enthusiastically in them for the half digested wild nuts and other tidbits.

Zouga could seldom resist him when Jan Cheroot looked up from his examination of the pad marks and said, 'A big bull, this one, walking heavy in the front quarters. Good teeth, I'd stake my sister's virtue on it.'

'A commodity which was staked and lost many years ago,' Zouga observed drily. 'But we will follow, none the less.'

Most evenings they could cut teeth and, having buried them, carry the bleeding heart to where they had left the porters, two men to carry the forty-pound hunk of raw flesh slung on a pole between them, a feast for the whole party. Because of the hunt, progress was slow and not always direct, but steadily Zouga identified and passed the landmarks that his father had described.

Then at last, knowing he was close, Zouga withstood the temptation to hunt, for the first time refusing to follow the fresh spoor of three fine bulls, and disappointing Jan Cheroot most grievously by doing so.

'You should never leave a good elephant, or a warm and willing lady,' he advised dolefully, 'because you never know where or when you are going to meet the next one.'

Jan Cheroot did not yet know the new object of their quest and Zouga's behaviour puzzled him. Zouga often caught him watching him with a quizzical sparkle in his bright little slitty eyes, but he avoided the direct question diplomatically and accepted Zouga's orders to abandon the spoor with only a little further grumbling, and they went on.

It was the porters who first baulked. Zouga never knew how they guessed, perhaps old Karanga had spoken of the Umlimo around the camp fire, or perhaps it was part of their tribal lore, although the gunbearers and most of the porters were from the Zambezi many hundreds of miles to the north. Yet Zouga had learned enough of Africa by now to recognize the strange, almost telepathic knowledge of far events and places. Whatever it was, and however they had acquired forewarning, there were thorns in the porters' feet for the first time in months.

At first Zouga was angry, and would have lived up to his nickname of 'Bakela', the Fist, but then he realized that their reluctance to continue towards the range of bald hills that showed above the horizon was confirmation that he was on a hot scent and close to his goal.

In camp that night, he drew Jan Cheroot aside and, speaking in English, explained what he was seeking and where. He was unprepared for the sickly expression that slowly spread over Jan Cheroot's wizened yellow features.

'Nie wat! Ik lol nie met daai goed nie!' The little Hottentot was driven in his superstitious terror to fall back on the bastard Cape Dutch. 'No what! I don't

mess around with that sort of thing,' he repeated in English, and Zouga smiled tauntingly across the camp fire at him.

'Sergeant Cheroot, I have seen you run, with a bare backside, right up to a wounded bull elephant, and wave your hat to turn him when he charged.'

'Elephants,' said Jan Cheroot without returning the smile, 'is one thing. Witches is another thing.' Then he perked up and twinkled like a mischievous gnome.

'Somebody must stay with the porters or they'll steal our traps and run for home.'

Zouga left them camped near a muddy little water-hole, within an hour's march of the northernmost granite kopje. At the water-hole he filled the big enamelled water bottle, and wet its thick covering of felt to keep the contents cool, slung a freshly charged powder sack on one hip and a food bag on the other, and, with the heavy smooth-bore elephant gun over his shoulder set out alone while the shadows were still long on the earth, and the grass wet with the dew.

The hills ahead of him were rounded domes of pearly grey granite, smooth as a bald man's pate and completely free of vegetation. As he trudged towards them across the lightly forested plain, his spirit quailed at the task ahead of him.

With each step the hills seemed to rise higher and steeper, the valleys between them deeper and more sheer, the thorny bush that choked the gorges and ravines more dense. It could take months to search all of this broken wilderness, and he did not have a guide as his father had had. Yet, in the end, it was so easy that he was irritated with his own lack of foresight.

His father had written in the journals 'Even Mzilikazi, that sanguine tyrant, sends gifts for her oracle.'

He struck the well-defined road, leading out of the west, broad enough for two men to walk along it, and aimed directly into the maze of smooth, granite hills. It could only be the road used by the emissaries of the Matabele king.

It led Zouga up the first gentle slope of ground, and then turned abruptly into one of the gorges between peaks. The path narrowed, and jinked between huge round granite boulders, the bush so thick on each side that he had to duck below the thorny branches that interlinked to form a gloomy tunnel overhead.

The valley was so deep that the sunlight did not penetrate to the floor, but the heat was thrown out by the granite as though it had been baked in an open fire, and the sweat soaked Zouga's shirt and slid in cool, tickling drops down his flanks. The bush thinned and the valley narrowed, and then pinched out into a narrow neck between the converging rock walls. It was a natural gateway where a few good spearsmen could have held a regiment. On a ledge high above was a small thatched watch hut, and beside it an idle blue tendril of smoke rising from a watchfire into the still hot air. But if there had been a guard he had deserted his post at Zouga's approach.

Zouga grounded the butt of his elephant gun, and leaned upon it to rest from the climb and at the same time surreptitiously to search the cliffs above him for a hidden enemy, or for the spot from which one could send the familiar boulders bounding and clanging down upon him.

The gorge was silent, hot and deserted. There was not even the chittering of birds or the murmur of insects in the undergrowth. The silence was more oppressive than the heat, and Zouga threw back his head and hallooed up at the deserted watch-hut.

The echoes, boomed grotesquely back and forth across the gorge, and then descended through confused whispers to the same foreboding silence. The last white man to pass this way was the Sword of God, in person, intent on decapitating the oracle, Zouga thought bitterly. He could not expect a hero's welcome.

He shouldered the gun again and went into the natural granite gateway, his instinct telling him that the bold approach was the only one open to him. The narrow passageway was floored with crunching grey sand, full of mica chips that sparkled like diamonds even in the subdued light. The passage curved gently until he could see neither the entrance behind him nor the end of it. He wanted to hurry, for this was like a cage, or a trap, but he controlled his feet and showed neither fear nor indecision in his tread.

Around the curve the passageway fanned open, and from one wall a small freshet rippled down the granite cliff, spilled with a tiny liquid gurgle into a natural basin of rock and then overflowed to run down into the hidden valley beyond. Zouga came out of the natural gateway and paused again to stare about him. It was a pleasant valley, probably a mile long and half as wide. The rivulet watered it, and the grass was cool green.

In the centre of the valley was a huddle of neatly thatched huts, around which scratched a few scrawny fowls. He went down to them. The huts were all deserted, although there was everywhere evidence of very recent occupation, even the porridge in the cooking pot was still hot.

Three of the largest huts were crammed with treasures, leather bags of salt, tools and weapons of iron, ingots of smelted red copper, a pile of small ivory tusks, and Zouga guessed that these were the tributes and gifts sent by petitioners and supplicants to the oracle. Payments made for her intercession with the rain gods, fees for a spell cast upon an enemy, or to soften a coquette's heart.

The fact that these treasures were left unguarded was proof of the Umlimo's power, and her own belief in that power. However, if Fuller Ballantyne's journal was the truth 'the foul and midnight hag' as he referred to her was long ago dead, and her severed skull crunched by the hyenas or bleaching somewhere in the hot African sun.

Zouga stooped out through the low entrance of the last hut, into the sunlight once more. He called again, but again there was no answer. There were people here, many of them, but to make contact with them, and then to learn from them the location of the 'burial place of the kings' was going to be more difficult than he expected.

Leaning on the long gun he turned his attention to the steep side of the valley, and again it was the pathway that caught his eye and led it to the entrance of the cave. For the path continued beyond the village, running down the centre of the valley and climbed the far slope of the valley, then came to an abrupt end against the granite cliff. The mouth of the cave was low and wide, a narrow horizontal gash in the base of the cliff like a toad's mouth and the path led directly into it.

Zouga climbed the gentle slope to the cave entrance. He had left his food bag and water bottle at the village, and, lightly burdened, he strode upwards, tall and lithe, his beard sparkling like gold thread in the sunlight, so that any hidden watcher could not have doubted that this was a chieftain and warrior to treat with respect.

He reached the cave entrance and checked, not from fatigue, for the climb had not taxed hime, but merely to take his bearings. The cave entrance was a hundred paces or so wide, and the roof so low that he could reach up and touch the rough rock.

There was a guard wall built to close off the opening, a wall of dressed granite blocks, fitted so closely that it would have been impossible to drive a knife blade between the joints, clearly the work of skilled masons, but done long ago for in places the wall had tumbled, the blocks piled upon each other in disarray.

The path led into one of these gaps, and disappeared into the gloom beyond. It was a most unwelcoming entrance. Going in he would have the light at his back, and his eyes would be unaccustomed to the poor light, there would be many places where a man could wait with spear or axe. Zouga felt his first ardour cooling as he peered into that forbidding opening, and he called again in the Matabele language.

'I come in peace!'

He was answered almost immediately, in a childish piping voice speaking the same language, close behind his shoulder, so close that his heart tripped, and he whirled.

'White is the colour of mourning and death,' piped the voice, and Zouga looked about him in confusion. There was no child, no human, no animal even, the valley behind him was deserted, silent. The voice had emanated from the very air.

Zouga felt his mouth drying, and the skin on his forearms and at the base of his skull crawled with the loathsome little insects of fear, and while he stared another voice screeched from the cliff above him.

'White is the colour of war.'

It was the voice of an old woman, a very old woman, quavering and shrill. Zouga's heart jumped again, and then raced as he looked up. The cliff face was bare and smooth. His heart was fluttering against his ribs like a trapped bird, and his breath rasped and sawed in his throat.

'White is the colour of slavery,' Sang a young girl's voice, filling the air about his head, having no direction and no substance, sweet and liquid as the burble of running water.

'She spoke in the voices of Belial and Beelzebub, the hideous voices of Azazel and Beliar, all Satan's myriad alter-egos,' his father had written, and Zouga felt the slow leaden spread of superstitious terror weighing down his legs.

Another voice, roaring like a bull, boomed from the mouth of the cave. 'The white eagle has cast down the stone falcons.'

He took a long slow breath, to bring his mutinous body under control, and he cast his mind back deliberately to a childhood memory. Brighton pier on August bank holiday, the small boy clutching his Uncle William's hand and staring up in wonder at the magician on the stage who made a doll come to life and speak in a quaint piping voice, answering the voice from the box too small to contain even a rabbit. The memory steadied him, and he laughed. It was a clear firm laugh, surprising himself even.

'Keep your tricks for the children, Umlimo. I come in peace to speak with you as a man.'

There was no reply, though he thought he caught the silken whisper of bare feet on stone, coming from the darkness beyond the ruined stone wall.

'See me, Umlimo! I lay aside my weapons.'

He unslung the powder bag and dropped it at his feet, and then he laid the elephant gun across it and holding his empty hands before him he advanced slowly into the cave.

As he reached the step in the wall, there was the crackling spitting snarl of an angry leopard from the shadows just ahead of him. It was a terrible sound, fierce and real, but Zouga had himself in hand now. He did not miss a pace but stooped under the sill through the gap, and straightened on the far side.

He waited for a minute while his eyes adjusted, and he could make out shapes and planes in the gloom. There were no other voices or animal sounds. There was a faint source of light somewhere ahead of him in the depths of the cave, and he could now make out a way amongst the scree and fallen rock that choked the cave, in some places as high as the low roof.

Zouga began to pick his way carefully forward. The light grew stronger, and Zouga realized that it was a single beam of sunlight, shining through a narrow crack in the roof.

Looking up, he stumbled and put out a hand to save himself. It was not rock that he touched but something sticklike that moved beneath his touch. There was a rattle, and a loose dry rush of debris. Zouga caught his balance and glanced down. A disembodied human skull gaped up at him from empty black eye sockets, the cheekbones still covered with a parchment of dried skin.

With a jolting little shock Zouga realized that what he had taken for loose scree and rock was instead piles of human remains, dried and desiccated corpses, lying in mounds and heaps, choking the passages and deepest recesses of the cave, here and there a single body, crouched or sprawled alone, bone shining dully from gaps in its covering of dark dried skin or through the rotting leather garments.

'That reeking charnel house,' Fuller Ballantyne had called it.

Instinctively Zouga wiped the hand that had touched the long-dead skeleton, and then went on towards the light. There was the smell of smoke now, and of human presence, and another sweet mousy odour that was hauntingly familiar but which Zouga could not place at that moment. The floor of the cave sloped downwards under his feet, and he turned a rocky shoulder and looked down into a small natural amphitheatre, with a floor of smooth granite.

In the centre of the floor burned a low fire of some aromatic wood, the smoke spiced the air and rose in a slow spiral towards the crack in the rocky roof, clouding the beam of sunlight with milky blue. There seemed to be other fingers of the cave leading further into the hillside, like the adits of a mine shaft, but Zouga's attention was focused on the figure that sat across the fire from him.

Zouga went slowly down on to the floor of the stone amphitheatre without taking his eyes from the figure.

'That foul and midnight hag,' his father had called the Umlimo, but this was no hag. She was young, in full physical prime, and as she knelt facing him Zouga realized that he had seldom seen such a fine-looking woman, certainly not in India or Africa, and very seldom, if ever, in the northern lands.

She had a long regal neck on which her head balanced like a black lily on its stem. Her features were Egyptian, with a straight fine nose and huge dark eyes above high moulded cheekbones. Her teeth were small and perfect, her lips chiselled like the flutes of a pink seashell.

She was naked, her body slim, her limbs long and fine, her hands and feet narrow and delicately shaped with tapered fingers and pale pink palms. Her small breasts rode high and were pefectly round, her waist narrow but flaring into tight hard buttocks and hips like the curve of a Venetian vase. Her sex was a wide triangle, deeply cleft, the inner lips bursting out unashamedly, like the wings of a dark exotic butterfly emerging from its woolly crysallis.

She was watching him with those huge dark eyes, and when he stopped across the fire from her, she made a slow gracious gesture with those delicately long fingers. Obediently Zouga squatted down opposite her and waited.

The woman took up one of the calabash gourds from the array beside her, holding it between the palms of her hands and poured from it into a shallow earthen bowl. It was milk. She set the calabash aside, and Zouga expected her to offer him the bowl, but she did not. She continued to watch him inscrutably.

'I come from the north,' Zouga said at last. 'Men call me Bakela.'

'Your sire slew the one before me,' said the woman. Her voice was compelling, for although the fluted lips barely moved, it was thrown with the power and timbre of the skilled ventriloquist. The sound of it seemed to quiver in the air long after she finished speaking and he knew now with certainty who had spoken in the voice of child and maid, of warrior and wild animal.

'He was a sick man,' Zouga replied, not questioning the source of her knowledge. Not querying how she had known that he was the son of the father.

Her words explained much to Zouga, and it was logical that the Umlimo was a hereditary duty, the office of high priestess being passed on down the years. This magnificent woman was the latest bearer of the title.

'My father was driven mad by the sickness in his blood. He did not know what he did,' Zouga explained.

'It was part of the prophecy.' The Umlimo's statement shimmered against the cave walls, but she did not stir while the silence spun out over many minutes.

'These,' Zouga spoke at last, indicating the dusty, crumbling piles of dead, 'who were they, and how did they die?'

They are the people of the Rozwi,' said the woman, 'and they died by fire and smoke.'

'Who laid the fire?' Zouga persisted.

'The black bull from the south. The Angoni.'

Zouga was silent again imagining the tribe fleeing here, to their holy place, their refuge, the women carrying the children, running like driven game ahead of the beaters, looking back over their shoulders for a glimpse of the waving tufts on the crowns of the warshields and the plumed headdresses of the Angoni *amadoda.*

He imagined them lying here in the darkness listening to the ring of axes and shouts of the besieging warriors as they cut the timber and piled it in the mouth of the cave, and then the crackle of the flames as they put fire to it and the first choking acrid clouds of smoke boiled into the cave.

He could hear again in his imagination the screams and cries of the choking, dying victims, and the shouts and the laughter of the men beyond the flaming, smoking barricade of timber.

'That too was part of the prophecy,' said the Umlimo and was silent. In the silence there was a soft rustling sound like a leaf blown by the breeze across the tiles at midnight, and Zouga's eyes turned towards the sound.

A dark thing flowed out of the shadows at the back of the cave, like a trickle of spilt blood, black in the gloom but catching the firelight in pinpricks of reflected light. It rustled softly across the stone floor, and Zouga felt his skin crawl and his nostrils flare at the sweetish mousy odour which he had noticed before, but which he recognized now.

It was the smell of snake.

Zouga stared at it, frozen with fascinated horror, for the reptile was as thick as his wrist and the full length of it was lost in the recesses of the cave. The head slid into the circle of orange firelight. The scales glittered with a marble lustre, the lidless eyes fixed Zouga with an unblinking stare and from the slyly grinning lipless mouth the silken black tongue vibrated as it tasted his scent upon the air.

'Sweet Christ!' Zouga whispered hoarsely and dropped his hand to the hilt of his hunting-knife on his belt, but the Umlimo did not move.

The snake lifted its head from the stone and dipped it over the bowl of milk. It began to drink.

It was a mamba, a black mamba, the most venomous of all the reptiles, the death it could inflict was swift but agonizing beyond all nightmares of pain. Zouga had not believed that a mamba could grow to such dimensions, for as he watched it drink half its length was still lost in the shadows.

After a minute the monstrous reptile lifted its head from the bowl and turned towards the Umlimo, it began to slide forward, the muscles under the glittering scales convulsing in little waves that came running down its length towards the broad spatulate head.

It touched the woman's bare knee with the flickering black tongue, seeming to use the tongue like a blind man uses his cane to grope its way along her thigh, licking briefly at the lips of her bulging sex, and then lifting itself up over her belly, over her breasts, still licking at her smoothly oiled skin, it rose up around her neck and then slid down over the other shoulder until it came to rest at last suspended around her neck, the head reaching out the length of a man's arm ahead of her at the level of her breasts; swaying slightly, it fixed Zouga once more with that cold ophidian stare.

Zouga licked his lips, and relaxed his grip on the hilt of the knife.

'I have come to seek wisdom,' he said hoarsely.

'I know what you seek,' replied the Umlimo. 'But you will find more than you seek.'

'Who will lead me?'

'Follow the little seeker of sweetness in the treetops.'

'I do not understand.' Zouga frowned, still watching the huge snake, and the Umlimo did not reply. Her silence was clearly an invitation to ponder the reply, and Zouga did so in silence, but found no explanation. He memorized the words, and would have asked another question but there was a silken rush out of the darkness near him, and he started half to his feet as a second snake slid swiftly past him.

It was another mamba, but a smaller snake, not much thicker than his thumb, and as long as twice the stretch of his arms. Half its length was raised arrow-straight in the air, and it sailed on its tail up to the kneeling woman with her grotesque living necklace.

The woman did not move, and the smaller snake stood before her, swaying gently from side to side, lowering itself gradually until it touched tongue to darting black tongue with the thick reptile around her neck.

Then it slid forward and began to roll itself around the body of the other snake, throwing turn after turn like a sailor lashing a sheet about a mast, and each time it rolled, it showed its soft white pulsating underbelly with the narrow scales reaching from flank to flank.

Neither the woman nor the bigger snake moved, nor removed their steadfast gaze from Zouga's fascinated pale face. The thinner lighter-coloured body of the second snake began a slow rhythmical and sensual movement, expanding and contracting about the thicker and darker body of the other and Zouga realized that they were a mating pair.

Two-thirds of the way down the underbelly of the male were the elongated scales that guarded the genital sac. As the male's excitement mounted so the scales gaped apart and the penis began to extrude. It was the colour and shape of the bloom of a night-flowering cactus, a pale lilac belled flower that gleamed like wet satin.

Insistently the male caressed the thick, dark body, and gradually his ardour was rewarded. The female rolled a portion of her own length, the white belly throbbing softly in acquiescence, exposing the scaled genital purse.

With a long shuddering movement the male slid his length down hers, white belly pressed to belly, and the swollen lilac flower prised open the female sexual purse, distorting the lips. The female mamba opened her mouth wide, and her throat was a lovely buttercup yellow. In her top jaw the small bony needles of her fangs were erect, each tipped with a pearly drop of venom, and she emitted a low sibilant hiss of ecstasy or pain as the male locked his penis deeply into her.

Zouga found he was sweating. A droplet slid down from his temple into his beard. The bizarre courtship and copulation had taken only minutes during which neither he nor the Umlimo had moved, but now she spoke.

'The white eagle has stooped on the stone falcons, and cast them to earth.' She paused. 'Now the eagle shall lift them up again and they will fly afar.'

Zouga leaned forward, listening intently.

'There shall be no peace in the kingdoms of the Mambos or the Monomatapas until they return. For the white eagle will war with the black bull until the stone falcons return to roost.'

While she spoke, the slow convulsing copulation of those interlocked bodies continued, giving to her words an obscene and evil weight.

'Generation will war with generation, the eaglet will strive against the bull calf – white against black, and black against black, until the falcons return. Until the falcons return.'

The Umlimo raised her narrow pink-palmed hands, and lifted the garland of intertwined serpents from off her own neck. She laid them gently on the stone floor of the cave and with a single flowing movement, she stood erect, and the firelight glinted upon her oiled satin body.

'When the falcons return,' she spread her arms, and the round breasts changed shape at the movement, 'when the falcons return, then once again the Mambos of Rozwi and the Monomatapa of Karanga will hold sway in the land.' She lowered her arms and her breasts sagged weightily. 'That is the prophecy. That is the whole prophecy,' she said, and turned away from the fire and, with a gliding walk, moved across the irregular stone floor, her back straight and her naked buttocks swaying in stately rhythm.

She disappeared into the dark shadows that shrouded one of the fingers of the cave beyond the amphitheatre.

'Wait!' Zouga called after her, scrambling to his feet and starting after her.

The huge female mamba hissed sharply, like the steam of a boiling kettle, and rose up as high as Zouga's head. The butter yellow mouth gaped again, and a crest of dark glittering scales came angrily erect down the length of her neck.

Zouga froze, and the snake hissed again and flared a little higher, the raised body arching gently into a taut 'S' shape. Zouga backed off, one pace and then another. The crest of scales subsided a little. He took another step backwards and the tense bow of the serpentine body relaxed, the head lowered a few inches. He moved steadily backwards towards the entrance of the cave, and before the amphitheatre was obscured by the shoulder of rock he saw the huge snake coiled in a knee-high pile of glinting scales still locked in sexual congress with her deadly consort.

The prophecy of the Umlimo, cryptic and unrevealed, stayed with Zouga during the long march back to where Jan Cheroot waited with his porters.

That night, by the firelight, Zouga copied it word for word into his journal, and afterwards the sweet smell of snakes haunted his nightmares – and lingered in his nostrils for long days after.

Now the wind turned fickle, sometimes completely still in the enervating hush and heat of noon, at other times dancing in the tall swaying vortex of the 'dust devils' across the plains, lifting leaves and dried blades of grass hundreds of feet in the yellow columns of dust, then again it gushed in turn from every point of the compass, one minute firm out of the north and the next as firmly from out of the south.

It was impossible to come up with elephant while the wind played so loosely. Often when the spoor was hot and true, and they had already laid aside their heavy traps and stripped down to light running order, Zouga would feel the cool touch of the breeze upon the back of his sweating neck and almost immediately afterwards hear the alarm squeal of an elephant ahead of them in the forest, and after that first alert, it was impossible to close with the herd, for they went into that long sloping gait that they could keep up for mile upon mile, hour upon hour, day upon night, that would kill a man who tried to match it for more than a few miles.

Thus they killed no elephant in the days following Zouga's meeting with the Umlimo, and once, when they had a good spoor which would have led them back into the north, away from the direction in which Zouga was convinced lay his quest, it was Zouga himself who called off the hunt. Jan Cheroot muttered bitterly for the rest of that day and the next while they made those seemingly aimless casts, eastward and then westward again, through the unmarked and uncharted wilderness.

Each day now the heat became fiercer, for the suicide month that ushers in the rains was upon them. Not even Zouga could march during the hours before and after noon. They would find the best shade and throw themselves down under it, sweating out the worst of the heat, trying to sleep when the buffalo flies would let them, but it was an effort to speak, an effort to wipe away the sweat that welled up on their bodies, and dried in white crystals on their skin and clothing. The salt rotted the fabric of Zouga's shirt and breeches so they tore like paper at the first touch of thorn or rock, and Zouga was gradually reduced to a beggar's rags, patched and stitched until little of the original material remained.

His boots had been resoled more than once with the raw-hide peeled from the inner surface of an elephant's ear, and his belt and webbing, the sling of his elephant gun renewed with uncured buffalo hide.

He made a strange gaunt figure, for hard hunting had burned all the fat and loose flesh from his body and limbs. His height was enhanced by his leanness and the breadth of his bony shoulders tapering sharply to his waist. The sun had burned his skin dark, yet bleached his hair and beard to white gold. His pale hair hung to his shoulders, and he tied it at the back of his neck with a leather thong. He kept his beard and whiskers trimmed neatly, using scissors to cut and the heated blade of his hunting knife to singe them.

The sense of well-being from his superb physical condition, together with the vaunting anticipation of a successful outcome to his search drove him onwards so that the days seemed too short for him and yet when the night fell he lay down on the hard earth and slept the deep dreamless refreshing sleep of a child, to awake again long before the dawn's first glimmering, impatient for what the new day would bring forth.

However, the time was passing. After each hunt, the powder bags were lighter, and though he dug the spent musket balls from the carcasses of his victims and recast them, there was always wastage.

The precious little store of quinine dwindled as swiftly, and the rains were coming. No white man could survive the rains without ammunition and quinine. Soon he would have to abandon the search for the ruined city with its idols decked in gold. He would have to march to beat the rains, south and west, five hundred miles or more, if his observations were still accurate, to cut his grandfather's road and follow it down to the mission station at Kuruman, which was the nearest outpost of European civilization.

The later he left it, the harder would be the march when he made it. Hard and fast, stopping for nothing, neither elephant nor gold, until he was out into the drier, safer land to the south.

The thought of leaving depressed him, for he knew with a certain deep gut feeling that there was something here, very close to where he now lay, and it irked him terribly that the oncoming rains would frustrate his search. But then he consoled himself that there would be another season, and he knew with the same deep gut certainty that he would return. There was something about this land – an insistent, irritating sound interrupted his thoughts. He pushed the cap up from his eyes and looked into the dense branches of the marula tree under which he lay. The harsh cries were repeated, and the drab little bird that uttered them hopped agitatedly from branch to branch, flirting its wings and tail with a sharp whirring. The bird was the size of a starling, its back dull brown and its chest and belly a muddy yellow.

Zouga rolled his head and saw that Jan Cheroot was awake also.

'Well?' he asked.

'I haven't tasted honey since we left Mount Hampden,' Jan Cheroot answered. 'But it's hot, and perhaps the bird is a liar, perhaps he will lead us to a snake or a lion.'

'He only leads you to a snake if you cheat him of his share of the comb,' Zouga told him.

'So they say,' Jan Cheroot nodded and then they were silent, considering the effort involved in following the honey guide, and weighing it against the possible rewards. The bird will very often lead a badger or a human being to a wild hive, and wait for its share of the wax and honey and bee grubs. The legend is that if his payment is not made, then next time he will lead the man who cheated him to a venomous snake or a man-eating lion.

Jan Cheroot's sweet tooth got the better of him. He sat up and the bird's cries were immediately shriller and more excited. It flashed away across the clearing to the next tree, flitting wings and tail noisily, calling them impatiently, and when they did not follow it darted back to the branches above them and continued its display.

'All right then, old fellow,' Zouga agreed resignedly, and stood up. Jan Cheroot took an axe from Matthew and the clay fire pot in its plaited bark carrying net.

'Make camp here,' Jan Cheroot told the bearers. 'We will bring you honey to eat tonight.'

Salt and honey and meat, the three greatest delicacies of the African bush. Zouga felt a twinge of guilt at wasting so much of the time that remained to him on this frivolous side-journey, but his men had worked hard and travelled fast and honey would revive their flagging spirits.

The little brown and yellow bird danced ahead of them, burring and rattling with a sound like a shaken box of Swan Vestas, darting from tree to bush, turning immediately it settled to make sure they were following.

For almost an hour it led them along a dry river course, and then it turned and crossed a rocky ridge of ground. At the saddle, they looked down into a heavily wooded valley bounded by the familiar rocky kopjes and hillocks.

'The bird is teasing us,' Jan Cheroot grumbled. 'How much further will he make us dance?'

Zouga shifted his elephant gun to the other shoulder. 'I think you are right,' he agreed, the valley ahead of him was forbidding, the floor choked with tall stands of the razor-edged elephant grass, higher than a man's head. It would be even hotter down there, and the dried seeds of the grass had arrowheads to them that could work themselves into the skin and cause festering little wounds.

'It comes to me that I am not so fond of honey as I thought I was,' Jan Cheroot cocked his head at Zouga.

'We will turn back,' he agreed. 'Let the bird find another dupe. We will look for a fat kudu cow on the way back, meat instead of honey.'

They started back down the ridge and instantly the bird flashed back, and renewed its entreaties above their heads.

'Go and find your friend the *rattel*' (honeybadger)! Jan Cheroot shouted at it, and the bird's contortions became frantic. It dropped lower and lower, until it was in the branches barely an arm's length above their heads, and its cries were irritating and distracting.

'*Voetsak!*' Jan Cheroot yelled at it. That bird's cries would alert all wild game for miles about to the presence of man, and thwart any chance of killing an animal for the night's meal. '*Voetsak!*' He stooped and picked up a stone to shy at the bird. 'Go away and leave us, little sugar mouth.'

The name stopped Zouga in his tracks. Jan Cheroot had used the bastard Dutch, '*klein Suiker bekkie*', and now he drew back his right arm to hurl the stone.

Zouga caught his wrist. 'Little sugar mouth,' he repeated, and the Umlimo's voice rang in his ears, that strange shimmering tone that he had memorized, 'the seeker of sweetness in the treetops.'

'Wait,' he told Jan Cheroot. 'Do not throw.'

It was ridiculous, of course it was. He would not make himself ludicrous by repeating the Umlimo's words to Jan Cheroot. He hesitated a moment. 'We have come so far, already,' he told the Hottentot reasonably, 'and the bird is so excited that the hive cannot be far.'

'It could be another two hours,' Jan Cheroot growled, but lowered his throwing arm. 'That makes six hours back to camp.'

'You don't want to grow fat and idle,' Zouga said. Jan Cheroot was lean as a whippet that had been coursing rabbit all season, and he had walked and run a hundred miles in the last two days. He looked pained at the accusation, but Zouga went on remorselessly, shaking his head in mock sympathy. 'But when a man grows older, he cannot march as far or as fast, and he is slower with the women too.'

Jan Cheroot dropped the stone, and went back up the ridge at a furious pace with the bird flitting and screeching ecstatically ahead of him.

Zouga followed him, smiling at the little man and at his own folly in placing any store on the words of that naked witch. Still the honey would be welcome, he consoled himself.

An hour later, Zouga was convinced that Jan Cheroot had been correct. The bird was a liar, and they were wasting what remained of the day, but there would be no turning Jan Cheroot now, he had been deeply insulted by Zouga's gibes.

They had crossed the valley, blundering through the stands of elephant grass, for the bird did not pick one of the game trails to follow. It moved on a direct line, and as they followed, the grass seeds showered upon them, working their way down the backs of their shirts and the sweat of their bodies activated them, as the first rains should have done, so that they began to worm like living things, trying to pierce the skin.

The view ahead was cut off by the tall grass, and they reached the far side of the valley with little prior warning. Suddenly there was a smooth rock cliff looming over them, almost obscured by the tall leafy trees of the forest, and by its own covering of lianas and dense climbing plants. It was not a very high prominence, perhaps forty feet, but it was sheer. They stopped below it and peered upwards.

The wild beehive was almost at the top of the cliff. The honey guide fluttered triumphantly above it, twisting its head to look down at them with a single bright beadlike eye.

The rock below the opening to the hive was stained with a dark dribble of old melted wax and the detritus of the hive, but it was almost entirely masked by a lovely creeping plant. The stem of the plant climbed the cliff, branching and twisting and doubling on itself, its pale leaves a cool green, but its flowers a lovely shade of cornflower blue.

The bees leaving and returning to the hive caught the sunlight like golden dust-motes, but their trajectory was swift and straight through the hot still air.

'Well, Sergeant, there is your hive,' Zouga said. 'The bird did not lie.' He felt a deep sense of disappointment. Although he had told himself to place no store on the Umlimo's words, yet there had been a sneaking anticipation, the forlorn hope persisting against common sense, and now that sense had prevailed, there was this regret.

Zouga leaned his gun against the bole of a tree, shed his traps, and threw himself down to rest and watch Jan Cheroot making his preparation to rob the hive. Jan Cheroot cut a square of bark from a mukusi tree, and rolled it into a smoking tube. He filled it with wood pulp scraped from a dead tree trunk.

Then he swung the clay fire pot on its carrying sling of bark rope, fanning it until the smouldering moss and wood chips that it contained burst into flame. He transferred fire to the smoking tube, and when it had fairly taken he hooked his axe over one shoulder and began climbing the interwoven branches of the flowering creeper up the sheer cliff.

The first of the defender bees buzzed fiercely about his head when he was a few feet from the opening to the hive, and pausing, Jan Cheroot lifted the bark tube to his mouth and blew a gentle stream of blue smoke towards his attacker. The smoke drove the insect away, and he resumed the climb.

Lying under the mukusi tree, idly swatting at the buffalo flies, picking at the grass under his shirt, and harbouring his disappointment, Zouga watched the Hottentot work.

Jan Cheroot reached the hive, and blew another stream of smoke over the hole in the cliff, stupefying the bees which had now formed a swirling defensive cloud about him. One of them darted in, despite the smoke, and stung him in the soft of the neck. Jan Cheroot swore bitterly, but he did not make the mistake of slapping at the attacker, or of trying to scratch away the barbed sting lodged in his flesh. He worked on calmly, unhurriedly, with the smoke tube.

Minutes later, the hive was sufficiently smoke-drugged to allow him to begin cutting away the screen of flowering branches that hid the entrance, and he balanced on a fork of the creeper, using both hands to swing the axe, perched like a little yellow monkey forty feet above where Zouga lay.

'What the thunder . . .' He stopped after a dozen axe blows, and stared at the cliff face that he had exposed. 'Master, there is devil's work here.'

The tone of his voice alerted Zouga, and he scrambled to his feet.

'What is it?'

Jan Cheroot's body obscured the object of his amazement, and impatiently Zouga crossed to the foot of the cliff and climbed hand over hand up the serpentine stem of the creeper.

He reached Jan Cheroot's side and clung to a handhold.

'Look!' Jan Cheroot exhorted him. 'Look at that!' He pointed at the stone face that he had exposed with the axe.

It took Zouga a few seconds to realize that the entrance to the hive was through a geometrically perfect, sculptured aperture, one of a series which pierced the cliff face in a broad horizontal band, that seemed to extend unbroken in both directions along the cliff face. The decorated band was in chiselled stone blocks, arranged in a chevron pattern, a lattice work that was without question the work of a skilled stonemason.

The realization jolted Zouga so that he almost missed his hand-hold, and immediately afterwards he saw something else that up to that moment had been hidden by the dense covering of climbing plants and the thick coating of old outpouring wax from the beehive.

The entire cliff face was formed of perfect blocks of dressed stone, small blocks, so neatly fitted that they had appeared on casual inspection to be a solid sheet of rock. Zouga and Jan Cheroot were suspended near the top of the massive stone wall, forty feet high, so thick and long that it had seemed to be a granite hillock.

It was a monumental work of stonemasonry, to compare with the outer wall of Solomon's temple, a vast fortification which could only be the periphery of a city, a city forgotten and overgrown with trees and creepers, undisturbed over the ages.

'*Nie wat!*' whispered Jan Cheroot. 'This is a devil's place – this is the place of Satan himself. Let us go, master,' he pleaded. 'Let us go far away, and very fast.'

The circuit of the walls took Zouga almost an hour, for the growth was thicker along the northern curve of the stone rampart. The wall seemed to be laid out in an almost perfect circle, and without openings. At tow or three likely points, Zouga hacked away the growth and searched the foot of the wall, looking for a postern or a gateway. He found none.

The decorative chevron pattern did not seem to extend around the entire circumference, but covered the eastern quadrant. Zouga wondered at the significance of that. The immediate explanation seemed to be that the decoration would face the rising sun. It seemed likely that the peoples who had built this massive edifice had been sun-worshippers.

Jan Cheroot trailed him reluctantly, prophesying the wrath of the devils and hobgoblins who guarded this evil place, while Zouga hacked and chopped his way around the walls, completely oblivious of his advice.

'There must be a gateway,' he grumbled. 'How did they get in and out?'

'Devils got wings,' Jan Cheroot pointed out broodingly. 'They fly. Me, I wish I had wings also, to fly the hell away from here.'

They came again to the point in the wall where they had discovered the beehive, and by then it was almost dark, the sun had disappeared below the treetops.

'We'll search for the gate in the morning,' Zouga decided.

'We are not going to sleep here?' Jan Cheroot demanded, horrified.

Zouga ignored the protest. 'Honey for supper,' he suggested mildly, and for once he did not sleep that deep hunter's sleep, but lay under his single blanket, his imagination filled with golden idols and treasure houses built out of massive worked stone blocks.

Zouga resumed the search again when it was light enough to see the top of the wall silhouetted against the misty pearl sky of dawn. The previous day he had been blinded by his own eagerness and careless in his haste. He had missed the area, only a few yards from where they were camped, where the creepers covering the wall had once been hacked away and then had regrown, even more thickly than before. Now, however, a looped branch beckoned him like a finger, the clean cut unmistakably made by an axe.

'Jan Cheroot,' Zouga called him from the cooking fire. 'Clean out this rubbish.' Zouga showed him the dense secondary growth, and Jan Cheroot sauntered away to fetch his axe.

While he waited for him to return, Zouga decided that only one person could possibly be responsible for these old overgrown and healed cut marks on the stems of the vine. Once again Fuller Ballantyne had been his guide, yet this time he did not resent it so fiercely; the experience of treading squarely in his father's footsteps was no longer new, and he had his excitement and anticipation to lessen the sting of it.

'Hurry,' he called to Jan Cheroot.

'It's been here a thousand years. It's not going to fall down now,' Jan Cheroot answered saucily, and spat on his palms before hefting the axe.

The little Hottentot was a great deal happier this morning. He had survived a night under the wall, without being assailed by even a single hobgoblin, and Zouga had passed the unsleeping hours in describing to him the treasures that might lie beyond that wall. Jan Cheroot's temporarily paralysed avarice had revived sufficiently to imagine himself with his pants filled with gold coin seated in his favourite tavern on the Cape Town dockside with a dozen butter yellow Hottentot beauties crowding close to him to hear the story, while the bartender prised the wax seal off another bottle of Cape Smoke. Now his entusiasm almost matched that of Zouga himself.

He worked swiftly and when Zouga stooped and peered into the passage that he had cut through the dense secondary growth that had sprung up behind Fuller Ballantyne's axe, he saw the outline of the curved portals of the gateway, and the chiselled granite steps that led up to the narrow opening.

The steps had been worn into a smooth dish shape by the passage of thousands of feet over the centuries, but the gateway had been deliberately blocked with stone and rubble, not the neat stonework of the main wall, but a careless and hurried attempt to seal the entrance, probably in the face of an advancing enemy, Zouga thought.

Somebody, probably Fuller Ballantyne, had pulled down this barrier sufficiently to enter. Zouga followed his tracks, the loose stone rolling under foot, he squeezed his way through the gateway, and found that it turned abruptly to the left, into a narrow vegetation-choked passage, between high walls open to the sky.

His disappointment was intense. He had hoped that once he forced the gateway, all the city and its wonders and treasures would lie before him. Instead there were many hours of hard sweating labour facing him. It had been years, four years at least, since Fuller Ballantyne had entered through this gate and passageway, and it was as though he had never been.

Where the stonework had collapsed, Zouga clambered over it gingerly, the thought and dread of snakes was very much with him since the cave of the Umlimo. The long narrow passage, obviously constructed as a defensive measure against intruders, followed the curve of the main wall until abruptly it opened into a clear space, again choked with dense green thorny growth, and dominated by a tall cylindrical tower of lichen-covered granit blocks. The tower was immense, seeming in Zouga's excitement to reach to the very clouds.

Zouga started across the intervening courtyard, hacking impatiently at the bush and creepers, and halfway across he saw that there was a second tower, an identical twin to the first that had until that moment obscured it. Now his heart was pounding fiercely against his ribs, not from the exertion of swinging the axe – but with an intuitive belief that the towers were the centre of this strange ancient city, and that they held the key to the mystery.

He stumbled in his haste, and went down on his knees, tearing another long rent in his breeches and abrading a strip of skin from his shin, so he swore in his impatience and his pain. He had lost the axe but when he groped for it in the tangled roots and interwoven branches, he found it almost immediately, and at the same time, uncovered the stone that had tripped him.

It was not the granite of which the walls and tower had been constructed. That fact caught his attention, and still on his knees he used the axe to clear the bush around the stone. He felt his nerves thrill as he realized that it was a work of sculpture.

Jan Cheroot had come up behind him, and now he knelt also and tore at the plants with his bare hands – then the two of them rocked back on their heels, and still squatting examined the statue that they had uncovered. It was not large, probably weighed less than a hundredweight. It was carved in satiny, greenish soapstone, sitting on that familiar ornamental plinth, the simple pattern of triangles, like a row of shark's teeth.

The head was smashed off the statue, seemingly by a blow from a sledge hammer, but more likely from a rock used as a hammer. The body of the statue was still intact, the body of the raptor, with the folded pointed wings of a bird of prey, crouching on the point of flight.

Zouga slipped his hand into the opening of his shirt and drew out the little ivory charm on its leather thong, that he had taken from the body of the Mashona chieftain he had killed at the pass of the elephant road.

He let it nestle in the palm of his hand, comparing it with the statue. Beside him Jan Cheroot murmured, 'It is the same bird!'

'Yes,' Zouga agreed softly. 'But what does it mean?' He dropped the ivory charm back inside his shirt.

'It iş from long ago,' Jan Cheroot shrugged. 'We will never know.' And dismissing it thus, he would have risen to his feet again, but something else caught his beady bright eye and he darted forward, his hand pecking at the loose earth beside the statue like a greedy hen, and held it up between thumb and forefinger to catch the slanted morning light.

It was a perfectly round bead of metal, pierced for the string of a necklace, a tiny bead only slightly bigger than the head of a wax Vesta, and it was irregular in shape, as though beaten out under the hammer of a primitive smithy, but the colour was red-yellow, and its surface was undulled by either tarnish or corrosion; there is only one metal that has that peculiar lustre and sheen.

Zouga held out his hand for it almost reverently, and it had the weight and the warmth of a living thing.

'Gold!' said Zouga, and beside him Jan Cheroot giggled ecstatically, like a young bride at her first kiss.

'Gold,' he agreed. 'Good yellow gold.'

Zouga was always aware of the very limited time left to him, and every hour or so as they worked he would lift his head to the sky with the sweat streaming down his face and neck, and greasing the flat hard muscles of his naked upper body, and always the clouds were taller and blacker, the heat more punishing, and the wind sullen as a captive tribe on the point of rebellion.

In the night he would start awake, breaking up through the drugged surface of exhausted sleep, to lie and listen to the thunder growling below the horizon like a man-killing monster.

Each dawn he shook his men from their blankets and drove them in a suppressed frenzy of impatience to their labour, and when Matthew, the gunbearer, refused to rise again after the short rest which Zouga allowed them in the hottest hour of the day, Zouga dragged him to his feet and hit him once, a short, perfectly timed chopping blow that sent him spinning backwards full length into his own excavation. Matthew crawled out again with blood dribbling from his chin, and picked up the crude sieve of plaited split bamboos with which he was sifting the earth from the digging, and began again working over the piles of loose earth and rubble.

Zouga drove himself harder than he drove his small band of temple plunderers. He worked shoulder to shoulder with them as they cut out all the undergrowth from the courtyard below the twin stone towers, exposing the broken cobbles, and piles of loose rubble amongst which lay the fallen statues.

He found six more of the bird carvings virtually undamaged, except for minor chips and the attrition of the ages, but there were the fragments of others that had been broken with a savagery which could only have been deliberate, so that he was uncertain of the original number of statues. Zouga spent little time puzzling over them. The loose earth and rubble on which they lay was rich ground for his band to pick over, though they were handicapped by the lack of tools. Zouga would have paid a hundred guineas for a set of good picks and spades and buckets. However, they had to make do with sharpened wooden stakes, the tips hardened in the fire, to dig out the loose stuff, and Jan Cheroot wove baskets of split bamboo, like the flat baskets used by the African women to winnow the stamped corn meal, and with these they sieved the fine earth after picking over it by hand.

It was tedious, back-breaking work, and the heat was murderous, but the harvest was rich. The gold was in small pieces, mostly in the pierced round beads, from which the string had long ago rotted away, but there were flakes and flecks of thinly beaten foil, which might once have been used to decorate a votive wooden carving, there were coils of fine gold wire, and more rarely small ingots of the metal the size and thickness of a child's finger.

Once the green stone birds must have stood in a circle, facing inwards like the granite columns of Stonehenge, and the gold had probably formed some part of the offerings and sacrifices made to them. Whoever had thrown down the statues had scattered and trampled the sacrifice, and time had corroded all except that lovely yellow incorruptible metal.

Within ten days of first hacking away the undergrowth that choked the inner courtyard, the temple yard, as Zouga called it, they had gleaned over fifty pounds weight of native gold, and the interior of the stone courtyard had been gutted, the earth rutted and harrowed as though a troop of wild bush pig had rooted it out.

Then Zouga turned his full attention to the twin towers. He measured them around the base, over a hundred paces, and inspected each joint in the masonry for a secret opening. There was none, so he built a rickety ladder of raw timber and bark rope and risking neck and limb reached the top of the tallest tower. From this vantage point he could look down into the roofless passageways and courtyards of the city. It was a maze, all of it choked with growth – but there was no other part as promising as the temple courtyard of the bird statues.

He turned his attention back to the tower on which he stood. There was again no sign of a secret opening, although he searched diligently for one. It puzzled him that the ancient architect would have built such a solid structure with no apparent use or motive, and the possibility occurred to him that it might be a sealed treasure house, built around an inner chamber.

The work of trying to penetrate the massive stonework, daunted even Zouga, and Jan Cheroot declared the attempt to be madness. But Zouga had exhausted the digging below the tower, and this seemed to be the only fruitful area left to him.

Complaining bitterly, a small team led by Matthew climbed the rickety ladder, and under Zouga's supervision began prising loose the small blocks from the summit of the tower. However, such was the skill and dedication of the original masons that progress in the demolition was painfully slow, and there was a long pause between each crash of one loose block into the courtyard below and the next. It needed three days' unremitting toil to break a jagged aperture through the first layer of dressed blocks and to discover that the interior of the tower consisted merely of a fill of the same grey granite.

Standing beside him on the summit of the tower, Jan Cheroot voiced Zouga's own disappointment.

'We are wasting our time. It's stone and more stone.' He spat over the side of the tower and watched the speck of phlegm float down into the ransacked courtyard. 'What we should look for is the place the gold came from.'

Zouga had been so obsessed by his search and plunder of the ruined and deserted city that he had paid no thought to the mines which must lie somewhere beyond the walls. Now he nodded his head thoughtfully.

'No wonder your mother loved you,' he said. 'Not only are you beautiful, but you are clever too.'

'Ja,' Jan Cheroot nodded smugly. 'Everybody tells me that.'

At that moment a fat weighty drop of rain struck Zouga's forehead, and ran down into his left eyeball so that his vision blurred. The drop was warm as blood, warm as the blood of a man racked by malarial fever.

Beyond the high walls there were other ruins, none of such proportions or importance as the inner city, however, and all of them so scattered, so overgrown and thrown down as to make detailed exploration of them out of the question in the time still available to Zouga.

The kopjes around the city had been fortified, but were deserted, the caves empty as the eye-sockets of a long dead skull, smelling of the leopards and rock rabbits who were the latest tenants, but Zouga concentrated his search on the ancient mine workings which he had convinced himself had formed the backbone of this vanished civilization. He imagined deep shafts driven into a hillside, and dumps of loose rock like the ancient Cornish tin mines, and he scoured the densely wooded country for miles in each direction, eagerly checking each irregularity of ground, each eminence that could possibly be an abandoned mine dump.

He left Jan Cheroot to oversee the scratching and sweeping up of the last tiny scraps of gold in the temple yard, and all the men profited by the new relaxed supervision. They shared views with Jan Cheroot on the role of menial work in the life of a warrior and hunter.

The first spattering of rain had been only a warning of the fury to come, and it had barely wet Zouga's shirt through to the skin before passing, but it was a warning that Zouga realized he was ignoring at his own peril. Yet still the hope of the ancient mine workings with their fat golden seams of the precious metal tantalized him, and he spun out the days until even Jan Cheroot began to worry.

'If the rivers spate, we will be trapped here,' he brooded beside the camp fire. 'Besides we have taken all the gold. Let us now live to spend it.'

'One more day,' Zouga promised him as he settled into his single blanket, and composed himself to sleep. 'There is a valley just beyond the southern ridge, it will take me only another day to search it – the day after tomorrow—' he promised sleepily.

Zouga smelled the snake first, the sweet sickening stench of it filled his nostrils, so he drew each breath with difficulty, yet trying not to gasp or choke lest he called the snake's attention. He could not move, he was pinned under an immense dark weight which threatened to crush his ribs and the smell of snake suffocated him.

He could barely turn his head towards the place from which he knew the snake would come, and it came flowing sinuously, coil upon thick undulating coil. Its head was lifted, its eyes were unblinking and glassily fixed in the cold and deadly reptilian stare, the ribbon of its tongue flickered in a soft black blur through the icy smile of its thin curved lips. Its scales scratched softly across the earth, and they glittered with a soft metallic sheen, the colour of the polished gold foil that Zouga had gleaned from the temple courtyard.

Zouga could not move nor cry out, his tongue had swollen with terror to fill his mouth and choke him, but the snake slid past him, close enough to touch if he had command of his arms to reach out. It slid on into the circle of soft wavering light, and the shadows drew back so the birds emerged from the darkness, each on its elevated perch.

Their eyes were golden and fierce, the cruel yellow curve of their beaks echoed by the proud pout of their russet-flecked breasts and the long pinions folded across their backs like crossed blades.

Though Zouga knew they were hunting falcons with belled tresses on their legs, yet they were the size of golden eagles. They were decked with garlands of flowers, crimson blossoms of King Chaka fire, and the snowy virginal white of arum lilies. They wore necklaces and chains of brightest gold about their arrogant necks, and as the serpent slid into the midst of the circle they stirred upon their perches.

Then as the serpent raised its glittering head with the crest of scales erect upon the back of its neck, the falcons burst into thunderous flight and the darkness was filled with the roar of their wings and the plaintive lament of their wild hunting cries.

Zouga lifted his hands to shield his face, and great wings beat all about him, as the flock of falcons took flight and the presence of the snake was no longer of significance – what was important was the departure of the birds. Zouga felt a tremendous sense of doom, of personal loss, and he opened his mouth, able to utter again. He shouted at the birds to call them back to roost.

He shouted into the darkness, after the soaring, buffeting thunder of the birds' wings and his own shouts and the cries of his servants woke him from the coils of the nightmare.

He woke to find the night was thunderous with the wind of the storm that swept down upon the camp. The trees tossed and thrashed their branches overhead, showering them with leaves and small twigs, and the rush of air was glacially cold. It stripped the thatch from their crudely built huts and it scattered ash and live coals from the fire. The coals, fanned into new life, were the only source of light, for overhead, the stars were obscured by the thick rolling banks of cloud that pressed close upon the earth.

Shouting to each other above the wind, they scrambled to collect their scattered equipment.

'Make sure the powder bags are kept dry,' Zouga bellowed, naked except for his tattered breeches, and barefooted as he groped for his boots. 'Sergeant Cheroot, where are you?'

The Hottentot's reply was lost in the cannon's roar of thunder that drove in their eardrums, and the flash of lightning that followed immediately seared their eyeballs, and imprinted on Zouga's vision the unforgettable picture of Jan Cheroot dancing stark naked on one foot, a red hot coal from the scattered fire stuck to the sole of the other, his wild curses lost in the drawn-out roll of the thunder and his face contorted like that of a gargoyle on the parapet of Notre

Dame cathedral. Then the darkness fell on them again, like an avalanche, and out of it came the rain.

It came in cutting horizontal sheets like the blade of a harvester's scythe, so thick that it filled the air with water so they coughed and gasped like drowning men, it came with such hissing force that it stung their naked skins as though coarse salt had been fired at them from a shotgun barrel, and the cold chilled them to the bone, so that they crawled into a forlorn huddle, crowding together for comfort and warmth with the sodden fur blankets pulled over their heads, and stinking like a pack of wet dogs.

The cold gloomy dawn found them still huddled from the silver streams of falling rain, under the swollen bruised sky that pressed down upon them like the belly of a pregnant sow. Scattered and sodden equipment floated or was submerged in the ankle-deep flood of water that poured through the wind-shattered camp.. The lean-to shelters had been wrecked, the camp fire was a muddy black puddle of ash, there was no prospect of rebuilding it, and with that went any chance of hot food or comfort for their stiff cold bodies.

Zouga had wrapped the powder bags in strips of oilskin, and he and Jan Cheroot had held them in their laps, like ailing infants, during the night. However, it was impossible to open the bags and check the contents for damp, for the rain still teemed down out of the low grey sky in long thin silver lances.

Slipping and sloshing in the muddy footing, Zouga drove his men to make up their loads for the outward march, while he made his own final preparations. In the middle of the morning they ate a miserable and hasty meal of cold millet cakes and the last scraps of smoked buffalo meat. Then Zouga stood, with a cloak of half-cured kudu skin draped over his head and shoulders, the rain dripping from his beard and plastering his patched clothing to his body.

'Safari!' he shouted. 'We march!'

'And not too damned soon either,' muttered Jan Cheroot, reversing his musket on its sling so the barrel pointed at the ground and the rain could not run into the muzzle.

It was then that the porters discovered the extra burden that Zouga had for them. It was lashed to carrying poles of mopani wood with bark rope, and protected by a plaited covering of elephant grass.

'They are not going to carry it,' Jan Cheroot told him, squeezing the rain from his woolly eyebrows with his thumb. 'I told you they would refuse.'

'They'll carry it.' Zouga's eyes were cold and green as cut emeralds, and his expression was fierce. 'They carry it – or they'll stay here with it, dead!'

He had carefully selected the best specimen of the carved stone birds, the only one that was completely undamaged and the one on which the carving was the most artistically executed, and he had packed and prepared it for porterage himself.

For Zouga the carving was physical proof of the existence of the ancient abandoned city, proof that could not be denied when even the most cynical critic read his account in far-away London. Zouga guessed that the intrinsic value of this relic probably surpassed the equivalent weight in pure gold. The value of the artefact was not the most important consideration in Zouga's determination to carry the carving out to civilization. The stone birds had come to have a special superstitious significance to him. They had come to symbolize for him the success of his endeavours, and by possessing one of them he had in some strange manner taken possession of this entire savage and beautiful land. He would return for the others, but he must have this single perfect specimen. It was his talisman.

'You and you.' He picked two of his strongest and his usually most willing porters, and when they still hesitated, he unslung the heavy elephant gun from his shoulder. They saw his expression and knew that his intention was serious, deadly serious. Sulkily they began breaking down their own loads and distributing them amongst their comrades.

'At least let us leave this other thundering piece of rubbish.' The rain and the cold had affected Jan Cheroot as much as the others, and he indicated the tin box that contained Zouga's dress uniform with a hatred and contempt usually reserved for animate objects. Zouga did not bother to reply, but gestured to Matthew to take it up.

It was noon before the bedraggled little column struggled through the long sodden grass that choked the valley floor and began to climb the far side, slipping and cursing in the mud.

It rained for five days and five nights, sometimes in thick drumming bursts that seemed to fall in solid sheets of water from the sky, at other times it was a cold drizzling mist, that swirled gently about them as they trudged on in the soft treacherous footing, a fine silver mist that blanketed and muted all sound except the eternal dripping of the forest and the soft sighing passage of the wind in the upper branches.

The fever vapours seemed to rise from the very ground, entering their lungs with each breath, and in the icy cold mornings they writhed and twisted like the wraiths of tormented souls down in the hollows of the valleys. The porters were the first to show the symptoms of the disease, for the fever was in their bones and the cold rain brought it out so they shivered in uncontrollable spasms and their teeth chattered in their jaws until it seemed they might crack like porcelain. However, they were seasoned to the rigours of the disease and they were still able to march.

The bulky statue in its ungainly packing of grass and bark was borne painfully up the rocky ridges and down the other side by half-naked men staggering like drunks from the fever boiling in their veins, and when they reached the bank of another water course they dropped it gratefully and fell in the mud to rest without the will to cover themselves from the relentless rain.

Where there had been dried river-beds, with drifts of white sand shining like alpine snowfields in the sun, with quiet pools of still green water, and with steep high banks in which the brilliant kingfisher and little jewelled bee-eaters burrowed to nest, there were now maddened torrents of racing brown water, which brimmed over the high banks and carved out the roots of tall trees, toppling them into the flood and whisking them away as though they were mere twigs.

There was no possible means by which a man could cross these racing, foaming deluges; the corpse of a drowned buffalo with bloated pink belly and its limbs sticking stiffly into the air was borne downstream at the speed of a galloping horse, while Zouga stood morosely on the bank, and knew that he had left it too late. They were trapped by the spate.

'We will have to follow the river,' he grunted, and wiped his streaming face on the sleeve of his sodden hunting jacket.

'It goes towards the west,' Jan Cheroot pointed out with morbid relish, and it was not necessary for him to expand on the thought.

To the west lay the kingdom of Mzilikazi, King of the Matabele, and already they must be close to that vaguely defined area that old Tom Harkness had marked on his map.

'The Burnt Land – here Mzilikazi's impis kill all travellers.'

'What do you suggest, my ray of golden Hottentot sunshine?' Zouga demanded bitterly. 'Have you got wings to fly this?' He indicated the broad expanse of wild water, where the curled waves stood as stationary as carved sculptures as they marked the position of submerged rocks and hidden snags. 'Or what about gills and fins?' Zouga went on. 'Let me see you swim, or if you have neither wings nor fins, then surely you have good advice for me?'

'Yes,' Jan Cheroot answered as bitterly. 'My advice is that you listen to good advice when first it is given, and second that you drop those in the river.' He indicated the bundled statue and the sealed uniform box. Zouga did not wait for the rest of it, but turned his back and shouted.

'Safari! On your feet, all of you! We march!'

They worked slowly west and a little south, but too much westward for even Zouga's peace of mind, though his route was dictated by the network of rivers and flooded valleys.

On the sixth day the rain relented, and the clouds broke open, revealing a sky of deep aquamarine blue and a fierce swollen sun that made their clothing steam, and stilled the fever shakes of the porters.

Even with the accuracy of his chronometer in doubt, Zouga was able to observe the meridian passage that local noon and establish his latitude. He was not as far south as he had calculated by dead reckoning, so he was probably even further west than his suspect calculations of longitude suggested.

'The land of the Mzilikazi is drier,' Zouga consoled himself, as he wrapped his navigational instruments in their oilskin covers, and I am an Englishman, and the grandson of Tshedi. Not even a Matabele would dare deny me passage, despite what old Tom writes. And he had his talisman, the stone bird, to add its protection.

Resolutely he faced west again, and drove his caravan onwards. There was one other misery to add to their sufferings. There was no meat, and there had been none since the day they left the abandoned city.

With the first onslaught of the rains, the great herds of game that had been concentrated upon the last few pools and waterholes had been freed to scatter widely across the vast land where every ditch and irregularity was now at last brimming with fresh sweet water and where the baked and sun-seared plains were already blooming green with tht tender first shoots of new growth.

In five days' march in the rain, Zouga had seen only one small herd of waterbuck, the least palatable of all African game with its rank turpentine-scented musk which permeates the flesh. The heavily built bull, in his shaggy plum-brown coat led his small troop of hornless females at a frantic gallop across Zouga's front with his wide lyre-shaped horns cocked high and the perfect white circle over his buttocks flashing with each bound. He tore through the drizzling rain and dense wild ebony bush not twenty paces from Zouga. Zouga threw up the heavy gun and led on his driving shoulder.

Behind him his hungry, exhausted porters yipped like a pack of hunting dogs with anticipation, and Zouga held his aim for an instant to make deadly certain and then squeezed off the trigger.

With a sharp crack, the cap exploded under the falling hammer, but there was not the long spurt of flame from the muzzle and the great clangour of the shot, followed by the heavy thumping impact of the lead ball into flesh. The gun had misfired and the handsome antelope led his harem away at full gallop, disappearing almost immediately into the bush and rain while the dwindling clatter of their hooves mocked Zouga. He swore with frustration as he laboriously drew the ball and charge with the corkscrew tool fitted to his ramrod, and found that the insidious rain had somehow entered the barrel, probably through the nipple and that the powder was as wet as though he had dipped it in the raging brown flood waters.

Those few hours of fierce sunlight on the sixth day gave Zouga and Jan

Cheroot an opportunity to spread the coarse grey contents of their powder bags on a flat rock and dry it out so there would be less chance of another disastrous misfire, and while they did so the porters let drop their packs and limped off to find a dry spot to stretch their aching limbs.

Then too swiftly the sunlight was blotted out once more, and hurriedly they scooped the powder back into the pouches and as the fat raindrops began to hiss and splat about them they wrapped them in the worn oilskins, tucked them under their voluminous leather capes and resumed the westward trudge, heads bowed, silent and hungry and cold and miserable, Zouga's ears singing with the quinine-buzz, the first apparent side-effect of massive doses of the drug taken over long periods. The quinine-buzz that can lead to eventual, irreversible deafness.

Despite the heavy daily doses of the bitter powder, the morning arrived at last when Zouga woke with the deep ache in the marrow of his bones, the dull weight like a heavy stone lying behind his eyes and by midday he was shaking and shivering with the alternate flood of fierce heat and deathly sepulchre cold through his veins.

'The seasoning fever,' Jan Cheroot told him philosophically, 'it kills you, or hardens you.'

'Some individuals would appear to have a natural resistance to the ravages of this disease,' his father had written in his treatise, *The Malarial Fevers of Tropical Africa: Their Causes, Symptoms and Treatment*, 'and there is evidence to suggest that this resistance is hereditary.'

'We'll see now if the old devil knew what he was talking about,' Zouga mumbled through chattering teeth, hugging the stinking wet leather coat around his shoulders. It never occurred to him even briefly to halt for his affliction; he had not accorded that courtesy to any of his men, and he did not expect it himself.

He trudged on grimly, with his knees giving a rubbery little bounce at each pace, his vision blurring and starring into little pinwheels of light, then emerging again though phantom worms and gnats still wriggled across his sight. Every now and then a touch upon his shoulder from the little Hottentot who marched behind him directed Zouga's stumbling feet back on to the path from which they had strayed.

The nights were hideous with the nightmares of his fever-inflamed brain, they were filled with the buffeting thunder of dark wings and the sickly stench of snakes so that he would wake panting and screaming, often to find Jan Cheroot holding him with a comforting arm around his shaking shoulders.

The lifting of that first bout of his seasoning fever coincided with the next brief break in the rains. It seemed that the bright sunlight, magnified by the lingering moisture in the air, burned away the mists from his mind and the poisonous miasma from his blood, leaving him clear-headed, with a fragile sense of well-being but a weakness in his legs and arms and a dull ache up under the right-hand side of his rib cage where his liver was still swollen and hard as a rock, the typical after-effect of the fever.

'You will be all right,' Jan Cheroot prophesied. 'You threw it off as quickly as I've seen any man with his first hit of the fever. Ja! You are a man of Africa – she will let you live here, my friend.'

It was while he still walked on wavering legs, light-headed, so that it felt as though his feet did not touch the muddy earth but danced inches above it, that they cut the spoor.

The weight of the great bull had driven the spoor a foot deep into the sticky red mud, so that it was a series of deep pot-holes, strung across the earth like beads on a necklace. The exact impression of the huge pads had been cast in the holes as though in plaster of Paris, each crack and fissure in the skin of the sole, each irregularity, even the outline of the blunt toe nails were there in precise detail, and at one place where the soft earth had been unable to bear his weight and the elephant had sunk almost belly deep, he had left the impression of his long thick ivories in the earth when he had used them to push himself free.

'It is him!' breathed Jan Cheroot, without looking up from the enormous spoor. 'I would know that spoor anywhere.' He did not need to say more to identify the great old bull that they had last seen so many months before on the high pass of the elephant road on the escarpment of the Zambezi river.

'Not an hour ahead of us,' Jan Cheroot went on in a reverential whisper, like a man at prayer.

'And the wind stands fair.' Zouga found he was whispering also. He remembered his premonition that he would encounter this animal again. Almost fearfully he looked up at the sky. In the east the storm clouds were rolling ponderously towards them once more, the brief respite was almost over. The next onslaught of the storm promised to be as fierce, and even those deep and perfect prints would soon dissolve into liquid mud and be washed into oblivion.

'They are feeding into the wind,' he went on, trying to put the threat of rain out of his mind and concentrating his still fever-dulled wits to the problem of the hunt.

The old bull and his remaining consort were feeding and moving forward with the wind into their faces. That way they would not walk into trouble. Yet these two old veterans, with their decades of accumulated experience, would not hold steadily into the wind for long, they would turn at intervals to get below the wind of a possible tracker.

Every minute now was of vital consideration, if the hunt was to suceed – for despite the weakness in his legs and the silliness in his head, Zouga had not for a single moment considered letting the spoor go. They might be a hundred miles within the borders of Mzilikazi's country with a Matabele impi of border guards closing swiftly, and the hours lost in following the two old bulls might make all the difference between escaping from these fever-haunted forests or leaving their bones here for the hyena to crunch, but neither Zouga nor Jan Cheroot hesitated. They began to shed their unneeded equipment, they would not need water bottles for the land was overflowing, the food bags were empty anyway, and the blankets sodden. They would shelter tonight against the old bull's massive carcass.

'Follow at your best pace,' Zouga shouted to his heavily burdened porters, dropping his unwanted equipment into the mud for them to pick up. 'You can fill your bellies with meat and fat tonight, if you put your feet to it now.'

They had to gamble all Zouga's remaining strength on the opening play, using speed to beat the rain and to reach the bulls before they made a turn into the wind and took the scent. They ran at the spoor, going hard from the first, knowing that even a healthy man could not hold that pace beyond an hour or two at the most before his heart broke.

In the first mile Zouga's vision was starring and fragmenting again, sweat drenched his lean body and he reeled like a drunkard as his legs threatened to give under him.

'Run through it,' Jan Cheroot counselled him grimly.

He did it, by a sheer effort of will. He drove himself through to that place beyond the pain. Quite suddenly his vision cleared and though there was no feeling at all in his legs they drove on steadily under him so he seemed to float over the ground without effort.

Running at his side Jan Cheroot recognized the moment when Zouga broke the shackles and went clear of his own weakness. He said nothing but glanced sideways at him, eyes bright with admiration and he nodded once. Zouga did not see that nod, for his head was up and his dreaming gaze was fixed far ahead.

They ran the sun to its zenith, Jan Cheroot not daring to break the rhythm for he knew that Zouga would drop like a man shot through the heart if they stopped to rest. They ran on as the sun began to drop, pursued by the ponderous cohorts of the oncoming storm that threatened it with extinction, and their own shadows danced ahead of them along the deeply driven elephant-spoor. In a tight bunch behind Zouga, his four gunbearers matched him pace for pace, ready to hand him a weapon at the instant he required it.

The hunter's instinct warned Jan Cheroot. He twisted his head every few minutes to look back along the trail they had already run. That was how he picked them up.

They were two grey shadows, merging softly into the darker acacia shadows below the dripping trees, but they were moving with steadfast purpose, circling to strike their own spoor again, throwing a loop about their pursuers and taking the wind from them.

The bulls were half a mile away, moving with that swinging deceptively leisurely gait that would bring them, within minutes, full on to the hot trail with which the small band of hunters had overlaid their own huge pug marks; the trail would be reeking with the rank odour of man, the air thick with it.

Jan Cheroot touched Zouga's arm, turning him back upon their own run without checking him nor breaking the driving rhythm of his numbed legs.

'We have to catch them before they cut our spoor,' he called softly. He saw Zouga's eyes come back into focus and the colour flare in his waxen pale cheeks as Zouga turned and saw for the first time the two huge shapes cruising serenely through the open forest, under the tall umbrella-shaped acacias, moving with a stately deliberation down towards the string of reeking man-prints in the red mud.

The big bull was leading, his gaunt frame too tall and bony for the wasted flesh over which the skin hung in deep folds and bags. The huge yellow tusks were too long and heavy for the ancient head, and his ears were ripped and torn into scarred tatters that dangled on to his creased cheeks. He had been wallowing in a mud hole and his body was slick and shining with wet red mud.

He stepped out on his long, heavily boned legs around which the thick loose skin bagged and drooped like a badly tailored pair of breeches, and close behind him strode his askari, a big heavily toothed elephant, but dwarfed by his leader.

Zouga and Jan Cheroot ran together, stride for stride, their breath hissing and gasping in their throats, as they spent their last reserves to get in gunshot range before the bulls took the scent.

They traded all stealth, any attempt at concealment for speed, trusting that the weak eyesight of the old bulls would betray them. This time, the vagaries of the weather favoured them, for as they ran, the storm burst about them again.

It had held off just long enough to allow them to come up, and now the thick streamers of pale grey rain were drawn across the forest like lace curtains and the bad light beneath the thick cloud banks gave them cover to cross the last few hundred yards unseen, and the tapping rain and the rush of the wind in the branches of the acacias muffled their racing footfalls.

A hundred and fifty yards ahead of Zouga the old bull hit the man spoor, and it stopped him as though he had run into the side of an invisible cliff of glass. He flared back on his hind quarters, his back humping and his wrinkled ivoried head flying up high, the ragged banners of his ears filling like the mainsail of a tall ship, and clapping thunderously as he flapped them against his shoulders.

He froze like that for a long moment, groping at the tainted earth with the tip of his trunk, then he lifted it to his mouth and sprayed the scent into the open pink buds of his olfactory organs. The dread and hated odour struck him like a physical force and he went back another pace, then his trunk lifted straight into the air above him, and he wheeled and like a well-trained pair of coach horses his tall askari wheeled with him, shoulder to shoulder, and flank to flank, they began to run – and Zouga was still a hundred yards behind them.

Jan Cheroot dropped on to one knee into the mud, and flung up his musket. At the same instant, the askari checked slightly and swung left, crossing his leader's rear. Perhaps it was unintentional, but neither Zouga nor Jan Cheroot believed that. They knew that the younger bull was drawing fire, protecting the other with his own body.

'You want it? Take it then, you thunder!' Jan Cheroot shouted angrily, he knew he had lost too much ground by pausing to fire.

Aiming for the younger bull, Jan Cheroot took the hip shot, and the bull staggered to it, flecks of red mud flying from his skin where the ball struck, and he broke his stride, favouring the damaged joint, swinging out of the line of his run, broadside to the hunters, while the great bull ran on alone.

Zouga could have killed the crippled bull with a heart shot, for the animal was down to a dragging, hump-backed trot and the range was less than thirty-paces, but Zouga ran straight past him, never checking, hardly glancing at him, knowing he could leave Jan Cheroot to finish that business. He ran after the big bull, but despite his utmost endeavour, losing ground to him steadily.

Ahead of them, the ground dipped into a shallow open saucer, and beyond that it rose to another ridge on which the wild teak trees stood like sentinels in the grey rain. The bull went down into the saucer, still in his initial burst of speed, stretching out so that his padfalls sounded like the steady beat of a bass drum, opening the gap between himself and his hunter – until he reached the bottom of the dip, and then he was almost halted.

His weight broke the surface of the swampy ground, and he sank through almost to his shoulders, and had to lunge for each step, with the glutinous mud sucking and squelching obscenely at each of his frantic movements.

Swiftly Zouga closed the range, and his spirits took wing, his exultation driving back his weakness and fatigue. He felt intoxicated with battle lust. He reached the swampy ground, and leapt from tussock to tussock of coarse swamp grass, while the bull struggled on ahead of him.

Closer and closer still Zouga came up to him, almost point-blank range, less than twenty yards and at last he stopped and balanced on one of the little islands of grass roots.

Just ahead of him the bull had reached the far side of the swamp, and was heaving himself out on to the firm ground at the foot of the slope. The bull's front legs were higher than his still-bogged hind-quarters, the whole slope of his back was exposed to Zouga, the knuckles of his massive spine stood out clearly through the mud-painted skin and the arched staves of his rib cage were like the frames of a Viking longboat. Zouga fancied he could actually see the pounding rhythm of the great heart beating against them.

There could be no mistake this time. In the months since their first encounter, Zouga had become a skilled huntsman, he knew the soft and vital places in the mountainous bulk of an elephant's body. At this range and from this angle, the heavy ball would shatter the spine between the shoulder blades without losing any of its velocity, and it would go on deep, to the heart, to those thick serpentine arteries that fed the lungs.

He touched the hair trigger, and with a pop like a child's toy the gun misfired. The great grey beast heaved himself clear of the mud, and went away up the slope, now at last settling into the swinging ground-eating gait which would carry him fifty miles before nightfall.

Behind him Zouga reached the firm ground and flung down the useless weapon, dancing with impatience as he screamed at his bearers to bring up the second gun.

Matthew was fifty paces behind him, slipping and staggering in the swampy ground. Mark, Luke and John were strung out behind him.

'Come on! Come on!' screamed Zouga, and snatched the second gun from Matthew, and dashed away up the slope. He had to catch the bull before he reached the crest of the slope, for down the other side he would go like an eagle on the wind.

Zouga ran now with all his heart, with all his will and the very last dregs of his strength, while behind him Matthew stopped, snatched up the misfired weapon from where Zouga had thrown it down, and, acting instinctively in the heat and excitement of the chase, he reloaded it.

He poured another handful of black powder on top of the charge and ball already in the barrel and tamped down a second quarter-pound ball of lead on top of it all. In so doing he changed the gun from a formidable weapon to a lethal bomb that could maim or even kill the man who attempted to fire it. Then Matthew slipped another percussion cap over the nipple and ran on up the slope after Zouga.

The bull was nearing the crest of the ridge, and Zouga was coming up on him, but slowly, the difference in their speed just barely discernible. At last Zouga's strength was failing, he could keep this pace for minutes more and he knew when he finally stopped he would be on the verge of total physical callapse.

His vision was swimming and wavering, and his feet stumbled and slipped on the wet lichen-covered rocks of the slope, and the rain beat into his face, almost blinding him. Sixty yards ahead of him the bull reached the crest, and there he did something that Zouga had never seen a hunted elephant do before – he turned broadside, flaring his ears, to look at his pursuers.

Perhaps he had been pushed too hard, perhaps he had been hunted too often and the hatred had accumulated like weed below the waterline of an old ship, perhaps this was his last defiance.

For a moment he stood tall, and glistening black with mud and rain, silhouetted against the low grey sky, and Zouga hit him in the shoulder, the gun ringing like a bronze cathedral bell, and the long lick of red flame blooming briefly in the gloom.

Both man and beast reeled to the shot, Zouga driven off-balance by the recoil and the bull taking the hardened lead ball through the ribs and going back on his haunches, the rheumy old eyes clenching tightly to the shock of it.

The bull kept his feet, though he was hard hit, and he opened his eyes and saw the man, that hated, evil-smelling and persistent animal that had persecuted him so relentlessly down the years.

He launched himself back down the slope, like an avalanche of dark grey granite, and his repeated blood squeals rang against the low sky, and Zouga turned and ran from the charging bull, while the earth trembled beneath his feet at the weight and nearness of the stricken beast.

Matthew stood his ground, even in the terrible press of the moment. Zouga loved him for that. He stood to do his duty, to deliver the second gun to his master.

Zouga reached him, just ahead of the charging bull, dropped his smoking weapon, snatched the second gun from Matthew, never suspecting that it had been double-shotted, and as he turned he thumbed the hammer back and swung up the long thick barrel.

The bull was on top of him, blotting out the rain-sodden sky, the long yellow ivories raised like roof-beams over his head, and the trunk already uncoiling to reach down and snatch Zouga up.

Zouga pressed the hair trigger, and this time the gun fired. With a shattering roar the barrel burst, the metal opening like the petals of a flower, and burning powder flew back into Zouga's face, singeing his beard and blistering the skin of his face. The hammer was blown clean off the barrel and it hit Zouga in the cheek, just under the right eye, cutting a jagged wound clean down to the bone. The shattered weapon flew out of his grasp, and slammed back into his shoulder with such force that he felt the ligaments and tendons tearing. Zouga was hurled into a backward somersault that carried him just beyond the grasp of the bull's questing trunk.

He fell heavily behind a pile of loose stone chips, and for a moment the elephant checked, going back on its hind legs to avoid the flashing flame and smoke of the explosion, blinded and unsighted for a moment – and then it saw the gunbearer still standing.

Matthew started to run, poor, loyal, brave Matthew, but the bull had him before he had gone a dozen paces. It took him about the waist with a single coil of its long trunk, and it threw him into the air as though he were light as a child's rubber ball. Matthew went up forty feet, with his arms and legs windmilling, his scream of terror unheard in the deafening squeals of the elephant. It sounded like the whistle of a steam engine blown by a crazed engineer, and Matthew seemed to rise very slowly into the air, hang for a long moment and then drop just as slowly downwards.

The bull caught him in mid-air and threw him again, this time even higher.

Zouga dragged himself into a sitting position. His right arm hung limply on its torn muscles and tendons, blood streamed from his ripped cheek into his beard and his eardrums were so tortured by the explosion that the elephant's squeals seemed muted and far off. He looked up groggily and saw Matthew high in the air, beginning to fall, saw him hit the ground, and the elephant begin to kill him.

Zouga dragged himself to his knees, and began to creep over the mound of loose stone towards the empty gun, the gun from which he had fired the first shot and which he had dropped when he snatched the double-shotted gun from Matthew, the gun which now lay five paces from him, five paces which seemed an infinite distance to drag his maimed body.

The elephant placed one foot on Matthew's chest and his ribs crackled like dry sticks in a fierce fire. It took his head in its trunk and plucked it from Matthew's shoulders, as easily as a farmer kills a chicken.

The elephant tossed Matthew's head aside and as it trundled down the slope close to where Zouga sat, he saw that Matthew's eyelids were blinking rapidly over his bulging eyeballs and that the nerves flickered under the skin of his cheeks.

Tearing his eyes from the gruesome object, Zouga lifted the empty gun into his lap and began to reload it. He had no use or feeling in his right arm, which still hung limply at his side.

Twenty paces away the elephant knelt over Matthew's decapitated body and drove one of the long yellow ivories through his belly.

Painfully Zouga poured a handful of powder into the gun muzzle, trying not to be distracted from his task.

Matthew hung impaled through the middle from the bloody tusk like a wet shirt on a laundry line, the elephant's trunk came up and coiled python-like about his battered body.

Zouga dropped a ball from his pouch into the barrel of the gun, and one-handed tamped it home with the ramrod.

The elephant tore an arm from the body, and Matthew slid from the point of the tusk and dropped once more to earth.

Moaning softly with the pain of each movement, Zouga primed the gun and hauled back the hammer against the powerful tension of the spring.

The elephant was kneeling with both front legs on what remained of Matthew, grinding him into a red mush against the rocky earth.

Dragging the gun with him, Zouga crawled back to the mound of rock chips behind which he had fallen. Using only his left hand, he balanced the stock of the big elephant gun over the top of the mound.

The elephant was still squealing in unabated fury as it crushed Matthew's corpse.

Grovelling flat on his belly, Zouga sighted over the thick barrel, but with only one hand it was almost impossible to hold the clumsy weapon true, and his vision swam and wavered with pain and exhaustion.

For an instant the shaking foresight aligned with the crude vee of the backsight, and he let the shot fly, in flame and a billowing cloud of burnt powder smoke.

The elephant's squeals stopped abruptly. As the powder smoke was blown aside on the cold breeze, Zouga saw that the bull had hoisted himself wearily upright and was swaying slowly from foot to foot. The massive head dropped under the weight of its blood-smeared tusks and its trunk hung as limply as Zouga's own damaged right arm.

The elephant was making a strange mournful humming sound deep in his chest, and from the second bullet wound just behind his bony shoulder joint, his heart blood spurted in short regular jets, to the beat of the huge heart, and poured down his body in a honey-thick stream.

The bull turned towards where Zouga lay, and shuffling like an old and very weary man came towards him, the tip of his trunk twitching with his last fading warlike instincts.

Zouga tried to drag himself away, but the bull came on faster than he could crawl, and the trunk reached out, touched Zouga's ankle, the vast bulk of the elephant filled the sky above Zouga, and he kicked out frantically but the trunk tightened its grip on his ankle with agonizing unbearable strength, and Zouga knew that it would tear his leg out of its socket at the hip.

Then the elephant groaned, a shuddering exhalation of air from the torn lungs, the grip on Zouga's ankle relaxed and the old bull died on his feet, his legs collapsed under him and he went down.

He fell with a weight and force that made the earth bounce and tremble under Zouga's prostrate body and with a thud that Jan Cheroot, who was crossing the swamp, heard clearly from a mile away.

Zouga dropped his head against the earth and closed his eyes, and the darkness overwhelmed him.

Jan Cheroot made no attempt to move Zouga from where he lay beside the old bull's carcass. He built a rough shelter of saplings and wet grass over him and then coaxed smoky flames from a fire at his head, and from another at his feet. This was all he could do to warm him until the porters came up with the blankets at sunset.

Then he helped Zouga into a sitting position, and between them they strapped the damaged arm.

'God Almighty,' croaked Zouga, as he prepared the needle and thread from his sewing kit, 'I'd give both the tusks for a dram of good malt whisky.'

Jan Cheroot held the hand mirror, and using one hand only Zouga stitched the flap of his torn cheek back into place, and as he pulled the last knot tight and snipped the thread, he collapsed back into his damp and stinking fur kaross.

'I will die rather than march again,' he whispered.

'That is your choice exactly,' Jan Cheroot agreed, without looking up from the chunks of elephant liver and heart that he had begun wrapping in yellow fat before stringing them on a green twig. 'You can march or die here in the mud.'

Outside the hut the porters were wailing and chanting the mourning dirge for Matthew. They had gathered the fragments of his horribly mutilated body and made a package of them, wrapping them in Matthew's own blanket and binding it up with bark rope.

They would bury him the following morning, but until then they would keep up the haunting cries of mourning.

Jan Cheroot scraped coals from the fire and began to grill the kebab of liver and fat and heart over them. 'They will be useless until they have buried him, and we must still cut the tusks.'

'I owe Matthew a night of mourning at least,' Zouga whispered. 'He stood the bull down. If he had run with the second gun ...' Zouga broke off, and groaned as a fresh stab of pain transfixed his shoulder. Using his good left hand, he scratched under the skin blanket on which he lay, moving the lumps of stone which had caused the discomfort.

'He was good – stupid, but good,' Jan Cheroot agreed. 'A wiser man would have run.' He turned the kebab slowly over the coals. 'It will take all day tomorrow to bury him and then cut the tusks from both elephants. But we must march the day after that.'

Jan Cheroot had killed his bull down on the plain, under the outspread branches of a giant acacia. Looking through the low opening of the hut Zouga could see the carcass of his own bull lying on its side not twenty feet away. Already it was swelling with trapped gas and the upper legs thrust out stiffly above the grey balloon of the belly. The tusks were unbelievable. Even as he stared at them Zouga thought they must be a fantasy of his exhaustion and agony. They were as thick as a girl's waist, and the spread of them must have been twelve feet from tip to tip.

'How much will they weigh?' he asked Jan Cheroot, and the Hottentot looked up and shrugged.

'I have never seen a bigger elephant,' he admitted. 'We will need three men to carry each of them.'

'Two hundred pounds?' Zouga asked, the conversation distracted him from the agony in his shoulder.

'More,' Jan Cheroot decided. 'You will never see another like him.'

'No,' Zouga agreed. 'That is true. There will never be another like him.' Deep regret blended with his pain, making it more intense. Regret for the magnificent beast and sorrow for the brave man who had died with him.

The pain and the sorrow would not let him sleep that night, and in the dawn when they gathered in the rain to bury Matthew, Zouga strapped his damaged arm into a bark sling and had two men help him to his feet, then he walked unaided but slowly and stiffly up the slope to the grave, using a staff to balance himself.

They had wrapped Matthew's body in his fur blanket and placed his possessions with him, his axe and spear, his food bowl and beer calabash, to serve him on the long journey ahead.

Singing the slow mournful song of the dead, they packed the rock over and around him so that the hyena would not dig him out. When they had finished, Zouga felt drained of strength and emotion. He staggered back to his hut and crawled under the dank blanket. He had only that day to gather his strength for the march that must be resumed in the dawn. He closed his eyes, but could not sleep for the thud of the axes into bone as Jan Cheroot supervised the chopping of the tusks from the casket of the old bull's skull.

Zouga rolled on to his back, and once again a loose rock chip dug into his aching body. He reached back and pulled it from under the blanket, was about to throw it aside when something caught his attention and he arrested the movement.

The rock was as white and as crystalline as the candied sugar that Zouga had loved so as a boy, a pretty little fragment, but that was not what had stopped his hand.

Even in the subdued light of the hut, the thin irregular seam of metal that wavered uncertainly between quartz crystals flicked a pinprick of bright gold into his eyes. Zouga stared at it numbly, twisting the lump of quartz to catch the light and make it twinkle. There was a sense of unreality about the moment, as there always is when something sought for and longed for is at last held in the hand.

He found his voice at last, a hoarse croak through his swollen, blistered, powder-scorched lips, and Jan Cheroot came almost immediately.

'The grave,' he whispered urgently, 'Matthew's grave, it was dug so swiftly in such rocky soil.'

'No,' Jan Cheroot shook his head. 'It was there. There are other holes like it along the ridge.'

Zouga stared at him for a long moment, his face lopsided with the scabbed and stitched wound, his one eye a mere slit in the puffed and bruised flesh. He had let himself sink low from the wound. It had been under his nose and he had almost missed it. He started to drag himself out of his blanket.

'Help me!' he ordered. 'I must see them. Show me these holes.'

Leaning on Jan Cheroot's shoulder, stooped to favour his shoulder, he dragged himself along the ridge in the rain, and when at last he was satisfied, he limped back to the hut and used the last feeble light of that day to scrawl in his journal, holding it in his lap and bowing over it to protect the pages from the drip of rain through the rough thatching, using his left hand so the writing was barely decipherable.

'I have named it the Harkness Mine, for this must be very similar to the ancient workings that old Tom described. The reef is white sugar quartz and runs along the back of the ridge. It would appear to be very narrow but rich, for there is visible gold in many of the samples. My injury prevents me crushing and panning these, but I would estimate values well in excess of two ounces of fine gold to the ton of quartz.

'The ancient miners have driven four shafts into the hillside. There may be more that I overlooked, for they are heavily overgrown and an attempt has been made to refill the shafts, possibly to conceal them.

'The shafts are large enough to admit a small man crawling on hands and knees. Probably they used child-slaves in the diggings and the conditions of labour in these rabbit warrens must have been infernal. In any event they were only able to go down as far as the water table, and without sophisticated machinery to pump the flooded working, they would have been abandoned. This is probably what happened here at the Harkness Mine and there is almost certainly a great amount of gold-bearing ore to be recovered by modern methods.

'The rock dump on which stands my rude hut is composed almost entirely of the gold matrix, awaiting crushing and refining, and the miners were probably driven away by an enemy before they could complete their labours.

'I am couched upon a mattress of gold, and like King Midas all around me

is the precious metal. Like that unfortunate King, there seems to be little profit
in it for me that I can perceive at this moment—'

Zouga paused, and laid his pen aside, warming his icy hands at the smoky
fire. He should have felt wildly elated. He picked up his pen once again. He
sighed and then wrote tortuously.

'I have a huge store of ivory, but it is spread across this land, buried in small
caches. I have fifty pounds and more of native gold in ingot and nugget, and I
have discovered the mother lode of untold fortune, but it cannot buy me a pound
flask of gunpowder nor an unguent for my grievous injuries.

'I will not know until tomorrow if I have the strength remaining to me to
continue the march to the south, or if I am destined to remain here with Matthew
and the great elephant as my only companions.'

Jan Cheroot shook him awake. It took a long time. Zouga seemed to be
swimming up from great depths through cold and murky water, and when at
last he surfaced, he knew immediately that his gloomy prophecy written in the
journal the previous evening had become reality. There was no feeling or
strength in his legs. His shoulder and arm were bound rock hard with spasmed
muscle.

'Leave me here,' he said to Jan Cheroot, and the Hottentot heaved him to a
sitting position, snarling at him when Zouga cried out at the agony of each
movement, and forced him to drink the steaming hot soup made from elephant
marrowbones.

'Leave one gun with me,' Zouga whispered.

'Here.' Jan Cheroot ignored the order and instead made him take the bitter
white powder. Zouga gagged on the quinine.

It took two porters to get him on his feet.

'I am leaving that stone.' Jan Cheroot pointed to the packaged statue. 'We
cannot carry both of you.'

'No!' Zouga whispered fiercely. 'If I go, the bird must go with me.'

'How?'

Zouga shrugged off their hands.

'I will walk,' he said. 'Carry the bird.'

They made less than five miles that day, but the following day the sun
emerged again to cheer them on. Once it warmed Zouga's abused muscles, he
could increase the pace.

That night he logged ten miles in his journal when they camped in open
grassland. In the dawn Zouga was able to crawl from his blankets and gain his
feet unaided. His injuries still stiff, he used the staff to leave the thron *scherm*
by its single gate and limp to the periphery of the camp. When he urinated his
water was a dark amber colour from the fever and the quinine, but he knew
now that he was going to be able to continue the march.

He looked up at the sky. It would rain again soon. They should start at once.
He was about to turn back to the camp and rouse the porters when movement
in the tall grass caught his attention.

For a moment he thought it might be a troop of wild ostrich passing the
camp, then suddenly he realized that the whole plain was alive with swift but
stealthy movement, the fluffy grass tops rustling and nodding with the passage
of many bodies, only now and again there was a brief glimpse of ruffled plumes
above the grass. The movement spread swiftly around both sides of the small
camp, where Zouga's men still slept.

Zouga stared uncomprehendingly, leaning on his staff, still muzzy with sleep and fever and anchored by his injuries, he did not move until the swift encircling movement had been completed, and then the stillness and silence descended again so for a moment he believed he had been imagining phantoms.

Then there was a soft fluting whistle, like a blast on Pan's pipe, sweet and hauntingly melodious in the dawn, and immediately there was movement again, an encroaching movement, like a strangler's hand upon the throat. Zouga saw the ostrich plumes clearly now, snowy white and dead black they swayed and danced above the grass tops, and immediately afterwards he saw the war shields, long oval shields of dappled black and white cowhide. The long shields – the Matabele.

Dread was a cold, heavy lump under his ribs, yet instinct warned him that to show it would mean death, just when he had once again believed in life.

There were a hundred, he calculated swiftly as he glanced around the closing ring of warriors. No, there were more than that, at least two hundred Matabele *amadoda* in full war plumage, only the plumes and their eyes showing above the tops of the long dappled shields. The grey dawn light glinted on the broad-bladed stabbing spears, held underhand so the points protruded beyond the ring of shields. The ring was unbroken, shield overlapped shield, the encircling horns of the bull, the classic tactics of the Matabele, the finest and most ruthless warriors that the continent of Africa had ever spawned.

'Here Mzilikazi's border impis kill all travellers,' Tom Harkness had written.

Zouga drew himself up and stepped forward, holding up his one good arm with the palm extended towards the ring of shields.

'I am an Englishman. A commander of the great white Queen, Victoria. My name is Bakela, son of Manali, son of Tshedi – and I come in peace.'

From the ranks stepped a man. He was taller than Zouga and his tossing ostrich plumes turned him into a giant. He swept aside his shield, and he was lean and muscled like a gladiator. On his upper arms he wore the tassels of cow tails, each one awarded him by his King for an act of valour. The cow tails were thick bunches, layer upon layer. His short kilt was of spotted civet cat tails, and there were more cow tails bound around his calves just below the knees. He had the handsome smooth moonface of the true Nguni, with a broad nose and full sculptured lips. His bearing was noble, the carriage of his head proud.

He looked at Zouga slowly and with grave attention. He looked at his tattered rags, at the untidy bindings that held his damaged arm, the staff on which he leaned like an old man.

He studied Zouga's singed beard, and powder-burned cheeks, the blisters on his lips and the black scabs that clung obscenely on his swollen discoloured cheek.

Then the Matabele laughed. It was a deep musical laugh, and then he spoke.

'And I,' he said, 'am Matabele. An Induna of two thousand. My name is Gandang, son of Mzilikazi, son of the high heavens, son of Zulu, and I come with a bright spear and a red heart.'

Robyn Ballantyne realized within the first day's march that she had seriously miscalculated her father's strength and resilience when she made the decision to try for the coast. Perhaps Zouga had divined instinctively what she a trained physician should have known. That thought made her angry with herself. She found that since parting with Zouga her hostility and sense of rivalry towards him had, if anything, increased. It made her angry that he should have given the correct advice.

By noon of that first day Robyn had been forced to call a halt and to go into camp. Fuller Ballantyne was very weak, weaker than he had been when first she found him. His skin was burning hot and dry to the touch. The movement of the litter, the jolting and bumping over uneven ground had aggravated Fuller's leg. It was grotesquely swollen, and so tender that he screamed and fought at the lightest touch upon the discoloured skin.

Robyn had one of the bearers begin work on a cradle of green twigs and bark to place over the leg and keep the fur blanket off it, and then she sat by the litter applying a damp, cool cloth to her father's forehead and speaking to little Juba and the Mashona woman, not expecting nor receiving advice from them, but taking comfort from the human contact.

'Perhaps we should have stayed at the cave,' she fretted. 'At least he would have been more comfortable there, but then for how long could we have stayed?' She spoke her thoughts aloud. 'The rains will be on us soon. We could not have stayed, and even if we march as slowly as this, we will still be trapped here by them. We simply must increase the pace – and yet I do not know if he can survive it.'

However, on the following day Fuller seemed stronger again, the fever had cooled, and they made a full day's march, but in the evening when they went into camp he had once more sunk very low.

When Robyn removed the dressing from the leg, it seemed to be less sensitive, and she was relieved – until she saw the colour of the skin around the ulceration. When she lifted the soiled dressing to her nose and sniffed it, she caught the taint that her professor of medicine at St. Matthew's had taught her to watch for. It was not the usual taint of benign pus, but a more pervasive odour, the smell of a decomposing corpse. Her alarm flared, and she threw the dressing on the fire and with dread returned to her examination of the leg.

From the inside of the groin, down the wasted thigh muscles, there were the unmistakable scarlet lines beneath the thin pale skin, and the extreme sensitivity of the area seemed to have passed. It was almost as though Fuller had no further feeling in the leg.

Robyn tried to console herself that the change and mortification in the leg was unconnected with having carried him two days in a litter over rough ground. But what other reasons were there? She could find no answer. Before the move, the ulceration had been stabilized, for it was almost eighteen months since the slaver's ball had shattered the bone.

The movement in the litter must have precipitated some serious change in the limb, and this was the result.

Robyn felt herself culpable. She should have listened to Zouga. She had brought this on her own father. Gas-gangrene. She could only hope that she was wrong, but she knew she was not. The symptoms were unmistakable. She could only continue the march and hope they would reach the coast and civilization before the disease swept to its inevitable climax – but she knew that hope was futile.

She wished that she had been able to develop the same philosophical acceptance that most of her fellow physicians cultivated in the face of disease or injury which were beyond their training and ability to alleviate. But she knew she never could, always she would be victim to this helpless sense of frustration, and this time the patient was her own father.

She bound up the leg in a hot compress and knew that it was a pathetic gesture, like trying to hold back the tide with a child's sandcastle. In the morning the leg felt cooler to the touch, and the flesh seemed to have lost resilience so that her fingers left depressions as though she had touched unleavened bread. The smell was stronger.

They made a full day's march, and Fuller was silent and comatose in the litter as Robyn walked beside it. He no longer chanted psalms and wild exhortations to the Almighty, and she thanked God that at least there was no pain.

In the late afternoon they met a broad pathway, well travelled and running east and west as far as Robyn could see it. It fitted exactly the description and the location that her father had written of in his journal. Little Juba burst into tears and was rendered almost helpless with terror when she saw the road.

They found an encampment of deserted and dilapidated huts, that might have been those used by the slave-traders, and Robyn ordered camp there. She left the Mashona woman and the still snivelling and shivering Juba to tend Fuller Ballantyne, and she took only old Karanga with her. He armed himself with his long spear, and strutted like an ancient peacock to be so honoured. Within two miles, the pathway climbed steeply to pass through a saddle in a line of low hills.

Robyn was seeking evidence that this was indeed the slave road, the Hyena Road, as Juba called it tearfully.

She found her evidence on the saddle, lying in the grass a few paces from the edge of the track. It was a double yoke, hewn from a forked tree trunk and roughly dressed with an axe.

Robyn had studied the sketches in her father's journal, and she recognized it immediately. When the slave-masters did not have chains and cuffs, they used these yokes to bind their captives around their necks; two slaves linked together and forced to do everything in concert, march, eat, sleep and defecate – everything except escape.

Now all that remained of the slaves who had once worn the yoke were a few fragments of bone that the vultures and hyena had overlooked. There was something terribly sad and chilling about that roughly carved fork of wood, and Robyn could not bring herself to touch it. She said a short prayer for the unfortunate slaves who had died on that spot and then, with her knowledge that she was on the slave road confirmed, she turned back towards the camp.

That night she held counsel with the Hottentot Corporal, old Karanga and Juba.

'This camp and road have not been used for this many days,' Karanga showed Robyn both hands twice with fingers spread, 'twenty days.'

'Which way did they go?' Robyn asked. She had come to have confidence in the old man's tracking ability.

'They were moving along the road towards the sunrise, and they have not yet returned,' quavered Karanga.

'It is even as he says,' Juba agreed, and it must have been an effort to agree with somebody for whom she had such disdain and jealousy. 'The slavers will make this the last caravan before the rains. There will be no trading after the rivers are full, and the Hyena Road will grow grass until the dry season comes again.'

'So there is a caravan of slavers ahead of us,' Robyn mused. 'If we follow the road we may overtake them.'

The Hottentot Corporal interrupted. 'That will not be possible, madam. They are weeks ahead of us.'

'Then we will meet them returning, after having sold their slaves.'

The Corporal nodded and Robyn asked him, 'Will you be able to defend us, if the slavers decide to attack our column?'

'Me and my men,' the Corporal drew himself to his full height, 'are a match for a hundred dirty slavers,' he paused and then went on, 'and you shoot like a man, madam!'

Robyn smiled. 'All right,' she nodded. 'We will follow the road down to the sea.'

And the Corporal grinned at her. 'I am sick of this country and its savages, I long to see the cloud on Table Mountain and wash the taste of dust from my throat with good Cape Smoke once again.'

The hyena was an old male. There were patches of fur missing from his thick shaggy coat, and his flat, almost snakelike head was covered with scars, his ears ripped away by thorns and a hundred snapping, snarling encounters over the decomposing carcasses of men and animals. His lip had been torn up into the soft of the nostril in one of these fights and had healed askew, so that the yellow teeth in one side of his upper jaw were exposed in a hideous grin.

His teeth were worn with age, so that he could no longer crush the heavy bones that made up the bulk of hyena diet, and unable to compete, he had been driven from the hunting-pack.

There had been no human corpses along the trail since the slave column had passed weeks before, and game was scarce in this dry country. Since then the hyena had subsisted on scrapings, the fresh dung of jackal and baboon, a nest of field mice, the long-abandoned and addled egg of an ostrich which had burst in a sulphurous geyser of gas and putrefied liquid when he pawed at it. However, even though the hyena was starving, he still stood almost three foot high at the shoulder and weighed 140 pounds.

His belly under the matted and scruffy coat was concave as that of a greyhound. From high ungainly shoulders, his spine slanted back in a bony ridge to his scraggy hindquarters.

He carried his head low, snuffling at the earth for offal and scourings, but when the scent came down on the wind to him, he lifted his head on high and flared his deformed nostrils.

There was the smell of wood smoke, of human presence, which he had grown to associate with a source of food, but sharper, clearer than all the others was a smell that made the saliva run from his twisted, scarred jaws in drooling silver ropes. He went lolloping into a swaying, uneven trot up into the wind following the tantalizing drift of that odour. The scent that had attracted the old dog hyena was the cloyingly sweet taint of a gangrenous leg.

The hyena lay on the outskirts of the camp. It lay like a dog, with its chin on its front paws and its hindlegs and its bushy tail drawn up under its belly, flat behind a clump of coarse elephant grass. It watched the activity about the smoking watch fires.

Only its eyes rolled in their sockets, and the ragged stumps of its ears twitched and cocked to the cadence of human voices, and the unexpected sounds of a bucket or an axe on a stump of firewood.

Once in a while a puff of wind would bring a whiff of the scent that had first attracted the hyena, and it would snuffle it, suppressing with difficulty the little anxious cries that rose in its throat.

As the evening shadows thickened, a human figure, a half-naked black woman, left the camp, and came towards its hiding-place. The hyena gathered itself to fly but before she reached the place where it lay, Juba paused and looked about her carefully without seeing the animal, then she lifted the flap of her beaded apron, lowered herself and squatted. The hyena cringed and watched her. When she stood and returned to the camp, the creature, emboldened by the oncoming night, crept forward and wolfed down that which Juba had left.

Its appetite was piqued and as the night fell, it inflated its chest, curled its bushy tail up over its back and uttered its drawn-out haunting cry, ascending sharply in key, 'Oooo-auw! Oooo-auw!' – a cry so familiar to every man and woman in the camp that hardly one of them bothered to look up.

Gradually the activity about the camp fires subsided, the sound of human voices became drowsy and intermittent, the fires faded, the flames sinking and the darkness crept in upon the camp, and the hyena crept in with it.

Twice a sudden loud voice put it to trembling flight and it galloped away into the bush, only to gather its courage at the renewed silence and creep back. It was long after midnight when the beast found a weak place in the protective *scherm* of thorn branches about the camp and quietly, furtively pushed its way through the opening.

The smell led it directly to an open-sided thatched shelter in the centre of the enclosure, and with its belly low to the earth the huge dog-like animal slunk closer and fearfully closer.

Robyn had fallen asleep beside her father's litter, still fully dressed and in a sitting position; she merely let her head fall forward on to her crossed arms and then overwhelmed by fatigue and worry and guilt she at last succumbed.

She awoke to the old man's shrill shrieks. There was complete darkness blanketing the camp, and Robyn thought for a moment that she was blinded by a nightmare. She scrambled wildly to her feet, not certain where she was and she stumbled over the litter. Her outflung arms brushed against something big and hairy, something that stank of death and excrement, a smell that blended sickeningly with the stench of her father's leg.

She screamed also, and the animal growled, a muffled sound through clenched jaws like a wolfhound with a bone. Fuller's shrieks and her screams had roused the camp, and somebody plunged a torch of dried grass into the ashes of the watch fire. It burst into flames, and after the utter blackness the orange light seemed bright as noonday.

The huge hump-backed animal had dragged Fuller from his litter in a welter of blankets and clothing. It had a grip on his lower body, and Robyn heard the sharp crack of bone splintering in those terrible jaws. The sound maddened her and she snatched up an axe that lay beside the pile of firewood and struck out at the dark misshapen body, feeling the axe strike solidly, and the hyena let out a choking howl.

The darkness and its own starvation had emboldened it. It had the taste in its mouth now, seeping through the blankets into its locked jaws and it would not relinquish its prey.

It turned and snapped at Robyn, its huge round eyes glowing yellow in the light of the flames and those terrible yellowed fangs clashing like the snap of a steel man-trap, closing on the axe handle inches from her fingers, jerking it out of her hand. Then it turned back to its prey, and once more locked its jaws onto the frail body. Fuller was so wasted that he was light as a child and the hyena dragged him swiftly towards the opening in the thorn *Scherm*.

Still screaming for help, Robyn stumbled after them and seized her father's shoulders, while the hyena had him by the belly. The woman and the animal fought over him, the blunted yellow teeth ripping and tearing throught the lining of Fuller's belly as the hyena strained back on its hindquarters, the neck stretched out at the pull.

The Hottentot Corporal dressed only in unlaced breeches, but brandishing his musket, ran towards them in the firelight.

'Help me,' screamed Robyn. The hyena had reached the thorn fence, her feet were slipping in the loose dust, she was not able to hold Fuller.

'Don't shoot!' Robyn screamed 'Don't shoot!' The danger from the musket was as great as from the animal.

The Corporal ran forward, reversing the musket and swung the butt at the hyena's head. It struck with a sharp crack of wood on bone, and the hyena released its grip. Finally, its natural cowardice overcame its greed. It turned and shambled through the opening in the thorn hedge and disappeared into the night.

'Oh, sweet merciful God,' Robyn whispered as they carried Fuller back to the litter, 'has he not suffered enough?'

Fuller Ballantyne lived out that night, but an hour after dawn that tenacious and tough old man at last relinquished his grip on life without having regained consciousness. It was as though a legend had passed, and an age had died with him. It left Robyn feeling numbed and disbelieving and she washed and dressed the frail and rotting husk for burial.

She buried him at the foot of a tall mukusi tree and carved into the bark with her own hand:

FULLER MORRIS BALLANTYNE
3rd Nov. 1788   17th Oct. 1860
'In those days there were giants upon the earth.'

She wished that she had been able to cut the words in marble. She wished that she had been able to embalm his body and carry it back to rest where it belonged in the great Abbey of Westminster. She wished that he had recognized and known who she was just once before he died, she wished she had been able to allay his suffering, and she was consumed with grief and guilt.

For three days she maintained the camp astride the Hyena Road, and she spent those days sitting listlessly beside the mound of newly turned earth under the mukusi tree. She drove old Karanga and even little Juba away, for she needed to be alone.

On the third day she knelt beside the grave and she spoke aloud. 'I make an oath to your memory, my dear father. I swear that I will devote my entire life to this land and its people, just as you did before me.'

Then she rose to her feet and her jaw-line hardened. The time for mourning was past. Now her duty lay plain before her – to follow this Hyena Road to the sea, and then to bear witness before all the world against the monsters who used it.

When the lions are hunting, the prey animals seem able to sense it. They are seized by a restlessness and will graze for only seconds at a time before throwing up their horned heads and freezing into that peculiar antelope stillness, only the wide trumpet-shaped ears moving incessantly; then, skittering like thrown dice, they rearrange themselves upon the grassy plains, snorting and nervous, aware of danger but uncertain of its exact source.

Old Karanga had the same instinct bred into him for he was Mashona, an eater of dirt, and as such he was natural prey. He was the first to become aware that there were Matabele somewhere close at hand. He became silent, nervous and watchful, and it infected the other bearers.

Robyn saw him pick a broken ostrich plume from the grass beside the path and study it gravely, puckering his lips and hissing quietly to himself. It had not fallen from the wing of a bird.

That night he voiced his fears to Robyn.

'They are here, the stabbers of women, the abductors of children—' He spat into the fire with a bravado that was hollow as a dead tree-trunk.

'You are under my protection,' Robyn told him. 'You and all the people in this caravan.'

But when they met the Matabele war party, it was without further warning, in the dawn when the Matabele always attack.

Suddenly they were there, surrounding the camp, a solid phalanx of dappled shields and nodding plumes, the blades of the broad stabbing assegai catching the early light. Old Karanga had gone in the night, and with him had gone all the other porters and bearers. Except for the Hottentots the camp was deserted.

Karanga's warning had not been in vain, however, and behind the thorn *scherm* all the Hottentot guards were standing to their muskets, with their bayonets fixed.

The encircling Matabele stood silent, and still as statues carved from black marble. There seemed to be thousands upon thousands of them – though common sense told Robyn that it was merely a trick of her heated imagination and the poor light. A hundred, at the most two hundred, she decided.

Beside her Juba whispered, 'We are safe, Nomusa. We are beyond the Burnt Land, beyond the border of my people. They will not kill us.'

Robyn wished she was as confident, and she shivered briefly, not merely from the dawn chill.

'See, Nomusa,' Juba insisted. 'The baggage boys are with them, and many of the *amadoda* carry their *isibamu* (firearms). If they intended to fight, they would not so burden themselves.'

Robyn saw that the girl was right, some of the warriors had rusty trade muskets slung upon their shoulders, and she remembered from her grandfather's writings that whenever the Matabele intended serious fighting they handed their muskets, which they neither trusted nor used with any accuracy, to the baggage boys and relied entirely upon the weapon that their ancestors had forged and perfected, the assegai of Chaka Zulu.

'The baggage boys carry trade goods, they are a trading party,' Juba whispered. The baggage boys were the young apprentice warriors, and beyond the ranks of fighting men they were still in column. As soon as Robyn recognized the boxes and bundles that the baggage boys carried balanced on their heads, her last qualms faded to be replaced by anger.

They were traders, that she was sure of now, and returning along the road from the east there was little doubt in Robyn's mind as to what they had traded for these paltry wares.

'Slavers!' she snapped. 'In God's name and mercy, these are the slavers we seek, returning from their filthy business. Juba, go and hide immediately,' she ordered.

Then, with her Sharps rifle tucked under her arm, she stepped out through the opening in the wall of thorn bush, and the nearest warriors in the circle lowered their shields a little and stared at her curiously. This small change in attitude confirmed Juba's guess, their intentions were not warlike.

'Where is your Induna?' Robyn called, her voice sharp with her anger, and now their curiosity gave way to astonishment. Their ranks swayed and rustled, until a man came from amongst them, one of the most impressive men she had ever laid eyes upon.

There was no mistaking his nobility of bearing, the arrogance and pride of a warrior tried in battle and covered in honours. He stopped before her and when he spoke his voice was low and calm. He did not have to raise it to be heard.

'Where is your husband, white woman?' he asked. 'Or your father?'

'I speak for myself, and all my people.'

'But you are a woman,' the tall Induna contradicted her.

'And you are a slaver,' Robyn flared at him, 'a dealer in women and children.'

The warrior stared at her for a moment, then lifted his chin and laughed, it was a low clear musical sound.

'Not only a woman,' he laughed, 'but an insolent one also.'

He shifted his shield on to his shoulder and strode past her. He was so tall that Robyn had to lift her chin to look up at him. He moved with a sinuous balance and assurance of carriage. The muscles in his back shone as though they were covered in black velvet, the tall plumes of his headdress nodded and the war rattles on his ankles whispered with each pace.

Swiftly he moved through the gap in the thorn hedge and at Robyn's gesture the Hottentot Corporal lifted the point of his bayonet into the 'present' position and stepped back to let the Induna pass.

With a sweeping gaze the Induna took in the condition of the camp and laughed again.

'Your bearers have run,' he said. 'Those Mashona jackals can smell a real man a day's march away.'

Robyn had followed him into the camp and now she demanded with anger that was not feigned.

'By what right do you enter my kraal and terrify my people?'

The Induna turned back to her.

'I am the King's man,' he said. 'On the King's business.' As though that was all the explanation that was necessary.

Gandang, the Induna, was a son of Mzilikazi, the King and Paramount Chief of the Matabele and all the subservient tribes.

His mother was of pure Zanzi blood, the old pure blood of the South, but she was a junior wife and as such, Gandang would never aspire to his father's estate.

However, he was one of his father's favourites. Mzilikazi, who mistrusted nearly all of his sons, and most of his hundreds of wives, trusted this son, not only because he was beautiful and clever and a warrior without fear, but because he lived in strict accordance with the law and custom of his people, and because of his unquestioned and oft-proven loyalty to his father and his King.

For this and for his deeds, he was covered in honours to which the ox-tail tassels on his arms and his legs bore witness. At four and twenty summers, he was the youngest *indona* ever to be granted the head-ring of the Induna and a place on the high council of the nation, where his voice was listened to with serious attention even by the old grey pates.

The ageing King, crippled with gout, turned more and more towards this tall and straight young man when there was a difficult task, or a bitter battle in the offing.

So when Mzilikazi learned of the treachery of one of his Indunas, a man who commanded the border guards of the south and eastern strip of the Burnt Land, he had not hesitated before summoning Gandang, the trusted son.

'Bopa, son of Bakweg, is a traitor.'

It was a mark of Gandang's favour that his father condescended to explain his orders as he issued them.

'At first, as he was ordered, he slew those who trespassed in the Burnt Land, then he grew greedy. Instead of killing, he took them as cattle and sold them in the east to the *Putukezi* (Portuguese) and the *Sulumani* (Arabs) and sent word to me that they were dead.' The old King shifted his swollen and painful joints and took snuff, before going on.

'Then because Bopa was a greedy man, and the men with whom he deals are greedy also, he began to seek other cattle to trade. On his own account, and secretly, he began to raid the tribes beyond the Burnt Land.'

Gandang, kneeling before his father, had hissed with astonishment. It was contrary to law and custom, for the tribes of the Mashona beyond the Burnt Land were the King's 'cattle', to be raided only at the King's direction. For another to usurp the powers and gather the booty that belonged to the King was the worst form of treason.

'Yes, my son,' the King agreed with Gandang's horror. 'But his greed was without frontiers. He hungered for the baubles and the trash which the *Sulumani* brought him, and when this supply of Mashona "cattle" was not enough, then he turned upon his own people.'

The King was silent and his expression one of deep regret, for though he was a despot with powers that were subject to neither check nor limitation, although his justice and his laws were savage, yet within those laws he was a just man.

'Bopa sent to me messengers accusing our own people, some of them nobles of Zanzi blood, one of treachery, another of witchcraft, another of stealing from the royal herds – and I sent the messengers back to Bopa ordering him to slay the offenders. But they were not slain. They, and all their people were taken along the road that Bopa had opened to the east. Now their bodies will not be buried in this land and their spirits will wander homelessly for all time.'

That was a terrible fate, and the King lowered his chin upon his chest, and brooded on it. Then he sighed and lifted his head. It was a small neat head and his voice was high-pitched, almost womanish, not that of a mighty conqueror and a warrior without fear.

'Take your spear to the traitor, my son, and when you have killed him, return to me.'

When Gandang would have crawled from his presence, the King halted him with one finger raised.

'When you have killed Bopa, you and those of your *amadoda* who are with you when the deed is done may go in to the women.'

It was the permission for which Gandang had waited for so many years, the highest privilege, the right to go in to the women and take wives.

Gandang shouted his father's praises as he crawled backwards from the royal presence.

Then Gandang, the loyal son, had done what his father commanded. He had carried his spear of retribution swiftly across all of Matabeleland, across the Burnt Land, and along the Hyena Road until he had met Bopa returning from the east laden with the spoils he so dearly coveted.

They had met at a pass through a line of granite hills, not a day's march from where Gandang now confronted Robyn Ballantyne.

Gandang's *Inyati* impi (buffalo) in their ostrich plumes and civet-tail skirts, carrying the dappled black and white oxhide shields had surrounded the slave-guards formed from selected warriors of Bopa's *Inhlambene* impi (the Swimmers). The slavers wore white egret plumes and kilts of monkey tails, while their war shields were of chocolate-red oxhide – but right was on the side of the Inyati, and after the swife *jikela* (encirclement) they raced in to crush the guilty and confused slave-guards in a few terrible unholy minutes of battle.

Gandang himself had engaged the grizzle-headed but powerfully built Bopa. He was a wily, scarred fighter and veteran of a thousand such conflicts. Their shields, the one dappled black and the other red, collided with a thud like charging bulls, and they wrestled for the advantage until Gandang, the younger and stronger, with a shift of weight and feet had hooked the point of his shield under the red shield of Bopa and prised it aside to open his enemy's flank.

'*Ngidla* – I have eaten!' Gandang sang out as he sent the broad blade cleaving

between Bopa's ribs, and when it was withdrawn against the reluctant cling of
flesh with a sucking noise like a man walking in thick ankle-deep mud, Bopa's
heart blood burst out behind it and splattered against Gandang's shield, drenching
the ox tail tassels on his arms and his legs.

Thus it was for good reason that Gandang had laughed when Robyn called
him 'Slaver'.

'I am on the King's business,' he repeated. 'But what do you do here, white
woman?' He knew very little of these strange people, for he had been a child
when the impis of Mzilikazi had fought them in the land to the south, and had
been driven by them northwards into what was now Matabeleland.

Gandang had met only one or two of them. They had been visitors to his
father's great kraal at Thabas Indunas, travellers and traders and missionaries
who had been 'given the road' by the King and allowed to cross the strictly
guarded frontiers.

Gandang was suspicious of them and their gaudy trade goods. He distrusted
their habit of breaking pieces off the rocks along their path, he disliked their
talk of a white man who lived in the sky and seemed to be in serious competition
with the 'Nkulu-kulu', the great God of the Matabele.

Had he met this woman and her followers in the Burnt Land, he would have
followed his orders without hesitation, and killed them all.

However, they were still ten days' march from the frontier and his interest
in them was casual; he was impatient to return to his father and report to him
the success of his expedition. He would not waste much further time.

'What is your business, woman?'

'I come to tell you that the Great Queen will no longer allow human beings
to be sold like cattle for a few beads. I come to put an end to this evil business.'

'That is man's work,' Gandang smiled. 'And besides, it has already been seen
to.'

The woman amused him, at another time he might have enjoyed bantering
with her.

He would have turned and strode from the camp when suddenly a small
movement seen through a gap in the thin thatch of one of the temporary shelters
caught his attention. With uncanny speed for such a big man, he ducked into
the hut and pulled the girl out by her wrist; holding her at arm's length he
studied Juba gravely.

'You are of the people, you are Matabele,' he said flatly.

Juba hung her head and her face had a pale greyish sheen of terror. For a
moment Robyn thought that Juba's legs would no longer bear her weight.

'Speak,' Gandang commanded in that low but imperious voice. 'You are
Matabele!'

Juba looked up at him and her whisper was so soft that Robyn hardly caught
it.

'Matabele,' she agreed, 'of Zanzi blood.'

The warrior and the maid considered each other carefully. Juba lifted her
chin, and the greyness vanished from her face.

'Your father?' Gandang asked at last.

'I am Juba, daughter of Tembu Tebe.'

'He is dead, and all his children, at the King's orders.'

Juba shook her head. 'My father is dead – but his wives and his children are
in the land of the *Sulumani* beyond the sea. I alone escaped.'

'Bopa!' Gandang said the name as though it were a curse. He considered a
moment. 'It is possible that your father was wrongly sentenced, for Bopa sent
false accusation to the King.'

Juba made no reply, but in the silence that followed, Robyn saw a subtle change coming over the girl, something altered in the carriage of her head, she shifted her weight, thrusting out one hip, a small but provocative movement.

Her eyes, when she looked up at the tall Induna, grew wider and softer, and her lips were held slightly apart so that the pink tip of her tongue just showed between them.

'What is this white woman to you?' Gandang asked, and there was just a trace of huskiness in his own voice. He held her wrist still, and she made no effort to pull away.

'She is as my mother was,' Juba replied, and as the Induna looked down from her face to her sweet young body the ostrich plumes fanned softly about his head, and Juba changed the angle of her shoulders slightly, offering up her breasts to his gaze.

'You are with her by your own will?' Gandang insisted, and Juba nodded.

'So be it.' It seemed to require an effort for the warrior to break his gaze, but he dropped Juba's wrist and turned back to Robyn. His smile was mocking once more.

'The slavers you seek are not far from here, white woman. You will find them at the next pass in the road.'

He went as swiftly and as silently as he had come, and his warriors followed him in a dense black column. Within minutes the last of them had disappeared along the winding narrow trail into the west.

Old Karanga was the first of the servants to return to the camp. He came in through the thorn *scherm* like a bashful stork on his thin legs.

'Where were you when I needed you?' Robyn demanded.

'Nomusa, I could not trust my temper with those Matabele dogs,' old Karanga quavered, but he could not meet her eyes.

Within the hour the other porters and bearers had crept down from the hills and out of the forest, all of them now endowed with amazing enthusiasm to continue the march in the opposite direction to that of the *Inyati* impi.

Robyn found the slavers where Gandang had promised her she would. They were scattered over the neck of the pass, they lay in knots and windrows, like leaves after the first storm of autumn. Nearly all of them had their death wounds in the chest or throat, proof that at the end they had fought like Matabele.

The victors had slit open the dead men's bellies to allow their spirits to escape, a last courtesy to men who had fought gallantly, but the vultures had used the openings to enter the belly pouches.

. The birds hopped and flapped and squabbled raucously over the cadavers, tugging and dragging at them so that their dead limbs kicked and twitched as though they were still alive, and dust and loose feathers flew around them. The croaking and squawking of the birds was deafening.

In the trees and on the cliffs above the pass, the birds that had already gorged crouched somnolently, puffing out their feathers and hunching their naked scaly heads and necks upon their shoulders, digesting the contents of their bulging crops before returning to the feast.

The little caravan passed slowly, in fascinated horror at the carnage, speechless in the raucous chorus of the scavengers, stepping carefully over the ragged, dust-covered remains of brave men, reminded by them of their own mortality.

Once they had crossed the pass they hurried down the far slope with fearful backward glances. There was a stream at the bottom of the slope, a tiny trickle of clear water springing from the slope and threading its way from pool to small shaded pool. Robyn went into camp upon the bank, and immediately called Juba to follow her.

She had to bathe herself, she felt as though death had touched her with its putrid fingertips and she needed to wash away the taint of it. She sat under the trickle of clear water, waist deep in the pool below the waterfall and let the stream flow over her head, her eyes closed trying to blank out the horrors of the battlefield. Juba was not so affected, she was no stranger to death in its most malevolent forms, and she splashed and played in the green water, completely absorbed in the moment.

At last Robyn waded to the bank, and pulled her shirt and breeches over her still-wet body. In that heat, her clothes would dry upon her within minutes, and while she twisted her wet hair into a rope on top of her head she called to Juba to come out of the pool.

In a mischievous and rebellious mood the girl ignored her, and remained rapt in her own game, singing softly as she picked wild flowers from a creeper that hung over the pool and plaited them into a necklace over her shoulders. Robyn turned away and left her, climbing back along the bank towards the camp, and the first turn hid her from view.

Now Juba looked up and hesitated. She was not certain why she had refused to obey, and she felt a little chill of disquiet at being alone. She was not yet accustomed to this new mood of hers, this strange and formless excitement, this breathless expectancy for she knew not what. With a toss of her head she returned to her song and her play.

Standing above the bank, half screened by the trailing creeper and mottled like a leopard by the slanting dappled sunlight through the leaves of the forest, a tall figure leaned against the bole of a wild fig tree and watched the girl.

He had stood there, unseen and unmoving since he had been led to the pool by the sound of splashing and singing. He had watched the two women, comparing their nakedness – the bloodless white against the luscious dark skin, the skinny angular frame against sweet and abundant flesh, the small pointed breasts tipped in the obscene pink of raw meat against the full and perfect rounds with their raised bosses, dark and shiny as new-washed coal, the narrow hips of a boy against the proud wide basin which would cradle fine sons, the mean little buttocks against the fullness and glossiness that was unmistakably woman.

Gandang was aware that by returning along the trail he was for the first time in his life neglecting his duty. He should have been many hours' march away from this place, trotting at the head of his impi into the west, yet there was this madness in his blood, that he had not been able to deny. So he had halted his impi and returned alone along the Hyena Road.

'I am stealing the King's time, just as surely as Bopa stole his cattle,' he told himself. 'But it is only a small part of a single day, and after all the years I have given to my father, he would not grudge me that.' But Gandang knew that he would, favourite son or not, Mzilikazi had only one punishment for disobedience.

Gandang was risking his life to see the girl again, he was risking a traitor's death to speak a few words to a stranger, daughter of one who had himself died a traitor's death.

'How many men have dug their graves with their own *umthondo*,' he mused, as he waited for the white woman to leave the pool, and when she had covered her skinny boy's body with those stiff and ugly garments and called to the lovely child in the pool to follow her, Gandang tried to reach out with his own will to hold Juba there.

The white woman, clearly piqued, turned and disappeared amongst the trees and Gandang relaxed slightly, giving himself once more to the pleasure of watching the girl in the water. The wild flowers were a pale yellow against her skin, and the waterdrops clung to her breasts and shoulders like stars against the midnight sky. Juba was singing one of the children's songs that Gandang knew so well, and he found himself humming the chorus under his breath.

Below him the girl waded to the bank and standing in the sugar-white sand began to wipe the water from her body; still singing she bent forward to wipe her legs, encircling them with long slim pink-lined fingers and running her hands slowly down from thigh to ankle. Her back was to Gandang, and as she stooped he gasped aloud at what was revealed to him, and instantly the girl flew erect and spun to face him. She was trembling like a roused fawn, her eyes huge and dark with fright.

'I see you, Juba, daughter of Tembu Tebe,' he said, there was a husky catch to his voice as he came down the bank to her.

The expression in her eyes changed, they glowed with golden lights like sunshine in a bowl of honey.

'I am a messenger of the King, and I demand the right of the road,' he said, and touched her shoulder. She shivered under his fingers. He saw the little goose bumps rise upon her skin.

The 'right of the road' was a custom from the south, from the old country beside the sea. It was the same right which Senzangakhona had demanded of Nandi, 'the sweet one', but Senzangakhona had not respected the law, and he had penetrated the forbidden veil. From this transgression one had been born, the bastard 'Chaka', 'the worm in the belly', who had grown to become both the King and the scourge of Zululand, the same Chaka from whose tyranny Mzilikazi had flown with his tribe to the north.

'I am a loyal maiden of the King,' Juba answered him shyly, 'and I cannot refuse to comfort one who follows the road on the King's business.' Then she smiled up at him. It was neither bold nor provocative, but a smile so sweet, so trusting and filled with admiration, that Gandang felt his heart squeezed afresh.

He was gentle with her, very gentle and calm and patient, so that she found herself impatient to render the service he desired, found herself desiring it as strongly as he so evidently did. When he showed her how to make a nest for him between her crossed thighs, she responded instantly to his word and touch, and there was something wrong with her throat and her breathing, for she was unable to answer him aloud.

While she held him in this nest she felt herself gradually overwhelmed by a strange wildness of heart and body. She tried to alter the angle of her pelvis, she tried to unlock her tightly crossed thighs and spread them for him, she strove to engulf him for she could no longer bear that dry and tantalizing friction against the inside of her upper legs. She wanted to feel him breast the warm and welcoming flood that she sent down for him and she wanted to feel him gliding upon it deeply up inside her. But his resolve, his respect for custom and law, was as powerful as that muscular body that drove above her, and he held her captive until the moment when she felt his grip break and his seed spring strongly from him to waste itself in the white sand beneath them. At that moment she felt such a sense of loss that she could have wept aloud.

Gandang held her still, his chest heaving and the sweat forming little shiny runnels across that smooth dark back and down the corded neck. Juba clung to him with both arms wrapped tightly about him, her face pressed into the hollow between his shoulder and his neck, and for a long time neither of them spoke.

'You are as soft and as beautiful as the first night of the new moon,' Gandang whispered at last.

'And you are as black and as strong as the bull of the *Chawala* festival,' she instinctively chose the simile that would mean most to a Matabele, the bull as the symbol of wealth and virility and the *Chawala* bull the most perfect specimen of all the King's herds.

'You will be only one of many wives,' Robyn was horrified at the thought.

'Yes,' agreed Juba. 'First of all of them, and the others will honour me.'

'I would have taken you with me to teach you many things and show you great wonders.'

'I have already seen the greatest wonder.'

'You will do nothing but bear children.'

Juba nodded happily. 'If I am truly lucky, I will bear him a hundred sons.'

'I will miss you.'

'I would never leave you, Nomusa, my mother, not for any person nor reason in the world, except this one.'

'He wants to give me cattle.'

'Since the death of my family, you are my mother,' explained Juba, 'and it is the marriage price.'

'I cannot accept payment – as though you were a slave.'

'Then you demean me. I am of Zanzi blood and he tells me that I am the most beautiful woman in Matabeleland. You should set the *lobola* as one hundred head of cattle.'

So Robyn called the Induna to her.

'The marriage price is one hundred head of cattle,' Robyn told him sternly.

'You make a poor bargain,' Gandang answered loftily. 'She is worth many times that amount.'

'You will keep the cattle at your kraal, against my coming. You will tend them carefully and see that they multiply.'

'It will be as you say, *amekazi*, my mother.' And this time Robyn had to return his smile, for it was no longer mocking and his teeth were so white and he was, as Jube has said, truly beautiful.

'Look after her well, Gandang.'

Robyn embraced the young woman and their tears mingled and smeared both their cheeks. Yet when she left Juba did not look back once, but trotted behind Gandang's tall erect figure carrying her rolled sleeping-mat balanced upon her head, and her buttocks jiggled merrily under the short beaded apron.

Man and woman reached the saddle of the pass and disappeared abruptly from view.

The Hyena Road led Robyn and her little party into the mountains, into the mist and the strangely desolate valleys of heather and fantastically shaped grey stone. It led her to the slave stockades which Juba had described to her, the meeting-place where the white man and black man made their trade for human life, where the slaves exchanged their carved yokes for cuff and chains. But now the stockades were deserted, the thatch already sagging and falling in untidy clumps, only the sour smell of captivity lingered, and the swarming vermin that infected the empty buildings. In a futile gesture, Robyn put fire to the buildings.

From the misty mountains the road led on, down through dark gorges and at last to the low littoral where once more the heat clamped down upon them from a sullen overcast sky and the grotesque baobab trees lifted their twisted arthritic branches to it like crippled worshippers at a healing shrine.

The rains caught them here upon the coastal plain. The flood swept three men away at a ford, four more, including one of the Hottentots, died of fever and Robyn herself was smitten with the first onslaught of the disease. Shivering, half demented by the phantoms of malaria, she toiled on along the rapidly overgrown trail, slipping and stumbling in the mud, and cursing the fever miasma that rose from the brimming swamps and hung like a silver wraith in the sickly green glades of fever trees through which they hurried.

Fever and the rigours of the last stage of the journey had tired and weakened them all. They knew that they were, at the most, only a few days' march from the coast, deep into Portuguese territory and therefore under the protection of a Christian king and a government of civilized men. It was for these reasons that the Hottentot sentries slept beside the smouldering watch fire of damp wood, and it was there that they died, their throats slit with a blade sharp enough to cut off the least cry.

So Robyn woke to rough hands upon her, twisting her arms up between her shoulder blades and a bony knee in the small of her back, while steel cuffs clicked coldly about her wrists. Then the hands released her and she was wrenched cruelly to her feet, and dragged from the leaky hut beside the Hyena Road.

The previous evening she had been too tired and feverish to undress, so now she was still clad in a stained and rumpled flannel shirt and patched moleskin breeches. She had even kept the cloth cap on her head, covering her hair, thus in the darkness her captors did not realize that she was a woman.

She was bound with her own porters and Hottentots, forced to wear the light marching chains which were proof, if proof was needed, as to who her captors were. The dawn revealed them to be half-breeds and blacks, all of them dressed in the cast-off finery of European style, but carrying modern weapons.

These were the men she had crossed half a continent to meet, but now she cowered in the rags that were her only disguise. She shuddered to think on her fate if they should discover her sex, and she berated herself for having so blithely believed that she and her entourage would be safe from these predators merely because she was white and English. Their prey was human flesh, of whatever colour and condition and that was all she was now, human flesh on the hoof. A chained creature, of little real value, a few dollars on the auction block, and she knew that her captors would think nothing of taking their pleasure upon her, or of leaving her beside the road with a ball through the temple if she provoked them in any way. She kept silent and obeyed instantly the least word or gesture from her captors. Slipping and dragging in the mud they were marched on eastwards, forced to carry their remaining stores and equipment which had now become slavers' booty.

They were closer to the coast than Robyn had calculated, they smelt the iodine and salt of the sea from afar, and later as night began to fall, they caught the smell of woodsmoke and the unmistakable odour of captive humanity. Then at last they saw the firelight flickering in the darkness ahead, and the awful loom of the barracoons.

Their captors marched between the dark stockades of pole and daubed mud, from which the chilling dirge rose of men without hope singing of a land they would never see again.

At last they came into the central square around which the barracoons were built. It was an open area of trampled mud where a raised platform of rough-sawn planks had been built. Its purpose was immediately clear, for the first of Robyn's servants was dragged up the steps and stood upon the platform, while the fires around the clearing were heaped with dry wood to light the scene. The platform was the auction block, and it seemed that the sale was to take place immediately.

The auctioneer was clearly of pure Portuguese stock, a little man with the wrinkled, sun-browned face of a vicious gnome. He had the bland smile and the unblinking eyes of a serpent. He was dressed in elegantly cut jacket and breeches, and his boots and belt were of the finest Iberian leather, ornately tooled and with solid silver buckles. He carried a pair of expensive pistols in his belt, and wore the wide-brimmed flat-crowned hat of a Portuguese gentleman upon his small wrinkled head.

Before climbing up on the block, he sent one of his personal slaves with a casual kick and cuff to the carved wooden drum at the edge of the clearing. On it the slave began pounding out a summons to the buyers. The slave went to it lustily, his bare torso gleaming with sweat and raindrops in the firelight.

And in answer to the urgent staccato rhythm of the drum, men came from out of the shadows of the grove and from the living huts between the barracoons. Some of them had been drinking, they came arm in arm brandishing their rum bottles and bellowing in drunken chorus, others came singly and silently – but they came from every direction and gathered in a circle about the auction block.

The men who formed the circle seemed to be of every hue that the human skin is capable of assuming, from purple black through all the shades of brown and yellow to dead shark's belly white, and their features were African and Arabic, Asian and European. Even their dress differed widely, from the flowing robes of Arabia to the faded finery of embroidered jackets and high boots. They had only one thing in common, the hawk-fierce eyes and merciless mien of those who deal in human misery.

One at a time Robyn's servants were prodded up on to the block, and their ragged clothing was ripped away to expose their physique to the buyers. One of these might come forward to feel the muscle tone, or force open a slave's mouth to examine the teeth, like a gypsy horse-dealer at the fair.

Then, when the buyers had satisfied themselves as to the quality of the wares on offer, the small Portuguese would step lightly to the front of the block and begin the bidding.

The men in the circle below him called him Alphonse and though they exchanged coarse banter with him, yet they all treated him with wary respect, there could be no clearer proof of the man's reputation than fear and respect from these men.

Under his control the sale went swiftly. The Hottentots, small wiry men, butter yellow and with flat pug-like features attracted little interest from the circle of buyers, knocked down for a few silver rupees apiece, while the porters, taller men and well muscled from many months of hard marching and porterage, fetched better prices – until they came to old Karanga, ancient and toothless, hobbling on to the block on storklike legs, seeming barely able to support the weight of his chains.

The laughter was derisive, and the little Portuguese pleaded in vain for a single bid before dismissing the old man with disgust. It was only when he was hauled down off the block and dragged away into the darkness beyond the fires that Robyn realized what was about to happen to him and, forgetting her resolve not to draw attention to herself, 'No – let him go!'

Hardly one of them glanced in her direction, and the man who held her chain hit her a careless open-handed blow across the side of her face that blinded her for a moment. She dropped to her knees in the mud, and through the buzzing in her ears heard the thud of a pistol shot from the darkness.

She began quietly to weep, and still weeping she was hoisted to her feet and in her turn dragged forward into the circle of firelight and hoisted by her chain on to the block.

'A young skinny one,' said the Portuguese. 'But white enough to make a choice bum-boy for the harems of Omani, once he has had his knackers clipped. Who will give me ten rupees?'

'Let's have a look at him,' a voice shouted from the circle, and the Portuguese turned to Robyn, hooked a finger into the top button of her flannel shirt and ripped it down to the level of her belt buckle.

She doubled over, trying to conceal her upper body, but the man behind her twisted the chain and forced her upright. Her breasts pushed out pertly through the torn shirt, and the ring of watchers growled and moved restlessly, the mood changing instantly.

Alphonse touched the butt of one of the pistols in his belt significantly, and the growl of comment died, the ring of men drew back a little.

'Ten rupees?' Alphonse Pereira asked.

From across the circle a powerfully-built man swaggered into the firelight. Robyn recognized him instantly. He wore a tall beaver hat tilted back on his head, and from under the brim curled thick shiny black hair. His teeth, when he opened his mouth, sparkled in the light of the flames. His face was flushed with excitement, his voice was thick with it.

'Gold,' he shouted. 'I'll bid gold, a gold mohur of the East India Company, and a plague on any of you that goes above that.'

'A gold mohur,' called Alphonse, the slave-master. 'A gold mohur bid by my brother Camacho Pereira, and good luck to him,' he chuckled. 'Come now, who wants to deny my brother Camacho a fair tup at the wench?'

One of his men slapped Camacho's back.

'Sweet Christ, you always were a hot one, at that price you can have my turn on top of her.'

And Camacho laughed delightedly, and came to the front of the block to stare up at Robyn, tipping the beaver hat forward he whispered,

'I've had to wait a long time—'

Robyn felt the little insects of loathing crawling over her skin, and she backed away to the limit of her chain.

'Come now,' Alphonse called. 'Who will go beyond a gold mohur for a fine piece—'

'She's mine,' Camacho told his brother. 'Strike the bargain.'

His brother lifted his hand to knock down the sale, when another voice stopped him.

'A double eagle, sir. Twenty golden dollars American bid.' The voice was not raised, yet it carried clearly to every man there, as it could carry from quarterdeck to maintop in a force eight gale.

Robyn started, and swung her chains disbelievingly in that direction; she would have known that lazy drawling inflection if she had not heard it for a lifetime. He stood at the very edge of the firelight, but as every head in the circle turned to him, he stepped forward.

The smile had frozen on Alphonse's face, and he hesitated.

'Call the bid!' The advancing figure in plain white shirt and dark breeches made the men about him seem small and grubby, and after a moment's hesitation, Alphonse obeyed him.

'A double eagle bid,' he said harshly. 'Captain Mungo St. John of the clipper *Huron* bids a double golden eagle.'

Robyn felt her legs start to sag under her with relief, but the men behind her jerked her upright by her chain. Camacho Pereira had whirled to face the American, and to stare at him furiously. Mungo St. John answered him with a smile, indulgent and patronizing. Robyn had never seen him look more handsome and dangerous, his dark wavy hair catching the firelight, and the gaze of his yellow-flecked eyes level and unflinching in the face of Camacho's fury.

'A thousand rupees, Camacho,' he said softly. 'Can you match it?'

Camacho hesitated, and then turned back quickly to his own brother, his voice low and urgent.

'Stake me?' he asked, and Alphonse laughed.

'I never lend money.'

'To a brother?' Camacho insisted.

'Especially not to a brother,' Alphonse answered. 'Let the wench go, you can buy a dozen better for fifty rupees each.'

'I must have her.' He whirled back to face Mungo St. John. 'I must have her. It is a matter of honour. Do you understand?' He took the beaver from his head, and spun it away. One of his men caught it, and Camacho ran both hands through his thick black locks, and then stretched his arms down at his sides, flexing the fingers like a conjurer about to perform a sleight of hand.

'I will make one more bid,' he said ominously. 'I bid one mohur of gold – and ten inches of Toledo steel.' The knife seemed to appear in his hand from out of the air, he lifted the point to the level of Mungo St. John's belt buckle.

'Walk away, Yankee, or I will take the woman *and* your gold double eagle.'

The watchers growled, a low blood-thirsty sound, and swiftly rearranged themselves into a ring about the two men, jostling for a better view.

'One hundred rupees says Machito slits the Yankee's guts.'

'Done!' And there was a rising hubbub as the wagers were called and accepted.

Mungo St. John had not stopped smiling, but now he held out his right hand without once taking his eyes off the Portuguese's face.

Out of the ranks of the watchers emerged a large, toadlike figure with a head as round and bald as a cannon ball. Tippoo moved with reptilian speed to Mungo St. John's right side. He placed a knife in the outstretched hand, and then unknotted the embroidered sash from his waist and handed that to his Captain. Mungo wrapped the sash around his left forearm, still smiling softly to himself.

He had not once looked up at Robyn, though she had not been able to tear her own eyes from his face.

He seemed godlike to her at that moment, everything about him, the darkly classical features, the wide shoulders under the white cloth of his shirt, the narrow waist clinched with a broad belt of polished leather, the strong straight legs in tightly fitted breeches and soft leather boots, seemed to have come down directly from Olympus. She would have gladly thrown herself at his feet and worshipped him.

Just below Robyn, Camacho was stripping off his own jacket and wrapping his guard arm with it. Then with the long knife in his right hand he made a low swift cut, forehand and then backhand, so the steel whispered as it dissolved into a silver blur like the wing of a dragonfly in flight. At each stroke he ducked his head slightly and flexed his knees, loosening and warming his muscles like an athlete before the contest.

Then he moved forward, stepping lightly in the treacherous mud and weaving the point of the knife to distract and intimidate his adversary.

The smile went from Mungo St. John's lips, to be replaced by a grave and attentive expression, like a mathematician considering a complex problem. He kept his own knife low, advancing his wrapped forearm, and balancing easily, stood his full height and turned gently to face the Portuguese as he circled. It reminded Robyn of the night she had watched him on the dance floor at Admiralty House, so tall and graceful, so balanced and controlled in each movement.

Now at last the watchers were silent, straining eagerly for the first glimpse of blood, but when Camacho charged they roared the way the crowd roars when the bull first bursts into the ring. Mungo St. John barely seemed to move, swaying his body at the hips so the knife slid past him, and then he was facing Camacho again.

Twice more the Portuguese attacked, and both times Mungo St. John moved effortlessly aside, but each time he gave a little ground, until he was backed up to the first rank of watchers, they began to fall back to give the American room to fight, but Camacho saw his opportunity as Mungo was crowded like a prize-fighter against the ropes and he swung back to attack. At the same moment, almost as though it had been rehearsed, a booted foot shot out from the crowd. Nobody was sure whose foot it was, for the throng was closely packed and the light uncertain, but the kick to the back of Mungo St. John's heel almost brought him down sprawling in the mud, he lunged to catch his balance, but before he could do so, Camacho hit him with the long bright blade. Robyn screamed and Mungo St. John spun away from the sting of the steel with scarlet spreading wetly down his shirt-front like rich Burgundy wine spilled on a damask tablecloth, and his own knife flicked out of his hand and was lost in the red mud.

The crowd bellowed, and Camacho swarmed in eagerly, following the wounded man the way a good dog hunts a pheasant with a broken wing.

Mungo was forced to give him ground, falling back, clutching the wound, dodging and weaving, catching a forehand slash on his wrapped guard arm so the embroidered cloth split almost to the flesh beneath it.

Skilfully Camacho herded him towards the auction block, and when Mungo felt the poles catch in the small of his back, he froze for a moment as he realized that he was trapped. Camacho drove in at him, going for the belly, his lips drawn back baring his perfect white teeth.

Mungo St. John caught the knife on his guard and then snatched a grip on the wrist with his right hand. The two men stood chest to chest, their arms entwined like vines on a trellis, swaying slightly as they strained together, and the effort brought a fresh flood of bright blood from Mungo's wound, but slowly he forced Camacho's knife hand upwards, bending it at the elbow, until the point was no longer aimed at Mungo's belly but at the night sky above them.

Mungo shifted his feet, gathering himself and then his face darkened, his jaw clenched and his breath sobbed with effort. Slowly Camacho's wrist gave to the pressure, and his eyes widened as the point of his own knife reversed towards him.

Now he also was wedged against the side of the auction block and could not break away, and infinitely slowly but inexorably, the long blade moved towards his own chest. Both men stared down at it, their hands and arms interlocked, pitting their strength to hold each other, but the point touched Camacho's chest, a drop of blood welled up at the tiny prick.

On the block beside Robyn, Alphonse Pereira drew the pistol from his belt with a furtive movement – but before she could shout a warning their was a blur of movement and Tippoo the mate towered beside him, his own huge smooth-bore pistol pressed to the side of Alphonse's skull. The little Portuguese rolled his eyes sideways at Tippoo, and then hurriedly returned the weapon to his belt, and Robyn could watch again with fascinated horror the contest at her feet.

Mungo St. John's face was congested with dark blood, every muscle in his shoulders and arms raised in knots under the thin shirt, his whole existence concentrated on the knife, and he slid his left foot back until it was anchored against the auction block, and then using it as a pivot hurled all his weight forward on to the knife, the final effort like the matador going over between the horns for the kill.

For a moment longer Camacho resisted him, and then the blade resumed its forward movement entering Camacho's chest as slowly as a python swallows a gazelle.

Camacho's mouth opened in a cawing burst of despair, and suddenly his fingers opened as all resistance and strength went out of them. His own blade with Mungo St. John's full weight behind it shot its length into his chest with such force that the cross piece of the hilt struck against his ribs with a sharp thump.

Mungo St. John released his grip and let him fall, face forward into the mud, while he himself caught at the edge of the auction block for support. Only then did he lift his chin to look up at Robyn.

'Your servant, ma'am,' he murmured, and Tippoo rushed forward to catch him before he fell.

Huron's seamen, all of them armed, formed a guard about them, and Tippoo led them holding aloft a bull's-eye lantern which he shone into the shadows as they hurried down the path.

Mungo St. John was on his feet, but supported by Nathaniel, his bosun, and Robyn had bound up the wound roughly with a strip of linen torn from a seaman's shirt and had used the rest of the shirt to make a sling for Mungo's right arm.

Through a grove of mangroves they reached the bank of the creek on which the barracoons had been built and in the centre of the stream, her bare masts and yards silhouetted against the starry sky, lay the lovely clipper.

She had lanterns in her rigging and an alert anchor watch, for at Tippoo's first hail the whaler swung away from her side and was rowed swiftly to the bank where they stood.

Mungo climbed the ship's side unaided, but sank down with a grateful sigh on to his bunk in the stern cabin, the bunk that Robyn remembered so vividly.

She tried to force the memory from her mind, and keep her manner brisk and businesslike.

'They have taken my medical chest,' she said as she rinsed her hands in the porcelain basin at the head of the bunk.

'Tippoo.' Mungo looked up at his mate, and the bald, scarred head bobbed once and then Tippoo ducked out of the cabin. Mungo and Robyn were alone, and she tried to remain remote and professional as she made her first examination of the wound in good lantern light.

It was narrow, but very deep. She did not like the angle of the thrust, just below the collar bone but angled in towards the point of the shoulders.

'Can you move your fingers?' she asked. He lifted his hand towards her face and touched her cheek lightly.

'Yes,' he said, as he stroked her. 'Very easily.'

'Don't,' she said weakly.

'You are sick,' he said. 'So thin and pale.'

'It is nothing – lower your arm, please.'

She was terribly conscious of her matted hair and filthy mud-stained clothing, of the yellow tinges of fever on her skin and the dark smudges of fatigue and terror under her eyes.

'Fever?' he asked quietly, and she nodded as she went on working on the wound.

'Strange,' he murmured. 'It makes you seem so young, so fragile,' he paused, 'so lovely.'

'I forbid you to talk like that.' She felt flustered, uncertain of herself.

'I said I would not forget you,' he ignored the instruction, 'and I did not.'

'If you don't stop, I will leave immediately.'

'When I saw your face tonight in the light of the fires, I could not believe it was you, and at the same time it was as though all our lives we had a rendezvous to keep here tonight, As though it had been destined from the moment of our births.'

'Please,' she whispered, 'please stop.'

'That's better – please is better. Now I will stop.'

But he watched her face attentively as she worked. In the ship's medical chest which he kept in the locker below his bunk Robyn found most of what she needed.

He neither flinched nor grimaced as she laid the stitches in the wound, but went on watching her.

'You must rest now,' she said as she finished, and he lay back on the bunk. At last he looked tired and drained, and she felt a rush of gratitude, of pity, and of that other emotion which she had believed that she had long ago subdued.

'You saved me.' She dropped her eyes, no longer able to look at him and busied herself with repacking the ship's chest. 'I will always be grateful for that, just as I will always hate you for what you are doing here.'

'What am I doing here?' he challenged her lightly.

'Buying slaves,' she accused. 'Buying human lives, just as you bought me on the slaving block.'

'But for a much lower price,' he agreed as he closed his eyes. 'At twenty dollars gold a head there is not much profit in it, I assure you.'

She awoke in the small cabin, the same cabin in which she had sailed the length of the Atlantic Ocean and in the same narrow uncomfortable bunk.

It was like homecoming, and the first thing she saw after her eyes had adjusted to the harsh beam of sunlight through the skylight were the chests of her medical instruments, her remaining medicines and her few personal possessions.

She remembered the unspoken command that Mungo had given to the mate the previous evening. Tippoo must have gone back ashore during the night, and she wondered what price he had paid or what threat he had made to get them back for her.

She rose swiftly from her bunk, ashamed of her sloth; whoever had left the chests, had also filled the enamel jug with fresh water. With relief she washed away the mud and filth and combed the tangles of her hair before finding worn but clean clothing in her chest. Then she hurried from her cabin down to the master's quarters. If Tippoo had been able to find her chests, then he might be able to find and free her people, the Hottentots and porters who had gone upon the auction block in the firelight.

Mungo's bunk was empty, the vest and bloodstained shirt bundled and thrown into a corner of the cabin, and the bedclothes in disarray. She turned swiftly for the deck, and as she came out into the sunlight she saw that it would be only a temporary respite from the monsoon, for already the thunderclouds were boiling up over the horizon.

She looked about her quickly. *Huron* lay in the centre of a broad estuary, with mangroves on each bank, and the bar and the open sea was not in sight, though the tide was ebbing, rustling down the ship's hull and leaving the mud flats half exposed.

There were other vessels in the roadstead, mostly big dhow-rigged buggaloos typical of the Arab coastal traders, but there was another fully rigged ship at anchor half a mile further downstream, flying the flag of Brazil at her peak. Even as Robyn paused to watch her, there came the clank of her capstan, and men ran up the ratlines and spread out along her yards. She was getting under way. Then Robyn realized that there was unusual activity all about her. Small boats were plying from the shore to the anchored dhows, and even on *Huron*'s deck there was a huddle of men on the quarter-deck.

Robyn turned towards them, and realized that the tallest of them was Mungo St. John. His arm was in a sling and he looked drawn and pale, but his expression was forbidding, the dark curved brows drawn together in a frown, and the mouth a thin cruel line as he listened attentively to one of his seamen. So absorbed was he that he did not notice Robyn until she was only a few paces away. Then he swung towards her, and all the questions and demands stayed behind her lips for his voice was harsh.

'Your coming was an act of God, Doctor Ballantyne,' he said.

'Why do you say that?'

'There is a plague in the barracoons,' he said. 'Most of the other buyers are cutting their losses, and leaving.' He glanced downstream to where the Brazilian schooner had set reefed main and jib and was running down towards the bar and the open sea, and there was activity aboard most of the other vessels.

'But I have over a thousand prime blacks afattening ashore – and I'll be damned if I'll run now. At least, not until I know what it is.'

Robyn stared at him. Her mind was a whirl of doubts and fears. 'Plague' was a layman's word, it covered everything from the Black Death to syphilis, the grand pox, as it was called.

'I will go ashore immediately,' she said, and Mungo St. John nodded.

'I thought you would say that,' he said, 'I will go with you.'

'No.' Her tone brooked no argument. 'You will aggravate that wound, and in your weakened condition you will be easy prey to this plague, whatever it is.' She glanced at Tippoo, and his face split laterally into that broad toadlike grin and he stepped up beside her.

'By God, ma'am, I've had them all,' said Nathaniel, the little pockmarked bosun. 'And none of them killed me yet.' And he stepped up to her other hand.

Robyn sat in the stern while Tippoo and Nathaniel handled the oars, and as they pulled across the ebb towards the shore the bosun explained what they would find ashore.

'Each of the traders has his own barracoon built and guarded by his own men,' he told Robyn. 'He buys from the Portos as the blackbirds are brought in.'

As Robyn listened to Nathaniel, she realized the answers to questions that had worried her and Zouga. This was the reason why Pereira had tried so desperately to persuade them not to bring the expedition south of the Zambezi river, and why, when all else had failed, he had attacked it with his armed brigands and tried to destroy it. He had been protecting his brother's trade routes and selling area. It was not mere avarice and lust, but a logical attempt to preserve this lucrative enterprise from discovery.

She went on listening to Nathaniel.

'Each trader fattens his wares ashore, like pigs for the market. That way they are stronger for the crossing, and he makes sure that they are healthy and not going to bring sickness aboard with them.

'There are twenty-three barracoons here, some small ones with twenty blacks or so, belonging to the small traders, right on up to the big ones like *Huron's*, with a thousand and more prime blackbirds in the cage.

'We have the slave-decks set up in *Huron's* hold, and we would have begun taking them aboard any day, but now—'

Nathaniel shrugged, and spat on the horny calloused palms of each hand in turn, and then plied himself to the oars once more.

'Are you a Christian, Nathaniel?' Robyn asked softly.

'That I am, ma'am,' he said proudly. 'As good a Christian as ever sailed out of Martha's Vineyard.'

'Do you think God approves of what you are doing here to these poor people?'

'Hewers of wood, ma'am, and drawers of water, like the Bible says,' the weather-beaten sailor told her, so glibly that she knew that the reply had been put in his mouth, and she guessed by whom.

Once they were ashore, Tippoo led the small party with Robyn in the centre and Nathaniel carrying her chest in the rear.

Captain Mungo St. John had chosen the best site available for his barracoon, on a rise of ground at a distance from the river. The sheds were well built, with floors of sawn timber raised above the mud and good roofs thatched with palmetto leaves.

Huron's guards had not deserted, proof of the discipline which Mungo St. John maintained and the slaves in the barracks had evidently been carefully chosen. They were all well set up men and women, and the copper cookers were filled with boiling farina so that their bellies bulged and their skins were glossy.

At Robyn's direction they were lined up and she passed swiftly down the ranks. There were some mild ailments, which she singled out for later treatment, but she found none of the symptoms which she so dreaded.

'There is no plague here,' she decided. 'Not yet.'

'Come!' said Tippoo.

He led her through the palm groves, and the next barracoon had been deserted by the traders who had built it and stocked it. Already the slaves were hungry and confused by their sudden liberation.

'You are free to go,' Robyn told them. 'Go back to your own land.'

She was not certain that they understood her. They squatted in the mud and stared at her blankly. It was as though they had lost all power of independent thought or action, and she knew that they would never be able to make their way back along the Hyena Road, even if they survived the coming epidemic.

With a flash of horror Robyn realized that without their slave-masters these poor creatures were doomed to a lingering death by starvation and disease. Their masters had cleared out the store rooms before they left, there was not a cupful of farina or corn meal left in any of the barracoons they visited that morning.

'We will have to feed them,' Robyn said.

'We have food for our own, that is all,' Tippoo told her impassively.

'He is right, ma'am,' Nathaniel confirmed. 'We feed them, then we'll starve our own blackbirds – besides, most of them are poor goods, not worth the price of a cup of farina.'

In the second barracoon Robyn thought that she had at last discovered the first plague victims, for the low thatched sheds were crammed with rows of prostrate naked figures, and their low moaning and whimpering was a heart-breaking sound, while the smell of corruption was thick and oily on the palate.

It was Tippoo who corrected her. 'China birds,' he grunted, and for a moment Robyn did not understand, and she stooped over the nearest body, then straightened immediately. Despite her training, cold blisters of sweat formed on her forehead.

By Imperial Decree from Peking, no black African slave could be landed on the shores of China unless he had been rendered incapable of reproducing his own kind. The Emperor was concerned that future generations would not be plagued by the growth of an alien population in their midst. The traders found it expedient to castrate their purchases in the barracoons, so that losses caused by the operation could be absorbed before the expense of the long voyage was incurred.

It was crudely done, a tourniquet applied to the root of the scrotum and then the entire scrotal sack removed at a single knife stroke and the wound cauterized immediately with a heated iron or a daub of hot pitch. About sixty per cent would survive the shock and subsequent mortification, but their price per capita was so enhanced that the trader could face forty per cent losses with equanimity.

There was nothing that Robyn could do for so many, she felt overwhelmed by the suffering and misery all around her, and she stumbled out on to the muddy pathway, blinded by her own tears. In the next barracoon, the one nearest to the central auction block, she found the first plague victims.

Once again the sheds had been deserted by the slave-masters, and the dimly lit thatched sheds were filled with naked figures, some squatting motionlessly, others lying on the damp earthen floor, knees drawn up, shaking with the cold of fever, and powerless to lift themselves out of their own bodily wastes. The sound of delirium and suffering was murmurous as of insects in an English orchard on a hot summer's day.

The first sufferer that Robyn touched was a young girl, just beyond puberty, and her skin was burning hot. She rolled her head from side to side, endlessly and senselessly, mouthing snatches of gibberish. Swiftly Robyn ran her fingertips down the girl's naked bulging stomach and immediately she felt the tiny lumps under the hot skin, like pellets of buckshot. There could be no doubt.

'Smallpox,' she said simply, and Tippoo drew back fearfully.

'Wait outside,' she told him, and he went swiftly and with obvious relief. She turned to Nathaniel. She had noticed the little pitted scars in his folded sun-toughened skin, and now there was no fear in his expression.

'When?' she asked.

'When I was a boy,' he said. 'It killed my old ma and my brothers.'

'We have work to do,' she told him.

In the gloomy stinking shed the dead were piled with the living, and on some of the wracked and furnace-heated black bodies the plague had already burst into full flower. They found it in all its stages. Papules beneath the skin had erupted into vesicles, bubbles of clear thin fluid that thickened into pustules, which in turn burst and released a custard-thick trickle of matter.

'These will live,' Robyn told Nathaniel. 'The plague is purging from their blood.' She found a man whose open pocks had already crusted over.

While Nathaniel held the man from moving, Robyn scraped away the crusty scabs with a spatula and gathered them in a wide-mouthed glass bottle that had once held quinine powder.

'This strain of the disease has been attenuated,' Robyn explained impatiently, and for the first time she saw fear in the flecked eyes of Mungo St. John. 'The Turks first used this method two hundred years ago.'

'I would prefer to sail away from it,' Mungo St. John said quietly, staring at the stoppered bottle which was half filled with damp yellow matter in which were small flecks of blood.

'It would be no use. The infection is already aboard.' Robyn shook her head firmly. 'In a week or less *Huron* would be turned into a stinking plague-ship filled with dying men.'

Mungo turned away from her and went to the ship's rail. He stood there with one hand clasped into a fist behind his back, the other still in its sling, staring at the shore where the thatched roofs of the barracoons just showed above the mangroves.

'You cannot leave those poor wretches,' Robyn said. 'They will starve. I alone could never find food to feed that multitude. You are responsible for them.'

He did not answer her for a moment, then he turned back to study her curiously.

'If *Huron* sailed, with her holds empty, would you stay here on this fever and smallpox-ridden coast to tend this multitude of doomed savages?' he asked.

'Of course.' She was still impatient, and he inclined his head. His eyes no longer mocked, but were sober, perhaps even filled with respect.

'If you will not stay for common humanity, then stay for self-interest.' She scorned him with her tone. 'A million dollars' worth of human cattle, and I will save them for you.'

'You would save them to be sold into captivity?' he insisted.

'Even slavery is better than death,' she replied.

Again, he turned away from her, taking a slow turn of the quarterdeck, frowning thoughtfully, puffing on the long black cheroot so that wreathes of tobacco smoke drifted behind him, and Robyn and half *Huron*'s crew watched him, some fearfully, others with resignation.

'You say that you have yourself undergone this – this thing.' His eyes were drawn back, with loathing fascination, to the little bottle that stood in the centre of his chart table.

For answer Robyn lifted the sleeve of her shirt and showed him the distinctive deeply pocked scar on her forearm.

A minute longer he hesitated, and she went on persuasively, 'I will give you a strain of the disease that is "passant" that has been weakened and attenuated by passage through another man's body, rather than the virulent form of the plague which you will breathe on the very air and which will kill most of you.'

'There is no risk?'

She hesitated and then replied firmly, 'There is always risk, but one hundred, nay a thousand times less risk, than if you take the disease from the air.'

With an abrupt gesture Mungo St. John ripped open the sleeve on his left arm with his teeth and offered it to her.

'Do it,' he said. 'But in God's name do it quickly, before my courage fails.'

She drew the point of her scalpel across the smooth deeply tanned skin of his forearm and the tiny crimson droplets rose behind it. He did not flinch, but when she dipped the scalpel into the bottle and scraped up a speck of the noisome yellow stuff, he blanched and made as if to jerk his arm away, then with an obvious effort controlled himself. She smeared the pus over the tiny wound, and he stepped back and turned from her.

'All of you.' His voice was rough with his horror and disgust. 'Every last one of you,' he told the gaping terrified seamen.

With Nathaniel, the bosun, there were three others who had survived the disease, and were speckled by the small dimpled scars which were its stigma.

Four men were not enough to help Robyn care for a thousand slaves, and her losses were much higher than she had expected. Perhaps this strain of the disease was more virulent, or perhaps the black men from the interior did not have the same resistance as the Europeans whose forbears had for generations been exposed to smallpox.

She introduced the crusted pus into the scratches on their limbs, working in the noon sunlight on into the gloom of dusk and then by the lantern's gleam, and they submitted with dumb resignation of the slave which she found pitiful and repugnant, but which none the less made her work much easier.

The reaction began within hours, the swelling and fever and the vomiting, and she went out into the other deserted barracoons to gather more of the loathsome pus from the bodies of those who had survived the smallpox and were now dying of starvation and neglect – resigning herself to the fact that she had only the strength and time to care for those in *Huron*'s barracoons, resigning herself to the fact that there was farina to feed them only, and closing her mind to the cries and entreaty, to the silent dying stare from wizened faces that streamed pus from open pocks.

Even in her own barracoon the four of them working hour after hour, night and day, could give only perfunctory attention to each of the slaves, a handful of the cold pasty farina and a mugful of water once a day during the period of the most violent reaction to the inoculation. Those who survived this were left to care for themselves, to crawl to the water bucket when they could or to wolf a lump of farina from the spadeful that Nathaniel left on a wooden platter at intervals between the rows of supine figures.

Then when they were strong enough to stand they were put to work at piling the rotting bodies of their less fortunate peers upon a gun carriage and dragging them out of the barracoon. There was not the remotest chance of either burying or burning the bodies, and there were too many for the bloated vultures. They piled the corpses in heaps in the coconut grove, well downwind of the barracoon and went back for more.

Twice a day Robyn went down to the edge of the creek and hailed the anchor watch on *Huron*'s deck and had the whaler row her out to the ship, and she spent an hour in the stern cabin.

Mungo St. John's reaction had been frighteningly severe, perhaps he had been weakened by the knife wound. His arm had swollen to almost twice normal size, and the scratch Robyn had inflicted turned into a hideous canker with a thick black crusty scab. His fever was intense, his skin almost painfully hot to the touch, and the flesh seemed to melt off his big-boned frame like candle wax under the flame.

Tippoo, himself suffering from a raging fever, his own arm swollen grotesquely, could not be made to leave the side of Mungo's bunk.

Robyn felt easier knowing that Tippoo was there, strangely gentle, almost like a mother with a child, to care for Mungo while she must go back ashore to the suffering multitude that choked the barracoons.

On the twelfth day when she went aboard *Huron*, Tippoo met her at the companionway with that wide toadlike grin which she had not seen for so long, and when she hurried into the cabin she saw why.

Mungo was propped up on the bolsters, thin and pale, his lips dry and dark purple bruises under his eyes, as though he had been beaten with a heavy club, but he was lucid and his skin cool.

'God's breath,' he croaked. 'You look awful!' And she felt like weeping with relief and chagrin.

When she had bathed and bandaged the shrinking canker on his forearm and was ready to leave, he took her wrist.

'You are killing yourself,' he whispered. 'When did you last sleep, and for how long?'

Only when he spoke did she realize the depth of her exhaustion – it had been two days previously and then only for a few hours that she had slept, and she felt *Huron*'s deck swing and lurch under her feet as though she rode a high sea and was not lying quietly at anchor in a placid creek.

Mungo drew her down gently beside him on to the bunk, and she did not have either the strength or will to resist. He made a cradle for her head on his shoulder, and almost immediately she was asleep, her last memory was the feel of his fingers smoothing back the dank ringlets from her temples.

She awoke with a guilty start, not sure how long she had slept, and still fuzzy with sleep struggled out of Mungo St. John's arms brushing the hair out of her eyes with her fingers, trying ineffectually to straighten her rumpled and sweat-dampened clothing.

'I must go!' she blurted groggily, still exhausted and half asleep. How many had died while she slept, she wondered. Before he could prevent it, she was stumbling up the companionway to the deck calling for Nathaniel to row her ashore.

The few hours of rest had refreshed her so that she looked about the estuary with a new and lively interest again. It was the first time that she became aware that one other vessel, besides *Huron*, was still lying at anchor in the river. It was one of the small dhow-rigged buggaloos, the coastal slavers similar to the one from which she had rescued Juba. On impulse, she had Nathaniel row her alongside, and when nobody answered her hail, she went aboard. The vessel had clearly been overwhelmed by the plague before she could flee, perhaps she was the vessel from which the original infection had been carried ashore.

Robyn found the same conditions prevailing aboard as there were ashore, the dead, the dying, and those who would recover. Although they were slavers she was still a physician, and she had taken the Hippocratic oath. What she could do was very little, but she did it and the Arab captain, stricken and weakened, thanked her from his sleeping-mat on the open deck.

'May Allah walk beside you,' he whispered, 'and may he give me the opportunity to return this kindness one day.'

'And may Allah show you the error of your ways,' Robyn told him tartly. 'I will send some fresh water, before nightfall, but now there are others more deserving.'

In the days that followed, the plague ran its inexorable course, the weaklings died, some of them consumed by the terrible thirsts of fever crawled from the abandoned barracoons on to the mud flats of the estuary to fill their bellies with the salt water. Their bodies were twisted into grotesque contortions by the cramps of the salt in their blood, and their insane rantings were like the cries of seabirds across the water, extinguished at last by the incoming tide. The surface of the river was troubled by the swirl and splash of the crocodile and the big sharks that had come upstream to gather this grisly harvest.

Others had crawled away into the forest and groves; they lay under every bush and even before they died they were covered with a red mantle of the fierce safari ants that overnight picked the skeleton to gleaming whiteness.

Some of those that survived, encouraged by Robyn, crept weakly away towards the west. Perhaps a few would complete the long hazardous journey back to their razed villages and devastated countryside, she hoped.

However, most of the survivors of the plague were to weak and confused and demoralized to move. They stayed on in the squalid stinking barracoons, pathetically dependent upon Robyn and her tiny band of helpers for every mouthful of water and farina, watching her with the eyes of dumb and suffering animals.

All this time the piles of corpses in the palm groves grew taller, and the stench more penetrating. Robyn knew too well what would happen next.

'The battlefield plagues,' she explained to Mungo St. John. 'They always follow when the dead are left unburied, when the rivers and wells are choked with bodies. If they strike now, then none will survive. All of us are weakened, we would be unable to resist the typhoid and enteric plagues. Now is the time to leave, for we have saved all those who are for saving. We must fly before the new onslaught, for unlike the smallpox, there is no defence against them.'

'Most of my crew are still sick and weak.'

'They will recover swiftly out on the open ocean.'

Mungo St. John turned to Nathaniel to ask, 'How many slaves have survived?'

'More than eight hundred, thanks to the missus here.'

'We will begin to take them aboard at dawn tomorrow,' he decided.

That night Robyn came back to his cabin after dark. She could not stay away, and he was waiting for her, she could tell by his expression and the quickness of his smile.

'I was beginning to fear that you preferred the company of eight hundred plague-ridden slaves,' he greeted her.

'Captain St. John, I wish to make one more appeal to you. As a Christian gentleman, will you not release these poor creatures and have them escorted and fed on the journey back to where they came—'

He interrupted her, his tone light and that smile hovering on his lips.

'And will you not call me Mungo, rather than Captain St. John?'

She ignored the interruption, and went on. 'After all they have suffered, that terrible march down from the highlands, the error and humiliation of slavery and now this plague. If you would consent to release them, I would lead them back to their homes.'

He rose from the canvas chair and came to stand over her. His leanness and pallor made him seem even taller.

'Mungo!' he insisted.

'God would forgive you, I am sure of that, he would forgive you the sins that you have already committed against humanity—'

'Mungo!' he whispered, and placed his hands upon her shoulders. She felt herself begin to tremble uncontrollably.

He drew her to his chest. She could feel his ribs, he was so thin, and her voice choked up in her throat when she tried to continue her appeal. Slowly he stooped over her, and she closed her eyes tightly, her arms stiff at her sides, her fists clenched.

'Say Mungo,' he commanded quietly, and his lips were cool and soft on hers. Her trembling became uncontrolled shaking.

Her lips opened under his, and her arms went up around his neck.

'Mungo,' she sobbed. 'Oh, Mungo, Mungo.'

She had been taught that her naked body was shameful, but it was the one lesson that she had learned imperfectly, and much of her shame had been mitigated, firstly in the lecture rooms and dissection rooms of St. Matthew's, and secondly in the company of Juba, the little Matabele dove, whose unaffected delight in her nudity she had transmitted to Robyn. Those childlike romps together in the cool green pools of an African river had served to blow away most of the cobwebs of shame.

Now Mungo St. John's delight in and admiration for her body gave her joy and, far from shame, brought her pride that she had never known before. Their love-making was no longer accompanied by pain, there were no longer barriers between them – so locked together they could ride the dips and swings of emotion from Himalayan heights where the great winds blew, down to the sweet languorous depths where they seemed to be drowning in honey, each movement slowed, every breath drawn out as though it would last forever, their bodies damp and hot, pressed together and without form, like clay in the hands of a child.

The night was too short, while the wick of the lantern guttered and smoked, neglected and untrimmed. In the dawn, their loving seemed to have filled them with new strength, to have driven away the weakness of fever and the exhaustion of the past weeks.

It was only the sound of the first slaves coming aboard that roused Robyn and brought her back from that far frontier to the hot and cramped little cabin on a slave ship in a fever creek on a wild and brutal continent.

She heard the whisper of bare feet and the clank and drag of slave chains, the sound of men's voices raised, hectoring and impatient, on the deck above.

'Hurry them, or we load for a week.' Tippoo's voice.

Robyn raised herself on her elbow and looked down at Mungo. His eyes were closed but he was not asleep, she knew.

'Now,' she whispered. 'Now you cannot but release them. After last night, I know that something has changed in you.'

She felt a strange joy, the zeal of the prophet looking down upon a convert for whose soul she had wrestled with the devil and won.

'Call Tippoo,' she insisted, 'and give him the order to free the slaves.'

Mungo opened his eyes, even after the long night in which neither of them had slept, his eyes were clear. There was the shadow of new beard, dense and dark, carpeting his bony jawline. He was magnificent and she knew then that she loved him.

'Call Tippoo,' she repeated, and he shook his head – a little gesture of perplexity.

'You still do not understand,' he answered her. 'This is my life. I cannot alter that, not for you nor for anybody.'

'Eight hundred souls,' she pleaded, 'and you have their salvation in your hands.'

'No.' He shook his head again. 'You are wrong, not eight hundred souls but eight hundred thousand dollars – that is what I have in my hands.'

'Mungo.' His name still felt awkward on her lips. 'Jesus has said that it is easier for a camel to pass through the eye of a needle than that a rich man should enter the kingdom of Heaven. Let them go, you cannot judge human lives in gold.'

He laughed and sat up.

'With eight hundred thousand bucks, I can bribe my way into Heaven, if I want to, but between us, my dear, it sounds an awfully dull place. I think the devil and I might have more to talk about.'

The mocking gleam was back in his eye again, and he swung his legs out over the edge of the bunk, and naked crossed to where his breeches hung on a wooden peg from the bulkhead.

'We have lain too long abed,' he said briskly. 'I must see to the loading, and you had best begin your own preparations for the voyage.' He belted his breeches and stuffed his shirt into them. 'It will take us three days to load, I would be obliged if you would test the water barrels.' He came to sit on the edge of the bunk and began dragging on his boots, talking the while in crisp businesslike fashion, detailing the preparations that she should make for the welfare of the slaves during the voyage. 'We will have less than a full cargo, which will make it easier to exercise them on deck and keep the holds clean.' He stood up and looked down at her.

With a rush like a roused fawn she threw off the blanket that covered her and knelt on the edge of the bunk, seizing him about the waist with both arms.

'Mungo,' she whispered urgently. 'You cannot torture us so.' She pressed the side of her face to his chest, feeling the harsh springing curls of his body hair even through the linen of his shirt. 'I cannot offend further against my God and my conscience – unless you free these poor damned souls, then I can never marry you.'

His expression changed swiftly, becoming tender and concerned. He lifted his hand to stroke the dense russet locks of her hair, still damp and tangled from the loving of the night.

'My poor darling,' his lips formed the words, soundlessly, but her face was still pressed to his chest and she could not see his lips. He drew a deep breath, and though his eyes were still marked with regret and his expression sober, his tone was light and casual.

'Then it is just as well that I have no intention of freeing a single one of them – for what would my wife say otherwise?'

The words took many seconds to make sense to Robyn, and then her whole body spasmed, her grip around his waist tightened and then slowly relaxed. She released him. Slowly she sat back on her heels, naked in the midst of his disordered bunk, and she stared at him with an expression of desolation and disbelief.

'You are married?' Robyn's voice echoed strangely in her own ears, as though from the end of a long bare corridor, and Mungo nodded.

'These ten years past,' he answered quietly. 'A French lady of aristocratic birth, a cousin of Louis Napoleon. A lady of great beauty who with the three fine sons she has borne me awaits my return to Bannerfield.' He paused and then went on with infinite regret. 'I am sorry, my dear, I never dreamed that you did not know.' And he reached out to touch her cheek, but she cringed away as though he held a poisonous serpent in his hand.

'Will you go away, please,' she whispered.

'Robyn—' he began, but she shook her head violently.

'No,' she said. 'Please don't say any more. Just go. Go away! Please go away.'

Robyn locked the door of her cabin and sat down at the sea chest which she used for a desk. There were no tears. Her eyes felt dry and burning as though blasted by a wind off the desert. She had very little paper left and had to tear the end sheets from her journal. They were speckled with mildew and distorted from the heat and dryness of the highlands and the humidity of the monsoon-ridden littoral.

She smoothed out the first sheet carefully on the lid of her writing case, dipped her pen in the remaining half-inch of India ink and headed the sheet with a hand that was calm and unshaken.

16th November, 1860.
Aboard the Slaver *Huron*.

And then in the same clear unhurried script began to write:

My Dear Captain Codrington,
    My trust in an all-merciful Providence and my belief in the true and one God, and in his gentle son and our Saviour Jesus convinces me that this will come into your hands while there is still time for you to act.
    Through a series of incredible adventures and misfortunes I now find myself devoid of friends or protectors, in the power of the notorious American Slave Master and trader Mungo St. John. Against both my will and my conscience I am being forced to act as the physician for this infamous vessel which is at this moment preparing for the voyage around the Cape of Good Hope, across the Atlantic Ocean for a port in the Southern States of America.
    As I write, I can hear the doleful sounds from the deck above me, and

from the hold below where the poor creatures, eight hundred forsaken souls in all, wearing only their chains are being brought aboard and incarcerated for the voyage which many of them will not survive.

We are lying at anchor in a hidden creek, concealed from the open sea by a sweep of the channel and the mangrove swamps, a perfect hide-away for the nefarious business in hand.

However, I have been able to study the ship's chart and from the navigator's markings learn the name of the estuary and its exact position. The river is the Rio Save, and it lies 20° 58' south latitude and 35° 03' east longitude.

I will do all in my power to delay the sailing of this vessel, though at this moment I cannot think what that will be. If this letter reaches you in time, there will be no difficulty for an officer of your courage and experience to blockade the river mouth and seize this slave ship when she attempts to leave the river.

If we have sailed before your arrival, then I implore you to follow in the same course as the Captain of the *Huron* must set to round Good Hope, and I will pray for adverse winds and weather that will enable you to come up with us.

Robyn went on pouring out the tale of her capture, of the plague that had swept through the barracoons, of her fear and hatred of the slavers, the detailed accounts of their barbaric practices and cruelties, and suddenly she realized that she had filled many pages with her account, and she began her last paragraph.

You were gracious enough to express your belief that our destinies were linked in some mysterious way. I know that you share with me the same hatred of this abominable trade, and for these reasons I have made bold enough to appeal to you, confident that you will hearken to my anguished cry.

Robyn paused again, and then searched swiftly in her pen case and found the pair of the earring which she had given to Clinton Codrington so many months ago.

I enclose with this letter a token of my friendship and trust which I hope you will recognize, and I will search every day to see the topsails of your fine ship hurrying to give succour to myself and to the other unfortunates who are my ship-mates on this cursed and iniquitous voyage.

She signed it with her bold, rounded signature and stitched the folded pages and the single item of cheap jewellery into a square of duck canvas.

There was only one address that she had for it. Clinton had told her that he was under orders to call at Zanzibar Island, and she knew that Her Majesty's Consul on the island was a man of substance and integrity, a staunch adversary of the slave trade, one of the few men that her father, Fuller Ballantyne, had ever written about with respect and affection.

When she had finished, she tucked the small canvas package up under her skirts, and went up on deck. Mungo St John was on his quarterdeck, gaunt and lean and pale, and he took a step towards her, but she turned from him immediately.

'Nathaniel,' she called to the bosun. 'I wish to visit the buggaloo.' She indicated the Arab dhow which was still anchored downstream from *Huron*.

'She's making ready to sail, ma'am.' Nathaniel knuckled his forehead. 'She'll be gone before we can get across—'

'She will if you continue talking,' Robyn told him briskly. 'I must see if there is aught they need, the poor devils, before they sail.'

Nathaniel glanced at his Captain, and after a moment's hesitation, Mungo nodded his assent and turned back to watch the stream of slaves coming aboard through the entry port.

The Arab Captain of the dhow, just strong enough to take his place at the tiller, greeted her respectfully and listened attentively while she spoke.

Nathaniel was waiting in the gig, out of sight below the level of the dhow's deck, and Robyn made sure that they were shielded from a casual watcher on Huron's deck before she passed the canvas package to the Arab, and followed it with a gold English sovereign.

'There will be another sovereign for you, from the man you deliver it to,' she told him, and the Arab bit the coin, and smiled wanly as he tucked it into a fold of his turban.

'And I am Matabele. Induna of two thousand. My name is Gandang, son of Mzilikazi, son of Zulu, and I come with a bright spear and a red heart.'

Zouga understood the words with difficulty, for they were spoken rapidly, in accents that were strange to his ears, but there was no misunderstanding the Induna's intention. His tone was clear, the murderous determination in his voice evident, and around him the circle of long black shields was unbroken and steadfast.

Unconsciously Zouga had straightened, forcing his aching muscles erect, and he held the Induna's gaze without flinching. They stared at each other, and Zouga found himself exerting all his will, all the force of his personality, trying to stay the Induna's spear arm. He knew it needed only for the bright broad blade to drop and two hundred amadoda would sweep into the rudimentary camp. It would be over so swiftly, the resistance that Zouga and his tiny band could offer would be so puny that they would not even earn the compliment of disembowelment from the victors.

He knew that only his steady gaze and the completely fearless mien that he offered to the Matabele had so far stayed the spear arm, but the silence was drawing out. At any second the spell would snap. He must chose his next action and words as though his life depended upon them, as indeed they did.

Gandang watched the strange pale man before him with his features impassive, yet for possibly the first time in his life while on his father's service, he was uncertain.

The man who called himself Bakela had spoken familiar names. Tshedi and Manali, they were names that his own father revered, yet that in itself would not have been enough to stay his hand, for the King's orders were clear: all who entered the Burnt Land must die. It was more than that. He knew who this man was. The maiden who he would soon take as wife had spoken of him. This was the brother of the white woman who had delivered Juba to his care, and who he had called amekazi, mother.

Juba had spoken of the man Bakela as she lay beside him on her sleeping-mat. She had spoken of him with admiration and awe, as a mighty hunter of elephant, as a warrior honoured by an all-powerful Queen who lived far beyond great waters. Juba had spoken of this man Bakela as a friend and a protector.

So Gandang paused before giving the order 'Bulala! Kill them!'

A Matabele Induna is never influenced by the words or whims of a woman, if he has fifty wives their voices are still as the chattering of the waters over the rocks in the shallow rapids of the Nyati river, and a man does not heed them, or rather it must never be apparent that he heeds them.

Juba had travelled to strange places and spoken of wonders and witchery, and Gandang while seeming not to listen had indeed listened and been impressed. The girl was not only comely and high bred, but sensible far beyond that mere simpering giggling sexuality to which he was accustomed in other girls of her age.

Gandang was learning that a Matabele Induna is never influenced by the whims and words of a woman, unless those words are spoken and the whims expressed on the privacy of the sleeping-mat, by a senior wife whose good sense has been proven.

Then it is folly not to hearken, for a senior wife can make a man's life unbearable, even if that man is an Induna of two thousand, and the favoured son of the most powerful monarch in Africa.

Behind the dark impassive mask of his handsome face, Gandang was thinking furiously. Instinct and Juba's words had warned him that it would be folly to slay this man, yet the warriors at his back knew his orders, and if he failed to carry them out, that failure would immediately be construed as weakness, and his treason reported to the King.

Before him the tattered figure took a pace forward, his whole being ludicrously arrogant. Gandang could see no trace of fear in the steady gaze of his strangely coloured eyes.

'I come as an emissary to the great King Mzilikazi, ruler of the Matabele people – and I bring greeting from the White Queen from across the waters.'

At the words Gandang felt a small warm flame of relief. The fact that the white man spoke the language of the people, albeit with a strange accent, made it more plausible that he was indeed an emissary. It was plausible, also, that this Queen of his would want to seek the protection and favour of a King as powerful as his father, and that she would be so ignorant as to send her emissary through the Burnt Land instead of along the open road from the south. Zouga saw the shift of mood in the Induna's eyes, that tiny crack in his determination.

'Wait,' he said. 'There is something that I have for you.'

In Zouga's writing-case still reposed the impressive handwritten letters, with seals of wax and scarlet ribbon, that had been provided him by the Under-Secretary at the Foreign Office, in the usual form.

In the name of Her Britannic Majesty, Ruler of Great Britain and Ireland, Empress of India – To the representatives of all foreign governments or to whosoever it may concern,

We do, by these presents, request and require that our beloved Morris Zouga Ballantyne be allowed to pass freely without let or hindrance and that he be afforded that assistance of which he may stand in need.

Zouga turned his back on the silent menacing ranks of spearsmen, and walked back slowly through the gap in the *scherm* of cut thorn branches.

Jan Cheroot was waiting for him, his face the colour of the watchfire ash. He and the gunbearers were crouched below the thorn barrier, staring through the chinks with expressions of such utter terror that Zouga felt emboldened in comparison.

'Lay down those guns,' he snapped, for all the weapons were cocked and primed and a nervous finger on a hair-trigger could let fly the shot that brought a solid black wave of Matabele sweeping through the camp.

Gandang suddenly found himself in a position of uncertainty. From being the merciless bearer of the King's justice, he found himself waiting like a timid suitor outside the gate in the thorn barrier, and every second detracted from his dignity.

Behind him he heard the stir of one of his men, the soft tap of assegai spear on hide shield. His men were growing restless already, sensing the passing of advantage to the little group of ragged starvelings they had surrounded. Gandang turned slowly, and his stony gaze passed over the ranks. They froze once more into utter stillness.

'Gandang, son of Mzilikazi, Induna of two thousand. Come forward.'

The hail from beyond the thorn barrier was unexpected and startlingly loud, but it came the moment before Gandang reached the limit of his patience and loosed his eager warriors. Gandang moved forward to the gateway. His plumes nodding about his head, his tread dignified, his carriage proud, so that no men might guess at his uncertainty. At the gateway he paused, and though his expression did not alter nor his gaze waver, he experienced a profound relief that his own wisdom and the words of his little dove had stayed his blade.

Before him stood a figure of almost incredible beauty. It took him many seconds to recognize the ragged individual of a few minutes previously. The figure wore cloth of that some peculiarly rich shade of red of the bushshrike's chest, brighter than the colour of freshly spilled blood. Though this was enough to stop a man's breath, it was not all. Bright metal ornaments on breast and shoulders sparkled in the morning sunlight, the belt buckle was of the same metal. The belt and cross-straps were of the same blinding whiteness as an egret's wing. The tall shakoe swept down to an elegant point between the eyes, and the helmet badge blazed like a sunrise upon the man's forehead.

There was no doubt now in Gandang's mind that here was indeed an important man, and a soldier of repute, as Juba had warned him, and he made a silent resolution to listen to her words in future with even greater attention. He felt a little shiver of dismay at the thought that he might have followed his first instincts and had this man cut down as though he was a worthless Mashona, a mere eater of dirt.

The magnificent figure took one pace towards him and lifted a hand to the peak of that beautiful helmet in a formal gesture that Gandang answered instinctively with a sweeping salute of his stabbing spear.

'I, Bakela, request that my token be conveyed to your father, the honoured and victorious Mzilikazi, and that he be informed that I request from him the right of the road,' said the man in his atrocious Sindebele and Gandang accepted the token from his hand, the small package with strange signs and marks upon it, bound up with strips of coloured cloth so beautiful that they would have delighted the heart of even the most vain and spoiled woman.

'It shall be done,' he agreed.

In the moments of his confrontation with Gandang, Zouga had been thinking as furiously as the Matabele and making his own calculations of survival. Now that he had fallen in with a border impi he knew he must put aside any thought of escaping southwards. Apart from the fact that they were completely surrounded and heavily outnumbered, he knew that no unmounted man could run ahead of these warriors. They were like machines built for the pursuit and the annihilation of an enemy.

The meeting had not taken him completely unprepared. There had been many a night in the preceding weeks when he had woken in the darkest hours, and he had lain on the hard earth and dreaded a moment such as this.

He had mentally rehearsed his actions – from the concealment of any fear while he won time to don his dress uniform, to the demand to be taken to the King's kraal. When it had gone as he planned it, when the tall Induna had agreed, 'It shall be done,' it had taken another enormous extension of Zouga's will not to show relief. He had stood aloof, disinterested, while Gandang had picked and called out five of his swiftest runners and had recited a long message that they must memorize, and take to Mzilikazi.

It began with a long recitation of the King's praises which began,

'Great black elephant who shakes the earth with his tread—' went on to list the deeds that Gandang had performed since leaving the great kraal at Thabas Indunas, the march eastward, the battle at the pass and the slaying of Bopa, the slave master, right up to this day's encounter with the white man. After a flowery description of the man's magnificent finery (which Gandang knew would intrigue his father), it ended with a repetition of Bakela's request to be 'given the road' to Thabas Indunas.

The chosen messengers, each in turn repeated the long message, and though he showed no change of expression Zouga was amazed that each of them had it word-perfect. It was an impressive demonstration of the developed memory of people who do not have the art of writing and reading.

Gandang handed them the sealed parchment envelope that contained Zouga's letter of credentials, and the messengers sprang to their feet from where they had squatted, saluted their Induna, formed file and trotted away towards the west.

Gandang turned back to Zouga. 'You will stay encamped here until the King sends word.'

'When will that be?' Zouga asked, and Gandang answered him sternly.

'Whenever the King is pleased to do so.'

Zouga's little party was left unmolested. Although there were a dozen Matabele *amadoda* positioned about the camp, guarding it day and night, not one of them attempted to enter the gateway in the thorn *scherm*. Until the moment when they might slaughter them, the persons and property of their prisoners were inviolate.

The main body of the impi camped a quarter of a mile downstream. Each evening the tall Induna visited Zouga and they sat for an hour or so across the fire from each other, speaking gravely and seriously.

As the days of waiting became weeks so the two men developed each for the other a deep respect, if not actual friendship. They were both warriors, and they had common ground when they spoke of old campaigns and of skirmishes and battles fought. They recognized in each other the strengths, the essential decencies of men who live by and respect the laws of their society, though those laws might diverge widely.

'I account him a gentleman,' Zouga wrote in his journal. 'One of nature's own.'

While Gandang, speaking to Juba on the sleeping-mat said merely, 'Bakela is a man.'

Gandang allowed Zouga's bearers to leave the enclosure, to cut and bring in thatch and timber to strengthen and improve the buildings, so that at last Zouga could sleep dry and warm. This, together with the rest and respite from endless marching brought an immediate improvement in Zouga's health. The deep wound in his cheek healed cleanly, leaving a pink shiny scar. The shoulder mended, the bruising abated, and he no longer needed a staff or a sling for his arm. Within a week he knew he was well enough to shoot the heavy four-to-the-pound.

One evening he proposed to Gandang that they hunt together, and the Induna who by this time was finding the waiting as tedious as Zouga was, agreed with alacrity. Gandang's *amadoda* surrounded a herd of Cape buffalo, and drove them down in a bellowing, stampeding black wave to where they waited. Zouga saw the tall Induna rise from cover and race in, bare-footed, shieldless, and kill a mature bull buffalo with a single thrust of the broad-bladed assegai through the ribs behind the heaving shoulder. Zouga knew that he lacked both the skill and courage to emulate that feat.

Gandang watched when Zouga stood to meet the squealing, thunderous charge of an enraged bull elephant, and when the beast went down to the crash of the shot, dropping on to its knees in a storm of dust, Gandang stepped past Zouga and touched the little black hole that punctured the elephant's thick grey hide an inch above the first crease at the top of the trunk.

Gandang inspected the smear of blood on the tip of his forefinger, and said 'Hau!' quietly but with force, which is an expression of deep amazement. For Gandang, himself, owned a musket, a Tower Musket manufactured in London in 1837. When he first acquired the weapon. Gandang had fired it at Buffalo, elephant and Mashona, all of whom had fled headlong, but unscathed.

Gandang understood that when firing it was necessary to close the eyes and the mouth firmly, to hold the breath and at the moment of discharge to shout a rebuke to the devil who lived in the gunpowder smoke, otherwise the devil could enter through the eyes or mouth and take possession of the marksman. In order to throw the musket ball to any distance, it was also necessary to pull the trigger with sudden and brutal force, as in hurling a spear. Furthermore, to minimize the recoil of the weapon, the butt should not touch the shoulder, but be held a hand's span from it. Despite all these precautions, Gandang had never succeeded in hitting the target at which he aimed, and had long abandoned the weapon to rust away, while he kept his assegai polished brightly.

Thus Gandang appreciated to the full the magnitude of the feat that Zouga performed with such apparent ease. So their mutual respect deepened with each day spent in each other's company, and became almost friendship. Almost, but not quite, there were chasms of culture and training between them that could never be bridged, and always the knowledge that on any day a swift runner might come from the west with a message for Gandang from his father.

'*Bulala umbuna!* Kill the white man!' And both of them knew that Gandang would hesitate not an instant longer.

Zouga had much time alone in camp, and he spent it planning his audience with the King. The longer he dwelt upon that the more ambitious became his plans. The memory of the ancient disused mine-shafts returned to plague these idle hours, and at first merely to amuse himself, and then with truly serious intent, Zouga began to draw up a document which he headed:

'Exclusive Concession to mine gold and hunt ivory in the Sovereign territory of Matabeleland.'

He worked on it each evening polishing and reshaping it in the gibberish that the layman takes for legal jargon and which he fondly believes will dignify his creation. 'Whereas I, Mzilikazi, ruler of Matabeleland, hereinafter referred to as the party of the first part—'

Zouga had completed this document to his entire satisfaction when a fatal flaw in his plans became evident. Mzilikazi could not sign his name. Zouga pondered this for a day and then the solution occurred to him. Mzilikazi should by this time have in hand the sealed package. The crimson wax seals must surely impress him, and in his writing-case Zouga had two full sticks of sealing wax.

Zouga began to design a great seal for King Mzilikazi. He sketched the design on the back cover of his journal, and the inspiration came from the first of the King's praise names.

'Great Black Elephant who shakes the earth.'

In Zouga's design the centre of the field depicted a bull elephant, with long tusks raised and ears spread wide. The upper border bore the legend, 'Mzilikazi

Nkosi Nkulu.' And the lower border carried the translation, 'Mzilikazi, King of the Matabele.'

He started experimenting with various materials, clay and wood, but the results did not please him – and the following day he asked Gandang for permission to send a party of his porters under Jan Cheroot back to the ancient workings at the Harkness mine to retrieve the ivory buried there.

It took two days of careful consideration for Gandang to agree, and when he did, he sent fifty of his men to accompany the caravan, with orders to kill them all at the first hint of flight or treachery. Jan Cheroot returned with the four huge tusks from the two bull elephants, and Zouga had not only the material from which to carve the King's great seal, but a gift fitting the King's importance.

Ivory was a treasure of which the Matabele had long ago realized the value in trade. It was, however, a scarce commodity, for even the bravest of men cannot kill a bull elephant with a stabbing spear. They had to rely on pick-ups from animals that had died of natural causes, or the very occasional victim of the pitfall.

Gandang's amazement when he saw the span and weight of the four tusks decided Zouga. The largest and most pleasingly shaped tusk would be Zouga's gift to Mzilikazi, if he were ever allowed to reach the great kraal at Thabas Indunas alive.

Not only was the threat of the King's wrath still hanging over him, but his supply of quinine powder was reduced to a few ounces. All around the camp steamed the swampy ground, fed each day by the interminable rains, and in the night he could even smell the evil fever-bearing vapours rising from the stagnant waters to waft over the camp. Yet he was forced to reduce his daily preventative dose of the bitter powder to perilously small quantities in an attempt to eke it out.

The inactivity and the dual threat of spear and disease wore on Zouga's nerves, until he found himself toying with suicidal plans to make an attempt to avoid the guarding impi and to escape on foot southwards. He thought of seizing Gandang and holding him as hostage, or using the remaining fifty pounds of black powder to manufacture a combustible with sufficient power to destroy the entire impi host at a blast. Reluctantly, one after another, he recognized these as plans of folly and abandoned them.

Gandang's impi came again in the dawn. Zouga was awakened by a stentorian voice calling him out of the thorn *scherm*. Zouga threw a fur kaross over his shoulders and went out into the grey and icy drizzle of rain, sloshing through the red mud to the gate, and he knew at a single glance that the King had at last sent his reply. The ranks of silent Matabele surrounded the camp, still as statues carved from the black wild ebony.

Zouga judged how swiftly he could reach the loaded gun beside his cot in the little thatched hut behind him, and guessed that he would probably be cut down before he could fire a single shot, yet he knew he would still make the attempt.

'I see you Bakela,' Gandang stepped from the dark and silent ranks.

'I see you Gandang.'

'The King's messenger has arrived –' Gandang paused a moment, solemn and stern, and then his perfectly square white teeth gleamed in the grey of dawn as he smiled. 'The King has given you the road, and bids you attend him at Thabas Indunas.'

The two men grinned at each other with relief, for both of them it meant life. The King had determined that Gandang had done his duty and correctly interpreted his commands, while Zouga had been accepted as an emissary and not as an enemy.

'We will march at once,' Gandang smiled still. 'Before the sun!' The King's summons brooked of no hesitations or delays.

'Safari!' Zouga roused his camp. 'We march at once!'

A natural delicacy and tact had made Gandang keep little Juba out of sight and hearing of Zouga's camp, nor had he mentioned the girl's name to Zouga while sentence of death still hung over the white man. However, that first night of the journey to Thabas Indunas after they had camped, he brought Juba to Zouga's hut, and she knelt and greeted him as 'Baba-father' and then with Gandang seated between them and listening attentively, he allowed them to talk for a short while.

Zouga was avid for news of his sister, and he listened in silence to the account of Fuller Ballantyne's death and his burial. It was better this way, and Zouga was already preparing his own fulsome tributes to the memory of his father.

While relieved also to hear that Robyn was safe, Zouga was less happy with the swift progress she seemed to be making. It must have been nearly three months since Juba last saw her, almost within sight of the eastern mountain range, and by this time Robyn must have surely reached the coast, and could be on board a Portuguese trade ship, well on her way to Good Hope and the Atlantic.

He did not know how long he would be delayed by the Matabele King, and then how long the overland journey down half the length of Africa might take him. Robyn's manuscript could be in London a year or even more before his own.

Zouga had exchanged one worry for another, and on the following day's march he chivvied his porters, heavily laden though they were, to keep up with their captors. It was of little avail, and they struggled along behind the trotting impi until Zouga demanded of Gandang that his own bearers be ordered to help with the load of ivory and the even greater weightier package of bark and plaited grass which contained the granite bird which Zouga had plundered from the tomb of the Kings.

With each day's travel towards the west, so the land became drier, and the forests thinned out and gave way to level pasturage with sparsely dotted acacias, graceful, mushroom-shaped trees from whose branches hung the big protein-rich, bean-shaped pods so dearly loved by game and domestic animals alike.

The relief from the driving and endless rain-storms lifted their spirits, and the impi sang on the march, winding like a thick black serpent through the lovely parklike lands below the bald and rounded kopjes of granite.

Soon they came across the first of the King's herds. The small hump-backed cattle whose origins lay far back beyond the veils of history, perhaps it had taken them and their drovers four thousand years to travel down from the valley of the Nile or from the fertile plains enclosed by the twin rivers of the Euphrates and the Tigris.

The cattle were sleek, for the grass was dense and sweet, even here in the drier lands the rains had been good. The animals were of every colour and pattern, chocolate-red and black and white and yellow, piebald and skewbald, solid black or pure snowy white. They watched with a blank bovine stare as the column of men trotted past, and the small herd boys, naked except for the tiny apron of the *beshu*, came scampering to stare in silent wide-eyed awe at the fighting men in plume and tassel, for they were already pining for the day that they would be called into their own regiments and in turn follow the warriors' road.

They reached the first of the Matabele towns. It was situated on the banks of the Inyati river. Gandang explained that it was the headquarters of his own impi, the Inyati impi, and that it was not the largest of the regimental towns. The settlement was laid out around the central cattle-pen, a vast enclosure large enough to hold ten thousand head of the King's herds. The dwellings were of identical thatched beehive construction in the tradition that the wandering tribe had preserved since leaving their native Zululand. The outer stockade was of cut mopani poles, set deep in the earth and forming a stout defensive wall. The villagers streamed out to welcome the returning impi, lining both sides of the route, a singing, clapping and laughing throng, mostly of women and children.

'Most of the men and the marriageable maidens have left already for Thabas Indunas. In the full of this moon, the *Chawala* dance begins, and all the nation will assemble at the King's kraal. We will rest here only one night and then take the road again to reach Thabas Indunas before the moon.'

The road from the Inyati westwards was now a populous highway, as the nation went in towards the King's capital city to celebrate the festival of the first fruits. The men marched in their regiments, their distinctive dress and ornaments, the colour of their war shields identifying each from afar, from the scarred and silverheaded veterans who had fought the Basuto, the Griquas and the Boer in the south, to the young bloods eager for their first kill, eager to learn in which direction the King would hurl his war-spear at the conclusion of the *Chawala* – for that was the direction in which they would find their reputation, their manhood, their glory and possibly their deaths.

The regiments of young unmarried women, interspersed those of the warriors, and as they passed each other on the road, the girls preened and giggled, casting languorous sloe-eyes at the unmarried men, and the men pranced and leapt in the pantomine of battle, the *Giya*, showing how they would wash their spears in blood and earn the privilege to 'go in to the women' and take wives.

With each day's march towards Thabas Indunas the roads became more congested, and their pace was reduced by the throng. They might wait half a morning to take their turn across a ford of the river, for the regiments drove the cattle which were their food supply ahead of them and dragged their baggage train behind. Each warrior's finery, his tassels and plumes and feathers, were carefully packed and carried by the young apprentice who was his personal bearer.

At last in the sweltering noon of high summer, Zouga's little party, still borne along on the river of humanity, came over a crest of ground and saw laid out ahead of them the great kraal and capital city of the Matabele.

It was spread out over many square miles of open plain below the bald-headed granite hills that gave it its name 'The Hills of the Chieftains'. The furthest hill was the 'Place of Killing', Bulawayo, and from its sheer cliffs those condemned to die were cast down.

The stockades formed concentric circles, dividing the city into its separate parts. Always the huge open cattle-pens were the centre of Matabele life, their cattle the source and store of their wealth, and now that the outlying herds had been brought in for the festival, every pen was filled with the multi-coloured herds of fat beasts.

Standing at Zouga's shoulder, Gandang used his stabbing-spear to point out with pride the city's features. There were sections for the unmarried girls, and the unblooded regiments, and another huge area for the married quarters; the huts were uniform in size and laid out in orderly patterns, the thatched roofs shining golden yellow in the sunlight. The earth between them was swept clean and beaten hard by the passage of bare feet.

'There is the King's hut.' Gandang pointed out a single huge conical structure in its own separate enclosure. 'And that is the compound of the King's wives,' a hundred other huts, within a high guarding stockade, 'and it is death to any man who enters that gate.'

Gandang led Zouga down to a small grove of acacia trees outside the main stockade. There was a stream within a few yards of it, and for the first time in days they were free of the close press of humanity. Although the plain without the city walls was thick with the temporary dwellings of the visiting impis, the area around the grove was empty, as if it had been placed out of bounds to the common people.

'When will I see the King?' Zouga asked.

'Not until after the festival,' Gandang answered. 'There is ritual and cleansing that the King must undergo, but he has sent you gifts, you are much honoured.' And he pointed with his blade at the line of young maidens that left a gate in the stockade. Each girl carried a large earthenware pot balanced easily upon her head, and she did not use a hand to maintain that balance.

The girls moved with that peculiar straight-backed grace, hips swinging in lazy rhythm, the hard unripe fruits of their breasts bouncing and jostling at each pace. They came in to Zouga's little camp in the grove and knelt to offer the gifts they bore.

Some pots contained thick millet beer, tart and effervescent, others the clotted and soured cow's milk, *imaas*, that was so much a staple of the Nguni diet, and others again big chunks of fatty beef, roasted on the open coals.

'You are much honoured by these gifts,' Gandang repeated, apparently himself surprised by the King's generosity. 'Yet Tshedi, your grandfather, was always his good and trusted friend.'

Once the camp was set up, Zouga found himself again the victim of idleness, with long days of waiting to fill. Here. however, he was free to roam about the city and its surrounds, save only the forbidden areas of the royal enclosure and women's quarters. He sketched the fascinating bustle of preparation for the festival. During the heat of the day the banks of the rivers were lined with men and women, their velvety black skins shimmering with water as they bathed and cleansed themselves for the dances. Every tree for miles about was hung with the kilts and furs, the feathers and plaited ornaments that were airing, the creases and rumples of travel and packing were being allowed to drop out of them as they billowed and flapped in the light breeze.

He passed groups of young girls plaiting each other's hair, smearing and rubbing each other's bodies with oil and coloured clays, and they giggled and waved at Zouga as he passed.

At first the problem of hygiene that this huge assembly presented puzzled Zouga, until he realized that there was an area of thick undergrowth beyond the city walls where both men and women went at dawn and in the short twilight. This area had its own population of crows and kites, of jackal and hyena that served as the city's cleansing service.

Interested further in the running of the city, he found that all bathing and washing of clothing was allowed only below a certain spot on the riverbanks marked by a distinctively large tree or other feature, and that the women filled the water pots for drinking and cooking above this point.

Even the huge cattle-pen in its very heart helped to keep the city clean. It acted as a vast fly-trap. The insects laid their eggs on the fresh cattle dung, but before they could hatch most of them were deeply trampled by the hooves of the milling herds. The brilliant sunlight and the untainted wind completed the process of keeping the area relatively clean and the smells interesting but not unbearable.

Zouga should have been content to have reached this haven, instead of leaving his assegai-riven corpse for a hyena's feast in the wilderness, but he was not.

He set himself tasks to fill the waiting days. He drew sketches and maps of the city, noting weaknesses in the fortifications, and where an attack would have the best chance of penetrating these and reaching the King's private quarters. He sketched the uniforms of the various impis. He noted the colours of their shields and other means of identifying them in the field. Asking innocent-seeming questions of Gandang, he was able to estimate the number of warriors each regiment contained, the ages and battle experience of the warriors, the names and personal idiosyncracies of their indunas, and the location of their regimental towns.

He found that much had changed in Matabeleland since old Tom Harkness had drawn his map, and Zouga noted these changes and drew his conclusions from them.

As a further exercise to pass the waiting days he began drawing up a battle plan for a campaign against the old King Mzilikazi, the requirements in men and weapons, the logistics of supply and resupply, the lines of march, and the most expedient methods of bringing the impis to battle – for Zouga was a soldier, a soldier with a dream which might one day become reality only through military action.

Unsuspecting, Gandang was flattered by Zouga's interest and he answered every question with pride in his nation's might and its achievements. Despite this work Zouga had given himself, the days dragged past.

'The King will not give you audience until after the festival,' Gandang repeated, but he was wrong.

The evening before the festival began, two elderly Indunas, blue heron feathers nodding above the silvery woollen caps of close-cropped hair, entered the camp in the acacia grove and Gandang greeted them with deep respect, listened to them attentively, and then came to Zouga.

'They have come to take you to the King,' he said simply.

There were three small fires burning before the King's hut, and over the middle one crouched a wizened ape-like figure, who crooned a low incantation through toothless gums, rocking on his haunches and occasionally adding a pinch of powder, or a sprig of herb into one of the large earthenware pots that bubbled over the flames.

The witchdoctor was festooned with the grisly accoutrements of his profession, the dried skins of reptiles, the claws of eagle and leopard, the inflated bladder of a lion, the skull of ape and the teeth of crocodile, small stoppered gourds of potions and powders, the horn of duiker to be used as a blooding cup, and other unidentifiable charms and elixirs.

He was the orchestrator of the entire festival, the most important event in the Matabele calendar, the gathering of the first fruits of the harvest, the blessing of the nation's herds, and the setting of the warlike campaigns which would occupy the *amadoda* during the coming dry season. Thus the assembled Indunas watched his preparations with attention and awe.

There were thirty or so men in the squatting circle of elders, the senior Indunas of the nation, the King's privy council. The small courtyard was crowded. The tall thatched sloping side of the King's hut towered thirty feet or so above them all, the top of it lost in darkness.

The thatching was skilfully done, with intricate patterns worked into the grass, and before the low doorway stood an armchair of European design and construction. With a small prick of recognition Zouga realized that this must be the same chair given to the King by his own grandfather Moffat, Tshedi, nearly twenty years before.

'Bayete! Mzilikazi, the bull elephant of the Matabele.'

Gandang had coached Zouga in the correct etiquette, the formal greetings and the behaviour which the King would expect.

As Zouga crossed the narrow yard of bare earth, he intoned the King's praise names, not shouting them aloud, not crawling on his knees as a subject would have done, for he was an Englishman and an officer of the Queen.

Nevertheless, at a distance of ten feet from the King's chair Zouga squatted down, his own head below the level of the King's, and waited.

The figure in the chair was much smaller than he had expected for a warrior of such fearsome reputation, and as his eyes adjusted to the gloom, Zouga saw that the King's feet and hands were small and delicately shaped, almost feminine, but that his knees were grotesquely swollen and distorted by the gout and arthritis that was attacking them.

The King was an old man now, nobody knew how old, but he had been a fighting warrior at the turn of the century. His once fine muscles had sagged so that his belly bulged out on to his lap, the skin stretched and riven with stria like that of a pregnant woman.

His head seemed too big for the narrow shoulders, and the neck hardly strong enough to support it, but the eyes which watched Zouga intently from the seams of wrinkles and loose, bagged skin, were black and bright and lively.

'How is my old friend Tshedi?' the King asked in a piping high-pitched voice.

Zouga had last seen his maternal grandfather twenty years previously; the only memory that persisted was of a long flowing white beard.

'He is well and happy,' Zouga replied. 'He sends you his greeting and respect.'

The old man in the armchair nodded the big ungainly head contentedly.

'You may present your gifts,' he said, and there was a buzz of comment from the Indunas, and even the witchdoctor at the fire looked up as the ivory tusk was carried in by three of Gandang's warriors, staggering under its weight, and laid before the King's chair.

The witchdoctor clearly resented this interruption of the ritual cleansing and the diversion of interest and attention from himself, and now with two of his assistants to help him he made an officious show of carrying one of the steaming pots from the fire and placing it between the King's feet.

Then he and his assistants raised a large kaross of stitched leopard skins and spread it like a tent over the King and his chair so the steam from the pot was trapped beneath it. Within a minute, there was a paroxysm of gasps and coughing from under the fur blanket, and when at last the witchdoctor removed it, the King was streaming sweat and choking for breath, his eyes inflamed and pouring tears, but any demons had been expelled by the coughing, and impurities washed away by the sweat and tears.

The gathering waited in respectful silence, while the King recovered his breath, and the witchdoctor withdrew to prepare the next potion. With his breath still wheezing and whistling in his throat, Mzilikazi reached into the small chest beside his chair and brought out the sealed package which Zouga had sent him.

'Speak the words.' The King handed it to Zouga, demanding that he read the letter.

Although he was illiterate, the King understood clearly the uses of the written word. For twenty years he had corresponded with Zouga's grandfather, who always sent one of his mission students to deliver his letters, to read them to the King, and to record the King's reply.

Zouga stood erect and opened the package. He read aloud, translating from the English as he went along, and adding a few small embellishments to the original text.

When he had finished, there was a respectful silence from the tribal elders, and even the King studied the tall and magnificently attired figure before him with new attention. The firelight danced on the burnished brass buttons and badges of Zouga's dress uniform, the scarlet cloth of his coat seemed to glow like the very flames of the fire.

The witchdoctor would have intervened again, coming forward with a brew of steaming medicine for the King to swallow, but Mzilikazi waved him away irritably.

Knowing that this was the moment when the King's interest was at its zenith, Zouga asked smoothly, 'Does the King see these signs of my Queen? They are her special marks, and every ruler should have such a mark to prove his power and the rocklike nature of his words.'

Zouga turned and beckoned the bearer who knelt in the gateway behind him and the terrified man crawled to Zouga's feet, not daring to look up at the King, and handed to Zouga the small tea caddy that contained the carved ivory seal and the sticks of wax.

'I have prepared one of these for the King, that his dignity and power may be known to all men.'

Mzilikazi was unable to contain his interest; he craned forward in his chair and called Zouga closer. Kneeling before him, Zouga prepared the wax, melting it on to the lid of the tea caddy with a taper lit from the fire. Then he made the impression of the seal upon it, and when it had hardened, handed it up to the King.

'It is an elephant.' The King recognized the beast with unconcealed amazement.

'The great black bull elephant of the Matabele,' Zouga agreed.

'Speak the words.' The King touched the lettering on the border, and commanded Zouga to translate it.

'Mzilikazi, Nkosi Nkulu!'

The King clapped his hands with delight, and passed the seal to his senior Induna. Soon they were all clucking and exclaiming over the imprint, the wax impression passing from hand to hand.

'Bakela,' the King told Zouga, 'you must come to me again on the day following the *Chawala* ceremony. You and I have much to discuss.'

Then with a wave of his hand he dismissed the splendid young man from his presence, and patiently, resignedly, gave himself up to the ministrations of the hovering doctor.

The full moon rose well past midnight, and the fires were stacked with new logs to welcome it, and the singing and drumming began. No man nor woman had dared to pick a single grain of corn from the harvest before this moment, for the rise of the moon heralded the *Chawala*, the dance of the first fruits, and the entire nation gave itself up to rejoicing.

The ceremony began in the middle of the first morning. The massed regiments assembled before their King, filing in column into the vast arena of the cattle stockade, and the earth shook to the crash of bare feet lifted in unison, twenty-five thousand at a time, lifted to the level of the shoulder and then brought down with the full force of the muscular, hardened bodies of highly trained warriors.

'Bayete!' they greeted the King with the royal salute.

'Bayete!' the crash of feet once more.

'Bayete!' a third time, and then the dancing began.

One regiment at a time coming forward in swaying, singing ranks, to perform before Mzilikazi's armchair throne. The perfect timing and execution of the intricate steps made it seem as though they were a single living organism, the shields interlocking and revolving and twisting together like the scales of some gigantic reptile, the dust rising and swirling through their ranks like smoke so that they appeared as wraiths, and their clocks of furs and their kilts of civets' tails and monkeyskins, of the pelts of foxes and cats, swirled about their legs so they appeared to be divorced from earth, suspended above it on the moving cloud of dust and the soft waves of fur.

From the ranks sprang the great champions and the heroes of each regiment, to *giya* in their pride. Leaping as high as their own heads, and stabbing furiously at the air, screaming challenge and triumph, the sweat greased their muscles and flew in explosive droplets in the sunlight.

Mzilikazi was caught up in the building sea of excitement, and he quaffed from the beer pots that the maidens brought him until his eyes rolled in his head and he could not contain himself further. He struggled from his chair, and hobbled out on his swollen and deformed legs, and the champions fell back to give him place.

'My father is the finest dancer in all of Matabeleland,' said Gandang, squatting beside Zouga.

The old King tried to leap, but his feet did not leave the ground. He shuffled back and forth, making little pawing gestures, hacking at the air with his toy war spear.

'Thus I struck down Barend the Griqua, and thus his sons died.'

The nation roared.

'The bull elephant dances, and the earth shakes.' And the slamming of ten thousand feet goaded the King to circle in a painful and pathetic parody of the young champions' wild gyrations.

'Thus I spurned the tyrant Chaka, and thus I cut the plumes from the headdress of his messengers and sent them back to him,' squealed Mzilikazi.

'Bayete!' thundered the nation. 'He the father of the world.'

Exhausted within minutes, the ancient King sank into the dust, and Gandang and two other of the King's sons leapt to their feet from the half circle of Indunas and raced to his side.

Gently they bore him up and carried him back to his chair, and Lobengula, the King's senior son, held a beer pot for him to drink from. The beer dribbled from his chin and ran down the King's heaving chest.

'Let the nation dance,' gasped the King, and Gandang returned to Zouga's side and squatted beside him.

'After war, my father loves best the dance,' he explained.

The maidens came, rank upon lovely rank, their naked skin shimmering in the glaring sunlight of noon. The tiny beaded apron that barely covered their little triangular sex was all they wore, and their singing was sweet and clear.

Mzilikazi hoisted himself from his chair once more, and hobbled out to dance with them, passing along the foremost rank, directing the singing with his ritual war-spear pointed to the skies. The King danced until he dropped once more, and was again carried back to his chair by his sons.

By nightfall, Zouga was exhausted. His sweaty neck was chafed by the high stock of his dress coat, and sweat had soaked through the thick scarlet serge in dark patches. His eyes were bloodshot and inflamed from the dust and the glare, his head ached from the cacophony of drums and the roar of Matabele voices, his tongue felt thick and furry from the draughts of sorghum beer that had been pressed upon him and his back and legs ached from the unfamiliar squatting attitude he had been forced into all that day – but the King was still dancing, hobbling and prancing and squeaking on those twisted and deformed legs of his.

The following morning Mzilikazi was on his throne again, so undaunted by the previous day's exertions, that when the *Chawala* bull was loosed into the arena his sons had bodily to restrain him from rushing out to slay it with his bare hands.

A champion from each regiment had been chosen, and stripped down to a loin-cloth. They waited in squatting ranks on each side of Mzilikazi's chair.

The bull came into the ring at the charge, horned head held high, red dust spurting from under his hooves, and his wild eyes glaring. He was pure, untainted black, with a huge humped back and glossy burnished hide.

Carefully picked from all the King's herds, he was the finest animal in the whole of Matabeleland and he made an arrogant circuit of the arena, stepping high, snorting and dropping his head to hook with curved horns at anything in his path.

The King, held by his sons, but struggling against their grip, was almost incoherent with excitement, and now he lifted his spear and his arms shook violently as he screamed.

'*Bulala inkunzi!* Kill the bull!'

The waiting men leapt to their feet, saluted the King, and then raced out, spreading into a half-moon-shape line, instinctively adopting the *jikela*, the movement of encirclement.

The black bull swung to meet them, came up short on locked front legs, his head swinging as he measured his charge; then the great rounded quarters bunched under him and he surged forward, picking a man in the centre of the line and thundering down on him.

The man he had chosen stood his ground, spreading his arms in a welcoming gesture and the bull dropped his head and hit him. Clearly Zouga heard the brittle snap of bone as the warrior absorbed the shock of impact against his chest, and then locked his arms around the animal's neck and held on.

The bull tried to toss him, hooking and throwing his head high, but the man held on, and was cruelly thrown about, but his body blocked the bull's sight and brought him to a halt. The racing line closed about him instantly, and abruptly the bull's great humped body was smothered by the rush of naked black men.

For long seconds the bull struggled to remain upright, but they bore him down and tore his legs out from under him so he hit the dusty earth with a heavy thump and a groaning bellow. A dozen men seized the long horns, and, using their leverage, began to twist them against the massive inert weight of his pinned body. Slowly, sweating and straining, they forced his head around, and the bull kicked his hooves in the air, his bellows becoming more desperate and strangled.

The King leapt up and down in his chair, screaming with excitement, and the roar of voices was like the sound of surf on a gale-driven coast of rock.

Inch by inch, the huge horned head revolved, and then suddenly there was no longer resistance. Zouga heard the crack of the vertebrae, sharp as a musket shot even above the thunder of the assembled nation. The horned head flicked through another half turn, the legs stiffened skywards for a moment, and the bull's bowels voided in a liquid green stream.

The sweat-drenched warriors lifted the carcass shoulder high and bore it bodily across the arena to lay it at Mzilikazi's feet.

On the third and last day of the ceremony, Mzilikazi stalked out into the centre of the cattle-pen. He made a frail and bent figure in the vast open space, and the noon sun burned down from above so that there was almost no shadow under him. The nation was quiet, forty thousand human beings watching one old man and there was not a whisper, nor a sound of breathing.

In the centre of the arena Mzilikazi paused and raised his war-spear above his head. The watching ranks stiffened as he revolved slowly, and then stopped facing towards the south. He drew back his spear arm, poised for a moment while the tension in the watchers was a palpable emanation from forty thousand charged bodies.

Then the King gave a little hop, and began slowly to revolve, the crowd sighed and swayed and then grew silent as again the King poised with his blade pointed towards the east. Then another little hop as he teased them deliberately, drawing out the moment with the timing of a natural showman.

Then suddenly his spear arm shot forward and the tiny toylike weapon flew from his hand in a high sparkling parabola, and dropped to bury its point in the baked earth.

'To the north!' thundered the nation. 'Bayete! The great bull has chosen the north!'

'We go northwards to raid the Makololo,' Gandang told Zouga. 'I will leave with my impi in the dawn.' He paused, and then smiled briefly. 'We will meet again, Bakela.'

'If the gods are kind,' Zouga agreed, and Gandang laid one hand on his shoulder, squeezed briefly, and then turned away.

Slowly, without looking back, Gandang walked away into the darkness which was clamorous with the singing and the sound of the drums.

'Your guns would be terrible weapons if they did not have to be reloaded,' Mzilikazi piped in his querulous old man's voice. 'But to fight with them a man must have a fast horse, so that he may fire and then gallop away to reload.'

Zouga squatted by the King's chair in the royal enclosure as he had for almost thirty successive days. The King sent for him each day, and he must listen to Mzilikazi's wisdom and eat huge quantities of half-raw beef washed down by pot after pot of beer.

'Without a horse my warriors will overrun them before they can reload, even as we did to the Griquas, and afterwards we picked up over three hundred of their precious guns from the battlefield.'

Zouga nodded his agreement, smiling inwardly as he imagined the *amadoda* trying those tactics on a square of British infantry.

Mzilikazi broke off to lift the beer pot, and then as he lowered it the sparkle of one of Zouga's tunic buttons caught his eye, and he leaned across to pluck at it. Resignedly Zouga took the clasp knife from his pocket and carefully cut the threads that held the button. He handed it to the King, and Mzilikazi grinned with pleasure and held it to the sunlight.

'Only five to go,' Zouga thought ironically. He felt like the Christmas turkey being plucked a feather at a time. His lapel badges and field officer's pips had long since been taken by the King, as had his belt buckles and helmet badge.

'The paper,' Zouga started and the King waved airily, dismissing the reference to the concession.

He might be on the verge of senility and certainly he was an alcoholic, drinking seven gallons of beer each day, by Zouga's count, but still Mzilikazi possessed a cunning and devious intellect with a natural grasp of his own bargaining weaknesses and strengths. He had teased Zouga for thirty days, just as he had teased the watching nation on the third day of the *Chawala*, while they had waited for him to hurl the war-spear.

Now the King turned away from Zouga at the mention of the concession, and transferred his attention to the young couple who knelt before him. They had been accused, and come before the King for judgement.

That day, in between chatting with Zouga, Mzilikazi had received emissaries bearing tribute from two of his vassal chieftains, he had rewarded a young herdboy for saving his herd from a marauding lion, he had sentenced to death another who had been seen drinking milk directly from the udder of one of his charges, he had listened to the reports of a messenger from the impis campaigning in the north against the Makololo, and now his attention was on the accused couple before him.

The girl was a lovely creature, with long delicately formed limbs and a sweetly rounded face with full flaring lips over small very white teeth. She kept her eyes tightly closed, so as not to look upon the King's wrath, and her body was shaken with tremors of terror as she knelt before him. The man was a finely muscled young warrior, from one of the unmarried regiments, who had still to win the honour of being allowed to 'go in to the women'.

'Rise up, woman, that the King may see your shame,' the voice of the accuser rang out, and hesitantly, timidly, still with her eyes tightly closed, the girl lifted her forehead from the dusty earth, and sat back on her heels.

Her naked stomach, drum tight and round as a ripening fruit, bulged out above the tiny bearded apron.

The King sat hunched in his chair, brooding silently for many minutes, then he asked the warrior.

'Do you deny this thing?'

'I do not deny it, Nkosi Nkulu.'

'Do you love this wench?'

'As I love life itself, my King.' The man's voice was low and husky, but firm and without a quaver to it.

The King brooded again.

Zouga had sat by and watched the King give judgement on a hundred such occasions. Sometimes the decision had been worthy of a black Solomon, at others Zouga had been appalled by the barbaric savagery of the sentence.

Now the King stared at the man before him, and he fiddled with the toy spear in his right hand, frowning and shaking his head softly, then he reached a decision, and leaning forward he proffered the weapon to the man who knelt before him.

'With this blade, open the womb of the woman you love, take out from it that which offends against law and against custom – and place it in my hands.'

Zouga did not sleep that night, and once he threw off his blankets and hurried to the fringe of the acacia grove to retch and heave, vomiting up his horror at what he had witnessed.

In the morning the memory of the girl's screams had not faded but the King was jocular and garrulous, pressing pot after pot of sour beer on Zouga's rebellious stomach, recounting episodes from his long and eventful life, describing vividly the scenes from his childhood and youth in far-off Zululand with a certain old man's wistful nostalgia.

Then suddenly, without any prior hint that he would do so, he commanded Zouga, 'Speak the words of your paper.'

He listened silently as Zouga translated the terms of the concession he was seeking, and at the end he mused a moment.

'To hunt elephant and to dig a hole,' he mumbled at last. 'It is not so very much you wish for. Write that you will do these things only in the land below the Zambezi, east of the Inyati River and above the Limpopo.'

Not quite convinced that the King was this time serious, Zouga quickly added the proviso to the foot of his home-grown legal document.

Then he directed the King's trembling hand to form the big uncertain cross below it.

'Mzilikazi: his mark.'

The King's pleasure in affixing the wax seal beside his mark was childlike and unaffected. After it was done he passed it to his Indunas to admire, and leaned forward towards Zouga.

'Now that you have what you want from me, you will wish to leave.' There was regret in the rheumy eyes, and Zouga felt a pang of guilt, but he replied directly.

'I cannot hunt in the rains, and there is much work for me to accomplish in my own land across the sea. I must go, but I shall return, Nkosi Nkulu.'

'I give you the road to the south, Bakela the Fist. Go in peace and return to me soon, for your presence pleases me, and your words are wise for one still so young.'

'Stay in peace, Great Elephant,' Zouga rose and left the King's courtyard, and his step was as light as his spirits were gay. He had the concession buttoned into the breastpocket of his tunic, fifty-six pounds of native gold in his chest, the stone bird of Zimbabwe, and three fine tusks of ivory to buy his way. The road to the south, to Good Hope and to England lay open before him.

The wind was offshore, a faint backlash of the monsoon, but the sky was low and grey and the twisting squalls of rain fell from it like pearl dust.

Ensign Ferris, *Black Joke*'s most junior officer, was taking his sights off the traverse board as the gunboat closed the land, calling them quietly to the signals yeoman who swiftly worked out the distance offshore, and wrote this down on the navigation slate, so that any moment the Captain could glance down at it to confirm his own observations.

There was a man in the bows with a leadline, chanting the depth as he read it from the markings on the line, then twirling the weight and hurling it out ahead of *Black Joke*'s creeping bows, letting it sink and then reading the mark again as the ship passed over it.

'By the deep six.'

Clinton Codrington was conning his ship in by the leadsman's chant, by the angles that Ferris was shooting off the land features which they had identified, by the colour shadings of the water, by the break and swirl of the tide on shoal and bank, and by a seaman's instinct. The chart surveyed thirty years previously by Captain Owen, R.N., he trusted not at all.

'Bring her around a point,' he told the helmsman quietly, and as the ship swung towards the land, they smelt it on the wind.

'Slave stink!' exclaimed Denham fiercely, and as he said it the masthead lookout sang out sharply,

'Smoke! Smoke from the right bank of the river.'

'How far up stream?'

'Two miles or more, sir!'

For the first time since sailing from Zanzibar harbour, Clinton allowed himself to believe that he was in time, that he had reached the Rio Save in time to answer the heartrending appeal of the woman he loved.

'We will clear for action, if you please, Mr. Denham, but don't run out the guns.' He kept his voice level and formal, but his Lieutenant grinned at him.

'A fair cop, by Jove. Congratulations, sir,' and the crew laughed and skylarked as they lined up at the arms chest to receive their pistol and cutlass.

As *Black Joke* breasted the breaking white water of the bar, touched sand bottom for a moment and then broke the grip of it, and surged forward into the dark green and still waters of the estuary, Clinton nodded at Denham.

'You may run out the guns now.'

He had delayed until this moment to avoid altering the ship's trim during the critical passage of the bar. With the carriages rumbling ominously, *Black Joke* bared her fangs and under fighting sail, her bronze propeller thrashing exultingly, her crew armed and eager, she went into the labyrinth of the Rio Save like a ferret into the warren.

Clinton took her around the first bend, following the deep green sweep of the channel between the paler sandbanks. It was two hours past low tide and the flood was pushing strongly, the leadsman calling good bottom and Clinton was trying to conceal his impatience and eagerness by the calm controlled tone in which he called his orders to the helm.

'Would you just look at that!' exclaimed Ferris, and pointed over the side. Beside them floated what looked like an ebony log. It was only as they passed and it bobbed and rolled in their wake that Clinton realized that it was a human corpse, stomach distended, round and shiny with gas and limbs twisted like the branches of a tree blasted by lightning. Clinton transferred his attention back to the ship, with a small grimace of distaste.

'Meet her,' he told the helmsman and then as they tore around the broad curve of water between the mangrove forests and the full stretch of the estuary opened ahead of them, he said 'Midships!'

His voice was flat, unemotional, neither triumphant nor dejected. Smoke rose from the bank of the river, and through his glass he could see the smouldering remains of a series of long low buildings, roofs burned through and collapsed inwards. They seemed to have been deliberately fired.

In the smoke soaring and circling on spread wings rose a host of birds, buzzards and kites and vultures and the carrion-eating marabou storks. They seemed to reach up with the smoke to the belly of the lowering monsoon clouds, dimming the light of day with their wings. The oppressive towering silence was broken only by the faint high cries of the birds, and the river was empty.

Clinton and his officers stared silently at the wide deserted sweep of the Rio Save, green and smooth from bank to mangrove-clad bank. No one spoke as *Black Joke* bore on, close in to the ruined and blackened barracoons. They stared at the piles of corpses, their faces stiff and expressionless, concealing their horror at the foul plague that lurked there in the palm groves, concealing also their disappointment and chagrin at finding the anchorage deserted and *Huron* gone.

'Stop engine,' Clinton broke the silence. 'Let go port anchor.'

Denham and Ferris turned to look at their Captain, their carefully controlled expressions cracking with disbelieving dread; he was going to send a party ashore. They would come back aboard carrying the plague with them, they would all be doomed.

The bow anchor hit the mud of the estuary bottom, and *Black Joke* turned sharply, the flow of the tide swinging her across the narrow channel in her own length, the anchor holding her head until she was pointed directly back down the river towards the sea. Immediately Clinton gave the order, 'Slow ahead,' and, as the ship breasted the tide, 'Up anchor,' and the steam winch clattered merrily. The officers relaxed visibly, and Denham allowed himself to smile with relief. The Captain had used the anchor merely to turn the ship as swiftly as possible without going through the dangerous business of backing and filling in the narrow channel against the push of the tide.

As the anchor came back aboard with the gluey black mud clinging to its flukes, Clinton gave another series of orders.

'Half ahead.' That was as fast as he dared push for the open sea.

'Secure from action stations.'

There was no enemy to fight and as the heavy long-barrelled thirty-two pounder guns were run in, *Black Joke* handled more easily.

'Mr. Ferris, we will fumigate the ship.'

The smoke from the pails of burning sulphur would redden all their eyes and for days would taint the food and water, but Clinton's dread of smallpox outweighed such small considerations as comfort, and, besides, he smiled wryly to himself, any change to the taste of *Black Joke*'s bullied beef and hard bread could only be an improvement.

The smile was fleeting. He was sickened by his brief glimpses of the barracoons, and his anger was a cold sharp thing like the blade of the cutlass on his belt.

'Mr. Denham,' he said quietly, 'please plot a course for Good Hope. We'll come on to it the moment we clear the land.'

He moved to the rail, half his mind on the job of conning *Black Joke* out of this stinking green river into the open sea, the other half of his mind running swiftly over the problem of bringing his ship into action against *Huron*.

How long was the start that the tall clipper had over his gunboat? Robyn Ballantyne's letter had been dated 16 November, today was the 27 November. Eleven days. That was too much. He could only hope that Robyn had been able to delay the sailing, as she had promised.

Clinton glanced back over his shoulder at the blue smoke column that blurred the horizon. How long had those fires in the barracoons been burning? Not more than three or four days, he guessed, with more hope than conviction. Yet even that was still too long a start. He had seen *Huron* on a wind and she was swift as a swallow, and light as a witch. Even with eight hundred slaves in her holds, and her water casks filled, she would toy with *Black Joke* in any wind better than a light breeze. His only advantage would be in the offing that *Huron* must make to get on the trades and weather the bulge of the continent, while *Black Joke* could cut across the other arm of the triangle, hugging the land. It was small advantage, a few hundred leagues, and in the end it would all depend on the wind.

Clinton found he was pounding his clenched fist on the ship's rail, that he was glaring ahead with such ferocity that the idle hands of the lee rail were watching him curiously.

With an effort he forced his features to relax, and linked his hands at the small of his back, beneath the tails of his uniform coat, but his eyes still glittered pale sapphire blue and his lips were chalky with stress. It seemed too long for his patience before he could at last bring *Black Joke* on to her true course, and bend to the engine room voice-tube.

'I want all the speed you can squeeze out of her,' he told his engineer. 'There is twenty thousand pounds of prize money just below the horizon, but it's running like a fox and I'll need every pound of steam you can give me.'

He straightened up and the wind whipped his pale golden hair against his sun-gilded cheeks and forehead. He glanced up at the sky and saw the ponderous role of the monsoon clouds on the wind.

Huron would have it full and boisterous on her port beam, with that hull and rigging it was probably her best point of sailing.

He knew that there was not the remotest chance of finding the clipper on the open sea, there were millions of square miles of ocean to cover – not even a battle fleet with a full squadron of frigates ideally placed ahead of the fugitive would have much chance of finding a single ship in that infinity of water.

Clinton knew that his only chance was to reach the southern tip of the continent ahead of *Huron* and to take up station athwart the narrow shipping-lane that was threaded around Cape Point. However, once *Huron* rounded the southern cape, the whole of the wide Atlantic would lie ahead of her and she would be gone again. Clinton's jawline clenched spasmodically at the thought of the American escaping into that limitless expanse of sea. If she had indeed eleven days' lead on him with this wind holding fair, she could even at this moment be raising the rocky cliffs of Cape Point. He put the thought from his mind and concentrated on coaxing every inch of speed from his ship over the long days and nights ahead.

Robyn had searched in vain for a subterfuge to delay *Huron*'s departure from the Rio Save, even though she knew that if she succeeded she would be endangering the lives of all aboard her. However, Mungo St. John had swiftly regained his energy and determination as his wound healed and the effects of the inoculation passed. Affected by Robyn's warning about the danger of battlefield plagues, he forced the pace of his crew in loading the slaves. They worked through the night by the light of tar-dipped rope torches, as well as by day, the crew every bit as eager as their Captain to be away from this cursed river. Four days after the loading began, *Huron*'s slave-decks were in place and her cargo of slaves aboard, and that evening at the full of the tide, using the last of the light and the first gusts of the offshore night breeze, *Huron* slipped over the bar, shook out her reefs and settled down to make her offing during the night.

At dawn they caught the steady push of the trades and Mungo brought her round on to a more southerly heading, close-hauled to make good their eastings before running for the bulge of Agulhas with the wind on the beam.

The sweet clean air of the open sea that had travelled thousands upon thousands of miles since last having touched land, swept through the ship, cleansing it of the dreadful stench of the plague barracoons, and Mungo's strict hygienic discipline helped to keep the holds free of the slave stink and impressed even Robyn, though reluctantly, with his forethought and his precautions.

By sacrificing a single slave deck, raising the space between each from the traditional 20 inches to 32 inches, he allowed not only greater comfort but easier access. In these mild conditions of wind and sea, the slaves were exercised during all of the daylight hours, the higher headroom and wider ladderways enabled even those in the lowest decks to be brought up on deck in batches of fifty at a time. On the maindeck they were forced to dance to the rhythm of a tribal drum beaten by a tattooed naked tribesman, the rattle and clink of their chains made a mournful background music to the drum and the sweet sound of the singing slaves.

'Funny business, that tattooing,' Nathaniel stopped to chat with Robyn as she stood watching the dismal show. 'They started tattooing their children to make them repulsive to us slavers, some of them file or knock out their teeth – like that one there.' He pointed at a muscular black man in the circle of dancing slaves whose teeth had been filed to sharp points like those of a shark. 'Some of them put bones through the noses of their daughters, and others stretch their tits –

begging your pardon at the plain speaking, ma'am – or they put rings of copper around their necks until they look like giraffes, all so the slavers will leave them alone. They do say now that these have become marks of beauty amongst the heathen. No accounting for taste, is there, ma'am?'

Robyn saw how the extra space and regular exercise would affect the well-being of the slaves, and while they were up on the maindeck, in the open air, their empty slave decks were flushed out with sea water from the ship's pumps and then scrubbed down with a strong lye mixture. Though even this was not enough to prevent the slave stink slowly impregnating the ship.

Each slave spent two hours on deck each second day, and while they were there, Robyn held clinic and examined each of them for any signs of disease or injury. Before going below once more, they were each forced to drink a decoction of molasses and lime juice to supplement the plain diet of boiled farina and water, and to ward off the dreaded scourge of the scurvy.

The slaves responded well to this treatment, and, incredibly, began to put on the weight that they had burned off during the fevers that were the result of the inoculation against the smallpox. The mood of the slaves was resigned and compliant, although there were isolated incidents. One morning, while a batch of slaves were being brought up, one of them, a fine-looking naked woman, managed to work free the shackle of her chain and the moment she reached the deck she rushed to *Huron*'s side and leapt over it, into the creaming blue wake of the racing clipper.

Despite the fact that she still wore the iron cuffs on her wrists, she managed to keep afloat for many long minutes; her struggles were pitiful to watch as she was slowly drawn down lower and lower in the water.

Robyn had run to the rail to watch the woman's efforts, expecting Mungo to heave-to and lower a boat to rescue her, but he remained detached and silent on his quarterdeck, barely glancing over the stern before occupying himself once more with the management of his ship, while *Huron* tore away and the woman's head dwindled to a speck on the blue water, then was drawn inevitably below the surface by the weight of her iron cuffs.

Although Robyn realized that it would have been impossible to stop the clipper and reach the woman before she drowned, yet she glared at Mungo across the length of the deck, wishing that there were words to express her fury and indignation.

That night she lay awake in her tiny cabin, hour after hour, racking her imagination for some ruse that could be used to delay the tall clipper's full flight towards the Southern Cape.

She thought of stealing one of the ship's boats and casting herself adrift during the night, forcing Mungo to turn back and to search for her. It took only a few minutes' reflection to realize that it would take a dozen strong men to free the whaler from its lashings and lower it on its davits over the ship's side – and even if she managed to accomplish that, it was far from certain that Mungo would delay even a minute. He was more likely to sail away and leave her, as he had left the slave woman.

She thought of setting fire to the ship, overturning a lantern in the mainsail locker, and creating so much damage that *Huron* would be obliged to call at the nearest port, Lourenço Marques or Port Natal, to effect repairs, and to give *Black Joke* an opportunity to come up with her. Then she imagined eight hundred chained slaves burning to death in the hold when the fire got out of control, and she shuddered, thrust that idea from her and hopelessly composed herself to a sleep which would not come.

In the end her opportunity came from a most unexpected source, Tippoo. The huge mate had a weakness, a single weakness that Robyn could observe.

He was a trencherman and, in his own taste, a gourmet. Half the lazaretto was filled with delicacies that Tippoo had hoarded and which he shared with no others. There were dried and smoked meats and sausages, cheeses the smell of which brought tears to the eyes, and wooden crates of cans and bottles of preserved foods, though as a strict Moslem, he took no alcohol. He made up what he lacked in the glass with his spoon.

His appetite was one of the ship's jokes, and Robyn had heard Mungo chaffing him across the wardroom table.

'Were it not for the tucker you brought aboard, Mr. Mate, we'd have room for another hundred blackbirds in our hold.'

'I'll wager that belly of yours costs you more to sustain than a harem of extravagant wives.'

'Sweet merciful heavens, Mr. Tippoo, but whatever you are eating should have been given a Christian burial a month ago.'

One of Tippoo's favourite appetizers was a particularly virulent bloater paste, packed in half-pound tins. The instruction printed on the tin read 'Spread thinly on biscuit or toast', and Tippoo would spoon it directly from the tin, consuming the entire half pound without once breaking the rhythmic dip and lift of his soup spoon, his eyes half closed and a cherubic smile buckling the wide line of his toad's mouth.

The fourth night out of the Rio Save he began his dinner with a can of bloater paste, but as he pierced the lid with his clasp knife, there was a sharp hiss of escaping gas, and Mungo St. John glanced up from his own plate of pea soup.

'It is blown, Mr. Tippoo. I would not eat it if I were you.'

'No,' Tippoo agreed. 'But you not me.'

They called Robyn a little before midnight. Tippoo was in convulsions, doubled up with agony, his belly swollen and hard as a yellow agate boulder. He had vomited until now he was retching only a little blood-flecked bile.

'It's ptomaine poisoning,' Robyn told Mungo St. John. It was the first time she had spoken directly to him since that morning in the Rio Save, and her voice was cool and formal. 'I do not have the medicines to treat it. You will have to put into a port where he can receive treatment. There is a military hospital at Port Natal.'

'Doctor Ballantyne,' Mungo answered her as formally, but his infuriating smile lurked behind the gold-flecked eyes. 'Mr. Tippoo's mother was an ostrich, he can digest stones, nails and lumps of broken glass. Your concern, touching as it may be, is entirely misplaced. He will be ready to fight, flog, or devour an ox by noon tomorrow.'

'And I tell you that without proper treatment he will be dead in a week.'

However, Mungo's prognosis proved to be correct, for by morning the vomiting and retching had abated and Tippoo seemed to have purged his bowels of the poisoned fish. Robyn was forced to a decision which she made on her knees in her cabin.

'Forgive me, oh Lord, but there are eight hundred of your children chained below decks in this foul prison, and I will not kill him – at least, with your help, I will not kill him.'

Then, off her knees she went briskly to work. She used a solution of peppermint tincture to disguise the taste, and let fall fifteen drops of essence of ipecacuanha into the medicine glass, which was three times the recommended dosage for the most powerful emetic known to the medical science.

'Drink it down,' she told Tippoo. 'It will soothe your stomach, and cure the diarrhoea.'

Late that afternoon she repeated the dose, but the wardroom steward had to help her lift Tippoo's head from the bolster and pour the draught down his throat. The effect was enough to alarm even Robyn.

An hour later she sent for Mungo, and the steward came back with the message, 'Captain says as how the ship's safety demands all his attention at the moment, begging your pardon, Doctor.'

When Robyn herself went on deck, Mungo was at the weather rail, sextant in hand, waiting for the sun to appear in a gap in the clouds.

'Tippoo is dying,' she told him.

'And this will be my first sight of the day,' Mungo replied without taking his eye from the eyepiece of the instrument.

'I at last believe that you are a monster with no human feelings,' she whispered fiercely, and at that moment blazing sunlight struck the deck, as the sun showed briefly through the ragged hole in the cloud.

'Stand by the chronometer,' Mungo called to the signals yeoman, and then 'Mark!' as he brought the sun's image down to bounce lightly as a green rubber ball on the dark line of the horizon.

'Excellent,' he murmured with satisfaction, as he lowered the sextant and read off the height of the sun, and called it to the yeoman to mark on his slate. Only then did he turn back to Robyn.

'I am sure you have misjudged the severity of Tippoo's ailment.'

'See for yourself,' she invited.

'That is my intention, Doctor.'

Mungo stooped into Tippoo's cabin, and paused. His expression changed, suddenly the light mocking smile was gone. It was evident that Tippoo was indeed dangerously ill.

'How are you, old friend?' Mungo asked quietly. It was the first time Robyn had ever heard him use that form of address. He lifted his hand and laid it on the mate's sweat-beaded forehead.

Tippoo rolled the bald yellow cannon ball of his head towards Mungo, and he tried to smile. It was a brave effort. Robyn felt a terrible guilty pang, at the suffering she was inflicting and at being the witness to this private, and strangely intimate, moment between these two hard and dangerous men.

Tippoo tried to lift himself, but the effort brought a long dragging groan rattling up his throat, and he clutched at his stomach with both hands, drawing his knees up with agony, and then desperately twisting his head as a fresh bout of heaving and retching racked his body.

Mungo snatched the bucket off the deck and with one arm around Tippoo's shoulders held it for him – but all that Tippoo could bring up was a little splash of blood and brown bile, and when he fell back on the bunk he was gasping unevenly, bathed in fresh sweat and his eyes rolled back in his skull until only a little half moon of the iris still showed.

Mungo stood beside his bunk for a full five minutes, bowed and attentive, swaying slightly to the ship's movement, but otherwise still and silent. His brow was creased with thought and his gaze remote, and watching him, Robyn knew he was making the dire decision – the throw of the dice of life, friendship against the loss of his ship and perhaps even his own liberty, for to go into a British port with slaves in his holds was an awful risk.

Strange, now that he was showing this gentler side of his nature, that her affection came flooding back at full strength, she felt mean and cheap for playing on his deepest emotions, and for torturing the huge yellow Moslem on the narrow bunk.

Mungo swore quietly but decisively, and, still stooped under the low deck, strode from the cabin.

Robyn's affection turned to disgust and disappointment. Disgust that even the life of an old and loyal friend meant nothing to this cruel and merciless man whom she was doomed to love, and intense disappointment that her ruse had failed, that she had inflicted this dangerous suffering on Tippoo to no avail.

She sank down wearily and bitterly beside his bunk, took a cloth soaked in sea water and bathed the sweat-basted yellow head.

During their long voyage down the Atlantic, Robyn had grown sensitive to all *Huron*'s moods, to the feel of the deck underfoot at every point of sailing, and to the sounds that her hull made in different sea and wind conditions, and now abruptly she felt the deck cant sharply beneath her. She heard the stamp of bare feet on the deck above as her yards were trained around and *Huron*'s action became easier, the sounds of her hull and rigging muted as she took the wind in over her stern quarter and rode more easily.

'He's altered course towards the west,' she breathed as she lifted her head to listen. 'It worked. He is going in to Port Natal. Oh thank you Lord, it worked.'

Huron anchored well offshore, out on the thirty-fathom line of the shelving coast, so that she could not benefit from the shelter of the huge whale-backed bluff that protected Port Natal's natural harbour. Even with a powerful telescope, a watcher on the shore would be unable to make out any significant details of *Huron*'s cargo, nor of her true occupation. However, the ship paid for her offshore berth by taking the unfettered scend of the sea and the wind. She pitched and she rolled and she jerked at her anchor chain.

At her peak she flew the stars and stripes of her country – and below that the yellow 'Quebec', the plague flag which warned, 'Stay away from me! I have plague on board!'

Mungo St. John placed an armed watch on both sides of the ship and others at her bow and stern, and, despite Robyn's strident protest, she was confined to her cabin for the duration of the ship's call, with another armed guard outside her door.

'You are very well aware of the reason, Doctor Ballantyne.' Mungo answered her protests calmly. 'I do not wish you to have any communication whatsoever with your countrymen ashore.'

The whaler, when it took Tippoo ashore, was rowed by men that Mungo selected personally, and they were instructed to inform the Harbour Master that there was smallpox aboard, and to request that no other vessel be allowed near *Huron*.

'I can only wait three days for you.' Mungo stooped over the litter on which Tippoo was carried on deck. 'That is all I can risk. If you are not sufficiently recovered by then, you will have to stay here until my return. That cannot be more than five months.' He tucked a leather draw-string purse under Tippoo's blanket. 'And that will pay your expenses in the meanwhile. Get well, Mr. Tippoo, I need you.'

Robyn had administered another dose of the peppermint and ipecacuanha a few minutes previously, and Tippoo could reply only in an agonized whisper.

'I will wait for you, Captain Mungo, as long as she takes.'

Mungo's voice was husky as he straightened and spoke to the seamen carrying the litter.

'Handle him easy, you hear me.'

For three days Robyn sweated and fretted in the stuffy little cabin, trying to occupy her time with writing up her journals but distracted by any loud noise from the deck above, her heart pounding as she both hoped for and dreaded the hail from a British gunboat, or the rush of a boarding-party coming in over *Huron*'s side.

On the third morning Tippoo was rowed back to the ship, and he climbed up the side and in through the entry port unaided. Without further doses of ipecacuanha, his recovery had amazed the military surgeons ashore, but he was so thin that the skin hung in folds from his jowls like a bulldog, his belly had shrunk so that he had tied his breeches with a length of rope to keep them from sinking down past his flattened belly, but still they flapped around his shrunken buttocks.

His skin was the pale yellow of ancient ivory, and he was so weak he had to pause to rest when he reached the deck.

'Welcome aboard, Mr. Tippoo,' Mungo called from the quarterdeck. 'And if you have finished your holiday ashore, I'll thank you to get this ship under way immediately.'

Twelve days later, having struggled with flukey and variable winds, Mungo St. John played the field of his glass down the open gaping maw of False Bay. On his right hand rose the distinctive curved black peak of Hangklip, shaped from this angle like a shark's dorsal fin, and directly opposite it across the mouth of the bay the southernmost tip of the African continent, Cape Point, with its light-house perched high above the steep wet cliffs.

It was a magnificent Cape summer's day, a light and fickle breeze scratching dark patches on the surface of the rolling dark blue sea, leaving the rest of it with a satiny gloss. There were seabirds working, their wings twinkling like flurrying snow flakes in the sunlight, huge flocks of them that stretched low across the horizon.

Creeping along on the breeze, lying for minutes at a time completely becalmed, *Huron* took half a day to round the point and came on to west-north-west and a point north, the course that would carry her up the Atlantic, across the equator and finally into Charleston Roads.

Once they were on their new course, Mungo St. John had leisure to inspect the other sails that were in sight. There were nine, no, ten other vessels in view now, for there was another far out to sea, just her topsails showing. They were small fishing craft out from Hout Bay and Table Bay, and the seabirds clouded the air about them, most of them were between *Huron* and the land, and all of them were bare-masted or under working sail as they plied their lines or their nets. Only the vessel furthest out was carrying topsails, and though she was hull down she gave to Mungo's seaman's eye the impression of being a bigger ship than the rest of the fishing fleet.

'There's a ship for you!' Tippoo exclaimed, touching Mungo's arm to draw his attention and when he swung his glass back towards the land Mungo murmured with pleasure as a square-rigged East Indiaman came into view around the headland that guarded the entrance to Table Bay itself.

She was as splendid a sight as *Huron* was herself, canvas piled to the sky and her paintwork gleaming in snowy white and Burgundy red, the two lovely ships on reciprocal courses passed each other by two cables' length, the officers eyeing each other through their telescopes with professional interest and appraisal as they paid passing honours.

Robyn was also at *Huron*'s rail, pining towards the land. The proximity of the beautiful ship interested her hardly at all, it was that flat-topped mountain from which she could barely tear her gaze. It was so very close, marking as it did her one hope of succour, her friends there, the British Governor and the Cape Squadron, if they only knew that she was a prisoner aboard this slave ship.

The thought was interrupted by an abrupt movement that she caught from the corner of her eye – strange how receptive she was to Mungo St. John's smallest movement, to his slightest change of expression – and now she saw that he had turned his back on the East Indiaman as she dwindled away astern, and instead he was peering intently over *Huron*'s port side, his expression rapt, his whole body seemed charged with latent energy, and the hands that gripped the barrel of the telescope were ivory knuckled with tension.

Quickly she followed his gaze, and for the first time noticed a tiny shred of white on the horizon that did not fade like the white caps of the waves, but stood constant and bright in the sunlight, though even as she watched it seemed to alter its shape slightly and – was it her imagination, or was it a thin dark wavering line that seemed to appear behind it and spread slowly away in the direction of the wind?

'Mr. Tippoo, what do you make of that sail?' She heard the timbre of concern and alarm in Mungo St. John's tone, and her heart leapt wildly, with hope and a Judas dread.

For Clinton Codrington it had been a desperate run down the eastern coastline of southern Africa, long days and sleepless nights of unceasing strain, when hope and despair pendulumed against each other. Each shift or change in the wind either alarmed or encouraged him, for it would either aid or hinder the tall clipper ship he was racing to head. The calms elated him, and the revival of the south-easterly prevailing winds sent his spirits plunging.

On the last days there was another worry to plague him. He had burned his coal like a spendthrift on the long thousand-mile run southwards, and his engineer came up on deck, a small red-headed Scot with the grease and coaldust etched into his skin so that he seemed to be suffering from some debilitating and incurable disease.

'The stokers' shovels be hitting the bottom of the bunkers already,' he told Clinton with mournful relish. 'I warned ye, sir, that we'd not make it if you—'

'Burn the ship's furniture if you must,' Clinton snapped at him. 'You can start with my bunk, I'll not be needing it.'

And when the engineer would have argued further Clinton added, 'I don't care how you do it, Mr. MacDonald, but I want a full head of steam on your boiler until I reach Cape Point, and another full head of steam when I bring this ship into action.'

They raised the Cape Point lighthouse a few minutes after midnight the following night, and Clinton's voice was hoarse with fatigue and relief as he stooped over the voice pipe.

'Mr. MacDonald, you can let your fires damp down, but keep your furnaces warmed and ready to stoke. When I ask for steam again, I'll need it in a hurry.'

'You'll be calling at Table Bay to take on fresh bunkers, of course, sir?'

'I'll let you know when,' Clinton promised him, and snapped the lid of the speaking tube closed and straightened up.

The Cape naval base, with all its amenities lay only a few hours steaming away. By dawn he could be filling *Black Joke* with coal and water and fresh vegetables.

However, Clinton knew that within minutes of dropping anchor in Table Bay, Admiral Kemp or one of his representatives would be on his way out to the ship, and Clinton's term of independent command would be over. He would revert to being a very junior commander, whose recent actions needed a great deal of explanation.

The closer that Clinton drew to Admiralty House, the louder the warnings of Sir John Bannerman rang in his ears, and the more soberly he was forced to review his own position. The excitement of storming Arab barracoons and of seizing slave-laden dhows on the high seas had long ago cooled, and Clinton realized that once he entered it he would not be able to escape again from Table Bay for weeks, or possibly months. It would not even suit his immediate plans to be seen and recognized from the land, for a boat would immediately be sent out by Admiral Kemp to order him in to face judgement and retribution.

Clinton felt not the least trepidation about the Navy's ultimate judgement, he was so indifferent to the threat hanging over his career that he surprised even himself. There was only one desire, one object in his mind, that overshadowed all else. He must have his ship in position to intercept *Huron* as she rounded the Cape, if she had not already done so. Nobody and nothing must prevent him from doing so. After that he would face his accusers with complete equanimity. *Huron* and Robyn Ballantyne first, beside them all else was pale and insignificant.

'Mr. Denham,' he called his Lieutenant across the dark deck. 'We will take up night patrol station ten miles off Cape Point, and I am to be called immediately the lights of any ship are sighted.'

As Clinton threw himself down, fully dressed and booted, upon his bunk, he experienced the first peace of mind since leaving Zanzibar harbour. He had done all that was in his power to reach Cape Point ahead of *Huron*, and now the rest was in the hands of God – and his trust in God was implicit.

He fell asleep almost instantly, and his steward woke him again an hour before dawn. He left the mug of coffee to grow cold beside his bunk and hurried on deck, reaching it a few seconds ahead of Lieutenant Denham.

'No ships during the night, sir,' Ferris, who had the watch, saluted him.

'Very well, Mr. Ferris,' Clinton acknowledged. 'We will take up our daylight patrol station immediately.'

By the time the light was strong enough for a watcher on the shore to make out any details, *Black Joke* had retreated tactfully below the horizon and it would have taken a sharp eye to pick out the occasional flash of her topsails, let alone to identify the gunboat and to speed a report to Admiral Kemp that his prodigal had returned.

From *Black Joke*'s masthead the land was a low irregular distortion of the horizon, but a ship rounding the Cape would be many miles closer than the land. *Huron*'s mainmast was almost one hundred and fifty feet tall, her sails would shine like a flaming beacon and as long as the fog did not come down, which was unlikely at this season of the year, Clinton was confident that she could not slip by him.

The only disquiet that scratched him like a burr as he paced his deck, and the gunboat settled down into the regular four-sided box-patterned legs of her patrol, was that *Huron* had long ago flown northwards on this fine wind that at last bore steadily out of the south-east at almost gale force, and that she was already lost in the endless watery green wastes of the southern Atlantic Ocean, leaving *Black Joke* to guard the gate of an empty cage.

He was not left long to brood, the first sighting was called down to the deck from the look-outs in the crow's nest at the main peak, and Clinton's nerves jumped tight and his expectations flared.

'What do you make of her?' he called up through the voice trumpet.

'Small lugger—' and his expectations plunged. A fishing-boat out of Table Bay, there would be many of them, but each time he could not control the wild surge of excitement when another sail was sighted, so that by nightfall his nerves were ragged, and his body ached with exhaustion as he gave the order for *Black Joke* to take up her inshore patrol station for the night.

Even then he could not rest, for three times during the night he was called from his bunk, and he stumbled owl-eyed on deck as *Black Joke* went down to investigate running lights that winked ruby red and emerald green out of the darkness.

Each time the same leap of expectation, the steeling of nerves for instant orders and swift action, and then the same let down as the lights proved to belong to small trading vessels, and the gunboat sheered away quickly, lest she be recognized and her presence off the Cape be reported in Table Bay.

In the dawn, Clinton was on deck again, as the gunboat moved further offshore to take up her daylight patrol station. He was distracted by the sighting reports as his masthead look-out picked up the first sails of the fishing fleet coming out for the day's business, and by the lugubrious report of his coal-stained Scottish engineer.

'Ye'll not last out the day, sir,' MacDonald told him. 'Even though I am burning just enough coal to keep the furnace warm – we've not more than a bucket or two left.'

'Mr. MacDonald,' Clinton interrupted him, trying to keep his temper under control and to disguise his exhaustion. 'This ship will stay on station until I give the order, I don't care what you burn, but you are to give me steam when I ask for it – or kiss good-bye to the fattest bundle of prize money that will ever come your way.'

Despite this brave promise and threat, Clinton's hopes were sinking swiftly. They had been on station for more than a day and a night already – he could not bring himself to believe that he had beaten the swift clipper to the Cape by that margin, not unless she had been somehow miraculously delayed, and every hour increased the certainty that she had run clear away from him, taking her cargo and the woman he loved out of his life for ever.

He knew he should go below to rest, but his cabin was stifling in the rising summer heat, and in it he felt like a trapped animal. He stayed on deck, unable to keep still for more than a few moments at a time, poring over the chart table and fiddling with the navigational instruments before throwing them down and resuming his nervous pacing, shooting quick glances up at the masthead, and then roaming the ship so obviously intent on finding fault or criticizing the ship's running that his officers followed his lanky figure with troubled expressions, while the watch on deck was silent and subdued, not one of them daring to glance in his direction until Clinton's voice rose in a coldly furious cry that froze them all.

'Mr. Denham,' the Lieutenant almost ran to the summons, 'this deck is a pig-sty. What animal is responsible for this filth?'

On the white holystoned deck planking was a brown splash of tobacco juice, and Denham stared at it for an instant before wheeling away to bellow a series of orders that had a dozen men scampering. The activity was so intense, the atmosphere electric, as Captain and Lieutenant stood over four men on their knees scrubbing furiously at the offending stain while others carried buckets of sea water and still others rigged the deck pump, that the hail from the masthead was almost ignored.

It was left to Ferris to acknowledge it, and to enquire through the voice trumpet,

'What do you make of her?'

'She's hull down, but she's a four-masted ship, square rigged—'

The activity on the deck ceased instantly, every head lifting as the look-out went on elaborating on his sighting.

'She's on a course to weather the Cape, now she's coming round on to a heading of north-north-west or thereabouts.'

Clinton Codrington was the first to move. He snatched the telescope out of Lieutenant Denham's hand and ran to the ratlines. With the telescope tucked in his belt he began to climb, hand over hand.

He went up steadily, never pausing nor faltering, not even when he reached the futtock shrouds and for a few moments hung over backwards one hundred feet above the swaying deck. However, when he reached the crow's nest at the main peak and tumbled into it thankfully, his breath was sawing dryly in his throat and the blood sang in his ears. He had not climbed like that since he had been a midshipman.

The look-out tried to make himself as small as possible, for they were crowded together in the canvas bucket, and he pointed out the ship to his Captain.

'There she be, sir.'

Black Joke's roll was emphasized up here on the tall pendulum of the mast, and the horizon swung giddily through the field of Clinton's telescope as he tried to keep it focused. It was an art that he had never completely mastered, but that was of little consequence for the first time the little regular white pyramids popped up in the field of his glass the last doubts were dispelled, and Clinton felt his heart leap fiercely against his ribs.

His voice was strangled with triumphant emotion as he shouted down at the tiny foreshortened figures on the gleaming white quarterdeck far below.

'Bring her round to due east, Mr. Denham. Order a full head of steam on the boiler—'

Though he had not yet fully recovered his breath, he threw himself out of the crow's nest and scrambled down faster than he had climbed. In his haste he slid the last fifty feet down the backstay and barely noticed the rough hempen rope scorching the palms of his hands.

By the time his feet hit the deck, *Black Joke* was coming around on to her new heading, and in anticipation of Clinton's next order, Denham had already called the watch below, and they came boiling out on to the deck.

'And we will clear for action, Mr. Denham, if you please,' gasped Clinton, his face dark with blood under his deepwater tan and the sapphire eyes alight with battle lust.

All *Black Joke*'s officers carried swords on their belts, only Clinton had selected a cutlass, for he preferred the stouter and heavier weapon, and he fiddled with the hilt even now as he spoke to them quietly and seriously.

'Gentlemen, I have documented proof that the ship ahead of us has a cargo of slaves aboard her,'

Denham coughed nervously and Clinton forestalled him. 'I am also aware that she is an American vessel, and in ordinary circumstances we would be helpless to oppose her passage.' Denham nodded with relief, but Clinton went on remorselessly, 'However, I have received an appeal from one of Her Majesty's subjects, Dr. Robyn Ballantyne whom you all know well, who is being abducted aboard the *Huron* against her will. I am certain what my duty is in these circumstances. I intend to board her, and if she resists me, I intend to fight her.' He paused and their faces were shocked, strained. 'Those of you who have objections to this course of action should immediately note them in the ship's log, and I will sign them.'

Their relief and gratitude was immediate, few other captains would be so lenient.

He signed his name neatly beneath the entry in the ship's log, and then returned the pen to its holder.

'Now that the formalities have been seen to, gentlemen, shall we get on with earning our hire?' And Clinton was smiling for the first time since they sailed from Zanzibar harbour as he indicated the pile of snowy white sails that was now clearly visible from the deck ahead of *Black Joke*'s bows, and as he spoke there was an eruption of dark tarry-smelling smoke from the tall single stack above them, and the engine telegraph clanged sharply as the pointer moved to

'Engine Standing By' position on the repeater. *Black Joke* had steam in her boiler.

Clinton stepped to the telegraph, thrust the handle fully around the dial to the 'Full ahead' position, and the deck vibrated under his feet as the propeller shaft began to spin and *Black Joke* lunged forward eagerly, breaking the swells off her shoulders in explosions of white spray.

'By God, he's got us pinned against the land—' Mungo drawled the words out nonchalantly, even smiling slightly at Tippoo as he lowered the glass from his eye for a moment and polished the lens on his shirt-sleeve. 'We'll have to run like the very devil to get round him, and make the open sea. Mr. Tippoo, will you be good enough to shake out every last reef and crack on all the sail we can carry, right up to the sky sails?' He lifted the glass to his eye again as Tippoo began bellowing the orders. 'It's a little bit too much luck for any one man,' Mungo murmured aloud. 'It's too much coincidence that the one man I would not wish to meet be lying in the one place on all the oceans where I would not wish to meet him.' Again he lowered the glass and strode to the poop rail to look down on to the maindeck.

Robyn Ballantyne was at the ship's side, staring out across the indigo blue waters at the sail and the smear of dark smoke, still far out to sea, but every moment converging on them, headed to a point far ahead of *Huron*'s elegant bows where the courses of the two ships would meet. She sensed Mungo's eyes upon her, and she lifted the shawl off her head so that her dark russet hair tumbled out and snapped and danced around her cheeks. Her skirts were flattened against her legs by the wind, so that she had to lean slightly forward to balance herself.

She lifted her chin and stared up at Mungo, her expression defiant and she watched him as he carefully bit the end off one of his long thin black cheroots and cupped his hands around the sulphurous flare of the Vesta match and lit the cheroot without once breaking the steady gaze that held her own.

Then he sauntered easily down the poop-ladder to her side.

'A friend of yours, Doctor Ballantyne?' The smile was on his lips alone. His eyes were frosty.

'I have prayed every night for him to come. Ever since I sent the letter that summoned him.'

'You do not deny the betrayal?'

'I am proud I was able to perform my Christian duty.'

'Who carried your letter?'

'No member of your crew, sir. I sent it by the master of the Omani buggaloo.'

'I see.' His voice was low, but stinging as dry ice. 'And what of Tippoo's illness, would a physician, per chance, stoop to poisoning a patient?'

She dropped her eyes, unable to meet that accusation.

'Will you be so kind, Doctor Ballantyne, as to return to your cabin immediately and stay there until I give you permission to leave it. There will be an armed guard at the door.'

'I am to be punished?'

'No man would blame me for dropping you over the side, and leaving you to be picked up by your countrymen. However, it is your safety I am thinking of. This deck could become an unhealthy spot in the very near future, and we will all be too much occupied to care for you.'

His attention left her, and he was staring ahead, and then glancing back at *Black Joke*'s smoke, judging speeds and angles with a seaman's eye. Then he smiled.

'Before you go, I would like you to know that all your efforts have really been a fine waste of time – look there!' He pointed ahead along the sheer and mountainous coastline, and following his arm she saw for the first time that ahead of them the sea was aa black and broken as new coal cut from the face, glittering with wild jumping wavelets, each flecked with pretty white crests.

'There is the wind,' Mungo said. 'That's where it comes through the mountains, and we will be into it before you are safely tucked up in your cabin.' He chuckled now comfortably, confidently. 'Once we get on that wind, there are few ships on all the oceans, either steam or sail, that would match *Huron* for a moment, and God knows, there are none who could run her down.' He gave her a small mocking bow, parody of gracious southern manners. 'Take a good look at that ugly little steam packet, before you go, ma'am, you'll not be seeing her again. And now, if you'll be good enough to excuse me—'

He turned from her and ran lightly back up the poop-ladder.

Tears of anger dimming her eyes, Robyn clutched the rail and stared across the narrowing strip of sea at the bustling, puffing little gunboat, already she could catch glimpses of the hull, and its painted chequer-board gun-ports. She began to hope that Mungo St. John's boast had been mere bravado, for *Black Joke* seemed to be keeping pace with the tall clipper, the wind was still a long, long way ahead.

There was a respectful touch on Robyn's shoulder, and old Nathaniel stood beside her.

'Captain's orders, ma'am, and I am to see you safe in your cabin.'

Clinton leaned forward, all his weight on the balls of his feet, almost as though he were trying to urge his ship on by the balance of his body, the way a rider leans forward into the jump. He also had seen the wind pattern on the surface of the sea, and knew what it heralded.

The tall clipper ship looked lazy now, indolent in her flounces and ruffles as a lady of high fashion, and *Black Joke* was snorting and snuffling busily down the short leg of the triangle. If they both maintained this speed and course they would meet about eleven nautical miles ahead. Clinton could visualize the exact spot clearly, just beyond the spit of land marked on his chart as 'Bakoven Point'.

Huron was committed to her present course. She could not bear up for the land lay close under her weather rail, and the chart showed breaking shoals well offshore – there was one of them now, close on her starboard beam, showing its round black granite back and blowing like a whale. *Huron* was in a trap, and her only escape would be to find the extra turn of speed which would carry her away out of gunshot range – and there it was, the wind, less than three miles ahead of her.

There was a loud banging from the deck below Clinton's feet, and he glanced irritably at Ferris.

'See what that is,' he snapped, and turned his full attention back to the clipper. Three short miles she had to go, but even as Clinton stared at her through his glass he saw her huge square mainsail quiver and then shake gently as she luffed in the flukey airs below the mountains.

'Please God!' Clinton whispered, and *Huron*'s speed bled off perceptively, all her sails were losing their taut clean shape and she checked away, baulking like a weary animal.

'She's found a hole in the wind,' Lieutenant Denham called exultantly. 'We've got her now, by God!'

'I'll thank you not to blaspheme on this quarterdeck, Mr. Denham,' Clinton told him sharply, and Denham's expression was instantly crestfallen.

'I beg your pardon, sir.' At that moment Ferris arrived breathlessly back on deck.

'The stokers, sir,' he panted. 'They are knocking out all the furniture from the officers' quarters. Your bunk's gone, sir, and your desk also.'

Clinton barely glanced at him, he was studying the clipper, evaluating each yard of difference in their speeds, judging as finely as he dared the angle of his interception.

Yes, he decided, with *Huron*'s loss of speed, he could edge in a touch more.

'Bring her up a point to starboard,' he told the helmsman, and then he glanced up at his own sails that were helping the big bronze screws under the stern to hurl *Black Joke* forward. The alteration of course had affected them.

'Mr. Ferris, see to the trim of your jib, if you please.'

Ferris bellowed an order to the foredeck watch, and watched critically as they hardened up the long triangular sail.

All *Huron*'s sails shivered, and then refilled, once more taking on their true shape, and she spurted away, a curl of white sparkling under her bows. The dark windswept water was much closer ahead of her.

It had been Denham's unnecessary blasphemy, Clinton was sure of it, and he glanced darkly at his Lieutenant, and then reluctantly gave the order.

'Let her fall off a point.' *Huron* was head-reaching again. If *Black Joke* held on she would be aiming to cut behind the clipper's stern. The alteration was an acknowledgement of the advantage changing hands once again.

The engine voice pipe squealed, and it was a relief to have even the small distraction.

'Engine room, Captain,' he snapped into the mouthpiece. 'Coal long ago gone, sir. Pressure down to 100 pounds, sir – and falling.'

'Burn everything you can find.'

'Wood goes up like paper, sir. No body to it – and it chokes the flue.' MacDonald seemed to relish the gloomy news, and Clinton felt his irritation turn to anger.

'Do your best, man, nobody can ask more than that,' and he snapped the voice pipe closed.

Was he close enough yet to try a shot with his bow-chaser, he wondered? The long sixteen-pounder had almost twice the range of the big thirty-two pounders that made up *Black Joke*'s main armament. A lucky shot might carry away one of the clipper's spars, might even bring down a yard – and at that moment he distinctly felt the change in the engine vibrations coming up through the deck, *Black Joke* was faltering, the steam in her boilers losing pressure.

'Mr. Ferris, break out the colours, if you please.'

As the Ensign unfurled at the peak, spread gloriously against the pale blue sky, crimson and silky white, shouting a challenge on the wind, Clinton felt that tightness in his chest, that swell of pride which never failed him.

'*Huron*'s replying,' Denham muttered, and Clinton lifted his glass, and watched the American's colours bloom like a flower high above her simmering piles of white canvas.

'And be damned,' Denham interpreted the show of colours. *Huron* was scorning their challenge.

'Mr. Ferris, we'll give her a gun now,' Clinton decided grimly. 'Put one over her bows.' And Ferris scrambled away to the bows to supervise the loading and laying of the bow-chaser.

The shot when it came was a puny little pop of sound, muted by the wind and the long spurt of grey powder smoke was whipped away almost before it could form. Though they were all watching avidly through the telescopes, not one of them could spot the fall of shot, and Denham spoke aloud for all of them.

'She's not altering. She's ignoring us.'

'Very well.' Clinton kept his voice low. 'We'll try one into her rigging.'

The sixteen-pounder banged again, like an unlatched door in a high wind, and this time they both exclaimed in unison. A pinprick of light appeared in one of the *Huron*'s studding sails, pierced by shot; it held its shape for an instant and then burst like a paper packet and was blown to tatters.

Clinton saw the bustle of *Huron*'s seamen on the decks and yards, and before the bow-chaser could be reloaded, the ruined sail was hauled down and another clean new sail spread open in its place. The speed with which the sail change was made impressed even Clinton.

'The devil is a good sailor, I'll grant him that—' And then he broke off, for *Huron* was turning boldly, seeming to aim to cut the gunboat's bows, and Clinton realized what her Captain was doing. He was anticipating the rush of the wind, and as Clinton watched it struck her.

It came roaring aboard the clipper, howling through her rigging, like a pack of hunting wolves, and the tall ship heeled and seemed almost to crouch, gathering herself like a blood stallion feeling the cut of the lash, and then she hurled herself forward and was away.

The dark wind-scoured sea burst open before the long lithe knifing hull, and joyously *Huron* tossed the dashing white spray over her bows.

'She's making twenty knots,' Denham cried with disbelief, as *Black Joke* seemed to come up dead in the water, a wallowing log when compared to the swift and lovely ship that cut daringly across her bows, just out of cannon shot, and dashed away into the open Atlantic Ocean.

Through his glass Clinton saw that the seamen who lined *Huron*'s yards were gambolling and waving their caps, mouths wide open and they cheered and jeered, and then he focused the glass on *Huron*'s deck.

There was a tall figure at *Huron*'s near rail, clad in a plain dark blue jacket. Clinton could not make out the man's features at this distance, but he recognized the set of wide shoulders, the arrogant carriage of head, that he had last seen over the sights of a duelling pistol.

The acid bile of hatred rose to scald his throat as the figure lifted a hand in a laconic salute, a taunting gesture of farewell, and then turned away from the rail unhurriedly.

Clinton snapped his telescope closed.

'Stern chase!' he ordered. 'We'll keep after her!'

He did not dare look at his officers' faces, lest one of them wore an expression of pity.

Lying on her bunk, her arms held stiffly at her sides and hands clenched painfully, Robyn heard the creak and squeal from the deck below her that meant *Huron* was altering course, and that the eight-inch thick rudder-lines were running through their blocks as the helmsman spun the wheel. It was a sound she had long become accustomed to, and she braced herself instinctively as the rudder lines attached to the pintles trained around the enormous wooden rudder under *Huron*'s stern and the ship altered her action through the water.

Seconds later there was a thunderous commotion from the deck above her, the blustering roar of the gale socking into the rigging, the crash of tackle coming up taut, the slam of the great sails as their awesome power was transferred into the hull, and Robyn was almost hurled from her bunk as *Huron* heeled wildly.

Then the cabin was filled with the exultant thrumming of the hull through water, as though she were the body of a violin as the bow was drawn across the bass strings, and *Huron* trembled with life, lifting and dropping to the new urgency of her run.

Very faintly Robyn could hear above it all the sound of men cheering. She jumped from the bunk and clutching for handholds crossed the cabin and pounded her fist upon the door.

'Nathaniel,' she called. 'Answer me this instant.'

'Captain says and how I'm not to talk to you.' His voice was muffled.

'You cannot torment me so,' Robyn yelled back. 'What is happening?'

A long pause while Nathaniel considered his duty and then weighed it against his affection for this spirited young woman.

'We are on the wind, ma'am,' he told her at last. 'And going like all the devils of hell with a crackerjack tied to their tails.'

'What of *Black Joke?*' she pleaded. 'What of the British gun-boat?'

'Ain't nothing will catch us now. Reckon the puffing Billy will be out of sight before nightfall. From here she looks like she's dropped her anchor.'

Slowly Robyn leaned forward until her forehead pressed against the planking of the door. She closed her eyes very tightly, and tried to fight down the black waves of despair that threatened to overwhelm her.

She stayed like that for a long time until Nathaniel's voice roused her. It was rough with concern.

'Are you all right then, missus?'

'Yes, thank you, Nathaniel. I'm just fine,' she replied tightly, without opening her eyes. 'I'm going to take a little nap now. Don't let anybody disturb me.'

'I'll be right here, missus. Ain't nobody going to get past me,' he assured her.

She opened her eyes and went back to the bunk, and knelt before it and began to pray – but for once she could not concentrate. Jumbled images kept intervening, and, when she closed her eyes, the face of Clinton Codrington was there, with those pale beautiful eyes in the darkly tanned mahogany of his face that accentuated the sun-bleached platinum of his hair. She longed for him as she had never done before – he had become a symbol for her that was good and clean and right.

Then her mind darted away and it was that distant mocking smile, the taunting gold-flecked eyes of Mungo St. John. She trembled with humiliation, the man who had violated her and turned her own emotions traitor, who had dallied with her and allowed her to hope, nay, to pray that she could bear his children and become his wife. Her despair turned to hatred once again, and hatred armed her.

'Forgive me, Lord – I'll pray later – but now I *have* to do something!'

She started to her feet, and the cramped little cabin was a cage, suffocating and unbearable. She hammered her fists on the door and Nathaniel replied immediately.

'Nathaniel, I cannot bear it in here a moment longer,' she cried. 'You must let me out.'

His voice was regretful but firm. 'Can't do that, missus. Tippoo would have a look at my back bone!'

She flung away from the door, angry, confused, her mind in a turmoil.

'I cannot let him carry me away to—' She did not go on, for she could not imagine what awaited her at the end of this voyage unless – and she had a vivid mental image of *Huron* coming into dock, while standing on the quay was a beautiful tall and aristocratic French woman in crinolines and velvets and pearls with three small sons standing at her side waving up at the tall arrogant figure on *Huron*'s quarterdeck.

She tried to close her mind to it, and she concentrated instead on the sound that *Huron* made as she bore away joyously on the wind, the drumming of her hull, and the pop and creak of her planking, the clatter of tackle and the stamp of bare feet on her deck as a party of seamen walked away with a fall, training one of the yards more finely to the wind. From beneath her feet came another muted squeal, like a rat in the cat's jaws, as the helmsman made a small adjustment to *Huron's* heading, and the rudder tackle ran protestingly through the blocks.

The sound triggered a memory, and Robyn froze, trembling again, but this time with anticipation. She remembered Clinton Codrington describing to her how as a young Lieutenant he had been in command of a cutting-out party sent into a river estuary that was crammed with small slaving craft, buggaloos and dhows.

'I didn't have enough men to take them all as prize at once, so we jumped from one to the other, cut their rudder lines and left them drifting helplessly, until we could pick 'em up later – those that hadn't gone aground, that is.'

Robyn roused herself from the memory and rushed to the corner of her cabin. She had to wedge her back against the bulkhead and push with both her feet to move her wooden chest into the centre of the cabin. Then she dropped to her hands and knees.

There was a small trap-door in the deck, so neatly fitted that its joints were knife edges, but there was a small iron ring let flush into the woodwork. Once on the long voyage down the Atlantic, she had been disturbed by a very apologetic carpenter's mate and she had watched with interest while he had dragged her chest aside and opened the hatch, to descend through it with a grease pot.

She tried now to open it, but the hatch was so tight-fitting, that it resisted her efforts. She snatched a woollen shawl from her chest, and threaded it through the iron ring. Now she could get a fairer purchase. Once more she strained back, and the hatch moved inchingly and then abruptly flew open with a crash that she was sure must have alerted Nathaniel. She froze again, listening for a half minute, but there was no sound from beyond the cabin door.

On her hands and knees again she peered into the open hatchway. There was a faint breeze of air coming up out of the dark square hole, and she could smell the thick grease, the reek of the bilges and the awful slave stink that not all the lye and scrubbing had been able to cleanse – her gorge rose at the taint. As her eyes adjusted, she made out the low and narrow tunnel that housed *Huron's* steering gear. It was just high enough for a man to crawl along, running fore and aft along the hull.

The rudder lines came down from the deck above, ran through heavy iron blocks bolted into one of *Huron's* main frames, and then changed direction and ran directly astern down the narrow wooden tunnel. The pulley wheels of the blocks were caked with black grease, and the rudder lines were of new yellow hemp. They seemed as thick as a man's leg, and she could sense the enormous strain on them, for they were as rigid as steel bars.

She looked around for a means of damaging them, a knife, one of her scalpels, perhaps, and almost immediately realized the futility of anything so puny. Even a strong man with a double-headed axe would be hard pressed to hack his way through those cables, and there was no room in which to swing an axe in that narrow tunnel. Even if a man had succeeded in severing one of them, he would have been cut to bloody tatters as the cable whiplashed.

There was only one means, one sure means, and she quailed at the thought of what would happen if it got out of control, and if *Black Joke* was not very swiftly alongside to render assistance with her steam-driven pumps and hoses. She had once already rejected the idea of using fire, but now with help so close astern, with the last chance rapidly fading, she was ready to accept any risk.

She reached across and pulled off the wooden bunk one of her grey woollen blankets and wadded it into a bundle, then she stood up and lifted the oil lamp from its gimbals in the deck above her. Her fingers were clumsy with haste as she unscrewed the cap of the oil reservoir in the base of the lamp.

She soaked the blanket, and then looked round for anything else that was inflammable – her journals? No, not them, but she pulled her medical manuals out of the chest and ripped the pages out of them, crumpling them so they would burn more readily, and she made a sack of the oil-soaked blanket and wadded the paper into it.

She stuffed it down the hatch and it fell across the straining rudder lines, and entangled itself in the iron pulleys.

The mattress on the bunk was filled with coir, the dry coconut fibre would burn fiercely; she dragged it off the bunk and pushed it into the hatch. Then the wooden slats off the bunk followed it, then the navigational books from the narrow bookshelf behind the door. She looked about her swiftly, but there was nothing else in the cabin that would burn.

The first Swan Vesta that she dropped burning down the hatchway flickered once and then went out. She tore the end sheet out of her journal and twisted it into a spill, when it was blazing strongly she let it fall into the dark square opening, and as it floated down it illuminated the gloomy recesses of *Huron*'s bilges, and the rough planking of her underbelly.

The burning spill landed on the oil-soaked blanket, and pale blue flames fluttered over it as the evaporating gases flashed off, then a crumpled ball of paper caught and little orange flames peaked up and danced merrily over the blanket and the linen covering of the mattress. A rush of heat came up through the hatchway, scorching Robyn's cheeks, and the sound of the flames was higher than that of the rushing seas along the outside of the hull.

Using all her strength, Robyn swung the hatch cover over and let it drop back on to its seating with a thump that alarmed her anew, but immediately the sound of the flames was cut off.

Panting with the effort and a savage excitement, Robyn backed away and leaned against the bulkhead to rest. Her heart was pounding so fiercely that the blood in her ears nearly deafened her, and suddenly she was afraid.

What if *Black Joke* had abandoned the unequal contest, and there was nobody to rescue the eight hundred miserable souls chained below *Huron*'s decks before the flames reached them?

That first wild assault of the wind, as it came boiling down off the mountains, had settled to a steady blast, not so furious, but constant and reliable.

'There will be no flukes or holes in this gale of wind,' Mungo thought with satisfaction, pausing in his pacing to look up at the small scudding wind-torn shreds of cloud that seemed to scrape the tops of his masts, and then turning to survey an indigo Atlantic that stretched to every corner of the horizon, dark with the wind rush and dappled with the prancing white horses that curled from every wave crest.

His leisurely survey ended over *Huron*'s stern rail. The land was already out of sight, so swiftly had *Huron* run the great flat-topped mountain below the horizon, and *Black Joke* was hull down. Only her topsails showed, not a trace of furnace smoke.

The absence of smoke puzzled Mungo a little and he frowned, considering it, and finding no plausible answer, he shrugged and resumed his pacing. *Black Joke* would be out of sight, even from *Huron*'s towering masthead, before sunset, and Mungo was planning the evolutions he would make during the night to confuse thoroughly any pursuit, before settling on to his final course to run through the doldrums and cross the equator.

'Deck, masthead.' A faint hail reached him, breaking his line of thought, and he stopped again, threw back his head and with both hands on his hips stared up at the masthead as it dipped and swung across the sky.

Tippoo answered the hail with a bull bellow, and the look-out's voice was strained, his anxiety evident even against the wind and at that remove.

'Smoke!'

'Where away?' Tippoo's voice was angry, the reply should have given both distance and bearing from *Huron* – already every man on *Huron*'s deck was twisting his head to sweep the horizon.

'Dead astern.'

'That will be the gunboat,' Mungo thought comfortably. 'She's got her boiler going again – and much good may it do her.' He dropped his fists from his hips and took one more pace before the look-out's voice rang out again.

'Smoke dead astern, we are trailing smoke!'

Mungo stopped dead in his tracks, his foot still an inch from the deck. He felt the icy spray of fear chill his guts.

'Fire!' bellowed Tippoo.

It was the one most dreaded word to men who lived their lives in the tinder hulls of wooden ships, whose seams were caulked with tar and pitch, and whose sails and rigging would burn like straw. Mungo completed that suspended pace, spinning on the ball of his foot as it struck the deck, and the next pace carried him to *Huron*'s rail. He leaned far out, peering back over the stern, and the smoke was a pale wisp, thin as sea fret, lying low against the dark blue sea, drifting away behind them, and dissipating even as he watched it.

Dry oak planks burn with a fine clean flame and little smoke, Mungo knew that, he knew also that the first thing he must do was starve the flames of air, heave the ship to, to reduce the wind of her passage while the extent of the flames could be explored and the ship's pumps—

He turned again, his mouth opening to begin shouting his commands. The quartermaster and his mate stood directly ahead of him, both of them balancing easily before the massive mahogany and brass wheel. Larger than the driving-wheel on a steam locomotive, it required the strength of two men to hold *Huron*'s head in this wind and on this point of sailing, for the huge spread of her canvas was opposed by the massive oak and copper rudder under her stern.

Down in the steering tunnel, the flames were being fed by the strong breeze that the canvas scoops on *Huron*'s foredeck were directing down into her own slave-decks in an attempt to keep them sweet.

The draught forced its way through the companionways and ladderways, through the ports and cracks in *Huron*'s bulkheads, and this steady breeze at last found its way into the long narrow tunnel that housed her steering-gear.

The bright rustling flames were almost smokeless, but intensely hot. They frizzled the loose fibres of hemp off the thick hairy rudder lines, and then swiftly blackened the golden brown cords, began to eat through them so that here a strand parted with a snap that was lost in the rising crackle of burning timbers and the strand unravelled, spinning upon itself and bursting in another tiny new explosion of light.

The two quartermasters were ten feet from where Mungo stood, poised to give his commands, composing the orders in his head, when suddenly the massive wheel no longer resisted the thrust of the brawny men who held it over.

Deep down in *Huron*'s hull, in the long wooden tunnel that had been turned into a raging blast furnace, the rudder lines had burned through, and as they snapped, they snaked and whipped viciously, smashing through the burning deck timbers, scattering flaming brands into the hold below, and letting in a fresh whistling gush of air that forced the flames higher.

Under the helmsman's hands the wheel dissolved in a spinning blur of glittering brass and the quartermaster was hurled the length of the deck, striking the bulwark with jarring force that dropped him to the planking wriggling feebly as a crushed insect. His mate was less fortunate, his right arm was caught in the polished mahogany spokes of the wheel and it twisted like a strip of rubber, the bone of his forearm breaking up into long sharp splinters whose points thrust out whitely through the tanned skin, and the head of the long humerus bone was plucked from its socket in the scapula and the whole upper arm screwed up in a twist of rubbery flesh.

With the press of the rudder under the stern no longer controlling the rush of *Huron*'s hull through the water, the tremendous pressure of the wind in her sails took over unopposed, and *Huron* became a giant's weathercock. She spun in almost her own length, her bows flying up into the wind and every man on her deck was hurled to the planking with stunning force.

The yards came crashing about, tackle snapping like cotton, one of the upper yards tearing itself loose, falling in a twisted web of its own canvas and rigging, and *Huron* was taken full aback, the neat geometrical pyramids of her sails disintegrating into flapping, fluttering chaos, wrapping around the stays and halyards, flogging against their own yards and masts.

With the gale of wind flying fully into the front of the sails, from the diametrically opposite direction to that for which they had been designed, the tall masts flexed and arched dangerously backwards, the backstays drooping slackly, adding to the confusion of sail and rigging, while all the forestays were humming with unbearable tension – and one of them parted with an ear-jarring crack and the foremast shifted a few degrees and then hung askew.

Mungo St. John dragged himself to his feet and clung to the rail. The screams of the maimed helmsman dinning in his ears, he looked about him, and disbelief turned to bitter despair, as he found his beautiful ship transformed to an ungainly shambles. Wallowing drunkenly, *Huron* was beginning to make sternway, as the wind pushed her backwards and the waves came tumbling aboard her.

For long seconds Mungo stared about him numbly. There was so much damage, so much confusion, and so much mortal danger, that he did not know where to begin, what his first order must be. Then over *Huron*'s heaving bows, in the opposite direction to which he had last seen it, the distant but suddenly dreadfully threatening speck that was *Black Joke*'s topsails showed in a pale flash above the horizon, and it galvanized Mungo.

'Mr. Tippoo,' Mungo called. 'We'll reef the mains and send down all her top hamper.'

The logical sequence of orders began to arrange themselves in his mind, and his voice was calm and clear, without the strained and panicky timbre they had expected.

'Mr. O'Brien, go below and give me a fire report, quick as you like.'

'Bosun, rig port and starboard pumps, and stand by to hose down the fire.'

'Mr. Tippoo, send a party to batten all her hatches and strike the air scoops.' They must try to prevent air reaching the flames, he was sealing the hull.

'Coxswain, have the whaler off her davits and launch her.' He would attempt to tow the heavy boat astern, to act as a drogue, a sea-anchor. He was not sure that it would provide a solution, but he intended to work *Huron*'s bows around with the delicate use of her forward sails – and with the drogue holding her tail in place of the rudder, he might be able to run directly before the wind. It was not his optimum course, and it would be fine and dangerous work with the deadly risk of gibing and broaching, but at the least it would give him respite while he rigged the emergency steering tackle to her useless rudder, and get *Huron* under control once more.

He paused for breath, but once more glanced forward. *Huron* was moving rapidly astern, dipping and staggering into the swells so they came flurrying aboard her in spray and solid green gouts of water, while over her bows the British gunboat was closer – so close that Mungo glimpsed a little silver of her painted hull, and it seemed that her action through the water was more boisterous and cocky, like a game rooster erecting its coxcomb and ruffling its feathers as it bounces across the sandy floor of the cockpit.

Unable to endure the company of his junior officers a moment longer, stifled and filled with a sense of helplessness by his inability to prevent the tall American clipper from romping away from him, desperate for some activity to help his nerves from fraying further, Clinton Codrington had taken his telescope and gone forward into *Black Joke*'s bows.

Oblivious to the spray that splattered over him, soaking the thin linen shirt and chilling him so that his teeth chattered even in the brilliant sunlight, Clinton clutched for a hand hold in the ratlines, balancing on the narrow bulwark and staring ahead through eyes that swam not only with the stinging spray and wind, but as much with humiliation and frustration.

Just perceptibly, *Huron*'s tower of canvas was sinking below the irregular watery horizon, by sunset she would be gone. She and Robyn Ballantyne. His chance had come and he had missed it. His spirits could sink no lower.

To add to his suffering, his streaming eyes were playing him false, and what he could still make out of the clipper became distorted, changing shape as he still stared after her. Then the hail from the look-out high above him broke the grip of his despair,

'Chase is altering!' Clinton could not yet believe the high-pitched shriek from the masthead. 'She's coming about!' The hail was almost incoherent with excitement and surprise.

Clinton whipped the telescope to his eye, and once again doubted his eyesight. *Huron*'s masts had been almost dead in line, but now they showed individually. She was coming about, already *Huron* was almost broadside, and Clinton stared. For a few moments more the orderly mass of sails retained their perfect snowy shape, and then the pattern began to break up. The ponderous belly of the mainsail wobbled and trembled, then began to flutter and shake like a pennant in the gale, it spilled its wind and collapsed like a bursting paper bag and lashed itself in a petulant fury around its own mainmast.

Huron was a shambles. Through the glass Clinton could see her beginning to tear herself to pieces, sails ripping, yards tumbling – her foremast sagging out of true, and he still could not believe it was happening.

'She's taken full aback.' He heard Denham's triumphant yell, and other voices took up the cry.

'She fast in irons!'

'We've got her, by God, we've got her now!'

Though his vision blurred and the wetness running down his cheeks was not all splattered spray, Clinton went on staring incredulously through the telescope.

'There is smoke, she's on fire!' Denham again, and Clinton picked up the fine pale mist of smoke spreading away from her; and at that moment a fresh burst of spray over the bows drenched the lens of his telescope, and he lowered it.

He took a silk bandanna from his hip pocket, and wiped his face and eyes of spray and the other wetness, then he blew his nose noisily, stuffed the handkerchief back into his pocket, jumped on to his deck and strode back to his quarterdeck.

'Mr. Ferris,' he said crisply, 'please send up a flag hoist under *Huron*'s name and make the following "I am sending a boarding party to you." ' The pale sapphire eyes shone with a zealot's intensity. ' "If you resist I shall fight you." '

It was a long message, and while Ferris called for the pennants from the flag locker, Clinton turned to Denham. His voice shook with passion.

'Please clear the ship for action, Mr. Denham – and we'll run out our guns now.'

Above the gale Clinton heard the clatter of the opening gunports, the rumble of the gun carriages, but all his attention was concentrated ahead upon the crippled slave ship.

He saw and understood the desperate attempts that her Captain was making to get her before the wind. He knew what a feat it had been to take down that tangled mast of canvas and rope in such a short time, yet he felt no admiration, only cold fighting fury.

Huron was showing only a storm jib.

St. John was clearly trying to break the grip of the gale upon her – for she was fast 'in irons' – her bows to the wind, and he was attempting to bring her round, but the tall ship that was usually so compliant and obedient was baulking, resisting him, and every minute *Black Joke* was swarming down upon her, closer and still closer.

'She's got serious structural damage,' Denham gloated aloud. 'I'd hazard a guess that she's lost her rudder.'

Clinton did not answer him, he strained ahead, half exultant, half fearful that St. John's efforts would succeed and he would watch helplessly as *Huron* turned her stern to him once more, and went plunging away at the speed which *Black Joke* could never hope to match.

Then, as he watched, it happened. *Huron* swung her long, low length nearly broadside to him, beam on to the wind once again, and hung there for infinite seconds, then she shuddered and shook herself free of the gale's grip and went through the eye of the wind. Instantly the scraps of sail on her foremast snapped open, she came around presenting her stern to *Black Joke* and was sailing again.

Even in his bitter chagrin, Clinton could at last feel admiration for that barely credible feat of seamanship, but beside him his officers were struck dumb, paralysed with disappointment to see their prey slipping away from them once more.

More sails bloomed upon her tall bare masts, and the gap between the two ships was no longer narrowing; instead, it began to widen once more; slowly, infinitely slowly, *Huron* was forging away, and the night was coming.

'She's streaming a warp behind her,' Denham lamented quietly.

'It's a small ship's boat,' Ferris corrected him. They were already close enough to make out such details, *Huron* was only three or four nautical miles ahead of them, all her hull was in plain sight and they could even make out the tiny human figures on her decks with the naked eye. 'Damned clever, what!' Ferris went on with professional interest. 'Who would have believed it would work. Like as not the damned Yankee has the legs of us still.'

Clinton's chagrin turned to anger at his junior's unnecessary commentary.

'Mr. Ferris, instead of chattering like a washerwoman, will you not read the signal *Huron* is flying?'

Huron's signal flags were blowing almost directly away from the watchers on *Black Joke*'s deck, making them difficult to spot and interpret, and Ferris, who had been fixing all his attention on the towing whaler, started guiltily, and then dived for his signal book and began busily scribbling on his slate.

'*Huron* sends under our name, "Stay clear of me, or I will fire upon you." '

'Good.' Clinton nodded and drew an inch of bare steel from the scabbard of his cutlass to make sure the weapon was free before thrusting it back to the hilt. 'Now we all know where we stand!'

But, slowly, inexorably, *Huron* even partially crippled, and steering only by the sails on her foremast, was drawing away from them, and she was still far out of random cannon shot.

'The fire has taken hold in the steering-gear under the doctor's cabin.' The third mate came hurrying back on deck to make his damage report. 'I got her out of there.' He jerked a thumb as Robyn came up on deck clutching her black leather valise into which she had hastily crammed her journals and other small valuables.

'It's got through into the cable tier and the lazaretto, it will be into the sternquarters in a minute.' The mate's arms and face streamed with oily sweat, and the soot had blackened them like a chimney sweep.

'Put the hoses in through the poop companionway,' Mungo told him calmly. 'And flood the stern section abaft the main hold.'

The mate hurried away and within seconds there was the tolling clangour of the pumps as a dozen men threw their combined weight on the handles and the canvas hoses filled and stiffened, ejaculating solid jets of seawater down the stifling ladderways where already the air was trembling with heat like a desert mirage. Almost immediately hissing clouds of white steam began to boil from the ports and stern lights.

Satisfied, Mungo turned away, shot one glance over the stern to make sure that the gunboat was still falling away behind the limping clipper, then let his gaze linger a moment longer on the thick hawser that was secured to the port stern stanchions and ran through the fairlead to the bobbing whaler that *Huron* was dragging half a cable's length astern. The whole complex arrangement of the wind and sails and drogue was critical and unstable, the slightest change might upset it. He decided he could not risk hoisting another square inch of canvas, nor could he send a party below to rig a jury tackle on the useless rudder until the fire was brought under control.

He lit a cheroot, frowning with concentration over the simple and familiar task, and then he raised his eyes to look directly at Robyn for the first time since she had come up on deck.

For a second they stared at each other, and then Robyn looked astern at the ugly little gunboat that was still plugging along after them.

'I keep making the mistake of trusting you,' Mungo said beside her.

'I only made that mistake once – with you,' she replied, and he inclined his head slightly, accepting the riposte.

'How did you get into the steering gear,' he began to enquire, then snapped his fingers irritably at his own oversight. 'Of course, the inspection hatch. Yet, your ingenuity, Doctor, has been of no avail. Your friends still cannot hold us and as soon as it is dark, I will have the rudder cables repaired.'

For the last minute Mungo had been studying her face, oblivious to the sea and the ship and the gale. He did not see the fresh squall racing down upon *Huron*. When it struck, there was no helmsman to hold her. She saw the flash of alarm in his eyes, the realization of danger. His voice, as he yelled an order down the length of the deck, had for the first time the crack of fear in it.

'Get the sails off her, Mr. Tippoo. Quick as you can!'

For the squall had upset the nice balance of *Huron*'s drogue and sail. The ship lunged forward sharply, the long bellied length of cable trailing astern lifted itself above the broken surface of the sea, straightening and coming under such strain that the seawater spurted from the hemp cords in tiny feathery jets.

The empty whaler, with her tarpaulin cover still lashed down over her in an attempt to keep her dry, was at that instant canted steeply over the crest of a breaking swell. The shattering impact transmitted by the taut cable to her bows pitched her forward and heaved her clear of the crest, so that for a moment she was airborne, like a leaping porpoise and then she struck bows first and was snatched below the surface.

For an instant *Huron* staggered to the enormous increase in drag upon the trailing cable, and then the whaler disintegrated in a boiling flurry of white disturbed water. Her broken planking popped to the surface and the cable freed of its wearying weight flicked high in the air like the tail of an angry lioness. Without restraint, *Huron* gibed fiercely, spinning once more across the wind, and this time being blown flat, her tall bare masts swinging over almost parallel to the sea's surface.

The lee rail dug deeply into the sea, and the water came aboard her in a sweeping torrent, like a bursting dam wall.

It caught Robyn and hurled her against Mungo St. John's chest; if it had not done so, she would have been carried overboard, but he caught her to him and held her as they were tumbled down the steeply canted deck – and then *Huron* was righting herself again, the water cascading off her in silver spouts.

She wallowed helplessly, taking the gale-driven seas on her beam, her desperate rolling accentuated by the pendulum of her high bare masts, but at least that drenching wall of sea water had poured into her hull through every opening and had extinguished her fires on the instant.

Mungo St. John dragged Robyn by the wrist across the flooded deck, sloshing and slipping knee deep with loose tackle slithering and floating around them.

At the break of the poop he stopped, both of them panting for breath, their clothing and hair streaming sea water, the deck heaving and dropping crazily under them so he had to cling to the weather rail for support. He stared across at *Black Joke*.

The race was run. The gunboat was crowding down upon them exultantly, so close that he could see the cannon protruding from her open ports and the heads of the gunners above the bulwarks. Her challenging flag hoist still flew in her rigging, gaudy and gay as Christmas decorations. She would be up to the wallowing clipper in minutes, long before Mungo could ever hope to get his ship sailing again.

Mungo shook the water from his sodden dark locks like a spaniel coming ashore, and he filled his lungs.

'Mr. O'Brien, a pair of slave cuffs here,' he bellowed, and Robyn, who had never heard him raise his voice, was stunned by the volume of sound that came up out of that muscular chest. She was still dazed and confused as she felt the cold kiss of iron on her wrists.

Mungo snapped the cuff on her left wrist, took two swift turns of chain around *Huron*'s rail and then snapped the second cuff on her right wrist.

'I have no doubt your friends will be delighted to see you – in the cannon's mouth,' he told her, his face still set with anger, the rims of his nostrils white as bone china. He turned from her, running his fingers through his dark curls, throwing the hair back from his forehead and eyes.

'Mr. O'Brien, muskets and pistols to every hand. Run out the guns and load with ball, we'll change to grape as the range closes.' The mate shouted his orders as he ran, and the crew scattered from the futile task of attempting to bring the clipper under control. They stumbled across the wave-swept deck, dodging fallen and broken tackle, hurrying to arm themselves and to man *Huron*'s guns.

'Mr. Tippoo!' Mungo's voice cut through the cacophony of gale and shouted orders.

'Captain Mungo!'

'Bring up the first deck of slaves.'

'We deep-sixing them?' Tippoo asked, for he had served before under slave captains, who, when capture by a naval vessel was imminent, would deep-six their cargo of blackbirds, drop them overboard, chains and all, and rid themselves of the most damning evidence against them.

'We'll chain 'em to the weather rail, Mr. Tippoo, with the woman.' Mungo used neither Robyn's title nor her name. 'Make the lime-juicer think a spell before he opens fire.' And Tippoo let an explosive chuckle of laughter come bouncing up his throat as he bounded away on those thick bowed legs, to get the gratings off the main hatch.

'Sir!' Denham's voice was incredulous, shocked. 'Sir!'

'Yes, Mr. Denham,' Clinton answered him quietly, without lowering his telescope. 'I have seen it—'

'But, sir, that's Doctor Ballantyne—'

'And black slaves.' Ferris could hold his tongue no longer. 'They're chaining them to the rail.'

'What manner of man is that Yankee!' Denham burst out again.

'A damned clever one,' Clinton answered him quietly. He was watching the woman he had come to rescue through the glass. He could already recognize her features. Her eyes seemed too large for her deathly white face, her sodden and rumpled clothing stuck to her body. Through a rent in her blouse he could see the pale skin of her shoulder and upper arm gleaming with a pearl-like lustre in the sunlight.

'Mr. Denham,' Clinton went on speaking. 'Warn the crew that we will be receiving fire in about five minutes, and we will be unable to return it.'

He watched the ranks of naked black slaves still coming up on to the clipper's maindeck and taking their place along the rail, their gaolers fussing about them, chivying them into place and securing their chains.

'We are fortunate in having a gale of wind, so we will be exposed to fire for a short period, but warn the men to lie flat upon the deck below the bulwark.'

Black Joke's fragile eggshell plating would give some protection at extreme range, but as they closed with the slave ship, he could expect even grape shot to penetrate their sides. One blessing, they would be spared the lethal flying splinters that were so much dreaded in wooden ships.

'I am going to lay her alongside the Yankee's stern,' Clinton went on. That way she would be exposed to the clipper's broadsides while the two ships were bound to each other. 'But she stands taller than we do. I want your best men with the grappling irons, Mr. Denham.' *Hruon*'s maindeck was ten feet higher than the gunboat's. There would be nice work ahead when they leapt the gap, and scrambled up *Huron*'s stern with its pronounced tumble home.

'By God! She's running out her guns. She means to fight us after all,' Denham cut in, and then, penitently, 'I beg your pardon, sir.' He excused himself for the interruption and the blasphemy.

Clinton lowered the telescope. They were so close now that he no longer needed it.

The clipper had six light cannons on each side of her, mounted on the maindeck. The barrels were almost twice as long as *Black Joke*'s own heavy carronades. However, the bore of the muzzles was much smaller in diameter, and as Clinton watched, they began to train around towards him, one at a time beginning at the stern.

Even without the glass, Clinton could make out the tall lean figure in the plain blue jacket moving at a deceptively leisurely pace from one gun to the next, laying each of them personally, gesturing at the gun crews to strain on the tackles and traverse the long cannon on to their target.

Clinton saw St. John reach the bow gun and make a careful adjustment, working over it a few seconds longer than he had the others, and then he leapt to the clipper's bulwark and balanced there with the assurance of an acrobat against the rudderless hull's unpredictable movements.

The scene engraved itself upon Clinton's mind, it seemed so theatrical, like the cast of a stage production lined up at the end of the performance to receive the applause of the spectators. The file of naked black bodies, standing almost shoulder to shoulder with their arms extended in unison, like the trained chorus, their wrists locked to the teak rail by the slave cuffs. Then the principal, the figure of the woman, slim and somehow delicate and tiny in their midst. The bodice of her dress, a buttercup yellow, was a gay spot of colour that drew Clinton's eye irresistibly. It was a distraction that he could not afford at this moment.

The American seemed to be watching Clinton, seemed to have singled him out from the group of officers, and even across the wide stretch of water that still separated them, Clinton was aware of the mesmeric pull of those golden-flecked eyes, the eyes of a predator, a leopard perhaps, poised with a lithe and patient grace upon the bough above the waterhole, awaiting the moment when the prey moved beneath him.

At the level of Mungo St. John's knees were the heads of his gun crews, little knots of pale tense faces, contrasting starkly with the quiescent rank of black slaves. They crouched over their weapons, and the long slim barrels were reduced to small dark circles as Clinton stared directly down the bores.

There were men also in *Huron*'s rigging, roosting in the cross-trees of the yards and masts, and the long barrels of their muskets were clear to see against the backdrop of the wind-driven sky. They would be picked marksmen, *Huron*'s best, and their preferred and special target would be the small group of officers on the gunboat's quarterdeck. Clinton hoped that the clipper's wild action in the gale would throw out their aim.

'Gentlemen, I advise you to take cover until we can bring the ship into action,' he told Denham and Ferris quietly, and felt a little prick of pride when neither of them moved. It was the tradition of Drake and Nelson not to flinch from the coming storm of fire, and Clinton himself went on standing at his ease, hands clasped at the small of his back, calling a small adjustment to the helm as *Black Joke* drove in eagerly, the terrier going for the hold on the bull's nose.

He saw the American move his head, a final judgement of range, considered against the clipper's rolling and beside him Ferris murmured the age-old blasphemy which Clinton this time could not find it in him to resent, for it was also a part of the great tradition.

'For what we are about to receive—' said Ferris, and as if he had heard the words, the American drew the sword from the scabbard on his belt, and raised it above his head. Involuntarily all three naval officers drew breath together and held it. *Huron* was at the bottom of her roll, her cannon pointing down into the sea close alongside, then she was coming up, the barrels rising – levelled, and the sword arm fell.

The six cannon leaped together, in perfect concert, and the startling white gusts of smoke shot fifty feet from her sides, completely silent, for the sound had not reached them, and for a fleeting part of a second they could believe that *Huron* had not loosed her broadside.

Then the very air beat in upon them, shocking the eardrums, seeming for a moment to suck their eyeballs from the sockets with the vast disruption of air caused by passing shot, and close above Clinton's head a stay parted with a whiplash crack.

That was one ball high, but under Clinton's feet, the deck jumped with the multiple impact of ball into her, and the hull rang like the strokes of a gigantic brass gong.

A single ball came through at deck level. It struck a burst of sparks from the steel hull, like Brocks fireworks at Crystal Palace, brilliant orange even in the strong sunlight, and the hole it tore through *Black Joke*'s plating was fringed with bare jagged tongues of metal like the petals of a silver sunflower.

A seaman in striped vest and baggy canvan breeches, who was kneeling behind the bulwark, took the ball full in his chest.

His severed limbs were strewn untidily across the gunboat's spotless deck and the ball went on to strike the foot of *Black Joke*'s mast, shivering it like a tall tree struck by lightning, and tearing a long white splinter from the seasoned Norwegian pine. Then, with its force mainly spent, the ball rolled the length of the deck, smoking and stinking of scorched metal until it thumped into the scuppers and rolled idly back and forth. Only then, seconds after the broadside struck, did the crash of the discharge reach their ears across the turbulent waters that separated the two vessels.

'Not bad shooting for a Yankee,' Ferris grudged them, raising his voice above the gun thunder, and Denham had his watch out and was timing how long it took for the clipper's gun crews to reload.

'Forty-five seconds,' Denham intoned, 'and not a single gun run out again. A bunch of fairground tinkers could do better.'

Clinton found himself wondering if it was merely bravado, or complete indifference to danger and violent death which allowed the two younger officers to chat so casually, while the seaman's severed arms still twitched on the deck, not twenty feet away.

Clinton was afraid, afraid of death and afraid of failing in his duty and afraid of being seen to be afraid, but then he was older than they, for despite their manly airs Ferris was a boy and Denham barely twenty – so perhaps it was not courage but ignorance and lack of imagination.

'Fifty-five seconds!' Denham grunted scornfully, as the next ragged broadside crashed into *Black Joke*'s iron hull, and somebody started to scream below decks, a high mindless keening like steam from a kettle.

'Send somebody to stop that fellow,' Ferris murmured to the seaman who crouched nearby, and doubled over still the man hurried away. Seconds later the screaming stopped abruptly.

'Good work,' Ferris told the seaman as he took his place at the bulwark again.

'Dead, sir, he is, poor devil.'

Ferris nodded without change of expression, and moved closer to listen to his Captain.

'Mr. Denham, I am going to lead the boarding-party. You are to be ready to sheer off and leave us to it, should there by any danger to the ship—' There was a sharp fluting sound, light the flight of a giant insect past their heads, and Clinton glanced up irritably. The marksmen in *Huron*'s rigging had opened fire, the pop of their muskets seemed muted and without menace. Studiedly Clinton ignored them and went on issuing his final orders, raising his voice to compete with the crash and roar of shot and the strike of it into the gunboat's hull.

As Clinton finished speaking, Denham blurted abruptly, 'It's hell not being able to reply.' He was staring across at the clipper whose silhouette was blurred with a bank of pale gunsmoke that even the gale could not disperse rapidly enough. 'It's bad for the men,' he corrected himself swiftly, and Clinton had his answer. Denham was afraid as he was, and the knowledge gave him no comfort at all. If only they could do something, anything, instead of having to stand here in the open and make studied conversation, while *Black Joke* tore across the last few hundred yards of white crested sea that still separated them.

The crash of cannon shot tearing into *Black Joke*'s vitals was almost continuous now as the fastest gunners aboard *Huron* outstripped the others. The bow cannon that the American Captain was supervising and laying was firing three times to the other's twice, Clinton had been counting the plumes of muzzle smoke, this would be the sixth ball they sent into the little gunboat since the American had given the order to fire as many minutes ago.

He watched the gunsmoke bloom again from the cannon's maw, and this time the gunboat's deck was swept as if by hail stones, but leaden hail stones as big as ripe grapes that pierced the thin steel bulwarks with pricks of sunlight and clawed chunks of wood from the maindeck, a deck that was now threaded with meandering scarlet snakes of blood and slick little puddles of it that spread from beneath the inert and crumpled figures that seemed to be scattered in purposeless profusion wherever Clinton looked.

Black Joke was taking merciless punishment, perhaps already more than she could afford, but they were close now, very close, seconds only left to go.

He could hear the cheering of the clipper's gun crews, the terrified wailing of the slaves who were huddled down in pathetic little heaps upon *Huron*'s decks, he could clearly hear the rumble of the sixteen-pounders run out against the straining tackles, and hear the shouted commands of the gun captains.

The girl at the rail still stood rigidly erect, staring white-faced across at him, and she had seen and recognized him now. She tried to raise a hand to wave a greeting, but the iron slave cuff on her wrist hampered the movement. As Clinton stepped forward the better to see her, something tugged sharply at the sleeve of his jacket and behind him Ferris gasped.

Clinton looked down at his arm, the sleeve was torn and the white lining showed in the tear – it was only then he realized that it was a musket ball fired from *Huron*'s crosstrees which might have struck him squarely had he not moved, and he turned quickly to Ferris.

The boy was pressing a wadded handkerchief to his chest, standing very upright.

'You are wounded, Mr. Ferris,' said Clinton. 'You may go below.'

'Thank you, sir,' wheezed Ferris. 'But I'd just as soon not miss the kill.' As he spoke, a droplet of blood formed in the corner of his mouth, and with a chilling little jolt, Clinton realized that the boy was probably mortally struck – blood in the mouth would almost certainly mean a lung hit.

'Carry on then, Mr. Ferris,' he said formally, and turned away. He must not let the doubts assail him now, he must not question whether his decision to board *Huron* had been correct, or if his execution of the attack had been properly carried out – or if he was responsible for those dismembered corpses that littered *Black Joke*'s deck, or for the dying lad who still determinedly kept erect. He must not let his resolve weaken.

Instead he slitted his eyes against the lowering sun that outlined *Huron*'s bare masts with golden haloes, and stared across at her with true hatred. It was then he realized suddenly that at last her bow cannons could no longer bear, the terrible battering of close-range grape shot was abating as they sailed into *Huron*'s stern quadrant.

'Bring her up two points,' he snapped, and the *Black Joke* cut in sharply under *Huron*'s stern. She loomed suddenly high above them and there was no more cannon fire from her while the clipper's tall hull shielded them from the gale. The sudden silence was ghostly, unnerving, as though the cannon fire had damaged his ears and he was rendered deaf.

Clinton shook off the sense of dreamlike unreality, and strode down the length of his deck.

'Up the jokers!' he shouted, and his crew rose from where they had been crouching under the fragile bulwark.

'You've shown you can take it, boys, now let's show those damned Yankees we can hand it out.'

'A tiger for Tongs!' yelled a voice, and suddenly they were all cheering, crowding the gunboat's side, so he had to cup his hands to his mouth to give the order.

'Helm a lee, let fly all!' and *Black Joke* spun up sharply under *Huron*'s counter, spilling her wind, while the seamen in her rigging stripped the canvas off her.

The two ships came together with a rending crackling crash, the gnashing of steel plate against timber and the shattering of glass in *Huron*'s sternlights.

A dozen of *Black Joke*'s sailors hurled the three-pronged grappling hooks high over the clipper's gunwale with the lines snaking up after them, and then heaved them up tight and made them fast to the portside cleats, and a swarm of seamen cheering wildly went up *Huron*'s stern, like a troop of vervet monkeys pursued into the trees by a hunting leopard.

'Take command, Mr. Denham,' Clinton shouted above the hubbub.

'Aye, aye, sir,' Denham's lips moved and he saluted as Clinton thrust his cutlass back into his scabbard and headed the next rush of his men, those who had been freed by the heaving-to of her sails.

The two hulls were working against each other as viciously as millstones, grinding and bumping, the gap opening and closing as the wind and the seas tore at them.

At *Huron*'s rail a dozen of her crew were hacking at the grappling lines with axes, the clunking of the blades into her timber blended with the popping of pistols and muskets as their mates blazed down on the swarm of seamen climbing up from the gunboat's deck.

One of *Black Joke*'s sailors climbed swiftly hand over hand, pushing off with his feet from the clipper's raked stern like a mountaineer, and he had almost reached the rail when an American sailor appeared above him, an axe held high and then sent thudding down into the woodwork, severing the line at a single blow.

The sailor dropped like a windblown fruit from the bough into the gap between the hulls. He floundered for an instant in the surging water and then the two ships came together again, with the shriek of rending timbers, chewing the man like a pair of monstrous jaws.

'More lines,' Clinton howled, and another grappling hook flew over his head, thrown by a stout British arm, and the line whipped around Clinton's shoulders.

He seized it, heaved once upon it to set the hook and then swung across the gap and his boots thudded on *Huron*'s stern. He had seen his seaman drop on the severed line, so he climbed with the strength and agility of terror and desperation, and only as he swung one leg over *Huron*'s rail did the battle rage seize him, the world changed colour before him, seen through a reddish haze of hatred and fury, hatred for the slave stink that rose to offend his soul and fury for the death and punishment that his ship and his seamen had suffered.

His cutlass sprang from its scabbard with metallic rasp, and there was a man rushing down upon him, and the man naked to the waist with a bulging hairy belly and thick heavily muscled arms. He was brandishing a double bladed axe above his head, and Clinton uncoiled his lanky frame as though it were the 'S' in an adder's body, straightening as it strikes. He drove the point of the cutlass through the axe man's furry silvered beard and the axe flew from his raised hands and went sliding away across the deck.

Clinton stood over the man he had killed, placed his foot on his chest and yanked the cutlass blade out of his throat. A bright scarlet carotid fountain followed the blade out, splattering Clinton's boot.

Half a dozen of his seamen had reached *Huron*'s deck ahead of Clinton, and without a word of command spoken, they bunched to guard the grappling lines over the stern, holding off *Huron*'s axe men with cutlass and point-blank pistol fire. Behind them, *Black Joke*'s men came swarming aboard, unopposed, surging forward, their cheers rising into a triumphant chorus.

'At 'em the Jokers!'

'All together, boys,' howled Clinton, the madness had taken complete hold of him now. There was no fear, no doubts, not even conscious thought. The madness was infectious, and his men howled with him, hunting as a pack like the wolf or the wild dog they swept across *Huron*'s deck to meet the wave of her own seamen rushing back from *Huron*'s bows.

The two waves of running, screaming men met just below the break of the poop, were transformed into a struggling mass of closely locked humanity, and their cries and curses mingled with the animal howl of terrified slaves. The pistols and muskets had all been discharged and there was no chance to reload. It was steel against steel now.

Black Joke's crew were battle-hardened, they had fought together fifty times in the past year, they had stormed glacis and barracoon and withstood fire and steel. They were blooded fighting men and proud of it.

Huron's men were commercial seamen, not warriors, most of them had never swung a cutlass nor fired a pistol at another man before, and the difference was evident almost immediately.

For a minute or less the closely engaged mass of men swayed and churned like the meeting of two strong currents at the tidal line of the ocean, and then *Black Joke*'s sailors began to forge forward.

'Up the Jokers!' They sensed their advantage.

'Hammer and tongs, boys. Give 'em hell!'

At only one point was the tide of British sailors checked, at the foot of *Huron*'s mainmast two men stood almost shoulder to shoulder.

Tippoo seemed immovable on the solid foundation of those massive bared legs. Like a Buddha carved from solid rock, he spurned the press of men around him, and their ranks parted and drew back.

His loin-cloth was drawn up between his legs, and his smooth belly bulged over it, again as hard as mountain rock, with the deep cyclops eye of his navel in its centre.

The golden thread of his embroidered gilet sparkled in the sunlight, and he held his great round head low on his shoulders as he swung a double-bladed axe as easily as though it were a lady's parasol, and the axe hissed fiercely at every stroke and *Black Joke*'s seamen gave him ground.

A pistol ball had nicked the scarred flesh of his bald head, and blood poured copiously from the shallow wound, turning his face to a glaring gory mask.

His wide toad's slit of a mouth opened as he laughed and shouted his contempt of the men who swarmed about him like pygmies about an ogre.

Beside him fought Mungo St. John. He had stripped off his blue jacket to free his sword arm, and his white linen shirt was open to the belt, the buttons torn from their threads by a clutching enemy hand. He had knotted a silk bandanna around his forehead to keep the sweat from running into his eyes, but sweat poured down his naked chest, and soaked through his shirt in patches. He had a sword in his right hand, a weapon with a plain silver steel guard and pommel, and he cut and parried and thrust without a break in the rhythm of his movements.

He was unmarked, the droplets of thrown blood that stained the full sleeve of his white shirt and which had been diluted by his sweat to a dirty brown, were not his blood.

'St. John!' Clinton called to him. They were both tall enough to look over the heads of the men between them, and they stared at each other for a moment.

Clinton's eyes were pale fanatical blue, and his lips white with fury. Mungo's expression was grave, thoughtful almost, and his gaze troubled, almost grieving, as though he knew he had lost his ship and that his life and the lives of most of his crew were forfeit.

'Fight me!' Clinton challenged him, his voice strident, ringing with triumph.

'Again?' Mungo asked, and the smile touched his lips fleetingly, then was gone.

Clinton shouldered his way roughly through the press of his own men. The last time it had been pistols, Mungo St. John's choice of weapon, but now Clinton had the familiar weight and balance of a naval cutlass in his right hand – his weapon, that he had first swung as a midshipman of fourteen years old, and the whip cord muscles in his long right arm were seasoned to the use of the blade, and every evolution in its use, every trick and subterfuge had been drilled until they were instinctive.

As they came together, Clinton feinted and cut backhanded and low, going for the hip to cripple and bring the man down. As the stroke was parried he felt the strenth of Mungo's sword arm for an instant before he disengaged, and switched his attack fluidly, going on the thrust leading with his right foot, a full stroke, and again the parry was strong and neat, but only just strong enough to hold the heavier, broader steel of the cutlass.

Those two brief contacts were enough for Clinton to judge his adversary and find his weakness, the wrist. He had felt it through the steel the way a skilled angler feels the weakness of the fish through line and rod – it was the wrist. St. John did not have the steely resilience that comes only from long and dedicated exercise and practice.

He saw the flare of alarm in St. John's strangely flecked eyes. The American, too, had felt his own inadequacy, and he knew he did not dare to draw out the encounter. He must try to end it swiftly, before the Englishman's superiority could wear him down.

With the swordsman's instinct, Clinton translated the little flicker of the golden yellow eyes. He knew that Mungo St. John was going on the attack, so that as the stroke came an instant later, he caught it on the broad curved blade of the cutlass; then he shifted his weight forward and, with a twist of his own iron wrist, prevented the disengagement, forcing St. John to roll his own wrist, the two blades milling across each other, the steel screeching sharply on a harsh abrasive note that set their teeth on edge. Clinton forced two and then three turns, the classic prolonged engagement from which Mungo St. John could not break without risking the thunderbolt of the riposte, and Clinton felt the other's wrist give under the strain. He lunged his weight against it, slid the guard of the cutlass high up the blade and used the rolling momentum of two blades and the leverage of his wrist and the curved guard of the cutlass to tear the hilt out of Mungo St. John's fingers.

The American's sword clattered to the deck between them, and Mungo St.

John threw up both hands, sucked in his belly and flung himself back against the mainmast in an attempt to avoid the thrust of the heavy cutlass blade which he knew would follow. In the fury of hatred that possessed Clinton, there was no thought of giving quarter to the man whom he had disarmed.

The thrust was full-blooded, driven by all the strength of wrist and arm, of shoulder and of Clinton's entire body weight, the killing stroke.

Clinton's whole being had been concentrated on the man before him, but now there was movement in the periphery of his vision. Tippoo had seen his Captain disarmed in the same instant that he had just completed a swing with the axe. He was off balance, it would take only a shaded instant to recover that balance, to raise the axe again, but that instant of time would be too long, for he saw the cutlass stroke already launched, and Mungo St. John trapped helplessly against the mainmast, his belly unprotected and his empty hands held high.

Tippoo opened his huge paws and let the axe go spinning away, like a cartwheel, and then he reached out and seized the gleaming cutlass blade in one bare hand.

He felt the blade run between his fingers and the terrible sting of the razor-sharp edge cutting down to the bone, still he heaved with all his weight, pulling the point away from the helpless man against the mainmast, deflecting it but unable to hold it for the tensed tendons in his lacerated fingers parted, and the blade ran on driven by the full weight of the tall platinum-headed naval officer.

Tippoo heard the point of the cutlass scrape over one of his ribs, and then a numbness filled his chest, and he felt the steel guard of the hilt strike his rib cage, a thud like that of a butcher's cleaver striking the chopping board, as the cutlass blade reached the limit of its travel.

Even the savage force of that blow was not enough to knock Tippoo off his feet, though it drove him back a pace. He stood solidly. His eyes screwed up into slits of skin, staring down at the blade that transfixed his chest, his bleeding hands still clutching the guard of the cutlass.

Only when Clinton leaned back and pulled the blade from his flesh, did Tippoo begin to sag slowly forward, his knees buckling, and he fell, his body slack and unresisting.

Clinton freed his cutlass blade, and it was thinly smeared along its full length, so that it blurred redly as he went on to the forehand cut, going once more for the man who was still pinned against the mainmast.

Clinton did not complete the stroke. He arrested it in mid-air, for Mungo St. John had been borne to the deck beneath a wave of struggling British seamen.

Clinton stepped back and rested on his cutlass. The fight was over, all around him the crew of *Huron* were throwing down their weapons.

'Quarter, for the love of God, quarter!'

They were dragging Mungo St. John to his feet, two seamen on each of his arms. He was unwounded, and Clinton's hatred was unabated. It took an enormous effort to prevent himself driving the point of the cutlass into Mungo's belly. Mungo was struggling to throw off the hands of the men who held him, straining to reach the massive body of the half-naked Moslem mate that lay at his feet.

'Let me free,' Mungo cried. 'I must see to my mate.' But they held him remorselessly, and Mungo looked up at Clinton.

'In the name of mercy,' he was pleading, and Clinton had never expected that. He took a deep ragged breath, the madness began to fade.

'I give you my word, sir,' Mungo was stricken, there was no mistaking his consuming grief, and Clinton hesitated. 'I am your prisoner,' Mungo told him. 'But this man is a friend—'

Clinton let out his breath slowly, and then he nodded to the seamen who held Mungo St. John.

'He has given his word.' And then to Mungo, 'You may have five minutes.' And the seamen released him. Mungo sank swiftly to his knees beside the inert figure.

'Old friend,' his whispered, as he tore the bandanna from off his own head and pressed it to the obscene little slit between Tippoo's ribs, 'old friend.'

Clinton turned away, slipping the cutlass back into its scabbard and he ran across the deck to the weather rail.

Robyn Ballantyne saw him coming and she strained towards him, unable to lift her arms for the slave cuffs that still bound her, but as he embraced her she put her face against his chest and her whole body trembled and shook as she sobbed.

'Oh, I give thanks to God—'

'Find the keys,' Clinton ordered brusquely, and as the cuffs fell from Robyn's wrists he snatched them up and handed them to one of his men. 'Use these on the slaver's Captain,' he ordered.

With that gesture, the last of his madness was gone.

'Forgive me, Doctor Ballantyne. We will speak later, but now there remains much to be done.' He bowed slightly and hurried away calling his orders.

'Carpenter's mate, go below immediately, I want the damage to this ship repaired at once. Bosun, disarm her crew, and have them sent below under lock and key with a guard on the companionway. Two men on her wheel, and a prize crew to work her. We'll sail her into Table Bay with the dawn, my boys, and there'll be prize money for your fancy.' His men were still drunk on excitement and battle lust, and they cheered him hoarsely as they rushed to obey the string of orders.

Rubbing her chafed wrists, Robyn picked her way across the littered deck and through the throngs of bustling British seamen as they hustled their captives and the still-chained files of slaves below.

Almost timorously she approached the ill-assorted pair at the foot of the ship's mainmast. Tippoo lay on his back, the mound of his naked belly pressing upwards like a woman in labour, the soiled bandanna hiding the wound. His eyes were wide, staring up at the mast that towered above him, and his lower jaw sagged.

Mungo St. John held the huge bald cannon-ball head on his lap. He sat with his legs thrust out straight ahead of him, his back against the mast and as Robyn approached, he closed the lids over Tippoo's staring eyes, one at a time, with his thumb. His head was bowed, his hands gentle as those of a mother with her infant as he lifted the bandanna and used it to bind up the sagging jaw.

Robyn went down on one knee and reached out to Tippoo's chest, to feel for the heart beat, but Mungo St. John raised his head and looked at her.

'Don't touch him,' he said softly.

'I am a doctor—'

'He no longer needs a doctor,' Mungo's voice was low and clear, 'especially if that doctor is you.'

'I am sorry.'

'Doctor Ballantyne,' he told her, 'you and I have no reason to apologize to each other, nor for that matter to speak to each other, ever again.'

She stared at him, and his face was cold and set, the eyes that stared back at her were devoid of all emotion, and it was in that moment she knew she had lost him, irrevocably and forever. She had thought that was what she wanted, but now the total knowledge left her devastated, without the strength to break her gaze, without the power of speech, and he stared back at her remotely, hard and unforgiving.

'Mungo,' she whispered, finding at last the strength and will to speak. 'I did not mean this to happen, as the Almighty is my witness, I did not mean it.'

Rough hands dragged Mungo St. John to his feet, so that Tippoo's dead head slipped from his lap and the skull thumped against the wooden deck.

'Captain's orders, me old cock, and you are to 'ave a taste of your own chains.'

Mungo St. John did not resist as the slave cuffs were fastened on his wrists and ankles. He stood quietly, balancing to *Huron*'s wild gale-driven lunges, looking about the fire-blackened ship with its decks covered with fallen and tangled rigging, stained with the blood of his crew, and though his expression did not change, there was a limitless grieving in his eyes.

'I am sorry,' whispered Robyn, still kneeling beside him. 'I am truly sorry.'

Mungo St. John glanced down at her, his wrists fastened at the small of his back by the cold black links of chain.

'Yes,' he nodded. 'So am I.' And a seaman thrust the palm of a horny hand between his shoulder blades, shoving him away towards the *Huron*'s forecastle, and the slave chains clanked about his ankles, as he staggered.

Within a dozen paces he had recovered his balance, and shrugged off the hands of his gaolers. He walked away with his back straight and his shoulders thrown back, and he did not look back at Robyn kneeling on the blood-stained deck.

Mungo St. John blinked at the brilliant sunlight as he followed the scarlet uniform coat and white cross-straps of his escort out into the courtyard of the Cape Town castle.

He had not seen the sun for five days; the cell in which he had been confined since he had been escorted ashore, had no external windows. Even in midsummer, the dark and chill of the past winter still lingered in the thick stone walls, and the air that entered through the single barred opening in the oaken door was stale and sullied by the gaol odours, the emanations from the dozen or so prisoners in the other cells.

Mungo filled his lungs now, and paused to look up at the ramparts of the castle. The British flag spread jauntily above the Katzenellenbogen redoubt, and beyond it the seagulls planed and volleyed on the fresh south-easterly wind. Force five and standing fair for a ship to clear the bay and make the open Atlantic, Mungo noted instinctively.

'This way please.' The young Subaltern who commanded the prison escort urged him on, but Mungo hesitated a moment longer. He could hear the murmurous song of the surf-break upon the beaches just beyond the castle walls, and from the ramparts he would have a clear view across Table Bay to Bloubergstrand on the far curve of the land.

Huron would be lying at anchor close inshore, still under her prize crew, and he longed for just a single glimpse of her, longed to know if the stern quarters were still smoke-blackened and gutted, or if O'Brien had been allowed to make the repairs to her hull and her steering-gear.

'If only Tippoo,' he began the thought, and then stopped himself, shivered briefly in the sunlight not only from the prison chill in his bones. He squared his shoulders and nodded to the Subaltern.

'Please lead the way,' he agreed, and the hobnailed boots of the escort gnashed the cobbles as they crossed the courtyard and then climbed the broad flight of steps to the Governor's suite of offices.

'Prisoner and escort, halt.'

Upon the portico a naval Lieutenant waited to receive them in his navy-blue and gold jacket, white breeches and cocked hat.

'Mr. St. John?' asked the Lieutenant. He was old for his rank, grey and worn-looking, with a weary disinterested eye, and Mungo nodded disdainfully.

The Lieutenant turned to the officer of the escort.

'Thank you, sir, I will take over from here,' and then to Mungo, 'Kindly follow me, Mr. St. John.'

He went in through the magnificent teak doors, carved by the master craftsman Anreith, into the Governor's antechamber with its polished floors of butter-coloured Cape deal, the high hewn rafters of the same timber, and with the thick walls hung with the treasures of the Orient gathered so assiduously by that great plunderer, the Dutch East India Company, which had in turn succumbed to an even more powerful predator.

The Lieutenant turned right, avoiding the brass and mahogany double doors of the Governor's private office to which Mungo had expected to be led; instead they went to a less pretentious single door set in a corner of the antechamber. At the Lieutenant's knock, a voice bade them enter, and they went in to a small office, clearly belonging to the Governor's Aide-de-camp whom Mungo had met before.

The Aide-de-camp sat at the plain oak desk facing the door, and he did not rise nor did he smile as Mungo entered. There were two other men in the room, both seated in armchairs.

'You know Admiral Kemp,' said the Aide-de-camp.

'Good morning, Admiral.'

Slogger Kemp inclined his head, but made no other gesture of recognition.

'And this is Sir Alfred Murray, Chief Justice of the Supreme Court of the Cape Colony.'

'Your servant, sir.' Mungo neither bowed nor smiled, and the judge leaned forward slightly in his armchair, both hands on the gold and amber handle of his walking-stick, and stared at Mungo from under beetling white brows.

Mungo was pleased that an hour previously his gaoler had provided him with hot water and razor and that he had been allowed to contract with the ex-slave Malay washerwoman who laundered for the castle's officers. His breeches were clean, his boots polished and his shirt crisply ironed and snowy white.

The Aide-de-camp picked up an official document from the desk before him.

'You are the Captain and owner of the clipper *Huron?*'

'I am.'

'The ship has been seized as prize by the Royal Navy under Articles Five to Eleven of the Treaty of Brussels, and presently lies under prize crew in British territorial waters.'

That did not need reply, and Mungo stood silently.

'The case has been considered by the Courts of Mixed Commission for the colony, under the presidency of the Chief Justice, and after hearing evidence from the Officer Commanding the Cape Squadron and others, the Court has determined that as the *Huron* was taken on the high seas, the Cape Colony has no jurisdiction in this matter. The Chief Justice has recommended to His Excellency, the Governor of Cape Colony, that the – ahem –' the Aide-de-camp paused significantly, 'the cargo of the clipper ship *Huron* be impounded by Her Majesty's Government, but that the clipper be released under the command and connaissance of its owner and that the owner be ordered to proceed with all despatch to place himself and his vessel under the jurisdiction of a properly constituted American Court and there to answer such charges as the President of the United States deems fit to bring against him.'

Mungo let out a long slow breath of relief. By God's breath, the Limeys were going to duck the issue! They were not about to chance the wrath of the new American President-elect. They had taken his slaves, eight hundred thousand dollars worth, but they were giving him back his ship and they were letting him go.

The Aide-de-camp went on reading without looking up.

'The Governor of Cape Colony has accepted the Court's recommendation and has so decreed. You are required to make your ship ready and safe for the voyage with all speed. In this respect, the officer commanding the Cape Squadron has agreed to place at your disposal the repair facilities of the Naval Station.'

'Thank you, Admiral.' Mungo turned to him, and Slogger Kemp's brows came together, his face mottled with passion, but his voice was very quiet and clear.

'Sixteen of my men dead, and as many maimed by your actions – sir – each day the smell of your filthy ship blows in to the windows of my office.' Admiral Kemp lifted himself with an effort from his armchair, and glared at Mungo St. John. 'I say rot you, and your thanks, Mr. St. John, and if I had my way we wouldn't be playing coy and cute with Mr. Lincoln, and I would have you swinging at the mainyard of a British man-of-war rather than sailing out of Table Bay in your stinking slaver.'

Slogger Kemp turned away and went to stare out of the single window, into the courtyard of the castle where his carriage waited. The Aide-de-camp seemed not to have noticed the outburst. He went on smoothly.

'A representative of the Royal Navy will accompany you aboard your ship and remain there until he determines that your vessel is seaworthy.'

The Aide-de-camp reached back and tugged the bell-pull behind his shoulder, and almost immediately the door opened and the naval Lieutenant reappeared.

'Just one other thing, Mr. St. John, the Governor has declared you to be an undesirable alien and you will immediately be arrested if you are ever again so rash as to set foot in Cape Colony.'

The tall figure came striding up the yellow gravel pathway, under the avenue of tall date palms, and Aletta Cartwright called gayly across the rose garden.

'Here comes your beau, Robyn. He is early today.'

Robyn straightened, the basket full of rose blossoms hanging on her arm, the wide straw hat shading her face from the flat glare of the Cape noonday. She watched Clinton coming towards her with the warmth of affection. He looked so gangling and boyish and impetuous, much too young ever to have led that rush of fighting seamen over *Huron*'s stern.

She had grown accustomed to him over the past weeks while she had been a guest once more of the Cartwright family, and each afternoon Clinton had walked up the hill from his modest lodgings in Waterkant Street. She looked forward to his visits, to their serious conversations after the frivolity and inconsequences of the Cartwright daughters. She found his admiration and his adoration flattering and deeply comforting. She felt it was something that would never change, something constant, a pole-star in the confusion and uncertainty that had been her life to this time.

She had learned to value his good sense, and his judgement. She had even allowed him to read the manuscript which was occupying most of her days now, and his comments and criticisms were always well based.

Then she had found that he filled a part of her life that had been empty for much too long. She needed something or someone to cherish and protect and comfort, somebody who needed her, someone on whom to lavish the bounty of her compassion.

'I do not believe I could ever live without you, my dear Doctor Ballantyne,' he had told her. 'I do not believe I could have endured this terrible period of my life without your help.'

She knew it was probably true, not just the hyperbole of the love-sick swain, and Robyn was entirely unable to resist the appeal of anybody in pain or in suffering.

It was many weeks since that heady day when *Black Joke* had sailed into Table Bay with her bulwarks and upperworks riddled with shot, her rigging in heroic and picturesque ruins, and her huge captive, blackened with smoke and limping under jury rigging and makeshift steering-gear, herded submissively under the menace of her carronades to an anchorage close inshore at Rogger Bay.

How the townsfolk had swarmed to the beachfront to gawk and exclaim, and how the other naval vessels in the bay had lined their rails and yards with seamen to cheer them in.

She had been standing at Clinton Codrington's side when the two contingents of naval officers from the Cape Squadron's headquarters had been rowed out to *Black Joke*'s anchorage. The first had been headed by a naval Commander, some years junior to Clinton.

'Captain Codrington,' he saluted. 'I am under orders to take over command of this ship from you forthwith, sir.'

Clinton accepted this without change of expression.

'Very well, sir, I will have my gear removed, and in the meantime we should complete the formalities, and I will introduce you to the remaining officers.'

When Clinton had shaken hands with his officers and his sea chest was at the entry port, the second longboat which had been lying on its oars a few yards off, now came alongside and a senior Captain came aboard. Everyone on *Black Joke*'s deck knew what was about to happen, and Denham stepped close to Clinton and said softly, 'Good luck, sir, you know you can count on me when the time comes.'

They both knew what he was referring to – the day they would meet again in the court-martial chamber.

'Thank you, Mr. Denham,' Clinton replied, then he went forward to where the senior Captain waited.

'Captain Codrington, it is my duty to inform you that you have been called upon by the Officer Commanding the Squadron to answer certain charges concerning the conduct of your duties. Therefore, you are to consider yourself under open arrest and to hold yourself in readiness to answer those charges as soon as a court-martial can be convened.'

'I understand, sir.'

Clinton saluted him, and then preceded him through the entry port and down the ladder into the waiting boat.

A single voice called out, 'Give 'em hell, Tongs.'

And suddenly they were all cheering, *Black Joke*'s crew lined her side and hung in her rigging and they cheered as though their throats would crack.

'Hammer and Tongs!' They tossed their caps on high.

'At 'em the Jokers!'

As the boat pulled away and rowed for the beach, Clinton Codrington stood in the stern and stared back at them without expression, and his bare head shone like a beacon fire in the sunlight.

That had been so many weeks ago. Still the opportunity of assembling enough senior officers in a small station like the Cape Colony to act as his judges might not occur for weeks still or even months.

Clinton had spent his nights in the cheap lodgings on Waterkant Street.

Ostracized by his brother officers, he had spent most of his days alone upon the waterfront staring out at the little gunboat that was making her repairs at the anchorage, and at the bar-masted clipper.

He had watched while the slaves were brought ashore from *Huron*'s holds, and their chains were struck off by a blacksmith from the castle. He had seen the bewildered blacks put their marks upon the indenture contracts, and then be led away by the Dutch and Huguenot farmers to learn their new duties, and he had wondered at this other fate to which he had delivered them.

Then in the afternoons he had climbed the hill to the Cartwright mansion set in its green and pleasant garden to pay his court to Robyn Ballantyne.

This day he was early, the noonday gun banged from the top of Signal Hill as Clinton came striding up the pathway, almost breaking into a run when he saw Robyn in the rose garden. He left the pathway and cut across the velvety green carpet of the lawn.

'Robyn! Doctor Ballantyne!' His voice was strange, and his pale eyes wild.

'What is it?' Robyn handed the basket to Aletta and hurried across the lawn to meet him.

'What is it?' she repeated with concern, and he seized both her hands in his.

'The slaver!' he was stuttering with the force of his emotion. 'The American – *Huron*!'

'Yes?' she demanded. 'Yes?'

'She is sailing – they are letting her go!'

It was a cry of outrage and despair, and Robyn froze, her face suddenly pale. 'I do not believe it.'

'Come!' said Clinton. 'I have a carriage at the gate.'

The coachman whipped the horses at the slope, with Clinton shouting to him to hurry still, and they came out on the crest of Signal Hill in a lather, with froth splattered on their chests and forelegs.

The moment the coach braked, Clinton jumped down and led Robyn to the side of the roadway facing down the steep hillside out over the bay. The tall American clipper slid silently and gracefully over a green sea that was speckled by the dancing white caps of the south-easterly wind.

As she cleared the low dark shape of Robben Island, she altered her heading a fraction and more sail bloomed upon her yards, white as the first flowers of spring. Silently, the man and the woman stared after the beautiful ship, and neither of them spoke as she merged with the milky sea fret, became a ghostly silhouette, and then quite suddenly was gone.

Still in silence the couple turned back and climbed into the waiting carriage, and neither of them spoke until it drew up before the gates of the Cartwright estate. Clinton looked at her face. It was completely bloodless, even her lips were ivory white and quivering with suppressed emotion.

'I know how you feel. After all we endured, to see that monster sail away. I share your distress,' he said quietly, but she shook her head once vehemently and then was still again.

'I have other news,' he told her when at last he judged she had recovered, and a little colour had returned to her cheeks.

'There is a Rear-Admiral on the passenger list of the East Indiaman that anchored in the bay yesterday. Slogger Kemp has asked him to make up the numbers at the court-martial. It begins tomorrow.'

Immediately she turned to face him, her expression softening with concern and alarm.

'Oh, I will pray for you every moment.' She reached out her hand impulsively, and he seized it with both of his, and clung to it.

It was as though the contact has loosened something in her that she had locked away tightly and at last the tears welled up in her hot dry eyes.

'Oh my dear Doctor Ballantyne,' Clinton whispered. 'Please do not fret for me.' But through the tears Robyn was still seeing the ghostly image of a tall and beautiful ship fading away into the pearly curtain of sea, fret, and the first sob shook her body.

The floor of the ballroom of Admiralty House was laid out in chessboard squares of black and white marble, and the human characters like chess pieces were ranged upon it haphazard, as though by the vagaries of a hard-fought end-game.

Robyn Ballantyne in skirt and blouse of sober green stood by the head of the board, a solitary queen, while arranged opposite her were the rooks of the legal council: two naval officers in full uniform and sword who were playing the roles of prosecutor and defender. They had been chosen arbitrarily, and neither of them relished the unfamiliar task.

They had isolated themselves from the rest of the company, and each of them busied himself with the sheaf of documents he carried, not looking at the man who they were destined to save or condemn, depending on the deliberations of the senior officers who were even now closeted behind the tall double doors at the far end of the ballroom.

The other witnesses, Denham of *Black Joke* bearing the ship's log under his arm, MacDonald the engineer hiding his grey coalstained hands behind his back, the colony's agent and Honorary Consul for the Sheikh of Omani, a prosperous Asian trader, were like the scattered pawns of the game around the edge of the board.

Only the officer accused and on trial for his life was not at rest. Captain Clinton Codrington paced at random about the ballroom floor, his heels clicking on the marble slabs, his cocked hat clasped under one arm, his pale blue eyes staring dead ahead. He paced without pattern, like the roving knight of the chess board.

The tension seemed to charge even this huge room, increasing rather than lessening with every minute. Only the two red-coated marines on each side of the double doors seemed totally unaffected.

They stood stolidly, their musket butts grounded beside the polished toe caps of their right boots, their expressions blank and their eyes fixed directly ahead.

Once Clinton stopped in front of Robyn and drew his watch.

'Fifty minutes,' he said.

'It could be hours yet,' she answered quietly.

'I can never thank you for the evidence you gave.'

'It was nothing but the truth.'

'Yes,' he agreed. 'But without it—' He broke off, and resumed his restless pacing.

The prosecuting officer who had attempted for the two previous days to damn him and send him to the gallows, glanced up at Clinton, and then hurriedly, almost guiltily, returned his eyes to the documents he held in his right hand. Robyn was the only one who watched him openly, and her eyes were dark with worry and concern, yet when he caught her eye again a few minutes later, she smiled at him bravely, trying to hide her doubts.

The four senior officers, before whom she had given her evidence, has listened attentively, but she had seen no warmth nor compassion in their faces.

'Madam,' Admiral Kemp had asked her at the end, 'is it true that you obtained a medical degree by impersonating a man, and if your answer is "Yes", would you not then believe us justified in doubting your allegiance to the truth?'

Robyn had seen the faces of the senior officers flanking Kemp harden, their eyes become remote. The Sultan's agent had been blatantly hostile, as the prosecuting officer had led him dutifully through a long list of aggressions and warlike acts against his master's sovereign territory and against his subjects.

Denham and MacDonald could only recite the facts, and their own repudiation of their Captain's orders was recorded in the ship's logbook.

The only thing that surprised Robyn was that the court had deliberated so long, and then she started involuntarily as, with a crash that echoed around the walls of the empty ballroom, the double doors were thrown open, and the two marine guards stamped to attention.

Through the doors she could see the naval officers seated down the length of the long dining-room table facing the ballroom. Their frogging and epaulettes gleamed with gold lace and Robyn was too far to be certain of their expressions. Though she took a step forward and craned to see the polished top of the table in front of the grim line of judges, she could not be certain of the hilt and point of the single weapon that lay upon it, and then her view was blocked by the backs of the three men who lined up facing the doors.

Clinton was in the centre with the prosecution and the defending officers flanking him. At a muttered command, they marched briskly through the open doors. The doors closed behind the trio, and still Robyn could not know which way the naval dirk on the table was pointing, whether it was in its sheath or if the blade was naked.

Clinton had explained to her the significance of that weapon. It was only placed upon the table when the judges had reached their decision. If the blade was sheathed, and if the hilt was pointed towards the prisoner when he entered, then the judgement was 'not guilty'. When the bare blade was pointed towards him, then he knew that the wrath of the service was about to descend upon him – and he might be called to pay his penalty upon the flogging grating, or upon the gallows itself.

Clinton kept his gaze fixed upon a point above Admiral Kemp's head, while the doors were banged closed behind him, and he and the officers flanking him came to attention five paces from the long polished table behind which sat his judges.

Only then did he allow himself to glance down at the dagger upon the table top. The bare blade glinted a bluish-silver in the late sunlight that slanted in from the tall french windows, and the bright point was aimed at Clinton's stomach.

He felt the cold drive of despair in his guts, as though the dagger had been plunged through them. The shock of the injustice of the verdict, the disbelief that his whole life had been brought down at a single stroke, the shame and disgrace of a career shattered and a reputation indelibly besmirched, left him numbed and blind to all but the wicked blade before him, and deaf to all but the voice of Admiral Kemp.

'Guilty of flagrant disregard of the orders of his superior officer.'

'Guilty of acts of piracy upon the high seas.'

'Guilty of destroying the property of the subjects of a friendly power.'

'Guilty of flouting the terms of a treaty between her Britannic Majesty's Government and the Sultan of the Omani Arabs.'

It must be death, Clinton realized, the verdict was too detailed, the list of his transgressions too long and his guilt too serious. It must be death by the noose.

He lifted his eyes from the accusing weapon, and he stared out of the french windows beyond his judges. The high stock of his uniform collar felt as tight as the hangman's noose as he tried to swallow.

'I have never feared death, Lord,' he prayed silently. 'There is only one thing I will regret – that I must leave the woman that I love.'

To be deprived of honour, and of life was sufficient punishment, but to lose his love as well was the final injustice.

'The Court has deliberated at length on the sentence,' Admiral Kemp paused and shot a sideways glance at a lean, tanned and silver-haired Rear-Admiral beside him, the passenger from the visiting East Indiaman, 'and has heard and been swayed by the eloquent arguments of Admiral Reginald Curry.'

He paused again and puffed out his lips, indicating clearly that he did not agree with those eloquent arguments, before going on.

'The sentence of this Court is that the prisoner be stripped of all rank, privileges and pay and that the Queen's Commission which he holds shall be withdrawn, and that he be *dishonourably* discharged from the naval service.'

Clinton steeled himself, the stripping of rank and discharge would precede the main body of the sentence.

'Furthermore,' Kemp paused and cleared his throat. 'Furthermore it is the sentence of the Court that the prisoner be taken from here to the castle and that he be there—'

The castle was the place of execution, the gallows would be erected on the parade ground before the main gates.

'That he be there imprisoned for a period of one year.'

The judges were standing up, were filing out of the room. As the lean silver-haired Admiral came level with Clinton, a small conspiratorial smile touched his lips, and for the first time Clinton realized that it was not death.

'A year,' said the Lieutenant who had prosecuted, as the door closed, 'not a flogging, nor a hanging – damned generous, I'd say.'

'Congratulations.' Clinton's defending officer was grinning incredulously. 'It was Curry, of course, he commanded the west coast anti-slavery squadron himself. What a stroke of luck to have him on the Board.'

Pale, voiceless, swaying slightly on his feet, Clinton was still staring blindly through the open windows.

'Come on, my dear fellow, a year will soon be past,' the defending officer touched his arm, 'and after that, no more bully beef and hard bread – do pull yourself together.'

Twenty miles a day since leaving grandfather Moffat's mission-station at Kuruman, Zouga had pushed the mules and his servants hard all the way, and now at the crest of the pass he reined in the tall sway-backed mule and stared out across the sweeping panorama of the Cape peninsula.

Directly below him was that strange pale hill of smooth rock, Die Paarl as the Dutch burghers had named it, 'the Pearl', and it shone with an almost translucent lustre in the Cape sunlight of high summer.

Beyond that the wheatlands and vineyards dotted the flat land that stretched away to the Paarde Berg, the Horse Mountains, where once the wild mountain zebra had roamed, and the Tyger Berg. The leopard to the Dutch burghers was a tiger and the zebra was a horse.

'Nearly home now, Sergeant,' Zouga called to Jan Cheroot.

'Just look at that—' The little Hottentot pointed to the smoky blue flat-topped mountain that stood up tall and massive against the southern horizon.

'We will be there before dark tomorrow night.'

Jan Cheroot puckered his lips and blew a kiss towards it. 'Pull the cork and tell the Cape Town ladies that my mama didn't call me big cheroot for nothing.'

His mule flicked its long hairy ears to the sound of his voice and gave a little half-hearted buck. 'You feeling it too, you old thunder!' Jan Cheroot chuckled. 'Let's go then!' and he whipped the animal up and went clattering away down the steep and rocky roadway.

Zouga stayed to watched the battered little two-wheeled Cape cart follow him at a more sedate pace, carrying its precious burden of ivory and sculptured green soapstone, as it had for a thousand miles and more.

It was a month before Robyn was allowed to pay her first visit to the castle. After the guard at the gates inspected her pass, she was led to a small whitewashed guard room, devoid of all furniture except three high-back uncushioned chairs.

She remained standing for ten minutes before the low door opposite her was opened and Clinton stooped through it. He stopped, facing her, and she was struck instantly by the prison pallor of his skin. His deepwater tan had faded to a tobacco stain of yellow, and the roots of his hair, no longer bleached by salt and strong sunlight, had darkened.

He looked older, tired and dejected.

'You at least have not deserted me in my disgrace,' he said simply.

The Subaltern of the guard took the third chair and tried to look as though he was not listening to their conversation. Robyn and Clinton sat facing each other stiffly, on the uncomfortable chairs, and their conversation was at first as stilted, a polite series of enquiries after each other's health.

Then Robyn asked, 'Have you received the newspapers?'

'Yes. The warder has been good to me.'

'Then you have read what the new American President has promised at his inauguration.'

'Lincoln was always a staunch enemy of the trade,' Clinton nodded.

'He has granted the ships of the Royal Navy the right of search at last.'

'And six of the Southern States have seceded already,' Clinton told her grimly. 'There will be fighting, if he tries to force it.'

'It's so unfair,' Robyn cried. 'Just a few short weeks and you would have been a hero instead of a—' she broke off with her hand to her mouth, 'I am sorry, Captain Codrington.'

'Captain no longer,' he said.

'I feel so much to blame – had I not send that letter—'

'You are so kind, so good,' then he blurted abruptly, 'and so beautiful that I can scarcely bear to look at you.'

Robyn found herself blushing hotly, and she glanced at the listening guard officer. He was studying the rough plaster ceiling of the cell.

'Do you know what I thought when I entered the chamber and saw the dirk pointed at me?' Clinton went on, and she shook her head. 'I thought I was going to lose you. That they would hang me and I would never see you again.' His voice was shaking with such emotion, that the listening officer rose to his feet.

'Doctor Ballantyne, I will leave the room for five minutes,' he said. 'Do I have your word that you will not attempt to pass a weapon or a tool to the prisoner in my absence?'

Robyn nodded jerkily and whispered, 'Thank you.'

The moment the door closed, Clinton launched himself across the gap between them and dropped to his knees before Robyn. He encircled her waist with both arms and pressed his cheek to her bosom.

'But now I have nothing to offer you, I have nothing to share with you but my disgrace.'

Robyn found herself stroking his hair as though he were a child.

'Soon I will go back to that beautiful land below the Zambezi river. I know now that is where my destiny lies,' she said quietly. 'To minister to the souls and the bodies of those who live there.'

She paused a moment and looked down fondly on the dense pale locks of his hair.

'You say you have nothing to offer, nothing to share, but I have something to offer you, and to share with you.'

He raised his head and looked up at her questioningly, hope starting to dawn in his pale sapphire eyes.

'Will you not offer yourself to be ordained in God's service as a missionary, and come with me into the wilderness, to the land of Zambezia?'

'To share my life with you, and with God.' His voice was husky and choked. 'I never dreamed I was worthy of such an honour.'

'The fellow is a prig,' said Zouga firmly. 'And, damn me, but now he is a gaol-bird to boot. Neither of you will be able to hold up your heads in society.'

'He has a true and noble spirit, and now he has found his true calling in God's service,' Robyn replied hotly. 'Neither of us intend spending much of our time in society, you may be certain of that.'

Zouga shrugged and smiled. 'Of course, that is your affair. At least he has made a pretty packet of prize money which they can't take away from him.'

'I assure you that money had nothing to do with my decision.'

'I will believe that.' Zouga's smile infuriated her, but before she could find a scathing enough retort, he turned away and sauntered the length of the long veranda under the trellised vines and stood with his hands thrust into his pockets, staring out across the Cartwright's gardens to the far glimpses of blue bay seen through the oaks and the rustling palms.

Robyn's anger subsided and gave way to regret. It seemed now that the two of them must always be squabbling, their desires and their motives always directly opposed.

At first her relief at his safety had been almost as strong as her sisterly delight at seeing him again. She had barely recognized him as he rode the bony sway-backed mule up the path to the Cartwright mansion. It was only when he dismounted and lifted the stained old hat from his head that she screamed with joy, leapt up from the luncheon table and ran down off the terrace to hug him.

He was so lean and hard and bronzed, and somehow endowed with new authority, charged with purpose and presence, that she glowed with pride as he recounted his experiences and all the company hung avidly on each word.

'He is like a Greek god!' Aletta Cartwright had whispered to Robyn, which was not an original description – but then Aletta did not run much to original thought, and Robyn had to agree that in this case it was accurate.

She had followed his description of the land of the Matabele, and of the long trek southward with all her attention, asking such acute questions that Zouga had asked sharply,

'I hope that you will not be using any of this in your own account, Sissy?'

'Of course not,' she assured him, but still that had been the first sour note, and he had not spoken further of his adventures, except to give her the greetings and news of their grandfather, Robert Moffat at Kuruman.

'You would never believe that he was seventy-five years old this past December. He is so bright and alive that he has just finished translating the Bible into the

Sechuan language. He gave me every courtesy and help, and it was he who arranged for mules and for the cart which made the last portion of the journey so much easier. He remembered you as a little girl of three years old, and he has received your letters and gave me this in reply.' It was a thick packet. 'He tell me that you have asked him about leading a missionary expedition to Zambezia or Matabeleland.'

'That is correct.'

'Sissy, I do not think that a woman on her own,' he had begun, but she had forestalled him.

'I shall not be alone. Captain Clinton Codrington has decided to seek ordination as a missionary, and I have consented to become his wife.'

That had led to the explosion which had once more marred their relationship. As her anger faded, she made another determined effort to avert the new clash of temperament.

'Zouga,' she went down the length of the terrace and took his arm. 'I would be grateful if you would consent to give me away at the wedding.'

Some of the hardness went out of his arm as his muscles relaxed.

'When will that be, Sissy?'

'Not for seven months. Clinton has that much longer of his sentence.'

Zouga shook his head. 'I will not be here. I have booked passage on the P. & O. steamer that sails for home at the beginning of next month.' They were both silent, and then Zouga went on, 'But I wish you joy and happiness – and I apologize for the remark I made about your future husband.'

'I understand.' She squeezed his arm. 'He is a different kind of man from you.'

Zouga almost exclaimed, 'Thank God for that,' but caught the blasphemy before it reached his lips, and again they were silent.

Zouga was considering the problem that had concerned him so intimately since his return to Cape Town – how to find out from Robyn what she had written in her manuscript, and if possible to influence her into amending those portions of it which might offend the family reputation.

Now that he had learned that she would not be returning to England, the natural opportunity had presented itself.

'Sissy, if your manuscript is prepared, I will be happy to take it with me and to make certain that it is delivered safely to Oliver Wicks.'

The voyage to England would give Zouga ample opportunity to study Robyn's work, and if the delivery was delayed for a month or so after his arrival, then Zouga's own published account of the expedition would skim the cream off the pool of interest and critical literary attention.

'Oh, did I not mention it to you?' Robyn lifted her chin, and her smile was spiced with a little spiteful relish. 'I sent my manuscript on the mail steamer a month before your arrival here. It will be in London already, and I should not be surprised if Mr. Wicks has not published it already. I expect he will have sent the reviews, and we will have them on the next mailship.'

Zouga jerked his arm out of her grip, and his eyes were steely as he glared down at her.

'I really should have mentioned it,' she added sweetly. His reaction confirmed her suspicions, and she knew that what last small chance they had was finished. From now on they would be enemies, and somehow she knew that the centre of their enmity would always be the land and peoples of that faraway country between two great rivers which Zouga had named Zambezia.

At the end of the Woodstock road, on the bank of the Liesbeeck river, not far from the domed roof of the Royal Astronomical Observatory, stands the Cartwright warehouse. It is a rambling white-washed building of unburnt Kimberley brick with a corrugated iron roof.

Against the rear wall of the main storeroom stood three articles left there in storage and for later collection by Major Morris Zouga Ballantyne, presently on passage aboard the Peninsular and Orient Steamship S.S. *Bombay* from India to the Pool of London. The three bulky articles were almost completely screened by the bays and hillocks of bales and crates, and of barrels and bags, which reached almost to the high ceiling.

The two huge elephant tusks formed a perfect frame with their curved yellow ivories for the third package. The carved soapstone figure was still contained in its protective covering of plaited elephant grass and twisted bark rope. It stood upright on its wide heavy base, and it was merely chance that it faced towards the north.

The grass covering had been torn away from the head by careless handling and long months of travel on the shoulders of porters and on the buckboards of an unsprung Cape cart.

The cruel proud head of the bird of prey protruded from its wrappings. The stony sightless eyes stared across forests and mountain and desert, one thousand five hundred miles, to a walled and ruined city and the words of the Umlimo's prophecy seemed to hover in the air above the graven head of the bird like living things.

'The white eagle has stooped on the stone falcons and cast them to earth. Now the eagle shall lift them up again and they will fly afar. There shall be no peace in the kingdoms of the Mambos or the Monomatapas until they return, or the white eagle will war with the black bull until the stone falcons return to roost.'

THE
DARK OF
THE SUN

Chapter One

'I don't like the idea,' announced Wally Hendry, and belched. He moved his tongue round his mouth getting the taste of it before he went on. 'I think the whole idea stinks like a ten-day corpse.' He lay sprawled on one of the beds with a glass balanced on his naked chest and he was sweating heavily in the Congo heat.

'Unfortunately your opinion doesn't alter the fact that we are going.' Bruce Curry went on laying out his shaving tackle without looking up.

'You should-a told them to keep it, told them we were staying here in Elisabethville – why didn't you tell them that, hey?' Hendry picked up his glass and swallowed the contents.

'Because they pay me not to argue.' Bruce spoke without interest and looked at himself in the fly-spotted mirror above the wash-basin. The face that looked back was sun-darkened with a cap of close-cropped black hair; soft hair that would be unruly and inclined to curl if it were longer. Black eyebrows slanting upwards at the corners, green eyes with a heavy fringe of lashes and a mouth which could smile as readily as it could sulk. Bruce regarded his good looks without pleasure. It was a long time since he had felt that emotion, a long time since his mouth had either smiled or sulked. He did not feel the old tolerant affection for his nose, the large slightly hooked nose that rescued his face from prettiness and gave him the air of a genteel pirate.

'Jesus!' growled Wally Hendry from the bed. 'I've had just about a gutsful of this nigger army. I don't mind fighting – but I don't fancy going hundreds of miles out into the bush to play nursemaid to a bunch of bloody refugees.'

'It's a hell of a life,' agreed Bruce absently and spread shaving-soap on his face. The lather was very white against his tan. Under a skin that glowed so healthily that it appeared to have been freshly oiled, the muscles of his shoulders and chest changed shape as he moved. He was in good condition, fitter than he had been for many years, but this fact gave him no more pleasure than had his face.

'Get me another drink, André.' Wally Hendry thrust his empty glass into the hand of the man who sat on the edge of the bed.

The Belgian stood up and went across to the table obediently.

'More whisky and less beer in this one,' Wally instructed, turned once more to Bruce and belched again. 'That's what I think of the idea.'

As André poured Scotch whisky into the glass and filled it with beer Wally hitched around the pistol in its webbing holster until it hung between his legs.

'When are we leaving?' he asked.

'There'll be an engine and five coaches at the goods yard first thing tomorrow morning. We'll load up and get going as soon as possible.' Bruce started to shave, drawing the razor down from temple to chin and leaving the skin smooth and brown behind it.

'After three months of fighting a bunch of greasy little Gurkhas I was looking forward to a bit of fun – I haven't even had a pretty in all that time – now the second day after the cease-fire and they ship us out again.'

'C'est la guerre,' muttered Bruce, his face twisted in the act of shaving.

'What's that mean?' demanded Wally suspiciously.

'That's war,' Bruce translated.

'Talk English, Bucko.'

It was the measure of Wally Hendry that after six months in the Belgian Congo he could neither speak nor understand a single word of French.

There was silence again, broken only by the scraping of Bruce's razor and the small metallic sounds as the fourth man in the hotel room stripped and cleaned his FN rifle.

'Have a drink, Haig,' Wally invited him.

'No, thanks.' Michael Haig glanced up, not trying to conceal his distaste as he looked at Wally.

'You're another snotty bastard – don't you want to drink with me, hey? Even the high-class Captain Curry is drinking with me. What makes you so goddam special?'

'You know that I don't drink.' Haig turned his attention back to his weapon, handling it with easy familiarity. For all of them the ugly automatic rifles had become an extension of their own bodies. Even while shaving Bruce had only to drop his hand to reach the rifle propped against the wall, and the two men on the bed had theirs on the floor beside them.

'You don't drink!' chuckled Wally. 'Then how did you get that complexion, Bucko? How come your nose looks like a ripe plum?'

Haig's mouth tightened and the hands on his rifle stilled.

'Cut it out, Wally,' said Bruce without heat.

'Haig don't drink,' crowed Wally, and dug the little Belgian in the ribs with his thumb, 'get that, André! He's a tee-bloody-total! My old man was a teetotal also; sometimes for two, three months at a time he was a teetotal, and then he'd come home one night and sock the old lady in the clock so you could hear her teeth rattle from across the street.'

His laughter choked him and he had to wait for it to clear before he went on.

'My bet is that you're that kind of teetotal, Haig. One drink and you wake up ten days later; that's it, isn't it? One drink and – pow! – the old girl gets it in the chops and the kids don't eat for a couple of weeks.'

Haig laid the rifle down carefully on the bed and looked at Wally with his jaws clenched, but Wally had not noticed. He went on happily.

'André, take the whisky bottle and hold it under Old Teetotal Haig's nose. Let's watch him slobber at the mouth and his eyes stand out like a pair a dog's balls.'

Haig stood up. Twice the age of Wally – a man in his middle fifties, with grey in his hair and the refinement of his features not completely obliterated by the marks that life had left upon them. He had arms like a boxer and a powerful set to his shoulders. 'It's about time you learned a few manners, Hendry. Get on your feet.'

'You wanta dance or something? I don't waltz – ask André. He'll dance with you –, won't you, André?'

Haig was balanced on the balls of his feet, his hands closed and raised slightly. Bruce Curry placed his razor on the shelf above the basin, and moved quietly round the table with soap still on his face to take up a position from which he could intervene. There he waited, watching the two men.

'Get up, you filthy guttersnipe.'

'Hey, André, get that. He talks pretty, hey? He talks real pretty.'

'I'm going to smash that ugly face of yours right into the middle of the place where your brain should have been.'

'Jokes! This boy is a natural comic.' Wally laughed, but there was something wrong with the sound of it. Bruce knew then that Wally was not going to fight. Big arms and swollen chest covered with ginger hair, belly flat and hard-looking, thick-necked below the wide flat-featured face with its little Mongolian eyes; but Wally wasn't going to fight. Bruce was puzzled: he remembered the night at the road bridge and he knew that Hendry was no coward, and yet now he was not going to take up Haig's challenge.

Mike Haig moved towards the bed.

'Leave him, Mike.' André spoke for the first time, his voice soft as a girl's. 'He was only joking. He didn't mean it.'

'Hendry, don't think I'm too much of a gentleman to hit you because you're on your back. Don't make that mistake.'

'Big deal,' muttered Wally. 'This boy's not only a comic, he's a bloody hero also.'

Haig stood over him and lifted his right hand with the fist, bunched like a hammer, aimed at Wally's face.

'Haig!' Bruce hadn't raised his voice but its tone checked the older man. 'That's enough,' said Bruce.

'But this filthy little—'

'Yes, I know,' said Bruce. 'Leave him!' With his fist still up Mike Haig hesitated, and there was no movement in the room. Above them the corrugated iron roof popped loudly as it expanded in the heat of the Congo midday, and the only other sound was Haig's breathing. He was panting and his face was congested with blood.

'Please, Mike,' whispered André. 'He didn't mean it.'

Slowly Haig's anger changed to disgust and he dropped his hand, turned away and picked up his rifle from the other bed.

'I can't stand the smell in this room another minute. I'll wait for you in the truck downstairs, Bruce.'

'I won't be long,' agreed Bruce as Mike went to the door.

'Don't push your luck, Haig,' Wally called after him. 'Next time you won't get off so easily.'

In the doorway Mike Haig swung quickly, but, with a hand on his shoulder, Bruce turned him again.

'Forget it, Mike,' he said, and closed the door after him.

'He's just bloody lucky that he's an old man,' growled Wally. 'Otherwise I'd have fixed him good.'

'Sure,' said Bruce. 'It was decent of you to let him go.' The soap had dried on his face and he wet his brush to lather again.

'Yeah, I couldn't hit an old bloke like that, could I?'

'No.' Bruce smiled a little. 'But don't worry, you frightened the hell out of him. He won't try it again.'

'He'd better not!' warned Hendry. 'Next time I'll kill the old bugger.'

No, you won't, thought Bruce, you'll back down again as you have just done, as you've done a dozen times before. Mike and I are the only ones who can make you do it; in the same way as an animal will growl at its trainer but cringe away when he cracks the whip. He began shaving again.

The heat in the room was unpleasant to breathe; it drew the perspiration out of them and the smell of their bodies blended sourly with stale cigarette smoke and liquor fumes.

'Where are you and Mike going?' André ended the long silence.

'We're going to see if we can draw the supplies for this trip. If we have any luck we'll take them down to the goods yard and have Ruffy put an armed guard on them overnight,' Bruce answered him, leaning over the basin and splashing water up into his face.

'How long will we be away?'

Bruce shrugged. 'A week – ten days'. He sat on his bed and pulled on one of his jungle boots. 'That is, if we don't have any trouble.'

'Trouble, Bruce?' asked André.

'From Msapa Junction we'll have to go two hundred miles through country crawling with Baluba.'

'But we'll be in a train,' protested André. 'They've only got bows and arrows, they can't touch us.'

'André, there are seven rivers to cross – one big one – and bridges are easily destroyed. Rails can be torn up.' Bruce began to lace the boot. 'I don't think it's going to be a Sunday school picnic.'

'Christ. I think the whole thing stinks,' repeated Wally moodily. 'Why are we going anyway?'

'Because,' Bruce began patiently, 'for the last three months the entire population of Port Reprieve has been cut off from the rest of the world. There are women and children with them. They are fast running out of food and the other necessities of life.' Bruce paused to light a cigarette, and then went on talking as he exhaled. 'All around them the Baluba tribe is in open revolt, burning, raping and killing indiscriminately. As yet they haven't attacked the town but it won't be very long until they do. Added to which there are rumours that rebel groups of Central Congolese troops and of our own forces have formed themselves into bands of heavily-armed *shufta*. They also are running amok through the northern part of the territory. Nobody knows for certain what is happening out there, but whatever it is you can be sure it's not very pretty. We are going to fetch those people in to safety.'

'Why don't the U.N. people send out a plane?' asked André.

'No landing field.'

'Helicopters?'

'Out of range.'

'For my money the bastards can stay there,' grunted Wally. 'If the Balubas fancy a little man steak, who are we to do them out of a meal? Every man's entitled to eat and as long as it's not me they're eating, more power to their teeth, say I.' He placed his foot against André's back and straightened his leg suddenly, throwing the Belgian off the bed on to his knees.

'Go and get me a pretty.'

'There aren't any, Wally. I'll get you another drink.' André scrambled to his feet and reached for Wally's empty glass, but Wally's hand dropped on to his wrist.

'I said *pretty*, André, not *drink*.'

'I don't know where to find them, Wally.' André's voice was desperate. 'I don't know what to say to them even.'

'You're being stupid, Bucko. I might have to break your arm.' Wally twisted the wrist slowly. 'You know as well as I do that the bar downstairs is full of them. You know that, don't you?'

'But what do I say to them?' André's face was contorted with the pain of his twisted wrist.

'Oh, for Christ's sake, you stupid bloody frog-eater – just go down and flash a banknote. You don't have to say a dicky bird.'

'You're hurting me, Wally.'

'No? You're kidding!' Wally smiled at him, twisting harder, his slitty eyes smoky from the liquor, and Bruce could see he was enjoying it. 'Are you going, Bucko? Make up your mind – get me a pretty or get yourself a broken arm.'

'All right, if that's what you want. I'll go. Please leave me, I'll go,' mumbled André.

'That's what I want.' Wally released him, and he straightened up massaging his wrist.

'See that she's clean and not too old. You hear me?'

'Yes, Wally. I'll get one.' André went to the door and Bruce noticed his expression. It was stricken beyond the pain of a bruised wrist. What lovely creatures they are, thought Bruce, and I am one of them and yet apart from them. I am the watcher, stirred by them as much as I would be by a bad play. André went out.

'Another drink, Bucko?' said Wally expansively 'I'll even pour you one.'

'Thanks,' said Bruce, and started on the other boot. Wally brought the glass to him and he tasted it. It was strong, and the mustiness of the whisky was ill-matched with the sweetness of the beer, but he drank it.

'You and I,' said Wally, 'we're the shrewd ones. We drink 'cause we want to, not 'cause we have to. We live like we want to live, not like other people think we should. You and I got a lot in common, Bruce. We should be friends, you and I. I mean us being so much alike.' The drink was working in him now, blurring his speech a little.

'Of course we are friends – I count you as one of my very dearest, Wally.' Bruce spoke solemnly, no trace of sarcasm showing.

'No kidding?' Wally asked earnestly. 'How's that, hey? Christ, I always thought you didn't like me. Christ, you never can tell, isn't that right? You just never can tell,' shaking his head in wonder, suddenly sentimental with the whisky. 'That's really true? You like me. Yeah, we could be buddies. How's that, Bruce? Every guy needs a buddy. Every guy needs a back stop.'

'Sure,' said Bruce. 'We're buddies. How's that, hey?'

'That's on, Bucko!' agreed Wally with deep feeling, *and I feel nothing*, thought Bruce, *no disgust, no pity – nothing. That way you are secure; they cannot disappoint you, they cannot disgust you, they cannot sicken you, they cannot smash you up again.*

They both looked up as André ushered the girl into the room. She had a sexy little pug face, painted lips – ruby on amber.

'Well done, André,' applauded Wally, looking at the girl's body. She wore high heels and a short pink dress that flared into a skirt from her waist but did not cover her knees.

'Come here, cookie.' Wally held out his hand to her and she crossed the room without hesitation, smiling a bright professional smile. Wally drew her down beside him on to the bed.

André went on standing in the doorway. Bruce got up and shrugged into his camouflage battle-jacket, buckled on his webbing belt and adjusted the holstered pistol until it hung comfortably on his outer thigh.

'Are you going?' Wally was feeding the girl from his glass.

'Yes.' Bruce put his slouch hat on his head; the red, green and white Katangese sideflash gave him an air of artificial gaiety.

'Stay a little – come on, Bruce.'

'Mike is waiting for me.' Bruce picked up his rifle.

'Muck him. Stay a little, we'll have some fun.'

'No, thanks.' Bruce went to the door.

'Hey, Bruce. Take a look at this.' Wally tipped the girl backwards over the bed, he pinned her with one arm across her chest while she struggled playfully and with the other hand he swept her skirt up above her waist.

'Take a good look at this and tell me you still want to go!'

The girl was naked under the skirt, her lower body shaven so that her plump little sex pouted sulkily.

'Come on, Bruce,' laughed Wally. 'You first. Don't say I'm not your buddy.'

Bruce glanced at the girl, her legs scissored and her body wriggled as she fought with Wally. She was giggling.

'Mike and I will be back before curfew. I want this woman out of here by then,' said Bruce.

There is no desire, he thought as he looked at her, *that is all finished*. He opened the door.

'Curry!' shouted Wally. 'You're a bloody nut also. Christ, I thought you were a man. Jesus Christ! You're as bad as the others. André, the doll boy. Haig, the rummy. What's with you Bucko? It's women with you, isn't it? You're a bloody nut-case also!'

Bruce closed the door and stood alone in the passage. The taunt had gone through a chink in his armour and he clamped his mind down on the sting of it, smothering it.

It's all over. She can't hurt me any more. He thought with determination, remembering her, the woman, not the one in the room he had just left but the other one who had been his wife.

'The bitch,' he whispered, and then quickly, almost guiltily, 'I do not hate her. There is no hatred and there is no desire.'

Chapter Two

The lobby of the Hotel Grand Leopold II was crowded. There were gendarmes carrying their weapons ostentatiously, talking loudly, lolling against walls and over the bar; women with them, varying in colour from black through to pastel brown, some already drunk; a few Belgians still with the stunned disbelieving eyes of the refugee, one of the women crying as she rocked her child on her lap; other white men in civilian clothes but with the alertness about them and the quick restless eyes of the adventurer, talking quietly with Africans in business suits; a group of journalists at one table in damp shirtsleeves, waiting and watching with the patience of vultures. And everybody sweated in the heat.

Two South African charter pilots hailed Bruce from across the room.

'Hi, Bruce. How about a snort?'

'Dave. Carl.' Bruce waved. 'Big hurry now – tonight perhaps.'

'We're flying out this afternoon.' Carl Engelbrecht shook his head. 'Back next week.'

'We'll make it then,' Bruce agreed, and went out of the front door into the Avenue du Kasai. As he stopped on the sidewalk the white-washed buildings bounced the glare into his face. The naked heat made him wince and he felt fresh sweat start out of his body beneath his battle-suit. He took the dark glasses from his top pocket and put them on as he crossed the street to the Chev three-tonner in which Mike Haig waited.

'I'll drive, Mike.'

'Okay.' Mike slid across the seat and Bruce stepped up into the cab. He started the truck north down the Avenue du Kasai.

'Sorry about that scene, Bruce.'

'No harm done.'

'I shouldn't have lost my temper like that.'

Bruce did not answer, he was looking at the deserted buildings on either side. Most of them had been looted and all of them were pock-marked with shrapnel from the mortar bursts. At intervals along the sidewalk were parked the burnt out bodies of automobiles looking like the carapaces of long-dead beetles.

'I shouldn't have let him get through to me, and yet the truth hurts like hell.'

Bruce was silent but he trod down harder on the accelerator and the truck picked up speed. *I don't want to hear*, he thought, *I am not your confessor – I just don't want to hear*. He turned into the Avenue l'Etoile, headed towards the zoo.

'He was right, he had me measured to the inch,' persisted Mike.

'We've all got troubles, otherwise we wouldn't be here.' And then, to change Mike's mood, 'We few, we happy few. We band of brothers.'

Mike grinned and his face was suddenly boyish. 'At least we have the distinction of following the second oldest profession – we, the mercenaries.'

'The oldest profession is better paid and much more fun,' said Bruce and swung the truck into the driveway of a double-storied residence, parked outside the front door and switched off the engine.

Not long ago the house had been the home of the chief accountant of Union Minière du Haut, now it was the billet of 'D' section, Special Striker Force, commanded by Captain Bruce Curry.

Half a dozen of his black gendarmes were sitting on the low wall of the verandah, and as Bruce came up the front steps they shouted the greeting that had become traditional since the United Nations intervention.

'U.N. – Merde!'

'Ah!' Bruce grinned at them in the sense of companionship that had grown up between them in the past months. 'The cream of the Army of Katanga!'

He offered his cigarettes around and stood chatting idly for a few minutes before asking, 'Where's Sergeant Major?' One of the gendarmes jerked a thumb at the glass doors that led into the lounge and Bruce went through with Mike behind him.

Equipment was piled haphazardly on the expensive furniture, the stone fireplace was half filled with empty bottles, a gendarme lay snoring on the Persian carpet, one of the oil paintings on the wall had been ripped by a bayonet and the frame hung askew, the imbuia-wood coffee table tilted drunkenly towards its broken leg, and the whole lounge smelled of men and cheap tobacco.

'Hello, Ruffy,' said Bruce.

'Just in time, boss.' Sergeant Major Ruffararo grinned delightedly from the armchair which he was overflowing. 'These goddam Arabs have run fresh out of folding stuff.' He gestured at the gendarmes that crowded about the table in front of him. 'Arab' was Ruffy's word of censure or contempt, and bore no relation to a man's nationality.

Ruffy's accent was always a shock to Bruce. You never expected to hear pure Americanese come rumbling out of that huge black frame. But three years previously Ruffy had returned from a scholarship tour of the United States with a command of the idiom, a diploma in land husbandry, a prodigious thirst for bottled beer (preferably Schlitz, but any other was acceptable) and a raving dose of the Old Joe.

The memory of this last, which had been a farewell gift from a high yellow sophomore of U.C.L.A., returned most painfully to Ruffararo when he was in his cups; so painfully that it could be assuaged only by throwing the nearest citizen of the United States.

Fortunately, it was only on rare occasions that an American and the necessary five or six gallons of beer were assembled in the same vicinity so that Ruffy's latent race antipathy could find expression. A throwing by Ruffy was an unforgettable experience, both for the victim and the spectators. Bruce vividly recalled that night at the Hotel Lido when he had been a witness at one of Ruffy's most spectacular throwings.

The victims, three of them, were journalists representing publications of repute. As the evening wore on they talked louder; an American accent has a carry like a well-hit golf ball and Ruffy recognized it from across the terrace. He became silent, and in his silence drank the last gallon which was necessary to tip the balance. He wiped the froth from his upper lip and stood up with his eyes fastened on the party of Americans.

'Ruffy, hold it. Hey!' – Bruce might not have spoken. Ruffy started across the terrace. They saw him coming and fell into an uneasy silence.

The first was in the nature of a practice throw; besides, the man was not aerodynamically constructed and his stomach had too much wind resistance. A middling distance of twenty feet.

'Ruffy, leave them!' shouted Bruce.

On the next throw Ruffy was getting warmed up, but he put excessive loft into it. Thirty feet; the journalist cleared the terrace and landed on the lawn below with his empty glass still clutched in his hand.

'Run, you fool!' Bruce warned the third victim, but he was paralysed.

And this was Ruffy's best ever, he took a good grip – neck and seat of the pants – and put his whole weight into it. Ruffy must have known that he had executed the perfect throw, for his shout of 'Gonorrhoea!' as he launched his man had a ring of triumph to it.

Afterwards, when Bruce had soothed the three Americans, and they had recovered sufficiently to appreciate the fact that they were privileged by being party to a record throwing session, they all paced out the distances. The three journalists developed an almost proprietary affection for Ruffy and spent the rest of the evening buying him beers and boasting to every newcomer in the bar. One of them, he who had been thrown last and farthest, wanted to do an article on Ruffy – with pictures. Towards the end of the evening he was talking wildly of whipping up sufficient international enthusiasm to have a man-throwing event included in the Olympic Games.

Ruffy accepted both their praise and their beer with modest gratitude; and when the third American offered to let Ruffy throw him again, he declined the offer on the grounds that he never threw the same man twice. All in all, it had been a memorable evening.

Apart from these occasional lapses, Ruffy had a more powerful body and happier mind than any man Bruce had ever known, and Bruce could not help liking him. He could not prevent himself smiling as he tried to reject Ruffy's invitation to play cards.

'We've got work to do now, Ruffy. Some other time.'

'Sit down, boss. We'll play just a couple of tricks, then we talk about work.' He shuffled the three cards back and forth between his hands.

'Sit down, boss,' Ruffy repeated, and Bruce grimaced resignedly and took the chair opposite him.

'How much you going to bet?' Ruffy leaned forward.

'Un mille.' Bruce laid a thousand-franc note on the table; 'when that's gone, then we go.'

'No hurry,' Ruffy soothed him. 'We got all day.' He dealt the three cards face down. 'The old Christian monarch is in there somewhere; all you got to do is find him and it's the easiest mille you ever made.'

'In the middle,' whispered the gendarme standing beside Bruce's chair. 'That's him in the middle.'

'Take no notice of that mad Arab – he's lost five mille already this morning,' Ruffy advised.

Bruce turned over the right-hand card.

'Mis-luck,' crowed Ruffy. 'You got yourself the queen of hearts.' He picked up the banknote and stuffed it into his breast pocket. 'She'll see you wrong every time that sweet-faced little bitch.' Grinning, he turned over the middle card to expose the Jack of spades with his sly eyes and curly little moustache. 'She's been shacked up there with the Jack right under the ole King's nose.' He turned the king face up. 'Look you at that dozy old guy – he's not even facing in the right direction.'

Bruce stared at the three cards and he felt that sickness in his stomach again. The whole story was there; even the man's name was right, but the Jack should have worn a beard and driven a red Jaguar and his queen of hearts never had such innocent eyes. Bruce spoke abruptly. 'That's it, Ruffy. I want you and ten men to come with me.'

'Where we going?'

'Down to Ordinance – we're drawing special supplies.'

Ruffy nodded and buttoned the playing cards into his top pocket while he selected the gendarmes to accompany them; then he asked Bruce. 'We might need some oil; what you think, boss?'

Bruce hesitated; they had only two cases of whisky left of the dozen they had looted in August. The purchasing power of a bottle of genuine Scotch was enormous and Bruce was loath to use them except in extraordinary circumstances. But now he realized that his chances of getting the supplies he needed were remote, unless he took along a substantial bribe for the quarter-master.

'Okay, Ruffy. Bring a case.'

Ruffy came up out of the chair and clapped his steel helmet on his head. The chin straps hung down on each side of his round black face.

'A full case?' He grinned at Bruce. 'You want to buy a battleship?'

'Almost,' agreed Bruce; 'go and get it.'

Ruffy disappeared into the back area of the house and returned almost immediately with a case of Grant's Standfast under one arm and half a dozen bottles of Simba beer held by their necks between the fingers of his other hand.

'We might get thirsty,' he explained.

The gendarmes climbed into the back of the truck with a clatter of weapons and shouted cheerful abuse at their fellows on the verandah. Bruce, Mike and Ruffy crowded into the cab and Ruffy set the whisky on the floor and placed two large booted feet upon it.

'What's this all about, boss?' he asked as Bruce trundled the truck down the drive and turned into the Avenue l'Etoile. Bruce told him and when he had finished Ruffy grunted non-committally and opened a bottle of beer with his big white chisel-blade teeth; the gas hissed softly and a little froth ran down the bottle and dripped on to his lap.

'My boys aren't going to like it,' he commented as he offered the open bottle to Mike Haig. Mike shook his head and Ruffy passed the bottle to Bruce.

Ruffy opened a bottle for himself and spoke again. 'They going to hate it like hell.' He shook his head. 'And there'll be even bigger trouble when we get to Port Reprieve and pick up the diamonds.'

Bruce glanced sideways at him, startled. 'What diamonds?'

'From the dredgers,' said Ruffy. 'You don't think they're sending us all that way just to bring in these other guys. They're worried about the diamonds, that's for sure!'

Suddenly, for Bruce, much which had puzzled him was explained. A half-forgotten conversation that he had held earlier in the year with an engineer from Union Minière jumped back into his memory. They had discussed the three diamond dredgers that worked the gravel from the bed of the Lufira swamps. The boats were based on Port Reprieve and clearly they would have returned there at the beginning of the emergency; they must still be there with three or four months' recovery of diamonds on board. Something like half a million sterling in uncut stones. That was the reason why the Katangese Government placed such priority on this expedition, the reason why such a powerful force was being used, the reason why no approaches had been made to the U.N. authorities to conduct the rescue.

Bruce smiled sardonically as he remembered the humanitarian arguments that had been given to him by the Minister of the Interior.

'It is our duty, Captain Curry. We cannot leave these people to the not-so-tender mercy of the tribesmen. It is our duty as civilized human beings.'

There were others cut off in remote mission stations and government outposts throughout southern Kasai and Katanga; nothing had been heard of them for months, but their welfare was secondary to that of the settlement at Port Reprieve.

Bruce lifted the bottle to his lips again, steering with one hand and squinting ahead through the windscreen as he drank. All right, we'll fetch them in and afterwards an ammunition box will be loaded on to a chartered aircraft, and later still there will be another deposit to a numbered account in Zurich. Why should I worry? They're paying me for it.

'I don't think we should mention the diamonds to my boys.' Ruffy spoke sadly. 'I don't think that would be a good idea at all.'

Bruce slowed the truck as they ran into the industrial area beyond the railway line. He watched the buildings as they passed, until he recognized the one he wanted and swung off the road to stop in front of the gate. He blew a blast on the hooter and a gendarme came out and inspected his pass minutely. Satisfied, he shouted out to someone beyond the gate and it swung open. Bruce drove the truck through into the yard and switched off the engine.

There were half a dozen other trucks parked in the yard, all emblazoned with the Katangese shield and surrounded by gendarmes in uniforms patchy with sweat. A white lieutenant leaned from the cab of one of the trucks and shouted.

'Ciao, Bruce!'

'How things, Sergio?' Bruce answered him.

'Crazy! Crazy!' Bruce smiled. For the Italian everything was crazy. Bruce remembered that in July, during the fighting at the road bridge, he had bent him over the bonnet of a Landrover and with a bayonet dug a piece of shrapnel out of his hairy buttocks – that also had been crazy.

'See you around,' Bruce dismissed him and led Mike and Ruffy across the yard to the warehouse. There was a sign on the large double doors *Dépôt*

Ordinance – Armée du Katanga and beyond them at a desk in a glass cubicle sat a major with a pair of Gandhi-type steel-rimmed spectacles perched on a face like that of a jovial black toad. He looked up at Bruce.

'Non,' he said with finality. 'Non, non.' Bruce produced his requisition form and laid it before him. The major brushed it aside contemptuously.

'We have not got these items, we are destitute. I cannot do it. No! I cannot do it. There are priorities. There are circumstances to consider. No, I am sorry.' He snatched a sheaf of papers from the side of his desk and turned his whole attention to them, ignoring Bruce.

'This requisition is signed by Monsieur le Président,' Bruce pointed out mildly, and the major laid down his papers and came round from behind the desk. He stood close to Bruce with the top of his head on a level with Bruce's chin.

'Had it been signed by the Almighty himself, it would be of no use. I am sorry, I am truly sorry.'

Bruce lifted his eyes and for a second allowed them to wander over the mountains of stores which packed the interior of the warehouse. From where he stood he could identify at least twenty items that he needed. The major noticed the gesture and his French became so excited that Bruce could make out only the repeated use of the word 'Non'. He glanced significantly at Ruffy and the sergeant major stepped forward and placed an arm soothingly about the major's shoulders; then very gently he led him, still protesting, out into the yard and across to the truck. He opened the door of the cab and the major saw the case of whisky.

A few minutes later, after Ruffy had prised open the lid with his bayonet and allowed the major to inspect the seals on the caps, they returned to the office with Ruffy carrying the case.

'Captain,' said the major as he picked up the requisition from the desk. 'I see now that I was mistaken. This is indeed signed by Monsieur le Président. It is my duty to afford you the most urgent priority.'

Bruce murmured his thanks and the major beamed at him. 'I will give you men to help you.'

'You are too kind. It would disrupt your routine. I have my own men.'

'Excellent,' agreed the major and waved a podgy hand around the warehouse. 'Take what you need.'

Chapter Three

Again Bruce glanced at his wrist watch. It was still twenty minutes before the curfew ended at 06.00 hours. Until then he must fret away the time watching Wally Hendry finishing his breakfast. This was a spectacle without much appeal, for Hendry was a methodical but untidy eater.

'Why don't you keep your mouth closed?' snapped Bruce irritably, unable to stand it any longer.

'Do I ask you your business?' Hendry looked up from his plate. His jowls were covered with a ginger stubble of beard, and his eyes were inflamed and puffy from the previous evening's debauchery. Bruce looked away from him and checked his watch again.

The suicidal temptation to ignore the curfew and set off immediately for the railway station was very strong. It required an effort to resist it. The least he could expect if he followed that course was an arrest by one of the patrols and a delay of twelve hours while he cleared himself; the worst would be a shooting incident.

He poured himself another cup of coffee and sipped it slowly. Impatience has always been one of my weaknesses, he reflected; nearly every mistake I have ever made stems from that cause. But I have improved a little over the years – at twenty I wanted to live my whole life in a week. Now I'll settle for a year.

He finished his coffee and checked the time again. Five minutes before six, he could risk it now. It would take almost that long to get out to the truck.

'If you are ready, gentlemen.' He pushed back his chair and picked up his pack, slung it over his shoulder and led the way out.

Ruffy was waiting for them, sitting on a pile of stores in one of the corrugated iron goods sheds. His men squatted round a dozen small fires on the concrete floor cooking breakfast.

'Where's the train?'

'That's a good question, boss,' Ruffy congratulated him, and Bruce groaned.

'It should have been here long ago,' Bruce protested, and Ruffy shrugged.

'*Should have been* is a lot different from *is*.'

'Goddammit! We've still got to load up. We'll be lucky if we get away before noon,' snapped Bruce. 'I'll go up to the station master.'

'You'd better take him a present, boss. We've still got a case left.'

'No, hell!' Bruce growled. 'Come with me, Mike.'

With Mike beside him they crossed the tracks to the main platform and clambered up on to it. At the far end a group of railway officials stood chatting and Bruce fell upon them furiously.

Two hours later Bruce stood beside the coloured engine driver on the footplate and they puffed slowly down towards the goods yard.

The driver was a roly-poly little man with a skin too dark for mere sunburn and a set of teeth with bright red plastic gums.

'Monsieur, you do not wish to proceed to Port Reprieve?' he asked anxiously.

'Yes.'

'There is no way of telling the condition of the permanent way. No traffic has used it these last four months.'

'I know. You'll have to proceed with caution.'

'There is a United Nations barrier across the lines near the old aerodrome,' protested the man.

'We have a pass.' Bruce smiled to soothe him; his bad temper was abating now that he had his transport. 'Stop next to the first shed.'

With a hiss of steam brakes the train pulled up beside the concrete platform and Bruce jumped down.

'All right, Ruffy,' he shouted. 'Let's get cracking.'

Bruce had placed the three steel-sided open trucks in the van, for they were the easiest to defend. From behind the breast-high sides the Bren guns could sweep ahead and on both flanks. Then followed the two passenger coaches, to be used as store rooms and officers' quarters; also for the accommodation of the refugees on the return journey. Finally, the locomotive in the rear, where it would be least vulnerable and would not spew smoke and soot back over the train.

The stores were loaded into four of the compartments, the windows shuttered and the doors locked. Then Bruce set about laying out his defences. In a low circle of sandbags on the roof of the leading coach he sited one of the Brens and made this his own post. From here he could look down over the open trucks, back at the locomotive, and also command an excellent view of the surrounding country.

The other Brens he placed in the leading truck and put Hendry in command there. He had obtained from the major at Ordinance three of the new walkie-talkie sets; one he gave to the engine driver, another to Hendry up front, and the third he retained in his emplacement; and his system of communication was satisfactory.

It was almost twelve o'clock before these preparations were complete and Bruce turned to Ruffy who sat on the sandbags beside him.

'All set?'

'All set, boss.'

'How many missing?' Bruce had learned from experience never to expect his entire command to be in any one place at any one time.

'Eight, boss.'

'That's three more than yesterday; leaves us only fifty-two men. Do you think they've taken off into the bush also?' Five of his men had deserted with their weapons on the day of the cease-fire. Obviously they had gone out into the bush to join one of the bands of *shufta* that were already playing havoc along the main roads: ambushing all unprotected traffic, beating up lucky travellers and murdering those less fortunate, raping when they had the opportunity, and generally enjoying themselves.

'No, boss, I don't think so, those three are good boys. They'll be down in the cité indigène having themselves some fun; guess they just forgot the time.' Ruffy shook his head. 'Take us about half an hour to find them; all we do is go down and visit all the knock-shops. You want to try?'

'No, we haven't time to mess around if we are going to make Msapa Junction before dark. We'll pick them up again when we get back.' Was there ever an army since the Boer War that treated desertion so lightly, Bruce wondered.

He turned to the radio set beside him and depressed the transmit button.

'Driver.'

'Oui, monsieur.'

'Proceed – very slowly until we approach the United Nations barrier. Stop well this side of it.'

'Oui, monsieur.'

They rolled out of the goods yard, clicking over the points; leaving the industrial quarter on their right with the Katangese guard posts on the Avenue du Cimetière intersection; out through the suburbs until ahead of them Bruce saw the U.N. positions and he felt the first stirring of anxiety. The pass he carried in the breast pocket of his jacket was signed by General Rhee Singh, but before in this war the orders of an Indian general had not been passed by a Sudanese captain to an Irish sergeant. The reception that awaited them could be exciting.

'I hope they know about us.' Mike Haig lit his cigarette with a show of nonchalance, but he peered over it anxiously at the piles of fresh earth on each side of the tracks that marked the position of the emplacements.

'These boys have got bazookas, and they're Irish Arabs,' muttered Ruffy. 'I reckon that's the maddest kind of Arab there is – Irish. How would you like a bazooka bomb up the throat, boss?'

'No, thanks, Ruffy,' Bruce declined, and pressed the button of the radio.

'Hendry!'

In the leading truck Wally Hendry picked up his set and, holding it against his chest, looked back at Bruce.

'Curry?'

'Tell your gunners to stand away from the Brens, and the rest of them to lay down their rifles.'

'Right.'

Bruce watched him relaying the order, pushing them back, moving among the gendarmes who crowded the forward trucks. Bruce could sense the air of tension that had fallen over the whole train, watched as his gendarmes reluctantly laid down their weapons and stood empty-handed staring sullenly ahead at the U.N. barrier.

'Driver!' Bruce spoke again into the radio. 'Slow down. Stop fifty metres this side of the barrier. But if there is any shooting open the throttle and take us straight through.'

'Oui, monsieur.'

Ahead of them there was no sign of a reception committee, only the hostile barrier of poles and petrol drums across the line.

Bruce stood upon the roof and lifted his arms above his head in a gesture of neutrality. It was a mistake; the movement changed the passive mood of the gendarmes in the trucks below him. One of them lifted his arms also, but his fists were clenched.

'U.N. – merde!' he shouted, and immediately the cry was taken up.

'U.N. – merde! U.N. – merde!' They chanted the war cry – laughing at first, but then no longer laughing, their voices rising sharply.

'Shut up, damn you,' Bruce roared and swung his open hand against the head of the gendarme beside him, but the man hardly noticed it. His eyes were glazing with the infectious hysteria to which the African is so susceptible; he had snatched up his rifle and was holding it across his chest; already his body was beginning to jerk convulsively as he chanted.

Bruce hooked his fingers under the rim of the man's steel helmet and yanked it forward over his eyes so that the back of his neck was exposed; he chopped him with a judo blow and the gendarme slumped forward over the sandbags, his rifle slipping from his hands.

Bruce looked up desperately; in the trucks below him the hysteria was spreading.

'Stop them – Hendry, de Surrier! Stop them for God's sake.' But his voice was lost in the chanting.

A gendarme snatched up his rifle from where it lay at his feet; Bruce saw him elbow his way towards the side of the truck to begin firing; he was working the slide to lever a round into the breech.

'Mwembe!' Bruce shouted the gendarme's name, but his voice could not penetrate the uproar.

In two seconds the whole situation would dissolve into a pandemonium of tracer and bazooka fire.

Poised on the forward edge of the roof, Bruce checked for an instant to judge the distance, and then he jumped. He landed squarely on the gendarme's shoulders, his weight throwing the man forward so his face hit the steel edge of the truck, and they went down together on to the floor.

The gendarme's finger was resting on the trigger and the rifle fired as it spun from his hands. A complete hush followed the roar of the rifle and in it Bruce scrambled to his feet, drawing his pistol from the canvas holster on his hip.

'All right,' he panted, menacing the men around him. 'Come on, give me a chance to use this!' He picked out one of his sergeants and held his eyes. 'You! I'm waiting for you – start shooting!'

At the sight of the revolver the man relaxed slowly and the madness faded from his face. He dropped his eyes and shuffled awkwardly.

Bruce glanced up at Ruffy and Haig on the roof, and raised his voice. 'Watch them. Shoot the first one who starts it again.'

'Okay, boss,' Ruffy thrust forward the automatic rifle in his hands. 'Who's it going to be?' he asked cheerfully, looking down at them. But the mood had changed. Their attitudes of defiance gave way to sheepish embarrassment and a small buzz of conversation filled the silence.

'Mike,' Bruce yelled, urgent again. 'Call the driver, he's trying to take us through!'

The noise of their passage had risen, the driver accelerating at the sound of the shot, and now they were racing down towards the U.N. barrier.

Mike Haig grabbed the set, shouted an order into it, and immediately the brakes swooshed and the train jolted to a halt not a hundred yards short of the barrier.

Slowly Bruce clambered back on to the roof of the coach.

'Close?' asked Mike.

'My God!' Bruce shook his head, and lit a cigarette with slightly unsteady hands. 'Another fifty yards—!' Then he turned and stared coldly down at his gendarmes.

'Canaille! Next time you try to commit suicide don't take me with you.' The gendarme he had knocked down was now sitting up, fingering the ugly black swelling above his eye. 'My friend,' Bruce turned on him, 'later I will have something for your further discomfort!' Then to the other man in the emplacement beside him who was massaging his neck, 'And for you also! Take their names, Sergeant Major.'

'Sir!' growled Ruffy.

'Mike.' Bruce's voice changed, soft again. 'I'm going ahead to toss the blarney with our friends behind the bazookas. When I give you the signal bring the train through.'

'You don't want me to come with you?' asked Mike.

'No, stay here.' Bruce picked up his rifle, slung it over his shoulder, dropped down the ladder on to the path beside the tracks, and walked forward with the gravel crunching beneath his boots.

An auspicious beginning to the expedition, he decided grimly, tragedy averted by the wink of an eye before they had even passed the outskirts of the city.

At least the Mickies hadn't added a few bazooka bombs to the altercation. Bruce peered ahead, and could make out the shape of helmets behind the earthworks.

Without the breeze of the train's passage it was hot again, and Bruce felt himself starting to sweat.

'Stay where you are, Mister.' A deep brogue from the emplacement nearest the tracks; Bruce stopped, standing on the wooden crossties in the sun. Now he could see the faces of the men beneath the helmets: unfriendly, not smiling.

'What was the shooting for?' the voice questioned.

'We had an accident.'

'Don't have any more or we might have one also.'

'I'd not be wanting that, Paddy.' Bruce smiled thinly, and the Irishman's voice had an edge to it as he went on. 'What's your mission?'

'I have a pass, do you want to see it?' Bruce took the folded sheet of paper from his breast pocket.

'What's your mission?' repeated the Irishman.

'Proceed to Port Reprieve and relieve the town.'

'We know about you.' The Irishman nodded. 'Let me see the pass.'

Bruce left the tracks, climbed the earth wall and handed the pink slip to the Irishman. He wore the three pips of a captain, and he glanced briefly at the pass before speaking to the man beside him.

'Very well, Sergeant, you can be clearing the barrier now.'

'I'll call the train through?' Bruce asked, and the captain nodded again.

'But make sure there are no more accidents – we don't like hired killers.'

'Sure and begorrah now, Paddy, it's not your war you're afighting either,' snapped Bruce and abruptly turned his back on the man, jumped down on to the tracks and waved to Mike Haig on the roof of the coach.

The Irish sergeant and his party had cleared the tracks and while the train rumbled slowly down to him Bruce struggled to control his irritation – the Irish captain's taunt had reached him. Hired killer, and of course that was what he was. Could a man sink any lower?

As the coach drew level with where he stood, Bruce caught the hand rail and swung himself aboard, waved an ironical farewell to the Irish captain and climbed up on to the roof.

'No trouble?' asked Mike.

'A bit of lip, delivered in music-hall brogue,' Bruce answered, 'but nothing serious.' He picked up the radio set.

'Driver.'

'Monsieur?'

'Do not forget my instructions.'

'I will not exceed forty kilometres the hour, and I shall at all times be prepared for an emergency stop.'

'Good!' Bruce switched off the set and sat down on the sandbags between Ruffy and Mike.

Well, he thought, here we go at last. Six hours run to Msapa Junction. That should be easy. And then – God knows, God alone knows.

The tracks curved, and Bruce looked back to see the last white-washed buildings of Elisabethville disappear among the trees. They were out into the open savannah forest.

Behind them the black smoke from the loco rolled sideways into the trees; beneath them the crossties clattered in strict rhythm, and ahead the line ran arrow straight for miles, dwindling with perspective until it merged into the olive-green mass of the forest.

Bruce lifted his eyes. Half the sky was clear and tropical blue, but in the north it was bruised with cloud, and beneath the cloud grey rain drifted down to meet the earth. The sunlight through the rain spun a rainbow, and the cloud shadow moved across the land as slowly and as darkly as a herd of grazing buffalo.

He loosened the chin strap of his helmet and laid his rifle on the roof beside him.

'You'd like a beer, boss?'

'Have you any?'

'Sure.' Ruffy called to one of the gendarmes and the man climbed down into the coach and came back with half a dozen bottles. Ruffy opened two with his teeth. Each time half the contents frothed out and splattered back along the wooden side of the coach.

'This beer's as wild as an angry woman,' he grunted as he passed a bottle to Bruce.

'It's wet anyway.' Bruce tasted it, warm and gassy and too sweet.

'Here's how!' said Ruffy.

Bruce looked down into the open trucks at the gendarmes who were settling in for the journey. Apart from the gunners at the Brens, they were lying or squatting in attitudes of complete relaxation and most of them had stripped down to their underwear. One skinny little fellow was already asleep on his back with his helmet as a pillow and the tropical sun beating full into his face.

Bruce finished his beer and threw the bottle overboard. Ruffy opened another and placed it in his hand without comment.

'Why we going so slowly, boss?'

'I told the driver to keep the speed down – give us a chance to stop if the tracks have been torn up.'

'Yeah. Them Balubas might have done that – they're mad Arabs all of them.'

The warm beer drunk in the sun was having a soothing effect on Bruce. He felt at peace now, withdrawn from the need to make decisions, to participate in the life around him.

'Listen to that train-talk,' said Ruffy, and Bruce focused his hearing on the clickety-clack of the crossties.

'Yes, I know. You can make it say anything you want it to,' agreed Bruce.

'And it can sing,' Ruffy went on. 'It's got real music in it, like this.' He inflated the great barrel of his chest, lifted his head and let it come.

His voice was deep but with a resonance that caught the attention of the men in the open trucks below them. Those who had been sprawled in the amorphous shapes of sleep stirred and sat up. Another voice joined in humming the tune, hesitantly at first, then more confidently; then others took it up, the words were unimportant, it was the rhythm that they could not resist. They had sung together many times before and like a well-trained choir each voice found its place, the star performers leading, changing the pace, improvising, quickening until the original tune lost its identity and became one of the tribal chants. Bruce recognized it as a planting song. It was one of his favourites and he sat drinking his lukewarm beer and letting the singing wash round him, build up into the chorus like storm waves, then fall back into a tenor solo before rising once more. And the train ran on through the sunlight towards the rain clouds in the north.

Presently André came out of the coach below him and picked his way forward through the men in the trucks until he reached Hendry. The two of them stood together, André's face turned up towards the taller man and deadly earnest as he talked.

'*Doll boy*,' Hendry had called him, and it was an accurate description of the effeminately pretty face with the big toffee eyes; the steel helmet he wore seemed too large for his shoulders to carry.

I wonder how old he is; Bruce watched him laugh suddenly, his face still turned upwards to Hendry; not much over twenty and I have never seen anything less like a hired killer.

'How the hell did anyone like de Surrier get mixed up in this?' His voice echoed the thought, and beside him Mike answered.

'He was working in Elisabethville when it started, and he couldn't return to Belgium. I don't know the reason but I guess it was something personal. When it started his firm closed down. I suppose this was the only employment he could find.'

'That Irishman, the one at the barrier, he called me a hired killer.' Thinking of Andre's position in the scheme of things had turned Bruce's thoughts back to his own status. 'I hadn't thought about it that way before, but I suppose he's right. That is what we are.'

Mike Haig was silent for a moment, but when he spoke there was a stark quality in his voice.

'Look at these hands!' Involuntarily Bruce glanced down at them, and for the first time noticed that they were narrow with long moulded fingers, possessed of a functional beauty, the hands of an artist.

'Look at them,' Mike repeated, flexing them slightly; 'they were fashioned for a purpose, they were made to hold a scalpel, they were made to save life.' Then he relaxed them and let them drop on to the rifle across his lap, the long delicate fingers incongruous upon the blue metal. 'But look what they hold now!'

Bruce stirred irritably. He had not wanted to provoke another bout of Mike Haig's soul-searching. Damn the old fool – why must he always start this, he knew as well as anyone that in the mercenary army of Katanga there was a taboo upon the past. It did not exist.

'Ruffy,' Bruce snapped, 'aren't you going to feed your boys.'

'Right now, boss.' Ruffy opened another beer and handed it to Bruce. 'Hold that – it will keep your mind off food while I rustle it up.' He lumbered off along the roof of the coach still singing.

'Three years ago, it seems like all eternity,' Mike went on as though Bruce had not interrupted. 'Three years ago I was a surgeon and now this—' The desolation had spread to his eyes, and Bruce felt his pity for the man deep down where he kept it imprisoned with all his other emotions. 'I was good. I was one of the best. Royal College. Harley Street. Guy's.' Mike laughed without humour, with bitterness. 'Can you imagine me being driven in my Rolls to address the College on my advanced technique of cholecystectomy?'

'What happened?' The question was out before he could stop it, and Bruce realized how near to the surface he had let his pity rise. 'No, don't tell me. It's your business. I don't want to know.'

'But I'll tell you, Bruce. I want to. It helps somehow, talking about it.'

At first, thought Bruce, I wanted to talk also, to try and wash the pain away with words.

Mike was silent for a few seconds. Below them the singing rose and fell, and the train ran on through the forest.

'It had taken me ten hard years to get there, but at last I had done it. A fine practice; doing the work I loved with skill, earning the rewards I deserved. A wife that any man would have been proud of, a lovely home, many friends, too many friends perhaps; for success breeds friends the way a dirty kitchen breeds cockroaches.'

Mike pulled out a handkerchief and dried the back of his neck where the wind could not reach.

'Those sort of friends mean parties,' he went on. 'Parties when you've worked all day and you're tired; when you need the lift that you can get so easily from a bottle. You don't know if you have the weakness for the stuff until it's too late; until you have a bottle in the drawer of your desk; until suddenly your practice isn't so good any more.'

Mike twisted the handkerchief around his fingers as he ploughed doggedly on. 'Then you know it suddenly. You know it when your hands dance in the morning and all you want for breakfast is *that*, when you can't wait until lunch time because you have to operate and that's the only way you can keep your hands steady. But you know it finally and utterly when the knife turns in your hand and the artery starts to spurt and you watch it paralysed – you watch it hosing red over your gown and forming pools on the theatre floor.' Mike's voice dried up then and he tapped a cigarette from his pack and lit it. His shoulders were hunched forward and his eyes were full of the shadows of his guilt. Then he straightened up and his voice was stronger.

'You must have read about it. I was headlines for a few days, all the papers. But my name wasn't Haig in those days. I got that name off a label on a bottle in a bar-room.

'Gladys stayed with me, of course, she was that type. We came out to Africa. I had enough saved from the wreck for a down payment on a tobacco farm in the Centenary block outside Salisbury. Two good seasons and I was off the bottle. Gladys was having our first baby, we had both wanted one so badly. It was all coming right again.'

Mike stuffed the handkerchief back in his pocket, and his voice lost its strength again, turned dry and husky.

'Then one day I took the truck into the village and on the way home I stopped at the club. I had been there often before, but this time it was different. Instead of half an hour, I stayed there until they threw me out at closing time and when I got back to the farm I had a case of Scotch on the seat beside me.'

Bruce wanted to stop him; he knew what was coming and he didn't want to hear it.

'The first rains started that night and the rivers came down in flood. The telephone lines were knocked out and we were cut off. In the morning—' Mike stopped again and turned to Bruce.

'I suppose it was the shock of seeing me like that again, but in the morning Gladys went into labour. It was her first and she wasn't so young any more. She was still in labour the next day, but by then she was too weak to scream. I remember how peaceful it was without her screaming and pleading with me to help. You see she knew I had all the instruments I needed. She begged me to help. I can remember that; her voice through the fog of whisky. I think I hated her then. I think I remember hating her, it was all so confused, so mixed up with the screaming and the liquor. But at last she was quiet. I don't think I realized she was dead. I was simply glad she was quiet and I could have peace.'

He dropped his eyes from Bruce's face.

'I was too drunk to go to the funeral. Then I met a man in a bar-room, I can't remember how long after it was, I can't even remember where. It must have been on the Copperbelt. He was recruiting for Tshombe's army and I signed up; there didn't seem anything else to do.'

Neither of them spoke again until a gendarme brought food to them, hunks of brown bread spread with tinned butter and filled with bully beef and pickled onions. They ate in silence listening to the singing, and Bruce said at last:

'You needn't have told me.'

'I know.'

'Mike—' Bruce paused.

'Yes?'

'I'm sorry, if that's any comfort.'

'It is,' Mike said. 'It helps to have – not to be completely alone. I like you, Bruce.' He blurted out the last sentence and Bruce recoiled as though Mike had spat in his face.

You fool, he rebuked himself savagely, *you were wide open then. You nearly let one of them in again.*

Remorselessly he crushed down his sympathy, shocked at the effort it required, and when he picked up the radio the gentleness had gone from his eyes.

'Hendry,' he spoke into the set, 'don't talk so much. I put you up front to watch the tracks.'

From the leading truck Wally Hendry looked round and forked two fingers at Bruce in a casual obscenity, but he turned back and faced ahead.

'You'd better go and take over from Hendry,' Bruce told Mike. 'Send him back here.'

Mike Haig stood up and looked down at Bruce.

'What are you afraid of?' his voice softly puzzled.

'I gave you an order, Haig.'

'Yes, I'm on my way.'

Chapter Four

The aircraft found them in the late afternoon. It was a Vampire jet of the Indian Air Force and it came from the north.

They heard the soft rumble of it across the sky and then saw it glint like a speck of mica in the sunlight above the storm clouds ahead of them.

'I bet you a thousand francs to a handful of dung that this Bucko don't know about us,' said Hendry with anticipation, watching the jet turn off its course towards them.

'Well, he does now,' said Bruce.

Swiftly he surveyed the rain clouds in front of them. They were close; another ten minutes' run and they would be under them, and once there they were safe from air attack for the belly of the clouds pressed close against the earth and the rain was a thick blue-grey mist that would reduce visibility to a few hundred feet. He switched on the radio.

'Driver, give us all the speed you have – get us into that rain.'

'Oui, monsieur,' came the acknowledgement and almost immediately the puffing of the loco quickened and the clatter of the crossties changed its rhythm.

'Look at him come,' growled Hendry. The jet fell fast against the back-drop of cloud, still in sunlight, still a silver point of light, but growing.

Bruce clicked over the band selector of the radio, searching the ether for the pilot's voice. He tried four wavelengths and each time found only the crackle and drone of static, but with the fifth came the gentle sing-song of Hindustani. Bruce could not understand it, but he could hear that the tone was puzzled. There was a short silence on the radio while the pilot listened to an instruction from the Kamina base which was beyond the power of their small set to receive, then a curt affirmative.

'He's coming in for a closer look,' said Bruce, then raising his voice, 'Everybody under cover – and stay there.' He was not prepared to risk another demonstration of friendship.

The jet came cruising in towards them under half power, yet incredibly fast, leaving the sound of its engine far behind it, sharklike above the forest. Then Bruce could see the pilot's head through the canopy; now he could make out his features. His face was very brown beneath the silver crash helmet and he had a little moustache, the same as the Jack of Spades. He was so close that Bruce saw the exact moment that he recognized them as Katangese; his eyes showed white and his mouth puckered as he swore. Beside Bruce the radio relayed the oath with metallic harshness, and then the jet was banking away steeply, its engine howling in full throttle, rising, showing its swollen silver belly and the racks of rockets beneath its wings.

'That frightened seven years' growth out of him,' laughed Hendry. 'You should have let me blast him. He was close enough for me to hit him in the left eyeball.'

'You'll get another chance in a moment,' Bruce assured him grimly. The radio was gabbling with consternation as the jet dwindled back into the sky. Bruce switched quickly to their own channel.

'Driver, can't you get this thing moving?'

'Monsieur, never before has she moved as she does now.'

Once more he switched back to the jet's frequency and listened to the pilot's excited voice. The jet was turning in a wide circle, perhaps fifteen miles away. Bruce glanced at the piled mass of cloud and rain ahead of them; it was moving down to meet them, but with ponderous dignity.

'If he comes back,' Bruce shouted down at his gendarmes, 'we can be sure that it's not just to look at us again. Open fire as soon as he's in range. Give him everything you've got, we must try and spoil his aim.'

Their faces were turned up towards him, subdued by the awful inferiority of the earth-bound to the hunter in the sky. Only André did not look at Bruce; he was staring at the aircraft with his jaws clenching nervously and his eyes too large for his face.

Again there was silence on the radio, and every head turned back to watch the jet.

'Come on, Bucko, come on!' grunted Hendry impatiently. He spat into the palm of his right hand and then wiped it down the front of his jacket. 'Come on, we want you.' With his thumb he flicked the safety catch of his rifle on and off, on and off.

Suddenly the radio spoke again. Two words, obviously acknowledging an order, and one of the words Bruce recognized. He had heard it before in circumstances that had burned it into his memory. The Hindustani word *'Attack!'*

'All right,' he said and stood up. 'He's coming!'

The wind fluttered his shirt against his chest. He settled his helmet firmly and pumped a round into the chamber of his FN.

'Get down into the truck, Hendry,' he ordered.

'I can see better from here.' Hendry was standing beside him, legs planted wide to brace himself against the violent motion of the train.

'As you like,' said Bruce. 'Ruffy, you get under cover.'

'Too damn hot down there in that box,' grinned the huge Negro.

'You're a mad Arab too,' said Bruce.

'Sure, we're all mad Arabs.'

The jet wheeled sharply and stooped towards the forest, levelling, still miles out on their flank.

'This Bucko is a real apprentice. He's going to take us from the side, so we can all shoot at him. If he was half awake he'd give it to us up the bum, hit the loco and make sure that we were all shooting over the top of each other,' gloated Hendry.

Silently, swiftly it closed with them, almost touching the tops of the trees. Then suddenly the cannon fire sparkled lemon-pale on its nose and all around them the air was filled with the sound of a thousand whips. Immediately every gun on the train opened up in reply. The tracers from the Brens chased each other out to meet the plane and the rifles joined their voices in a clamour that drowned the cannon fire.

Bruce aimed carefully, the jet unsteady in his sights from the lurching of the coach; then he pressed the trigger and the rifle juddered against his shoulder. From the corner of his eye he saw the empty cartridge cases spray from the breech in a bright bronze stream, and the stench of cordite stung his nostrils.

The aircraft slewed slightly, flinching from the torrent of fire.

'He's yellow!' howled Hendry. 'The bastard's yellow!'

'Hit him!' roared Ruffy. 'Keep hitting him.'

The jet twisted, lifted its nose so that the fire from its cannons passed harmlessly over their heads. Then its nose dropped again and it fired its rockets, two from under each wing. The gunfire from the train stopped abruptly as everybody ducked for safety; only the three of them on the roof kept shooting.

Shrieking like four demons in harness, leaving parallel lines of white smoke behind them, the rockets came from about four hundred yards out and they covered the distance in the time it takes to draw a deep breath, but the pilot had dropped his nose too sharply and fired too late. The rockets exploded in the embankment of the tracks below them.

The blast threw Bruce over backwards. He fell and rolled, clutching desperately at the smooth roof, but as he went over the edge his fingers caught in the guttering and he hung there. He was dazed with the concussion, the guttering cutting into his fingers, the shoulder-strap of his rifle round his neck strangling him, and the gravel of the embankment rushing past beneath him.

Ruffy reached over, caught him by the front of his jacket and lifted him back like a child.

'You going somewhere, boss?' The great round face was coated with dust from the explosions, but he was grinning happily. Bruce had a confused conviction that it would take at least a case of dynamite to make any impression on that mountain of black flesh.

Kneeling on the roof Bruce tried to rally himself. He saw that the wooden side of the coach nearest the explosions was splintered and torn and the roof was covered with earth and pebbles. Hendry was sitting beside him, shaking his head slowly from side to side; a small trickle of blood ran down from a scratch on his cheek and dripped from his chin. In the open trucks the men stood or sat with stunned expressions on their faces, but the train still raced on towards the rain storm and the dust of the explosions hung in a dense brown cloud above the forest far behind them.

Bruce scrambled to his feet, searched frantically for the aircraft and found its tiny shape far off above the mass of cloud.

The radio was undamaged, protected by the sandbags from the blast. Bruce reached for it and pressed the transmit button.

'Driver, are you all right?'

'Monsieur, I am greatly perturbed. Is there—'

'Not you alone,' Bruce assured him. 'Keep this train going.'

'Oui, monsieur.'

Then he switched to the aircraft's frequency. Although his ears were singing shrilly from the explosions, he could hear that the voice of the pilot had changed its tone. There was a slowness in it, a breathless catch on some of the words. He's frightened or he's hurt, thought Bruce, but he still has time to make another pass at us before we reach the storm front.

His mind was clearing fast now, and he became aware of the complete lack of readiness in his men.

'Ruffy!' he shouted. 'Get them on their feet. Get them ready. That plane will be back any second now.'

Ruffy jumped down into the truck and Bruce heard his palm slap against flesh as he began to bully them into activity. Bruce followed him down, then climbed over into the second truck and began the same process there.

'Haig, give me a hand, help me get the lead out of them.'

Further removed from the shock of the explosion, the men in this truck reacted readily and crowded to the side, starting to reload, checking their weapons, swearing, faces losing the dull dazed expressions.

Bruce turned and shouted back, 'Ruffy, are any of your lot hurt?'

'Couple a scratches, nothing bad.'

On the roof of the coach Hendry was standing again, watching the aircraft, blood on his face and his rifle in his hands.

'Where's André?' Bruce asked Haig as they met in the middle of the truck.

'Up front. I think he's been hit.'

Bruce went forward and found André doubled up, crouching in a corner of the truck, his rifle lying beside him and both hands covering his face. His shoulders heaved as though he were in pain.

Eyes, thought Bruce, he's been hit in the eyes. He reached him and stooped over him, pulling his hands from his face, expecting to see blood.

André was crying, his cheeks wet with tears and his eyelashes gummed together. For a second Bruce stared at him and then he caught the front of his jacket and pulled him to his feet. He picked up André's rifle and the barrel was cold, not a single shot had been fired out of it. He dragged the Belgian to the side and thrust the rifle into his hands.

'De Surrier,' he snarled, 'I'm going to be standing beside you. If you do that again I'll shoot you. Do you understand?'

'I'm sorry, Bruce.' André's lips were swollen where he had bitten them; his face was smeared with tears and slack with fear. 'I'm sorry. I couldn't help it.'

Bruce ignored him and turned his attention back to the aircraft. It was turning in for its next run.

He's going to come from the side again, Bruce thought; this time he'll get us. He can't miss twice in a row.

In silence once more they watched the jet slide down the valley between two vast white mountains of cloud and level off above the forest. Small and dainty and deadly it raced in towards them.

One of the Bren gunners opened up, rattling raucously, sending out tracers like bright beads on a string.

'Too soon,' muttered Bruce. 'Much too soon; he must be all of a mile out of range.'

But the effect was instantaneous. The jet swerved, almost hit the tree tops and then over-corrected, losing its line of approach.

A howl of derision went up from the train and was immediately lost in the roar as every gun opened fire. The jet loosed its remaining rockets, blindly, hopelessly, without a chance of a hit. Then it climbed steeply, turning away into the cloud ahead of them. The sound of its engines receded, was muted by the cloud and then was gone.

Ruffy was performing a dance of triumph, waving his rifle over his head. Hendry on the roof was shouting abuse at the clouds into which the jet had vanished, one of the Brens was still firing short ecstatic bursts, someone else was chanting the Katangese war cry and others were taking it up. And then the driver in the locomotive came in with his whistle, spurting steam with each shriek.

Bruce slung his rifle over his shoulder, pushed his helmet on to the back of his head, took out a cigarette and lit it, then stood watching them sing and laugh and chatter with the relief from danger.

Next to him André leaned out and vomited over the side; a little of it came out of his nose and dribbled down the front of his battle-jacket. He wiped his mouth with the back of his hand.

'I'm sorry, Bruce. I'm sorry, truly I am sorry,' he whispered.

And they were under the cloud, its coolness slumped over them like air from

an open refrigerator. The first heavy drops stung Bruce's cheek and then rolled
down heavily washing away the smell of cordite, melting the dust from Ruffy's
face until it shone again like washed coal.

Bruce felt his jacket cling wetly to his back.

'Ruffy, two men at each Bren. The rest of them can get back into the covered
coaches. We'll relieve every hour.' He reversed his rifle so the muzzle pointed
downwards. 'De Surrier, you can go, and you as well, Haig.'

'I'll stay with you, Bruce.'

'All right then.'

The gendarmes clambered back into the covered coaches still laughing and
chattering, and Ruffy came forward with a groundsheet and handed it to Bruce.

'The radios are all covered. If you don't need me, boss, I got some business
with one of those Arabs in the coach. He's got near twenty thousand francs on
him; so I'd better go and give him a couple of tricks with the cards.'

'One of these days I'm going to explain your Christian monarchs to the boys.
Show them that the odds are three to one against them,' Bruce threatened.

'I wouldn't do that, Boss,' Ruffy advised seriously. 'All that money isn't good
for them, just gets them into trouble.'

'Off you go then. I'll call you later,' said Bruce. 'Tell them I said "well done",
I'm proud of them.'

'Yeah. I'll tell them,' promised Ruffy.

Bruce lifted the tarpaulin that covered the set.

'Driver, desist before you burst the boiler!'

The abandoned flight of the train steadied to a more sedate pace, and Bruce
tilted his helmet over his eyes and pulled the groundsheet up around his mouth
before he leaned out over the side of the truck to inspect the rocket damage.

'All the windows blown out on this side and the woodwork torn a little,' he
muttered. 'But a lucky escape all the same.'

'What a miserable comic-opera war this is,' grunted Mike Haig. 'That pilot
had the right idea: why risk your life when it's none of your business.'

'He was wounded,' Bruce guessed. 'I think we hit him on his first run.'

Then they were silent, with the rain driving into their faces, slitting their eyes
to peer ahead along the tracks. The men at the Brens huddled into their brown
and green camouflage groundsheets, all their jubilation of ten minutes earlier
completely gone. They are like cats, thought Bruce as he noticed their dejection,
they can't stand being wet.

'It's half past five already.' Mike spoke at last. 'Do you think we'll make
Msapa Junction before nightfall?'

'With this weather it will be dark by six.' Bruce looked up at the low cloud
that was prematurely bringing on the night. 'I'm not going to risk travelling in
the dark. This is the edge of Baluba country and we can't use the headlight of
the loco.'

'You going to stop then?'

Bruce nodded. What a stupid bloody question, he thought irritably. Then he
recognized his irritation as reaction from the danger they had just experienced,
and he spoke to make amends.

'We can't be far now – if we start again at first light we'll reach Msapa
before sun-up.'

'My God, it's cold,' complained Mike and he shivered briefly.

'Either too hot or too cold,' Bruce agreed; he knew that it was also the reaction
that was making him garrulous. But he did not attempt to stop himself. 'That's
one of the things about this happy little planet of ours: nothing is in moderation.
Too hot or too cold, either you are hungry or you've overeaten, you are in love
or you hate the world—'

'Like you?' asked Mike.

'Dammit, Mike, you're as bad as a woman. Can't you conduct an objective discussion without introducing personalities?' Bruce demanded. He could feel his temper rising to the surface, he was cold and edgy, and he wanted a smoke.

'Objective theories must have subjective application to prove their worth,' Mike pointed out. There was just a trace of an amused smile on his broad ravaged old face.

'Let's forget it then. I don't want to talk personalities,' snapped Bruce; then immediately went on to do so. 'Humanity sickens me if I think about it too much. De Surrier puking his heart out with fear, that animal Hendry, you trying to keep off the liquor, Joan—' He stopped himself abruptly.

'Who is Joan?'

'Do I ask you your business?' Bruce flashed the standard reply to all personal questions in the mercenary army of Katanga.

'No. But I'm asking you yours – who is Joan?'

All right. I'll tell him. If he wants to know, I'll tell him. Anger had made Bruce reckless.

'Joan was the bitch I married.'

'So, that's it then!'

'Yes – that's it! Now you know. So you can leave me alone.'

'Kids?'

'Two – a boy and a girl.' The anger was gone from Bruce's voice, and the raw naked pain was back for an instant. Then he rallied and his voice was neutral once more.

'And none of it matters a damn. As far as I'm concerned the whole human race – all of it – can go and lose itself. I don't want any part of it.'

'How old are you, Bruce?'

'Leave me alone, damn you!'

'How old are you?'

'I'm thirty.'

'You talk like a teenager.'

'And I feel like an old, old man.'

The amusement was no longer on Mike's face as he asked.

'What did you do before this?'

'I slept and breathed and ate – and got trodden on.'

'What did you do for a living?'

'Law.'

'Were you successful?'

'How do you measure success? If you mean, did I make money, the answer is yes.'

I made enough to pay off the house and the car, he thought bitterly, and to contest custody of my children, and finally to meet the divorce settlement. I had enough for that, but, of course, I had to sell my partnership.

'Then you'll be all right,' Mike told him. 'If you've succeeded once you'll be able to do it again when you've recovered from the shock; when you've rearranged your life and taken other people into it to make you strong again.'

'I'm strong now, Haig. I'm strong *because* there is no one in my life. That's the only way you can be secure, on your own. Completely free and on your own.'

'Strong!' Anger flared in Mike's voice for the first time. 'On your own you're *nothing,* Curry. On your own you're so weak I could piss on you and wash you away!' Then the anger evaporated and Mike went on softly, 'But you'll find out – you're one of the lucky ones. You attract people to you. You don't have to be alone.'

'Well, that's the way I'm going to be from now on.'

'We'll see,' murmured Mike.

'Yes, we'll see,' Bruce agreed, and lifted the tarpaulin over the radio.

'Driver, we are going to halt for the night. It's too dark to proceed with safety.'

Chapter Five

Brazzaville Radio came through weakly on the set and the static was bad, for outside the rain still fell and thunder rolled around the sky like an unsecured cargo in a high sea.

'—Our Elisabethville correspondent reports that elements of the Katangese Army in the South Kasai province today violated the cease-fire agreement by firing upon a low-flying aircraft of the United Nations command. The aircraft, a Vampire jet fighter of the Indian Air Force, returned safely to its base at Kamina airfield. The pilot, however, was wounded by small arms fire. His condition is reported as satisfactory.

'The United Nations Commander in Katanga, General Rhee, has lodged a strong protest with the Katangese government—' The announcer's voice was overlaid by the electric crackle of static.

'We winged him!' rejoiced Wally Hendry. The scab on his cheek had dried black, with angry red edges.

'Shut up,' snapped Bruce, 'we're trying to hear what's happening.'

'You can't hear a bloody thing now. André, there's a bottle in my pack. Get it! I'm going to drink to that coolie with a bullet up his—'

Then the radio cleared and the announcer's voice came through loudly.

'—at Senwati Mission fifty miles from the river harbour of Port Reprieve. A spokesman for the Central Congolese Government denied that Congolese troops were operating in this area, and it is feared that a large body of armed bandits is taking advantage of the unsettled conditions to—' Again the static drowned it out.

'Damn this set,' muttered Bruce as he tried to tune it.

'—stated today that the removal of missile equipment from the Russian bases in Cuba had been confirmed by aerial reconnaissance—'

'That's all that we are interested in.' Bruce switched off the radio. 'What a shambles! Ruffy, where is Senwati Mission?'

'Top end of the swamp, near the Rhodesian border.'

'Fifty miles from Port Reprieve,' muttered Bruce, not attempting to conceal his anxiety.

'It's more than that by road, boss, more like a hundred.'

'That should take them three or four days in this weather, with time off for looting along the way,' Bruce calculated. 'It will be cutting it fairly fine. We must get through to Port Reprieve by tomorrow evening and pull out again at dawn the next day.'

'Why not keep going tonight?' Hendry removed the bottle from his lips to ask. 'Better than sitting here being eaten by mosquitoes.'

'We'll stay,' Bruce answered. 'It won't do anybody much good to derail this lot in the dark.' He turned back to Ruffy. 'Three-hour watches tonight, Sergeant Major. Lieutenant Haig will take the first, then Lieutenant Hendry, then Lieutenant de Surrier, and I'll do the dawn spell.'

'Okay, boss. I'd better make sure my boys aren't sleeping.' He left the compartment and the broken glass from the corridor windows crunched under his boots.

'I'll be on my way also.' Mike stood up and pulled the groundsheet over his shoulders.

'Don't waste the batteries of the searchlights, Mike. Sweep every ten minutes or so.'

'Okay, Bruce.' Mike looked across at Hendry. 'I'll call you at nine o'clock.'

'Jolly good show, old fruit.' Wally exaggerated Mike's accent. 'Good hunting, what!' and then as Mike left the compartment, 'Silly old bugger, why does he have to tâlk like that?'

No one answered him, and he pulled up his shirt behind.

'André, what's this on my back?'

'It's a pimple.'

'Well, squeeze it then.'

Bruce woke in the night, sweating, with the mosquitoes whining about his face. Outside it was still raining and occasionally the reflected light from the searchlight on the roof of the coach lit the interior dimly.

On one of the bottom bunks Mike Haig lay on his back. His face was shining with sweat and he rolled his head from side to side on the pillow. He was grinding his teeth – a sound to which Bruce had become accustomed, and he preferred it to Hendry's snores.

'You poor old bugger,' whispered Bruce.

From the bunk opposite, André de Surrier whimpered. In sleep he looked like a child with dark soft hair falling over his forehead.

Chapter Six

The rain petered out in the dawn and the sun was hot before it cleared the horizon. It lifted a warm mist from the dripping forest. As they ran north the forest thickened, the trees grew closer together and the undergrowth beneath them was coarser than it had been around Elisabethville.

Through the warm misty dawn Bruce saw the water tower at Msapa Junction rising like a lighthouse above the forest, its silver paint streaked with brown rust. Then they came round the last curve in the tracks and the little settlement huddled before them.

It was small, half a dozen buildings in all, and there was about it the desolate aspect of human habitation reverting to jungle.

Beside the tracks stood the water tower and the raised concrete coal bins. Then the station buildings of wood and iron, with the large sign above the verandah:

'MSAPA JUNCTION. Elevation 963m.'

An avenue of casia flora trees with very dark green foliage and orange flowers; and beyond that, on the edge of the forest, a row of cottages.

One of the cottages had been burned, its ruins were fire blackened and tumbled; and the gardens had lost all sense of discipline with three months' neglect.

'Driver, stop beside the water tower. You have fifteen minutes to fill your boiler.'

'Thank you, monsieur.'

With a heavy sigh of steam the loco pulled up beside the tower.

'Haig, take four men and go back to give the driver a hand.'

'Okay, Bruce.'

Bruce turned once more to the radio.

'Hendry.'

'Hello there.'

'Get a patrol together, six men, and search those cottages. Then take a took at the edge of the bush, we don't want any unexpected visitors.'

Wally Hendry waved an acknowledgement from the leading truck and Bruce went on:

'Put de Surrier on.' He watched Hendry pass the set to André. 'De Surrier, you are in charge of the leading trucks in Hendry's absence. Keep Hendry covered, but watch the bush behind you also. They could come from there.'

Bruce switched off the set and turned to Ruffy. 'Stay up here on the roof, Ruffy. I'm going to chase them up with the watering. If you see anything, don't write me a postcard, start pooping off.'

Ruffy nodded. 'Have some breakfast to take with you.' He proffered an open bottle of beer.

'Better than bacon and eggs.' Bruce accepted the bottle and climbed down on to the platform. Sipping the beer he walked back along the train and looked up at Mike and the engine driver in the tower.

'Is it empty?' he called up at them.

'Half full, enough for a bath if you want one,' answered Mike.

'Don't tempt me.' The idea was suddenly very attractive, for he could smell his own stale body odour and his eyelids were itchy and swollen from mosquito bites. 'My kingdom for a bath.' He ran his fingers over his jowls and they rasped over stiff beard.

He watched them swing the canvas hose out over the loco. The chubby little engine driver clambered up and sat astride the boiler as he fitted the hose.

A shout behind him made Bruce turn quickly, and he saw Hendry's patrol coming back from the cottages. They were dragging two small prisoners with them.

'Hiding in the first cottage,' shouted Hendry. 'They tried to leg it into the bush.' He prodded one of them with his bayonet. The child cried out and twisted in the hands of the gendarme who held her.

'Enough of that.' Bruce stopped him from using the bayonet again and went to meet them. He looked at the two children.

The girl was close to puberty with breasts like insect bites just starting to show, thin-legged with enlarged knee-caps out of proportion to her thighs and calves. She wore only a dirty piece of trade cloth drawn up between her legs and secured round her waist by a length of bark string, and the tribal tattoo marks across her chest and cheeks and forehead stood proud in ridges of scar tissue.

'Ruffy.' Bruce called him down from the coach. 'Can you speak to them?'

Ruffy picked up the boy and held him on his hip. He was younger than the girl – seven, perhaps eight years old. Very dark skinned and completely naked, as naked as the terror on his face.

Ruffy grunted sharply and the gendarme released the girl. She stood trembling, making no attempt to escape.

Then in a soothing rumble Ruffy began talking to the boy on his hip; he smiled as he spoke and stroked the child's head. Slowly a little of the fear melted and the boy answered in a piping treble that Bruce could not understand.

'What does he say?' urged Bruce.

'He thinks we're going to eat them,' laughed Ruffy. 'Not enough here for a decent breakfast.' He patted the skinny little arm, grey with crushed filth, then he gave an order to one of the gendarmes. The man disappeared into the coach and came back with a handful of chocolate bars. Still talking, Ruffy peeled one of them and placed it in the boy's mouth. The child's eyes widened appreciatively at the taste and he chewed quickly, his eyes on Ruffy's face, his answers now muffled with chocolate.

At last Ruffy turned to Bruce.

'No trouble here, boss. They come from a small village about an hour's walk away. Just five or six families, and no war party. These kids sneaked across to have a look at the houses, pinch what they could perhaps, but that's all.'

'How many men at this village?' asked Bruce, and Ruffy turned back to the boy. In reply to the question he held up the fingers of both hands, without interrupting his chewing.

'Does he know if the line is clear through to Port Reprieve? Have they burnt the bridges or torn up the tracks?' Both children were dumb to this question. The boy swallowed the last of his chocolate and looked hungrily at Ruffy, who filled his mouth again.

'Jesus,' muttered Hendry with deep disgust. 'Is this a crèche or something. Let's all play ring around the roses.'

'Shut up,' snapped Bruce, and then to Ruffy, 'Have they seen any soldiers?' Two heads shaken in solemn unison.

'Have they seen any war parties of their own people?'

Again solemn negative.

'All right, give them the rest of the chocolate,' instructed Bruce. That was all he could get out of them, and time was wasting. He glanced back at the tower and saw that Haig and the engine driver had finished watering. For a further second he studied the boy. His own son would be about the same age now; it was twelve months since – Bruce stopped himself hurriedly. That way lay madness.

'Hendry, take them back to the edge of the bush and turn them loose. Hurry up. We've wasted long enough.'

'You're telling me!' grunted Hendry and beckoned to the two children. With Hendry leading and a gendarme on each side they trotted away obediently and disappeared behind the station building.

'Driver, are your preparations complete?'

'Yes, monsieur, we are ready to depart.'

'Shovel all the coal in, we've gotta keep her rolling.' Bruce smiled at him, he liked the little man and their stilted exchanges gave him pleasure.

'Pardon, monsieur.'

'It was an imbecility, a joke – forgive me.'

'Ah, a joke!' The roly-poly stomach wobbled merrily.

'Okay, Mike,' Bruce shouted, 'get your men aboard. We are—'

A burst of automatic gunfire cut his voice short. It came from behind the station buildings, and it battered into the heat-muted morning with such startling violence that for an instant Bruce stood paralysed.

'Haig,' he yelled, 'get up front and take over from de Surrier.' That was the weak point, and Mike's party ran down the train.

'You men.' Bruce stopped the six gendarmes. 'Come with me.' They fell in behind him, and with a quick glance Bruce assured himself that the train was safe. All along its length rifle barrels were poking out protectively, while on the roof Ruffy was dragging the Bren round to cover the flank. A charge by even a thousand Baluba must fail before the fire power that was ready now to receive it.

'Come on,' said Bruce and ran, with the gendarmes behind him, to the sheltering wall of the station building. There had been no shot fired since that initial burst, which could mean either that it was a false alarm or that Hendry's party had been overwhelmed by the first rush.

The door of the station master's office was locked. Bruce kicked and it crashed open with the weight of his booted foot behind it.

I've always wanted to do that, he thought happily in his excitement, ever since I saw Gable do it in *San Francisco*.

'You four – inside! Cover us from the windows.' They crowded into the room with their rifles held ready. Through the open door Bruce saw the telegraph equipment on a table by the far wall; it was clattering metallically from traffic on the Elisabethville–Jadotville line. Why is it that under the stimulus of excitement my mind always registers irrelevances? Which thought is another irrelevancy, he decided.

'Come on, you two, stay with me.' He led them down the outside wall, keeping in close to its sheltering bulk, pausing at the corner to check the load of his rifle and slip the selector on to rapid fire.

A further moment he hesitated. What will I find around this corner? A hundred naked savages crowded round the mutilated bodies of Hendry and his gendarmes, or?

Crouching, ready to jump back behind the wall, rifle held at high port across his chest, every muscle and nerve of his body cocked like a hair-trigger, Bruce stepped sideways into the open.

Hendry and the two gendarmes stood in the dusty road beyond the first cottage. They were relaxed, talking together, Hendry reloading his rifle, cramming the magazine with big red hands on which the gingery hair caught the sunlight. A cigarette dangled from his lower lip and he laughed suddenly, throwing his head back as he did so and the cigarette ash dropped down his jacket front. Bruce noticed the long dark sweat stain across his shoulders.

The two children lay in the road fifty yards farther on.

Bruce was suddenly cold, it came from inside, a cramping coldness of the guts and chest. Slowly he straightened up and began to walk towards the children. His feet fell silently in the powder dust and the only sound was his own breathing, hoarse, as though a wounded beast followed close behind him. He walked past Hendry and the two gendarmes without looking at them; but they stopped talking, watching him uneasily.

He reached the girl first and went down on one knee beside her, laying his rifle aside and turning her gently on to her back.

'This isn't true,' he whispered. 'This can't be true.'

The bullet had taken half her chest out with it, a hole the size of a coffee cup, with the blood still moving in it, but slowly, oozing, welling up into it with the viscosity of new honey.

Bruce moved across to the boy; he felt an almost dreamlike sense of unreality.

'No, this isn't true.' He spoke louder, trying to undo it with words.

Three bullets had hit the boy; one had torn his arm loose at the shoulder and the sharp white end of the bone pointed accusingly out of the wound. The other bullets had severed his trunk almost in two.

It came from far away, like the rising roar of a train along a tunnel. Bruce could feel his whole being shaken by the strength of it, he shut his eyes and listened to the roaring in his head, and with his eyes tight closed his vision was filled with the colour of blood.

'Hold on!' a tiny voice screamed in his roaring head. 'Don't let go, fight it. Fight it as you've fought before.'

And he clung like a flood victim to the straw of his sanity while the great roaring was all around him. Then the roar was muted, rumbling away, gone past, a whisper, now nothing.

The coldness came back to him, a coldness more vast than the flood had been.

He opened his eyes and breathed again, stood up and walked back to where Hendry stood with the two gendarmes.

'Corporal,' Bruce addressed one of the men beside Hendry; and with a shock he heard that his own voice was calm, without any trace of the fury that had so nearly carried him away on its flood.

'Corporal, go back to the train. Tell Lieutenant Haig and Sergeant Major Ruffararo that I want them here.'

Thankfully the man went, and Bruce spoke to Wally Hendry in the same dispassionate tone.

'I told you to turn them loose,' he said.

'So they could run home and call the whole pack down on us – is that what you wanted, Bucko?' Hendry had recovered now, he was defiant, grinning.

'So instead you murdered them?'

'Murdered! You crazy or something, Bruce? They're Balubes, aren't they? Bloody man-eating Balubes!' shouted Hendry angrily, no longer grinning. 'What's wrong with you, man? This is war, Bucko, war. C'est la guerre, like the man said, c'est la guerre!' Then suddenly his voice moderated again. 'Let's forget it. I did what was right, now let's forget it; what's two more bloody Balubes after all the killing that's been going on. Let's forget it.'

Bruce did not answer, he lit a cigarette and looked beyond Hendry for the others to come.

'How's that, Bruce? You willing we just forget it?' persisted Hendry.

'On the contrary, Hendry, I make you a sacred oath, and I call upon God to witness it.' Bruce was not looking at him, he couldn't trust himself to look at Hendry without killing him. 'This is my promise to you: I will have you hanged for this, not shot, hanged on good hemp rope. I have sent for Haig and Ruffararo so we'll have plenty of witnesses. The first thing I do once we get back to Elisabethville will be to turn you over to the proper authorities.'

'You don't mean that!'

'I have never meant anything so seriously in my life.'

'Jesus, Bruce—!'

Then Haig and Ruffy came; they came running until they saw, and then they stopped suddenly and stood uncertainly in the bright sun, looking from Bruce to the two frail little corpses lying in the road.

'What happened?' asked Mike.

'Hendry shot them,' answered Bruce.

'What for?'

'Only he knows.'

'You mean he – he just killed them, just shot them down?'

'Yes.'

'My God,' said Mike, and then again, his voice dull with shock, 'my God.'

'Go and look at them, Haig. I want you to look closely so you remember.'

Haig walked across to the children.

'You too, Ruffy. You'll be a witness at the trial.'

Mike Haig and Ruffy walked side by side to where the children lay, and stood staring down at them. Hendry shuffled his feet in the dust awkwardly and then went on loading the magazine of his rifle.

'Oh, for Chrissake!' he blustered. 'What's all the fuss. They're just a couple of Balubes.'

Wheeling slowly to face him Mike Haig's face was a yellowish colour with only his cheeks and his nose still flushed with the tiny burst veins beneath the surface of the skin, but there was no colour in his lips. Each breath he drew sobbed in his throat. He started back towards Hendry, still breathing that way, and his mouth was working as he tried to force it to speak. As he came on he unslung the rifle from his shoulder.

'Haig!' said Bruce sharply.

'This time – you – you bloody – this is the last—' mouthed Haig.

'Watch it, Bucko!' Hendry warned him. He stepped back, clumsily trying to fit the loaded magazine on to his rifle.

Mike Haig dropped the point of his bayonet to the level of Hendry's stomach.

'Haig!' shouted Bruce, and Haig charged surprisingly fast for a man of his age, leaning forward, leading with the bayonet at Hendry's stomach, the incoherent mouthings reaching their climax in a formless bellow.

'Come on, then!' Hendry answered him and stepped forward. As they came together Hendry swept the bayonet to one side with the butt of his own rifle. The point went under his armpit and they collided chest to chest, staggering as Haig's weight carried them backwards. Hendry dropped his rifle and locked both arms round Haig's neck, forcing his head back so that his face was tilted up at the right angle.

'Look out, Mike, he's going to butt!' Bruce had recognized the move, but his warning came too late. Hendry's head jerked forward and Mike gasped as the front of Hendry's steel helmet caught him across the bridge of the nose. The rifle slipped from Mike's grip and fell into the road, he lifted his hands and covered his face with spread fingers and the redness oozed out between them.

Again Hendry's head jerked forward like a hammer and again Mike gasped as the steel smashed into his face and fingers.

'Knee him, Mike!' Bruce yelled as he tried to take up a position from which to intervene, but they were staggering in a circle, turning like a wheel and Bruce could not get in.

Hendry's legs were braced apart as he drew his head back to strike again, and Mike's knee went up between them, all the way up with power into the fork of Hendry's crotch.

Breaking from the clinch, his mouth open in a silent scream of agony, Hendry doubled up with both hands holding his lower stomach, and sagged slowly on to his knees in the dust.

Dazed, with blood running into his mouth, Mike fumbled with the canvas flap of his holster.

'I'll kill you, you murdering swine.'

The pistol came out into his right hand; short-barrelled, blue and ugly.

Bruce stepped up behind him, his thumb found the nerve centre below the elbow and as he dug in the pistol dropped from Mike's paralysed hand and dangled on its lanyard against his knee.

'Ruffy, stop him,' Bruce shouted, for Hendry was clawing painfully at the rifle that lay in the dust beside him.

'Got it, boss!' Ruffy's huge boot trod down heavily on the rifle and Hendry struggled ineffectually to pull it out from under him.

'Take his pistol,' Bruce ordered.

'Got that too!' Ruffy stooped quickly over the crawling body at his feet, in one swift movement opened the flap of the holster, drew the revolver and the lanyard snapped like cotton as he jerked on it.

They stood like that: Bruce holding Haig from behind, and Hendry crouched at Ruffy's feet. The only sound for several seconds was the hoarse rasping of breath.

Bruce felt Mike Haig relaxing in his grip as the madness left him; he unclipped his pistol from its lanyard and let it drop.

'Leave me, Bruce. I'm all right now.'

'Are you sure? I don't want to shoot you.'

'No, I'm all right.'

'If you start it again, I'll have to shoot you. Do you understand?'

'Yes, I'll be all right now. I lost my senses for a moment.'

'You certainly did,' Bruce agreed, and released him.

They formed a circle round the kneeling Hendry, and Bruce spoke.

'If either you or Haig start it again you'll answer to me, do you hear me?' Hendry looked up, his small eyes slitted with pain. He did not answer.

'Do you hear me?' Bruce repeated the question and Hendry nodded.

'Good! From now on, Hendry, you are under open arrest. I can't spare men to guard you, and you're welcome to escape if you'd like to try. The local gentry would certainly entertain you most handsomely, they'd probably arrange a special banquet in your honour.'

Hendry's lips drew back in a snarl that exposed teeth with green slimy stains on them.

'But remember my promise, Hendry, as soon as we get back to—'

'Wally, Wally, are you hurt?' André came running from the direction of the station. He knelt beside Hendry.

'Get away, leave me alone.' Hendry struck out at him impatiently and André recoiled.

'De Surrier, who gave you permission to leave your post? Get back to the train.'

André looked up uncertainly, and then back to Hendry.

'De Surrier, you heard me. Get going. And you also, Haig.'

He watched them disappear behind the station building before he glanced once more at the two children. There was a smear of blood and melted chocolate across the boy's cheek and his eyes were wide open in an expression of surprise. Already the flies were settling, crawling delightedly over the two small corpses.

'Ruffy, get spades. Bury them under those trees.' He pointed at the avenue of casia flora. 'But do it quickly.' He spoke brusquely so that how he felt would not show in his voice.

'Okay, boss. I'll fix it.'

'Come on, Hendry,' Bruce snapped, and Wally Hendry heaved to his feet and followed him meekly back to the train.

Chapter Seven

Slowly from Msapa Junction they travelled northwards through the forest. Each tree seemed to have been cast from the same mould, tall and graceful in itself, but when multiplied countless million times the effect was that of numbing monotony. Above them was a lane of open sky with the clouds scattered, but slowly regrouping for the next assault, and the forest shut in the moist heat so they sweated even in the wind of the train's movement.

'How is your face?' asked Bruce and Mike Haig touched the parallel swellings across his forehead where the skin was broken and discoloured.

'It will do,' he decided; then he lifted his eyes and looked across the open trucks at Wally Hendry. 'You shouldn't have stopped me, Bruce.'

Bruce did not answer, but he also watched Hendry as he leaned uncomfortably against the side of the leading truck, obviously favouring his injuries, his face turned half away from them, talking to André.

'You should have let me kill him,' Mike went on. 'A man who can shoot down two small children in cold blood and then laugh about it afterwards—!' Mike left the rest unsaid, but his hands were opening and closing in his lap.

'It's none of your business,' said Bruce, sensitive to the implied rebuke. 'What are you? One of God's avenging angels?'

'None of my business, you say?' Mike turned quickly to face Bruce. 'My God, what kind of man are you? I hope for your sake that you don't mean that!'

'I'll tell you in words of one syllable what kind of man I am, Haig,' Bruce answered flatly. 'I'm the kind that minds my own bloody business, that lets other people lead their own lives. I am ready to take reasonable measures to prevent others flouting the code which society has drawn up for us, but that's all. Hendry has committed murder; this I agree is a bad thing, and when we get back to Elisabethville I will bring it to the attention of the people whose business it is. But I am not going to wave banners and quote from the Bible and froth at the mouth.'

'That's all?'

'That's all.'

'You don't feel sorry for those two kids?'

'Yes I do. But pity doesn't heal bullet wounds; all it does is distress me. So I switch off the pity – they can't use it.'

'You don't feel anger or disgust or horror at Hendry.'

'The same thing applies,' explained Bruce, starting to lose patience again. 'I could work up a sweat about it if I let myself loose on an emotional orgy, as you are doing.'

'So instead you treat something as evil as Hendry with an indifferent tolerance?' asked Mike.

'Jesus Christ!' grated Bruce. 'What the hell do you want me to do?'

'I want you to stop playing dead. I want you to be able to recognize evil and to destroy it.' Mike was starting to lose his temper also; his nerves were taut.

'That's great! Do you know where I can buy a secondhand crusader outfit and a white horse, then single-handed I will ride out to wage war on cruelty and ignorance, lust and greed and hatred and poverty—'

'That's not what I—' Mike tried to interrupt, but Bruce overrode him, his handsome face flushed darkly with anger and the sun. 'You want me to destroy evil wherever I find it. You old fool, don't you know that it has a hundred heads and that for each one you cut off another hundred grow in its place? Don't you know that it's in you also, so to destroy it you have to destroy yourself?'

'You're a coward, Curry! The first time you burn a finger you run away and build yourself an asbestos shelter—'

'I don't like being called names, Haig. Put a leash on your tongue.'

Mike paused and his expression changed, softening into a grin.

'I'm sorry, Bruce. I was just trying to teach you—'

'Thank you,' scoffed Bruce, his voice still harsh; he had not been placated by the apology. 'You are going to teach me, thanks very much! But what are you going to teach me, Haig? What are you qualified to teach? "How to find success and happiness" by Laughing Lad Haig who worked his way down to a lieutenancy in the black army of Katanga – how's that as a title for your lecture, or do you prefer something more technical like: "The applications of alcohol to spiritual research—" '

'All right, Bruce. Drop it, I'll shut up,' and Bruce saw how deeply he had wounded Mike. He regretted it then, he would have liked to unsay it. But that's one thing you can never do.

Beside him Mike Haig was suddenly much older and more tired looking, the pouched wrinkles below his eyes seemed to have deepened in the last few seconds, and a little more of the twinkle had gone from his eyes. His short laughter had a bitter humourless ring to it.

'When you put it that way it's really quite funny.'

'I punched a little low,' admitted Bruce, and then, 'perhaps I should let you shoot Hendry. A waste of ammunition really, but seeing that you want to so badly,' Bruce drew his pistol and offered it to Mike butt first, 'use mine.' He grinned disarmingly at Mike and his grin was almost impossible to resist; Mike started to laugh. It wasn't a very good joke, but somehow it caught fire between them and suddenly they were laughing together.

Mike Haig's battered features spread like warm butter and twenty years dropped from his face. Bruce leaned back against the sandbags with his mouth wide open, the pistol still in his hand and his long lean body throbbing uncontrollably with laughter.

There was something feverish in it, as though they were trying with laughter to gargle away the taste of blood and hatred. It was the laughter of despair.

Below them the men in the trucks turned to watch them, puzzled at first, and then beginning to chuckle in sympathy, not recognizing the sickness of that sound.

'Hey, boss,' called Ruffy. 'First time I ever seen you laugh like you meant it.'

And the epidemic spread, everyone was laughing, even André de Surrier was smiling.

Only Wally Hendry was untouched by it, silent and sullen, watching them with small expressionless eyes.

They came to the bridge over the Cheke in the middle afternoon. Both the road and the railway line crossed it side by side, but after this brief meeting they diverged and the road twisted away to the left. The river was padded on each bank by dense dark green bush; three hundred yards thick, a matted tangle of thorn and tree fern with the big trees growing up through it and bursting into flower as they reached the sunlight.

'Good place for an ambush,' muttered Mike Haig, eyeing the solid green walls of vegetation on each side of the lines.

'Charming, isn't it,' agreed Bruce, and by the uneasy air of alertness that had settled on his gendarmes it was clear that they agreed with him.

The train nosed its way carefully into the river bush like a steel snake along a rabbit run, and they came to the river. Bruce switched on the set.

'Driver, stop this side of the bridge. I wish to inspect it before entrusting our precious cargo to it.'

'Oui, monsieur.'

The Cheke river at this point was fifty yards wide, deep, quick-flowing and angry with flood water which had almost covered the white sand beaches along each bank. Its bottle-green colour was smoked with mud and there were whirlpools round the stone columns of the bridge.

'Looks all right,' Haig gave his opinion. 'How far are we from Port Reprieve now?'

Bruce spread his field map on the roof of the coach between his legs and found the brackets that straddled the convoluted ribbon of the river.

'Here we are.' He touched it and then ran his finger along the stitched line of the railway until it reached the red circle that marked Port Reprieve. 'About thirty miles to go, another hour's run. We'll be there before dark.'

'Those are the Lufira hills.' Mike Haig pointed to the blue smudge that only just showed above the forest ahead of them.

'We'll be able to see the town from the top,' agreed Bruce. 'The river runs parallel to them on the other side, and the swamp is off to the right, the swamp is the source of the river.'

He rolled the map and passed it back to Ruffy who slid it into the plastic map case.

'Ruffy, Lieutenant Haig and I are going ahead to have a look at the bridge. Keep an eye on the bush.'

'Okay, boss. You want a beer to take with you?'

'Thanks.' Bruce was thirsty and he emptied half the bottle before climbing down to join Mike on the gravel embankment. Rifles unslung, watching the bush on each side uneasily, they hurried forward and with relief reached the bridge and went out into the centre of it.

'Seems solid enough,' commented Mike. 'No one has tampered with it.'

'It's wood.' Bruce stamped on the heavy wild mahogany timbers. They were three feet thick and stained with a dark chemical to inhibit rotting.

'So, it's wood?' enquired Mike.

'Wood burns,' explained Bruce. 'It would be easy to burn it down.' He leaned his elbows on the guard rail, drained the beer bottle and dropped it to the surface of the river twenty feet below. There was a thoughtful expression on his face.

'Very probably there are Baluba in the bush' – he pointed at the banks – 'watching us at this moment. They might get the same idea. I wonder if I should leave a guard here?'

Mike leaned on the rail beside him and they both stared out to where the river took a bend two hundred yards downstream; in the crook of the bend grew a tree twice as tall as any of its neighbours. The trunk was straight and covered with smooth silvery bark and its foliage piled to a high green steeple against the clouds. It was the natural point of focus for their eyes as they weighed the problem.

'I wonder what kind of tree that is. I've never seen one like it before.' Bruce was momentarily diverted by the grandeur of it. 'It looks like a giant blue gum.'

'It's quite a sight,' Mike concurred. 'I'd like to go down and have a closer—'
Then suddenly he stiffened and there was an edge of alarm in his voice as he pointed.

'Bruce, there! What's that in the lower branches.'

'Where?'

'Just above the first fork, on the left—' Mike was pointing and suddenly Bruce saw it. For a second he thought it was a leopard, then he realized it was too dark and long.

'It's a man,' exclaimed Mike.

'Baluba,' snapped Bruce; he could see the shape now and the sheen of naked black flesh, the kilt of animal tails and the head-dress of feathers. A long bow stood up behind the man's shoulder as he balanced on the branch and steadied himself with one hand against the trunk. He was watching them.

Bruce glanced round at the train. Hendry had noticed their agitation and, following the direction of Mike's raised arm he had spotted the Baluba. Bruce realized what Hendry was going to do and he opened his mouth to shout, but before he could do so Hendry had snatched his rifle off his shoulder, swung it up and fired a long, rushing, hammering burst.

'The trigger-happy idiot,' snarled Bruce and looked back at the tree. Slabs of white bark were flying from the trunk and the bullets reaped leaves that fluttered down like crippled insects, but the Baluba had disappeared.

The gunfire ceased abruptly and in its place Hendry was shouting with hoarse excitement.

'I got him, I got the bastard.'

'Hendry!' Bruce's voice was also hoarse, but with anger, '—Who ordered you to fire?'

'He was a bloody Baluba, a mucking big bloody Baluba. Didn't you see him, hey? Didn't you see him, man?'

'Come here, Hendry.'

'I got the bastard,' rejoiced Hendry.

'Are you deaf? Come here!'

While Hendry climbed down from the truck and came towards them Bruce asked Haig:

'Did he hit him?'

'I'm not sure. I don't think so, I think he jumped. If he had been hit he'd have been thrown backwards, you know how it knocks them over.'

'Yes,' said Bruce, 'I know.' A .300 bullet from an FN struck with a force of well over a ton. When you hit a man there was no doubt about it. All right, so the Baluba was still in there.

Hendry came up, swaggering, laughing with excitement.

'So you killed, hey?' Bruce asked.

'Stone dead, stone bloody dead!'

'Can you see him?'

'No, he's down in the bush.'

'Do you want to go and have a look at him, Hendry? Do you want to go and get his ears?'

Ears are the best trophy you can take from a man, not as good as the skin of a black-maned lion or the great bossed horn of a buffalo, but better than a scalp. The woolly cap of an African scalp is a drab thing, messy to take and difficult to cure. You have to salt it and stretch it inside out over a helmet; even then it smells badly. Ears are much less trouble and Hendry was an avid collector. He was not the only one in the army of Katanga; the taking of ears was common practice.

'Yeah, I want them.' Hendry detached the bayonet from the muzzle of his rifle. 'I'll nip down and get them.'

'You can't let anyone go in there Bruce. Not even him,' protested Haig quietly.

'Why not? He deserves it, he worked hard for it.'

'Only take a minute.' Hendry ran his thumb along the bayonet to test the edge. My God! he really means it, thought Bruce; he'd go into that tangled stuff for a pair of ears – he's not brave he's just stupendously lacking in imagination.

'Wait for me, Bruce, it won't take long.' Hendry started back.

'You're not serious, Bruce?' Mike asked.

'No,' agreed Bruce, 'I'm not serious,' and his voice was cold and hard as he caught hold of Hendry's shoulder and stopped him.

'Listen to me! You have no more chances – that was it. I'm waiting for you now, Hendry. Just once more, that's all. Just once more.'

Hendry's face turned sullen again.

'Don't push me, Bucko.'

'Get back to the train and bring it across,' said Bruce contemptuously and turned to Haig.

'Now we'll have to leave a guard here. They know we've gone across and they'll burn it for a certainty, especially after that little fiasco.'

'Who are you going to leave?'

'Ten men, say, under a sergeant. We'll be back by nightfall or tomorrow morning at the latest. They should be safe enough. I doubt there is a big war party here, a few strays perhaps, but the main force will be closer to the town.'

'I hope you're right.'

'So do I,' said Bruce absently, his mind busy with the problem of defending the bridge. 'We'll strip all the sandbags off the coaches and build an emplacement here in the middle of the roadway, leave two of the battery-operated searchlights and a case of flares with them, one of the Brens and a couple of cases of grenades. Food and water for a week. No, they'll be all right.'

The train was rolling down slowly towards them – and a single arrow rose from the edge of the jungle. Slowly it rose, curving in flight and falling towards the train, dropping faster now, silently into the mass of men in the leading truck.

So Hendry had missed and the Baluba had come up stream through the thick bush to launch his arrow in retaliation. Bruce sprang to the guard rail and, using it as a rest for his rifle, opened up in short bursts, searching the edge of the jungle blindly, firing into the green mass and seeing it tremble with his bullets. Haig was shooting also, hunting the area from which the arrow had come.

The train was up to them now and Bruce slung his rifle over his shoulder and scrambled up the side of the truck. He pushed his way to the radio set.

'Driver, stop the covered coaches in the middle of the bridge,' he snapped, and then he switched it off and looked for Ruffy.

'Sergeant Major, get all those sandbags off the roof into the roadway.' While they worked, the gendarmes would be protected from further arrows by the body of the train.

'Okay, boss.'

'Kanaki.' Bruce picked his most reliable sergeant. 'I am leaving you here with ten men to hold the bridge for us. Take one of the Brens, and two of the lights—'

Quickly Bruce issued his orders and then he had time to ask André:

'What happened to that arrow? Was anyone hit?'

'No, missed by a few inches. Here it is.'

'That was a bit of luck.' Bruce took the arrow from André and inspected it quickly. A light reed, crudely fletched with green leaves and with the iron head bound into it with a strip of rawhide. It looked fragile and ineffectual, but the barbs of the head were smeared thickly with a dark paste that had dried like toffee.

'Pleasant,' murmured Bruce, and then he shuddered slightly. He could imagine it embedded in his body with the poison purple-staining the flesh beneath the skin. He had heard that it was not a comfortable death, and the iron-tipped reed was suddenly malignant and repulsive. He snapped it in half and threw it out over the side of the bridge before he jumped down from the truck to supervise the building of the guard post.

'Not enough sandbags, boss.'

'Take the mattresses off all the bunks, Ruffy.' Bruce solved that quickly. The leather-covered coir pallets would stop an arrow with ease.

Fifteen minutes later the post was completed, a shoulder-high ring of sandbags and mattresses large enough to accommodate ten men and their equipment, with embrasures sited to command both ends of the bridge.

'We'll be back early tomorrow, Kanaki. Let none of your men leave this post for any purpose; the gaps between the timbers are sufficient for purposes of sanitation.'

'We shall enjoy enviable comfort, Captain. But we will lack that which soothes.' Kanaki grinned meaningly at Bruce.

'Ruffy, leave them a case of beer.'

'A whole case?' Ruffy made no attempt to hide his shocked disapproval of such a prodigal order.

'Is my credit not good?'

'Your credit is okay, boss,' and then he changed to French to make his protest formal. 'My concern is the replacement of such a valuable commodity.'

'You're wasting time, Ruffy!'

Chapter Eight

From the bridge it was thirty miles to Port Reprieve. They met the road again six miles outside the town; it crossed under them and disappeared into the forest again to circle out round the high ground taking the easier route into Port Reprieve. But the railroad climbed up the hills in a series of traverses and came out at the top six hundred feet above the town. On the stony slopes the forest found meagre purchase and the vegetation was sparser; it did not obscure the view.

Standing on the roof Bruce looked out across the Lufira swamps to the north, a vastness of poisonous green swamp grass and open water, disappearing into the blue heat haze without any sign of ending. From its southern extremity it was drained by the Lufira river. The river was half a mile wide, deep olive-green, ruffled darker by eddies of wind across its surface, fenced into the very edge of the water by a solid barrier of dense river bush. In the angle formed by the swamp and the river was a headland which protected the natural harbour of Port Reprieve. The town was on a spit of land, the harbour on one side and a smaller swamp on the other. The road came round the right-hand side of the hills, crossed a causeway over the swamp and entered the single street of the town from the far side.

There were three large buildings in the centre of the town opposite the railway yard, their iron roofs bright beacons in the sunlight; and clustered round them were perhaps fifty smaller thatched dwellings.

Down on the edge of the harbour was a long shed, obviously a workshop, and two jetties ran out into the water. The diamond dredgers were moored alongside; three of them, ungainly black hulks with high superstructures and blunt ends.

It was a place of heat and fever and swamp smells, an ugly little village by a green reptile river.

'Nice place to retire,' Mike Haig grunted.

'Or open a health resort,' said Bruce.

Beyond the causeway, on the main headland, there was another cluster of buildings, just the tops showing above the forest. Among them rose the copper-clad spire of a church.

'Mission station,' guessed Bruce.

'St. Augustine's,' agreed Ruffy. 'My first wife's little brudder got himself educated there. He's an attaché to the ministry of something or other in Elisabethville now, doing damn good for himself.' Boasting a little.

'Bully for him,' said Bruce.

The train had started angling down the hills towards the town.

'Well, I reckon we've made it, boss.'

'I reckon also; all we have to do is get back again.'

'Yessir, I reckon that's all.'

And they ran into the town.

There were more than forty people in the crowd that lined the platform to welcome them.

We'll have a heavy load on the way home, thought Bruce as he ran his eye over them. He saw the bright spots of women's dresses in the throng. Bruce counted four of them. That's another complication; one day I hope I find something in this life that turns out exactly as expected, something that will run smoothly and evenly through to its right and logical conclusion. Some hope, he decided, some bloody hope.

The joy and relief of the men and women on the platform was pathetically apparent in their greetings. Most of the women were crying and the men ran beside the train like small boys as it slid in along the raised concrete platform. All of them were of mixed blood, Bruce noted. They varied in colour from creamy yellow to charcoal. The Belgians had certainly left much to be remembered by.

Standing back from the throng, a little aloof from the general jollification, was a half-blooded Belgian. There was an air of authority about him that was unmistakeable. On one side of him stood a large bosomy woman of his own advanced age, darker skinned than he was; but Bruce saw immediately that she was his wife. At his other hand stood a figure dressed in a white open-necked shirt and blue jeans that Bruce at first thought was a boy, until the head turned and he saw the long plume of dark hair that hung down her back, and the unmanly double pressure beneath the white shirt.

The train stopped and Bruce jumped down on to the platform and laughingly pushed his way through the crowds towards the Belgian. Despite a year in the Congo, Bruce had not grown accustomed to being kissed by someone who had not shaved for two or three days and who smelled strongly of garlic and cheap tobacco. This atrocity was committed upon him a dozen times or more before he arrived before the Belgian.

'The Good Lord bless you for coming to our aid, Monsieur Captain.' The

Belgian recognized the twin bars on the front of Bruce's helmet and held out his hand. Bruce had expected another kiss, so he accepted the handshake with relief.

'I am only glad that we are in time,' he answered.

'May I introduce myself – Martin Boussier, district manager of Union Minière Corporation, and this is my wife, Madame Boussier.' He was a tall man but, unlike his wife, sparsely fleshed. His hair was completely silver and his skin folded, toughened and browned by a life under the equatorial sun. Bruce took an instant liking to him. Madame Boussier pressed her bulk against Bruce and kissed him heartily. Her moustache was too soft to cause him discomfort and she smelled of toilet soap, which was a distinct improvement, decided Bruce.

'May I also present Madame Cartier,' and for the first time Bruce looked squarely at the girl. A number of things registered in his mind simultaneously: the paleness of her skin which was not unhealthy but had an opaque coolness which he wanted to touch, the size of her eyes which seemed to fill half her face, the unconscious provocation of her lips, and the use of the word *Madame* before her name.

'Captain Curry – of the Katanga Army,' said Bruce. She's too young to be married, can't be more than seventeen. She's still got that little girl freshness about her and I bet she smells like an unweaned puppy.

'Thank you for coming, monsieur.' She had a throatiness in her voice as though she were just about to laugh or to make love, and Bruce added three years to his estimate of her age. That was not a little girl's voice, nor were those little girl's legs in the jeans, and little girls had less under their shirt fronts.

His eyes came back to her face and he saw that there was colour in her cheeks now and sparks of annoyance in her eyes.

My God, he thought, I'm ogling her like a matelot on shore leave. He hurriedly transferred his attention back to Boussier, but his throat felt constricted as he asked:

'How many are you?'

'There are forty-two of us, of which five are women and two are children.'

Bruce nodded, it was what he had expected. The women could ride in one of the covered coaches. He turned and surveyed the railway yard.

'Is there a turn-table on which we can revolve the locomotive?' he asked Boussier.

'No, Captain.'

They would have to reverse all the way back to Msapa Junction, another complication. It would be more difficult to keep a watch on the tracks ahead, and it would mean a sooty and uncomfortable journey.

'What precautions have you taken against attack, monsieur?'

'They are inadequate, Captain,' Boussier admitted. 'I have not sufficient men to defend the town – most of the population left before the emergency. Instead I have posted sentries on all the approaches and I have fortified the hotel to the best of my ability. It was there we intended to stand in the event of attack.'

Bruce nodded again and glanced up at the sun. It was already reddening as it dropped towards the horizon, perhaps another hour or two of daylight.

'Monsieur, it is too late to entrain all your people and leave before nightfall. I intend to load their possessions this evening. We will stay overnight and leave in the early morning.'

'We are all anxious to be away from this place; we have twice seen large parties of Baluba on the edge of the jungle.'

'I understand,' said Bruce. 'But the dangers of travelling by night exceed those of waiting another twelve hours.'

'The decision is yours,' Boussier agreed. 'What do you wish us to do now.'

'Please see to the embarkation of your people. I regret that only the most essential possessions may be entrained. We will be almost a hundred persons.'

'I shall see to that myself,' Boussier assured him, 'and then?'

'Is that the hotel?' Bruce pointed across the street at one of the large double-storied buildings. It was only two hundred yards from where they stood.

'Yes, Captain.'

'Good,' said Bruce. 'It is close enough. Your people can spend the night there in more comfort than aboard the train.'

He looked at the girl again; she was watching him with a small smile on her face. It was a smile of almost maternal amusement, as though she were watching a little boy playing at soldiers. Now it was Bruce's turn to feel annoyed. He was suddenly embarrassed by his uniform and epaulettes, by the pistol at his hip, the automatic rifle across his shoulder and the heavy helmet on his head.

'I will require someone who is familiar with the area to accompany me, I want to inspect your defences,' he said to Boussier.

'Madame Cartier could show you,' suggested Boussier's wife artlessly. I wonder if she noticed our little exchange, thought Bruce. Of course she did. All women have a most sensitive nose for that sort of thing.

'Will you go with the captain, Shermaine?' asked Madame Boussier.

'As the captain wishes.' She was still smiling.

'That is settled then,' said Bruce gruffly. 'I will meet you at the hotel in ten minutes, after I have made arrangements here.' He turned back to Boussier. 'You may proceed with the embarkation, monsieur.' Bruce left them and went back to the train.

'Hendry,' he shouted, 'you and de Surrier will stay on board. We are not leaving until the morning but these people are going to load their stuff now. In the meantime rig the searchlights to sweep both sides of the track and make sure the Brens are properly sited.'

Hendry grunted an acknowledgement without looking at Bruce.

'Mike, take ten men with you and go to the hotel. I want you there in case of trouble during the night.'

'Okay, Bruce.'

'Ruffy.'

'Sa!'

'Take a gang and help the driver refuel.'

'Okay, boss. Hey, boss!'

'Yes.' Bruce turned to him.

'When you go to the hotel, have a look-see maybe they got some beer up there. We're just about fresh out.'

'I'll keep it in mind.'

'Thanks, boss.' Ruffy looked relieved. 'I'd hate like hell to die of thirst in this hole.'

The townsfolk were streaming back towards the hotel. The girl Shermaine walked with the Boussiers, and Bruce heard Hendry's voice above him.

'Jesus, look what that pretty has got in her pants. What ever it is, one thing is sure: it's round and it's in two pieces, and those pieces move like they don't belong to each other.'

'You haven't any work to do, Hendry?' Bruce asked harshly.

'What's wrong, Curry,' Hendry jeered down at him. 'You got plans yourself. Is that it, Bucko?'

'She's married,' said Bruce, and immediately was surprised that he had said it.

'Sure,' laughed Hendry. 'All the best ones are married; that don't mean a thing, not a bloody thing.'

'Get on with your work,' snapped Bruce, and then to Haig, 'Are you ready? Come with me then.'

Chapter Nine

When they reached the hotel Boussier was waiting for them on the open verandah. He led Bruce aside and spoke quietly.

'Monsieur, I don't wish to be an alarmist but I have received some most disturbing news. There are brigands armed with modern weapons raiding down from the north. The last reports state that they had sacked Senwati Mission about three hundred kilometres north of here.'

'Yes,' Bruce nodded, 'I know about them. We heard on the radio.'

'Then you will have realized that they can be expected to arrive here very soon.'

'I don't see them arriving before tomorrow afternoon; by then we should be well on our way to Msapa Junction.'

'I hope you are right, monsieur. The atrocities committed by this General Moses at Senwati are beyond the conception of any normal mind. He appears to bear an almost pathological hatred for all people of European descent.' Boussier hesitated before going on. 'There were a dozen white nuns at Senwati. I have heard that they—'

'Yes,' Bruce interrupted him quickly; he did not want to listen to it. 'I can imagine. Try and prevent these stories circulating amongst your people. I don't want to have them panic.'

'Of course,' Boussier nodded.

'Do you know what force this General Moses commands?'

'It is not more than a hundred men but, as I have said, they are all armed with modern weapons. I have even heard that they have with them a cannon of some description, though I think this unlikely. They are travelling in a convoy of stolen vehicles and at Senwati they captured a gasoline tanker belonging to the commercial oil companies.'

'I see,' mused Bruce. 'But it doesn't alter my decision to remain here overnight. However, we must leave at first light tomorrow.'

'As you wish, Captain.'

'Now, monsieur,' Bruce changed the subject, 'I require some form of transport. Is that car in running order?' He pointed at a pale green Ford Ranchero station wagon parked beside the verandah wall.

'It is. It belongs to my company.' Boussier took a key ring from his pocket and handed it to Bruce. 'Here are the keys. The tank is full of gasoline.'

'Good,' said Bruce. 'Now if we can find Madame Cartier—'

She was waiting in the hotel lounge and she stood up as Bruce and Boussier came in.

'Are you ready, madame?'

'I await your pleasure,' she answered, and Bruce looked at her sharply. Just a trace of a twinkle in her dark blue eyes suggested that she was aware of the double meaning.

They walked out to the Ford and Bruce opened the door for her.

'You are gracious, monsieur.' She thanked him and slid into the seat. Bruce went round to the driver's side and climbed in beside her.

'It's nearly dark,' he said.

'Turn right on to the Msapa Junction road, there is one post there.'

Bruce drove out along the dirt road through the town until they came to the last house before the causeway. 'Here,' said the girl and Bruce stopped the car. There were two men there, both armed with sporting rifles. Bruce spoke to them. They had seen no sign of Baluba, but they were both very nervous. Bruce made a decision.

'I want you to go back to the hotel. The Baluba will have seen the train arrive; they won't attack in force, we'll be safe tonight. But they may try and cut a few throats if we leave you out here.'

The two half-breeds gathered together their belongings and set off towards the centre of town, obviously with lighter hearts.

'Where are the others?' Bruce asked the girl.

'The next post is at the pumping station down by the river, there are three men there.'

Bruce followed her directions. Once or twice as he drove he glanced surreptitiously at her. She sat in her corner of the seat with her legs drawn up sideways under her. She sat very still, Bruce noticed. I like a woman who doesn't fidget; it's soothing. Then she smiled; this one isn't soothing. She is as disturbing as hell! She turned suddenly and caught him looking again, but this time she smiled.

'You are English, aren't you, Captain?'

'No, I am a Rhodesian,' Bruce answered.

'It's the same,' said the girl. 'You speak French so very badly that you had to be English.'

Bruce laughed. 'Perhaps your English is better than my French,' he challenged her.

'It couldn't be much worse,' she answered him in his own language. 'You are different when you laugh, not so grim, not so heroic. Take the next road to your right.'

Bruce turned the Ford down towards the harbour.

'You are very frank,' he said. 'Also your English is excellent.'

'Do you smoke?' she asked, and when he nodded she lit two cigarettes and passed one to him.

'You are also very young to smoke, and very young to be married.'

She stopped smiling and swung her legs off the seat.

'Here is the pumping station,' she said.

'I beg your pardon. I shouldn't have said that.'

'It's of no importance.'

'It was an impertinence,' Bruce demurred.

'It doesn't matter.'

Bruce stopped the car and opened his door. He walked out on to the wooden jetty towards the pump house, and the boards rang dully under his boots. There was a mist coming up out of the reeds round the harbour and the frogs were piping in fifty different keys. He spoke to the men in the single room of the pump station.

'You can get back to the hotel by dark if you hurry.'

'Oui, monsieur,' they agreed. Bruce watched them set off up the road before he went to the car. He spun the starter motor and above the noise of it the girl asked:

'What is your given name, Captain Curry?'

'Bruce.'

She repeated it, pronouncing it 'Bruise,' and then asked:

'Why are you a soldier?'

'For many reasons.' His tone was flippant.

'You do not look like a soldier, for all your badges and your guns, for all the grimness and the frequent giving of orders.'

'Perhaps I am not a very good soldier.' He smiled at her.

'You are very efficient and very grim except when you laugh. But I am glad you do not look like one,' she said.

'Where is the next post?'

'On the railway line. There are two men there. Turn to your right again at the top, Bruce.'

'You are also very efficient, Shermaine.' They were silent again, having used each other's names. Bruce could feel it between them, a good feeling, warm like new bread. But what of her husband, he thought, I wonder where he is, and what he is like. Why isn't he here with her?

'He is dead,' she said quietly. 'He died four months ago of malaria.'

With the shock of it, Shermaine answering his unspoken question and also the answer itself, Bruce could say nothing for a moment, then:

'I'm sorry.'

'There is the post,' she said, 'in the cottage with the thatched roof.'

Bruce stopped the car and switched off the engine. In the silence she spoke again.

'He was a good man, so very gentle. I only knew him for a few months but he was a good man.'

She looked very small sitting beside him in the gathering dark with the sadness on her, and Bruce felt a great wave of tenderness wash over him. He wanted to put his arm round her and hold her, to shield her from the sadness. He searched for the words, but before he found them, she roused herself and spoke in a matter of fact tone.

'We must hurry, it's dark already.'

At the hotel the lounge was filled with Boussier's employees; Haig had mounted a Bren in one of the upstairs windows to cover the main street and posted two men in the kitchens to cover the back. The civilians were in little groups, talking quietly, and their expressions of complete doglike trust as they looked at Bruce disconcerted him.

'Everything under control, Mike?' he asked brusquely.

'Yes, Bruce. We should be able to hold this building against a sneak attack. De Surrier and Hendry, down at the station yard, shouldn't have any trouble either.'

'Have these people,' Bruce pointed at the civilans, 'loaded their luggage?'

'Yes, it's all aboard. I have told Ruffy to issue them with food from our stores.'

'Good.' Bruce felt relief; no further complications so far.

'Where is old man Boussier?'

'He is across at his office.'

'I'm going to have a chat with him.'

Unbidden, Shermaine fell in beside Bruce as he walked out into the street, but he liked having her there.

Boussier looked up as Bruce and Shermaine walked into his office. The merciless glare of the petromax lamp accentuated the lines at the corners of his eyes and mouth, and showed up the streaks of pink scalp beneath his neatly combed hair.

'Martin, you are not still working!' exclaimed Shermaine, and he smiled at her, the calm smile of his years.

'Not really, my dear, just tidying up a few things. Please be seated, Captain.'

He came round and cleared a pile of heavy leather-bound ledgers off the chair and packed them into a wooden case on the floor, went back to his own chair, opened a drawer in the desk, brought out a box of cheroots and offered one to Bruce.

'I cannot tell you how relieved I am that you are here, Captain. These last few months have been very trying. The doubt. The anxiety.' He struck a match and held it out to Bruce who leaned forward across the desk and lit his cheroot. 'But now it is all at an end; I feel as though a great weight has been lifted from my shoulders.' Then his voice sharpened. 'But you were not too soon. I have heard within the last hour that this General Moses and his column have left Senwati and are on the road south, only two hundred kilometres north of here. They will arrive tomorrow at their present rate of advance.'

'Where did you hear this?' Bruce demanded.

'From one of my men, and do not ask me how he knows. There is a system of communication in this country which even after all these years I do not understand. Perhaps it is the drums, I heard them this evening, I do not know. However, their information is usually reliable.'

'I had not placed them so close,' muttered Bruce. 'Had I known this I might have risked travelling tonight, at least as far as the bridge.'

'I think your decision to stay over the night was correct. General Moses will not travel during darkness – none of his men would risk that – and the condition of the road from Senwati after three month's neglect is such that he will need ten or twelve hours to cover the distance.'

'I hope you're right.' Bruce was worried. 'I'm not sure that we shouldn't pull out now.'

'That involves a risk also, Captain,' Boussier pointed out. 'We know there are tribesmen in close proximity to the town. They have been seen. They must be aware of your arrival, and might easily have wrecked the lines to prevent our departure. I think your original decision is still good.'

'I know.' Bruce was hunched forward in his chair, frowning, sucking on the cheroot. At last he sat back and the frown evaporated. 'I can't risk it. I'll place a guard on the causeway, and if this Moses gentleman arrives we can hold him there long enough to embark your people.'

'That is probably the best course,' agreed Boussier. He paused, glanced towards the open windows and lowered his voice. 'There is another point, Captain, which I wish to bring to your attention.'

'Yes?'

'As you know, the activity of my company in Port Reprieve is centred on the recovery of diamonds from the Lufira swamps.'

Bruce nodded.

'I have in my safe' – Boussier jerked his thumb at the heavy steel door built into the wall behind his desk – 'nine and a half thousand carats of gem-quality diamonds and some twenty-six thousand carats of industrial diamonds.'

'I had expected that.' Bruce kept his tone non-committal.

'It may be as well if we could agree on the disposition and handling of these stones.'

'How are they packaged?' asked Bruce.

'A single wooden case.'

'Of what size and weight?'

'I will show you.'

Boussier went to the safe, turned his back to them and they heard the tumblers whirr and click. While he waited Bruce realized suddenly that Shermaine had not spoken since her initial greeting to Boussier. He glanced at her now and she smiled at him. I like a woman who knows when to keep her mouth shut.

Boussier swung the door of the safe open and carried a small wooden case across to the desk.

'There,' he said.

Bruce examined it. Eighteen inches long, nine deep and twelve wide. He lifted it experimentally.

'About twenty pounds weight,' he decided. 'The lid is sealed.'

'Yes,' agreed Boussier, touching the four wax imprints.

'Good,' Bruce nodded. 'I don't want to draw unnecessary attention to it by placing a guard upon it.'

'No, I agree.'

Bruce studied the case a few seconds longer and then he asked:

'What is the value of these stones?'

Boussier shrugged. 'Possibly five hundred million francs.' And Bruce was impressed; half a million sterling. Worth stealing, worth killing for.

'I suggest, monsieur, that you secrete this case in your luggage. In your blankets, say. I doubt there will be any danger of theft until we reach Msapa Junction. A thief will have no avenue of escape. Once we reach Msapa Junction I will make other arrangements for its safety.'

'Very well, Captain.'

Bruce stood up and glanced at his watch. 'Seven o'clock, as near as dammit. I will leave you and see to the guard on the causeway. Please make sure that your people are ready to entrain before dawn tomorrow morning.'

'Of course.'

Bruce looked at Shermaine and she stood up quickly. Bruce held the door open for her and was just about to follow her when a thought struck him.

'That mission station – St. Augustine's, is it? I suppose it's deserted now?'

'No, it's not.' Boussier looked a little shamefaced. 'Father Ignatius is still there, and of course the patients at the hospital.'

'Thanks for telling me.' Bruce was bitter.

'I'm sorry, Captain. It slipped my mind, there are so many things to think of.'

'Do you know the road out to the mission?' he snapped at Shermaine. *She* should have told him.

'Yes, Bruce.'

'Well, perhaps you'd be good enough to direct me.'

'Of course.' She also looked guilty.

Bruce slammed the door of Boussier's office and strode off towards the hotel with Shermaine trotting to keep pace with him. You can't rely on anyone, he thought, not anybody!

And then he saw Ruffy coming up from the station, looking like a big bear in the dusk. With a few exceptions, Bruce corrected himself.

'Sergeant Major.'

'Hello, boss.'

'This General Moses is closer to us than we reckoned. He's reported two hundred kilometres north of here on the Senwati road.'

Ruffy whistled through his teeth. 'Are you going to take off now, Boss?'

'No, I want a machine-gun post on this end of the causeway. If they come we can hold them there long enough to get away. I want you to take command.'

'I'll see to it now.'

'I'm going out to the mission – there's a white priest there. Lieutenant Haig is in command while I'm away.'

'Okay, boss.'

Chapter Ten

'I'm sorry, Bruce. I should have told you.' Shermaine sat small and repentant at her end of the Ranchero.

'Don't worry about it,' said Bruce, not meaning it.

'We have tried to make Father Ignatius come in to town. Martin has spoken to him many times, but he refuses to move.'

Bruce did not answer. He took the car down on to the causeway, driving carefully. There were shreds of mist lifting out of the swamp and drifting across the concrete ramp. Small insects, bright as tracer in the headlights, zoomed in to squash against the windscreen. The froggy chorus from the swamp honked and clinked and boomed deafeningly.

'I have apologized,' she murmured.

'Yes, I heard you,' said Bruce. 'You don't have to do it again.'

She was silent, and then:

'Are you always so bad-tempered?' she asked in English.

'*Always*,' snapped Bruce, 'is one of the words which should be eliminated from the language.'

'Since it has not been, I will continue to use it. You haven't answered my question: are you always so bad tempered?'

'I just don't like balls-ups.'

'What is *balls-up*, please?'

'What has just happened: a mistake, a situation precipitated by inefficiency, or by somebody not using his head.'

'You never make balls-up, Bruce?'

'It is not a polite expression, Shermaine. Young ladies of refinement do not use it.' Bruce changed into French.

'You never make mistakes?' she corrected herself. Bruce did not answer. That's quite funny, he thought – never make mistakes! Bruce Curry, the original balls-up.

Shermaine held one hand across her middle and sat up straight.

'Bonaparte,' she said. 'Cold, silent, efficient.'

'I didn't say that—' Bruce started to defend himself. Then in the glow from the dash light he saw her impish expression and he could not stop himself; he had to grin.

'All right, I'm acting like a child.'

'You would like a cigarette?' she asked.

'Yes, please.'

She lit it and passed it to him.

'You do not like—' she hesitated, 'mistakes. Is there anything you do like?'

'Many things,' said Bruce.

'Tell me some.'

They bumped off the end of the causeway and Bruce accelerated up the far bank.

'I like being on a mountain when the wind blows, and the taste of the sea. I like Sinatra, crayfish thermidor, the weight and balance of a Purdey Royal, and the sound of a little girl's laughter. I like the first draw of a cigarette lit from a wood fire, the scent of jasmine, the feel of silk; I also enjoy sleeping late in the morning, and the thrill of forking a queen with my knight. Shadows on the floor of a forest please me. And, of course, money. But especially I like women who do not ask too many questions.'

'Is that all?'

'No, but it's a start.'

'And apart from – mistakes, what are the things you do not like.'

'Women who ask too many questions,' and he saw her smile. 'Selfishness except my own, turnip soup, politics, blond pubic hairs, Scotch whisky, classical music and hangovers.'

'I'm sure that is not all.'

'No, not nearly.'

'You are very sensual. All these things are of the senses.'

'Agreed.'

'You do not mention other people. Why?'

'Is this the turn off to the mission?'

'Yes, go slowly, the road is bad. Why do you not mention your relationship to other people?'

'Why do you ask so many questions? Perhaps I'll tell you some day.'

She was silent a while and then softly:

'And what do you want from life – just those things you have spoken of? Is that all you want?'

'No. Not even them. I want nothing, expect nothing; that way I cannot be disappointed.'

Suddenly she was angry. 'You not only act like a child, you talk like one.'

'Another thing I don't like: criticism.'

'You are young. You have brains, good looks—'

'Thank you, that's better.'

'—and you are a fool.'

'That's not so good. But don't fret about it.'

'I won't, don't worry,' she flamed at him. 'You can—' she searched for something devastating, 'You can go jump out of the lake.'

'Don't you mean into?'

'Into, out of, backwards, sideways. I don't care!'

'Good, I'm glad we've got that settled. There's the mission, I can see a light.'

She did not answer but sat in her corner, breathing heavily, drawing so hard on her cigarette that the glowing tip lit the interior of the Ford.

The church was in darkness, but beyond it and to one side was a long low building. Bruce saw a shadow move across one of the windows.

'Is that the hospital?'

'Yes.' Abruptly.

Bruce stopped the Ford beside the small front verandah and switched off the headlights and the ignition.

'Are you coming in?'

'No.'

'I'd like you to present me to Father Ignatius.'

For a moment she did not move, then she threw open her door and marched up the steps of the verandah without looking back at Bruce.

He followed her through the front office, down the passage, past the clinic and small operating theatre, into the ward.

'Ah, Madame Cartier.' Father Ignatius left the bed over which he was stooping and came towards her.

'I heard that the relief train had arrived at Port Reprieve. I thought you would have left by now.'

'Not yet, Father. Tomorrow morning.'

Ignatius was tall, six foot three or four, Bruce estimated, and thin. The sleeves of his brown cassock had been cut short as a concession to the climate and his exposed arms appeared to be all bone, hairless, with the veins blue and prominent. Big bony hands, and big bony feet in brown open sandals.

Like most tall, thin men he was round-shouldered. His face was not one that you would remember, an ordinary face with steel-rimmed spectacles perched on a rather shapeless nose, neither young nor old, nondescript hair without grey in it, but there was about him, that unhurried serenity you often find in a man of God. He turned his attention to Bruce, scrutinizing him gently through his spectacles.

'Good evening, my son.'

'Good evening, Father.' Bruce felt uncomfortable; they always made him feel that way. If only, he wished with envy, I could be as certain of one thing in my life as this man is certain of everything in his.

'Father, this is Captain Curry.' Shermaine's tone was cold, and then suddenly she smiled again. 'He does not care for people, that is why he has come to take you to safety.'

Father Ignatius held out his hand and Bruce found the skin was cool and dry, making him conscious of the moistness of his own.

'That is most thoughtful of you,' he said smiling, sensing the tension between them. 'I don't want to seem ungrateful, but I regret I cannot accept your offer.'

'We have received reports that a column of armed bandits are only two hundred kilometres or so north of here. They will arrive within a day or two. You are in great danger, these people are completely merciless,' Bruce urged him.

'Yes,' Father Ignatius nodded. 'I have also heard, and I am taking the steps I consider necessary. I shall take all my staff and patients into the bush.'

'They'll follow you,' said Bruce.

'I think not.' Ignatius shook his head. 'They will not waste their time. They are after loot, not sick people.'

'They'll burn your mission.'

'If they do, then we shall have to rebuild it when they leave.'

'The bush is crawling with Baluba, you'll end up in the cooking pot.' Bruce tried another approach.

'No.' Ignatius shook his head. 'Nearly every member of the tribe has at one time or another been a patient in this hospital. I have nothing to fear there, they are my friends.'

'Look here, Father. Don't let us argue. My orders are to bring you back to Elisabethville. I must insist.'

'And my orders are to stay here. You do agree that mine come from a higher authority than yours?' Ignatius smiled mildly. Bruce opened his mouth to argue further; then, instead, he laughed.

'No, I won't dispute that. Is there anything you need that I might be able to supply?'

'Medicines?' asked Ignatius.

'Acriflavine, morphia, field dressings, not much I'm afraid.'

'They would help, and food?'

'Yes, I will let you have as much as I can spare,' promised Bruce.

One of the patients, a woman at the end of the ward, screamed so suddenly that Bruce started.

'She will be dead before morning,' Ignatius explained softly. 'There is nothing I can do.'

'What's wrong with her?'

'She has been in labour these past two days; there is some complication.'

'Can't you operate?'

'I am not a doctor, my son. We had one here before the trouble began, but he is here no longer – he has gone back to Elisabethville. No,' his voice seemed to carry helpless regret for all the suffering of mankind, 'No, she will die.'

'Haig!' said Bruce.

'Pardon?'

'Father, you have a theatre here. Is it fully equipped?'

'Yes, I believe so.'

'Anaesthetic?'

'We have chloroform and pentothal.'

'Good,' said Bruce. 'I'll get you a doctor. Come on, Shermaine.'

Chapter Eleven

'This heat, this stinking heat!' Wally Hendry mopped at his face with a grubby handkerchief and threw himself down on the green leather bunk. 'You notice how Curry leaves me and you here on the train while he puts Haig up at the hotel and he goes off with that little French bit. It doesn't matter that me and you must cook in this box, long as he and his buddy Haig are all right. You notice that, hey?'

'Somebody's got to stay aboard, Wally,' André said.

'Yeah, but you notice who it is? Always you and me – those high society boys stick together, you've got to give them that, they look after each other.' He transferred his attention back to the open window of the compartment. 'Sun's down already, and still hot enough to boil eggs. I could use a drink.' He unlaced his jungle boots, peeled off his socks and regarded his large white feet with distaste. 'This stinking heat got my athlete's foot going again.'

He separated two of his toes and picked at the loose scaly skin between. 'You got any of that ointment left, André?'

'Yes, I'll get it for you.' André opened a flap of his pack, took out the tube and crossed to Wally's bunk.

'Put it on,' instructed Wally and lay back offering his feet. André took them in his lap as he sat down on the bunk and went to work. Wally lit a cigarette and blew smoke towards the roof, watching it disperse.

'Hell, I could use a drink. A beer with dew on the glass and a head that thick.' He held up four fingers, then he lifted himself on one elbow and studied André as he spread ointment between the long prehensile toes.

'How's it going?'

'Nearly finished, Wally.'

'Is it bad?'

'Not as bad as last time, it hasn't started weeping yet.'

'It itches like you wouldn't believe it,' said Wally.

André did not answer and Wally kicked him in the ribs with the flat of his free foot.

'Did you hear what I said?'

'Yes, you said it itches.'

'Well, answer me when I talk to you. I ain't talking to myself.'

'I'm sorry, Wally.'

Wally grunted and was silent a while, then:

'Do you like me, André?'

'You know I do, Wally.'

'We're friends, aren't we, André?'

'Of course, you know that, Wally.'

An expression of cunning had replaced Wally's boredom.

'You don't mind when I ask you to do things for me, like putting stuff on my feet?'

'I don't mind – it's a pleasure, Wally.'

'It's a pleasure, is it?' There was an edge in Wally's voice now. 'You like doing it?'

André looked up at him apprehensively. 'I don't mind it.' His molten toffee eyes clung to the narrow Mongolian ones in Wally's face.

'You like touching me, André?'

André stopped working with the ointment and nervously wiped his fingers on his towel.

'I said, do you like touching me, André? Do you sometimes wish I'd touch you?'

André tried to stand up, but Wally's right arm shot out and his hand fastened on André's neck, forcing him down on to the bunk.

'Answer me, damn you, do you like it?'

'You're hurting me, Wally,' whispered André.

'Shame, now ain't that a shame!'

Wally was grinning. He shifted his grip to the ridge of muscle above André's collar bone and dug his fingers in until they almost met through the flesh.

'Please, Wally, please,' whimpered André, wriggling face down on the bunk.

'You love it, don't you? Come on, answer me.'

'Yes, all right, yes. Please don't hurt me, Wally.'

'Now, tell me truly, doll boy, have you ever had it before? I mean for real.' Wally put his knee in the small of André's back, bearing down with all his weight.

'No!' shrieked André. 'I haven't. Please, Wally, don't hurt me.'

'You're lying to me, André. Don't do it.'

'All right. I was lying.' André tried to twist his head round, but Wally pushed his face into the bunk.

'Tell me all about it – come on, doll boy.'

'It was only once, in Brussels.'

'Who was this beef bandit?'

'My employer, I worked for him. He had an export agency.'

'Did he throw you out, doll boy? Did he throw you out when he was tired of you?'

'No, you don't understand!' André denied with sudden vehemence. 'You don't understand. He looked after me. I had my own apartment, my own car, everything. He wouldn't have abandoned me if it hadn't been for – for what happened. He couldn't help it, he was true to me. I swear to you – he loved me!'

Wally snorted with laughter, he was enjoying himself now.

'Loved you! Jesus wept!' He threw his head back, for the laughter was almost strangling him, and it was ten seconds before he could ask: 'Then what happened between you and your true blue lover? Why didn't you get married and settle down to raise a family, hey?' At the improbability of his own sense of humour Wally convulsed with laughter one more.

'There was an investigation. The police – ooh! you're hurting me, Wally.'

'Keep talking, mamselle!'

'The police – he had no alternative. He was a man of position, he couldn't afford the scandal. There was no other way out – there never is for us. It's hopeless, there is no happiness.'

'Cut the crap, doll boy. Just give me the story.'

'He arranged employment for me in Elisabethville, gave me money, paid for my air fare, everything. He did everything, he looked after me, he still writes to me.'

'That's beautiful, real true love. You make me want to cry.'

Then Wally's laughter changed its tone, harsher now. 'Well, get this, doll boy, and get it good. I don't like queers!' He dug his fingers in again and André squealed.

'I'll tell you a story. When I was in reform school there was a queer there that tried to touch me up. One day I got him in the shower rooms with a razor, just an ordinary Gillette razor. There were twenty guys singing and shouting in the other cubicles. He screamed just like they were all screaming when the cold water hit them. No one took any notice of him. He wanted to be a woman, so I helped him.' Hendry's voice went hoarse and gloating with the memory. 'Jesus!' he whispered. 'Jesus, the blood!' André was sobbing now, his whole body shaking.

'I won't – please, Wally. I can't help it. It was just that one time. Please leave me.'

'How would you like me to help you, André?'

'No,' shrieked André. And Hendry lost interest; he released him, left him lying on the bunk and reached for his socks.

'I'm going to find me a beer.' He laced on his boots and stood up.

'Just you remember,' he said darkly, standing over the boy on the bunk. 'Don't get any ideas with me, Bucko.' He picked up his rifle and went out into the corridor.

Wally found Boussier on the verandah of the hotel talking with a group of his men.

'Where's Captain Curry?' he demanded.

'He has gone out to the mission station.'

'When did he leave?'

'About ten minutes ago.'

'Good,' said Wally. 'Who's got the key to the bar?'

Boussier hesitated.

'The captain has ordered that the bar is to remain locked.'

Wally unslung his rifle.

'Don't give me a hard time, friend.'

'I regret, monsieur, that I must obey the captain's instructions.'

For a minute they stared at each other, and there was no sign of weakening in the older man.

'Have it your way then,' said Wally and swaggered through the lounge to the bar-room door. He put his foot against the lock and the flimsy mechanism yielded to the pressure. The door flew open and Wally marched across to the counter, laid his rifle on it and reached underneath to the shelves loaded with Simba beer.

The first bottle he emptied without taking it from his lips. He belched luxuriously and reached for the second, hooked the cap off with the opener and inspected the bubble of froth that appeared at its mouth.

'Hendry!' Wally looked up at Mike Haig in the doorway.

'Hello, Mike.' He grinned.

'What do you think you're doing?' Mike demanded.

'What does it look like?' Wally raised the bottle in salutation and then sipped delicately at the froth.

'Bruce has given strict orders that no one is allowed in here.'

'Oh, for Chrissake, Haig. Stop acting like an old woman.'

'Out you get, Hendry. I'm in charge here.'

'Mike,' Wally grinned at him, 'you want me to die of thirst or something?' He leaned his elbows on the counter. 'Give me a couple more minutes. Let me finish my drink.'

Mike Haig glanced behind him into the lounge and saw the interested group of civilians who were craning to see into the bar-room. He closed the door and walked across to stand opposite Hendry.

'Two minutes, Hendry,' he agreed in an unfriendly tone, 'then out with you.'

'You're not a bad guy, Mike. You and I rubbed each other up wrong. I tell you something, I'm sorry about us.'

'Drink up!' said Mike. Without turning Wally reached backwards and took a bottle of Remy Martin cognac off the shelf. He pulled the cork with his teeth, selected a brandy balloon with his free hand and poured a little of the oily amber fluid into it.

'Keep me company, Mike,' he said and slid the glass across the counter towards Haig. First without expression, and then with his face seeming to crumble, Mike Haig stared at the glass. He moistened his lips, again older and tired-looking. With a physical wrench he pulled his eyes away from the glass.

'Damn you, Hendry.' His voice unnaturally low.

'God damn you to hell.' He hit out at the glass, spinning it off the counter to shatter against the far wall.

'Did I do something wrong, Mike?' asked Hendry softly. 'Just offered you a drink, that's all.'

The smell of spilt brandy, sharp, fruity with the warmth of the grape, and Mike moistened his lips again. The saliva jetting from under his tongue, and the deep yearning aching want in his stomach spreading outwards slowly, numbing him.

'Damn you,' he whispered. 'Oh, damn you, damn you,' pleading now as Hendry filled another glass.

'How long has it been, Mike? A year, two years? Try a little, just a mouthful. Remember the lift it gives you. Come on, boy. You're tired, you've worked hard. Just one – there you are. Just have this one with me.'

Mike wiped his mouth with the back of his hand, sweating now across the forehead and on his upper lip, tiny jewels of sweat squeezed out of the skin by the craving of his body.

'Come on, boy.' Wally's voice hoarse with excitement; teasing, wheedling, tempting.

Mike's hand closed round the tumbler, moving of its own volition, lifting it towards lips that were suddenly slack and trembling, his eyes filled with mingled loathing and desire.

'Just this one,' whispered Hendry. 'Just this one.'

Mike gulped it with a sudden savage flick of his arm, one swallow and the glass was empty. He held it with both hands, his head bowed over it.

'I hate you. My God, I hate you.' He spoke to Hendry, and to himself, and to the empty glass.

'That's my boy!' crowed Wally. 'That's the lad! Come on, let me fill you up.'

Chapter Twelve

Bruce went in through the front door of the hotel with Shermaine trying to keep pace with him. There were a dozen or so people in the lobby, and an air of tension amongst them. Boussier was one of them and he came quickly to Bruce.

'I'm sorry, Captain, I could not stop them. That one, that one with the red hair, he was violent. He had his gun and I think he was ready to use it.'

'What are you talking about?' Bruce asked him, but before Boussier could answer there was the bellow of Hendry's laughter from behind the door at the far end of the lobby; the door to the bar-room.

'They are in there,' Boussier told him. 'They have been there for the past hour.'

'Goddam it to hell,' swore Bruce. 'Now of all times. Oh, goddam that bloody animal.'

He almost ran across the room and threw open the double doors. Hendry was standing against the far wall with a tumbler in one hand and his rifle in the other. He was holding the rifle by the pistol grip and waving vague circles in the air with it.

Mike Haig was building a pyramid of glasses on the bar counter. He was just placing the final glass on the pile.

'Hello, Bruce, old cock, old man, old fruit,' he greeted Bruce, and waved in an exaggerated manner. 'Just in time, you can have a couple of shots as well. But Wally's first, he gets first shot. Must abide by the rules, no cheating, strictly democratic affair, everyone has equal rights. Rank doesn't count. That's right, isn't it, Wally?' Haig's features had blurred; it was as though he were melting, losing his shape. His lips were loose and flabby, his jowls hung pendulously as an old woman's breasts, and his eyes were moist.

He picked up a glass from beside the pyramid, but this glass was nearly full and a bottle of Remy Martin cognac stood beside it.

'A very fine old brandy, absolutely exquisite.' The last two words didn't come out right, so he repeated them carefully. Then he grinned loosely at Bruce and his eyes weren't quite in focus.

'Get out of the way, Mike,' said Hendry, and raised the rifle one-handed, aiming at the pile of glasses.

'Every time she bucks, she bounces,' hooted Haig, 'and every time she bounces you win a coconut. Let her rip, old fruit.'

'Hendry, stop that,' snapped Bruce.

'Go and get mucked,' answered Hendry and fired. The rifle kicked back over his shoulder and he fell against the wall. The pyramid of glasses exploded in a shower of fragments and the room was filled with the roar of the rifle.

'Give the gentleman a coconut!' crowed Mike.

Bruce crossed the room with three quick strides and pulled the rifle out of Hendry's hand.

'All right, you drunken ape. That's enough.'

'Go and muck yourself,' growled Hendry. He was massaging his wrist; the rifle had twisted it.

'Captain Curry,' said Haig from behind the bar, 'you heard what my friend said. You go and muck yourself sideways to sleep.'

'Shut up, Haig.'

'This time I'll fix you, Curry,' Hendry growled. 'You've been on my back too long – now I'm going to shake you off!'

'Kindly descend from my friend's back, Captain Curry,' chimed in Mike Haig. 'He's not a howdah elephant, he's my blood brother. I will now allow you to persecute him.'

'Come on, Curry. Come on then!' said Wally.

'That's it, Wally. Muck him up.' Haig filled his glass again as he spoke. 'Don't let him ride you.'

'Come on then, Curry.'

'You're drunk,' said Bruce.

'Come on then; don't talk, man. Or do I have to start it?'

'No, you don't have to start it,' Bruce assured him, and lifted the rifle butt-first under his chin, swinging it up hard. Hendry's head jerked and he staggered back against the wall. Bruce looked at his eyes; they were glazed over. That will hold him, he decided; that's taken the fight out of him. He caught Hendry by the shoulder and threw him into one of the chairs. I must get to Haig before he absorbs any more of that liquor, he thought, I can't waste time sending for Ruffy and I can't leave this thing behind me while I work on Haig.

'Shermaine,' he called. She was standing in the doorway and she came to his side. 'Can you use a pistol?'

She nodded. Bruce unclipped his Smith & Wesson from its lanyard and handed it to her.

'Shoot this man if he tries to leave that chair. Stand here where he cannot reach you.'

'Bruce—' she started.

'He is a dangerous animal. Yesterday he murdered two small children and, if you let him, he'll do the same to you. You must keep him here while I get the other one.'

She lifted the pistol, holding it with both hands and her face was even paler than was usual.

'Can you do it?' Bruce asked.

'Now I can,' she said and cocked the action.

'Hear me, Hendry.' Bruce took a handful of his hair and twisted his face up. 'She'll kill you if you leave this chair. Do you understand. She'll shoot you.'

'Muck you and your little French whore, muck you both. I bet that's what you two have been doing all evening in that car – playing "hide the sausage" down by the river side.'

Anger flashed through Bruce so violently that it startled him. He twisted Hendry's hair until he could feel it coming away in his hand. Hendry squirmed with pain.

'Shut that foul mouth – or I'll kill you.'

He meant it, and suddenly Hendry knew he meant it..

'Okay, for Chrissake, okay. Just leave me.'

Bruce loosened his grip and straightened up.

'I'm sorry, Shermaine,' he said.

'That's all right – go to the other one.'

Bruce went to the bar counter, and Haig watched him come.

'What do you want, Bruce? Have a drink.' He was nervous. 'Have a drink, we are all having a little drink. All good clean fun, Bruce. Don't get excited.'

'You're not having any more; in fact, just the opposite,' Bruce told him as he came round the counter. Haig backed away in front of him.

'What are you going to do?'

'I'll show you,' said Bruce and caught him by the wrist, turning him quickly and lifting his arm up between his shoulder-blades.

'Hey, Bruce. Cut it out, you've made me spill my drink.'

'Good,' said Bruce and slapped the empty glass out of his hand. Haig started to struggle. He was still a powerful man but the liquor had weakened him and Bruce lifted his wrist higher, forcing him on to his toes.

'Come along, buddy boy,' instructed Bruce and marched him towards the back door of the bar-room. He reached round Haig with his free hand, turned the key in the lock and opened the door.

'Through here,' he said and pushed Mike into the kitchens. He kicked the door shut behind him and went to the sink, dragging Haig with him.

'All right, Haig, let's have it up,' he said and changed his grip quickly, thrusting Haig's head down over the sink. There was a dishtowel hanging beside it which Bruce screwed into a ball; then he used his thumbs to open Haig's jaws and wedged the towel between his back teeth.

'Let's have all of it.' He probed his finger down into Haig's throat. It came up hot and gushing over his hand, and he fought down his own nausea as he worked. When he had finished he turned on the cold tap and held Haig's head under it, washing his face and his own hand.

'Now I've got a little job for you, Haig.'

'Leave me alone, damn you,' groaned Haig, his voice indistinct beneath the rushing tap. Bruce pulled him up and held him against the wall.

'There's a woman in childbirth at the mission. She's going to die, Haig. She's going to die if you don't do something about it.'

'No,' whispered Haig. 'No, not that. Not that again.'

'I'm taking you there.'

'No, please not that. I can't – don't you see that I can't. The little red and purple veins in his nose and cheeks stood out in vivid contrast to his pallor. Bruce hit him open-handed across the face and the water flew in drops from his hair at the shock.

'No,' he mumbled, 'please, Bruce, please.'

Bruce hit him twice more, hard. Watching him carefully, and at last he saw the first flickering of anger.

'Damn you, Bruce Curry, damn you to hell.'

'You'll do,' rejoiced Bruce. 'Thank God for that.'

He hustled Haig back through the bar-room. Shermaine still stood over Hendry, holding the pistol.

'Come on, Shermaine. You can leave that thing now. I'll attend to him when we get back.'

As they crossed the lobby Bruce asked Shermaine, 'Can you drive the Ford?'

'Yes.'

'Good,' said Bruce. 'Here are the keys. I'll sit with Haig in the back. Take us out to the mission.'

Haig lost his balance on the front steps of the hotel and nearly fell, but Bruce caught him and half carried him to the car. He pushed him into the back seat and climbed in beside him. Shermaine slid in behind the wheel, started the engine and U-turned neatly across the street.

'You can't force me to do this, Bruce. I can't, I just can't,' Haig pleaded.

'We'll see,' said Bruce.

'You don't know what it's like. You can't know. She'll die on the table.' He held out his hands palms down. 'Look at that, look at them. How can I do it with these?' His hands were trembling violently.

'She's going to die anyway,' said Bruce, his voice hard. 'So you might as well do it for her quickly and get it over with.'

Haig brought his hands up to his mouth and wiped his lips.

'Can I have a drink, Bruce? That'll help. I'll try then, if you give me a drink.'

'No,' said Bruce, and Haig began to swear. The filth poured from his lips and his face twisted with the effort. He cursed Bruce, he cursed himself, and God in a torrent of the most obscence language that Bruce had ever heard. Then suddenly he snatched at the door handle and tried to twist it open. Bruce had been waiting for this and he caught the back of Haig's collar, pulled him backwards across the seat and held him there. Haig's struggles ceased abruptly and he began to sob softly.

Shermaine drove fast; across the causeway, up the slope and into the side road. The headlights cut into the darkness and the wind drummed softly round the car. Haig was still sobbing on the back seat.

Then the lights of the mission were ahead of them through the trees and Shermaine slowed the car, turned in past the church and pulled up next to the hospital block.

Bruce helped Haig out of the car, and while he was doing so the side door of the building opened and Father Ignatius came out with a petromax lantern in his hand. The harsh white glare of the lantern lit them all and threw grotesque shadows behind them. It fell with special cruelty on Haig's face.

'Here's your doctor, Father,' Bruce announced.

Ignatius lifted the lantern and peered through his spectacles at Haig.

'Is he sick?'

'No, Father,' said Bruce. 'He's drunk.'

'Drunk? Then he can't operate?'

'Yes, he damn well can!'

Bruce took Haig through the door and along the passage to the little theatre. Ignatius and Shermaine followed them.

'Shermaine, go with the Father and help him bring the woman,' Bruce ordered, and they went; then he turned his attention back to Haig.

'Are you so far down there in the slime that you can't understand me?'

'I can't do it, Bruce. It's no good.'

'Then she'll die. But this much is certain: you are going to make the attempt.'

'I've got to have a drink, Bruce.' Haig licked his lips. 'It's burning me up inside, you've got to give me one.'

'Finish the job and I'll give you a whole case.'

'I've got to have one now.'

'No.' Bruce spoke with finality. 'Have a look at what they've got here in the way of instruments. Can you do it with these?' Bruce crossed to the sterilizer and lifted the lid, the steam came up out of it in a cloud. Haig looked in also.

'That's all I need, but there's not enough light in here, and I need a drink.'

'I'll get you more light. Start cleaning up.'

'Bruce, please let me—'

'Shut up,' snarled Bruce. 'There's the basin. Start getting ready.'

Haig crossed to the hand basin; he was more steady on his feet and his features had firmed a little. You poor old bastard, thought Bruce, I hope you can do it. My God, how much I hope you can.

'Get a move on, Haig, we haven't got all night.'

Bruce left the room and went quickly down the passage to the ward. The windows of the theatre were fixed and Haig could escape only into the passage. Bruce knew that he could catch him if he tried to run for it.

He looked into the ward. Shermaine and Ignatius, with the help of an African orderly, had lifted the woman on to the theatre trolley.

'Father, we need more light.'

'I can get you another lantern, that's all.'

'Good, do that then. I'll take the woman through.'

Father Ignatius disappeared with the orderly and Bruce helped Shermaine manoeuvre the trolley down the length of the ward and into the passage. The woman was whimpering with pain, and her face was grey, waxy grey. They only go like that when they are very frightened, or when they are dying.

'She hasn't much longer,' he said.

'I know,' agreed Shermaine. 'We must hurry.'

The woman moved restlessly on the trolley and gabbled a few words; then she sighed so that the great blanket-covered mound of her belly rose and fell, and she started to whimper again.

Haig was still in the theatre. He had stripped off his battle-jacket and, in his vest, he stooped over the basin washing. He did not look round as they wheeled the woman in.

'Get her on the table,' he said, working the soap into suds up to his elbows.

The trolley was of a height with the table and, using the blanket to lift her, it was easy to slide the woman across.

'She's ready, Haig,' said Bruce. Haig dried his arms on a clean towel and turned. He came to the woman and stood over her. She did not know he was there; her eyes were open but unseeing. Haid drew a deep breath; he was sweating a little across his forehead and the stubble of beard on the lower part of his face was stippled with grey.

He pulled back the blanket. The woman wore a short white jacket, open-fronted, that did not cover her stomach. Her stomach was swollen out, hard-looking, with the navel inverted. Knees raised slightly and the thick peasant's thighs spread wide in the act of labour. As Bruce watched, her whole body arched in another contraction. He saw the stress of the muscles beneath the dark greyish skin as they struggled to expel the trapped foetus.

'Hurry, Mike!' Bruce was appalled by the anguish of birth. I didn't know it was like this; in sorrow thou shalt bring forth children – but this! Through the woman's dry grey swollen lips burst another of those moaning little cries, and Bruce swung towards Mike Haig.

'Hurry, goddam you!'

And Mike Haig began his examination, his hands very pale as they groped over the dark skin. At last he was satisfied and he stood back from the table.

Ignatius and the orderly came in with two more lanterns. Ignatius started to say something, but instantly he sensed the tension in the room and he fell silent. They all watched Mike Haig's face.

His eyes were tight closed, and his face was hard angles and harsh planes in the lantern light. His breathing was shallow and laboured.

I must not push him now, Bruce knew instinctively, I have dragged him to the lip of the precipice and now I must let him go over the edge on his own.

Mike opened his eyes again, and he spoke.

'Caesarian section,' he said, as though he had pronounced his own death sentence. Then his breathing stopped. They waited, and at last the breath came out of him in a sigh.

'I'll do it,' he said.

'Gowns and gloves?' Bruce fired the question at Ignatius.

'In the cupboard.'

'Get them!'

'You'll have to help me, Bruce. And you also Shermaine.'

'Yes, show me.'

Quickly they scrubbed and dressed. Ignatius held the pale green theatre gowns while they dived into them and flapped and struggled through.

'That tray, bring it here,' Mike ordered as he opened the sterilizer. With a pair of long-nosed forceps he lifted the instruments out of the steaming box and laid them on the tray naming each one as he did so.

'Scalpel, retractors, clamps.'

In the meantime the orderly was swabbing the woman's belly with alcohol and arranging the sheets.

Mike filled the syringe with pentothal and held it up to the light. He was an unfamiliar figure now; his face masked, the green skull cap covering his hair, and the flowing gown falling to his ankles. He pressed the plunger and a few drops of the pale fluid dribbled down the needle.

He looked at Bruce, only his haunted eyes showing above the mask.

'Ready?'

'Yes,' Bruce nodded. Mike stooped over the woman, took her arm and sent the needle searching under the soft black skin on the inside of her elbow. The fluid in the syringe was suddenly discoloured with drawn blood as Mike tested for the vein, and then the plunger slid slowly down the glass barrel.

The woman stopped whimpering, the tension went out of her body and her breathing slowed and became deep and unhurried.

'Come here.' Mike ordered Shermaine to the head of the table, and she took up the chloroform mask and soaked the gauze that filled the cone.

'Wait until I tell you.'

She nodded. Christ, what lovely eyes she has, thought Bruce, before he turned back to the job in hand.

'Scalpel,' said Mike from across the table, pointing to it on the tray, and Bruce handed it to him.

Afterwards the details were confused and lacking reality in Bruce's mind.

The wound opening behind the knife, the tight stretched skin parting and the tiny blood vessels starting to squirt.

Pink muscle laced with white; butter-yellow layers of subcutaneous fat, and then through to the massed bluish coils of the gut. Human tissue, soft and pulsing, glistening in the flat glare of the petromax.

Clamps and retractors, like silver insects crowding into the wound as though it were a flower.

Mike's hands, inhuman in yellow rubber, moving in the open pit of the belly. Swabbing, cutting, clamping, tying off.

Then the swollen purple bag of the womb, suddenly unzipped by the knife.

And at last, unbelievably, the child curled in a dark grey ball of legs and tiny arms, head too big for its size, and the fat pink snake of the placenta enfolding it.

Lifted out, the infant hung by its heels from Mike's hand like a small grey bat, still joined to its mother.

Scissors snipped and it was free. Mike worked a little longer, and the infant cried.

It cried with minute fury, indignant and alive. From the head of the table Shermaine laughed with spontaneous delight, and clapped her hands like a child at a Punch and Judy show. Suddenly Bruce was laughing also. It was a laugh from long ago, coming out from deep inside him.

'Take it,' said Haig and Shermaine cradled it, wet and feebly wriggling in her arms. She stood with it while Haig sewed up. Watching her face and the way she stood, Bruce suddenly and unaccountably felt the laughter snag his throat, and he wanted to cry.

Haig closed the womb, stitching the complicated pattern of knots like a skilled seamstress, then the external sutures laid neatly across the fat lips of the wound, and at last the white tape hiding it all. He covered the woman, jerked the mask from his face and looked up at Shermaine.

'You can help me clean it up,' he said, and his voice was strong again and proud. The two of them crossed to the basin.

Bruce threw off his gown and left the room, went down the passage and out into the night. He leaned against the bonnet of the Ford and lit a cigarette.

Tonight I laughed again, he told himself with wonder, and then I nearly cried. And all because of a woman and a child. It is finished now, the pretence. The withdrawal. The big act. There was more than one birth in there tonight. I laughed again, I had the need to laugh again, and the desire to cry. A woman and a child, the whole meaning of life. The abscess had burst, the poison drained, and he was ready to heal.

'Bruce, Bruce, where are you?' She came out through the door; he did not answer her for she had seen the glow of his cigarette and she came to him. Standing close in the darkness.

'Shermaine—' Bruce said, then he stopped himself. He wanted to hold her, just hold her tightly.

'Yes, Bruce.' Her face was a pale round in the darkness, very close to him.

'Shermaine, I want—' said Bruce and stopped again.

'Yes, me too,' she whispered and then, drawing away, 'come, let's go and see what your doctor is doing now.' She took his hand and led him back into the building. Her hand was cool and dry, with long tapered fingers in his.

Mike Haig and Father Ignatius were leaning over the cradle that now stood next to the table on which lay the blanket-covered body of the Baluba woman. The woman was breathing softly, and the expression on her face was of deep peace.

'Bruce, come and have a look. It's a beauty,' called Haig.

Still holding hands Bruce and Shermaine crossed to the cradle.

'He'll go all of eight pounds,' announced Haig proudly. Bruce looked at the infant; new-born black babies are more handsome than ours – they have not got that half-boiled look.

'Pity he's not a trout,' murmured Bruce. 'That would be a national record.' Haig stared blankly at him for a second, then he threw back his head and laughed; it was a good sound. There was a different quality in Haig now, a new confidence in the way he held his head, a feeling of completeness about him.

'How about that drink I promised you, Mike?' Bruce tested him.

'You have it for me, Bruce, I'll duck this one.' He isn't just saying it either, thought Bruce, as he looked at his face; he really doesn't need it now.

'I'll make it a double as soon as we get back to town.' Bruce glanced at his watch. 'It's past ten, we'd better get going.'

'I'll have to stay until she comes out from the anaesthetic,' demurred Haig. 'You can come back for me in the morning.'

Bruce hesitated. 'All right then. Come on, Shermaine.'

They drove back to Port Reprieve, sitting close together in the intimate darkness of the car. They did not speak until after they had reached the causeway, then Shermaine said:

'He is a good man, your doctor. He is like Paul.'

'Who is Paul?'

'Paul was my husband.'

'Oh.' Bruce was embarrassed. The mention of that name snapped the silken thread of his mood. Shermaine went on, speaking softly and staring down the path of the headlights.

'Paul was of the same age. Old enough to have learned understanding – young men are so cruel.'

'You loved him.' Bruce spoke flatly, trying to keep any trace of jealousy from his voice.

'Love has many shapes,' she answered. Then, 'Yes, I had begun to love him. Very soon I would have loved him enough to—' She stopped.

'To what?' Bruce's voice had gone rough as a wood rasp. *Now it starts*, he thought, *once again I am vulnerable*.

'We were only married four months before he – before the fever.'

'So?' Still harsh, his eyes on the road ahead.

'I want you to know something. I must explain it all to you. It is very important. Will you be patient with me while I tell you?' There was a pleading in her voice that he could not resist and his expression softened.

'Shermaine, you don't have to tell me.'

'I must. I want you to know.' She hesitated a moment, and when she spoke again her voice had steadied. 'I am an orphan, Bruce. Both my Mama and Papa were killed by the Germans, in the bombing. I was only a few months old when it happened, and I do not remember them. I do not remember anything, not one little thing about them; there is not even a photograph.' For a second her voice had gone shaky but again it firmed. 'The nuns took me, and they were my family. But somehow that is different, not really your own. I have never had anything that has truly belonged to me, something of my very own.'

Bruce reached out and took her hand; it lay still in his grasp. You have now, he thought, you have me for your very own.

'Then when the time came the nuns made the arrangements with Paul Cartier. He was an engineer with Union Minière du Haut here in the Congo, a man of position, a suitable man for one of their girls.

'He flew to Brussels and we were married. I was not unhappy, for although he was old – as old as Doctor Mike – yet he was very gentle and kind, of great understanding. He did not—' She stopped and turned suddenly to Bruce, gripping his hand with both of hers, leaning towards him with her face serious and pale in the half-darkness, the plume of dark hair falling forward over her shoulder and her voice full of appeal. 'Bruce, do you understand what I am trying to tell you?'

Bruce stopped the car in front of the hotel, deliberately he switched off the ignition and deliberately he spoke.

'Yes, I think so.'

'Thank you,' and she flung the door open and went out of it and up the steps of the hotel with her long jeaned legs flying and her hair bouncing on her back.

Bruce watched her go through the double doors. Then he pressed the lighter on the dashboard and fished a cigarette from his pack. He lit it, exhaled a jet of smoke against the windscreen, and suddenly he was happy. He wanted to laugh again.

He threw the cigarette away only a quarter finished and climbed out of the Ford. He looked at his wrist watch; it was after midnight. My God, I'm tired. Too much has happened today; rebirth is a severe emotional strain. And he laughed out loud, savouring the sensation, letting it come slowly shaking up his throat from his chest.

Boussier was waiting for him in the lounge. He wore a towelling dressing-gown, and the creases of sleep were on his face.

'Are all your preparations complete, monsieur?'

'Yes,' the old man answered. 'The women and the two children are asleep upstairs. Madame Cartier has just gone up.'

'I know,' said Bruce, and Boussier went on, 'As you see, I have all the men here.' He gestured at the sleeping bodies that covered the floor of the lounge and bar-room.

'Good,' said Bruce. 'We'll leave as soon as it's light tomorrow.' He yawned, then rubbed his eyes, massaging them with his finger tips.

'Where is my officer, the one with the red hair?'

'He has gone back to the train, very drunk. We had more trouble with him after you had left.' Boussier hesitated delicately. 'He wanted to go upstairs, to the women.'

'Damn him.' Bruce felt his anger coming again. 'What happened?'

'Your sergeant major, the big one, dissuaded him and took him away.'

'Thank God for Ruffy.'

'I have reserved a place for you to sleep.' Boussier pointed to a comfortable leather armchair. 'You must be exhausted.'

'That is kind of you,' Bruce thanked him. 'But first I must inspect our defences.'

Chapter Thirteen

Bruce woke with Shermaine leaning over the chair and tickling his nose. He was fully dressed with his helmet and rifle on the floor beside him and only his boots unlaced.

'You do not snore, Bruce,' she congratulated him, laughing her small husky laugh. 'That is a good thing.'

He struggled up, dopey with sleep.

'What time is it?'

'Nearly five o'clock. I have breakfast for you in the kitchen.'

'Where is Boussier?'

'He is dressing; then he will start moving them down to the train.'

'My mouth tastes as though a goat slept in it.' Bruce moved his tongue across his teeth, feeling the fur on them.

'Then I shall not kiss you good morning, mon capitaine,' She straightened up with the laughter still in her eyes. 'But your toilet requisites are in the kitchen. I sent one of your gendarmes to fetch them from the train. You can wash in the sink.'

Bruce laced up his boots and followed her through into the kitchen, stepping over sleeping bodies on the way.

'There is no hot water,' Shermaine apologized.

'That is the least of my worries.' Bruce crossed to the table and opened his small personal pack, taking out his razor and soap and comb.

'I raided the chicken coop for you,' Shermaine confessed. 'There were only two eggs. How shall I cook them?'

'Soft boiled, one minute.' Bruce stripped off his jacket and shirt, went to the sink and filled it. He sluiced his face and lifted handfuls of water over his head, snorting with pleasure.

Then he propped his shaving mirror above the taps and spread soap on his face. Shermaine came to sit on the draining board beside him and watched with frank interest.

'I will be sorry to see the beard go,' she said. 'It looked like the pelt of an otter, I liked it.'

'Perhaps I will grow it for you one day.' Bruce smiled at her. 'Your eyes are blue, Shermaine.'

'It has taken you a long time to find that out,' she said and pouted dramatically. Her skin was silky and cool-looking, lips pale pink without make-up. Her dark hair, drawn back, emphasized the high cheek bones and the size of her eyes.

'In India "sher" means "tiger",' Bruce told her, watching her from the corner of his eye. Immediately she abandoned the pout and drew her lips up into a snarl. Her teeth were small and very white and only slightly uneven. Her eyes rolled wide and then crossed at an alarming angle. She growled. Taken by surprise, Bruce laughed and nearly cut himself.

'I cannot abide a woman who clowns before breakfast. It ruins my digestion,' he laughed at her.

'Breakfast!' said Shermaine and uncrossed her eyes, jumped off the draining board and ran to the stove.

'Only just in time.' She checked her watch. 'One minute and twenty seconds, will you forgive me?'

'This once only, never again.' Bruce washed the soap off his face, dried and combed his hair and came to the table. She had a chair ready for him.

'How much sugar in your coffee?'

'Three, please.' Bruce chopped the top off his egg, and she brought the mug and placed it in front of him.

'I like making breakfast for you.' Bruce didn't answer her. This was dangerous talk. She sat down opposite him, leaned forward on her elbows with her chin in her hands.

'You eat too fast,' she announced and Bruce raised an eyebrow. 'But at least you keep your mouth closed.'

Bruce started on his second egg.

'How old are you?'

'Thirty,' said Bruce.

'I'm twenty – nearly twenty-one.'

'A ripe old age.'

'What do you do?'

'I'm a soldier,' he answered.

'No, you're not.'

'All right, I'm a lawyer.'

'You must be clever,' she said solemnly.

'A genius, that's why I'm here.'

'Are you married?'

'No – I was. What is this, a formal interrogation?'

'Is she dead?'

'No.' He prevented the hurt from showing in his face, it was easier to do now.

'Oh!' said Shermaine. She picked up the teaspoon and concentrated on stirring his coffee.

'Is she pretty?'

'No – yes, I suppose so.'

'Where is she?' Then quickly, 'I'm sorry it's none of my business.'

Bruce took the coffee from her and drank it. Then he looked at his watch.

'It's nearly five fifteen. I must go out and get Mike Haig.'

Shermaine stood up quickly.

'I'm ready.'

'I know the way – you had better get down to the station.'

'I want to come with you.'

'Why?'

'Just because, that's why.' Searching for a reason. 'I want to see the baby again.'

'You win.' Bruce picked up his pack and they went through into the lounge. Boussier was there, dressed and efficient. His men were nearly ready to move.

'Madame Cartier and I are going out to the mission to fetch the doctor. We will be back in half an hour or so. I want all your people aboard by then.'

'Very well, Captain.'

Bruce called to Ruffy who was standing on the verandah. 'Did you load those supplies for the mission?'

'They're in the back of the Ford, boss.'

'Good. Bring all your sentries in and take them down to the station. Tell the engine driver to get steam up and keep his hand on the throttle. We'll shove off as soon as I get back with Lieutenant Haig.'

'Okay, boss.'

Bruce handed him his pack. 'Take this down for me, Ruffy.' Then his eyes fell on the large heap of cardboard cartons at Ruffy's feet. 'What's that?'

Ruffy looked a little embarrassed. 'Coupla bottles of beer, boss. Thought we might get thirsty going home.'

'Good for you!' grinned Bruce. 'Put them in a safe place and don't drink them all before I get back.'

'I'll save you one or two,' promised Ruffy.

'Come along, tiger girl,' and Bruce led Shermaine out to the Ford. She sat closer to him than the previous day, but with her legs curled up under her, as before. As they crossed the causeway she lit two cigarettes and passed one to him.

'I'll be glad to leave this place,' she said, looking out across the swamp with the mist lifting sluggishly off it in the dawn, hanging in grey shreds from the fluffy tops of the papyrus grass.

'I've hated it here since Paul died. I hate the swamp and the mosquitoes and the jungle all around. I'm glad we're going.'

'Where will you go?' Bruce asked.

'I haven't thought about it. Back to Belgium, I suppose. Anywhere away from the Congo. Away from this heat to a country where you can breathe. Away from the disease and the fear. Somewhere so that I know tomorrow I will not have to run. Where human life has meaning, away from the killing and the burning and the rape.' She drew on her cigarette almost fiercely, staring ahead at the green wall of the forest.

'I was born in Africa,' said Bruce. 'In the time when the judge's gavel was not the butt of an FN rifle, before you registered your vote with a burst of gunfire.' He spoke softly with regret. 'In the time before the hatred. But now I don't know. I haven't thought much about the future either.'

He was silent for a while. They reached the turn-off to the mission and he swung the Ford into it.

'It has all changed so quickly; I hadn't realized how quickly until I came here to the Congo.'

'Are you going to stay here, Bruce? I mean, stay here in the Congo?'

'No,' he said, 'I've had enough. I don't even know what I'm fighting for.'

He threw the butt of his cigarette out of the window.

Ahead of them were the mission buildings.

Bruce parked the car outside the hospital buildings and they sat together quietly.

'There must be some other land,' he whispered, 'and if there is I'll find it.'

He opened the door and stepped out. Shermaine slid across the seat under the wheel and joined him. They walked side by side to the hospital; her hand brushed his and he caught it, held it and felt the pressure of his fingers returned by hers. She was taller than his shoulder, but not much.

Mike Haig and Father Ignatius were together in the women's ward, too engrossed to hear the Ford arrive.

'Good morning, Michael,' called Bruce. 'What's the fancy dress for?'

Mike Haig looked up and grinned. 'Morning, Bruce. Hello, Shermaine.' Then he looked down at the faded brown cassock he wore.

'Borrowed it from Ignatius. A bit long in the leg and tight round the waist, but less out of place in a sick ward than the accoutrements of war.'

'It suits you, Doctor Mike,' said Shermaine.

'Nice to hear someone call me that again.' The smile spread all over Haig's face. 'I suppose you want to see your baby, Shermaine?'

'Is he well?'

'Mother and child both doing fine,' he assured her and led Shermaine down between the row of beds, each with a black woolly head on the pillow and big curious eyes following their progress.

'May I pick him up?'

'He's asleep, Shermaine.'

'Oh, please!'

'I doubt it will kill him. Very well, then.'

'Bruce, come and look. Isn't he a darling?' She held the tiny black body to her chest and the child snuffled, its mouth automatically starting to search. Bruce leaned forward to peer at it.

'Very nice,' he said and turned to Ignatius. 'I have those supplies I promised you. Will you send an orderly to get them out of the car?' Then to Mike Haig, 'You'd better get changed, Mike. We're all ready to leave.'

Not looking at Bruce, fiddling with the stethoscope round his neck, Mike shook his head. 'I don't think I'll be going with you, Bruce.'

Surprised, Bruce faced him.

'What?'

'I think I'll stay on here with Ignatius. He has offered me a job.'

'You must be mad, Mike.'

'Perhaps,' agreed Haig and took the infant from Shermaine, placed it back in the cradle beside its mother and tucked the sheet in round its tiny body, 'and then again, perhaps not.' He straightened up and waved a hand down the rows of occupied beds. 'There's plenty to do here, that you must admit.'

Bruce stared helplessly at him and then appealed to Shermaine.

'Talk him out of it. Perhaps you can make him see the futility of it.'

Shermaine shook her head. 'No, Bruce, I will not.'

'Mike, listen to reason, for God's sake. You can't stay here in this disease-ridden backwater, you can't—'

'I'll walk out to the car with you, Bruce. I know you're in a hurry—'

He led them out through the side door and stood by the driver's window of the Ford while they climbed in. Bruce extended his hand and Mike took it, gripping hard.

'Cheerio, Bruce. Thanks for everything.'

'Cheerio, Mike. I suppose you'll be taking orders and having yourself made into a fully licensed dispenser of salvation?'

'I don't know about that, Bruce. I doubt it. I just want another chance to do the only work I know. I just want a last-minute rally to reduce the formidable score that's been chalked up against me so far.'

'I'll report you "missing, believed killed" – throw your uniform in the river,' said Bruce.

'I'll do that.' Mike stepped back. 'Look after each other, you two.'

'I don't know what you mean,' Shermaine informed him primly, trying not to smile.

'I'm an old dog, not easy to fool,' said Mike. 'Go to it with a will.'

Bruce let out the clutch and the Ford slid forward.

'God speed, my children.' That smile spread all over Mike's face as he waved.

'Au revoir, Doctor Michael.'

'So long, Mike.'

Bruce watched him in the rear-view mirror, tall in his ill-fitting cassock, something proud and worthwhile in his stance. He waved once more and then turned and hurried back into the hospital.

Neither of them spoke until they had almost reached the main road. Shermaine nestled softly against Bruce, smiling to herself, looking ahead down the tree-lined passage of the road.

'He's a good man, Bruce.'

'Light me a cigarette, please, Shermaine.' He didn't want to talk about it. It was one of those things that can only be made grubby by words.

Slowing for the intersection, Bruce dropped her into second gear, automatically glancing to his left to make sure the main road was clear before turning into it.

'Oh my God!' he gasped.

'What is it, Bruce?' Shermaine looked up with alarm from the cigarette she was lighting.

'Look!'

A hundred yards up the road, parked close to the edge of the forest, was a convoy of six large vehicles. The first five were heavy canvas-canopied lorries painted dull military olive, the sixth was a gasoline tanker in bright yellow and red with the Shell Company insignia on the barrel-shaped body. Hitched behind the leading lorry was a squat, rubber-tyred 25-pounder anti-tank gun with its long barrel pointed jauntily skywards. Round the vehicles, dressed in an assortment of uniforms and different styled helmets, were at least sixty men. They were all armed, some with automatic weapons and others with obsolete bolt-action rifles. Most of them were urinating carelessly into the grass that lined the road, while the others were standing in small groups smoking and talking.

'General Moses!' said Shermaine, her voice small with the shock.

'Get down,' ordered Bruce and with his free hand thrust her on to the floor. He rammed the accelerator flat and the Ford roared out into the main road, swerving violently, the back end floating free in the loose dust as he held the wheel over. Correcting the skid, meeting it and straightening out, Bruce glanced at the rear-view mirror. Behind them the men had dissolved into a confused pattern of movement; he heard their shouts high and thin above the racing engine of the Ford. Bruce looked ahead; it was another hundred yards to the bend in the road that would hide them and take them down to the causeway across the swamp.

Shermaine was on her knees pulling herself up to look over the back of the seat.

'Keep on the floor, damn you!' shouted Bruce and pushed her head down roughly.

As he spoke the roadside next to them erupted in a rapid series of leaping dust fountains and he heard the high hysterical beat of machine-gun fire.

The bend in the road rushed towards them, just a few more seconds. Then with a succession of jarring crashes that shook the whole body of the car a burst of fire hit them from behind. The windscreen starred into a sheet of opaque diamond lacework, the dashboard clock exploded powdering Shermaine's hair with particles of glass, two bullets tore through the seat ripping out the stuffing like the entrails of a wounded animal.

'Close your eyes,' shouted Bruce and punched his fist through the windscreen. Slitting his own eyes against the chips of flying glass, he could just see through the hole his fist had made. The corner was right on top of them and he dragged the steering-wheel over, skidding into it, his off-side wheels bumping into the verge, grass and leaves brushing the side of the car.

Then they were through the corner and racing down towards the causeway.

'Are you all right, Shermaine?'

'Yes, are you?' She emerged from under the dashboard, a smear of blood across one cheek where the glass had scratched her, and her eyes bigger than ever with fright.

'I only pray that Boussier and Hendry are ready to pull out. Those bastards won't be five minutes behind us.'

They went across the causeway with the needle of the speedometer touching eighty, up the far side and into the main street of Port Reprieve. Bruce thrust his hand down on the hooter ring, blowing urgent warning blasts.

'Please God, let them be ready,' he muttered. With relief he saw that the street was empty and the hotel seemed deserted. He kept blowing the horn as they roared down towards the station, a great billowing cloud of dust rising behind them. Braking the Ford hard, he turned it in past the station buildings and on to the platform.

Most of Boussier's people were standing next to the train. Boussier himself was beside the last truck with his wife and the small group of women around him. Bruce shouted at them through the open window.

'Get those women into the train, the *shufta* are right behind us, we're leaving immediately.'

Without question or argument old Boussier gathered them together and hurried them up the steel ladder into the truck. Bruce drove down the station platform shouting as he went.

'Get in! For Chrissake, hurry up! They're coming!'

He braked to a standstill next to the cab of the locomotive and shouted up at the bald head of the driver.

'Get going. Don't waste a second. Give her everything she's got. There's a bunch of *shufta* not five minutes behind us.'

The driver's head disappeared into the cab without even the usual polite, 'Oui, monsieur.'

'Come on, Shermaine.' Bruce grabbed her hand and dragged her from the car. Together they ran to one of the covered coaches and Bruce pushed her half way up the steel steps.

At that moment the train jerked forward so violently that she lost her grip on the hand rails and tumbled backwards on top of Bruce. He was caught off balance and they fell together in a heap on the dusty platform. Above them the train gathered speed, pulling away. He remembered this nightmare from his childhood, running after a train and never catching it. He had to fight down his panic as he and Shermaine scrambled up, both of them panting, clinging to each other, the coaches clackety-clacking past them, the rhythm of their wheels mounting.

'Run!' he gasped, 'Run!' and with the panic weakening their legs he just managed to catch the hand rail of the second coach. He clung to it, stumbling along beside the train, one arm round Shermaine's waist. Sergeant Major Ruffararo leaned out, took Shermaine by the scruff of her neck and lifted her in like a lost kitten. Then he reached down for Bruce.

'Boss, some day we going to lose you if you go on playing around like that.'

'I'm sorry, Bruce,' she panted, leaning against him.

'No damage done.' He could grin at her. 'Now I want you to get into that compartment and stay there until I tell you to come out. Do you understand?'

'Yes, Bruce.'

'Off you go.' He turned from her to Ruffy. 'Up on to the roof, Sergeant Major! We're going to have fireworks. Those *shufta* have got a field gun with them and we'll be in full view of the town right up to the top of the hills.'

By the time they reached the roof of the train it had pulled out of Port Reprieve and was making its first angling turn up the slope of the hills. The sun was up now, well clear of the horizon, and the mist from the swamp had lifted so that they could see the whole village spread out beneath them.

General Moses's column had crossed the causeway and was into the main street. As Bruce watched, the leading truck swung sharply across the road and stopped. Men boiled out from under the canopy and swarmed over the field gun, unhitching it, man-handling it into position.

'I hope those Arabs haven't had any drill on that piece,' grunted Ruffy.

'We'll soon find out,' Bruce assured him grimly and looked back along the train. In the last truck Boussier stood protectively over the small group of four women and their children, like an old white-haired collie with its sheep. Crouched against the steel side of the truck, André de Surrier and half a dozen gendarmes were swinging and sighting the two Bren guns. In the second truck also the gendarmes were preparing to open fire.

'What are you waiting for?' roared Ruffy. 'Get me that field gun – start shooting.'

They fired a ragged volley, then the Bren guns joined in. With every burst André's helmet slipped forward over his eyes and he had to stop and push it back. Lying on the roof of the leading coach, Wally Hendry was firing short businesslike bursts.

The *shufta* round the field gun scattered, leaving one of their number lying in the road, but there were men behind the armour shield – Bruce could see the tops of their helmets.

Suddenly there was a long gush of white smoke from the barrel, and the shell rushed over the top of the train, with a noise like the wings of a giant pheasant.

'Over!' said Ruffy.

'Under!' to the next shot as it ploughed into the trees below them.

'And the third one right up the throat,' said Bruce. But it hit the rear of the train. They were using armour-piercing projectiles, not high explosive, for there was not the burst of yellow cordite fumes but only the crash and jolt as it struck.

Anxiously Bruce tried to assess the damage. The men and women in the rear trucks looked shaken but unharmed and he started a sigh of relief, which changed quickly to a gasp of horror as he realized what had happened.

'They've hit the coupling,' he said. 'They've sheared the coupling on the last truck.'

Already the gap was widening, as the rear truck started to roll back down the hill, cut off like the tail of a lizard.

'Jump,' screamed Bruce, cupping his hands round his mouth. 'Jump before you gather speed.'

Perhaps they did not hear him, perhaps they were too stunned to obey, but no one moved. The truck rolled back, faster and faster as gravity took it, down the hill towards the village and the waiting army of General Moses.

'What can we do, boss?'

'Nothing,' said Bruce.

The firing round Bruce had petered out into silence as every man, even Wally Hendry, stared down the slope at the receding truck. With a constriction of his throat Bruce saw old Boussier stoop and lift his wife to her feet, hold her close to his side and the two of them looking back at Bruce on the roof of the departing train. Boussier raised his right hand in a gesture of farewell and then he dropped it again and stood very still. Behind him, André de Surrier had left the Bren gun and removed his helmet. He also was looking back at Bruce, but he did not wave.

At intervals the field gun in the village punctuated the stillness with its deep boom and gush of smoke, but Bruce hardly heard it. He was watching the *shufta* running down towards the station yard to welcome the truck. Losing speed it ran into the platform and halted abruptly as it hit the buffers at the end of the line. The *shufta* swarmed over it like little black ants over the body of a beetle and faintly Bruce heard the pop, pop, pop of their rifles, saw the low sun glint on their bayonets. He turned away.

They had almost reached the crest of the hills; he could feel the train increasing speed under him. But he felt no relief, only the prickling at the corners of his eyes and the ache of it trapped in his throat.

'The poor bastards,' growled Ruffy beside him. 'The poor bastards.' And then there was another crashing jolt against the train, another hit from the field gun. This time up forward, on the locomotive. Shriek of escaping steam, the train checking its pace, losing power. But they were over the crest of the hills, the village was out of sight and gradually the train speeded up again as they started down the back slope. But steam spouted out of it, hissing white jets of it, and Bruce knew they had received a mortal wound. He switched on the radio.

'Driver, can you hear me? How bad is it?'

'I cannot see, Captain. There is too much steam. But the pressure on the gauge is dropping swiftly.'

'Use all you can to take us down the hill. It is imperative that we pass the level crossing before we halt. It is absolutely imperative – if we stop this side of the level crossing they will be able to reach us with their lorries.'

'I will try, Captain.'

They rocketed down the hills but as soon as they reached the level ground their speed began to fall off. Peering through the dwindling clouds of steam Bruce saw the pale brown ribbon of road ahead of them, and they were still travelling at a healthy thirty miles an hour as they passed it. When finally the train trickled to a standstill Bruce estimated that they were three or four miles beyond the level crossing, safely walled in by the forest and hidden from the road by three bends.

'I doubt they'll find us here, but if they do they'll have to come down the line from the level crossing to get at us. We'll go back a mile and lay an ambush in the forest on each side of the line,' said Bruce.

'Those Arabs won't be following us, boss. They've got themselves women and a whole barful of liquor. Be two or three days before old General Moses can sober them up enough to move them on.'

'You're probably right, Ruffy. But we'll take no chances. Get that ambush laid and then we'll try and think up some idea for getting home.'

Suddenly a thought occurred to him: Martin Boussier had the diamonds with him. They would not be too pleased about that in Elisabethville.

Almost immediately Bruce was disgusted with himself. The diamonds were by far the least important thing that they had left behind in Port Reprieve.

Chapter Fourteen

André de Surrier held his steel helmet against his chest the way a man holds his hat at a funeral, the wind blew cool and caressing through his dark sweat-damp hair. His hearing was dulled by the strike of the shell that had cut the truck loose from the rear of the train, he could hear one of the children crying and the crooning, gentling voice of its mother. He stared back up the railway line at the train, saw the great bulk of Ruffy beside Bruce Curry on the roof of the second coach.

'They can't help us now.' Boussier spoke softly. 'There's nothing they can do.' He lifted his hand stiffly in almost a military salute and then dropped it to his side. 'Be brave, ma chère,' he said to his wife. 'Please be brave,' and she clung to him.

André let the helmet drop from his hands. It clanged on to the metal floor of the truck. He wiped the sweat from his face with nervous fluttering hands and then turned slowly to look down at the village.

'I don't want to die,' he whispered. 'Not like this, not now, please not now.' One of his gendarmes laughed, a sound without mirth, and stepped across to the Bren. He pushed André away from it and started firing at the tiny running figures of the men in the station yard.

'No,' shrilled André. Don't do that, no, don't antagonize them. They'll kill us if you do that—'

'They'll kill us anyway,' laughed the gendarme and emptied the magazine in one long despairing burst. André started towards him, perhaps to pull him away from the gun, but his resolve did not carry him that far. His hands dropped to his sides, clenching and unclenching. His lips quivered and then opened to spill out his terror.

'No!' he screamed. 'Please, no! No! Oh, God have mercy. Oh, save me, don't let this happen to me, please, God. Oh, my God.'

He stumbled to the side of the truck and clambered on to it. The truck was slowing as it ran into the platform. He could see men coming with rifles in their hands, shouting as they ran, black men in dirty tattered uniforms, their faces working with excitement, pink shouting mouths, baying like hounds in a pack.

André jumped and the dusty concrete of the platform grazed his cheek and knocked the wind out of him. He crawled to his knees, clutching his stomach and trying to scream. A rifle butt hit him between the shoulder-blades and he collapsed. Above him a voice shouted in French.

'He is white, keep him for the general. Don't kill him.' And again the rifle butt hit him, this time across the side of the head. He lay in the dust, dazed, with the taste of blood in his mouth and watched them drag the others from the truck.

They shot the black gendarmes on the platform, without ceremony, laughing as they competed with each other to use their bayonets on the corpses. The two children died quickly, torn from their mothers, held by the feet and swung head first against the steel side of the truck.

Old Boussier tried to prevent them stripping his wife and was bayoneted from behind in anger, and then shot twice with a pistol held to his head as he lay on the platform.

All this happened in the first few minutes before the officers arrived to control them; by that time André and the four women were the only occupants of the truck left alive.

André lay where he had fallen, watching in fascinated skin-crawling horror as they tore the clothing off the women and with a man to each arm and each leg held them down on the platform as though they were calves to be branded, hooting with laughter at their struggling naked bodies, bickering for position, already unbuckling belts, pushing each other, arguing, some of them with fresh blood on their clothing.

But then two men, who by their air of authority and the red sashes across their chests were clearly officers, joined the crowd. One of them fired his pistol in the air to gain their attention and both of them started a harangue that slowly had effect. The women were dragged up and herded off towards the hotel.

One of the officers came across to where André lay, stooped over him and lifted his head by taking a handful of hair.

'Welcome, mon ami. The general will be very pleased to see you. It is a pity that your other white friends have left us, but then, one is better than nothing.'

He pulled André into a sitting position, peered into his face and then spat into his eyes with sudden violence. 'Bring him! The general will talk to him later.'

They tied André to one of the columns on the front verandah of the hotel and left him there. He could have twisted his head and looked through the large windows into the lounge at what they were doing to the women, but he did not. He could hear what was happening; by noon the screams had become groans and sobbing; by mid-afternoon the women were making no sound at all. But the queue of *shufta* was still out of the front door of the lounge. Some of them had been to the head of the line and back to the tail three or four times.

All of them were drunk now. One jovial fellow carried a bottle of Parfait Amour liqueur in one hand and a bottle of Harpers whisky in the other. Every time he came back to join the queue again he stopped in front of André.

'Will you drink with me, little white boy?' he asked. 'Certainly you will,' he answered himself, filled his mouth from one of the bottles and spat it into André's face. Each time it got a big laugh from the others waiting in the line. Occasionally one of the other *shufta* would stop in front of André, unsling his rifle, back away a few paces, sight along the bayonet at André's face and then charge forward, at the last moment twisting the point aside so that it grazed his cheek. Each time André could not suppress his shriek of terror, and the waiting men nearly collapsed with merriment.

Towards evening they started to burn the houses on the outskirts of town. One group, sad with liquor and rape, sat together at the end of the verandah and started to sing. Their deep beautiful voices carrying all the melancholy savagery of Africa, they kept on singing while an argument between two *shufta* developed into a knife fight in the road outside the hotel.

The sweet bass lilt of singing covered the coarse breathing of the two circling, bare-chested knife fighters and the shuffle, shuffle, quick shuffle of their feet in the dust. When finally they locked together for the kill, the singing rose still deep and strong but with a triumphant note to it. One man stepped back with his rigid right arm holding the knife buried deep in the other's belly and as the loser sank down, sliding slowly off the knife, the singing sank with him, plaintive, regretful and lamenting into silence.

They came for André after dark. Four of them less drunk than the others.

They led him down the street to the Union Minière offices. General Moses was there, sitting alone at the desk in the front office.

There was nothing sinister about him; he looked like an elderly clerk, a small man with the short woollen cap of hair grizzled to grey above the ears and a pair of horn-rimmed spectacles. On his chest he wore three rows of full-dress medals; each of his fingers was encased in rings to the second joint, diamonds, emeralds and the occasional red glow of a ruby; most of them had been designed for women, but the metal had been cut to enlarge them for his stubby black fingers. The face was almost kindly, except the eyes. There was a blankness of expression in them, the lifeless eyes of a madman. On the desk in front of him was a small wooden case made of unvarnished deal which bore the seal of the Union Minière Company stencilled in black upon its side. The lid was open, and as André came in through the door with his escort General Moses lifted a white canvas bag from the case, loosened the draw string and poured a pile of dark grey industrial diamonds on to the blotter in front of him.

He prodded them thoughtfully with his finger, stirring them so they glittered dully in the harsh light of the petromax.

'Was this the only case in the truck?' he asked without looking up.

'Oui, mon général. There was only the one,' answered one of André's escorts.

'You are certain?'

'Oui, mon Général. I myself have searched thoroughly.'

General Moses took another of the canvas bags from the case and emptied it on to the blotter. He grunted with disappointment as he saw the drab little stones. He reached for another bag, and another, his anger mounting steadily as each yielded only dirty grey and black industrial diamonds. Soon the pile on the blotter would have filled a pint jug.

'Did you open the case?' he snarled.

'Non, mon général. It was sealed. The seal was not broken, you saw that.'

General Moses grunted again, his dark chocolate face set hard with frustration. Once more he dipped his hand into the wooden case and suddenly he smiled.

'Ah!' he said pleasantly. 'Yes! yes! what is this?' He brought out a cigar box, with the gaudy wrappers still on the cedar wood. A thumb nail prised the lid back and he beamed happily. In a nest of cotton wool, sparkling, breaking the white light of the petromax into all the rainbow colours of the spectrum, were the gem stones. General Moses picked one up and held it between thumb and forefinger.

'Pretty,' he murmured. 'Pretty, so pretty.' He swept the industrial stones to one side and laid the gem in the centre of the blotter. Then one by one he took the others from the cigar box, fondling each and laying it on the blotter, counting them, smiling, once chuckling softly, touching them, arranging them in patterns.

'Pretty,' he kept whispering. 'Bon – forty-one, forty-two. Pretty! My darlings! Forty-three.'

Then suddenly he scooped them up and poured them into one of the canvas bags, tightened the draw string, dropped it into his breast pocket above the medals and buttoned the flap.

He laid his black, bejewelled hands on the desk in front of him and looked up at André.

His eyes were smoky yellow with black centres behind his spectacles. They had an opaque, dreamlike quality.

'Take off his clothes,' he said in a voice that was as expressionless as the eyes.

They stripped André with rough dispatch and General Moses looked at his body.

'So white,' he murmured. 'Why so white?' Suddenly his jaws began chewing nervously and there was a faint shine of sweat on his forehead. He came round from behind the desk, a small man, yet with an intensity about him that doubled his size.

'White like the maggots that feed in the living body of the elephant.' He brought his face close to André's. 'You should be fatter, my maggot, having fed so long and so well. You should be much fatter.'

He touched André's body, running his hands down his flanks in a caress.

'But now it is too late, little white maggot,' he said, and André cringed from his touch and from his voice. 'For the elephant has shaken you from the wound, shaken you out on to the ground, shaken you out beneath his feet – and will you pop when he crushes you?'

His voice was still soft though the sweat oozed in oily lines down his cheeks and the dreaminess of his eyes had been replaced by a burning black brightness.

'We shall see,' he said and drew back. 'We shall see, my maggot,' he repeated, and brought his knee up into André's crotch with a force that jerked his whole frame and flung his shoulders back.

The agony flared through André's lower body, fierce as the touch of heated steel. It clamped in on his stomach, contracting it in a spasm like childbirth, it rippled up across the muscles of his chest into his head and burst beneath the roof of his skull in a whiteness that blinded him.

'Hold him,' commanded General Moses, his voice suddenly shrill. The two guards took André by the elbows and forced him to his knees, so that his genitals and lower belly were easily accessible to the general's boots. They had done this often.

'For the times you gaoled me!' And General Moses swung his booted foot into André's body. The pain blended with the other pain, and it was too strong for André to scream.

'This, for the insults,' and André could feel his testicles crush beneath it. Still it was too strong – he could not use his voice.

'This, for the times I have grovelled.' The pain had passed its zenith, this time he could scream with it. He opened his mouth and filled his empty lungs.

'This, for the times I have hungered.' Now he must scream. Now he must – the pain, oh, sweet Christ, I must, please let me scream.

'This, for your white man's justice.' Why can't I, please let me. Oh, no! No – please. Oh, God, oh, please.

'This, for your prisons and your Kiboko!'

The kicks so fast now, like the beat of an insane drummer, like rain on a tin roof. In his stomach he felt something tear.

'And this, and this, and this.'

The face before him filled the whole field of his vision. The voice and the sound of boot into him filled his ears.

'This, and this, and this.' The voice high-pitched and within him the sudden warm flood of internal bleeding.

The pain was fading now as his body closed it out in defence, and he had not screamed. The leap of elation as he knew it. *This last thing I can do well, I can die now WITHOUT SCREAMING.* He tried to stand up, but they held him down and his legs were not his own, they were on the other side of the great numb warmth of his belly. He lifted his head and looked at the man who was killing him.

'This for the white filth that bore you, and this, and this—'

The blows were not part of reality, he could feel the shock of them as though he stood close to a man who was cutting down a tree with an axe. And André smiled.

He was still smiling when they let him fall forward to the floor.

'I think he is dead,' said one of the guards. General Moses turned away and walked back to his seat at the desk. He was shaking as though he had run a long way, and his breathing was deep and fast. The jacket of his uniform was soaked with sweat. He sank into the chair and his body seemed to crumple; slowly the brightness faded from his eyes until once more they were filmed over, opaque and dreamy. The two guards squatted down quietly on each side of André's body; they knew it would be a long wait.

Through the open window there came an occasional shout of drunken laughter, and the red flicker and leap of flames.

Chapter Fifteen

Bruce stood in the centre of the tracks and searched the floor of the forest critically. At last he could make out the muzzle of the Bren protruding a few inches from the patch of elephant grass. Despite the fact that he knew exactly where to look for it, it had taken him a full two minutes to find it.

'That'll do, Ruffy,' he decided. 'We can't get it much better than that.'

'I reckon not, boss.'

Bruce raised his voice. 'Can you hear me?' There were muffled affirmatives from the bush on each side, and Bruce continued.

'If they come you must let them reach this spot before you open fire. I will mark it for you.' He went to a small shrub beside the line, broke off a branch and dropped it on the tracks.

'Can you see that?'

Again the affirmatives from the men in ambush. 'You will be relieved before darkness – until then stay where you are.'

The train was hidden beyond a bend in the line, half a mile ahead, and Bruce walked back with Ruffy.

The engine driver was waiting for them, talking with Wally Hendry beside the rear truck.

'Any luck?' Bruce asked him.

'I regret, mon capitaine, that she is irreparably damaged. The boiler is punctured in two places and there is considerable disruption of the copper tubing.'

'Thank you,' Bruce nodded. He was neither surprised nor disappointed. It was precisely what his own judgment had told him after a brief examination of the locomotive.

'Where is Madame Cartier?' he asked Wally.

'*Madame* is preparing the luncheon, *monsir*,' Wally told him with heavy sarcasm. 'Why do you ask, Bucko? Are you feeling randy again so soon, hey? You feel like a slice of veal for lunch, is that it?'

Bruce snuffed out the quick flare of his temper and walked past him. He found Shermaine with four gendarmes in the cab of the locomotive. They had scraped the coals from the furnace into a glowing heap on the steel floor and were chopping potatoes and onions into the five gallon pots.

The gendarmes were all laughing at something Shermaine had said. Her usually pale cheeks were flushed with the heat; there was a sooty smudge on her forehead. She wielded the big knife with professional dexterity. She looked up and saw Bruce, her face lighting instantly and her lips parting.

'We're having a Hungarian goulash for lunch – bully beef, potatoes and onions.'

'As of now I am rating you acting second cook without pay.'

'You are too kind,' and she put her tongue out at him. It was a pink pointed little tongue like a cat's. Bruce felt the old familiar tightening of his legs and the dryness in his throat as he looked at it.

'Shermaine, the locomotive is damaged beyond repair. It is of no further use.' He spoke in English.

'It makes a passable kitchen,' she demurred.

'Be serious.' Bruce's anxiety made him irritable. 'We're stranded here until we think of something.'

'But, Bruce, you are the genius. I have complete faith in you. I'm sure you'll think of some truly beautiful idea.' Her face was solemn but she couldn't keep the banter out of her eyes. 'Why don't you go and ask General Moses to lend you his transportation.'

Bruce's eyes narrowed in thought and the black inverted curves of his eyebrows nearly touched above the bridge of his nose.

'The food better be good or I'll break you to third cook,' he warned, clambered down from the cab to the ground and hurried back along the train.

'Hendry, Sergeant Major, come here, please. I want to discuss something with you.'

They came to join him and he led the way up the ladder into one of the covered coaches. Hendry dropped on to the bunk and placed his feet on the wash basin.

'That was a quick one,' he grinned through the coppery stubble of his beard.

'You're the most uncouth, filthy-mouthed son of a bitch I have ever met, Hendry,' said Bruce coldly. 'When I get you back to Elisabethville I'm going to beat you to pulp before I hand you over to the military authority for murder.'

'My, my,' laughed Hendry. 'Big talker, hey? Curry, big, big talker.'

'Don't make me kill you now – don't do that, please, I still need you.'

'What's with you and that Frenchy, hey? You love it or something? You love it, or you just fancy a bit of that fat little arse? It can't be her titties – she ain't got much there, not even a handful each side.'

Bruce started for him, then changed his mind and swung round to stare out of the window. His voice was strangled when he spoke.

'I'll make a bargain with you, Hendry. Until we get out of this you keep off my back and I'll keep off yours. When we reach Msapa Junction the truce is off. You can do and say whatever you like and, if I don't kill you for it, I'll try my level best to see you hanged for murder.'

'I'm making no bargain with you or nobody, Curry. I play along until it suits me, and I won't give you no warning when it doesn't suit me to play along any more. And let me tell you now, Bucko, I don't need you and I don't need nobody. Not Haig or you, with your fancy too-good-to-kiss-my-arse talk; when the time comes I'm going to trim you down to size – just remember that, Curry. And don't say I didn't warn you.' Hendry was leaning forward, hands on his knees, body braced and his whole face twisting and contorted with the vehemence of his speech.

'Let's make it now, Hendry.' Bruce wheeled away from the window, crouching slightly, his hands stiffening into the flat hard blades of the judo fighter.

Sergeant Major Ruffararo stood up from the opposite bunk with surprising grace and speed for such a big man. He interposed his great body.

'You wanted to tell us something, boss?'

Slowly Bruce straightened out of his crouch, his hands relaxing. Irritably he brushed at the damp lock of dark hair that had fallen on to his forehead, as if to brush Wally Hendry out of his mind with the same movement.

'Yes,' controlling his voice with an effort, 'I wanted to discuss our next move.' He fished the cigarette pack from his top pocket and lit one, sucking the smoke down deep. Then he perched on the lid of the wash basin and studied the ash on the tip of the cigarette. When he spoke again his voice was normal.

'There is no hope of repairing this locomotive, so we have to find alternative transport out of here. Either we can walk two hundred miles back to Msapa Junction with our friends the Baluba ready to dispute our passage, or we can ride back in General Moses's trucks!' He paused to let it sink in.

'You going to pinch those trucks off him?' asked Ruffy. 'That's going to take some doing, boss.'

'No, Ruffy, I don't think we have any chance of getting them out from under his nose. What we will have to do is attack the town and wipe him out.'

'You're bloody crazy,' exclaimed Wally. 'You're raving bloody mad.'

Bruce ignored him. 'I estimate that Moses has about sixty men. With Kanaki and nine men on the bridge, Haig and de Surrier and six others gone, we have thirty-four men left. Correct, Sergeant Major?'

'That's right, boss.'

'Very well,' Bruce nodded. 'We'll have to leave at least ten men here to man that ambush in case Moses sends a patrol after us, or in case of an attack by the Baluba. It's not enough, I know, but we will just have to risk it.'

'Most of these civilians got arms with them, shotguns and sports rifles,' said Ruffy.

'Yes,' agreed Bruce. 'They should be able to look after themselves. So that leaves twenty-four men to carry out the attack, something like three to one.'

'Those *shufta* will be so full of liquor, half of them won't be able to stand up.'

'That's what I am banking on: drunkenness and surprise. We'll hit them and try and finish it before they know what's happened. I don't think they will have realized how badly we were hit; they probably expect us to be a hundred miles away by now.'

'When do you want to leave, boss?'

'We are about twelve miles from Port Reprieve – say, six hours' march in the dark. I want to attack in the early hours of tomorrow morning, but I'd like to be in position around midnight. We'll leave here at six o'clock, just before dark.'

'I'd better go and start sorting the boys out.'

'Okay, Ruffy. Issue an extra hundred rounds to each man and ten grenades. I'll want four extra haversacks of grenades also.' Bruce turned to Hendry and looked at him for the first time. 'Go with the sergeant major, Hendry, and give him a hand.'

'Jesus, this is going to be a ball,' grinned Wally in anticipation. 'With any luck I'll get me a sackful of ears.' He disappeared down the corridor behind Ruffy, and Bruce lay back on the seat and took off his helmet. He closed his eyes and once again he saw Boussier and his wife standing together in the truck as it rolled back down the hill, he saw the huddle of frightened women, and André standing bareheaded staring back at him with big brown gentle eyes. He groaned softly. 'Why is it always the good ones, the harmless, the weak?'

A tap on the door roused him and he sat up quickly.

'Yes?'

'Hello, Bruce.' Shermaine came in with a multiple-decked metal canteen in one hand and two mugs in the other. 'It's lunchtime.'

'Already!' Bruce checked his watch. 'Good Lord, it's after one.'

'Are you hungry?'

'Breakfast was a century ago.'

'Good,' she said, lowered the collapsible table and began serving the food.

'Smells good.'

'I am a chef Cordon Bleu. My bully beef goulash is demanded by the crowned heads of Europe.'

They ate in silence for both of them were hungry. Once they looked at each other and smiled but returned to the food.

'That was good,' sighed Bruce at last.

'Coffee, Bruce?'

'Please.'

As she poured it she asked, 'So, what happens now?'

'Do you mean what happens now we are alone?'

'You are forward, monsieur. I meant how do we get out of here.'

'I am adopting your suggestion: borrowing General Moses's transportation.'

'You make jokes, Bruce!'

'No,' he said, and explained briefly.

'It will be very dangerous, will it not? You may be hurt?'

'Only the good die young.'

'That is why I worry. Please do not get hurt – I am starting to think I would not like that.' Her face was very serious and pale. Bruce crossed quickly and stooped over her, lifting her to her feet.

'Shermaine, I—'

'No, Bruce. Don't talk. Don't say anything.' Her eyes were closed with thick black lashes interlaced, her chin lifted exposing the long smooth swell of her neck. He touched it with his lips and she made a soft noise in her throat so he could feel the skin vibrate. Her body flattened against his and her fingers closed in the hair at the back of his head.

'Oh, Bruce. My Bruce, please do not get hurt. Do not let them hurt you.'

Wanting now, urgently, his mouth hunted upwards and hers came to meet it, willing prey. Her lips were pink and not greased with make-up, they parted to the pressure of his tongue, he felt the tip of her nose cool upon his cheek and his hand moved up her back and closed round the nape of her neck, slender neck with silky down behind her ears.

'Oh, Bruce—' she said into his mouth. His other hand went down on to the proud round, deeply divided thrust of her buttocks, he pulled her lower body against his and she gasped as she felt him – the arrogant maleness through cloth.

'No,' she gasped and tried to pull away, but he held her until she relaxed against him once more. She shook her head, 'Non, non,' but her mouth was open still and her tongue fluttered against his. Down came his hand from her neck and twitched her shirt tails loose from under her belt, then up again along her back, touching the deep lateral depression of her spine so that she shuddered, clinging to him. Stroking velvet skin stretched tight over rubber-hard flesh, finding the outline of her shoulder-blades, tracing them upwards then back to the armpits, silky-haired armpits that maddened him with excitement, quickly past them to her breasts, small breasts with soft tips hardening to his touch.

Now she struggled in earnest, her fists beating on his shoulders and her mouth breaking from his, and he stopped himself, dropped the hand away to encircle her waist. Holding her loosely within his arms.

'That was not good, Bruce. You get naughty very quick.' Her cheeks flamed with colour and her blue eyes had darkened to royal, her lips still wet from his, and her voice was unsteady, as unsteady as his when he answered.

'I'm sorry, Shermaine. I don't know what happened then. I did not mean to frighten you.'

'You are very strong, Bruce. But you do not frighten me, only a little bit. Your eyes frighten me when they look at me but do not see.'

You really made a hash of that one, he rebuked himself. Bruce Curry, the gentle sophisticated lover. Bruce Curry, the heavyweight, catch-as-catch-can, two-fisted rape artist.

He felt shaky, his legs wobbly, and there was something seriously wrong with his breathing.

'You do not wear a brassière,' he said without thinking, and immediately regretted it, but she chuckled, soft and husky.

'Do you think I need to, Bruce?'

'No, I didn't mean that,' he protested quickly, remembering the saucy tilt of that small breast. He was silent then, marshalling his words, trying to control his breathing, fighting down the madness of desire.

She studied his eyes. 'You can see again now – perhaps I will let you kiss me.'

'Please,' he said and she came back to him.

Gently now, Bruce me boy.

The door of the compartment flew back with a crash and they jumped apart. Wally Hendry stood on the threshold.

'Well, well, well.' His shrewd little eyes took it all in. 'That's nice!'

Shermaine was hurriedly tucking in her shirt tail and trying to smooth her hair at the same time.

Wally grinned. 'Nothing like it after a meal, I always say. Gets the digestion going.'

'What do you want?' snapped Bruce.

'There's no doubt what you want,' said Wally. 'Looks like you're getting it too.' He let his eyes travel up from Shermaine's waist, slowly over her body to her face.

Bruce stepped out into the corridor, pushing Hendry back and slammed the door.

'What do you want?' he repeated.

'Ruffy wants you to check his arrangements, but I'll tell him you're busy. We can put the attack off until tomorrow night if you like.'

Bruce scowled at him. 'Tell him I'll be with him in two minutes.'

Wally leaned against the door. 'Okay, I'll tell him.'

'What are you waiting for?'

'Nothing, just nothing,' grinned Wally.

'Well, bugger off then,' snarled Bruce.

'Okay, okay, don't get your knickers in a knot, Bucko.'

He sauntered off down the corridor.

Shermaine was standing where Bruce had left her, but with her eyes bright with tears of anger.

'He is a pig, that one. A filthy, filthy pig.'

'He's not worth worrying about.' Bruce tried to take her in his arms again, but she shrugged him off.

'I hate him. He makes everything seem so cheap, so dirty.'

'Nothing between you and I could be cheap and dirty,' said Bruce, and instantly her fury abated.

'I know, my Bruce. But he can make it seem that way.' They kissed, gently.

'I must go. They want me.' For a second she clung to him.

'Be careful. Promise me you'll be careful.'

'I promise,' said Bruce and she let him go.

Chapter Sixteen

They left before dark, but the clouds had come up during the afternoon and now they hung low over the forest, trapping the heat beneath them.

Bruce led, with Ruffy in the middle of the line and Hendry in the rear.

By the time they reached the level crossing the night was on them and it had started to rain, soft fat drops weeping like a woman exhausted with grief, warm rain in the darkness. And the darkness was complete. Once Bruce touched the top of his nose with his open palm, but he could not see his hand.

He used a staff to keep contact with the steel rail that ran beside him, tapping along it like a blind man, and at each step the gravel of the embankment crunched beneath his feet. The hand of the man behind him was on his shoulder, and he could sense the presence of the others that followed him like the body of a serpent, could hear the crunch of their steps and the muted squeak and rattle of their equipment. A man's voice was raised in protest and immediately quenched by Ruffy's deep rumble.

They crossed the road and the gradient changed beneath Bruce's feet so that he had to lean forward against it. They were starting up the Lufira hills.

I will rest them at the top, he thought, and from there we will be able to see the lights of the town.

The rain stopped abruptly, and the quietness after it was surprising. Now he could distinctly hear the breathing of the man behind him above the small sounds of their advance, and in the forest nearby a tree frog clinked as though steel pellets were being dropped into a crystal glass. It was a sound of great purity and beauty.

All Bruce's senses were enhanced to compensate for his lack of sight; his hearing; his sense of smell, so that he could catch the over-sweet perfume of a jungle flower and the heaviness of decaying wet vegetation; his sense of touch, so that he could feel the raindrops on his face and the texture of his clothing against his body; then the other animal sense of danger told him with sickening, stomach-tripping certainty that there was something ahead of him in the darkness.

He stopped, and the man following him bumped into him throwing him off balance. All along the line there was a ripple of confusion and then silence. They all waited.

Bruce strained his hearing, half crouched with his rifle held ready. There was something there, he could almost feel it.

Please God, let them not have a machine-gun set up here, he thought; they could cut us into a shambles.

He turned cautiously and felt for the head of the man behind him, found it and drew it towards him until his mouth was an inch from the ear.

'Lie down very quietly. Tell the one behind you that he may pass it back.'

Bruce waited poised, listening and trying to see ahead into the utter blackness. He felt a gentle tap on his ankle from the gendarme at his feet. They were all down.

'All right, let's go take a look.' Bruce detached one of the grenades from his webbing belt. He drew the pin and dropped it into the breast pocket of his jacket. Then feeling for the cross-ties of the rails with each foot he started forward. Ten paces and he stopped again. Then he heard it, the tiny click of two pebbles just ahead of him. His throat closed so he could not breathe and his stomach was very heavy.

I'm right on top of them. My God, if they open up now—

Inch by inch he drew back the hand that held the grenade.

I'll have to lob short and then get down fast. Five-second fuse – too long, they'll hear it and start shooting.

His hand was right back, he bent his legs and sank slowly on to his knees.

Here we go, he thought, and at that instant sheet lightning fluttered across the sky and Bruce could see. The hills were outlined black below the pale grey belly of the clouds, and the steel rails glinted in the sudden light. The forest was dark and high at each hand, and – a leopard, a big golden and black leopard, stood facing Bruce. In that brief second they stared at each other and then the night closed down again.

The leopard coughed explosively in the darkness, and Bruce tried desperately to bring his rifle up, but it was in his left hand and his other arm was held back ready to throw.

This time for sure, he thought, this time they lower the boom on you.

It was with a feeling of disbelief that he heard the leopard crash sideways into the undergrowth, and the scrambling rush of its run dwindle into the bush.

He subsided on to his backside, with the primed grenade in his hand, the hysterical laughter of relief coming up into his throat.

'You okay, boss?' Ruffy's voice lifted anxiously.

'It was a leopard,' answered Bruce, and was surprised at the squeakiness of his own voice.

There was a buzz of voices from the gendarmes and a rattle and clatter as they started to stand up. Someone laughed.

'That's enough noise,' snapped Bruce and climbed to his feet; he found the pin in his pocket and fitted it back into the grenade. He groped his way back, picked up the staff from where he had dropped it, and took his position at the head of the column again.

'Let's go,' he said.

His mouth was dry, his breathing too quick and he could feel the heat beneath the skin of his cheeks from the shock of the leopard.

I truly squirted myself full of adrenalin that time, Bruce grinned precariously in the dark, I'm as windy as hell. And before tonight is over I shall find fear again.

They moved on up the incline of the hills, a serpent of twenty-six men, and the tension was in all of them. Bruce could hear it in the footsteps behind him, feel it in the grip of the hand upon his shoulder and catch it in the occasional whiffs of body smell that came forward to him, the smell of nervous sweat like acid on metal.

Ahead of them the clouds that had crouched low upon the hills lifted slowly, and Bruce could see the silhouette of the crests. It was no longer utterly dark for there was a glow on the belly of the clouds now. A faint orange glow of reflected light that grew in strength, then faded and grew again. It puzzled Bruce for a while, and thinking about it gave his nerves a chance to settle. He plodded steadily on watching the fluctuations of the light. The ground tilted more sharply upwards beneath his feet and he leaned forward against it, slogging up the last half mile to the pass between the peaks, and at last came out on the top.

'Good God,' Bruce spoke aloud, for from here he could see the reason for that glow on the clouds. They were burning Fort Reprieve. The flames were well established in the buildings along the wharf, and as Bruce watched one of the roofs collapsed slowly in upon itself in a storm of sparks leaving the walls naked and erect, the wooden sills of the windows burning fiercely. The railway buildings were also on fire, and there was fire in the residential area beyond the Union Minière offices and the hotel. Quickly Bruce looked towards St. Augustine's. It was dark, no flames there, no light even, and he felt a small lift of relief.

'Perhaps they have overlooked it, perhaps they're too busy looting,' and as he looked back at Port Reprieve, his mouth hardened. 'The senseless wanton bastards!' His anger started as he watched the meaningless destruction of the town.

'What can they possibly hope to gain by this?' There were new fires nearer the hotel. Bruce turned to the man behind him.

'We will rest here, but there will be no smoking and no talking.'

He heard the order passed back along the line and the careful sounds of equipment being lowered and men settling gratefully down upon the gravel embankment. Bruce unslung the case that contained his binoculars. He focused them on the burning town.

It was bright with the light of fires and through the glasses he could almost discern the features of the men in the streets. They moved in packs, heavily armed and restless. Many carried bottles and already the gait of some of them was unsteady. Bruce tried to estimate their numbers but it was impossible, men kept disappearing into buildings and reappearing, groups met and mingled and dispersed.

He dropped his glasses on to his chest to rest his eyes, and heard movement beside him in the dark. He glanced sideways. It was Ruffy, his bulk exaggerated by the load he carried; his rifle across one shoulder, on the other a full case of ammunition, and round his neck half a dozen haversacks full of grenades.

'Looks like they're having fun, hey, boss?'

'Fifth of November,' agreed Bruce. 'Aren't you going to take a breather?'

'Why not?' Ruffy set down the ammunition case and lowered his great backside on to it. 'Can you see any of those folks we left behind?' he asked.

Bruce lifted the glasses again and searched the area beyond the station buildings. It was darker there but he made out the square shape of the truck standing among the moving shadows.

'The truck's still there,' he murmured, 'but I can't see—'

At that moment the thatched roof of one of the houses exploded upwards in a column of flame, lighting the railway yard, and the truck stood out sharply.

'Yes,' said Bruce, 'I can see them now.' They were littered untidily across the yard, still lying where they had died. Small and fragile, unwanted as broken toys.

'Dead?' asked Ruffy.

'Dead,' confirmed Bruce.

'The women?'

'It's hard to tell.' Bruce strained his eyes. 'I don't think so.'

'No.' Ruffy's voice was soft and very deep. 'They wouldn't waste the women. I'd guess they've got them up at the hotel, taking it in turn to give them the business. Four women only – they won't last till morning. Those bastards down there could shag an elephant to death.' He spat thoughtfully into the gravel at his feet. 'What you going to do, boss?'

Bruce did not answer for a minute; he swung the glasses slowly back across the town. The field gun was still standing where he had last seen it, its barrel pointing accusingly up towards him. The transports were parked before the

Union Minière offices; he could see the brilliant yellow and red paint and the Shell sign on the tanker. I hope it's full, Bruce thought, we'll need plenty of gasoline to get us back to Elisabethville.

'Ruffy, you'd better tell your boys to keep their bullets away from that tanker, otherwise it'll be a long walk home.'

'I'll tell them,' grunted Ruffy. 'But you know these mad Arabs – once they start shooting they don't stop till they're out of bullets, and they not too fussy where those bullets go.'

'We'll split into two groups when we get to the bottom of the hill. You and I will take our lot through the edge of the swamp and cross to the far side of the town. Tell Lieutenant Hendry to come here.' Bruce waited until Wally came forward to join them, and when the three of them crouched together he went on.

'Hendry, I want you to spread your men out at the top of the main street – there in the darkness on this side of the station. Ruffy and I are going to cross the edge of the swamp to the causeway and lay out on the far side. For God's sake keep your boys quiet until Ruffy and I hit them – all we need is for your lot to start pooping off before we are ready and we won't need those lorries, we'll need coffins for the rest of our journey. Do you understand me?'

'Okay, okay, I know what I'm doing,' muttered Wally.

'I hope so,' said Bruce, and then went on. 'We'll hit them at four o'clock tomorrow morning, just before first light. Ruffy and I will go into the town and bomb the hotel – that's where most of them will be sleeping. The grenades should force the survivors into the street and as soon as that happens you can open up – but not before. Wait until you get them in the open. Is that clear?'

'Jesus,' growled Hendry. 'Do you think I'm a bloody fool, do you think I can't understand English?'

'The crossfire from the two groups should wipe most of them out.' Bruce ignored Wally's outburst. 'But we mustn't give the remainder a chance to organize. Hit them hard and as soon as they take cover again you must follow them in – close with them and finish them off. If we can't get it over in five to ten minutes then we are going to be in trouble. They outnumber us three to one, so we have to exploit the element of surprise to the full.'

'Exploit the element of surprise to the full!' mimicked Wally. 'What for all the fancy talk – why not just murder the bastards?'

Bruce grinned lightly in the dark. 'All right, murder the bastards,' he agreed. 'But do it as quickly as bloody possible.' He stood up and inclined the luminous dial of his wrist watch to catch the light. 'It's half past ten now – we'll move down on them. Come with me, Hendry, and we'll sort them into two groups.'

Bruce and Wally moved back along the line and talked to each man in turn.

'You will go with Lieutenant Hendry.'

'You come with me.'

Making sure that the two English-speaking corporals were with Wally, they took ten minutes to divide them into two units and to redistribute the haversacks of grenades. Then they moved on down the slope, still in Indian file.

'This is where we leave you, Hendry,' whispered Bruce. 'Don't go jumping the gun – wait until you hear my grenades.'

'Yeah, okay – I know all about it.'

'Good luck,' said Bruce.

'Your bum in a barrel, Captain Curry,' rejoined Wally and moved away.

'Come on, Ruffy.' Bruce led his men off the embankment down into the swamp. Almost immediately the mud and slime was knee deep and as they worked their way out to the right it rose to their waists and then to their armpits, sucking and gurgling sullenly as they stirred it with their passage, belching little evil-smelling gusts of swamp gas.

The mosquitoes closed round Bruce's face in a cloud so dense that he breathed them into his mouth and had to blink them out of his eyes. Sweat dribbled down from under his helmet and clung heavily in his eyebrows and the matted stems of the papyrus grass dragged at his feet. Their progress was tortuously slow and for fifteen minutes at a time Bruce lost sight of the lights of the village through the wall of papyrus; he steered by the glow of the fires and the occasional column of sparks.

It was an hour before they had half completed their circuit of Port Reprieve. Bruce stopped to rest, still waist deep in swamp ooze and with his arms aching numb from holding his rifle above his head.

'I could use a smoke now, boss,' grunted Ruffy.

'Me too,' answered Bruce, and he wiped his face on the sleeve of his jacket. The mosquito bites on his forehead and round his eyes burnt like fire.

'What a way to make a living,' he whispered.

'You go on living and you'll be one of the lucky ones,' answered Ruffy. 'My guess is there'll be some dying before tomorrow.'

But the fear of death was submerged by physical discomfort. Bruce had almost forgotten that they were going into battle; right now he was more worried that the leeches which had worked their way through the openings in his anklets and were busily boring into his lower legs might find their way up to his crotch. There was a lot to be said in favour of a zip fly, he decided.

'Let's get out of this,' he whispered. 'Come on, Ruffy. Tell your boys to keep it quiet.'

He worked in closer to the shore and the level fell to their knees once more. Progress was more noisy now as their legs broke the surface with each step and the papyrus rustled and brushed against them.

It was almost two o'clock when they reached the causeway. Bruce left his men crouched in the papyrus while he made a stealthy reconnaissance along the side of the concrete bridge, keeping in its shadow, moving doubled up until he came to dry land on the edge of the village. There were no sentries posted and except for the crackle of the flames the town was quiet, sunk into a drunken stupor, satiated. Bruce went back to call his men up.

He spread them in pairs along the outskirts of the village. He had learned very early in this campaign not to let his men act singly; nothing drains an African of courage more than to be on his own, especially in the night when the ghosts are on the walk-about.

To each couple he gave minute instructions.

'When you hear the grenades you shoot at anybody in the streets or at the windows. When the street is empty move in close beside that building there. Use your own grenades on every house and watch out for Lieutenant Hendry's men coming through from the other side. Do you understand?'

'It is understood.'

'Shoot carefully. Aim each shot – not like you did at the road bridge, and in the name of God do not hit the gasoline tanker. We need that to get us home.'

Now it was three o'clock, Bruce saw by the luminous figures on his wrist watch. Eight hours since they had left the train, and twenty-two hours since Bruce had last slept. But he was not tired, although his body ached and there was that gritty feeling under his eyelids, yet his mind was clear and bright as flame.

He lay beside Ruffy under a low bush on the outskirts of Port Reprieve and the night wind drifted the smoke from the burning town down upon them, and Bruce was not tired. For I am going to another rendezvous with fear.

Fear is a woman, he thought, with all the myriad faces and voices of a woman. Because she is a woman and because I am a man I must keep going back to her. Only this time the appointment is one that I cannot avoid, this time I am not deliberately seeking her out.

I know she is evil, I know that after I have possessed her I will feel sick and shaken. I will say, 'That was the last time, never again.'

But just as certainly I know I will go back to her again, hating her, dreading her, but also needing her.

I have gone to find her on a mountain – on Dutoits Kloof Frontal, on Turret Towers, on the Wailing Wall, and the Devil's Tooth.

And she was there, dressed in a flowing robe of rock, a robe that fell sheer two thousand feet to the scree slope below. And she shrieked with the voice of the wind along the exposed face. Then her voice was soft, tinkling like cooling glass in the Berg ice underfoot, whispering like nylon rope running free, grating as the rotten rock moved in my hand.

I have followed her into the Jessie bush on the banks of the Sabi and the Luangwa, and she was there, waiting, wounded, in a robe of buffalo hide with the blood dripping from her mouth. And her smell was the sour-acid smell of my own sweat, and her taste was like rotten tomatoes in the back of my throat.

I have looked for her beyond the reef in the deep water with the demand valve of a scuba repeating my breathing with metallic hoarseness. And she was there with rows of white teeth in the semicircle of her mouth, a tall fin on her back, dressed this time in shagreen, and her touch was cold as the ocean, and her taste was salt and the taint of dying things.

I have looked for her on the highway with my foot pressed to the floorboards and she was there with her cold arm draped round my shoulders, her voice the whine of rubber on tarmac and the throaty hum of the motor.

With Colin Butler at the helm (a man who treated fear not as a lover, but with tolerant contempt as though she were his little sister) I went to find her in a small boat. She was dressed in green with plumes of spray and she wore a necklace of sharp black rock. And her voice was the roar of water breaking on water.

We met in darkness at the road bridge and her eyes glinted like bayonets. But that was an enforced meeting not of my choosing, as tonight will be.

I hate her, he thought, but she is a woman and I am a man.

Bruce lifted his arm and turned his wrist to catch the light of the fires.

'Fifteen minutes to four, Ruffy. Let's go and take a look.'

'That's a good idea, boss.' Ruffy grinned with a show of white teeth in the darkness.

'Are you afraid, Ruffy?' he asked suddenly, wanting to know, for his own heart beat like a war drum and there was no saliva in his mouth.

'Boss, some questions you don't ask a man.' Ruffy rose slowly into a crouch. 'Let's go take a look around.'

So they moved quickly together into the town, along the street, hugging the hedges and the buildings, trying to keep in shadow, their eyes moving everywhere, breathing quick and shallow, nerves screwed up tight until they reached the hotel.

There were no lights in the windows and it seemed deserted until Bruce made out the untidy mass of humanity strewn in sleep upon the front verandah.

'How many there, Ruffy?'

'Dunno – perhaps ten, fifteen.' Ruffy breathed an answer. 'Rest of them will be inside.'

'Where are the women – be careful of them.'

'They're dead long ago, you can believe me.'

'All right then, let's get round the back.' Bruce took a deep breath and then moved quickly across the twenty yards of open firelit street to the corner of the hotel. He stopped in the shadow and felt Ruffy close beside him. 'I want to take a look into the main lounge, my guess is that most of them will be in there,' he whispered.

'There's only four bedrooms,' agreed Ruffy. 'Say the officers upstairs and the rest in the lounge.'

Now Bruce moved quickly round the corner and stumbled over something soft. He felt it move against his foot.

'Ruffy!' he whispered urgently as he teetered off balance. He had trodden on a man, a man sleeping in the dust beside the wall. He could see the firelight on his bare torso and the glint of the bottle clutched in one outflung hand. The man sat up, muttering, and then began to cough, hacking painfully, swearing as he wiped his mouth with his free hand. Bruce regained his balance and swung his rifle up to use the bayonet, but Ruffy was quicker. He put one foot on the man's chest and trod him flat on his back once more, then standing over him he used his bayoneted rifle the way a gardener uses a spade to lift potatoes, leaning his weight on it suddenly and the blade vanished into the man's throat.

The body stiffened convulsively, legs thrust out straight and arms rigid, there was a puffing of breath from the severed windpipe and then the slow melting relaxation of death. Still with his foot on the chest, Ruffy withdrew the bayonet and stepped over the corpse.

That was very close, thought Bruce, stifling the qualm of horror he felt at the neat execution. The man's eyes were fixed open in almost comic surprise, the bottle still in his hand, his chest bare, the front of his trousers unbuttoned and stiff with dried blood – not his blood, guessed Bruce angrily.

They moved on past the kitchens. Bruce looked in and saw that they were empty with the white enamel tiles reflecting the vague light and piles of used plates and pots cluttering the tables and the sink. Then they reached the bar-room and there was a hurricane lamp on the counter diffusing a yellow glow; the stench of liquor poured out through the half-open window, the shelves were bare of bottles and men were asleep upon the counter, men lay curled together upon the floor like a pack of dogs, broken glass and rifles and shattered furniture littered about them. Someone had vomited out of the window leaving a yellow streak down the whitewashed wall.

'Stand here,' breathed Bruce into Ruffy's ear. 'I will go round to the front where I can throw on to the verandah and also into the lounge. Wait until you hear my first grenade blow.'

Ruffy nodded and leaned his rifle against the wall; he took a grenade in each fist and pulled the pins.

Bruce slipped quickly round the corner and along the side wall. He reached the windows of the lounge. They were tightly closed and he peered in over the sill. A little of the light from the lamp in the bar-room came through the open doors and showed up the interior. Here again there were men covering the floor and piled upon the sofas along the far wall. Twenty of them at least, he estimated by the volume of their snoring, and he grinned without humour. My God, what a shambles it is going to be.

Then something at the foot of the stairs caught his eye and the grin on his face became fixed, baring his teeth and narrowing his eyes to slits. It was the mound of nude flesh formed by the bodies of the four women; they had been discarded once they had served their purpose, dragged to one side to clear the floor for sleeping space, lying upon each other in a jumble of naked arms and legs and cascading hair.

No mercy now, thought Bruce with hatred replacing his fear as he looked at the women and saw by the attitudes in which they lay that there was no life left in them. *No mercy now!*

He slung his rifle over his left shoulder and filled his hands with grenades, pulled the pins and moved quickly to the corner so that he could look down the length of the covered verandah. He rolled both grenades down among the sleeping figures, hearing clearly the click of the priming and the metallic rattle against the concrete floor. Quickly he ducked back to the lounge window, snatching two more grenades from his haversack and pulling the pins, he hurled them through the closed windows. The crash of breaking glass blended with the double thunder of the explosions on the verandah.

Someone shouted in the room, a cry of surprise and alarm, then the windows above Bruce blew outwards, showering him with broken glass and the noise half deafening him as he tossed two more grenades through the gaping hole of the window. They were screaming and groaning in the lounge. Ruffy's grenades roared in the bar-room bursting through the double doors, then Bruce's grenades snuffed out the sounds of life in the lounge with violent white flame and thunder. Bruce tossed in two more grenades and ran back to the corner of the verandah unslinging his rifle.

A man with his hands over his eyes and blood streaming through his fingers fell over the low verandah wall and crawled to his knees. Bruce shot him from so close that the shaft of gun flame joined the muzzle of his rifle and the man's chest, punching him over backwards, throwing him spreadeagled on to the earth.

He looked beyond and saw two more in the road, but before he could raise his rifle the fire from his own gendarmes found them, knocking them down amid spurts of dust.

Bruce hurdled the verandah wall. He shouted, a sound without form or meaning. Exulting, unafraid, eager to get into the building, to get amongst them. He stumbled over the dead men on the verandah. A burst of gunfire from down the street rushed past him, so close he could feel the wind on his face. Fire from his own men.

'You stupid bastards!' Shouting without anger, without fear, with only the need to shout, he burst into the lounge through the main doors. It was half dark but he could see through the darkness and the haze of plaster dust.

A man on the stairs, the bloom of gunfire and the sting of the bullet across Bruce's thigh, fire in return, without aiming from the hip, miss and the man gone up and round the head of the stairs, yelling as he ran.

A grenade in Bruce's right hand, throw it high, watch it hit the wall and bounce sideways round the angle of the stairs. The explosion shocking in the confined space and the flash of it lighting the building and outlining the body of the man as it blew him back into the lounge, lifting him clear of the banisters, shredded and broken by the blast, falling heavily into the room below.

Up the stairs three at a time and into the bedroom passage, another man naked and bewildered staggering through a doorway still drunk or half asleep, chop him down with a single shot in the stomach, jump over him and throw a grenade through the glass skylight of the second bedroom, another through the third and kick open the door of the last room in the bellow and flash of the explosions.

A man was waiting for Bruce across the room with a pistol in his hand, and both of them fired simultaneously, the clang of the bullet glancing off the steel of Bruce's helmet, jerking his head back savagely, throwing him sideways against the wall, but he fired again, rapid fire, hitting with every bullet, so that the man seemed to dance, a jerky grotesque twitching jig, pinned against the far wall by the bullets.

On his knees now Bruce was stunned, ears singing like a million mad mosquitoes, hands clumsy and slow on the reload, back on his feet, legs rubbery but the loaded rifle in his hands making a man of him.

Out into the passage, another one right on top of him, a vast dark shape in the darkness – kill him! kill him!

'Don't shoot, boss!'

Ruffy, thank God, Ruffy.

'Are there any more?'

'All finished, boss – you cleaned them out good.'

'How many?' Bruce shouted above the singing in his ears.

'Forty or so. Jesus, what a mess! There's blood all over the place. Those grenades—'

'There must be more.'

'Yes, but not in here, boss. Let's go and give the boys outside a hand.'

They ran back down the passage, down the stairs, and the floor of the lounge was sodden and sticky, dead men everywhere; it smelt like an abattoir – blood and ripped bowels. One still on his hands and knees, creepy-crawling towards the door. Ruffy shot him twice, flattening him.

'Not the front door, boss. Our boys will get you for sure. Go out the window.'

Bruce dived through the window head first, rolled over behind the cover of the verandah wall and came to his knees in one movement. He felt strong and invulnerable. Ruffy was beside him.

'Here come our boys,' said Ruffy, and Bruce could see them coming down the street, running forward in short bursts, stopping to fire, to throw a grenade, then coming again.

'And there are Lieutenant Hendry's lot.' From the opposite direction but with the same dodging, checking run, Bruce could see Wally with them. He was holding his rifle across his hip when he fired, his whole body shaking with the juddering of the gun.

Like a bird rising in front of the beaters one of the *shufta* broke from the cover of the grocery store and ran into the street unarmed, his head down and his arms pumping in time with his legs. Bruce was close enough to see the panic in his face. He seemed to be moving in slow motion, and the flames lit him harshly, throwing a distorted shadow in front of him. When the bullets hit him he stayed on his feet, staggering in a circle, thrashing at the air with his hands as though he were beating off a swarm of bees, the bullets slapping loudly against his body and lifting little puffs of dust from his clothing. Beside Bruce, Ruffy aimed carefully and shot him in the head, ending it.

'There must be more,' protested Bruce. 'Where are they hiding?'

'In the offices, I'd say.'

And Bruce turned his attention quickly to the block of Union Minière offices. The windows were in darkness and as he stared he thought he saw movement. He glanced quickly back at Wally's men and saw that four of them had bunched up close behind Wally as they ran.

'Hendry, watch out!' he shouted with all his strength. 'On your right, from the offices!'

But it was too late, gunfire sparkled in the dark windows and the little group of running men disintegrated.

Bruce and Ruffy fired together, raking the windows, emptying their automatic rifles into them. As he reloaded Bruce glanced back at where Wally's men had been hit. With disbelief he saw that Wally was the only one still on his feet; crossing the road, sprinting through an area of bullet-churned earth towards them, he reached the verandah and fell over the low wall.

'Are you wounded?' Bruce asked.

'Not a touch – those bastards couldn't shoot their way out of a French letter,'

Wally shouted defiantly, and his voice carried clearly in the sudden hush. He snatched the empty magazine off the bottom of his rifle, threw it aside and clipped on a fresh one. 'Move over,' he growled, 'let me get a crack at those bastards.' He lifted his rifle and rested the stock on top of the wall, knelt behind it, cuddled the butt into his shoulder and began firing short bursts into the windows of the office block.

'This is what I was afraid of.' Bruce lifted his voice above the clamour of the guns. 'Now we've got a pocket of resistance right in the centre of the town. There must be fifteen or twenty of them in there – it might take us days to winkle them out.' He cast a longing look at the canvas-covered trucks lined up outside the station yard. 'They can cover the lorries from there, and as soon as they guess what we're after, as soon as we try and move them, they'll knock out that tanker and destroy the trucks.'

The firelight flickered on the shiny yellow and red paint of the tanker. It looked so big and vulnerable standing there in the open. It needed just one bullet out of the many hundred that had already been fired to end its charmed existence.

We've got to rush them now, he decided. Beyond the office block the remains of Wally's group had taken cover and were keeping up a heated fire. Bruce's group straggled up to the hotel and found positions at the windows.

'Ruffy.' Bruce caught him by the shoulder. 'We'll take four men with us and go round the back of the offices. From that building there we've got only twenty yards or so of open ground to cover. Once we get up against the wall they won't be able to touch us and we can toss grenades in amongst them.'

'That twenty yards looks like twenty miles from here,' rumbled Ruffy, but picked up his sack of grenades and crawled back from the verandah wall.

'Go and pick four men to come with us,' ordered Bruce.

'Okay, boss. We'll wait for you in the kitchen.'

'Hendry. Listen to me.'

'Yeah. What is it?'

'When I reach that corner over there I'll give you a wave. We'll be ready to go then. I want you to give us all the cover you can – keep their heads down.'

'Okay,' agreed Wally and fired another short burst.

'Try not to hit us when we close in.'

Wally turned to look at Bruce and he grinned wickedly.

'Mistakes happen, you know. I can't promise anything. You'd look real grand in my sights.'

'Don't joke,' said Bruce.

'Who's joking?' grinned Wally and Bruce left him. He found Ruffy and four gendarmes waiting in the kitchen.

'Come on,' he said and led them out across the kitchen yard, down the sanitary lane with the steel doors for the buckets behind the outhouses and the smell of them thick and fetid, round the corner and across the road to the buildings beyond the office block. They stopped there and crowded together, as though to draw courage and comfort from each other. Bruce measured the distance with his eye.

'It's not far,' he announced.

'Depends on how you look at it,' grunted Ruffy.

'There are only two windows opening out on to this side.'

'Two's enough – how many do you want?'

'Remember, Ruffy, you can only die once.'

'Once is enough,' said Ruffy. 'Let's cut out the talking, boss. Too much talk gets you in the guts.'

Bruce moved across to the corner of the building out of the shadows. He waved towards the hotel and imagined that he saw an acknowledgement from the end of the verandah.

'All together,' he said, sucked in a deep breath, held it a second and then launched himself into the open. He felt small now, no longer brave and invulnerable, and his legs moved so slowly that he seemed to be standing still. The black windows gaped at him.

Now, he thought, now you die.

Where, he thought, not in the stomach, please God, not in the stomach.

And his legs moved stiffly under him, carrying him half way across.

Only ten more paces, he thought, one more river, just one more river to Jordan. But not in the stomach, please God, not in my stomach. And his flesh cringed in anticipation, his stomach drawn in hard as he ran.

Suddenly the black windows were brightly lit, bright white oblongs in the dark buildings, and the glass sprayed out of them like untidy spittle from an old man's mouth. Then they were dark again, dark with smoke billowing from them and the memory of the explosion echoing in his ears.

'A grenade!' Bruce was bewildered. 'Someone let off a grenade in there!'

He reached the back door without stopping and it burst open before his rush. He was into the room, shooting, coughing in the fumes, firing wildly at the small movements of dying men.

In the half darkness something long and white lay against the far wall. A body, a white man's naked body. He crossed to it and looked down.

'André,' he said, 'it's André – he threw the grenade.' And he knelt beside him.

Chapter Seventeen

Curled naked upon the concrete floor, André was alive but dying as the haemorrhage within him leaked his life away. His mind was alive and he heard the crump, crump of Bruce's grenades, then the gunfire in the street, and the sound of running men. The shouts in the night and then the guns very close, they were in the room in which he lay.

He opened his eyes. There were men at each of the windows, crouched below the sills, and the room was thick with cordite fumes and the clamour of the guns as they fired out into the night.

André was cold, the coldness was all through him. Even his hands drawn up against his chest were cold and heavy. His stomach only was warm, warm and immensely bloated.

It was an effort to think, for his mind also was cold and the noise of the guns confused him.

He watched the men at the windows with a detached disinterest, and slowly his body lost its weight. He seemed to float clear of the floor and look down upon the room from the roof. His eyelids sagged and he dragged them up again, and struggled down towards his own body.

There was suddenly a rushing sound in the room and plaster sprayed from the wall above André's head, filling the air with pale floating dust. One of the men at the windows fell backwards, his weapon ringing loudly on the floor as it dropped from his hands; he flopped over twice and lay still, face down within arm's length of André.

Ponderously André's mind analysed the sights his eyes were recording. Someone was firing on the building from outside. The man beside him was dead and from his head wound the blood spread slowly across the floor towards him. André closed his eyes again, he was very tired and very cold.

There was a lull in the sound of gunfire, one of those freak silences in the midst of battle. And in the lull André heard a voice far off, shouting. He could not hear the words but he recognized the voice and his eyelids flew open. There was an excitement in him, a new force, for it was Wally's voice he had heard.

He moved slightly, clenching his hands and his brain started to sing.

Wally has come back for me – he has come to save me. He rolled his head slowly, painfully, and the blood gurgled in his stomach.

I must help him, I must not let him endanger himself – these men are trying to kill him. I must stop them. I mustn't let them kill Wally.

And then he saw the grenades hanging on the belt of the man that lay beside him. He fastened his eyes on the round polished metal bulbs and he began to pray silently.

'Hail, Mary, full of grace, the Lord is with thee.'

He moved again, straightening his body.

'Blessed art thou among women, and blessed is the fruit of thy womb, Jesus.'

His hand crept out into the pool of blood, and the sound of the guns filled his head so he could not hear himself pray. Walking on its fingers, his hand crawled through the blood as slowly as a fly through a saucer of treacle.

'Blessed is the fruit of thy womb, Jesus. Oh, Jesus. Pray for me now, and at the hour. Full of grace.'

He touched the smooth, deeply segmented steel of the grenade.

'Us sinners – at the day, at the hour. This day – this day our daily bread.'

He fumbled at the clip, fingers stiff and cold.

'Hallowed be thy— Hallowed be thy—'

The clip clicked open and he held the grenade, curling his fingers round it.

'Hail, Mary, full of grace.'

He drew the grenade to him and held it with both hands against his chest. He lifted it to his mouth and took the pin between his teeth.

'Pray for us sinners,' he whispered and pulled the pin.

'Now and at the hour of our death.'

And he tried to throw it. It rolled from his hand and bumped across the floor. The firing handle flew off and rattled against the wall. General Moses turned from the window and saw it – his lips opened and his spectacles glinted above the rose-pink cave of his mouth. The grenade lay at his feet. Then everything was gone in the flash and roar of the explosion.

Afterwards in the acrid swirl of fumes, in the patter of falling plaster, in the tinkle and crunch of broken glass, in the small scrabbling noises and the murmur and moan of dying men, André was still alive. The body of the man beside him had shielded his head and chest from the full force of the blast.

There was still enough life in him to recognize Bruce Curry's face close to his, though he could not feel the hands that touched him.

'André!' said Bruce. 'It's André – he threw the grenade!'

'Tell him—' whispered André and stopped.

'Yes, André—?' said Bruce.

'I didn't, this day and at the hour. I had to – not this time.' He could feel it going out in him like a candle in a high wind and he tried to cup his hands around it.

'What is it, André? What must I tell him?' Bruce's voice, but so far away.

'Because of him – this time – not of it, I didn't.' He stopped again and gathered all of what was left. His lips quivered as he tried so hard to say it.

'Like a man!' he whispered and the candle went out.

'Yes,' said Bruce softly, holding him. 'This time like a man.'

He lowered André gently until his head touched the floor again; then he stood upright and looked down at the terribly mutilated body. He felt empty inside, a hollowness, the same feeling as after love.

He moved across to the desk near the far wall. Outside the gunfire dwindled like half-hearted applause, flared up again and then ceased. Around him Ruffy and the four gendarmes moved excitedly, inspecting the dead, exclaiming, laughing the awkward embarrassed laughter of men freshly released from mortal danger.

Loosening the chin straps of his helmet with slow steady fingers, Bruce stared across the room at André's body.

'Yes,' he whispered again. 'This time like a man. All the other times are wiped out, the score is levelled.'

His cigarettes were damp from the swamp, but he took one from the centre of the pack and straightened it with calm nerveless fingers. He found his lighter and flicked it open – then, without warning, his hands started to shake. The flame of the lighter fluttered and he had to hold it steady with both hands. There was blood on his hands, new sticky blood. He snapped the lighter closed and breathed in the smoke. It tasted bitter and the saliva flooded into his mouth. He swallowed it down, nausea in his stomach, and his breathing quickened.

It was not like this before, he remembered, even that night at the road bridge when they broke through on the flank and we met them with bayonets in the dark. Before it had no meaning, but now I can feel again. Once more I'm alive.

Suddenly he had to be alone; he stood up.

'Ruffy.'

'Yes, boss?'

'Clean up here. Get blankets from the hotel for de Surrier and the women, also those men down in the station yard.' It was someone else speaking; he could hear the voice as though it were a long way off.

'You okay, boss?'

'Yes.'

'Your head?'

Bruce lifted his hand and touched the long dent in his helmet.

'It's nothing,' he said.

'Your leg?'

'Just a touch, get on with it.'

'Okay, boss. What shall we do with these others?'

'Throw them in the river,' said Bruce and walked out into the street. Hendry and his gendarmes were still on the verandah of the hotel, but they had started on the corpses there, using their bayonets like butchers' knives, taking the ears, laughing also the strained nervous laughter.

Bruce crossed the street to the station yard. The dawn was coming, drawing out across the sky like a sheet of steel rolled from the mill, purple and lilac at first, then red as it spread above the forest.

The Ford Ranchero stood on the station platform where he had left it. He opened the door, slid in behind the wheel, and watched the dawn become day.

Chapter Eighteen

'Captain, the sergeant major asks you to come. There is something he wants to show you.'

Bruce lifted his head from where it was resting on the steering wheel. He had not heard the gendarme approach.

'I'll come,' he said, picked up his helmet and his rifle from the seat beside him and followed the man back to the office block.

His gendarmes were loading a dead man into one of the trucks, swinging him by his arms and legs.

'Un, deux, trois,' and a shout of laughter as the limp body flew over the tailboard on to the gruesome pile already there.

Sergeant Jacque came out of the office dragging a man by his heels. The head bumped loosely down the steps and there was a wet brown drag mark left on the cement verandah.

'Like pork,' Jacque called cheerily. The corpse was that of a small grey-headed man, skinny, with the marks of spectacles on the bridge of his nose and a double row of decorations on his tunic. Bruce noted that one of them was the purple and white ribbon of the military cross – strange loot for the Congo. Jacque dropped the man's heels, drew his bayonet and stooped over the man. He took one of the ears that lay flat against the grizzled skull, pulled it forward and freed it with a single stroke of the knife. The opened flesh was pink with the dark hole of the eardrum in the centre.

Bruce walked on into the office and his nostrils flared at the abattoir stench.

'Have a look at this lot, boss.' Ruffy stood by the desk.

'Enough to buy you a ranch in Hyde Park,' grinned Hendry beside him. In his hand he held a pencil. Threaded on to it like a kebab were a dozen human ears.

'Yes,' said Bruce as he looked at the pile of industrial and gem diamonds on the blotter. 'I know about those. Better count them, Ruffy, then put them back in the bags.'

'You're not going to turn them in?' protested Hendry. 'Jesus, if we share this lot three ways – you, Ruffy and I – there's enough to make us all rich.'

'Or put us against a wall,' said Bruce grimly. 'What makes you think the gentlemen in Elisabethville don't know about them?' He turned his attention back to Ruffy. 'Count them and pack them. You're in charge of them. Don't lose any.'

Bruce looked across the room at the blanket-wrapped bundle that was André de Surrier.

'Have you detailed a burial squad?'

'Yes, boss. Six of the boys are out back digging.'

'Good,' Bruce nodded. 'Hendry, come with me. We'll go and have a look at the trucks.'

Half an hour later Bruce closed the bonnet of the last vehicle.

'This is the only one that won't run. The carburettor's smashed. We'll take the tyres off it for spares.' He wiped his greasy hands on the sides of his trousers.

'Thank God, the tanker is untouched. We've got six hundred gallons there, more than enough for the return trip.'

'You going to take the Ford?' asked Hendry.

'Yes, it may come in useful.'

'And it will be more comfortable for you and your little French thing.' Heavy sarcasm in Hendry's voice.

'That's right,' Bruce answered evenly. 'Can you drive?'

'What do you think? You think I'm a bloody fool?'

'Everyone is always trying to get at you, aren't they? You can't trust anyone, can you?' Bruce asked softly.

'You're so bloody right!' agreed Hendry.

Bruce changed the subject. 'André had a message for you before he died.'

'Old doll boy!'

'He threw that grenade. Did you know that?'

'Yeah. I knew it.'

'Don't you want to hear what he said?'

'Once a queer, always a queer, and the only good queer is a dead queer.'

'All right.' Bruce frowned. 'Get a couple of men to help you. Fill the trucks with gas. We've wasted enough time already.'

They buried their dead in a communal grave, packing them in quickly and covering them just as quickly. Then they stood embarrassed and silent round the mound.

'You going to say anything, boss?' Ruffy asked, and they all looked at Bruce.

'No.' Bruce turned away and started for the trucks.

What the hell can you say, he thought angrily. Death is not someone to make conversation with. All you can say is, 'These were men; weak and strong, evil and good, and a lot in between. But now they're dead – like pork.'

He looked back over his shoulder.

'All right, let's move out.'

The convoy ground slowly over the causeway. Bruce led in the Ford and the air blowing in through the shattered windscreen was too humid and steamy to give relief from the rising heat.

The sun stood high above the forest as they passed the turn-off to the mission.

Bruce looked along it, and he wanted to signal the convoy to continue while he went up to St. Augustine's. He wanted to see Mike Haig and Father Ignatius, make sure that they were safe.

Then he put aside the temptation. If there is more horror up there at St. Augustine's, if the *shufta* have found them and there are raped women and dead men there, then there is nothing I can do and I don't want to know about it.

It is better to believe that they are safely hidden in the jungle. It is better to believe that out of all this will remain something good.

He led the convoy resolutely past the turn-off and over the hills towards the level crossing.

Suddenly another idea came to him and he thought about it, turning it over with pleasure.

Four men came to Port Reprieve, men without hope, men abandoned by God.

And they learned that it was not too late, perhaps it is never too late.

For one of them found the strength to die like a man, although he had lived his whole life with weakness.

Another rediscovered the self-respect he had lost along the way, and with it the chance to start again.

The third found – he hesitated – yes, the third found love.

And the fourth? Bruce's smile faded as he thought of Wally Hendry. It was a neat little parable, except for Wally Hendry. What had he found? A dozen human ears threaded on a pencil?

Chapter Nineteen

'Can't you get up enough steam to move us back to the crossing – only a few miles.'

'I am desolate, m'sieur. She will not hold even a belch, to say nothing of a head of steam.' The engine driver spread his pudgy little hands in a gesture of helplessness. Bruce studied the rent in the boiler. The metal was torn open like the petals of a flower. He knew it had been a forlorn request.

'Very well. Thank you.' He turned to Ruffy. 'We'll have to carry everything back to the convoy. Another day wasted.'

'It's a long walk,' Ruffy agreed. 'Better get started.'

'How much food have we?'

'Not too much. We've been feeding a lot of extra mouths, and we sent a lot out to the mission.'

'How much?'

'About two more days.'

'That should get us to Elisabethville.'

'Boss, you want to carry everything to the lorries? Searchlights, ammunition, blankets – all of it?'

Bruce paused for a moment. 'I think so. We may need it.'

'It's going to take the rest of the day.'

'Yes,' agreed Bruce. Ruffy walked back along the train but Bruce called after him.

'Ruffy!'

'Boss?'

'Don't forget the beer.'

Ruffy's black moon of a face split laterally into a grin.

'You think we should take it?'

'Why not?' Bruce laughed.

'Man, you talked me right into it!'

And the night was almost on them before the last of the equipment had been carried back from the abandoned train to the convoy and loaded into the trucks.

Time is a slippery thing, even more so than wealth. No bank vault can hold it for you, this precious stuff which we spend in such prodigal fashion on the trivialities. By the time we have slept and eaten and moved from one place to the next there is such a small percentage left for the real business of living.

Bruce felt futile resentment as he always did when he thought about it. And if you discount the time spent at an office desk, then how much is there left? Half of one day a week, that's how much the average man lives! That's how far short of our potential is the actuality of existence.

Take it further than that: we are capable of using only a fraction of our physical and mental strength. Only under hypnosis are we able to exert more than a tenth of what is in us. So divide that half of one day a week by ten, and the rest is waste! Sickening waste!

'Ruffy, have you detailed sentries for tonight?' Bruce barked at him.

'Not yet. I was just—'

'Well, do it, and do it quickly.'

Ruffy looked at Bruce in speculation and through his anger Bruce felt a qualm of regret that he had selected that mountain of energy on which to vent his frustration.

'Where the hell is Hendry?' he snapped.

Without speaking Ruffy pointed to a group of men round one of the trucks at the rear of the convoy and Bruce left him.

Suddenly consumed with impatience Bruce fell upon his men. Shouting at them, scattering them to a dozen different tasks. He walked along the convoy making sure that his instructions were being carried out to the letter; checking the siting of the Brens and the searchlights, making sure that the single small cooking fire was screened from Baluba eyes, stopping to watch the refuelling of the trucks and the running maintenance he had ordered. Men avoided catching his eye and bent to their tasks with studied application. There were no raised voices or sounds of laughter in the camp.

Again Bruce had decided against a night journey. The temptation itched within him, but the exhaustion of those gendarmes who had not slept since the previous morning and the danger of travelling in the dark he could not ignore.

'We'll leave as soon as it's light tomorrow,' Bruce told Ruffy.

'Okay, boss,' Ruffy nodded, and then soothingly, 'you're tired. Food's nearly ready, then you get some sleep.'

Bruce glared at him, opening his mouth to snarl a retort, and then closed it again. He turned and strode out of the camp into the forest.

He found a fallen log, sat down and lit a cigarette. It was dark now and there were only a few stars among the rain clouds that blackened the sky. He could hear the faint sounds from the camp but there were no lights – the way he had ordered it.

The fact that his anger had no focal point inflamed it rather than quenched it. It ranged restlessly until at last it found a target – himself.

He recognized the brooding undirected depression that was descending upon him. It was a thing he had not experienced for a long time, nearly two years. Not since the wreck of his marriage and the loss of his children. Not since he had stifled all emotion and trained himself not to participate in the life around him.

But now his barrier was gone, there was no sheltered harbour from the storm surf and he would have to ride it out. Furl all canvas and rig a sea anchor.

The anger was gone now. At least anger had heat but this other thing was cold; icy waves of it broke over him, and he was small and insignificant in the grip of it.

His mind turned to his children and the loneliness howled round him like a winter wind from the south. He closed his eyes and pressed his fingers against the lids. Their faces formed in the eye of his mind.

Christine with pink fat legs under her frilly skirt, and the face of a thoughtful cherub below soft hair cropped like a page boy.

'I love you best of all,' said with much seriousness, holding his face with small hands only a little sticky with ice cream.

Simon, a miniature reproduction of Bruce even to the nose. Scabs on the knees and dirt on the face. No demonstrations of affection from him, but in its place something much better, a companionship far beyond his six years. Long discussions on everything from religion, 'Why didn't Jesus used to shave?' to politics, 'When are you going to be prime minister, Dad?'

And the loneliness was a tangible thing now, like the coils of a reptile squeezing his chest. Bruce ground out the cigarette beneath his heel and tried to find refuge in his hatred for the woman who had been his wife. The woman who had taken them from him.

But his hatred was a cold thing also, dead ash with a stale taste. For he knew that the blame was not all hers. It was another of his failures; perhaps if I had tried harder, perhaps if I had left some of the cruel things unsaid, perhaps – yes, it might have been, and perhaps and maybe. But it was not. It was over and finished and now I am alone. There is no worse condition; no state beyond loneliness. It is the waste land and the desolation.

Something moved near him in the night, a soft rustle of grass, a presence felt rather than seen. And Bruce stiffened. His right hand closed over his rifle. He brought it up slowly, his eyes straining into the darkness.

The movement again, closer now. A twig popped underfoot. Bruce slowly trained his rifle round to cover it, pressure on the trigger and his thumb on the safety. Stupid to have wandered away from the camp; asking for it, and now he had got it. Baluba tribesmen! He could see the figure now in the dimness of starlight, stealthily moving across his front. How many of them, he wondered. If I hit this one, there could be a dozen others with him. Have to take a chance. One quick burst and then run for it. A hundred yards to the camp, about an even chance. The figure was stationary now, standing listening. Bruce could see the outline of the head – no helmet, can't be one of us. He raised the rifle and pointed it. Too dark to see the sights, but at that range he couldn't miss. Bruce drew his breath softly, filling his lungs, ready to shoot and run.

'Bruce?' Shermaine's voice, frightened, almost a whisper. He threw up the rifle barrel. God, that was close. He had nearly killed her.

'Yes, I'm here.' His own voice was scratchy with the shock of realization.

'Oh, there you are.'

'What the hell are you doing out of the camp?' he demanded furiously as anger replaced his shock.

'I'm sorry, Bruce, I came to see if you were all right. You were gone such a long time.'

'Well, get back to the camp, and don't try any more tricks like that.'

There was a long silence, and then she spoke softly, unable to keep the hurt out of her tone.

'I brought you something to eat. I thought you'd be hungry. I'm sorry if I did wrong.'

She came to him, stooped and placed something on the ground in front of him. Then she turned and was gone.

'Shermaine.' He wanted her back, but the only reply was the fading rustle of the grass and then silence. He was alone again.

He picked up the plate of food.

You fool, he thought. You stupid, ignorant, thoughtless fool. You'll lose her, and you'll have deserved it. You deserve everything you've had, and more.

You never learn, do you, Curry? You never learn that there is a penalty for selfishness and for thoughtlessness.

He looked down at the plate in his hands. Bully beef and sliced onion, bread and cheese.

Yes, I have learned, he answered himself with sudden determination. I will not spoil this, this thing that is between this girl and me. That was the last time; now I am a man I will put away childish things, like temper and self-pity.

He ate the food, suddenly aware of his hunger. He ate quickly, wolfing it. Then he stood up and walked back to the camp.

A sentry challenged him on the perimeter and Bruce answered with alacrity.

At night his gendarmes were very quick on the trigger; the challenge was an unusual courtesy.

'It is unwise to go alone into the forest in the darkness,' the sentry reprimanded him.

'Why?' Bruce felt his mood changing. The depression evaporated.

'It is unwise,' repeated the man vaguely.

'The spirits?' Bruce teased him delicately.

'An aunt of my sister's husband disappeared not a short throw of a spear from my hut. There was no trace, no shout, nothing. I was there. It is not a matter for doubt,' said the man with dignity.

'A lion perhaps?' Bruce prodded him.

'If you say so, then it is so. I know what I know. But I say only that there is no wisdom in defying the custom of the land.'

Suddenly touched by the man's concern for him, Bruce dropped a hand on to his shoulder and gripped it in the old expression of affection.

'I will remember. I did it without thinking.'

He walked into the camp. The incident had confirmed something he had vaguely suspected, but in which previously he had felt no interest. The men liked him. A hundred similar indications of this fact he had only half noted, not caring one way or the other. But now it gave him intense pleasure, fully compensating for the loneliness he had just experienced.

He walked past the little group of men round the cooking fire to where the Ford stood at the head of the convoy. Peering through the side window he could make out Shermaine's blanket-wrapped form on the back seat. He tapped on the glass and she sat up and rolled down the window.

'Yes?' she asked coolly.

'Thank you for the food.'

'It is nothing.' The slightest hint of warmth in her voice.

'Shermaine, sometimes I say things I do not mean. You startled me. I nearly shot you.'

'It was my fault. I should not have followed you.'

'I was rude,' he persisted.

'Yes.' She laughed now. That husky little chuckle. 'You were rude but with good reason. We shall forget it.' She placed her hand on his arm. 'You must rest, you haven't slept for two days.'

'Will you ride in the Ford with me tomorrow to show that I am forgiven?'

'Of course,' she nodded.

'Good night, Shermaine.'

'Good night, Bruce.'

No, Bruce decided as he spread his blankets beside the fire, I am not alone. Not any more.

Chapter Twenty

'What about breakfast, boss?'

'They can eat on the road. Give them a tin of bully each – we've wasted enough time on this trip.'

The sky was paling and pinking above the forest. It was light enough to read the dial of his wrist watch. Twenty minutes to five.

'Get them moving, Ruffy. If we make Msapa Junction before dark we can drive through the night. Home for breakfast tomorrow.'

'Now you're talking, boss.' Ruffy clapped his helmet on to his head and went off to rouse the men who lay in the road beside the trucks.

Shermaine was asleep. Bruce leaned into the window of the Ford and studied her face. A wisp of hair lay over her mouth, rising and falling with her breathing. It tickled her nose and in her sleep it twitched like a rabbit.

Bruce felt an almost unbearable pang of tenderness towards her. With one finger he lifted the hair off her face. Then he smiled at himself.

If you can feel like this before breakfast, then you've got it in a bad way, he told himself.

Do you know something, he retorted. I like the feeling.

'Hey, you lazy wench!' He pulled the lobe of her ear. 'Time to wake up.'

It was almost half past five before the convoy got under way. It had taken that long to bully and cajole the sleep out of sixty men and get them into the lorries. This morning Bruce did not find the delay unbearable. He had managed to find time for four hours' sleep during the night. Four hours was not nearly enough to make up for the previous two days.

Now he felt light-headed, a certain unreal quality of gaiety overlaying his exhaustion, a carnival spirit. There was no longer the same urgency, for the road to Elisabethville was clear and not too long. Home for breakfast tomorrow!

'We'll be at the bridge in a little under an hour.' He glanced sideways at Shermaine.

'You've left a guard on it?'

'Ten men,' answered Bruce. 'We'll pick them up almost without stopping, and then the next stop, room 201, Grand Hotel Leopold II, Avenue du Kasai.' He grinned in anticipation. 'A bath so deep it will slop over on to the floor, so hot it will take five minutes to get into it. Clean clothes. A steak that thick, with French salad and a bottle of Liebfraumilch.'

'For breakfast!' protested Shermaine.

'For breakfast,' Bruce agreed happily. He was silent for a while, savouring the idea. The road ahead of him was tiger-striped with the shadows of the trees thrown by the low sun. The air that blew in through the missing windscreen was cool and clean-smelling. He felt good. The responsibility of command lay lightly on his shoulders this morning; a pretty girl beside him, a golden morning, the horror of the last few days half-forgotten – they might have been going on a picnic.

'What are you thinking?' he asked suddenly. She was very quiet beside him.

'I was wondering about the future,' she answered softly. 'There is no one I know in Elisabethville, and I do not wish to stay there.'

'Will you return to Brussels?' he asked. The question was without significance, for Bruce Curry had very definite plans for the immediate future, and these included Shermaine.

'Yes, I think so. There is nowhere else.'

'You have relatives there?'

'An aunt.'

'Are you close?'

Shermaine laughed, but there was bitterness in the husky chuckle. 'Oh, very close. She came to see me once at the orphanage. Once in all those years. She brought me a comic book of a religious nature and told me to clean my teeth and brush my hair a hundred strokes a day.'

'There is no one else?' asked Bruce.

'No.'

'Then why go back?'

'What else is there to do?' she asked. 'Where else is there to go?'

'There's a life to live, and the rest of the world to visit.'

'Is that what you are going to do?'

'That is exactly what I'm going to do, starting with a hot bath.'

Bruce could feel it between them. They both knew it was there, but it was too soon to talk about it. I have only kissed her once, but that was enough. So what will happen? Marriage? His mind shied away from that word with startling violence, then came hesitantly back to examine it. Stalking it as though it were a dangerous beast, ready to take flight again as soon as it showed its teeth.

For some people it is a good thing. It can stiffen the spineless; ease the lonely; give direction to the wanderers; spur those without ambition – and, of course, there was the final unassailable argument in its favour. Children.

But there are some who can only sicken and shrivel in the colourless cell of matrimony. With no space to fly, your wings must weaken with disuse; turned inwards, your eyes become short-sighted; when all your communication with the rest of the world is through the glass windows of the cell, then your contact is limited.

And I already have children. I have a daughter and I have a son.

Bruce turned his eyes from the road and studied the girl beside him. There is no fault I can find. She is beautiful in the delicate, almost fragile way that is so much better and longer-lived than blond hair and big bosoms. She is unspoilt; hardship has long been her travelling companion and from it she has learned kindness and humility.

She is mature, knowing the ways of this world; knowing death and fear, the evilness of men and their goodness. I do not believe she has ever lived in the fairy-tale cocoon that most young girls spin about themselves.

And yet she has not forgotten how to laugh.

Perhaps, he thought, perhaps. But it is too soon to talk about it.

'You are very grim.' Shermaine broke the silence, but the laughter shivered just below the surface of her voice. 'Again you are Bonaparte. And when you are grim your nose is too big and cruel. It is a nose of great brutality and it does not fit the rest of your face. I think that when they had finished you they had only one nose left in stock. "It is too big," they said, "but it is the only nose left, and when he smiles it will not look too bad." So they took a chance and stuck it on anyway.'

'Were you never taught that it is bad manners to poke fun at a man's weakness?' Bruce fingered his nose ruefully.

'Your nose is many things, but not weak. Never weak.' She laughed now and moved a little closer to him.

'You know you can attack me from behind your own perfect nose, and I cannot retaliate.'

'Never trust a man who makes pretty speeches so easily, because he surely makes them to every girl he meets.' She slid an inch further across the seat until they were almost touching. 'You waste your talents, mon Capitaine. I am immune to your charm.'

'In just one minute I will stop this car and—'

'You cannot.' Shermaine jerked her head to indicate the two gendarmes in the seat behind them. 'What would they think, Bonaparte? It would be very bad for discipline.'

'Discipline or no discipline, in just one minute I will stop this car and spank you soundly before I kiss you.'

'One threat does not frighten me, but because of the other I will leave your poor nose.' She moved away a little and once more Bruce studied her face. Beneath the frank scrutiny she fidgeted and started to blush.

'Do you mind! Were you never taught that it is bad manners to stare?'

So now I am in love again, thought Bruce. This is only the third time, an average of once every ten years or so. It frightens me a little because there is always pain with it. The exquisite pain of loving and the agony of losing.

It starts in the loins and it is very deceptive because you think it is only the old thing, the tightness and tension that any well-rounded stern or cheeky pair of breasts will give you. Scratch it, you think, it's just a small itch. Spread a little of the warm salve on it and it will be gone in no time.

But suddenly it spreads, upwards and downwards, all through you. The pit of your stomach feels hot, then the flutters round the heart. It's dangerous now; once it gets this far it's incurable and you can scratch and scratch but all you do is inflame it.

Then the last stages, when it attacks the brain. No pain there, that's the worst sign. A heightening of the senses: your eyes are sharper, your blood runs too fast, food tastes good, your mouth wants to shout and legs want to run. Then the delusions of grandeur: you are the cleverest, strongest, most masculine male in the universe, and you stand ten feet tall in your socks.

How tall are you now, Curry, he asked himself. About nine feet six and I weigh twenty stone, he answered, and almost laughed aloud.

And how does it end? It ends with words. Words can kill anything. It ends with cold words; words like fire that stick in the structure and take hold and lick it up, blackening and charring it, bringing it down in smoking ruins.

It ends in suspicion of things not done, and in the certainty of things done and remembered. It ends with selfishness and carelessness, and words, always words.

It ends with pain and greyness, and it leaves scar tissue and damage that will never heal.

Or it ends without fuss and fury. It just crumbles and blows away like dust on the wind. But there is still the agony of loss.

Both these endings I know well, for I have loved twice, and now I love again.

Perhaps this time it does not have to be that way. Perhaps this time it will last. Nothing is for ever, he thought. Nothing is for ever, not even life, and perhaps this time if I cherish it and tend it carefully it will last that long, as long as life.

'We are nearly at the bridge,' said Shermaine beside him, and Bruce started. The miles had dropped unseen behind them and now the forest was thickening. It crouched closer to the earth, greener and darker along the river.

Bruce slowed the Ford and the forest became dense bush around them, the road a tunnel through it. They came round one last bend in the track and out of the tunnel of green vegetation into the clearing where the road met the railway line and ran beside it on to the heavy timber platform of the bridge.

Bruce stopped the Ranchero, switched off the engine and they all sat silently, staring out at the solid jungle on the far bank with its screen of creepers and monkey-ropes hanging down, trailing the surface of the deep green swift-flowing river. They stared at the stumps of the bridge thrusting out from each bank towards each other like the arms of parted lovers; at the wide gap between with the timbers still smouldering and the smoke drifting away downstream over the green water.

'It's gone,' said Shermaine. 'It's been burnt.'

'Oh, no,' groaned Bruce. 'Oh, God, no!'

With an effort he pulled his eyes from the charred remains of the bridge and turned them on to the jungle about them, a hundred feet away, ringing them in. Hostile, silent. 'Don't get out of the car,' he snapped as Shermaine reached for the door handle. 'Roll your window up, quickly.'

She obeyed.

'They're waiting in there.' He pointed at the edge of the jungle.

Behind them the first of the convoy came round the bend into the clearing. Bruce jumped from the Ford and ran back towards the leading truck.

'Don't get out, stay inside,' he shouted and ran on down the line, repeating the instruction to each of them as he passed. When he reached Ruffy's cab he jumped on to the running board, jerked the door open, slipped in on to the seat and slammed the door.

'They've burnt the bridge.'

'What's happened to the boys we left to guard it?'

'I don't know but we'll find out. Pull up alongside the others so that I can talk to them.'

Through the half-open window he issued his orders to each of the drivers and within ten minutes all the vehicles had been manoeuvred into the tight defensive circle of the laager, a formation Bruce's ancestors had used a hundred years before.

'Ruffy, get out those tarpaulins and spread them over the top to form a roof. We don't want them dropping arrows in amongst us.'

Ruffy selected half a dozen gendarmes and they went to work, dragging out the heavy folded canvas.

'Hendry, put a couple of men under each truck. Set up the Brens in case they try to rush us.'

In the infectious urgency of defence, Wally did not make his usual retort, but gathered his men. They wriggled on their stomachs under the vehicles, rifles pointed out towards the silent jungle.

'I want the extinguishers here in the middle so we can get them in a hurry. They might use fire again.'

Two gendarmes ran to each of the cabs and unclipped the fire-extinguishers from the dashboards.

'What can I do?' Shermaine was standing beside Bruce.

'Keep quiet and stay out of the way,' said Bruce as he turned and hurried across to help Ruffy's gang with the tarpaulins.

It took them half an hour of desperate endeavour before they completed the fortifications to Bruce's satisfaction.

'That should hold them.' Bruce stood with Ruffy and Hendry in the centre of the laager and surveyed the green canvas roof above them and the closely packed vehicles around them. The Ford was parked beside the tanker, not included in the outer ring for its comparative size would have made it a weak point in the defence.

'It's going to be bloody hot and crowded in here,' grumbled Hendry.

'Yes, I know.' Bruce looked at him. 'Would you like to relieve the congestion by waiting outside?'

'Funny boy, big laugh,' answered Wally.

'What now, boss?' Ruffy put into words the question Bruce had been asking himself.

'You and I will go and take a look at the bridge,' he said.

'You'll look a rare old sight with an arrow sticking out of your jack,' grinned Wally. 'Boy, that's going to kill me!'

'Ruffy, get us half a dozen gas capes each. I doubt their arrows will go through them at a range of a hundred feet, and of course we'll wear helmets.'

'Okay, boss.'

It was like being in a sauna bath beneath the six layers of rubberized canvas. Bruce could feel the sweat squirting from his pores with each pace, and rivulets of it coursing down his back and flanks as he and Ruffy left the laager and walked up the road to the bridge.

Beside him Ruffy's bulk was so enhanced by the gas capes that he reminded Bruce of a prehistoric monster reaching the end of its gestation period.

'Warm enough, Ruffy?' he asked, feeling the need for humour. The ring of jungle made his nervous. Perhaps he had underestimated the carry of a Baluba arrow – despite the light reed shaft, they used iron heads, barbed viciously and ground to a needle point, and poison smeared thickly between the barbs.

'Man, look at me shiver,' grunted Ruffy and the sweat greased down his jowls and dripped from his chin.

Long before they reached the access to the bridge the stench of putrefaction crept out to meet them. In Bruce's mind every smell had its own colour, and this one was green, the same green as the sheen of putrefaction on rotting meat. The stench was heavy so he could almost feel it bearing down on them, choking in his throat and coating his tongue and the roof of his mouth with the oily over-sweetness.

'No doubt what that is!' Ruffy spat, trying to get the taste out of his mouth.

'Where are they?' gagged Bruce, starting to pant from the heat and the effort of breathing the fouled air.

They reached the bank and Bruce's question was answered as they looked down on to the narrow beach.

There were the black remains of a dozen cooking fires along the water's edge, and closer to the high bank were two crude structures of poles. For a moment their purpose puzzled Bruce and then he realized what they were. He had seen those cross-pieces suspended between two uprights often before in hunting camps throughout Africa. They were paunching racks! At intervals along the crosspieces were the bark ropes that had been used to string up the game, heels first, with head and forelegs dangling and belly bulging forward so that at the long abdominal stroke of the knife the viscera would drop out easily.

But the game they had butchered on *these* racks were men, his men. He counted the hanging ropes. There were ten of them, so no one had escaped.

'Cover me, Ruffy. I'm going down to have a look.' It was a penance Bruce was imposing upon himself. They were his men, and he had left them here.

'Okay, boss.'

Bruce clambered down the well-defined path to the beach. Now the smell was almost unbearable and he found the source of it. Between the racks lay a dark shapeless mass. It moved with flies; its surface moved, trembled, crawled with flies. Suddenly, humming, they lifted in a cloud from the pile of human debris, and then settled once more upon it.

A single fly buzzed round Bruce's head and then settled on his hand. Metallic blue body, wings cocked back, it crouched on his skin and gleefully rubbed its front legs together. Bruce's throat and stomach convulsed as he began to retch. He struck at the fly and it darted away.

There were bones scattered round the cooking fires and a skull lay near his feet, split open to yield its contents.

Another spasm took Bruce and this time the vomit came up into his mouth, acid and warm. He swallowed it, turned away and scrambled up the bank to where Ruffy waited. He stood there gasping, suppressing his nausea until at last he could speak.

'All right, that's all I wanted to know,' and he led the way back to the circle of vehicles.

Bruce sat on the bonnet of the Ranchero and sucked hard on his cigarette, trying to get the taste of death from his mouth.

'They probably swam downstream during the night and climbed the supports of the bridge. Kanaki and his boys wouldn't have known anything about it until they came over the sides.' He drew on the cigarette again and trickled the smoke out of his nostrils, fumigating the back of his throat and his nasal passages. 'I should have thought of that. I should have warned Kanaki of that.'

'You mean they ate all ten of them – Jesus!' even Wally Hendry was impressed. 'I'd like to have a look at that beach. It must be quite something.'

'Good!' Bruce's voice was suddenly harsh. 'I'll put you in charge of the burial squad. You can go down there and clean it up before we start work on the bridge.' And Wally did not argue.

'You want me to do it now?' he asked.

'No,' snapped Bruce. 'You and Ruffy are going to take two of the trucks back to Port Reprieve and fetch the materials we need to repair the bridge.'

They both looked at Bruce with rising delight.

'I never thought of that,' said Wally.

'There's plenty of roofing timber in the hotel and the office block,' grinned Ruffy.

'Nails,' said Wally as though he were making a major contribution. 'We'll need nails.'

Bruce cut through their comments. 'It's two o'clock now. You can get back to Port Reprieve by nightfall, collect the material tomorrow morning and return here by the evening. Take those two trucks there – check to see they're full of gas and you'll need about fifteen men. Say, five gendarmes, in case of trouble, and ten of those civilians.'

'That should be enough,' agreed Ruffy.

'Bring a couple of dozen sheets of corrugated iron back with you. We'll use them to make a shield to protect us from arrows while we're working.'

'Yeah, that's a good idea.'

They settled the details, picked men to go back, loaded the trucks, worked them out of the laager, and Bruce watched them disappear down the road towards Port Reprieve. An ache started deep behind his eyes and suddenly he was very tired, drained of energy by too little sleep, by the heat and by the emotional pace of the last four days. He made one last circuit of the laager, checking the defences, chatting for a few minutes with his gendarmes and then he stumbled to the Ford, slid on to the front seat, laid his helmet and rifle aside, lowered his head on to his arms and was instantly asleep.

Chapter Twenty-One

Shermaine woke him after dark with food unheated from the cans and a bottle of Ruffy's beer.

'I'm sorry, Bruce, we have no fire to cook upon. It is very unappetizing and the beer is warm.'

Bruce sat up and rubbed his eyes. Six hours' sleep had helped; they were less swollen and inflamed. The headache was still there.

'I'm not really hungry, thank you. It's this heat.'

'You must eat, Bruce. Try just a little,' and then she smiled. 'At least you are more gallant after having rested. It is "Thank you" now, instead of "Keep quiet and stay out of the way".'

Ruefully Bruce grimaced. 'You are one of those women with a built-in recording unit; every word remembered and used in evidence against a man later.' Then he touched her hand. 'I'm sorry.'

'I'm sorry,' she repeated. 'I like your apologies, mon capitaine. They are like the rest of you, completely masculine. There is nothing about you which is not male, sometimes almost overpoweringly so.' Impishly she watched his eyes; he knew she was talking about the little scene on the train that Wally Hendry had interrupted.

'Let's try this food,' he said, and then a little later, 'not bad – you are an excellent cook.'

'This time the credit must go to M. Heinz and his fifty-seven children. But one day I shall make for you one of my tournedos au Prince. It is my special.'

'Speciality,' Bruce corrected her automatically.

The murmur of voices within the laager was punctuated occasionally by a burst of laughter. There was a feeling of relaxation. The canvas roof and the wall of vehicles gave security to them all. Men lay in dark huddles of sleep or talked quietly in small groups.

Bruce scraped the metal plate and filled his mouth with the last of the food.

'Now I must check the defences again.'

'Oh, Bonaparte. It is always duty.' Shermaine sighed with resignation.

'I will not be long.'

'And I'll wait here for you.'

Bruce picked up his rifle and helmet, and was half-way out of the Ford when out in the jungle the drum started.

'Bruce!' whispered Shermaine and clutched his arm. The voices round them froze into a fearful silence, and the drum beat in the night. It had a depth and resonance that you could feel; the warm sluggish air quivered with it. Not fixed in space but filling it, beating monotonously, insistently, like the pulse of all creation.

'Bruce!' whispered Shermaine again; she was trembling and the fingers on his arm dug into his flesh with the strength of terror. It steadied his own leap of fear.

'Baby, baby,' he soothed her, taking her to his chest and holding her there.

'It's only the sound of two pieces of wood being knocked together by a naked savage. They can't touch us here, you know that.'

'Oh, Bruce, it's horrible – it's like bells, funeral bells.'

'That's silly talk.' Bruce held her at arms' length. 'Come with me. Help me calm down these others, they'll be terrified. You'll have to help me.'

And he pulled her gently across the seat out of the Ford, and with one arm round her waist walked her into the centre of the laager.

What will counteract the stupefying influence of the drum, the hypnotic beat of it, he asked himself. Noise, our own noise.

'Joseph, M'pophu—' he shouted cheerfully picking out the two best singers amongst his men. 'I regret the drumming is of a low standard, but the Baluba are monkeys with no understanding of music. Let us show them how a Bambala can sing.'

They stirred; he could feel the tension diminish.

'Come, Joseph—' He filled his lungs and shouted the opening chorus of one of the planting songs, purposely off-key, singing so badly that it must sting them.

Someone laughed, then Joseph's voice hesitantly starting the chorus, gathering strength. M'pophu coming in with the bass to give a solid foundation to the vibrant, sweet-ringing tenor. Half-beat to the drum, hands clapped in the dark; around him Bruce could feel the rhythmic swinging of bodies begin.

Shermaine was no longer trembling; he squeezed her waist and felt her body cling to him.

Now we need light, thought Bruce. A night lamp for my children who fear the darkness and the drum.

With Shermaine beside him he crossed the laager.

'Sergeant Jacque.'

'Captain?'

'You can start sweeping with the searchlights.'

'Oui, Captain.' The answer was less subdued. There were two spare batteries for each light, Bruce knew. Eight hours' life in each, so they would last tonight and tomorrow night.

From each side of the laager the beams leapt out, solid white shafts through the darkness; they played along the edge of the jungle and reflected back, lighting the interior of the laager sufficiently to make out the features of each man. Bruce looked at their faces. They're all right now, he decided, the ghosts have gone away.

'Bravo, Bonaparte,' said Shermaine, and Bruce became aware of the grins on the faces of his men as they saw him embracing her. He was about to drop his arm, then stopped himself. The hell with it, he decided, give them something else to think about. He led her back to the Ford.

'Tired?' he asked.

'A little,' she nodded.

'I'll fold down the seat for you. A blanket over the windows will give you privacy.'

'You'll stay close?' she asked quickly.

'I'll be right outside.' He unbuckled the webbing belt that carried his pistol. 'You'd better wear this from now on.'

Even at its minimum adjustment the belt was too large for her and the pistol hung down almost to her knee.

'The Maid of Orleans.' Bruce revenged himself. She pulled a face at him and crawled into the back of the station wagon.

A long while later she called softly above the singing and the throb of the drum.

'Bruce.'

'Yes?'

'I wanted to make sure you were there. Good night.'

'Good night, Shermaine.'

Bruce lay on a single blanket and sweated. The singing had long ago ceased but the drum went on and on, never faltering, throb-throb-throbbing out of the jungle. The searchlight swept regularly back and forth, at times lighting the laager clearly and at others leaving it in shadow. Bruce could hear around him the soft sounds of sleep, the sawing of breath, a muted cough, a gabbled sentence, the stirring of dreamers.

But Bruce could not sleep. He lay on his back with one hand under his head, smoking, staring up at the canvas. The events of the preceding four days ran through his mind: snatches of conversation, André dying, Boussier standing with his wife, the bursting of grenades, blood sticky on his hands, the smell of dead, the violence and the horror.

He moved restlessly, flicked away his cigarette and covered his eyes with his hands as though to shut out the memories. But they went on flickering through his mind like the images of a gigantic movie projector, confused now, losing all meaning but retaining the horror.

He remembered the fly upon his arm, grinning at him, rubbing its legs together, gloating, repulsive. He rolled his head from side to side on the blanket. I'm going mad, he thought, I must stop this.

He sat up quickly hugging his knees to his chest and the memories faded. But now he was sad, and alone. So terribly alone, so lost, so without purpose.

He sat alone on the blanket and he felt himself shrinking, becoming small and frightened.

I'm going to cry, he thought, I can feel it there heavy in my throat. And like a hurt child crawling into its mother's lap, Bruce Curry groped his way over the tailboard of the station wagon to Shermaine.

'Shermaine!' he whispered, blindly searching for her.

'Bruce, what is it?' She sat up quickly. She had not been sleeping either.

'Where are you?' There was panic in Bruce's voice.

'Here I am – what's the matter?'

And he found her; clumsily he caught her to him.

'Hold me, Shermaine, please hold me.'

'Darling.' She was anxious. 'What is it? Tell me, my darling.'

'Just hold me, Shermaine. Don't talk.' He clung to her, pressing his face into her neck. 'I need you so much – oh, God! How I need you!'

'Bruce.' She understood, and her fingers were at the nape of his neck, stroking, soothing.

'My Bruce,' she said and held him. Instinctively her body began to rock, gentling him as though he were her child.

Slowly his body relaxed, and he sighed against her – a gusty broken sound.

'My Bruce, my Bruce.' She lifted the thin cotton vest that was all she wore and, instinctively in the ageless ritual of comfort, she gave him her breasts. Holding his mouth to them with both her arms clasped around his neck, her head bowed protectively over his, her hair falling forward and covering them both.

With the hard length of his body against hers, with the soft tugging at her bosom, and in the knowledge that she was giving strength to the man she loved, she realized she had never known happiness before this moment. Then his body was no longer quiescent; she felt her own mood change, a new urgency.

'Oh yes, Bruce, yes!' Speaking up into his mouth, his hungry hunting mouth
and he above her, no longer child, but full man again.

'So beautiful, so warm.' His voice was strangely husky, she shuddered with
the intensity of her own need.

'Quickly, Bruce, oh, Bruce.' His cruel loving hands, seeking, finding.

'Oh, Bruce – quickly,' and she reached up for him with her hips.

'I'll hurt you.'

'No – yes, I want the pain.' She felt the resistance to him within her and cried
out impatiently against it.

'Go through!' and then, 'Ah! It burns.'

'I'll stop.'

'*No, No!*'

'Darling. It's too much.'

'Yes – I can't – oh, Bruce. My heart – you've touched my heart.'

Her clenched fists drumming on his back. And in to press against the taut,
reluctantly yielding springiness, away, then back, away, and back to touch the
core of all existence, leave it, and come long gliding back to it, nuzzle it, feel it
tilt, then come away, then back once more. Welling slowly upwards, scalding,
no longer to be contained, with pain almost – and gone, and gone, and gone.

'I'm falling. Oh, Bruce! Bruce! Bruce!'

Into the gulf together – gone, all gone. Nothing left, no time, no space, no
bottom to the gulf.

Nothing and everything. Complete.

Out in the jungle the drum kept beating.

*Afterwards, long afterwards, she slept with her head on his arm and her face
against his chest. And he unsleeping listened to her sleep. The sound of it was
soft, so gentle breathing soft that you could not hear it unless you listened very
carefully – or unless you loved her, he thought.*

Yes. I think I love this woman – but I must be certain. In fairness to her and
to myself I must be entirely certain, for I cannot live through another time like
the last, and because I love her I don't want her to take the terrible wounding
of a bad marriage. Better, much better to leave it now, unless it has the strength
to endure.

*Bruce rolled his head slowly until his face was in her hair, and the girl nuzzled
his chest in her sleep.*

But it is so hard to tell, he thought. It is so hard to tell at the beginning. It
is so easy to confuse pity or loneliness with love, but I cannot afford to do that
now. So I must try to think clearly about my marriage to Joan. It will be
difficult, but I must try.

Was it like this with Joan in the beginning? It was so long ago, seven years,
that I do not know, *he answered truthfully.* All I have left from those days are
the pictures of places and the small heaps of words that have struck where the
wind and the pain could not blow them away.

A beach with the sea mist coming in across it, a whole tree of driftwood half
buried in the sand and bleached white with the salt, a basket of strawberries
bought along the road, so that when I kissed her I could taste the sweet tartness
of the fruit on her lips.

I remember a tune that we sang together, 'The mission bells told me that I
mustn't stay, South of the border, down Mexico way.' I have forgotten most of
the words.

And I remember vaguely how her body was, and the shape of her breasts
before the children were born.

But that is all I have left from the good times.

The other memories are clear; stinging, whiplash clear. Each ugly word, and the tone in which it was said. The sound of sobbing in the night, the way it dragged itself on for three long grey years after it was mortally wounded, and both of us using all our strength to keep it moving because of the children.

The children! Oh, God, I mustn't think about them now. It hurts too much. Without the children to complicate it, I must think about her for the last time; I must end this woman Joan. So now finally and for all to end this woman who made me cry. I do not hate her for the man with whom she went away. She deserved another try for happiness. But I hate her for my children and for making shabby the love that I could have given Shermaine as a new thing. Also, I pity her for her inability to find the happiness for which she hunts so fiercely. I pity her for her coldness of body and of mind, I pity her for her prettiness that is now almost gone (it goes round the eyes first, cracking like oil paint) and I pity her for her consuming selfishness which will lose her the love of her children.

My children – not hers! My children!

That is all, that is an end to Joan, and now I have Shermaine who is none of the things that Joan was. I also deserve another try.

'Shermaine,' he whispered and turned her head slightly to kiss her. 'Shermaine, wake up.'

She stirred and murmured against him.

'Wake up.' He took the lobe of her ear between his teeth and bit it gently. Her eyes opened.

'Bon matin, madame.' He smiled at her.

'Bon jour, monsieur,' she answered and closed her eyes to press her face once more against his chest.

'Wake up. I have something to tell you.'

'I am awake, but tell me first if I am still dreaming. I have a certainty that this cannot be reality.'

'You are not dreaming.'

She sighed softly, and held him closer.

'Now tell me the other thing.'

'I love you,' he said.

'No. Now I am dreaming.'

'In truth,' he said.

'No, do not wake me. I could not bear to wake now.'

'And you?' he asked.

'You know it—' she answered. 'I do not have to tell you.'

'It is almost morning,' he said. 'There is only a little time.'

'Then I will fill that little time with saying it—' He held her and listened to her whispering it to him.

No, he thought, now I am certain. I could not be that wrong. This is my woman.

Chapter Twenty-Two

The drum stopped with the dawn. And after it the silence was very heavy, and it was no relief.

They had grown accustomed to that broken rhythm and now in some strange way they missed it.

As Bruce moved around the laager he could sense the uneasiness in his men. There was a feeling of dread anticipation on them all. They moved with restraint, as though they did not want to draw attention to themselves. The laughter with which they acknowledged his jokes was nervous, quickly cut off, as though they had laughed in a cathedral. And their eyes kept darting back towards the ring of jungle.

Bruce found himself wishing for an attack. His own nerves were rubbed sensitive by contact with the fear all around him.

If only they would come, he told himself. If only they would show themselves and we could see men not phantoms.

But the jungle was silent. It seemed to wait, it watched them. They could feel the gaze of hidden eyes. Its malignant presence pressed closer as the heat built up.

Bruce walked across the laager to the south side, trying to move casually. He smiled at Sergeant Jacque, squatted beside him and peered from under the truck across open ground at the remains of the bridge.

'Trucks will be back soon,' he said. 'Won't take long to repair that.'

Jacque did not answer. There was a worried frown on his high intelligent forehead and his face was shiny with perspiration.

'It's the waiting, Captain. It softens the stomach.'

'They will be back soon,' repeated Bruce. If this one is worried, and he is the best of them, then the others must be almost in a jelly of dread.

Bruce looked at the face of the man on the other side of Jacque. Its expression shrieked with fear.

If they attack now, God knows how it will turn out. An African can think himself to death, they just lie down and die. They are getting to that stage now; if an attack comes they will either go berserk or curl up and wail with fear. You can never tell.

Be honest with yourself – you're not entirely happy either, are you? No, Bruce agreed, it's the waiting does it.

It came from the edge of the clearing on the far side of the laager. A high-pitched inhuman sound, angry, savage.

Bruce felt his heart trip and he spun round to face it. For a second the whole laager seemed to cringe from it.

It came again. Like a whip across aching nerves. Immediately it was lost in the roar of twenty rifles.

Bruce laughed. Threw his head back and let it come from the belly.

The gunfire stammered into silence and others were laughing also. The men who had fired grinned sheepishly and made a show of reloading.

It was not the first time that Bruce had been startled by the cry of a yellow hornbill. But now he recognized his laughter and the laughter of the men around him, a mild form of hysteria.

'Did you want the feathers for your hat?' someone shouted and the laughter swept round the laager.

The tension relaxed as the banter was tossed back and forth. Bruce stood up and brought his own laughter under control.

No harm done, he decided. For the price of fifty rounds of ammunition, a purchase of an hour's escape from tension. A good bargain.

He walked across to Shermaine. She was smiling also.

'How is the catering section?' He grinned at her. 'What miracle of the culinary art is there for lunch?'

'Bully beef.'

'And onions?'

'No, just bully beef. The onions are finished.'

Bruce stopped smiling.

'How much is left?' he asked.

'One case – enough to last till lunchtime tomorrow.'

It would take at least two days to complete the repairs to the bridge; another day's travel after that.

'Well,' he said, 'we should all have healthy appetites by the time we get home. You'll have to try and spread it out. Half rations from now on.'

He was so engrossed in the study of this new complication that he did not notice the faint hum from outside the laager.

'Captain,' called Jacque. 'Can you hear it?'

Bruce inclined his head and listened.

'The trucks!' His voice was loud with relief, and instantly there was an excited murmur round the laager.

The waiting was over.

They came growling out of the bush into the clearing. Heavily loaded, timber and sheet-iron protruding backwards from under the canopies, sitting low on their suspensions.

Ruffy leaned from the cab of the leading truck and shouted.

'Hello, boss. Where shall we dump?'

'Take it up to the bridge. Hang on a second and I'll come with you.'

Bruce slipped out of the laager and crossed quickly to Ruffy's truck. He could feel his back tingling while he was in the open and he slammed the door behind him with relief.

'I don't relish stopping an arrow,' he said.

'You have any trouble while we were gone?'

'No,' Bruce told him. 'But they're here. They were drumming in the jungle all night.'

'Calling up their buddies,' grunted Ruffy and let out the clutch. 'We'll have some fun before we finish this bridge. Most probably take them a day or two to get brave, but in the end they'll have a go at us.'

'Pull over to the side of the bridge, Ruffy,' Bruce instructed and rolled down his window. 'I'll signal Hendry to pull in beside us. We'll off-load into the space between the two trucks and start building the corrugated iron shield there.'

While Hendry manoeuvred his truck alongside, Bruce forced himself to look down on the carnage of the beach.

'Crocodiles,' he exclaimed with relief. The paunching racks still stood as he had last seen them, but the reeking pile of human remains was gone. The smell and the flies, however, still lingered.

'During the night,' agreed Ruffy as he surveyed the long slither marks in the sand of the beach.

'Thank God for that.'

'Yeah, it wouldn't have made my boys too joyful having to clean up that lot.'

'We'll send someone down to tear out those racks. I don't want to look at them while we work.'

'No, they're not very pretty.' Ruffy ran his eyes over the two sets of gallows. Bruce climbed down into the space between the trucks.

'Hendry.'

'That's my name.' Wally leaned out of the window.

'Sorry to disappoint you, but the crocs have done the chore for you.'

'I can see. I'm not blind.'

'Very well then. On the assumption that you are neither blind nor paralysed, how about getting your trucks unloaded?'

'Big deal,' muttered Hendry, but he climbed down and began shouting at the men under the canvas canopy.

'Get the lead out there, you lot. Start jumping about!'

'What were the thickest timbers you could find?' Bruce turned to Ruffy.

'Nine by threes, but we got plenty of them.'

'They'll do,' decided Bruce. 'We can lash a dozen of them together for each of the main supports.' Frowning with concentration, Bruce began the task of organizing the repairs.

'Hendry, I want the timber stacked by sizes. Put the sheet-iron over there.' He brushed the flies from his face. 'Ruffy, how many hammers have we got?'

'Ten, boss, and I found a couple of handsaws.'

'Good. What about nails and rope?'

'We got plenty. I got a barrel of six-inch and—'

Preoccupied, Bruce did not notice one of the coloured civilians leave the shelter of the trucks. He walked a dozen paces towards the bridge and stopped. Then unhurriedly he began to unbutton his trousers and Bruce looked up.

'What the hell are you doing?' he shouted and the man started guiltily. He did not understand the English words, but Bruce's tone was sufficiently clear.

'Monsieur,' he explained, 'I wish to—'

'Get back here!' roared Bruce. The man hesitated in confusion and then he began closing his fly.

'Hurry up – you bloody fool.'

Obediently the man hastened the closing of his trousers. Everyone had stopped work and they were all watching him. His face was dark with embarrassment and he fumbled clumsily.

'Leave that.' Bruce was frantic. 'Get back here.'

The first arrow rose lazily out of the undergrowth along the river in a silent parabola. Gathering speed in its descent, hissing softly, it dropped into the ground at the man's feet and stuck up jauntily. A thin reed, fletched with green leaves, it looked harmless as a child's plaything.

'Run,' screamed Bruce. The man stood and stared with detached disbelief at the arrow.

Bruce started forward to fetch him, but Ruffy's huge black hand closed on his arm and he was helpless in its grip. He struck out at Ruffy, struggling to free himself but he could not break that hold.

A swarm of them like locusts on the move, high arcing, fluting softly, dropping all around the man as he started to run.

Bruce stopped struggling and watched. He heard the metal heads clanking on to the bonnet of the truck, saw them falling wide of the man, some of the frail shafts snapping as they hit the ground.

Then between the shoulders, like a perfectly placed banderilla, one hit him.

It flapped against his back as he ran and he twisted his arms behind him, vainly trying to reach it, his face twisted in horror and in pain.

'Hold him down,' shouted Bruce as the coloured man ran into the shelter. Two gendarmes jumped forward, took his arms and forced him face downwards on to the ground.

He was gabbling incoherently with horror as Bruce straddled his back and gripped the shaft. Only half the barbed head had buried itself – a penetration of less than an inch – but when Bruce pulled the shaft it snapped off in his hand leaving the steel twitching in the flesh.

'Knife,' shouted Bruce and someone thrust a bayonet into his hand.

'Watch those barbs, boss. Don't cut yourself on them.'

'Ruffy, get your boys ready to repel them if they rush us,' snapped Bruce and ripped away the shirt. For a moment he stared at the crudely hand-beaten iron arrow-head. The poison coated it thickly, packed in behind the barbs, looking like sticky black toffee.

'He's dead,' said Ruffy from where he leaned over the bonnet of the truck. 'He just ain't stopped breathing yet.'

The man screamed and twisted under Bruce as he made the first incision, cutting in deep beside the arrowhead with the point of the bayonet.

'Hendry, get those pliers out of the tool kit.'

'Here they are.'

Bruce gripped the arrow-head with the steel jaws and pulled. The flesh clung to it stubbornly, lifting in a pyramid. Bruce hacked at it with the bayonet, feeling it tear. It was like trying to get the hook out of the rubbery mouth of a cat-fish.

'You're wasting your time, boss!' grunted Ruffy with all the calm African acceptance of violent death. 'This boy's a goner. That's no horse! That's snake juice in him, fresh mixed. He's finished.'

'Are you sure, Ruffy?' Bruce looked up, 'Are you sure it's snake venom?'

'That's what they use. They mix it with kassava meal.'

'Hendry, where's the snake bite outfit?'

'It's in the medicine box back at the camp.'

Bruce tugged once more at the arrow-head and it came away, leaving a deep black hole between the man's shoulder-blades.

'Everybody into the trucks, we've got to get him back. Every second is vital.'

'Look at his eyes,' grunted Ruffy. 'That injection stuff ain't going to help him much.'

The pupils had contracted to the size of match heads and he was shaking uncontrollably as the poison spread through his body.

'Get him into the truck.'

They lifted him into the cab and everybody scrambled aboard. Ruffy started the engine, slammed into reverse and the motor roared as he shot backwards over the intervening thirty yards to the laager.

'Get him out,' instructed Bruce. 'Bring him into the shelter.'

The man was blubbering through slack lips and he had started to sweat. Little rivulets of it coursed down his face and naked upper body. There was hardly any blood from the wound, just a trickle of brownish fluid. The poison must be a coagulant, Bruce decided.

'Bruce, are you all right?' Shermaine ran to meet him.

'Nothing wrong with me.' Bruce remembered to check his tongue this time. 'But one of them has been hit.'

'Can I help you?'

'No, I don't want you to watch.' And he turned from her. 'Henry, where's that bloody snake bite outfit?' he shouted.

They had dragged the man into the laager and laid him on a blanket in the shade. Bruce went to him and knelt beside him. He took the scarlet tin that Hendry handed him and opened it.

'Ruffy, get those two trucks worked into the circle and make sure your boys are on their toes. With this success they may get brave sooner than you expected.' Bruce fitted the hypodermic needle on to the syringe as he spoke.

'Hendry, get them to rig some sort of screen round us. You can use blankets.' With his thumb he snapped the top off the ampoule and filled the syringe with the pale yellow serum.

'Hold him,' he said to the two gendarmes, lifted a pinch of skin close beside the wound and ran the needle under it. The man's skin felt like that of a frog, damp and clammy.

As he expelled the serum Bruce was trying to calculate the time that had elapsed since the arrow had hit. Possibly seven or eight minutes; mamba venom kills in fourteen minutes.

'Roll him over,' he said.

The man's head lolled sideways, his breathing was quick and shallow and the saliva poured from the corners of his mouth, running down his cheeks.

'Get a load of that!' breathed Wally Hendry, and Bruce glanced up at his face. His expression was a glow of deep sensual pleasure and his breathing was as quick and shallow as that of the dying man.

'Go and help Ruffy,' snapped Bruce as his stomach heaved with disgust.

'Not on your Nelly. This I'm not going to miss.'

Bruce had no time to argue. He lifted the skin of the man's stomach and ran the needle in again. There was an explosive spitting sound as the bowels started to vent involuntarily.

'Jesus,' whispered Hendry.

'Get away,' snarled Bruce. 'Can't you let him die without gloating over it?'

Hopelessly he injected again, under the skin of the chest above the heart. As he emptied the syringe the man's body twisted violently in the first seizure and the needle snapped off under the skin.

'There he goes,' whispered Hendry, 'there he goes. Just look at him, man. That's really something.'

Bruce's hands were trembling and slowly a curtain descended across his mind.

'You filthy swine,' he screamed and hit Hendry across the face with his open hand, knocking him back against the side of the gasoline tanker. Then he went for his throat and found it with both hands. The wind pipe was ropy and elastic under his thumbs.

'Is nothing sacred to you, you unclean animal,' he yelled into Hendry's face. 'Can't you let a man die without—'

Then Ruffy was there, effortlessly plucking Bruce's hands from the throat, interposing the bulk of his body, holding them away from each other.

'Let it stand, boss.'

'For that—' gasped Hendry as he massaged his throat. 'For that I'm going to make you pay.'

Bruce turned away, sick and ashamed, to the man on the blanket.

'Cover him up.' His voice was shaky. 'Put him in the back of one of the trucks. We'll bury him tomorrow.'

Chapter Twenty-Three

Before nightfall they had completed the corrugated iron screen. It was a simple four-walled structure with no roof to it. One end of it was detachable and all four walls were pierced at regular intervals with small loopholes for defence.

Long enough to accommodate a dozen men in comfort, high enough to reach above the heads of the tallest, and exactly the width of the bridge, it was not a thing of beauty.

'How you going to move it, boss?' Ruffy eyed the screen dubiously.

'I'll show you. We'll move it back to the camp now, so that in the morning we can commute to work in it.'

Bruce selected twelve men and they crowded through the open end into the shelter, and closed it behind them.

'Okay, Ruffy. Take the trucks away.'

Henry and Ruffy reversed the two trucks back to the laager, leaving the shelter standing at the head of the bridge like a small Nissen hut. Inside it Bruce stationed his men at intervals along the walls.

'Use the bottom timber of the frame to lift on,' he shouted. 'Are you all ready? All right, lift!'

The shelter swayed and rose six inches above the ground. From the laager they could see only the boots of the men inside.

'All together,' ordered Bruce. 'Walk!'

Rocking and creaking over the uneven ground the structure moved ponderously back towards the laager. Below it the feet moved like those of a caterpillar.

The men in the laager started to cheer, and from inside the shelter they answered with whoops of laughter. It was fun. They were enjoying themselves enormously, completely distracted from the horror of poison arrows and the lurking phantoms in the jungle around them.

They reached the camp and lowered the shelter. Then one at a time the gendarmes slipped across the few feet of open into the safety of the laager to be met with laughter, and back-slapping and mutual congratulation.

'Well, it works, boss,' Ruffy greeted Bruce in the uproar.

'Yes.' Then he lifted his voice. 'That's enough. Quiet down all of you. Get back to your posts.'

The laughter subsided and the confusion became order again. Bruce walked to the centre of the laager and looked about him. There was complete quiet now. They were all watching him. I have read about this so often, he grinned inwardly, the heroic speech to the men on the eve of battle. Let's pray I don't make a hash of it.

'Are you hungry?' he asked loudly in French and received a chorus of hearty affirmatives.

'There is bully beef for dinner.' This time humorous groans.

'And bully beef for breakfast tomorrow,' he paused, 'and then it's finished.'

They were silent now.

'So you are going to be truly hungry by the time we cross this river. The sooner we repair the bridge the sooner you'll get your bellies filled again.'

I might as well rub it in, decided Bruce.

'You all saw what happened to the person who went into the open today, so I don't have to tell you to keep under cover. The sergeant major is making arrangements for sanitation – five-gallon drums. They won't be very comfortable, so you won't be tempted to sit too long.'

They laughed a little at that.

'Remember this. As long as you stay in the laager or the shelter they can't touch you. There is absolutely nothing to fear. They can beat their drums and wait as long as they like, but they can't harm us.'

A murmur of agreement.

'And the sooner we finish the bridge the sooner we will be on our way.'

Bruce looked round the circle of faces and was satisfied with what he saw. The completion of the shelter had given their morale a boost.

'All right, Sergeant Jacque. You can start sweeping with the searchlights as soon as it's dark.'

Bruce finished and went across to join Shermaine beside the Ford. He loosed the straps of his helmet and lifted it off his head. His hair was damp with perspiration and he ran his fingers through it.

'You are tired,' Shermaine said softly, examining the dark hollows under his eyes and the puckered marks of strain at the corners of his mouth.

'No. I'm all right,' he denied, but every muscle in his body ached with fatigue and nervous tension.

'Tonight you must sleep all night,' she ordered him. 'I will make the bed in the back of the car.'

Bruce looked at her quickly. 'With you?' he asked.

'Yes.'

'You do not mind that everyone should know?'

'I am not ashamed of us.' There was a fierceness in her tone.

'I know, but—'

'You said once that nothing between you and I could ever be dirty.'

'No, of course it couldn't be dirty. I just thought—'

'Well then, I love you and from now on we have only one bed between us.' She spoke with finality.

Yesterday she was a virgin, he thought with amazement, and now – well, now it's no holds barred. Once she is roused a woman is more reckless of consequences than any man. They are such wholesale creatures. But she's right, of course. She's my woman and she belongs in my bed. The hell with the rest of the world and what it thinks!

'Make the bed, wench.' He smiled at her tenderly.

Two hours after dark the drum started again. They lay together, holding close, and listened to it. It held no terror now, for they were warm and secure in the afterglow of passion. It was like lying and listening to the impotent fury of a rainstorm on the roof at night.

Chapter Twenty-Four

They went out to the bridge at sunrise, the shelter moving across the open ground like the carapace of a multi-legged metallic turtle. The men chattered and joked loudly inside, still elated by the novelty of it.

'All right, everybody. That's enough talking,' Bruce shouted them down. 'There's work to do now.'

And they began.

Within an hour the sun had turned the metal box into an oven. They stripped to the waist and the sweat dripped from them as they worked. They worked in a frenzy, gripped by a new urgency, oblivious of everything but the rough-sawed timber that drove white splinters into their skin at the touch. They worked in the confined heat, amidst the racket of hammers and in the piney smell of sawdust. The labour fell into its own pattern with only an occasional grunted order from Bruce or Ruffy to direct it.

By midday the four main trusses that would span the gap in the bridge had been made up. Bruce tested their rigidity by propping one at both ends and standing all his men on the middle of it. It gave an inch under their combined weight.

'What do you think, boss?' Ruffy asked without conviction.

'Four of them might just do it. We'll put in king-posts underneath,' Bruce answered.

'Man, I don't know. That tanker weighs plenty.'

'It's no flyweight,' Bruce agreed. 'But we'll have to take the chance. We'll bring the Ford across first, then the trucks and the tanker last.'

Ruffy nodded and wiped his face on his forearm; the muscles below his armpits knotted as he moved and there was no flabbiness in the powerful bulge of his belly above his belt.

'Phew!' He blew his lips out. 'I got the feeling for a beer now. This thirst is really stalking me.'

'You've got some with you?' Bruce asked as he passed his thumbs across his eyebrows and squeezed the moisture from them so it ran down his cheeks.

'Two things I never travel without, my trousers and a stock of the brown and bubbly.' Ruffy picked up the small pack from the corner of the shelter and it clinked coyly. 'You hear that sound, boss?'

'I hear it, and it sounds like music,' grinned Bruce. 'All right, everybody.' He raised his voice. 'Take ten minutes.'

Ruffy opened the bottles and passed them out, issuing one to be shared between three gendarmes. 'These Arabs don't properly appreciate this stuff,' he explained to Bruce. 'It'd just be a waste.'

The liquor was lukewarm and gassy; it merely aggravated Bruce's thirst. He drained the bottle and tossed it out of the shelter.

'All right.' He stood up. 'Let's get these trusses into position.'

'That's the shortest ten minutes I ever lived,' commented Ruffy.

'Your watch is slow,' said Bruce.

Carrying the trusses within it, the shelter lumbered out on to the bridge. There was no laughter now, only laboured breathing and curses.

'Fix the ropes!' commanded Bruce. He tested the knots personally, then looked up at Ruffy and nodded.

'That'll do.'

'Come on, you mad bastards,' Ruffy growled. 'Lift it.'

The first truss rose to the perpendicular and swayed there like a grotesque maypole with the ropes hanging from its top.

'Two men on each rope,' ordered Bruce. 'Let it down gently.' He glanced round to ensure that they were all ready.

'Drop it over the edge, and I'll throw you bastards in after it,' warned Ruffy.

'Lower away!' shouted Bruce.

The truss leaned out over the gap towards the fire-blackened stump of bridge on the far side, slowly at first, then faster as gravity took it.

'Hold it, damn you. Hold it!' roared Ruffy with the muscles in his shoulders humped out under the strain. They lay back against the ropes, but the weight of the truss dragged them forward as it fell.

. It crashed down across the gap, lifted a cloud of dead wood ash as it struck, and lay there quivering.

'Man, I thought we'd lost that one for sure,' growled Ruffy, then turned savagely on his men.

'You bastards better be sharper with the next one – if you don't want to swim this river.'

They repeated the process with the second truss, and again they could not hold its falling length, but this time they were not so lucky. The end of the truss hit the far side, bounced and slid sideways.

'It's going! Pull, you bastards, pull!' shouted Ruffy.

The truss toppled slowly sideways and over the edge. It hit the river below them with a splash, disappeared under the surface, then bobbed up and floated away downstream until checked by the ropes.

Both Bruce and Ruffy fumed and swore during the lengthy exasperating business of dragging it back against the current and manhandling its awkward bulk back on to the bridge. Half a dozen times it slipped at the crucial moment and splashed back into the river.

Despite his other virtues, Ruffy's vocabulary of cursing words was limited and it added to his frustration that he had to keep repeating himself. Bruce did much better – he remembered things that he had heard and he made up a few.

When finally they had the dripping baulk of timber back on the bridge and were resting, Ruffy turned to Bruce with honest admiration.

'You swear pretty good,' he said. 'Never heard you before, but no doubt about it, you're good! What's that one about the cow again?'

Bruce repeated it for him a little self-consciously.

'You make that up yourself?' asked Ruffy.

'Spur of the moment,' laughed Bruce.

'That's 'bout the dirtiest I ever heard.' Ruffy could not conceal his envy. 'Man, you should write a book.'

'Let's get this bridge finished first,' said Bruce. 'Then I'll think about it.'

Now the truss was almost servile in its efforts to please. It dropped neatly across the gap and lay beside its twin.

'You curse something good enough, and it works everytime,' Ruffy announced sagely. 'I think your one about the cow made all the difference, boss.'

With two trusses in position they had broken the back of the project. They carried the shelter out and set it on the trusses, straddling the gap. The third and fourth trusses were dragged into position and secured with ropes and nails before nightfall.

When the shelter waddled wearily back to the laager at dusk, the men within it were exhausted. Their hands were bleeding and bristled with wood splinters, but they were also mightily pleased with themselves.

'Sergeant Jacque, keep one of your searchlights trained on the bridge all night. We don't want our friends to come out and set fire to it again.

'There are only a few hours' life left in each of the batteries.' Jacque kept his voice low.

'Use them one at a time then.' Bruce spoke without hesitation. 'We must have that bridge lit up all night.'

'You think you could spare a beer for each of the boys that worked on the bridge today?'

'A whole one each!' Ruffy was shocked. 'I only got a coupla cases left.'

Bruce fixed him with a stern eye and Ruffy grinned.

'Okay, boss. Guess they've earned it.'

Bruce transferred his attention to Wally Hendry who sat on the running-board of one of the trucks cleaning his nails with the point of his bayonet.

'Everything under control here, Hendry?' he asked coolly.

'Sure, what'd you think would happen? We'd have a visit from the archbishop? The sky'd fall in? Your French thing'd have twins or something?' He looked up from his nails at Bruce. 'When are you jokers going to get that bridge finished, instead of wandering around asking damn-fool questions?'

Bruce was too tired to feel annoyed. 'You've got the night watch, Hendry,' he said, 'from now until dawn.'

'Is that right, hey? And you? What're you going to do all night, or does that question make you blush?'

'I'm going to sleep, that's what I'm going to do. I haven't been lolling round camp all day.'

Hendry pegged the bayonet into the earth between his feet and snorted.

'Well, give her a little bit of sleep for me too, Bucko.'

Bruce left him and crossed to the Ford.

'Hello, Bruce. How did it go today? I missed you,' Shermaine greeted him, and her face lit up as she looked at him. It is a good feeling to be loved, and some of Bruce's fatigue lifted.

'About half finished, another day's work.' Then he smiled back at her. 'I won't lie and say I missed you – I've been too damn busy.'

'Your hands!' she said with quick concern and lifted them to examine them. 'They're in a terrible state.'

'Not very pretty, are they?'

'Let me get a needle from my case. I'll get the splinter out.'

From across the laager Wally Hendry caught Bruce's eye and with one hand made a suggestive sign below his waist. Then, at Bruce's frown of anger, he threw back his head and laughed with huge delight.

Chapter Twenty-Five

Bruce's stomach grumbled with hunger as he stood with Ruffy and Hendry beside the cooking fire. In the early morning light he could just make out the dark shape of the bridge at the end of the clearing. That drum was still beating in the jungle, but they hardly noticed it now. It was taken for granted like the mosquitoes. 'The batteries are finished,' grunted Ruffy. The feeble yellow beam of the searchlight reached out tiredly towards the bridge.

'Only just lasted the night,' agreed Bruce.

'Christ, I'm hungry,' complained Hendry. 'What could I do to a couple of fried eggs and a porterhouse steak.'

At the mention of food Bruce's mouth flooded with saliva. He shut his mind against the picture that Wally's words had evoked in his imagination.

'We won't be able to finish the bridge and get the trucks across today,' he said, and Ruffy agreed.

'There's a full day's work left on her, boss.'

'This is what we'll do then,' Bruce went on. 'I'll take the work party out to the bridge. Hendry, you will stay here in the laager and cover us the same as yesterday. And Ruffy, you take one of the trucks and a dozen of your boys. Go back ten miles or so to where the forest is open and they won't be able to creep up on you. Then cut us a mountain of firewood; thick logs that will burn all night. We will set a ring of watch fires round the camp tonight.'

'That makes sense,' Ruffy nodded. 'But what about the bridge?'

'We'll have to put a guard on it,' said Bruce, and the expressions on their faces changed as they thought about this.

'More pork chops for the boys in the bushes,' growled Hendry. 'You won't catch me sitting out on the bridge all night.'

'No one's asking you to,' snapped Bruce. 'All right, Ruffy. Go and fetch the wood, and plenty of it.'

Bruce completed the repairs to the bridge in the late afternoon. The most anxious period was in the middle of the day when he and four men had to leave the shelter and clamber down on to the supports a few feet above the surface of the river to set the king-posts in place. Here they were exposed at random range to arrows from the undergrowth along the banks. But no arrows came and they finished the job and climbed back to safety again with something of a sense of anticlimax.

They nailed the crossties over the trusses and then roped everything into a compact mass.

Bruce stood back and surveyed the fruit of two full days' labour.

'Functional,' he decided, speaking aloud. 'But we certainly aren't going to win any prizes for aesthetic beauty or engineering design.'

He picked up his jacket and thrust his arms into the sleeves; his sweaty upper body was cold now that the sun was almost down.

'Home, gentlemen,' he said, and his gendarmes scattered to their positions inside the shelter.

The metal shelter circled the laager, squatting every twenty or thirty paces like an old woman preparing to relieve herself. When it lifted and moved on it left a log fire behind it. The ring of fires was completed by dark and the shelter returned to the laager.

'Are you ready, Ruffy?' From inside the shelter Bruce called across to where Ruffy waited.

'All set, boss.'

Followed by six heavily armed gendarmes, Ruffy crossed quickly to join Bruce and they set off to begin their all-night vigil on the bridge.

Before midnight it was cold in the corrugated iron shelter, for the wind blew down the river and they were completely exposed to it, and there was no cloud cover to hold the day's warmth against the earth.

The men in the shelter huddled under their gas capes and waited. Bruce and Ruffy leaned together against the corrugated iron wall, their shoulders almost touching, and there was sufficient light from the stars to light the interior of the shelter and allow them to make out the guard rails of the bridge through the open ends.

'Moon will be up in an hour,' murmured Ruffy.

'Only a quarter of it, but it will give us a little more light,' Bruce concurred, and peered down into the black hole between his feet where he had prised up one of the newly laid planks.

'How about taking a shine with the torch?' suggested Ruffy.

'No.' Bruce shook his head, and passed the flashlight into his other hand. 'Not until I hear them.'

'You might not hear them.'

'If they swim downstream and climb up the piles, which is what I expect, then we'll hear them all right. They'll be dripping water all over the place,' said Bruce.

'Kanaki and his boys didn't hear them,' Ruffy pointed out.

'Kanaki and his boys weren't listening for it,' said Bruce.

They were silent then for a while. One of the gendarmes started to snore softly and Ruffy shot out a huge booted foot that landed in the small of his back. The man cried out and scrambled to his knees, looking wildy about him.

'You have nice dreams?' Ruffy asked pleasantly.

'I wasn't sleeping,' the man protested, 'I was thinking.'

'Well, don't think so loudly,' Ruffy advised him. 'Sounds though you sawing through the bridge with a cross cut.'

Another half hour dragged itself by like a cripple.

'Fires are burning well,' commented Ruffy, and Bruce turned his head and glanced through the loophole in the corrugated iron behind him at the little garden of orange flame-flowers in the darkness.

'Yes, they should last till morning.'

Silence again, with only the singing of the mosquitoes and the rustle of the river as it flowed by the piles of the bridge. Shermaine has my pistol, Bruce remembered with a small trip in his pulse, I should have taken it back from her. He unclipped the bayonet from the muzzle of his rifle, tested the edge of the blade with his thumb, and slid it into the scabbard on his web-belt. Could easily lose the rifle if we start mixing it in the dark, he decided.

'Christ, I'm hungry,' grunted Ruffy beside him.

'You're too fat,' said Bruce. 'The diet will do you good.' And they waited.

Bruce stared down into the hole in the floorboards. His eyes began weaving fantasies out of the darkness; he could see vague shapes that moved, like things seen below the surface of the sea. His stomach tightened and he fought the impulse to shine his flashlight into the hole. He closed his eyes to rest them. I will count slowly to ten, he decided, and then look again.

Ruffy's hand closed on his upper arm; the pressure of his fingers transmitted alarm like a current of electricity. Bruce's eyelids flew open.

'Listen,' breathed Ruffy.

Bruce heard it. The stealthy drip of water on water below them. Then something bumped the bridge, but so softly that he felt rather than heard the jar.

'Yes,' Bruce whispered back. He reached out and tapped the shoulder of the gendarme beside him and the man's body stiffened at his touch.

With his breath scratching his dry throat, Bruce waited until he was sure the warning had been passed to all his men. Then he shifted the weight of his rifle from across his knees and aimed down into the hole.

He drew in a deep breath and switched on the flashlight. The beam shot down and he looked along it over his rifle barrel.

The square aperture in the floorboards formed a frame for the picture that flashed into his eyes. Black bodies, naked, glossy with wetness, weird patterns of tattoo marks, a face staring up at him, broad sloped forehead above startlingly white eyes and flat nose. The long gleaming blade of a panga. Clusters of humanity clinging to the wooden piles like ticks on the legs of a beast. Legs and arms and shiny trunks merged into a single organism, horrible as some slimy sea-creature.

Bruce fired into it. His rifle shuddered against his shoulder and the long orange spurts from its muzzle gave the picture a new flickering horror. The mass of bodies heaved, and struggled like a pack of rats trapped in a dry well. They dropped splashing into the river, swarmed up the timber piles, twisting and writhing as the bullets hit them, screaming, babbling over the sound of the rifle.

Bruce's weapon clicked empty and he groped for a new magazine. Ruffy and his gendarmes were hanging over the guard rails of the bridge, firing downwards, sweeping the piles below them with long bursts, the flashes lighting their faces and outlining their bodies against the sky.

'They're still coming!' roared Ruffy. 'Don't let them get over the side.'

Out of the hole at Bruce's feet thrust the head and naked upper body of a man. There was a panga in his hand; he slashed at Bruce's legs, his eyes glazed in the beam of the flashlight.

Bruce jumped back and the knife missed his knees by inches. The man wormed his way out of the hole towards Bruce. He was screaming shrilly, a high meaningless sound of fury.

Bruce lunged with the barrel of his empty rifle at the contorted black face. All his weight was behind that thrust and the muzzle went into the Baluba's eye. The foresight and four inches of the barrel disappeared into his head, stopping only when it hit bone. Colourless fluid from the burst eyeball gushed from round the protruding steel.

Tugging and twisting, Bruce tried to free the rifle, but the foresight had buried itself like the barb of a fish hook. The Baluba had dropped his panga and was clinging to the rifle barrel with both hands. He was wailing and rolling on his back upon the floorboards, his head jerking every time Bruce tried to pull the muzzle out of his head.

Beyond him the head and shoulders of another Baluba appeared through the aperture.

Bruce dropped his rifle and gathered up the fallen panga; he jumped over the writhing body of the first Baluba and lifted the heavy knife above his head with both hands.

The man was jammed in the hole, powerless to protect himself. He looked up at Bruce and his mouth fell open.

Two-handed, as though he were chopping wood, Bruce swung his whole body into the stroke. The shock jarred his shoulders and he felt blood spatter his legs. The untempered blade snapped off at the hilt and stayed imbedded in the Baluba's skull.

Panting heavily, Bruce straightened up and looked wildly about him. Baluba were swarming over the guard rail on one side of the bridge. The starlight glinted on their wet skins. One of his gendarmes was lying in a dark huddle, his head twisted back and his rifle still in his hands. Ruffy and the other gendarmes were still firing down over the far side.

'Ruffy!' shouted Bruce. 'Behind you! They're coming over!' and he dropped the handle of the panga and ran towards the body of the gendarme. He needed that rifle.

Before he could reach it the naked body of a Baluba rushed at him. Bruce ducked under the sweep of the panga and grappled with him. They fell locked together, the man's body slippery and sinuous against him, and the smell of him fetid as rancid butter.

Bruce found the pressure point below the elbow of his knife arm and dug in with his thumb. The Baluba yelled and his panga clattered on the floorboards. Bruce wrapped his arm round the man's neck while with his free hand he reached out for his bayonet.

The Baluba was clawing for Bruce's eyes with his fingers, his nails scored the side of Bruce's nose, but Bruce had his bayonet out now. He placed the point against the man's chest and pressed it in. He felt the steel scrape against the bone of a rib and the man redoubled his struggles at the sting of it. Bruce twisted the blade, working it in with his wrist, forcing the man's head backwards with his other arm.

The point of the bayonet scraped over the bone and found the gap between. Like taking a virgin, suddenly the resistance to its entrance was gone and it slid home full length. The Baluba's body jerked mechanically and the bayonet twitched in Bruce's fist.

Bruce did not even wait for the man to die. He pulled the blade out against the sucking reluctance of tissue that clung to it and scrambled to his feet in time to see Ruffy pick another Baluba from his feet and hurl him bodily over the guard rail.

Bruce snatched the rifle from the gendarme's dead hands and stepped to the guard rail. They were coming over the side, those below shouting and pushing at the ones above.

Like shooting a row of sparrows from a fence with a shotgun, thought Bruce grimly, and with one long burst he cleared the rail. Then he leaned out and sprayed the piles below the bridge. The rifle was empty. He reloaded with a magazine from his pocket. But it was all over. They were dropping back into the river, the piles below the bridge were clear of men, their heads bobbed away downstream.

Bruce lowered his rifle and looked about him. Three of his gendarmes were killing the man that Bruce had wounded, standing over him and grunting as they thrust down with their bayonets. The man was still wailing.

Bruce looked away.

One horn of the crescent moon showed above the trees; it had a gauzy halo about it.

Bruce lit a cigarette and behind him those gruesome noises ceased.

'Are you okay, boss?'

'Yes, I'm fine. How about you, Ruffy?'

'I got me a terrible thirst now. Hope nobody trod on my pack.'

About four minutes from the first shot to the last, Bruce guessed. That's the way of war, seven hours of waiting and boredom, then four minutes of frantic endeavour. Not only of war either, he thought. The whole of life is like that.

Then he felt the trembling in his thighs and the first spasm of nausea as the reaction started.

'What's happening?' A shout floated across from the laager. Bruce recognized Hendry's voice. 'Is everything all right?'

'We've beaten them off,' Bruce shouted back. 'Everything under control. You can go to sleep again.'

And now I have got to sit down quickly, he told himself.

Except for the tattoos upon his cheeks and forehead the dead Baluba's features were little different from those of the Bambala and Bakuba men who made up the bulk of Bruce's command.

Bruce played the flashlight over the corpse. The arms and legs were thin but stringy with muscle, and the belly bulged out from years of malnutrition. It was an ugly body, gnarled and crabbed. With distaste Bruce moved the light back to the features. The bone of the skull formed harsh angular planes beneath the skin, the nose was flattened and the thick lips had about them a repellent brutality. They were drawn back slightly to reveal the teeth which had been filed to sharp points like those of a shark.

'This is the last one, boss. I'll toss him overboard.' Ruffy spoke in the darkness beside Bruce.

'Good.'

Ruffy heaved and grunted, the corpse splashed below them and Ruffy wiped his hands on the guard rail, then came to sit beside Bruce.

'Goddam apes.' Ruffy's voice was full of the bitter tribal antagonism of Africa. 'When we get shot of these U.N. people there'll be a bit of sorting out to do. They've got a few things to learn, these bloody Baluba.'

And so it goes, thought Bruce, Jew and Gentile, Catholic and Protestant, black and white, Bambala and Baluba.

He checked the time, another two hours to dawn. His nervous reaction from physical violence had abated now; the hand that held the cigarette no longer trembled.

'They won't come again,' said Ruffy. 'You can get some sleep now if you want. I'll keep an eye open, boss.'

'No, thanks. I'll wait with you.' His nerves had not settled down enough for sleep.

'How's it for a beer?'

'Thanks.'

Bruce sipped the beer and stared out at the watch fires round the laager. They had burned down to puddles of red ash but Bruce knew that Ruffy was right. The Baluba would not attack again that night.

'So how do you like freedom?'

'How's that, boss?' The question puzzled Ruffy and he turned to Bruce questioningly.

'How do you like it now the Belgians have gone?'

'It's pretty good, I reckon.'

'And if Tshombe has to give in to the Central Government?'

'Those mad Arabs!' snarled Ruffy. 'All they want is our copper. They're going to have go get up early in the morning to take it. We're in the saddle here.'

The great jousting tournament of the African continent. I'm in the saddle, try to unhorse me! As in all matters of survival it was not a question of ethics and political doctrine (except to the spectators in Whitehall, Moscow, Washington and Peking). There were big days coming, thought Bruce. My own country, when she blows, is going to make Algiers look like an old ladies' sewing circle.

Chapter Twenty-Six

The sun was up, throwing long shadows out into the clearing, and Bruce stood beside the Ford and looked across the bridge at the corrugated iron shelter on the far bank.

He relaxed for a second and let his mind run unhurriedly over his preparations for the crossing. Was there something left undone, some disposition which could make it more secure?

Hendry and a dozen men were in the shelter across the bridge, ready to meet any attack on that side.

Shermaine would take the Ford across first. Then the lorries would follow her. They would cross empty to minimize the danger of the bridge collapsing, or being weakened for the passage of the tanker. After each lorry had crossed, Hendry would shuttle its load and passengers over in the shelter and deposit them under the safety of the canvas canopy.

The last lorry would go over fully loaded. That was regrettable but unavoidable.

Finally Bruce himself would drive the tanker across. Not as an act of heroism, although it was the most dangerous business of the morning, but because he would trust no one else to do it, not even Ruffy. The five hundred gallons of fuel it contained was their safe-conduct home. Bruce had taken the precaution of filling all the gasoline tanks in the convoy in case of accidents, but they would need replenishing before they reached Msapa Junction.

He looked down at Shermaine in the driver's seat of the Ford.

'Keep it in low gear, take her over slowly but steadily. Whatever else you do, don't stop.'

She nodded. She was composed and she smiled at him. Bruce felt a stirring of pride as he looked at her, so small and lovely, but today she was doing man's work. He went on. 'As soon as you are over, I will send one of the trucks after you. Hendry will put six of his men into it and then come back for the others.'

'Oui, Monsieur Bonaparte.'

'You'll pay for that tonight,' he threatened her. 'Off you go.'

Shermaine let out the clutch and the Ford bounced over rough ground to the road, accelerated smoothly out on to the bridge.

Bruce held his breath, but there was only a slight check and sway as it crossed the repaired section.

'Thank God for that.' Bruce let out his breath and watched while Shermaine drew up alongside the shelter.

'Allez,' Bruce shouted at the coloured engine driver who was ready at the wheel of the first truck. The man smiled his cheerful chubby-faced smile, waved, and the truck rolled forward.

Watching anxiously as it went on to the bridge, Bruce saw the new timbers give perceptibly beneath the weight of the truck, and he heard them creak loudly in protest.

'Not so good,' he muttered.

'No—' agreed Ruffy. 'Boss, why don't you let someone else take the tanker over?'

'We've been over that already,' Bruce answered him without turning his head. Across the river Hendry was transferring his men from the shelter to the back of the truck. Then the shelter started its tedious way back towards them.

Bruce fretted impatiently during the four hours that it took to get four trucks across. The long business was the shuttling back and forth of the corrugated iron shelter, at least ten minutes for each trip.

Finally there was only the fifth truck and the tanker left on the north bank. Bruce started the engine of the tanker and put her into auxiliary low, then he blew a single blast on the horn. The driver of the truck ahead of him waved an acknowledgement and pulled forward.

The truck reached the bridge and went out into the middle. It was fully loaded, twenty men aboard. It came to the repaired section and slowed down, almost stopping.

'Go on! Keep it going, damn you,' Bruce shouted in impotent anger. The fool of a driver was forgetting his orders. He crawled forward and the bridge gave alarmingly under the full weight, the high canopied roof rocked crazily, and even above the rumble of his own engine Bruce could hear the protesting groan of the bridge timbers.

'The fool, oh, the bloody fool,' whispered Bruce to himself. Suddenly he felt very much alone and unprotected here on the north bank with the bridge being mutilated by the incompetence of the truck driver. He started the tanker moving.

Ahead of him the other driver had panicked. He was racing his engine, the rear wheels spun viciously, blue smoke of scorched tyres, and one of the floorboards tore loose. Then the truck lurched forward and roared up the south bank.

Bruce hesitated, applying the brakes and bringing the tanker to a standstill on the threshold of the bridge.

He thought quickly. The sensible thing would be to repair the damage to the bridge before chancing it with the weight of the tanker. But that would mean another day's delay. None of them had eaten since the previous morning. Was he justified in gambling against even odds, for that's what they were? A fifty-fifty chance, heads you get across, tails you dump the tanker in the middle of the river.

Then unexpectedly the decision was made for him.

From across the river a Bren gun started firing. Bruce jumped in his seat and looked up. Then a dozen other guns joined in and the tracer flew past the tanker. They were firing across towards him, close on each side of him. Bruce struggled to drag from his uncomprehending brain an explanation of this new development. Suddenly everything was moving too swiftly. Everything was confusion and chaos.

Movement in the rear-view mirror of the tanker caught his eye. He stared at it blankly. Then he twisted quickly in his seat and looked back.

'Christ!' he swore with fright.

From the edge of the jungle on both sides of the clearing Baluba were swarming into the open. Hundreds of them running towards him, the animal-skin kilts swirling about their legs, feather head-dresses fluttering, sun bright on the long blades of their pangas. An arrow rang dully against the metal body of the tanker.

Bruce revved the engine, gripped the wheel hard with both hands and took the tanker out on to the bridge. Above the sound of the guns he could hear the shrill ululation, the excited squealing of two hundred Baluba. It sounded very close, and he snatched a quick look in the mirror. What he saw nearly made him lose his head and give the tanker full throttle. The nearest Baluba, screened from the guns on the south bank by the tanker's bulk, was only ten paces away. So close that Bruce could see the tattoo marks on his face and chest.

With an effort Bruce restrained his right foot from pressing down too hard, and instead he bore down on the repaired section of the bridge at a sedate twenty miles an hour. He tried to close his mind to the squealing behind him and the thunder of gunfire ahead of him.

The front wheels hit the new timbers, and above the other sounds he heard them groan loudly, and felt them sag under him.

The tanker rolled on and the rear wheels brought their weight to bear. The groan of wood became a cracking, rending sound. The tanker slowed as the bridge subsided, its wheels spun without purchase, it tilted sideways, no longer moving forward.

A sharp report, as one of the main trusses broke, and Bruce felt the tanker drop sharply at the rear; its nose pointed upwards and it started to slide back.

'Get out!' his brain shrieked at him. 'Get out, it's falling!' He reached for the door handle beside him, but at that moment the bridge collapsed completely. The tanker rolled off the edge.

Bruce was hurled across the cab with a force that stunned him, his legs wedged under the passenger seat and his arms tangled in the strap of his rifle. The tanker fell free and Bruce felt his stomach swoop up and press against his chest as though he rode a giant roller coaster.

The sickening drop lasted only an instant, and then the tanker hit the river. Immediately the sounds of gunfire and the screaming of Baluba were drowned out as the tanker disappeared below the surface. Through the windscreen Bruce saw now the cool cloudy green of water, as though he looked into the windows of an aquarium. With a gentle rocking motion the tanker sank down through the green water.

'Oh, my God, not this!' He spoke aloud as he struggled up from the floor of the cab. His ears were filled with the hiss and belch of escaping air bubbles; they rose in silver clouds past the windows.

The truck was still sinking, and Bruce felt the pain in his eardrums as the pressure built up inside the cab. He opened his mouth and swallowed convulsively, and his eardrums squeaked as the pressure equalized and the pain abated. Water was squirting in through the floor of the cab and jets of it spurted out of the instrument panel of the dashboard. The cab was flooding.

Bruce twisted the handle of the door beside him and hit it with his shoulder. It would not budge an inch. He flung all his weight against it, anchoring his feet on the dashboard and straining until he felt his eyeballs starting out of their sockets. It was jammed solid by the immense pressure of water on the outside.

'The windscreen,' he shouted aloud. 'Break the windscreen.' He groped for his rifle. The cab had flooded to his waist as he sat in the passenger's seat. He found the rifle and brought it dripping to his shoulder. He touched the muzzle to the windscreen and almost fired. But his good sense warned him.

Clearly he saw the danger of firing. The concussion in the confined cab would burst his eardrums, and the avalanche of broken glass that would be thrown into his face by the water pressure outside would certainly blind and maim him.

He lowered the rifle despondently. He felt his panic being slowly replaced by the cold certainty of defeat. He was trapped fifty feet below the surface of the river. There was no way out.

He thought of turning the rifle on himself, ending the inevitable, but he rejected the idea almost as soon as it had formed. Not that way, never that way!

He flogged his mind, driving it out of the cold lethargic clutch of certain death. There must be something. Think! Damn you, think!

The tanker was still rocking; it had not yet settled into the ooze of the river bottom. How long had he been under? About twenty seconds. Surely it should have hit the bottom long ago.

Unless! Bruce felt hope surge into new life within him. The tank! By God, that was it.

The great, almost empty tank behind him! The five-thousand-gallon tank which now contained only four hundred gallons of gasoline – it would have a displacement of nearly eighteen tons! It would float.

As if in confirmation of his hope, he felt his eardrums creak and pop. The pressure was falling! He was rising.

Bruce stared out at green water through the glass. The silver clouds of bubbles no longer streamed upwards; they seemed to hang outside the cab. The tanker had overcome the initial impetus that had driven it far below the surface, and now it was floating upwards at the same rate of ascent as its bubbles.

The dark green of deep water paled slowly to the colour of Chartreuse. And Bruce laughed. It was a gasping hysterical giggle and the sound of it shocked him. He cut it off abruptly.

The tanker bobbed out on to the surface, water streamed from the windscreen and through it Bruce caught a misty distorted glimpse of the south bank.

He twisted the door handle and this time the door burst open readily, water poured into the cab and Bruce floundered out against its rush.

With one quick glance he took in his position. The tanker had floated down twenty yards below the bridge, the guns on the south bank had fallen silent, and he could see no Baluba on the north bank. They must have disappeared back into the jungle.

Bruce plunged into the river and struck out for the south bank. Vaguely he heard the thin high shouts of encouragement from his gendarmes.

Within a dozen strokes he knew he was in difficulties. The drag of his boots and his sodden uniform was enormous. Treading water he tore off his steel helmet and let it sink. Then he tried to struggle out of his battle-jacket. It clung to his arms and chest and he disappeared under the surface four times before he finally got rid of it. He had breathed water into his lungs and his legs were tired and heavy.

The south bank was too far away. He would never make it. Coughing painfully he changed his objective and struck upstream against the current towards the bridge.

He felt himself settling lower in the water; he had to force his arms to lift and fall forward into each stroke.

Something plopped into the water close beside him. He paid no attention to it; suddenly a sense of disinterest had come over him, the first stage of drowning. He mistimed a breath and sucked in more water. The pain of it goaded him into a fresh burst of coughing. He hung in the water, gasping and hacking painfully.

Again something plopped close by, and this time he lifted his head. An arrow floated past him – then they began dropping steadily about him.

Baluba hidden in the thick bush above the beach were shooting at him; a gentle pattering rain of arrows splashed around his head. Bruce started swimming again, clawing his way frantically upstream. He swam until he could no longer lift his arms clear of the surface and the weight of his boots dragged his feet down.

Again he lifted his head. The bridge was close, not thirty feet away, but he knew that those thirty feet were as good as thirty miles. He could not make it.

The arrows that fell about him were no longer a source of terror. He thought of them only with mild irritation.

Why the hell can't they leave me alone? I don't want to play any more. I just want to relax. I'm so tired, so terribly tired.

He stopped moving and felt the water rise up coolly over his mouth and nose.

'Hold on, boss. I'm coming.' The shout penetrated through the grey fog of Bruce's drowning brain. He kicked and his head rose once more above the surface. He looked up at the bridge.

Stark naked, big belly swinging with each pace, thick legs flying, the great dangling bunch of his genitals bouncing merrily, black as a charging hippopotamus, Sergeant Major Ruffararo galloped out along the bridge.

He reached the fallen section and hauled himself up on to the guard rail. The arrows were falling around him, hissing down like angry insects. One glanced off his shoulder without penetrating and Ruffy shrugged at it, then launched himself up and out, falling in an ungainly heap of arms and legs to hit the water with a splash.

'Where the hell are you, boss?'

Bruce croaked a water-strangled reply and Ruffy came ploughing down towards him with clumsy overarm strokes.

He reached Bruce.

'Always playing around,' he grunted. 'Guess some guys never learn!' His fist closed on a handful of Bruce's hair.

Struggling unavailingly Bruce felt his head tucked firmly under Ruffy's arm and he was dragged through the water. Occasionally his face came out long enough to suck a breath but mostly he was under water. Consciousness receded and he felt himself going, going.

His head bumped against something hard but he was too weak to reach out his hand.

'Wake up, boss. You can have a sleep later.' Ruffy's voice bellowed in his ear. He opened his eyes and saw beside him the pile of the bridge.

'Come on. I can't carry you up here.'

Ruffy had worked round the side of the pile, shielding them from arrows, but the current was strong here, tugging at their bodies. Without the strength to prevent it Bruce's head rolled sideways and his face flopped forward into the water.

'Come on, wake up.' With a stinging slap Ruffy's open hand hit Bruce across the cheek. The shock roused him, he coughed and a mixture of water and vomit shot up his throat and out of his mouth and nose. Then he belched painfully and retched again.

'How's it feel now?' Ruffy demanded.

Bruce lifted a hand from the water and wiped his mouth. He felt much better.

'Okay? Can you make it?'

Bruce nodded.

'Let's go then.'

With Ruffy dragging and pushing him, he worked his way up the pile. Water poured from his clothing as his body emerged, his hair was plastered across his forehead and he could feel each breath gurgle in his lungs.

'Listen, boss. When we get to the top we'll be in the open again. There'll be more arrows – not time to sit around and chat. We're going over the rail fast and then run like hell, okay?'

Bruce nodded again. Above him were the floorboards of the bridge. With one hand he reached up and caught an upright of the guard rail, and he hung there without strength to pull himself the rest of the way.

'Hold it there,' grunted Ruffy and wriggled his shiny wet bulk up and over.

The arrows started falling again; one pegged into the wood six inches from Bruce's face and stood there quivering. Slowly Bruce's grip relaxed. I can't hold on, he thought, I'm going.

Then Ruffy's hand closed on his wrist, he felt himself dragged up, his legs dangled. He hung suspended by one arm and the water swirled smoothly past twenty feet below.

Slowly he was drawn upwards, his chest scraped over the guard rail, tearing his shirt, then he tumbled over it into an untidy heap on the bridge.

Vaguely he heard the guns firing on the south bank, the flit and thump of the arrows, and Ruffy's voice.

'Come on, boss. Get up.'

He felt himself being lifted and dragged along. With his legs boneless soft under him, he staggered beside Ruffy. Then there were no more arrows; the timbers of the bridge became solid earth under his feet. Voices and hands on him. He was being lifted, then lowered face down on to the wooden floor of a truck. The rhythmic pressure on his chest as someone started artificial respiration above him, the warm gush of water up his throat, and Shermaine's voice. He could not understand what she was saying, but just the sound of it was enough to make him realize he was safe. Darkly through the fog he became aware that her voice was the most important sound in his life.

He vomited again.

Hesitantly at first, and then swiftly, Bruce came back from the edge of oblivion.

'That's enough,' he mumbled and rolled out from under Sergeant Jacque who was administering the artificial respiration. The movement started a fresh paroxysm of coughing and he felt Shermaine's hands on his shoulders restraining him.

'Bruce, you must rest.'

'No.' He struggled into a sitting position. 'We've got to get out into the open,' he gasped.

'No hurry, boss. We've left all the Balubes on the other bank. There's a river between us.'

'How do you know?' Bruce challenged him.

'Well—'

'You don't!' Bruce told him flatly. 'There could easily be another few hundred on this side.' He coughed again painfully and then went on. 'We're leaving in five minutes, get them ready.'

'Okay.' Ruffy turned to leave.

'Ruffy!'

'Boss?' He turned back expectantly.

'Thank you.'

Ruffy grinned self-consciously. ' 'At's all right. I needed a wash anyway.'

'I'll buy you a drink when we get home.'

'I won't forget,' Ruffy warned him, and climbed down out of the truck. Bruce heard him shouting to his boys.

'I thought I'd lost you.' Shermaine's arm was still round his shoulders and Bruce looked at her for the first time.

'My sweet girl, you won't get rid of me that easily,' he assured her. He was feeling much better now.

'Bruce, I want to – I can't explain—' Unable to find the words she leaned forward instead and kissed him, full on the mouth.

When they drew apart, Sergeant Jacque and the two gendarmes with him were grinning delightedly.

'There is nothing wrong with you now, Captain.'

'No, there isn't,' Bruce agreed. 'Make your preparations for departure.'

From the passenger seat of the Ford Bruce took one last look at the bridge.

The repaired section hung like a broken drawbridge into the water. Beyond it on the far bank were scattered a few dead Baluba, like celluloid dolls in the sunlight. Far downstream the gasoline tanker had been washed by the current against the beach. It lay on its side, half-submerged in the shallows and the white Shell insignia showed clearly.

And the river flowed on, green and inscrutable, with the jungle pressing close along its banks.

'Let's get away from here,' said Bruce.

Shermaine started the engine and the convoy of trucks followed them along the track through the belt of thick river bush and into the open forest again.

Bruce looked at his watch. The inside of the glass was dewed with moisture and he lifted it to his ear.

'Damn thing has stopped. What's your time?'

'Twenty minutes to one.'

'Half the day wasted,' Bruce grumbled.

'Will we reach Msapa Junction before dark?'

'No, we won't. For two good reasons. Firstly, it's too far, and secondly, we haven't enough gas.'

'What are you going to do?' Her voice was unruffled, already she had complete faith in him. I wonder how long it will last, he mused cynically. At first you're a god. You have not a single human weakness. They set a standard for you, and the standard is perfection. Then the first time you fall short of it, their whole world blows up.

'We'll think of something,' he assured her.

'I'm sure you will,' she agreed complacently and Bruce grinned. The big joke, of course, was that when she said it he also believed it. Damned if being in love doesn't make you feel one hell of a man.

He changed to English so as to exclude the two gendarmes in the back seat from the conversation.

'You are the best thing that has happened to me in thirty years.'

'Oh, Bruce.' She turned her face towards him and the expression of trusting love in it and the intensity of his own emotion struck Bruce like a physical blow.

I will keep this thing alive, he vowed. I must nourish it with care and protect it from the dangers of selfishness and familiarity.

'Oh, Bruce, I do love you so terribly much. This morning when – when I thought I had lost you, when I saw the tanker go over into the river—' She swallowed and now her eyes were full of tears. 'It was as though the light had gone – it was so dark, so dark and cold without you.'

Absorbed with him so that she had forgotten about the road, Shermaine let the Ford veer and the offside wheels pumped into the rough verge.

'Hey, watch it!' Bruce cautioned her. 'Dearly as I love you also, I have to admit that you're a lousy driver. Let me take her.'

'Do you feel up to it?'

'Yes, pull into the side.'

Slowly, held to the speed of the lumbering vehicles behind them, they drove on through the afternoon. Twice they passed deserted Baluba villages beside the road, the grass huts disintegrating and the small cultivated lands about them thickly overgrown.

'My God, I'm hungry. I've got a headache from it and my belly feels as though it's full of warm water,' complained Bruce.

'Don't think you're the only one. This is the strictest diet I've ever been on, must have lost two kilos! But I always lose in the wrong place, never on my bottom.'

'Good,' Bruce said. 'I like it just the way it is, never shed an ounce there.' He looked over his shoulder at the two gendarmes. 'Are you hungry?' he asked in French.

'Mon Dieu!' exclaimed the fat one. 'I will not be able to sleep tonight, if I must lie on an empty stomach.'

'Perhaps it will not be necessary.' Bruce let his eyes wander off the road into the surrounding bush. The character of the country had changed in the last hundred miles. 'This looks like game country. I've noticed plenty of spoor on the road. Keep your eyes open.'

The trees were tall and widely spaced with grass growing beneath them. Their branches did not interlock so that the sky showed through. At intervals there were open glades filled with green swamp grass and thickets of bamboo and ivory palms.

'We've got another half hour of daylight. We might run into something before then.'

In the rear-view mirror he watched the lumbering column of transports for a moment. They must be almost out of gasoline by now, hardly enough for another half hour's driving. There were compensations however; at least they were in open country now and only eighty miles from Msapa Junction.

He glanced at the petrol gauge – half the tank. The Ranchero still had sufficient to get through even if the trucks were almost dry.

Of course! That was the answer. Find a good camp, leave the convoy, and go on in the Ford to find help. Without the trucks to slow him down he could get through to Msapa Junction in two hours. There was a telegraph in the station office, even if the junction was still deserted.

'We'll stop on the other side of this stream,' said Bruce and slowed the Ford, changed into second gear and let it idle down the steep bank.

The stream was shallow. The water hardly reached the hub-caps as they bumped across the rocky bottom. Bruce gunned the Ford up the far bank into the forest again.

'There!' shouted one of the gendarmes from the back seat and Bruce followed the direction of his arm.

Standing with humped shoulders, close beside the road, bunched together with mournfully drooping horns, heads held low beneath the massive bosses, bodies very big and black, were two old buffalo bulls.

Bruce hit the brakes, skidding the Ranchero to a stop, reaching for his rifle at the same instant. He twisted the door handle, hit the door with his shoulder and tumbled out on to his feet.

With a snort and a toss of their ungainly heads the buffalo started to run.

Bruce picked the leader and aimed for the neck in front of the plunging black shoulder. Leaning forward against the recoil of the rifle he fired and heard the bullet strike with a meaty thump. The bull slowed, breaking his run. The stubby forelegs settled and he slid forward on his nose, rolling as he fell, dust and legs kicking.

Turning smoothly without taking the butt from his shoulder, swinging with the run of the second bull, Bruce fired again, and again the thump of bullet striking.

The buffalo stumbled, giving in the legs, then he steadied and galloped on like a grotesque rocking horse, patches of baldness grey on his flanks, big-bellied, running heavily.

Bruce shifted the bead of the foresight on to his shoulder and fired twice in quick succession aiming low for the heart, hitting each time, the bull so close he could see the bullet wounds appear on the dark skin.

The gallop broke into a trot, with head swinging low, mouth open, legs beginning to fold. Aiming carefully for the head Bruce fired again. The bull bellowed – a sad lonely sound – and collapsed into the grass.

The lorries had stopped in a line behind the Ford, and now from each of them swarmed black men. Jabbering happily, racing each other, they streamed past Bruce to where the buffalo had fallen in the grass beside the road.

'Nice shooting, boss,' applauded Ruffy. 'I'm going to have me a piece of tripe the size of a blanket.'

'Let's make camp first.' Bruce's ears were still singing with gunfire. 'Get the lorries into a ring.'

'I'll see to it.'

Bruce walked up to the nearest buffalo and watched for a while as a dozen men strained to roll it on to its back and begin butchering it. There were clusters of grape-blue ticks in the folds of skin between the legs and body.

A good head, he noted mechanically, forty inches at least.

'Plenty of meat, Captain. Tonight we eat thick!' grinned one of his gendarmes as he bent over the huge body to begin flensing.

'Plenty,' agreed Bruce and turned back to the Ranchero. In the heat of the kill it was a good feeling: the rifle's kick and your stomach screwed up with excitement. But afterwards you felt a little bit dirtied; sad and guilty as you do after lying with a woman you do not love.

He climbed into the car and Shermaine sat away from him, withdrawn.

'They were so big and ugly – beautiful,' she said softly.

'We needed the meat. I didn't kill them for fun.' But he thought with a little shame, I have killed many others for fun.

'Yes,' she agreed. 'We needed the meat.'

He turned the car off the road and signalled to the truck drivers to pull in behind him.

Chapter Twenty-Seven

Later it was all right again. The meat-rich smoke from a dozen cooking fires drifted across the camp. The dark treetops silhouetted against a sky full of stars, the friendly glow of the fires, and laughter, men's voices raised, someone singing, the night noises of the bush – insects and frogs in the nearby stream – a plate piled high with grilled fillets and slabs of liver, a bottle of beer from Ruffy's hoard, the air at last cooler, a small breeze to keep the mosquitoes away, and Shermaine sitting beside him on the blankets.

Ruffy drifted across to them, in one hand a stick loaded with meat from which the juice dripped and in the other hand a bottle held by the throat.

'How's it for another beer, boss?'

'Enough.' Bruce held up his hand. 'I'm full to the back teeth.'

'You're getting old, that's for sure. Me and the boys going to finish them buffalo or burst trying.' He squatted on his great haunches and his tone changed. 'The trucks are flat, boss. Reckon there's not a bucketful of gas in the lot of them.'

'I want you to drain all the tanks, Ruffy, and pour it into the Ford.'

Ruffy nodded and bit a hunk of meat off the end of the stick.

'Then first thing tomorrow morning you and I will go on to Msapa in the Ranchero and leave everyone else here. Lieutenant Hendry will be in charge.'

'You talking about me?' Wally came from one of the fires.

'Yes, I'm going to leave you in charge here while Ruffy and I go on to Msapa Junction to fetch help.' Bruce did not look at Hendry and he had difficulty keeping the loathing out of his voice. 'Ruffy, fetch the map will you?'

They spread it on the earth and huddled round it. Ruffy held the flashlight.

'I'd say we are about here.' Bruce touched the tiny black vein of the road. 'About seventy, eighty miles to Msapa.' He ran his finger along it. 'It will take us about five hours there and back. However, if the telegraph isn't working we might have to go on until we meet a patrol or find some other way of getting a message back to Elisabethville.'

Almost parallel to the road and only two inches from it on the large-scale map ran the thick red line that marked the Northern Rhodesian border. Wally Hendry's slitty eyes narrowed even further as he looked at it.

'Why not leave Ruffy here, and I'll go with you.' Hendry looked up at Bruce.

'I want Ruffy with me to translate if we meet any Africans along the way.' Also, thought Bruce, I don't want to be left on the side of the road with a bullet in my head while you drive on to Elisabethville.

'Suits me,' grunted Hendry. He dropped his eyes to the map. About forty miles to the border. A hard day's walk.

Bruce changed to French and spoke swiftly. 'Ruffy, hide the diamonds behind the dashboard of your truck. That way we are certain they will send a rescue party, even if we have to go to Elisabethville.'

'Talk English, Bucko,' growled Hendry, but Ruffy nodded and answered, also in French.

'I will leave Sergeant Jacque to guard them.'

'NO!' said Bruce. 'Tell no one.'

'Cut it out!' rasped Hendry. 'Anything you say I want to hear.'

'We'll leave at dawn tomorrow,' Bruce reverted to English.

'May I go with you?' Shermaine spoke for the first time.

'I don't see why not.' Bruce smiled quickly at her, but Ruffy coughed awkwardly.

'Reckon that's not such a good idea, boss.'

'Why?' Bruce turned on him with his temper starting to rise.

'Well, boss,' Ruffy hesitated, and then went on, 'you, me and the lady all shoving off towards Elisabethville might not look so good to the boys. They might get ideas, think we're not coming back or something.'

Bruce was silent, considering it.

'That's right,' Hendry cut in. 'You might just take it into your head to keep going. Let her stay, sort of guarantee for the rest of us.'

'I don't mind, Bruce. I didn't think about it that way. I'll stay.'

'She'll have forty good boys looking after her, she'll be all right,' Ruffy assured Bruce.

'All right then, that's settled. It won't be for long, Shermaine.'

'I'll go and see about draining the trucks.' Ruffy stood up. 'See you in the morning, boss.'

'I'm going to get some more of that meat.' Wally picked up the map carelessly.
'Try and get some sleep tonight, Curry. Not too much grumble and grunt.'

In his exasperation, Bruce did not notice that Hendry had taken the map.

Chapter Twenty-Eight

It rained in the early hours before the dawn and Bruce lay in the back of the
Ranchero and listened to it drum on the metal roof. It was a lulling sound and
a good feeling to lie warmly listening to the rain with the woman you love in
your arms.

He felt her waking against him, the change in her breathing and the first
slow movements of her body.

There were buffalo steaks for breakfast, but no coffee. They ate swiftly and
then Bruce called across to Ruffy.

'Okay, Ruffy?'

'Let's go, boss.' They climbed into the Ford and Ruffy filled most of the seat
beside Bruce. His helmet perched on the back of his head, rifle sticking out
through the space where the windscreen should have been, and two large feet
planted securely on top of the case of beer on the floor.

Bruce twisted the key and the engine fired. He warmed it at a fast idle and
turned to Hendry who leaned against the roof of the Ford and peered through
the window.

'We'll be back this afternoon. Don't let anybody wander away from camp.'

'Okay.' Hendry breathed his morning breath full into Bruce's face.

'Keep them busy, otherwise they'll get bored and start fighting.'

Before he answered Hendry let his eyes search the interior of the Ford
carefully and then he stood back.

'Okay,' he said again. 'On your way!'

Bruce looked beyond him to where Shermaine sat on the tailboard of a truck
and smiled at her.

'Bon voyage!' she called and Bruce let out the clutch. They bumped out on
to the road amid a chorus of cheerful farewells from the gendarmes round the
cooking fires and Bruce settled down to drive. In the rear-view mirror he watched
the camp disappear round the curve in the road. There were puddles of rain
water in the road, but above them the clouds had broken up and scattered across
the sky.

'How's it for a beer, boss?'

'Instead of coffee?' asked Bruce.

'Nothing like it for the bowels,' grunted Ruffy and reached down to open the
case.

Wally Hendry lifted his helmet and scratched his scalp. His short red hair
felt stiff and wiry with dried sweat and there was a spot above his right ear that
itched. He fingered it tenderly.

The Ranchero disappeared round a bend in the road, the trees screening it
abruptly, and the hum of its motor faded.

Okay, so they haven't taken the diamonds with them. I had a bloody good look around. I guessed they'd leave them. The girl knows where they are like as not. Perhaps – no, she'd squeal like a stuck pig if I asked.

Hendry looked sideways at Shermaine; she was staring after the Ranchero.

Silly bitch! Getting all broody now that Curry's giving her the rod. Funny how these educated Johnnies like their women to have small tits – nice piece of arse though. Wouldn't mind a bit of that myself. Jesus, that would really get to Mr. High Class Bloody Curry, me giving his pretty the business. Not a chance though. These niggers think he's a God or something. They'd tear me to pieces if I touched her. Forget about it! Let's get the diamonds and take off for the border.

Hendry settled his helmet back on to his head and strolled casually across to the truck that Ruffy had been driving the day before.

Got a map, compass, coupla spare clips of ammo – now all we need is the glass.

He climbed into the cab and opened the cubbyhole.

Bet a pound to a pinch of dung that they've hidden them somewhere in this truck. They're not worried – think they've got me tied up here. Never occurred to them that old Uncle Wally might up and walk away. Thought I'd just sit here and wait for them to come back and fetch me – take me in and hand me over to a bunch of nigger police aching to get their hands on a white man.

Well, I got news for you, Mr. Fancy-talking Curry!

He rummaged in the cubbyhole and then slammed it shut.

Okay, they're not there. Let's try under the seats. The border is not guarded, might take me three or four days to get through to Fort Rosebery, but when I do I'll have me a pocket full of diamonds and there's a direct air service out to Ndola and the rest of the world. Then we start living!

There was nothing under the seats except a greasy dust-coated jack and wheel spanner. Hendry turned his attention to the floorboards.

Pity I'll have to leave that bastard Curry. I had plans for him. There's a guy who really gets to me. So goddam cocksure of himself. One of them. Makes you feel you're shit – fancy talk, pretty face, soft hands. Christ, I hate him.

Viciously he tore the rubber mats off the floor and the dust made him cough.

Been to university, makes him think he's something special. The bastard. I should have fixed him long ago – that night at the road bridge I nearly gave it to him in the dark. Nobody would have known, just a mistake. I shoulda done it then. I shoulda done it at Port Reprieve when he ran out across the road to the office block. Big bloody hero. Big lover. Bet he had everything he ever wanted, bet his Daddy gave him all the money he could use. And he looks at you like that, like you crawled out of rotting meat.

Hendry straightened up and gripped the steering wheel, his jaws chewing with the strength of his hatred. He stared out of the windscreen.

Shermaine Cartier walked past the front of the truck. She had a towel and a pink plastic toilet bag in her hand; the pistol swung against her leg as she moved.

Sergeant Jacque stood up from the cooking fire and moved to intercept her. They talked, arguing, then Shermaine touched the pistol at her side and laughed. A worried frown creased Jacque's black face and he shook his head dubiously. Shermaine laughed again, turned from him and set off down the road towards the stream. Her hair, caught carelessly at her neck with a ribbon, hung down her back on to the rose-coloured shirt she wore and the heavy canvas holster emphasized the unconsciously provocative swing of her hips. She went out of sight down the steep bank of the stream.

Wally Hendry chuckled and then licked his lips with the quick-darting tip of his tongue.

'This is going to make it perfect,' he whispered. 'They couldn't have done things to suit me better if they'd spent a week working it out.'

Eagerly he turned back to his search for the diamonds. Leaning forward he thrust his hand up behind the dashboard of the truck and it brushed against the bunch of canvas bags that hung from the mass of concealed wires.

'Come to Uncle Wally.' He jerked them loose and, holding them in his lap, began checking their contents. The third bag he opened, contained the gem stones.

'Lovely, lovely grub,' he whispered at the dull glint and sparkle in the depths of the bag. Then he closed the draw string, stuffed the bag into the pocket of his battle-jacket and buttoned the flap. He dropped the bags of industrial diamonds on to the floor and kicked them under the seat, picked up his rifle and stepped down out of the truck.

Three or four gendarmes looked up curiously at him as he passed the cooking fires. Hendry rubbed his stomach and pulled a face.

'Too much meat last night!'

The gendarme who understood English laughed and translated into French. They all laughed and one of them called something in a dialect that Hendry did not understand. They watched him walk away among the trees.

As soon as he was out of sight of the camp Hendry started to run, circling back towards the stream.

'This is going to be a pleasure!' He laughed aloud.

Chapter Twenty-Nine

Fifty yards below the drift where the road crossed the stream Shermaine found a shallow pool. There were reeds with fluffy heads around it and a small beach of white river sand, black boulders, polished round and glossy smooth, the water almost blood warm and so clear that she could see a shoal of fingerlings nibbling at the green algae that coated the boulders beneath the surface.

She stood barefooted in the sand and looked around carefully, but the reeds screened her, and she had asked Jacque not to let any of his men come down to the river while she was there.

She undressed, dropped her clothes across one of the black boulders and with a cake of soap in her hand waded out into the pool and lowered herself until she sat with the water up to her neck and the sand pleasantly rough under her naked behind.

She washed her hair first and then lay stretched out with the water moving gently over her, soft as the caress of silk. Growing bold the tiny fish darted in and nibbled at her skin, tickling, so that she gasped and splashed at them.

At last she ducked her head under the surface and, with the water streaming out of her hair into her eyes, she groped her way back to the bank.

As she stooped, still half blinded, for her towel Wally Hendry's hand closed over her mouth and his other arm circled her waist from behind.

'One squeak out of you and I'll wring your bloody neck.' He spoke hoarsely into her ear. She could smell his breath, warm and sour in her face. 'Just pretend I'm old Bruce – then both of us will enjoy it.' And he chuckled.

Sliding quickly over her hip his hand moved downwards and the shock of it galvanized her into frantic struggles. Holding her easily Hendry kept on chuckling.

She opened her mouth suddenly and one of his fingers went in between her teeth. She bit with all her strength and felt the skin break and tasted blood in her mouth.

'You bitch!' Hendry jerked his hand away and she opened her mouth to scream, but the hand swung back, clenched, into the side of her face, knocking her head across. The scream never reached her lips for he hit her again and she felt herself falling.

Stunned by the blows, lying in the sand, she could not believe it was happening, until she felt his weight upon her and his knee forced cruelly between hers.

Then she started to struggle again, trying to twist away from his mouth and the smell of his breath.

'No, no, no.' She repeated it over and over, her eyes shut tightly so she did not have to see that face above her, and her head rolling from side to side in the sand. He was so strong, so immensely powerful.

'No,' she said, and then, 'Ooah!' at the pain, the tearing stinging pain within, and the thrusting heaviness above.

And through the pounding, grunting, thrusting nightmare she could smell him and feel the sweat drip from him and splash into her upturned unprotected face.

It lasted forever, and then suddenly the weight was gone and she opened her eyes.

He stood over her, fumbling with his clothing, and there was a dullness in his expression. He wiped his mouth with the back of his hand and she saw the fingers were trembling. His voice when he spoke was tired and disinterested.

'I've had better.'

Swiftly Shermaine rolled over and reached for the pistol that lay on top of her clothes. Hendry stepped forward with all his weight on her wrist and she felt the bones bend under his boot and she moaned. But through pain she whispered. 'You pig, you filthy pig,' and he hit her again, flat-handed across the face, knocking her on to her back once more.

He picked up the pistol and opened it, spilling the cartridges into the sand, then he unclipped the lanyard and threw the pistol far out into the reed bed.

'Tell Curry I say he can have my share of you,' he said and walked quickly away among the reeds.

The white sand coated her damp body like icing sugar. She sat up slowly holding her wrist, the side of her face inflamed and starting to swell where he had hit her.

She started to cry, shaking silently, and the tears squeezed out between her eyelids and matted her long dark lashes.

Chapter Thirty

Ruffy held up the brown bottle and inspected it ruefully.

'Seems like one mouthful and it's empty.' He threw the bottle out of the side window. It hit a tree and burst with a small pop.

'We can always find our way back by following the empties,' smiled Bruce, once more marvelling at the man's capacity. But there was plenty of storage space. He watched Ruffy's stomach spread on to his lap as he reached down to the beer crate.

'How we doing, boss?'

Bruce glanced at the milometer.

'We've come eighty-seven miles,' and Ruffy nodded.

'Not bad going. Be there pretty soon now.'

They were silent. The wind blew in on to them through the open front. The grass that grew between the tracks brushed the bottom of the chassis with a continuous rushing sound.

'Boss—' Ruffy spoke at last.

'Yes?'

'Lieutenant Hendry – those diamonds. You reckon we did a good thing leaving him there?'

'He's stranded in the middle of the bush. Even if he did find them they wouldn't do him much good.'

'Suppose that's right.' Ruffy lifted the beer bottle to his lips and when he lowered it he went on. 'Mind you, that's one guy you can never be sure of.' He tapped his head with a finger as thick and as black as a blood-sausage. 'Something wrong with him – he's one of the maddest Arabs I've found in a long time of looking.'

Bruce grunted grimly.

'You want to be careful there, boss,' observed Ruffy. 'Any time now he's going to try for you. I've seen it coming. He's working himself up to it. He's a mad Arab.'

'I'll watch him,' said Bruce.

'Yeah, you do that.'

Again they were silent in the steady swish of the wind and the drone of the motor.

'There's the railway.' Ruffy pointed to the blue-gravelled embankment through the trees.

'Nearly there,' said Bruce.

They came out into another open glade and beyond it the water tank at Msapa Junction stuck up above the forest.

'Here we are,' said Ruffy and drained the bottle in his hand.

'Just say a prayer that the telegraph lines are still up and that there's an operator on the Elisabethville end.'

Bruce slowed the Ford past the row of cottages. They were exactly as he remembered them, deserted and forlorn. The corners of his mouth were compressed into a hard angle as he looked at the two small mounds of earth beneath the casia flora trees. Ruffy looked at them also but neither of them spoke.

Bruce stopped the Ford outside the station building and they climbed out stiffly and walked together on to the verandah. The wooden flooring echoed dully under their boots as they made for the door of the office.

Bruce pushed the door open and looked in. The walls were painted a depressing utility green, loose paper was scattered on the floor, the drawers of the single desk hung open, and a thin grey skin of dust coated everything.

'There she is,' said Ruffy and pointed to the brass and varnished wood complexity of the telegraph on a table against the far wall.

'Looks all right,' said Bruce. 'As long as the lines haven't been cut.'

As if to reassure him, the telegraph began to clatter like a typewriter.

'Thank God for that,' sighed Bruce.

They walked across to the table.

'You know how to work this thing?' asked Ruffy.

'Sort of,' Bruce answered and set his rifle against the wall. He was relieved to see a Morse table stuck with adhesive tape to the wall above the apparatus. It was a long time since he had memorized it as a boy scout.

He laid his hand on the transmission key and studied the table. The call sign for Elisabethville was 'EE'.

He tapped it out clumsily and then waited. Almost immediately the set clattered back at him, much too fast to be intelligible and the roll of paper in the repeater was exhausted. Bruce took off his helmet and laboriously spelled out, 'Transmit slower.'

It was a long business with requests for repetition. 'Not understood' was made nearly every second signal, but finally Bruce got the operator to understand that he had an urgent message for Colonel Franklyn of President Tshombe's staff.

'Wait,' came back the laconic signal.

And they waited. They waited an hour, then two.

'That mad bastard's forgotten about us,' grumbled Ruffy and went to the Ford to fetch the beer crate. Bruce fidgeted restlessly on the unpadded chair beside the telegraph table. He reconsidered anxiously all his previous arguments for leaving Wally Hendry in charge of the camp, but once again decided that it was safe. He couldn't do much harm. Unless, unless, Shermaine! No, it was impossible. Not with forty loyal gendarmes to protect her.

He started to think about Shermaine and the future. There was a year's mercenary captain's pay accumulated in the Crédit Banque Suisse at Zurich. He made the conversion from francs to pounds – about two and a half thousand. Two years' operating capital, so they could have a holiday before he started working again. They could take a chalet up in the mountains, there should be good snow this time of the year.

Bruce grinned. Snow that crunched like sugar, and a twelve-inch-thick eiderdown on the bed at night.

Life had purpose and direction again.

'What you're laughing at, boss?' asked Ruffy.

'I was thinking about a bed.'

'Yeah? That's a good thing to think about. You start there, you're born there, you spend most of your life in it, you have plenty of fun in it, and if you're lucky you die there. How's it for a beer?'

The telegraph came to life at Bruce's elbow. He turned to it quickly.

'Curry – Franklyn,' it clattered. Bruce could imagine the wiry, red-faced little man at the other end. Ex-major in the third brigade of the Legion. A prime mover in the O.A.S., with a sizeable price still on his head from the De Gaulle assassination attempt.

'Franklyn – Curry,' Bruce tapped back. 'Train unserviceable. Motorized transport stranded without fuel. Port Reprieve road. Map reference approx—' He read the numbers off the sheet on which he had noted them.

There was a long pause, then:

'Is U.M.C. property in your hands?' The question was delicately phrased.

'Affirmative,' Bruce assured him.

'Await air-drop at your position soonest. Out.'

'Message understood. Out.' Bruce straightened from the telegraph and sighed with relief.

'That's that, Ruffy. They'll drop gas to us from one of the Dakotas. Probably tomorrow morning.' He looked at his wrist watch. 'Twenty to one, let's get back.'

Bruce hummed softly, watching the double tracks ahead of him, guiding the Ford with a light touch on the wheel.

He was contented. It was all over. Tomorrow the fuel would drop from the Dakota under those yellow parachutes. (He must lay out the smudge signals this evening.) And ten hours later they would be back in Elisabethville.

A few words with Carl Engelbrecht would fix seats for Shermaine and himself on one of the outward-bound Daks. Then Switzerland, and the chalet with icicles hanging from the eaves. A long rest while he decided where to start again. Louisiana was under Roman-Dutch Law, or was it Code Napoléon? He might even have to rewrite his bar examinations, but the prospect pleased rather than dismayed him. It was fun again.

'Never seen you so happy,' grunted Ruffy.

'Never had so much cause,' Bruce agreed.

'She's a swell lady. Young still – you can teach her.'

Bruce felt his hackles rise, and then he thought better of it and laughed.

'You going to sign her up, boss?'

'I might.'

Ruffy nodded wisely. 'Man should have plenty wives – I got three. Need a couple more.'

'One I could only just handle.'

'One's difficult. Two's easier. Three, you can relax. Four, they're so busy with each other they don't give you no trouble at all.'

'I might try it.'

'Yeah, you do that.'

And ahead of them through the trees they saw the ring of trucks.

'We're home,' grunted Ruffy, then he stirred uncomfortably in his seat. 'Something going on.'

Men stood in small groups. There was something in their attitude: strain, apprehension. Two men ran up the road to meet them. Bruce could see their mouths working, but could not hear the words.

Dread, heavy and cold, pushed down on the pit of Bruce's gut.

Gabbled, incoherent, Sergeant Jacque was trying to tell him something as he ran beside the Ford.

'Tenente Hendry – the river – the madam – gone.' French words like driftwood in the torrent of dialect.

'Your girl,' translated Ruffy. 'Hendry's done her.'

'Dead?' The question dropped from Bruce's mouth.

'No. He's hurt her. He's – you know!'

'Where's she?'

'They've got her in the back of the truck.'

Bruce climbed heavily out of the car. Now they were silent, grouped together, not looking at him, faces impassive, waiting.

Bruce walked slowly to the truck. He felt cold and numb. His legs moved automatically beneath him. He drew back the canvas and pulled himself up into the interior. It was an effort to move forward, to focus his eyes in the gloom.

Wrapped in a blanket she lay small and still.

'Shermaine.' It stuck in his throat.

'Shermaine,' he said again and knelt beside her. A great livid swelling distorted the side of her face. She did not turn her head to him, but lay staring up at the canvas roof.

He touched her face and the skin was cold, cold as the dread that gripped his stomach. The coldness of it shocked him so he jerked his hand away.

'Shermaine.' This time it was a sob. The eyes, her big haunted eyes, turned unseeing towards him and he felt the lift of escape from the certainty of her death.

'Oh, God,' he cried and took her to him, holding the unresisting frailty of her to his chest. He could feel the slow even thump of her heart beneath his hand. He drew back the blanket and there was no blood.

'Darling, are you hurt? Tell me, are you hurt?' She did not answer. She lay quietly in his arms, not seeing him.

'Shock,' he whispered. 'It's only shock,' and he opened her clothing. With tenderness he examined the smoothly pale body; the skin was clammy and damp, but there was no damage.

He wrapped her again and laid her gently back on to the floor.

He stood and the thing within him changed shape. Cold still, but now burning cold as dry ice.

Ruffy and Jacque were waiting for him beside the tailboard.

'Where is he?' asked Bruce softly.

'He is gone.'

'Where?'

'That way.' Jacque pointed towards the south-east. 'I followed the spoor a short distance.'

Bruce walked to the Ford and picked up his rifle from the floor. He opened the cubbyhole and took two spare clips of ammunition from it.

Ruffy followed him. 'He's got the diamonds, boss.'

'Yes,' said Bruce and checked the load of his rifle. The diamonds were of no importance.

'Are you going after him, boss?'

Bruce did not answer. Instead he looked up at the sky. The sun was half way towards the horizon and there were clouds thickly massed around it.

'Ruffy, stay with her,' he said softly. 'Keep her warm.'

Ruffy nodded.

'Who is the best tracker we've got?'

'Jacque. Worked for a safari outfit before the war as a tracker boy.'

Bruce turned to Jacque. The thing was still icy cold inside him, with tentacles that spread out to every extremity of his body and his mind.

'When did this happen?'

'About an hour after you left,' answered Jacque.

Eight hours start. It was a long lead.

'Take the spoor,' said Bruce softly.

Chapter Thirty-One

The earth was soft from the night's rain and the spoor deep trodden, the heels had bitten in under Hendry's weight, so they followed fast.

Watching Sergeant Jacque work, Bruce felt his anxiety abating, for although the footprints were so easy to follow in these early stages that it was no test of his ability, yet from the way he moved swiftly along – half crouched and wholly absorbed, occasionally glancing ahead to pick up the run of the spoor, stooping now and then to touch the earth and determine its texture – Bruce could tell that this man knew his business.

Through the open forest with tufted grass below, holding steadily south by east, Hendry led them straight towards the Rhodesian border. And after the first two hours Bruce knew they had not gained upon him. Hendry was still eight hours ahead, and at the pace he was setting eight hours' start was something like thirty miles in distance.

Bruce looked over his shoulder at the sun where it lay wedged between two vast piles of cumulus nimbus. There in the sky were the two elements which could defeat him.

Time. There were perhaps two more hours of daylight. With the onset of night they would be forced to halt.

Rain. The clouds were swollen and dark blue round the edges. As Bruce watched, the lightning lit them internally, and at a count of ten the thunder grumbled suddenly. If it rained again before morning there would be no spoor to follow.

'We must move faster,' said Bruce.

Sergeant Jacque straightened up and looked at Bruce as though he were a stranger. He had forgotten his existence.

'The earth hardens.' Jacque pointed at the spoor and Bruce saw that in the last half hour the soil had become gritty and compacted. Hendry's heels no longer broke the crust. 'It is unwise to run on such a lean trail.'

Again Bruce looked back at the menace of gathering clouds.

'We must take the chance,' he decided.

'As you wish,' grunted Jacque, and transferred his rifle to his other shoulder, hitched up his belt and settled the steel helmet more firmly on his head.

'Allez!'

They trotted on through the forest towards the south-east. Within a mile Bruce's body had settled into the automatic rhythm of his run, leaving his mind free.

He thought about Wally Hendry, saw again the little eyes and round them the puffy folded skin, and the mouth below, thin and merciless, the obscene ginger stubble of beard. He could almost smell him. His nostrils flared at the memory of the rank red-head's body odour. Unclean, he thought, unclean mind and unclean body.

His hatred of Wally Hendry was a tangible thing. He could feel it sitting heavily at the base of his throat, tingling in his finger-tips and giving strength to his legs.

And yet there was something else. Suddenly Bruce grinned: a wolfish baring of his teeth. That tingling in his fingertips was not all hatred, a little of it was excitement.

What a complex thing is a man, he thought. He can never hold one emotion – always there are others to confuse it. Here I am hunting the thing that I most loathe and hate, and I am enjoying it. Completely unrelated to the hatred is the thrill of hunting the most dangerous and cunning game of all, man.

I have always enjoyed the chase, he thought. It has been bred into me, for my blood is that of the men who hunted and fought with Africa as the prize.

The hunting of this man will give me pleasure. If ever a man deserved to die, it is Wally Hendry. I am the plaintiff, the judge and the executioner.

Sergeant Jacque stopped so suddenly that Bruce ran into him and they nearly fell.

'What is it?' panted Bruce, coming back to reality.

'Look!'

The earth ahead of them was churned and broken.

'Zebra,' groaned Bruce, recognizing the round uncloven hoof prints. 'God damn it to hell – of all the filthy luck!'

'A big herd,' Jacque agreed. 'Spread out. Feeding.'

As far ahead as they could see through the forest the herd had wiped out Hendry's tracks.

'We'll have to cast forward.' Bruce's voice was agonized by his impatience. He turned to the nearest tree and hacked at it with his bayonet, blazing it to mark the end of the trail, swearing softly, venting his disappointment on the trunk.

'Only another hour to sunset,' he whispered. 'Please let us pick him up again before dark.'

Sergeant Jacque was already moving forward, following the approximate line of Hendry's travel, trying vainly to recognize a single footprint through the havoc created there by the passage of thousands of hooves. Bruce hurried to join him and then moved out on his flank. They zigzagged slowly ahead, almost meeting on the inward leg of each tack and then separating again to a distance of a hundred yards.

There it was! Bruce dropped to his knees to make sure. Just the outline of the toecap showing from under the spoor of an old zebra stallion. Bruce whistled, a windy sound through his dry lips, and Jacque came quickly. One quick look, then:

'Yes, he is holding more to the right now.' He raised his eyes and squinted ahead, marking a tree which was directly in line with the run of the spoor. They went forward.

'There's the herd.' Bruce pointed at the flicker of a grey body through the trees.

'They've got our wind.'

A zebra snorted and then there was a rumbling, a low blurred drumming of hooves as the herd ran. Through the trees Bruce caught glimpses of the animals on the near side of the herd. Too far off to show the stripes, looking like fat grey ponies as they galloped, ears up, black-maned heads nodding. Then they were gone and the sound of their flight swindled.

'At least they haven't run along the spoor,' muttered Bruce, and then bitterly: 'Damn them, the stupid little donkeys! They've cost us an hour. A whole priceless hour.'

Desperately searching, wild with haste, they worked back and forth. The sun was below the trees; already the air was cooling in the short African dusk. Another fifteen minutes and it would be dark.

Then abruptly the forest ended and they came out on the edge of a vlei. Open as wheatland, pastured with green waist-high grass, hemmed in by the forest, it stretched ahead of them for nearly two miles. Dotted along it were clumps of ivory palms with each graceful stem ending in an untidy cluster of leaves. Troops of guinea-fowls were scratching and chirruping along the edge of the clearing, and near the far end a herd of buffalo formed a dark mass as they grazed beneath a canopy of white egrets.

In the forest beyond the clearing, rising perhaps three hundred feet out of it, stood a kopje of tumbled granite. The great slabs of rock with their sheer sides and square tops looked like a ruined castle. The low sun struck it and gave the rock an orange warmth.

But Bruce had no time to admire the scene; his eyes were on the earth, searching for the prints of Hendry's jungle boots.

Out on his left Sergeant Jacque whistled sharply and Bruce felt the leap of excitement in his chest. He ran across to the crouching gendarme.

'It has come away.' Jacque pointed at the spoor that was strung ahead of them like beads on a string, skirting the edge of the vlei, each depression filled with shadow and standing out clearly on the sandy grey earth.

'Too late,' groaned Bruce. 'Damn those bloody zebra.' The light was fading so swiftly it seemed as though it were a stage effect.

'Follow it.' Bruce's voice was sharp with helpless frustration. 'Follow it as long as you can.'

It was not a quarter of a mile farther on that Jacque rose out of his crouch and only the white of his teeth showed in the darkness as he spoke.

'We will lose it again if we go on.'

'All right.' Bruce unslung his rifle with weary resignation. He knew that Wally Hendry was at least forty miles ahead of them; more if he kept travelling after dark. The spoor was cold. If this had been an ordinary hunt he would long ago have broken off the chase.

He looked up at the sky. In the north the stars were fat and yellow, but above them and to the south it was black with cloud.

'Don't let it rain,' he whispered. 'Please God, don't let it rain.'

The night was long. Bruce slept once for perhaps two hours and then the strength of his hatred woke him. He lay flat upon his back and stared up at the sky. It was all dark with clouds; only occasionally they opened and let the stars shine briefly through.

'It must not rain. It must not rain.' He repeated it like a prayer, staring up at the dark sky, concentrating upon it as though by the force of his mind he could control the elements.

There were lions hunting in the forest. He heard the male roaring, moving up from the south, and once his two lionesses answered him. They killed a little before dawn and Bruce lay on the hard earth and listened to their jubilation over the kill. Then there was silence as they began to feed.

That I might have success as well, he thought. I do not often ask for favours, Lord, but grant me this one. I ask it not only for myself but for Shermaine and the others.

In his mind he saw again the two children lying where Hendry had shot them. The smear of mingled blood and chocolate across the boy's cheek.

He deserves to die, prayed Bruce, so please don't let it rain.

As long as the night had been, that quickly came the dawn. A grey dawn, gloomy with low cloud.

'Will it go?' Bruce asked for the twentieth time, and this time Jacque looked up from where he knelt beside the spoor.

'We can try now.'

They moved off slowly with Jacque leading, doubled over to peer short-sightedly at the earth and Bruce close behind him, bedevilled by his impatience and anxiety, lifting his head every dozen paces to the dirty grey roof of cloud.

The light strengthened and the circle of their vision opened from six feet to as many yards, to a hundred, so they could make out the tops of the ivory palms, shaggy against the grey cloud.

Jacque broke into a trot and ahead of them was the end of the clearing and the beginning of the forest. Two hundred yards beyond rose the massive pile of the kopje, in the early light looking more than ever like a castle, turreted and sheer. There was something formidable in its outline. It seemed to brood above them and Bruce looked away from it uneasily.

Cold and with enough weight behind it to sting, the first raindrop splashed against Bruce's cheek.

'Oh, no!' he protested, and stopped. Jacque straightened up from the spoor and he too looked at the sky.

'It is finished. In five minutes there will be nothing to follow.'

Another drop hit Bruce's upturned face and he blinked back the tears of anger and frustration that pricked the rims of his eyelids.

Faster now, tapping on his helmet, plopping on to his shoulders and face, the rain fell.

'Quickly,' cried Bruce. 'Follow as long as you can.'

Jacque opened his mouth to speak, but before a word came out he was flung backwards, punched over as though by an invisible fist, his helmet flying from his head as he fell and his rifle clattering on the earth.

Simultaneously Bruce felt the bullet pass him, disrupting the air, so the wind of it flattened his shirt against his chest, cracking viciously in his ears, leaving him dazedly looking down at Sergeant Jacque's body.

It lay with arms thrown wide, the jaw and the side of the head below the ear torn away; white bone and blood bubbling over it. The trunk twitched convulsively and the hands fluttered like trapped birds. Then flat-sounding through the rain he heard the report of the rifle.

The kopje, screamed Bruce's brain, *he's lying in the kopje*!

And Bruce moved, twisting sideways, starting to run.

Chapter Thirty-Two

Wally Hendry lay on his stomach on the flat top of the turret. His body was stiff and chilled from the cold of the night and the rock was harsh under him, but the discomfort hardly penetrated the fringe of his mind. He had built a low parapet with loose flakes of granite, and he had screened the front of it with the thick bushy stems of broom bush.

His rifle was propped on the parapet in front of him and at his elbow were the spare ammunition clips.

He had lain in this ambush for a long time now – since early the preceding afternoon. Now it was dawn and the darkness was drawing back; in a few minutes he would be able to see the whole of the clearing below him.

I coulda been across the river already, he thought, *coulda been fifty miles away.* He did not attempt to analyse the impulse that had made him lie here unmoving for almost twenty hours.

Man, I knew old Curry would have to come. I knew he would only bring one nigger tracker with him. These educated Johnnies got their own rules – man to man stuff, and he chuckled as he remembered the two minute figures that he had seen come out of the forest in the fading light of the previous evening.

The bastard spent the night down there in the clearing. Saw him light a match and have hisself a smoke in the night – well, I hope he enjoyed it, his last.

Wally peered anxiously out into the gradually gathering dawn.

They'll be moving now, coming up the clearing. Must get them before they reach the trees again. Below him the clearing showed as a paleness, a leprous blotch, on the dark forest.

The bastard! Without preliminaries Hendry's hatred returned to him. *This time he don't get to make no fancy speeches. This time he don't get no chance to be hoity-toity.*

The light was stronger now. He could see the clumps of ivory palms against the pale brown grass of the clearing.

'Ha!' Hendry exclaimed.

There they were, like two little ants, dark specks moving up the middle of the clearing. The tip of Hendry's tongue slipped out between his lips and he flattened down behind his rifle.

Man, I've waited for this. Six months now I've thought about this. And when it's finished I'll go down and take his ears. He slipped the safety catch; it made a satisfying mechanical click.

Nigger's leading, that's Curry behind him. Have to wait till they turn, don't want the nigger to get it first. Curry first, then the nigger.

He picked them up in his sights, breathing quicker now, the thrill of it so intense that he had to swallow and it caught in his throat like dry bread.

A raindrop hit the back of his neck. It startled him. He looked up quickly at the sky and saw it coming.

'Goddam it,' he groaned, and looked back at the clearing. Curry and the nigger were standing together, a single dark blob in the half-light. There was no chance of separating them. The rain fell faster, and suddenly Hendry was overwhelmed by the old familiar feeling of inferiority; of knowing that everything, even the elements, conspired against him; the knowledge that he could never win, not even this once.

They, God and the rest of the world.

The ones who had given him a drunk for a father.

A squalid cottage for a home and a mother with cancer of the throat.

The ones who had sent him to reform school, had fired him from two dozen jobs, had pushed him, laughed at him, gaoled him twice – They, all of them (and Bruce Curry who was their figurehead), they were going to win again. Not even this once, not even ever.

'Goddam it,' he cursed in hopeless, wordless anger against them all.

'Goddam it, goddam it to hell,' and he fired at the dark blob in his sights.

Chapter Thirty-Three

As he ran Bruce looked across a hundred yards of open ground to the edge of the forest.

He felt the wind of the next bullet as it cracked past him.

If he uses rapid fire he'll get me even at three hundred yards.

And Bruce jinked his run like a jack-rabbit. The blood roaring in his ears, fear driving his feet.

Then all around him the air burst asunder, buffeting him so he staggered; the vicious whip-whip-whip of bullets filled his head.

I can't make it.

Seventy yards to the shelter of the trees. Seventy yards of open meadow land, and above him the commanding mass of the kopje.

The next burst is for me – it must come, now!

And he flung himself to one side so violently that he nearly fell. Again the air was ripping to tatters close beside him.

I can't last! He must get me!

In his path was an ant-heap, a low pile of clay, a pimple on the open expanse of earth. Bruce dived for it, hitting the ground so hard that the wind was forced from his lungs out through his open mouth.

The next burst of gunfire kicked lumps of clay from the top of the ant-heap, showering Bruce's back.

He lay with his face pressed into the earth, wheezing with the agony of empty lungs, flattening his body behind the tiny heap of clay.

Will it cover me? Is there enough of it?

And the next hail of bullets thumped into the ant-heap, throwing fountains of earth, but leaving Bruce untouched.

'I'm safe.' The realization came with a surge that washed away his fear.

But I'm helpless, answered his hatred. *Pinned to the earth for as long as Hendry wants to keep me here.*

The rain fell on his back. Soaking through his jacket, coldly caressing the nape of his neck and dribbling down over his jaws.

He rolled his head sideways, not daring to lift it an inch, and the rain beat on to the side of his face.

The rain! Falling faster. Thickening. Hanging from the clouds like the skirts of a woman's dress.

Curtains of rain. Greying out the edge of the forest, leaving no solid shapes in the mist of falling liquid mother-of-pearl.

Still gasping but with the pain slowly receding, Bruce lifted his head.

The kopje was a vague blue-green shape ahead of him, then it was gone, swallowed up by the eddying columns of rain.

Bruce pushed himself up on to his knees and the pain in his chest made him dizzy.

Now! he thought. *Now, before it thins*, and he lumbered clumsily to his feet.

For a moment he stood clutching his chest, sucking for breath in the haze of water-filled air, and then he staggered towards the edge of the forest.

His feet steadied under him, his breathing eased, and he was into the trees.

They closed round him protectively. He leaned against the rough bark of one of them and wiped the rain from his face with the palm of his hand. The strength came back to him and with it his hatred and his excitement.

He unslung the rifle from his shoulder and stood away from the tree with his feet planted wide apart.

'Now, my friend,' he whispered, 'we fight on equal terms.' He pumped a round into the chamber of the FN and moved towards the kopje, stepping daintily, the weight of the rifle in his hands, his mind suddenly sharp and clear, vision enhanced, feeling his strength and the absence of fear like a song within him, a battle hymn.

He made out the loom of the kopje through the dripping rain-heavy trees and he circled out to the right. There is plenty of time, he thought. I can afford to case the joint thoroughly. He completed his circuit of the rock pile.

The kopje, he found, was the shape of a galleon sinking by the head. At one end the high double castles of the poop, from which the main deck canted steeply forward as though the prow were already under water. This slope was scattered with boulders and densely covered with dwarf scrub, an interwoven mass of shoulder-high branches and leaves.

Bruce squatted on his haunches with the rifle in his lap and looked up the ramp at the twin turrets of the kopje. The rain had slackened to a drizzle.

Hendry was on top. Bruce knew he would go to the highest point. Strange how height makes a man feel invulnerable, makes him think he is a god.

And since he had fired upon them he must be in the turret nearest the vlei, which was slightly the higher of the two, its summit crowned by a patch of stunted broom bush.

So now I know exactly where he is and I will wait half an hour. He may become impatient and move; if he does I will get a shot at him from here.

Bruce narrowed his eyes, judging the distance.

'About two hundred yards.'

He adjusted the rear-sight of the FN and then checked the load, felt in the side pocket of his jacket to make sure the two extra clips of ammunition were handy, and settled back comfortably to wait.

'Curry, you sonofabitch, where are you?' Hendry's shout floated down through the drizzling rain and Bruce stiffened. *I was right – he's on top of the left-hand turret.*

'Come on, Bucko. I've been waiting for you since yesterday afternoon.'

Bruce lifted the rifle and sighted experimentally at a dark patch on the wall of the rock. It would be difficult shooting in the rain, the rifle slippery with wet, the fine drizzle clinging to his eyebrows and dewing the sights of the rifle with little beads of moisture.

'Hey, Curry, how's your little French piece of pussy? Man, she's hot, that thing, isn't she?'

Bruce's hands tightened on the rifle.

'Did she tell you how I gave her the old business? Did she tell you how she loved it? You should have heard her panting like a steam engine. I'm telling you, Curry, she just couldn't get enough!'

Bruce felt himself start to tremble. He clenched his jaws, biting down until his teeth ached.

Steady, Bruce my boy, that's what he wants you to do.

The trees dripped steadily in the silence and a gust of wind stirred the scrub on the slope of the kopje. Bruce waited, straining his eyes for the first hint of movement on the left-hand turret.

'You yellow or something, Curry? You scared to come on up here? Is that what it is?'

Bruce shifted his position slightly, ready for a snap shot.

'Okay, Bucko. I can wait, I've got all day. I'll just sit here thinking about how I mucked your little bit of French. I'm telling you it was something to remember. Up and down, in and out, man it was something!'

Bruce came carefully up on to his feet behind the trunk of the tree and once more studied the layout of the kopje.

If I can move up the slope, keeping well over to the side, until I reach the right-hand turret, there's a ledge there that will take me to the top. I'll be twenty or thirty feet from him, and at that range it will all be over in a few seconds.

He drew a deep breath and left the shelter of the tree.

Wally Hendry spotted the movement in the forest below him; it was a flash of brown quickly gone, too fast to get a bead on it.

He wiped the rain off his face and wriggled a foot closer to the edge.

'Come on, Curry. Let's stop buggering about,' he shouted, and cuddled the butt of his rifle into his shoulder. The tip of his tongue kept darting out and touching his lips.

At the foot of the slope he saw a branch move slightly, stirring when there was no wind. He grinned and snuggled his hips down on to the rock. *Here he comes*, he gloated, *he's crawling up, under the scrub.*

'I know you're sitting down there. Okay, Curry, I can wait also.'

Half-way up the slope the top leaves of another bush swayed gently, parting and closing.

'Yes!' whispered Wally, 'Yes!' and he clicked off the safety catch of the rifle. His tongue came out and moved slowly from one corner of his mouth to the other.

I've got him, for sure! There – he'll have to cross that piece of open ground. A couple a yards, that's all. But it'll be enough.

He moved again, wriggling a few inches to one side, settling his aim into the gap between two large grey boulders; he pushed the rate-of-fire selector on to rapid and his forefinger rested lightly on the trigger.

'Hey, Curry, I'm getting bored. If you are not going to come up, how about singing to me or cracking a few jokes?'

Bruce Curry crouched behind a large grey boulder. In front of him were three yards of open ground and then the shelter of another rock. He was almost at the top of the slope and Hendry had not spotted him. Across the patch of open ground was good cover to the foot of the right-hand turret.

It would take him two seconds to cross and the chances were that Hendry would be watching the forest at the foot of the slope.

He gathered himself like a sprinter on the starting blocks.

'Go!' he whispered and dived into the opening, and into a hell storm of bullets. One struck his rifle, tearing it out of his hand with such force that his arm was paralysed to the shoulder, another stung his chest, and then he was across. He lay behind the far boulder, gasping with the shock, and listened to Hendry's voice roaring triumphantly.

'Fooled you, you stupid bastard! Been watching you all the way up from the bottom.'

Bruce held his left arm against his stomach; the use of it was returning as the numbness subsided, but with it came the ache. The top joint of his thumb had caught in the trigger guard and been torn off; now the blood welled out of the stump thickly and slowly, dark blood the colour of apple jelly. With his right hand he groped for his handkerchief.

'Hey, Curry, your rifle's lying there in the open. You might need it in a few minutes. Why don't you go out and fetch it?'

Bruce bound the handerkerchief tightly round the stump of his thumb and the bleeding slowed. Then he looked at the rifle where it lay ten feet away. The foresight had been knocked off, and the same bullet that had amputated his thumb had smashed into the breech, buckled the loading handle and the slide. He knew that it was damaged beyond repair.

'Think I'll have me a little target practice,' shouted Hendry from above, and again there was a burst of automatic fire. Bruce's rifle disappeared in a cloud of dust and flying rock fragments and when it cleared the woodwork of the rifle was splintered and torn and there was further damage to the action.

Well, that's that, thought Bruce, *rifle's wrecked, Shermaine has the pistol, and I have only one good hand. This is going to be interesting.*

He unbuttoned the front of his jacket and examined the welt that the bullet had raised across his chest. It looked like a rope burn, painful and red, but not serious. He rebuttoned the jacket.

'Okay, Bruce Baby, the time for games is over. I'm coming down to get you.' Hendry's voice was harsh and loud, filled with confidence.

Bruce rallied under the goading of it. He looked round quickly. *Which way to go? Climb high so he must come up to get at you. Take the right-hand turret, work round the side of it and wait for him on the top.*

In haste now, spurred by the dread of being the hunted, he scrambled to his feet and dodged away up the slope, keeping his head down, using the thick screen of rock and vegetation.

He reached the wall of the right-hand turret and followed it round, found the spiral ledge that he had seen from below and went on to it, up along it like a fly on a wall, completely exposed, keeping his back to the cliff of granite, shuffling sideways up the eighteen-inch ledge with the drop below him growing deeper with each step.

Now he was three hundred feet above the forest and could look out across the dark green land to another row of kopjes on the horizon. The rain had ceased but the cloud was unbroken, covering the sky.

The ledge widened, became a platform and Bruce hurried across it round the far shoulder and came to a dead end. The ledge had petered out and there was only the drop below. He had trapped himself on the side of the turret – the summit was unattainable. If Hendry descended to the first floor and circled the kopje he would find Bruce completely at his mercy, for there was no cover on the narrow ledge. Hendry could have a little more target practice.

Bruce leaned against the rock and struggled to control his breathing. His throat was clogged with the thick saliva of exhaustion and fear. He felt tired and helpless, his thumb throbbed painfully and he lifted it to examine it once more. Despite the tourniquet it was bleeding slowly, a wine-red drop at a time.

Bleeding! Bruce swallowed the thick gluey stuff in his throat and looked back along the way he had come. On the grey rock the bright red splashes stood out clearly. He had laid a blood spoor for Hendry to follow.

All right then, perhaps it is best this way. At least I may be able to come to grips with him. If I wait behind this shoulder until he starts to cross the platform, there's a three hundred foot drop on one side, I may be able to rush him and throw him off.

Bruce leaned against the shoulder of granite, hidden from the platform, and tuned his ears to catch the first sound of Hendry's approach.

The clouds parted in the eastern sector of the sky and the sun shone through, slanting across the side of the kopje.

It will be better to die in the sun, thought Bruce, *a sacrifice to the Sun god thrown from the roof of the temple*, and he grinned without mirth, waiting with patience and with pain.

The minutes fell like drops into the pool of time, slowly measuring out the ration of life that had been allotted to him. The pulse in his ears counted also, and this breath that he drew and held and gently exhaled – how many more would there be?

I should pray, he thought, *but after this morning when I prayed that it should not rain, and the rains came and saved me, I will not presume again to tell the Old Man how to run things. Perhaps he knows best after all.*

Thy will be done, he thought instead, and suddenly his nerves jerked tight as a line hit by a marlin. The sound he had heard was that of cloth brushing against rough rock.

He held his breath and listened, but all he could discern was the pulse in his ears and the wind in the trees of the forest below. The wind was a lonely sound.

Thy will be done, he repeated without breathing, and heard Hendry breathe close behind the shoulder of rock.

He stood away from the wall and waited. Then he saw Hendry's shadow thrown by the early morning sun along the ledge. A great distorted shadow on the grey rock.

Thy will be done. And he went round the shoulder fast, his good hand held like a blade and the weight of his body behind it.

Hendry was three feet away, the rifle at high port across his chest, standing close in against the cliff, the cup-shaped steel helmet pulled low over the slitty eyes and little beads of sweat clinging in the red-gold stubble of his beard. He tried to drop the muzzle of the rifle but Bruce was too close.

Bruce lunged with stiff fingers at his throat and he felt the crackle and give of cartilage. Then his weight carried him on and Hendry sprawled backwards on to the stone platform with Bruce on top of him.

The rifle slithered across the rock and dropped over the edge, and they lay chest to chest with legs locked together in a horrible parody of the love act. But in *this* act we do not procreate, we destroy!

Hendry's face was purple and swollen above his damaged throat, his mouth open as he struggled for air, and his breath smelt old and sour in Bruce's face.

With a twist towards the thumb Bruce freed his right wrist from Hendry's grip and, lifting it like an axe, brought it down across the bridge of Hendry's nose. Twin jets of blood spouted from the nostrils and gushed into his open mouth.

With a wet strangling sound in his throat Hendry's body arched violently upwards and Bruce was thrown back against the side of the cliff with such force that for a second he lay there.

Wally was on his knees, facing Bruce, his eyes glazed and sightless, and the strangling rattling sound spraying from his throat in a pink cloud of blood. With both hands he was fumbling his pistol out of its canvas holster.

Bruce drew his knees up on to his chest, then straightened his legs in a mule kick. His feet landed together in the centre of Hendry's stomach, throwing him backwards off the platform. Hendry made that strangled bellow all the way to the bottom, but at the end it was cut off abruptly, and afterwards there was only the sound of the wind in the forest below.

For a long time, drained of strength and the power to think, Bruce sat on the ledge with his back against the rock.

Above him the clouds had rolled aside and half the sky was blue. He looked out across the land and the forest was lush and clean from the rain. *And I am still alive*. The realization warmed Bruce's mind as comfortably as the early sun was warming his body. He wanted to shout it out across the forest. *I am still alive!*

At last he stood up, crossed to the edge of the cliff and looked down at the tiny crumpled figure on the rocks below. Then he turned away and dragged his beaten body down the side of the turret.

It took him twenty minutes to find Wally Hendry in the chaos of broken rock and scrub below the turret. He lay on his side with his legs drawn up as though he slept. Bruce knelt beside him and drew his pistol from the olive-green canvas holster; then he unbuttoned the flap of Hendry's bulging breast pocket and took out the white canvas bag.

He stood up, opened the mouth of the bag and stirred the diamonds with his forefinger. Satisfied, he jerked the draw string closed and dropped them into his own pocket.

In death he is even more repulsive than he was alive, thought Bruce without regret as he looked down at the corpse.

The flies were crawling into the bloody nostrils and clustering round the eyes. Then he spoke aloud.

'So Mike Haig was right and I was wrong – you can destroy it.'

Without looking back he walked away. The tiredness left him.

Chapter Thirty-Four

Carl Engelbrecht came through the doorway from the cockpit into the main cabin of the Dakota.

'Are you two happy?' he asked above the deep drone of the engines, and then grinning with his big brown face, 'I can see you are!'

Bruce grinned back at him and tightened his arm around Shermaine's shoulders.

'Go away! Can't you see we're busy?'

'You've got lots of cheek for a hitch-hiker – bloody good mind to make you get out and walk,' he grumbled as he sat down beside them on the bench that ran the full length of the fuselage. 'I've brought you some coffee and sandwiches.'

'Good. Good. I'm starving.' Shermaine sat up and reached for the thermos flask and the greaseproof paper packet. The bruise on her cheek had faded to a shadow with yellow edges – it was almost ten days old. With his mouth full of chicken sandwich Bruce kicked one of the wooden cases that were roped securely to the floor of the aircraft.

'What have you got in these, Carl?'

'Dunno,' said Carl and poured coffee into the three plastic mugs. 'In this game you don't ask questions. You fly out, take your money, and let it go.' He drained his mug and stood up. 'Well, I'll leave you two alone now. We'll be in Nairobi in a couple of hours, so you can sleep or something!' He winked. 'You'll have to stay aboard while we refuel. But we'll be airborne again in an hour or so, and the day after tomorrow, God and the weather permitting, we'll set you down in Zurich.'

'Thanks, old cock.'

'Think nothing of it – all in the day's work.'

He bent forward and disappeared into the cockpit, closing the door behind him.

Shermaine turned back to Bruce, studied him for a moment and then laughed. 'You look so different – now you look like a lawyer!'

Self-consciously Bruce tightened the knot of his Old Michael-house tie.

'I must admit it feels strange to wear a suit and tie again.' He looked down at the well-cut blue suit – the only one he had left – and then up again at Shermaine.

'And in a dress I hardly recognize you either.' She was wearing a lime-green cotton frock, cool and crisp looking, white high-heel shoes and just a little make-up to cover the bruise. A damn fine woman, Bruce decided with pleasure.

'How does your thumb feel?' she asked, and Bruce held up the stump with its neat little turban of adhesive tape.

'I had almost forgotten about it.'

Suddenly Shermaine's expression changed, and she pointed excitedly out of the perspex window behind Bruce's shoulder.

'Look, there's the sea!' It lay far below them, shaded from blue to pale green in the shallows, with a rind of white beach and the wave formation moving across it like ripples on a pond.

'That's Lake Tanganyika.' Bruce laughed. 'We've left the Congo behind.'

'Forever?' she asked.

'Forever!' he assured her.

The aircraft banked slightly, throwing them closer together, as Carl picked out his landmarks and altered course towards the north-east.

Four thousand feet below them the dark insect that was their shadow flitted and hopped across the surface of the water.

THE SUNBIRD

The Sunbird

For my wife, Danielle

Part One

It cut across the darkened projection room and exploded silently against the screen – and I did not recognize it. I had waited fifteen years for it, and when it came I did not recognize it. The image was swirled and vague, and it made no sense to me for I had expected a photograph of some small object; a skull perhaps, or pottery, or an artefact, a piece of gold work, beads – certainly not this surrealistic pattern of grey and white and black.

Louren's voice, tight with excitement, gave me the clue I needed. 'Taken at thirty-six thou. at six forty-seven on the fourth of Sept,' that was eight days ago, 'exposed in a 35 mm. Leica.'

An aerial photograph then. My eyes and brain adjusted, and almost instantly I felt the first tickle of my own excitement begin as Louren went on in the same crisp tone.

'I've got a charter company running an aerial survey over all my concession areas. The idea is to pick the strike and run of geographical formations. This photograph is only one of a couple of hundred thousand of the area – the navigator did not even know what he was photographing. However, the people in analysis spotted it, and passed it on to me.'

His face turned towards me, pale and solemn in the glare of the projector. 'You can see it, can't you, Ben? Just off centre. Top right quarter.'

I opened my mouth to reply, but my voice caught in my throat and I had to turn the sound I made into a cough. With surprise I found I was trembling, and my guts seethed with an amalgam of hope and dread.

'It's classic! Acropolis, double enclosure and the "phallic towers".' He was exaggerating, they were faint outlines, indistinct and in places disappearing, but the general shape and configuration was right.

'North,' I blurted. 'Where is north?'

'Top of picture – she's right, Ben. Facing north. Could the towers be sun-orientated?'

I did not speak again. The reaction was coming swiftly now. Nothing in my life had been this easy, therefore this was suspect and I searched for the flaws.

'Stratification,' I said. 'Probably limestone in contact with the country granite. Throwing surface patterns.'

'Oh bull!' Louren cut in, the excitement still bubbling in his voice. He jumped up and strode to the screen, picked up an ebony pointer from the lectern and used it to spot the cell-like stippling around the outline of what he was pleased to presume was the main enclosure. 'You tell me where you've ever seen geological patterns like that.'

I didn't want to accept it. I didn't want to make myself vulnerable again with hope.

'Perhaps,' I said.

'Damn you.' He laughed now, and the sound was good for he did not often laugh these days. 'I should have known you'd fight it. You are without doubt the most miserable bloody pessimist in Africa.'

'It could be anything, Lo,' I protested. 'A trick of light, of shape and shade. Even conceding that it is man-made – it could be recent gardens or agriculture—'

'A hundred miles from the nearest surface water? Forget it, Ben! You know as well as I do that this is the—'

'Don't say it,' I almost shouted, and was out of the padded leather chair, across the projection room and had hold of his arm before I realized I had moved.

'Don't say it,' I repeated. 'It's – it's bad luck.' I always stutter when I am excited, but it is the least of my physical disabilities and I have long ago ceased worrying about it.

Louren laughed again, but with the trace of uneasiness he shows whenever I move quickly or unleash the strength of my arms. He stooped over me now, and eased my fingers that were sunk into the flesh of his forearm.

'Sorry – did I hurt you?' I released the grip.

'No.' But he massaged his arm as he moved to the control panel and doused the projector, then turned the wall switch and we stood blinking at each other in the light.

'My little Yiddish leprechaun,' he smiled. 'You cannot fool me. You are wetting yourself.'

I looked up at him, ashamed of my outburst now, but still excited.

'Where is it, Lo? Where did you find it?'

'I want you to admit it first. I want you to go out on a limb for once in your life. I want you to say it – before I'll tell you another thing,' he teased.

'All right.' I looked away and picked my words. 'It looks, at first glance, quite interesting.'

And he threw back the great golden head and bellowed with bull laughter.

'You're going to have to do a lot better than that. Let's try again.'

His laughter I cannot resist, and my own followed immediately. I was aware of its birdlike quality against his.

'It looks to me,' I wheezed, 'as though you may have found – it.'

'You beauty!' he shouted. 'You little beauty.'

It was years since I had seen him like this. The solemn banker's mask stripped away, the cares of the Sturvesant financial empire forgotten in this moment of promise and achievement.

'Now tell me,' I pleaded. 'Where did you find it?'

'Come,' he said, serious again, and we went to the long table against the wall. There was a chart spread and pinned on the green baize. It was a high table, and I scrambled quickly on to a chair and leaned across it. Now I was almost on equal terms with Louren who stood beside me. We pored over the chart.

'Aeronautical Series A. Southern Africa. Chart 5. Botswana and Western Rhodesia.'

I searched it quickly, looking for some indication – a cross, or pencil mark perhaps.

'Where?' I said. 'Where?'

'You know that I've got twenty-five thousand square miles of mineral concession down here south of Maun—'

'Come *on*, Lo. Don't try and sell me shares in Sturvesant Minerals. Where the hell is it?'

'We've put a landing-strip in here that will take the Lear jet. Just finished it.'

'It can't be that far south of the gold series.'

'It isn't,' Louren reassured me. 'Throttle back, you'll rupture something.' He was enjoying himself tormenting me.

His finger moved across the chart, and stopped suddenly – my heart seemed to stop with it. It was looking better and better. The latitude was perfect, all the clues I had so painstakingly gathered over the years pointed to this general area.

'Here,' he said. 'Two hundred and twelve miles south-east of Maun, fifty-six miles from the south-western beacon of the Wankie game reserve, tucked below a curve of low hills, lost in a wilderness of rock and dry land scrub.'

'When can we leave?' I asked.

'Wow!' Louren shook his head. 'You do believe it. You really do!'

'Someone else could stumble on it.'

'It's been lying there for a thousand years – another week won't—'

'Another week!' I cried in anguish.

'Ben, I can't get away before then. I've got the Annual General Meeting of Anglo-Sturvesant on Friday, and on Saturday I have business in Zürich – but I'll cut it short, especially for you.'

'Cut it altogether,' I begged. 'Send one of your bright young men.'

'When somebody lends you twenty-five million, it's only polite to go fetch the cheque yourself, not send the office boy.'

'Christ, Lo. It's only money – this is really important.'

For a moment Louren stared at me, the pale blue eyes bemused and reflective.

'Twenty-five million is only money?' He shook his head slowly and then wonderingly as though he had heard a new truth spoken. 'I suppose you are right.' He smiled, gently now, the smile of affection for a well-loved friend. 'Sorry, Ben. Tuesday. We'll fly at dawn, I promise you. We'll recce from the air. Then land at Maun. Peter Larkin – you know him?'

'Yes, very well.' Peter ran a big safari business out of Maun. Twice I'd used him on my Kalahari expeditions.

'Good. I've been on to him already. He will service the expedition. We will go in light and fast – one Land-Rover and a pair of three-ton Unimogs. I can only spare five days – and that's a squeeze – but I'll get a charter helicopter to fetch me out, and I'll leave you to scratch around—' As he talked Louren led me out of the projection room into the long gallery.

Sunlight spilled in through the high windows, giving good light to the paintings and sculptures that decorated the gallery. Here works of the leading South African artists mingled easily with those of the great internationals living and dead. Louren Sturvesant, and his ancestors before him, had spent money wisely. Even now in the urgency of the moment, my eyes were tugged aside by the soft fleshy glow of a Renoir nude.

Louren paced easily over the sound-deadening pile of Oriental carpets, and I matched him stride for stride. My legs are as long as his and as powerful.

'If you turn up what we are both hoping for, then you can go in full-scale. A permanent camp, airstrip, assistants of your choice, a full crew, and any equipment you call for.'

'Please God, let it happen,' I said softly and at the head of the staircase we paused. Louren and I grinned at each other like conspirators.

'You know what it could cost?' I asked. 'We might be digging for five or six years.'

'I hope so,' he agreed.

'It could run into – a couple of hundred thousand.'

'It's only money, like the man said.' And again that great bull laugh started me off. We went down the staircase roaring and tittering, each in his own way. Elated and hyper-tense, we faced each other in the hall.

'I'll be back at seven-thirty Monday evening. Can you meet me at the airport, Alitalia flight 310 from Zürich? In the meantime you get your end arranged.'

'I'll need a copy of that photograph.'

'I've already had an enlargement delivered by hand to the Institute. You have got a week to gloat over it.' He glanced at the gold Piaget on his wrist. 'Damn. I'm late.'

He turned to the doorway at the moment that Hilary Sturvesant came through it from the patio. She wore a short white tennis dress, and her legs were long and achingly beautiful. A tall girl with gold-brown hair hanging shiny and soft to her shoulders.

'Darling, you aren't going?'

'I'm sorry, Hil. I meant to tell you I wouldn't be staying for lunch, but Ben will need somebody to hold him down.'

'You've shown him?' She turned and came to me, stooped to kiss me on the lips easily and naturally, with not the least sign of revulsion, and then she stepped back and smiled full into my eyes. Every time she does that she makes me her slave for another hundred years.

'What do you think of it, Ben? Is it possible?' But before I could answer Louren had slipped his arm about her waist and they both smiled down at me.

'He's doing his nut. He's frothing at the mouth and doing back flips. He wants to rush into the desert now, this minute.' Then he pulled Hilary to him and kissed her. For a long minute they were oblivious of my presence as they embraced. They are, for me, the epitome of beautiful woman and manhood, both of them tall and strong and well-favoured. Hilary is younger than he is by twelve years, his fourth wife and the mother of only the youngest of his seven children. In her middle twenties she has the maturity and poise of a much older woman.

'Give Ben some lunch, my darling. I'll be home late.' Louren pulled away from the embrace.

'I'll miss you,' Hilary said.

'And I you. I'll see you Monday, Ben. Cable Larkin if you think of anything special we will need. So long, partner.' And he was gone.

Hilary took my hand and led me out on to the wide flagged patio. Five acres of lawn and dazzling flowerbeds sloped gently down to the stream and artificial lake. Both tennis courts were occupied and a shrieking mob of small near-naked bodies thrashed the water of the swimming-pool to sun-sparkled white. Two uniformed servants were laying out a cold buffet on the long patio trestle-table, and with a small squirming twinge of dread I saw a half-dozen young matrons in tennis dress sprawled in the lounging chairs beside the outside bar. They were flushed with exertion, perspiration dampened the crisp white dresses and they sipped at long dewy, fruit-laden glasses of Pimms No. 1.

'Come,' said Hilary, and led me towards them. I steeled myself, trying to draw myself up an extra inch of height as we moved towards the group.

'Girls – we've got a man to keep us company. I want you to meet Dr. Benjamin Kazin, Dr. Kazin is the Director of the Institute of African Anthropology and Prehistory. Ben, this is Marjory Phelps.'

I turned to each of them as she spoke their names, and I acknowledged the slightly over-effusive greetings; giving each my eyes and voice, they are my good things. It was as difficult for them as it was for me. You do not expect your hostess to spring a hunchback on you with the pre-lunch drinks.

The children rescued me. Bobby spotted me and came at a run, shrieking, 'Uncle Ben! Uncle Ben!' She flung her cold wet arms around my neck and pressed her sopping bathing-costume to my new suit, before dragging me away to become overwhelmed by the rest of the Sturvesant brood and their hordes of young friends. I find it easier with children, they either do not seem to notice or they come straight out with it. 'Why do you walk all bent over like that?'

For once I was not very good value, I was too preoccupied to give them my full attention – and soon they drifted away, all but Bobby – for she is ever loyal. Then Hilary took over from her stepdaughter and I was returned to the league of young mothers where I made a better impression. I cannot resist pretty women, once the first awkwardness wears off. It was three o'clock before I left for the Institute.

Bobby Sturvesant pours Glen Grant malt whisky with the same heavy thirteen-year-old hand she uses to pour Coca-Cola. Consequently I floated into the Institute feeling very good indeed.

The envelope was on my desk marked 'Private and Confidential' with a note pinned to one corner, 'This came for you at lunch-time. Looks exciting! Sal.'

With a quick stab of jealousy I inspected the seal of the envelope. It was unbroken. Sally hadn't been into it – but I knew it must have taken all her self-control for she has an almost neurotic curiosity. She calls it a fine inquiring scientific mind.

I guessed she would arrive within the next five minutes so I found the packet of Three X peppermints in my top drawer and slipped one into my mouth to smother the whisky fumes before I opened the envelope and drew out the glossy twelve-by-twelve enlargement, switched on the desk light and adjusted it and the magnifying table lens over the print. Then I looked around at the hosts of the past that crowd my office. All four walls are lined with shelves, and from floor to shoulder height – my shoulder height – these are filled with books: the tools of my trade, all bound in brown and green calf-skin, and titled in gold leaf. It is a big room, and there are many thousands of volumes. The shelves above the books carry the plaster busts of all the creatures that preceded man. Head and shoulders only. Australopithecus, Proconsul, Robusta, Rhodesian Man, Peking – all of them up to Neanderthal and finally Cro-Magnon himself – *homo sapiens sapiens* in all his glory and infamy. The shelves to the right of my desk are laden with busts of all the typical ethnic types found in Africa, Hamites, Arabs, pygmies, the negroids, Boskops, bushmen, Griqua, Hottentot and all the others. They watched me attentively, with their bulging glass eyes as I addressed them.

'Gentlemen,' I said, 'I think we are on to something good.' I only speak aloud to them when I am excited or drunk, and now I was more than a little of each.

'Who are you talking to?' asked Sally from the doorway, making me leap in my seat. It was a rhetorical question, she knew damn well who I was talking to. She lounged against the jamb, her hands thrust deeply into the pockets of her grubby white dust-coat. Dark hair drawn back with a ribbon from the deep bulging forehead, large green eyes well spaced beside the pert nose. High cheek-bones, wide sensual smiling mouth. A big girl with long well-muscled legs in the tight-fitting blue jeans. Why do I always like them big?

'Good lunch?' she asked, starting the slow sidling approach across the carpet towards my desk that would put her in position to check what was going on. She can read documents upside-down, as I have proved to my cost.

'Great,' I answered, deliberately covering the photograph with the envelope. 'Cold turkey, lobster salad, smoked trout, and a very good duck and truffles in aspic.'

'You bastard,' she whispered softly. She loves good food, and she had noticed my play with the envelope. I don't allow her to talk to me like that, but then I can't stop her either.

Five feet from me she sniffed, 'And peppermint-flavoured malt whisky! Yummy!'

I blushed, I can't help it. It's like my stutter – and she burst out laughing and came to perch on the edge of my desk.

'Come on, Ben.' She eyed the envelope frankly. 'I've been bursting since it arrived. I would have steamed it open – but the electric kettle is broken.'

Dr. Sally Benator has been my assistant for two years, which is coincidently the exact period of time that I have been in love with her.

I moved aside making room for her behind the desk and uncovered the photograph. 'All right,' I agreed, 'let's see what you make of it.'

She squeezed in beside me, her upper arm touching my shoulder – a contact that shivered electrically through my whole body. In two years she had become like the children, she didn't seem to notice the hump. She was easy and natural, and I had a time-table worked out – in another two years our relationship would have ripened. I had to go slowly, very slowly, so as not to alarm her, but in that time I would have accustomed her to the thought of me as a lover and husband. If the last two years had been long – I hated to think about the next two.

She leaned over the desk peering into the magnifying lens, and she was still and silent for a long time. Reflected light was thrown up into her face, and when she at last looked up her expression was rapt, the green eyes sparkled.

'Ben,' she said. 'Oh Ben – I'm so glad for you!' Somehow her easy acceptance and presumption annoyed me.

'You are jumping the gun,' I snapped. 'There could be a dozen natural explanations.'

'No.' She shook her head, smiling still. 'Don't try and knock it. It's true, Ben, at last. You've worked so long and believed so long, don't be afraid now. Accept it.'

She slipped out from behind the desk and crossed quickly to the shelf of books under the label 'K'. There are twelve volumes there that bear the author's name 'Benjamin Kazin'. She selected one, and opened it at the fly-leaf.

'*Ophir*,' she read, 'by Dr. Benjamin Kazin. *A personal investigation of the prehistoric gold-working civilization of Central Africa, with special reference to the city of Zimbabwe and to the legend of the ancients and the lost city of the Kalahari.*'

She came to me smiling. 'Have you read it?' she asked. 'It's quite entertaining.'

'There's a chance, Sal. I agree. Just a chance, but—'

'Where does it lie?' she cut in. 'In the mineralized series, as you predicted?'

I nodded. 'Yes, it's in the gold belt. But it could, it just could, produce so much more than Langebeli and Ruwane.'

She grinned triumphantly, and bent over the lens again. With her finger she touched the indian ink arrow in the corner of the photo that gave the northerly bearing.

'The whole city—'

'If it is a city,' I cut in.

'The whole city,' she repeated with emphasis, 'faces north. Into the sun. With the acropolis behind it – sun and moon, the two gods. The phallic towers – there are four, five – six. Perhaps seven of them.'

'Sal, those aren't towers, they are just dark patches on a photograph taken from 36,000 feet.'

'Thirty-six thousand!' Sal's head jerked up. 'Then it's huge! You could fit Zimbabwe into the main enclosure half a dozen times.'

'Easy, girl. For God's sake.'

'And the lower city outside the walls. It stretches for miles. It's enormous, Ben – but I wonder why it's crescent-shaped like that?' She straightened up, and for the first time – the very first wonderful time – she spontaneously threw her arms around my neck and hugged me. 'Oh, I'm so excited, I could die. When do we leave?'

I didn't answer, I hardly heard the question, I just stood there and revelled in the feel of her big warm breasts pressing against me.

'When?' she asked again, pulling back to look into my face.

'What?' I asked. 'What did you say?' I was both blushing and stuttering – and she laughed.

'When do we leave, Ben? When are we going to find your lost city?'

'Well,' I considered how to phrase it delicately, 'Louren Sturvesant and I will go in first. We leave on Tuesday. Louren didn't mention an assistant – so I don't think you will be coming along on the recce.'

Sally stepped back and placed her clenched fists on her hips, she looked at me unkindly and asked with deceptive gentleness: 'Do you want to bet on that?'

I like reasonable odds when I do bet, so I told Sally to pack. A week was too long for the job, for she is a professional and travels light. Her personal effects filled a single small valise and a shoulder-strapped carry-all. Her sketch-books, and paints, were more bulky, but we pooled our books to avoid duplication. My photographic equipment was another big item, and then the sample bags and boxes together with my one canvas case made a formidable pile in the corner of my office. We were ready in twenty-four hours, and for the next six days we killed time by arguing, agonizing, squabbling and poring over the photograph which was starting to lose a little of its gloss. When our tensions built up to explosion point, then Sally would lock herself in her own office and try to work on the translation of the rock-engraving from Drie Koppen or the painted symbols from the Witte Berg. Rock-paintings, engravings and the translation of the ancient writings are her speciality.

I would wander fretfully around the public rooms, trying to find dust on the exhibits, dreaming up some novel way of displaying the treasures that filled our warehouse and upstairs store-rooms, counting the names in the visitors' book, playing guide to parties of schoolchildren – doing anything but work. Finally I would go upstairs to tap on Sally's door. Sometimes it was, 'Come in, Ben.' And then again it might be, 'I'm busy. What do you want?' Then I would drift through to spend an hour in the African languages section with my dour giant, Timothy Mageba.

Timothy started at the Institute as a sweeper and cleaner, that was twelve years ago. It took me six months to discover that apart from his own southern Sotho he spoke sixteen other dialects. I taught him to speak English fluently in eighteen months, to write it in two years. He matriculated two years later, graduated Bachelor of Arts in another three, Master's degree in the required further two years – and he is working on his doctorate in African languages. He now speaks nineteen languages including English, which is one more than I do, and he is the only man I know, apart from myself – spent nine months in the desert, living with the little yellow men – who speaks the dialects of both the northern and Kalahari bushmen.

For a linguist, he is a peculiarly silent man. When he does speak it is in *basso profundo* which matches well his enormous frame. He stands six foot five inches tall and he is muscled like a professional wrestler and yet he moves with the grace of a dancer.

He fascinates me, and frightens me a little. His head is completely hairless, the rounded pate shaven and oiled to gleam like a midnight-black cannon ball. The nose broad and flat with flaring nostrils, the lips a thick purple black and behind them gleam big strong white teeth. From behind this impassive mask a chained animal ferocity glowers through the eye slits, and once in a while flashes like distant summer lightning. There is a satanical presence about him, despite the white shirt and dark business suit he wears, and though for twelve years I have spent much of my time in his presence I have never fathomed the dark depths beneath those dark eyes and darker skin.

Under my loose surveillance he runs the African languages department of the Institute. Five younger Africans, four men and a girl, work under him and, so far, they have published authoritative dictionaries of the seven main African languages spoken in southern Africa. They have also accumulated written and taped material to keep them busy for the next seven years.

On his own initiative, with just a little of my help and encouragement, he has published two volumes of African history which have raised a storm of hysterical abuse from white historians, archaeologists and reviewers. As a child Timothy was apprenticed to his grandfather, the witchdoctor and historical custodian of the tribe. As part of his initiation into the mysteries his grandfather placed Timothy under hypnosis and taped the entire tribal history on his brain. Even now, thirty years later, Timothy is able to throw himself into a trance and establish total recall of this mass of legend, folk-lore, unwritten history and magical doctrine. Timothy's grandfather was tried by an unsympathetic white judge and hanged for his part in a series of ritual murders the year before Timothy had completed his training and been entered into the priesthood. However, his legacy to Timothy is a formidable mountain of material – much of it palpably spurious, a great deal of it unpublishable as being either too obscene or too explosive, and the remainder fascinating, puzzling or downright scary.

I have drawn on much of Timothy's unpublished material for my own book *Ophir* – particularly those unscientific and 'popular' sections which deal with the legend of the ancients, a race of fair-skinned golden-haired warriors from across the sea, who mined the gold, enslaved the indigenous tribes, built walled cities and flourished for hundreds of years before vanishing almost without trace.

I am aware that Timothy edits the information he passes on to me – some of it is too secret, the taboos which surround it too powerful to disclose to other than an initiate of the mysteries. I am sure that much of this withheld information relates to the legend of the ancients. I, however, never abandon my attempts to milk him.

On the Monday morning of Louren's return from Switzerland, Sally was so overwrought by the possibility that Louren would veto her inclusion in the preliminary expedition that her company was unbearable. To escape her and to kill the last long waiting hours, I went down to Timothy.

He works in a tiny room – we are a little pressed for space at the Institute, which is congested with neatly stacked pamphlets, books, folders, and piles of loose paper that reach almost to the ceiling – and yet there is room for my chair. This is a long-legged affair like a bar-room stool. For although my legs and arms are regulation size, or better, my trunk is squashed and humped so that from the seat of an ordinary chair I have trouble seeing over the top of a desk.

'Machane! Blessed one!' Timothy rose with his usual greeting as I entered. According to Bantu lore those of us with club feet, albino pigmentation, squint eyes, and humped backs are blessed by the spirits and endowed with psychic powers. I derive a sneaky sort of pleasure from this belief, and Timothy's greeting always gives me a lift.

I hopped up on my chair, and began a desultory conversation which flicked from subject to subject and changed from language to language. Timothy and I are proud of our talents – and I suppose we do show off a little. There is no other man living, of this I am convinced, who could follow one of our conversations from beginning to end.

'It will be strange,' I said at last in I forget what language, 'not to have you along on a journey. It will be the first time in ten years, Timothy.'

He was immediately silent and wary. He knew I was going to start again on the lost city. I had shown him the photograph five days before, and had been pumping him steadily ever since for some significant comment. I changed into English.

'Anyway, you are probably not missing anything. Another groping for shadows. God knows there have been many of those. If only I knew what to look for.'

I broke off and froze with expectancy. Timothy's eyes had glazed. It is a physical thing, an opaque blueish film seems to cover the eyeballs. His head sinks down on the thick corded column of the neck, his lips twitch – and the goose flesh runs up my arms and the hair on the back of my neck fans erect.

I waited. As often as I had seen it I could never shake off the supernatural thrill of watching Timothy going into trance. Sometimes it is involuntary – a word, a thought will trigger it, and the reflex is almost instantaneous. Then again it can be a deliberate act of auto-hypnosis, but this involves preparation and ritual.

This time it was spontaneous, and I waited eagerly knowing that if the material was taboo it would be but a few seconds only before Timothy broke the spell with a deliberate effort of will.

'Evil—' he spoke in the quavering, high-pitched voice of an old man. The voice of his grandfather. A little spittle wet the thick purple lips, '—an evil to be cleaned from the earth and from the minds of men, for ever.'

His head jerked, the conscious mind intervening, his lips worked loosely. The brief internal struggle – and suddenly his eyes cleared. He looked at me and saw me.

'I'm sorry,' he murmured in English, turning his eyes away now. Embarrassed by the involuntary display, and the need to exclude me. 'Would you like some coffee, Doctor? They have repaired the kettle at last.'

I sighed. Timothy had switched off, there would be no more communication that day. He was closed up and defensive. To use his own expression, he had 'turned nigger' on me.

'No thanks, Timothy.' I looked at my watch and slipped off the stool. 'Still some last-minute things to do.'

'Go in peace, Machane, and the spirits guide your feet.' We shook hands.

'Stay in peace, Timothy, and if the spirits are kind I will send for you.'

Standing on the rail of the coffee bar in the main hall of Jan Smuts Airport
I had a good view of the entrance to the international terminal.

'Damn it,' I swore.

'What is it?' Sal asked anxiously.

'B.Y.M. – a whole platoon of them.'

'What are B.Y.M.?'

'Bright young men. Sturvesant executives. There, you see the four of them
beside the bank counter.'

'How do you know they are Sturvesant men?' she asked.

'Haircuts, short back and sides. Uniforms, dark cashmere suits and plain
ties. Expressions, tense and ulcer-ridden but poised to blossom as the big man
appears.' And then I added in an unaccustomed fit of honesty, 'Besides, I
recognize two of them. Accountants. Friends of mine – have to prise money
out of them every time I want a roll of toilet paper for the Institute.'

'Is that him?' asked Sally, and pointed.

'Yes,' I said, 'that's him.'

Louren Sturvesant came out of the doors of the international terminal, the
first of the Zürich flight through customs and immigration, the airport public
relations officer trotting to keep pace with him. Two other B.Y.M. a pace
behind him on either side. Probably a third taking care of his luggage. The
four waiting men broke into smiles that seemed to light the hall and hurried
forward in order of seniority for a brief handclasp and then fell into formation
around Louren. Two of them running interference ahead of him, the others
closing in at either hand. The public relations officer fell back bewildered to
the tail of the field, and Anglo-Sturvesant drove across the crowded floor like
an advancing Panzer division.

In their midst Louren stood out by a golden curly head, his sun-bronzed
features grim in contrast to the artificial smiles around him.

'Come on!' I caught Sally's hand and dove into the crowd. I am good at
this. I go in at the level of their legs – and the pressure from this unexpected
level cleaves them open like the waters of the Red Sea. Sally ran through
behind me like the Israelites.

We intercepted Anglo-Sturvesant at the glass exit doors, and I dropped
Sally's hand to crack the inner circle. I broke through at the first attempt and
Louren nearly tripped over me.

'Ben.' I saw immediately how tired he was. Pale beneath the gold skin,
purply smudges under the eyes – but a warm smile cleared the fatigue for a
moment. 'I'm sorry. I should have warned you not to come. Something has
come up. I am on my way to a meeting now.'

He saw the expression on my face, and clasped my shoulder quickly.

'No. Don't jump to conclusions. It's still on. Be at the airfield at five o'clock
tomorrow morning. I'll meet you there. I must go now. I'm sorry.'

We shook hands quickly.

'All the way, partner?' he asked.

'All the way,' I agreed, grinning at the schoolboy inanity and then they
swept on by and disappeared through the glass doors.

We were half-way back to Johannesburg before Sally spoke.

'Did you ask him about me? Is it fixed?'

'There wasn't time, Sal. You saw that. He was so rushed.'

Neither of us spoke again until I turned into the grounds of the Institute
and parked the Mercedes beside her little red Alfa in the empty car park.

'Would you like a cup of coffee?' I asked.

'It's late.'

'It isn't. You won't sleep anyway – not tonight. We could have a game of chess.'

'All right.'

I let us in at the front door and we went through the public rooms, crowded with glass cases and wax figures, to the private staircase that led to my office and flat.

Sal lit the fire and set out the chessmen while I made coffee. When I came back from the kitchen she was sitting cross-legged on a tooled leather pouffe, brooding over the ivory and ebony chessboard. I caught my breath at the fresh dimension of her loveliness that the light and setting presented to me. She wore a patchwork poncho, as brilliantly coloured as the Oriental carpets strewn on the floor about her – and the gentle sidelighting glowed on the soft sun-touched olive of her skin. Watching her, I thought my heart might burst.

She looked up with those big soft eyes. 'Come,' she said, 'let's play.'

If I can weather the storm of her first lightning, volatile attacks then I can smother and wear her down with pawn play and superior development. She calls it the creeping death.

At last she toppled her queen with a little groan of exasperation and stood up to pace restlessly about the room, hugging her own shoulders under the vivid poncho. I sipped coffee and watched her with covert pleasure until suddenly she swirled and faced me with long legs astride and clenched fists on her hips, her elbows tenting the poncho around her.

'I hate the bastard,' she said in a tight, strangled voice. 'A big arrogant god-man. I knew the type as soon as I saw him. Why, in the name of all that's holy, does he have to come with us? If we make any significant discovery, you can guess who will hog all the glory.'

I knew immediately she was talking of Louren – and I was startled by the acid and gall in her tone. Later I would remember it, and know the reason. But now I was stunned and then angry.

'What on earth are you talking about?' I demanded.

'The face, the walk, the flock of idolaters, the condescending air with which he dispenses favours, the immense overpowering conceit of the man—'

'Sally!'

'The casual, unthinking cruelty of his presumption—'

'Stop it, Sally.' I was on my feet now.

'Did you see those poor little men of his – shaking with fright?'

'Sally, you'll not talk of him like that – not in front of me.'

'Did you see yourself? One of the gentlest, kindest, most decent men I have ever known. One of the finest brains I have ever been privileged to work with. Did you see yourself, scampering and tail-wagging – God, you were rolling on your back at his feet – offering your belly to be tickled—' She was almost hysterical now, crying, tears of anger running down her face, shaking, white-faced. 'I hated you – and him! I hated you both. He was demeaning you, making you cheap and, and—'

I could not answer her. I stood stricken and numb – and her temper changed. She lifted her hand and pressed it to her mouth. We stared at each other.

'I must be mad,' she whispered. 'Why did I say those things? Ben, oh Ben. I'm sorry. So very sorry.'

And she came and knelt before me, her arms went around my body and she hugged me to her. I stood like a statue. I was cold with fear, dread of what was to come. For although this was what I had long prayed for, yet it had come so suddenly, without a moment's warning, and now I had been thrust far beyond the point of no return, into unknown territory. Sally lifted her head, still clinging to me, and looked up into my face.

'Forgive me, please.'

I kissed her, and her mouth was warm and salty with tears. Her lips opened under mine, and my fear was gone.

'Make love to me, Ben – please.' She knew instinctively that I must be led. She took me to the couch.

'The lights,' I whispered harshly, 'please switch off the lights.'

'If that's what you want.'

'Please, Sally.'

'I will,' she said. 'I know, my darling.' And she switched off the lights.

Twice in the darkness she cried out: 'Oh, please Ben – you're so strong. You are killing me. Your arms are – your arms.'

Then not long after, she screamed, an incoherent cry without form or meaning, and my own hoarse cry blended with it. Then there was only the ragged sound of our breathing in the darkness.

I felt as though my mind had broken free from my body and floated in warmth and darkness. For the first time in my life I was completely at rest, contented and secure. There seemed to be so many first times with this woman. When at last Sally spoke, her voice came as a small shock.

'Will you sing for me, Ben?' And she switched on the lights on the table beside the couch. We blinked at each other, owl-eyed in the muted glow. Her face was flushed rosily, and her hair a dark unruly tumble.

'Yes,' I said, 'I want to sing.' I went through into my dressing-room and took the guitar from the cupboard, and as I closed the door there was my reflection in the full-length mirror.

I looked with full attention, for a stranger stood before me. The coarse black hair framed a square face, with dark eyes and girlishly long lashes, a heavy simian jaw and a long pale forehead. The stranger was smiling at me, half shy – half proud.

I glanced down the strange, telescoped body over which I had agonized since childhood. The legs and arms were over-developed, thick and knotted with slabs of muscle, the limbs of a giant. Instinctively I glanced at the body-builder's weights in the corner of the room – and then back to the mirror. I was perfect around the edges – but in the centre was this squat, humped, toad-like torso, covered in a shaggy pelt of curly black hair. I looked at that remarkable body, and again for the first time in my life, I did not hate it.

I went back to where Sally still lay on the soft monkey-skin kaross that covered the couch. I hopped up, and squatted cross-legged beside her with the guitar in my lap.

'Sing sad – please, Ben,' she whispered.

'But I'm happy, Sal.'

'Sing a sad song – one of your own sad ones,' she insisted, and as I picked out the first notes she closed her eyes. I was grateful, for I had never had a woman's body to gloat over. I leaned forward and as I touched the singing strings, I caressed the long smooth length of her with my eyes, the pale planes and rounds and secret shadows. Flesh that had cradled mine – how I loved it! I sang:

> 'In the lonely desert of my soul,
> The nights are long,
> And no other traveller journeys there.

O'er the lonely oceans of my mind
The winds blow strong—'

And in a short while a tear squeezed out between her closed lids for there is a magic in my voice which can call up tears or laughter. I sang until my throat was rough and my picking finger tender. Then I lay the guitar aside and went on looking at her. Without opening her eyes she turned her head slightly towards me.

'Tell me about you and Louren Sturvesant,' she said. 'I would like to understand about that.'

The question took me by surprise, and I was silent for a moment. She opened her eyes.

'I'm sorry, Ben. You don't have to—'

'No,' I answered quickly. 'I'd like to talk about it. You see, I think you were wrong about him. I don't think you can apply ordinary standards to them – the Sturvesants. Louren and his father, when he was alive, that is. My own father worked for them. He died of a broken heart a year after my mother. Mr. Sturvesant had heard of my academic record, and of course my father had been a loyal employee. There are a few of us, the Sturvesant orphans. We have nothing but the best. I went to Michaelhouse, the same school as Louren. A Jew at a church school, and a cripple at that – you can imagine how it was. Small boys are such utterly merciless little monsters. Louren dragged me out of the urinal where four of them were trying to drown me. He beat the daylights out of them, and after that I was his charge. I have been ever since. He finances this Institute, every penny of it. At first it was something just for me, but little by little he has become more and more involved. It's his hobby and my life – you will be surprised how knowledgeable he is. He loves this land, just as you and I do. He is caught up in its history and future more than you or I will ever be—' I broke off, for she was staring at me in a way that seemed to pierce my soul.

'You love him, Ben, don't you?'

I blushed then, and dropped my eyes. 'How do you mean that—'

'Oh, for God's sake, Ben,' she interrupted impatiently. 'I don't mean queer. You just proved the opposite. But I mean love, in the biblical sense.'

'He has been father, protector, benefactor and friend to me. The only friend I've ever had. Yes, you could say I love him.'

She reached up and touched my cheek.

'I'll try to like him. For your sake.'

It was still dark when we drove in through the gates of Grand Central Airport. Sal was huddled into her coat, silent and withdrawn. I was light-headed and brittle-feeling from a night of love and talk without sleep. There were floodlights picking out the private Sturvesant hangar at the east end of the runway, and as we approached I saw Louren's Ferrari parked in his reserved bay, and beside it another half-dozen late model saloons gleaming in the floods.

'Oh God,' I groaned. 'He's got the whole team with him.'

I parked beside the Ferrari, and Sal and I began unloading our equipment from the boot. She picked up her easel and slung it over her shoulder, then with a huge folder of parchment in one hand and a box of paints in the other she ducked through the wicket gate into the hangar. I should have gone with her, of course, but I was so absorbed in checking my luggage that it was three or four minutes before I followed her. By then it was too late.

As I stepped through the low aperture into the brightly lit hangar, my stomach churned with alarm. The gleaming sharklike silhouette of the Lear jet formed a backdrop for a tension-charged tableau. Seven of Louren's bright young men clad in the regulation casual garb – smartly cut safari suits and fleece-lined car coats – stood in a discreet circle about the two protagonists.

Louren Sturvesant very rarely loses his temper, and when he does it is only after severe and prolonged provocation. However, in less than two minutes Sally Benator had managed to achieve what many experts before her had never accomplished. Louren was in a towering, shaking, tight-lipped rage, which had his seven B.Y.M. awed and slack-mouthed.

Sally had dropped her load of equipment on the concrete floor and was standing with clenched fists on her hips and bright explosions of colour burning in her cheeks, trading Louren glare for glare.

'Dr. Kazin told me I could come.'

'I don't care if the goddam King of bloody England told you that you could come. I'm telling you that the plane is full – and that I have no intention of dragging a female with me on the first break I've had in six months.'

'I didn't realise it was a pleasure jaunt—'

'Will somebody throw this bitch out of here?' shouted Louren, and the B.Y.M. roused themselves and made a tentative advance. Sally picked up the heavy wooden easel, and held it in both hands. The advance petered out. I scuttled into the void and grabbed Louren's arm.

'Please, Lo. Can we talk?' I almost dragged him into the flight office – although I thought I detected a twinge of relief from Louren as I rescued him.

'Look I'm terribly sorry about this, Lo. I didn't have a chance to explain—'

Five minutes later Louren strode out of the office, and without a glance at either Sal or the frozen group of B.Y.M., climbed into the jet and a moment later his head appeared beside that of the pilot in the window of the cockpit as he adjusted his earphones.

I went to the junior B.Y.M. and gave him the word of the law.

'Mr. Sturvesant asked me to tell you to arrange a charter to Gaberones for yourself.' Then I turned to the others. 'I wonder if you could give us a hand with the luggage.'

While a gang of the most highly paid stevedores in Africa carried in Sally's luggage, she preened with shameless triumph. I managed to whisper a harsh warning.

'Back seat,' I snapped. 'And try and make yourself invisible. You will never know how close that was. Not only did you nearly miss the trip, but you almost talked yourself out of a job.'

We had been airborne for ten minutes before the pilot came back along the aisle. He stopped beside us and looked at Sal with open admiration.

'Jesus, lady.' He shook his head. 'I would have given a month's salary not to miss that! You were great.'

Sally, who had been suitably subdued since my warning, immediately perked up.

'With boys that size I don't even spit out the bones,' she declared, and a couple of B.Y.M. who heard it swivelled in their seats with startled expressions.

The pilot laughed delightedly and turned to me. 'The man wants to speak to you, Doctor. I'll change places with you.'

Louren was chit-chatting with flight control over the radio, but he waved me into the co-pilot's seat and I squeezed behind the wheel and waited. Louren ended his transmission and turned to me.

'Breakfast?'

'I've eaten.'

He ignored it and passed me a leg of cold turkey, and a huge slice of chicken and egg pie from the hamper beside him.

'Coffee in the Thermos. Help yourself.'

'Did you get your £25 million loan?' I asked with a full mouth.

'Yes – despite a last-minute panic.'

'I didn't think you needed to borrow, Lo. Have you fallen on hard times?'

'Oil prospecting.' He laughed at my suggestion. 'Risk money. I prefer to gamble with other people's money, and play the certainties with my own.' He changed the subject smoothly. 'Sorry about the detour. I am dropping the boys off at Gaberones. They've a series of meetings with the Botswana government. Routine stuff, just settling the details of the concession. Anyway, it's not too far off our course. Then we can press on alone.' He filled his mouth with turkey and spoke around it. 'Met. report is lousy, Ben. Thick cloud down on the deck over the whole northern area. Happens about once in three years that you get low overcast in the desert – but today's the day. Anyway we'll have a stab at picking up the hills and the ruins, no harm done if we can't though. We'll not learn anything more from the air.' He was relaxed and easy, not a trace of his early rage, he could switch it on or off as he wished, and we talked and laughed together. I knew his mood, it was holiday and release. He was truly looking forward to it. Lost city or no lost city, it was an excuse to get out into the wild country that he loved.

'This is like the old days. God, Ben, how long is it since we got away together? Must be all of ten years. Remember the canoe trip down the Orange River – when was that? 1956 or '7? And the expedition to find the wild bushmen.'

'We must do it more often, Lo.'

'Yes,' he said, really meaning it; as though he had a choice. 'We must, but there is so little time. It's running out so quickly – I'll be forty years old next year.' And his voice was wistful. 'God, if only we could buy time with money!'

'We've got five days,' I said, heading the conversation away from the quicksands, and he picked it up eagerly. It was another half an hour before he mentioned Sally.

'That assistant of yours, the prize fighter. What's her name?' And I told him.

'Are you having it away with her?' he asked. It was said so naturally, so casually, that for an instant I did not realize what had been said. Then I felt my vision blur with red rage, felt the blood pound in my temples and heat my throat and face. I think I could have killed him then, but instead I lied in a thick, shaken voice.

'No,' I said.

'Just as well,' he grunted. 'She's a wild one. Well, as long as she doesn't mess up the trip.' If only I had told him then, but it was too private a thing – too precious and fragile to despoil with words, especially the words he had chosen. Then the moment was passed, and I was sitting trembling and shaky as he talked on lightly about the five days ahead.

As we flew the cloud solidified beneath us, congealing into a dirty greyish blanket that stretched away in all directions to the horizon. We crossed the border between South Africa and the independent African state of Botswana. At Gaberones the ceiling was down to a thousand feet when we landed. Despite Louren's assurance that we would be speedily airborne once more, there was a deputation of senior government officials, and an invitation to drinks and food in a private dining-room of the airport. Hot, sticky weather with intent white faces talking softly and greedily to shiny intent black faces – all of them sweating in the heat and whisky fumes, and the thick swirls of cigar and cigarette smoke.

Three hours more before the Lear jet with just four of us aboard slashed up into the cloud cover, then burst through into the high bright sunshine.

'Wow!' said Louren. 'An expensive little party. That black bastard Ngelane has just raised the price of his honour by another 20,000. I'll have to square him, of course. He could squash the whole deal. It has to go through his ministry.'

Louren flew northwards with the map on his lap and a stopwatch in his hand. His eyes darted from compass to airspeed indicator and back to the watch.

'Okay, Ben. You'd better let Roger take over the controls. We'll go down into the porridge and take a look-see.'

With Louren and the pilot, Roger Van Deventer, at the controls and Sal and I braced in the doorway of the cockpit behind them, the jet slanted down towards the floor of dirty cloud. A few wisps of the stuff flickered past and then suddenly the sun was gone and we were enfolded in the dark grey mist.

Roger was flying, his attention completely on the instrument panel, and as the needle of the altimeter slowly unwound I saw his hands tightening on the wheel. We dropped steadily lower through the grey filth. Now Roger pulled on the flaps and airbrakes and throttled back. The three of us staring forward and down for the first glimpse of the earth. Down we sank, and still down. The pilot's tension turned to active fear. I could smell it, the rank greasy tang of it. It was infectious. If he, the hardened fly-bird, was afraid, then I was prepared to be terrified. I knew suddenly that rather than risk Louren's wrath he would fly us straight into the ground. I decided to intervene, and opened my mouth. It was unnecessary.

'Overflown,' grunted Louren, checking the stop-watch. 'Ease up, Rog.'

'Sorry, Mr. Sturvesant, there is no bottom to this stuff.' Roger said it like a sigh, and lifted the Lear's nose. He opened the throttle and let off the airbrakes.

'No go!' I murmured with relief. 'Forget it, Lo. Let's go on to Maun.'

Louren turned to look back at me, and instead looked into Sally's face. She stood behind his shoulder. I could not see her expression, but I could guess what it was by the tone in which she asked softly, 'Chicken?'

Louren stared at her a moment longer, then he grinned. I could have turned Sally over my knee and beaten that luscious backside to a pulp. The warm active fear I had felt the minute before, turned now to cold numbing terror for I had seen Louren grin like that before.

'Okay, Roger,' he said, slipping the map and stop-watch into the pocket beside his seat. 'I've got her.' And the Lear stood on one wing as he pulled her around in a maximum-rate turn. It was so finely executed that Sally and I merely sagged a little at the knees as gravity caught us.

He levelled out and flew for three minutes on even keel, retracing our course. I stole a glance at Sally's face. It was bright-eyed, and flushed with excitement – she was staring ahead into the impenetrable murk.

Again Louren banked the aircraft steeply and came out of the turn flying the reciprocal of our previous course and eased the nose downwards. This was no cautious groping with flaps and half throttle. Louren flew us in boldly and fast. Sally's hand groped for mine and squeezed. I was afraid and angry with both of them, I was too old for these children's games, but I returned her grip. As much for my own comfort as hers.

'Christ, Lo,' I blurted. 'Take it easy, will you!' And no one took the least notice of me. Roger was frozen in his seat, hands gripping the armrests, staring ahead. Louren was deceptively relaxed behind the controls, as he hurtled us into mortal danger – and Sally, damn her, was grinning all over her face and hanging on to my icy hand like a child on a roller coaster.

Suddenly we were into rain, pearly strings and snakes of it writhing back over the rounded Perspex windscreen. I tried to protest again, but my voice stuck somewhere in my parched throat. There was wind outside now. It buffeted the sleek gleaming body of the Lear, and the wings rocked. I felt like crying. I didn't want to die now. Yesterday would have been fine, but not after last night.

Before my own reflexes had even registered, Louren had seen the ground and caught the headlong plunge of the jet. With a soft shudder that threw Sally and I gently together he pulled us up level with the earth.

This was even more terrifying than the blind fall through space. The dark hazy outlines of the low scrubby tree-tops flicked by our wingtips close enough to touch, while ahead of us through the rain-mist an occasional big baobab tree loomed and Louren eased the jet over its greedily clutching branches. Seconds that seemed like a lifetime passed, then abruptly the filthy curtains of rain and cloud were stripped aside and we burst into a freak hole in the weather.

There before us, full in our path and washed by watery sunlight, stood a rampart of red stone cliffs. It was only the merest fleeting glimpse of red rock rushing down on us, then Louren had dragged the jet up on its tail and the rock seemed almost to scrape our belly as we slid over the crest and arrowed upwards into the clouds with the force of gravity squashing me down on buckling knees.

No one spoke until we had plunged out into the sunlight high above. Sally softly disengaged her hand from mine as Louren turned in his seat to look at us. I noticed with grim satisfaction that both he and Sally were looking slightly greenish with reaction. They stared at each other for a moment. Then Louren snorted with laughter.

'Look at Ben's face!' he roared and Sally thought that was very funny. When they finished laughing, Sally asked eagerly, 'Did anyone see the ruins? I just got a glimpse of the hills, but did anyone see the ruins?'

'The only thing I saw,' muttered Roger, 'was my own hairy little ring.' And I knew how he felt.

The cloud was breaking up by the time we reached Maun. Roger took us in through a gap and put us down sedately, and Peter Larkin was waiting for us.

Peter is one of the very few left. An anachronism, complete with fat cartridges looped to the breast of his bush jacket and his trousers tucked into the tops of mosquito boots. He has a big red beefy face and huge hands, the right index finger scarred by the recoil of heavy rifles. His single level of communication is a gravelly, whisky-raddled shout. He has no feelings and very little intelligence, so consequently never experiences fear. He has lived in Africa all his life and never bothered to learn a native language. He uses the lingua franca of South Africa, the bastard Fanagalo, and emphasizes his points with boot or fist. His knowledge of the animals on which he preys is limited to how to find them and where to aim to bring them down. Yet there is something appealing about him in an elephantine oafish way.

While his gang of hunting boys loaded out gear into the trucks he shouted amiable inanities at Louren and me.

'Wish I was coming with you. Got this bunch of yanks arriving tomorrow – with a big sack of green dollars. Short notice, you gave me, Mr. Sturvesant. But I'm giving you my best boys. Good rains in the south, be plenty of game in the area. Should run into gemsbok this time of year. And jumbo, of course, shouldn't be surprised if you get a simba or two—'

The coy use of pet names for game animals sickens me, especially when the intention is to blast them with a high-velocity rifle. I went to where Sally was supervising the packing of our gear.

'It's after one o'clock already,' she protested. 'When do we get cracking?'

'We'll probably push through to the top end of the Makarikari Pan tonight. It's about 200 miles on a fair road. Tomorrow we'll bash off into the deep bush.'

'Is Ernest Hemingway coming with us?' she asked, eyeing Peter Larkin with distaste.

'No such luck,' I assured her. I was trying to form some idea of those who were accompanying us. Two drivers, their superior status evident in the white shirts, long grey slacks and shod feet, with paisley-patterned scarves knotted at the throat. One for each of the three-ton trucks. Then there was the cook, carrying a lot of weight from his sampling, skin glossy from good food. Two gnarled and grey-headed gunboys who had jealously taken out Louren's sporting rifles from the other luggage, had unpacked them from their travelling cases, and were now fondling and caressing them lovingly. These were the elite and took no part in the frenzied scurryings of the camp boys as they packed away our gear. Bamangwatos most of them, I listened briefly to their chattering. The gunboys were Matabele, as was to be expected and the drivers were Shangaans. Good, I would understand every word spoken on this expedition.

'By the way, Sal,' I told her quietly, 'don't let on that I speak the language.'

'Why?' She looked startled.

'I like to monitor the goings-on and if they know I understand they'll freeze.'

'Svengali!' She pulled a face at me. I don't think I'd have laughed if anyone else had called me that. It was a bit too close to the bone. We went to shake hands and say goodbye to Roger, the pilot.

'Don't frighten the lions,' Roger told Sally. Clearly she had made another conquest. He climbed into the jet and we stood in a group and watched him taxi out to the end of the runway and then take off and wing away southwards.

'What are we waiting for?' asked Louren.

'What indeed,' I agreed.

Louren took the wheel of the Land-Rover and I climbed in beside him. Sally was in the back seat with the gunbearers on the bench seats.

'With you two – I feel a damned sight safer on the ground,' I said.

The road ran through open scrubland and baobab country. Dry and sun-scorched. The Land-Rover lifted a pale bank of drifting dust, and the two trucks followed us at a distance to let it settle.

There were occasional steep, rock-strewn dry river-beds to cross, and at intervals we passed villages of mud and thatched huts where the naked pot-bellied piccaninnies lined the side of the road to wave and sing as though we were royalty. Sally soon ran out of pennies, throwing them to watch the resulting scramble, and clapping her hands with delight. When she started tossing our lunch out of the window I pulled my guitar from its case to distract her.

'Sing happy, Ben,' Sally instructed.

'And bawdy,' added Louren, I think it was to needle her, or perhaps test her.

'Yes,' Sally agreed readily. 'Make it meaty and happy.'

And I started with the saga of the Wild, Wild Duck, with Sal and Louren shouting the chorus at the end of each verse.

We were children going on a picnic that first day out, and we made a good run of it to the pan. The sun was a big fat ball of fire amongst the tattered streamers of cloud on the horizon when we came out on the edge of the pan. Louren parked the Land-Rover and we climbed out to wait for the trucks and stared out with silent awe across that sombre, glistening salt plain that stretched away to the range of the eye.

When the trucks arrived they spilled their load of black servants before they had properly stopped, and I timed it at seventeen and a half minutes to when the tents were pitched, the camp-beds made up and the three of us sitting around the fire, drinking Glen Grant malt on the rocks of glistening ice that dewed the glasses. From the cooking fire drifted the tantalizing smell of the hunter's pot as our cook reheated it and tossed in a dash more garlic and origanum. They were a good, cheerful gang that Larkin had given us and after we had eaten they gathered around their own fire fifty yards away and sweetened the night with the old hunting songs.

I sat and listened half to them, and half to the involved and heated argument between Sal and Louren. I could have warned her that he was playing the devil's advocate, needling her again, but I enjoyed the interplay of two good minds. Whenever the discussion threatened to degenerate into personal abuse and actual physical violence, I intervened reluctantly and herded them back to safety.

Sally was staunchly defending the premise of my book *Ophir* that postulated an invasion of southern central Africa by Phoenician or Carthaginian colonizers in about 200 B.C. and which flourished until about A.D. 450, before disappearing abruptly.

'They were not equipped for a major voyage of discovery as early as that,' Louren challenged. 'Let alone a colonizing . . .'

'You will find, Mr. Sturvesant, that Herodotus records a circumnavigation of Africa in the reign of King Necho. It was led by six Phoenician navigators as early as 600 B.C. or thereabouts. They started at the apex of the Red Sea and in three years returned through the Pillars of Hercules.'

'A single voyage,' Louren pointed out.

'Not a single voyage, Mr. Sturvesant. Hanno sailed from Gibraltar to a point south in the west coast of Africa in about 460 B.C. a voyage from which he returned with bartered ivory and gold sufficient to whet the appetites of all the merchant adventurers.'

Still Louren attacked her dates. 'How do you get a date of 200 B.C., when the very earliest carbon-datings from the foundations of Zimbabwe are mid-fifth century A.D. and most of them are later?'

'We aren't concerned with Zimbabwe, but with the culture that preceded it,' Sally came back at him. 'Zimbabwe could have been built towards the end of the ancients' reign, probably only occupied for a short time before they disappeared; that would fit neatly with your carbon-dating of around A.D. 450. Besides the carbon-dating from the ancient mines at Shala and Inswezwe show results at 250 and 300 B.C.' Then she ended it with fine feminine logic.

'Anyway, carbon-dating isn't *that* accurate. It could be out by hundreds of years.'

'The mines were worked by the Bantu,' declared Louren. 'And Caton-Thompson – and of course, more recently, Summers – said—'

Fiercely she attacked Louren. 'Did the Bantu, who only probably arrived in the area about A.D. 300 suddenly conceive of a brilliant prospecting talent which enabled them to locate the metal lodes where not a scrap of it showed in the ore as visible gold or copper? Did they at the same time develop engineering know-how that enabled them to remove 250,000,000 tons of ore from rock at depth – remember they had never demonstrated these talents before – and did they abruptly forget or cease to use them for another thousand years?'

'Well, the Arab traders – they may have—' Louren began but Sally rode over him without a check.

'Why did they mine it at such risk and expenditure of energy? Gold has no value to the Bantu—cattle are their standard of wealth. Where did they learn how to dress and use rock for building? The Bantu had never done it before. Suddenly the art was fully fledged and highly skilled, and then instead of becoming more refined, the art *deteriorated* rapidly and then died out.'

With assumed reluctance Louren retreated steadily before her onslaughts, but he made his final stand when my own theory of incursion from the west instead of the east came under discussion. Louren had read the views and arguments of all my many detractors and critics and he repeated them now.

The accepted theory was that the point of entry was from the Sofala coast, or the mouth of the Zambezi. I had put forward the theory, based on the evidence of early texts and extensive excavations of my own, that a Mediterranean people left that sea through the Pillars of Hercules, and voyaged steadily down the western coast of Africa, probably establishing trading stations on the Gold, Ivory and Nigerian coasts, until their southward explorations led them into an unpeopled vacuum. I guessed at a river mouth long since dried and silted or altered in its course and depth in the present day. A river that drained what then would have been the huge lakes of Makarikari, Ngami, and others long since disappeared, shrivelled by the progressive desiccation of southern Africa. They entered the river, possibly the Cunene or the Orange, journeyed up it to the source, and from there sent their metallurgists overland to discover the ancient mines of Manica – and who knows but they discovered the diamonds in the gravel of the lakes and rivers, and certainly they would have hunted the vast herds of elephant that roamed the land. Sufficient wealth to justify the establishment of a city, a great walled fortress and trading station. Where would they site this city? Clearly at the limit of water-borne travel. On the shores of the furthest lake. Makarikari, perhaps? Or the lake that overflowed the present boundaries of the great salt pan.

Sally and Louren argued with increasing acrimony and bitterness. Sally called him 'an impossible man', and he countered with 'madam know-it-all'. Then suddenly Louren capitulated and the next minute all three of us were joyously anticipating the discovery of the lost city of Makarikari.

'The lake would have spread at least fifty miles beyond the boundaries of the present pan,' Louren pointed out. 'Only a hundred years ago Burchell describes Lake Ngami as an inland sea, and nowadays it's a puddle you can jump across without straining yourself. It's altogether probable that the ancient lake extended to the foot of the hills on which our ruins are placed. We have plenty of evidence of the gradual desiccation and drying up of southern Africa, read Cornwallis Harris' description of the forests and rivers which no longer exist.

'Ben.' Sally grabbed my arm with excitement. 'The crescent-shape of the city, do you remember me puzzling on it? It could be the shape of the ancient harbour with the town following the shoreline!'

'God,' Louren whispered. 'I can hardly wait for tomorrow.'

It was after midnight, and the whisky bottles had taken a terrible beating before Louren and Sally went off to their tents. I knew I could not sleep so I left the camp, passing the fire around which lay the blanket-cocooned bodies of our servants, and I walked out onto the surface of the pan. The stars lit the salt a ghastly grey, and it crunched crisply with each pace I took. I walked for a long time, stopping once to listen to the distant roaring of a lion, from the edge of the bush. When I returned to the camp a lantern still burned in Sally's tent, and her silhouette was magnified against the pale canvas, a huge, dark portrait of my love. She was reading, sitting cross-legged upon her camp-bed, but as I watched she reached across and extinguished the lantern.

I waited awhile, gathering my courage, then I went to her tent, and my heart threatened to hammer its way out of its malformed rib-cage.

'Sal?'

'Ben?' she answered my whisper softly.

'May I come in?' She hesitated before she replied.

'All right – just for a minute.'

I went into the tent, and in the gloom her nightdress was a pale blur. I groped for her face, and touched her cheek.

'I came to tell you that I love you,' I said softly, and I heard her little catch of breath in the dark. When she answered her voice was gentle.

'Ben,' she whispered. 'Dear, sweet Ben.'

'I would like to be with you tonight.'

And it seemed to me there was regret in her voice as she replied, 'No, Ben. Everyone would know about it. I don't want that.'

The morning started off as the previous day had ended. Everybody was in high spirits, laughing at the breakfast table. The servants sky-larked as they broke camp and repacked the trucks – and by seven o'clock we had left the road and were following the edge of the pan. The Land-Rover leading and the truck following our tracks through scrub and rank grass, and across the dry ravines which meandered down to the pan.

We had been going for an hour when I saw a flash of pale movement among the trees ahead of us, and three stately gemsbok broke out onto the open pan and trotted in single file away from us. They moved heavily, like fat ponies, the pale mulberry of their coats and the elaborate black and white face masks standing out clearly against the grey of the pan surface.

Louren slammed the brakes on the Land-Rover, and with the smoothly executed timing of the professional the old Matabele gunbearer put the big .375 Magnum Holland and Holland into Louren's hand and he was gone, running doubled-up behind the fringe of grass that lined the edge of the pan.

'Is he going to kill them?' asked Sally in her little-girl voice. I nodded and she went on, 'Why – but why?'

'It's one of the things he likes doing.'

'But they are so beautiful,' she protested.

'Yes,' I agreed. Out on the pan, about six hundred yards from the Land-Rover, the gemsbok had stopped. They were standing broadside to us. Staring at us intently with heads held high, and long slender horns erect.

'What's he doing?' Sal pointed at Louren who was still running along the edge of the pan.

'He's playing the rules,' I explained. 'It's an offence to fire within 500 yards of a vehicle.'

'Jolly sporting,' she muttered, biting her lip and glancing from Louren to the distant gemsbok. Then suddenly she had jumped from the Land-Rover and clambered up onto the engine bonnet. She cupped her hands around her mouth and yelled.

'Run, you fools. Run, damn you!'

She snatched her hat and waved it over her head, jumping up and down on the bonnet and howling like a banshee. Out on the pan the gemsbok erupted into startled flight, galloping diagonally away from us in a bunch. I glanced at Louren's small figure, and saw him drop into a sitting position with elbows braced on his knees, head cocked over the telescopic sight. The rifle jerked, and smoke spurted from the muzzle – but it was a second or two before the flat report of the shot reached us. Out on the pan the leading gemsbok slid over his nose and rolled in a drift of white dust. Louren fired again, and the second animal tumbled with legs kicking to the sky. The last gemsbok ran on alone.

Behind me the old gunbearer spoke to the other in Sindebele. 'Hou! This is much man.'

Sally climbed down off the bonnet, and sat silently while I drove to where Louren waited. He handed the rifle to the gunbearer, and as I relinquished the wheel to him the bitter tang of burnt cordite filled the cab of the Land-Rover. He glanced at Sally. 'Thanks,' he said, 'I prefer a running shot.'

'Why didn't you kill all three of them?' Her tone was neutral, without rancour.

'You are only allowed two on a licence.'

'Christ,' said Sally in a voice that now reeked of anger and outrage, 'how bloody touching. It's not often you meet a true gentleman.'

And Louren drove us out to where the dead animals lay. While the servants skinned and butchered the carcasses, Sally remained in the back seat with her face averted, her hat pulled down low over her forehead, and her eyes glued to a book.

I stood beside Louren in the bright sunlight, that was intensified by the glare of the white salt surface, and watched the gunboys cut the incisions in the skin and flay the gemsbok with the skill of a pair of Harley Street surgeons.

'You might have warned me we had one of *them* on this trip,' Louren told me bitterly. 'Am I ever regretting having given in to you and letting her come along!'

I didn't reply and he went on. 'I've a bloody good mind to send her back to Maun on one of the trucks.' The suggestion was so unworkable that it didn't give me even a twinge, and Louren went on immediately. 'She's your assistant – try and keep her under control, will you!'

I moved away, giving him time to recover his temper, and took the map-case from the seat beside Sally. She didn't look up from her book. I walked around the vehicle and spread the aeronautical large-scale map on the bonnet of the Land-Rover, and within two minutes Louren was with me. Navigation is one of his big things, and he fancies himself no end.

'We'll leave the pan here,' he pointed to where a dry river-bed joined the eastern extremity of the pan, 'and strike in on a compass-bearing.'

'What kind of going will we meet, I wonder.'

'Sand veld, like as not. I've never been in there before.'

'Let's ask the drivers,' I suggested.

'Good idea.' Louren called the two of them across and the gunboys, who had by now finished the skilled work and were leaving the rest to the camp boys, joined us as was their right.

'This is where we want to go to.' Louren pointed it out on the map. 'These hills here. They haven't got a name marked, but they run in line with the edge of the pan, like this.'

It took a moment or two for the drivers to figure out their bearings on the chart, and then a remarkable change came over both of them. Their features dissolved into blank masks of incomprehension.

'What kind of country is it between the pan and the hills?' Louren asked. He had not sensed the change in them. The drivers exchanged furtive glances.

'Well?' asked Louren.

'I do not know that country. I have never heard of these hills,' Joseph, the elder driver, muttered, and then went on to give himself the lie. 'Besides there is much sand, and there are river-beds which one cannot cross.'

'There is no water,' agreed David, the second driver. 'I have never been there. I have never heard of these hills either.'

'What do the white men seek?' asked the old gunboy in Sindebele. It was obvious that maps meant nothing to him.

'They want to go to Katuba Ngazi,' the driver explained quickly. They were all convinced by now that neither Louren nor I had mastery of the language, and that they could speak freely in front of us. This then was the first time I heard the name spoken. Katuba Ngazi – the Hills of Blood.

'What have you told them?' demanded the gunbearer.

'That we do not know the place.'

'Good,' the gunbearer agreed. 'Tell them that there are no elephant there, that the wild animals are south of the pan.' The driver dutifully relayed this intelligence, and was disappointed in our obvious lack of dismay.

'Well,' Louren told them pleasantly, 'you will learn something today. For the first time you will see these hills.' He rolled up the map. 'Now get the meat loaded and let us go on.'

In five minutes the whole tone of the expedition had changed. Sally and the entire staff were all in the deepest depression. The smiles and horse-play were gone, there were sulky faces and meetings in muttering groups. The tempo of work dropped to almost zero, and it took almost half an hour to load the butchered gemsbok. While this was happening I led Louren away from the cluster of vehicles out of earshot and quickly told him of the exchange between the African servants.

'Hills of Blood! Wonderful!' Louren enthused. 'It means that almost certainly they know about the ruins – there is probably a taboo on them.'

'Yes,' I agreed. 'But now we are going to have to watch for attempts to sabotage the trip. Look at them.' We turned to watch the slow-motion, almost somnambulistic movements of our staff. 'My guess is that it's going to take longer to reach the Hills of Blood than we allowed for.'

We got off the pan once more, for the going is suspect with soft places beneath the crust that will bog a vehicle, and we followed the firm but sandy ground along the edge. We crossed another of the steep ravines, after having scouted for a place where the banks were flattened, and drove on for twenty minutes before we realized that neither of the trucks were following us. After waiting ten minutes, with both Louren and I fuming impatiently, we turned back and retraced our course to the dry river-bed.

One truck was hanging half over the edge of the ravine, one front wheel and one rear wheel not touching earth, but its belly heavily grounded. The other truck was parked nearby, and fourteen grown men were sitting or standing around in various attitudes of relaxation without making the least attempt to free the stranded truck.

'Joseph,' Louren called the driver. 'How did this happen?'

Joseph shrugged his shoulders disinterestedly, but he was having difficulty hiding his satisfaction.

'All right, gentlemen, let's get it out,' Louren suggested with heavy irony. Half an hour later, despite the ladylike efforts of all fourteen of them, and despite Joseph's hearty clashing of gears and desperate engine racing and stalling, the truck still hung over the edge of the ravine. Finally they all climbed out of the ravine and looked at Louren and me with interest.

'Okay, Ben?' Louren turned to me as he began to strip his bush jacket.

'All right, Lo,' I agreed. I was delighted to see how well Louren had taken care of himself. His body looked rock-hard, and denuded of fatty tissue. At six foot two he carried a mass of muscle whose outlines beneath the skin were unblurred.

I kept my shirt on. My body, although it has the same utility as Louren's, is not so good to look at.

'Front end first,' Louren suggested.

The truck had been unloaded, petrol tank about half filled, I estimated the front end weight at a little over two thousand pounds. I windmilled my arms as I looked at the problem, loosening up cold muscles. The servants looked puzzled, and one of them giggled. Even Sally put aside her book and climbed out of the Land-Rover to watch.

Louren and I went to the front of the truck and stooped to it, placing our hands carefully, bending at the knee, spreading our legs a little.

'All the way, partner?'

'All the way, Lo.' I grinned back at him, and we began the lift. I started slow, just taking up the slack in my muscles, bringing on the strain evenly and letting it build up in shoulders, thighs and belly. It was a dead unmoving mass and I started to burn the reserves, feeling the tension turn to pain and my breathing start to scald my throat.

'Now,' grunted Louren beside me, and I let it all come, rearing back against it with my vision starting to star and pinwheel. It came away smoothly in our hands, and I heard the gasps and startled explanations from the watchers.

We lifted the front of the truck clear of the ravine, went around to the back and did the same there. Then we started to laugh, a little shakily at first, but building up to a full gale. Louren put his arm around my shoulder and led me back to face our retinue of retainers who were looking discomforted and uneasy.

'You are—' Louren told them, still laughing, '—a bunch of frail old women and giggling virgins. Translate that for them, Joseph.'

I noticed that Joseph gave them a correct rendition of this pleasantry.

'And as for you, Joseph, you are a fool.' Louren stepped away from me towards Joseph, one quick dancing step, and hit him with an open hand across the side of the head. The sound of it was shockingly loud, and the force of it spun Joseph fully around in a tight circle before throwing him to the ground. He sat up groggily, with a thin trickle of blood running out of the corner of his mouth where teeth had cut into the thick under lip.

'You see that I am still laughing,' Louren pointed out to his startled audience. 'I am not even angry yet. Think a while on what may happen to anyone who makes me really angry.'

The truck was reloaded with alacrity and we went on.

'Well,' said Sally, 'we can be sure of full co-operation for the rest of this trip. Why didn't the big white bwana use a sjambok, rather than soiling his hands?'

'Tell her, Ben.' Louren did not look around at either of us, while I told Sally quickly about the campaign of deliberate obstruction that we had run into.

'I'm sure Louren didn't enjoy hitting the man, Sal. But he ditched the truck deliberately. We've got three and a half days left to get to these Hills of Blood, and we can't afford any more tricks.'

Sally immediately forgot her concern for Joseph. 'Hills of Blood,' she gloated. 'My God, it conjures up visions of human sacrifice and—'

'More likely it's merely the red colour of the cliffs,' I suggested.

'And this taboo thing.' She ignored me. 'It must be because of the ruins! Oh God, I can feel it in my blood – temples stuffed with treasures, relics and written records of a whole civilization, tombs, weapons—'

'You will notice my assistant's unbiased, unromantic and thoroughly scientific approach,' I pointed out to Louren, and he grinned.

'It irks me like hell, but for once I feel the way she does,' Louren admitted.

'For once that makes you smart, dearie,' Sally told him tartly.

It was two in the afternoon before we reached the point on the eastern extremity of the pan where we were to cut off on compass for the hills, and almost immediately it became apparent that we would not reach them that day. The going was heavy, sand-veld clutched at the wheels of the vehicles and reduced our rate of progress to a low-gear slog. Half a dozen times the trucks bogged in the thick sand, and had to be dragged out by the four-wheel transmission of the Land-Rover. Each time this happened there was a profuse offering of apologies from the driver and crew concerned.

The sand had absorbed all traces of the recent rains, but they showed in the new growth of green that decked the thorn and acacia trees – and more dramatically in the display of wild flowers that were spread everywhere in carpets and thick banks.

Their seeds and bulbs had lain dormant for three long years of drought, waiting for this time of plenty – and now the bright crimson of King Chaka's fire burned brilliantly among the fields of Namaqua daisies. Star lilies, Ericas, golden Gazanias and twenty other varieties made a royal show, and helped to lessen the frustrations of our snail's progress.

At every enforced halt, I left the cursing and hustling to Louren, and wandered away from the vehicles with my camera.

Sunset found us still fifteen miles from the hills, and when I climbed into the top branches of the flat-topped acacia under which we camped, I could see their low outlines on the eastern horizon. The cliffs caught the last slanted rays of the sun, and glowed orange-red. I sat in the fork of the main trunk and watched them until the sun was gone and the hills melted into the dark sky.

A strange mood gripped me as I watched the far hills. A mystic sense of pre-destiny filled me with a languid melancholy – a sense of unease and disquiet.

When I climbed down into the camp, Louren sat alone by the fire, staring into the flames and drinking whisky.

'Where's Sally?' I asked.

'Gone to bed. In a sulk. We got into a discussion about blood sports and beating up blacks.' Louren glanced at her tent which glowed with internal lantern light. There was no singing from the servants' fire as Louren and I ate grilled gemsbok liver and bacon, washed down with warm red Cape wine. We sat in silence for a while after we had eaten, and finished the wine.

'I'm bushed,' Louren said at last, and stood up. 'I'll just call Larkin. I promised to check in every second night. See you in the morning, Ben.'

I watched him cross to the Land-Rover and switch on the two-way radio set. I heard Larkin's boozy voice through the buzz and crackle of static. I listened for a few minutes, while Louren made his report. Then I stood up also and moved away from the camp-fire.

Restless, and still under the spell of my mood of disquiet, I wandered into the dark again. The gemsbok carcasses had attracted a pack of hyena to the camp, and they giggled and screeched out among the thorn trees. So I kept close to camp, passing Sally's tent and pausing for a while to draw comfort from her nearness, then walked on towards the servants' fire. My feet made no sound in the soft sand, and one of the old gunbearers was speaking as I approached. He had the attention of all the others who squatted in a circle about the low fire. His words came to me clearly, and stirred my memory. I felt the tingle of them run along my spine, and the ghost fingers stroked my arms and neck bringing the hair erect.

'This evil to be cleaned from the earth and from the minds of men, for ever.'

The words were exactly those that Timothy Mageba had spoken – the same words, but in a different language. I stared fascinated at the lined and time-quarried features of the old Matabele. It was as though he sensed my scrutiny for he looked up and saw me standing in the shadows.

He spoke again, warning them. 'Be careful, the spider is here,' he said. They had named me for my small body and long limbs. His words released them from the spell that held them, they shuffled their feet and coughed, glancing at me. I turned and moved away, but the old Matabele's words stayed with me. They troubled me, increasing my restless mood.

Sally's tent was dark now, and Louren's also. I went to my own bed and lay awake far into the night, listening to the hyenas and pondering what tomorrow would bring. One thing was certain, by noon we would know if the patterns on the photograph were natural or man-made, and with that thought I at last fell asleep.

We could see the hills from the front seat of the Land-Rover by ten the following morning. They showed orange-red beyond the tops of the taller acacias, stretching across our front, higher at the centre of our horizon then dwindling in size as they strung out on either hand.

I took over the driving from Louren while he pored over map and photograph, directing me in towards the highest point of the cliffs. There was a distinctive clump of giant candelabra euphorbia trees on the skyline of the cliff – and these showed up clearly in the photograph. Louren was using them to orientate our approach.

The cliffs were between two and three hundred feet high, their exposed fronts furrowed and weather-worn, rising almost sheer to the crests. Later I was to find that they were a form of hardened sandstone heavily pigmented with mineral oxides. Below the cliffs grew a small grove of big trees, and it was clear that there was underground water trapped there to nourish these giants. Their exposed roots twisted and writhed up the face of the cliff like frenzied pythons, and their dense, dark green foliage was a welcome relief from the drab greenish grey of the thorn and acacia. In a strip about half a mile wide, the ground before the cliffs was open and sparsely covered with a low growth of scrub and pale grass.

I threaded the Land-Rover through the scrub towards the cliffs in a silence which momentarily grew more strained. Closer we crawled towards the towering red cliffs, until we had to crane our necks to look up at them.

Sally broke the silence at last, voicing our disappointment and chagrin. 'Well, we should be within the great walls of the main enclosure now – if there was one.'

We parked at the foot of the cliff and climbed out stiffly to look around us, subdued and reluctant to meet each other's eyes. There was no trace of a city, not a single dressed block of stone, not a raised mound of earth nor the faintest outline of wall or keep. This was virgin African bush and kopje, untouched and unmarked by man.

'You're sure this is the right place?' Sally asked miserably, and we did not answer her. The trucks came up and parked. The servants climbed down in small groups, peering up at the cliffs and talking in hushed tones.

'All right,' said Louren. 'While they set up the camp we will scout the area. I will go along the cliff that way. You two go the other way – and, Ben, take my shotgun with you.'

We picked our way along the base of the cliff, through the grove of silent trees. Once we startled a small troop of vervet monkeys in the high branches and they fled through the treetops in shrieking consternation. Their antics couldn't raise a smile from either Sally or me. We paused to examine the cliff at intervals, but there was little enthusiasm or hope in our efforts. Three or four miles from camp we stopped to rest, sitting on a block of sandstone that had fallen out from the cliff face.

'I could cry,' said Sal. 'I really could.'

'I know. I feel the same way.'

'But the photograph. Damn it, there was definitely *something* showing. You don't think it's his idea of a joke, do you?'

'No.' I shook my head. 'Lo wouldn't do that. He was just as keen as we were.'

'Then what about the photograph?'

'I don't know. It was clearly some sort of optical illusion. The shadow from the cliff, and cloud perhaps.'

'But those patterns!' she protested. 'They are geometrical and symmetrical.'

'Light can play funny tricks, Sal,' I said. 'Remember that photograph was taken at six o'clock in the evening – almost sunset. Low sun throwing shadows, you could get almost any effect.'

'I think this is the most disappointing thing that has ever happened to me.' She really did look as though she might burst into tears, and I went to her shyly and put one long arm around her.

'I'm sorry,' I said, and she pulled a face and offered her lips to be kissed.

'Wow!' she said at last. 'Dr. Kazin, you do carry on!'

'You ain't seen nothing yet.'

'I've seen too much.' She broke away gently. 'Come on, Ben. Let's circle back to camp, away from the cliff. There may be something out there.'

We tramped slowly through the heat. The flowers were out here also, and I noticed the bees crawling busily into the blossoms, their back legs thick with yellow pollen. We found where the recent rains had scoured a shallow ravine, although there was no remaining trace of moisture. I climbed down into the ravine and examined the exposed layers of stone and earth. Three feet from the surface the pebbles were rounded and water-worn.

'Good guess, Sal,' I told her as I picked out a few pebbles and found the shell of a bivalve encrusted in the half-formed sandstone. 'That proves at least a little of our theory. At one time this was the bed of a lake – look.'

Eagerly Sal clambered down beside me. 'What is it?'

'A type of *unionidae*, fresh-water African mussel.'

'I wish,' said Sally, 'that it were something a little more exciting.' She dropped the ancient shell in the sand.

'Yes,' I agreed, and climbed out of the ravine.

My only excuse is that my reasoning was clouded by intense disappointment and my recent physical excitement with Sally. I do not usually behave in such a cavalier fashion with scientific clues. Nor do I usually miss as many as four hints in the space of an hour. We walked away without a backward glance.

The camp was fully set up and functioning smoothly when Sal and I trailed in, sweaty and dusty, and sat down to lunch of tinned ham and Windhoek beer.

'Anything?' asked Louren, and we shook our heads in unison and lifted our beer glasses.

'Warm!' Sally spoke with disgust at her first taste of the beer.

'Cook has got the refrigerator going. It'll be cold by tonight.'

We ate in silence until Louren spoke. 'I raised Larkin on the radio while you were away. He will send in a helicopter tomorrow. We'll have a last search from the air. That will settle it once and for all. If there's nothing doing, I will fly out. Some things are brewing back in Johannesburg, and there is only one passenger seat, I'm afraid. You two will have to bus out the hard way.'

It was at that moment that a deputation arrived, headed by Joseph, to tell us that some unknown and foolish person had left the taps open on four of the water tanks. We had thirty-five gallons of water between seventeen people to last the rest of the trip.

'Therefore,' added Joseph, with evident relish, 'we will have to leave this place tomorrow, and return to the nearest water on the Maun road.'

There were a few expressions of disgust at this latest, clearly deliberate setback, but none of us could work up any real anger.

'All right, Joseph,' Louren agreed with resignation. 'Break camp tomorrow morning. We will leave before lunch.' There was an immediate improvement in employer-employee relations. I even noticed a few smiles, and heard a little laughter from the cooking fire.

'I don't know what you two intend doing this afternoon,' Louren lit a cigar as he spoke, 'but I noticed elephant spoor when I did my little recce this morning. I'm taking the Land-Rover and the gunbearers. Don't worry if I don't arrive back tonight, we may get hung up on the spoor.'

Sally looked up quickly; for a moment I thought she was going to start her anti-blood sport campaign again, but instead she merely frowned and went back to her ham. I watched the Land-Rover drive off along the base of the cliff before I suggested to Sally:

'I'm going to try and find a path up to the top – do you want to come along?'

'Deal me out, Ben,' she answered. 'I think I'll do some sketching this afternoon.'

Hiding my disappointment as best I could, I set off along the base of the cliff, and within half a mile I had found a game trail leading into one of the bush-choked gullies that furrowed the face of red rock.

It was a steep climb and I toiled up with the sun burning onto my back and bouncing off the rock into my face. From cracks and crannies in the cliff-face an army of furry little rock rabbits watched my endeavours with avid interest. It was forty minutes before I came out on the top, my arms scratched by the thorny undergrowth of the gully and sweat soaking my shirt.

I found a good vantage point on the front edge of the cliff under the spreading shade of a giant euphorbia, and my first concern was to sweep with the binoculars for any trace of ruins. The thorn bush at the base of the cliff below me was fairly open and scantily grassed, and immediately it was obvious that there was no trace of any human habitation or cultivation. I shouldn't really have hoped for more, but disappointment gave a sickening little lurch in my guts. Then I dismissed it, and. turned the glasses towards the camp far below. A Bantu was cutting firewood, and for a while I amused myself by watching the axe-stroke, then listening for the sound of the blow seconds later. I searched further from the camp and picked up Sally's rose-coloured blouse at the edge of the grove. She had obviously given up all hope of a major discovery and, sensible girl, was deriving what other enjoyment she could from the expedition. I watched her for a long time, trying to decide how exactly to proceed with my campaign to make her my own. I had spent one night with her, but I was not so naïve as to believe that this proved a breathless and undying passion on behalf of a sophisticated highly intelligent and extravagantly educated modern Miss. Angel that she was, yet I was pretty damned certain that my Sally had played the game with other men before Dr. Ben stumbled starry-eyed into her bed. The odds were extremely high she had been motivated by respect for my mind rather than my body, pity, and possibly a little perverse curiosity. However, I was almost certain she had not found the experience too repulsive, and I had only to keep working on her to change respect and pity into something a little deeper and more permanent.

A good quiet sense of peace came over me as I sat there in the high kranz; slowly I realized that this whole journey had been worthwhile and I found myself wishing that I could stay longer at these haunting Hills of Blood, with their mystery and silent beauty. Sally and I together here in the wilderness where I could teach her to love me.

A flicker of movement in the corner of my eye made me turn my head slowly, and within six feet of where I sat a marico sunbird was sucking the nectar from the blossoms of a wild aloe, its metallic green head shimmering as it dipped the long curved bill into the fiery red blossoms. I watched it with an intense pleasure, and when it was gone on quick darting wings I felt as though I had missed something. The feeling became stronger, making me restless, there was a message somewhere that was trying to come through to me but it was being blocked. I let my brain relax, and had the feeling that it was just there at the very fringe of my conscious mind. Another second and I would have it.

Dull on the hot breathless hush of afternoon the double boom-boom of distant heavy gunfire jerked my attention away. I sat up and listened for another thirty seconds – then it came again, boom, and again. Louren had found his elephant.

I picked Sally up in the field of the binoculars. She had heard it also, and was standing away from her easel staring out into the bush. I stood up also, my sudden restlessness still persisting, and started down the cliff path again. I could not shake off the mood, and it grew stronger. There is *something* here, I thought, something strange and inexplicable.

'You and I are lucky, my friend,' Timothy Mageba had told me once. 'We are marked by the spirits and we have the eye within that can see beyond, and the ear that can catch the sounds of silence.'

It was cool now in the heavily shaded gully and my shirt was still damp with sweat. I felt the goose pimples rising on my skin but not entirely from the chill. I began to hurry, I wanted to get back to the camp and Sally.

For dinner that night we ate grilled elephant heart sliced thin and covered with a biting pepper sauce, served with potatoes roasted in their jackets. The beer was icy cold as Louren had promised, and he was in an expansive mood. It had been a good day's hunt, fully compensating him for the other disappointments. Lying in the lantern light beyond the fire were four long, curved yellow tusks of ivory.

When Louren sets out to be charming, he is irresistible. Although Sally tried to maintain a disapproving attitude at first, she soon succumbed to his charisma and she laughed with us when Louren gave us the toast. 'To the city that never was, and the treasure we didn't find.'

I went to bed a little drunk, and I dreamed strange dreams – but I woke in the morning clear-headed and with an unformed sense of excitement buoying me, as though today something good was going to happen.

The helicopter came out of the south an hour before noon, drawn to us by the smudge fires of oil-soaked rag; it sank noisily down towards the camp on its glistening silver rotor, and raised a whirlwind of dust and debris.

There was a brief conference with the dark-haired young pilot, then Louren climbed into the seat beside him and the ungainly craft lifted into the air once more and began a series of sweeps along the cliffs, rising higher with each pass until it was a dark insect speck in the aching blue of that hot high sky. Its manoeuvres were so clearly indicative of failure, that Sally and I soon lost interest and went to sit in the shade of the dining tent.

'Well,' she said, 'that is that, I guess.'

I didn't answer her, but went to the refrigerator and brought us each a can of Windhoek. For the first time in days the fabled Kazin brain began running on all cylinders. Thirty gallons of water shared between two persons meant a gallon a day for two weeks. Water? There was something else about water in the back of my mind. Sally and water.

The helicopter landed once more on the outskirts of the camp, and Louren and the pilot came to the tent. Louren shook his head.

'No go. Nothing. We'll have a bite of lunch and be on our way. Leave you to make the best of it home.'

I nodded agreement, not telling him my plans to forestall any argument.

'Well, Ben, I'm sorry about this. I just can't understand it.' Louren began building himself a sandwich of bread and cold slices of roast gemsbok fillet, smearing it with mustard. 'Anyway, it won't be the last disappointment we will ever have in our lives.'

Twenty minutes later Louren's essential luggage was packed in the helicopter and while the pilot started the motor we said our farewells.

'See you back in jolly Jo'burg. Look after those tusks for me.'

'Good trip, Lo.'

'All the way, partner?'

'All the way, Lo.'

Then he was ducking under the spinning rotor and climbing into the passenger's seat of the helicopter. It rose in the air like a fat bumble-bee and clattered away over the tree-tops. Bumble-bee? Bee? Bee! My God, that was what had been niggling me.

Bees, birds and monkeys!

I grabbed Sally's arm, my excitement startling her.

'Sally, we're staying.'

'What?' She gaped at me.
'There are things here we've overlooked.'
'Like what?'
'The birds and the bees,' I told her.
Why, you randy old thing', she said.

We split the water fifteen to twenty gallons. That would give the servants a little over half a gallon a day each for two days, sufficient to get them out safely. Sally and I would have a full gallon a day for ten days. I kept the Land-Rover, making sure the petrol tanks were full, and there were twenty-five gallons in the emergency cans. I kept also the radio, one tent, bedding; a selection of tools including spade, axe and pick, rope, gas lanterns and spare cylinders, torches and spare batteries, tinned food, Louren's shotgun and half a dozen packets of shells, together with all of Sally's and my personal gear. All the rest of the equipment was loaded onto the two trucks and when the servants were all on board I took the old Matabele gunbearer aside.

'My old and respected father,' I spoke in Sindebele, 'I have heard you speak of a great mystery that lives in this place. I ask you now as a son, and a friend, to speak to me of these things.'

It took him a few seconds to get over his astonishment. Then I went on to speak a sentence that Timothy Mageba had given me. It is a secret code, a recognition signal used at a high level among the initiates to the mysteries. The old man gasped. He could not question me now, nor ignore my appeal.

'My son,' he spoke softly 'If you know those words then you should know of the legend. At a time when the rocks were soft and the air was misty,' an expression of the uttermost antiquity, 'there was an abomination and an evil in this place which was put down by our ancestors. They placed a death curse upon these hills and commanded that this evil be cleaned from the earth and from the minds of men, for ever.'

Again those fateful words, repeated exactly.

'That is the whole legend?' I asked. 'There is nothing else?'

'There is nothing else,' the old man told me, and I knew it was the truth. We went back to the waiting lorries and I spoke to Joseph first in Shangaan.

'Go in peace, my friend. Drive carefully and care well for those who ride with you – for they are precious to me.' Joseph gaped at me, his wits scattered. I turned to the camp boys and changed to Sechuana.

'The Spider gives you greetings and wishes you peace.' There was consternation amongst them as I used my nickname, but when they drove away they had recovered from the shock and were laughing delightedly at the joke. The trucks disappeared amongst the thorn trees, and the sound of their motors dwindled into the eternal silence of the deep bush.

'You know,' Sally murmured reflectively, 'I think I've been took! Here I am stranded 200 miles from anywhere with a man whose morals are definitely suspect.' Then she giggled. 'And isn't it lovely?' she asked.

I had found the spot on the top of the cliff where I could lean out over the drop, supported by a hefty young baboon apple tree, and obtain a good view of the rock screen on either side, as well as over the open plain below. Sally was down beyond the silent grove, and I could see her clearly.

The sun seemed at the right angle for her, although it was shining directly into my eyes. It was only ten or fifteen degrees above the horizon now and the golden rays brought out new soft colours from rock and foliage.

'Yoo hoo!' Sally's shout carried faintly up to me, and she held both hands straight up towards the sky. It was the signal we had evolved to mean, 'Come back towards me.'

'Good,' I grunted. She must have picked them up. I had explained to her carefully how to shade her eyes against the slant of the sun's rays and to watch for the arrow-straight flight of the tiny golden motes of light. It was an old trick used by bee hunters to find the hive, a bushman had taught it to me.

I pulled back from the cliff, and began working my way through the thorns and thick bush that clogged the crest. I had guessed where to begin the search, for the chances were enormously in favour of the hive being located in this tall wall of red rock with its many gullies and crevices, and now with Sally calling the range for me from below, it was only a matter of fifteen minutes before she windmilled her arms and I heard her call.

'That's it! Right under you.' Again I leaned out over the edge, and now I picked up the swift sunlit flight of the returning bees as they homed in on the cliff below me.

Leaning far out I could make out the entrance to the hive; a long diagonal crack the edges of which were discoloured by old wax. It must have been an enormous hive, judging by the number of workers coming in, and by the extent of the waxing around the entrance. In such an inaccessible position it had probably remained undisturbed by man or beast for hundreds of years. A rarity in this land where honey is so highly prized.

I tied my white handkerchief to an overhanging branch to mark the spot and in the swiftly falling dark I went down to Sally on the plain. She was very excited by our small success, and we discussed the implications of it over our dinner.

'You are really quite clever, Doc Ben.'

'On the contrary, I was as slow as doomsday. I had to beat my head against all the signs for two whole days before I tumbled to it,' I told her smugly. 'The place is thick with birds, animals and bees, all of which must have a good permanent supply of surface water. There is supposed to be no permanent water for two hundred miles – well, that's wrong for sure.'

'Where will we find it, I wonder?' She was all big-eyed and enthusiastic again.

'I can't even guess, but when we do I promise you something interesting.'

That night when I came into the tent in my pyjmas, having modestly changed outside, she was already in her bed with the sheets up under her chin. I hesitated in the space between the two camp-beds, until with a mischievous grin she took pity on me and lifted the blankets beside her in invitation.

'Come to Mama,' she said.

In the chilly darkness before dawn I huddled in my leather jacket on the cliff above the hive, and waited for the sun. I was a very happy man again, some of my doubt dispelled during the night.

Down on the dark plain there was a flash of light. Sally at her place beyond the grove again, probably lonely and a little scared in the African darkness with its night rustlings and animal cries. I flashed my torch down at her to reassure her, and the dawn started coming on quickly.

Dawn was a thing of soft pinks and roses, misty mauves and mulberry – then the sun burst up above the horizon and the bees began to fly. For twenty minutes I watched them to decide the pattern and purpose of their flight. There was a fan of workers winging wide out over the plain. These were the pollen-gatherers. I established this by leaning out and watching their return, through the binoculars, checking the bunches of yellow pollen on their hind legs as they alighted on the protruding bulge of the crack.

In so doing I discovered another pattern of flight that I might have missed. A steady stream of workers was dropping almost vertically down towards the dark foliage of the silent grove below me – and on their return there was no pollen on their legs. Water-carriers then! I signalled Sally in towards the base of the cliff, this morning our roles were reversed by the slant and angle of the sun's rays. After a while she waved to let me know she had spotted them, and I began the laborious climb down to the plain.

She had to point out to me the indistinct flight of bees down the cliff towards the grove, but even then the shadow cast by the cliff caused them to vanish before we could establish their exact destination within the grove. We watched them for thirty minutes, then gave it up and went into the trees to search at random.

By noon I could swear that there was no sign of surface water within the environs of the grove. Sally and I flopped down side by side with our backs to the sturdy trunk of one of the mhoba-hoba trees, the wild loquat tree that legend states the ancients brought with them from their homeland, and we looked at each other in despair.

'Another blank!' She was perspiring in a light dew across her forehead and temples and a dark curl was plastered to the skin. With one finger I pushed it gently back and tucked it behind her ear.

'It's here, somewhere. We'll find it,' I told her with the confidence I did not feel. 'It's got to be here. It just has to be.'

She was about to answer me, when I pressed my fingers to her lips to silence her. I had seen movement beyond the last trees of the grove. We watched the troop of vervet monkeys crossing the open plain at a gallop with their tails in the air. As they reached the grove they shot up the trunk of the nearest tree with comical relief. Their little black faces peered down anxiously from the massed green foliage, but they did not notice us sitting quietly at the base of the mhoba-hoba.

Confidently now they moved across the tree-tops towards the cliff, the big males leading while the mothers, with infants slung beneath their bodies, and the rabble of half-grown youngsters followed them.

They reached the top branches of a gargantuan wild fig tree, one of those whose roots and trunk were embedded in the vertical cliff wall of red rock, and whose branches spread wide and green fifty feet above the earth – and they began to disappear.

It was an astonishing phenomenon, sixty monkeys went into the tree and dwindled swiftly until the branches were deserted. Not a single monkey was left.

'What happened to them?' whispered Sally. 'Did they go up the cliff?'

'No, I don't think so.' I turned to her grinning happily. 'I think we've found it, Sal. I think this is it, but let's just wait for the monkeys to come back.'

Twenty minutes later the monkeys suddenly began reappearing in the branches of the wild fig again. The troop moved off in a leisurely fashion along the cliff, and we waited until they were all out of sight before we went forward.

The convoluted and massed roots of the wild fig formed a flight of irregular steps up towards the point where the trunk emerged from the cliff. We climbed up and began examining the trunk, working our way around it, peering up into the branches high overhead. The trunk was gigantic, fully thirty feet around, deformed and flattened by its contact with the uneven wall of red rock. Even then we might have missed it, had there not been a smoothly polished footpath leading into the living rock – a path worn by the passage of feet and paws and hooves over the course of thousands of years. The path squeezed between the gross yellow trunk of the wild fig, and the wall of rock. In the same manner as there is often a cave behind a waterfall hidden by the falling water, so our wild fig screened the entrance.

Sally and I peered into the darkened recess behind the trunk, and then we looked at each other. Her eyes were sparkling bright and her cheeks flushed a dull rose.

'Yes!' she whispered, and I nodded, unable to speak.

'Come on!' She took my hand and we went in.

The opening was a long vertical crack in the cliff and good light came in from high above. Looking up I saw how the rock was polished by the paws of the monkeys who came in that way.

We moved on down the passage, the wall rising twenty feet on each side of us to a narrow vee of a roof. Immediately it was clear that we were not the first human beings that had entered here. The smooth red walls were covered with a profusion of magnificent bushman rock paintings. The most beautiful and well preserved that I had ever seen.

'Ben! Oh Ben! Just look at them!' One of Sally's specialities is bushman art. 'It's a treasure house. Oh, you wonderful clever man!' Her eyes shone in the gloom like lamps.

'Come on!' I tugged at her hand. 'There will be plenty of time for that later.'

We moved slowly along the narrow passage as it slanted steadily downwards for another hundred feet. The roof above us climbed progressively higher, until it was lost in the gloom above. We heard the squeak of bats from the dark recesses of the passage.

'There is light ahead,' I said, and we went on into an open chamber, rounded, perhaps 300 feet across with sheer walls which rose 200 feet upwards. Like the interior walls of a cone, they narrowed into a small aperture high above which gave a view of cloudless blue sky beyond.

I saw immediately that this was an intrusion of limestone into the red sandstone, and that it was a typical sink-hole formation, very similar to the Sleeping Pool at Sinoia in Rhodesia.

Here also the floor of the cavern was a basin which led down to a pool of water. The water was crystal clear, obviously very deep as the pale greenish colour showed, perhaps 150 feet across, the surface mirror-smooth and still.

Sally and I stood and stared at it. The beauty of this great cavern had paralysed us. Through the tiny aperture 200 feet above us the sun's rays poured in like the beam of a searchlight, striking the walls of shimmering limestone and lighting the entire cavern with an eerie reflected glow. From the arched roof and walls hung great butterfly wings and stalactites of sparkling white.

The walls of the main chamber were also decorated to a height of fifteen feet or more with the lovely bushman art. In places water seeping from the rock had destroyed the graceful figures and designs, but mostly it was well preserved. I guessed there was two years' work for Sally and me in this wondrous place.

Slowly she disengaged her hand from mine and I walked down to the edge of the emerald pool. I stayed where I was in the mouth of the tunnel, watching her with rapt attention as she stood at the edge of the pool and leaned forward to peer down into the still water.

Then she straightened and slowly, with deliberate movements, began to strip off her clothing. She stood naked at the edge of the pool and her skin was as pale and translucent as the limestone cliffs. Her body, for all its size and strength, had a delicacy of line and texture to it that reminded me of the Chinese carvings in old ivory.

Like a priestess of some old pagan religion, she stood beside the pool and lifted her arms. With a strange atavistic thrill this gesture brought to my mind an ancient forgotten ritual. There was something deep in me that I wanted to cry out, a blessing perhaps, or an invocation.

Then she dived, a long graceful curve of white body and flowing dark hair. She struck the water and went on down, deep. The sweet clean shape of her showed clearly through the crystal water, then she came up slowly from the depths and broke the surface. Her long dark hair was slicked down over her neck and shoulders, she lifted one slender arm and waved at me.

I felt like crying out aloud with relief. I realized then that I had not expected her to come up again from those mysterious green depths. I went down to the edge of the pool to help her out of the water.

Presently we moved slowly around the walls of the cavern and passage, awed by the profusion of paintings and engravings Sally with her damp hair hanging to her shoulders and her face shining with wonder.

'There is work here spread over 2,000 years, Ben. This must have been a very holy place to the little yellow men.' The light failed before we had completed half the tour of the cavern, and it was chilly and scary in the passage as we groped our way out. It was only then that I realized we had not eaten that day.

While Sally warmed up a hash of bully beef and onions, I raised Peter Larkin on the radio and was relieved to hear that the two trucks had returned safely to Maun. I ended the transmission by asking Larkin to get a message through to Louren. 'Tell him we have found some very interesting rock paintings and will be staying on here indefinitely.'

'How are you for water?' bellowed Larkin, his voice distorted by static and Scotch whisky.

'Fine. We managed to find an adequate supply here.'

'You found water?' roared Larkin. 'There isn't any water there!'

'A small catchment in a rock basin from the last rain.'

'Oh, I see. Okay then. Keep in touch. Over and out.'

'Thanks, Peter. Over and out.'

'You are a fibber.' Sally grinned at me as I switched off the set.

'All in a good cause,' I agreed, and we began to prepare lanterns, and cameras, and sketching equipment for the following day.

The old bull elephant was mortally wounded. Blood, slick and shiny, poured from the wounds in throat and shoulder and the shafts of fifty arrows pin-cushioned his massive frame. He stood at bay, with his back humped in agony, while around him swarmed the brave little yellow hunters with drawn bows, and pelting arrows. A dozen of their number were strewn back along the path of the hunt, their frail bodies crushed and broken beneath the great round pads and cruel ivory shafts – but the others were closing in for the kill.

The ancient artist had filled his canvas of red rock with such movement and drama that I felt myself a witness to the actual hunt. However, the light was tricky and the best reading I could get was F.11. at 1/10th of a second.

Reluctantly I decided to use flash. I try to avoid it where possible for it tends to distort colour and throw in false highlights. I began setting up tripod and camera when Sally called.

'Ben! Come here, please!'

The echo effect and distortion caused by the lofty cavern could not disguise the urgency and excitement in her voice, and I went quickly.

She was in the main cavern beyond the emerald pool, where the rear wall cut back steeply to form a low recess. It was gloomy in there and Sally's torch beam jumped quickly over the smooth rock surface.

'What is it, Sal?' I asked as I came up beside her.

'Look.' She moved the torch beam down and I stared at the representation of a massive human figure before me.

'Good God!' I gasped. 'The White Lady of the Brandberg!* It's the same!'

Sally played the beam of the torch down across the figure until it spotlighted the vaunting erection that thrust from its thighs.

'That *lady* is beautifully hung,' she murmured, 'if you get the point.'

The figure was six feet tall, dressed in yellow breastplate and ornate helmet with a high arched crest. On his left shoulder he carried a rounded shield on which yellow ornamental rosettes were set in a circle about the central boss. In his other hand he carried a bow and sheaf of arrows, and from his waist hung sword and battle-axe. His shins were protected by greaves of the same yellow metal and on his feet were light open sandals.

The figure's skin was depicted as deathly white, but a fiery bush of red beard hung onto his chest. The display of his sexual parts was clearly a stylized indication of his dominant and lofty status. The effect was in no way obscene, but gave to the figure a masculine pride and arrogance.

'A white man,' I whispered. 'Armour and rounded shield, bow and battle-axe. Could it be—'

'A Phoenician king,' Sally finished for me.

'But the Phoenician type is more likely to have been dark-haired, hook-nosed. This man would have been an unusual figure among the ancients, to say the least. A throw-back, perhaps, to some north Mediterranean ancestor. How old is it, Sal?'

'I can't be sure yet, but I'd say 2,000 years. This wall of paintings is the most ancient in the whole cavern.'

'Look, Sal'. I pointed eagerly.

Beyond the central figure was an army of stick figures that followed the king. They were not executed in such detail, but the swords and helmets were unmistakable.

'And look there.' Sally directed the beam of the torch onto a row of white-robed figures that stood at the king's feet. Tiny figures, perhaps nine inches tall.

'Priests, perhaps – and, oh Ben! Look! Look!'

She played the beam across the stone canvas, and for a moment I did not recognize it – then my heart jumped. Like a huge frieze, that was obliterated in places by moisture, moss and lichens, or that was obscured by the myriad figures of men and animals drawn over it, and that yet managed to maintain

---

* The White Lady of the Brandberg is one of the most celebrated and controversial rock paintings yet discovered in Africa. Its date is agreed at about A.D. 0–200, but its interpretation is the subject of much dispute. One source claims it is a Xhosa circumcision candidate daubed with white clay (one thousand miles from the territory of the Xhosa). The famous Abbé Breuil named it a lady, and Credo Mutwa in his recent book *Idaba My Children* gives an intriguing interpretation in which he concludes '— It is not a Lady, but a strikingly handsome young white man, one of the great emperors who ruled the African Empire of the Ma-iti (Phoenicians) for nearly two centuries.'

its imposing majesty and power, swept the drawing of a stone fortress wall. It was built in blocks with the joints clearly shown, and along its summit was the decorative pattern of chevrons, identical to the one that graces the main temple wall at the ruins of Zimbabwe. Beyond the wall rose outlines of the phallic towers we had expected to find.

'It's our city, Ben. Our lost city.'

'And our lost king, Sally, and his priests, and warriors and – oh, my God! Sally, look at that!'

'Elephants!' she squealed. 'War elephants with archers on their backs, just like Hannibal used against the Romans. Carthaginian – Phoenician!'

There was so much of it, a curved wall 100 feet long and ten to fifteen feet high and every square inch of it thick with bushman paintings. The figures and forms were interwoven, some of the earlier pictures overlaid and smothered; others, like our white king, standing proudly untouched and unspoiled. It would be a major undertaking to unravel those portraits which related to our lost civilization, from the great mass of traditional cave art. This was Sally's special skill, my camera could only capture the whole confused scene, while she would patiently and painstakingly pick out a figure or group of particular interest that was almost entirely obliterated and recreate and restore it on her rolls of wax paper.

However, there was no suggestion of such work beginning now. Sally and I spent what was left of the day climbing and crawling along the back wall peering and probing and exclaiming with wonder and delight.

When we got into camp that night we were physically and emotionally exhausted. Peter Larkin had a message for us from Louren:

'He says to wish you good luck, and that one of the oil helicopters will be in your area within the next few days. Is there anything you need, and if so give me a list. They will drop it to you.'

The next ten days were the happiest of my entire life. The helicopter came as Louren had promised with the name 'Sturvesant Oil' blazoned across its fuselage. It carried a full load of necessities and luxuries for us, another tent, folding chairs, a surveyor's theodolite, gas for the lamps, food, extra clothing for both of us, more paper and paints for Sally, film for me, and even a few bottles of Glen Grant malt whisky, that sovereign specific for all the ills of man. A note from Louren enjoined me to carry on with what I was doing as long as it looked promising. He would give me his full support, but I was not to keep him in the dark too long as he was 'dying of curiosity'.

I sent him my thanks, a roll of film showing the paintings which had no ancients in them, and a batch of Polythene bags containing samples of pigments from the cavern for carbon-14 dating. Then the helicopter flew away and left us to our idyll.

We worked from early each morning until dark each evening, mapping the cavern in plan and elevation, and photographing an overlapping run of the walls and relating this to our map. Sally alternated between assisting me and continuing with her own task of isolating our ancient figures. We worked in complete harmony and understanding, breaking off now and then to eat our lunch beside the emerald pool, or to swim naked together in its cool limpid water, or at times just to lie idly on the rocks and talk.

At first our occupation of the cavern seriously affected the ecology of the local fauna, but as we hoped would happen, they soon adapted. Within days the birds were dropping down through the hole in the cavern roof to drink and bathe at the edge of the pool. Soon they ignored us as they went about their noisy and vigorous ablutions, shrieking and chattering and spraying water, while we paused in our labours to watch them.

Even the monkeys, driven by thirst, at last crept in through the rock passage to snatch a mouthful of water before darting away again. Rapidly these timid forays became bolder, until at last they were a positive nuisance, stealing our lunch, or any loose equipment that was left unguarded. We forgave them, for their antics were always appealing and entertaining.

They were wonderful days of satisfying work, good loving companionship, and the deep peace of that beautiful place. There was only one day on which anything happened to ruffle the surface of my happiness. As Sally and I were sitting below the portrait of our wonderful white king, I said: 'They won't be able to deny this, Sal. The bastards are going to have to change their narrow little minds now!'

She knew I was talking about the debunkers, the special pleaders, the politico-archaeologists, who could twist any evidence to fill the needs of their own beliefs, the ones who had castigated me and my books.

'Don't be so certain of that, Ben,' Sally warned. 'They will not accept this. I can hear their carping little voices now. It's secondhand observation by bushmen, open to different interpretations – don't you remember, Ben, how they accused the Abbé Breuil of retouching the paintings in the Brandberg?'

'Yes. That's the great pity of it – it *is* secondhand. When we show them the paintings of the fortified walls, they will say, "Yes, but where are the walls themselves?"'

'And our king, our beautiful virile warrior king,' she looked up at him, 'they'll emasculate him. He will become another "White Lady". His war shield will become a bouquet of flowers, his milky white skin will change to ceremonial clay, his fiery red beard will suddenly turn into a scarf or a necklace, and when they reproduce his portrait it will be subtly altered in all those ways. The *Encyclopaedia Britannica* will still read,' she changed her voice, mimicking a pedantic and pompous lecturer, ' "modern scientific opinion is that the ruins are the work of some Bantu group, possibly the Shona or Makalang."'

'I wish – oh, how I wish we had found some definite proof,' I said miserably. I was facing for the first time the prospect of delivering our discovery to my learned brothers in science, and the idea was as appealing as climbing into a pit full of black mambas. I stood up. 'Let's have a swim, Sal.'

We swam side by side, an easy breast stroke, back and forth across the pool. When we climbed out to sit in the spot of bright sunlight that fell from the roof above, I tried to alleviate my unhappiness by changing the subject. I touched Sally's arm, and with all the finesse of a wounded rhinoceros, I blurted out, 'Will you marry me, Sally?'

She turned a startled face to me, her cheeks and eyelashes still bejewelled with water droplets, and she stared at me for fully ten seconds before she began to laugh.

'Oh, Ben, you funny old-fashioned thing! This is the twentieth century. Just because you done me wrong – doesn't mean you have to marry me!' And before I could protest or explain she had stood up and dived once again into the emerald pool.

For the rest of that day she was completely occupied with her paints and brushes, and she had no time to even look in my direction, let alone talk to me. The message was received my end loud and clear – there were some areas of discussion that Sally had put the death curse on. Matrimony was one of them.

It was a very bad day, but I learned the lesson well, and decided to clutch at what happiness I now had without pressing for more.

That evening Larkin had another message from Louren:

'Your samples 1–16 give C.14 average result of 1620 years ± 100. Congratulations. Looks good. When do I get in on the secret? Louren.'

I perked up at this news. Assuming our old bushman artist had been an eye-witness of the subjects he had drawn, then somewhere between A.D. 200 and A.D. 400 an armed Phoenician warrior had led his armies and war-elephants across this beloved land of mine. I felt guilty about excluding Louren from the secrets of the cavern, but it was still too soon. I wanted to have it to myself a little longer – to gloat upon it, to have its peace and beauty to myself, unsullied by other eyes. More than that, it had become the temple of my love for Sally. Like the old bushmen, it had become a very holy place to me.

On the following day, it was as though Sally was determined to make up for the unhappiness she had caused me. She was teasing, and loving, and mischievous all at once. At noon with the beam of sunlight burning down on us, we made love on the rocks beside the pool. Sally skilfully and gently taking the initiative once again. It was a shattering and mystic experience that scoured the sadness from the cup of my soul and filled it to the brim with happiness and peace.

We lay together softly entwined, murmuring sleepily, when suddenly I was aware of another presence in the cavern. Alarm flared through me, and I struggled up on one elbow and looked to the entrance tunnel.

A golden-brown human figure stood in the gloomy mouth of the tunnel. He was dressed in a short leather loin-cloth, a quiver and short bow stood up behind his shoulder, and around his neck hung a necklace of ostrich egg-shell beads and black monkey beans. The figure was tiny, the size of a ten-year-old child, but the face was that of a mature man. Slanted eyes, and high flat cheek-bones gave it an Asiatic appearance, but the nose was flattened and the lips were full and voluptuously chiselled. The small domed skull was covered by a pelt of tight black curls.

For an instant we looked into each other's eyes and then, like the flash of a bird's wing, the little manikin was gone, vanished into the dark passage in the rock.

'What is it?' Sally stirred against me.

'Bushman,' I said. 'Here in the cavern. Watching us.'

She sat up quickly, and peered fearfully about her.

'Where?'

'He's gone now. Get dressed – quickly!'

'Is he dangerous, Ben?' Her voice was husky.

'Yes. Very!' I was pulling on my clothes quickly, trying to decide on our best course of action, running over in my mind the words I would speak. Although it was a little rusty I found the language was still on my tongue, thanks to sessions of practice with Timothy Mageba. They would be northern bushmen here, not Kalahari, the languages were similar but distinctly different.

'They wouldn't attack us, would they, Ben?' Sally was dressed.

'If we do the wrong thing now, they will. We don't know how holy this place is to them. We mustn't frighten them, they have been persecuted and hunted for 2,000 years.'

'Oh, Ben.' She moved closer to me, and even in my own alarm I enjoyed her reliance upon me.

'They wouldn't – kill us, would they?'

'They are wild bushmen, Sally. If you threaten or molest a wild thing it will attack you. I've got to get an opportunity to talk to them.' I looked around for something to use as a shield, something strong enough to turn a reed arrow with a poisoned tip. Poison that would inflict a lingering but certain death of the most unspeakable agony.

I selected the leather theodolite case, and tore it open along the seams with my hands, flattening it out to give it maximum area.

'Follow me down the passage, Sal. Keep close.'

Her hand was on my shoulder as I led her slowly along the rock passage, using the four-cell torch to search every dark corner and recess before moving on. The light alarmed the bats and they fluttered and squeaked about our heads. The grip of Sally's hand on my shoulder became painfully tight, but we reached the tree-trunk that guarded the entrance to the cavern.

We crouched by the narrow slit between rock and tree-trunk, and the bright sunlight beyond was painful to my eyes. Minutely I examined each tree-trunk in the grove, each tuft of grass, each hollow or irregularity of earth – and there was nothing. But they were there, I knew, hidden, waiting with the patience and concentration of the earth's most skilful hunters.

We were prey, there was no escaping this fact. The accepted laws of behaviour did not apply out here on the fringe of the Kalahari. I remembered the fate of the crew of a South African Air Force Dakota that force-landed in the desert ten years before. They hunted down the family of bushmen that did it, and I flew to Gaberones to interpret at the trial. In the dock they wore the parachute silk as clothing, and their faces were childlike, trusting, without guilt or guile as they answered my question.

'Yes. We killed them,' they said. Locked in a modern gaol, like caged wild birds, they were dead within twelve months – all of them. The memory was chilling now and I thrust it aside.

'Now listen to me carefully, Sally. You must stay here. No matter what happens. I will go out to them. Talk to them. If,' I choked on the words, and cleared my throat, 'if they hit me with an arrow I'll have half an hour or so before—' I rephrased the sentence, '—I'll have plenty of time to get the Land-Rover and come back for you. You can drive. You'll have no trouble following the tracks we made back to the Makarikari Pan.'

'Ben – don't go. Oh God, Ben – please.'

'They'll wait, Sal – until dark. I have to go now, in the daylight.'

'Ben—'

'Wait here. Whatever happens, wait here.' I shrugged off her hands and stepped to the opening.

'Peace,' I called to them in their own tongue. 'There is no fight between us.'

I took a step out into the sunlight.

'I am a friend.'

Another slow step, down over the twisted roots of the wild fig, holding the flattened leather case low against my hip.

'Friend!' I called again. 'I am of your people. I am of your clan.'

I went slowly down into the silent hostile grove. There was no response to my words, no sound nor movement. Ahead of me lay a fallen tree. I began sidling towards it, my guts a hard tight ball of tension and fear.

'I carry no weapon,' I called, and the grove was quiet and sinister in the hush of afternoon.

I had almost reached the fallen tree, when I heard the twang of the bow string and I dived for the shelter of the dead trunk. Close beside my head the arrow fluted, humming in the silence, and I went down. My face was pressed into the dry earth, my heart frozen with fear at the close passage of such hideous death.

I heard footsteps, running, from behind me and I rolled over on my side ready to defend myself.

Sally was running down the wild fig roots towards me, ignoring my instructions, her face a pale mask of deathly terror, her mouth open in a silent scream. She had seen me fall and lie still, and the thought of me dead had triggered her panic. Now as I moved she realized her mistake, and she faltered in her run, suddenly aware of her own vulnerability.

'Get back, Sal,' I yelled. 'Get back!' Her uncertainty turned to dismay and she stopped, stranded half-way between the cavern entrance and my dead tree-trunk, undecided on which way to move.

In the edge of my vision I saw the little yellow bushman rise from a patch of pale grass. There was an arrow notched to his bow and the feathered flights were drawn back to his cheek as he aimed. He was fifty paces from where Sally hovered, and he held his aim for a second.

I dived forward across the space that separated Sally from me at the instant the bushman released the arrow. The arrow and I flew on an interception course, two sides of a triangle with Sally at the apex.

I saw the humming blur of the arrow flash in belly-high at Sally and I knew I could not reach her before it struck. I threw the flattened leather case with a despairing underhand flick of my wrist as I dived towards her. It cart-wheeled lazily, spinning in the air – and the arrow slapped into it. The deadly iron tip, with the poison-smeared barbs, bit into the tough leather of the case. Arrow and case fell harmlessly at Sally's feet, and I picked her up in my arms and spinning on my heels, doubled up under her weight, I raced back towards the cover of the dead tree-trunk.

The bushman was still on his knees in the grass ahead of me. He reached over his shoulder and pulled another arrow from his quiver, in one smoothly practised movement he had notched and drawn.

This time there was no hope of dodging, and I ran on grimly. The bow-string sang, the arrow flew, and instantly I felt a violent jerk at my neck. I knew I was hit, and with Sally still in my arms we fell behind the dead tree-trunk.

'I think I'm hit, Sal.' I could feel the arrow dangling against my chest as I rolled away from her. 'Break off the shaft – don't try and pull it out against the barbs.'

We lay facing each other, our eyes only a few inches apart. Strangely, now that I was a dead man I felt no fear. The thing was done, even if I was hit a dozen more times, my fate would be unaltered. It remained only to get Sally safely away before the poison did its work.

She reached out with shaking hands and took the frail reed arrow, lifting it gingerly – and then her face cleared.

'Your collar, Ben, it's lodged in the collar of your jacket. It hasn't touched you.'

Relief washed through me as I ran my hands up the shaft of the arrow, and found that I was not dead. Carefully lying on my side while Sally held the tip of the arrow from my flesh, I shrugged off my light khaki jacket. For a moment I stared in revulsion at the hand-forged iron arrow-head with the sticky toffee-coloured material clogging the wicked barbs, then I threw jacket and arrow aside.

'God, that was close,' I whispered. 'Listen, Sal, I think there is only one of them here. He's a young man, panicky, probably as afraid as we are. I will try to talk to him again.'

I wriggled forward against the reassuring solidity of the dead tree, and raised my voice in the most persuasive tones that would pass my parched throat.

'I am your friend. Though you fly your arrows at me, I will not war with you. I have lived with your people, I am one with you. How else do I speak your language?'

A deathly, impenetrable silence.

'How else do I speak the tongue of the people?' I asked again, and strained my ears for a sound.

Then the bushman spoke, his voice a high-pitched fluting, broken up with soft clucking and clicking sounds.

'The devils of the forest speak in many tongues. I close my ears to your deceits.'

'I am no devil. I have lived as one of yours. Did you never hear of the one named the Sunbird,' I used my bushman name, 'who stayed with the people of Xhai and became their brother?'

Another long silence followed, but now I sensed that the little bushman was undecided, puzzled, no longer afraid and deadly.

'Do you know of the old man named Xhai?'

'I know of him,' admitted the bushman, and I breathed a little easier.

'Did you hear of the one they called the Sunbird?'

Another long pause, then reluctantly, 'I have heard men speak of it.'

'I am that one.'

Now the silence went on for ten minutes or more. I knew the bushman was considering my claim from every possible angle. At last he spoke again.

'Xhai and I hunt together this season. Even now he comes, before darkness he will be here. We will wait for him.'

'We will wait for him,' I agreed.

'But if you move I will kill you,' warned the bushman, and I took him at his word.

Xhai the old bushman came to my shoulder, and heaven knows I am no giant. He had the characteristically flattened features, with high cheek-bones and oriental eyes, but his skin was dry and wrinkled, like an old yellow raisin. The wrinkling extended over his entire body as though he were covered with brittle parchment. The little peppercorns of hair on his scalp were smoky-grey with age, but his teeth were startling white and perfect, and his eyes were black and sparkling. I had often thought that they were pixie eyes, alive with mischief and intelligent curiosity.

When I told him how his friend had tried to kill us, he thought it an excellent joke and went off into little grunting explosions of laughter, at the same time shyly covering his mouth with one hand. The younger bushman's name was Ghal, and he was married to one of Xhai's daughters, so Xhai felt free to josh him mercilessly.

'Sunbird is a white ghost!' he wheezed. 'Shoot him, Ghal, quickly! Before he flies away.' Overwhelmed by his own humour, Xhai staggered in mirth-racked circles giving an imitation of how he thought a ghost would look as it flew away. Ghal was very embarrassed and looked down at his feet as he shuffled them in the dust. I chuckled weakly, the sound of flighted arrows very fresh in my memory.

Xhai stopped laughing abruptly, and demanded anxiously, 'Sunbird, have you got tobacco?'

'Oh, my God!' I said in English.

'What is it?' Sally was alarmed by my tone, expecting that something else horrifying had happened.

'Tobacco,' I said. 'We haven't any.' Neither Sally nor I used the stuff, but it is very precious to a bushman.

'Louren left a box of cigars in the Land-Rover,' Sally reminded me. 'Is that any use?'

Both Ghal and Xhai were intrigued with the aluminium cylinders in which Romeo and Juliette cigars were packed. After I showed them how to open them and remove the tobacco, they cooed and chattered with delight. Then Xhai sniffed the cigar like the true connoisseur he was, nodded approvingly and took a big bite. He chewed a while and then tucked the wad of sodden cigar up under his top lip. He passed the stub to Ghal who bit into it and followed Xhai's example. The two of them squatted on their haunches, positively glowing with contentment and my heart went out to them. It took so little to make them happy.

They stayed with us that night, cooking on our fire a meal of bush-rats threaded on a stick like kebabs, and grilled over the open coals without gutting or removal of the skin. The hair frizzled off in the fire and stank like burning rags.

'I think I'm going to throw up,' murmured Sally palely as she watched the relish with which our two friends ate, but she didn't.

'Why do they call you Sunbird?' she asked later, and I repeated her question to Xhai.

He jumped up and did his celebrated imitation of a sunbird, darting his head and fluttering his hands. It was convincingly done, for bushmen are wonderful observers of nature.

'They say that's how I act when I get excited,' I explained.

'Yes!' Sally exclaimed, clapping her hands with delight as she recognized me, and then they were all laughing.

In the morning we went to the cave together, all four of us, and in that setting the little men were completely at home. I photographed them, and Sally sketched them as they sat on the rocks by the pool. She was fascinated by their delicate little hands and feet, and their enlarged buttocks, a recognized anatomical peculiarity named steatopygia, which enabled them to store food, like a camel stores water, against the contingencies of the wilderness. Ghal remarked to Xhai on the activity in which Sally and I had been engaged beside the pool when he discovered us the previous day, and this led to much earthy comment and laughter. Sally wanted to know the source of it, and when I told her she blushed like a sunset, which was a pleasant change, for I am usually the blusher.

The bushmen were enthusiastic over Sally's sketches, and this enabled me to lead them naturally to the rock paintings.

'They are the paintings of our people,' Xhai boasted. 'This has been our place from the beginning.'

I pointed out the portrait of the white king and Xhai explained frankly, without any of the reserve or secrecy I had expected.

'He is the king of the white ghosts.'

'Where did he live?'

'He lives with his army of ghosts on the moon,' Xhai explained – and my critics accuse *me* of being a romantic!

We discussed this at some length, and I learned how the ghosts fly between moon and earth, how they are well disposed towards the bushmen, but care should be taken as the common forest devils will sometimes masquerade as white ghosts. Ghal had mistaken me for one of these.

'Have the white ghosts ever been men?' I asked.

'No, certainly not.' Xhai was a little put out by the question. 'They were always ghosts, and they have always lived on the moon and these hills.'

'Have you ever seen them, Xhai?'

'My grandfather saw the ghost king.' Xhai avoided the question with dignity.

'And this, Xhai,' I pointed out the drawing of the stone wall with its chevrons and towers, 'what is this?'

'That is the Moon City,' Xhai answered readily.

'Where is it – on the moon?'

'No. It is here.'

'Here?' I demanded, my blood starting to race. 'You mean on these hills?'

'Yes.' Xhai nodded, and took another bite of his five-dollar cigar.

'Where, Xhai? Where? Can you show it to me?'

'No.' Xhai shook his head regretfully.

'Why not, Xhai? I am your brother. I am of your clan,' I pleaded. 'Your secrets are my secrets.'

'You are my brother,' Xhai agreed, 'but I cannot show you the City of the Moon. It is a ghost city. Only when the moon is full and the white ghosts come down, then the city stands upon the plain below the hills – but in the morning it is gone.'

My blood no longer raced, and my excitement cooled.

'Have you seen the Moon City, Xhai?'

'My grandfather saw it, once long ago.'

'Grandpa was a big mover,' I remarked bitterly in English.

'What is it?' Sally wanted to know.

'I'll explain later, Sal,' I said, and turned back to the old bushman. 'Xhai, in all your life have you ever seen such a city as this? A place of tall stone walls, of round stone towers? I don't mean here at these hills, but anywhere. In the north, by the great river, in the desert of the west – anywhere?'

'No,' said Xhai, 'I have never seen such a place.' And I knew that there was no lost city north of the great Pan or south of the Zambezi, for if there were, Xhai would have come across it in seventy years of ceaseless wandering.

'It was probably some old bushman who wandered 270 miles east of here and saw the temple at Zimbabwe,' I suggested to Sally that night as we sat around the fire and discussed the old bushman's story. 'He was so impressed that on his return he painted it.'

'Then how do you explain your white king?'

'I don't know, Sal,' I told her honestly. 'Perhaps it *is* a white lady with a bouquet of flowers.'

It seems that whenever I receive a serious disappointment – Sally's rejection of my proposal, and the story of the Moon City were both serious – my brain ceases to function for a period. I missed the clue completely, and the link-up was so obvious. I mean, for God's sake, I have a tested I.Q. of 156 – I'm a god-damned genius!

In the morning the two bushmen went, back to the families they had left by the Pan. They took with them the treasures we lavished upon them. A hatchet, Sally's make-up mirror, two knives and half a box of Romeo and Juliette cigars. They trotted away into the vastness of the Kalahari, without a backward glance, and left us poorer for their going.

The helicopter came the following week, bringing in a full load of supplies and the special equipment I had asked Louren to send us.

Sally and I carried the rubber dinghy up to the cavern and inflated it beside the pool, taking it in turns to blow until we felt dizzy.

Sally launched it and paddled happily around the pool while I assembled the rest of the equipment. There was a short glass-fibre fishing-rod, a heavy one, twenty-five ounces, and in the case which held a 12/0 Penn Senator fishing-reel was a note from Louren: 'What are you after, for crying out aloud? Sand fish, or desert trout? "L" '

I fitted the reel to rod, threaded the line through the runners, and attached the five-pound lead weight to the end of it. Sally paddled us out into the centre of the pool. I dropped the lead weight over the side, disengaged the clutch on the reel, and let the line start running out.

As I had requested, the plaited Dacron line was marked at intervals of fifty feet, and as each marker of coloured cotton disappeared into the luminous green water, we counted aloud.

'Five, six, seven – my God, Ben. It's bottomless.'

'These limestone sink-holes can go down to tremendous depths.'

'Eleven, twelve, thirteen.'

'I hope we've got enough line.' Sally eyed what remained on the spool dubiously.

'We have got 800 yards here,' I told her. 'It will be more than enough.'

'Sixteen, seventeen.' Even I was impressed, I had guessed at a depth of around 400 feet, the same as the Sleeping Pool at Sinoia, but still the line unwound steadily from the big-game fishing-reel.

At last I felt the weight bump on the bottom, and the line went slack. We looked at each other with awe.

'A little over 850 feet,' I said.

'It makes me feel scary, hanging over a hole in the earth that deep.'

'Well,' I said with finality, 'I had plans to explore the bottom with a Scuba, but that's out now. Whatever is down there will stay there for ever. Nobody can dive that deep.'

Sally looked down into the green depths, and the dappled, moving, reflected light illuminated her face weirdly. There were shadows in her eyes, and her expression was dazed. Suddenly she shook herself violently, a shudder that went through her whole body, and she tore her eyes away from the green surface.

'Oh! I felt funny then. A really creepy sensation, as though something walked over my grave.'

I began to wind in the fishing-line, and Sally lack back flat on the floor of the dinghy staring up at the rock roof high above. It was a laborious task to recover all that line, but I worked away steadily.

'Ben.' Sally spoke suddenly. 'Look up there.' I stopped winding and looked up. We had never looked up at the opening in the roof from this angle. The shape of the opening was different.

'There, Ben. On the side,' Sally pointed. 'That piece of rock sticking out. It's square, too regular to be natural, surely?'

I studied it for a while.

'Perhaps.' I was dubious.

'You know we have never tried to find where the cavern opens out onto the top of the hills, Ben.' Sally sat up excitedly. 'Can't we do that. Let's go up and look at that piece of square stone. Can we, Ben?'

'Of course,' I agreed readily.

'Today. Now! Can we go now?'

'Hell, Sal. It's after two o'clock already. We will be out after dark.'

'Oh, come on! We can take torches with us.'

The growth of vegetation at the crest of the hills was dense and spiny. I was glad of the machete I had with me, and I hacked a path for us through it. We had marked the approximate position of the hole from the plain below, but even then we blundered about in the undergrowth for two hours before I nearly walked into it.

Suddenly the earth opened at my feet in that frightening black shaft, and I threw myself backwards, nearly knocking Sally down.

'That was a near one.' I was shaken, and I kept a respectful distance from the edge as we worked our way around to where a slab of stone jutted squarely out into the void.

I knelt on the lip to examine the stone. Far below, the surface of the emerald pool glowed in the gloomy depths. I do not like exposed heights, and I felt distinctly queasy as I leaned out to touch the flat surface of the stone.

'It is certainly regular, Sal.' I ran my hands over it. 'But I can't feel any chisel marks. It's been badly weathered though, perhaps—'

I looked up and froze with horror. Sally had walked out onto the stone platform as though it were a diving-board. She stood now with her toes over the edge, and as I watched in horror she lifted her hands above her head. She pointed them straight at the sky with all her fingers and both thumbs extended stiffly in that same gesture she had used when first she saw the emerald pool.

'Sally!' I screamed, and her head jerked. She swayed slightly. I scrambled to my knees.

'Don't, Sally, don't!' I screamed again, for I knew she was about to plunge into the hungry stone mouth. Slowly she leaned out over the gap. I ran out onto the stone platform and as she went forward beyond the point of balance my hand closed on her upper arm. For brief unholy seconds we teetered and struggled together on the lip of stone, then I dragged her back, and pulled her to safety.

Suddenly she was shaking and weeping hysterically, and I clung to her, for I also was badly scared. Something had happened that was beyond my understanding, something mystical and deeply disturbing.

When Sally's sobs had abated, I asked her gently, 'What happened, Sal? Why did you do it?'

'I don't know. I just felt dizzy, and there was a black roaring in my head, and – oh, I don't know, Ben. I just don't know.'

It was another twenty minutes before Sally seemed sufficiently recovered to begin the journey back to camp, and by then the sun was setting. Before we reached the path down the cliff face it was completely dark.

'The moon will be up in a few minutes, Sal. I don't fancy going down the cliff in the dark. Let's wait for it.'

We sat on the edge of the cliff huddled together, not for warmth, for the air was still hot and the rocks were sunbaked, but because both of us were still a little shaken from the experience we had just come through. The moon was a big silver glow beneath the horizon, then it pushed up fat and yellow and round above the trees, and washed the land with a soft pale light.

I looked at Sally. Her face was silver-grey in the moonlight with dark bruised eyes, and her expression was remote and infinitely sad.

'Shall we go, Sal?' I hugged her lightly.

'In a minute. It's so beautiful.' I turned to stare out over the moon-silver plain. Africa has many moods, many faces, and I love them all. Here, before us, she put on one of her more enchanting displays. We were silent and engrossed for a long time.

Suddenly I felt Sally stir against me, half rising.

'Ready?' I asked her, rising with her.

'Ben!' Her hand closed on my wrist with surprising strength, she was shaking my arm.

'Ben! Ben!'

'What is it, Sal?' I was seized with dread that her earlier mood had returned.

'Look, Ben. Look!' Her voice was choked with emotion.

'What is it, Sal? Are you all right?'

With one hand she was shaking my arm, with the other she was pointing down at the plain below us.

'Look, Ben, there it is!'

'Sally!' I put both arms around her to restrain her. 'Easy, my dear. Just sit down quietly.'

'Don't be a fool, Ben. I'm perfectly all right. Just look down there.'

Still holding her securely, I did as she asked. I stared and saw nothing.

'Do you see it, Ben?'

'No.' And then, like the face in the picture-puzzle, it was there. It was there, as it should have been from the beginning.

'Can you see it?' Sally was trembling. 'Tell me you can see it too, Ben. Tell me I'm not imagining it.'

'Yes,' I mumbled, still not certain, 'yes, I think—'

'It's the City of the Moon, Ben. The ghost city of the bushmen – it's our lost city, Ben. It is. It is – it must be!'

It was vague, hazy. I shut my eyes tightly and opened them again. It was still there.

The double enclosure around the silent grove, vast symmetrical tracings on the silver plain, dark shadowy lines. There were the dark circles that marked the spots on which the phallic towers had stood, some of them obscured by the trees of the grove. Beyond the walls were the honeycomb cells of the lower city, crescent-shaped and spread around the shores of the ancient, vanished lake.

'The moon,' I whispered. 'Low angle. Picking up the outline of the foundations. They must be so flattened that we have walked over them, lived on top of them for a month! The light of the full moon is just the right strength to cast shadows where the remains stand slightly proud.'

'The photograph!'

'Yes. From 36,000 feet, the light low enough and soft enough to give the same effect,' I agreed.

'We probably wouldn't have seen it from such a low altitude, the helicopter didn't go high enough,' Sally suggested.

'And it was noon,' I agreed. 'High-angle sun, no shadows. That is why Louren didn't see it from the helicopter.' It was so simple, and I had missed it. Some bloody genius – they must have botched the tests.

'But there are no walls, Ben, no towers, nothing. Only the foundations. What happened to it? What happened to our city?'

'We will find out, Sal,' I promised. 'But now let's mark it, before it disappears again.'

I handed her the one torch from the knapsack, 'One flash means "come towards me"; two flashes, "move away from me"; three, "move left"; four, "move right"; and a windmill means "you're on it".' Quickly we agreed a simple code. 'I'll go down onto the plain and you signal me. Put me on top of the large tower first, then guide me around the perimeter of the outer walls. We had better work fast we don't know how long the effect will last. Give me a flat cut-out sign when it goes.'

It lasted a little over an hour with me scampering about on the plain in obedience to Sally's signals, and then the city faded, and slowly vanished as the moon rose towards its zenith. I went up to fetch Sally down from the cliff. I was bare to the waist, having ripped my shirt to shreds and tied strips of it onto clumps of grass and shrubs as markers.

Back in camp we built a huge fire and I got out the Glen Grant to celebrate. We were so elated, and there was so much to discuss and marvel over, that sleep was long delayed.

We went over the lighting phenomenon again in greater detail, agreeing how it worked and ruefully remembering how close we had come to the truth when we discussed the low sun effect on our very first day, the day we discovered the fresh-water mussel shells. We discussed the shells and their new significance. 'I swear here and now, with all the gods as my witness, that I will never again toss a piece of vital scientific evidence over my shoulder.' I made oath and testament.

'Let's drink to that,' suggested Sal.

'What a wonderful idea,' I agreed, and refilled the glasses.

Then we went on to the old bushman's story.

'It just goes to show you that every piece of legend, every piece of folklore is based on some fact, however garbled.' Sally becomes all philosophical after one shot of Glen Grant.

'And let's face facts, my blood brother Xhai is a champion garbler of facts from way back – the City of the Moon, forsooth.'

'It's a lovely name. Let's keep it,' Sally suggested. 'And what do you think about Xhai's grandfather actually meeting one of the white ghosts?'

'He probably saw one of the old hunters or prospectors, remember, we nearly had ghost status awarded us.'

'Literally and figuratively,' Sally reminded me.

The talk went on and on while the moon made its splendid transit of the sky above us. Every now and then serious discussion degenerated into effusive outbursts of, 'Oh, Ben. Isn't it wonderful. We've got a whole Phoenician city to excavate. All to ourselves.' Or, 'My God, Sal. All my life I've dreamed of something like this happening to me.'

It was long past midnight before we got our feet back on the earth, and Sally brought up the subject of practical procedure.

'What do we do, Ben? Do we tell Louren Sturvesant now?'

I poured another drink slowly, while I considered this.

'Don't you think, Sal, we should sink a pothole, a small one, of course, on the foundations. Just to be certain we're not making fools of ourselves?'

'Ben, you know that's the first rule. Don't go scratching around haphazardly. You might destroy something valuable. We should wait until we can go in on an orderly, organized basis.'

'I know, Sal. But I just can't help myself. Just one tiny little hole?'

'Okay,' she grinned. 'Just one tiny little hole.'

'I suppose we'd better try and get some sleep now, it's past two o'clock.'

Just before we finally drifted off, Sally murmured against my chest, 'I still wonder what happened to our city. If the bushman picture was correct then huge walls and towers of masonry have vanished into thin air.'

'Yes. It's going to be exciting to find out.'

With that strength of character which I am able occasionally to conjure up, I firmly thrust aside the temptation to open a trench within the temple enclosure, and instead I chose a spot upon the foundations of the outer wall where I hoped I would do minimum damage.

With Sally watching avidly, and volunteering more than her share of advice, I marked out with tapes torn from my sheets the outline of the intended excavation. A narrow trench three foot wide and twenty foot long, set at a right-angle to the run of the foundations so as to open a cross-section of the horizon.

We numbered the tapes at intervals of one foot, and Sally cross-referenced her notebook to the markings on the tapes. I fetched the cameras, tools and tarpaulin from the Land-Rover. Our trench was only thirty yards from the tents. We had camped almost on top of the ancient wall.

I spread the tarpaulin ready to receive the earth removed from the trench, and then I pulled off my shirt and threw it aside. I was no longer ashamed to expose my body in front of Sally. I spat on the palms of my hands, straddled the tapes, hefted the pick, and glanced at Sally, sitting attentively on the tarpaulin with a big floppy-brimmed hat on her head.

'Okay?' I grinned at her.

'All the way, partner?' she said, and I was startled. The words jarred, they were Louren's and mine. We didn't say them to other people. Then suddenly I thought, what the hell! I love her also.

'All the way, girl!' I agreed and swung the pick. It was good to feel the pick feather-light in my hands, and the head clunking deep into the sandy earth. I worked steadily swinging pick and shovel easily, but soon the sweat was running in rivulets down my body and soaking my breeches. As I shovelled the earth from the trench and piled it on the tarpaulin, Sally began sifting it carefully. She chattered away happily as she worked, but my only reply was the grunt at each swing of pick.

By noon I had opened the trench along its full length to a depth of three feet. The sandy soil gave way at a depth of eighteen inches to a dark reddish loam which still held the damp of the recent rains. We rested and I ate a mess of canned food and drank a bottle of Windhoek to replace some of my lost moisture.

'You know,' Sally looked me over thoughtfully, 'once you get used to it, your body has a strange sort of beauty,' she said, and I blushed until my eyes watered.

I worked for another hour, and then suddenly the bite of the pick turned up black. I swung again – still black. I dropped the pick, and knelt in the trench. 'What is it?' Sally was there immediately.

'Ash!' I said. 'Charcoal!'

'An ancient hearth,' she guessed.

'Perhaps.' I didn't commit myself, luckily, so that later I could chide her for her presumption. 'Let's take some samples for dating.'

I worked more carefully now, trying to expose the layer of ash without disturbing it. We sampled it and found that it varied between a quarter of an inch and two inches deep across the full horizon of the trench. Sally noted the depth from surface, and the position of each of the carbon samples we took, while I photographed the trench and tapes.

Then we straightened up and looked at each other.

'Too big for a hearth,' she said, and I nodded. 'We shouldn't go deeper, Ben. Not like this, crashing in with pick and shovel.'

'I know,' I said. 'We will stop on half the trench, leave the layer of ash undisturbed – I'll make that concession to the rules – but I am sure as hell going down on the rest of it, to bedrock, if I can!'

'I'm glad you said that,' Sally applauded my decision. 'It's exactly what I feel as well.'

'You begin at the far end, I'll start here and we will work towards each other,' I instructed, and we began lifting the layer of ash from half the trench. I found that immediately below it was a floor of hard clay and, though I didn't say so, I guessed it was a building filler. A transported layer, not occurring naturally.

'Go carefully,' I cautioned Sally.

'Quoth the pick-and-shovel man,' she muttered sarcastically without looking up, and almost immediately she made the first discovery from the ruins of the City of the Moon.

As I write I have her notebook in front of me, with her grubby, earthy fingerprints upon the pages and her big school-girlish handwriting filling it.

Trench 1. Reference AC. 6. II.4. Depth 4'2½".
Item: One glass bead. Oval. Blue. Circum. 2½ mm.
             Pierced. Slightly heat-distorted.
Remarks: Found in layer of ash at Level I.
Index No. CM. 1.

This laconic notation can give no idea of our jubilation, the way we hugged each other and laughed in the sun. It was a typical blue Phoenician trade bead, and I cupped the tiny pellet of glass in my one hand.

'I'm going to take it and stick it up their backsides,' I threatened, referring of course to my critics.

'If that end is as narrow as their minds, Ben dear, then it will be a pretty tight fit.'

I started using a small pick and fifteen minutes later I made the next discovery. A charred fragment of bone.

'Human?' Sally asked.

'Possibly,' I said. 'Head of a human femur – the shaft has been burned away.'

'Cannibalism? Cremation?' Sally hazarded.

'You do run on,' I said.

'What do you think then?' she challenged. I was silent for a long time, then I made up my mind, and came out with it.

'I think at this level the City of the Moon was sacked and burned, its inhabitants were slaughtered, the walls thrown down and its buildings obliterated.'

Sally whistled softly, staring at me in mock amazement. 'On the evidence of one bead, and a piece of bone – that just has to be the greatest flyer of all time!'

That evening, in reply to Larkin's bellowed queries, I replied, 'Thanks, Peter. We are fine. No, we don't need anything. Yes. Good. Please tell Mr. Sturvesant there is no change here, nothing to report.'

I switched off the set, and avoided Sally's eyes.

'Yes,' she told me sternly. 'After a stinking one like that, you should look guilty!'

'Well, you said yourself it's only one bead and a piece of bone.'

But by the evening two days later, I had no such excuse, for I had sunk my trench seven feet five inches and there I uncovered the first of four courses of dry packed masonry. The stones were skilfully dressed, and squared. The joints between each block were so tight that a knife-blade would not go between them. The stones were bigger than those of Zimbabwe, clearly intended to support the weight of a substantial edifice; the average size was approximately four feet, by two, by two. They were cut from red sandstone similar to that of the cliffs and as I examined the workmanship I knew beyond any doubt that they were the work of artisans from a powerful and wealthy civilization.

That night I spoke to Larkin again.

'How soon can you get a message through to Mr. Sturvesant, Peter?'

'He should have got back from New York today. I can put a phone call through this evening.'

'Please ask him to come right away.'

'You mean you want him to drop everything and come running – that's a laugh.'

'Just do it, please.'

The helicopter arrived at three o'clock the following afternoon, and I ran to meet it, pulling on my shirt.

'What have you got for me, Ben?' Louren demanded as he climbed, big and blond, out of the cabin.

'I think you are going to like it,' I told him, as we shook hands.

Five hours later we sat around the fire and Louren smiled over the rim of his glass at me.

'You were right, lad. I do like it!' This was the first opinion he had expressed since his arrival. He had followed Sal and me from excavation to cavern to cliff-top, listening attentively to our explanations, shaking his head with a rueful grin when I explained our theory of low-angle light on the ruins, firing a question occasionally in the same tone I had heard him use in a directors' meeting. Each time the question was relevant, incisive and searching, as though he were evaluating a business deal.

When Sally spoke he stood close to her, looking frankly into her face, those marvellous classical features of his rapt and still. Once she touched his arm to enforce a point and they smiled at each other. I was happy to see them so friendly at last, for they were the two people in the world I loved.

He knelt with me in the bottom of the trench and caressed the worked stone with his hands, he held the charred bone and melted glass bead in his palm and frowned at them as though trying to draw their secrets from them by sheer force of concentration.

Just before sunset, at Louren's insistence, we returned to the cavern and went to the rear wall. I lit one of the gas lanterns and placed it so that its light fell full on the painting of the white king. Then the three of us sat around it in a semi-circle and studied it in every detail. The king's head was in profile and Sally pointed out the features, the long straight nose and high forehead.

'A face like that never came out of Africa,' she said, and as a contrast she picked out the painting of another figure further down the wall. 'Look at that. It's a Bantu and no mistaking it. The artist was skilled enough to differentiate between the features of each type.'

However, Louren's attention never wavered from his scrutiny of the king. Again he seemed to be trying to wrest its secrets from it, but the king was regally aloof and at last Louren sighed and stood up. He was about to turn away when his glance dropped to the white-robed priest figures below the king.

'What are those?' he asked.

'We have named them the priests,' I told him, 'but Sally feels they could be Arab traders or—'

'The figure in the centre—' he pointed out the central priest figure, and his voice was sharp, almost alarmed, 'what is he doing?'

'Bowing to the king,' Sally suggested.

'Even though he is bowing, he stands taller than the others?' Louren protested.

'Size was the bushman artist's way of showing importance. See the relative size of the king – although they are pygmies they always show themselves as giants – the size of the central priest would signify that he was the High Priest, or the leader of the Arabs, if Sally is right.'

'If he is bowing, it's with the top third of his body only and he is the only one doing it. The others are erect.' Louren was still not convinced. 'It's almost as though—' his voice trailed away, and he shook his head. Then suddenly he shivered briefly, and I saw the gooseflesh appear on the smooth tanned skin of his upper arms.

'It's become cold in here,' he said, folding his arms across his chest. I had not noticed any drop in temperature, but I stood up also.

'Let's get back to camp,' Louren said, and it was only after I had built up the fire to a cheerfully crackling, spark-flying blaze that he spoke again.

'You are right, lad. I do like it!' And he took a swallow of the malt whisky. 'Now let's start talking prices,' he suggested.

'Set it out for us, Lo,' I agreed.

'I will negotiate with the Botswana Government. I can put a little leverage on them. We'll have to have a formal agreement drawn up, probably split any finds fifty-fifty, they'll have to guarantee us access and exclusive rights. That sort of thing.'

'Good. That's certainly your bag of tricks, Lo.'

'Knowing you, Benjamin, you have a list of your requirements, the men you want, equipment – am I right?'

I laughed and unbuttoned my top pocket. 'As a matter of fact—' I admitted as I handed him three foolscap sheets. He glanced over them quickly.

'Very Spartan, Ben,' he congratulated me. 'But I think we can go in a bit bigger than this. I'll want at least a rough landing-strip here to start with, something to handle a Dakota. The hot weather is coming. You'll die living out under canvas. We'll need solid accommodation, also office and storage space with air-conditioning. That means a generator for lighting and to pump water down from the pool.'

'No one can ever accuse you of being half-arsed, Lo,' I told him, and we all laughed. Sally refilled my glass. I was jubilant and mightily pleased with myself that evening. I had much to be proud of, ferreting out a secret so well hidden for millennia, and Louren was going to back me all the way, partner. The whisky went down my throat like water.

I used to drink a lot of whisky. It was a way of forgetting certain things and making others easier to accept. Then about six years ago I found I hadn't worked on a book for a year, that my memory and intellect were blurry and unreliable, and my hands shook in the morning. I still drink a tot or two of an evening, and occasionally I take on a full blast of the stuff. But now I drink because I am happy not because I am sad.

'Come on, Ben. Tonight we've got something to celebrate.' Sally laughed and poured me another heavy portion.

'Wow! Gently, Doctor,' I protested weakly, but that night I got drunk, pleasantly, contentedly, floating drunk. With dignity I refused Louren's offer of assistance and made my own way to the tent wherein Sally had discreetly segregated me since Louren's arrival. I fell on top of my bed fully clothed and went to sleep. I half woke when Louren came in and climbed into his bed across the tent. I remember opening one eye and seeing the glow of the waning moon through the fly of the tent – or was it the first glow of dawn? It didn't seem important then.

The personnel for the project was the most important consideration, and here I was lucky. Peter Willcox was due for his sabbatical leave from Cape Town University. I flew down to see him, and in six hours convinced him that he wouldn't enjoy the fleshpots of Europe at all. Heather, his wife, was a little harder to sway, until I showed her the photographs of the white king. Like Sally, rock art is one of her big things.

They were good people to have on a dig. We had been together on the excavation of the Slangkop caves. They were both in their thirties; he a little paunchy and balding with steel-rimmed spectacles and trousers always on the point of falling down. He had to keep tugging at the waistband. She was thin and angular, with a wide laughing mouth and a snub, heavily freckled nose. They were childless, cheerful, knowledgeable and hard-working. Peter plays a very jazzy accordion and Heather has a voice that harmonizes well with mine.

Peter introduced me to two of his postgraduate students whom he recommended without reservation. I was startled at my first meeting with them. Ral Davidson was a young man of twenty-one – although the fact that he was a man was not immediately obvious. However, Peter assured me that beneath all the untidy hair lurked a promising young archaeologist. His fiancée was an intense bespectacled young woman, who had graduated at the head of her year. Although she was depressingly plain and I prefer my women beautiful, Leslie Johns endeared herself to me immediately by whispering breathlessly, 'Dr. Kazin, I think your book, *Ancient Africa*, is the most exciting thing I've ever read.'

This display of good taste secured the job for them.

Peter Larkin found me forty-six African labourers from the southern territories of Botswana, who had never heard of the Hills of Blood nor of any curse upon them.

My only disappointment was with Timothy Mageba. I spent five days at the Institute in Johannesburg on my way back from Cape Town, mostly trying to convince Timothy that I needed him at the Hills of Blood.

'Machane,' he said, 'there is work here that no one else can do.' I was to remember those words later. 'Where you are going there is work that many men are capable of. You have these men and women already, specialists all of them. You do not need me.'

'Please, Timothy. It would be for six months or so. Your work here can wait.'

He shook his head vehemently , but I hurried on.

'I really want you, and need you. There are things that you alone can explain. Timothy, there are over fifteen thousand square feet of paintings on the rocks. Much of it is symbol, stylized emblems which only you—'

'Dr Kazin, you could send me copies of them. I can still give you my interpretation.' Timothy switched to English, which with him was always a discouraging sign. 'I hope you don't insist that I leave the Institute now. My assistants cannot work without my direction.'

We stared at each other for a few seconds. It was a deadlock. I could order him to come, but an unwilling helper is worse than none at all. There was a rebellious, independent spirit smouldering in Timothy's dark eyes and I knew that there was some deeper reason why he refused to accompany me.

'Is it—' I hesitated. I was about to ask him if the ancient curse was the reason for his refusal. It was always disquieting to find superstition influencing an intelligent and well-educated man. I was reluctant to come straight out with it, for even an African like Timothy the direct question is considered gauche and discourteous.

'There are always reasons within reasons, Doctor. Please believe me when I tell you it would be better if I did not accompany you this time.'

'All right, Timothy, 'I agreed with resignation, and stood up. Again we locked glances, and it seemed to me that he was different. The flickering fires burned brighter, and again I felt the stirring of unease, of fear even, deep within me.

'I promise you, Doctor, that my work here is at a critical stage.'

'I will be very interested to see it when you are ready, Timothy.'

My four new assistants arrived on the commercial flight from Cape Town the following morning and we drove directly to the Sturvesant hangar where the Dakota transport was waiting for us.

The flight in was noisy and gay. Peter had his accordion along, and I never travel without my old guitar. We hit a couple of easy ones like 'Abdul Abulbul Emir', and 'Green grow the rushes, oh!', and I discovered with delight that Ral Davidson whistled with a clarity and purity that was truly beautiful, and that Leslie had a sweet little soprano.

'When we've finished this dig, I'm going to take you lot on tour,' I told them, and began teaching them some of my own compositions.

It was three weeks since I had left the Hills of Blood, and as we circled it I could see that changes had taken place in my absence. The landing-strip, complete with wind-sock, had been gouged out of the dusty plain. Near it stood a cluster of prefabricated buildings. One long central bungalow with the residential quarters grouped around it. A skeletal metal tower supported a 2,000-gallon galvanized iron water-tank, and beyond that was the encampment which housed the African labour force.

Sally was waiting for us at the landing-strip, and we piled our luggage into the Land-Rover and went to look at our new home. I expected Louren to be there but Sally told me he had gone the previous day after a stay of a few days.

Proudly Sally showed us over the camp. The central air-conditioned bungalow was divided into a small common room and lounge at the one end, in the centre was a large office and beyond that a storage warehouse. There were four residential huts, air-conditioned, but sparsely furnished. Sally had allotted one to the Willcoxes, one for Leslie and herself, one for Ral and me, and the fourth for Louren or other visitors, pilots, and overnight guests.

'I could think of a few improvements in the sleeping arrangements,' I muttered bitterly.

'Poor Ben.' Sally smiled cruelly. 'Civilization has caught up with you. By the way, I hope you remembered to bring your bathing costume, no skinny dips in the pool any more.'

And perversely I regretted all that Louren had done for me. The Hills of Blood were no longer a lonely, mysterious place in the wilderness, but a bustling little community, with aircraft landing regularly, Land-Rovers kicking up the dust and even the clatter of an electric water-pump shattering the dreaming silence of the cavern and disturbing the still green waters of the emerald pool.

Quickly my group settled into their allotted tasks. Sally worked on at the cavern, with a single young African assistant. Each of the other four was placed in charge of a team of ten labourers and assigned an area in which to work.

Peter and Heather shrewdly elected to work outside the main walls, in the ruins of the lower city. It was here that the ancients would have disposed of their rubbish, broken pottery, old weapons, discarded beads and the fascinating debris of a vanished civilization.

Ral and Leslie with dreams of gold and treasure jumped at the chance of excavating within the enclosure, an area which the ancients would have kept swept and scrupulously clean, and therefore much less likely to yield finds of interest. That is the difference between experience and inexperience, between the impetuosity of youth and the cool calculations of an older head.

I kept myself free, on a supervisory and advisory capacity. Spending my time at those places where it could do the most good. Anxiously I watched Ral and Leslie to assure myself that their approach and technique was satisfactory, then I relaxed as Peter Willcox's recommendation proved correct. They were clever, enthusiastic youngsters and, more important, they knew their way around an archaeological dig.

The four teams shook themselves out as the dullards amongst the African labourers were sorted from the bright ones. In a shorter time than I had hoped for, the firm of Kazin and Company was breaking ground and doing good business.

It was slow, painstaking and thoroughly satisfying work. Each evening, before the nightly singsong in the common room, the day's work was discussed and any discoveries evaluated and related to their place in the general picture of the site.

The first conclusive discovery we made was that the ash layer at Level I persisted throughout the site, even in the lower city. It was by no means evenly distributed, but showed up in patches of varying thickness. Carbon-dating, however, gave a fairly constant result, and we settled at a date of A.D. 450. This date seemed to be concurrent or to slightly pre-date the oldest bushman paintings in the cavern.

We were agreed that bushman occupation of the cavern would have followed immediately after the departure or disappearance of the ancients from the city. Scrupulously we referred to the first occupations as 'ancients,' considering the term 'Phoenician' as yet unproven. A condition which it was my most dearly-held hope would soon be altered.

Associated with the ash layer were haunting scraps of human remains. Ral uncovered an incisor in the ash against the base of the main tower, Peter a complete humerus together with many other unidentifiable bone fragments. These unburied human remains went a long way to ensuring a general acceptance of my theory of a violent end to the City of the Moon.

This was reinforced by the baffling disappearance of walls and towers, which we could reasonably accept once stood on these bases of clay, with their vestigial stone foundations which occurred spasmodically along the outline of the temple enclosure.

Ral hesitantly suggested an enemy so crazed with hatred, that he had set out to obliterate all trace of the ancients from the earth. We could all accept this.

'Fair enough. But what happened to thousands of tons of massive masonry?' Sally spoke for all of us.

'They scattered it out across the plain,' Ral hazarded.

'A Herculean task, besides the plain was a lake in those days. To get rid of it they would have scattered it along the area between cliff and lake. There is no sign of it.'

Apologetically Peter Willcox reminded us of the account in Credo Mutwa's book *Indaba My Children* of how an ancient city was carried by its people, block by block, out of the west, and how the city was rebuilt at Zimbabwe.

'This is red sandstone,' Sally cut in brusquely. 'Zimbabwe is granite, quarried from the rock on which it stands. Zimbabwe is 275 miles east of here. The labour involved is unthinkable. I will accept that the building skills and techniques were transported, but not the material itself.'

There were no more ideas forthcoming and we could turn from theories to facts. At the end of six weeks Louren Sturvesant visited us for the first time. All digging and other work was suspended as for two days we held a seminar, with myself as Chairman, in which we presented Louren with all our accomplishments and conclusions to date.

These were very impressive. To begin with, the list of artefacts, pottery sherds, and other relics filled 127 typewritten foolscap pages. Peter and Heather were responsible for most of these and they opened the seminar.

'So far all excavation without the enclosure has been confined to the area north of it, and lying within 1,000 feet of the outer perimeter. In the main it seems to have been a complex of small rooms and buildings built from adobe clay and roofed with poles and thatch—'

Peter described the area in detail, giving the average size of the rooms and the exact position of each object discovered. Louren started thrashing around in his chair, and fiddling with his cigar. Peter is meticulous, almost old-maidish, in his approach to his work. Finally he reached his conclusions. 'It seems, therefore, that this area was an extensive bazaar and market.' And he led us through into the warehouse to examine the finds from this area. There were fragments of badly rusted iron, a bronze comb, the handle of a knife fashioned in the shape of a woman's body, fourteen rosettes of bronze that we guessed had embossed a leather shield, twenty-five pounds' weight of bronze discs, and stars and sun objects which were clearly ornaments, sixteen shaped and beaten bronze plates that we hoped might comprise part of a suit of body armour, a magnificent bronze dish twenty-four inches in diameter chased with a sun image and set around with an intricate border pattern, and another forty pounds' weight of bronze scraps and fragments so badly battered and damaged as to be unidentifiable.

'These are all the bronze objects so far recovered,' Peter told Louren. 'The workmanship is crude, but not recognizably Bantu in conception and execution. It would relate more closely to what we know of Phoenician craftsmanship. Unlike the Romans and Greeks, they placed little value on the arts. Their artefacts, like their buildings, were massive and roughly executed. One other fact that emerges is the veneration of the sun. It was clearly a generally polytheistic community but one in which sun-worship predominated. In this settlement, it appears that Baal, the Phoenician male deity, was personified by the sun.'

I thought Peter was verging on the mistake of special pleading but I let him continue without interruption. After discussing each item separately, Peter led us to the next row of tables that carried all the glass and pottery.

'One hundred and twenty-five pounds' weight of glass beads – the colours are predominantly blue and red. Phoenician colours, with greens and whites and yellows recovered only in Levels I and II. In other words, later than A.D. 50 which coincides approximately with the final phase of absorption of Phoenician civilization by the Romans in the Mediterranean area, and its gradual disappearance.'

I interrupted. 'The Romans were so thorough in their absorption of Phoenicia and all her works, that we know very little of them. . . .'

My attention wandered to Sally. She was in a sparkling mood, a complete change from the previous six weeks when she had been moody and withdrawn. She had washed her hair and it was shiny and springing with soft lights. Her skin also shone with golden hues where the sun had touched it, and she had coloured her lips and dramatized her eyes. Her beauty squeezed my heart. I forced my mind back to the row of tables.

'. . . A case in point is this recovery of pottery,' Peter was saying. He indicated the huge display of fragments, portions, and a very few complete pieces. 'On all of this, with one exception, there is not a single inscription. This is the exception.' He picked up a sherd which was set out in a place of honour, and passed it to Louren. Although we had all gloated over it before, we crowded around Louren as he examined it. There was a symbol cut into the baked clay.

'A chip from the lip of a cup, or vase. The symbol could conceivably be a Punic T.'

Louren burst in impulsively, turning to me and laying a hand on my shoulder, 'Conclusive, Ben. They must accept that, surely?'

'By no means, Lo.' I shook my head regretfully. 'They will cry, "Imported." The old trick of discrediting anything you can't explain, or which doesn't support your theories, by saying that it was brought in during the course of trade.'

'Looks as though you can't win, Ben,' Louren sympathized, and I grinned.

'At least we haven't uncovered any fourteenth-century Nanking – or a chamber pot with Queen Victoria's portrait on it!'

Laughing we moved on to the next display of copper and copperware. There were bangles and brooches, green-encrusted and eaten away. Bales of copper wire and, significantly, ingots cast into the shape of a St. Andrew's Cross each weighing twelve pounds.

'Those aren't something new,' Louren remarked.

'No,' I agreed. 'They turn up all over central and southern Africa. And yet the shape is exactly that of the ingots taken from the tin mines of Cornwall by the Phoenicians – or the copper ingots from the ancient mines on Cyprus.'

'Still not conclusive?' Louren looked at me and I shook my head, leading him on to see the iron work we had recovered. All of it was so badly rusted and damaged that the original shape was a matter of conjecture and guesswork. There were hundreds of arrow-heads, mostly associated with Levels I and II, spear-heads and sword-blades, axe-heads and knives.

'Judging by the quantities of weapons, or what we take to be weapons, the ancients were a warlike people. Alternatively they were a people fearful of attack and well armed against it,' I suggested, and there was a general murmur of agreement. From the iron section we went on to a display of my photographs, showing each stage of the excavations, views of the lower city, the temple, the acropolis and the cavern.

'Pretty good, Ben,' Louren admitted. 'Is that all you have for me?'

'The best comes last.' I couldn't help a little showmanship in my presentation, and I had screened off the end of the warehouse. I led him beyond the first screen with all my team hovering anxiously to judge his reaction. It was gratifying.

'God God!' Louren stopped short and stared at the phallic columns with their ornamental tops. 'Zimbabwe birds!'

There were three of them. Although incomplete, they stood about five foot high, and were thirty inches in circumference. Only one of them was relatively undamaged, the other two had been mutilated so as to be hardly recognizable. The carving on top of each pillar had obviously originally depicted a vulturine bird shape with heavy beak, hunched shoulders, and predatory claws. They were similar in design and execution to those recovered from Zimbabwe by Hall, MacIver, and others.

'Not Zimbabwe birds,' I corrected Louren.

'No,' Sally affirmed. 'These are the ones from which the Zimbabwe birds were copied.'

'Where did you find them?' Louren asked as he moved in for a closer scrutiny of the green soapstone figures.

'In the temple,' I smiled at Ral and Leslie, who looked suitably modest, 'within the inner enclosure. They are probably religious objects – you see the sun symbols around the collar of the column – clearly they are associated with the worship of Baal as the sun god.'

'We have named them the sunbirds,' Sally explained, 'as Ben felt a name like the birds of Ophir was a bit too pretentious.'

'Why have they been damaged like this?' Louren indicated where deliberate blows had shattered the brittle green stone.

'That's anybody's guess.' I shrugged away the question. 'But we know that they had been toppled and were lying without design or direction in the layer of ash at Level I.'

'That's very interesting, Ben.' Louren's eyes were drawn to the final screen at the end of the warehouse. 'Now come on, you secretive old bastard, what have you got behind there?'

'What the whole city and colonization was based on —' I opened the screen, '— gold!'

There is something about that beautiful buttery metal that holds the imagination captive. A hush came over the party as we stared at it. The objects had been carefully cleaned, and the surfaces shone with the special soft radiance which is unmistakably gold.

To coldly itemize the collection detracts in some way from its excitement and mystery. The gross weight of the pieces was 683 fine ounces. There were fifteen rods of native gold as thick and as long as a man's finger. There were forty-eight pieces of crudely wrought jewellery, pins, brooches and combs. There was a statuette of a female figure four and a half inches tall—

'Astarte – Tanith,' Sally whispered as she stroked it, 'Goddess of the moon and the earth.'

In addition there were a handful of gold beads with the string long ago disintegrated, dozens of sun discs and many chips, tacks and flakes and buttons of no definite shape or discernible purpose.

'And then,' I said, 'there is this,' picking up the heavy chalice of solid gold. It had been crushed and flattened, but the base was undamaged. 'Look,' I said, pointing to the design worked into it with uncommon delicacy of line.

'Ankh? The Egyptian sign of eternal life?' Louren looked to me for confirmation, and I nodded.

'For the Christians and heathens amongst you. We know that the Pharaohs on occasions used the Phoenicians to supply treasure for their empire. Was this,' and I turned the chalice in my hands, 'a gift from a Pharaoh to the King of Ophir?'

'And do you remember the cup in the right hand of the White Lady of the Brandberg?' Sally asked.

It was enough to keep us arguing and locked in discussion into the early hours, and the next day Sally, helped by Heather Willcox, presented her drawings and paintings from the cavern. When she showed the tracing of the white king, that frown of concentration again creased Louren's brow, and he stood up and went to examine it more closely. We waited for a long time in silence, before he looked up at Sally.

'I would like to make a copy of this, for my own personal collection. Would you mind?'

'With the greatest of pleasure.' Sally smiled happily at him. The mood of sparkle and smile was still strong upon her and she was enjoying the sensation that the display of her work was causing. Sally, like most beautiful women, is not completely averse to standing in the limelight. She knew her work was damned good, and she liked the plaudits.

'Now I haven't been able to decide what these are.' Sally smiled as she hung a new sheet on the common-room board. 'There are seventeen symbols similar to this which I have so far isolated. Heather calls them the walking cucumbers, or the double walking cucumbers. Have you any ideas?'

'Tadpoles?' Ral tried.

'Centipedes?' Leslie was a bit more feasible.

That was the end of our imagination, and we were silent.

'No more offers?' Sally asked. 'I thought that with the formidable collection of academic qualification and worldly wisdom we have assembled here we could do better—'

'A bireme!' Louren said softly. 'And a trireme.'

'By Jove.' I saw it immediately. 'You're right!'

' "Quinquereme of Nineveh, from distant Ophir," ' Peter quoted joyously.

'The shape of a ship's hull, and the banks of oars,' I enlarged upon it. 'Of course – if we are right then vessels like that must have plied regularly across the lakes.'

We could accept it, but others certainly would not.

After lunch we went for a tour of the excavations, and Louren again distinguished himself with an inspired guess. A series of large regular cell-like rooms had been uncovered by Peter's team in the angle formed by the cliff and the enclosure wall. They were joined by a long corridor, and there was evidence of paved floors and a system of drainage. Each room was approximately twenty-five feet square, and it seemed that these were the only buildings outside the enclosure which had been made of stone blocks and not adobe clay.

The closest we could come to a purpose for these cells was to call them 'the prison'.

'Do I have to do all the work around here?' Louren sighed. 'When you've just shown me pictures of the war elephants?'

'Elephant stables?' I asked.

'Very quick, lad!' Louren clapped me on the shoulder and I blushed. 'But I believe they are called elephant lines in India.'

After dinner I worked for an hour in my dark room, developing three rolls of film, and when I was finished I went to look for Louren. He was leaving again early the following morning and there was much for us to discuss.

He wasn't in the guest room, nor in the lounge, and when I asked for him, Ral told me, 'I think he has gone up to the cavern, Doctor. He borrowed a torch from me.'

Leslie looked at him in a way which was clearly meant to be highly significant, a frown and a quick little shake of the head, but it meant as much to him as it did to me. I went to fetch my own torch, and set off through the silent grove, picking my way carefully around the open excavations. No light showed from the entrance of the tunnel beyond the great wild fig tree.

'Louren!' I called. 'Are you there?' And my voice bounced hollowly from cliff and rock. There was silence once the echoes died, and I went forward into the tunnel. Flashing my torch into the darkness ahead, ducking my head under the zooming flight of the bats, and hearing my own footsteps magnified in the silence.

I could see no light, and I stopped and called again.

'Louren!' My voice boomed around the cavern. There was no reply, and I went on down the passage.

As I stepped out from the mouth of the tunnel, suddenly the beam of a powerful torch flashed from across the cavern shining full in my eyes.

'Louren?' I asked. 'Is that you?'

'What do you want, Ben?' he demanded from the darkness behind the torch. He sounded irritable, angry even.

'I want to talk to you about the plans for the next step.' I shielded my eyes from the beam.

'It can wait until tomorrow.'

'You are leaving early – let's talk now.'

I started to cross the cavern towards him, averting my eyes from the dazzling beam.

'Point that light somewhere else, won't you,' I protested mildly.

'Are you deaf!' Louren's voice rasped, the voice of a man used to being obeyed. 'I said tomorrow, damn you.'

I stopped dead, stunned, confused. He had never spoken to me like that in my life before.

'Lo, are you all right?' I asked anxiously. There was something wrong here in the cavern. I could sense it.

'Ben,' his voice crackled, 'just turn around and walk out of here, will you. I'll see you tomorrow morning.'

I hesitated a moment longer. Then I turned and walked back down the passage. I hadn't even had a glimpse of Louren in the darkness beyond the torch.

In the morning Louren was as charming as only he can be. He apologized handsomely for the previous evening. 'I just wanted to be alone, Ben. I'm sorry. I get like that sometimes.'

'I know, Lo. I am the same.'

In ten minutes we had agreed that although the circumstantial evidence of a Phoenician occupation of the city was most encouraging, it was not conclusive. We would not make any public announcement yet, but in the meantime Louren gave me complete *carte blanche* to proceed with a full-scale excavation and investigation.

He flew out with the dawn, and I knew he would be in London for breakfast the following morning.

The weeks that followed Louren's departure were dissatisfying for me. Although the work on the ruins went forward steadily, and my assistants never faltered in their enthusiasm and industry – yet the results were uniformly disappointing.

There were other finds, many of them, but they were repetitive. Pottery, beads, even the occasional gold fragment or ornament no longer thrilled me as it had before. There was nothing that added a scrap of knowledge to the store we had accumulated already. I roved the site restlessly, anxiously hovering over a new trench or exposed level, praying that the next spadeful of earth turned would expose an inscribed pallet or the headstone to a burial vault. Somewhere here was the key to the ancient mystery, but it was well hidden.

Apart from the lack of progress on the excavation, my relationship with Sally had deteriorated in some subtle fashion which I was at a loss to explain. Naturally there had been no opportunity for any physical intimacy since the arrival of the others at the City of the Moon. Sally was adamant in her determination not to allow our affair to become common knowledge. My amateurish manoeuvrings to get her alone were deftly countered. The nearest I came to success was when I visited her at the cavern during the day. Even here she had her assistant with her, and often Heather Willcox as well.

She seemed withdrawn, taciturn, even surly. She worked over her easel with a fierce concentration during the day, and she usually slipped away to her hut immediately after dinner. Once I followed her, knocking softly on the door of her hut, then hesitantly pushing the door open when there was no reply. She was not there. I waited in the shadows, feeling like a peeping Tom, and it was after midnight before she returned, slipping out of the silent grove like a ghost and going directly to her room where Leslie had long ago switched out the light.

It was distressing for me to see my laughing Sally so withdrawn, and finally I visited her at the cavern.

'I want to talk to you, Sal.'

'What about?' She looked at me with mild surprise, as though it were the first time in days that she had noticed me. I sent the young African assistant away and prevailed on Sally to join me on the rocks beside the emerald pool, hoping that its beauty and associations would soften her mood.

'Is something wrong, Sal?'

'Good Lord, should there be?' It was an awkward unsatisfying conversation. Sally seemed to feel I was prying into affairs that did not concern me. I felt my anger rising, and I wanted to shout at her,

'I am your lover, damn you, and everything you do concerns me!'

But good sense prevailed, for I am sure presumption of that magnitude from me would have severed the last tenuous threads of our relationship. Instead I took her hand and, hating myself for the blush that burned my cheeks, I told her softly, 'I love you, Sally. Just remember that – if there is ever anything I can do—'

I think it was probably the best thing I could have said, for immediately her hand tightened on mine and her face softened, her eyes went slightly misty.

'Ben, you are a sweet dear person. Don't take any notice of me for a while. I've just got the blues, there is nothing anybody can do about it. They will go on their own, if you don't fuss.'

For a moment she was my old girl again, a smile quivering precariously on the corner of her mouth, and in those great green eyes.

'Let me know when it's over, won't you?' I stood up.

'That I will, Doctor. You'll be the first to know.'

The following week I flew back to Johannesburg. There was the Annual General Meeting of the trustees of the Institute which I could not avoid, and I was committed to a series of lectures for the Faculty of Archaeology at the University of Witwatersrand.

I was scheduled to be away from the site for eleven days. I left it all in Peter Willcox's safe hands, after extracting from him a promise that he would cable me immediately if any new development broke.

The three girls fussed around me, packing my case, making a picnic lunch for me to eat on the plane, and lining up to kiss me goodbye at the airstrip. I must admit that I rather enjoyed all the attention.

I have often found that living too close to any problem narrows one's view of the whole. Three hours after leaving the City of the Moon, I made a minor breakthrough. If there had been walls and towers standing on the ruined foundations, then the rock must have been brought from nearby. The obvious place was from the cliffs themselves. Somewhere in those cliffs, close to the city, there was a quarry.

I would find it, and from its extent I would calculate the actual size of the city.

For the first time in weeks I felt good, and the days that followed were gratifying and solidly enjoyable. The meeting of the trustees was the type of festive affair which can be expected when funds are unlimited and prospects are favourable. From the Chair Louren was most complimentary when he renewed my contract as Director of the Institute for a further twelve months. To celebrate the thirty per cent rise in my remuneration, he invited me to a dinner at his home where forty people sat down at the yellow wood table in the huge dining-room, and I was the guest of honour.

Hilary Sturvesant, in a gown of yellow brocade silk and wearing the fabled Sturvesant diamonds, gave me her almost undivided attention during the meal. I have a weakness for beautiful things, particularly if they are women. There were twenty of them there that night, and in the drawing-room afterwards I held court like royalty. The wine had loosened my tongue, and washed away my confounded shyness. No matter that Hilary and Louren had probably primed the other guests to make a fuss of me, for when at two o'clock in the morning I went down to the Mercedes with Hilary and Louren escorting me I swaggered along seven feet tall.

This new-found confidence carried me through the series of four lectures at the University of the Witwatersrand. The first of which was attended by twenty-five students and faculty members, the latter outnumbering the former two to one. The word got out, however, and my final venue was changed to one of the main lecture theatres to handle the audience of 600 that turned up. I was an unqualified success. I was prevailed upon to return at an early date – and there was an unsubtle hint from the Vice-Chancellor of the University that the Archaeology Chair would fall vacant the following year.

For the last three days of my visit I spent every minute at the Institute. With relief I found that not much had suffered in my absence, and my multitudinous staff had kept things running smoothly.

The bushman exhibition in the Kalahari Room was completed, and open to the public. It was magnificently executed, and the central figure of the main group reminded me sharply of my little friend Xhai. The model was depicted in the act of painting on the stone wall of a cave abode. With his stoppered buck-horn paint pots, and reed pipes and brushes, I imagined that this was how the artist who had painted my white king had worked. It gave me an odd sensation, as though two millennia had rolled away, as though I could send my mind back along the years. I spoke of it to Timothy Mageba.

'Yes, Machane. I have told you before that you and I are marked. We have the sign of the spirits on us, and we have the sight.'

I smiled and shook my head. 'I don't know about you, Timothy, but I've never been able to pick a winner—'

'I am serious, Doctor,' Timothy rebuked me. 'You have the gift. It is merely that you have not been taught to develop it.'

I will accept hypnotism, but talk of clairvoyance, necromancy, mantology and the like leaves me feeling embarrassed. To divert the conversation from me and my gifts, I asked, 'You have told me before that you are also marked by the spirits . . .'

Timothy looked at me steadily from out of those disturbing black eyes. At first I thought I had insulted him by my thinly disguised question, but suddenly he nodded that cannon-ball head. He stood up, closed and locked the door of his office before returning to his seat. Quickly he stripped shoe and sock from his right foot, and showed it to me.

The deformity was shocking, although I had seen photographs of it before. It was of fairly common occurrence among the Batonga tribe of the Zambezi Valley. There had been a paper on it published in the *British Medical Journal* during 1969. The condition was known as 'ostrich-footed', and consisted of a massive division between the metatarsus of the big toe and the second toe. The effect was to make the foot resemble the claw of an ostrich or predatory bird. Timothy was obviously very sensitive about his deformity, and almost immediately replaced his sock and shoe. I realized later that he had shown it to me in a deliberate attempt to enlist my sympathy, to create a bond between us.

'Both feet?' I asked, and he nodded. 'There are many people in the Zambezi Valley with feet like that,' I told him.

'My mother was a Batonga woman,' he answered. 'It was this mark that qualified me for training in the mysteries.'

'Does it hinder you at all?' I asked.

'No,' he answered brusquely, and then went on almost defiantly in Batonga. 'We men of the cloven feet outrun the fleetest antelope.'

It was a beneficial mutation then, and I would have enjoyed discussing it further but I was warned by Timothy's expression. I realized the effort it had taken him to show me.

'Will you have some tea, Doctor?' He reverted to English, closing the subject. When one of his young African assistants had poured cups of strong black tea for us, Timothy asked, 'Please tell me how the work at the City of the Moon is progressing, Doctor.'

We chatted for another half hour, then I left him.

'You must excuse me now, Timothy. I am flying back tomorrow morning early and there is still much to do.'

I was awakened by a soft but insistent knocking on the door of my suite in the Institute. I switched on the bedside light and saw that the time was three o'clock in the morning.

'Who is there?' I called and the knocking stopped. I slipped out of bed, shrugged into a dressing-down and slippers, and started for the front door, when I realized the risk I was taking. I went back to my bedroom and took the big ugly automatic ·45 from the drawer. Feeling a little melodramatic, I pumped a round into the chamber and went back to the front door.

'Who is it?' I repeated.

'It's me, Doctor. Timothy!'

I hesitated a moment longer – anybody could call themselves Timothy.

'Are you alone?' I asked in Kalahari bushman.

'I am alone, Sunbird,' he answered in the same language, and I slipped the pistol into my pocket and opened the door.

Timothy was dressed in dark blue slacks and a white shirt with a windcheater thrown over his shoulders and I noticed immediately that there were spots of fresh blood on the shirt and that there was a rather grubby cloth wrapped around his left forearm. He was clearly much agitated, his eyes wide and staring in the light, and his movements jerky and nervous.

'Good God, Timothy, are you all right?'

'I've had a terrible night, Doctor. I had to see you right away.'

'What have you done to your arm?'

'I cut it on the window pane of my front door, I fell in the dark,' he explained.

'You'd better let me have a look at it.' I went towards him.

'No, Doctor. It's only a scratch. What I have come to tell you is more important.'

'Sit down at least,' I told him. 'Can I get you a drink?'

'A drink, thank you, Machane, as you can see I am upset and nervous. That is how I came to injure my arm.'

I poured both of us whisky, and he took his glass in his right hand and continued moving nervously around my sitting-room while I sat in one of the big leather armchairs.

'What is it, Timothy?' I prompted him.

'It is difficult to begin, Machane, for you are not a believer. But I must convince you.'

He broke off and drank whisky, before turning to face me.

'Yesterday evening we spoke at length about the City of the Moon, Doctor, you told me how there are mysteries there that still baffle you.'

'Yes.' I nodded encouragement.

'The burial grounds of the ancients,' Timothy went on. 'You cannot find them.'

'That is true, Timothy.'

'Since then I have thought heavily on this matter.' He changed into Venda, a language better suited for the discussion of the occult. 'I went back in my memory over all the legends of our people.' I imagined vividly how he must have thrown himself into hypnotic trance to search. 'And there was something there, like a shadow beyond the firelight, a dark memory that eluded me.' He shook his head and turned away, pacing restlessly, sipping at his drink, muttering softly to himself as though he still searched in the dark archives of his mind.

'It was no use, Doctor. I knew it was there, but I could not grasp it. I despaired of it, and at last I slept. But it was a sleep greatly troubled by the dream demons – until at last ...' he hesitated, ' ... my grandfather came to me.'

I stirred uneasily in my chair. Timothy's grandfather had lain twenty-five years in a murderer's grave.

'All right, Doctor.' Timothy saw my small movement of disbelief, and changed smoothly to English. 'I know you do not believe such things can happen. Let me explain it in terms you can accept. My imagination, heated by my search for a long forgotten fragment of knowledge, threw up a dream image of my grandfather. The one from whom the knowledge was learned in the first place.'

I smiled to cover my spooky feelings; at this time of night with this half-demented black man talking of dark things, I felt myself falling under his spell.

'Go on, Timothy.' I tried to say it lightly, but my voice croaked a little.

'My grandfather came to me, and he touched my shoulder and he said. "Go with the blessed one, to the Hills of Blood and there I will make the mysteries known to you and open up the secret places." '

I felt my skin prickle. Timothy had said 'The Hills of Blood', and nobody had told him that name.

'The Hills of Blood,' I repeated.

'That is the name he used,' Timothy agreed. 'I can only believe he meant your City of the Moon.'

I was silent; reasonable man at war with primitive superstitious man within me.

'You want to come with me tomorrow, Timothy?' I asked.

'I will go with you,' Timothy agreed. 'And perhaps I will be able to show you something for which you search – then again I may not be able to.'

There was certainly nothing to lose. Timothy was obviously sincere, he was still tense and nervously aware.

'I have already invited you to join me, Timothy, and I was very disappointed when you refused. Of course, you may come with me – we can certainly see if the sight of the ruins stirs something in your memory.'

'Thank you, Doctor. What time will you leave?'

I glanced at my watch.

'Good Lord, it's four o'clock already. We will leave at six.'

'Then I must hurry home and pack.' Timothy replaced his glass on my cabinet, then he turned to me. 'There is a small snag, Doctor. My travel papers have expired and we will have to cross an international border into Botswana.'

'Oh, damn it,' I muttered, deeply disappointed. 'You will have to get them renewed and come up with me on the next trip.'

'As you wish, Doctor,' he agreed readily. 'Of course, it will take two or three weeks – and by then the whole thing might have faded from my memory.'

'Yes,' I nodded, but I felt a prick of temptation. I am usually a law-abiding person, but now as I thought about it I saw that no harm could come from what I intended. The chance that Timothy might lead me to the burial grounds of the ancients was worth any risk.

'Would you like to take a chance, Timothy?' I asked. Formalities concerned with the coming and going of Sturvesant aircraft had been reduced to a minimum. There were daily arrivals and departures, and a phone call to the airport authorities was all that was necessary before departure. The Sturvesant name carried such weight, that there was never a head count on arrival or departure. At the City of the Moon Louren had arranged special status with the Botswana Government, and we were virtually free from bothersome red tape.

I could have Timothy in and out within three days with nobody the wiser and no damage done. Roger van Deventer would accept my word that Louren had sanctioned the flight. I could see no problems.

'Very well, Doctor, if you think it's safe.' Timothy agreed to my proposal.

'Be at the Sturvesant hangar before six.' I sat down to scribble a note. 'If you are questioned at the airport gate, which I doubt, show them this. It's a note authorizing you to deliver goods to the Sturvesant hangar. Park your car behind the flight office, and wait for me in the office.'

Quickly we made our arrangements, and when I stood at the window of my bedroom and watched Timothy's old blue Chevy pull out of the Institute car park I felt a mixture of elation and apprehension. Idly I wondered what the penalty was for aiding illegal exit and entry, then dismissed the thought and went to make myself some coffee.

Timothy's Chevy was in one of the parking bays when Roger van Deventer and I drove up in the Mercedes. We went through into the hangar. The big sliding doors were open and the ground crew was readying the Dakota for the flight, and through the glass doors of the flight office I saw Timothy sitting hunched at the desk. He looked up and smiled at me.

'I'll get the clearance, Roger,' I suggested smoothly. 'You go and start the engines.'

'Okay, Doctor.' He handed me the flight dossier. We had done this before, and I had banked on the same procedure. Roger climbed up through the door of the fuselage, while I went quickly into the office.

'Hello, Timothy.' I looked at him and felt a twinge of concern. He was huddled into his blue windcheater, and there were lines of pain cut into his forehead and the corners of his nostrils. His skin was grey and his lips pale purplish blue. 'Are you all right?'

'My arm is a little painful, Doctor.' He opened the front of his jacket. The arm was in a sling, freshly bandaged. 'But it will be all right. I've had it attended to.'

'Do you feel up to this trip?'

'I'll be all right, Doctor.'

'Are you sure?'

'Yes, I'm sure.'

'All right, then.' I sat down at the desk and picked up the phone. It was answered at the first ring.

'Airport police!'

'This is Dr. Kazin – from Sturvesant, Africa.'

'Oh, good morning, Doctor. How are you this morning?'

'Fine, thank you. I want to clear a flight to Botswana on ZA-CEE.'

'Hold on, Doctor. Let me get the particulars. Who are the passengers?'

'One passenger, myself – and the pilot is Roger van Deventer as usual.'

I dictated while the constable on the other end took it down in laborious shorthand. Until finally he said: 'That's okay, Doctor. Have a good flight. I'll give your clearance to control.'

I hung up and smiled at Timothy.

'All clear.' I stood up. 'Let's go.' And I led the way out of the office. The engines of the Dakota were ticking over. The three black ground crew inexplicably left their positions beside the landing gear and began walking rapidly towards me.

'Doctor!' Timothy's voice behind me, and I turned back towards him. It took me four or five seconds to realize that he had a short-barrelled Chinese model machine-pistol in his uninjured hand and the muzzle was pointing into my belly. I gaped at him.

'I am sorry, Doctor,' he said softly, 'but it is necessary.'

The ground crew closed in on each side of me, they gripped my arms.

'Please believe me, Doctor, when I tell you that I will not hesitate to kill you if you do not co-operate.' He raised his voice without taking his eyes off me. 'Come,' he called in Venda.

Five others came through the outer door of the hangar. I immediately recognized two of the young Bantu assistants from the Institute, and one of the girls. All of them carried those stubby, lethal-looking machine-pistols and between them they supported a badly wounded stranger. His feet dangled loosely, and blood-soaked bandages covered his chest and neck.

'Get him into the plane,' Timothy ordered crisply.

All this time I had stood dumbly, paralysed with shock, but now the party carrying the wounded man squeezed past between my captors and the side wall. They were blanketing each others' line of fire, the whole group was off balance and at that moment I regained my wits. I braced my legs, leaned forward slightly and heaved. The men on my arms shot forward like thrown darts, crashing headlong into Timothy and knocking him down in a floundering heap.

'Roger!' I shouted. 'Radio! Get help!' Hoping my voice would carry over the sound of the aircraft engines. The third ground crew leaped on my back, one arm locking around my throat. I reached up, took him at wrist and elbow and wrenched against the joint. His elbow went with a rubbery popping sound and he screamed like a girl, his arm loose and flabby in my grip.

'Don't shoot,' shouted Timothy. 'No noise.'

'Help!' I screamed, the engines drowning my cry. They dropped the wounded man and came at me. I ducked and went in low. I kicked for the groin of the leader, and felt my boot sock into him, fleshy and soft. He doubled over and I swung my other knee up into his face. It crunched as the gristle of his nose collapsed.

Timothy and the ground crew were scrambling to their feet.

'No shooting.' Timothy's voice was desperate. 'No noise.' I went for him. Leopard-mad with rage, hating him for this betrayal, with the full strength of my being, wanting to see his blood splash and feel his bones break in my hands.

One of the girls hit me with the steel butt of the machine-pistol, as I brushed past her. I felt the sharp edges of it cut into the flesh of my scalp, it threw me off balance. One of the ground crew grappled with me, and I took him to my chest and hugged him. He screamed, and I felt his ribs buckling in my grip.

They hit me again, steel biting into the bone of my skull. Blood poured warmly down my face, blinding me. My arms went soft, I dropped the man I was crushing and turned to charge into the others. Blinded with my own blood, my maniacal roars deafening me, they hit me again, crowding around me as I flailed and groped for them. The blows rained on my head and my shoulders. My knees collapsed, and I went down. I was still conscious, hot waves of anger buoying me. The boots started then, crashing into my chest and belly. I doubled up, blind, rolled into a ball on the cold oily concrete, trying to ride that storm of booted feet.

'Enough, leave him.' Timothy's voice. 'Get him to the aircraft.'

'My arm. I'll kill him.' The voice pig-squealing with agony.

'Stop that.' Timothy again, and the sound of a palm slapping against a face. 'We need hostages. Get him into the plane.'

They dragged me across the floor, many hands. I was lifted and thrown heavily onto the metal floor of the fuselage. The door slammed closed, muting the engine noise.

'Tell the pilot to take off,' Timothy ordered. 'Get the Doctor into the radio compartment.'

I was hustled down the length of the aisle. Blinking the blood out of my eyes, I saw the white ground engineer and his black ground crew lying bound and gagged against the wall of the fuselage. They were stripped of their overalls, which the gang had used to impersonate them.

Rough hands forced me into the steel chair in the radio compartment, and they tied me so tightly that the ropes bit painfully into my flesh. My face felt swollen and numb, and the taste of my own blood was thick and metallic in my mouth.

I turned my head, looking into the cockpit. Roger van Deventer was at the controls. There was a livid red swelling under his eye, and his grey hair was rumpled, his face pale and terrified. One of them stood over him with the muzzle of a machine-pistol pressed firmly against the back of his head.

'Take off,' instructed Timothy. 'Observe all routine procedures. Do you understand?'

Roger nodded jerkily. I felt sorry for him, I had guessed he was not cast in the heroic mould.

'Sorry, Doctor,' he tried to explain. 'They jumped me the moment I stepped aboard.' His full attention was on the job of taxiing the big aircraft out onto the still dark airfield. He did not look at me. 'I didn't have a chance.'

'That's all right, Roger. I didn't do so good either,' I replied thickly. 'I only got in two good kicks.'

'That is enough talking for now, please, Doctor. Mr. van Deventer must attend to the business of take-off,' Timothy admonished me, and I turned to give him the most expressive glare of hatred that I could force from my numbed features.

Roger asked for and received control clearance, and the take-off was routine and uneventful. The tense, anxious black faces relaxed and there were a few nervous laughs.

'You will fly on course for Botswana,' Timothy instructed Roger. 'Once you are over the border I will give you a new course.'

Roger nodded stiffly, the machine-pistol still held at his head. I was assessing the strength of the gang, I had already formed a working idea of their motives. Apart from Timothy and the eight who had overwhelmed me, there were five others. These were the ones who had captured and guarded Roger and the ground crew. The wounded man and the two I had damaged were laid out on the floor of the cargo hold. The two girls were working over them, both girls from the Institute, they were fitting a splint and changing bloody bandages.

As I watched, the gang members began changing from civilian clothing into camouflage paratrooper battle-dress. I saw the red star shoulder flashes, and my last doubts were dispelled. I turned my head and found Timothy was watching me.

'Yes, Doctor.' He nodded. 'Soldiers of freedom.'

'Or the bringers of darkness, depending how you look at it.'

Timothy frowned at my retort. 'I had always believed you to be a man of humanity, Doctor. You, I would have expected, could understand and sympathize with our aspirations.'

'I find it hard to sympathize with gangsters carrying guns in their hands.'

We stared at each other for a few moments. Then abruptly he stood up and came to the radio equipment beside my chair. He switched on the set, glanced at his watch, and began sweeping the bands. The station came on loudly, and immediately all movement in the aircraft arrested, all attention fixed on the announcer's voice:

'This is the South African Broadcasting Corporation. The time is seven o'clock and here is the news. A spokesman for the South African Police states that at 2.15 a.m. this morning a detachment of the Security Police, acting on information received, raided a farm house on the outskirts of Randburg, a suburb of Johannesburg. A pitched battle between police and a large gang of unidentified persons armed with automatic weapons ensued. Elements of the gang escaped in four motor-cars, and after a chase by the police, two vehicles managed to evade pursuit. Initial reports are that eight of the gang were shot dead, and four were captured wounded or unhurt. It is anticipated that many of those escaping were also wounded. A full-scale police hunt is now in progress, and all roads out of the Witwatersrand area are under surveillance, together with all airports. It is with deep regret that we announce the death of three members of the South African Police Force, and the critical wounding of two—'

A ragged cheer rang out through the aircraft, and one or two of the gang clenched their fists over their heads in the Communist salute.

'Congratulations,' I murmured sarcastically to Timothy and he looked down at me.

'Death is ugly, slavery is worse,' he said evenly. 'Doctor, there is a bond between us.'

'My head is sore, my face is too painful to listen to your Communistic cant,' I told him, 'don't give me fancy words, you bastard. You want to burn my land and soak it in blood. You want to tear down everything I hold dear and sacred. It is my country and with all its faults I love it. You are my enemy. There is no bond between us – except that of the knife.'

Again we held each other's eyes for a long moment, then he nodded. 'To the knife then,' he agreed and turned away. The Dakota bore on steadily into the north, and my injuries began to ache. I closed my eyes, and rode the long dizzy swells of pain that rose up out of my guts and exploded in my head.

The Mirage jet came up out of the east and flashed silvery sleek across our nose, and as it passed with incredible speed I saw the Air Force roundels and the goggled face of the pilot staring at us. Then it was gone, but immediately the Tannoy crackled into life.

'ZA-CEE. This is Air Force Red Striker Two. Do you read me?' I stared out of the window beside my head, and saw the Mirage turn sparkling in the sunlight high above us. Timothy came running forward to the set beside me and stared at it for a moment. The atmosphere was hushed and tense. Timothy could not reply, his Bantu accent was too thick for deception.

Again the jet howled across our front. The gunman crouched low behind Roger's seat hidden from view.

'ZA-CEE.' Again the call was repeated. Timothy was sweating lightly, his face blue-grey with strain and the pain of the arm-wound. He turned from the set and motioned to two of his men.

'Bring him,' he pointed to the white ground engineer. They dragged him into the radio compartment and held him in front of me. His face was pale and shiny with sweat, his terrified eyes held mine in pitiful appeal, the gag cut into his mouth. One of them stood behind him and pulled his head back, exposing his throat and stretching the pale skin so that the arteries showed blue and pulsing. He reached around in front of the man, and laid the glistening blade of a trench knife against his throat.

'I am serious, Doctor.' Timothy assured me as he freed the rope from my arms and put the microphone of the radio transmitter into my hand. 'Reassure them. Tell them there are only two aboard, and that you are bound for the City of the Moon on a routine flight.' He placed his finger on the transmit switch of the set ready to cut it off.

The terrified engineer moaned into his gag, the knife pressed to the softly throbbing skin of his throat. They pushed him towards me, closer so that I could see his face clearly.

'Air Force Striker Two this is ZA-CEE standing by.' I croaked into the mike, staring fascinated into the engineer's terrified face.

'Report your complement and destination.'

'This is Dr. Kazin of Sturvesant, Africa on a routine flight from—' As I spoke I saw them relax, the tension eased and Timothy's hand moved from the transmit switch of the set. The engineer's eyes held mine and I wanted to tell him that I was sorry, that I wished I could save him. I wanted to explain that I was trading his life for those of fourteen of my country's most dangerous enemies, that the sacrifice was worthwhile, and that I would willingly add my own life to the price. Instead I shouted into the handset:

'Hi-jacked by terrorists! Fire into us! Disregard our safety.' Timothy's hand darted to the transmit switch, and at the same moment he turned towards the hostage. I think he was going to intervene, to try and stop it. He was too late.

The knife slashed across the tensed throat, slitting it deeply beneath the line of the jaw. The blood burst forth like a ruptured garden hose, it sprayed out in a red fountain that drenched both Timothy and me. It pumped in great liquid jets that splashed against the roof of the cabin, then dribbled in thick cords and strings to the floor. The engineer was keening a high wailing sound like steam from a kettle, and the air from his lungs burst from the severed windpipe in a pink froth, that spattered the radio set.

The Tannoy was squawking, 'Reverse your course! Conform to me! Conform to me immediately, or I will fire into you.'

Timothy was cursing as he wrestled the microphone out of my hand: I was screaming and fighting against the ropes.

'You animals! You filthy murdering bloody animals.'

One of the gang lifted his machine-pistol to hit me in the face, but Timothy knocked his arm away.

'Get him out of here!' He jerked his head towards the still twitching, kicking corpse of the engineer – and they dragged him out into the cargo hold.

'Mirage is attacking!' shouted Roger, from the cockpit, and we saw it coming from ahead of us, a silvery flash as it bore in on a head-on interception course.

Timothy snatched the microphone to his mouth. I saw that his face was speckled with the engineer's blood.

'Hold your fire!' he shouted. 'We have hostages aboard.'

'Attack!' I screamed, tearing and jerking at my bonds. 'They'll murder us anyway! Open fire!'

The Mirage jet pulled up steeply ahead of us, without opening fire, and howled a few feet over our heads. The Dakota rocked violently in the slipstream. I was still screaming and struggling to tear myself loose. I wanted to get at them. The steel chair was rocking from side to side. I got my feet against the side of the fuselage and heaved with all my strength. The seat buckled a little, and again the guard lifted his machine-pistol.

'No,' shouted Timothy. 'We need him alive. Tell Mary to bring the morphine.'

The Mirage sheered off, then circled in to take up station a hundred feet off our starboard wingtip. I could see the pilot staring helplessly across the gap at us.

'You have spoken to Dr. Kazin,' Timothy warned the pilot of the jet. 'And we have four other hostages. We have already executed one white hostage and we will not hesitate to execute another if you take any further hostile action.'

'They're going to kill us anyway,' I shouted, but Timothy broke the contact.

It took five of them to hold me still for the hypodermic, but at last they got it into my arm, and though I tried to resist the drug, I felt myself going muzzy and misty. I tried to maintain my struggles, but my movements became lethargic and uncoordinated and slowly I drifted off into unconsciousness. My last waking memory was hearing Timothy giving Roger a new course to fly.

Pain and thirst woke me. My mouth was thick and scummy and my head was a mass of solid blinding agony. I tried to sit up and cried out aloud.

'Are you all right, Doctor? Take it easy.' Roger van Deventer's voice, and I focused my eyes on him.

'Water?' I asked.

'Sorry, Doc.' He shook his head, and I looked around the bare white-washed room. Four wooden bunks and a lavatory bucket were all the furnishings, and the door was barred and grilled. The three Bantu ground crew sat on one of the bunks across the room, looking lost and unhappy.

'Where are we?' I whispered.

'Zambia. Some sort of military camp. We landed an hour ago.'

'What happened to the Air Force jet?'

'It turned back when we crossed the Zambezi. Nothing they could do.'

And there was nothing we could do, either. For five days we sat in the airless, oven-like room with its stinking bucket, until on the fifth day our guards came to fetch me. With much shouting and many unnecessary shoves and blows I was marched down a corridor and into a sparsely furnished office whose main furnishing was a portrait of Chairman Mao. Timothy Mageba rose from behind the desk and motioned my guards to leave.

'Sit down, Doctor, please.' He wore paratrooper camouflage, and the bars and stars of a Colonel in the Chinese People's Army.

I sat on the wooden bench, and my eyes fastened on the half-dozen bottles of Tusker beer that stood on a tray. The bottles were bedewed with cold, and I felt my throat contracting.

'I know how fond you are of a bottle of cold beer, Doctor.' Timothy opened one of the bottles, and offered it to me. I shook my head.

'No, thank you. I don't drink with murderers.'

'I see.' He nodded, and I saw the little shadows of regret in those dark brooding eyes. He lifted the bottle to his own lips and drank a mouthful. I watched him thirstily.

'The engineer,' he said, 'the execution, it was not intended. I did not mean it to happen. Please understand that, Doctor.'

'Yes. I understand. And when the smoke of our burning land blackens the skies, and the stink of our dead sickens even your dark spirits, will you cry out, *I did not mean it to happen?*'

Timothy turned away and went to stand at the window, looking out over a parade ground where squads of uniformed Bantu drilled under a dazzling sun.

'I have been able to arrange for your release, Doctor. You will be allowed to return in the Dakota.' He came back to stand before me, and then he changed from English into Venda. 'My heart cries out to see you go, Machane, for you are a man of gentleness, and strength, and great courage. Once I hoped that you might join us.'

In Venda I answered, 'My heart weeps also, for a man who was a friend, one I trusted, one who I believed was a man of goodwill, but he is gone now into the half-world of the criminals and the destroyers. He is dead to me, and my heart weeps.'

It was true, I realized. It was not just an attempt to shame him. Beneath my hatred and anger, there was a sense of sorrow, of loss. I had believed in him. I had seen in a man such as he was, a hope for the future of this poor tormented continent of ours. We looked at each other wistfully, regretfully across a space of four feet that was as wide as the span of the heavens and as deep as the chasms of Hell.

'Goodbye, Doctor,' he said softly. 'Go in peace, Machane.'

They took us in the covered back of a three-ton truck to the airstrip, bare-footed and stripped to our underclothes.

They formed a double line from the truck to the Dakota. There were perhaps 200 of them in paratrooper uniform, and we were forced to walk down the narrow aisle with jeering black faces on each side of us. There were Chinese instructors with them, their lank black hair flopping out from under the cloth uniform caps, grinning hugely as we passed. I was bitterly aware of the mocking eyes and jibes aimed at my crooked exposed back, and I hurried towards the refuge of the Dakota. Suddenly one of them stepped out of the ranks in front of me. Deliberately he spat at me, and a storm of laughter went up from them. With a thick gob of yellow phlegm plastered in my hair, I scrambled up into the cabin of the aircraft.

The Air Force Mirages picked us up an hour after we crossed the Zambezi river and they escorted us to the military airfield at Voortrekker Hoogte. However, my almost hysterical relief at our safe home-coming was shortlived. Once a doctor had cleaned and dressed the clotted and suppurating gashes in my head, I was hustled away in a closed car to a meeting with four unsmiling, grimly polite, officers of the police and military intelligence.

'Dr. Kazin, is this your signature?'

It was my recommendation for the issue of Timothy Mageba's passport.

'Dr. Kazin, do you remember this man?'

A Chinaman I had met when I visited Timothy at London University.

'Are you aware that he is an agent of the Communist Chinese government, Doctor?'

There was a photograph of the three of us drinking beer on the tow-path beside the Thames.

'Can you tell us what you spoke about, please, Doctor?'

Timothy had told me that the Chinaman was an anthropology major, and we had discussed Leakey's discoveries at Olduvai Gorge.

'Did you recommend Mageba for the Sturvesant travel scholarship, Doctor?'

'Did you know that he went to China and received training as a guerrilla leader?'

'Did you sign these order forms for twenty-seven drums of fuller's earth from Hong Kong, Doctor – and these customs declarations?'

They were standard Institute forms, I could recognize my signature on the customs form across the desk. I did not remember the shipment.

'Were you aware that this shipment contained 150 lb. of plastique explosives, Doctor?'

'Do you recognize these, Doctor?'

Pamphlets in a dozen African languages. I read the first line of one of them. Terrorist propaganda. Exhortations to kill, burn and destroy.

'Were you aware that these were printed on your press at the Institute, Doctor?'

The questions went on endlessly, I was tired, confused, and began contradicting myself. I pointed out the wounds on my head, the rope burns at my wrists and ankles, and the questions went on. My head throbbed, my brain felt like a battered jelly.

'Do you recognize these, Doctor?'

Machine-pistols, ammunition.

'Yes!' I shouted at them. 'I had pistols like that against my head, in my belly!'

'Did you know that these were imported in cases of books addressed to your Institute?'

'When you obtained police clearance for the Dakota flight, Doctor, you stated—'

'They jumped me after the phone call. I've explained that a dozen times, damn you!'

'You've known Mageba for twelve years. He was a protégé of yours, Doctor.'

'Do you mean to tell us that you were never approached by Mageba? Never discussed politics with him?'

'I'm not one of them! I swear it—' I remembered the blood spraying against the cabin roof, the crunch of steel biting into the bone of my skull, the spittle clinging in my hair. 'You've got to believe me, please! Oh God, please!' And I think I must have fainted, it went all dark and warm in my head and I slumped sideways off the chair onto the floor.

I woke in a hospital room, between clean crisp sheets – and Louren Sturvesant sat beside the bed.

'Lo, oh thank God.' I felt all choked up with relief. Louren was here, and it would be all right now.

He leaned forward, unsmiling, that marvellous face cold and hard as though it had been cast in bronze. 'They think you were one of the gang. That you set it up, that you were using the Institute as the headquarters for a terrorist organization.'

I stared at him, and he went on remorselessly, 'If you have betrayed me and your country, if you have gone over to our enemies, then you can expect no mercy from me.'

'Not you also, Lo. I don't think I can stand that.'

'Is it true?' he demanded.

'No!' I shook my head. 'No! No!' And suddenly there were tears streaming down my face and I was shaking and blubbering like a baby. Louren leaned forward and gripped my shoulder hard.

'Okay, Ben.' He spoke with infinite gentleness and pity. 'It's okay, partner. I'll fix it. It's all over now, Ben.'

Louren would not let me go back to my bachelor quarters at the Institute, and I was installed in a guest suite at Kleine Schuur, the Sturvesant residence.

The first night Louren woke me from a screaming nightmare of blood and mocking black faces. He was in a dressing-gown, with his golden curls disordered from sleep. He sat on the side of my bed, and we talked of the good, sane things we had done together and the things we would do together in the future, until at last I slipped off into untroubled sleep.

For ten lazy, idyllic days I stayed at Kleine Schuur, spoiled by Hilary and fussed by the children, protected from the news-hungry Press, and sheltered from the realities and alarums of the outside world. The bruises faded, the scabs dried and fell away, and I found it more and more difficult to respond to the children's cry of 'Story' with something new. They shouted the punchlines in chorus, and corrected me on the details. It was time to go back into the stream.

In one unpleasant day-long session I told the story of the hi-jacking at the public inquiry, and afterwards faced the Press of the world. Then Louren flew me north in the Lear jet, back to the City of the Moon.

On the way I told him how I intended to find the stone quarries – and then the tombs of the ancients.

When he grinned and told me, 'That's the tiger - get in there, boy, and tear the bottom out of it!' I realized that I had been enthusing and emoting a little. I remembered old Xhai's imitation of the Sunbird, and put my fluttering hands firmly back in my lap.

A hero's welcome was waiting for me at the City of the Moon, they had followed my adventures on the radio. But now they opened a case of Windhoek beer and sat round me in a circle while I told the whole story again.

'That Timothy, he always gave me a funny feeling.' Solemnly Sally demonstrated her amazing gift of hindsight. 'I could have told you there was something fishy about him.' Then she stood up and came to kiss me on the forehead in front of them all, while I blushed crimson. 'Anyway, we are glad you're safe, Ben. We were so worried about you.'

The next morning, after I had driven Louren to the airstrip and watched him take off, I went looking for Ral Davidson. I found him in the bottom of a trench measuring a slab of sandstone. He was covered by a skimpy pair of shorts and a mass of hair that almost completely obscured his features, but he was burned a deep mahogany brown by the sun and was lean and fit. I had become very fond of him. We sat on the edge of the trench dangling our feet over the side, and I explained to him about the quarry.

'Gee, Doc! Why didn't we think of that before?' he enthused. That evening we drew up an elaborate search pattern, with a schedule to enlarge the area of search in expanding spirals each day. Ral's gang was temporarily withdrawn from the excavations within the temple, and armed with machetes for the assault on the thick, spiny vegetation on top of the cliffs.

The whole search was planned like a military operation. I had been dying to find an opportunity to use the walkie-talkie radio sets with which Louren had, unbidden, supplied us. This was it. Ral and I checked the radios, shouting things like 'Over to you' and 'Roger!' and 'Read you five five!' at each other.

Peter Willcox muttered something about 'boy scouts', but I think he was a little jealous that he hadn't been invited to join the search. Leslie and Sally, however, were infected by our enthusiasm and they victualled the expedition with sufficient food and drink to keep an army bloated and drunk for a week. They turned out in a pink dawn, still in their pyjamas and dressing-gowns, Leslie with her hair in curlers, to wave us off and wish us luck. At the head of my gang of stalwarts, laden with food and equipment, feeling a little like Scott or bold Cortez, I led them towards the gap in the cliffs which had become our regular route to the top – and ten hours later, sweaty, bedraggled, scratched by thorns, stung by hippo fly and other insects, broiled by the sun and in a filthy temper, I led them down again.

We repeated this routine daily for the next ten days, and on the tenth evening when we paused half-way down the gap in the cliff to rest, Ral suddenly looked at the steep sides of the gap and said in a voice of wonder:

'Gee, Doc! This is it!'

For ten days we had been using the steps cut by the ancients into their quarry. Thick growth had covered the neat terraces from which they had sawn the red stone. We found some of the half-formed blocks of masonry still *in situ*, only a little undercut and almost unweathered in this protected gully. The marks of the saws were fresh upon them as though the workmen had laid down their tools the day before, instead of 2000 years ago. Then there were blocks, cut in the rough, and abandoned half-way through the process of dressing. Others were completed, ready for transporting – yet others were in transit, discarded haphazard along the floor of the gully.

We cleared the undergrowth from around them and were then able to follow each fascinating step of the process of manufacture. The whole team came up to assist. They were jubilant with this new success, for we had all been a little put down with the recent total lack of progress. We sketched and mapped, measured and photographed, argued and theorized, and there was an evident renaissance of enthusiasm in all of us. The feeling that we had reached a dead end in the investigation was dispelled. I have a photograph, taken by one of the Bantu foremen who thought us all mad. We are clowning it up, posing on one of the bigger blocks of masonry. Peter strikes a Napoleonic attitude, hand in the breast of his jacket. Ral's hairy visage is adorned with a ferocious squint, and he poises a pick-axe murderously above Peter's head. Leslie is coyly showing a little cheesecake, and that is almost as bad as Ral's squint, with those legs she could kick elephants to death. I am sitting on Heather's lap, sucking my thumb. Sally has Peter's glasses on her nose and my hat pulled down over her ears, she is trying to look hideous, but failing resoundingly. This photograph illustrates the mood of those days.

After their assistance was no longer needed, the others were back to their separate tasks with renewed energy. Ral and I stayed on in the quarry. I brought up my theodolite and we set about calculating its extent and the amount of masonry removed from it. It was impossible to measure accurately the irregular excavation, but we decided that approximately a million and a half cubic yards of rock had been removed.

Then by a study of the method of quarrying and using the volume of abandoned blocks as a very rough guide, we guessed that the ratio of dressed finished blocks to waste material would be about 40:60. Finally we arrived at a figure of 600,000 cubic yards.

Up to this point we had been working with fairly factual figures, but now we pushed off into an ocean of conjecture.

'At least it's not as bad as drawing a dinosaur from its footprints,' Ral defended us, as we used the map of the foundations of the temple together with our calculation of rock volumes to reconstruct a complete elevation of the vanished City of the Moon.

'Here, let me do that!' Irritably Sally took the paint brush out of my hand on the first evening, after she had watched my efforts for ten minutes.

'I think the batter of the main walls is a little excessive,' Peter murmured critically, watching her, 'if you compare the walls of the elliptical building at Zimbabwe—'

'Yes, but take the temple of Tarxien at Malta,' Heather interceded. 'Or the main walls of Knossos.' And before Ral and I could do a thing to prevent it, the project had become a group effort that replaced the nightly song-fest in the common room.

With everybody contributing from their own particular area of the dig, and from their own specialized talents and interests, we built up a series of pictures of our city.

Massive red walls, ornamented with the chevron patterns of the waves that made Phoenicia great. Red walls that caught the rays of the setting sun, the evening blessing of the great sun god Baal. The tall towers, symbols of fertility and prosperity, rising from the dark green foliage of the silent grove. Beyond it, the vertical gash in the cliffs that led through a secret passage into the mysterious cavern. Again a symbol of the organs of reproduction. Surely this must have been sacred to Astarte – more commonly worshipped by the Carthaginians as Tanith – goddess of earth and moon, and so ranks of white-clad priests wound in procession through the grove, past the towers and into the secret cavern.

We knew that the Phoenicians made human sacrifice to their gods and goddesses. The Old Testament describes the infants delivered to the flaming belly of Baal, and we wondered what dreadful ritual our peaceful emerald pool had seen, depicting the victim dressed in gold and finery and poised on the edge of the pool with the high priest lifting the sacrificial knife.

'If only it weren't so deep!' Sally exclaimed. 'Ben wanted to get divers to go down, but he says they couldn't work so deep.'

In the area between the inner and outer walls of the temple, where the layer of ash lay thick and where the majority of golden beads and richer ornaments had been discovered, we drew in the quarters of the priests and priestesses. This would be a maze of mud walls with thatched roofs. We reconstructed the streets and courts of the priests and nobles.

'What about the king and his court?' Peter demanded. 'Wouldn't they live within the main walls also?'

So we divided the area between the quarters of the priests and the court of the king, drawing on what little we knew of Knossos, Carthage and Tyre and Sidon to give our paintings life. Ral had found the gate through the outer wall, it was the only opening and it looked towards the west.

'From it a road would have led directly down to the harbour.' Sally drew it in.

'Yes, but there would have been a market, a place of trade beside the harbour,' Ral suggested, and pointed to the map. 'This would be it. The area Peter has been puzzling over.'

'Can you imagine the piles of ivory and copper and gold,' Leslie sighed.

'And slaves standing on the blocks to be sold,' Heather agreed.

'Hold it! Hold it! This is supposed to be a scientific investigation.' I tried to restrain them.

'And the ships lying on the beach.' Sally started to paint them in. 'Huge biremes with their prows shaped like rams' heads, covered in gilt and enamel.'

The walls and towers rose again, the lake refilled with bright waters, and the harbours and taverns were peopled with hosts dead for two thousand years. Warriors strutted, and slaves whined, noble ladies rode in their litters, caravans poured in from the land to the east laden with gold and treasure, and a white king strode out through the great stone gates with a rosetted shield on his shoulder and his armour asparkle in the sun.

The project was fun, and it served also to prod our imagination. By the time Sally had put the last touches to our painting, four weeks had passed, and as a direct result of it Peter had discovered the shipyards suggested by Sally's biremes beached below the city.

There was the keel of a ship laid on the slip, with the main frames in place. The unfinished vessel had been burned, and its charred parts scattered. Only imagination and faith could recognize it as a ship. I knew my scientific opponents would challenge it, but carbon 14 on the charred wood gave us an approximate date of A.D. 300, the date which we had defined as that of the 'great fire'.

The project gave me an excuse to spend more of my time with Sally. I began taking my lunch and bathing costume up to the cavern. At first there was an awkwardness between us, but I worked hard at setting Sally at ease and soon we were back in that friendly bantering relationship that made us such a good working team. Only once I referred back to our more intimate association.

'Have you still got the blues, Sal?' I asked, and she gave me a long frank gaze before replying.

'Please give me time, Ben. There is something I have to work out with myself.'

'Okay.' I smiled as cheerfully as I could, and resigned myself to a long, long wait.

Sometimes the others joined our lunch-time sessions at the pool, for even when the heat was a hissing 115° outside, it was cool in the cavern. We splashed and shouted, and the echoes boomed back at us. One of my indelible memories is that of Leslie clad in a frilly little pink bikini romping skittishly around the pool like a lady hippopotamus in the mating season, pursued by the indefatigable Ral.

Five weeks after my return I went up to the cavern with good news.

'I just received a radio message from Larkin, Sal, Louren is arriving tomorrow.'

I was disappointed in her negative reaction, because I was sure she had overcome her initial dislike of Louren for my sake – and that she had begun to like him.

I went to meet Louren at the airstrip, and I was shocked. He had lost 20 lb in weight, and his skin which usually glowed with golden health was now chalky grey. Beneath his eyes were smears of dark plum that looked like bruises.

'Ben!' He put an affectionate arm around my shoulder and squeezed. 'It's good to see you, you old bastard.' But his voice was weary and I noticed the threads of silver at his temples which were newly acquired.

'My God, Lo, you look terrible.'

'Thanks.' He grinned wryly, and slung his bags into the back of the Land-Rover.

'Seriously, Lo. Are you sick or something?' I was distressed to see him looking so ill and haggard.

'I've been on a rough one, Ben,' he confided as he climbed into the Land-Rover beside me. 'Four weeks at the bargaining table, I had to do it all myself – could not trust anyone else to handle it. The other side sent in teams, changing them when they were worn out.'

'You're going to kill yourself,' I scolded him, sounding a little like a nagging wife. And he leaned across, punched my arm lightly, and laughed.

'You're a shot in the arm, partner.'

'Was it worth it? What was it about?'

'It's big, Ben! E – bloody – normous! Copper and iron, South West Africa, near the Cunene River, massive ore bodies lying in association, low-grade copper and high-grade iron – together they are a treasure chest.' The weary tone was gone from his voice. 'I put those little Jap bastards over the table and I roasted their arses. They will put in the finance for a deep-water harbour and a railway line to get the stuff out. That will cost them 150 million.' He was exultant, colour coming back into the pale cheeks. 'One of my companies will do the construction work, of course.' He touched a finger to his lips in a conspiratory gesture and I giggled delightedly. I enjoyed him in this mood. 'I'll put up for the pelletization plant and . . .' He went on to outline the scheme, laughing and punching my arm when he recounted each bargaining point on which he had scored.

'What will it make for you?' I asked at last, and he looked at me, slightly put down.

'You mean in terms of money?' he asked.

'Sure! What else?'

'Hell, Ben. I've explained it before. That's not the important thing. It's not money, it's exports and employment, and opening up new resources, and building for the future, realizing the potential of our country and – and—'

'And getting one hell of a kick out of it,' I suggested.

He laughed again. 'You are too shrewd, Ben. I suppose that's a lot of it. The game not the score.'

'Have you seen last week's *Time* magazine?' I asked. I knew it would needle him.

'Oh, for God's sake, Ben,' he protested.

'Your name is on the list of the world's thirty richest men.'

'Those bastards,' he muttered darkly. 'Now everybody doubles their prices. Why don't they mind their own business and let me get on with mine.'

'And in the process you are killing yourself.'

'You're right, Ben. I do feel a little spent, so I'm taking a week. A whole week's holiday.'

'Big deal,' I sneered, 'a holiday with your B.Y.M. arriving every half-hour for conferences, and the rest of the time with you hanging over the radio set.'

'Forget it,' he smiled. 'I'm getting away, and you're coming with me.'

'What do you mean, Lo?' I asked.

'Tell you later.' He avoided the question for we were approaching the branch in the dirt track, and I automatically slowed to turn down to the huts.

'Straight on, Ben,' Louren instructed. 'I want to go up to the cavern. I've been thinking of that place for weeks.' His voice went soft and reflective. 'When things got really tough there at the table, I'd think about the peace and tranquillity of that place. It seemed to . . .' He stopped, and coughed with embarrassment. Louren doesn't often talk that way.

Sally was working at the rear wall of the cavern. She wore a green silk blouse and tailored khaki slacks, with her hair loose and shiny. As she looked up to greet Louren, I saw with mild surprise that she wore lipstick for the first time in weeks.

She noticed his haggard features immediately, and I saw the concern in her eyes although she said nothing about it. Her greeting was subdued, almost offhand, and she turned back to her easel. Louren went immediately to the portrait of the white king. I drifted across to join him and we sat in a friendly relaxed silence examining the strange figure. Louren spoke first.

'Do you get the feeling he's trying to tell you something, Ben?'

It was a fanciful question for Louren, but I treated it with respect for he was clearly in deadly earnest.

'No, Lo, I can't say that I do.'

'There is something here, Ben,' he said with certainty. 'Something you – we have overlooked. The key to this place, the whole secret of it is in this cavern.'

'Well, Lo, we could . . .' I began but he wasn't listening. Sally left her easel and came to join us, she sat beside Louren and watched his face with complete attention.

'This feeling has never let me down, Ben. Do you remember the Desolation Valley mine? My geologists gave it a thumbs down, but I had this feeling. Do you remember?'

I nodded. Desolation Valley was now yielding twenty thousand carats of gem diamonds a month.

'There is something here. I am sure of it, but where?' He turned to stare at me, as though I had hidden whatever he was searching for. 'Where is it, Ben? The floor, the walls, the roof?'

'And the pool,' I said.

'All right, let's start with the pool,' he agreed.

'It's too deep, Lo. No diver—'

'What do you know about diving?' he demanded.

'Well, I've dived a couple of times.'

'Oh, for God's sake, Ben!' he interrupted brusquely. 'When I need a heart operation I go to Chris Barnard, not the local vet. Who is the best diver in the world?'

'Cousteau, I suppose.'

'Fine. I'll get my people onto him. That takes care of the pool. Now the floor.'

Dealing with Louren is like being caught in a hurricane. At the end of an hour, he had outlined a scheme for a thorough investigation of the cavern, and at last he suggested casually, 'Okay, Ben. Why don't you go on back to camp. I'd like an hour or so alone here.' I was reluctant to miss a minute of his company but I stood up immediately.

'Are you coming, Sal?' I asked. Louren wanted to be alone.

'Oh, Ben. I'm in the middle of—'

'That's okay, Ben,' Louren told me, 'she won't disturb me.' And I left them in the cavern.

The guest hut was long ago prepared, but I went with one of the servants to supervise the unpacking of Louren's bags. I noticed that someone had cut a spray of the wild cave-lilies that grew under the cliffs, and placed them in a beer tankard beside the bed. I meant to compliment the Matabele who acted as our cook, butler and housekeeper for this thoughtful little touch. It relieved the bleakness of the hut.

After checking Louren's accommodation I went down to the big bungalow and made sure there was ice in the refrigerator and plenty of cold water. Then I cracked the seal on a fresh bottle of Glen Grant – Louren and I have a common fondness for this nectar. While I was busy with the whisky bottle, Ral and Leslie came in off the dig and I heard them clump into the office next door. I did not intend eavesdropping, but the partition walls were paper-thin.

Ral growled like an enraged beast, and Leslie squealed.

'Oh, you are naughty!' she cried breathlessly, and it was clear that she had been physically molested. 'Some one will catch you doing that.'

'As long as they don't catch me doing what I'm going to do tonight,' Ral declared.

'Shh!' Leslie enjoined silence, but to no avail.

'Five weeks. I thought he'd never come. I was going mad.'

'Oh, Rally Dally darling,' wheezed Leslie in high passion.

'Toodles, my little Toodles,' Ral replied, and I blushed for them. Silently I set down the bottle and stole from the room. I was slightly puzzled as to how Louren's arrival, for that was obviously what Ral was referring to, could make such a dramatic improvement in their physical relationship, and I envied them for I had no such expectation.

We were all of us sick to the stomach with a diet of canned and preserved food. Louren had brought with him a full load of fresh fruit, vegetables and meat. That night we had a suckling pig, golden brown in its suit of crackling, with roast potatoes, green peas and a gigantic bowl of fresh salad. There was very little conversation at the dinner-table.

Once the dishes were cleared, Louren lit a cigar. I refilled the glasses and we all settled down in a circle about Louren. First I reported to Louren the discovery of the quarry, and the deductions we had made from it. This led on to an exhibition of Sally's reconstruction of the city.

I had not expected Louren to react the way he did. I had thought he might be mildly amused, as we were, not that he would accept our fantasy as proven fact. He worked himself into a fever of excitement, jumping up from his chair to examine each illustration, firing his abrupt searching questions at us, or simply sitting hunched forward in his seat staring at the painting with glitter-eyed concentration. His face was still pale and ravaged, which gave an almost demented intensity to his expression.

Sally, with a touch of canny showmanship, had kept the painting of the white king for the last. As she lifted it onto the board I saw Louren stiffen in his seat. The white king was in full battle armour, helmet and breastplate in glistening bronze, shield slung, and a short sword girt around his waist. His red-gold beard was curled and clubbed, and his bearing regal. His attendants followed him through the gates of the high outer wall, one carried his battle-axe, another his bow and a quiver of arrows, a third bore the golden chalice of eternal life.

Sally had lavished patient skill upon this particular illustration, and it was the most impressive of the whole series. We all stared at it in silence until suddenly I uncrossed my legs and leaned forward quickly, spilling a little of my whisky in my surprise. I had not noticed it before, the golden beard had masked it, but now I realized suddenly whom Sally had used as her model for the white king. I turned to stare at Louren, and there was the same deep forehead, the noble brow above wide-set piercing pale blue eyes, the same straight nose with delicately chiselled nostrils, and the proud curve of mouth with the slightly sensual pout of the lower lip.

'Ben!' His voice was husky, he did not take his eyes off the portrait. 'This is remarkable – I hadn't realized until this evening what this meant. Up to now it was just intriguing blocks of stone, and a few beads and scraps of gold. I never really thought about the people. That's the important thing, Ben! These men that voyaged to the ends of their world; that built something magnificent in the wilderness—' He broke off, and shook his head slowly, considering the magnitude, the grandeur of it. Then he turned to me.

'Ben. We have got to find out what happened to them, and their city. I don't care how long it takes, how much it costs. I have got to know.'

Now he stubbed out his cigar and jumped up from his chair, began pacing with a barely controlled violence.

'It's about time we announced this, Ben. I will set up a press conference. I'll want you all there to explain it. The world must know about these men.'

My stomach dropped steeply with alarm, and I stuttered a protest.

'But, Lo, we can't do that. Not now, not yet – please!'

'Why not?' He wheeled on me belligerently.

'We haven't got enough proof yet.' I went chill with horror, as I thought how my critics would hang, draw and quarter me if I went out on the stage with such a sorry script. 'They'll scalp us, Lo. They'll tear us to pieces.'

'We'll show them these.' He pointed at the paintings.

'God!' I shuddered at the thought. 'Those are just conjecture, fantasy, in that picture the only single detail we could substantiate would be the chalice.'

Louren stared at me, but I saw the madness fading in his eyes. Suddenly he laughed guiltily, and struck his forehead with the heel of his hand.

'Wow!' he laughed. 'I must be tired! For a moment there those paintings were real, from life!' He went to stand before the painting again and examined it wistfully. 'I've got to know, Ben,' he said again, 'I've just got to know.'

The following day, while we ate lunch beside the emerald pool, Louren told me how he and I were to get away together. He used Sally's charcoal stick to draw on the flat surface of a rock.

'Here we are, and here sixty-five miles to the north-east are the ruins at

Domboshaba. If your theories are correct then there was an ancient caravan route between the two cities. You and I are going to take the Land-Rover, and go cross-country, trying to pick up the old trail.'

'It's pretty rough country,' I pointed out, without enthusiasm. 'Completely unexplored, no roads, no water.'

'And no B.Y.M.,' Louren smiled.

'That makes it irresistible.' I returned his smile, remembering that this was therapeutic not scientific. 'When do we leave?'

'Tomorrow morning at first light.'

It was still dark when I awoke, and my bedside clock showed four-thirty. It was too late to go back to sleep and too early to get up. I was pondering the problem when the door of the hut opened stealthily and, as I prepared to repel burglars, Ral's hairy head silhouetted by the moonlight appeared around the jamb.

He had given me a fright so I shouted at him, 'What are you doing?'

If I had been frightened, it was as nothing to Ral's reaction to my question. Letting out a howl of terror he leapt about three feet in the air with his arms flapping, rather like a crested crane doing its mating dance. It took him a minute or two to recover himself sufficiently to shamble across to his bed and reply in a shaky voice, 'I've been to the toilet.' Which was just as well, I thought, otherwise my challenge could have had disastrous consequences. I got up, dressed and went out to check the Land-Rover. I suppose I guessed that Ral had been with Leslie, but I did not realize the implications of this.

It took Louren and me most of the first day to find a way over the Hills of Blood that the Land-Rover could negotiate. We followed the line of cliffs northward until they dwindled away and broke up into low kopjes and we could climb one of the gullies between them. It was a rugged ascent that taxed even that sturdy vehicle, but once on the top the going was through open savannah and scattered acacia forest and we made good progress, swinging away southward again to pick up the caravan route that Louren had hopefully drawn in on his large scale map.

That night we camped astride it, or at least where we hoped it might have been. With the amount of gasoline and water aboard, there was scant room for the luxuries of camp life. Besides it was meant to be a rough trip to dispel the smogs and grimes of civilization, a nostalgic return to the expeditions we had made together in our youth.

We grilled a brace of sand-grouse over the coals, and drank Glen Grant and sun-warmed water from enamel mugs. Then with hollows scraped from the hard earth for hip and shoulder we rolled into our sleeping bags beside the Land-Rover and chatted drowsily and contentedly for an hour before falling asleep.

In the dawn Louren massaged his back and gingerly worked the stiffness out of his muscles.

'I've just remembered I'm not twenty any longer,' he groaned, but by the third day he was looking it. The sun coloured him again, the bruises under his eyes were gone and he laughed freely.

Our progress was slow. Often it was necessary to retrace our spoor out of broken ground whose kopjes and ridges denied us passage. Then we would leave the Land-Rover and go in on foot to try and pioneer a way through. There was no hurry, however, so we could fully enjoy each mile as we groped our way north and east through country that changed its character and mood with the bewitching rapidity that is Africa's alone.

Each hour of eastward travel rewarded us with more evidence of bird and animal life. The dry-land birds gave way for guinea fowl, francolin, and the

gigantic korrie bustard. While amongst the mopani and masasa trees there
was the occasional silver-grey flash of a running kudu, with his long
corkscrew horns laid flat along his back.

'Water not far away,' Louren commented as we stopped the Land-Rover at
the edge of one of those open glades of yellow grass and watched a herd of
sable antelope move away into the trees on the far side. The most stately
antelope in Africa, proud heads holding the curved scimitar horns high and
the dazzling contrast of snowy breast against black body.

'Another endangered species,' I remarked sadly. 'Making way for the greed
and excesses of man.'

'Yes,' Louren agreed. 'And you know something, there's not one single
specimen of *homo sapiens* that's half as beautiful, and that,' he said, 'includes
Raquel Welch.'

That night we camped in a grove of masasa trees, clad in their outlandish
spring foliage which has the colours of no other tree on earth – pinks, soft
shiny beige, and flaming reds. Louren had shot a young impala ram during
the day and he wrapped the fillets in bacon and roasted them in a heavy iron
pot while I made a sauce of onions and tomato and plenty of garlic. We ate
it with thick slices of brown bread and yellow tinned butter and it tasted like
no other food I had ever known.

'If you ever need a job, Lo, you can come cook for me,' I told him around
a mouthful. He grinned and went to the Land-Rover to switch on the radio.

'What was the deal?' I asked.

'Just the news.' He had the grace to look guilty. 'Can't lose touch entirely.'

We listened to the strivings and strugglings of a world gone mad. Somehow,
in this remote and tranquil place the affairs of man seemed unimportant,
petty and transient.

'Switch if off, Lo,' I said. 'Who needs it?'

He reached for the control knob of the set, but checked his hand as the
voice of the announcer spoke a familiar name.

'Lusaka Radio reports that the leader of the terrorist gang which yesterday
ambushed a detachment of police in the Wankie district of Rhodesia, killing
four and wounding two others, is the self-styled "Colonel" Timothy Mageba
who two months ago made world headlines in his dramatic hi-jacking bid. A
spokesman for the Rhodesian police said that Mageba is probably one of the
most dangerous terrorists in Africa. A reward of 10,000 Rhodesian dollars has
been offered for information leading to his death or capture.'

With a savage gesture Louren switched off the set and came back to the
fire. He sipped his whisky before speaking.

'He's operating only 100 miles or so north of here. I'd give anything to get
a chance at that one.'

News of Timothy disturbed me deeply, and that night I lay long awake
with my hands behind my head staring up at the starry splendour of the night
sky. Venus had dropped below the horizon before I fell into a sleep troubled
with ugly dreams.

The morning sun lit the crests of the kopjes a fresh gold and inflamed the
sky with virulent reds and purples, driving away dark thoughts and we talked
and laughed together as we picked our way slowly towards the east.

In the middle of the morning we saw the vultures circling off towards the
north, a vast wheel of specks turning slowly beneath the hard blue sky.
Following the flight of these grotesque scavengers is one of the most intriguing
invitations that Africa has to offer. For every time they will lead you to the
scene of some desperate incident in the never-ending drama of the wilderness.

'A couple of miles off,' Louren commented, peering eagerly ahead through the windscreen. I shared his curiosity. The hell with ruined cities and lost civilizations, this was the stark, raw rule of tooth and claw we were going to witness.

A quarter of a mile ahead of us we saw the hunch-backed bird shapes squatting obscenely in the tree tops, thick as some devil's fruit in the orchards of hell.

'They are off the kill.' Louren was jubilant. 'Something's keeping them up in the trees and sky.'

He stopped the Land-Rover, and switched off the ignition. We climbed out, and Louren checked the load of his big .375 magnum, changing the solid bullets for soft-nosed ones that would deliver a heavier knock-down blow.

'We'll walk up,' he said. 'I'd love a chance at a big black-maned lion.' He snapped the bolt of the rifle closed. 'Take the shotgun, Ben, load with buckshot.'

This is my sort of thinking. If a lion is far enough away to warrant the use of a rifle then he and I have got no quarrel; closer than that I like a weapon that I can't miss with.

Louren set off through the waist-high grass, I followed him, keeping out on his flank to open my line of fire, the shotgun loaded for lion and my pockets bulging with spare shells. We moved in slowly, trying to find the focal point of this gathering of vultures for they were scattered in the trees over an area of half a square mile.

Every step heightened our tension with the expectation of walking on top of a pride of lions lying in the grass. Louren signalled each change of direction to me, as we quartered carefully back and forth over the ground. From the trees around us the birds launched into flight, changing miraculously from ungainly repose into something graceful and beautiful as they entered their true element.

My throat was dry with excitement, and a pleasurable fear. I could see Louren was sweating through the back of his shirt, not entirely from the heat. His every movement was charged with restrained energy, ready to explode at the first sign of the quarry. I loved this part of the hunt, for there is the atavistic urge of hunter still hidden in most of us, it was only the killing that repulsed me.

Louren froze, rifle at high port. He was staring ahead, and I braced myself for the heavy detonation of the shot that I knew must follow; but the seconds passed slowly as dripping oil and still Louren stood with only the slightest movements of his head as he searched.

Quietly I moved up beside him. Ahead of us was an area of flattened and trampled grass. In the centre of it lay the body of a dead buffalo, his belly bloated with gas, and big shiny green flies swarming over his dead eyes and into his open mouth. I could see no marks of claws in the thick hide, with its coarse black hair blotched with patches of shiny baldness and rough scab.

I looked down at the ground, not wishing to tread on a twig as I moved again, and I saw the small childlike human footprint in a patch of ant-turned earth.

I felt the hair at the back of my neck prickle, we had walked into something a damned sight more dangerous than a pride of lions. Quickly I looked back to the dead buffalo, and for the first time noticed two inches of a frail reed stalk protruding from the folded skin of the neck. The flesh around it was swollen tight and hard.

'Lo!' I croaked huskily. 'Let's get the hell out of here – this is a bushman kill.'

Louren's head jerked around and he stared at me. I saw the rim of his nostrils fade to china white.

'How do you know?' he demanded hoarsely.

'Footprints at your feet.' He glanced down. 'Arrow in the buffalo's neck.'

He was convinced. 'This is your shauri, Ben. What do we do?' Now he was sweating as heavily as I was.

I said 'Slowly, slowly! Don't turn your back and don't move suddenly. They are watching us, Lo. Probably right here.'

We began backing off, clutching our weapons with sweat-greasy hands, eyes darting restlessly from side to side.

'Talk to them, for God's sake, Ben!' Louren whispered. I found time to examine the discovery that the threat of poison could turn even a man like Louren into a coward.

'Can't take the chance. Anything could trigger them.'

'They may be behind us.' His voice shook, and I felt my skin between the shoulder blades cringe as I listened for the flute of the arrow. With each pace backwards I felt my fear shrinking, and fifty yards from the kill I risked hailing them.

'Peace,' I called. 'We mean you no harm.'

The reply came immediately, birdlike and disembodied, seeming to emanate from the heated air itself.

'Tell the big white-head to lay down his weapon, for we do not know him.'

'Xhai,' I cried out my relief and delight. 'My brother!'

'His eye was bright as the yellow moon,
His hoof struck fire from the iron hills.'

We sang the buffalo song together, the men squatting around the leaping fire, clapping out the complicated rhythm with our hands. The women danced in an outer circle around us, swaying and shuffing, miming the buffalo and his gallant hunter. The firelight shone on their golden-yellow skins, their tiny childlike bodies with the startling bulge of buttocks and the fat little yellow breasts joggling to the dance rhythm.

'The arrow-bird flew from my hand
Swift as a bee, or a stooping hawk.'

The branches of the trees around us were heavy with festoons of raw meat, hung out to dry, and beyond the firelight the jackal and hyena howled their frustrations to the star-bright heavens, as they snuffed the tantalizing odours.

'The blood when it flowed was bright as a flower
And sweet as wild honey was the flesh of his body.'

The dance ended at last, and the women giggled and trilled as they flocked to the fire to cram more meat into their little round bellies. Bushmen and women, are awed by physical size, and to them Louren was a huge golden giant. They discussed him in a frank and intimate manner, starting at his golden head and working downwards until I laughed out aloud.

'What's so funny?' Louren demanded, and I told him.

'My God, they didn't say that!' Louren was shocked, staring at the women in horror, and they covered their mouths with their hands as they giggled.

I sat between Xhai and Louren, one of them smoking and the other eating a Romeo and Juliette cigar, and I translated for them. They spoke of the animals and the birds for they had a common love of the chase.

'My grandfather told me that when he was a young man the buffalo in this land below the great river were as locusts, black upon the earth – but then the red sickness came.'

'Rinderpest,' I explained to Louren.

'And they died so that they fell one upon the other, so thick that the vultures could not fly with the load of their bellies, and their bones lay in the sun like the fields of white Namaqua daisies in the spring time.'

They talked on after the women and children had curled up and fallen asleep like little yellow puppies in the dust. They spoke of noble animals and great hunts, and they became friends beside the fire so that at last Xhai told me shyly, 'I should like to share the hunt with such a one. I could show him an elephant, like those that my grandfather knew, with teeth as thick as my waist and as long as the shaft of a throwing spear.'

And there goes any further pretence of looking for ruins and caravan routes, I thought, as I watched Louren's face light up at the suggestion.

'But,' I added, 'he says you must leave the Land-Rover here. They heard us coming for half an hour before we arrived today and he says this elephant is old and cunning. Which means we will have to get some sleep now. We've got a hell of a day ahead of us tomorrow.'

By the time the sun came up we had been on the march for three hours, dew had soaked our trousers to the knees but we had walked the night's chill out of our joints and were extending ourselves, stepping out with full stride to keep the two tiny brown figures in view. Xhai and Ghal were into that loose-limbed trot that would eat away the miles all day without flagging, their little brown forms danced ahead of us through the thickening thorns and jessie bush.

'How you doing, Ben?'

I grunted and changed the shotgun to my other shoulder.

'The little bastards can certainly foot it.'

'Brother, you have only just started,' I warned him. They led us into bad, broken country where harsh black ridges of ironstone thrust from the earth and the thorn was grey and spiny and matted, where deep ravines rent the walls of steep tableland outcrops and the heat was a fierce dazzling thing that sucked the moisture from our bodies and dried it in rings of white salt on our shirts. It was the type of country that a canny old elephant bull, pursued by men all his life, might choose as a retreat.

We rested for half an hour at noon, seeking shade in the lee of a boulder whose black surface was scalding to the touch and drinking a few mouthfuls of lukewarm water, then we went on and almost immediately cut the spoor.

'There and there.' With the point of a poison arrow, Xhai traced the outline of a padmark on the iron-hard earth. 'Do you not see it?' he asked with exasperation, and though we circled the area, tilting our heads learnedly, neither of us could make it out.

'If that's an elephant spoor,' muttered Louren, 'I'm a Chinese tinker.' But Xhai set off confidently on a new bearing through the thorns, and we climbed one of the rocky tablelands, following a trail that Louren and I could not even see. Near the crest of the hill, lay a pile of elephant dung, still moist despite the furnace-dry heat, and a cloud of yellow and orange butterflies hovered over it attracted by the wetness. The dung looked like the contents of a coir mattress.

'Velly solly,' I whispered to Louren, 'please fixee pottee – chop chop.'

'The man's a bloody magician.' Louren shook his head in amazement, as he unslung the heavy rifle from his shoulder and tucked it under his arm.

We went on again, but slowly now, pausing frequently while Xhai and Ghal searched the impenetrable thickets of thorn ahead of us. It was a gut-aching business in this close bush, each step planned and made only at a signal from Xhai's dainty pink-palmed hand, moving forward when the hand beckoned and freezing when it froze.

'Come,' said the hand and we went on again, then abruptly—

'Stop!' A quick cut-out sign, with the hand like a blade, then balling into a fist and pointing ahead, bad luck to point with a finger at the quarry.

We stood still as death, sweat-shiny faces staring ahead into the wall of thorn – and then suddenly the elephant loomed ghostly grey amongst the grey thorn, moving from us in a leisurely sway-backed shamble, grey skin wrinkled and old, hanging in bags and pouches at the belly and in the crotch of his back legs, the tail bare of tuft hair, the knuckles of the spine showing clearly through the ridged skin on his back. Old elephant. Big elephant.

'Stay here!' Xhai's hand pointed at Ghal and me, and I nodded in acknowledgement.

'Come with me!' Xhai's forefinger crooked at Louren, and they went on together, circling out on the elephant's flank through the thorn. The bushman doll-like beside Louren's bulk, leading him around for a clean shot at the head or shoulder.

The elephant paused, and began feeding from one of the thickets, delicately plucking the pale green shoots with the tip of his trunk, stuffing them into his mouth, completely unaware of danger – while out on his flank Louren reached a firing stance and braced himself, legs spread, leaning forward to meet the recoil of the heavy rifle.

The shot was stunningly loud, shocking in the heat-drugged silence. I heard the bullet slap into flesh, and the elephant spun away from the impact, turning to face Louren, with its long yellow ivories lifted high, the huge grey ears cocked back, and it squealed as it saw the man. It squealed in anger, and a long smouldering hatred now burst into flame.

It crabbed sideways as it began the charge, blanketing Louren's line of fire with a thicket of thorns. I saw Louren turn and run out to the side, trying to open his front for a clear shot. His foot hit an ant-bear hole and he fell in full run, going down heavily, the rifle flying from his hand, lying stunned full in the path of the charge.

'Louren!' I screamed, and then I was running also, armed with only a shotgun, racing to head the charge of a wounded bull elephant.

'Here!' I screamed at it as I ran. 'Here!' Trying to lead it off him, in the corner of my vision I saw Louren on hands and knees crawling painfully towards his rifle.

'Yah! Yay!' I screamed with all the strength of my lungs, and the bull checked his charge, his head swinging towards me, piggy eyes seeking me, trunk questing for my scent.

I threw up the shotgun, and at thirty yards' range I aimed for his little eyes, hoping to blind him.

Blam! Blam! I fired left and right into his face, and he came at me. I felt a vast sense of relief as his charge exploded towards me, I had taken him off Louren – that was all that counted. With clumsy fingers I groped for fresh cartridges, knowing that before I could reload he would be upon me.

'Run, Ben, run!' Louren's voice, high above the ground-thudding charge of the bull. But I found my legs would not function, and I stood in the path of the charge, groping stupidly for cartridges which were useless as thrown peppercorns against this grey mountain of flesh.

The blast of Louren's rifle beat against my numbed brain, once – twice, it crashed out and like an avalanche the grey mountain fell towards me, dead already, the brain shattered like an overripe fruit at the passage of the heavy bullet.

My feet were rooted to the earth, I could not move, could not dodge, and the outflung trunk hit me with savage force. I felt myself thrown through air, and then the cruel impact of earth and my brain burst into bright colours and stabbing lights as I went out.

'You silly bastard! Oh, you silly brave little bastard.' I heard Louren's voice speaking to me down a long dark tunnel, and the sound of it echoed strangely in my head. Cool wetness splashed over my face, blessed wetness on my lips and I opened my eyes. Louren was sitting on the ground, my head was cradled in his lap and he was splashing water from the bottle into my face.

'Who are you calling a bastard?' I croaked up at him, and the expression of relief that flooded over his worried features was one of the most satisfying things I have ever seen.

I was stiff and sore, bruised of shoulder and across the small of my back, and there was a lump above my temple that was too painful to touch.

'Can you walk?' Louren fussed over me.

'I can try.' It wasn't too painful, and I even found the inclination to photograph the huge dead beast as it knelt in a prayerful attitude with the head supported on the curved yellow tusks. Louren and the bushman sat on its head.

'We will camp tonight at the Water-In-The-Rocks,' Xhai told me, 'and tomorrow we will return and take the teeth.'

'How far is it?' I asked dubiously.

'Close!' Xhai assured me. 'Very close.' And I scowled at him uncertainly. I had heard him use the same words to describe a march of fifty miles.

'It had bloody well better be,' I said in English, and to my surprise it was much closer than I had expected – and a lot of other things I had not expected either.

We crossed one ridge with me hobbling along on Louren's arm and then came out on a wide granite sheet, a great curved dome of rock almost four acres in extent. I took one look at it, at the lines of shallow rounded holes that dimpled the entire surface, and I let out a whoop of joy. Suddenly I no longer needed Louren's support, and both of us ran down onto the stone floor, chortling with glee, as we examined the regular lines of worn depressions

'It must have been a big one, Ben,' Louren exulted, he made a guess at the number of holes. 'A thousand?'

'More!' I said. 'More like two thousand.'

I paused then, imagining the long regular lines of naked slaves kneeling on the rock floor, each beside one of the smooth depressions, each of them linked to his neighbours by the iron slave chains, each of them with a heavy iron pestle in his hands, pounding away at the gold-bearing ore in the stone mortar between his knees.

I saw in my imagination the slave masters walking along the lines, the leather whips in their hands as they checked that the rock was crushed to a fine powder. I saw the endless columns of slaves with ore baskets balanced on their heads coming up from the workings.' All this had happened here nearly 2,000 years before.

'I wonder where the mine is.' Louren was paralleling my thoughts.

'And the water?' I added. 'They'd need water to wash the gold out.'

'The hell with the water,' Louren shouted. 'It's the mine I want, those old boys only worked values of three ounces and over and they stopped at water level – there's a bloody treasure house around here somewhere.'

This was how all the ancient mines had been destroyed. It was a credit to the skill of the ancient metallurgists that the site of nearly every modern mine in central Africa had been discovered by them 2,000 years before. The modern miners ripped out all trace of the ancient workings in their haste to expose the abandoned reef. I made a vow that at the least I would be first into this one, before the vandals with their drills and dynamite.

The water was at the bottom of a fifty-foot well, cut cleanly through the living rock, its walls lined with masonry. It was the finest example of an ancient well I had ever seen; clearly it had been kept in good repair by the bushmen, and I gloated over it while Xhai fetched a raw-hide rope and leather bucket from a hiding place among the rocks. He brought the bucket up brimming with clear water in which floated a few dead frogs and a drowned bush rat. I made a resolution to boil every drop before it passed my lips.

Louren spent a full thirty seconds in admiring the well, before he set off into the narrow valley between the two ridges of granite. I watched him disappear amongst the trees searching diligently, and twenty minutes later his faint shouts drifted up to me.

'Ben! Come here! Quickly!' I dragged myself off the coping of the well and limped down into the valley.

'Here it is, Ben.' Louren was wild with excitement and I was struck again by the power that gold has to quicken the most sluggish pulse, and to put the glitter of avarice in even the most world-weary eye. I am not a materialistic person, but the lure and magic of it quickened my own breathing as I stood beside Louren and we looked upon the mine of the ancients.

It was not an impressive sight in itself, a shallow depression, a trench sunk about three or four feet below the level of the surrounding earth, its banks gently rounded, it meandered away amongst the trees like a footpath that had been worn into the earth.

'Open stope,' Louren told me. 'They followed the strike of the reef.'

'And back-filled.' I commented on the peculiar habit that the ancients had of filling in all their workings before abandoning them. This shallow trench was caused by the subsidence of the loose soil with which they had filled it.

'Come on,' said Louren. 'Let's follow it.'

For a mile and a half we followed the old stope through the forest before it petered out.

'If only we could find one of their dumps,' Loren muttered as we searched the rank vegetation for a pile of loose rock. 'Or at least a piece of the ore that they overlooked.'

My back was hurting so I sat on a fallen log to rest, and left Louren to continue the search. He moved away through the trees leaving me alone, and I could enjoy the sense of history which enveloped me when I was alone in a place such as this.

The water level in the well was fifty feet, so I guessed that this was the depth to which the ancients had worked their stope. They did not have the pumps or equipment to evacuate the workings, and as soon as water started pouring in they refilled it and left to find another reef.

This mine had been an open trench, one and a half miles long and fifty feet deep by six feet wide, hacked from the earth with adzes of iron and iron wedges pounded into the grain of the rock with stone hammers. When the rock was hard enough to resist this method, then they built fires upon it and poured water mixed with sour wine on the heated surface to shatter it. This was the same method that Hannibal used to break up the boulders that blocked the passage of his elephants across the Alps – a Carthaginian trick, you might call it. From the sheet of reef they prised lumps of gold quartz and packed it into baskets to be hauled to the surface on raw-hide ropes.

Using these methods they removed an estimated 700 tons of fine gold from workings spread over 300,000 square miles of central and southern Africa, together with vast quantities of iron and copper and tin.

'That's 22 million ounces of gold at $40 an ounce, 880 million dollars.' I worked it out aloud, then added, 'And that's a big loaf of bread.'

'Ben, where are you?' Louren was coming back through the trees. 'I found a piece of the reef.' He had a lump of rock in his hand and he handed it to me.

'What do you make of that?'

'Blue sugar quartz,' I said. And I licked at it to wet the surface, then held it to catch the sunlight. 'Wow!' I exclaimed as the native gold sparkled wetly back at me, filling the cracks and tiny fissues in the quartz like butter in a sandwich.

'Wow, indeed!' Louren agreed. 'This is good stuff. I'll send a couple of my boys in to peg the whole area.'

'Lo, don't forget about me,' I said, and he frowned quickly.

'You'll be cut in on it, Ben, Have I ever tried—'

'Don't be a clot, Lo. I didn't mean that. I just don't want your rock hounds tearing up the countryside before I've had a chance to go over it.'

'Okay, Ben. I promise,' he laughed. 'You can be here when we reopen the workings.' He juggled the lump of quartz in his hand. 'Let's get back, I want to pan this and get some idea of its value.'

Using one of the stone mortars in the granite cap and a lump of ironstone as a pestle, Louren pounded a piece of the quartz to a fine white powder. This he collected in our cooking pot, and with well-water washed off the powdered stone. Swirling the contents of the pot with an easy circular motion, letting a little spill over the rim of the pot with each turn. It took him fifteen minutes to separate the 'tail' of gold. It lay curled around the bottom of the pot, greasy shiny yellow.

'Pretty,' I said.

'They don't come prettier!' Louren grinned. 'This stuff will go five ounces to the ton.'

'You are an avaricious bastard, aren't you,' I teased him.

'Put it this way, Ben,' he was still grinning, 'the profits from this will probably keep your Institute running for another twenty years. Don't kick it, partner, money isn't the root of all evil if you use it right.'

'I won't kick it,' I promised him.

We camped that night beside the well, feasting on boiled elephant tongue and potatoes and keeping a bonfire going to compensate for our lack of blankets. We spent the following morning cutting out the tusks. These we buried beneath a huge pile of rocks to keep off the hyenas, and it was after noon before we started back for the Land-Rover.

Night caught us out again, but we reached the Land-Rover in the middle of the following morning. I had blisters on my heels the size of grapes and my lumps and bruises ached abominably. I collapsed thankfully into the passenger seat of the Land-Rover.

'Up to this moment I have never truly appreciated the invention of the internal combustion engine,' I announced gravely. 'You can take me home now, James.'

We left Xhai and his small tribe to their eternal wanderings in the wilderness and we arrived back at the City of the Moon eight days after we left it. We were blackened by the sun and an accumulation of dirt, we had sprouted beards, and our hair was stiff with dust and grime. Louren's beard came out a burnished red-gold that glistened in the sunlight.

He had been AWOL for three days, and the pack was clamorous. A tall pile of messages waited for him in the radio shack, and before he could shave or bath he had to spend an hour on the radio taking care of the most urgent matters that had arisen in his absence.

'I should get on back to the salt mines right away,' he told me as he came out of the shack. 'It's four-thirty. I could make it.' He hesitated a moment, then his resolve hardened. 'No, damn it! I'm going to steal one more night. Get out the Glen Grant while I take a bath.'

'Now you are talking sense.' I laughed.

'All the way, partner.' He punched my shoulder.

'All the way, Lo,' I assured him.

We talked a lot, and sang a little, and drank whisky until after midnight.

'Bed!' said Louren then, and rose to go, but suddenly he paused. 'Ben you promised to let me have some photographs of the "White king" painting to take back with me.'

'Sure, Lo.' I stood up a little unsteadily and went through into the office. I took a sheaf of nine-by-six-inch glossy prints from my files and went back with them to Louren. Standing under the light he shuffled through them.

'What's wrong with this one, Ben?' he asked suddenly, and handed it to me.

'What? I can't see anything.'

'The face, Ben. There is a mark.'

I saw it then; a faint shadowy cross which marred the death-white face of the king. I studied it a moment. It puzzled me. I hadn't noticed it before – like a dark grey hot cross bun.

'It's probably a flaw in the printing, Lo,' I guessed. 'Is it on the others?' He glanced through the other prints quickly.

'No. Just that one.'

I handed it back to him. 'Just a faulty print,' I said.

'Okay.' Louren accepted my explanation. 'Good night.'

I poured myself a nightcap while Sally and the others trooped off after Louren, and I drank it slowly, sitting alone, running over in my mind the plans that Louren and I had formulated for the thorough investigation of the cavern.

I will admit that I never gave the mark on the white king's face another thought. My excuse is that I was more than a little drunk.

The next two months passed swiftly. Ral and I devoted ourselves to a thorough excavation of the floor of the cavern.

The results were surprising only in their paucity. The cavern had never been used for human habitation, there was no midden or hearth level. We found an accumulation of animal detritus that extended down to bed-rock. On the bed-rock itself we found a single square block of dressed stone, and that was the total bag.

Our excavations had given the cavern a forlorn and gutted appearance, and the bed-rock was uneven limestone, so I had the dig refilled and neatly levelled. Then we used the ancient blocks to lay a pavement around the emerald pool. I saw this as a concession to the convenience of the thousands of future visitors who would come to view this wonderful gallery of bushman art once its existence was known to the world.

As he had promised, Louren radioed me when his company was ready to begin re-opening the ancient mine we had discovered on the hunt for the elephant. A helicopter fetched me and I spent three weeks with the engineers who were doing the work.

The reef was there below the water-table as we had hoped, and although its values varied widely from place to place along its length, yet the average was exceptionally high. Secretly I was glad of my ten per cent interest in the mine, despite my non-materialist values. We recovered many hundreds of artefacts, mostly mining tools. There were badly rusted adzes and wedges, stone hammers, scraps of chain, a few well-preserved fibre baskets and the usual beads and pottery.

Of these I was most pleased with the fibre baskets which enabled us to obtain a carbon-14 date from the laboratories. This was slightly prior to, if not concurrent with, the date of the great fire, and served to link the elephant mine with the City of the Moon.

However, the most interesting find at the elephant mine was that of fifteen human skeletons lying like a string of beads along the stope at its deepest point. The arrangement of the bodies was so regular as to preclude the idea that they may have been killed in a rockfall. Although the skeletons had been flattened by the weight of earth from above, I was able to determine that five of them were female and ten were males. All of them were elderly, and one of them showed traces of arthritis, another had lost an arm between elbow and wrist but the bone had encysted, proving that it had not been a recent injury. Most of them had lost teeth. On all of them I found traces of iron chains, and the picture I had was that of fifteen elderly and infirm slaves laid deliberately along the bottom of the stope before it was filled.

After supervising the cataloguing, packing and despatch to the Institute of all these finds, I returned to the City of the Moon, and I went immediately to the cavern. As I had hoped, Sally was hard at work there. I do not think her pleasure was affected as she came to meet me and kissed me.

'Oh, Ben. I've missed you.' Then she launched immediately into a technical discussion, and while I made the right answers my thoughts were far from bushman paintings.

I watched the way she crinkled her nose as she spoke, and the way she kept pushing her hair back from her cheek with the back of her hand, and my whole being throbbed with love of her. Down in my stomach I felt a squirming of dread. Our work at the City of the Moon was almost finished, soon we would be returning to Johannesburg and the hushed halls of the Institute. I wondered how this would affect Sally and me.

'We'll be leaving soon, Sal.' I gave expression to my thoughts.

'Yes,' she agreed, immediately sobered. 'The thought saddens me. I've been so happy here. I'm going to miss it.'

We sat in silence for a while, then Sally stood up and went to stand before the portrait of the white king. She stared at it moodily, her arms folded tightly across her breast.

'We've learned so much here,' she paused for a moment, and then went on, 'and yet there was so much that was denied us. It was like chasing clouds, often I felt we were so close to having it in our hands.' She shook her head, angrily. 'There are so many secrets still locked away from us, Ben. Things we will never know.'

She turned and came back to where I sat; she knelt in front of me with her hands on her knees, staring into my face.

'Do you know that we haven't got proof, Ben! Do you realize there is nothing we have found here that can't be discredited by the old arguments.' She leaned closer towards me. 'We have a symbol on a scrap of pottery. Imported in the course of trade, they will say. We have the golden chalice, the work of native goldsmiths using the Ankh motif by chance, they will say. We have the paintings – hearsay is not evidence, they will say.'

She sat back on her haunches and stared at me.

'Do you know what we've got, Ben, after it's all been sifted and sorted? We've got a big fat *nothing*.'

'I know,' I said miserably.

'We haven't even a single fact to knock them off their smug little perch. Our City of the Moon – our beautiful city – will be simply another culture of obscure Bantu origin, and there isn't a damn thing we can do about it. We will never know what happened to the great walls and towers, and we will never know where our white king lies buried.'

I planned to shut down the dig on the 1st of August, and we spent the last weeks of July tidying it all, leaving the foundations exposed for others who might follow us, packing our treasures with loving care, making the last entries in the piles of notebooks, typing the long lists of catalogues and attending to the hundreds of other finicky details.

The field investigation was over, but ahead of me lay months of work, filing and correlating everything we had discovered, fitting each fact into its niche and comparing it with evidence gathered by others at other sites and finally there would be the summation and the book. Months before, I had hoped I might be able to entitle my book *The Phoenicians in Southern Africa*. Now I would have to find another title.

The Dakota arrived to take away the first load of crates, and with it went Peter and Heather Willcox. They would still have two or three months of their European holiday, but we were sorry to see them go, for we had been a happy group.

That evening Louren spoke to me over the radio.

'We have got hold of Cousteau at last, Ben. He's been cruising in the Pacific but my office in San Francisco spoke with him. He thinks he may be able to help, but there is no chance that he will be able to come before next year. He has a full schedule for the next eight months.'

That was my last excuse for staying on at the City of the Moon, and I began packing my own private papers. Sally offered to help me. We worked late, sorting through the thousands of photographs. Now and then we would pause to examine a print of particular interest, or laugh over one that had been taken in fun, remembering the good times we had spent together over the months.

Finally we came to the file of prints of the white king.

'My beautiful mysterious king,' Sally sighed. 'Isn't there anything more you can tell us? Where did you come from? Who did you love? Into what battles did you carry your war shield, and who wept over your wounds when they carried you home from the field?'

We went slowly through the thick pile of prints. They were taken from every angle, with every type of variation in lighting, exposure and printing technique.

A detail of one of the prints caught my eye. I suppose that subconsciously I was alerted to pick it up. I stared at it, with eyes that began to see for the first time. I felt something fluttering inside of me like a trapped bird, felt the electric tickle run up my arms.

'Sal,' I said and then stopped.

'What is it, Ben?' She picked up the quaver of suppressed excitement in my voice.

'The light!' I said. 'Do you remember how we found the city in the moonlight? The angle and intensity of the light?'

'Yes,' she nodded eagerly.

'Do you see it, Sal?' I touched the white king's face. 'Do you remember the print I gave to Lo? Do you remember the mark on it?'

She stared at the photograph. It was fainter than on Louren's print, but it was there, the same shadowy cross shape superimposed upon the death-white face.

'What is it?' Sally puzzled, turning the photograph in her hands to catch the light.

'I don't know,' I said as I hurried across the room to the equipment cupboard, and began scratching around in it, 'but I'm damned well going to find out.'

I came out of the cupboard and handed her one of the four-cell torches. 'Take this and follow me, Watson.'

'We always seem to do our best work at night,' Sally began, and then realized what she had said. 'I didn't mean it that way!' She forestalled any ribald comment.

The cavern was as still as an ancient tomb, and our footsteps echoed loudly off the paving as we skirted the pool and went to the portrait of the white king. The beams of our torches danced upon him and he stared down at us, regal and aloof.

'There's no mark on his face,' Sally said, and I could hear the disappointment in her voice.

'Wait.' I took my handkerchief from my pocket. Folding it in half, and in half again, I masked the glass of my torch. The bright beam was reduced to a steady glow through the cloth. I climbed up onto the timber framework that had been left in position.

'Switch yours off,' I ordered Sally, and in the semi-darkness I stepped up to the portrait and began examining the face with the dimmer light.

The cheek was white, flawless. Slowly I moved the light, lifting higher, lowering it, moving it in a wide circle around the king's head.

'There!' we cried together, as suddenly the hazy mark of the cross appeared over the pale features. I steadied the light in its correct position and examined the mark.

'It's a shadow, Sal,' I said. 'I think there must be an irregularity beneath the paint. A sort of groove, or rather two grooves intersecting each other at right angles to form a cross.'

'Cracks in the rock?' Sally asked.

'Perhaps,' I said. 'But they seem to be too straight the angles too precise to be natural.'

I unmasked my torch, and turned to her.

'Sal, have you an article of silk with you?'

'Silk?' She looked stunned, but recovered quickly. 'My scarf.' Her fingers went to her throat.

'Lend it to me, please.'

'What are you going to do with it?' she demanded, holding her hand protectively over the scrap of pretty cloth that showed in the neck of her blouse. 'It's genuine Cardin. Cost me a ruddy king's ransom.'

'I won't spoil it,' I promised.

'You'll buy me a new one if you do,' she warned me, as she unknotted the scarf and passed it up to me.

'Give a light,' I requested and she directed her torch onto the king. I spread the scarf over the king's head, holding it in position with the fingers of my left hand.

'What on earth are you doing?' she demanded.

'If you are ever buying a second-hand car, and you want to be sure it has never been in a smash, then this is the way you feel for blemishes that the eye can't see.'

With the finger-tips of my right hand I began feeling the surface of the painting through the silk. The cloth allowed my finger-tips to slip easily over the rock, and seemed to magnify the feel of the texture. I found a faint groove, followed it to a cross-roads, moved down the south axis to another cross-roads, moved east, north, and back to my starting point. My finger-tips had traced a regular oblong shape, measuring about nine by six inches.

'Do you feel anything?' Sally could not contain her impatience. I did not answer her for my heart was in my mouth, and my fingers were busy, running all over the rock beneath the silk, moving well away from the portrait, down almost to floor level, and up as high as I could reach.

'Oh, Ben. Do tell me! What is it?'

'Wait!' My heart was drumming like the flight of a startled pheasant, and the track of my finger-tips trembled with excitement.

'I will not wait, damn you,' she shouted. 'Tell me!'

I jumped down off the framework and grabbed her hand. 'Come on.'

'Where are we going?' she demanded as I dragged her across the cavern.

'To get the camera.'

'What on earth for?'

'We are going to take some photographs.'

I had two rolls of Kodak Ektachrome Aero-film type 8443 in the small refrigerated cabinet which housed my stock of films. I had ordered this infra-red film to experiment with photographing the unexcavated foundations of the city from the top of the cliffs, but the results had not been encouraging. There were too many rock strata and too much vegetation confusing the prints.

I filled my Rolleiflex with a roll of the infra-red film, and I fitted a Kodak No. 12 Wratten filter over the lens. Sally pestered me while I worked, but I replied to all her queries with, 'Wait and see!'

I took up two arc-lights, and we arrived back at the cavern a little after midnight.

I used a direct frontal lighting, plugging the arc-lights into the switch-board of the electric water-pump beside the pool. I set the Rolleiflex on a tripod and made twenty exposures at varying speeds and aperture-settings. By this time Sally was on the point of expiring with curiosity, and I took mercy on her.

'This is the technique they use for photographing canvases and picking out the signatures and details over-laid by layers of other paints, for aerial photography through cloud, for photographing the currents of the sea, things which are invisible to the human eye.'

'It sounds like magic.'

'It is,' I said, clicking away busily. 'The filter takes out everything but the infra-red rays, and the film is sensitive to it. It will reflect any temperature or texture differences in the subject and show them in differing colours.'

There was an hour's work in the dark room before I could project the images onto our viewing screen. All colours were altered, becoming weird and hellish. The king's face was a virulent green and his beard purple. There were strange dapplings, speckles, and spots which we had never noticed before. These were irregularities in the surface, extraneous materials in the paint pigments, colonies of lichens and other imperfections. They glowed like outlandish jewels.

I hardly noticed these. What held all my attention, and set my pulses pounding, was the grid of regular oblong shapes that underlaid the entire image. An irregular chequer-board effect; they showed in lines of pale blue.

'We've got to get Louren here immediately,' I blurted.

'What is it? I still don't understand. What does it mean?' Sally pleaded, and I turned to her with surprise. It was so clear to me that I had expected her to understand readily.

'It means, Sal, that beyond our white king is an opening in the rock wall which has been closed off by a master mason with perfectly laid blocks of sandstone. The white king has been painted over it.'

Louren Sturvesant stood before the rock wall in the cavern and stared angrily at the white king. His hands were clasped behind his back. He was balanced on the balls of his feet, with his jaw thrust out aggressively. We stood around him in a semi-circle, Ral, Sally, Leslie and I, and we watched his face anxiously.

Suddenly Louren tore the cigar out of his own mouth and hurled it onto the paved floor. Savagely he ground the stub to powder, then he swung away and went to the edge of the emerald pool and stared down into its shadowy depths. We waited in silence.

He came back, drawn to the painting like a moth to the candle.

'That thing,' he said, 'is one of the world's great works of art. It's two thousand years old. It's irreplaceable. Invaluable.'

'Yes,' I said.

'It doesn't belong to us. It's part of our heritage. It belongs to our children, to generations not yet born.'

'I know,' I said, but I knew more than that. I had watched Louren over the months as his feelings towards the portrait grew. It had developed some deep significance for him, which I could only guess at.

'Now you want me to destroy it,' he said.

We were all silent. Louren swung away and began pacing, back and forth, in front of the portrait. All our heads swung to watch him, like spectators at a tennis match. He stopped abruptly, in front of me.

'You and your fancy bloody photographs,' he said, and began pacing again.

'Couldn't we—' Leslie began timidly, but her voice faded out as Louren spun around and glared at her.

'Yes?' he demanded.

'Well, could you sort of go round behind it, I mean, well—' Her voice faded and then grew stronger again. 'Drill a passage in the wall off to one side, and then turn back behind the king?'

For the first time in my life I felt like throwing my arms around her neck and kissing her.

Louren flew up one of his mine captains with a crack team of five Mashona rock-breakers from the Little Sister gold mine near Welcome. They brought with them an air-compressor, pneumatic drills, jumper bars, and all the other paraphernalia of their trade. The mine captain was a big, ginger-haired man, with cheerful cornflower-blue eyes, and a freckled baby face. His name was Tinus van Vuuren, and he threw himself wholeheartedly into the project.

'Reckon we will be able to cut her fairly easy. Doctor. This sandstone is like cheese, after the serpentine and quartz that I am used to.'

'I want the smallest opening you can work in,' Sally told him sternly. 'I want as little damage as possible done to the paintings.'

'Man,' Tinus turned to her earnestly, 'I'll cut you one no bigger than a mouse's—' he cut the word off, and substituted another, '— ear-hole.'

Sally and I taped the outline of the mouth of the shaft on the wall of the cavern. We positioned it carefully to avoid the most beautiful and significant paintings. Though we took Tinus at his word and made the opening a mere two feet wide by four high – yet we would destroy part of a lovely group of giraffe, and a dainty little gazelle with big listening ears.

We kept thirty feet away from the white king, to avoid undue vibrations from the drills which may have loosened flakes of stone or paint pigments. Tinus would go in for thirty feet, then turn his shaft at right angles to the face and cut in behind the king. Tinus was set to begin first thing the following morning, but that night we entertained him in the common room. The atmosphere was similar to that of a fighter squadron mess on the eve of a dangerous sortie. We were all voluble and tense, and all of us were drinking a little too much.

To begin with, Tinus was very reserved, clearly overawed by the company of the legendary Louren Sturvesant, but the brandy loosened him up and he joined in the conversation.

'What do you want the respirators for, Doc?' he asked. 'You expecting gas or a fire?'

'Respirators?' Louren broke off a private conversation with Sally. 'Who ordered respirators?'

'They specially told me six respirators.' Tinus looked dismayed at Louren's direct questioning. 'They told me that, sir.'

'That's right, Lo.' I rescued the poor man. 'I asked for them.'

'Why?'

'Well, Lo. What we are all hoping to find is a passage, a—' I was about to say tomb, but I did not want to tempt the gods, '—cave of some sort.'

He nodded. They were all watching me – and with a receptive audience I can seldom resist a touch of the theatrical.

'That cave will have been sealed, airtight, for two thousand years or so, which means there could be a danger of—'

'The Curse of the Pharaohs!' Sally interjected. 'Of course, do you remember what happened to the men who first entered Tutankhamen's tomb?' She drew a finger across her own throat and rolled her eyes horribly. She was onto her second Glen Grant.

'Sally, you ought to know better,' I cut in severely. 'The Curse of the Pharaohs is of course a myth. But there is a danger of a peculiarly unpleasant lung disease.'

'Well, I must say, I don't believe in curses and all that sort of bulldust,' Tinus laughed, a little too loudly. His inhibitions were way down around his ankles.

'That makes two of us,' agreed Ral Davidson.

'It's not a supernatural thing,' Leslie told them primly. 'It's a fungus disease.'

I seemed to have lost control of the situation completely, so I raised my voice.

'If you are all finished, I'll go on,' which got their attention back to me.

'The conditions would have been ideal for the development of *cryptococcus neuromyces*, a fungoid saphrophitic growth whose air-borne spores are the cause of a fatal disease.'

'What does it do?' Tinus asked.

'The spores are breathed into the lungs, and in the warm moist conditions they germinate almost immediately and develop into dense granulitic colonies.'

'Sies!' said Tinus, which is an expression of the deepest disgust. 'You mean it starts growing on your lungs like that green stuff on mouldy bread?'

'What are the consequences?' Louren asked.

I had it word perfect. 'Primarily they are extensive lesions of the lung tissue, with haemorrhage, high temperature and rapidly painful breathing, but then the fungoid colonies begin generating wastes which are readily absorbed into the blood and carried to the brain and central nervous system.'

'My God!' Tinus was blanched and horrified, his blue eyes stared out of the white freckled face. 'Then what happens?'

'Well, the wastes act as a virulent neurotoxin and induce hallucination. There is inflammation of the meninges, and severe brain malfunction, similar to the effects of lysergic acid or mescalin.'

'Groovy!' said Ral, and Leslie kicked his shin.

'You mean it drives you crazy?' Tinus demanded.

'Clean out of your little skull,' Sally assured him.

'Fatal?' asked Louren.

'Seventy-five per cent, depending on individual immunity and the rate of antibody formation.'

'In the event of survival, is there permanent damage?'

'Scarring of the lungs similar to healed tuberculosis.'

'Brain damage?'

'No.' I shook my head.

'Hell, man,' said Tinus carefully, setting his glass down. 'I don't know that I am so keen on this deal. Rock falls, methane gas, pressure bursts – those don't worry me. But this fungus thing,' he shuddered, 'it is creepy, man. Just plain bloody creepy.'

'What precautions are you going to take, Ben?' Louren asked.

'The first party in will be protected by respirators.' I explained. 'I will take air and dust samples for microscopic examination.'

Louren nodded, and smiled at Tinus.

'Satisfied?'

'What will you do if you don't find it – but it's sort of lurking there? Like, ready to pounce, you know. Like in those science fiction books,' Tinus hedged.

'If it's there, it will be thick. Every dust sample will be full of it. You can't miss it under the microscope. A black, three-ball structure like a pawnbroker's sign.'

'Are you sure, Doc?'

'I'm sure, Tinus.'

He took a deep breath, hesitated a moment longer, then nodded. 'Okay, Doc. I'll trust you,' he said.

The buffeting, fluttering roar of the rock drills chased my agonized brain into a corner of my skull and started kicking it to a jelly. The party had ended in the early hours.

'How are you feeling, Doc?' Tinus van Vuuren came across to where I stood watching the work and shouted above the din. My nerves vibrated like guitar strings. Tinus looked as fresh and baby-faced as though his night cap had been hot milk and honey and he had slept twelve hours. I knew the type – Louren was one of them.

'I feel bloody awful, thanks,' I shouted back.

'There won't be anything to see here for a couple of days,' Tinus told me. 'Why don't you go lie down for a bit, Doc.'

'I'll stick around,' I said, which seemed to be the general sentiment. Louren piloted the course of the Sturvesant empire from the radio shack, unable to tear himself away from the City of the Moon. Sally made a few desultory attempts at cataloguing and filing, but these never lasted more than an hour or two and then she was back at the cavern. Ral and Leslie made no pretence, and spent all day in the cavern, except for brief simultaneous absences which Louren and I guessed were exercise periods.

Tinus was a top man in his trade, and his team cut the tunnel swiftly and skilfully. The walls were shaped smoothly and precisely. They were shored with heavy timber baulks, and electric lights were strung along the roof. Thirty feet in, Tinus constructed a large chamber from which a new drive was made, aimed at the area behind the painting of the white king.

Tinus and I had made careful measurements and calculations, and we had decided exactly where we could expect to strike whatever the wall of masonry concealed.

The Bantu drill-men were warned of the need for respirators, and Tinus and I crouched behind them in the cramped rock tunnel as they began the assault on the last few feet of rock. Their backs were naked glistening bunches of black muscles as they worked the heavy drills. The noise in the confined space was thunderous, and despite the ventilation fans circulating air, the heat was appalling. The sweat poured down inside the face mask of my respirator, and the eye goggles were fogged and blurry.

The tension was becoming almost painful as the long steel bit of the drill hammered itself into the rock, sinking in inch by inch, the muddy lubricating water running back from the drill hole. I glanced sideways at Tinus. He appeared monstrous in the black rubber mask, but the blue eyes twinkled out of the eye glasses and he winked and held up a thumb in a gesture of assurance.

Suddenly the drill-man was thrown off balance, as the drill ran away with him. It slid, unresisted, into its hole, and he staggered wildly as he tried to control the enormous weight of steel. Tinus slapped his shoulder, and he slammed the valve of the drill closed. The silence was almost painful, and our laboured breathing was the only sound.

Through, I thought, *we've holed through into God knows what.*

I saw my own excitement reflected in Tinus' blue eyes. I nodded at him, and he turned and tapped the drill-men's shoulder's and jerked his thumb in a gesture of dismissal. They shuffled back, bowed in the low tunnel, and disappeared around the bend.

The two of us went forward and crouched at the face. Gingerly we withdrew the drill steel from its hole, and a wisp of fine dust followed it out, smoking in the harsh glare of the electric lights. Tinus and I exchanged glances. Then I jerked my head at Tinus. He nodded, and followed his gang back along the tunnel. I worked on alone at the face.

I used the long plastic rod, with a piece of sterile white cloth attached to the end of it, to probe the drill hole to its limit. It ran fourteen feet into the rock. before meeting resistance, and when I withdrew it the cloth was thick with grey floury dust. I dropped it into the sample bottle, and attached another cloth to the rod. In all I collected six separate samples, before I followed Tinus back along the passage. There was a bench and an angle-poise lamp set up ready for me in the rock chamber. The microscope was under the light, with its mirror adjusted and it was the work of only a few minutes to smear my dust samples onto the slides and spread the red dye over them.

It was difficult to get a view into the eyepiece of the microscope through my befogged goggles. One quick scrutiny was sufficient, but I doggedly inspected all six samples before I ripped off my respirator and sucked big relieved breaths. Then I scampered down the passage and out into the cavern.

They were all waiting for me, crowding around me eagerly.

'We've drilled into a cavity,' I shouted, 'and it's clean!'

Then they were on me, pounding my back and shaking my hand, laughing and chattering excitedly.

Louren would let no one else work with me at the face, though Ral and Sally were clearly breaking their hearts to do so.

The two of us worked carefully, slowly chipping away at the drill hole with chisel and four-pound hammer, enlarging it gradually until we had exposed a slab of dressed masonry. It was a massive slab of red sandstone which blocked off the end of our tunnel from floor to roof, and from wall to wall. It was obviously the lining of the cavity into which the drill had bored.

The drill hole cut through the centre of it like a single black eye-socket. All our efforts to peer through it were rewarded with a vista of impenetrable darkness and we had to content ourselves with the slower pains-taking approach.

For three days we worked shoulder to shoulder, stripped to the waist, chipping steadily at the living rock until, despite our gloves, our hands were mushy with blisters and smeared skin. Slowly we exposed the massive slab over its full width and height, to find that it butted on either side against identical slabs and that it appeared to carry across its summit the cross-pieces of an equally massive stone lintel.

We used two fifty-ton hydraulic jacks to take the strain of the lintel off the slab. Then we drilled and attached ring bolts to the slab itself and hooked steel chains to them. We jammed a brace of steel H-sections across the tunnel to anchor the chains and with two heavy ratchet winches we began to haul the slab bodily out of its seating.

We knelt side by side, each of us straining against one of the winches, taking up the pull one pawl at a time. With each click of the ratchet the strain on the chains increased until they were as rigid as solid steel bars. Now the handles of the winches were almost immovable.

'Okay, Ben. Let's both get onto one of them,' Louren panted. His golden curls were dark and heavy with sweat and dirt, plastered against his skull, and the sweat highlighted his great shoulder muscles and the straining, swollen biceps as we heaved together at the winch.

'Clank!' went the ratchet and the chain moved a sixteenth of an inch.

'Clank!' Again she moved. Our breathing hissed and whistled in the silence.

'All the way, partner,' Louren gasped beside me.

'All the way, Lo.' And my body arched like a drawn bow, I felt the muscles in my back begin to tear, my eyes strained from their sockets.

Then with a soft grating sound the great slab of sandstone swung slowly out of the face, and then fell with a heavy thump to the floor of the tunnel, and beyond it we saw the square black opening.

We lay together side by side, fighting for breath, sweat trickling down our faces and bodies, our muscles still quivering and twitching from our exertions and we stared into that sinister hole.

There was a smell; a stale, long-dead, dry smell as the air that had been trapped in there for 2,000 years gushed out.

'Come!' Louren was the first to move, he scrambled to his feet and snatched up one of the electric bulbs in its little wire cage, the extension cable slithered after him like a snake as he went forward. I followed him quickly, and we crawled through the opening.

It was a jump of four feet down to the floor of the chamber beyond. We stood side by side, Louren holding the light above his head, and we peered around us into the moving mysterious shadows.

We were in a long commodious passage that ran straight and undeviatingly 155 feet from the cavern end to terminate against a blank wall of stone. The passage was eight foot six inches high, and ten foot wide.

The roof was lined with lintels of sandstone laid horizontally from wall to wall, and the walls themselves were tiled with blocks similar to the one we had removed from its seating. The floor was paved with square flags of sandstone.

Let into the walls on each side of the passage were stone-lined cupboards. These were seven feet wide and five feet deep and reached from floor to roof height. Each of these recesses was fitted with shelves of stone slab, rank upon rank of them, three feet apart and upon the shelves stood hundreds upon hundreds of pottery jars.

'It's some sort of store room,' Louren said, holding the light high and moving slowly down the passage.

'Yes, probably wine or corn in the jars.' I have never learned not to guess aloud. My heart was hammering with excitement and my head swivelled from side to side, as I tried to take in every detail.

There were twenty of these recesses, ten on each side of the passage, and I guessed again.

'Must be two or three thousand pots,' I said.

'Let's open one.' Louren was consumed by a layman's impatience.

'No, Lo, we can't do that until we are ready to work properly.'

There was a thick soft shroud of pale dust over everything, it softened the outlines and edges of all shapes. It rose lazily around our legs like a sea mist as our movements stirred it.

'We will have to clean up before we can do anything else,' I said, and sneezed as the dust found its way into my nostrils.

'Move slowly,' Louren told me. 'Don't stir it up.' He took a further pace and then stopped.

'What's this?' Scattered along the passage floor were dozens of large shapeless objects, their identity concealed by the blanketing dust. They were lying singly, or in heaps, strange fluid shapes that teased my memory. Compared with the orderly ranks of jars on their shelves, the objects were strewn with a careless abandon.

'Hold the lamp,' I told Louren, and crouched over one of them. I touched it gently, running my fingers through the velvety dust, brushing it softly aside until I recognized what it was and I drew back with an involuntary exclamation of surprise.

Through the soft mist of dust and ages a face stared up at me. A long-dead, mummified face over which was stretched dry tobacco-brown skin. The eyes were empty dark holes, and the lips had dried and shrunken to expose the grinning yellow teeth.

'Dead men,' Louren said. 'Dozens of them.'

'Sacrifices?' I pondered. 'No, this is something else.'

'It looks like a battle. As though they had been killed in a fight.'

Now that we knew what they were, it was possible to make out the way the bodies were piled upon each other like the debris of a hurricane, or were thrown loosely about the stone floor. A corpse in a mantle of grey dust sat with his back to the wall, his head sagged forward on his chest, and one outflung arm had knocked four of the jars from their shelf – they lay on the floor beside him like fat rolls of French bead.

'It must have been a hell of a fight,' I said with awe.

'It was,' said Louren softly, and I turned to him with surprise. His eyes glowed with some intense inner excitement, and his lips were parted, a reckless half smile on his lips.

'What do you mean?' I demanded. 'How do you know that?'

Louren looked at me. For a second or two he did not see me, then his eyes focused.

'Hey?' he said, puzzled.

'Why did you say that, as though you knew?'

'Did I?' he asked. 'I don't know. I meant – it must have been.'

He moved on slowly down the passage, stepping over the wind-rows of dead men, peering in each recess as he passed, and I followed him slowly. My mind was thrashing around like a corralled bull, charging madly at each fleeting idea that crossed its path, spinning back on its track and charging again. I knew there was no chance of it being capable of calm, logical thought until this first surging excitement waned.

Of one thing, and one thing only, I was certain. This was big. This was something to rank with Leakey's discoveries at Olduvai Gorge, something to startle and dazzle the world of archaeology. Something that I had prayed for and dreamed about for twenty years.

We had reached the end of the passage. The end wall was another panel of sandstone, but this was decorated. A swirling, stylized engraving of the sun image. Three feet in diameter, it looked like a Catherine wheel with the rays radiating from its circumference. The image evoked in me a strange sense of reverential awe, a hushed feeling of the spirit such as I experience sometimes in a synagogue or the cloisters of a Christian cathedral. Louren and I stood and stared at the image for a long time, then suddenly he turned and looked back to the bricked-in wall 155 feet away.

'Is that all?' he asked, and there was an irritable tone to his voice. 'Just this passage and pots and old bones? There must be something more!'

It came as a shock to me to realize that he was actually disappointed. For me the universe could hold no richer prize, this was the culminating moment of my life – and Louren was disappointed. I felt anger start to hiss and bubble within me.

'What the hell do you want?' I demanded. 'Gold and diamonds and ivory sarcophagi and—'

'Something like that.'

'You don't even know what we've got here yet, and already it's not enough.'

'Ben, I didn't say that.'

'You know what's wrong with you, Louren Sturvesant? You're bloody well spoiled. You've got everything, so nothing is good enough for you.'

'Now, listen here!' I saw my own anger reflected in his eyes, but I rushed on regardlessly.

'I've planned and saved and worked for this all my life. And now I achieve it, and what do you do?'

'Hey, Ben!' I saw comprehension in his eyes suddenly. 'I didn't mean it that way. I'm not knocking your achievement. I really think it's the most incredible discovery ever made in Africa, I was just—'

It took him a few minutes of hard talking to mollify me, but at last I grinned reluctantly.

'Okay,' I relented, 'just don't go saying things like that, Lo. All my life the bastards have been putting down my discoveries and theories, so don't you start!'

'One thing they'll never be able to say about you is that you're frightened to speak your mind!' He punched my shoulder lightly. 'Come on, Ben, let's see what we've got in these pots.'

'We shouldn't disturb them, Lo.' I was ashamed of my outburst now, and eager to make it up to him. 'Not until we have mapped and charted—'

'A couple of them are lying on the floor, knocked off the shelves,' Louren pointed. 'There are thousands of the bloody things. We will just snaffle one of them. Hell, Ben, it won't do that much harm!'

He was not asking permission, not Louren Sturvesant, he was merely giving an order in the pleasantest possible fashion. Already he was making his way back to where the jars were lying beside the dusty bowed corpse, and I hurried after him.

'Okay,' I agreed unnecessarily, in an attempt to keep nominal control of my find. 'We will remove one of them only.' I felt a sneaking sense of relief that the wrong decision had been made for me. I was also in a fever of impatience to find out what was in the jars.

The jar stood in the centre of the work-shop bench in our pre-fabricated warehouse. Night had fallen outside, but the overhead lights were all on. We stood around the bench, Sally, Ral, Leslie and I. Tinus van Vuuren was still up at the cavern, his status having changed from mine captain to night watchman. Louren had decided to place a twenty-four-hour armed guard over the entrance to the tunnel, and Tinus was it – until we could get others.

Through the thin partition walls of the hut I could hear Louren's voice as he shouted into the microphone of the radio.

'A vacuum cleaner. *Vacuum cleaner.* VACUUM CLEANER! V for Venereal, A for Alcoholic – that's *right*. Vacuum cleaner. You know the heavy-duty model for cleaning factories. Two of them. Have you got that? Good! Now I want you to get on to Robeson, Head of Security at Sturvesant Diamond Mines. He is to send me his two best men, with half a dozen Bantu guards. Yes, that's right. Yes, I want them armed.'

None of us paid attention to Louren's voice, we were all staring in mesmerized fascination at the earthenware jar.

'Well, it's not filled with gold.' Ral was certain. 'Not heavy enough.'

'Nor is it liquid – not wine or oil,' Leslie agreed. And we relapsed into silence. The pot was about eighteen inches high, and thick around as a pickle jar. It was of unglazed red pottery, without inscription or ornamentation, and the lid was like that of a teapot with a small knob for a handle. It was sealed with a layer of black substance, probably gum or wax.

'Get that lot on the Dakota first thing tomorrow morning, do you hear?' Louren was still busy next door.

'I wish he'd hurry up!' Sally stirred impatiently. 'I'm dying to find out what it is.'

Suddenly I was afraid. I didn't want to know – I didn't want to find the jar filled with African millet or some other indigenous grain. I could hear my critics howling like wolves out there in the wilderness. Suddenly I was doubting my own premonition of some momentous discovery and I sat on the edge of my stool, miserably rubbing my grimy hands together and staring at the jar. Perhaps Louren was right, perhaps we would echo his cry, 'Is that all?'

From the radio shack we heard Louren's voice end the transmission, and he came through into the warehouse. He was still filthy from the work in the tunnel, and his golden hair was stiff with dust and dried sweat. Yet the grime and unruly curls gave him an air of romance, the jaunty look of an old-time pirate. He stood in the doorway with his thumbs hooked into his belt, and all our attention was on him. He grinned at me.

'Okay, Ben. What have you got for us?' he asked and sauntered across the room to stand behind my shoulder. Instinctively the others drew closer, crowding into a circle around me and I picked up the surgical scalpel and touched the point of it to the joint of the lid.

The first touch told me that my guess had been correct.

'Bee's wax, I think.'

Carefully I scraped it away, then laid the scalpel aside and gently tried the lid. It came away with surprising ease.

All heads craned forward, but the first view of the contents was disappointing. An amorphous mass of substance that was stained dirty yellow-brown by time.

'What is it?' Louren demanded of his experts, but none of us could answer him. I was not sure whether to be disappointed or relieved. It certainly wasn't corn.

'It smells,' said Sally. There was a faintly unpleasant, but familiar odour.

'I know that smell,' I said.

'Yes,' agreed Leslie.

We stared at the pot trying to place it. Then suddenly I remembered.

'It smells like a tannery works.'

'That's it!' agreed Sally.

'Leather?' asked Louren.

'Let's see,' I said, and carefully tipped the jar onto its side with the mouth facing me. Gently I began easing the contents out of the jar. It became immediately clear that it held something cylindrical in shape and of a hard, brittle texture.

It seemed to have stuck to the inside of the jar, but I twisted carefully and with a faint rending sound it was loose. I inched it out of the jar, and as it emerged, there was a running commentary from the watchers.

'It's a long round thing.'

'Looks like a polony sausage.'

'It's wrapped in cloth.'

'Linen, I hope!'

'It's woven anyway. That will take some explaining away as Bantu culture!'

'The cloth is rotten, it's falling away in patches.'

I laid it on the table, and as I stared at it I knew all my dreams had become reality. *I knew what it was.* A treasure beyond all the gold and diamonds Louren had hoped for. I looked up quickly at Sally to see if she had guessed, her expression was eager but puzzled. Then her eyes met mine and my jubilation must have been obvious.

'Ben!' She guessed then. 'It isn't? Oh, Ben, it couldn't be! Open it, man! For God's sake, open it!'

I took up a pair of tweezers, but my hands were too unsteady to work. I clenched my fists, and drew a couple of deep breaths to try and calm the racing of my blood and the pounding of it in my ears.

'Here, let me do it,' said Ral, and reached to take the tweezers from my grip.

'No!' I snatched my hand away. I think I would have struck him if he had persisted. I saw the shock on Ral's face, he had never before seen the violence that lurks in my depths.

They all waited until I had got control of my hands again. Then carefully I began to peel the wrappings of brittle yellow cloth from the cylinder. I saw it appear from under the wrappings, and there were no more doubts. I heard Sally's little gasp from across the bench, but I did not look up until it was done.

'Ben!' she whispered, 'I'm so happy for you.' And I saw that she was crying, big fat tears sliding slowly down her cheeks. This was what triggered me, I am certain that if she hadn't started it I would have been all right, but suddenly my own eyes were burning and my vision blurred with moisture.

'Thanks, Sal,' I said, and my voice was soggy and nasal. When I felt the droplets start to spill on to my cheeks I struck them away with an angry hand, and groped for my handkerchief. I blew my nose like a bugler sounding the charge, and my heart sang as loudly.

It was a tightly rolled cylindrical scroll of leather. The outer edges of the scroll were tattered and eaten by decomposure. The rest of it, however, was miraculously preserved. There were lines of writing running like columns of little black insects along the length of the scroll. I recognized the symbols immediately, identifying the individual letters of the Punic alphabet. It was written in a flowing Punic script, of which the first thirty lines were exposed on the roll of ancient leather. The language was not one I understood, but I looked up at Sally again. This was her speciality, she had worked with Hamilton at Oxford.

'Sal, can you read it? What is it?'

'It's Carthaginian,' she spoke with complete certainty. 'Punic!'

'Are you sure?' I demanded.

In reply she read aloud in a voice that was still choked up and muffled with tears, *Into Opet this day a caravan from the*' she hesitated, 'that piece is obscure but it goes on, *In fingers of fine gold one hundred and twenty-seven pieces, of which a tenth part unto—*'

'What the hell is going on?' Louren demanded. 'What does all this mean?'

I turned to him. 'It means we have found the archives of our city – completely intact and decipherable. We have the whole written history of our city, of our dead civilization, written by the people themselves in their own language. Their own words.'

Louren was staring at me. It was clear that the significance of our discovery had not yet occurred to him.

'This, Lo, is what every archaeologist prays for. This is proof in its most absolute form, in its most detailed and elaborate form.'

He still didn't seem to understand.

'In one line of writing we have proved conclusively the existence of a people who spoke and wrote the ancient Punic of Carthage, who traded gold, who called their city Opet, who—'

'And that's only in one line of writing,' Sally interrupted. 'There are thousands of jars, each with its scroll of writings. We will know the names and deeds of their kings, their religion, their ceremonial—'

'Their battles and strivings, where they came from and when.' I took the verbal ball from Sally, but just as adroitly she snatched it back.

'And where they went to and why!'

'My God!' Louren understood at last. 'This is everything we've been looking for, Ben. It's the whole bloody shebang and shooting-match rolled into one!'

'The works!' I agreed. 'The whole ruddy lot!'

Within an hour of my triumph, right at the zenith of my career when nothing but the prospect of fame and brilliant success lay ahead of me, Dr. Sally Benator managed to bring it all crashing down around me.

We were sitting in the same tight circle around the scroll, still talking eagerly, one of those talk sessions which could only end in the early morning, for already the Glen Grant bottle was out and all our throats were oiled, the words pouring out smoothly.

Sally had translated all the writing visible on the scroll. It was an accounting of trade into the city, a cataloguing of goods and values that in itself held intriguing references to places and peoples.

'*Twenty large amphora of the red wines of Zeng, taken by Habbakuk Lal of which a tenth part to the Gry-Lion.*'

'What's a gry-lion?' Louren's hunter's instincts were roused.

'Gry is a superlative,' Sally explained. 'So a gry-lion is a great lion. Probably a title of the king or governor of the city.'

From the grass seas of the south one hundred and ninety-two large tusks of ivory in all two-hundred and twenty-one talents in weight of which a tenth part to the Gry-Lion and the balance outwards on the bireme of Al-Muab Adbm.'

'How much is a talent?' Louren asked.

'About 56 pounds avoirdupois.'

'My God, that's over 10,000 lb. of ivory, in one load,' Louren whistled. 'They must have been great little hunters.'

We had discussed in detail every line of exposed writing, and again Louren's impatience came to the surface.

'Let's unroll a little more,' he suggested.

'That's a job for an expert, Lo.' I shook my head regretfully. 'That leather has been rolled up for nearly 2,000 years. It's so dry and brittle it will fall to pieces if it isn't done correctly.'

'Yes,' Sally agreed with me. 'It will take me weeks to do each one.'

Her presumption left me flabbergasted. Her practical knowledge of palaeography and ancient writings was limited to three years as a third assistant to Hamilton, I doubted if she had actually done much work on preservation and preparation of leather or papyrus scrolls. She could read Punic with about the same aplomb as the average ten-year-old can read Shakespeare, and she was taking it for granted that she would be placed in sole control of one of the greatest hoards of ancient writings ever discovered.

She must have read my expression, for her own alarm showed clearly.

'I *am* to do the work, aren't I, Ben?'

I tried to make it easier for her, I do not like hurting anyone, let alone the girl I love.

'It's an enormous and difficult job, Sal. I really think we should try and get someone like Hamilton himself, or Levy from Tel Aviv, even Rogers from Chicago.' I saw her face starting to fall to pieces, the lips drooping and trembling, the eyes clouding, and I went on hurriedly. 'But I'm sure we can arrange for you to become first assistant to whoever does the work.'

There was a deadly silence for five seconds, and during that time Sally's despair changed swiftly to a blind all-consuming rage. I saw it coming like a build-up of storm clouds but I was powerless to divert it.

'Benjamin Kazin,' she began with deceptive softness of voice, 'I think you are the most unmitigated bastard it has ever been my misfortune to meet. For three long difficult years I have given you my complete and unswerving loyalty—'

Then she lost control and it was a splendid spectacle. Even while her words lashed my soul raw and bleeding I could still admire the flashing eyes, the flushing cheeks and the masterly choice of invective.

'You are a *little* man, in mind as well as body.' She used the adjective deliberately, and I gasped. No one should ever call me that, it is a word that eats away the fabric of my soul and she knew it. 'I hate you. I hate you, you *little* man.'

I felt the blood rush to my face, and I stuttered, trying to find the words to defend myself, but before I could do so Sally had turned on Louren. Her rage still blazed, her tone was not moderated in the least as she shouted at him.

'Make him give it to me. Tell him to do it!'

Even in my distress I felt alarm for poor Sally. This wasn't a crippled, soft-hearted little doctor of archaeology she was talking to now. This was like prodding a black mamba with a short stick, or throwing stones at a man-eating lion. I could not believe that Sally would be so stupid, would presume so upon the mildly friendly attitude which Louren had shown to her. I could not believe that she would dare that tone with Louren, as though she had some special right to his consideration, as though there was some involvement of emotions or of loyalties which she could call upon in such imperious terms. Even I who had such rights would never misuse them in such a fashion, I knew no one else who would.

Louren's eyes flashed cold blue light, like the glinting of spearheads. His lips drew into grim lines, and the rims of his nostrils flared and turned pale as bone china.

'Woman!' His voice crackled like breaking ice. 'Hold your tongue.'

If it were possible then my despair plunged even deeper as Louren responded precisely as I had expected. Now the two persons I loved were on collision course, and I knew each of them so well, knew their pride and pig-headedness, that neither would deviate. Disaster was certain, inevitable.

I wanted to cry out to Sally, 'Don't, please don't. I'll do what you ask. Anything to prevent this happening.'

And Sally's bravado collapsed. All the fight and anger went out of her. She seemed to cringe beneath the lash of Louren's voice.

'Go to your room and stay there until you learn how to behave.' Louren gave the order in the same coldly furious tone.

Sally stood up and with eyes downcast she left the room.

I could not believe it had happened. I gaped at the door through which she had gone – my saucy, rebellious Sally – as meekly as a chastened child. Ral and Leslie were writhing in a sea of agonized embarrassment.

'Bedtime, I think,' Ral muttered. 'Please excuse us. Come, Les. Good night, all.' And they were gone, leaving Louren and me alone.

Louren broke the long silence. He stood up as he spoke in an easy natural voice. His hand dropped on my shoulder in a casually affectionate gesture.

'Sorry about that, Ben. Don't let it worry you. See you in the morning.' And he strolled out into the night.

I sat alone with my suddenly worthless roll of old leather, and my breaking heart.

'I hate you, you *little* man!' Her voice echoed through the lonely wastes of my soul, and I reached for the Glen Grant bottle.

It took me a long time to get completely drunk, to the stage where the words had lost some of their sting, and when I staggered down the steps into the bright silver moonlight, I knew what I was going to do. I was going to apologize to Sally, and let her do the work. Nothing was important enough to warrant her displeasure.

I went to the hut where Sally now slept alone. Leslie had moved into Peter and Heather's old room. I scratched softly on the door, and there was no reply from within. I knocked louder, and called her name.

'Sally! Please, I must talk to you.'

At last I tried the door, and it opened into the darkened room. I almost went on in, but then my courage deserted me. I closed the door softly, and staggered to my own hut. I fell face down across the bed, and still dirty and fully dressed I found oblivion.

'Ben! Ben! Wake up.' Sally's voice and her hand shaking me gently but insistently. I turned my head and opened my burning eyes. It was bright morning. Sally sat on the edge of my bed, leaning over me. She was fully dressed, although her skin glowed from the bath and her hair was freshly brushed and gay with a scarlet ribbon, yet her eyes were puffy and swollen as though she had slept badly, or had been crying.

'I've come to apologize for last night, Ben. For the stupid, hateful things I said, and my disgusting behaviour—' As she talked the shattered pieces of my life fell back into place, and the pain in my head and heart abated.

'Even though you've probably changed your mind, and I don't deserve it anyway, I'd be honoured to act as first assistant to Hamilton or whoever does the work.'

'You've got the job.' I grinned at her. 'That's a promise.'

Our first task at the archives was to clean away the thick accumulation of grey dust that blanketed everything. I was puzzled as to the source of this dust in a sealed and airless space like the passage, but I soon found that the joints of the roof lintels were not as tight as those of the walls, and during the centuries a fine sprinkling of dust had filtered down through these cracks.

When the equipment which Louren had ordered arrived on the Dakota, along with a detachment of Louren's security police, we could begin the work.

The security police set up a hut at the entrance to the tunnel, where there was a permanent guard posted. Only the five of us were allowed to enter.

The vacuum equipment simplified the removal of dust from the archives. Ral and I worked from the outer end of the passage like a pair of busy housewives, and the suffocating clouds of grey dust made it necessary to wear respirators until the job was finished.

We were then able to assess our discovery more accurately. There were 1,142 sealed jars of pottery in the stone recesses. Of these 148 had been knocked from their niches and 127 were broken or cracked, with their scrolls exposed to the air and obviously much the worse for it. These we sprayed with paraffin wax to prevent them crumbling, before lifting, labelling and packing them.

We then turned our full attention to the evidence of the deadly battle that had raged through the archives, and wrought the damage to the shelves of jars.

There were thirty-eight corpses strewn down the passage between the shelves in all the abandoned attitudes of sudden and violent death, and their state of preservation was quite remarkable. A few of them had crawled away into the recesses to die, groaning out their last breaths, and clutching the terrible wounds that still gaped in their mummified bodies. Their dying agonies were clearly stamped into their contorted features. Others had died swiftly, and most of these had received hideous wounds that had severed limbs, or split their skulls down to the shoulders, or, in a few cases, had struck the head clean from the trunk and sent it rolling yards away.

There was evidence here of a diabolical fury, the unleashing of an almost superhuman destructive strength.

All the victims were clearly negroid in type, and wore loin cloths or aprons of tanned leather, with beadwork or bone decorations. On their feet were light leather sandals, and on their heads caps or head-dresses of leather, feathers or plaited fibre also decorated with beads, shells or bones.

Around them were strewn their weapons; crudely forged iron spearheads bound on shafts of polished hardwood. Many of these shafts were broken, or severed by the blows of some razor-sharp weapon. With them lay hundreds of reed arrows, fledged with the feathers of wild duck and tipped with wickedly barbed heads of hand-forged iron. The arrows had nicked and chipped the soft sandstone walls, and it was easy to determine that they had been fired from outside the mouth of the passage before it had been sealed off. Not one of them had found a mark in a human body, and so we reasoned that a barrage of arrows had preceded the attack by these men who lay scattered in death down the length of the passage.

Fifteen feet from the sealed mouth of the passage there was evidence of a large bonfire which had blackened the walls, roof and floor around it. A pile of charred logs still lay where the lack of air had stifled the fire when the mouth of the tunnel was sealed. This fire puzzled us until Louren reconstructed the battle for us. He paced restlessly back and forth along the passage, his footsteps ringing on the stone slabs, his shadow falling grotesque and monstrous on the stone walls.

'They drove them into this place, the last of our men of Opet, a small party of the strongest and the bravest.' His voice rang with the truth of it, like a troubadour singing the legends of the old heroes. 'They sent in their champions to finish the slaughter but the men of Opet cut them down and the others fled. Then they drew up their archers at the mouth of the passage, and fired volleys of arrows into it. Again they went in, but the men of Opet were there waiting for them and again they died in their dozens.'

He turned and came down the passage to stand beside me under the swaying electric bulb, and we were silent for a moment imagining it.

'My God, Ben. Think of it. What a fight to end with. What glory these men won on that last day.'

Even I, a man of peace, was stirred by it. I felt my heartbeat quicken and I turned to him like a child at story-time. 'What happened then?' I asked.

'They were dying already, weak with a dozen wounds each. There was no strength left in them to continue and they stood shoulder to shoulder, companions in life, and now in death also, leaning wearily on their weapons, but the enemy would not come again. Instead, they built a fire in the mouth of the passage to smoke them out, and when that did not do it, they abandoned the attack and bricked up the entrance turning it into a tomb for the dead and the living alike.'

We were all silent then, thinking about Louren's story. It made sense, it fitted the evidence in all but one respect. I did not want to say it, did not want to spoil such a stirring tale, but Sally had no such compunction.

'If that's true, then what happened to your band of heroes – did they change into moonbeams and flit away?' Her tone was slightly derisive, but of course she was right. I wished she was not.

Louren laughed, a little embarrassed chuckle. 'So *you* think of something better,' he challenged her.

Of the heroes of this ancient drama there was no trace, except that which lay at the foot of the passage below the graven sun image of Baal. It was blanketed by the thick grey dust and it was the final discovery on the archives floor. It was a battle-axe. A weapon of striking beauty and utility. When first I took it up from the paving where it had lain for almost 2,000 years, my hand closed snugly around the haft, the grooves in the handle fitted my fingers as though they had been moulded from them. A broken wrist-strap of leather dangled from the end of the handle.

The haft was forty-seven inches long, and fashioned from lengths of rhinoceros horn that had been laminated into a solid rod of steely resilience and strength. The handle was of ivory and the whole had been bound with electrum wire to reinforce its already surpassing strength and to protect the shaft from the cuts of enemy blades. The blade was shaped like a double crescent moon, each side exposing seven and a half inches of razor edge. From its extreme end protruded an unbarbed spike twelve inches long, thus the weapon could be used on the cut as well as the thrust.

The head was exquisitely worked and engraved, with the shapes of four vultures with wings spread, one on each side of the double blade. The birds were rendered in such detail that every feather was shown, and beyond the figures a sun rose in a burst of rays like a flower. The engravings were inlaid with electrum, an alloy of gold and silver, and from the silvery sheen of the blades it was clear that they had been tempered. The weapon was caked and dulled with what must have been dried blood, it was obviously the author of those horrible wounds that bloomed upon so many of the corpses scattered along the passage.

Holding the beautiful weapon in my hand I was infected by a sudden madness. I was not truly aware of my own intention until the axe was flying in a wide glittering circle around my head. The balance and weight of the great axe was so pure and sweet that no effort was involved as I swung it high, and then into a long overhand killing stroke. The blade whickered eagerly at the kiss of moving air across its bright edge. The flexing of the handle seemed to bring it alive in my hand, alive again after nearly 2,000 long years of sleep.

From some deep atavistic depths of my soul I felt a cry rising, an exultant yell which seemed the natural accompaniment to the deadly song of the axe. With an effort I checked the flight of the axe and the cry before it reached my lips, and looked around at the faces of the others.

They were staring at me as though I had begun raving and frothing at the mouth. Quickly I lowered the axe. I stood there feeling utterly foolish, appalled at my treatment of such a rare treasure. The horn handle could easily have become brittle, and snapped at such harsh usage.

'I was just testing it,' I said lamely. 'I'm sorry.'

That night we pondered and puzzled the riddle of the archives until well after midnight. We found no answer and afterwards Louren walked with me to my hut.

'The Lear is coming to pick me up tomorrow morning, Ben. I've been here two weeks already, and I just cannot stay another day. God, when I think of how I've neglected my responsibilities since we started on this dig!'

We stopped at the door of my hut and Louren lit a cigar.

'What is it about this place that makes us all act so strangely, Ben? Do you feel it also? This strange sense of,' he hesitated, 'of destiny.'

I nodded, and Louren was encouraged.

'That axe. It did something to you, Ben. You weren't yourself for a few minutes there today.'

'I know.'

'I am desperate to discover the contents of the scrolls, Ben. We must start on that as soon as possible.'

'There is ten years' work there, Lo. You will have to be patient.'

'Patience is not one of my virtues, Ben. I was reading of the discovery of Tutankhamen's tomb last night. Lord Carnarvon made the discovery possible, and yet he died before he could look on the sarcophagus of the dead Pharaoh.'

'Don't be morbid, Lo.'

'All right,' Louren agreed. 'But don't waste time, Ben.'

'You get Hamilton for me,' I said. 'We can't do a thing without him.'

'I'll be in London on Friday,' Louren told me. 'I'll see him myself.'

'He is a difficult old codger,' I warned him.

Louren grinned. 'Leave him to me. Now, listen to me, Benjamin my boy, if you find anything else here, you let me know immediately, you understand? I want to be here when it happens.'

'When what happens?'

'I don't know – something. There is something else here, Ben. I know it.'

'I hope you are right, Lo.' And he clapped my shoulder and walked away into the night towards his own hut.

While we worked on in the archives, lifting the human remains and the piles of weapons, a construction crew arrived on the site by Dakota to erect a repository for the scrolls. This was another large prefabricated warehouse, fitted with airtight doors and a powerful air-conditioning unit to maintain the scrolls in an atmosphere of optimum temperature and humidity. A high barbed-wire fence was erected around the building for security reasons, and every precaution for the safety of the scrolls was taken.

At the same time the construction crew erected another half-dozen living quarters for the expanded team, and the first inhabitants of these were four high officials of the Botswana Government. It was the Government who had forbidden the removal of the scrolls from the territory and made the erection of the new buildings necessary. The Government deputation stayed for two days, and left satisfied that their interests in the discovery would be adequately protected, but not before I had exacted a solemn promise of secrecy. The announcement of the site would be at my signal only.

We began labelling and removing the pottery jars from their shelves. Taking the greatest pains to record, both photographically and by written notes, the exact position of each. It seemed likely that they had been stacked in chronological order, and this would assist the work of interpretation.

On the Monday I received a crippling blow to my plans in the form of a laconic message from Louren.

'Hamilton unavailable. Please suggest alternative.'

I was disappointed, hurt and angry. Disappointed because Hamilton was the best in the world, and his presence would have immediately given weight and authenticity to my site. I was hurt because Hamilton obviously believed my claims were spurious, my reputation had been damaged by the vicious attacks of my critics and scientific opponents, Hamilton had clearly been influenced by this. He did not want to be party to some mistaken or blatantly fraudulent discovery of mine. Finally, I was angry because Hamilton's refusal to undertake the work was a direct insult. He had put the mark of the pariah on me and it would discourage others from giving the assistance I desperately needed. I might find myself discredited before I had even started.

'He didn't even give me a chance,' I protested to Sally. 'He didn't even want to listen to me. Christ, I didn't realize I was such a professional leper. Even talking to me can ruin a reputation!'

'He's a skinny, bald-headed old goat!' Sally agreed. 'He's a lecherous old feeler of bottoms, and—'

'And the greatest living authority on ancient writings in the world,' I told her bitterly. There was no reply to that, and we sat in forlorn silence for a while.

Then Sally perked up. 'Let's go and fetch him!' she suggested.

'He might refuse to see us,' I gloomed.

'He won't refuse to see me,' Sally assured me, and behind the words was an untold story that set my jealousy coursing corrosively through my veins. Sally had worked for him three years, and I could only console myself that her standards were high enough to exclude Eldridge Hamilton.

Seventy-two hours later I sat in the front lounge of the Bell at Hurley with a pint of good English bitter in front of me, and watched the car park anxiously. It was only a fifteen-minute drive from Oxford and Sally should have been here long ago.

I felt tired, irritable and depressed from that soul-destroying overnight flight from Johannesburg to Heathrow. Sally had phoned Hamilton from the airport.

'Professor Hamilton, I do hope you don't mind me phoning you,' she had cooed.

'Sally Benator, do you remember I worked under you in 1966. That's right, Sally Green-Eyes.' And she giggled coyly.

'Well, I am on my way through England. Just here for a day or two. I felt so lonely and nostalgic – those were wonderful times.' Her tone had a hundred intimate shades of invitation and promise.

'Lunch? That's wonderful, Professor. Why don't I pick you up. I have a hire car.' She gave me a triumphant thumbs-up sign.

'The Bell at Hurley? Yes, of course, I remember. How could I forget.' She made a sick face at me. 'I so look forward to it.'

The silver Jaguar slid into the car park, and I saw Sally at the wheel. With a scarf in her hair and laughter on her lips, she didn't look like a girl who had sat fourteen hours in the cramped seat of an intercontinental jet.

She slid out of the car, giving me a flash of those wonderful sun-browned thighs, and then she was coming towards me. Hanging on the arm of Eldridge Hamilton, and laughing gaily.

Hamilton was a tall stoop-shouldered man in his fifties, a baggy Harris tweed suit with leather patches on the elbows hung like a sack on his gaunt frame. His nose was beaky, and his bald pate shone in the pale sunlight as though it had been buffed up with a good wax polish. All in all he was not formidable competition, but his little eyes sparkled behind the heavy horn-rimmed glasses and his lips were slack with desire, exposing a mouthful of bad teeth, as he looked at Sally. I found it a hard price to pay for his services.

Sally led him to my table, and he was six feet from me before he recognized me. He stopped dead, and I saw him blink once. He knew instantly that he had been taken, and for a moment the whole project hung in the balance. He could so easily have turned on his heel and walked out.

'Eldridge!' I leapt to my feet, crooning seductively. 'How wonderful to see you.' And while he still hesitated, I had him by the elbow in a grip like a velvet-lined vice. 'I've ordered you a large Gilbey's gin and tonic – that's your poison, isn't it?'

It was five years since last we had met, and my memory of his personal tastes mollified him slightly. He allowed Sally and I to ease him into a seat and place the gin convenient to his right hand. While Sally and I bombarded him with all our considerable combined charm he maintained a suspicious silence, until the first gin had gone down. I ordered another and he began to thaw, half-way through the third he became skittish and voluble.

'Did you read Wilfred Snell's reply to your book *Ophir* in the *Journal?*' he asked. Wilfred Snell was the most vociferous and merciless of all my scientific adversaries. 'Jolly amusing, what?' And Eldridge neighed like a randy stallion, and clutched at one of Sally's beautiful thighs.

I am a man of peace, but at that moment I was having difficulty remembering it. My expression must have been a sickly grin, my finger nails were driven like claws into the flesh of my palms as I fought down the temptation to drag Eldridge around the room by his heels.

Sally wriggled out from his exploring hand, and I suggested in a strangled voice, 'Let's go through to lunch, shall we?'

There was a quick game of musical chairs at the dining-room table, as

Eldridge tried to get a seat within clutching distance of Sally and I tried to prevent it.

We out-foxed him on a cunning double play, allowing him to settle down triumphantly beaming over the top of his menu at Sally who was backed into a corner beside him, before I cried, 'Sally, you are in a draught there.' And smoothly as a pair of ballet dancers we changed seats.

Then I could relax and give the pheasant the attention it deserved, although the burgundy that Eldridge suggested was nothing if not gauche.

With characteristic tact Eldridge brought up the subject we had all been flirting with.

'Met a friend of yours the other day, big flashy chap like a cross between a male model and a professional wrestler. Accent like an Australian with the 'flu. Had some cock-and-bull story about scrolls you'd found in a cave outside Cape Town.' And Eldridge neighed again at a volume that momentarily stopped all other conversation in the room. 'Damned man had the cheek to offer me money. I know the type, not a bean to bless himself with, and talks like he's made of the stuff. He had "shyster" written all over him in letters two feet high.'

Sally and I gaped at him, struck dumb by his astute grasp of the facts and his masterly summation of Louren Sturvesant's character.

'Sent him packing of course,' said Eldridge with relish, and stuffed his mouth with breast of pheasant.

'You probably did the right thing,' I murmured. 'Incidentally the site is in northern Botswana – 1,500 miles from Cape Town.'

'Oh, yes?' Eldridge asked, expressing disinterest as politely as one can with a mouthful of pheasant and rotten teeth.

'And Louren Sturvesant was on *Time* Magazine's list of the thirty richest men in the world,' murmured Sally. Eldridge stopped chewing with his mouth ajar, and afforded us a fine view of a semi-masticated pheasant-breast.

'Yes,' I affirmed. 'He is bank-rolling my dig. He has put in 200,000 dollars already, and he has set no limit.'

Eldridge turned a stricken face towards me. That sort of patron of scientific research was almost as rare as the unicorn, and Eldridge realized suddenly that he had been within range of one and let him escape. All the bumptiousness was gone out of Professor Hamilton.

I signalled the waitress to clear my plate, and I swear that I felt true compassion in my heart for Eldridge as I unlocked my briefcase and took from it a cylindrical bundle wrapped in its protective canvas jacket.

'I have an appointment with Ruben Levy in Tel Aviv tomorrow, Eldridge.' I opened the canvas wrapping.

'We have 1,142 of these leather scrolls. So Ruby will be pretty busy for the next few years. Of course, Louren Sturvesant will make a donation of 100,000 dollars to the Tel Aviv University Faculty of Archaeology for their co-operation, and I shouldn't be surprised if the faculty doesn't have some of the scrolls given to them as well.'

Eldridge swallowed his mouthful of pheasant as though it were broken glass. He wiped his fingers and mouth with his napkin, before leaning forward to examine the scroll.

'*From out of the southern plains of grass,*' he whispered as he read, and I noticed the difference from Sally's translation, '*received 192 large ivory tusks, weighing 221 talents—*' His voice died but his lips moved as he read on. Then he began speaking again, and his voice quavered with excitement.

'Punic in the style of the second century B.C., do you see the use of ligatures to join the median "m", still using the hang of the characters from the line, that's definitely pre-first century B.C. Here, Sally, do you see the archaic crossing of the "A"?'

'We have over a thousand of these scrolls, preserved in chronological order – Levy is very excited,' I interrupted this flow of technicalities with a gentle untruth. Levy didn't know they existed.

'Levy,' Eldridge snorted, and his spectacles flashed with outrage. 'Levy! Take him outside Hebrew and Egyptian and he's a babe in the bloody woods!' He had hold of my wrist now.

'Ben. I insist, I absolutely insist on doing this work!'

'What about Wilfred Snell's criticism of my theories? You seemed to find it amusing.' I had him by the ackers now, and I could afford to be a little cocky. 'How do you feel about working with somebody whose views are so suspect?'

'Wilfred Snell,' said Eldridge earnestly, 'is a monumental jackass. Where did he ever find a thousand Punic scrolls?'

'Waiter,' I called, 'please bring us two large Cordon Argent brandies.'

'Make that three,' said Sally.

As the brandy diffused a gentle warmth through my body, I listened to Eldridge Hamilton effusing about the scrolls and demanding of Sally information as to exactly where, when and how we had discovered them. I found myself beginning to like the man. It was true that he had teeth like the stumps of a pine forest devastated by fire, but then I am not a perfect physical specimen myself. It was also true that he had a weakness for Gilbey's gin and pretty girls – but then he differed from me only in his choice of liquor, and who am I to hold that Glen Grant is in any way superior?

No, I decided, despite my prejudices, I would be able to work with him, just as long as he kept his bony little claws off Sally.

Eldridge followed us out a week after our return to the City of the Moon, and we met him at the airstrip. I was concerned that he might find that the transition from a northern winter to our 110°F summer impaired his abilities. I need not have worried. He was one of those Englishmen who, solar topee cocked, go out in the midday sun without raising a sweat. His luggage consisted of a single small valise which contained his personal effects and a dozen large packing-cases filled with chemicals and equipment.

I gave him the Grade 'A' tour of the site, trying without success to fan his interest in the city and the cavern. Eldridge was a single-minded specialist.

'Yes,' he said. 'Jolly interesting – now where are the scrolls?' I think even then he had doubts, but I took him into the archives and he purred like an angular old tom cat as he moved down the burdened stone shelves.

'Ben,' he said, 'there's just one thing still to settle. I write the paper on the actual scrolls, agreed?' We are a strange breed, we work not for the gold but for the glory. Eldridge was making certain of his share.

'Agreed.' We shook hands.

'Well then there is nothing to stop me beginning right away,' he said.

'No,' I said, 'there isn't, is there.'

The treatment of the scrolls was an art form more than an exact science. For each of them the treatment varied, depending on their state of preservation, the quality of the leather, the composition of the ink and other inter-related factors. Sally admitted to me in a weak moment that she would not have been able to handle the task, it required a fund of acquired experience which she did not have at her command.

Eldridge worked like a medieval alchemist, steaming and soaking and spraying and painting. His domain stank of chemicals and other weird smells, and his and Sally's fingers were stained. Sally reported that his absorption with the task had reduced his animal instincts to the level where he made only spasmodic and half-hearted clutches at the protruding parts of her anatomy.

As each scroll was unrolled, its contents were evaluated and the detailed translation begun. One after the other they proved to be either books of account on the city's trade, or proclamations made by the Gry-Lion and the council of the nine families. The authors were nameless clerks, and their style was brisk and economical with little time for poetic flights or unnecessary descriptive passages. This starkly utilitarian outlook echoed the life style which we had so far reconstructed from our finds on the site. We discussed it at the nightly talk sessions.

'It's typically Punic,' Eldridge agreed. 'They had little taste in the visual arts, their pottery was coarse and mass-produced. In my opinion their sculpture, what little there was, was downright hideous.'

'It requires wealth and leisure and security to produce art,' I suggested.

'That's true – Rome and Greece are examples of that. Carthage and, earlier, Phoenicia were often threatened, on occasion struggling for survival – they were the bustlers and hustlers. Traders and warriors, more concerned with wealth and the acquisition of power than the niceties of living.'

'You don't have to go back that far, modern art comes from the great wealthy and secure nations.'

'And we white Africans are like the old Carthaginians,' Sally said, 'when there's gold in them thar hills who gives a hoot about painting pictures.'

The scrolls reinforced the theory. Gold from Zimbao and Punt, ivory from the southern plains of grass or from the forests along the great river, hides and dried meat, salted fish from the lakes, wine and oil from the terraced gardens of Zeng, copper from the hills of Tuya, and salt from pans along the west shores of the lakes, tin from the juncture of the two rivers, corn from the middle kingdom in baskets of woven cane, sun stones from the southern river of the crocodile, iron bars from the mines of Sala – and slaves, thousands upon thousands of human beings treated as domestic animals.

The chronicle was dated from some undisclosed point in time, we suspected this as the date of the founding of the city, and each entry was prefaced by such datings as, 'In year 169 the month of the elephant.' From these we deduced a ten-month year based on a calendar of 365 days.

Once the nature of the scrolls had been established, I suggested to Eldridge that rather than work systematically through the collection from beginning to end, we sample them and try to establish the overall history of our city.

He fell in with my wishes, and there evolved a picture of a widespread colonization of central and southern Africa by a warlike and energetic people, based on the city of Opet, and ruled by a hereditary king, the 'Gry-Lion', and an oligarchy of nine noble families. The decrees of this Council covered a range as wide as the measures adopted for dredging the channels of the lake and preventing the encroachment of water weed, to the choice of messengers to be sent to the gods Baal and Astarte. Here Astarte seemed to have taken precedence over the more usual Carthaginian form Tanith. 'Messengers', we suspected, were human sacrifices.

We discovered carefully recorded family trees, based like the Jewish system on a matrilinear system. Each noble man or woman could trace his or her line back to the founding of the city. It was also clear from the chronicle that their religion was part of their scheme of living, and we could reasonably guess that it was a conventional form of polytheism, with leading male and female godheads, Baal and Astarte.

As we moved forward in time so we found new factors intruding, new contingencies occupying the attention of the ruling king. The rapid shrinking of the waters of the lake of Opet began to threaten the city's life line, and in the year 296 the Gry-Lion sent 7,000 slaves to assist with the work of keeping the channels open to the sea. He also despatched a column of 1,000 of his own guards under the war-captain Ramose with orders to 'venture eastwards towards the rising sun stopping not, nor failing in determination' until he had reached the eastern sea and had discovered the route to the lands of the north whose existence was postulated by the sea captain and navigator, Habbakuk Lal.

A year later Ramose returns, with only seventy men, the others having perished in a land of pestilential swamps and putrid fevers. He had, however, reached the eastern sea and there found a city of traders and seafarers 'dark men, and bearded, dressed in fine linens, and binding their brows with the same material'. They come from a land beyond the eastern sea, and Ramose is rewarded with twenty fingers of gold and twenty slaves. Our men of Opet have made their first contact with the Arabs, known to them as 'the Dravs', who are colonizing the Sofala coast.

We learned how the Gry-Lion's search for a new source of slave-labour becomes desperate. Orders are despatched to the mine overseers to take all measures to prolong the working lives of their slaves. Rations of meat and corn are increased, inflating the cost of production but increasing the life expectancy of the slaves. Owners are enjoined to breed all female slaves regularly, and the practice of infibulation is discontinued. The slaving expeditions are sent further and further afield, as the Yuye are hunted down. From the description of these yellow-skinned Yuye we guessed they were the ancestors of Hottentot people.

Then suddenly the Gry-Lion is delighted by the return of a northerly expedition with 500 'savage Nubians, both tall and strong' and the leader of the expedition is rewarded with ten fingers of gold. This delight fades slowly over the following hundred years as a solid mass of black humanity builds up north of the great river. The vast Bantu migrations have begun and now the concern of the Gry-Lion is to dam the flood southwards and his legions march constant patrol upon the northern border.

Our samplings gave us these fleeting glimpses into the past, but they were recorded as bland impersonal statements of fact. How we longed to find the writings of a Pliny or Livy to give flesh and breath to these meticulous records of acquired wealth.

Each fact seemed to present us with a hundred unanswered questions. Of these the most pressing was: where did they come from these men of Opet, and when? Where did they go to and why? We hoped the answers to the major questions were here somewhere in this maze of writings, and in the meantime we occupied ourselves with finding the lesser answers.

It was easy enough to locate the places mentioned in the chronicles, Zimbao and Punt were the southern and northern territories of modern Rhodesia, the great river was the Zambezi, the lakes had disappeared, the gardens of Zeng were clearly the hundreds and thousands of acres of terraced hillsides in the Inyanga area of eastern Rhodesia, the hills of Tuya must be the copper-rich country above Sinoia; step by step we established the presence of our men of Opet at nearly all of the ancient sites, and at the same time we had a picture of the building-up of an immense treasure. For although the bulk of this wealth was sent 'outwards' yet there re-occurred the words 'a tenth part to the Gry-Lion'.

Where had this treasure been stored, and what had become of it? Had it perished with the city, or was it still here in some secret storehouse carved from the red rock cliffs of the Hills of Blood?

As a mental exercise I made an estimate of the extent of this treasure.

Assuming that a 'finger' of gold was one of the finger-like rods of the precious metal we had discovered among the foundations of the city, I listed the total inflow of gold recorded in twenty odd sample years beginning in the year 345 and ending in the year 501. I found that previous estimates had been hopelessly inadequate. Instead of 750 tons of gold, I found that the total recovery from the ancient mines could not have been less than 4,000 tons – of which a tenth part to the Gry-Lion.

Assuming half of this 400 tons had been spent on the maintenance of his army, the building of the temple and other public works, this still left the staggering figure of 200 tons of gold that might be hidden in or near the city – 200 tons represents a fortune of almost £80,000,000.

When I showed my calculations to Louren on his next visit to the site, I saw the gold-greed glitter in the pale blue eyes. He took away the sheet of paper with my workings on it, and the following morning as he was about to board the Lear for Johannesburg, he remarked casually, 'You know, Ben, I really think that you and Ral should spend more time exploring the area along the cliffs, rather than living in those archives.'

'What should we look for, Lo?' As if I didn't know.

'Well, those old boys were dab hands at hiding things away. They must have been the most secretive people in history, and we still haven't found their burial grounds.'

'So you want me to go grave-hunting.' I grinned at him, and he laughed.

'Of course, Ben, if you happened to stumble on their treasury I wouldn't hate you for it. After all eighty Big M's are a nice piece of petty cash.'

We had transferred 261 jars from the archives to the repository and Eldridge and Sally had sufficient material to keep them busy for the next two or three months, so I decided to follow Louren's suggestion and suspend work in the archives and undertake another detailed search of the area. My timing was impeccable, Ral was within five feet of where the small jars with the sunbird seals on their lids were standing in the darkest corner of the last recess. They were tucked away behind the front rank of jars twice their size and so effectively hidden by them that we had not included them in our original count. Ral was working his way steadily towards them, another three days would have been enough, but I took him away to search the cliffs.

This was November which we call the 'suicide month' in Africa. The sun was a hammer, and the earth an anvil but we worked the cliffs despite it. We rested only for two hours in the middle of the day, when the heat was murderous and the cool green waters of the emerald pool were irresistible.

We were alert now to the tricks and subterfuges of the ancient men of Opet. Having learned from bitter experience how skilfully they could cover their tracks and how cunningly their masons could conceal the joints in their masonry, I went back over ground I had already covered. I used my own tricks to try and out-think them. Ral and I re-photographed every inch of the cavern walls, but this time with infra-red film. We found no more concealed passages.

From there we worked outwards. Each day I marked off a 300-foot section and we combed this minutely. Not content merely to eye-ball the rocks, we searched by sense of touch also. Groping our way over them like blind men.

Each day brought its small adventures, I was chased by a black mamba, eight feet of irritability and sudden death, with eyes like glass beads and a flicking black tongue, that resented my prodding around in the crack which was its home and castle. Ral was very impressed with my turn of speed over broken ground, and suggested I took it up professionally.

A week later I could return his sallies in kind by remarking on the improvement that twenty wild bee stings made to his appearance. His face looked like a hairy pumpkin, and his eyes were slits in the swollen flesh. For five days poor Ral was of no use to me at all.

November passed and in mid-December we had a quarter of an inch of rain, which is about par for the course in this part of Africa. It laid the dust for an hour or so, and that was the end of the rainy season. I guessed that the ancient lake of Opet would have ensured a higher and more regular rainfall for the area. Open water encourages rain, both by its evaporation and by cooling the air to aid precipitation.

Ral and I worked on without results, but also without any diminution of our determination or enthusiasm. Despite our days of wearing labour under the killer sun, we spent most of our evenings poring over the map of the foundations of the city. By a process of guess, deduction and elimination, we tried to work out where the ancients would have sited their tombs. I had by now become extremely fond of Ral Davidson, and I saw in this big gangling indefatigable youth the makings of one of the giants of our profession. There would be a permanent post for him at the Institute once this dig was finished, I would see to that.

In contrast to our results, Eldridge Hamilton, assisted by Sally, and Leslie, continued to reap the rich and enchanting harvest of the scrolls. Each evening I would spend an hour in the air-conditioned repository with them, reviewing the day's work. Steadily the sheets of typed translation piled up, the margins thick with notes and references in Eldridge's spidery and untidy hand.

Christmas came and we sat out under a moon as big as a silver gong, exchanging gifts and companionship. I gave them 'White Christmas' in the style of Bing Crosby, even though the night temperature was in the high eighties. Then Eldridge and I did 'Jingle Bells' as a duet. Eldridge had forgotten the words, all except the jingling part. He was a great little jingler was our Eldridge, especially after ten large gins. He was still jingling away merrily when Ral and I carried him off to bed.

Early in the new year we had what amounted to a royal visit. Hilary Sturvesant had at last prevailed on Louren to bring her to see the site. We had a week to prepare for the family. Hilary was bringing the elder children with her and I was beside myself with excitement at the prospect of having all my favourite women at the City of the Moon. I left the search of the cliffs to Ral, while I rushed about re-arranging the accommodation and checking our stores for such essentials as Coca-Cola and chocolates. Commodities which make life bearable for Bobby Sturvesant.

They arrived in time for the lunch of cold meats and salads which I had personally prepared, and immediately the visit began souring. Sally Benator was not at the meal, she sent a message that she had a headache and was going to lie down. However, I saw her sneaking off with towel and bathing costume towards the emerald pool.

Eldridge Hamilton and Louren Sturvesant took one look at each other, and remembered their last meeting. They were as hostile as a pair of rutting stags. I recalled Eldridge's boast that he had sent Louren packing. They began making elaborately offensive remarks at each other, and I was fully extended in trying to prevent active physical violence breaking out, and when Eldridge spoke about people with 'more money than either breeding or sense', I thought I had lost my expert on ancient writings.

As if this was not sufficient, it was also obvious that Hilary and Louren were engaged in a domestic dispute which made it impossible for them to address each other directly. All communication was conducted through the agency of Bobby Sturvesant and was preceded by remarks of the order, 'Please ask your step-mother if' or 'If your father wants . . .'

Hilary wore dark glasses at the lunch-table, and I could guess her eyes bore the traces of recent weeping. She was silent and reserved, as were both Ral and Leslie. The two youngsters were overcome with shyness in the presence of the Sturvesants, and when Louren and Eldridge also subsided into a smouldering truce, there were only two of us left articulate, Bobby Sturvesant and me.

Bobby took full advantage of the temporary breakdown in parental control to become an utterly impossible little bitch. She spent the entire meal either showing off shamelessly or being insolent to her step-mother. I would dearly have loved to turn her over my knee and paddle her stern.

Immediately after the meal dragged to its tortured conclusion, Eldridge retreated to his repository, Ral and Leslie muttered excuses and fled. Louren asked me for the keys of the Land-Rover and I saw him take his shotgun and drive away towards the north, leaving Hilary and the children to me. I took Hilary through the site museum and she soon forgot her unhappiness in the fascination of our exhibits.

I had carefully cleaned and polished the great battle-axe. It glittered silver, gold and ivory, and we examined the craftsmanship of its manufacture together before going across to the repository of the scrolls. Sally was too busy to talk to us. She hardly lifted her head when we entered, but Hilary turned her gentle charisma on to Eldridge Hamilton and he was not proof against it. When we left an hour later Hilary had another devoted admirer.

We went up to the cavern, and sat together above the emerald pool while the children splashed and shrieked in the cool green water. We talked together like the old and dear friends we were, but even then it was some time before Hilary could bring herself to mention that which was troubling her.

'Ben, have you noticed anything different about him?' The old question of an unhappy woman, and I made the old excuse for him.

'He works so hard, Hil.' And she snatched at it.

'Yes, he's been tied up in this hotel business for months. He's building a chain of luxury vacation hotels across the islands of the Indian Ocean. Comores, Seychelles, Madagascar, ten of them. He is exhausting himself.'

Then as we walked down towards the huts in the dusk, she said suddenly, 'Do you think he has found another woman, Ben?'

I was startled. 'Good Lord, Hil. What on earth makes you think that?'

'I don't know. Nothing I suppose. It's just that—' She stopped and sighed.

'Where would he find more than he has now?' I asked softly, and she took my hand and squeezed it.

'My dear Ben. What would we do without you?'

When I went to tuck Bobby up and kiss her good night, I told her what I thought of her behaviour at lunch and she snuffled a bit and said she was sorry. Then we kissed and hugged and agreed that we still loved each other. She was asleep before I had switched out the light, and with dread in my heart I went across to the common room for a repeat of the midday performance.

At the threshold I blinked with surprise. Louren, Eldridge and Sally were in a friendly and animated huddle over the typed pile of translation sheets, while Ral and Leslie were eagerly discussing their marriage plans with Hilary. The transformation was miraculous. I made my way with relief towards the Glen Grant bottle, and poured a medium-sized one.

'One for me also.' Sally came across to me. I could see no evidence of headache. Her mouth was a hectic slash of bright lipstick, and the silk dress she wore was draped to expose her strong brown back and shoulders. She had piled her hair up on her head, and I thought I had seldom seen her look so lovely.

I poured her a drink, and we went to join the discussion of the scrolls. In contrast to his earlier mood, Louren was at his most charming, and even Eldridge could not resist him.

'Professor Hamilton has done a most remarkable job here, Ben,' he greeted me. 'I can only congratulate you on your choice of a colleague.' Eldridge preened modestly.

'There is something we cannot put off much longer, Ben,' Louren went on. 'We are going to have to make an announcement soon. We can't keep this a secret much longer.'

'I know,' I agreed.

'Have you had any thoughts on it, yet?'

'Well, as a matter of fact—' I hesitated. I hate having to ask Louren to spend money. 'I was thinking of something on a rather grand scale.'

'Yes?' Louren encouraged me.

'Well, I thought if we could have the Royal Geographical Society convene a special symposium on African pre-history. Eldridge is a member of the Council, I'm sure he could arrange it.'

We looked at him, and he nodded.

'Then perhaps Sturvesant International could play host to the delegates, fly them to London and pay their expenses to make sure they all attend, or at least some of them.'

Louren threw his head back and laughed delightedly. 'You are a scheming son-of-a-gun, Ben. I see your plan exactly. You are going to get all your critics and enemies together in one bunch within the hallowed precincts of the R.G.S., and you are going to play the Al Capone of archaeology in a scientific St. Valentine's day massacre. In the jargon, you are going to murder da bums. That's right, isn't it?'

I blushed at having my plans so readily exposed.

'Well,' and then I grinned sheepishly and nodded, 'I guess that's about it, Lo.'

'I love it.' Sally clapped her hands with delight. 'We will draw up a guest list.'

'We will do this in style,' Louren promised. 'We'll fly them in first class and we'll put them at the Dorchester. We'll give a champagne lunch to lull them and then we'll turn Ben and Eldridge loose amongst them like a pack of ravening wolves.' He had entered fully into the spirit of the thing and he turned to Eldridge.

'How long would it take to arrange?'

'Well, it would have to go before the Council for approval. We would have to give them some idea of the agenda, but of course your offer to pay the expenses would make it a lot easier. I will lobby a couple of the other Council members.' Eldridge was enjoying it also. There is a rather perverse thrill to be had out of planning and executing the professional assassination of one's enemies. 'I think we could arrange it for April.'

'April the first,' I suggested.

'Lovely,' laughed Louren.

'We must have Wilfred Snell,' Sally pleaded.

'He's top of the list,' I assured her.

'And that slimy little Rogers.'

'And De Vallos.'

We were still gloating and scheming when we sat down to eat the fiery curry of wild pheasant that I hoped would make the sultry night air seem cool by comparison. There were pitchers of cold draught beer to go with it, and the meal developed into a festive occasion. We were still gloating on the discomfort of our scientific enemies and planning the confrontation in detail, when Sally turned suddenly to Hilary who had been sitting quietly beside me.

'You must forgive us, Mrs. Sturvesant. This must be terribly boring for you. I don't suppose a word of it makes sense to you.' Sally's tone was honeyed and solicitous. I was as surprised as Hilary, for I understand enough of the secret language of women to recognize this as an open declaration of war. I hoped that I was mistaken, but five minutes later Sally attacked again.

'You must find the heat and primitive conditions here most trying, Mrs. Sturvesant. Not the sort of weather for your tennis parties, is it?'

The way she said it made tennis seem the pastime of a spoiled and ineffectual social butterfly. But this time Hilary was ready for her, and with a face like an angel and tones every bit as sugary as Sally's, she ripped back in a devastating counter-attack.

'I'm sure it can be most unhealthy, especially after any length of time, Dr. Benator. The sun can play havoc with one's skin, can it not? And you are still looking peaky from your headache. We were very worried about you. I do hope you are feeling better now.'

Sally found that despite her gentle nunlike air, Hilary was an opponent worthy of her steel. She changed her attack. She turned all her attention onto Louren, laughing gaily at his every word and not taking her eyes from his face. Hilary was helpless in the face of these tactics. I seemed to be the only one in the party aware of this duel in progress, and I sat silently trying to puzzle out the meaning of it all – until Hilary played her trump.

'Louren, darling, it has been such a busy, exciting day. Won't you take me to bed now, please.

She swept off the field on Louren's arm, and reluctantly I had to admit that my Sally had received the treatment she deserved.

I woke to the awareness of somebody else in my bedroom with me, and I tensed myself for sudden violent action as I rolled my head stealthily and looked towards the door. It was open. The moonlight outside was bright and clear. Sally stood in the opening.

She wore a flimsy nightdress, which did not conceal the lovely outline of her nude body against the silver moonlight. The long legs, the swelling womanly hips, the nip-in of waist and flare of breast, the long gazelle neck with tilt of dainty head.

'Ben?' she asked softly.

'Yes.' I sat up, and she came quickly to me. 'What is it, Sal?'

In reply she kissed me with open mouth and probing tongue. I was taken completely by surprise, frozen in her arms and she laid her cheek against mine. In a small gusty voice she whispered, 'Make love to me, Ben.'

There was something wrong here, desperately wrong. I felt no awakening of desire, only a warm rise of compassion for her.

'Why, Sal?' I asked. 'Why now?'

'Because I need it, Ben.'

'No, Sally. I don't think you do. I think that is the very last thing in the world you need now.'

And suddenly she was crying, big broken silent sobs. She cried for a long time, and I held her. When she was quiet I laid her on the pillow and covered her with the blankets.

'I am a bitch, aren't I, Ben?' she whispered, and went to sleep. I stayed awake all that night, watching over her. I think I knew then what was happening, but I did not want to admit it to myself.

At breakfast Louren abruptly announced that the family would return immediately to Johannesburg, rather than stay the extra day as had been originally planned. I found it hard to hide my disappointment, and when I asked Louren for a reason as soon as we were alone, he merely looked towards the heavens and shrugged with exasperation.

'You are plain lucky you never married, Ben. My God – women!'

Life at the City of the Moon returned to its normal satisfying routine for a week, during which Ral and I pursued our search for the tombs and the others worked steadily at the scrolls. Then while Ral and I sat in a sizzling midday sun under the meagre shade of a camel thorn, a little puckish figure rose from the grass seemingly at my feet.

'Sunbird,' said Xhai softly, 'I have travelled many days to seek the sunshine of your presence.' He turns the prettiest compliment, and my heart went out to him.

'Ral,' I said, 'let me have your tobacco pouch, please.'

We sat together all that afternoon under the camel thorn and we talked. The conversations of primitive Africa are an art form, with elaborate rituals of question and answer, and it was late before Xhai reached the subject which he had come to discuss.

'Does Sunbird remember the water-in-the-rock at the place where we slew the elephant?'

Sunbird remembered it well.

'Does Sunbird remember the little holes that the white ghosts made in the rock?'

Sunbird would never forget them.

'These holes gave Sunbird and the big golden one much pleasure, did they not?'

They did indeed.

'Since that day I have looked with fresh eyes upon the rocks as I hunted. Would Sunbird wish to visit another place where there are many such holes?'

Would I!

'I will lead you there,' Xhai promised.

'And I will give you as much tobacco as you can carry away,' I promised him in return, and we beamed at each other.

'How far is this place?' I asked, and he began to explain. It was beyond the 'big wire' he told me. This was the 300-mile-long game fence along the Rhodesia border which was erected to control movements of the wild animals as a precaution against foot and mouth disease. We would need clearance from the Rhodesians, and when Xhai went on to describe an area which seemed fairly close to the Zambezi river border with Zambia, I knew I would have to ask Louren to arrange an expedition. It was obviously squarely within the zone of terrorist activity.

Xhai refused to accompany me back to a camp which was filled with his traditional enemies, the Bantu. Instead we arranged to meet under the camel thorn three days later, once Xhai had completed the rounds of his trap line.

I was fortunate enough that evening to find Louren had returned an hour before from Madagascar.

'What's the trouble, Ben?' His voice boomed above the radio static.

'No trouble, Lo. Your little bushman friend has found another ancient gold working site. He's happy to take me to it.'

'That's great, Ben. The elephant mine is in production already, and looking very good indeed.'

'There is only one problem, Lo. It's in Rhodesia, in the closed area.'

'No problem, Ben. I'll fix it.' And the following evening we spoke again.

'It's set up for Monday week. There will be a Rhodesian police escort to meet us at the Panda Matenga border gate.'

'Us?' I asked.

'I'm stealing a couple of days off, Ben. Just couldn't resist it. You take the bushman with you, go by Land-Rover through to Panda Matenga. I will come in from Bulawayo by helicopter. See you there. Monday week, morning, okay?'

The commander of the police escort was one of those beefy,. boyish young Rhodesians with impeccable manners, and an air of quiet competence which I found most reassuring. He was an assistant inspector with an askari sergeant and five constables under him. His rank and the composition of the escort gave me some indication of the level to which Louren had applied for co-operation.

We had two Land-Rovers, both with mounted medium machine-guns on the bonnet, and the armament of the rest of the party was impressive, as was to be expected on the borders of a country subjected to unceasing harassment by terrorist infiltrators from the north.

'Dr. Kazin.' The inspector saluted and we shook hands. 'My name's Mac-Donald. Alaistair MacDonald. May I introduce my men?'

They were Matabeles, all of them. The big moon-faced descendants of Chaka's fighting impis, led here 150 years ago by the renegade general, Mzilikazi. They were dressed in camouflage fatigues with soft jungle hats, and they stood to rigid attention as MacDonald led me down the single rank.

'This is Sergeant Ndabuka.' And when I acknowledged the introduction in fluent Sindebele, the stern military expressions dissolved into huge flashing smiles.

Xhai was obviously very ill at ease in this company. He followed on my heels like a puppy.

'Did you know, Doctor, that there is still a field order issued to the British South Africa Police that hasn't been rescinded,' MacDonald told me, as he looked Xhai over with interest. 'It is an instruction to shoot all bushmen on sight. This is the first one I've ever seen. Poor little blighters.'

'Yes.' I had heard of that order which was maintained as a curiosity, but too faithfully reflected the attitude of the last century. The time of the great bushmen hunts, when a hundred mounted men would band together into a commando to hunt and kill these little yellow pixies as though they were dangerous animals.

White and black had hunted them mercilessly. The atrocities committed against them were legion. Shot and speared – and worse. In 1869 King Khama had enticed a whole tribe of them to a feast of reconciliation, and while they sat at his board, with their weapons laid aside, his warriors seized them. The king had supervised the subsequent torture personally. The last bushman died on the fourth day. With this history to remember it was no wonder that Xhai stayed within arm's length of me, and watched these colossal strangers with frightened Chinese eyes.

I explained to MacDonald our approximate destination, pointing out the general area on his map as accurately as I could reckon it from Xhai's description, and the inspector looked grave. He picked a shred of sun-burned skin from the tip of his nose before replying.

'That's not a very good area, Doctor.' And he went off to talk to his men.

It was midday before the helicopter came clattering over the tree-tops from the south-east. Louren jumped from the cabin lugging his own bag.

'Sorry I'm late, Ben. I had to wait for a phone call from New York.'

MacDonald came forward and touched his cap-brim.

'Afternoon, sir.' His attitude was deferential. 'The prime minister asked me to give you his respects, Mr. Sturvesant, and I am to place myself at your disposal.'

We left the track before we reached the ranching country near Tete, and we swung away northwards towards the Zambezi. MacDonald was in the leading Land-Rover with a driver and a trooper on the machine-gun. We followed in the central spot, Louren driving and another trooper riding shotgun in the passenger seat. Xhai and I together in the back. The second police Land-Rover took the rearguard with Sergeant Ndabuka in command.

The slow miles ground past, as the column wound through forests of morpane, and climbed the low ranges of granite. At any hesitation in our advance, Xhai's arm would signal the direction and we would move forward, jolting and pitching over the rough places or humming swiftly through open glades of brown grass. I realized that Xhai was guiding us along the elephant trail, the migratory road that the huge beasts had beaten out from the river to the sanctuary of the Wankie game reserve in the south. Skilled trail blazers, they had picked a route that required the minimum effort to negotiate. Always it was the easy gradient, the low pass through the hills, and the river drifts with gentle sloping banks that they chose.

We camped beside one of these drifts. The river bed was dry, choked with polished black boulders that glittered like reptiles in the sunset. There were banks of sugar-white sand, patches of tall reeds and a pool of slimy green water overhung with the branches of fever trees.

Beyond the river the ground rose steeply in another of those rocky ridges dotted with marula trees and patches of scrub. However, on this side the bush was open, offering a clear field of fire around our camp. MacDonald drew the three vehicles into a defensive triangle, and while he placed his sentries, Louren and I, followed by Xhai, went down the bank to the pool.

We sat on the rocks and watched a colony of yellow weaver birds chattering and fluttering around their nests of woven grass that hung from the fever trees over the green water.

Louren gave Xhai a cigar, and while we talked the little bushman's eyes never left our faces, like those of a faithful dog. The talk was fitful, changing from one subject to another without design. Louren told me about the hotel project on the islands. He was very certain of its success.

'It's one of my really good ones, Ben.' And when I thought about his other good ones – the cattle ranches, the diamond mines, gold, chrome and copper – I knew how big it must be.

I touched lightly on his difficulties with Hilary.

'My God, Ben. If only they understood that they don't buy you with the marriage certificate!' There were three others who had found that out the hard way, I hoped that Hilary would not be the fourth.

It was almost dark when MacDonald came down the bank.

'Excuse me, Mr. Sturvesant. Could I ask you to come into the perimeter now. I don't like taking unnecessary chances.' And with good grace Louren flicked the stub of his cigar into the pool, and stood up.

'This used to be a country where a man could range to the full extent of his fancy. Times are changing, Ben.'

When we entered the camp there was coffee brewing on a low screened fire, and while we sipped from the steaming mugs I saw the precautions MacDonald had taken for our safety and I realized that his competent looks were not deceiving. He finished his sentry rounds and came to sit with us.

'I should have asked you sooner, but do you gentlemen know how to use the FN rifle and the 60-calibre machine-gun?' Louren and I both told him we did.

'Good.' MacDonald looked out towards the north. 'The closer we get to the border the more chance there is of a clash. There has been a big step-up in the terrorist activity recently. Something brewing up there.'

He poured a mug of coffee and sipped before he asked:

'Well, gentlemen, what are your plans for tomorrow? How far are we from our destination?'

I looked at Xhai. 'How far is it to the holes in the rock, my brother?'

'We will be there before the sun stands so,' indicating noon with one delicate little hand, 'my people are camped at the waterhole near the holes in the rock. We will go there to find them first, for they have long awaited my coming.'

I stared at him, realizing for the first time the extent of Xhai's friendship. Then I turned to Louren. 'Do you realize, Lo, that this little devil has made a trek of 150 miles on foot merely to tell us something that might give us pleasure.'

'What do you mean?'

'As soon as he discovered the old workings he left his tribe and set off to find me.'

That night Xhai slept between Louren and me. He still didn't trust the big Matabele troopers one little bit.

It was eleven o'clock the following morning when we saw the vultures in the northern sky. MacDonald halted the column, and came back to our vehicle.

'Something up ahead. Probably only a lion kill, but we had better not take any chances.'

Xhai slipped off the seat and clambered up on to the roof of the Land-Rover. For a minute he watched the distant birds, then he came down to me.

'My people have killed a large animal. Perhaps even a buffalo, for the birds are above my camp. There is nothing to fear. Let us go forward.'

I translated for MacDonald, and he nodded.

'Okay, Doctor. But we'll keep our eyes peeled all the same.'

The bushmen had erected five rude shelters beside a hole of mud and filthy water. They had merely bent a number of saplings inwards to form the framework, and then thatched it roughly with leaves and grass. There was no smoke and no sign of the little yellow people as we drove towards the encampment. Xhai was looking puzzled, darting little birdlike glances into the thick bush, and whistling softly through his teeth. The vultures sat in the tree-tops all around the camp, and as we approached there was a sudden commotion from amongst the huts and twenty or thirty of the big ugly birds flapped into the air.

Xhai let out a soft wailing cry. I did not understand what had happened, it merely seemed odd that the vultures were on the ground amongst the huts, but Xhai had guessed it. He began rocking slowly on the seat, hugging his chest and emitting that low-pitched wail.

MacDonald stopped his Land-Rover and climbed out. He stooped over something on the ground, then he straightened up and shouted an order. His troopers jumped from the vehicle and spread out with their weapons held ready. Louren parked our Land-Rover and we went to where MacDonald was standing amongst the huts. Xhai remained in the back seat, still rocking and wailing.

For the Bantu the bushman girls are an object of peculiar lust. I do not know why this should be so, perhaps it is their golden yellow colour, or it may be their tiny doll-like bodies. They had raped Xhai's women, all of them, even the little immature girls. Then they had bayoneted them and left them lying in that pathetically vulnerable attitude of love. Ghal and the other two males they had shot. Bursts of automatic fire had smashed their bodies so that slivers and chips of bone protruded from the mangled flesh. The blood had dried in black splashes and puddles. There were flies everywhere, big green metallic flies that buzzed like hiving bees and came to settle on my lips and eyes. I struck them away angrily. The birds had been at the bodies, that was the truly horrible part of it, the birds.

'God,' said Louren. 'Oh God. Why? Why did they do it?'

'It's their style,' MacDonald answered. 'Frelimo, Mau-Mau, all of them hit their own people hardest.'

'But why?' repeated Louren.

'They've got guns. They want to use them. This is easier than going for white ranchers or police posts.' Two of the police troopers carried a tarpaulin from one of the Land-Rovers. They began wrapping the bodies. I walked back to our vehicle and leaned against the door. Suddenly I was sick, an acid bitter flood gushing up my throat, and I retched painfully.

When I was finished I wiped my mouth on my sleeve and looked up to find Xhai watching me. He was a man deprived of everything except the breath of life. There was such agony in those dark eyes, such sorrow twisted that mouth that I felt my own heart breaking for him.

'Let us find who has done this thing, Sunbird,' he whispered, and he led me into the short grass around the camp. He worked quickly, like a gundog.

There were spills of the bright brass cartridge cases scattered on the sandy earth. Shoddily manufactured, and stamped with Chinese characters, hundreds of them. The gunners had fired with childish gusto, pouring a torrent of bullets into the camp. Their boots had left the characteristic chevron-patterned imprints. There seemed to be hundreds of them, for the earth was churned and the grass flattened.

'They came in the night,' Xhai explained softly. 'See! Here is where they waited.' He pointed to the scuffed places amongst the bushes. 'There were many of them.' And he showed both his hands with fingers spread, three times. Thirty of them. A big party. 'They struck in the dawn. Yesterday at dawn.' Thirty-two hours ago. They would be miles away now, I realized. When we returned to the encampment the nine bodies were wrapped in canvas and laid out in a neat line, like parcels ready for posting. Four of the troopers were digging a shallow communal grave.

Xhai went to squat beside the line of dead. He was silent now, and the silence was more distressing than his despairing wail. Once he leaned forward and timidly touched one of the green canvas-wrapped bundles. How many of these little men had squatted like this in the sun to mourn the massacre of their tribe, I wondered. It is at times such as this that I hate the savage ferocity of this land of ours. I could not watch Xhai's grief and I turned away and went to where Louren and MacDonald stood together talking quietly.

'It's a big party, Ben,' Louren greeted me as I came up.

'Xhai says there are thirty of them,' I told him, and he nodded.

'Very likely. The inspector feels we should turn back, and I reckon I agree with him.'

MacDonald explained, 'Should we run into them, they outnumber us heavily, Doctor. These swine are well trained and armed with the most modern weapons. It's not like a few years ago when they sent in a half-baked rabble. They are really dangerous now, and we aren't an offensive patrol. I think we must get out as quickly as possible, and call in the helicopters. Once they locate them the Hunter jets will give them a whiff of napalm.'

'Yes,' I agreed. The ancient workings were no longer important in the face of this horror. I looked across to where the troopers were lifting the bundles down into the grave. Xhai stood watching them. When the grave was filled with loose earth I went across to Xhai and placed an arm around his shoulder.

'Come, little brother,' I said and led him to the Land-Rover. The column turned and in the same order made its way back into the south.

The journey slowly developed into a nightmare of tension and straining nerves. The revving and gear-changing that was necessary to negotiate the rough and broken ground broadcast our progress far ahead of us. Every mile there was a location ideal for an ambush, with thick cover pressing in closely on either hand. Our trail was laid clearly, and we must follow it on our return. They would know this and wait for us there. It was possible they carried landmines and we watched anxiously for disturbed earth in the trail ahead. The strain was on all of us. Louren drove in grim silence, with an unlit stub of cigar rolling restlessly in the corner of his mouth.

The trooper beside him rode with the butt of the machine-gun pulled into his shoulder, and occasionally he traversed the heavy weapon experimentally. All our heads moved constantly, swinging slowly from side to side, searching, searching.

'Have you noticed there is no sign of game, Ben?' Louren asked suddenly. He was correct. Since leaving the bushman encampment we had seen none of the wild life which had enlivened our outward journey, not even a herd of the dainty brown impala.

'I don't like it, Lo.'

'Join the club,' Louren grunted.

'In thirty-two hours the bastards could have moved miles. They could be anywhere.' I fiddled restlessly with the rate of fire selector on the rifle in my lap. MacDonald had insisted on us taking the spare weapons from two of the troopers on the heavy machine-guns. I was glad of it now. There was much comfort to be drawn from that hunk of wood and steel.

Suddenly the Land-Rover ahead of us skidded to a halt, and Louren slammed on his own brakes and snatched the automatic rifle from the bracket behind him. We sat with our weapons poised, peering into the wilderness of rock and scrub around us. Waiting for the sudden shuddering roar of machine-guns. The slow seconds passed and my own pulse drummed in my ears deafening me.

'Sorry,' MacDonald called from up front. 'False alarm!'

The engines revved, hideously loud in the vast silence of Africa, and we went on.

'For Christ's sake stop fiddling with that bloody thing!' Louren snapped at me with unnecessary violence. I had not realized that I had been clicking the selector of the rifle.

'Sorry,' I muttered guiltily. The tension was infectious. Louren's outburst was a symptom of it, but almost immediately he glanced over his shoulder and grinned apologetically.

'This is bloody murder.'

It seemed hours later that we crossed a ridge and went twisting down amongst the trees to the pool in the dry water course where we had camped the previous night. MacDonald signalled the column to a halt on the far bank, and he came back to us.

'We will top up the fuel tanks here, Mr. Sturvesant. I'll see to that. Will you take a party down to the pool and refill the water containers.'

Louren went down the bank with two of the troopers lugging the five-gallon jerry cans while I watched MacDonald begin refuelling. The gasoline fumes swirled like a mirage in the heat, and the smell was biting in my throat. One of the troopers splashed the liquid in a spurt down the side of the lead vehicle and MacDonald reprimanded him sharply.

'Stay here,' I told Xhai. 'Do not move.' And he nodded at me from the back seat of the Land-Rover.

I left him and followed Louren down to the edge of the pool. It was a tranquil scene, so typical of Africa. Tall reeds languidly drooping their fluffy heads, black mud, pocked with the hooves of a thousand beasts, water green and thick with slime bubbling sulkily with marsh gas, the weaver birds hanging upside down below their swinging basket nests. The two troopers were talking quietly as they filled the jerry cans, Louren standing over them with the automatic rifle.

'Another hour's travel will see us in the clear,' he remarked as I joined him. He took a cigar from his top pocket and began unwrapping it without interrupting his search of the surrounding trees and brush.

There was a fleck of white on the rocks at the water's edge. It caught my eye and I glanced at it, and was about to dismiss it as a splash of bird droppings. Then I noticed something else, and I felt the first cool draught of apprehension blow down my spine. Casually, I strolled along the edge of the pool averting my eyes from the white object until it was at my feet. Then I glanced down, and my breath jammed in my throat. My first impulse was to scream a warning to Louren and run for the Land-Rover, but I controlled the urge and forced myself to look away casually. Despite the racing of my heart and the difficulty I had in breathing I managed to stoop and pick up a pebble from the water's edge and toss it out into the pool where it fell with a plop in a widening ring of ripples. Quickly I glanced down again.

The white fleck was a piece of domestic soap, with a wet lacework of bubbles still frothing around it. There were damp marks on the rocks, that the sizzling sun had not yet dried, and in the mud at the water's edge, amongst all the thousands of hoof marks was a print. A strange half-human print, like that of a giant bird. The big toes deeply divided from the rest of the foot, split half-way back to the heel, and I knew that Timothy Mageba was watching me over the sights of an automatic weapon.

My skin prickled as from the stings of the myriad insects of fear. They crawled over my body and along the strings of my nerves. Slowly I walked back to Louren. The cigar was in his mouth and he struck a match as I approached. It flared in a puff of blue nitrous smoke in his cupped hands, and he bowed over it.

'Lo,' I said softly. 'Don't do anything suddenly. Behave as naturally as you can. They are here. Right here, watching us.'

He puffed four times then waved the match to extinguish it, and he looked around naturally.

'Where?' he asked.

'I don't know, but they are very close. We must show ourselves here until Mac is ready.'

'Tell the troopers,' Lo said.

The troopers were recapping the jerry cans, and as they moved back past us I stopped them.

'Go very gently. Do not run. Do not look behind you. The evil ones are here. Go to the inspector. Tell him to start the engines, when we hear them we will come running.'

They nodded, expressionlessly, understanding immediately, and I knew then why these were famed as the finest native troops in Africa. They went calmly up the bank, leaning away from the weight of the jerry cans.

'I feel like one of those little mechanical ducks in a shooting gallery,' I said, and tried to smile. It hung all crookedly on my face. 'What are they waiting for?' I asked.

'They probably didn't have time to set it up properly.' Louren laughed, a very good effort. It rang convincingly. 'They'll be moving into position now. Then they will wait until we are all together in a bunch, not spread out like this.'

'God, I wish I knew where they are, where to expect it to come from.'

'What tipped you?' Louren asked, anything to keep this conversation flowing naturally.

'Piece of soap, and wet footprints on the rocks. They were bathing when they heard us coming.'

Louren tapped ash from his cigar, and glanced at the rocks seeing the soap. Then his eyes flicked back to me. Above the bank we heard the starters whirring loudly in the silence, and then the engines running steadily. One, two, and the third one.

Louren ground the fresh cigar into the mud at the edge of the pool then turned to me. He let his hand fall onto my shoulder.

'All the way, partner?' he asked.

'All the way, Lo.' And we whirled together and went for the path up the bank, unslinging the rifles as we ran. I felt a lift of relief, the waiting was over. It had begun.

I had the strange sensation of not moving, of marking time, rather than running. The climb up the bank seemed endless, my feet dragged leadenly and a hot hushed silence persisted in which the engines of the Land-Rovers seemed muted, but our footsteps pounded like stampeding hooves.

We came out on top of the bank.

Sergeant Ndabuka was at the wheel of our vehicle swinging in towards us, slowing up for the pick up.

The other two Land-Rovers were backing up, ready to cover us, turning for the path with the gunners traversing the heavy machine-guns.

'Jump!' shouted MacDonald. 'Let's hit out!'

I leapt for the side of the Land-Rover and Louren piled in beside me.

'Go!' he snapped urgently at the sergeant. The engine roared and we surged forward. From the moment when we started to run to the moment we boarded the speeding vehicle perhaps six seconds had elapsed. It had all gone very quickly, and I scrambled onto my knees, pushing the automatic rifle forward to cover one flank. In that instant they opened on us. The air around me was torn by the sound of a thousand bull whips, while the gunfire sounded like a stick dragged swiftly across a corrugated-iron fence.

MacDonald's vehicle was leading us out, back along our tracks. It was drawing fire also. I saw the gunner hit. His head snapping backwards as though from a heavy punch and his hat flying from his head. He collapsed over the seat, his untended weapon spiralling idly on its mounting.

They were below the river bank, lining it, hidden in the reeds and scrub there. I saw the muzzle flashes, glinting like swords. I let off a burst, swinging on them, but with the Land-Rover bucking I was low. Dust flew in a line below the bank as though a whiplash had churned the dust. I corrected my aim and fired, the weapon shuddering in my hands. Seeing the reeds shake and tremble as my bullets raked them. Someone screamed, a thin passionless sound, and my weapon clicked empty.

I snatched for a fresh magazine, looking ahead, to estimate how much longer we must receive fire. MacDonald was just entering the forest, there were big trees on either side of the path indicating the passage. I saw the loose earth in the path ahead of MacDonald swept neatly, and I knew then why they had held their fire until it served to drive us into the trap.

I opened my mouth to scream a warning, but it was lost in the continuous clamour of gunfire and engine roar.

MacDonald hit the landmines they had laid for us across our old tracks and the detonation was a burst of bright white light that seared the retina of the eye. The concussion slammed painfully into my eardrums, and MacDonald's Land-Rover reared like a wounded lion. Its front end was smashed in, one of the wheels spinning lazily through the air. It toppled backwards, crushing the occupants beneath it. The second Land-Rover drove into it at thirty miles an hour. There was a rending screeching sound of metal as the two came together.

'Look out!' shouted Louren and the sergeant swung the wheel violently to avoid colliding with the mass of wrecked vehicles. Our Land-Rover hung over on two wheels, then flopped over on its side. We were thrown out on to the rocky earth.

There was a silence that lasted for three or four seconds. A stunned silence, even the enemy frozen by the suddenness of the havoc they had created. We were perhaps fifty yards from the river-bed where Timothy's men lay. The intervening ground was sparsely studded with fever trees. These and the bodies of the vehicles gave us a little cover.

I had lost my rifle and as I groped for it I found Xhai huddled next to me. I had one glimpse of his terrified face, as I crawled towards Louren.

'Are you all right?'

For answer he pointed. 'Look!' Twenty feet away Alaistair MacDonald lay on his back with the full weight of the Land-Rover lying across his pelvis. He was pushing at the mass of metal with weak fluttering hands. He moaned then softly.

I stood up to go to him, and at that moment the guns opened again. Flailing us, rattling and clanging against the Land-Rovers, lashing billows of dust and storms of stone fragments, ricocheting with the sound of tearing silk – and Louren dragged me down.

I was aware of movement beside me and as I turned towards it little Xhai wailed softly like a restless baby. I put out my hand to calm him, but my touch galvanized him. He jumped to his feet, his dark amber eyes ablaze with terror, and he ran.

'Wait, little brother,' I shouted, and I scrambled up to follow him. Louren grabbed and held me and I watched as Xhai ran out into that hell storm.

He drew all their fire immediately. They hunted him, hosing bullets at him. He ran like a rabbit caught in a car's headlights, making no attempt to hide. I struggled in Louren's grip.

'No!' I shouted. 'Leave him! No! No!' And they hit him, knocking him down so he rolled across the stony earth like a small brown ball. He came up on his feet again, still running but his left arm was shot away above the elbow, holding only by a tatter of wet flesh and it bounced loosely against his flank. They hit him again, squarely this time, between the shoulder blades and he went down hard and skidded on his face. He lay very still and small in the harsh white sunlight. I was quiet in Louren's grip, while around me the surviving troopers crawled into position to return the enemy fire. Louren rolled away from me, lying prone and fired a burst around the tailboard of the overturned Land-Rover.

The storm of bullets returned to sweep over us, and MacDonald was still moaning. Nobody could reach him across that bullet-swept space. I knelt on the hard earth staring at Xhai's frail little body, and I felt the hot winds of my rage blow through my soul. They came from deep and far, crescendoed and overwhelmed my reason.

I jumped up and ran to the mined Land-Rover, I tore the pin from the mounting and hefted the heavy machine-gun out of its seating. Then I threw four loops of the cartridge-belt over my shoulders, draping myself with death as though it were an Hawaiian lei. Then, with the gun on my hip, I went after them, running towards the river-bed, straight at the centre of their line.

I heard myself screaming, and the violent disruption of the air around me as shot passed close, buffeted my ears and fanned my face with a hot dry wind. I

ran screaming and the gun shook my body as though it were a giant fist. The
spent cartridge cases spewed from the breech in a glittering stream, ringing like
silver bells as they bounced off the stony earth. I saw the lip of the bank dissolve
in spurting, swirling clouds of dust as I traversed it, saw one of them hit and
flung backwards.

Their fire was shrivelling, I saw movement in the reeds as they ran. One of
them leapt to his feet and fired a burst. Beside me slabs of white bark exploded
from the trunk of a fever tree, and I swivelled the gun onto him. He was in
camouflage battledress, a pudding-basin helmet of steel on his head and he
crouched over his weapon, the muzzle winked its hot red eye at me and I
wondered that it could miss me at such close range.

One of my bullets caught him in the mouth, spinning his helmet away and
the contents of his skull blew out of the back of his head in a pink cloud. He
dropped below the bank.

'Follow him! Cover him!' I heard Louren yelling somewhere behind me, but
I did not care. I reached the bank of the river and looked down into the dry bed.
They were running, panicky, for the far bank and I turned the gun on them.
Watching as they fell, with the white sand dancing in sudden soft fountains
amongst them. I was still screaming.

The last loop of cartridges flipped off my shoulder and fed into the hungry
breech of my weapon. The gun went dead and useless in my hands, and I hurled
it after them. Rage and sorrow had driven me far beyond the boundaries of
reason and fear. I stood unarmed and unafraid and from the far bank Timothy
Mageba turned back towards me. He had a pistol in his right fist, and he aimed
at me. I felt the passage of the bullet close beside my head.

'Murderer!' I screamed, and he fired again, twice. It was as though the angels
of death had draped their wings around me, shielding me, for I did not even
hear the bullets. I saw him glaring at me, those terrible smoky eyes, the great
cannon-ball head like that of some wounded beast at bay.

Then suddenly Louren was beside me, he threw up his rifle and snapped a
shot at Timothy. I think Louren may have nicked him, for I saw him wince and
stagger slightly, but then he was gone into the thick scrub that covered the high
ground on the far bank. The police troopers went past us, moving forward in
line of skirmishers down the bank and across the river-bed where the dead men
lay. They fired a few rounds into the bush, then Louren called them back.

Louren turned to stare at me with a look of disbelief. 'They didn't touch you,'
he said with wonder. 'Not a single bullet – my God, Ben, my God!' He shook
his head. 'You frightened me, you crazy bastard. You frightened the hell out of
me.' He put his arm around my shoulder and led me back to the vehicles.

MacDonald was still moaning softly. We lifted the side of the Land-Rover,
Louren and I between us. MacDonald screamed as the troopers drew him out
from under the vehicle. His legs were twisted at an odd angle and his face was
very pale, his tan a dirty brown over it and little beads of sweat dewed his upper
lip.

I left Louren to administer morphine and try to splint the badly shattered
bone, and I went across to where Xhai still lay.

The entry hole was a blue black pucker in the centre of his back, there was
no bleeding from it. Yet he lay in a puddle of thick gelatinous blood, and I knew
what hideous damage the exit of the bullet from his chest must have caused. I
did not turn him over. I could not bring myself to do it, but his head was twisted
sideways and I squatted beside him. With my finger-tips I closed the lids over
those staring Chinese eyes.

'Go in peace, little brother,' I whispered.

'Come on, Ben. They'll be back. We must hurry,' Louren called.

Two of our troopers were dead, and the sergeant rolled them in their blankets. 'The bushman also,' I told him. He hesitated, but then he saw my expression and went quickly.

We rolled the third vehicle back onto its wheels and while the troopers lifted our dead and wounded aboard, Louren and I checked it out. Two of the tyres were shot through, the petrol tank was riddled, the steering box was severed by a bullet and another had shattered the engine sump cover. Oil poured from it, stinking in the heat.

Quickly Louren placed the sergeant and the three remaining troopers in a defensive perimeter amongst the fever trees and we pushed the crippled Land-Rover into the lee of the wrecked vehicles giving ourselves some cover to work behind.

There was a tool box in MacDonald's Land-Rover. We changed the wheels as quickly as a pair of Grand Prix mechanics, cannibalizing from the wrecks. As we tightened the last wheel bolts the sniping began. It was long range, from the far ridge a quarter of a mile away. They had learned their lesson well, and kept a respectful distance now. Our troopers answered, blazing away with the two heavy machine-guns to discourage them further.

In the middle of a fire fight Louren and I worked, greasy to the elbows. Smearing skin from knuckles on sharp steel in our haste, burning blisters into our skin on the red-hot manifold and exhaust system.

We pulled the sump cover off the capsized Land-Rover, and lay on our backs with hot oil dripping into our faces as we bolted it back onto our vehicle. The gasket was torn, it would leak, but it would hold oil long enough to get us clear.

Louren changed the steering-box, while I found a cake of soap in my pack and plugged the bullet holes in the fuel tank. As we worked, I blessed the Chinese artisans who had manufactured those shoddy weapons on the far ridge, with their limited range and accuracy.

We refuelled and replaced the engine oil, standing by necessity fully exposed to the marksmen on the hill, forcing ourselves to work methodically and trying to shut from our ears the terrifying sound of passing shot.

Louren jumped into the driver's seat, and pressed the starter; it whirled dismally, on and on, and I closed my eyes tight and prayed. Louren released the starter button and in the silence I heard him swearing with bitter vehemence. He tried again, the battery was weakening now, the whirring of the engine slowed and faltered.

A stray bullet smashed the windscreen spraying us with glittering glass fragments. Louren was still swearing. In despair I glanced at the setting sun, only half an hour or so of daylight left. In the darkness the hyenas would come down from the ridge. As though they had read my thoughts the fire from up there intensified. I heard a bullet whine away off the metal of the Land-Rover. Louren jumped out of the driver's seat and opened the bonnet again, as he worked I shouted across to Ndabuka.

'Why aren't you firing, Sergeant? You are letting them have target practice. Keep their heads down, dammit!'

'The ammunition is almost finished, sir,' he called back, and a coldness closed about my guts. No ammunition, and darkness coming on fast.

Louren slammed the bonnet closed, and ducked back into the driver's seat. He looked at me through the shattered windscreen.

'Say another prayer, Ben. The last one was no damned good.' And he pressed the starter. It wheezed wearily but the engine would not turn.

'We've had it, Ben,' Louren told me. 'Both the other batteries are *kaputt*.'

'Sergeant – all of you. Shove,' I shouted. 'Come on, help me.'

They ran to me at the rear of the Land-Rover.

'Try her in second,' I shouted at Louren, and a burst of bullets kicked around my legs stinging them with fragments of stone.

We threw our combined weight on the Land-Rover and it bumped over rough ground, back towards the river.

'Now,' I shouted at Louren. The Land-Rover juddered and slowed and we hurled ourselves against it, keeping it moving against compression.

It fired once. 'Keep going!' I gasped. And abruptly the engine roared into life and we howled with triumph.

'Climb on,' Louren yelled and swung the Land-Rover back towards the trail, but I ran beside him.

'Matches!' I panted.

'What?'

'Give me your matches, damn you.' I snatched them from his hand and ran to the tangled wreckage. Gasoline was dribbling from one of the ruptured tanks and I flicked a match at it. The sucking, roaring torrent of flame licked across my face singeing my eyelashes away, and I turned and ran after the Land-Rover, scrambling in over the tailboard, falling face forward onto the pile of dead and wounded men in the back.

Louren smashed a new route through a belt of scrub thorn, avoiding the mined trail, and then angled back to pick it up further out.

The firing from the ridge died away as the forest blanketed us. I watched the column of black sooty smoke climbing up into the flushed evening sky, pleased that I had denied them the spoils of victory, and suddenly I found myself shaking like a man in high fever. Icy waves of shock and reaction engulfed me.

'Are you all right, Ben?' Louren called to me.

'Yes, I'm fine,' I answered and looked down at the pathetic blanket-wrapped bundles at my feet.

All that night we crawled southwards, jolting and bumping over the rough ground, often losing the track and having to search for it, shivering in the cold of an African night when the wind blew through the shattered windscreen.

In a dawn that was grape-purple and smoky blue I asked Louren to stop the Land-Rover. The troopers helped me to dig a shallow grave in the sandy bottom land between two kopjes. I lifted Xhai out of the Land-Rover still wrapped in the dark grey police blanket and he was as light as a sleeping child in my arms. I laid him in the earth and we stood around in a circle and looked down at him. Blood had soaked through the blanket and dried in a black stain.

I nodded at the troopers. 'All right. Cover him.' They did it quickly and went back to the Land-Rover. It was still cold, and I shivered in my thin cotton shirt. Up on the kopje an old bull baboon barked, his cry boomed across the valley.

I followed the troopers back to the Land-Rover and climbed up beside them. As we drove on I looked back, and saw a herd of buffalo moving down out of the bush. They were grazing, heads down and tails swinging towards Xhai's grave. This was where my brother belonged, with the animals in the wilderness he loved.

'I'm very much afraid that they have slipped back across the river,' the assistant commissioner of police told me. 'There is nothing we would have liked more than to get our hands on this fellow Mageba.'

We had flown out with MacDonald in the police helicopter to Bulawayo two days before. Louren had left me to help the Rhodesian police as best I could while he sent for the Lear and went on direct to Johannesburg. Now I was having a final debriefing at police headquarters, while a charter flight stood by to take me back to the City of the Moon.

The assistant commissioner was a tall man with a military set to his shoulders, and a brush of closely cropped grey hair. His face was seamed and furrowed and burned darkly by a thousand suns. There were ribbons on his chest that I recognized, the emblems of courage and honour.

'He is top of our list of the chaps we'd like to meet, actually. A nasty piece of work, but then you'd know that as well as anybody.' And he turned those steely grey eyes onto me, giving me the feeling that I was being interrogated.

'I know him,' I agreed. My part in the hi-jacking incident was common knowledge.

'What do you make of the man?'

'He is an intelligent man, and he has a presence. There is something about him.' I tried to find the words to describe him. 'He's the type of man who sets out to get what he wants, and the type that other men will follow.'

'Yes,' the assistant commissioner nodded. 'That's a fair summation of our own intelligence. Since he joined them there has been an escalation of hostile activity from our friends across the river.' He sighed, and massaged his iron-grey temples. 'I thought we might have got him this time. They left their dead unburied, and made a run for the river. We could only have missed them by minutes.'

He walked down with me to where a police car waited under the jacaranda trees with their clouds of purple blossom.

'What news have you of MacDonald?' I asked as we stood beside the police car.

'He will be all right. They saved both legs.'

'I am glad.'

'Yes,' agreed the assistant commissioner. 'He is a good type. Wish we had more of them. By the way, Doctor, we would rather you kept mum about this business. We don't like to make too much fuss about these incidents. Rather playing into their hands, you know. Gives them the publicity they want.'

We shook hands and he turned and strode back into the building. As we drove through the busy streets and I saw the smiles on the faces around me I wondered why anybody should want to destroy this society – and if they succeeded, with what would they replace it?

It seemed natural to think then of the City of the Moon. A great civilization, a nation which held dominion over an area the size of Europe, a people who built great cities of stone and sent their ships in trade to the limits of the known world. All that remained of them were the few poor relics which we had so laboriously gleaned. No other continent was so fickle in the succour it gave to men, to raise them up so swiftly and then to pluck them down and devour them so that they were denied even a place in her memory. A cruel land, a savage and merciless land. It was a wonder that so many of us loved her so deeply.

My return to the City of the Moon was disappointing. After the events of the last few days it was an anti-climax. It seemed that the others had hardly noticed my absence.

'Did you enjoy yourself?' Sally asked over the typewriter and a pile of translation sheets.

'Well, it was interesting.'

'That's good. What happened to your eyelashes?' she asked and without waiting for an answer began pounding the keyboard with two fingers, biting her tongue with concentration, pausing only to push her hair off her cheek with the back of one hand.

'Glad you are back, Ben,' said Eldridge Hamilton. 'I've been wanting to talk to you about this.' And he led me to a table on which a portion of one of the scrolls was spread. I didn't seem to be able to concentrate. Suddenly, for the first time in my life I felt that it was ancient and unimportant compared with the blood that I so recently had seen spurt fresh and red.

Ral and Leslie had obviously used my absence to scheme out an approach. Ral spoke for both of them, with Leslie prompting him when he faltered. 'So you see, Doctor, we don't feel it's right to marry until at least one of us has a steady job. So, well, we thought we'd sort of ask your advice. I mean we love it here, both of us. We'd like to stay on, but we'd also like to get married. It's just that, well, we've got such a high opinion of you, Doctor. We wouldn't like to miss the rest of the investigation, but—'

I spoke to Louren that evening and then called them from the supper table.

'The job is worth three and a half thousand, and Leslie will get two. Of course, there is a free flat at the Institute and I'll help you with the furnishing, as a wedding present.'

Leslie kissed Ral, and then me. A novel way in which to accept the offer of employment, I felt.

Ral threw himself into the search of the cliffs with renewed energy, but I spent little time with him. Instead, I began to prepare my address to the Royal Geographical Society. This should have been a labour of love and excitement, but I found myself floundering. There was so much detail in the scrolls, but all of it seemed irrelevant to those unanswerable questions: where did they come from and when, where did they go to, and why?

Each time, my efforts became so long-winded and convoluted that they bored even me. Then I would rip the sheets from my typewriter, ball them and hurl them at the wall. There is no more lonely place in the world than a blank sheet of paper, and it frightened me that my unruly emotions should intrude and prevent me marshalling my thoughts and facts in orderly ranks. I told myself that it was reaction from the horrors of our journey to the north, that Sally's enigmatic behaviour was worrying me deeply, that it was merely the fear of the imminent confrontation with my enemies.

I tried all the tricks, forcing myself to sit at the typewriter until I had completed 10,000 words or rising at midnight to try and shake loose a flow of words from my stalled brain.

The address remained unwritten, and I found myself mooning about my office polishing the great battle-axe until it gleamed and glittered, painful to the eye, or strumming fitfully on my guitar and composing new songs which all seemed sad and mournful. At other times I would sit for hours before the painting of the white king, dreaming and withdrawn, or I would wander all day along the cliffs, oblivious of the sun and the heat, and it seemed that often a little bird-like presence was near me, moving like a mischievous brown sprite just beyond the fringe of my vision. Or again, I would sit alone in the dim depths of the archives, deep in a trance of despair as I remembered the hatred in Timothy's smoky eyes as he glared at me across the water-course where the dead men lay. Neither Timothy nor I were all of what we seemed to be, there were dark and ugly depths in both of us. I remembered the savagely mauled bodies of the tiny bushmen left lying for the birds, and my own screaming madness as I cut down the running men on the white sand of the river-bed. I do not know how long my despondency might have lasted except for the discovery which uncovered the answer to so many of the mysteries that still shrouded our city.

Eldridge's team had been countering my apathy by an accelerated advance through the scrolls. Practice had sharpened Sally's grasp of the language, until she was as quick and as fluent as Eldridge himself. Even Leslie was now able to make an appreciable contribution to the work, while Eldridge had arrived by a process of trial and error at the most suitable method of unrolling and preserving our scrolls and he was now saving a great deal of time in this procedure.

At breakfast, which seemed to be the only time we spent together these days, Eldridge asked me to resume the work of removing the pottery jars from the archives. To be truthful I welcomed the excuse not to have to face the blank accusing stare of the sheet of paper in my typewriter, and Ral seemed as pleased to have a change from his fruitless search of the cliffs.

In the cool, peaceful gloom of the archives we worked in our established routine, photographing and marking the position of each jar after we had labelled it and entered it in the master notebook. The work was unexacting, and Ral did most of the talking for my mood of lethargy still persisted. Ral lifted down another of the jars from its slab, and then he peered curiously into the space beyond where the wall opened into a square stone cupboard.

'Hello,' Ral exclaimed. 'What's this?' And I felt my lethargy fall away like a discarded article of clothing. I hurried across to him and I had a feeling of pre-knowledge as I stared at the row of smaller, squatter jars of the same pottery which had been hidden away in this carefully prepared recess. I knew that we had made another major advance, a significant step forward in our search for the ancient secrets. This idea came into my mind fully formed, it was as though I had simply mislaid these small jars and now I had rediscovered them.

Ral moved the arc-light to obtain a better lighting of the recess, and immediately we noticed another unusual feature. Each of the jars that we could see were sealed – a loop of plaited gold wire linked lid and body of the jar, and a clay seal bore the imprinted figure of a bird. I leaned forward and gently blew away the dust that obscured the impression on the seal. It was of the crouching vulture, the classical soapstone bird of the Zimbabwe culture with its base of sun discs and rays. It came as a distinct shock to find this emblem of modern Rhodesia upon a seal of indisputably Punic origin 2,000 years old, as it would be to find the lion and unicorn of the British coat of arms in an Egyptian tomb of the twentieth dynasty.

We worked as quickly as was reconcilable with accuracy; labelling and photographing the large jars which obscured the recess, and when we lifted them down we discovered that there were five of the smaller jars concealed behind them. All this time my excitement had been increasing, my hope of a major discovery becoming more certain. The concealment of the jars, and the seals indicated their importance. It was as though I had been marking time, waiting for these jars, and my spirits surged. When finally we were ready to remove them from the recess, I reserved this honour for myself despite Ral's protests of, 'But I found them!'

Balancing on the top rungs of the step-ladder, I reached in and attempted to lift the first of them.

'It's stuck,' I said, as the jar sat immovably on its slab of stone. 'They must have bolted it down.' And I leaned further into the recess and carefully groped behind the jar for the fixings which held it in place. I was surprised to find that there were none.

'Try one of the others,' Ral suggested, breathing heavily on the back of my neck from his lofty perch atop those lanky legs. 'Can I give you a hand?'

'Look, Ral, if you don't give me a bit of room you're going to suffocate me.'

'Sorry, Doc,' he muttered, moving back a full quarter of an inch.

I tried the next jar and found that it was also solidly anchored to the shelf, as were the next three.

'That's very odd,' Ral understated the position, and I returned to the first jar, and bracing my elbows on the edge of the shelf I began to twist it in an anti-clockwise direction. It required my full strength, and the muscles bulged and knotted in my forearms before the jar moved. It slid towards me an inch, and immediately I realized that the jar was held down on the slab not by bolts but by its own immense weight. It was fifty times heavier than the jars twice its size.

'Ral,' I said. 'You are going to have to give me a hand, after all.'

Between us we moved the jar to the front edge of the shelf, and then I cradled it in my arms like a new-born infant and lifted it down. Later we found that it weighed 122 pounds avoirdupois, and was not much bigger than a magnum of champagne.

Gently Ral helped me to settle it into the fibre-glass cradle we had designed for transporting the jars. We each took a handle and carried it down the archives, out through the access tunnel and past the guard post at the entrance. I was surprised to find it was already dark, and the stars were pricks of light in the high opening above the emerald pool.

Our disparity of heights made it awkward carrying the cradle, but we hurried down the rock passage and down towards the camp. I was relieved to see that lights still burned in the repository. When Ral and I carried in our precious burden the others hardly glanced up from their work.

I winked at Ral, and we carried the jar to the main workbench. Concealing it with our bodies, we lifted it out of the cradle and stood it in the centre of the bench. Then I turned back to the three bent heads across the room.

'Eldridge, would you mind having a look at this one.'

'One moment.' Eldridge went on poring over an unrolled scroll with his magnifying glass, and Ral and I waited patiently until at last he laid the glass aside and looked up. Like I had, he reacted immediately. I saw the glitter of his spectacles, the rosy glow suffuse his bald pate like sunset on the dome of the Taj Mahal. He came quickly to the bench.

'Where did you find it? How many are there? It's sealed!' His hand was actually trembling as he touched the clay tablet. His tone alerted the girls and they almost ran to join us. We stood about the jar in a reverent circle.

'Open it.' Sally broke the short silence.

'It's almost dinner-time.' I glanced at my watch. 'We had better leave it until tomorrow,' I suggested mildly, and both girls turned on me furiously.

'We can't,' Sally began, then she saw my expression, and relief flooded her face. 'You shouldn't joke about things like that,' she told me sternly.

'Well, Professor Hamilton, what are we waiting for?' I asked.

'What indeed?' he demanded, and the two of us went to work on the seal. We used a pair of side-cutters to nip the gold wire, and then carefully worked the seal loose. The lid lifted easily, and there was the usual linen-wrapped cylinder. However, there was not a suggestion of the unpleasant leathery odour. Eldridge, whose arms are like a pair of thin white candles, was unable to lift the jar. I tilted it carefully onto its side, and while he steadied it I withdrew the weighty roll. The wrapping was well preserved and folded off in one piece.

Nobody spoke as we stared at the exposed cylinder. I had guessed what it would contain. There is only one material which is that heavy, but it was still a delicious thrill to have my expectations realized.

It was another writing scroll, but it was not of leather. This scroll was a continuous rolled sheet of pure gold. It was one-sixteenth of an inch thick, eighteen inches wide and a fraction over twenty-eight feet long. It weighed 1,954 fine ounces with an intrinsic value of over $85,000. There were five of them – $425,000, but this was a fraction of the value of the contents.

The beautifully mellow metal unrolled readily as though eager to impart its ancient secrets to us. The characters had been cut with a craftsman's skill into the metal with a sharp engraver's tool, but the reflected light from its surface dazzled the reader.

We all watched with complete fascination as Eldridge spread lamp black across the blinding surface and then carefully wiped off the excess. Each character stood out now, etched in black against the golden background. He adjusted his spectacles, and pored deliberately over the cramped lines of Punic. He started making non-committal grunts and murmurs, while we crowded closer, like children at story-time.

I think I spoke for all of us when at last I blurted out, 'For God's sake, read the bloody thing!'

Eldridge looked up, and grinned wickedly at me. 'This is very interesting.' He kept us all in aching suspense for a few seconds longer while he lit a cigarette. Then he began to read. It was immediately clear that we had chosen the first scroll in a series, and that Eldridge was reading the author's note.

'Go thou unto my store and take from thence five hundred fingers of the finest gold of Opet. Fashion therefrom a scroll that will not corrupt, that these songs may live for ever. That the glory of our nation may live for ever in the words of our beloved Huy, son of Amon, High Priest of Baal and favourite of Astarte, bearer of the cup of life and Axeman of all the Gods. Let men read his words and rejoice as I have rejoiced, let men hear his songs and weep as I have wept, let his laughter echo down all the years and his wisdom live for ever.

'Thus spoke Lannon Hycanus, forty-seventh Gry-Lion of Opet, King of Punt and the four Kingdoms, ruler of the southern seas and keeper of the waterways, lord of the plains of grass and the mountains beyond.'

Eldridge stopped reading, and looked about the circle of our intent faces. We were all silent. This was something far removed from the dry accounts, the list of trade and the Council orders. This scroll was imbued with the very breath, the essence of a people and a land.

'Wow!' Ral whispered. 'They had a pretty good press agent.' And I felt irritation scratch across my nerves at this irreverence.

'Go on,' I said, and Eldridge nodded. He crushed out the stub of his cigarette in the ashtray at his elbow and began to read again. Pausing only to unroll and lamp-black each new turn of the scroll, he read on steadily while we listened, completely entranced. The hours fled on nimble feet, as we heard the poems of Huy Ben-Amon sung again after 2,000 years.

Opet had produced her first philosopher and historian. As I listened to the words of this long-dead poet, I felt a curious kinship of the spirit with him. I understood his pride and petty conceits, I admired his bold vision, forgave his wilder flights of fancy and his more obvious exaggerations, and was held captive by the story-web he wove about me.

His story began with Carthage surrounded by the wolves of Rome, besieged and bleeding, as the legions of Scipio Aemilianus pressed forward on her walls to the chant of 'Carthage must die'.

He told us how Hasdrubal sent a swift ship flying along the shore of the Mediterranean to where Hamilcar, the last scion of the Barcas, a family long since fallen from power and politics, lay with a war fleet of fifty-seven great ships off Hippo on the north African coast.

How the besieged leader called for succour and of the storm and adverse winds that denied it to him. Scipio broke through into the city, and Hasdrubal died with a reeking sword in his hand hacked to pieces by the Roman legionaries below the great altar in the temple of Ashmun upon the hill.

As Eldridge paused, I spoke for the first time in half an hour.

'That gives us our first date. The third Punic war and the final destruction of Carthage, 146 B.C.'

'I think you'll find that is also about the date point for the Opet calendar,' Eldridge agreed.

'Go on,' said Sally. 'Please go on.'

Two biremes escaped the carnage, the sack and rape of Carthage. They fled with the great winds to where Hamilcar lay fretting and storm-bound at Hippo and they told him how Hasdrubal had died and how Scipio had dedicated the city to the infernal gods, had burned it and thrown down the walls, how he had sold the 50,000 survivors into slavery and had sowed the fields with salt and forbidden under pain of death any man to live amongst the ruins.

'So great a hatred, so cruel a deed, could only spring from the heart of a Roman,' cried the poet, and Barca Hamilcar mourned Carthage for twenty days and twenty nights before he sent for his sea captains.

They came to him all nine of them, and Huy the poet named them, Zadal, Hanis, Philo, Habbakuk Lal and the others. Some would fight but most would fly, for how could this pitiful remnant of Carthaginian power stand against the legions of Rome and her terrible fleet of galleys?

There seemed to be no sanctuary for a Carthaginian, Rome ground all the world beneath her armoured heels. Then Habbakuk Lal, the old sea lion and master navigator, reminded them of the voyage that Hanno had made 300 years before beyond the gates of Hercules to a land where the seasons were inverted, gold grew like flowers upon the rocks, and elephants lived in great herds upon the plains. They had all of them read the account that Hanno had written of his voyage inscribed on tablets in the great temple of Baal Hammon at Carthage, now destroyed by Rome. They recalled how he spoke of a river and a mighty lake, where a gentle yellow people had welcomed him and traded gold and ivory for beads and cloth, and how he had lingered there to repair his ships and plant a harvest of corn.

'It is a good land,' he had written. 'And rich.'

Thus in the first year of the exodus Barca Hamilcar had led a fleet of fifty-nine great ships, each with 150 oarsmen and officers aboard, westward beneath the towering gates of Hercules and then southward into an unknown sea. With him went 9,000 men, women and children. The voyage lasted two years, as they made slow progress down the western coast of Africa. There were a thousand hardships and dangers to meet and overcome. Savage tribes of black men, animals and disease when they landed, and shoals and currents, winds and calms upon the sea.

Two years after setting out they sailed into the mouth of a wide, placid river and journeyed up it for sixteen days, dragging their ships bodily through the shallows, until finally they reached the mighty lake of which Hanno had written. They landed upon the furthest shore under a tall red cliff of stone, and Barca Hamilcar died of the shaking fever which he had carried with him from the pestilential lands of the north. His infant son Lannon Hamilcar was chosen as the new king and the nine admirals were his councillors. They named their new land Opet, after the legendary land of gold, and they began to build their first city at a place where a deep pool of water sprang from the cliffs. The pool and the city were dedicated to the goddess Astarte.

'My God, it's four o'clock.' Ral Davidson broke the spell which had held us all for most of the night, and I realized how tired I was, emotionally and physically exhausted, but well content. I had found my Pliny, now I could go to London in triumph. I had it all.

How swiftly the days passed now. I was at work each morning before sunrise. My typewriter clattered steadily and the filled sheets piled up beside it. I worked until noon each day, and spent the afternoons and evenings in the repository. Listening to the songs from the golden books of the poet Huy. There was no question that the translation could be completed before April the first. Indeed we would be lucky to have the two first scrolls out of the five completed by then. There was equally no possibility that we could postpone the symposium that had been approved by the Council of the Royal Geographical Society for that date. The public relations office of the London branch of Anglo-Sturvesant had completed the arrangements, invitations had been issued and accepted, accommodation, transport and a hundred other details had been arranged and confirmed.

It was in a race to marshal and present as much of this incredible plethora of facts and legend as I could in the time left to me. Always I must guard against the temptation to romanticize my subject. The words of Huy were inflammatory to my emotions, I wanted to copy his ebullient style, to laud his heroes and castigate the villains as he did. All of us at the City of the Moon were becoming deeply involved in the story, even Eldridge Hamilton, who was the only one of us not of Africa, was caught up in the grandeur of it. While to the rest of us for whom Africa was, academically and emotionally, the well of our existence, these songs were a compulsive living cavalcade.

How often I found our recent history but an echo of the endeavours and adventures of these men of Opet. How closely they seemed linked to us despite the passage of nearly 2,000 years.

For the first five years the settlement on the shores of the lake prospered. The buildings were of log and mud, the men of Opet came to terms with their new land. They fell into a trading relationship with the Yuye. These were the yellow people that Hanno had described 300 years before, tall graceful men with slanted eyes and delicate features. Clearly they were the ancestors of the Hottentots. They were a pastoral people, with herds of goats and small scrub cattle. They were also hunters and trappers, and gatherers of the flakes of alluvial gold from the gravel beds of the rivers. In the name of the infant king, Habbakuk Lal concluded a treaty with Yuye, King of the Yuye. A treaty that granted all the land between the great river and the hills of Tuya to the men of Opet in return for five bolts of linen and twenty swords of iron.

Well satisfied, Habbakuk Lal, to whom the set and scent of the sea were as the coursing of blood through his own veins, returned with five of his swiftest ships laden with the gold and ivory of Opet to the middle sea. He completed the return journey in nine months, setting up staging posts along the western shores of Africa, and returned with a cargo of beads and linen and the luxuries of civilization. He had pioneered the trade route along which the treasures of southern Africa would pour to the known world, but ever wary of Rome's vengeful eye he covered his tracks like the crafty old sea-fox he was.

He brought with him also new recruits for the colony at Opet. Metallurgists, masons, shipbuilders and gentlemen adventurers. However, the trickle of Yuye gold and ivory shrivelled as the accumulated stores of ages were exhausted. Habbakuk Lal led a company of 100 men to the city of Yuye. He sought the right to prospect and hunt throughout the kingdom of the Yuye, and the king agreed readily, placing his mark at the foot of a leather scroll covered with characters he did not understand. Then he called a feast to entertain his honoured guests. The beer was brought in great gourds, the oxen roasted whole over the pits of glowing coals, and the lithe Yuye maids danced naked, their yellow bodies glistening with oil in the sunlight.

At the height of the revelry Yuye, the king, stood, and pointed his fist at the men whose demands became ever more excessive.

'Kill the white devils,' he cried, and his warriors who had lain in readiness without the mud walls of the city fell upon them.

Habbakuk Lal cut himself a road to safety, his battle-axe swinging in a furious arc about him. Three of his men followed him out, but the rest of them were dragged down and their skulls crushed beneath the war clubs of the Yuye.

Habbakuk Lal and his gallant three outran the warriors that pursued them, and reached the bank of the great river where their ship was moored. Flying on white sails they carried the warning to Opet. When the Yuye regiments, 40,000 strong, swarmed down through the pass of the red cliffs, they found 5,000 men of Opet standing to meet them.

All that day the yellow horde broke like the waves of the sea on the ranks of the Opet archers, and all that day the arrows flew like clouds of locusts. Then at the moment when the Yuye drew back exhausted, their resolve broken, Habbakuk Lal opened his ranks and let his axemen run. Greyhounds on the rabbit, wolves on the sheep herds, they pursued until darkness halted the slaughter. Yuye died in the flames of his burning city, and his people were taken into slavery. This is the law of Africa, a land that favours the strong, where the lion alone walks proud.

Now suddenly the colony which had been quietly establishing itself, putting down its roots and making sure of its base, exploded into growth and bloom.

Her metallurgists sought out the mother lodes of metal, her hunters ranged widely, her ranchers bred the scrub cattle of the Yuye to the blood bulls that Habbakuk Lal's ships brought from the north. Her farmers sowed the corn, and watered it from the lake. To protect her citizens and her gods a start was made on the walls of Opet. The land and its treasures were divided amongst the nine noble families, the sea captains of the exodus, who were now the members of the king's council.

Habbakuk Lal, with his huge frame twisted and tortured by arthritis, and with the flaming red beacon of his hair and beard long ago changed to grey ash, died at last. But his eldest son, already admiral of the fleet of Opet, took his father's name. Another Habbakuk Lal directed the growing fleet of Opet in trade and exploration. His ships still beat the well-worn sea-lanes to the north, but also they voyaged southwards to where the land turned back upon itself and a great flat-topped mountain guarded the southern Cape. Here a sudden gale out of the north-west smashed half the Opet fleet upon the rocks below the mountain. The priests read this as an omen from the gods, and never again would a ship of Opet venture this far southwards.

The centuries pass. Kings take the throne and then pass from it. New customs arise, the ways of the gods and their worship are altered to suit this land, a new breed of man arises from the mixed blood of Opet and Yuye. He is a citizen, but only the noble families may govern. He may enjoy all the privileges and carry all the responsibilities of citizenship, except that of directing the affairs of state. This is reserved for those of the old blood, pure and untainted. As an offshoot of this nobility a clan of warrior priests arises. These are the sons of Amon, and it amused me to learn that the clan has its origin in a man from the old kingdom of Canaan. These priests probably spring from Jewish stock. You cannot keep us out of a good proposition, can you?

New heroes spring up and fight along the borders, or crush a rising of slaves, or slay the wild beasts. The old art of elephant-training is revived, and the king's elephants spearhead his army and lighten the heavy labours of building and mining.

From the golden books we had an occasional exciting flash of physical contact with the past. Huy describes the lay-out of the walls, and the towers of Baal. They tally exactly with the foundations we had exposed. Huy gives the dimensions of walls thirty-five feet high and fifteen thick, and again we wonder how they had disappeared.

At another place he describes a gift of treasure from the Egyptian agents at Cadiz to the Gry-Lion, as the king is now called; amongst the items is a gold cup marvellously worked with the signs of eternal life. It is our chalice found among the ruins of the temple, and that night I went to examine it again. Seeing its battered beauty with new eyes.

Always running through the songs of Huy was the puzzle game of guessing the modern names of the animals and places he mentions. Towns and garrisons had long since gone, or had been reduced to those mysterious piles of old stone which dot the landscape of central Africa. However, we were enthralled to hear how the men of Opet began a search for land where the vine and olive will grow. The oils and wines from the north were more precious than their weight in gold by the time they had completed the journey in the ships of the fifth Habbakuk Lal.

The Gry-Lion's horticulturists and viticulturists discover a range of high mountains far to the east. Mountains of mist and cool pure air. The terracing and developing of the benign slopes begins, with tens of thousands of slaves employed in the project. Living plants in pottery jars are sped southwards in the swiftest ships, then carried on the backs of elephants to the mountains of Zeng, and from them come the sweet red wines of Zeng which the poet Huy so loudly and lovingly extols. Here then is a description of the building of those terraced gardens which cover the Inyanga mountains to this day.

From the descriptions of the animals and wild birds of Punt and the four Kingdoms we could recognize most of them. The sacred sunbird, who carried offerings of meat to Baal, flying upwards into a cloudless sky until it disappeared beyond the range of the human eye was obviously the vulture. Then we realized the significance of the carved vulture birds and the seal on the golden scrolls. The vulture had been taken as the emblem of the warrior priests, the sons of Amon, Ben-Amon. Huy had placed his personal seal on the jars which contained the scrolls.

There were other animals described by the poet which could only be extinct species, types which had vanished in the intervening 2,000 years. Chief of these was the Gry-Lion. For we learned that the king took his title from a real beast. This was a large predatory cat which lived along the southern shores of the lake amongst the reed beds that grew there. As early as the year of Opet 216, laws were passed to protect this animal, already threatened by extinction. This protection was afforded it because of the role it played in the ritual of coronation of a new king; a ceremony which Huy referred to as 'taking the Gry-Lion'. He described it as reddish roan-brown in colour with a face masked in lines of black and white, and standing five feet high at the shoulder. Its eye teeth protruded from its jaw in a set of great curved fangs ten inches long. Despite the doubts of the others as to Huy's veracity, I thought I recognized a description of the giant sabre-toothed lynx. A skeleton of this animal had been discovered amongst the upper level of bones at Sterkfontein caves.

Huy describes how the trade in live animals begins. Their ancient enemy, Rome, is denuding north Africa of lion and rhinoceros and elephant, for use in her circuses. Hanis, the hunter of the southern plains of grass, develops a method of capturing these animals alive and drugging them with a distillation of the seeds of the wild hemp. In a comatose state they are placed aboard the ships of Habbakuk Lal, and sped swiftly northwards from staging-post to post along the coast. Huy reports an unexpectedly high survival rate of fifty per cent, and these fetch atronomical prices for the entertainment of the sensation-hungry populace of Rome.

In the Opet year of 450, the nation is at the zenith of her wealth and power, but she has outgrown herself. Her boundaries are extended, her slave population hardly sufficient to support her multifarious enterprises. In desperation the Gry-Lion sends a slaving expedition for ten days' march to the north of the great river. Hasmon Ben-Amon returns with 500 superb black Nubian captives, and claims his reward from the Gry-Lion.

We had reached the end of Huy Ben-Amon's second golden book, and the Lear was waiting for us. Reluctantly we had to interrupt our readings and go.

Leaving Ral and Leslie to supervise the site, Eldridge, Sally and I flew out to meet the international flight from Luanda. We had to pay the excess on 200 lb. of overweight luggage, and the fare of the Botswana Police Inspector sent by his Government to guard their interests in the ancient relics we carried with us.

In London we had one free day, one precious day to ourselves and as usual I tried to do it all. The crocuses were out on the lawns of Lincolns Inn Fields, the bitter at the Barley Mow in Duke Street tasted better than I remembered, and the new crop of girls in the King's Road were prettier than the last. When the National Gallery closed at six o'clock Sally and I took a cab directly to San Lorenzo in Beauchamp Place and ate Lorenzo's wonderful ossobucco washed down with red Chianti. We were only just in time for the curtain at the Queen's Theatre. It was all so different from our life at the City of the Moon.

By the time we returned to the Dorchester it was after midnight, but Sally was still wrought-up with the first impact of that fabulous city.

'I'm too excited to sleep yet, Ben. What shall we do?'

'Well, I've got a bottle of champagne in my suite,' I hinted, and she looked at me with an amused twinkle in her eyes.

'Ben Kazin, my favourite boy scout. Always prepared. Okay, let's go drink it.'

It was Krug, very pale and dry. When the bottle was half finished we made love for the first time in six months. If it were possible this was for me a more cataclysmic experience than our first time. Afterwards I lay exhausted physically and spiritually, and it was Sally who took the empty glasses and carried them through into the lounge. She came back with the brimming pale wine and stood over me naked, and lovely.

'I don't know why I did that,' she said, and gave me a tulip-shaped glass.

'Are you sorry?' I asked.

'No, Ben. I have never regretted anything between us. I only wish—' But she stopped and instead she sipped at her glass and sat down beside me on the bed.

'You know that I love you,' I said.

'Yes.' She looked at me with an expression I could not fathom.

'I will always love you,' I said.

'No matter what?' she asked.

'No matter what,' I told her.

'I believe you, Ben,' she nodded, her eyes dark brooding green. 'Thank you.'

'Sally—' I began again, but she placed one long tapered finger on my lips, and shook her head so the soft dark wings of her hair swung against her cheeks.

'Be patient, Ben. Please be patient.' But I lifted her finger from my mouth.

'Sally—' She leaned forward and silenced my lips with hers. Still holding the kiss she placed her glass on the floor beside my bed, she took mine from my unresisting fingers and placed it beside hers. Then she made love to me with such devastating skill and subtlety that there were no questions nor protests left in me.

At nine o'clock the next morning I got Sally into a taxi headed for Elizabeth Arden in Bond Street, a little apprehensive as to what would happen to that dark silky head of hers. What some of those faggots do to a pretty girl they should be hanged for. Then I climbed into another taxi and headed for the M4 and Heathrow to become snarled in one of those traffic jams which make British motoring such a leisurely and soothing experience.

Louren's flight had landed by the time I paid off my taxi and ran through into the International Terminal, that seething cauldron of humanity.

I heard someone in the crowd exclaim, 'It must be Dicky and Liz!' and I was immediately alerted to the whereabouts of the Sturvesant party. With the limited horizon that I have from my altitude above ground, I am forced to rely on these gratuitous sighting reports.

I fought my way through to the entourage which had been mistaken for that of the Burtons, and realized that the error was excusable. This was Louren Sturvesant travelling heavy, in the grand manner, with his fore-riders running interference and clearing a path for the doors. There was a light screen of the gentlemen of the Press skirmishing along the flanks of the advance, but unable to break through the ranks of B.Y.M. Their methods were too conventional. I got into a head-on position and went in low and dirty, and there were a few yelps and cries of, 'Watch that one,' and, 'Get him,' which changed quickly to, 'Sorry, Doctor.'

And I was through into the soft centre. Bobby Sturvesant let out a shriek and landed around my neck, and the entire advance broke down for the minute it took for us to accomplish the greeting ceremony. Hilary was in a soft wrap of honey mink which was made to look shabby by the lustre of her hair, and over her towered Louren, his mane of hair sun-bleached to white gold and his face burned dark nut-brown.

'Ben, you old bastard.' He grabbed me around the shoulder. 'Thank God you made it. Will you look after Hil and the kids for me. I've got a few things to clear up, then I'll see you back at the Dorchester.' ·

There were two long shiny black limousines waiting under the portico and the party split neatly, but not before Louren had doubled back to tell me proudly, 'I got a black marlin in the Seychelles – 900-pounder, Ben. A real beauty.'

'That's the tiger,' I congratulated him.

'Get out the Glen Grant, sport. I won't be long.'

I sat in the jump seat opposite Hilary, having beaten one of the B.Y.M. to it, and I was delighted to see how radiant she looked. It was that bright shiny look of happiness which you cannot fake with cosmetics and eye-liner.

'We had ten days on the islands, Ben. It was wonderful.' She went all misty and soft at the memory. 'Our anniversary. Look!' And she held up her left hand which was overburdened with a ring of red gold and a solitaire diamond. I was accustomed to Louren's style of living, but even I blinked. The diamond was bluey-white in colour and looked good, it was certainly not a shade less than twenty-five carats.

'It's beautiful, Hilary.' And for no good reason I thought, 'The deeper the guilt, the bigger the gift.'

When we reached the Dorchester Hilary gasped and covered her mouth with surprise at the baroque super-abundance of the Oliver Messel suite.

'It's not true, Ben,' she laughed. 'It just can't be!'

'Don't laugh,' I warned her. 'We must be costing Louren over £100 per day.'

'Wow!' She flopped into one of the enormous armchairs. 'You can get a drink, Ben, my love. I need it.'

While I poured I asked unnecessarily, 'Your problems were of a temporary nature then, Hil?'

'I have forgotten I ever had any, Ben. He's better than he ever was.'

When Louren arrived I saw what she meant. He was in high humour, laughing and restless with energy, sleek and hard and tanned. He disposed of the last two B.Y.M. while I poured him a Glen Grant, then he threw his coat and tie over a chair, rolled his sleeves up over brown bulging muscle and settled with the drink.

'Okay, Ben. Show it to me.' And we plunged into an examination and discussion of the scrolls and their translation.

Louren picked on the first line of the first page.

'Go thou unto my store and take from thence five hundred fingers of the finest gold—' He repeated the line, then looked up at me. 'That's right from the old boy's mouth, Ben. *My store*! That's his treasury. That clot Hamilton mistranslated it. It should read "treasury".'

'Suddenly your Punic is pretty hot,' I commended him.

'Well, for cat's sake, Ben, when did you ever send down to a store for your gold?' He tasted the Glen Grant. 'If your theories are correct—'

'Don't give me that *if* bit, Lo. Your name is not Wilfred Snell.'

'All right, let's accept that there was a violent and sudden death to our city. Fire and dead men, the archives which they obviously held so dear are untouched, then there is a better than ever chance the treasury was untouched also. We've just got to find it.'

'Great!' I nodded, and grinned sarcastically. 'This is a major breakthrough. I've been breaking my heart searching for it these last six months.'

'It's there, Ben.' He did not answer my grin.

'Where, Lo? Where?'

'Close. Somewhere within the main walls, probably within the cavern area.'

'Hell, Lo. I've been over every inch of it fifty times.' I spoke with mild but rising irritation.

'And when you've been over it for the hundredth time, you'll realize how blind you've been.'

'Damn it, Lo!' I started. 'I don't think—'

'Get yourself a drink, partner, before you blow up.'

I did as he advised, and Louren went on. 'I'm not knocking what you've done, Ben. But let me just remind you that in 1909 Theodore Davis ended his book by saying, "I fear that the valley of the kings is now exhausted."'

'Yes, I know, Lo, but—'

Ignoring me Louren went on, 'And it was thirteen years later that Howard Carter discovered the tomb of Tutankhamen, the greatest treasure that the valley had ever yielded.'

'Nobody is talking about giving up the search, Lo. I'll go on just as long as you keep paying.'

'And I'll bet that my cheque book is more tenacious than your resolve.'

'That's a bad bet,' I warned him, and we were laughing again.

We parted in the middle of the afternoon. Louren being borne away in a flood of B.Y.M., across the lobby to where a black Rolls waited in front of the hotel, and I slipping out the side entrance to hail my own taxi in Park Lane.

Eldridge Hamilton was waiting for me on the pavement outside the Royal Geographical Society, having motored up from Oxford in his bright red mini.

He was dressed as always in his tweed with the elbow patches, but was feverish with anticipation of the morrow.

'I can hardly wait for it, Ben,' he chortled with malicious glee. 'Have they arrived at the hotel yet?'

'No, but Snell is due in this evening.'

Eldridge did a little hop and skip of excitement and said. 'Like a hippopotamus lumbering into the dead fall.' Cruel but apt, I thought, and we went up through the double oaken doors into the panelled hall which is a high temple of our profession. There is a hushed dignity about the building which I find reassuring and permanent in this insane and transitory modern world.

Side by side we climbed the sweeping staircase, past the portraits of great men and the lists of former medallists honoured by the Society.

'You'll have to give some thought as to who should paint you, Ben.' Eldridge indicated the portraits. 'They do say this foreign Johnny – what's his name, Annigoni? – is not too bad.'

'Don't talk tripe,' I snapped, and he let out one of those startling neighs of laughter that rang like a bugle call through the hallowed precincts. I was irritated by Elddrige's assault on one of my most private and treasured fantasies. I am a modest and almost painfully retiring person, but the very first time I had entered here, and looked up at the portraits, I had imagined my own dark visage peering down from the wall of honour. I had even selected the pose – seated to avoid undue emphasis on my body, with my head turned half away. I have a good right-hand profile. There would be a flecking of dignified grey at the temples, a gay little ribbon of some foreign decoration in my lapel, Legion of Honour, perhaps. The expression pensive, the brow furrowed . . .

'Come on,' said Eldridge, and we went to where the President and a handful of Council Members waited for us with sherry and biscuits, and not a decent whisky in sight. Nevertheless, I was aware that these gentlemen had it in their power to make into reality my imaginings of a few minutes previously. I set out to be as affable and charming as is possible, and it seemed to have the desired effect.

We discussed the opening of the symposium, which was set for two-thirty the following afternoon.

'His Grace will make the opening address,' one of them explained. 'We've asked him to keep it down to forty-five minutes, and if possible to avoid reference to orchid-growing or steeple-chasing.'

I would then read my paper. It would rank as a follow-on to the one I had read six years earlier, 'The Mediterranean Influence on Central and Southern Africa of the Pre-Christian Era', the paper which had afforded Wilfred Snell and his pack so much sport. They had set aside four hours for me.

Eldridge would read his paper the following morning, 'Certain ancient writings and symbols of south-western African origin.' The title Eldridge had chosen was purposely vague, so as not to telegraph my punch.

Eldridge and I reassured ourselves that the exhibits we had brought with us from Africa were safe in the strong-room of the Society, then Eldridge gave me a bad attack of the shakes by driving me back to the Dorchester through London's rush-hour traffic in his satanical red mini. We were carried around Hyde Park Corner four times, with Eldridge cursing fluently and his bald head shining like a warning beacon while I hung terrified to the door handle ready to bale out, before Eldridge managed to break out of the traffic stream into Park Lane.

I led him, both of us still palpitating, into the cocktail bar and shot a pair of double Gilbeys into him, and then left him. I had plans for the evening and it was already past six.

Sally came out of the lifts as I approached them. I mentally apologized to her hairdresser. He had let it lie, still loose and cloudy. They had wrought some sort of magic with her face also. It was all eyes and soft pink mouth. She had on a full-length dress of a floating green material that picked up the green of those eyes.

'Ben,' she came to me quickly. 'I'm so glad I found you. I left a note for you under your door. About this evening, I'm terribly afraid that I won't be able to make it, Ben. I'm sorry.'

'That's all right, Sal. It wasn't definite anyway.' I told her, hiding my disappointment behind a grin as my plans collapsed like soggy pastry.

'I have to see them. They are old friends, Ben. They've come all the way from Brighton.'

I went up to Louren's suite, and hung around waiting for him to return, chatting to Hilary and the children. At seven-thirty he phoned, and Hilary put me on after she had spoken to him.

'I was hoping we could have had dinner, Ben, but I'm screwed up here for heaven knows how long. They have made a complete hash of the tax clause in the contract. We are trying to redraft it. Why don't you take Hilary for dinner, instead?'

But she pleaded exhaustion, and announced her intentions of making it an early night. I ate alone at Isow's, a real kosher meal begun with chopped liver and onions. Afterwards I crossed the alley to Raymond's, and for five pounds watched the loveliest girls in London taking off their clothes. It was a distressing experience. It made me feel even more lonely and despondent, and afterwards, though I am not a lecher, I teetered on the edge of temptation when the girls beckoned from the dark doorways in Wardour Street.

I rang Sally's room when I got in a few minutes before midnight, and again an hour later when I had given up my efforts at sleep. Neither call was answered, and the telephone buzzed dismally like an insect sending out an unanswered mating call. It was almost morning before I found sleep.

Louren woke me, boorishly healthy and hearty at eight, bellowing into the phone, 'It's the big day, Ben. Come and have breakfast up here. I'll order it now, what do you want?'

'Coffee,' I mumbled, and when I arrived in his suite he had a huge platter of steak and bacon, kidneys and eggs, with smoked kippers and porridge to start and toast, marmalade and coffee to end it. An average sort of breakfast for Louren.

'You are going to need your strength, partner. Get in there and eat, boy.'

With my spirits bolstered by this solid bulwark, I was carried through the morning on a cresting wave of expectation and I felt like a lion when we went down to meet our guests at noon. When I say lion, I mean a man-eating lion. I had anointed my smoothly shaven cheeks with a double handful of Dior aftershave, I wore my dark cashmere suit with a white shirt and maroon tie, and Hilary had found a carnation for my button-hole. I smelt like a rose garden, and there was an eager snap to my step and the hunter's warm thrill in my belly.

Louren and I entered the private lounge together, and the buzz of conversation dwindled. I don't pretend that my entrance to a room can command silence, but Louren's certainly can. Only one voice continued raised; in a convincing imitation of the British upper class, it brayed across the lounge. Wilfred Snell stood in a circle of his sycophants, towering above them much bigger than life size, almost like a badly executed monument to himself. His legs were set apart and his body braced in the stance of a heavily pregnant woman to counter-balance his monstrous gut. It was as though he carried a half-filled winesack under his vest. The expanse of pearl-grey suiting material necessary to cover this bulge was as vast as a theatre curtain. His face hung down on his chest in a series of chins like the ripples on a pond. It was white and soft-looking as though a plastic skin had been filled with dirty milk. His mouth was a deep purple gash in the whiteness, loose, perpetually open, even when he was not talking, which was seldom. His hair was a wild curling bush from which a gentle white rain of dandruff sifted down onto his shoulders and lapels, and he was hung with things – a pair of reading glasses around his neck like a tank commander's binoculars, a golden cigar-cutter from his money pocket, from his lapel a monocle on a black ribbon, a watch chain and key ring.

I approached him obliquely, stopping to greet friends, to chat with colleagues, but moving in on him steadily. Someone put a glass in my hand and I looked around.

'Scotch courage,' Sally smiled at me.

'I don't need it, luv.'

'Let's go talk to him,' she suggested.

'I was sort of making the pleasure last.'

We looked at him openly, this self-appointed drummer of archaeology, whose half-dozen books had sold 500,000 copies, books that aimed at and struck squarely in the centre of popular tastes. Books in which he flirted dangerously with the laws of plagiarism and criminal libel; books in which cant masqueraded as erudition, and facts were squeezed, ignored or subtly altered to suit the argument.

I am not a bitter man, not one who bears grudges, but when I looked at this great bloated executioner, this torturer, this – well, when I looked at him I felt the blood bubble and fizz behind my eyes. I started towards him directly.

He saw me coming, but ignored it. The entire room was aware of what was happening, had probably been anticipating this confrontation since the day they received their invitations. The circle about the master opened giving me space to approach the presence.

'There is no doubt—' Wilfred brayed, his gaze passing several feet over my head. He usually precedes each of his statements with an advertising plug.

'As I have always said—' his voice carried to the furthest corners, and I waited patiently. I have a carefully rehearsed smile which I use at times like this. It is shy, self-effacing.

'It is generally agreed—' Such a recommendation from Wilfred usually means that the theory in question is the subject of a racing controversy.

'To tell the truth—' And he went on to tell a blatant lie.

At last he glanced down, stopped in mid-sentence, screwed his monocle into his eye, and to his delight and surprise, discovered his old friend and colleague Dr. Benjamin Kazin.

'Benjamin, my dear little fellow,' he cried, and the diminutive stung like a dart in the hump of the bull. 'How very good to see you!'

Then Wilfred Snell did a very rash thing. He dangled his great soft white hairy paw languidly in my direction. For an instant I could not believe my good fortune; at the same instant Wilfred remembered the last time we had shaken hands six years before and tried to snatch it back. His reactions are no match for mine, and I had him.

'Wilfred,' I cooed, 'my dear, dear chap.' His hand felt like a glove full of warm jelly, it was only when my fingers had cut in for an inch or two that you could actually feel the bones.

'We were absolutely delighted that you could come,' I told him, and he made a little mooing sound. A few loose drops of spittle spattered from the slack purple lips.

'Did you have a good trip?' I asked, still smiling shyly. Wilfred had begun to do a little jig, skipping from foot to foot. My fingers had almost disappeared in the soft white flesh, I could now feel every knuckle very clearly. It was rather like playing a jelly fish on a trout rod.

'We must make time for a little private chat before the end of the symposium,' I said, and the air started to leak out of Wilfred. He was making a soft hissing sound, and he seemed to shrink, like a punctured balloon. Suddenly I was disgusted with my brutality, my weakness in giving in to it. I let him go, and the return of blood to the abused hand must have been more painful than my treatment of it. He held it tenderly to his chest, his big pansy eyes were filled with tears and his lips trembled like those of a petulant child.

'Come,' I told him gently. 'Let me get you another drink.' And I led him away unprotesting like an elephant and its mahout. However, Wilfred Snell is nothing if not resilient, and he came back strongly. Throughout the luncheon snatches of his monologue carried across to our table. He was 'making no bones about it' and 'letting them in on a little secret' in his best form. From what I could hear he was repeating his conviction as to the medieval age and Bantu origin of the central African ruin system, and was lightly and amusingly debunking my own writings. At one stage I glanced across to see that he had *Ophir* open beside his plate and was reading from it to the general merriment of his table companions.

However, I had another crisis threatening which took all my skill to avert. Sally was my lunch partner and we sat opposite the Sturvesants. Within five seconds of seating ourselves, Sally noticed Hilary's new diamond. She could hardly overlook it, it was throwing slivers of light about the room, bright as arrows. Sally was silent for half the meal, but her eyes were drawn to that flaming jewel every few seconds. The rest of us were vying for an opportunity to speak, and there was much laughter and excited banter. Louren seemed to be especially attentive to Hilary, but suddenly there was a momentary silence.

Sally leaned forward, and in her sweetest voice, told Hilary, 'What a pretty ring. You are so lucky to be able to wear costume jewellery, my dear. My bones are too small. It doesn't suit me, I'm afraid.' And she turned back to me and started chattering brightly. She had ruined the mood with one expert thrust. I saw Louren frown, and flush angrily. Hilary pursed her lips, and I saw a hundred retorts pass in review behind her eyes but she withheld them. I plunged gamely into the void, but even my charm and social grace could not restore the mood. I was relieved when at last Louren glanced at his watch, then looked across at the B.Y.M. who was in charge of the arrangements and nodded. Immediately this gentleman was on his feet, shepherding the unwieldy party out to where the cavalcade of cars waited. As we passed through the lobby, Wilfred Snell cleaved a path to my side with a swarm of his admirers following him in grinning anticipation.

'I was glancing through your book again during lunch. I had forgotten how amusing it was, my dear chap.'

'Thank you, Wilfred,' I replied gratefully. 'That's jolly decent of you to say so.'

'You must sign it for me.'

'I will. I will.'

'Looking forward to your paper this afternoon, my dear little chap.' And again I shuddered with the effort of suppressing my feelings and keeping my voice mild.

'I hope you'll find it as amusing.'

'I am sure I will, Benjamin.' He let go a fruity chuckle and moved off like a crowd. I heard him saying to De Vallos as they climbed into their limousine, 'Mediterranean influence! My God, why not Eskimo while he is about it.'

We went through the park like the mourners at a state funeral, a convoy of black limousines, and turned out of the second gate into Kensington Gore.

We were set down at the door of the Society, and moved into the lecture hall. The speakers and Council Members were on the platform, and the body of the hall filled solidly. Wilfred was in his place, front centre, where I could watch every expression on his face. He was surrounded by his hatchet men.

They led in His Grace, smelling of cigars and good port. They pointed him at the audience like a howitzer, and let him go. In forty-five minutes he had covered orchids, and the steeple-chase season. The President began tugging discreetly at his coat-tails, but it was another twenty minutes before I had my chance.

'Six years ago I had the honour of addressing this Society. My subject was "The Mediterranean Influence on Central and Southern Africa of the Pre-Christian Era". I come before you now with the identical subject, but armed with further evidence that has come to light in the intervening period.'

Every few minutes Wilfred would heave himself around in his seat to address a remark to either Rogers or De Vallos in the row behind him. He used a stage whisper, covering his mouth with his programme. I ignored the distraction and ploughed through my introduction. It was a resumé of all the previously known evidence, and the various theories that had been applied to them. I made it purposely dull, pedestrian, letting Wilfred and his party believe that I had nothing further to support my views.

'Then in March of last year a photograph was shown to me by Mr. Louren Sturvesant.' Now I changed my delivery, let a little electricity come into my tone. I saw a flare of interest in faces which had taken on glazed expressions. I fanned it steadily. Suddenly, I was telling them a detective story. There were longer intervals between Wilfred's pompous asides. The snickers from his admirers died away. I had the audience by the throat now, they were there with Sally and me in the moonlight looking down on the ghostly outlines of a long-dead city. They shared our thrill as we exposed the first blocks of dressed stone.

At the moment when I needed it, the lights were turned down into darkness and the first image was flashed upon the screen behind me.

It was the white king, proud and aloof, regal in his rampant maleness and golden armour. Out of the darkness the images flashed upon the screen. The audience sat in rapt silence, their fascinated faces lit by the reflected glow of the screen, the only movement was the frantic scribbling of the Pressmen in the front row as my voice went on weaving spells about them.

I carried the story to the point where we had investigated the plain and cavern, but had not yet discovered the walled-up tunnel beyond the portrait of the white king.

At my signal the lights went up, and the audience stirred back to the present, all except His Grace who had succumbed to the port and was sleeping like a dead man. He was the only one of two hundred who I had not captivated by my tale. Even Wilfred looked groggy and shaken, like a badly beaten prize fighter trying to rouse himself to meet the gong. I had to accord him a grudging admiration, the man was game to the core. He heaved himself around towards De Vallos and in a penetrating whisper told him:

'Typical Bantu stonework of the thirteenth century A.D., of course. But very interesting. Reinforces my theories about the dating of the immigrations.'

I waited silently, clenched fists on the lectern, my head bowed over it. Sometimes I believe I could have been a truly great motion picture actor. I lifted my head slowly and stared at Wilfred, my expression was desolate. He took heart from it.

'The painting means nothing, of course. To tell you the truth it's probably a Bantu initiation candidate, similar to the White Lady of the Brandberg.'

I maintained my silence, letting him take out line as though he were a marlin. I wanted him to swallow it down deep, before I set the hook.

'There is no new evidence here, I'm afraid.'

He looked around him with a satisfied smirk, and his followers' heads started nodding and grinning like puppets.

I addressed him directly then.

'As Professor Wilfred Snell has just remarked, fascinating as all of this was, it presented no new evidence.' They all nodded more vigorously. 'And so, I determined to look deeper.'

And I was away again into a description of the discovery of the blocked tunnel, the decision to preserve the white king and cut through living rock, the hole through into the tunnel and again I paused, and looked at Wilfred Snell. Suddenly I felt sorry for him; where before he had been my implacable enemy, an open running canker in my professional life, now he was just a fat and rather ridiculous figure.

Like the poet Huy, Axeman of all the Gods, I hacked into him then. Cutting him to pieces with my account of the scrolls, the vulture axe, and the five golden books.

As I spoke, one of the attendants wheeled in a barrow covered with a green velvet cloth. It pulled all their eyes, and at my signal he drew aside the cloth and there lay the great gleaming battle-axe and one of the scrolls.

Wilfred Snell slumped in his seat with his gut in his lap and his purple mouth hanging open slackly while I read the opening words of the first golden book of Huy.

' "Let men read his words and rejoice as I have rejoiced, let men hear his songs and weep as I have wept." '

I ended and looked around at them. They were gripped by the heart strings, every one of them. Even Louren, Hilary and Sally who knew it all were leaning forward in their seats, shiny-eyed and intent.

It was after seven-thirty, I noticed with surprise. I had overrun my time by an hour and there had been no rebuke from the President beside me.

'Our time is finished, but not the story. Tomorrow morning Professor Eldridge Hamilton will read his paper on the scrolls and their contents. I hope you will be able to attend. Your Grace, President, ladies and gentleman, I thank you.'

The silence was complete, nobody moved nor spoke for a full ten seconds, then suddenly they were on their feet applauding wildly. It was the first time since the formation of the Society in 1830 that a paper had been applauded as though it were a stage performance. They came out of their seats, crowding around me to shake my hand and ask their questions which I could not hope to answer. From my vantage-point on the dais I saw Wilfred Snell rise from his seat and lumber ponderously towards the door. He walked alone, his band of followers had left him to join the crowd around me. I wanted to call out to him, to tell that I felt sorry for him, that I wished I could have spared him, but there was nothing to say,. He had said it all a hundred times before.

Every single national paper had it the following morning, and even *The Times* had allowed itself a touch of the dramatic. 'Discovery of Carthaginian Treasure,' it stated, 'one of archaeology's most significant finds since the tomb of Tutankhamen.'

Louren had sent out for them all, and we sat in a sea of newsprint as we ate another of those gargantuan breakfasts. I was touched by Louren's pride in my achievements. He read each article aloud, interspersing his own comments:

'You rocked them, partner.'

'Ben, you murdered the bums.'

'The way you told it, you even had me wetting my pants, and, hell! I was there!'

He picked one of the left-wing tabloids from the pile and opened it. His expression changed immediately. Suddenly he was scowling furiously, a look of such concentrated venom that I asked quickly, 'What is it, Lo?'

'Here.' He almost flung the sheet at me. 'Read it for yourself, while I finish changing.' He went through into the bedroom and slammed the door.

I found it almost immediately. A full-page of photographs under a big banner 'The forces of freedom'- Black men with guns, with tanks. Black men marching, rank upon endless rank. Eggshell helmets like evil toadstools of hatred, modern automatic weapons slung on camouflaged shoulders, booted feet swinging. It was not these that held me. In the centre of the page was a picture of a tall man with shoulders wide as the crosstree of a gallows, and a bald cannon-ball head that shone in the bright African sunshine. He walked unsmiling between two grinning Chinamen in those shabby rumpled uniforms that look like pyjamas.

The caption was in bold lettering: 'The Black Crusader. Major-General Timothy Mageba, the newly appointed commander of the people's Liberation Army with two of his military advisors.'

I felt a sinking sensation of dread as I looked at the brooding hatred in that face, the power and terrible purpose in those set shoulders and thrusting gait.

In some inexplicable fashion it seemed to detract from my own personal triumph. What had happened 2,000 years ago seemed of lessened importance when I looked at the picture of this man, and I thought of the dark forces in movement through the length of my land.

Yet it came to me then that this man was not unique, Africa had bred many like him. The dark destroyers who had strewn her plains with the white bones of men, Chaka, Mzilikazi, Mamatee, Mutesa, and hundreds of others that history had forgotten. Timothy Mageba was only the latest in a long line of warriors which stretched back beyond the shadowy, impenetrable veils of time.

Louren came out of the bedroom, and with him was Hilary. She came to kiss me and congratulate me again, and I dropped the sheet of newspaper from my hand, but not my mind.

'I'm sorry I can't be with you to hear your friend Eldridge this morning, Ben. I can't get out of this meeting. Please look after Hil for me. Give her a good lunch, will you?' Louren told me as the three of us went down in the lift.

Eldridge, in his tweeds and elbow patches, massacred his subject. For three and a half hours he mumbled about 'hangs' and 'abridgements', occasionally letting fly with that laugh of his, a sound which woke the sleepers. I was grateful to him as I looked around the slowly emptying hall, and the doodling yawning members of the Press. He certainly wasn't stealing my glory from me.

An hour before lunch Sally slipped me a note from her seat behind me. 'I can't take any more. Going out to do some shopping. See you. S.'

And I smiled as I watched her slide gracefully out of the side exit. Hilary turned and winked at me, and we both smiled.

Eldridge ground to a slow, inconclusive halt and beamed around at his depleted audience.

'Well,' he said, 'I think that covers just about everything.' And there followed a relieved scramble for the doors.

In the lobby of the Society I was once more surrounded by an enthusiastic mob, and we made slow progress towards the door and our lunch.

When at last we reached the taxi, with Eldridge and myself flanking Hilary on the seat, I was just about to give the driver the address of the Trattoria

Terrazza when Hilary looked down at her hands in her lap and gave a little stricken cry.

'My ring!' And for the first time we noticed that the great jewel was no longer flamed upon her hand. I stared aghast at the naked finger, a fortune beyond my dreams was missing. That diamond must certainly be worth £30,000.

'When did you last have it?' I demanded of her, and after a second's thought a look of relief replaced her worried frown.

'Oh, I remember now. At the hotel, I was painting my nails. I put it in the alabaster cigarette box beside my chair.'

'Which room? Which chair?'

'The lounge, the tapestry chair beside the television set.'

'Eldridge, will you take Mrs. Sturvesant on to the restaurant, please. I'd better take another cab and dash back to the hotel before one of the cleaning staff discovers it. Have you your key with you, Hil?'

She dug into her handbag and came out with the key.

'Ben, you are an old sweetheart. I'm so sorry about this.' And she handed it to me.

'Damsels in distress are my speciality.' I stepped out onto the pavement. They pulled away and for five minutes I behaved like a berserk semaphorist towards the passing stream of taxis. I can never tell if those little yellow lights on top are burning or not, so I flag them all.

I let myself into the Oliver Messel suite with Hilary's key and hurried down that long passage past the bedrooms. With a little grunt of relief I found the ring amongst the cigarettes in the alabaster box. With it in my hand I moved across to the light from the window to admire it for a moment. It was a thing of such brilliant beauty that my stomach turned within me. I felt a fleeting envy, a twinge of unhappiness that I should never own an object of such pure enchantment. Then I pushed the feeling aside and quickly tied the ring into the corner of my handkerchief, and I started back down the passage.

As I came level with the bedroom door I noticed that it was slightly ajar, and I paused with my hand going out towards the handle to draw it closed.

From the room beyond came a woman's voice, a voice husky with emotion, a voice broken by the panting of breath aroused and tremulous.

'Yes, oh God, yes. Do it! Do it!' And a man's voice blended with it, a voice rising in a hoarse cry like a wounded animal.

'Darling! My darling!' The voices washed, and swirled and broke together, the high surf of passion driven by the storm winds of love. With it was another sound, rhythmic, urgent, pounding out the pulse of creation, a sound as old as man, as unchanging as the courses of the stars. As I stood frozen, my hand still out-stretched towards the door handle, the thudding heart-beat of love was arrested and then there was only the sound of ragged breathing and the small sighs and moans of emotions spent and exhausted.

I turned away like a sleep walker. Silently I went to the front door and silently I closed it behind me.

I sat quietly through a lunch I do not remember eating, through conversations I do not remember hearing, for the voices I had heard beyond that door were those of Sally Benator and Louren Sturvesant.

I do not remember the return to the Royal Society, and only vague snatches of the concluding papers and ceremonial remain with me.

I sat in my seat in the front row, hunched down in my chair and stared at a crack in the polished wooden floor. My mind cast back, working over the past like a gun-dog hunting a hidden bird.

I remembered a night at the City of the Moon when I had gone drunk to bed, drunk on whisky poured for me by Sally's own hand. I remembered waking when Louren came into the tent, and seeing the pale flush of dawn in the sky beyond the tent-flap.

I remembered my visit to the cavern in the night, when Louren had dazzled me with the torch beam and sent me away.

I remembered that conversation overheard between Ral and Leslie. I remembered Sally's friends from Brighton, her violent unreasonable attacks on Hilary, her moods and silences, her sudden gaiety and even more sudden depressions, the half-statements, the hovering upon the verge of revelation, the midnight visit to my bedside, and a hundred other clues and hints – and I marvelled at my own blindness. How could I not have seen it, nor sensed it.

My name had been spoken, and I struggled to rouse myself, to try and listen to what was said. It was Graham Hobson, the President of the Society, speaking and looking down at me, smiling. Around me heads were craning, smiling also, friendly kind faces.

'Awarded the Society's Patron's and Founder's Medal,' said Hobson. 'In addition, my Council has instructed me to announce that a sum has been set aside from the fund provided, and that a commission will be awarded to a leading artist to paint a portrait of Dr. Kazin. At an appropriate ceremony the portrait will be hung—'

I shook my head to clear it. I felt fuzzy and stupid. Hobson's voice kept fading and I tried to concentrate. Then gentle but insistent hands were pulling me to my feet, pushing me towards the stage.

'Speech!' they called, laughing, applauding.

I stood before them. I felt dizzy, the room turned and steadied again, blurred and refocused.

'Your Grace,' I began and choked, my throat felt flannelly, the words came out thickly. 'I am honoured.' I stopped and groped for words, they wre silent, expectant. I looked desperately about the hall, seeking deliverance or inspiration.

Sally Benator was standing beside the side entrance. I did not know how long she had been there. She was smiling, white teeth in her sun-brown and lovely face, dark hair hanging in shining wings to her shoulders, her cheeks aflame and eyes sparkling, a girl freshly arisen from the bed of her lover.

I stared at her. 'I am thankful,' I mumbled, and she nodded and smiled encouragement at me – and my heart broke; it was a physical thing, a sharp pain, tissue tearing in my chest, so intense that I caught my breath. I had lost her, my love, my only love, and all these honours, all this acclaim was meaningless.

I stared across at her, desolate and bereft of purpose. I felt the tears flood and burn my eyes. I did not want them all to see it, and I stumbled from the stage towards the door. The applause swelled again, and I heard voices in the tumult.

'Poor fellow, he's completely overcome.'

'How touching.'

'He's overwhelmed.'

And I ran out into the street. It was raining a soft drizzle and I ran wildly. Like a wounded animal I wanted to be alone to recover from this hurt. The cold rain soothed my burning eyes.

I craved solitude and surcease from pain, and I found both at the City of the Moon. Eldridge had a month's lecturing commitments to meet in England, and Sally had disappeared. I had not spoken to her since that night, but Louren told me casually that she had taken two weeks of her accumulated vacation time and had joined a tour to Italy and the Greek Islands. At the City of the Moon an airmail letter from Sally reached me, postmarked Padua, confirming this and regretting that her efforts to see me before I left London had failed. This was not surprising, for I had not returned to the Dorchester, but had my luggage sent to Blue Bird House and flown out on the early morning flight for Africa. Sally sent her congratulations, and ended by saying she would return to Johannesburg at the end of the month and take advantage of the first flight to the City of the Moon.

Reading her letter gave me a feeling of unreality, like receiving a message from beyond the grave. For she was dead to me, gone beyond my reach for ever. I burned the letter.

Louren visited the site for one day. I found that I had nothing to say to him. It was as though we were strangers, his features once so well remembered and beloved, were unfamiliar to me now.

He sensed the gap that separated us, and tried to reach across it. I could not respond, and he cut short his visit and left. I knew his puzzlement, and vaguely I regretted it. I could not find it in myself to blame or hate him.

Ral and Leslie were shadowy figures on the borders of my solitude. They did not intrude in the private world in which I now lived.

This was the world of Huy Ben-Amon, a place beyond pain and sorrow. During the time that Eldridge worked upon the scrolls, I had followed daily each detail of his translation. Language is my greatest talent, it comes to me without effort. Lawrence of Arabia learned to speak Arabic in four days – in ten I had taught myself Punic, and in so doing had gained the key to the fairyland of the golden books of Huy.

The third book was a continuation of the history of Opet up to the lifetime of the poet. This was as fascinating a document as the two that preceded it, but the true magic for me was in the remaining two golden books.

These were the poems and songs of Huy, poems and songs in the modern sense of the words. This was Huy, the warrior, the Axeman of all the Gods, writing an ode to the shiny wing of the bird of the sun, his battle-axe.

He described the ore brought from the mines of the south, and its smelting in the womb-shaped furnace, the smell of the glowing charcoal and the trickle of the molten metal.

How it was purged, and alloyed, forged and shaped, its edging and engraving, and when he described the figures of the four vultures and the four suns I looked up at the great axe that hung above my working desk with wonder.

With Huy I heard the gleaming blade moan in flight, heard the snick of the edge into bone, the sucking withdrawal from living flesh. I read wih awe the list of the enemies who had died beneath it, and wondered at their crimes and transgressions.

Then Huy's mood changed and he was a roistering fellow, tipping back the jug of red Zeng wine, roaring with laughter in the fire light with his companions in arms.

Now he was the dandy dressed in white linen, perfumed with sweet oils, his beard twisted and plaited into ropes.

Now the priest, walking with his gods. Sure of them, tending to their mysteries, and rendering unto them their portion of the sacrifice. Huy kneeling alone in silent prayer, Huy in the dawn lifting his arms in greeting to Baal, the sun-god. Huy in a frenzy of religious revelation.

Then again Huy is the friend, the true companion, describing his joy in the company of another man. The interlock of personalities, the spice of shared pleasures, dangers faced together and overcome. There is a strong hint in this poem that Huy is a hero-worshipper, blind to the faults of his friend, describing his physical beauty with an almost womanly insight. He details the breadth of shoulder, the regal curve of flaming red beard down onto a chest where the muscle bulges smooth and hard as the boulder upon the hills of Zambao, the legs like strong saplings, the smile like the warm blessing of the sun-god Baal, and he ends with the line, 'Lannon Hycanus you are more than King of Opet, you are my friend.' Reading it, I felt that to have the friendship of Huy was to have something of value.

The mood of the poet changes again and he is the observer of nature, the hunter, describing his quarry with loving care, missing no detail, from the curve in the ivory tusk to the creamy softness of a lioness's underbelly.

Then he is a lover, bemused by the beauty of his sweetheart.

Tanith whose wide brow is shining white and full as the moon whose hair blows soft and light as the smoke from the great papyrus fires in the swamps, whose eyes shine green as the deep pool in the temple of the goddess Astarte.

Then suddenly Tanith is dead, and the poet cries his grief, seeing her death as the flight of a bird, her ivory arms gleaming like spread wings, her last cry echoing across the vault of heaven to touch the hearts of the gods themselves. Huy's lament was mine, his voice was mine, his terrors and triumphs became my own, and it seemed that Huy was me, and I was Huy.

I rose early and retired late, I ate little and my face grew gaunt and pale, a haunted face that stared back at me from my mirror with wild eyes.

Then suddenly reality caught up with me, shattering the fragile crystal walls of my fairyland. On the same aircraft Louren and Sally arrived together at the City of the Moon. The torment which I had for so long avoided had now begun again.

Again I tried to hide. I chose the archives as my sanctuary, and spent each day there trying to avoid all contact with either Sally or Louren. Still there was that dreaded hour of the evening meal, trying to smile my way through it and join in the banter and discussion, trying not to notice the private intimate exchange of glances and smiles between Louren and Sally until I could reasonably leave.

Twice Louren came to me.

'There is something wrong, Ben.'

'No, Louren. No. I swear to you. You are mistaken.' And I escaped to the stillness of the archives.

There was Ral's quiet company and the physical labour of cataloguing, photographing and packing the jars, and besides these I found another distraction. This cavern sealed for almost 2,000 years had been sterile, devoid of any life form when first we opened it. Now it was establishing it own ecology, first the tiny midge flies, then sand fleas, ants, spiders, moths, and finally the little brown gecko lizards. I had started making a film record of this colonization of the archives.

I spent many hours a day sitting quietly with my camera poised, waiting to obtain some difficult close-up shot of fly or insect and it was thus that I made the last major discovery at the City of the Moon.

I was working alone at the furthest end of the archives, close by the wall on which was graven the image of the sun. One of the gecko lizards ran down the wall, and across the stone floor. At the spot where the great battle-axe had lain when we discovered it, the lizard stopped. It stood poised, the soft skin of its throat pulsing and its little black beady eyes shiny with expectation. I noticed then the insect it was stalking. A white moth that sat quietly with spread wings on the sun image.

Quickly I reached for my camera, and set the flashbulb and exposure. I was anxious to record one of the lizards in the moment of its kill. Slowly I moved into a position from which I could focus on the moth, and I waited while the lizard approached in a series of swift dashes. Twelve inches from the moth it stopped again, and seemed to gather itself for the final assault. I waited breathlessly, my finger on the trigger button. The lizard shot forward and I exploded the bulb.

The lizard froze with the body of the moth crammed in its mouth. Then it turned and darted head-down towards the floor; when it reached the corner formed by wall and floor it disappeared and I laughed at its ludicrous fright.

I wound the film, replaced the flash bulb, returned the camera to its case, and was about to resume my work when a thought occurred to me. I went back to the end wall of the cavern, to the point where the lizard had disappeared and stooped to examine the juncture of floor and wall. It seemed solid, and I could see no hole or crack for the lizard to use as a refuge. Intrigued now by the lizard's disappearance, I went to fetch one of the electric arc-lights on its cable and I set it so that the beam fully illuminated the wall.

Then on hands and knees I crawled along the wall. I felt my heart start to pound like a war drum, and the hum of blood in my ears, the warmth of it in my cheeks. My hand as I reached for my pen-knife was unsteady, and I nearly broke my thumbnail as I tried to open the blade.

Then I was probing the faint crack line, plugged with dust, that separated wall and floor. The blade of my knife slipped into the crack to its full length.

I rocked back on my heels and stared at the wall, seeing the image of the sun throwing weird shadows in the arc-light.

'Perhaps,' I whispered aloud, 'it's just possible . . .' And then I was grovelling again beneath the image of Baal, almost as though I were one of his worshippers. Frantically I probed the crack, following it along the floor, until abruptly it turned ninety degrees, and climbed the wall. Here the crack was secret-jointed, riveted and turned back onto itself, making it all but invisible. The cunning skill with which this joint had been concealed convinced me that it hid something vital. The workmanship of this piece of the wall was a far cry from the rough joints on the roof slabs through which the dust had filtered down.

Now I jumped up and paced restlessly back and forth before the blank wall. I was alive again for the first time since my return to the City of the Moon. My skin tingled, my step was full of spring, my fists clenched and unclenched and my brain was racing with excitement.

'Louren,' I thought suddenly. 'He should be here.' I almost ran back down the archives, and out through the tunnel. In the wooden guard hut which enclosed the entrance to the tunnel one of the security guards was sprawled in a chair with his boots on the desk. The collar of his blue uniform was unbuttoned, his cap pushed back on his head. On the wall behind him his gunbelt hung from a hook, with the black butt of the revolver sticking out of the holster. He looked up from his paperback Western, a thick beaky-nosed face with cold eagle eyes.

'Hi, Doc. You in a hurry?'

'Bols, can you get hold of Mr. Sturvesant for me? Ask him to come up here right away.'

I was on my knees below the sun image when Louren arrived.

'Lo, come over here. I want to show you something.'

'Hey, Ben!' Louren laughed, and it seemed to me that his expression was one of relieved pleasure. 'That's the first time I've seen you really smile in two weeks. God, I was worried about you.' He slapped my shoulder, still laughing. 'This is more like the old Ben again.'

'Lo, look at this.' And he knelt beside me.

Ten minutes later he was no longer smiling, his face was cold and intent. He was staring at the wall with those pale blue eyes as though he were seeing through the solid rock.

'Lo,' I began, but he waved me to silence with a peremptory gesture. He never took his eyes from the wall and now it seemed to me that he was listening to a voice I could not hear, I watched that cold god-like face with a sudden feeling of almost superstitious awe. I had a premonition of something unnatural about to happen.

Slowly, step by step, Louren approached the sun image. His hand went out and lay against the centre of the great disc. His fingers were spread, seeming to echo the shape of the image. He began to press against the wall, I saw the tips of his fingers flatten against the rock, changing shape beneath the pressure of his hand.

For a few long seconds nothing happened, then suddenly the wall began to move. There was no sound, no grating or squeal of protesting hinge, but the whole wall began to revolve upon a concealed axis. A ponderous, deliberate movement that revealed the square dark opening to a further passageway concealed beyond the image of Baal.

Staring into that dark prehistoric opening I whispered without glancing at Louren, 'How did you do that, Lo? How did you guess?'

His tone as he replied was puzzled. 'I knew – I just knew, that's all.' We were both silent again, staring into the opening. I was seized by a sudden unaccountable dread of what we would find in there.

'Get the light, Ben,' Louren ordered without taking his eyes from the doorway. I fetched the portable arc-light, and Louren took it from my hand. I followed him as he walked through the doorway.

Before us a passageway slanted down into the earth at an angle of forty-five degrees. The passage was seven foot six inches high, and nine feet wide. There was a flight of stone steps cut into the floor. Each step was worn, with edges smoothed and rounded. The walls and roof of the tunnel were of unadorned stone, and the depths of the tunnel were hidden from us by shadow and darkness.

'What's this?' Louren pointed at two large circular objects which lay at the head of the staircase. I saw the gleam of bronze rosettes upon them.

'Shields,' I told him. 'War shields.'

'Someone dropped them in a hurry.'

We stepped over them carefully and started down the staircase. There were 106 steps, each six inches high.

'No dust in here,' Louren remarked.

'No,' I agreed. 'The seal of the door was tight.'

His words should have acted as a warning, but I was lost in the wonder and excitement of this new discovery. The surface of the stairs was as clean as though freshly swept.

At the bottom of the staircase we reached a T-junction. On our right the passage led to a gate of barred ironwork which was closed and bolted. On the left it descended another twisting staircase that disappeared into the living rock.

'Which way?' Louren asked.

'Let's see what's behind the gate,' I suggested in a voice choking with excitement, and we went to it.

The heavy bolts were not locked but a thread of gold wire was twisted around the jamb of the gate, and a heavy clay seal closed the entrance.

The figure on the seal was of a crudely wrought animal, and the words, 'Lannon Hycanus. Gry-Lion of Opet, King of Punt and the four kingdoms.'

'Give me your knife,' Louren said.

'Lo, we can't,' I began.

'Give it to me, damn you.' His voice was shaking, thick with a peculiar lust and passion. 'You know what this is? It's the treasury, the gold vaults of Opet!'

'Wait, let's do it properly, Lo,' I pleaded, but he took the seal in his bare hands and ripped it from the gate.

'Don't do it, Lo,' I protested, but he pulled the bolts open, and flung his weight against the gate. It was rusted closed, but he attacked it with all his weight, It gave, swinging back far enough for Louren to squeeze through. He ran forward, and I ran after him. The tunnel turned again at right angles and led directly into a large chamber.

'God!' shouted Louren. 'Oh God! Look at it, Ben. Just look at it.'

The treasury of Opet lay before us with all its fabulous wealth untouched. Later we could count and weigh and measure it, but now we stood and stared.

The chamber was 186 feet long and 21 wide. The ivory was stacked along most of one wall. There were 1,016 large elephant tusks. The ivory was rotten and crumbly as chalk, but in itself must have been a vast treasure 2,000 years ago.

There were over 900 large amphorae, sealed with wax. The contents of precious oils had long since evaporated into a congealed black mass. There were bolts of imported linen and silk, rotted now so that they crumbled to dust at the touch.

The metals were stacked along the opposite wall of the vault – 190 tons of native copper cast into ingots shaped like the cross of St. Andrew; 3 tons of tin, cast into the same shape; 16 tons of silver; 96 of lead; 2 of antimony.

We walked down the aisle along the centre of the vault, staring about us at this incredible display of wealth.

'The gold,' Louren muttered. 'Where is the gold?'

There was a stack of wooden chests, carved from ebony, the lids decorated with ivory and mother-of-pearl inlay. These were the only objects of an artistic nature in the vault, and even they were crudely executed battle scenes or hunting scenes.

'No, don't do it, Lo,' I cried another protest as Louren began ripping open the lids.

They were filled with semi-precious stones, amethyst, beryl, tigers' eyes, jade and malachite. Some of these were crudely cut and incorporated in gold jewellery, thick clumsy pieces, collars, brooches, necklaces and rings.

Louren hurried on down the aisle, and then stopped abruptly. In another recess that led off the main chamber, behind another iron gate, the gold was stacked in neat piles. Cast in the usual 'finger' moulds. The piles of precious metal were insignificant in bulk, but when, months later, it was all weighed the total was over sixty tons.

Its value was in excess of £60,000,000 sterling. In the same recess as the gold were two small wooden chests. These yielded 26,000 carats of uncut and rough-cut diamonds of every conceivable colour and shape. Not one of these was smaller than one and a half carats, and the largest was a big sulky yellow monster of thirty-eight carats, and this added a further £2,000,000 to the intrinsic value of the treasure.

Here was the wealth of forty-seven kings of Opet, accumulated painstakingly over the course of 400 years. No other treasure of antiquity could compare with this profusion.

'We'll have to be bloody careful, Ben. No word of this must leak out. You understand what might happen if it did?' He stood with a finger of solid gold in each hand, looking down on the piles of treasure. 'This is enough to kill for, to start a war!'

'What do you want me to do, Lo? I must have help in here. Ral or Sally even.'

'No!' He turned on me ferociously. 'No one else will be allowed in here. I will leave orders with the guards, no one but you and I.'

'I need help, Lo. I can't do it myself, there is too much here.'

'I'll help you,' Louren said.

'It will take weeks.'

'I'll help you,' he repeated. 'No one else. Not a word to anyone else.'

Until six o'clock that evening Louren and I explored the treasure vault.

'Let's find out where the other branch of the tunnel leads to,' I suggested.

'No,' Louren stopped me. 'I want to keep normal hours here. I don't want the others to guess that we are up to something. We will go down to the camp now. Tomorrow we will have a look at the other fork of the tunnel. It can't be anything like this anyway.'

We closed the stone door behind us, sealing off the secret passage, and at the guard post Louren made his orders clear, repeating them and writing them on the guard's instruction sheet. Ral's and Sally's names were removed from the list of those allowed into the tunnel. And later he mentioned it to them at dinner. He explained it away as an experiment that he and I were attempting. It was a difficult evening for me. I was overwrought by the day's excitement, and now that I had shaken off my mood of apathy I was over-reacting to the normal stimuli of living. I found myself laughing too loudly, drinking too much, and the agony of my jealousy returned more intensely than ever.

When Louren and Sally looked at each other like that, I wanted to shout at them, 'I know. I know about it, and damn you, I hate you for it.'

But then I knew it was not true. I did not hate them. I loved them both and this made it all the harder to bear.

There was no chance of sleep for me, that night. When I get myself into a certain state of nervous tension, then I can go for two or three nights without being able to still the racing of my overheated brain. I did not mean to spy on her. It was a mere coincidence that I was standing at the window of my hut staring out from my darkened room at the moonlit night when Sally left her own hut.

She wore a long pale-coloured dressing-gown and her hair was let down in a dark cloud around her shoulders. She paused in the doorway of her own hut and looked around carefully, making sure that the camp was asleep. Then guiltily, quickly, she hurried across the open moonlit yard to the hut in which Louren was living. She opened the door and went in without hesitating and for me a long harrowing vigil had begun.

I stood by my window for two hours, watching the moon shadows change shape, watching the patterns of the stars swing and turn across the heavens, stars as fat and bright as they are only in the sweet clean air of the wilderness. The beauty of it was wasted on me this night. I was watching Louren's hut, imagining each whispered word, each touch, each movement, and hating myself and them. I thought of Hilary and the children, wondering what madness it is that makes a man gamble his all on a few hours of transient pleasure. In that darkened hut how many confidences were those two betraying, how many people's happiness were they risking.

Then suddenly I realized that I was assuming that this affair was merely play on Louren's part, and I faced the possibility that he was serious. That he would desert Hilary and go to Sally. I found this thought intolerable. I could no longer watch and wait, I must have some distraction and I dressed quickly and hurried across to the repository.

The night-watchman greeted me sleepily and I unlocked the door and went to the vault in which the golden books were kept. I took out the fourth book of Huy. I carried it across to my own office, and before I settled down to read I went to fetch a bottle of Glen Grant. My two opiates, words and whisky.

I opened the scroll at random and re-read Huy's ode to his battle-axe, the gleaming wing of the bird of the sun. When I had finished I was taken by an impulse and I lifted the great axe down from its place of honour. I caressed the shimmering length of it, studying it with new attention. I was convinced that this was the weapon of the poem. Could there be another answering the description so accurately? I held it in my lap, wishing that I could draw from it the story of the last days of Opet. I was sure it was involved intimately in the final tragedy. Why had it been left abandoned, a thing so well beloved and yet thrown carelessly aside to lie uncared for and discarded for nearly 2,000 years? What had happened to the Axeman Huy and his king and his city?

I read and dreamed, disturbed less frequently by thoughts of Sally and Louren. However, at every pause in my readings they came to me with a sick little slide of jealousy and despair in my guts. I was torn beween the present and the distant past.

I read on, sampling those portions of the scroll which were still unknown territory while the level in the whisky bottle sank slowly and the long night passed.

Then when midnight had flown and the new day was being born, I came upon a small piece of writing which touched a new depth of response in me. Huy makes a sudden heart-felt cry from the depths of his being. It is as though some long-suppressed emotion will no longer be contained and must come out in this appeal to have his physical form discounted when his value is assessed. From base earth flowers the purest gold, Huy cries, in his own poor distorted clay there were treasures concealed.

I re-read the passage half a dozen times, making sure of my translation before I could accept that Huy Ben-Amon was like me. *A cripple.*

Dawn's first promise was tracing a silouette of the cliff tops with a pale rose colour when I laid the golden book away in its vault and walked slowly back to my hut.

Sally stepped out of Louren's doorway and came towards me in the darkness. Her gown was ghostly pale and she seemed to float above the ground. I stood still, hoping she would not see me. There was a chance for I stood in the deeper shadow of her hut and I turned my face away, standing quietly.

I heard the rustle of her skirts, the whisper of her feet in the dust very close in the dark, then her startled gasp as she saw me. I looked at her then. She had seen but not recognized me. Her face was a pale moon of fear and her hands were at her mouth.

'All right, Sally,' I said. 'It's only me.'

I could smell her now. On the clean night air of the desert it was a perfumed smell like crushed rose petals, and mingled with it the warm-smell of perspiration and love. My heart slid in my chest.

'Ben?' she said, and we were both silent staring at each other.

'How long have you been here?'

'Long enough,' I answered, and again the silence.

'You know, then?' It was said in a small voice, shy and sad.

'I didn't mean to spy,' I said, and another silence.

'I believe you.' She began to move away. Then she turned back. 'Ben, I want to explain.'

'You don't have to do that,' I said.

'Yes, I do. I want to.'

'It doesn't matter, Sal.'

'It does matter.' And we faced each other. 'It does matter,' she repeated. 'I don't want you to think that I, well, that I am so terrible.'

'Forget it, Sally.' I said.

'I tried not to, Ben. I swear to you.'

'It's all right, Sally.'

'I couldn't help it, truly. I tried so hard to fight it. I didn't want it to happen.' She was crying now, silently, her shoulders shaking as she sobbed.

'It doesn't matter,' I said, and went to her. I took her gently to her room and put her to bed. In the light I saw how her lips were swollen and kiss-inflamed.

'Oh, Ben, I would have given anything for it to be different.'

'I know, Sally.'

'I tried so hard, but it was too much for me. He had me in some kind of spell, from the very first moment I saw him.'

'That evening at the airport?' I could not help but ask the question, remembering now how she had watched Louren that first time she met him and how later she had ranted against him.

'That's why – later, with me – that's why we – ' I did not want to hear her answer, and yet I must know if she had first come to me inflamed with thoughts of another man.

'No, Ben.' She tried to deny it, but she saw my eyes, and turned her face away. 'Oh, Ben, I'm sorry. I didn't want to hurt you.'

'Yes,' I nodded.

'I truly didn't want to hurt you. You are so good, so gentle, so different from him.' There were dark shadows of sleeplessness beneath her eyes, and the peach-coloured velvet of her cheek was rubbed pink by Louren's unshaven skin.

'Yes,' I said with my heart breaking.

'Oh, Ben, what shall I do?' she cried in distress. 'I am caught in this thing. I cannot escape.'

'Does Lo – has he said what he is going to do? Has he told you he, well, that he will leave Hilary, and marry you?'

'No.' She shook her head.

'Has he given you reason —'

'No! No!' She caught my hand. 'Oh, Ben. It's just fun for him. It's just a little adventure.'

I said nothing, watching her lovely tortured face, glad at least that she knew about Louren. Realized that he was a hunter and she the quarry. There had been many Sallys in Louren's life, and there would be many more. The lion must kill regularly.

'Is there anything I can do, Sally?' I asked at last.

'No, Ben. I don't think so.'

'If there is, tell me,' I said and moved towards the door.

'Ben,' she stopped me, and sat up. 'Ben, do you still love me?'

I nodded without hesitation. 'Yes, I still love you.'

'Thank you, Ben,' she sighed softly. 'I don't think I could have taken it if you had turned away from me.'

'I'll never do that, Sally,' I said, and walked out into the lemon and rose glow of dawn.

Louren and I descended the staircase beyond the sun image. We went first to the treasure vault. While Louren gloated over the stacks of golden fingers, I watched his face. I was light-headed from lack of sleep, and I could taste the spirits I had drunk in the back of my throat. Watching Louren, I tried to find hatred for him in my heart, I searched diligently without success. When he looked up and smiled at me, I could not but answer him with a smile.

'This will keep, Ben,' he said. 'Let's go and have a look at the rest of it.'

I had guessed what we would find beyond the junction of the tunnels, and once we had descended the last spiralling stairs and come into another short level passage I had my last doubts dispelled.

The passage ended against another solid stone wall. Here, however, there was no attempt at concealment, for carved into the stone was an inscription. We stood before it, and Louren held the arc-lamp full upon it.

'What does it say?' he asked.

I read it through slowly. Even with all my practice I read slowly, for in Punic there are no symbols for the vowels and each must be guessed from the context of the word.

'Come on,' Louren muttered impatiently.

' "You who come here to interrupt the sleep of the kings of Opet, and to despoil their tomb, do so at your peril, and may the curse of Astarte and great Baal hound you to your own graves." '

'Read it again,' Louren commanded, and I did. He nodded.

'Yes,' he said, and stepped to the stone door. He began to seek the pivot point which we knew would trigger the mechanism. Here we were not so fortunate as we had been at the threshold of the sun door. After two hours, our way was still barred by that solid slab of uncompromising stone.

'I'm going to blow the bloody thing open,' Louren warned, but I knew he would not commit such an atrocity in this sacred place. We rested and discussed the problem, before returning to the door. It had to be another simple leverage system, but the trick was to find the pressure point and the angle of movement.

When we found it at last, I cursed my own stupidity. It should have been my first attempt. The symbol for the name of the sun-god Baal was once more the pressure point.

The door swung open, ponderous and slow, and we went through into the tomb of the kings of Opet.

There is only one other place I have known with the same atmosphere. That is Westminster Abbey which contains the tombs of so many of the kings of England. There was the same hushed cathedral sense of time past and history reborn.

Neither of us spoke as we went to the centre of the long narrow vaulted tomb. The silence was an oppressive weight upon my ear drums. Utter silence, so complete as to be sinister and threatening. Here again the air was long disused, but with an even heavier musty quality to it. I thought I detected the faint, stale smell of dust and mushrooms.

Along each wall, parallel to it, stood the sarcophagi of the kings of Opet. They were carved of massive granite. Solid, squat and grey. The lids were held in place by their own immense weight, and the upper surface had been polished and engraved with the name and style of the body that lay within. The mighty names that had echoed through the golden books of Huy. I recognized them, Hamilcar, Hannibal, Hycanus. Forty-seven great coffins, but the last was empty, its lid propped against the wall beside it. Its interior cut into a man's shape, ready to swallow the last king of Opet.

At the foot of the great stone coffin a man lay stretched upon his back on the floor of the tomb. His helmet was missing and his red-gold hair and beard formed a soft frame for the wizened, mummified features. His breast-plate had been removed exposing the dried parchment skin stretched over the skeletal rib-cage. The broken shaft of an arrow protruded from a long-dead chest. He wore a kilt of leather, studded with bronze rosettes and on his shins were greaves of bronze, on his feet light sandals.

His arms lay at his side, his heels were together. The dead body had been laid out with care and obvious love.

Over him stood another figure, kneeling like a man in prayer. A figure in full armour, with only the war helmet and breast-plate discarded on the floor beneath the empty sarcophagus. Long black hair hung forward to conceal his bowed face. Both hands clutched at his chest at the level of the diaphragm. From his chest a blade of steel protruded, a reversed sword, with its hilt securely anchored against the stone slabs of the floor, the pivot driven up under the ribs and lodged in his vitals.

Here was a man in the attitude of final escape from the shame of defeat, a man who in despair had fallen upon his own sword. The weapon had supported his weight these many centuries, propping him up in that kneeling position.

Neither Louren nor I could speak, as we drew closer to this tableau of ancient tragedy. For me there was no doubt as to the identity of these dried-out human husks.

Lannon Hycanus, the last King of Opet, lay stretched on the cold stone floor. Above him knelt this friend and high priest Huy Ben-Amon.

I felt choked with a sense of destiny, with a cold aching dread – for Huy Ben-Amon, the Axeman of the Gods, was a *hunchback*.

I had to see his face. I had to see it! I ran forward, and knelt beside him.

I touched his gaunt bony shoulder, covered by a tunic of brittle yellow linen. It was the lightest touch, a breath almost, but it was enough to shatter that delicately poised mummy.

The corpse of Huy Ben-Amon slid forward and crashed down on the body of the king. Steel and bronze rang on the stone floor, and echoed about the vaulted tomb of Opet.

The two figures burst into dust at the impact, a soft yellow explosion of mustard-yellow dust, swirling like smoke in the arc-light. There was nothing left of them but the metal of armour and sword, and two hanks of gold and sable hair in the puddle of talcum-soft dust.

I stood up, choking with the yellow dust. My eyes were swimming with tears of wonder and burning with the dust. The dust smelled of mushrooms.

Louren Sturvesant and I stared at each other without speaking. We had witnessed a miracle.

I awoke from a screaming nightmare of blood and flame and smoke, a horror of shining black faces and sweat-polished bodies lit by crackling roaring flames and the scream of the dying and the animal roar of blood-crazed voices. I woke panting and choking from the memory, and the terror and the horror of it stayed with me long after I had found myself alone in my quiet hut in the silent night.

I switched on the bedside light and looked at my watch. It was still early, a little before eleven. I threw back my sheets and stood up, surprised to find my legs shaky and my breathing ragged. There was a twinge of pain at each breath I drew, and a dull tight sensation behind my eyes. My body felt hot, fever hot. I went to the wash-stand across the hut, and shook three aspirin from the bottle. I swallowed them with a mouthful of water, and then the tickling sensation in my lungs grew stronger. I coughed as though I was on sixty cigarettes a day, and the effort left me sweaty and trembling. My skin seemed to be aflame.

Without really knowing why, I took my dressing-gown off the hook behind the door, pulled it on and went out into the yard. There was a half moon in the sky, horned and yellow. The shadows under the trees and around the buildings were very dark and ugly. I felt the lingering dread and horror of my nightmare still upon me as I hurried across towards my office, and I glanced about me nervously. I could smell the tinge of smoke on the night air, and it troubled me also. I sniffed at it feeling the faint sting deep in my lungs.

I reached the door of my office, and there was something waiting for me in the deep shadow beside the building. I saw it rush at me from the corner of my vision, a big dark thing, rounded and shapeless and deadly silent. I spun to face it, falling against the wall of the hut, weak with terror. A scream bubbled and died in my throat for there was nothing there. It was gone, I had imagined it, but now the pain in my head beat like hammer blows on the anvil.

I pulled the door open, and fell into my office, slammed the door behind me, locked it, gasping with unnamed and baseless fear. Something scratched against the door from the outside, a terrifying clawing animal sound that ripped my quivering nerves.

I backed away from the door towards my desk, crouching there, trembling, shaking and weak.

The sound came again, but from the wall beside me, I spun to face it, and I heard myself whimper.

I needed a weapon, I looked around desperately and the great battle-axe of Huy hung on the wall above my desk. I snatched it down and backed into a corner, holding it ready, at the present position across my chest. I coughed.

There was a thick sheaf of white paper on my desk. It moved and I felt the gooseflesh crawl all over my hot body. The white square of paper quivered and wavered, it changed shape, crawled across my desk, and spread white bats' wings. Then suddenly it launched into flight, wings whispering, and it flew at my face. I saw the wide open mouth ringed with needle vampire teeth, heard the shrill squeaks as it attacked. I shouted with horror, and struck with the axe. The white thing fluttered and squeaked against my throat and face, and I fought and shouted, striking it down onto the floor where it crawled and slithered loathsomely. I struck with the edge of the axe, and inky black blood spurted from the thing and puddled the wooden floor of the hut.

I backed away from the thing, and lay against the wall. I felt weak, and terribly afraid. I began to cough. The cough took hold of my whole body and shook it, rocking me, doubling me against the wall. I coughed until my vision burst into bright lights, and there was a salty taste in my mouth.

I sank to my knees against the wall, my mouth was filled with warm wetness and I spat a thick gob of bright blood onto the floor. I stared at it, not understanding what was happening to me. I lifted my hand to my mouth and wiped my lips. My hand came away smeared with blood.

I knew then what it was. Louren and I had passed beyond two sealed doorways into the depths of a tomb closed for 2,000 years – and we had breathed air loaded with the spores of *cryptococcus neuromyces,* the curse of the Pharoahs.

It was too late now for me to berate myself for overlooking the precautions. I had believed that because the archives were safe, the rest of it was also. In my eagerness and excitement I had not given another thought to the fungus danger, even when Louren and I had discussed the door seals and even when I had smelled the mushroom odour in the tomb of the kings.

Now my lungs were clogged with the horrible colonies of living fungus, a growing living thing within me, feeding on the soft tissues of my body, and pouring out its poisons into my blood to be carried to my brain.

'Treatment,' I gasped, 'got to find the treatment.' And I staggered across to my bookshelves. I tried to read the letters on the spines of the books, but they changed to little black insects and crawled away. Suddenly a thick mottled snake uncoiled from the top shelf, and dangled down towards my face, a thick bloated puff-adder with a flicking black tongue. I backed away, then turned and fled into the night.

The smoke was thick, swirling around me, choking me so that I coughed wildly. The flames around me lit all with a lurid satanic glow, a flickering glow. There were dark shapes and strange sounds. I saw Louren's hut, and ran towards it.

'Louren,' I screamed, bursting in through the door. 'Louren!' panting, coughing.

The light went on. Sally was alone in Louren's bed, she sat up, sleepy, soft-eyed, naked, and looked at me with unfocused vision.

'Where is he?' I shouted at her. She looked confused, not understanding.

'Ben, what is it? You're bleeding!'

'Where is Lo?' It was desperately urgent. I had to find him. He had been exposed to the fungus also. I had to find him.

Sally looked down at the bed beside her. There was the indentation on the pillow where Louren's head had lain.

'I don't know,' she said, big-eyed, puzzled. 'He was here. He must have gone out.'

I coughed, great choking sobs, and felt fresh blood in my mouth. Sally was fully awake now. She stared at me.

'Ben, what is it?'

'Neuromyces,' I told her, and she gasped seeing the blood streaming down my chin.

'Louren and I have opened a secret passage beyond the sun image in the archives. It's infected with the spores. We took no precautions. It has got us. I'm sure he's there now. I'm going to him.' I stopped to breathe. Sally was out of bed slipping into her gown, coming to me.

'Get Ral Davidson. Respirators. Take all precautions. Follow us. I will prop the doors open. Down steps. Turn left at bottom. Follow us. Louren will have it also, drives you mad. Crazy. Terrible things. Come quickly – do you understand?'

'Yes, Ben.'

'Get Ral,' I said and turned. I ran out into the smoke and flames and darkness, running for the cliffs and the cavern. The great walls of the temple towered above me, walls long gone. The great phallic towers of Baal pointed to the moon, lit by the flames of a burning city. Towers that stood again after so long. They were screaming, the women, burning alive with their children. Dead men lay strewn in my path, cut down like the harvest of the devil, their dead faces terrible in the moonlight.

'Louren,' I shouted and ran on through the temple. They were in my path, dark and savage, crowding forward to oppose me. Dark, shapeless, terrifying, and I flew at them with a strange battle cry yelled from a blood-glutted throat. The mighty axe spun its silver circles in the firelight, and I was through them, running.

I reached the cavern, saw it lit by the guttering torches, saw the pavement of stone bordering the circular green beauty of the emerald pool. The rows of stone benches, rising in tiers around it as they had 2,000 years before. With a last enormous effort of will, I forced my brain to discount this fantasy and to recognize reality.

The wooden guard hut stood across the cavern from me. I staggered towards it. The guard sat at his desk reading. He looked up, his expression changing to surprise and incredulity.

'Good God, are you all right, Doctor?'

'Mr Sturvesant, is he in the tunnel?'

'Yes.'

'When did he go in?'

'An hour ago.' The guard came towards me. 'Is something wrong? You are bleeding, Doctor!'

'Wait here,' I told him. 'The others are coming. They know what to do.'

I hurried on into the archives, smelling the smoke still and hearing the clamour of a dying city ring in my ears.

Before the image of the sun-god I let the great battle-axe slip from my hand and left it lying on the stone floor. I pushed the stone door open, and propped it with one of the war shields to prevent it swinging closed behind me.

I ran down the staircase. Half-way down I saw the glow of light from the tomb below.

The inscribed doorway with its graven curse of the gods stood open, jammed in the hinge by the cable of the arc-light.The light lay on its side in the centre of the tomb where Louren had dropped it. The bulb still burned, lighting the tomb vividly.

Louren lay on his back at the foot of the huge granite sarcophagus of Lannon Hycanus, the last king of Opet.

He was naked to the waist. His face was deathly pale, his eyes closed, and bright blood stained the corners of his mouth and ran back down his cheeks into his ears and hair.

With the last of my strength I staggered to where he lay and dropped on to my knees beside him. I stooped over him and tried to lift him, my arms around his shoulders.

His skin was moist and burning hot, and his head flopped helplessly backwards. A new bright gush of blood ran out of his mouth, wetting my hands.

'Louren,' I cried, holding him to my chest. 'Oh please, God, help me! Help me!'

There was still life in him, just the last flicker of it. He opened his eyes, those pale blue eyes with the first shadows of death darkening them.

'Ben,' he whispered, choking with his own blood. He coughed, spattering droplets of the bright lung blood.

'Ben,' he whispered so softly I could scarcely hear it. 'All the way?'

'All the way, Lo,' I whispered, holding him like a sleepy child. His head of golden curls cradled against my shoulder. He was quiet for a little while, then suddenly he stirred again, and when he spoke it was in a clear strong voice.

'Fly!' he said. 'Fly for me, bird of the sun.' And the life went out of him, he turned to nothing in my arms, the great wild spirit flown – gone.

I knelt over him, feeling my own senses reel. The world turned and swung beneath me. I slipped over the edge of it, down into the swirling darkness of time. Down into a kind of death, a kind of life, for in my dying I dreamed a dream. In my poisoned sleep of death which lasted a moment and a million years I dreamed of long-dead men in a time long passed . . .

Part Two

Of the thirty days of the prophecy there were but two remaining when Lannon Hycanus and his train came at last to the Bay of the Little Fish on the furthest southerly shores of the great lake. It was already dark when ten ships of the fleet anchored in the shallow waters of the bay, and their torches and lamps smeared long ruddy paths of light across the black waters.

Lannon stood beside the wooden gunwale of his steering-deck, and looked out across the fields of papyrus and hidden waterways to the south where the open country began and spread away endlessly into the unknown. He knew that here lay his destiny and that of the nation. For twenty-eight days he had hunted and now he felt an unaccustomed chill of fear fan his arms and neck, fear not of the terrible animal he had come to find, but of the consequences of the animal continuing to evade him.

Behind him there were light footsteps on the wooden deck and Lannon turned quickly. His hand on the hilt of the dagger beneath his leather cloak relaxed as he saw the unmistakable shape of the man in the light of the torches.

'Huy,' he greeted him.

'Highness, you must eat now and sleep.'

'Have they come yet?'

'Not yet, but they will before morning,' replied the hunchback, moving closer to his prince. 'Come now. You will have need of a steady hand and clear eye on the morrow.'

'Sometimes it seems I have ten wives, not nine,' laughed Lannon, and regretted the jest when he saw the blood darken the face of the hunchback; quickly he went on. 'You pamper me, old friend, but I think that tonight I will hunt sleep with as little success as I have hunted the gry-lion these twenty-eight days since my father's funeral.' He turned back to the bridge rail and looked across at the other nine ships. The ships of the nine families, come to watch him make good his claim to the throne of Opet and the four kingdoms, come to watch him take his gry-lion.

'Look at them, Huy.' And his friend came to his side. 'How many of them have made sacrifices to the gods for my failure?'

'Three of them, certainly – you know which I mean. There are perhaps more of them.'

'And those who are loyal to house Barca, those we can count upon without question?'

'You know them also, my lord. Habbakuk Lal will stand with you until the seas turn to sand, house Amon, House hasmon—'

'Yes,' Lannon interrupted. 'I know them, Huy, every one of them, for and against. I was but talking to have the comfort of your voice.' He touched the hunchback's shoulder in a gesture of affection, before turning away to gaze once more into the southern wilderness.

'When the prophecy was made did they ever foresee the day when the great gry-lion would pass from the land? When a prince might search for all thirty of the days allotted to the task without seeing even the marks of the beasts' paws in the earth of Opet?' Lannon spoke with sudden anger. He flung his cloak back over his shoulder and folded his arms across his naked chest. His skin was freshly oiled and the muscles glowed in the torch light, he kneaded his own flesh with the long powerful fingers.

'My father killed on the twenty-fifth day, and that was forty-six years ago. They said even then that the gry-lion was finished. Since then how many have the scouts reported?'

'My Lord, the gods will decide,' Huy tried to soothe him.

'We have hunted every covert where the gry-lion has been seen in the last 200 years. Five full legions have swept the swamps in the north, three more along the great river.' He broke off and began pacing the deck, pausing to look down into the hull where the tiers of naked slaves slept chained upon their benches, leaning on the mighty oars in the position in which they would die. The stench of the rowing decks came up to him as a solid thing in the humid night. He turned back to Huy.

'This reach of the swamps is the last place in the whole of my kingdoms which might hide a gry-lion. If it does not, then what will happen, Huy? Is there no other way in which I might prove my right? Is there no escape in the scrolls?'

'None, my lord.' Huy shook his head with regret.

'The kingship must fall?'

'Unless there is a gry-lion taken then Opet will have no king.'

'Who will rule without a king?'

'The Council of Nine, alone.'

'And the royal house? What will become of house Barca?'

'Let us not talk of it,' Huy suggested softly. 'Come, my lord. A slave is preparing a jug of hot spiced wine and a stew of fish. The wine will help you to sleep.'

'Will you make an oracle for tomorrow, my priest of Baal?' Lannon asked suddenly.

'If the oracle is unfavourable, will it help you sleep?' asked Huy, and Lannon stared at him a moment before barking with harsh laughter.

'You are right, as always. Come then, I am hungry.'

Lannon ate with vast appetite from the bowl of fish, sitting naked on his fur-covered bed. He had let his hair loose and it hung to his shoulders, curling and gleaming strangely golden in the light of the hanging lamp. He was a god-like figure among his dark-haired people.

The leather awnings were opened, and a light breeze came up from the south-east to cool the cabin and blow out the galley stench. The ship moved to the breeze and the light chop of the surface, her timber popped and creaked softly, a slave cried out in nightmare, and from the deck above came the steps of the night guard – all the familiar comforting sounds of the flagship at sea.

Lannon wiped out the bowl with a piece of millet bread, popped it into his mouth, and washed it down with the last of the wine. He sighed with content, and smiled at Huy.

'Sing for me, my bird of the sun.'

Huy Ben-Amon squatted on the deck at the foot of the prince's bed. He held his lute in his lap, and crouched over it. The curve of his back exaggerated the attitude, the long tar-black tresses of hair hung forward to hide his face, his massively developed arms seemed too powerful for the long delicate fingers that held the lute. He struck a note, and a listening hush fell upon the night. The footsteps overhead ceased, two slave girls ceased their work and came to kneel beside Lannon's bed, the arguing voices from the ship anchored alongside quieted, and Huy sang.

His voice rang sweetly across the dark waters, and the prince and the fleet listened. Dark shapes moved to the rails of the nearest ships and stood quietly there looking across at the flagship. On the cheeks of one of the pretty slave girls stood tear-drops that glistened in the lamp light, when Huy sang of a lost love. Then she smiled through her tears when Huy changed the song to one of the bawdy marching tunes of the Sixth Legion.

'Enough.' Huy looked up from his lute at last. 'There will be work tomorrow, my lord.'

Lannon nodded and touched one of the slave girls on the cheek. Immediately she stood up and loosed the shoulder strap of her linen tunic, letting it fall from her body. She was young and lithe, her body almost boyishly slim in the lamp light. She stooped and gathered her robe, dropped it across the bench beside the door and stepped naked into Lannon's bed. The other girl went to snuff the lamp, and Huy rose from the deck with his lute slung on his shoulder.

A voice hailed from the darkness, a great bull bellow from the edge of the papyrus beds that carried across the water to the flagship.

'Open your lines for a friend!'

'Who calls himself friend?' One of the guards shouted a challenge, and the reply was bellowed hoarsely.

'Mursil, huntmaster of house Barca.' And Lannon was out of his bed in one bound.

'He has come!' he exclaimed, flinging his cloak over his shoulders and hurrying to the companion ladder with Huy scampering beside him.

A small canoe bumped alongside and Mursil came up through the entry-port as Lannon and Huy reached the deck, a huge figure, gross and apelike with his big beefy round face ruddy from sun and wine.

The ship was awake now. Her officers swarming up onto the deck, new torches flaring to light the scene as day, the bustle and hum of excitement affecting them all.

Mursil saw Lannon and hurried to him down the aisle which opened for him across the crowded deck. He was followed closely by a pygmy figure, a tiny brown naked manikin that looked about him from slanted eyes in obvious terror at these unfamiliar surroundings.

'My lord.' Mursil opened his cloak and dropped heavily to one knee in front of Lannon. 'I bring good news.'

'Then you are welcome.'

'This one,' Mursil reached behind him and dragged the little bushman forward, 'this one has found what we seek.'

'You have seen it?' Lannon demanded.

'The tracks of his paws only, but this one has seen the beast itself.'

'If it is true, you will be well rewarded, both of you,' promised Lannon Hycanus and turned to grin triumphantly at Huy.

'The gods have decided. House Barca will have its chance once more.'

The sky was only a shade lighter than the black brooding swampland, the dawn-flighting duck ghost-whistled unseen overhead and each minute the light strengthened.

Half a mile out on the open plain a herd of buffalo grazed in a dark bunch. Heads down, tails swinging lazily, they moved back steadily towards the tall dense banks of papyrus reed.

They moved faster as the light strengthened, hurrying to reach the sanctuary of the reed-beds, 200 huge bovine shapes with their armoured heads and bunched black shoulders. Dawn's first light showed the white tick birds which hovered above the dark herd in a cold pink sheen. The swampy earth smoked with mist and the endless banks of papyrus stood frozen in the hush of dawn, for once their fluffy white heads were not nodding and dancing – except where something moved amongst the reeds.

Following its track the papyrus stirred, an opening and closing movement that set them nodding briefly before settling into stillness once more. The movement was sedate and yet so weighty that it betrayed the size of the animal which stalked beneath it.

The big bull buffalo that led the herd, stopped suddenly fifty yards from the edge of the papyrus bed. He lifted his nose high and spread his ears wide beneath the heavy boss of horn. With little suspicious piggy eyes he examined the bed of reeds ahead of him. Behind him the herd stopped also, alerted by his stillness.

The gry-lion came out of the reeds at full charge, a blur of soft roan-brown, an animal as tall and almost as heavy as the quarry it hunted. It crossed the open ground so swiftly that the bull had only begun to turn away before the gry-lion was on him.

It landed on his back, curved yellow claws hooked through thick black skin and flesh at shoulder and haunch. The long fangs sank into the back of the buffalo's neck, holding it steady while one paw reached forward and grasped the bull's nose. A single powerful wrench twisted the black neck back against the holding fangs, the spine snapped with a sharp retort and the bull folded in full run.

Before he went down the gry-lion had left him, dropping lightly to the ground, seeming hardly to touch it before he was in the air again, a long arcing leap, flashing soft brown against the pink dawn sky to land easily across the back of an old black cow that ran beside the bull.

Lightly as a humming bird flashing from flower to flower, the gry-lion had killed again. Bone breaking sharply in the dawn, the victim carrying the great lion forward in the press of galloping buffalo, and as the cow died the gry-lion was gone, flitting to the next, killing again in one fleeting movement and flitting again.

Six times the gry-lion killed before the surging, plunging, panicking herd had run 300 paces. Then he let them run, the thunder of their hooves dwindled, a far bank of papyrus swallowed them and they were gone.

The gry-lion stood in the silky light of dawn. His long, black-tufted tail still slashed from side to side with the thrill of the hunt. Every muscle was tight and swollen and the great beast half crouched, the flat snakelike head lifted as though to counter the weight of those long white fangs that curved down almost to touch the fluffy fur of his chest.

The face mask was elaborately patterned in black and startling white, an effect that enhanced the golden glowing savagery in the wide-set eyes, but the whiskers and eyelashes were long white bristle, and seemed to soften the animal's expression. However, when it stood up from its crouch, with the short ruff of mulberry-brown mane along its back still fully erect, any illusion of softness vanished.

As tall as a man, and as heavy as a horse, armed with those legendary fangs and claws, this was the most dangerous cat that all nature's wits and evolutions had ever produced.

The cat turned and paced back to where its last victim lay in the short grass of the plain. It stood over the dead buffalo, and it seemed impossible that such a large animal could move as swiftly as this one had at the height of the hunt.

The gry-lion lifted its head, the massive jaws parted, the long pink tongue curled out between those unbelievable fangs, and it roared.

It was a sound that seemed to shake the purple skies of dawn, that made the earth shudder and ruffled the quiet waters of the great lake.

In the dawn, upon the narrow muddy beach beside the reed banks, Huy Ben-Amon greeted his god. Huy wore light hunting armour of leather, a leather breastplate and arm-guards over a short linen tunic and bronze-studded leather kilt, but his weapons were laid aside, for he was about to offer the sacrifice, to send a messenger to great Baal. A messenger to carry the request of Lannon Hycanus to his god. The prince and his nobles were gathered in a half circle about the priest, all of them facing the eastern sky. Baal showed the tip of his fiery orb above the horizon, and they lifted their hands to him. Fingers spread in the sun-sign.

'Great Baal,' Huy called the greeting in sweet shimmering tones that seemed must carry to the sky. 'Your children greet you!' Huy's swarthy, beak-nosed features were lit by a mystic glow which gave him a strange beauty.

'We have come to this place to choose a king for your people and we ask your blessing on our endeavours.' Huy knew his gods intimately, and though he loved them yet he knew their all too human weaknesses. They were vain, inconsistent, touchy, greedy and sometimes bone-lazy. They must be flattered and cajoled, bribed and jollied along, they needed special ceremony and display to capture their jaded interest and attention, sacrifice which Huy personally found revolting, to assuage their lust for warm blood. It was not enough that sacrifice was made, it must be made in all the correct forms before the gods would accept it, and as one of his lesser priests led the white bull forward Huy wondered if he had done the right thing in persuading Lannon to offer an animal rather than a slave. The gods preferred human blood, but Huy had argued with Lannon that a bull now and the promise of a slave later might be more effective. Huy had no compunction in bargaining with the great immortals, especially if it delayed the moment when he must look into the terrified pleading eyes of a doomed slave. In the five years that Huy had directed the religious life of Opet, not more than 100 human messengers had been sent to the gods. Whereas there had been times in the city's history when that number had been sent at a single ceremony.

'We send you a fine white bull to carry our message.' Huy turned and approached the animal. It was of the short stocky Opet type, white and grey dappled, with a fat hump on its shoulders and wide straight horns. It stood quietly as Huy took the vulture axe from one of his priests. The circle of nobles drew back a little, giving the axe space to swing and the blood to spurt.

'Great Baal, receive our messenger!' Huy shouted, and the axe went up, reflecting the low rays of the sun from its flashing blade. It hissed angrily as it fell, and the bull's thick neck severed cleanly, the head seeming to leap from the trunk. Headless, the body fell to its knees and the blood pumped and gushed.

Huy leaned upon his weapon in the typical stance of the resting axeman.

'A sign, great Baal!' Huy shouted, making it more a demand than a request. 'Give your children a sign!' And his voice was tiny in the immensity of swamp and sky and water. The timeless silence of the swamps fell upon them, the silence of the ages in the smoky purple dawn.

A flight of spur-winged geese passed overhead, wings beating heavily, long necks out-stretched, silhouetted darkly against the rosy streamers of sun-touched mist. Huy watched them hopefully, tempted to claim them as god-forms.

'A sign, great Baal!' He thrust aside the temptation, but his irritation was increasing. The sacrifice had been meticulously performed right down to the single clean stroke of the axe – was this to be one of those occasions when the god's attention had wandered, or was he being obstinate, pig-headed? A hippopotamus splashed and snorted out in the bay, and Huy turned towards it expectantly, but the fat grey sea-cow merely fluttered its ears like bees' wings, then submerged with a swirl.

'A sign, great Baal!' The third and final request, and almost immediately it was answered.

A sound rose from beyond the papyrus beds that startled the water birds into flight, that shook the fluffy white heads of the reeds, that seemed to roll across the heavens like thunder. A sound such as none of them had ever heard before. The roaring of the gry-lion.

Huy's dark scowl vanished beneath a beatific smile, and he turned those long-lashed gazelle eyes on his prince.

'The gods have answered you, Lannon Hycanus.' He was seeing the faces of the priests and nobles and warriors and huntsmen, the superstitious awe with which they gazed at him. He would sacrifice privately to Baal later, nothing ostentatious or expensive, a chicken perhaps, as a gesture of thanks for this magnificent co-operation. It would rank with one of his best performances ever. Huy was so delighted with his success that he could not resist a further histrionic gesture.

'Go out, Prince of Opet, and take your gry-lion,' said Huy.

The little bushman led them along one of the buffalo paths. It was a green tunnel of reeds, the papyrus closing overhead to hide the sky, the damp peaty swamp earth underfoot, the musty animal swamp smell in their nostrils. They came out at last into the open grassland. Short, bright green grass cropped down by the countless herds of buffalo that infested this reach of the shore.

The bushman turned and led them along the edge of the papyrus-beds. They were an unwieldy procession, four or five hundred strong, for some of the noble nine would not come ashore to look for the gry-lion without a thick screen of archers and axemen around them. They trailed far behind Lannon's party which consisted of Mursil the huntmaster, smelling richly of fruity Zeng wine, the bushman, Huy, the prince and his two arms-bearers.

The gods were as good as their promise that morning. The bushman led them around a bank of papyrus that thrust out into the plain like an accuser's finger, and as they turned the point of it they came upon another bay of open grassland. It was a natural arena, fenced on three sides by the stands of dark reeds, a huge circular extent of lush grass about half a mile across.

Down the centre of this opening, lying at regular intervals, were six large dark objects, clearly visible on the open plain, but the range was too long for immediate identification.

Mursil, the huntmaster, spoke quickly to the pygmy scout in a formless dialect. Huy made a note to study this language, it was the only spoken word in all the four kingdoms in which he was not fluent.

'My lord, he says they are dead buffalo killed by the gry-lion,' Mursil translated on a warm wave of wine fumes.

'Where is the beast?' Lannon asked, and the bushman pointed.

'It is there, behind the second carcass. It has seen and heard us, and it is lying hidden,' Mursil explained.

'Can he see it?' Lannon demanded.

'Yes, my lord. He can see the tips of its ears and its eyes. It is watching us.'

'At that distance?' Lannon asked with disbelief, looking down at the bushman. 'I do not believe it.'

'It is true, my lord. He has the eyes of an eagle.'

'At your peril, if he is mistaken,' Lannon warned.

'At my peril,' Mursil agreed readily, and Lannon turned to Huy.

'Make ready, my bird of the sun.'

While they stripped Lannon of his armour, bound his loins in a cloth of linen, and set light hunting sandals on his feet, the rest of the party straggled up. Some of the older nobles were in litters. Asmun, looking frail and white-haired, stopped his bearers beside Lannon.

'A clean kill,' he wished the prince. 'Like the one your father made.' And they carried him to where he could have a view of the field. The party spread out along the edge of the reed bank, their arms and armour glinting in the sunlight, their robes purple and white and red, spots of gay colour against the dark reed-beds. A silence fell upon them as Lannon stepped forward and turned to face them.

His body was naked but for the loin-cloth, and the skin was smooth and startlingly white except where the sun had gilded his face and limbs. It was a beautiful body, tall and gracefully proportioned, heavy in the shoulder and narrow at waist and belly. His curls were bound with a purple headband and his red-gold beard was clubbed and turned up against his throat.

He looked at the waiting ranks before him.

'I make claim to the city of Opet, and all the four kingdoms,' he said with simplicity, and his voice carried clearly to every one of them.

Huy took his weapons to him. The shield. Hide of the buffalo, shaped in a long oval, tall as a man and as wide as his shoulders. In its centre were the 'eyes', a pair of fierce owl eyes painted in white and yellow. When these were exposed to a beast they represented the natural aggressive stare which would usually trigger the charge of a predator.

'May this shield cover you well,' Huy told him softly.

'Thank you, old friend.'

Next Huy offered him the lion spear. This was such a heavy cumbersome weapon that only a powerful man could handle it. The shaft was of carefully selected hard wood, fire-treated, and bound with green leather which had been allowed to dry and shrink upon it. It was as thick as Lannon's wrist, and twice as tall as he was.

The unbarbed blade was in proportion wide and heavy, bound into the shaft with leather strips, the round point honed to a razor edge. It was designed to allow the maximum penetration into flesh and, once buried, to open a massive wound that would induce heavy bleeding.

'May this blade find the heart,' Huy whispered, and then louder. 'Roar for me, Gry-Lion of Opet.'

Lannon reached out and touched the priest's shoulder. He squeezed it briefly.

'Fly for me, bird of the sun,' he said and turned away. With the shield on his back, careful not to show the 'eyes', Lannon walked out towards the waiting beast. He walked tall and proud in the sunlight, a king in all but name, and Huy's heart went with him. Quietly Huy began to pray, hoping that the gods were still attentive.

Lannon strode through the soft grass that brushed his knees. As he went he remembered the advice of the oldest and best of his huntmasters, rehearsing each move, each word of it.

'Wait until he growls before you show him the eyes.'

'Make him come to you at an angle.'

'He charges with head held low. You must open his chest from the side.'

'The skull is like iron, the bones of the shoulder will turn the finest metal.'

'There is one place only. The base of the neck, between spine and shoulder.'

Then the words of the only man amongst them all who had ever faced the gry-lion, Hamilcar Barca, the forty-sixth Gry-Lion of Opet, 'Once the spear is in, hold it, my son, cling to it with your life. For the gry-lion is still alive and that shaft is all that will keep him from you until he dies.'

Lannon walked on steadily watching the black swollen-bellied carcass of the buffalo, seeing no sign of the beast he was hunting.

'They are mistaken,' he thought. 'There is nothing here.'

He could hear his own heart beating in the silence, his own footfalls, and the hiss and suck of his breath. He watched the dead buffalo and walked on, tucking the butt of the lion spear more firmly under his right armpit.

'There is nothing here. The gry-lion has gone,' he thought, then suddenly he saw movement ahead of him. Just the flick of two ears held erect for a moment then flattened again, but he knew that it was there waiting for him. He felt his steps begin to drag, feet heavy with fear, but he forced himself onwards.

'Fear is the destroyer,' he thought, and tried to force it down, but it was a cold heavy thing like oil in his guts. He walked on, and suddenly the gry-lion stood up beside the carcass of the buffalo. It stood facing him, with ears erect, its tail swinging lazily, head up, watching him, and Lannon gasped aloud. He had not expected it to be so large. He missed a step, hesitating. It was huge, unbelievable, like something from a nightmare.

He was 200 paces from it, and he walked on towards it, concealing the 'eyes', and watching the giant cat's tail swish faster with agitation as he approached.

A hundred paces from it, and now the tail began to slash angrily, like a whip against the gry-lion's flanks. The cat crouched a little, the ears flattening against the skull. Lannon could see the eyes now, hot yellow eyes in the patterned face-mask.

He walked on, and the gry-lion's ruff of mane came erect, swelling out the shape of its head, it sank a little lower into its crouch. Its tail slashed furiously, and Lannon walked on towards it.

Fifty paces separated them now, and the gry-lion growled. It was muttering menace of distant thunder, the drumming of the earth in quake, a belly-jarring sound like the crash of surf on a storm-swept beach. Lannon stopped, he could not walk on with that sound in his ears. He stood frozen, staring at this terrible animal in its mounting rage.

Long seconds he hesitated, then with an abrupt movement born of fear he swept the shield from his back and showed the 'eyes'. The glaring roundels were all that was needed to precipitate the beast's anger. The black tufted tail froze rigid, lifted slightly above the level of its back, the head dropped low against its chest, and it charged.

At the same moment as the charge began Lannon went up on his toes, and jumped forward. The shackles of fear fell from his limbs, and he bounded towards the charging cat with long light strides. He was angling his run across the gry-lion's front, forcing it to keep turning towards him, bringing it in at an angle, exposing the neck and the side of the chest.

As Lannon ran the spear blade danced above the earth ahead of him, like a firefly of light in the sun.

The gry-lion came fast, and low, head down so that the incredible fangs almost touched its chest, curved and ivory pale. It seemed to snake against the grass as it closed for the kill, and its enormous bulk filled the whole of Lannon's vision.

At the last possible instant Lannon lifted the spear-tip slightly, centring it on the vital spot at the base of the neck, and the gry-lion came on to the spear with its whole weight driving it.

The blade plunged into the brown furry body, sucked into unresisting flesh, and the shock of the impact drove up the shaft and hurled Lannon backwards on to his knees – but he held on to the spear.

A storm raged about him, great waves of sound engulfed him, battering his eardrums, as the gry-lion roared out its death throes. The shaft of the lion-spear whipped and thrashed in his grip, smashing against his ribs, crushing and bruising his flesh, shaking him so his teeth clashed together in his skull lacerating his tongue. He clung to the spear.

He was lifted from his feet, riding high on the shaft of the spear as the gry-lion reared, then he was smashed down on to the earth again as the great cat plunged. He felt muscle and sinew tear in his arm and shoulders, felt the gry-lion's claws raking the flimsy leather shield, felt weakness in his body and darkness in his head, but still the storm raged and shook him.

Once more the gry-lion roared and reared. Lannon felt himself hurled towards the heavens, the shaft of the lion-spear snapped like a brittle twig, and Lannon was thrown with the butt of it still in his hands. He flew for long seconds, bird free, then earth thumped the breath from his lungs. Painfully he dragged himself into a sitting position, and looked around him stunned, clutching the broken shaft of the spear to his chest.

Ten paces away the gry-lion was crawling towards him through the grass. The broken hilt of the spear protruded from the exact spot in the neck where Lannon had aimed. The gry-lion's throes had worked the blade mercilessly in its own flesh, opening a hideous wound from which the bright heart blood pumped, but the gry-lion's yellow eyes were still upon him, and those great curved fangs gleamed for his flesh.

Slowly it crawled towards him, its breath drumming in the mighty throat, dragging its paralysed hind quarters, dying but still deadly.

'Die,' thought Lannon, watching it with fascination, crushed by the conflict, unable to move. 'Die,' he thought. 'Please die.' And suddenly the final spasm caught the giant cat. Its back arched, the legs stiffened, claws ripping into the earth, the mouth opened wide and pink, and it groaned. One last long pitiful groan, and it died.

The half circle of watchers shouted, a cheer that was lost in the great silence of the swamps, and they began moving forward slowly towards the tiny figure of the king out on the grassy plain. But Huy was running. On legs too long for his crumpled trunk he seemed to dance over the ground, his long black tresses flowing out behind him and the vulture axe on his shoulder.

He was half-way to where Lannon sat bowed in the grass when the second gry-lion stood up from where it had lain concealed behind the carcass of the nearest buffalo. Huy saw it and shouted as he ran.

'Lannon! Behind you! Beware!'

Lannon looked back and saw it. It was the female, lighter in colour, daintier in build, but notoriously more savage than the male. It moved towards Lannon with the deadly concentration of a stalking cat.

'Baal speed me!' Huy prayed as he ran towards his prince, and saw him trying to struggle to his feet. The gry-lion was slinking low along the ground, moving forward in short dashes.

Huy ran with all his might, driven by horror and fear for his prince. Lannon was on his feet now, reeling weakly away from the stalking cat. The movement triggered the hunting reflex of the gry-lion, it closed remorselessly.

Huy shouted at it. 'Here!' he yelled. 'Come!' And the cat noticed him for the first time. It lifted its head and looked at him. The fangs glinting long and pale, the eyes yellow and splendid.

'Yes!' shouted Huy. 'Here I am!' He saw Lannon stagger and fall, dropping out of sight into the grass, but he watched the beast. Saw the tail stiffen and the head drop. It began its charge, and Huy checked his.

He stood to meet the gry-lion, braced on long powerful legs, with the axe on his shoulder, and he let the cat come straight.

As it closed he fastened his gaze on the black diamond pattern between the gry-lion's eyes, and he adjusted his grip on the axe, settling it carefully.

The axe went up and the gry-lion covered the last few paces in a soft roan-coloured blur of fluid movement, towering over the little hunchback.

'For Baal!' howled Huy and the axe moaned in flight. The blade cracked into skull, buried in the gry-lion's brain and was instantly torn from his grip as the full weight of the dead beast smashed into his chest.

Huy came back from deep down and far away along a tunnel of roaring darkness, and when he opened his eyes Lannon Hycanus, the forty-seventh Gry-Lion of Opet, knelt over him in the sunlight.

'The fool,' said the King, his own face bruised and swollen, caked with drying blood. 'Oh! The brave little fool.'

'Brave, yes,' whispered Huy painfully. 'But fool never, majesty.' And saw the relief dawn in Lannon's eyes.

They spread the wet skins of the two gry-lions on the main mast of the flagship, and Lannon Hycanus received the oaths of allegiance from the heads of the nine houses of Opet while reclining on a couch of soft fur beneath them. Huy Ben-Amon carried the cup of life, despite the protests of his king.

'You must rest, Huy. You are badly wounded, I believe the ribs of your chest are stove—'

'My lord, I am the cup-bearer. Would you deny me that honour?'

Asmun was the first of the nine to make oath. His sons helped him from the litter, but he shrugged away their hands as he approached Lannon.

'In respect of the snow upon your brow, and the scars of your body, you need not kneel, Asmun.'

'I will kneel, my king,' replied Asmun, and went down on the deck in the sunlight. Baal must witness the oath of this frail old man. When Huy held the cup of life to his lips he sipped it, and Huy carried the cup to the king. He drank and then offered it back to Huy.

'Drink also, my priest.'

'It is not the custom,' Huy demurred.

'The King of Opet and the four kingdoms makes the custom. Drink!'

Huy hesitated a moment longer, then lifted the cup and took a long draught. By the time Habbakuk Lal, the last of the nine, came forward the cup had been refilled five times with the heavy sweet wine of Zeng.

'Do your wounds still trouble you?' Lannon asked softly as Huy brought the cup to him for the last time.

'Majesty, I feel no pain,' Huy replied and then giggled suddenly and spilled a drop of wine down the king's chest.

'Fly high, Sunbird,' laughed Lannon.

'Roar loudly, Gry-Lion,' said Huy, and laughed with him. Lannon turned to the nobles who crowded the steering deck.

'There is food and drink.' The ceremony was over, Lannon Hycanus was king. 'Habbakuk Lal!' Lannon picked out the big ginger-bearded seaman with his freckled and sea-brined face.

'My lord.'

'Will you weigh, and set for Opet?'

'A night run?'

'Yes, I wish to reach the city before noon tomorrow, and I trust your seamanship.'

Habbakuk Lal inclined his head at the compliment and the heavy gold earrings dangled against his cheek. Then he turned on his heel, and stumped across the deck, bellowing orders at his officers.

The anchors came up over the stern, and the drummer on the forecastle of the flagship struck the hollow tree trunk with the wooden drumstick, beating out the rhythm for the racing start.

Three swift, two slow, three swift. The bank of oars dipped and swung and rose and swung forward and dipped to the beat. In perfect unison, an undulating movement, like the wet silver wing-beats of a great water bird. The long narrow hull slicing boldly through the sunset blush of lake water, the clean run of the wake streaming out behind her, the standard of house Barca hoisted at the crosstree of her masthead and her high castles fore and aft standing tall and proud above the papyrus banks on either hand.

As she swept past the other vessels of the fleet they dipped their standards, and fell in behind the flagship. Each of them holding their station meticulously in line ahead, the steersmen leaning on the rudder oar and the drum-beats booming out across the lake.

His hobbling gait was all that betrayed Huy's discomfort as he moved from group to group upon the torch-lit deck, with each of them he pointed the bottom of the wine bowl to the starry bright night sky, and bounced the ivory dice across the deck.

'Damn your luck,' laughed Philo, but the laughter did not hide the anger in his brooding gypsy dark features. 'Am I mad to dice with a favourite of the gods?' But he stacked gold upon the board, covering Huy's pile, and Huy scooped the dice and threw the three black fish again. Philo pulled his robes closer about him and moved away with the laughter and the shouted gibes of the watchers following him.

The bright white star of Astarte had set when at last Lannon and Huy stood together beneath the spread skins of the gry-lions and looked about the deck. It was a battlefield when the battle is spent. The bodies lay strewn about in the torch light, lying where they had fallen, loose and senseless. A wine bowl rolled back and forth with the easy motion of the ship that still sped on into the darkness.

'Another victory,' Lannon spoke thickly, peering blearily around at the carnage.

'A notable victory, Majesty.'

'I think,' Lannon began, but did not finish. His legs buckled under him. He swayed and swung forward. Huy caught him neatly as he fell, and settled him across one shoulder. Ignoring the pain in his chest he lifted the king and carried him down to the main cabin below the deck. He dropped Lannon on the bed, and arranged his limbs and head more comfortably. A moment longer he stayed, hanging over the supine figure.

'Sweet sleep, my beautiful king,' he blurted and turned to stagger away to his own cabin. The slave girl rose at his entrance.

'I have set out your writing pallet,' she told him, and Huy peered at the scroll, ink bowl and stylus under the hanging lamp.

'Not tonight.' He started towards the bed, lost direction, crashed into the bulkhead and bounced backwards. The slave girl ran to help him, and steered him into port.

Huy lay on his back and looked up at her. She was one of Lannon's household. Huy wished he could afford one like her, but she would fetch ten fingers of gold at the least.

'Is there anything else, my lord?' she asked. She was a pretty little thing with dark soft hair and pale ivory-yellow skin. Huy closed one eye the better to focus on her.

'Perhaps,' he said shyly. 'If you will help a little.' But his aspirations were too ambitious, and in a few moments his snores shook the ship to its keel. The girl rose, pulled on her robe and for a moment smiled down at him before she slipped out of the cabin.

In the darkness before dawn Huy stood on the forecastle of the galley and worked the axe, keeping it in flight, humming and hissing in the gloom. He felt the sluggish old wine in his veins begin to course faster, the sweat broke out on his body that the cool lake air could not quench. He changed hands smoothly on the cut, and the great axe sang. The dullness in his head lightened and the sweat poured now, streaming down his muscled legs and arms, over the bull-humped back, soaking the loin cloth, running into his eyes, and Huy began to dance, lightly he spun and leapt and weaved, and still the axe flew.

Dawn was pinking the sky when at last he stopped and leaned upon the axe. His breath steamed and gasped in the cold stream of air, but his blood raced through his body and he felt like a man again.

In the cabin one of Lannon's slave girls scraped the sweat from his body with the gold strigil that was a gift from Lannon. Then she rubbed him down with perfumed oil, plaited and set his hair and beard, and held a loose unbelted robe of white linen for him.

He came up on the steering-deck just as the order to heave to was passed to the fleet, and they swung towards the east to await the coming of the sun with the slave oarsmen collapsing thankfully over their oars. As the sun showed over the horizon Huy led the praise chant to Baal. Then there was breakfast on the open deck with the company squatting on mats of plaited reeds. Huy looked at their faces, grey and crumpled, baggy-eyed and bad-tempered. Even Lannon was pale and his hands shook as he breakfasted on a bowl of warm milk and honey.

Huy started on millet cakes dripping with oil and honey, then he ate a large smoked and salted lake bream, and when he called for a broiled duck reeking with rank wild garlic and more millet cakes the company watched him with awe. Huy ripped the duck to pieces and forced an expression of relish as he ate, for he was jealous of his reputation.

Philo spoke for them all when he cried at last 'Great Baal! You insult not only your own belly but mine as well.' And he jumped up and hurried below.

'He is right,' Lannon laughed for the first time that day. 'You look like a child who has drunk nothing more poisonous than his mother's milk.'

'He was weaned on red Zeng wine, and he cut his teeth on the blade of a battle-axe.'

'If the lake was wine he would lower the level so we could walk across.'

Huy twinkled at them like a mischievous gnome, and tore another leg from the carcass of the duck.

In the middle morning they reached the shallows and Habbakuk Lal went forward to pilot the ship through the narrow channel. Water hyacinth, papyrus and a dozen other varieties of vegetation threatened to clog the life-line of Opet. The channel boats pulled out of the lane as the ten great ships flew past on their silver-wet wings. The officers saluted the standard of Barca at the masthead with a clenched fist, but the slave gangs who were doomed for ever to fight the lake weed stood dumbly and watched with patient animal eyes.

Closer to Opet now they began passing the fishing fleet, the nets coming in over the side with fish shining silver in the mesh like captured stars, and the white clouds of gulls shrieking and fussing overhead.

Then the cliffs came up on the horizon, glowing dusky red in the sunlight and the rail was crowded with those who were enjoying this moment of homecoming.

Mursil, the huntmaster, came to Lannon on the steering deck and knelt briefly.

'You sent for me, Majesty.'

'Yes – and the pygmy.'

'He is here, King.'

'I promised you a reward. Name it.'

'My lord, I have three wives. All of them avaricious.'

'Gold?'

'If it please you, my lord.'

'Huy, write an order on the treasury for five fingers of gold.'

'May Baal shine upon you always!'

'What of the pygmy?'

Mursil called the little yellow bushman to him, and Lannon examined him with interest.

'What is he named?'

'Xhai, my lord.'

'Does he not understand the language?'

'No, my lord, he speaks only his own primitive tongue.'

'Ask him what he desires – freedom, perhaps?'

'He does not understand the idea of freedom. He is like a dog, Majesty. Deprive him of a master and you deprive him of the reason for life.'

'Ask him what he wants.'

Mursil and the bushman spoke for a long while in that birdlike chittering tongue, before the huntmaster turned back to the king.

'It is a strange request.'

'Name it.'

'He wishes to hunt with the slayer of the gry-lion.'

Lannon stared at the bushman, who grinned at him with the beguiling candour of a child.

'He thinks, my lord, and you will forgive the impertinence,' Mursil was sweating a little, ill at ease, 'he thinks you are a God, and he wants to belong to you.'

Lannon let out a bull roar of laughter and slapped his thigh.

'So be it then. He is elevated to a master of the royal hunt – with the pay and privileges. Take him, Huy. Teach him to speak the language, or failing that learn to speak his!'

'All the strays and cripples,' thought Huy ruefully. His household was filled with them, whenever he had accumulated sufficient gold for a luscious young slave maid it went on another who was too old or infirm to justify his keep and who was consigned by his master to the pool of Astarte. At least the pygmy would have his pay as a huntmaster to help with the costs.

Lannon dismissed the subject and turned back to the rail. The mother city came up over the horizon at last. The walls of the temple shone a ruddy rose in the sunlight, and the lower city was brilliant white, the walls of the houses painted with the ash of the lake shell-fish.

The war fleet of Opet streamed out from the harbour to meet them. The shields and helmets of the legionaries sparkled in the sun as each ship in turn wheeled across the flagship's bows with the gilt work on her arrow-sharp prow catching the sunlight. They saw the raw skins hanging below the standard of house Barca and a cheer roared out across the water.

The flagship led them into the harbour. Still scudding to the drive of her banked oars. Habbakuk Lal aimed at the stone jetty below the city where the crowds thronged the shore. The entire population of the city was out in their best and most brilliant robes, shrieking and cheering their new king from 100,000 throats.

At the last possible moment Habbakuk Lal dropped his hand in a signal to the drummer and steersman. The ship spun on her heel, with every oar clawing at the water to drag her to a halt, her side lightly touching the stone jetty. Lannon Hycanus and his train stepped ashore.

Lannon's wives were the first to greet him. Nine of them, one from each of the noble houses, young matrons of the blood, proud and beautiful. Each one came forward to kneel before Lannon, and call him 'sire' for the first time.

Huy looked at them with a heart that ached. These were not the pliant, brainless slave girls whose company was all he had ever known. These were full women. He needed someone like that to share a life with, and he had tried so hard. He had carried his suit to every one of the great houses of Opet, and had it rejected. They could see no further than his back, and he could not blame them for it.

The dignity of the occasion was abruptly shattered by a loud chorus of 'Hoo! Hoo!' and the twins broke away from their nursemaids and raced each other across the jetty. Ignoring their father and the gathered nobles, they ran to Huy and danced about him, tugging at his robe and demanding his attention. When he picked them up they competed so fiercely for his kisses that it developed into a hair-pulling bout. The nursemaids flew to the rescue and dragged them away.

Imilce's hands still locked in Helanca's golden tresses, and from the scowl on Lannon's face Huy knew that there would be retribution and that those plump little bottoms would soon be glowing red. He wished there was some way he could prevent it.

Huy slipped away into the crowd. On the way to the temple he haggled for a chicken with one of the merchants and struck a good bargain. After he had sacrificed he went to his own house in the precinct of the priests between the outer and inner wall of the temple. His household were all there to meet him, doting and doddering, fussing about him with their grey heads and toothless gums. All agog for the news of his latest exploits, demanding the story of the hunt, while they bathed and fed him.

When at last he escaped to his sleeping quarters to rest, he had not lain for long when the four eldest princesses arrived. Aged from ten to six, they broke through the feeble defences of his slaves and invaded his room as if by right.

With a sigh Huy abandoned rest and sent one of them to fetch his lute, and as he began to sing the slaves, one at a time, crept into the room and sat quietly along the wall. Huy Ben-Amon was home again.

In the year 533 from the founding of Opet, six months after he had taken the gry-lion and claimed the four kingdoms, Lannon Hycanus, the head of house Barca, left the city of Opet and went out to march around his borders, a custom that would bind his claim irrevocably. He was twenty-nine years old in that spring, a year older than his high priest.

He marched with four of his wives, the childless ones, hoping to change their status upon the two-year journey. He took with him two legions each of 6,000 hoplites, light infantry, axemen and archers. The legions were composed mostly of Yuye freedmen with officers from the noble families of Opet. These legions were organized along the Roman lines, in the manner that Hannibal had adopted during his campaign in Italia. There were ten cohorts to a legion and six centuries to a cohort. They were uniformed in leather body armour with conical iron helmets and circular leather shields studded with bronze rosettes. On their legs and feet they wore leather greaves and nailed sandals, and they sang as they marched.

The officers were more magnificently appointed as befitted their noble origins. Their armour was of bronze and their cloaks were of fine linen dyed purple and red, and they marched at the head of their divisions.

There was no cavalry. In 500 years no attempt to bring horses from the north had succeeded. Every one of the animals had succumbed to the sea voyage, or surviving that had died soon after arrival at Opet of a mysterious disease that made their coats stand on end and turned their eyeballs to bloody red jelly.

In place of cavalry were the elephants. Huge, ugly-tempered beasts, who struck terror into the hearts of the enemies of Opet when they charged with the archers in the castle upon their backs loosing a shower of arrows as they came on. In battle frenzy, however, they could wreak as much havoc amongst their own army as that of the enemy, and their handlers were equipped with a mallet and a spike to drive into the brains of the berserk animals. Lannon took twenty-five of these beasts upon his march.

With him went his high priest and a dozen lesser priests, engineers, physicians, armourers, cooks, slaves and a huge flock of camp followers: merchants, prospectors, gamblers, soothsayers, liquor-sellers and prostitutes. The bullock train carrying the tentage and supplies stretched for seven miles, while the whole unwieldy column spread out over fifteen miles. This was no problem in the huge unpeopled grass plains of the south with their plentiful supplies of water and forage, but when Huy Ben-Amon stood on a low hill with his king and saw the slow straggling mass coming down out of the north he thought of the time when they would turn north again in a great circle amongst the forests and broken country along the great river. Such a collection of wealth would be a sore temptation to the pagan war bands from the unknown land beyond the river. He told Lannon his misgivings and Lannon laughed, crinkling his pale blue eyes into the sun.

'You think more like a soldier than a priest.'

'I am both.'

'Of course.' Lannon dropped a hand on his shoulder. 'Not for nothing the command of the sixth legion – well, Huy, I have thought much of this march. In the past, it has always been a great time-waster and a sorry expense on the treasury of Opet. My march will be different. I intend to turn a profit.'

Huy smiled at that magic word, the one understood by all in Opet, noble or commoner, king or priest.

'I intend to make this a different type of march. In the south kingdom we will hunt – hunts such as you have never conceived, and the meat will be smoked and dried and sold to the houses and mines to feed their slaves. We will hunt also for elephant. I would like my army to have 200 of these animals to meet the threats from the north of which you have just reminded me.'

'I had wondered at the multitude of empty wagons that follow us.'

'They will be filled before we turn northwards again,' Lannon promised. 'And when we pass through the gardens of Zeng, I will change the garrisons there, leaving these men in their place. Troops who stay too long in one billet grow lazy and corrupt. At Zeng I will meet the emissaries of the Dravs from the east and renew our treaty with them.'

'But what of the north?' Huy came back to his original question.

'From Zeng we will march north in battle array. The women and the others will be sent home to Opet along the road through the middle kingdom. We will come to the river with two full legions to reinforce the two already there, and we will cross the river on a burning and slave-taking raid that will warn the tribes beyond that a new king reigns in Opet.'

Lannon turned and glared towards the north, and his mane of golden and red hair and beard shone in the sunlight.

'For a hundred years now they have plagued us, and we have been too soft with them. Each year they have grown more numerous, more daring. I will show them the iron of my hand, Sunbird. I will show them that the river is held by a barrier of bright steel, and they will press against it at their cost.'

'Where do they come from, I wonder, and how many of them are there?' Huy asked softly.

'They are the hosts of darkness, black because they are not of the sun-god Baal as we are. They were spawned in darkness in the forests of eternal night to the north, and when you can number the greedy locusts then you will count them also.'

'Are you afraid, Lannon?' Huy asked, and the king turned to him with a fiery anger darkening his face.

'You presume, priest,' he snarled.

'Call me friend, not priest – and I do presume to show you that unreasoning hatred is based on fear.'

Lannon's anger faded, and he fiddled with the hilt of his sword, glancing about to make sure that his aides were out of earshot.

'There is reason for fear,' he said at last.

'I know,' said Huy.

Huy led the praise chant to Baal in the dawn, but they kept the volume of their voices low so as not to alarm the nearest herds, and afterwards Huy asked the gods to look with favour upon the hunt, promising that a part of the spoils would be left for the Sunbirds to carry on high. Then Huy and Lannon drank a bowl of wine and ate a dry millet cake together as they waited for the hunt to develop.

Mursil, the huntmaster of the south, had chosen the ground with cunning and care. From where they sat on the low line of the escarpment they could look down the vast funnel-shaped plain hemmed in by hills on either hand; along the summit of the hills the signal fires smoked in the early morning to show that the warriors were in position there to run any of the game that tried to cross out of the valley.

In the distance, beyond the range of the eye the two legions were spread out across the plain. Already they were moving forward, 10,000 men, sweeping the grassland like a wave across the beach. The dust of their advance rose palely against the eggshell blue of the morning sky, and below the pall an occasional flash of light came from helmet or spear.

'It has begun,' said Lannon with satisfaction.

Huy looked out on the tens of thousands of grazing animals scattered in herds about the plain. This was the tenth great hunt in fifty days, and the slaughter was beginning to sicken him a little.

He glanced down to where the plain narrowed and the river that bisected it ran down into the neck. At the base, squeezed into a wedge shape by the hills, was a gap of 500 paces which promised escape to the limitless expanse of grassland beyond. The whole plain was thinly scattered with tall flat-topped acacia trees.

Even from where they sat above the gap they could barely see the treble line of concealed pits across the gap that joined the spurs of the two ranges of hills. A thousand of Lannon's archers lay in ambush there, each with a bundle of 300 arrows and a spare bow.

Beyond them still was a double line of netting, heavy woven mesh standing on flimsy poles that would collapse when a heavy body charged into it, smothering the animal in its folds until one of the hoplites could jump up from his hiding-place and run forward with a javelin to despatch the animal and reset the net. Here another 1,000 javelin throwers lay in waiting.

'We should go down now.' Lannon finished the last of the wine and brushed a few crumbs from his cloak.

'A little longer,' Huy suggested. 'I should like to watch this.'

A restlessness was running through the herds upon the plain, beginning with the animals nearest the lines of beaters. The long lines of gnu began running in aimless circles with their noses almost raking the ground, black bodies with long flowing manes kicking and frolicking. The herds of zebra grouped themselves in compact masses of some 200 or 300 animals and looked curiously towards the line of approaching beaters. Their close relatives, the quagga, short and sturdier, assembled in lesser herds, a darker bay colour then the grey zebra. Mixed with them were herds of brilliant yellow and red hartebeest, purple sassaby, and the great bovine eland, striped and maned and majestic. This vast multitude began a stirring and moving, a general slow retreat down the valley towards the gap – and the dust rose around them.

'Ah,' said Lannon. 'What a booty.'

'There could never have been a greater in the history of the hunt,' Huy agreed.

'How many, do you think?' Lannon asked.

'I do not know – fifty, a hundred thousand – it would not be possible to count them.'

Now the long-necked giraffe were infected by the growing alarm, they left the shelter of the acacia trees and their calves followed them as they joined the mass movement down the valley. Amongst the host trotted an occasional rhinoceros, big and cumbersome, horned and snorting, lifting his massive hooves high as he ran.

Like a flux holding the entire mass together moved the smoky brown herds of dainty springbok. They came on down the valley, moving more urgently, like flood waters, and the dust rose thicker, swirling up in choking clouds. The hills squeezed the herds into a denser mass, and when the hartebeest and sassaby tried to cross the ridges on either hand there was a line of screaming, weapon-brandishing men to meet and turn them from the crest. They charged down the slope again carrying and spreading the panic through the closely packed herds below.

They surged forward, and the sound of their hooves rose like the sound of storm, surf and wind. The ground began to shake. 'Come,' shouted Lannon and he jumped up and went bounding down the slope. For a moment longer Huy watched that unbelievable phalanx of living creatures thundering down on the gap, then he shouldered his axe and went racing down the slope after Lannon. His long black hair streamed out behind him, and he ran goat-footed, rabbit fast, so that he and Lannon came out on the plain together and Huy led the way into the centre of the gap where a pit had been dug for them and a dozen bundles of javelins lay ready.

Lannon jumped down beside him. 'There was no gold on that race,' he laughed.

'There should have been,' said Huy, and they went to the front lip of the pit and looked up the valley. It was a terrifying sight. The entire valley from side to side was clogged with a great tide of living things, and above them rose a high brown wall of dust through which the low sun glared balefully.

The heads and manes of the lead animals tossed and heaved like the surface of a torrent, and above them rose the stick-like necks of the giraffe and ostrich.

The whole bore down upon them, and the earth trembled beneath them and they stared in awe and wonder.

Lannon was judging his moment carefully, waiting for the first wave of game to cross his range-markers. The moment came and he snapped an order to his trumpeter. The single urgent note of the attack rang out, repeated stridently over and over again.

From the earth at the feet of the advancing wall of living things rose the line of archers. They loosed four times before the wall swept over them. Four thousand arrows in twenty seconds and those that followed fell over the wind-rows of dead animals, screaming with the agony of broken bone and arrow-impaled flesh.

Borne by the weight of their own forward momentum the masses of game pressed onwards while flight after flight of arrows decimated their ranks, and the corpses and wounded piled in ridges and huge mounds.

The smaller game were wiped out by the archers, but the larger thick-skinned animals came through with the arrows bristling in their flanks. Great grey rhinoceros, lumbering wild-eyed towards the line of nets, tossing their long curved nose horns. Giraffe galloping long-legged and terror-driven. A squadron of black buffalo running in a mass, shoulder to shoulder like a team in span.

They came into the nets, and fell struggling and screaming. The javelins whipped into them as they rolled and roared, smothered in the folds of heavy netting. Desperately Lannon and his men worked to clear the dead from the netting and reset the poles, but it was effort wasted. There were too many of them now, and there was death out there in the open beyond the security of the pits. Arrow-maddened, the wounded game charged for any man who showed himself.

Huy saw a soldier tossed by an angry rhinoceros. He cartwheeled in the air, and fell on the hard earth to be kicked and trampled to a muddy pulp in the dust by the hordes that followed.

From the pit now Lannon hurled his javelins with an uncanny accuracy and power, aiming each bolt for the soft ribs behind the shoulder of the passing game. He piled the bodies about the pit, shouting and laughing in the frenzied excitement of the hunt.

Huy also was infected by it. He danced and shouted and waved his axe, guarding Lannon's back and flank, hurling a javelin when some huge animal seemed about to crash into the pit on top of them.

Both he and Lannon were soaked with their own sweat and caked with the swirling dust; a stone flung by a dashing hoof had cut Huy's forehead open to the bone of the skull and he ripped the hem from his tunic and bound the wound quickly, hardly interrupting his dance of excitement.

In front of them the archers had been overwhelmed by the sheer weight of animal flesh. With their arrows exhausted they cowered in their pits and let the solid ranks pour over them.

Huy saw the fresh ranks driving down on them and he grabbed his blood-crazed king and dragged him struggling to the floor of the pit, and they lay with their heads covered by their arms while the edges of the pit crumbled in on top of them under the impact of hooves. Earth smothered them and they covered their faces with the hems of their tunics and gasped for breath.

A young zebra stallion fell into the pit on top of them, kicking and neighing in terror with its powerful yellow teeth snapping indiscriminately, it was a deadly danger.

Huy rolled away from its flying razor-sharp hooves. He paused a moment to aim and then shot his right arm upwards. The spiked head of the vulture axe lanced up under the terrified animal's jaw, entering the brain cleanly. It collapsed warm and limp and shivering on top of them, and its corpse was a protection from the storm of hooves that raged about them.

The storm dwindled, passed over, and rumbled away into the distance. In the quiet that followed, Huy rolled towards Lannon.

'Are you safe?' And Lannon crawled with difficulty from under the dead zebra. They dragged themselves from the pit and looked about them with wonder.

Across a front of 500 paces, and to a depth of the same distance the ground was covered by a thick carpet of dead and dying game. From their pits amongst this terrible carnage the archers and javelin-throwers climbed and stood staring with the dazed air of drunken men.

The line of beaters seemed to wade towards them out of a swamp of hanging dust, even the sky was dulled with the dust, and the pitiful cries and the bleating of the dying and wounded animals shamed the silence.

The beaters came forward in lines through the fields of bleeding flesh and their swords rose and fell as they killed the wounded. Huy reached under his tunic and brought out a leather flask of Zeng wine.

'I can always trust you for comfort.' Lannon grinned, and drank greedily. The wine drops shone like blood in his dusty beard.

'Was there ever a hunt like that?' he asked as he handed the flask to Huy.

Huy drank and then looked about him at the field. 'I cannot believe there ever was,' he said softly.

'We will smoke and dry this kill – and then hunt again,' Lannon promised and strode away to order the butchery.

A high dome of orange light hung over the plain, light reflected from 10,000 fires. All afternoon and all that night the army worked to butcher the enormous bag. To cut the flesh into strips and hang it on the racks over the smoking fires. The smell of sweet raw flesh, the musty reek of split entrails, and the sizzle of the cooking meat drifted across the camp where Huy sat beneath the awning of his leather tent and worked by the fluttering light of an oil lamp.

Lannon came out of the darkness, still filthy with dust and dried blood.

'Wine! Sunbird, for the love of a friend.' He pretended to stagger with thirst, and Huy passed both amphora and bowl to him. Scorning the bowl Lannon drank directly from the neck of the jug and wiped his beard on his arm.

'I come with news,' he grinned. 'The bag was 1,700 head.'

'How many of them men?'

'Fifteen men died, and there are some wounded – but was it not worth it?'

Huy did not answer, and Lannon went on.

'There is more news. Another of my javelins has struck the mark. Annel has missed her moon.'

'The southern air must be beneficial. All four of them with child in two months.'

'It is not the air, Sunbird,' Lannon laughed and drank again.

'I am pleased,' said Huy. 'More of the old blood for Opet.'

'When did you ever care for blood, Huy Ben-Amon? You are pleased to have more of my brats to spoil – I know you.' Lannon came to stand behind Huy. 'You are writing,' he said, unnecessarily. 'What is it?'

'A poem,' said Huy modestly.

'What of?'

'The hunt – today's hunt.'

'Sing it to me,' commanded Lannon and dropped onto Huy's fur bed, with the amphora still grasped by the neck.

Huy fetched his lute, and squatted on the reed mat. He sang, and when he had finished Lannon lay quietly on the bed staring out through the opening of the tent into the night.

'I did not see it like that,' he said at last. 'To me it was just a taking, a harvest of flesh.'

He was silent again.

'I have displeased you?' Huy asked, and Lannon shook his head.

'Do you truly believe that what we did today has destroyed something that will never be replaced?' he asked.

'I do not know, perhaps not – but if we hunted like that every day, or even once every ten days, would we not soon turn this land into a desert?'

Lannon brooded quietly over the half-empty amphora for a long while, then he looked up at Huy and smiled.

'We have taken sufficient meat. We will not hunt again this year – only for ivory.'

'My lord, has the wine jug stuck to your hand?' Huy asked softly, and Lannon stared at him for a moment then laughed.

'A trade, Sunbird, another song and I will give you wine.'

'A fair trade,' Huy agreed.

When the amphora was empty, Huy sent one of his ancient slaves for another.

'Bring two,' suggested Lannon. 'It will save time later.'

At midnight Huy was soft from the wine, and desolated by the beauty of his own voice and the sadness of his own song. He wept, and Lannon seeing him weep, wept with him.

'I will not have such beauty recorded on the skin of beasts,' cried Lannon with the tears cutting runnels through the dust on his cheeks and pouring into his beard. 'I will have a scroll made of the finest gold, and on it you will inscribe your songs, my Sunbird. Then they will live for ever to delight my children and my children's children.'

Huy stopped weeping. The artist in him aroused, his mind quickly assimilating the offer which he knew Lannon would not remember in the morning.

'I am truly honoured, my lord.' Huy went to kneel at the side of the bed. 'Will you sign the treasury order now?'

'Write it, Huy, write it now, this instant,' Lannon commanded. 'I will sign it.'

And Huy ran for his writing pallet.

The column moved on slowly in a great circle to the south and east through the southern plains of grass. It was a land of such limitless dimensions that the fifteen-mile column was as significant as a file of safari ants. There were rivers and ranges of hills, forests and plains teeming with game. The only men they met were the garrisons of the king's hunting camps. Their task was primarily to provide a steady supply of dried meat for the multitude of slaves that were the foundation of the nation's prosperity.

They crossed the river of the south* six months after departure from the city of Opet and 100 miles beyond they reached the range of thickly forested blue mountains† which marked the border of the southern kingdom.

They went into camp at the mouth of a dark rocky gorge that tore its way through the heart of the mountains, and Lannon and Huy with a cohort of infantry and archers took the precipitous path through the gorge. It was an eerie

* Limpopo River.
† Zoutpansberg.

place of tall black stone cliffs hanging high above the roaring frothing torrent in the depths below. It was a cold dark place where the warmth of the sun seldom penetrated. Huy shivered, not from the cold, and clutched his axe firmly. He prayed almost continually during the three days that they marched through the mountains for it was most certainly a place frequented by demons.

They camped on the southern slopes of the mountains and built signal fires, sending the smoke aloft in tall columns that could be seen for fifty miles. To the southward stretched a land as vast as that to the north.

Looking out across its golden rolling grasslands and its dark green forests, Huy felt a sense of awe. 'I would like to go down into that land,' he told Lannon.

'You would be the first,' Lannon agreed. 'I wonder what it holds. What treasures, what mysteries?'

'We know there is a Cape to the far south with a flat-topped mountain where the fleet of Hycanus IX was destroyed, but that is all we know.'

'I have a mind to defy the prophecy and lead an expedition southwards beyond these mountains – what say you, Huy?'

'I would not counsel it, my lord,' Huy answered formally. 'No good ever comes of challenging the gods, they have damnably long memories.'

'I expect you are right,' Lannon conceded. 'Yet I am sorely tempted.'

Huy changed a subject which was making him uncomfortable, he should never have broached it.

'I wonder when they will come.' He looked up at the smoke from the signal fires streaming up into the calm blue of the midday sky.

'They will come when they are ready,' Lannon shrugged. 'But I wish they would make it soon. Whilst we wait, we will hunt the leopard.'

For ten days they hunted the big spotted cats which abounded in the misty cliffs and woody gorges of the mountains. They hunted with specially trained hounds and lion-spears. They would run the quarry with the pack, until it was cornered or bayed and they would then surround it and close in until the charge was provoked.

Then the man selected by the leopard would take the snarling, slashing animal on the point of his spear. Two of the hunters were killed in those ten days – and one of them was a grandson of Asmun, the old nobleman. He was a fine brave lad and they all mourned, although it was a good and honourable death. They cremated his body, for he had died in the field, and Huy sacrificed for a safe passage of his soul to the sun.

On the eleventh day, in the dawn after Huy had greeted Baal, and they had breakfasted and were dressing and arming for the hunt, Huy noticed the agitation and restlessness of the little bushman huntmaster, Xhai.

'What is it that troubles you, Zhai?' he asked him in his own language, which he now spoke with authority.

'My people are here,' the bushman told him.

'How do you know that?' Huy demanded.

'I know it!' Xhai answered simply, and Huy hurried through the camp to Lannon's tent.

'They have come, my lord,' he told him.

'Good.' Lannon laid aside his lion-spear and began stripping his hunting armour. 'Call the stone-finders.' And the royal geologists and metallurgists came hurrying to the summons.

The meeting place was at the foot of the mountains where thick forest ended abruptly at the edge of a wide glade.

Lannon led his party down amongst the rocks and at the edge of the glade they halted, and threw out a protective screen of archers. In the centre of the glade, well out of arrow-shot of the forest edge or the rocky slope, a pole had been driven into the soft earth and the tail of a reed buck dangled from it like a standard. It was the sign that the trade could begin.

Lannon nodded to his senior stone-finder, Aziru, and Rib-Addi, master of the royal treasury. The two of them walked out into the glade unarmed and with two slaves following them. The slaves each carried a leather bag.

At the foot of the pole was a dried gourd which contained a handful of bright pebbles and stones of various colours ranging from glassy to fiery red.

The two officials examined each stone, rejecting some by dropping them in a neat pile on the earth, selecting others by returning them to the gourd. Then from the leather bags they doled out glass beads into a pottery jar which they placed beside the gourd. They withdrew to the rocky slope where Lannon and his archers stood.

They waited until a dozen tiny figures left the edge of the forest and approached the pole. The troop of little bushmen squatted beside the gourd and jar and there was a long heated debate before they withdrew to the forest once more. The two officials went out into the glade and found gourd and jar untouched. The offer had been refused. They added a dozen iron arrow heads to the offering.

At the third attempt a bargain was struck when the bushmen accepted the beads and arrow heads and copper bangles, leaving the stones to be collected.

Then another batch of stones was set out beside the pole and haggled over. It was a tedious business which occupied four whole days, and while they waited Huy added considerably to his knowledge of geology.

'From where do these sun-stones come?' he asked Aziru, as he examined a yellow diamond the size of an acorn which had been traded for a pound's weight of glass beads.

'When sun and moon show together in the sky, then it may happen that their rays mingle and become hot and heavy. They fall to earth, and if they strike water then they are quenched and freeze into one of these sun stones.' Huy found this explanation utterly convincing.

'A love-drop of Baal and Astarte,' he whispered with reverence. 'No wonder then that they are so beautiful.' He looked up at Aziru. 'Where do the pygmies find them?'

'It is said that they search in the gravel beds of the rivers, and also the edge of the lakes,' Aziru explained. 'But they are not adept at recognizing the true sun-stone and their offerings contain many common stones.'

When the bushmen had traded their entire gathering of diamonds, they offered for sale the unwanted children of the tribe. These little yellow mites were left bound and shivering with terror beside the trading pole. The slave masters, experts in appraising human flesh, went out to examine them and offer payment. The pygmies were much in demand as slaves, for they were tractable, loyal and hardy. They made excellent hunters, guides, entertainers, and, strangely, children's companions.

Xhai stood behind his tall yellow-haired king and watched the trade, exactly the bargaining which had been conducted over him as a child.

At the end of the fourth day the treasury of Opet had acquired five large pottery jars of fine diamonds. Trade in these stones was a jealously guarded monopoly of the ruling house of Barca. In addition there were eighty-six bushman children between the ages of five and fifteen years. They were wild slaves, and had to be bound until tamed.

Huy devoted himself almost entirely to their welfare during the return across the mountains. With the help of Xhai and the other tame bushmen he was able to save most of them. Only a dozen of the tiny creatures died of terror and heartbreak before they could be handed over to the slave women of the main camp.

Lannon broke the camp under the southern mountains and they turned north and east, recrossing the river and picking up the mountains of Bar-Zeng* on the horizon. They began passing through the populous kingdom of the east, where the Yuye peasants farmed the corn lands along the Lion River.†

At each settlement the freedmen turned out to welcome them, and make tribute to their new king. They were a cheerful throng, and the mud-walled villages were clean and prosperous-looking. Even the slaves in the fields were sleek and well cared for, only a fool would abuse a valuable possession. The slaves were mostly blacks, taken in the north, but amongst them were those of mixed blood, sired by their own masters, or by selected stud slaves. They were unbound, differing little in dress or ornament from their masters.

Along their way the legionaries who had completed their military service left their regiments and returned to their villages. Their places in the ranks were filled by the young recruits.

They camped each night at one of the walled and fortified garrisons that studded the road to the mountains of Zeng. They were passing now through the fringes of the wide gold belt that ran east and west across the middle kingdom. It was this belt on which the wealth of Opet was based, and the king's stone-finders had developed an almost supernatural ability to find the enriched reefs in which the gold was hidden. The results of their efforts were numerous mines where the ore was prised from the earth by platoons of black slaves working naked in the narrow stifling stopes. At the surface it was crushed and the powdered rock washed from the grains of native gold in specially designed copper basins.

Lannon paused in his march to inspect many of these works, and Huy was impressed by the ingenuity of the engineers who overcame the problems that the extraction of the ore presented at each separate site.

Where the gold-bearing reef was narrow, they kept the head-room in the stopes as low as possible by using only women and children in the workings.

They employed elephants for hauling the ore baskets to the surface, and for carrying water to the mines situated in the drier areas.

They had developed a method of undermining massive ore bodies and collapsing them under their own weight. It was a dangerous procedure, and at one of the mines practising this method Lannon and Huy were kept from sleep the entire night by the mourning wailing from the slave compound. During the day an ore body had collapsed prematurely and over a hundred slaves with a few slave-masters had been crushed beneath it. Huy wondered how much of that hideous sound was on account of the dead slave-masters.

Driven by his insatiable curiosity, Huy had himself lowered in one of the ore baskets to the lower levels of one of the workings. It was a hellish place of foul air, and heat and sweat, lit by the flickering oil lamps. The naked slaves toiled in cramped and dangerous chambers hacked from the living rock. Huy watched an intrusive outcrop of harder rock demolished by the means Hannibal had used hundreds of years before to clear his passage across the alps. A slow fire was lit and kept burning upon the rock until it had heated to a dull glow. It was quenched then with buckets of liquid, a mixture of water and sour wine, that exploded in a swirling cloud of steam, and split the rock into chunks which were hacked out and dragged away by the slaves. Huy went to the face where he saw

* The Chimanimani Mountains.
† The Sabi River.

the native gold shine in the mother lode, rich and yellow, and he mused at the price that must be paid for its extraction.

When Huy was again hoisted to the surface he was soaked with sweat, and filthy with dirt from the stopes.

Lannon shook his head. 'What did you want to do that for? Have the birds got your brain, that you must grovel around in the earth?'

At one of the mines the ore had been exhausted above the level of the subterranean water. It was impossible to go down below this level, for no method had yet been devised to clear the water from the workings. Bucket chains of slaves were seldom able to lower the level by more than a few inches. The mine must be returned to Astarte the mother of moon and earth. She had given of her bounty, and in return she must receive.

Lannon, as was his right, selected the messengers, conferring with his slave-masters to decide which fifteen slaves would be the least loss to the labour force. The gods were not particular about the quality of the sacrifice. To them a life was a life, and therefore acceptable.

Huy's heart went out to them as they were led down into the workings for the last time. They wore the symbolic chains of the sacrifice, and they shuffled along, stooped and maimed and coughing with the lung disease of the miners.

Huy delegated one of his priests to supervise the sending, and when his emissary emerged from that evil dark pit Huy led the praise chant to Astarte, and the work of refilling the mine began. It would continue for many weeks because of the amount of rock that must be carefully repacked into the caverns.

This refilling was necessary to placate the earth mother further and also to allow new gold to grow.

Aziru explained the need for this. 'This is benevolent ground, suitable for the growth of gold. We replace rock in the earth and the action of the sun upon it will, in time, engender a fresh growth of the precious metal.'

'All life is in Baal,' Huy intoned formally.

'Our children's children will one day thank us for this seeding of the earth,' Aziru predicted smugly, and Huy was impressed with this forethought – and he recorded every detail of it all in his neatly flowing script.

Three hundred days after leaving the city of Opet, the column climbed the foothills of the Zeng Mountains.* The air was cool and fresh after the heat of the lowlands, and at night the mist hung heavily along the slopes and woke the fever in men's bones so that they shivered and huddled in their cloaks about the camp-fires.

Those hills were the gardens of Opet, where tens of thousands of acres of land had been terraced and cultivated, and where tens of thousands of slaves tended the olive groves and vineyards. The centre and citadel of these gardens was a fortified hilltop town named after the twelfth Gry-Lion of Opet, Zeng-Hanno. Here there were temples to both Baal and Astarte, the religious strongholds of the eastern kingdom, and Huy spent twenty days in synod with his priests and priestesses. Huy also exercised and inspected his own personal legion, the sixth Ben-Amon, which was the only one of the eight legions of Opet composed entirely of warriors of the blood. Their standard was a golden vulture set on a shaft of polished ebony.

These religious activities were interrupted when Lannon summoned Huy to accompany him on a short journey to the east, from whence word had come that the Dravs awaited Lannon to renew the five-year treaty.

* Inyanga Mountains.

Three sheikhs of the Drav met them when they descended the mountains of Zeng towards the eastern sea. They were tall, brown-skinned men with fierce eagle features and dark glittering eyes. They wore headdresses of white over their long black hair, and they dressed in full-length robes belted with sashes of filigree and semi-precious stones. Each carried a magnificent broad curved dagger at his waist, and wore slippers with long pointed toes.

Their warriors dressed differently, wearing baggy pantaloons, on their heads onion-shaped helmets, body armour of silver breast-plates; and they were armed with round iron shields and long curved scimitars, spears and short oriental bows. Most of them were Negroes, but they had clearly adopted the Drav manner of speech and dress. Two hundred years of relentless warfare had preceded the treaty between the Drav and the kings of Opet.

The two armies bivouacked on each side of a wide valley, with a stream of clear water overhung with shady green trees separating the camps.

Under these trees the council tents were pitched, and here for five days the two delegations feasted and bargained and manoeuvred diplomatically.

Huy spoke the language of the Dravs and he translated for Lannon the negotiations towards a treaty of unrestricted trade and mutual military aid.

'My lord, Prince Hassan is concerned to know how many warriors Opet could put into the field in the event of a threat to the security of the two nations.'

They sat on piles of silken cushions and lovely woven woollen rugs of vivid design and colour, drinking sherbet, for the Drav would not touch even the finest wines, eating a dish of mutton and fish spiced with herbs, smiling at each other and not trusting each other further than the range of the eye.

'Prince Hassan,' replied Lannon, nodding and smiling at him, 'is concerned to know with what force we would oppose an attempt to seize the gardens of Zeng and the gold mines of the middle kingdom.'

'Of course,' Huy agreed. 'What shall I tell him?'

'Tell him I can field fourteen regular legions, as many auxiliaries, and 400 elephants.'

'He will not believe those figures, my lord.'

'Of course not, no more do I believe his. Tell him anyway.' And so the bargaining proceeded in an atmosphere of mutual trust.

They agreed to secure each other's flanks, combine to hold the line of the great river in the north against invasion by the migrant black tribes, and to come to each other's assistance if that border was violated.

'The prince would like to revolve the unit of trade, my lord. He suggests that 500 mikthals should equal one Opet finger of gold.'

'Tell him politely to swing on his own testicles,' Lannon replied, smiling at the prince, and the prince nodded and smiled back at him, the gem stones sparkling and glittering on his fingers.

They set the rate of exchange at 590 mikthals per finger, and went on to negotiate the slaving agreement, and the cotton and silk clauses. On the fifth day they ate salt together and exchanged extravagant gifts, while the armies gave displays of archery and swordsmanship and drill. These were intended to impress the other side.

'Their archers are ineffectual,' Lannon appraised them.

'The bow is too short, and they draw to the waist not the chin,' Huy agreed. 'They limit their range and accuracy.'

Then later when the infantry drilled:

'Their infantry are lighter armed and armoured, my lord. They have no axemen, and I doubt those breastplates would turn an arrow.'

'And yet they move fast, and they have a fiery spirit – do not dismiss them lightly, my Sunbird.'

'No, my lord. I will not do that.'

The elephants charged across the open ground with the archers in their castles spraying a shower of arrows ahead of the line. The huge grey beasts tossed and trampled the lines of straw dummies and their squeals and trumpets rang against the crest of the hills.

'See their faces,' Lannon murmured. 'The prince seems to be looking on the eternal seas!' And it was true that the Dravs were silent and subdued for they had no elephants of their own, they had not mastered the art of training them.

They parted and when Lannon and Huy looked back into the valley they saw the Drav army winding away eastwards in column, with the sunlight sparkling on helmets and spear-heads.

'Our eastern border is secure for five more years,' Lannon declared with satisfaction.

'Or until the princes change their minds,' Huy qualified.

'No, Sunbird. They must honour the treaty – it is in their own best interest. Trust me, old friend.'

'You, I trust,' said Huy.

On the return to Zeng-Hanno the legions assembled and preparations began for the burning which Lannon planned to lead across the great river.

Huy's legion was one of those chosen, and he spent much time with his priest-officers. They dined with him in the spendid quarters set aside for him within the enclosure of the temple of Baal. Huy invited the reverend priestesses of Astarte, and provided magnificent fare for he had hunted the day before and there was game to add to the beef and chicken and fish seasoned with spices traded from the Drav, while the gardens of Zeng provided the best of their fruits and wines.

Lannon was the guest of honour, and they were all decked with wreaths of flowers and boisterous with wine.

'Reverend Mother,' one of Huy's priests, a handsome young rake named Bakmor, called across the board to the High Priestess of Astarte. 'Is it true that you have discovered a new oracle among your novices to replace the Lady Imilce who died two years ago of the shivering sickness?'

The reverend mother turned wise old eyes on the young officer. She had pale, brittle-looking skin and her hair was fine and fluffy white. Her arms were thin and pale also and her hands skeletal and corded with blue veins. Up until now she had sat withdrawn from the revelry.

'It is true that one of the temple novices shows wisdom and wit beyond her years or training, it is true also that she has seen beyond the veil and made prophecy, but the sisterhood has not yet decided to send her to the High Priest for examination.'

'Is there doubt then, Reverend Mother?' Bakmor insisted.

'There is always doubt, my son,' the priestess answered, in a tone that clearly rebuked his presumption and the youngster sat back discomforted.

'I have not heard of this,' Huy remarked with interest and a trace of accusation in his tone. For two years the priesthood had been without the services of an oracle, and the search had been diligent. Fees for divination and prophecy formed a significant proportion of the temple income, and there were also political reasons why Huy was anxious to find a successor to Lady Imilce.

'Forgive me, Holy Father. I had determined to discuss this with you privately,' the High Priestess spoke confidentially, but Lannon leaned across Huy to join the discussion.

'Send for the wench,' he said, speaking thickly with wine. The priestess stiffened at his choice of words. 'Send for her, let her entertain us with her prophecies.'

'My lord,' Huy wished to remonstrate but Lannon brushed his protest aside, and raised his voice.

'Send for the oracle – let her speak on the outcome of the campaign to the north.'

Huy turned back to the priestess with an apology in his eyes.

'The king commands,' he said, and the priestess inclined her head then turned to whisper to her body slave. The slave hurried from the hall.

When she came the loud voices and laughter stilled, and they stared at her with curiosity. She was a tall girl with finely boned wrists and ankles. She wore the long green robes of the temple novice which left her arms bare, and her skin had a lustre and smoothness which made it glow in the lamp light. Her hair was dark and soft, so that it floated cloudlike to her shoulders. She wore the gold crescent moon emblem of Astarte on her deep bulging forehead, dangling from a fine chain of gold, and her ear-rings were two small sun-stones that shone like the stars of heaven.

Her eyes were green, a colour that reminded Huy of the pool of Astarte in the cavern of the temple of Opet. Her lips were full and quivered faintly, betraying her agitation at his unexpected summons, while there were spots of colour in her cheeks. However, her manner was calm and controlled, and she moved with dignity to where Huy sat. He saw then that she was very young.

'Pray for me, Holy Father,' she greeted him and bowed her head. Huy studied her avidly, taken with her direct manner and her dignity.

'Greet your king, my child,' he murmured and the girl turned to Lannon. While she made the formal greeting Huy continued to examine her.

'What is your name?' he asked, and the girl turned back to Huy and fixed him with those solemn green eyes.

'Tanith,' she answered. It was the ancient name of the goddess, from the days of the old city of Carthage.

'It is a pretty name,' Huy nodded. 'I have always loved it.' And the girl smiled at him. It was a smile that took him by surprise, for it was as warm and uplifting as the dawn of Baal.

'You are kind, Holy Father,' she said, smiling at him and Huy Ben-Amon fell in love. He felt the bottom fall out of his stomach, and his vitals sucked downwards in a long sliding sensation. He stared at Tanith, unable to speak, feeling his cheeks flush with hot blood, searching desperately for the right word but not finding it.

Lannon broke the spell by shouting at a slave, 'Bring a cushion.' And they seated Tanith before the king and priests.

'Make an oracle,' Lannon commanded, and leaned towards her, breathing heavily and with the wine flushing his face. Tanith looked at him calmly with the faintest trace of a smile on her lips.

'If it were within my power, I would speak an oracle for you, lord, but then there would be a matter of fee and question.'

'What is the fee?' Lannon demanded, he had flushed a little darker with the first stirring of anger. He was not accustomed to this treatment.

'Holy Father, would you set the fee?' Tanith asked of Huy – and the devil took Huy.

'One hundred fingers of fine gold,' he spoke before he realized what he had done. It was an enormous fee, and it constituted a challenge to Lannon, daring him to back down or pay. Tanith smiled again now, a provocative dimple appeared in her cheek and she held Lannon's scowl with a cool amused stare. Huy was suddenly aware that he had placed the girl in a position of peril.

Lannon would not forgive this readily, and Huy hastened to give Lannon a graceful escape.

'For this fee the Gry-Lion may put as many questions as he has fingers on his sword hand.'

Lannon hesitated, Huy could see that he was still angry but slightly placated by Huy's amendment.

'I doubt that the wisdom of a child will be worth that much, but it amuses me to test this wench,' Lannon mumbled, looking anything but amused. He took up his wine bowl and drank deeply, then he wiped his beard and looked at Tanith.

'I go northwards on a mission. Speak to me of the outcome,' he ordered, and Tanith settled herself on the leather cushion, spreading her green robe about her. She lowered her head slightly, and her green eyes seemed to look inwards. There was an expectant hush on the guests now, and they watched her eagerly. Huy noticed that her cheeks paled, and her lips also rimmed with white.

'There will be a mighty harvest,' Tanith whispered hoarsely in a strange unnatural monotone, 'more than the Gry-Lion expects or realizes.'

The guests stirred, glancing at each other, whispering, pondering the answer. Lannon frowned over the girl's words.

'Do you speak of a harvest of death?' Lannon asked.

'You will take death with you, but death will return with you unknown and secretly,' Tanith replied. It was an unfavourable oracle, the young officers were restless, sobering rapidly. Huy wanted to intervene – he was regretting the whole business. He knew his king, knew he would not readily forget or forgive.

'What must I fear?' Lannon asked.

'Blackness,' Tanith answered readily.

'How will I find death?' Lannon was shaking with anger now, his voice guttural and his pale blue eyes deadly.

'At the hand of a friend.'

'Who will reign in Opet after me?'

'He who kills the gry-lion,' Tanith replied, and Lannon struck the wine bowl aside and it shattered on the earthen floor, the red wine splattering the feet of a waiting slave.

'The gry-lion is finished,' he shouted. 'I killed the last of them – do you dare prophesy the death of house Barca?'

'That is your sixth question, my lord.' Tanith looked up. 'I cannot see the answer to it.'

'Get her out of here,' Lannon roared. 'Take the witch away.'

And Huy signalled quickly for the High Priestess to take her, for a slave to replace Lannon's wine bowl, and for another to fetch his lute.

After Huy's third song Lannon laughed again.

On the eve of the departure of the legions from Zeng-Hanno, Huy sent for the priestess and the novice Tanith. It was five days since her disastrous prophecies to Lannon Hycanus, and it had taken all Huy's strength of will not to send for her earlier.

When she came she was fresher and lovelier than he remembered. While the priestess sat in the shade, Huy walked with Tanith upon the walls of the city, looking down on the one hand upon the streets and courtyards with the bustle of the army preparing for its march, while on the other hand they looked across the wooded hills and terraces where the slaves tended the neatly laid out vineyards and orchards.

'I have instructed the reverend mother that you will join the convoy to Opet through the middle kingdom. You will travel with the wives of the king, and at Opet you will enter the sisterhood of Astarte – and await my return.'

'Yes, my lord.' Her humble tone was at odds with her saucy expression. Huy stopped and looked into her green eyes, she held his gaze easily, smiling a little.

'Do you truly possess the sight, Tanith?'

'I do not know, my lord.'

'The words you spoke to the king, what did they mean?'

'I do not know. They are words that came into my mind unbidden. I cannot explain them.'

Huy nodded, and paced on in silence. There was an appealing innocence about this girl, coupled with a bright mind and a sunny disposition it was impossible to resist. Huy stopped again, and she waited for him to speak.

'Do you love the gods, Tanith?'

'I do.'

'Do you believe that I am their appointed one?'

'I do, Holy Father,' she answered with such conviction, with such transparent honesty and respect, that Huy's reservations were set at rest. There was no doubt that she was an instrument which could be used, as long as it was used with skill.

'What is your destiny, Tanith?' he asked suddenly.

'I cannot see it,' she answered, but she hesitated then and for the first time Huy knew she was uncertain. 'But this I know, that this – this meeting between you and me is part of that destiny.'

Huy felt his heart swell, but his voice was gruff as he replied. 'Caution, child. You are a priestess, dedicated to the goddess. You know better than to speak like that to a man.'

Tanith dropped her eyes and colour stained her skin a dusky rose. The soft wing of dark hair swung forward against her cheek, and she pushed it away with her hand. Huy felt his soul shrivel with despair. Her presence was a physical agony, for no matter how great his need of her it could never be slaked. She belonged to the gods, forbidden, untouchable.

'You know that,' Huy warned her sternly. 'Do not trifle with the gods.'

She looked up at him demurely, but Huy could have sworn there were glints of laughter and teasing mockery in the green eyes.

'Holiness, you wrong me. I did not mean as man and maid.'

'How then?' demanded Huy, disappointed and with a hollow feeling in his guts at the denial.

'We will find the answer to that when we meet at Opet, Holiness,' she murmured and Huy knew that the months until then would pass slowly.

Lannon stood over a clay box in which was modelled a relief map of the great river area. In the west rose the Clouds of Baal, a mighty waterfall where the river fell hundreds of feet into a dark gorge and the spray from the torrent rose high into the heavens, a perpetual cloud that stood upon the plain.* From here the river flowed into a deep valley, a hot unhealthy place where rough and rocky ramparts rose on each bank, heavily forested and rich with the ivory-bearing herds. Six hundred miles further east the river entered the territory of the Dravs, and ran though a wide alluvial plain which was inundated in the season of rain. Then at last the river joined the eastern sea through a dozen fan-shaped mouths.

Lannon pointed out the main features of this country on the model to his

* Victoria Falls.

generals, occasionally turning for verification to his garrison commanders who had held the river during the past year. There were twenty men in the large leather tent, and the sides were lifted to allow a dry breeze to enter – and to show the view across the wide valley below the camp. The great river itself was obscured by the tall dark green growth of trees along its bank. There was an occasional flash of reflected sunlight from the water amongst the trees. Far to the north the opposite escarpment of the valley rose in smoky blue tiers of hills.

'Our spies have marked the main towns at which the tribes are gathered. They are mostly on the high ground, a day's march beyond the river, and it is important that each tribe be attacked on the same day.'

He went on to assign a target to each of his commanders, a crossing place over the river, and a return route.

'There will be no danger of attack on the return march, as long as you break their spirit on the first day. Each of the tribes is at war with the others, and they will not rally to the assistance of each other. The only way in which we can fail is if warning is carried to the barbarians and they scatter before our thrust.'

He explained the plan in detail, dwelling on the logistics of supply and routes of march, until at last Lannon set a date for the attack.

'Twelve days from now. That will give each of your legions time to march to the crossing places, and reach the towns of the barbarians.'

From the camp on the escarpment of the valley, Huy marched the Sixth Ben-Amon to the garrison fort on the banks of the great river at Sett, and here he put the legion into camp in a forest of mopane trees which would screen them from observers on the opposite bank. Fires were forbidden during the day and were carefully screened at night and the men were kept busy building the rafts for the crossing. Heavy rains in the west had swollen the river and the ford was impassable.

Mago Tellema, the garrison commander, was a tall balding disillusioned man with the yellowish skin and eyes of the shivering sickness which was endemic along the river. He seemed pathetically glad of Huy's company during the waiting days, and Huy found his information valuable, so they dined together every evening – Huy provided the wine out of the ample stocks he had brought from Zeng.

'I have kept my patrols on their usual routine, as you ordered.'

'Good,' Huy nodded over a bowl of baked river fish and wild rice. 'Have they noticed any increase in activity since my arrival?'

'No, Holiness. A war party of a few hundred crossed last night and attacked one of my outposts. We drove them off readily enough, killing fifty of them.'

'What do they gain by these raids?'

'Weapons, and an appraisal of our strength.'

'Is the whole border so active?'

'No, Holy Father. But here at Sett we oppose one of the more warlike tribes, the Vendi – they are exceptional. You recall how four years ago they crossed in strength, 20,000 of them overwhelmed the garrison here and left the valley—'

'Yes,' Huy interrupted. 'I was with the legions when we met them at Bhor.'

'Ah! Of course. I remember now that your legion's number was on the honour list.' The commander chuckled. 'Of that 20,000 not one returned across the river.'

'They fought well, though – for pagans,' Huy conceded.

'Indeed, Holiness, they are exceptional in that respect also and in the years since then they have become more formidable.'

'Have you seen their town?'

'No, Holiness, but I have many spies. It is set on the first slopes of the northern escarpment, where the tributary river Kal comes down from the plateau.'

'What is the population?'

'I believe them to number 50,000.'

'So large!' Huy looked up with a mouthful of fish and stared at the commander.

'They are a numerous tribe – not all of them live in the town. They tend large herds of cattle and are spread over a vast area.'

'Is the town fortified?'

'It is a large and sprawling huddle of huts, Holiness. Some of the huts are ringed with primitive palisades, but these are defence against wild animals only.'

A slave refilled Huy's wine bowl and took away his empty dish. Huy cupped the bowl in his hands and stared moodily into the dark red liquid. His silence discomforted the commander who at last blurted, 'Is it true that the king will arrive here on the morrow?'

'Yes. Lannon Hycanus will march with my legion in the raid.'

'I have never been presented to him,' the man murmured, and Huy had a penetrating insight into the career of an elderly officer doomed to a minor outpost in the wilderness without patron or prospects.

'I will commend you to him,' Huy promised, and saw the pathetic gratitude in the man's eyes.

One of the biremes that patrolled the river landed a century of axeman and archers on the far bank in the night, and before dawn they had rigged the lines across the river.

The river was 300 paces wide at this point, a dirty green flow of water between steep banks which were thickly wooded and covered with reed and dense vegetation. The rafts were carried down on to the river's edge and attached to the looped lines. The legion boarded in groups of fifty, and the elephants walked away with the lines drawing the rafts smoothly across the river.

The crossing went with well-drilled precision – it was not the first time a legion had crossed the great river. There were a few minor incidents – two hoplites fell from their rafts and sank swiftly beneath the weight of their armour, one of the rafts capsized a struggling mass of men and equipment into the shallow water beside the bank but all waded to safety, a legionary entangled his arm in one of the lines and had it neatly severed below the elbow – but the crossing was completed before mid-afternoon and Lannon turned to Huy:

'Bravely done, my Sunbird. Now explain to me your order of march.'

Huy left a cohort to hold the crossing, and to act as a base for his stores, a pile of dried meat and corn in leather bags. His legion would be tired, hungry, and perhaps hard pressed on its return and if all went as was planned, there would also be many thousands of extra mouths to feed.

Then behind a screen of light infantry and archers he began his march on the barbarian town of Kal. Here the weeks of training and hardening during the march from Zeng-Hanno showed. For although the ground was broken and heavily forested, the legion moved swiftly in compact columns, covering the ground at a pace that pushed a steady five miles behind them every hour. Ahead of them the scouts ensured that no one would carry a warning to the town. The few hundred herders and hunters and root gatherers that were met with by the scouts were despatched with a silent shower of arrows or a swift clean axe stroke. Their bodies lay where they had fallen beside the track, and the columns trudged on past them with hardly a sidelong glance. Huy saw that they were well-formed men and women, dressed in kilts of animal skins and with tribal scars on their cheeks and breasts. Like most of the tribes from the north their skins were a very dark blueish black. Some of them had mutilated their teeth by filing them to a sharp point like those of a shark, and the men were armed with throwing spears and light axes with half-moon-shaped blades.

The legion halted after dark, and ate cold cooked meat and corn cakes from their pouches while the wine-carriers moved amongst them filling the bowls.

'Look.' Huy touched Lannon's shoulder and pointed towards the northern hills. The sky glowed, as though the moon was rising from the wrong direction. It was the reflected light from thousands of cooking fires.

'A rich harvest,' Lannon nodded. 'Just as the witch prophesied.'

Huy stirred uncomfortably at the mention of Tanith, but remained silent.

'Her words have troubled me – I've spent many nights pondering them.' Lannon wiped his greasy fingers and lips, before he reached for the wine bowl. 'She preaches death and darkness and betrayal by a friend.' He rinsed his mouth with wine and spat it on the ground before drinking.

Huy murmured, 'She did not preach, Majesty – she replied to a question.'

But Lannon said, 'I believe she is evil.'

'Sire!' Huy protested quickly.

'Do not be misled by a pretty face, Huy.'

'She is young, innocent,' he began but saw Lannon leaning towards him and peering into his face, and he stopped.

'What is this witch to you, my Sunbird?'

'As a maid, she means nothing. How could she, she belongs to the goddess,' Huy denied his love, and Lannon leaned back and grunted sceptically.

'It is as well – you are wise in all things but women, my friend. You must let me guide you.'

'You are always kind,' Huy muttered.

'Keep away from that one, Huy. Be warned by one who loves you, she will bring you nothing but sorrow.'

'We have rested long enough.' Huy stood up and settled the strap of his axe about his wrist. 'It is time to march.'

After midnight they crested the low line of hills that formed the first slope of the escarpment, and before them spread a wide-open basin of land through which the dark river Kal meandered. The basin was moon-washed silver and blue, and the smoke from 10,000 cooking fires spread like a pale sea mist across the river, lying in layers in the still night air.

The fires had died to pin-points of dull red that specked the town, and the huts were dark and shapeless, scattered thickly without plan or pattern, a vast agglomeration of primitive dwellings.

'He estimated 50,000 – and he's not far wrong.' Huy looked out across the basin, and beside him Lannon asked?

'How will you proceed?' And Huy smiled in the moonlight.

'You taught me how to hunt game, my king.'

His cohort commanders came for their orders, cloaked and helmeted and grim. Huy ordered out a thin screen of light infantry and covering bowmen to the east. During the day the scouts had captured 4,000 of the rangy little scrub cattle belonging to the Vendi.

'Take the cattle with you. You remember Hannibal's ruse in Italia, it will serve us as well upon the great river.'

Lannon laughed delightedly and clapped Huy's shoulder when he had explained it. 'Fly for me, Sunbird.'

'Roar for me, Gry-Lion,' Huy grinned back at him as he settled and buckled his helmet.

Silently Huy led 4,500 of his heavy infantry and axemen around to the west and lay them in a crescent shape at the edge of the forest beyond the town. Huy slept for an hour and when one of his centurions shook him awake he was stiff and cold with the night dew.

'Stand to!' he ordered quietly, and the word was passed from mouth to mouth. There was a stirring and a dark movement along the edge of the forest as the legionaries slung their axes and swords and bows, and took up instead the slavers' wooden clubs.

Huy and Lannon hurried to the command position at the centre of the line, shrugging off their cloaks and flexing cold muscles.

Huy looked out across the sleeping town and the smell of it was wood smoke and cooking food and human excrement, a great sour smell of humanity that wrinkled his nostrils. The town was silent except for the lonely barking of a cur, and the petulant wail of a sleepless baby.

Huy said softly. 'The time is now.' And Lannon nodded. Huy turned and gave the order to one of his centurions and the man stooped over a clay fire pot and blew flame to life on the bunch of pitch-dipped rags that tipped the signal arrow. When the flame had caught and blossomed he notched the arrow and loosed it in a high arching parabola against the dark sky. From along the line the signal was repeated, orange flame soaring briefly in the darkness, but the silence was unbroken and the town slept on.

'They have set no guards, no picket, nothing,' Lannon remarked scornfully.

'They are barbarians,' Huy pointed out mildly.

'They deserve slavery,' Lannon said.

'They will fare better as slaves than free men,' Huy agreed.

'We will dress them and feed them and show them the true gods.'

Lannon nodded. 'We have come to lead them out of the darkness and into the sun.' And he shifted the heavy slaving club into his right hand.

From the east, appearing suddenly out of the edge of the forest, stampeded a mass of bellowing, maddened cattle. On their horns burned torches of pitch and grass, behind them they dragged flaming dry branches and they were driven by their own terror and by a line of yelling whooping warriors. The whole scene was hellish with dust and smoke and flame. The line of cattle crashed into the town, knocking down the flimsy grass huts, leaving fire to bloom and spread in their wake, trampling the sleep-drugged naked Vendi that stumbled into their path. Behind them ran the warriors, clubbing down the survivors and leaving them lying in the hoof-churned dust.

Huy heard a steady climbing wail from the town, the sound of thousands of terrified voices. He heard the drumming of running hooves and saw the explosions of yellow flame and sparks mount into the night sky as the tinder-dry huts burned.

'Hold your line,' he called to the men in the darkness around him. 'Leave no gaps in the net for the fish to slip through.'

The night was filled with movement and sound and flame. The flames spread quickly lighting the scene with a great flickering orange light, and the Vendi darted and milled and screamed as the grim line of marauders moved down upon them. The clubs rose and fell and the sound of the blows against bone was that of woodsmen working in a forest. They fell black and naked, and lay in the glaring firelight, or crawled and wriggled and wailed.

One woman with her infant clutched to her breast saw the relentless line bearing down on her, and she whirled like a doe startled from covert and ran into the tall bellowing flames of burning thatch. She burned like a torch, her hair exploding, and she screamed once and then fell scorched and unrecognizable into the flames. Huy saw it, and his blood madness cooled, congealing into revulsion and disgust.

'Hold!' he shouted. 'Lighten your blows!' And slowly out of this terrible confusion order emerged. The slave-masters were there ordering the captives into squatting lines, the infantry swept the town clear, and the flames burned themselves out, leaving only black mounds of smoking ash.

The dawn came up, a red and angry dawn – across which drifted banks of dark smoke. When Huy led the praise chant to Baal, the cries and wailing of the captives rose with the voice of the legion.

Huy hurried through the devastation ordering and organizing the retreat. Already two cohorts under the young Bakmor had started back towards the great river driving an uncounted herd of captured cattle before them. Huy guessed there might be as many as 20,000 head of the scrubby little beasts. Bakmor had Huy's orders to swim the cattle across the river and return immediately to cover the retreat.

Now his concern was to get the slow unwieldy columns of slaves moving. The approach march that his legion had made in half a day and night would surely take two or three days on the return. The newly captured slaves must be chained, and unaccustomed to their bonds they would move but slowly, retarding the march. Every hour's delay was dangerous, and would make the heavily encumbered legion more vulnerable to attack or reprisal.

One of his centurions accosted him, his tunic blackened with smoke and his beard singed. 'My lord!'

'What is it?'

'The slaves. There are few young men amongst them.'

Huy turned to examine one of the masses of squatting black humanity. They were festooned with the light marching chains, shackled at the neck like hunting dogs in leash.

'Yes.' He saw it now, they were mostly women and immature youths. The slave-masters had weeded out the old and infirm, but there were very few men of warrior age and status. Huy picked a bright-looking youngster from the squatting ranks and spoke to him in vernacular.

'Where are the warriors?' The youth looked startled at being addressed in his own language, but he dropped his eyes sullenly and would not answer. The centurion half drew his sword, and at the scrape of steel in the scabbard the boy glanced up fearfully.

'A drop more blood will mean nothing,' Huy warned him, and the boy hesitated before replying.

'They have gone to the north to hunt the buffalo.'

'When will they return?' Huy demanded.

'I do not know,' the slave shrugged expressively, and Huy now had a more telling reason for haste. The fighting regiments of the Vendi were intact, and this towering beacon of smoke would draw them as meat draws the vultures.

'Get them up, and moving,' he ordered the centurion and hurried away. Lannon came out of the smoke followed by his armour-bearers and men-at-arms. Once glance at his face was enough to warn Huy, for it was flushed and scowling.

'Did you order the slave-masters to spare those they reject?'

'Yes, sire.' Suddenly Huy was impatient with the king's rages and tantrums, there were more important matters to occupy him now.

'By what authority?' Lannon demanded.

'By the authority of a commander of a Royal Legion in the field,' Huy answered him.

'I commanded a burning.'

'But not a massacre of the aged and infirm.'

'I want the tribes to know that Lannon Hycanus passed this way.'

'I leave witnesses to it,' Huy told him shortly. 'If these old ones would burden us, will they not also be a burden upon their tribe?' Lannon drew himself up, Huy saw his rage boil over – and he took Lannon's arm in unexpectedly conspiratorial grip.

'Majesty, there is something of importance I must tell you.' And before Lannon could give vent to his rage Huy had led him aside. 'The regiments of Vendi have escaped us, they are in the field and out in battle array.'

Lannon's rage was forgotten. 'How close are they?'

'I do not know – except that the longer we talk the closer they come.'

It was past noon before the long files of shuffling slaves were all tallied and moving. The slave-masters reported in to Huy's command post, and the final count was almost 22,000 human beings.

Despite Huy's orders to keep the column bunched and under control, the files of chained Vendi stretched over four miles and their pace was that of the slowest. At a laboured crawl like a crippled centipede, they wound through the hills and down into the bad broken ground of the valley bottom.

The first attack hit them a little after midnight on the first night. It came as a shock to Huy, for although he had taken every precaution for a night camp in enemy territory, he had not expected anything like this from the tribes. A few sentries with slit throats, a flight of arrows from ambush, even a swift rush and withdrawal at some weak spot along the line, but not a full-scale night attack which showed every evidence of planning and control, and which was pressed home with murderous intent.

Only training and discipline held his legion together before that howling torrent that hurled itself upon them from the darkness. for two hours they closed up and fought, with the trumpets blowing the standfast and the rallying cries of the centurions ringing out in the darkness.

'On me, the Sixth.'

'Steady, the Sixth.'

'Hold hard, the Sixth.'

When the moon came out and lit the field, the attackers melted away into the forests and Huy could stride among his cohorts and assess his position.

The dead tribesmen were piled chest deep about the square where the cohorts had stood. In the torch light the skirmishers were finishing the enemy wounded with quick sword thrusts, while others were tending their own wounded and laying out their dead for cremation. Huy was relieved to see how small a toll the enemy had exacted from the defence, and how grievous a price they had paid themselves.

In the confusion of the battle many of the files of slaves had responded to the calls of the attackers and, with a concerted rush, had broken out of the square and escaped into the night still linked together. But there were still more than 16,000 of them howling with terror and hunger and thirst.

The legion lit its cremation fires in the dark and sang the praise chant to Baal on the march. Before the sun had been up an hour, it was clear what tactics the Vendi had decided upon for that day. Each feature along the route was contested by groups of archers and spearmen. They had to be laboriously dislodged, always falling back before the charges of Huy's axemen, but at the same time the flanks of the column and the rear were harried and tested by repeated attacks in considerable strength.

'I have never heard of this happening before,' protested Lannon during a lull while he unbuckled his helmet to air his sweat-sodden curls, and wash his mouth out with wine. 'They behave like drilled and trained troops.'

'It is something new,' Huy agreed as he accepted a cloth one of his armour-bearers had wetted for him. Huy's arms and face were speckled with droplets of thrown blood, and blood had dried black and crusty on the blade and shaft of the vulture axe.

'They have direction and purpose – I have never known tribesmen regroup after a charge has broken them. I have never known them come back after a mauling.'

Lannon spat red wine upon the ground. 'We may have better sport than we had bargained for before the day is out,' he laughed with anticipation and passed the wine bowl to Huy.

There was a place where the track crossed a narrow stream and then passed between two symmetrical rounded maiden's breast hills. There was a ford at the stream and on the approaches to it sixteen spears had been set in the earth and spiked upon them were the severed heads of legionaries who had been with Bakmor's cohorts that had gone ahead with the cattle.

'Bakmor has not got through unscathed either,' Huy remarked, as he watched the heads taken down and hurriedly wrapped in leather cloaks.

'Sixteen from twelve hundred is hardly a disaster to rank with Lake Trasimene,' Lannon remarked easily. 'And with their grisly display they have warned us of their intention to hold the ford – weak tactics, Sunbird.'

'Perhaps, my lord,' Huy conceded, but he had noticed the faces of his men who had seen the ragged red throats and the dull staring eyes of the trophy heads. Their stomachs had cooled a little.

The ford was held as Lannon had predicted. It was held by a force that Huy guessed was not less than twice his own, and while they attempted to hack their way through the attacks upon the flanks and rear never let up. Twice Huy pulled his axemen and infantry out of the reddened mud of the ford to rest and reform. By now the day was baking hot and the legionaries were tiring.

Lannon had received a spear-thrust in the face which had opened his cheek to the bone, a wound that looked uglier than it really was and his beard was thick with blood and dust. A physician was stitching the wet lips of the wound closed when Huy joined the group around the king, and Lannon dismissed his anxious inquiry with a chuckle.

'It will leave an interesting scar.' Then without moving his head he told Huy, 'I have discovered the solution to the mystery, Huy, and there it is!' He pointed across the stream to the closest of the two hills. The crest was just out of random arrow range, perhaps 500 paces away. Although the slopes of the hill were forested the crest was a dome of rounded bare granite, and upon the dome stood a small group of men. They were gathered about a central figure.

Huy would always remember him as he was that fateful noon on the hilltop beside the ford. The distance did not dwarf him as it did the men about him. In some strange fashion it made his physical presence more imposing. He was a huge man, fully a head and shoulder taller than his companions. The sun shone on the oiled black muscles of his chest and arms, and a tall head-dress of blue heron feathers stood wind-tossed and proud upon his head. He wore a short kilt of leopard tails around his waist, but Huy did not need that to know he was a king.

'Ah!' he said softly, and he felt something stir in him, a cold sliding thing like an uncoiling snake. On the hilltop the Vendi king made a sweeping gesture, and then stabbed towards the ford with his heavy war spear. It was clearly the delivery of a command, and from the group around him a messenger broke away and raced down the slope of the hill carrying the order.

'At last the tribes have found a leader,' said Huy. 'I should have guessed it earlier.'

'Take him for me,' Lannon commanded. 'I want him. Nothing else is important. Take that man for me.' And Huy heard a new tone in Lannon's voice. It puzzled him and he glanced at his king. He saw it then. It was not the pain of his crudely stitched cheek that made dark shadows play in the pale blue eyes. For the first time in all the years Huy knew that Lannon was afraid.

Huy timed it carefully for the last hour before dark, for the last of the day when the shadows were long and the light uncertain. During the afternoon he skirmished at the ford in half-cohort strength, but in the thick forest on the banks of the stream he held his main strength in reserve. He let them rest during the heat of the afternoon, let them eat and drink and sharpen their blades while he made his preparations. He chose fifty of his finest, selecting them by name from the ranks and he took them well back where they would be screened from prying eyes on the heights beyond the stream.

From the bottoms of the cooking-pots they scraped the thick black soot and mixed it into a thick paste with cooking oil. There was not enough to darken the skins of fifty men so for their arms and legs they used the black mud from the river. They were all of them stripped stark naked when the slave chains were shackled about their throats, but instead of the iron pins a thin dry twig was used to close the links on every collar. They could not take shields with them, and they smeared their weapons with a thick coating of black mud to hide the twinkle and flash of naked metal, then they strapped them to their backs so they could run empty-handed.

'You are slaves, not legionaries,' Huy told them. 'Run like a slave, scamper like a beaten dog.'

When they broke from the trees and ran for the river with half a century of legionaries in pursuit, they howled with terror and the carefully aimed arrows pattered around them. They reached the bank 500 paces upstream from the ford. As they blundered across, still linked together by the slave chain, the Vendi king from his vantage point saw their escape and sent two large parties of archers and spearmen to screen their crossing.

A fierce bloody little battle flared up on the river bank, and under cover of the tumult Huy got his group over the river and into the shelter of the forest on the far bank. There was a thin detachment of tribesmen in set positions amongst the trees, but by the time they realized the deception Huy's band had dropped their chains and cut into them in'a silent murderous rush.

Then they were through with nothing opposing them to the foot of the command hill. Bunched up, and hidden by the forest, Huy led them at a run around the back of the hill. They had moved fast, and he rested them here for a few minutes. The mud had washed from legs and arms during the crossing of the river and the soot and oil was streaky with sweat giving them a wild and desperate appearance.

The clamour of the fighting at the river had died away and the forest was silent and still as Huy led his band up the back slope of the hill. There were sentries posted here, but they were inattentive and did not see the weird blackened figures amongst the forest shades until it was too late.

Below the bare dome of granite Huy waited again, listening for the diversion which Lannon had promised. The distant yells and tiny scraping sound of metal from the ford were almost blanketed by the distance and the intervening bulk of the hill.

Huy said softly, 'Now. All together.' And they burst from the forest edge and went racing away up the granite dome. Huy led them easily, bounding ahead with the loping long-armed gait of an old bull baboon.

When he was twenty paces from the crest, the Vendi king sensed his presence and turned to face Huy. He shouted a warning to his staff, and Huy went at him like a terrier at the throat of a lion. Two of the king's bodyguard leapt to intervene, but Huy flicked a casual axe stroke at them, rolling his wrist slightly in mid-stroke so the blade whimpered as it changed direction, killing the one guard cleanly and taking the spear arm of the other away above the elbow with a single cut. They fell aside and Huy went on to take the king.

He was a big man, perhaps the biggest Huy had ever met, and his skin was a shiny purplish black. The muscles of shoulder and arms were bunched and knotted. The sinews of his neck stood out starkly, corded into the heavy bone of his jaw. His head was round as a river-washed boulder, and without head-dress the scalp was bald and polished black.

He moved to meet Huy, sliding in on thick black legs with his leopard-skin kilts swirling, crouching slightly with the stabbing spear held underhand, the blade glistening hungrily for the softness of Huy's belly. He moved with leopard speed, reacting instantly to Huy's attack, and there was a sense of savage power and energy about him that checked Huy's charge and made him whirl instinctively to the side, just as the blade of the stabbing spear slashed upwards through nothingness where Huy's belly should have been.

The huge black man grunted as his stroke died in air, and his tawny yellow eyes fastened on Huy. He struck again and Huy hopped aside as the point hissed past him, and Huy reached out as he sprang and ran the stabbing point of the axe across the giant's exposed ribs. The purple black skin opened and for an instant white bone showed in the depths of the wound before the rush of dark blood obscured it. The king bellowed at the sting of it, and he struck and slashed and cut at the dancing gadfly before him. Each stroke wilder, each charge more reckless as Huy goaded him, watching for his moment. It came and suddenly Huy was through the circle of the spear. With the point of the axe he probed for the femoral artery in the giant's groin, running the engraved steel into the tight flesh half an inch too far to the right, missing the artery but dropping the king to one knee. Huy twisted out of close contact. The axe flew high and Huy went into the kill stroke aiming at the round black skull of the kneeling king, a stroke which would split him to the chest.

'For Baal!' he shouted, sending the axe down from on high. Then in full stroke he changed. He never knew what impulse it was that made him check, made him twist the weapon, presenting the flat of the blade and not the edge, holding the stroke half back so that the side of the axe cracked against the king's skull with enough force to topple him forward senseless onto his face but not enough to stove in the bone of the great round head.

Huy jumped back and with one quick glance made certain that the Vendi king's train were all lying lifeless on the dome of granite, and his legionaries were grouped around him resting on their bloody swords. The surprise had been complete and overwhelming.

Huy turned and ran to the highest point of the hill. Naked and filthy with soot and mud he brandished his axe above his head, and his band cheered and waved their weapons also. From the ford a trumpet began to blare the advance, and immediately the call was taken up and shrilled from cohort to cohort.

Huy watched Lannon lead the first wave across the ford. The legion crashed into the leaderless tribesmen who opposed them, and drove through them with scarcely a check, splitting them and driving them back·against the hills in a disorganized rabble. They had seen their king cut down and there was no spirit left in any of them.

From the hilltop Huy watched Lannon commit his last two reserve cohorts at exactly the right moment. The tribesmen broke and made a rout of it.

Throwing aside their weapons they streamed back in a wailing panic-stricken mob into the bottle-neck between the hills.

At that moment the handsome young Bakmor, with the two cohorts which had driven the captured cattle to the great river, marched out of the forest. He deployed the cohorts neatly across the only line of retreat open to the tribes. His return was timely indeed, and Huy watched him with grudging professional approval as he made his dispositons. As the sun touched the horizon in a splendour of red and purple the trumpets sounded the advance once again, and the slaughter and the slave-taking lasted until after midnight.

Huy crossed his legion and the host of wild slaves, using the elephant-drawn rafts at Sett. After the battle at the ford the return march had been unopposed. The regiments of the Vendi had been shattered, all their war chiefs killed or captured and Lannon was jubilant.

He told Huy, 'My Sunbird! It was more than I asked of you. Even I did not guess that such a dangerous enemy had grown up upon my borders. If we had left him another year, only the gods know how deadly he might have become.'

'Baal smiled upon me,' Huy disclaimed modestly.

'And so does Lannon Hycanus,' Lannon assured him. 'What was the harvest, Sunbird? Has old Rib-Addi made the accounting yet?'

'I hope so, my lord.'

'Send for him,' Lannon commanded, and Rib-Addi came with his scrolls and his ink-stained fingers and his untrusting little book-keeper's eyes. He read out the lists of cattle and slaves of each grade, every one of them carefully categorized by the slave-masters.

'The prices will be much depressed, sire,' Rib-Addi pointed out pessimistically. 'For the other legions have taken a great tribute from all the tribes across the river. It will be two or three years before the markets of Opet have absorbed this mass of wealth.'

'Nevertheless, the prize money taken by the Sixth Ben-Amon must be considerable, Rib-Addi.'

'As my lord says.'

'How much?' Lannon demanded.

Rib-Addi looked alarmed. 'I could only hazard a guess, Majesty.'

'Guess, then,' Lannon invited him.

'It could be as much as 25,000 fingers – and as low as—'

'You would smell dung in an alabaster jar of perfume,' Lannon chided the old man. 'Do not give me your low figure.'

'As my lord pleases.' Rib-Addi bowed, and Lannon turned to Huy and clasped his shoulder.

'Your share is one part in a hundred, Sunbird. Two hundred and fifty fingers – you are a rich man at last! How does it feel?'

'It does not sicken me,' Huy grinned at him, and Lannon laughed delightedly as he turned back to Rib-Addi.

'Write in your book, old man. Write that Lannon Hycanus sets aside half of his share of the prize. He makes it over as an award to the legion commander, Huy Ben-Amon, for his conduct of the campaign.'

'My lord, that is one part in twenty,' Rib-Addi protested vehemently. 'It is an award of over 1,000 fingers!'

'I have learned my figures also,' Lannon assured him, and the book-keeper might have protested further, but he saw Lannon's expression.

'It shall be written,' he mumbled, and Huy came to kneel before his king in gratitude.

'Up!' Lannon ordered him, smiling. 'Do not grovel for me, old friend.' And Huy went to stand beside Lannon's stool, as the king called each of the officers who had acted with distinction and made the awards.

Huy was lost in a trance of avarice, hardly able to credit his fortune. He was rich – rich! He must sacrifice to the gods this very day. A white bull, at the least. As Rib-Addi had pointed out, the market was flooded and Huy would be able to get one cheaply. Then he remembered that he no longer had to stint.

He could afford any luxury he had ever coveted, and still have enough over for an estate on the terraces of Zeng, a share in one of Habbakuk-Lal's trading galleys. A seat on one of the gold-mining syndicates, a secure income for life. No more patches in his tunics, no more bullying his household to cut down on the consumption of meat, no more of the cheap sour wines from the harbour taverns. And then his mind jumped, no more reliance on Lannon's hospitality and on the goodwill of his young slave girls. He would have one of his own – no, damn it, two – three! Young and pretty and pliant. He felt his body stir. He could afford a wife now, even the daughters of the noble houses might turn a blind eye to his back when dazzled by such a pile of the golden metal.

Then suddenly he remembered Tanith, and the phantom slave girls and wives faded back into the mists of his imagining. His spirits plunged sickeningly. The priestesses of Astarte were dedicated to the goddess, they could never marry. Suddenly Huy did not feel as rich as he had a moment before.

'Do you not hear your king when he speaks?' Lannon demanded, and Huy started guiltily.

'My lord, I was dreaming. Forgive me.'

'It is no longer necessary to dream,' Lannon told him.

'What was it the Gry-Lion asked?'

'I said we should send for the barbarian – we can deal with him before the legion assembles.'

Huy looked around at his cohorts drawn up in an open square before the leather awning under which Lannon sat. The legions' standards glittered in the sunlight, and the officers stood at ease before their men. They waited expectantly, and Huy sighed quietly.

'As the Gry-Lion wishes.'

'Order it so,' Lannon commanded.

They had chained him at wrists and ankles, as well as at the throat. The slave-masters could pick a dangerous one at a glance, and two of them held him in leash by the chains from his throat collar.

He was as big as Huy remembered, and his skin ever darker, but he was a young man. This came as a shock to Huy, he had thought of him as being in his prime years but this was an illusion. The man's physical bulk and his commanding presence made him older than his years.

Huy saw how he had fought against his bonds, tearing his own flesh, smearing the skin on the unyielding iron shackles, and the wound in his groin had been crudely dressed with leaves and bark. There were the first watery yellow discharges of putrefaction soiling the dressing, and the flesh around it looked hard and swollen. Although he limped, although the chains jangled mockingly at every pace, and although the slave-masters braced against him as though he were a captured animal, there was no mistaking that he was a king. He stood before Lannon and lowered his head slightly on the thick sinewed neck. His eyes were ferocious, even the whites were smoking yellow and covered with a fine lacework of blood vessels, and he stared at his captors with a hatred that was a palpable thing.

'You captured this – this great black beast, Huy?' Lannon returned the giant's stare. 'Without help, you took him?' Lannon shook his head with wonder and turned to Huy, but Huy was watching the Vendi king.

'What is your name?' Huy asked softly, and the big round head swivelled towards him, the fierce eyes held his.

'How do you have the tongue of Vendi?'

'I have many tongues,' Huy assured him. 'Who are you?'

'Manatassi, King of the Vendi.' And Huy translated for Lannon.

'Tell him he is king no longer,' Lannon snapped, and Manatassi shrugged and smiled. His smile was a frightening thing for although the thick purple lips drew back to expose strong white teeth, yet his eyes still smoked with hatred.

'Fifty thousand warriors of Vendi call me king still,' he answered.

'A slave king of a slave people,' Lannon laughed, and then to Huy. 'What of him, Huy? Is he not a dangerous enemy? Can we afford to let him live?'

Huy tore his gaze from the slave king and considered the question, trying to think logically but finding it difficult. Huy had conceived a sudden but powerful proprietary interest in Manatassi. He was impressed with the man's power and presence, with the military skills he had displayed, with the cunning and cleverness and the strange smouldering depths of him. Huy had taken him, he could claim him, even from Lannon, and he was strongly tempted to do so now, for he sensed that here was some extraordinary opportunity. To take this man and educate him, civilize him – what might be made of him! He felt an excitement as a new idea tried to struggle to the surface of his mind.

'I think not,' Lannon answered himself. 'From the first moment I saw him, on the hill above the ford, I knew he was dangerous. Deadly dangerous. I do not think we can let him live, Huy. He would make a fine messenger to the gods. We will dedicate him to Baal and send him as a messenger to express our gratitude for the outcome of the campaign.'

'My lord,' Huy dropped his voice for Lannon alone, 'I have a feeling about this man. I feel I could enlighten him, teach him the true gods. He is young, my lord, I could work upon him, and when we are ready we could return him to his people.'

'Have the birds picked out your brain?' Lannon looked at Huy in astonishment. 'Why should we return him to his people, when we have spent so much effort on capturing him?'

'We could use him as an ally then.' Huy was trying desperately to get his idea over. 'Through him we could make a treaty with the tribes. We could win him over and use him to secure our northern borders.'

'Treaties with barbarians!' Lannon was angry now. 'What nonsense is this? Secure our northern borders, you say? One thing, and one thing only will secure our northern borders, and that is a sharp sword in a strong hand.'

'My lord, please hear me out.'

'No, Huy. I will have no more of it. He must die – and quickly.' Lannon stood up. 'Tonight at sunset. Prepare to send him.' And Lannon strode away.

'Dismiss the legion,' Huy ordered his commanders, and nodded to the slave-masters to lead the captive away. But Manatassi stepped forward dragging the slave-masters with him on the chains.

'High born!' Manatassi called Huy, who turned back to him with surprise. He had not expected a title of respect.

'What is it?' Huy looked at him.

'Is it death?' Manatassi asked, and Huy nodded.

'It is death,' he admitted.

'But you argued for me?' Manatassi insisted, and again Huy nodded.

'Why?' demanded the slave king, and Huy could not answer. He spread his hands, a gesture of weariness and incomprehension.

'Twice already,' the slave king said. 'First you turned the blade which should
have killed, and now you speak for me. Why?'

'I do not know. I cannot explain.'

'You feel the bond – the bond between us,' Manatassi declared, and his voice
sank low, rumbling and soft. 'The bond of the spirits. You felt it.'

'No.' Huy shook his head, and hurried away to his tent. He worked on his
scrolls for most of the afternoon, recording the campaign, describing the burning
and the battle at the ford, listing the battle honours and the slaves taken, the
booty and the glory – but he could not bring himself to describe Manatassi. The
man would soon be dead, let his memory die with him, let it not linger on to
haunt the living. A phrase that Lannon had used stuck in his mind, 'the black
beast', and he used it as the only reference to the doomed slave king.

He ate the noon meal with Bakmor and a few others of his young officers,
but his mood infected them all and the meal was awkward, the conversation
trivial and stilted. Afterwards Huy spent an hour with his adjutant and
quartermaster ordering the legion's affairs, then he worked with the axe until
his sweat ran down his body in streams. He scraped and oiled and changed into
fresh robes for the sacrifice, and went to Lannon's tent. Lannon was in
conference, a group of his advisers and officials sitting in a half-circle around
him on the skins and cushions. Lannon looked up and smiled and called Huy
to him.

'Sit by me, my Sunbird. There is something here on which I would value
your thoughts.' And Huy sat and listened to Lannon directing the affairs of the
four kingdoms with a quick and confident logic. He made decisions which would
have tormented Huy for days, and he made them easily, without doubts or
hesitations. Then he dismissed his court, and turned to Huy.

'A bowl of wine with me, Huy. It will be many days before we have the
chance again, for in the morning I leave you.'

'Whither, my lord?'

'I return to Opet, but at speed. I will leave you and your slaves and herds to
make the best of it.'

They drank together, exchanging the seemingly easy desultory talk of old
friends, but Huy was manoeuvring for an opening to speak of Manatassi, and
Lannon was deftly denying it to him. At last Huy in desperation approached
the subject directly.

'The Vendi king, my lord.' And he got no further, for Lannon slammed the
wine bowl down so that it cracked and a ruby gush of the lees spurted on to the
furs on which they sat.

'You presume on friendship. I have ordered his death. Except for the axe-
stroke the matter is settled.'

'I believe it is a mistake.'

'To let him live will be a greater mistake.'

'My lord—'

'Enough, Huy! Enough, I say! Go out now and send him.'

In the sunset they brought the Vendi king to a clear place on the river bank
below the garrison walls of Sett. He was dressed in a cloak of leather, worked
with the symbols of Baal, and he wore the symbolical chains of the sacrifice.
Huy stood with the priests and nobles, and when they led the doomed king
forward his eyes fastened on Huy's. Those terrible yellow eyes seemed almost
to hook into his flesh, seemed to draw Huy's soul out through his eye sockets.

Huy began the ritual, chanting the offertory, making the obeisance to the
flaming god image in the western sky and all the while he could feel those eyes
eating into the core of his existence.

Huy's assistant offered him the vulture axe, polished and glinting red and gold in the last rays of the sunset. Huy went to where Manatassi stood, and looked up at him.

The slave-masters stepped forward and lifted the cloak from the shoulders of the sacrifice. Except for the golden chains he was naked and magnificent. They had removed the raw-hide sandals from his feet. The slave-masters waited with the chains in their hands, at Huy's signal they would jerk the sacrifice off his feet and stretch him out upon the ground. His neck drawn out for the axe blade.

Huy hesitated, unable to force himself to give the order, held fascinated by those fierce yellow eyes. With an effort he tore his gaze free and looked downwards. He had started to give the signal, but his hand froze. He was staring at Manatassi's bare feet.

Around him the watchers stirred restlessly, glancing towards the horizon where the sun was rapidly sliding below the trees. Soon it would be too late.

Still Huy stared at Manatassi's feet.

'The sun goes, priest. Strike!' Lannon called abruptly, angrily in the silence and the sound of his voice seemed to arouse Huy. He turned to Lannon.

'My lord, there is something you must see.'

'The sun is going,' Lannon called impatiently.

'You must see it,' Huy insisted, and Lannon strode forward to stand beside him.

'Look!' Huy pointed at the Vendi king's feet, and Lannon frowned on a quick intake of breath.

Manatassi's feet were monstrously deformed, deeply divided between the toes so that they resembled the claws of some preternatural bird. Involuntarily Lannon stepped backwards, making the full-handed sun sign to avert evil.

'He is bird-footed,' Huy said, 'he has the feet of the sacred sunbird of Baal.' And there was a rustle and murmur from the watchers. They craned forward with a ghoulish, superstitious curiosity.

Huy raised his voice. 'I declare this man god-marked. He is favoured by the gods – and cannot be sent as a messenger.'

As he spoke the sun dropped below the rim of the world and there was a chill and a dankness in the air.

Lannon was in a towering, shaking rage that paled his lips and face so that the black clotted scab of his wound stood out clearly on his cheek.

'You defied me!' he said it softly, but in a voice that trembled with his rage.

'He is god-marked!' Huy protested.

'Do not try to hide behind your gods, Priest. You and I both know that many of Baal's decisions are made by Huy Ben-Amon, for Huy Ben-Amon.'

'Majesty,' Huy gasped at the accusation, at the dreadful blasphemy of it.

'You defied me,' Lannon repeated. 'You think to place this barbarian beyond my reach, you aspire to play the game of power and politics with me.'

'It is not true, my lord. I would not dare.'

'You *would* dare, Priest. You would dare to steal the teeth from the mouth of the living Gry-Lion, if the fancy came upon you.'

'My lord, I am your true, your most loyal—'

'Tread lightly, Priest. I warn you. You fly high in the four kingdoms, but remember always that you do so by my favour alone.'

'I know this well.'

'I who exalted you, have it in my power to throw you down as readily.'

'I know this also, my lord,' said Huy humbly.

'Then give me this barbarian,' Lannon demanded, and Huy looked up at him with an expression of deep regret.

'He is not mine to give, my lord. He belongs to the gods.'

Lannon let out a bellow of frustrated rage, and snatched up a heavy amphora of wine. He hurled it at Huy's head, and Huy ducked nimbly. The amphora slapped into the leather side of the tent, cushioning the impact and it dropped to the ground without breaking, wine gurgled from the mouth and soaked into the dry earth.

Lannon was on his feet now, towering over Huy, holding out towards him fists bunched into bony clubs, the muscles in his forearms knotted and ridged with exasperation. He held those fists under Huy's nose, and his eyes were pale glittering blue and deadly, the thick red-golden ringlets danced on his shoulders as he shook with the tempests of his rage.

'Go!' he said in a strangled voice. 'Go quick – before – before I—'

Huy did not wait to hear the rest of it.

Lannon Hycanus marched from Sett with a bodyguard of 200 men, and Huy watched him go from the walls of the garrison. He felt a chill of apprehension, vulnerable now and lonely without the king's favour.

Huy watched the small travelling party march out between the ranks of the legion, and saw that Lannon wore only a light tunic and that he was bareheaded in the early morning sunlight, his hair shining like a beacon fire. His armour-bearers followed him with helmet and breastplate, bow and sword and javelins. At Lannon's heels followed the little pygmy huntmaster, Xhai the bushman; he was attentive as a shadow to the king.

The legion cheered Lannon away, their voices ringing from the escarpment of the valley, and Lannon moved through the gates. He stood taller than those that surrounded him, smiling and proud and beautiful.

He looked up and saw Huy on the wall, and the smile changed to a quick fierce scowl; ignoring Huy's hesitant salute he marched out through the gates and took the road that ran southwards into the pass, and over the hills to the middle kingdom.

Huy watched until the forest hid him from sight, and then he turned away, feeling very alone. He went down to where the slave king lay dying on a bed of dry straw in a corner of Huy's own tent.

In the rising heat of the morning the smell of the wound was the rank, fetid odour of fever swamps and things long dead.

One of the old slave women was bathing his body, trying to lower the fever. She looked up as Huy entered and answered his query with a shake of her head. Huy squatted beside the pallet, and touched the slave king's skin. It was burning hot and dry, and Manatassi moaned in delirium.

'Send for a slave-master,' Huy ordered irritably. 'Have him strike away these chains.'

It was amazing to watch the fever eat away the flesh from that huge black frame, to see the bone appear beneath the skin, to watch the face collapse, and the skin change colour from shiny purple black to dry dusty grey.

The wound in his groin swelled up hot and hard, with a crusty evil-smelling scab from which a watery greenish-yellow fluid wept slowly. Each hour the slave king's hold on life seemed to slacken, his body grew hotter, the wound swelled to the size of a man's bunched fist.

In the noon of the second day Huy left the camp alone and climbed to a high place upon the escarpment where he could be alone with his god. Here in the valley of the great river the sun-god's presence seemed all-pervading and his usually warm benevolent countenance was oppressive. It seemed to fill the entire sky, and to beat down upon the earth like the hammer of a smith upon the anvil.

Huy sang the prayer of approach, but he did so in a perfunctory fashion, gabbling out the last lines, for Huy was very angry with his gods, and he wanted them to be aware of his displeasure.

'Great Baal,' he omitted the more flowery titles, and came swiftly to the main body of his protest, 'following your evident wishes, I have saved this one who bears your marks. Although I do not wish to complain, nor to question your motives, yet you should know that this has been no easy task. I have made serious sacrifices. I have weakened the position of the High Priest of Baal in the king's favour – I think not of myself, naturally, but only of my influence as your agent and servant. What weakens me, weakens the worship of the gods.' Huy said this with relish, that must surely catch their attention, and Huy was delighted with it. He felt it was entirely justified, it was high time that certain things were said and that the reciprocal duties of loyalty were stated.

'You know of old that no command of yours is too difficult of execution, no burden you place upon me but I shoulder it cheerfully, for always I have been secure in the certainty of your wisdom and purpose.'

Huy paused for breath, and thought. He was angry, but he must not let anger run away with his tongue. He had offended the king, best not offend the gods also. Quickly he moderated his closing address.

'However, in the matter of this marked barbarian I have no such certainty. I have saved him at great cost – to what purpose? Is it your intention that he must now die?' Huy paused again, letting his point sink in.

'I ask you now, most humbly,' Huy spread a drop of honey, 'most humbly, to make your intentions plain to your always attentive and obedient servant.'

Huy paused once more, should he dare the use of stronger terms? He decided against it, and instead spread both hands in the sun sign and sang the praise of Baal, with all the skill and beauty at his command. The sound of his voice shimmering and aching sweet in the breathless heat-hush of the wilderness was enough to make the gods weep, and when the last pure note had died upon the heated air Huy went down to the camp and with a bronze razor he lanced the grotesque swelling in the slave king's loin. Manatassi screamed with pain even in his delirium, and the poison gushed out thick and yellow and stinking. Huy poulticed the open wound with boiled corn wrapped in a linen cloth, scalding hot to drain the poisons.

By evening the fever had passed, and Manatassi lay in exhausted, but natural sleep. Huy stood over him smiling and nodding happily. He felt that he had won this wasted giant, wrested him from death's dark jaws with prayer and endeavour. He experienced a proud warmth of ownership and when the old slave crone brought him a brimming bowl of good Zeng wine, Huy lifted it in a salute to the sleeping giant.

'The gods have given you to me. You are mine. You live under my protection now, and I pledge it to you.' And he drained the bowl.

The weakness of his body smothered him, pressing him down on the hard mattress of straw. It was an effort to lift head or hand, and he hated his body that had failed him now. He rolled his head slowly and opened his eyes.

Across the tent, on a mat of woven reeds sat the strange little man. Manatassi watched him with a quick flaring of interest. He was stooped over a roll of the strange glowing metal that had been beaten out into a thin pliable length, and with a pointed knife he was scratching and cutting marks into the soft surface. He spent many hours of each day at this unusual activity. Manatassi watched him, noticing the quick nervous birdlike movements of head and hands that set the golden ear-rings jangling and the thick black plaits of hair dangling down his back.

The head seemed too large for the oddly hunched body, and the legs and arms were long and thick and brutal-looking, dark hair grew on the forearms and the back of the long tapered hands – and Manatassi remembered the speed and strength of that body in battle. He lifted his head slightly and glanced down at the linen bandages which swathed his lower body.

At the movement Huy was on his feet in one swift movement, and he came to the pallet and stooped over him, smiling.

Huy said, 'You sleep like a breast-fed baby.' And Manatassi looked up at him, wondering that a man could speak such a deadly insult to the paramount king of Vendi – and smile as he said it.

'Aia, bring food,' Huy shouted for the old slave woman, and settled down on a cushion beside Manatassi's couch. While Manatassi ate with huge appetite he listened with only a small part of his attention to a ridiculous description of the moon as a white-faced woman. He wondered that such a skilled warrior could be so naïve. It was only necessary to look at the moon to see that it was a cake of ground corn, and as the Mitasi-Mitasi the one great god devoured it, so the shape of his bite could clearly be seen cut from the round cake.

'Do you understand this?' Huy asked with deep concern, and Manatassi answered readily,

'I understand, high-born.'

'You believe it?' Huy insisted.

'I believe it.' Manatassi gave the answer which he knew would please, and Huy nodded happily. His efforts to teach the slave king were most rewarding. He had explained the theory of symbolic representation very carefully, showing Manatassi that the moon was not Astarte but her symbol, her coin, her sign and promise. He had explained the waning and waxing as the symbolic subjugation of the female to the male, repeated in the human female by the periodic moon-sickness.

'Now, the great god Baal,' Huy said, and Manatassi sighed inwardly. He knew what was coming. This strange person would now talk about the hole in the sky through which Mitasi-Mitasi made his entrance and exits. He would try to make Manatassi believe that this was a man with a flowing red beard. What a contradictory people they were, these pale ghost-like beings. On the one hand they had weapons and clothes and wonderful possessions and almost magical skills in civil and military matters. He had seen them fight and work, and it had amazed him. Yet these same people could not recognize truths that even the unweaned infants of his tribe understood completely.

Manatassi's first conscious thoughts when he had emerged from the hot mists of fever had been of escape. But now, forced by his weakness into the role of observer, he had time to reconstruct his plans. He was safe here, this hunch-backed manikin wielded some strange power, and he was under its protection. He knew this now. No one would touch him as long as his new master held his shield over him.

The other thing he knew was that there was much to learn here. If he could acquire the skills and knowledge of this people, he would be armed a thousand times. He would be the greatest war chief the tribes had ever known. They had used these skills to defeat him, he would defeat them with the same skills that he learned from them.

'Do you understand?' Huy asked earnestly. 'Do you understand that Baal is the master of the whole of heaven and earth?'

'I understand,' said Manatassi.

'Do you accept Astarte and great Baal as gods?'

'I accept them,' Manatassi agreed, and Huy looked very pleased.

'They have placed their mark upon you. It is right that you should be dedicated to their service. When we reach the city I will perform the ceremony in the temple of great Baal. I have chosen a god-name for you – you will no longer use the old style.'

'As you wish, high-born.'

'From henceforth you will be called Timon.'

'Timon,' the slave king tested the sound of it.

'He was the priest-warrior in the reign of the fifth Gry-Lion. A great man.'

Timon nodded, not understanding but content to watch and wait and learn.

'High-born,' he asked softly, 'the marks you scratch upon the yellow metal – what are they?'

Huy jumped up and fetched the golden scroll to the couch.

'This is how we store words and stories and ideas.' He plunged into an explanation of the writing process, and was rewarded by Timon's quick grasp of the principle of the phonetic alphabet.

On a scrap of leather he wrote Timon's name in sooty black ink, and in unison they spelled it out aloud, Timon laughing delightedly at his first achievement.

'Yes,' he thought, 'there is much to learn here – and so little time.'

Across the clay box Caius Terentius Varro, Consul of Rome, fought once more, pressing his legions into Hannibal's soft centre. The centre gave, with the sucky reluctance of dough, the Spaniards and Gauls there withdrew at Hannibal's design.

'Do you see it, Timon? The beauty of it, the sheer genius of it!' Huy called excitedly, speaking in Punic now, manipulating the counters.

'And where was Marhabal now?' Timon demanded as excitedly in the same language. After two years his Punic was fluent, with only the dragging vowels marring its perfection.

'He was here,' Huy touched the cavalry counters, 'holding his horse on a short rein.' Timon understood a horse to be a swift animal like a zebra on whose back armed men rode.

'Varro is entangled now?' Timon asked.

'Yes! Yes! Hannibal has crumpled his front and enveloped him – then what does he do, Timon?'

'The reserves?' Timon guessed.

'Yes! You have it! The Numidians and African reserves.' Huy was hopping up and down in his agitation. 'With the timing of the great master, he unleashes them. Taking Varro in the flanks, squeezing him in a vice, packing his ranks so they cannot manoeuvre nor wield their weapons. Then what, Timon, what then?'

'The cavalry?'

'Ah! The cavalry – Marhabal! The faithful brother. The master of horse, who has waited all that long day. Go! cries Hannibal.' Huy threw his arm in a wide gesture. 'Go! My brother, ride with your wild Iberians! They crash into them, Timon. It is the moment, the exact moment. Five minutes earlier is too soon – five minutes later and it is too late. Timing! Timing! The talent of the great military commander, timing! Of the statesman, the lover, the businessman, the merchant. The right action, at the right time.'

'And the result, high-born, what was the result?' Timon pleaded, in an agony of suspense. 'Was it victory?'

'Victory?' Huy asked. 'Yes, Timon. It was victory. Victory and massacre.

Eight legions of vaunting Rome wiped out to the man, two entire consular armies.'

'Eight legions, high-born.' Timon marvelled. 'Forty-eight thousand men in a single battle?'

'More than that, Timon. The auxiliaries were lost also. Sixty thousand men!' Huy swept his hand across the board, exterminating the Roman legions. 'We won the battles, Timon, but they won the wars. Three of them. Three bloody wars, that crushed us—' Huy broke off. His voice choking. He turned away quickly and went to the water jug. Timon hurried across and held the basin for him while Huy washed his hands and combed his beard. 'That brings us to the end of our study of Hanibal's campaigns, Timon. I kept the battle of Cannae for the last.'

'Who will we study next, high-born?'

'The one who Hannibal himself rated the most skilful General of all history.'

'Who was that?'

'Alexander III,' Huy said, 'King of Macedonia, who smashed the Persian Empire – whom the oracle at Delphi proclaimed invincible, and men called the Great.'

Timon held Huy's cloak for him, and Huy fastened the clasp as he left the precincts of the temple college through the small gate in the inner wall. Timon followed a pace behind him, wearing the short blue tunic of Huy's household with a light gold chain, dagger and purse belting his waist, the mark of high trust as a body slave. He walked a pace behind Huy's left shoulder, so as not to mask his master's sword arm, and he kept his hand on the dagger.

'High-born, the manner in which Hannibal invested Varro?'

'Yes?' Huy encouraged him.

'Could he not have advanced his flanks, and held his centre firm?'

'It is the difference between defence and offence,' Huy explained, and they plunged into discussion of battle tactics and strategy until they left the main gate in the outer wall of the temple area. From here any conversation was impossible, for the crowds spotted this strange couple. Giant black slave and diminutive gnomelike master. They cheered Huy, crowding around him to touch his arm in greeting, to listen to his banter and perhaps receive an alms coin from the purse on Timon's belt.

Huy loved his popularity. He smiled and joked and pushed his way gently through the press. A successful General – there had been two other campaigns since the great slave-taking – a well-beloved priest, a noted wit and song-writer, and a rich philanthropist (Huy's investments had prospered exceedingly in the last two years), he was the object of popular adulation throughout the city.

They crossed the market-place with its fascinating smells and sights and sounds of hides and humanity, of spices and open sewers. On one of the slave blocks was a light-skinned girl of mixed Yuye blood, and the auctioneer spotted Huy in the crowd and called out to him.

'My lord, a work of art for you. A statue in yellow ivory,' opening the girl's cloak to display her body.

Huy laughed and waved a hand in refusal. They moved along the stone jetty at the lakeside where the ships lay with stern almost touching stern, their hatches open and a boiling of stevedores running over them, loading and unloading the merchandise. From the taverns and wineshops flanking the jetty came the sour stench of cheap wine and gusts of drunken laughter. The street girls beckoned from the narrow lanes between the shops. The uncertain light of dusk softened their raddled features and hectic painted cheeks and lips – Huy wondered what solace a man could find with the likes of them.

Beyond the bustle of the harbour area lay the town houses of the noble families and rich merchants, each protected by the high mud outer wall and a heavy carved wooden gate. Huy's new residence was one of the least pretentious of these, with the entrance off a narrow walled lane, and a view from the flat roof over the lake.

Once through the gate Huy shed his sword and cloak and handed them to Timon with a sigh of pleasure at the moment of homecoming, and he went through into the paved central courtyard.

The princes and princesses were waiting for him, fourteen of them, headed by the twins, Helanca and Imilce. The two of them had grown in the past years, and they were stranded now in that awkward period between girlhood and womanhood. Too young to giggle, yet too old to greet Huy with a kiss.

There were no such inhibitions upon the younger members of house Barca, and they swarmed forward to engulf Huy. The religious instruction of the children of the royal house was a duty Huy had imposed upon himself, and despite the estrangement between king and priest, Lannon had not interfered with this arrangement. He had not sanctioned it, but he had not forbidden it. Huy led his students through into the airy living-room of the house.

In the courtyard one of the royal nursemaids waited until her charges had followed the priest before she turned and her eyes sought those of Timon. She was a tall girl with strong shoulders, long-waisted and with fruitful hips. Her legs also were straight and strong, but her hands were narrow and pink-palmed and delicately shaped. She wore her hair oiled and dressed in the manner of the Vendi, for she was of Timon's tribe. Taken in the great raid, she was not slave born, not of the humble dependent breed that had known nothing but captivity. There was a fierce spirit in her to match Timon's. Her skin was a shade lighter than his, her face was round, moon-shaped, her nose flat and broad, her lips full and pouting, but her teeth were small and even, and very white when she smiled at Timon.

Timon inclined his head sharply in a command, and Sellene the slave girl nodded in acknowledgement. When Timon left the courtyard and went through the kitchens into the slave quarters she followed him.

He was waiting for her in his own tiny room with its single pallet of reed mat and furs. She went to him without hesitation, and lay against the great hard muscles of his chest and belly and thighs. Her round breasts jutting through the purple tunic of house Barca pressed against Timon.

They held their faces together, sniffing softly but eagerly at each other's eyes and mouth and nostrils, clinging to each other in the need and wanting.

'When I hold you, then once again I am King of Vendi, and no slave dog,' Timon whispered, and the girl groaned against him with her love.

With gentle hands that could crush the life from a man Timon loosened her tunic and carried her to the pallet. He laid her upon the bed, and as he came over her he said, 'You shall be the first of all my wives. You shall be my queen and the mother of my sons.'

'When shall it be?' she asked him and her voice shook with the emotions locked within her.

'Soon,' he promised. 'Very soon now. I have what I came for, and I will take you back beyond the river. I shall be the greatest king the tribes have ever known, and you shall be my queen.'

'I believe you,' whispered Sellene.

'My royal lords and fair ladies.' The children squealed with glee, it was one of their jokes when Huy addressed them that way. 'Today I have a special treat for you!' Again pandemonium broke out. Huy's treats were usually something special indeed.

'What is it?' Imilce demanded breathlessly.

'This evening you will meet the oracle of Opet,' Huy announced, and the uproar subsided swiftly. The small ones not understanding but none the less infected by the solemnity of their elders. The bigger children had heard of the oracle, their nurses often frightened them into obedience with the name. Now that they were about to meet this mythical creature the atmosphere was charged with tension. They were all of them suffering from an onset of the creeps and ghostlies.

Anna spoke for all of them when she asked in a very subdued voice, 'She won't eat us, will she?'

When Tanith came she seated herself amongst them, and threw the hood of her cloak back from her face. She smiled at the children, and said softly, 'I am going to tell you a story.' The smile and the promise were enough to ease the tension and they edged in closer to her. 'It's the story of the marriage of the great god Baal to the goddess Astarte.'

Tanith began the tale from religious mythology which was the basis of the Festival of the Fruitful Earth, a festival celebrated every five years. This year of Opet 538 was the 106th ceremony since the founding of the city, and the following day would begin the festivities that would last for ten days.

Tanith held her young audience enthralled, speaking in the compelling voice which Huy had trained so carefully, using the mannerisms and gestures he had taught her. Huy watched her with an unusual mixture of professional appraisal and the adulation of a besotted lover.

In two years she had lost the last traces of gawkiness and uncertainty, and although she was not yet twenty years of age, there was an inner calm, a serenity of mind and expression, that befitted her role of seeress and occult adviser to a nation. No matter that her pronouncements were carefully coached and rehearsed by Huy Ben-Amon, it was she that made the delivery, and made it convincingly. Much of Huy's material success in the last two years stemmed from the questions and requests for guidance addressed to Tanith by the rich merchants and trading syndicates of Opet – and Tanith's replies. The supplicants were usually well satisfied with Tanith's advice, though it was always couched in terms of ambiguity to ensure against recriminations. Did it matter that Huy Ben-Amon was also well satisfied?

In the same way Huy, despite his loss of the king's ear, kept a guiding hand on the rudder of the ship of state. Huy was certain that Lannon Hycanus was fully aware of the ultimate source of the advice and guidance which he received from Tanith. In any event, Lannon visited the oracle regularly in her shrine in the grotto beside the silent green pool of Astarte.

On the morrow Lannon's visit to the oracle would be his first official act that would signal the commencement of the Festival of the Fruitful Earth. This was the true reason why Huy had summoned Tanith to his residence. He must brief her carefully on the replies she would make to the king's queries. Huy knew with a high degree of accuracy what these would be, for his informers were close to the king and again Huy guessed that Lannon intentionally leaked his questions in advance, certain that they would reach Huy and that the replies would come through the oracle.

Thinking of Lannon always brought on a mood of deep melancholy. Two years Huy had been without solace of Lannon's smile and hand clasp and companionship, and during that time the sharp edge of his loss had not blunted but grown keener. He would wait for hours for a passing glimpse of his old friend, he would pester others for accounts of the banquets at the palace to which he was not invited. On each anniversary of the king's birth, and also on his throne day Huy had composed a sonnet and sent it with a handsome gift to the palace. The gift had been unacknowledged and the sonnet unsung – as far as he knew.

Huy tore himself out of this sad mood, and looked instead at his love. The children had crowded her now, silent and big-eyed and intent. Four-year-old Hannibal, named after his illustrious ancestor, had crawled into Tanith's lap and was sucking his thumb as he stared up into her face.

Tanith's mask of solemnity had slipped a little, with these children she was childlike, her expression animated and her voice excited. Seeing her thus seemed to add a new dimension to Huy's feelings for her, and his heart swelled in his chest until it seemed his chest must burst. How much longer must he wait, he wondered, and for what? If it had taken two long carefully planned years to win her confidence, how much longer to win her heart, and having won it what could he hope for – for she was dedicated to the goddess and could never belong to mortal man.

Tanith's story ended, and the children exclaimed and clamoured for more, besieging her with demands and entreaties and bribery kisses – but Huy feigned outrage, and scolded them while they laughed and clapped their hands with delight. He shouted for the nursemaids and they came – among them that tall brooding fiery woman who always made Huy feel disquiet when she looked at him from those unfathomably dark eyes.

He said to her. 'Sellene, darkness falls, tell Timon to carry a lamp for you to the palace gate.' And she acknowledged him with an inclination of the head, showing no gratitude at the order nor resentment either.

After the children had gone they ate the evening meal, the three of them, Tanith, Huy and Aina the ancient priestess who was Tanith's chaperone. Huy had selected her for two good reasons. She was half blind and completely deaf. Huy had tested her by making obscene gestures at her from a range of twenty paces. Aina had shown no reaction, nor had she when Huy crept up behind her and shouted a rude name in her ear. She was just the type of chaperone that Huy wanted.

They ate with the lamps trimmed low and the food served by one of the ancient slaves, and when they were finished Huy led Tanith up the outside staircase to the roof and they sat together below the parapet on reed mats and leather cushions. The night wind off the lake was cool and the stars very yellow and bright. Huy crouched over his lute, and strummed softly the rippling tune which he had trained Tanith's unconscious mind to accept as the signal for hypnotic concentration. Before he had finished the last bars of the tune she was breathing slowly and evenly, her body still and her eyes dark green and unseeing.

While his fingers ran over the strings of the instrument repeating the tune again and again, Huy began to speak. He kept his voice at a monotonous sing-song tone, speaking softly but insidiously and Tanith sat in the starlight and listened with an inner ear.

On the first day of the 106th Festival of the Fruitful Earth, Lannon Hycanus the forty-seventh Gry-Lion of Opet went in procession to the temple of Astarte to take the oracle.

He passed through the enclosure of the temple of Baal where the sacred towers pointed to the sun, guarded by the carved sunbird monoliths, and where the silent populace of the city waited, but when he reached the cleft in the red cliffs that guarded the entrance to the sacred grotto he unbuckled his sword and handed it to his little pygmy huntmaster, his shield and helmet he gave to his armour bearers, and bareheaded and unarmed he entered the opening in the cliff.

He passed through the paved tunnel and into the silent beauty of the grotto. The surrounds of the pool were paved with slabs of sandstone and the pool itself was edged with a rounded coping of the same material. Tiers of stone benches rose against the sheer walls of the grotto, and against the far wall the shrine of Astarte was built into the living rock. Its portals were columned in the Hellenic style, and it contained the cells of the priestesses and the chamber of the oracle.

Beyond the stone throne of the oracle was concealed the entrance to the city archives cut into the rock, and beyond that again, guarded by a massive stone door and the curse of the gods, was the treasury and the tomb of the kings.

Lannon paused beside the pool, and the priestesses came forward to meet him and escort him to the edge of the pool. Here they helped him to shed his armour and under garments.

He stood tall and naked, golden-headed and beautifully formed, at the head of the steps leading down into the green water. His body was finely muscled as that of a trained athlete, although there was heavy bunched muscle in the shoulders and neck, the mark of the swordsman. His belly and flanks, however, were lean with the shape of muscle beneath the skin but lightly stated. A gilding of red-gold hair ran down from his navel across the flat stomach to explode in a sunny burst of curls in the angle of his legs. The legs were shapely, long and moulded, and balanced his regal bulk easily.

The High Priestess blessed him, and called down the goddess's favour upon him. Then Lannon went down the steps and immersed himself in the sacred, life-giving water.

While two young novices dried his body and dressed the king in robes of fresh linen, Huy Ben-Amon sang the praise chant to the goddess and when it ended all eyes looked up to the opening in the roof of the cavern high above the green pool.

Lannon called out in a loud voice. 'Astarte, mother of moon and earth, receive the messenger we send you – and hear our plea with favour.'

The throng about the pool lifted their hands high in the sign of the sun, and at the signal the body of the sacrifice plunged from the slab that jutted into the opening in the grotto roof. The wail of the doomed soul echoed briefly about the cavern, until he struck the water and was dragged down swiftly into the green depths by the weight of the chains he wore.

Lannon turned from the pool, and passed between the ranks of the priestesses into the entrance of the shrine. The audience chamber of the oracle was only a little larger than the living-room of a rich man's house. The lamps burned with a steady light. The flames were tinted an unnatural greenish hue, and the incense of burning herbs was heavy and oppressive. There were draperies beyond the oracle's throne hanging from roof to flagged floor.

The oracle sat upon the throne, a small figure completely swathed in white robes, the face hidden in the shadows of her hood.

Lannon halted in the centre of the chamber and before he spoke he admired for a moment the arrangements that put the interviewer at such a disadvantage. Barefooted, damp from the pool, stripped of weapons and finery, dressed in strange robes and forced to look up at the figure on the throne while he inhaled the subtly drugged air – he must be off balance. Lannon felt his anger stir, and his voice was harsh as he made the formal greeting and asked the first question.

Huy watched from his place of concealment behind the draperies. He revelled in the closeness of his friend's physical presence, remembering his mannerisms and voice tones, watching the familiar and well-loved face, smiling at an expected change of expression, the quick smoulder of anger in the pale blue eyes, the quickening of interest at a warning, the glimmer of a smile as he recognized good advice.

Tanith spoke in the same sing-song cadence as Huy had used, picking the answers from the wide selection with which Huy had armed her.

When Lannon was finished and would have left the chamber, Tanith's voice stopped him.

'There is more.'

Lannon turned back with surprise, for he was not accustomed to unsolicited – and unpaid for – counsel from the oracle. But Tanith spoke, 'The lion had faithful jackal to warn him of the hunter's approach, but drove the jackal away.

'The sun had a bird to carry the sacrifices on high, but turned his countenance away from the bird.

'The hand had an axe to defend it, but cast the axe aside.

'Oh, proud lion! Oh, faithless sun! Oh, careless hand!'

Behind the drapery Huy held his breath. It had sounded very clever when he had composed it, but now spoken out in the bare stone chamber it shocked even him.

Lannon's pale eyes seemed to glaze over as he puzzled the riddle, but it was not that subtle and as the import struck him his eyes cleared to the chill sparkle of sapphire and the blood engorged his face and neck.

'Damn you, witch,' he shouted. 'Must I have it from you also? That cursed priest plagues me at every turn. I cannot walk the streets of my city but I hear the crowds sing his piddling songs. I cannot dine in my own banquet-room but my guests will repeat his empty mouthings. I cannot fight, nor drink a bowl of wine, nor toss a dice but his shadow stands at my shoulder.' Lannon was panting with anger, as he stamped across the audience chamber and shook his fist in the oracle's startled face. 'My children even, he bewitches them also.'

Behind the drapes Huy felt his spirits soar on bright wings, this was not an enemy speaking.

'He struts and lords it in the streets of my city, his name echoes through my kingdoms.'

Lannon's anger was changing to righteous indignation.

'They cheer him when he passes, I have heard it, and, by great Baal, they cheer him louder than they do their own king.'

Lannon swung away from the throne, unable to control his agitation. His eyes swept over the draperies and for an instant seemed to stare into Huy's soul. Huy drew back with a quick intake of breath, but Lannon paced quickly about the chamber before approaching the oracle again.

'He does all this, mark you, *without my favour*. He should be an outcast a—' He broke off and paced again, and nis voice changed, the cutting edge of it dulled, and he said almost inaudibly, 'How I miss that terrible little man.'

Huy doubted for a moment that the words had been spoken, but almost immediately Lannon's voice rose in a bellow.

'But he defied me. He took from me what was mine, and that I cannot overlook!'

Lannon whirled and stormed from the shrine. His gentleman-at-arms and his huntmaster saw the expression on his face and they signalled the warnings ahead of the king's furious progress back to the palace.

On the final day of the festival Lannon Hycanus prayed in the temple of great Baal, alone in the sacred grove among the towers and the sunbird monoliths. Then he emerged to receive the renewed pledges of loyalty from his subjects. Each of the nine noble families would be represented, as well as the order of priesthood, the guilds of craftsmen and the powerful trading syndicates of the kingdom. They would restate their oaths of allegiance to the throne, and present gifts to the Gry-Lion.

Huy Ben-Amon was absent from the ceremony. Bakmor made the oath for the priesthood and presented the gift. Lannon growled softly at the young warrior priest as he made obeisance before him.

'Where is the Holy Father of Ben-Amon?'

'My lord, I speak for him and all the priests of great Baal.' Bakmor avoided the question as Huy had coached him, and Lannon could protest no further in the presence of his assembled nobles.

The ceremony ended the festival and Opet plunged into an orgy of food and wine and frolic and licence. While Lannon feasted with his nobles in the palace, the commoners thronged the narrow streets singing and dancing. The wine vendors passed freely amongst them, but during the daylight hours the restraints of custom and law checked the behaviour of the crowds. Darkness would bring on the lewd and wanton revels which characterized the festival. In the night the noble matrons and their pretty daughters would slip out, cloaked and hooded, into the streets to join the debauchery – or at the very least to watch it with shining eyes and breathless laughter. For a day and night the rules of society were suspended, and no husband nor wife could demand explanation or accounting from their spouses. It happened but once every five years, and when the festival ended there were wine-sore heads, pale faces and shaking hands, as well as smug and secret smiles.

By the middle of the afternoon Lannon was drunk, expansively and happily drunk, as were most of his guests. The banquet-room of the palace was sweltering. The sun beat down fiercely upon the flat mud roof, while the body heat of 500 excited nobles, and the heat from the steaming dishes of rich food turned it into an oven.

The roar of voices drowned the valiant efforts of the musicians, and the artistry of the naked girl dancers was impaired by a barrage of ripe grapes aimed by a group of young and noble knights. Hits upon various parts of the girls' anatomy scored for the marksmen in a contest upon which large amounts of gold were wagered.

Deep in wine and talk, Lannon was not aware of the change in the feast until almost complete silence had descended upon the hall. He looked up, frowning quickly, and saw that the musicians' hands had frozen upon their instruments, the dancers stood paralysed, and the guests gawked.

Lannon's frown deepened to a scowl as he saw Huy Ben-Amon approaching him down the hall. Huy was dressed in a blue tunic with a border of woven gold wire. He wore a gold belt, and a jewelled dagger. His hair and beard were carefully oiled and curled, and golden ear-rings dangled to his shoulders.

His expression was solemn as he knelt quickly before Lannon, and his voice rang golden and sweet to every corner of the hall.

'My king, I come to renew my allegiance to you. Let all men know that I honour you above all things, and my loyalty is unto death and beyond.'

Lannon was caught off balance, as Huy had intended. His brain was fuddled with surprise and wine. He fumbled for words, but before he found them, Huy had risen swiftly.

'As a mark of my faith, I offer a gift.' He signalled with one hand behind his back, and all heads in the hall swung to the main doors.

The towering figure of Timon stalked into the hall, passed down its length and stopped beside Huy. He stared into Lannon's face with those ferocious smoky eyes.

Huy whispered. 'Down!' And nudged the giant slave, and slowly Timon lowered himself to one knee and bowed his head.

'But he belongs to the gods,' Lannon challenged harshly. 'You declared him god-marked, priest.'

And Huy gathered his resolve, steeling himself to tell the lie, to commit this sacrilege. Despite the fact that he had already explained it to the gods and to Timon, he was uneasy. It was necessary to regain the king's favour, Huy had explained, there was but one way of doing so. Lannon was bound by his pride. He could not move to break the deadlock. Huy must make the offer. He asked great Baal for permission to deny the bird-footed marking of the slave. He asked aloud, while pacing the roof of his house in the noon day. A distant muttering of summer thunder had been all the answer Huy needed. The gods had answered, but Huy felt nervous, the answer had been in a very minor key, and not without ambiguity. It was also very difficult for Huy to admit that he was wrong – it jarred the very foundations of his soul.

'My lord,' said Huy. 'I was mistaken. The gods have shown me that the markings are not sacred.'

Lannon stared at Huy. He shook his head slightly, as though he doubted the evidence of his own ears.

'You mean – you give him to me without reservation? I can have him despatched immediately, if I wish to?' He leaned forward staring at Huy. 'Do you give him to me without conditions?'

'I have declared my love for the king,' said Huy, and with his foot he nudged Timon.

In a great rumbling bass, Timon spoke his lines in near perfect Punic. 'I come to you as a living proof of that love.'

Lannon rocked back on his cushions. He thought about it, and the scowl reappeared, as he saw it.

'You seek to chain me! There are still conditions – only better concealed,' he growled.

'Nay, my lord. Not chains, but the silken threads of friendship,' Huy told him softly. They held each other's eyes. Lannon beginning to flush with anger, Huy steady and calm.

Then suddenly Huy's face cracked, and the dark eyes sparkled. The ringlets on his cheeks began to dance with suppressed laughter. Lannon opened his mouth to bellow at him, to reject the gift and the offer of friendship. Instead, laughter rattled up his throat and burst from his open lips. He laughed, until the tears poured down his cheeks and between gusts of laughter he moaned with the pain of his aching belly muscles.

'Fly for me, bird of the sun,' he sobbed, and Huy flopped down beside him on the cushions and shook and quivered with laughter.

'Roar for me, Lion of Opet,' he cried and a slave girl filled a wine bowl and brought it to him. Huy quaffed half of it, then passed the bowl to Lannon. He drained it. A little wine ran from the corners of his mouth into his golden beard. He smashed the bowl on the stone floor, then clasped Huy about the shoulders.

'We have wasted much time, my Sunbird. Let us make up for it. What shall we do first?'

'Drink,' said Huy.

'Ah!' cried Lannon. 'And then what?'

'Hunt,' suggested Huy, choosing those activities dearest to the king.

'Hunt!' Lannon echoed. 'Send for my huntmasters – we march tomorrow to hunt the elephant!'

'Astarte, mother of earth, your beauty is multiplied until it floods my soul,' muttered Huy, swaying gracefully, as he looked up at the night sky. He reeled backwards, but fell against a wall. It steadied him, and he went on studying the astronomical phenomena in the heavens. Four silver moons hung above the night-revelling city. Huy closed one eye, and three of the moons vanished – he opened it and they reappeared.

'Astarte, guide your servant's footsteps,' Huy entreated, pushed himself away from the wall and went on down the narrow lane towards the harbour. He stumbled over a body lying in the shadows, and stooped unsteadily to check for signs of life.

The body snored and grunted as he rolled it onto its back, and a warm fruity gust of winey breath came up to Huy. It reminded him of the recumbent figures he had left strewn about the banquet hall at the palace. Lannon chief among them, smiling as he slept.

'Tonight you are in good company, citizen of Opet,' Huy chuckled, and went tottering onwards down the lane. In an angle of the wall a dark shape moved. Huy peered at it curiously, saw one body, two heads, heard broken gusty breathing, soft incoherent cries. The movements were small, but unmistakable. Huy smiled, tripped and nearly fell. He saw a startled girl's face turn towards him from the gloom. 'Let all things be fruitful,' he told her solemnly and went on, and as he went another figure slipped silently from the dark lane and followed Huy. The figure was cloaked and hooded in rough woven brown cloth, and its movements were stealthy and deliberate.

The quayside of the harbour was crowded with revellers, and there were bonfires burning here. The reflections of the flames smeared ruddy and bright upon the still black waters of the lake. Around them, arms linked in a circle, danced the crowds. Some of the women were past all restraint, stripped naked to the waist, spilled wine snaking down their white bodies like blood.

Huy stopped to watch them a while, and the following figure hung back, mingling with the throng of merry-makers.

When Huy started forward, the cloaked figure hurried forward also. The lane that led up to Huy's house was in deep darkness, but a lamp burned dimly in a niche above the gate, left there to welcome the master home.

As Huy groped his way towards the light, the following figure closed with him silently and swiftly. The blundering sounds of his own progress blanketed the rustle of cloth and the light footfalls behind him.

Huy reached the gate, and he stood in the dim lamplight. His dagger was under his cloak, and his sword hand reached out for the latch of the gate. In that instant while he was unready and off balance, the dark figure flew at him from out of the darkness. A hand closed on his wrist, and he was thrown back against the wall beside the gate. Wine had slowed his reflexes, he twisted his face upwards in surprise and alarm. He saw the dark figure, with its face hidden in the recesses of the hood, come at him – and before he could shout soft lips were pressed against his, and a little muffled chuckle broke through these lips into his startled mouth – and he felt warm breasts and thighs moving against him.

The shock of it paralysed Huy. For long seconds he stood utterly still while lips and cunning hands teased and goaded him. Then with a hoarse cry he reached for the taut warm woman shape, and immediately it was gone, slipping away beyond his reach.

He lunged for it wildly, his hands groping air, and the shape danced away, swirled through the gateway into Huy's house and slammed the gate closed.

Cursing desperately, Huy struggled with the gate, wrenched it open at last and ran into the entrance court.

There was a flash of dark movement across the court, disappearing into the house, and Huy raced after it, tripped over a cushion and fell full length, knocked over a stool on which a house slave had left an amphora and wine bowl. They shattered loudly, splashing wine across the mud floor. A mocking whisper of laughter, from the dim recesses of the house, sent Huy scrambling to his feet and charging onwards. He saw the cloaked figure silhouetted against the lamplit doorway of his sleeping quarters.

'Wait!' he shouted. 'Who are you?' And his house slaves roused by the uproar came running, still half asleep, panicky and hastily armed.

'Be gone!' Huy shouted at them furiously. 'All of you – the first one I catch out of his room before morning, I will have flogged.' And they retreated to their quarters, not seriously alarmed by the threat. Huy maintained his dignity until the last of them had disapppeared, then he turned and charged towards the doorway of his sleeping quarters.

There was a night lamp burning here also, on a low stool beside his bed. The wick was trimmed low, a soft orange puddle of light which left the furthest reaches of the room in darkness. Beside the lamp stood the cloaked woman. She stood motionless and the face within the hood was completely hidden although Huy thought he caught the sheen of reflected light off watching eyes.

The force of Huy's charge carried him half across the room, but in the wrong direction. He swung towards her, and at that moment she stooped and snuffed the lamp flame. The room was plunged into darkness, and Huy's charge ended against the wall. He gathered himself quickly, he was sobering fast now, and he crouched beside the wall listening.

He heard the rustle of cloth, and he pounced. His fingers closed on a hem of the cloak. There was a muted shriek of surprise, and the fold of material was plucked from his fingers. He swore bitterly, and with arms widespread groped like a blind man about the room.

He sensed movements near him, the lightest breathing, the softest stirring in the darkness. He reached out quickly, and his fingers brushed against smooth skin. He recognized the shape of a nude back, and the plump warm bulge of a buttock. A soft chuckle and it was gone again. Huy froze with his heart hammering at his ribs, and his physical arousal making him momentarily dizzy.

Whoever she was, she had discarded the cloak. He was alone with a woman who was elusive as a darting lake pike, and as naked as a new-born babe. Like a stalking leopard he went after her, stripping his own tunic and breech clout as he went, dropping them carelessly on the floor, until, except for the gold rings in his ears, he was as bare as his own passion.

She was panicky in the darkness now, unable to control the gasps and nervous giggles. And Huy hunted her by ear, closing in on her, driving her into the corner beside the bed.

She nearly escaped again, ducking under his searching hands but one of his long arms whipped around her waist and he lifted her easily. She squealed now, kicking like a captive animal, her fists beating against his face and chest.

He carried her to the thick pile of furs that made up his bed.

Huy woke with a sense of peace, a feeling of deep happiness.

His body seemed softened and enervated, but his mind was clear and sharply focused. The soft pinks of dawn suffused his chamber and the cry of the winging lake birds carried clearly to him.

He raised himself on one elbow and looked down at the girl who slept beside him in the storm-tossed bed. She had cast aside her covering in the warm spring night. Her hair was moist at the temples, and a fine sheen of moisture shone on her softly pouting upper lip. Her eyes were closed, and she slept so lightly that her breathing barely stirred the mass of soft dark hair which lay upon her cheeks.

One arm was thrown over her head, pulling the surprisingly large breasts out of shape. Her breasts were big and full and round for the long slim length of her body, and the tips were still flushed dark red from the loving of the night. Her skin was smooth and pale creamy olive, with violent puffs of black silky hair in her armpits and at the base of her belly.

Huy saw all of this in his first startled glance, before his eyes fastened on her calm and sleeping face.

Incredulously Huy stared at her, all sound locked away in his throat. He felt horror, and awe, and superstitious terror.

The girl opened her eyes, and saw him and smiled.

'Baal's blessings on you, Holy Father,' she said softly.

'Tanith!' gasped Huy.

'Yes, my lord.' She was still smiling.

'This is sacrilege,' Huy whispered. 'This is an offence against the goddess.'

'To deny my love for you would have been an offence against all nature.' Tanith sat up on the bed, and kissed him without remorse, without the least sign of guilt.

'Love?' Huy asked, his misgivings temporarily forgotten.

'Yes, my lord,' Tanith nodded, and kissed him again.

'But—' Huy stuttered, and his cheeks turned bright as bush fires. 'You cannot – how can you love me?'

'How can I not, my lord?'

'But my body – my back.'

'Your back I love because it is part of you, part of your goodness and kindness and wisdom.'

He stared at her for many seconds, then clumsily he took her in his arms and buried his face in the fragrant dark cloud of her hair.

'Oh, Tanith,' he whispered. 'What are we going to do?'

Huy stood on the hilltop in the dawn and waited for his god. Below him the camp stirred. The cooking fires paled in the growing light of day. Small sounds carried up to him, the sounds of 6,000 men preparing for the hunt. The 6,000 warriors of Huy's legion, and the king's train, and the slaves and the women and the elephants and the baggage train. Small wonder that the camp filled the entire valley on both sides of the small river that flowed down the escarpment of the hills. Thirty miles away to the north lay the sluggish green ribbon of the great river, sweltering in its hot and unhospitable valley. One of Lannon's legions was camped there already, and for days now they had been harassing the elephant herds that were feeding along the river. They had attacked them with archers, and javelin-throwers and war elephants.

Under this harassment the herds would leave the valley, taking to their ancient roads out over the escarpment. Lannon was encamped now astride these well-blazed trails, and scouts from the valley had reported the previous evening that the herds were already on the move. They were massing and moving in towards the escarpment wall, and in the next few days they would come pouring up out of the valley in long majestic files, as the old bulls led them to sanctuary from the persistent hunters who plagued them.

Huy Ben-Amon pondered this as he stood in the dawn. He wore light hunting armour and running sandals, and he leaned comfortably on the shaft of the vulture axe. The splendid blade was covered with a soft leather sheath to protect the finely honed edge and the delicate engravings. It seemed to Huy that the gods had so arranged circumstances as to provide him with this opportunity.

For two weeks, ever since that last night of the Festival of the Fruitful Earth, Huy had spent most of his waking moments pondering his dilemma. He had spent hours poring over the sacred books, examining the roles of priest and priestess, their duties and relationship to the gods, and to each other. He thought that from all this research he had built up a case for his behaviour. He could not bring himself to call it sacrilege. He had come now to plead his case, and to receive judgement.

The sun shot its first golden lance against the crest of the hill, and Huy sang the praise chant with all the beauty at his command. Then he made his plea. It was complicated dialectic, based on the concept of earthly representation, and amounting to a line of reasoning which supposed that what was good behaviour between Baal and his mate Astarte would be equally justifiable between their earthly representatives – although, of course, not between a priestess and any other person than the High Priest of Baal. Huy glossed over the more evidently weak spots in his case.

He ended, 'It may be, however, great Baal and heavenly Astarte, that I am mistaken in my reasoning. It may well be that I have sinned. If this is the case then I deserve your full wrath and, despite my life of service and faithful duty, I deserve the most dire punishment!'

Huy paused for effect. 'I go now to hunt the elephant. I swear on my life that wherever the chase is hottest, there I shall be. Wherever the danger is deadliest, there I shall be.

'If I have sinned – then let the tusked beasts strike me down. If I have not sinned then let me live and return to the bosom of your priestess. If you grant me life and love – I swear my duty and service will last to the end of my days, and no man nor woman will ever know of the dispensation you have granted me.' He was quiet a while longer then he spoke again, 'You who have loved, take pity on one who loves also.'

Huy came down the hill well satisfied with his bargain. He would give the gods full measure. He would not hang back in distaste from the slaughter today, the gods would have every opportunity to demonstrate their outrage. In any event, Huy was well aware that only death could keep him out of Tanith's arms. The taste of that fruit had been too sweet for him ever to deny it.

'Huy,' Lannon shouted as Huy entered the camp. 'Where have you been?' He was armed and striding impatiently back and forth outside his tent. He came towards Huy quickly. 'The day wastes away,' he cried. 'Already from the hills our look-outs have seen the approach of the herds.'

The war elephants were ready, drivers sitting on their necks and the tall castles on their backs. Lannon's hunting party was assembled about the tent. Among them Huy noticed some of the king's most renowned huntmasters: Mursil, with his purple boozy face, the lean and saturnine Zadal, Huya the celebrated bowman, and the diminutive yellow Xhai whose fame as a tracker had grown apace in the last few years. Beyond them amongst the horde of body slaves towered the colossal black bulk of Timon. Huy smiled at him, and then he hurried beside Lannon to the elephant lines.

Lannon told him, 'You will ride with me, Sunbird.' And Huy replied, 'I am honoured, my lord.'

Mursil handed Huy one of the elephant bows. Few men could draw these massive weapons. Carved from solid baulks of wild ebony, they were as thick at the centre as a man's wrist and strung with twisted strands of lion gut. It required immense strength in the arms and chest to draw one of the five-foot arrows, that were armed with a heavy steel head and flighted with wild duck feathers. However, once drawn to the limit and loosed, they could fly 100 paces and bury the arrow up to its feathers in the living flesh of an elephant. They could reach the mighty heart in its castle of ribs, they could cut deep into the massive pink lungs, or loosed with skill they could cut through the ear-hole in the great bony skull and find the brain.

'I know you prefer the bow to the spear, Holy Father,' Mursil murmured respectfully. 'As for me, my old arm can no longer draw.'

'Thank you, huntmaster.'

'The quivers are full. I have tested and selected each of the arrows,' Mursil assured him, and Huy followed Lannon to where his war elephant knelt. It was a rangy old cow, more steady than the bull in the heat of battle, more reliable and even-tempered than the bull in the hunt.

Huy followed Lannon up into the castle. There was room for three men in the wooden box. The arrow quivers were fitted to the outside, but with the arrow-heads standing up ready to the hand. The javelins were racked on the front of the castle and Lannon selected one and tested it thoughtfully.

'A nice balance,' he judged it, and then looked down to where his huntmasters waited anxiously. Each of them eager for the honour of riding with the Gry-Lion. Lannon glanced over them, but his eye stopped on Xhai. He nodded, and with pathetic gratitude the pygmy scrambled up the elephant's side.

With a heavy lurch that threw Huy against the edge of the castle, the elephant came up on its feet. They looked down from the majestic height of nearly eighteen feet, and the driver goaded the old cow into a stately swaying walk. They took the trail down towards the escarpment of the valley.

'I have selected a good place for it,' Lannon told Huy. 'Where the steep path comes out suddenly into a small flat bowl. We will wait for them there.'

Huy looked back and saw the other war elephants following them. Twenty of them in single file, ears flapping, trunks swinging they trundled sedately along. The huntsmen in the castles were checking and testing their weapons, and chattering excitedly.

'For what do we hunt, my lord?' Huy asked. 'Calves or ivory?'

'Calves first. The elephant trainers have asked for two dozen youngsters between five and ten years old. We will capture those this morning, for it will be the breeding herds that come up out of the valley first. Then later we will hunt for ivory. The scouts report many fine bulls scattered along the great river.'

The saucer which Lannon had selected was hemmed in with steep broken ground. It was circular in shape, perhaps 500 paces across. The elephant road came into it through a narrow rocky pass, crossed the saucer and climbed out of it up a steep pitch to the high ground above. The saucer was thickly wooded, and Lannon placed his war elephants in ambush, concealing them about the perimeter of the bowl in the good cover. The war elephants were forced to kneel for better concealment, and while they waited Huy and Lannon breakfasted on cold corn cakes, cheese and roast salt beef washed down with red wine. It was a hunter's meal, taken in cover with the mounting excitement of the chase sharpening their appetites, and as they ate they kept glancing up at the lookouts on the high ground above the saucer whose task it was to watch for and to signal the approach of the herds.

The dew was still on the grass when a figure waved frantically from the skyline above them, and Lannon grunted with satisfaction and wiped the grease from his fingers and lips.

'Come, my Sunbird,' he said, and they mounted the kneeling elephant once more.

It was a long wait that stretched and tightened their nerves, then suddenly little Xhai stirred expectantly beside Huy and his dark amber eyes snapped.

'They are here,' he whispered, and almost immediately a single wild elephant came out through the rocky portals of the pass and paused on the lip of the saucer. It was an old cow, grey and lean and tuskless. Suspiciously she looked about the saucer, lifting her trunk to sample the air and then blowing the sample into her mouth against the olfactory glands in her upper lip. The breeze was behind her, a soft dry movement of air that carried the smell of waiting men away from her, and she lowered her trunk and moved forward.

From the pass behind her poured an avalanche of great grey bodies.

'Breeding herd,' murmured Lannon, and Huy saw the calves at heel. They ranged in size from almost full grown to not much bigger than a large pig. The smaller they were the more noisy and mischievous, squealing and frolicking and chasing between the legs of their mothers. Huy smiled at the attempts of one to suckle from his moving mother, groping for the teats between her front legs with his miniature trunk until in exasperation the mother picked up a fallen branch and swatted him mercilessly across the rump. The calf squealed and fell in at her heels again, demure and chastened.

The saucer was full of wild elephants now, their grey humped backs showing above the thick bush as they streamed along the ancient road to safety.

Lannon leaned forward and touched the driver on the shoulder, and the war elephant rose beneath them lifting them high so that they could look down from their castle upon the quarry. All around the saucer, the war elephants rose from cover with the armed men upon their backs. They closed in on the herd quietly, the squealing and uproar from the calves blanketing their approach until they were right in amongst the herd.

Lannon selected a young cow with a half-grown calf and leaning out from the castle he hurled his javelin into her neck, aiming for the great arteries there. The cow squealed in pain and alarm, and bright red arterial blood blew in a cloud from the tip of her trunk. She reeled backwards, mortally wounded, and from the other castles a torrent of missiles flew into the herd. Hundreds of huge bodies burst into flight and the forest shook and rang with their trumpeting and their frantic efforts at escape.

Despite his promise to the gods, Huy did not raise his bow, but watched in awful fascination the slaughter of the terrified beasts. He saw an old cow, bristling with arrows and javelins, charge one of the war elephants and knock it down on its knees; the men were hurled from the castle to fall beneath stampeding hooves, and the old cow tottered away to fall and die, still in her battle rage. He saw a calf, hit in error, trying to tear the arrow from its own flank and squealing pitifully as the barbs clung stubbornly in the flesh. He saw another calf attempting vainly to rouse its dead mother, tugging at her with its little trunk.

Lannon was shouting with excitement, hurling his javelins into the neck and spine with that deadly accuracy that dropped the great grey bodies in profusion about them.

One of the herd mothers charged them from the side; a bad-tempered old queen as big and as strong as their mount, she bore down on them. Lannon swung to face her, braced himself and threw, but the old queen lifted her trunk and the javelin struck it squarely, biting deep into that pulpy sensitive member just below the level of her eyes. She squealed in agony but never faltered in her run, and regretfully Huy lifted his bow. He knew she would charge home, and that only death would stop her.

The old queen lifted her head and trunk high, bracing herself for the impact of her charge. Her mouth was wide open, with the pointed lower lip dangling, and Huy drew and loosed his shaft into the back of her throat. All five feet of the arrow disappeared into her gaping mouth, and he knew the point had found the brain for she reeled back on to her haunches, shuddering and quivering, a strangled gurgling cry bubbling from her throat. The lids of her eyes twitched violently and she fell forward and was still.

They killed forty-one cows, thirty of them with calf. However, nine of the calves were adjudged by the trainers too young for survival as orphans and they were put down with a single merciful arrow. The others were cut out and rounded up by specially trained nursing cows and led away from the mountainous bleeding carcasses of their mothers. By noon the work was done, and the slaves could busy themselves in butchering the carcasses and carrying the meat away to the smoking racks. The saucer was a reeking charnel-house, and the vultures turned overhead in a dark cloud that almost obscured the sun.

Lannon ate the midday meal with his nobles and huntmasters. Fresh grilled elephant tripe seasoned with hot pepper sauce, broiled elephant heart stuffed with wild rice and olives, platters of golden corn cakes and the inevitable earthen amphorae of Zeng wine made it a meal fit for a hunter's appetite.

Lannon was in a high good humour, striding amongst his men, laughing and jesting with them, picking out one or another for a special commendation. He was still wrought up by the excitement of the chase, and when he paused beside Huy he meant to chaff him when he said:

'My poor Sunbird, you loosed but one arrow during the whole hunt.' And Huy was about to answer lightly that one arrow for one elephant was as good a score as any, when suddenly Zadal the huntmaster from the middle kingdom laughed.

'Was the bow too strong for you, Holiness, or the game too fierce?'

There was sudden and deathly silence on the entire group, and all their faces turned towards the lean dark man with the thin sneering mouth and bright acquisitive eyes.

It took a few seconds of the silence for Zadal to realize what he had said, then he glanced quickly about the circle of watching faces. With a small chill he saw they were looking at him with that same detached curious expression that men looked upon those doomed to sacrifice. Beside him a noble said softly but matter of factly, 'You are a dead man.'

Swiftly, with real alarm, Zadal looked back at Huy Ben-Amon. Too late he recalled the reputation of this priest. It was said that no man still lived who had sneered at his back or his height or his courage. With relief he saw that the priest was smiling slightly, and delicately wiping his fingers on the hem of his tunic.

'Thank you, great Baal,' Huy prayed silently, smiling a little. 'It was right that you remind me of my promise. I held back from the hunt. Forgive me, great Baal. I will give you your chance now.'

Zadal's relief was short-lived for when Huy looked directly at him he saw the smile was on the priest's lips only. His eyes were bright and black and cold.

'Zadal,' Huy said softly, and the crowd pressed closer to hear his words. 'Will you fly with me on the wings of the storm?'

They stirred at the challenge, a quick buzz of comment and they watched Zadal's face. It had paled to a dirty yellow, and his lips compressed into a thin white line.

'I forbid it,' said Lannon loudly. 'I will not let you do this, Huy. You are too valuable to me to waste your life in—'

Huy interrupted him quietly, 'Majesty, it is a matter of honour. This one called me coward.'

'But no man has hunted in that manner for fifty years,' Lannon protested.

'Fifty years is too long,' Huy smiled, 'is it not, Zadal? You and I will revive the custom.'

Zadal stared at him, hating his own unruly tongue.

Huy still smiled at him. 'Or is it that the game is too fierce for you?' he asked softly. For long moments it seemed that Zadal might refuse, then he nodded curtly, his lips still white.

'As you wish, Holiness.' And he knew they were right, he was a dead man.

In two large baskets, slaves had collected from one of the elephant carcasses the contents of the lower intestines. As Huy and Zadal, stripped naked, smeared their bodies with the yellow dung he overheard young Bakmor discussing the hunt with Mursil.

'I do not believe it is possible to kill a full-grown bull elephant with a battle-axe. It sounds to me like an unpleasant form of suicide.'

'That's why they call it flying on the wings of the storm.'

The elephant dung had a rank odour, strong enough to mask the man smell. It was the one protection the hunters would have. Their one chance of getting into close contact with the great beasts without being discovered. The sharp sense of smell of the elephant is its main defence, for its vision is weak and near sighted.

Timon came over from the king's entourage and assisted Huy, spreading the dung across his back. Quickly Timon had understood the method that they would use.

'High-born, I fear for you,' he said softly.

'I fear for myself,' Huy admitted. 'Spread the dung thickly, Timon. I would prefer to stink, rather than die.'

Huy looked down the steep slope which stretched down into the valley from the saucer. The elephant road zig-zagged up through the sparse forest. They would intercept the next herd here, before it was alarmed by the smell of blood in the saucer.

Huy glanced around him and saw that the huntsmen had spread out along the ridge, selecting vantage points from which to view the sport. His eyes met those of Zadal. The huntmaster was daubed with the yellow filth from his head to his feet, and he gripped the handle of his axe too hard. There was fear in those dark eyes, and fear in the taut manner in which he held himself. Huy smiled at him, enjoying his discomfort, and Zadal looked away. His lips quivered.

'Are you ready, huntmaster?' Huy asked, and Zadal nodded. He could not trust his voice.

'Come,' said Huy, and started down the slope, but Lannon stepped into his path. There was a foreboding in his eyes, and his smile was unconvincing.

'That fool Zadal spoke in haste and without meaning it. No man here doubts your courage, Huy, except you yourself. Do not seek to prove it too convincingly. Life will hold little for me without my Sunbird.'

'My lord,' Huy's voice was hoarse. He was touched to the heart by Lannon's concern.

'The first cut is the dangerous one, Huy. Be careful that when he drops, he does not fall upon you.'

'I will remember.'

'Remember also to bathe before you dine with me this evening.' Lannon smiled and stepped aside.

Twice during the afternoon small herds of elephant passed them, moving swiftly up the slope amongst the trees. Each time Huy shook his head at Zadal and let them pass for they were cows and calves and immature bulls.

The day drew towards its close, and Huy felt an uneasy sense of relief. Perhaps the gods had decided in his favour and would not seek to put him to the test.

There was an hour of light left now. Huy and Zadal sat quietly beside the path, hidden by a screen of monkey apple vines that hung from one of the trees.

The dung had dried upon their bodies, making Huy's skin feel stiff and uncomfortable. He sat with the vulture axe across his lap and watched the path, hoping that nothing would come up it before darkness and he could abandon this mad adventure to which he was committed by honour and hasty choice. It was strange how inactivity dulled even the brightest passion, Huy thought, and grinned wryly as he fondled the handle of the axe.

He saw movement far down the slope, a grey drifting movement like smoke amongst the trees and he felt his skin prickle. Zadal had seen it also, he stopped his restless fidgeting and sat woodenly beside Huy.

They waited, and suddenly two elephants came out of the trees. Two big old bulls, with heavy ivory, stepping lightly up the slope. They were a hundred paces apart, spaced out on the path and there was an alertness and a sense of purpose in their tread that warned Huy they had been freshly disturbed, possibly wounded, by the huntsmen down in the valley.

'We will take these two,' Huy whispered. 'Choose one.'

Zadal was silent a moment, watching the two bulls with an experienced eye. The leading bull was older, and his one tusk was broken off at the lip. He was leaner and rangier-looking than his companion, and his leading position showed he was the more experienced, the more alert, and the broken tusk would make him meaner and his temper more uncertain.

'The second one,' Zadal whispered, and Huy nodded. He had expected it.

'I will move back now. We must try to attack at the same moment.' He left the cover of the hanging vines, and slipped back along the path opening a gap between him and Zadal approximately equal to that between the bulls.

Huy dropped into a patch of coarse grass beside the trail, and looked back. The elephants were striding steadily up towards them. The leading bull passed Zadal's hiding place, and came on. Huy saw that the gap between the two bulls had closed. Zadal's elephant would reach him before Huy's came level with the clump of grass where he lay.

If one of the hunters launched his attack prematurely the other bull would be alerted, and the danger multiplied many times. Huy knew he could not rely on consideration from Zadal. The man would think only of his own best interests.

As the thought came to him he saw Zadal leave the shelter of the vines, and run silently out into the path behind the second bull. Huy's elephant was still fifty paces from where he lay, and it was facing him.

Zadal was following his elephant, running close upon its heels. Huy felt a moment's admiration for him. Perhaps he had misjudged him. Perhaps Zadal would follow the second bull and wait for Huy to get into position.

Then Huy saw the huntmaster's axe go up and glint at the top of its swing; as it flashed down, Huy transferred all his attention to the leading bull.

There was a squeal of pain and alarm as Zadal's axe struck, and Huy's bull burst into a full run. Sweeping down on him until it seemed to fill the whole field of Huy's vision, an animal as large as the very earth it sprang from.

As Huy rose from his hide he knew he had a few fleeting seconds in which to strike. Then the bull would be gone.

He went bounding along beside the bull, keeping uphill of him for when he fell he would roll down the slope. The pace stretched Huy's long legs to the full, and he was losing ground swiftly, falling back to the bull's hindquarters.

With every pace, as the huge weight of the grey body fell on the hind legs, so the hamstring tendons running down the back of the leg from knee to heel tightened under the coarse eroded skin. The tendon was a thick cord, that flexed and bulged, thick as a girl's wrist; it carried the whole weight of the bull at each stride.

Huy swerved in his run, crossing behind the bull and as the tendon in the nearest leg tightened he slashed the blade of the vulture axe across it, severing it cleanly so that the sound of it was a sharp snapping, like the sheet of a sail parting in a gale.

The bull lunged off balance as the leg collapsed under him, he teetered wildly on the edge of the path, his weight held only on the good leg.

'For Baal!' Huy shouted with excitement and the axe went high as he swung. The second tendon parted as sharply, and the huge grey beast dropped heavily. The sound of its fall carried clearly to the watchers on the ridge, and a cloud of dust boiled up from the dry earth. Huy had danced back from under the rolling body and that terrible flailing trunk.

He steeled himself for the final act, as he danced about the rearing floundering animal, knowing he had only seconds to exploit his surprise, seconds before the maimed animal braced itself and saw him, and he searched for his opening desperately.

The bull reared up on its front legs, dragging its crippled hind legs behind it. In its unreasoning rage it was tearing at the trees, and slashing its terrible trunk in wild circles, gouging the earth with its single tusk.

But its back was turned to Huy, it had not recognized its attacker yet. Lightly Huy ran in, ducking under the flailing trunk. He vaulted up on the bull's wide back, landing on his knees with the axe high above his head.

The knotted spine stood out clearly through the wrinkled dry skin, great knuckles of bone braced for the blade. Huy struck, the killing stroke that crashed through the bone, and severed the soft yellow core of the spinal tissue. The bull shrieked, and collapsed, kicking and shaking spasmodically in its death throes.

Huy jumped down from its pulsating body and danced back out of danger from the legs and trunk of the dying beast. He felt a soaring sense of triumph and relief. It was done, he had flown upon the wings of the storm—and lived through it.

He heard the wild shrill trumpeting of the other bull, and he spun around. One glance showed him that the task was not yet completed, the gods were not finished with him.

Zadal had blundered. His second cut had missed the tendon and the bull was on three legs, but moving with agility and speed as it hunted the man. Zadal had thrown his axe aside, and was running, dodging up the slope with the bull close upon him. The bull was shrieking with rage, its trunk out-stretched, gaining swiftly on the fleeing man.

As Huy started forward it caught him. It wrapped its trunk around Zadal's body and flung him high in the air, above the tops of the tallest trees and his body spun loosely in the air.

He fell face down on the rocky earth, and the bull placed one foot in the small of his back while with its trunk it plucked his head from his body, the way a farmer kills a chicken, and it tossed the head aside. It bounced and rolled down the slope like a child's ball.

Huy ran towards the bull, scrambling up the slope. The bull knelt on the mangled corpse and drove one tusk through Zadal's chest. It was so preoccupied with the mutilation of Zadal's body that Huy came up easily behind it.

He saw the deep gash in the back of the bull's knee where Zadal's stroke had failed to find the tendon, and the vulture axe moaned softly in flight. This time there was no mistake.

'I give you a new title.' Lannon lifted his wine bowl, and silence fell expectantly on the nobles and knights who sat about his board. 'I give a battle honour for the man who has flown on the wings of the storm.'

Huy dropped his eyes modestly, blushing a little in the torch light under the leather awning of Lannon's campaign tent.

'Huy Ben-Amon – Axeman of the Gods!' Lannon shouted the title, and the nobles echoed it, saluting Huy with clenched fists.

'Drink, Huy! Drink, my Sunbird!' Lannon offered Huy his own wine bowl. Huy sipped the wine, smiling around at the company. Tonight he would not look too deeply into the wine bowl. He did not want to cloud or befuddle this sense of joy. The gods had answered him, and he sat quietly smiling in the midst of noisy revelry, hardly hearing the laughter and the banter, listening instead to the voice deep inside him which sang, 'Tanith! Tanith!'

When he rose to leave, Lannon was outraged, dragging him down into his seat by the hem of his tunic.

'You'll not leave here on your feet, Axeman. You deserve to be carried to your couch this night! Come, I challenge you to a bout with the wine cups.'

Huy shrugged aside the challenge, laughing and shaking his head.

'One challenge a day, my lord, I beg of you.'

Outside the night was still, and the sky was brilliant with the stars. The heat of the day was cooling, and the feel of the night wind in his face was like the caress of Tanith's silky tresses against his cheek.

'Astarte!' The goddess rose out of the valley, the golden disc of her countenance lighting the land with a soft radiance. 'Mother of earth. I thank you,' Huy whispered, and felt the tears of happiness flood his eyes.

He moved on through the camp towards his own tent, hugging the warmth of his love secretly to him.

'Tanith,' he whispered, 'Tanith.'

He moved on through the shadows until movement caught his attention, and he stopped. Beside one of the cooking fires crouched a figure, a slave woman working on the grinding stone, crushing corn for cakes.

The firelight caught her handsome features, and shone on the dark skin of her strong arms. It was the nurse Sellene.

Huy was about to move on, when the slave girl looked up expectantly. A man came towards her out of the darkness, and the girl's face lit with such a look of adoration, such unashamed love, that Huy felt his heart go out to her.

The man stepped into the firelight, and it needed only one glance at the powerful body and rounded bald head for Huy to recognize Timon.

Sellene stood up and went quickly to meet Timon, and they embraced. They sniffed at each other's face in the strange love greeting of the pagans, holding each other closely. Huy smiled tenderly, feeling the warm sympathy of the lover for all other lovers.

Timon drew back from the girl, holding her at arm's length and he spoke softly. Huy could not catch the words. He heard only the soft rumble of Timon's voice, and the girl nodded quickly.

Timon left her and disappeared amongst the tents. Sellene went to the grinding stone and filled a leather bag with ground corn, then she glanced about furtively and followed Timon into the darkness. Huy watched her go, and smiled.

'I must talk to Lannon,' he thought. 'I could arrange a pairing between those two.'

In his own tent Huy took the golden scroll and spread it upon his writing pallet. He adjusted the lamp wicks, picked up his engraving tool, and began to write the poem to Tanith.

'Her hair is dark and soft as the smoke from the papyrus fires upon the great lake,' he wrote, and the incident between Timon and Sellene was forgotten.

Exhaustion overcame him a little after midnight, and he fell forward across his writing pallet and he slept with one cheek pressed to the love poem to Tanith on the golden scroll. The lamp flames smoked and faded and died.

Rough hands shook him awake in the dawn, and he looked up groggily. It was Mursil, the huntmaster.

'The Gry-Lion sends for you, Holiness. The hounds are in leash, and the slave-masters assembled. Two of the king's slaves have run, and the king bids you join the chase.'

Even in his half-wakening state, Huy knew who the running slaves were, and he felt the sick sliding of his guts.

'The fools,' his whispered. 'Oh, the stupid fools.' Then he looked at Mursil. 'No,' he said. 'I cannot – I will not go with him. I am sick, tell him I am sick.'

Sellene stood in the shadows and listened to the drunken bellowing and laughter from the king's tent. Beneath the short cloak was concealed the leather grain-bag, a bundle of smoked meat dried into hard black sticks, and a small earthen cooking pot. There was food for two of them for four days, and by then they would be across the great river. She was fearful, and elated at the same time. They had planned this moment for two years, and many emotions played behind her round impassive face as she waited.

Timon came at last; quietly he appeared beside her with such suddenness that she gasped with fright. He took her hand, and led her away towards the perimeter of the camp. She saw that he wore a cloak also, and that a bow and quiver stood behind his shoulder and a short iron sword was belted at his waist. These were weapons forbidden to a slave, and death was the penalty for carrying them.

There were two guards at the gate of the stockade, and while Sellene spoke with them, offering favours, Timon came from the darkness behind them. He broke their necks with his bare hands. Taking one in each hand and shaking them the way a dog will shake a rat. There was no outcry, and Timon laid the bodies gently beside the stockade gate and they went through.

They passed through the saucer where the elephant had been butchered, and the night was hideous with the snarling and yammering of the scavengers. Hyena and jackal fought over the bloody scraps and bone chips. With the sword bared in one hand Timon led Sellene through, and though the slinking hump-shouldered hyena followed them, moaning and sniggering, they reached the pass and started down the elephant road into the valley. The moon gave them good light, and they moved fast. They stopped only once at the ford of the stream to rest and drink a little water, then they hurried on towards the north.

Once they came upon a lion in the path. A big male whose body was ghostly grey in the moonlight, with a dark ruff of mane. They stared at each other for long seconds before the lion grunted softly and leapt into the undergrowth beside the path. He had fed recently, and the two human shapes did not interest him.

The moon, four days past full, wheeled across the star-furry sky and sank towards the dark horizon. When it set, there was only the indistinct glow of the stars to light their way, and at a steep and broken place in the path Sellene fell heavily.

Timon heard her cry out and he turned back quickly. She was lying on her side, making a soft moaning sound.

'Are you hurt?' he asked as he dropped to his knees beside her.

'My ankle,' she whispered, agony making her voice husky and Timon groped down her leg. Already the ankle was hot to the touch, and as he held it he could feel it swelling, blowing up into a hard hot ball.

With the sword Timon cut strips from his cloak, and he bound the ankle tightly as Huy had taught him. He worked with frantic haste, and the worms of dread were already gnawing his guts.

When he lifted Sellene to her feet, she cried out as her weight came on the injured foot.

'Can you walk on it?' Timon asked, and she tried a few painful hobbling steps. She was panting with pain and her breathing whistled in her throat. She clung to Timon and shook her head hopelessly.

'I cannot go on. Leave me here.' Timon lowered her to the ground, and then straightened up as he discarded his weapons and her provisions. He kept only the short sword. He folded and knotted the two leather cloaks into a sling seat for Sellene, and placed it about her body. Then he looped the end over his neck and shoulder and lifted her. She was in his arms, with her own clasped about his shoulders. Half of her weight was taken by the sling, hanging about Timon's neck. He started forward, striding out down the steep path towards the valley floor.

By mid-morning the sling had rubbed the skin from his neck, a weeping pink graze through the dark skin. The heat was strong now, the heavy oppressive heat of the valley floor sucking away the last of his energy. The spring had long gone from Timon's step, and he reeled forward with spirit outlasting his physical strength.

On the edge of one of the glades of open grass, Timon stopped and leaned against the trunk of a mhoba-hoba tree. He was afraid to lower the girl's body to the ground lest he could not find the strength to lift it again. His lips were white and rimmed with dried spittle, and his eyes were laced with red veins. His chest heaved and shook with his breathing.

'Leave me, Timon,' Sellene whispered. 'This way both of us will die.'

Timon did not answer, but gestured her to silence with an impatient inclination of his head. He held his breath and listened. She heard it also then, the faint and distant baying of the hound pack.

He said, 'It is too late for that.' And he looked about quickly for a place to stand. They could not hope to outrun the dogs.

'You can still escape,' she urged him. 'The river is not far.'

'Without you there is no escape,' he said, and she clung to him as he carried her across the glade to a place where the mother rock outcropped. A jumble of fragmented granite like the ruins of an ancient castle.

He laid her gently amongst the rocks, with her back against one of the slabs. He folded her cloak and placed it as a pillow for her head, then he squatted beside her and caressed her face and neck with a surprisingly gentle touch for so big a man.

'They will kill us,' Sellene said. 'They always kill those who run.'

Timon did not answer, but his fingers stroked her cheek lightly.

'They kill in the worst way,' Sellene said, turning her head to look at him. 'Would it not be better if we died now, before the dogs come?' But he did not answer, and after a while she went on.

'You have the sword, Timon. Will you not use it?'

'If the little priest is with them, then we have a chance. He has power over the king – and there is a thing between him and me. There is a bond. He will save us.'

The dogs were closer now, and it seemed that their baying had become more urgent as the scent ran hotter. Timon stood up and unsheathed the sword. He went out amongst the rocks and looked back towards the escarpment. Half a mile back the pack streamed from the forest into the glade. There were thirty of the tall sinewy hounds, long-legged and with rough ginger-brown coats and the heads and fangs of wolves. They were bred to chase and drag down the quarry.

Timon felt his skin tighten and prickle as he watched them string out across the glade towards him. Behind them, running on the heels of the pack were the handlers, with their distinctive green tunics and the dog-whips over their shoulders.

Beyond them again came the war elephants, five of them with the knights and slave-masters in their castles. The elephants followed the pack easily, in that ambling gait which could cover fifty miles in a day.

Timon shaded his eyes and tried to pick out the distinctive figure of the priest amongst the men in the castles. They were too far off still, but the hounds were closing swiftly.

He wrapped his cloak carefully about his left forearm, and settled his grip on the sword. Swinging the weapon in a short arc to stretch his muscles.

The leading hounds saw him amongst the rocks, and immediately the deep regular baying changed to an excited yammering. Their ears flattened as they ran, and long pink tongues flopped over white fangs in the wolf jaws, and they fanned out across his front.

Timon stepped back into the opening where Sellene lay, guarding her from the vicious clamouring rush of brown bodies.

The first hound rushed in at him, with its jaws snapping, and it leapt at his face.

Timon took him on the point, in the base of his throat, killing the dog instantly, but before he could clear his blade another had sprung at him. He thrust his cloaked arm into its jaws, and hacked at a third hound.

They swarmed over him as he stabbed and hacked and thrust. He swung the hound that hung on his arm against the rock beside him, crushing in its ribs, but another had locked its fangs in his calf and was tugging him cruelly off balance. He drove the point into its shaggy back and the hound shrieked and released him.

Another went for his face and he struck at its head with the sword hilt. A great furry body smashed into his chest, a fang ripped his shoulder muscles.

There were too many of them, overwhelming him, ripping and tearing at him, smothering him with their weight and strength. He went down on his knees, holding a frothing slavering animal away from his throat and face with one hand, strangling it – but he felt other teeth slashing at his back and belly and thighs.

Then abruptly the dog-handlers were there, whipping the pack away from him, shouting to the animals by name, dragging them back and leashing them in the strangling collars.

Slowly Timon pulled himself up on to his feet. He had lost his sword and blood streamed down his shining black body from the deep cuts and lacerations that covered him.

He looked up at the war elephant which towered over him. His last hope faded as he saw that Huy Ben-Amon was not amongst the hunters – and that Lannon Hycanus, the Gry-Lion of Opet was laughing.

'A good run, slave,' Lannon laughed. 'I thought that you might reach the river.' He looked beyond Timon to where Sellene lay. 'My huntmasters were correct, then. They judged by the sign that the woman had damaged her leg and that you were carrying her. A noble gesture, slave, most unusual for a pagan. All the same it will cost you dear.' Lannon looked away to one of his slave-masters. 'There seems little to be gained by returning with them. Execute them here.'

Timon looked up at the king and spoke in a strong clear voice.

'I am the living symbol of that love,' he said, and Lannon's head jerked around as he remembered the words. With the laughter gone from his lips he stared at the bleeding slave king, meeting those smoky yellow eyes. For long seconds, Timon's life teetered on the verge of extinction, then suddenly Lannon's eyes dropped away from those of Timon.

'Very well,' he nodded. 'You remind me of my duty to a friend. I will honour it, but I swear you will live to curse the moment you spoke those words. You will live – but in life you will long for the sweetness of death.' Lannon's face was a mask of cold anger, as he turned back to his slave-masters. 'This man will not be executed, but he is declared "incorrigible" and he will be chained with a weight of two talents.' Almost a hundred pounds' weight of chains to be carried night and day, waking and sleeping. 'Send him to the mines at Hulya, tell the overseer there that he is to be used at the deep levels.'

Lannon watched Timon's face as he went on. 'The woman cannot claim my protection, but we will take her back with us, none the less. Let her be chained to the castle of one of the war elephants and marched.'

For the first time Timon showed emotion. He stepped forward and in appeal lifted one badly savaged arm from which the dark tattered flesh hung.

'My lord, the woman is hurt. She cannot walk.'

'She will walk,' said Lannon. 'Or she will be dragged. You will ride upon the elephant and encourage her. You will have time to decide if the swift death I offered you would not have been preferable to the life you have chosen.'

They chained Sellene at the wrists with a light marching chain twenty paces long. The other end of the chain was shackled to the rear wall of the elephant castle.

Timon, wearing his massive chains at neck and ankles, was seated in the castle. He was made to face backwards to where Sellene stood swaying slightly on one leg, favouring her grotesquely swollen ankle. Her face was greyish with pain, but she tried to smile up at Timon.

The first jerk of the chain as the elephant started forward pulled her face downwards on the hard earth, with its sharp shales and harsh clumps of razor grass. She was dragged fifty paces before she managed to roll on to her feet again and hop and stumble after the striding elephant. Her knees and elbows were raw, and there were scratches across her belly and breasts.

She fell and regained her feet a dozen times, each time her body was more battered and torn. She went down for the last time a little before sunset.

As Timon sat in the castle, draped in his chains, he swore an oath. In his anger and grief and pain he swore an oath of vengeance, watching Sellene's lifeless body bounce and slide over the rough places, leaving a damp brown smear across the dry red African earth. Then Timon wept, for the last time in his life he succumbed to tears. They ran down his face and dripped from his chin to mingle with the blood and dust that caked his body.

Huy filled a wine bowl from one of his choice amphorae, one that he had set aside for a rare occasion. He was humming softly to himself, and there was a small smile which came and went upon his lips and made his dark eyes sparkle.

He had returned to Opet in the middle of the night, slept five hours and now, bathed and dressed in his best linen, he had sent a slave to summon the oracle of Opet to meet with him. All the blood and passion of these last weeks upon the escarpment of the great river were forgotten now in his anticipation of his reunion with Tanith. Forgotten were the memories of Sellene's mutilated corpse dragged into camp behind the war elephant, the tall figure of Timon bowed beneath his chains and grief, led away by the slave-masters, those terrible accusing eyes turned towards Huy, the manacled wrists lifted in a gesture of menace or of appeal – Huy could not guess which. Then the slave-master's whip hissing and snapping across the purple black shoulders, lifting a welt as thick as a finger without cutting the skin. For the first time since it had happened Huy was free of it, his whole being taken up with the joy of his love.

Pursing his lips thoughtfully he let four drops of the clear liquid drip from the blue glass vial into the wine. He stoppered the bottle and stirred the wine with his forefinger, sucking his finger thoughtfully and wrinkling his nose at the faint musty taste of the opiate. He added a little wild honey to mask it, tasted again and at last satisfied he set the bowl on one of the wooden stools beside the pile of cushions. There was a dish of cakes and sweetmeats there already. Huy covered the wine bowl with a silken cloth, then surveyed his preparations with pleasure. He picked up his lute and climbed the staircase to the parapet of the roof and seated himself. He tuned the instrument and strummed upon it, loosening his voice and fingers, watching the narrow lane that led up to the front gate.

In the bright morning sunlight the lake waters were a cheery blue, only slightly darker than the sky. The breeze had flecked the surface with little floppy waves, and one of Habbakuk Lal's galleys had shipped her oars and was running in towards the harbour under a big lateen sail. The sea birds followed her, planing and soaring across her stern.

High above the lake the midday clouds were building tall, frothy thunderheads. There would be rain before sunset, Huy thought, feeling the thunder in the air, in the touch of his garments upon his skin and the curl of his beard.

His breath caught, and the music died under his fingers as two figures turned into the lane and came up towards the gate. They wore the coarse brown-hooded robes that the priestesses of Astarte affected while travelling abroad. However, the bulky garment could not disguise the quick step and youthful carriage of the taller figure that hurried ahead, nor the age and aggravation of the bent figure that hobbled after her. The ancient voice, breathless and high, called with exasperation.

'My lady, slower! I pray you.' And Huy grinned. A slave opened the gate, and as they crossed the courtyard Huy struck a single authorative note on the lute, and Tanith stopped dead. The old chaperone, unhearing, moved on into the house mumbling and muttering while Tanith looked up at Huy upon the parapet of the roof.

He began to sing, and the girl below him lifted the hood from her face and let it fall back on her shoulders. She shook her hair loose, watching his face with large green eyes and her expression was rapt and solemn. He sang the song he had written in the wilderness, the song to Tanith inscribed in the golden book, and as he let the last sweet note fall on the bright morning, Tanith's cheeks were flushed and her lips trembled.

Huy went down the staircase and stood close to her, without touching her.

'You are my soul,' he said gently, and she swayed towards him as if drawn by a force beyond her control.

'My lord, I cannot trust myself to be with you where other eyes may see us. I fear I shall betray my love to the blindest of them. Be strong for me.'

Huy touched her elbow, guiding her towards the house. As they passed through into the main room, Tanith stumbled slightly, for a moment pressed against him.

'Oh! I cannot bear it,' she said, and Huy's voice shook as he answered.

'In a while, my love. In a very short while.'

The old priestess was seated on the cushions already, mouthing a cake with bald gums, dropping crumbs and spittle down her robe and mumbling bitterly about her pains and aches.

Huy moved around behind her, and picked up the prepared wine bowl in both hands. Secure in the old priestess's deafness he asked Tanith, 'Is she strong?'

'As strong as most men,' Tanith smiled. 'Though she'll not admit it.'

'She does not complain of chest pains or shortness of breath?'

'Never.' Tanith was intrigued. 'Why do you ask?'

'I have placed star-drops in her wine,' Huy explained. 'But I do not want her sleep to be eternal.'

Tanith's smile flamed, lighting the green depths of her eyes and sparkling on her teeth. 'Oh, Holy Father, how clever of you.' She clapped her hands, a childlike gesture that never failed to touch Huy to the core of his being.

'How many drops?' Tanith demanded.

'Four,' Huy admitted.

'Perhaps a few more would not hurt her,' Tanith said. 'I have not seen you in many weeks, Holiness. There is much to discuss.'

During this exchange the old priestess had been nodding and grimacing intelligently, quite as though she had understood every word. Huy studied her a moment, then firmly thrust aside the temptation.

'No,' he said. 'Four is sufficient.' And he came around in front of the priestess. The wrinkled monkey-like face split into a hugh toothless grin and she reached for the bowl with a pair of bony claws, on which the old-age blotches and blue veins stood out clearly.

'You have a kind heart, Holiness,' she keened.

They seated themselves in front of her, and while they talked they watched her anxiously. The crone was drawing out her pleasure, sipping the wine and rolling it noisily around her mouth before swallowing and smacking her gums.

'Since we have been apart, I have thought much upon what has happened between us,' Huy admitted, without looking at Tanith.

'I have thought of nothing else.'

'As a man whose life is devoted to the service of the gods, I was greatly troubled that we had sinned against them,' Huy told her.

'There can be no sin in something which gives so much pleasure and happiness.'

'I asked the gods to set a test for me, a trial of my sins.' Huy had still not looked at her, but Tanith glanced at him sharply and her voice snapped.

'You did not indulge in foolish risk, did you?'

'The trial was a fair one – the gods were not cheated.' Huy wanted her to understand, and she understood too well.

'I forbid you to do these stupid male things. I shiver to think of what madness you committed out there in the wilderness.' She was angry now.

'It was necessary. They must have the opportunity to express their wrath.'

'They could as readily express their wrath with a lightning bolt or a falling tree! I will not have you provoking them to destroy you.'

'Tanith, please let me—'

'I can see, my lord, that you will require stricter supervision in the future. I want a lover not a hero.'

'But, Tanith, the gods' answer was favourable. Don't you see, now we need feel no guilt.'

'I never felt guilt, then or now. But, Holiness, I will feel wrath beside which that of the gods will pale if again you risk your life needlessly.'

Huy turned to her, and shook his head with mock sorrow.

'Oh Tanith, what would I ever do without you?' And her stern expression softened.

'My lord, that question will never arise.' And at that moment the empty wine bowl slipped from the old priestess's fingers and spun on one end across the mud floor. Its circles narrowed, until it settled into silence and the priestess let out a long contented snore and bowed forward. Huy caught her and eased her backwards onto the cushions. He laid her out comfortably, and arranged her robe modestly about her. She was smiling and burbling and whistling in her sleep.

Huy straightened up and Tanith stood close beside him. They turned to each other and embraced, coming together slowly and carefully. Her lips had a glossy feeling, cool and firm. Her soft hair brushed his cheeks, and her body pressed boldly against his.

'Tanith,' he whispered. 'Oh Tanith, there is so much I want to tell you.'

'My Lord, your voice is the most beautiful I have ever heard. Your wisdom and wit are celebrated throughout the four kingdoms – but please do not talk now.'

Tanith pulled gently out of his embrace, took his hand and led him softly from the room.

Over the months that followed, Tanith's chaperone developed a peculiar taste for Huy's wine. At the temple feasts she was wont to disparage the quality of the wine served by the Reverend Mother, comparing it most unfavourably against the other, and she would always end with a word of praise for the Holy Father himself.

'A dear, dear man,' she would tell her audience. 'None of the nonsense you find with some of the others. Did I ever tell you about Rastafa Ben-Amon, the Holy Father in the reign of the forty-fourth Gry-Lion when I was a novice. Now there was a one!' Her old eyes went a little misty, and she drooled a thread of saliva.

'Drink!' She said with outraged virtue. 'Fight! And other things.' Then she nodded sagely. 'A terrible, terrible man!' And she grinned fondly at her ancient memories.

From the leather pipe, with its pitch-sealed joints, feeble gusts of air puffed like the dying breaths of a dinosaur. Driven by the great bellows at the surface, the circulation of fresh air had lost most of its force here, seventy feet below.

Timon leaned against the sweating rock surface, pressing his face to the hose outlet gasping at that scanty trickle of air in the hellish heat and sulphurous atmosphere of the underground workings. He was lean, every rib showed clearly through the black skin, each sinewy muscle was outlined. His head was skull-like, with gaunt cheek-bones and deep eye-sockets in which the smouldering fires of his indomitable spirit still burned.

All fat and spare flesh had been burned off him by the ceaseless toil and the heat. Even now a sheen of moisture squeezed from the pores of his skin, highlighting the scars which criss-crossed his back and curled around his rib cage – scars that patterned his arms and legs, scars long healed into thick ridges and shiny grooves, scars fresh and pink, scars still thick-scabbed and oozing. The chain shackles hung loosely at his neck and wrists and ankles. They had rubbed coarse calloused circles around his neck and limbs, slave marks that he would carry to his grave.

He sucked in the air, his chest pumping, swelling and subsiding, the ribs beneath the skin fanning open and closing. Around him the smoke swirled, dipping the lamp flames. The heat was a violent shimmering thing, and the rock at the face glowed still, although the fires had burned to thick beds of ash.

For five days now they had been attempting to break up this intrusion of hard green serpentine rock which was obscuring the gold reef. Sixteen men had died in the attempt, suffocated by the steam and smoke, struck down by flying shards of exploding rock or merely overcome by the heat to fall swooning on to the glowing floor and to sizzle while their flesh stuck to the hot rock and came away in stinking slabs from the bone.

From the shaft above him, dangling on a plaited reed rope, one of the water-bladders was lowered to him. Made from the whole skin of an ox, carefully stitched and with the joints waterproofed with pitch the bladder contained forty gallons of liquid, a mixture of sour wine and water.

Timon doused his leather cloak in the filthy warm water of the wooden trough beside him, then one at a time he lifted his feet and dipped them into the trough, soaking his leather leggings and the sandals. The soles of the sandals were reinforced with five thicknesses of leather to withstand the heat of the rock floor. Timon drew the cloak across his shoulders, bound the linen cloth over his mouth and nose, took one last breath from the air pipe and held it. Then he ducked under the dangling water bladder and took the weight on his shoulders. Reaching up, he jerked loose the tail of the knot that held it, and, bowed under the weight of liquid, he staggered up the tunnel.

As he approached the face, the wet soles of his sandals began spluttering and stinking. He could feel the heat through the thick leather. Heat from the rock walls hammered at him, a physical force against which he had to fight his way forward.

There was little time in which to work. Already his abused lungs were pumping painfully, but he dared not draw a breath of this poisonous smoke-laden air. The heat was scalding the exposed skin on his arms and face, his feet were agony as the rock burned away the protective soles.

Against the face of the drive, he eased the bladder from his shoulder. He moaned with the pain as his careless elbow touched the rock, searing away an inch of skin and leaving the pink raw flesh exposed.

He lowered the bladder to the floor, whirled and ran back through swirling fumes and heat down the tunnel with his chains jangling loosely under the cloak. This was the moment when men died, when the hot rock ate through the water bladder too swiftly, before the bearer was out of the danger area.

Behind Timon the bladder popped, forty gallons of liquid drenched the hot rock, the sudden contraction of the strata shattered the surface, the rock burst explosively and a sharp sliver of it hit Timon in the back of the head, a glancing razor touch that sliced down to the bone of his skull. He staggered, knowing that to fall on this burning floor was to die horribly. He kept his feet while with his senses reeling he reached the water trough and plunged his head quickly into the filthy scummy water. Then with dirty water and fresh blood streaming down his back, he clutched the air pipe with both hands and panted into it. He was coughing and retching and his eyes were blinded with the tears of pain.

It took him minutes to recover a little of his strength, and he staggered to the ladder that led to the level above. As he climbed, the next water bladder was being lowered, and he squeezed himself against the side of the narrow shaft to allow it past. He climbed fifty feet in darkness and then crawled over the edge into a dimly lit low-roofed cavern.

The slave-master saw him grovelling on the lip of the shaft.

'Why have you left your station?' And the long lash of the hippo-hide kiboko curled wickedly around Timon's ribs. He writhed at the sting of it.

'My head,' he gasped. 'I'm hurt.' And the slave-master stepped closer to him, stooping to examine the clotted cut in the back of Timon's scalp from which dark blood still welled. He grunted impatiently.

'Rest, then.' And turned to a row of ten squatting slaves. They were all incorrigibles, wearing the same heavy chains as Timon, and their bodies were also scarred and abused. The slave-master selected one of them, prodding him with the sharpened point of the whip.

'You next. Quickly now.' The slave stood, and shuffled to the mouth of the shaft, moving stiffly for the damp of the workings was in all their bones. At the edge of the shaft the slave paused and peered fearfully into that dreadful fuming pit.

'Move!' grunted the slave-master and the kiboko whistled and clapped against his flesh. He went down the ladder.

Timon dragged himself to the low bench against the wall. He sat with his elbows on his knees and his face in his hands. His lungs ached with the smoke and the cut in his scalp burned and stung. None of the other slaves looked at him. Each man was sunk in his own private hell, uncaring and silent. Beside Timon a man began to cough, a monotonous hacking sound, and a little bloody saliva wet his lips and glistened in the lamp light. He was dying of the lung sickness of the miners. The dust of powdered rock had filled his lungs, solidifying like concrete and turning his lungs to stone. None of them moved, none of them spoke.

The younger slave-master paced restlessly back and forth before them. He was a swarthy bearded man, part Yuye, a freedman as like as not. He wore a linen tunic with light body armour, enough to turn a dagger's point, and an iron helmet to protect his skull from the rough roof of the tunnel. At his waist were belted a short iron sword and a slave club studded with iron nails. He was tall and hard-looking, with flat sinewy muscle in his arms and legs. A cruel man, selected to work with the incorrigibles because of his brutality. There were always two of them. The other slave-master was an older man with a frosting of grey in his beard and a pale sickly-looking face. But he was big in the shoulder, and dangerous, as cruel as the younger man and more experienced. From above, five bladders of liquid were lowered into the shaft, and five times a thick rush of steam swirled from the dark mouth as they were used to quench the heated rock.

'Enough!' the younger slave-master bellowed down, and the slave crawled up out of the pit and lay on the edge coughing and retching. He was filthy with ash and sweat and mud, and he vomited a little yellow bile into the mud.

'Take him away,' ordered the slave-master and two of them shambled forward and dragged him away to the bench.

The younger slave-master's eyes travelled along the row, and they stiffened into awareness, each trying to will the choice away from himself.

'You.' The sharp point of the whip dug spitefully into Timon's ribs. 'You did not finish your shift.'

There was no right of appeal, protest was folly, Timon had learned long ago. He stood up, and shuffled to the shaft. He steeled himself to the descent, but the delay was too long, and the hippo-hide whip seared its white flash of agony across the tenderness beneath his armpit.

It began as a reflex of pain, Timon lifted his arms to protect himself and the chains swung. In a sudden orgasm of anger and pain, Timon whirled the heavy links just as the slave-master swung the next whip stroke. The chain wrapped about the slave-master's forearm and the bone snapped with a sharp brittle sound.

He backed away with a startled cry, and his broken arm dangled loosely at his side. Beside him the older man drew his sword. It came out of the scabbard with a harsh rasp. He was fifty paces away down the tunnel.

Two of them now, for the younger man was groping left-handed for his sword. Somewhere beneath the slave dullness, the blankness of the slave animal mind, a spark burned. Huy Ben-Amon's training came back to Timon: of two enemies – separate them and attack the weaker first.

Flailing the chain Timon leapt at the younger slave-master, and the man went down in the mud.

Timon leapt over him, and caught the second man's sword stroke on the iron shackle at his wrist. The blow jarred him to the shoulder, and numbed his arm, but he ran in under the next stroke and threw a twist of the chain about the man's throat. He drew tight and held it.

The older man dropped his sword and clutched desperately at Timon's hands, at the links of iron that were strangling him.

Timon found that he was growling like a dog as he jerked and twisted the chain tighter. Suddenly the slave-master's hands dropped away, his tongue fell out between slack and swollen lips and there was the sharp acrid odour of faeces as his sphincter muscle relaxed. Timon let him down on to the floor, and picked up his sword from the mud.

He turned to the younger slave-master who had crawled to his knees, still stunned. He had lost his helmet, and he was cradling his broken arm against his chest.

Timon stood over him and with the short sword chopped his skull open. The slave-master fell face downwards into the mud.

Timon stood back and looked about the drive quickly. From the first blow to the last only ten seconds had passed, and there had been no outcry.

Timon looked down at the sword in his hand, the blade was dulled with mud and blood, but he felt the despondency of abject slavery fall away. He felt the spark burst into flame, felt himself become a man again.

He looked at the other slaves sitting on the bench. Not one of them had moved. Their eyes were dull, incurious. They were not men. Timon felt a chill as he looked at them. He needed men. He must have men.

There was one of them. His name was Zama. A young man of Timon's age. A wild slave, taken beyond the river. He had not worn his chains for a year yet. Timon stared at him, and saw his eyes come into focus, saw his chin lift and the muscles in his jaw clench.

'Hammer!' Timon commanded. 'Bring a hammer!' Zama stirred. It was an effort of will for him to break the pattern of slavery.

'Hurry,' said Timon. 'There is little time.'

Zama picked up one of the short-handled iron-headed mining adzes, and stood up from the bench.

Timon felt his heart soar within him. He had found a man. He held out his wrists, with the bloody sword in his hand.

'Strike off these chains,' he said.

Lannon Hycanus was pleased, but trying not to make it obvious. He stood by the window, and looked down towards the harbour where five galleys lay against the stone jetty. Lannon twisted a curl of his beard about one finger, and smiled secretly.

In the room behind him Rib-Addi was reading in his prim and precise voice, combing his fingers through his scraggily grey beard.

'Into Opet this day from the southern plains of grass, fifty-eight large tusks of ivory, in all sixty-nine talents.'

Lannon turned quickly, a scowl masking his pleasure.

'You attended the weighing?' he demanded.

'As always, my lord,' Rib-Addi assured him, and his clerks looked up from their writings, saw the Gry-Lion's expression soften and they grinned and bobbed their heads ingratiatingly.

'Ah!' Lannon grunted, and turned back to the window, while Rib-Addi resumed his reading. The voice was monotonous, and Lannon found his attention wandering although his subconscious was alert for a false note in the bookkeeper's voice. Rib-Addi had the habit of raising his voice slightly whenever he reached a portion of the accounting which might cause the Gry-Lion's displeasure – a lower return, an estimate unfulfilled – and immediately Lannon pounced on him. This convinced Rib-Addi that the Gry-Lion was a financial genius, and that he could hide nothing from him.

Lannon's mind drifted away, picking idly at stray thoughts, turning over mental stones to see what scurried out from under. He thought of Huy, and felt a cold breeze ruffle the surface of his contentment. There was a flaw in their friendship. Huy had changed towards Lannon, and he searched for the reason. He discarded the thought that it might be the aftermath of their long estrangement. It was something else. Huy was withdrawn, secretive. Seldom would he spend his nights in the palace, sharing the dice and wine and laughter with Lannon. Often when Lannon sent for him in the night, instead of Huy arriving with his lute slung on his shoulder and a new ballad to sing, the slave would return with a message that Huy was sick or sleeping or writing.

Lannon frowned now, and at that moment he heard the tell-tale rise in Rib-Addi's voice and he swung around and glared at them.

'What?' he bellowed, and their faces were yellow-white with fright. The clerks ducked their heads over their scrolls.

'My lord, there was a heavy fall of rock in the southern end of the mine,' Rib-Addi stuttered. It ceased to amaze him that from a mass of figures Lannon would instantly pounce on a ten per cent decrease of output from one of the dozens of tiny mines of the middle kingdom.

'Who is the overseer?' Lannon demanded, and ordered the man replaced.

'It is carelessness, and I will not have it so,' Lannon told him. 'The yield is affected, valuable slaves wasted. I would rather spend more on shoring timber, it is cheaper so in the end.'

Rib-Addi dictated the order to one of the clerks, and Lannon turned back to the window and his thoughts of Huy. He remembered how it had been before, how Huy's presence had provided the zest that made each triumph more valuable, and each disappointment or disaster easier to surmount. All the good things happened when Huy was there.

In a rare moment of self-honesty Lannon realized that Huy Ben-Amon was the only human being that he could look upon as a friend.

His position had isolated him from all others. He could not approach them for the warmth and comfort that even a king needs. His wives, his children feared him. They were uneasy in his presence, and left it with obvious relief.

In all his kingdom there was only one person with the blend of courage, honesty, and disregard of consequence which allowed him to live in the king's presence without shrivelling.

'I need him,' Lannon thought. 'I need him much more than he needs me. Everybody loves him, but he is the only one who truly loves me.' And he grimaced as he remembered how Huy had defied him, and it was he, Lannon Hycanus the forty-seventh Gry-Lion of Opet, who had suffered most during the estrangement.

'I will not let him go again,' he vowed. 'I will not let him draw away from me like this.' And his self-honesty persisted. He saw that he was jealous of his priest. 'I will destroy anything which comes between us. I need him.'

He thought of this latest journey of Huy Ben-Amon's. Was it truly a matter of such urgency that the High Priest must travel 400 miles, taking with him two cohorts of his legion and the priestess and oracle of Opet, to consecrate some minor shrine to the goddess at a desolate garrison outpost in the northern kingdom? Lannon thought it more likely that Huy was leaving Opet for some devious reason of his own, and the result was that Lannon was bored, lonely and irritable. Huy knew that Lannon had planned a feast for his name-day.

The clash of urgent armoured feet interrupted Lannon's thoughts. He turned from the window as three of his high officers burst into the room. With them was a centurion in dusty cloak and unburnished armour. There was dust in his beard and dust coated his sandals and greaves. He had travelled fast.

'My lord. News of the worst possible kind.'

'What is it?'

'A slave rising.'

'Where?'

'At Hulya.'

'How many?'

'A great many. We are not sure. This man,' indicating the centurion, 'has seen it.'

Lannon turned to the weary officer. 'Speak!' he ordered.

'I was on patrol, Majesty. Fifty men on a sweep to the north. We saw the smoke, but by the time we returned to the mine it was finished. They had opened the compounds, slaughtered the garrison.' He paused, remembering the dead men with their bowels ripped open and the bloody mush of castration between their legs. 'They had gone, all except the sick and the lame. Those they left.'

'How many?'

'About 200.'

'What did you do with them?'

'We put them to the sword.'

'Good!' Lannon nodded. 'Continue.'

'We followed after the main party of slaves. There were more than 5,000 when they left Hulya, and they moved northwards.'

'Northwards,' Lannon growled. 'The river, of course.'

'They are moving slowly, very slowly. And they plunder and burn as they go. We could follow them by the smoke and the vultures. The population ahead of them flees, leaving all to them. They devour the land like locusts.'

'How many? How many?' Lannon demanded. 'We must know!'

'They have opened the compounds at Hulya, and Tuye and a dozen other mines – all the field slaves have flocked to join them,' the centurion answered.

One of the officers hazarded. 'There must be 30,000 of them, then?'

'At least, Majesty,' the centurion agreed.

'Thirty thousand, in Baal's holy name,' whispered Lannon. 'Such a multitude!' Then his anger came and he spoke harshly. 'What force have we to oppose their march? How many legions are mobilized.'

'There are two legions at Zeng,' an officer volunteered.

'We could not move them in time,' Lannon answered.

'One legion here at Opet.'

'Too far, too far,' Lannon growled.

'And two more along the south bank of the great river.'

'And they are scattered in garrisons spread over a distance of 500 miles. All the others are disbanded?' Lannon asked. 'How long to call them up?'

'Ten days.'

'Too long,' Lannon snapped. 'We must put down this rising with the uttermost ruthlessness. Rebellion is a plague, it spreads like fire in dry papyrus beds. We must isolate it, and quench it. Every spark of it. What other force have we?'

'There is His Holiness,' one of the officers murmured diffidently, and Lannon stared at him. He had forgotten Huy. 'He is at Sinal, directly in the slaves' line of march to the north.'

'Huy!' said Lannon softly, and then was silent while his officers plunged into an animated discussion.

'He has only two cohorts with him – 1,200 men – he would not engage an army of 30,000.'

'No army, but a slave rabble.'

'Thirty thousand, none the less.'

'We cannot reinforce him in time.'

'It would be folly to try odds like that – and, my lord, Ben-Amon is no fool.'

'The nearest reserves are at Sett on the river.'

'Ben-Amon will not fight,' one of them declared, and they looked to Lannon for his opinion.

Lannon smiled. 'Content yourselves. Ben-Amon will fight. At a time and a place of his own choosing His Holiness will fight.' Then the smile was gone. 'I will march in four hours with all available troops to support Ben-Amon. Issue mobilization orders to all the disbanded legions, send runners to Zeng.'

'Will there be a battle?' Tanith asked. Her eyes sparkled green with anticipation, and her lips were parted expectantly. 'I mean, a real battle like the ones you sing about?'

Huy grunted without looking up from his writing pallet where he was formulating his orders to the garrison commander at Sett.

'Gather to you all troops within your sector and hold them within your walls. Account to me for your store of javelins, arrows and other weapons. What force of elephant do you command? Command the galleys of the river patrol to anchor beneath your walls and await my orders. Inform me of the level of the river. What fords are passable?

'I will join you within six days to assume command. It is my intention to dispute the enemies' passage of the river at—'

Tanith slipped off the couch and crossed the tent. She came up behind Huy and put a finger in his ear.

'My lord,'

'Please, Tanith. I am busy on affairs of moment. This is urgent.'

'No more urgent than a reply to my question – will there be a battle?'

'Yes,' Huy replied testily. 'Yes, there will.'

'Oh, good!' Tanith clapped her hands. 'I have never watched a real battle.'

'Nor will you now!' replied Huy grimly as he resumed his writing. 'You will leave tomorrow morning on a war elephant with an escort of fifty men. You are going home to Opet until this trouble is over.'

Tanith returned to the couch and plumped herself down upon it with the skirts of her tunic drawn up wantonly about her smooth thighs. She glared at the back of Huy's head, and her lips compressed into a stubborn line.

'That, Holy Father,' she whispered inaudibly, 'may be *your* plan!'

Tanith lay unsleeping and listened to the voices of Huy and his officers as they planned the campaign. Her tent was placed conveniently close to that of the High Priest, and the unlit space between them could be crossed without observation by the sentries. This journey to Sinal had been planned by Huy as a love tryst, an escape for them from the restraints of Opet.

Across the tent from her, Aina, the ancient priestess, burbled and muttered in her sleep. Tanith picked up one of her sandals from beside the couch and threw it at her. Aina hiccupped and subsided into silence.

Tanith was too excited by the momentous events in which she had been caught up for her to even contemplate sleep. A savage slave army was trundling down upon them, tens of thousands of wild men, leaving behind them a wide swathe of rape and slaughter and fire-blackened earth.

All that day the refugees had poured into the camp, each of them bringing fresh tales of horror and death. To oppose these savages was Huy Ben-Amon and his small band of heroes, outnumbered twenty to one. It was the stuff of legend, and Tanith would not miss a moment of it. In her mind the outcome was assured, in the ballads the hero always triumphed. He was the favourite of the gods, and therefore invincible. It was a pity merely that the favourite of the gods in the usual masculine fashion was being tiresome, but Tanith had laid her plans.

It was long after midnight before Tanith heard the officers taking loud leave of Huy, and clumping away to their own tents. She sat up, and started to induce tears to flood her eyes. She could usually achieve this by remembering a puppy she had owned as a child. A leopard had taken it. Tonight the trick would not work and she had to resort to rubbing her eyes with her knuckles.

Huy lay on his couch, with the lamp wick trimmed low so the corners of the tent were in darkness. He came up quickly on one elbow when Tanith slipped in through the tent flap, and before he could speak she had thrown herself on the couch beside him and wrapped her arms about his neck. She was shivering violently.

'What is it, my heart?' Huy was alarmed.

'Oh my lord, a dream. A dream of ill omen.' And Huy felt icy little prickles of dread upon the back of his neck. In two years he had learned that Tanith was truly possessed of the gift of prescience. She was capable of vivid glimpses of the future, from small incidents to matters of the gravest moment. If Huy primed her on the course her prophesies should take, it was only on the more mundane consultations. He had, however, developed a hearty respect for her abilities. Tanith knew this as she whispered, 'I walked upon a night field lit only by the funeral fires.' And Huy held her closer, feeling the chill spreading through his body – night, funeral fires, ill-omens indeed.

'I was weeping, my lord. I do not know why, but there was a great sense of loss. There had been a battle. The field was littered with weapons, and broken shields. I came upon the standard of the sixth legion, the sunbird, broken and discarded in the dirt.' Huy shuddered with awe, the sunbird thrown down! It was not only the symbol of his legion, but his own personal totem.

'Then our Lady Astarte was with me. She also was weeping. Silver tears that ran down across her white face. She was very beautiful and very sad. She spoke to me, chiding me sorrowfully. "You should have stayed with him, Tanith. This would never have happened if you had stayed with him." '

Huy felt the quick stab of doubt through his superstitious awe. He placed his hands on Tanith's shoulders and held her away to study her face. Her eyes were reddened, and tears had washed her cheeks, but still he was suspicious. It seemed a little too neat, and he had learned that when Tanith set her heart on something she was not easily put off.

'Tanith,' he said severely. 'You know how grave a matter it is to misrepresent the words of the gods.'

Tanith nodded fervently. 'Oh yes, my lord.'

'As a seeress you have a sacred duty,' Huy insisted, and Tanith wiped her cheeks and remembered how Huy had used that sacred duty to steer the political and economic life of the nation, not to mention his personal profit. She could not deny herself a wicked pleasure in paying him in his own coin.

'I know it well, Holy Father.' Huy stared at her but could find no evidence of guile. Unable to withstand the scrutiny of those dark eyes a moment longer, Tanith buried her face in his neck once more and waited silently. The silence lasted a long time, before Huy finally admitted defeat.

'Very well,' he gruffed. 'I will keep you with me, if that is what the goddess wants.' And Tanith hugged him closer and smiled triumphantly into Huy Ben-Amon's curly beard.

For five days Huy probed and tested that moving mass of humanity as it flowed on towards the great river like a vast black jelly-fish. Always he moved back, retreating ahead of it. keeping his tiny force compact and well under his hand, using it with economy and purpose.

On the fifth day he linked up with the garrison at Sett. Mago, the elderly commander, placed himself under Huy with 1,800 archers and light infantry, 12 war elephants, 2 patrol galleys of 100 oars each, and the garrison's considerable arsenal.

Huy greeted him in the heated noonday on a small hill a dozen miles south of the river, and he led Mago aside out of earshot of the staff.

'I am honoured to serve under you, Holy Father. They say there is glory for those that follow the standard of the Sunbird.'

'There will be enough glory for all here, I warrant you,' Huy told him grimly, and pointed across the open forest land. 'There they are.'

The slave army moved like a thick column of foraging ants, and a pale mist of dust rose above the trees.

'What thought comes first to your mind, Captain?' Huy asked quietly, and Mago studied the distant army.

'From here, my lord, they look like any other army on the march,' he muttered doubtfully.

'And does that not strike you as odd? This is not an army, Mago, it is a rabble of escaped slaves. Yet it moves like an army.'

Mago nodded quickly, understanding. 'Yes! Yes! They are in hand, you can see it. It is true, you would not expect such control.'

'There is more to it than that,' Huy told him. 'You will see it demonstrated in a moment, for I have arranged a little entertainment. I believe in giving these slaves plenty of pepper in their diet. We will raid their baggage in a moment, and then you will see what I mean.'

They were silent for a moment, watching the enemy move slowly down towards them.

Then Huy asked, 'What is the state of the river, Mago?'

'My lord, it is very low.'

'The ford is passable?' Huy insisted. 'How deep is it?'

'It can be crossed on foot. The water at the deepest is neck-deep, but flowing fast. I have had the guide ropes cut.'

Huy nodded. 'They are moving towards the ford at Sett. I have been sure of that from the moment when they chose the Lulule pass of the escarpment.' Huy was silent a moment longer. 'That is where I will destroy them,' he went on firmly, and Mago glanced sideways at him. 'Destroy' seemed a strange word for a General of 3,000 men to use in connection with an army of 30,000.

'My lord!' one of Huy's officers shouted. 'The attack begins!' And Huy hurried across to join the group.

'Ah!' he said with satisfaction. 'Bakmor has chosen his moment well.'

From their carefully prepared ambush, Bakmor's 500 heavy infantry men charged into the flank of the column. Huy's favourite had picked a weak spot in the protective screen of black spearmen. His axemen hacked their way through to the baggage train, and the drivers of the bullock wagons jumped from their seats and ran, the women bearers dropped the baskets of grain from their heads and followed them in a shrieking panic.

Swiftly the attackers slaughtered the oxen in their traces, and piled the grain baskets in heaps. Fire from the earthenware pots was fanned to life and within minutes the plundered food stores of the slave army was ablaze.

'Look!' Huy pointed out to Mago the response of the slaves to this sudden onslaught. From head and tail of the column formations of spearmen were doubling back and forward in the classical manoeuvre of envelopment. The movement was not executed with any of the precision of a trained legion. It was slow and unwieldy, a mere parody of the correct formations, but it was recognizable.

'Remarkable!' Mago exclaimed. 'A soldier commands them, one at least who has read the military statutes. Your officer must be careful now.'

'Bakmor knows what to do,' Huy assured him, and as he spoke the distant axemen formed up quickly into the testudo formation, an armoured tortoise of shields, and they trotted out between the enclosing arms of spearmen, beating the encircling movement with minutes to spare. Behind them the baggage train burned, smearing black smoke across the tree-tops.

'Good! Good!' Huy grinned his pleasure and relief, slapping his thigh with pleasure. 'Sweetly done! Now, let the slave commander show if he is as great a quartermaster as he is a tactician! There will be growling bellies in the enemy camp tonight.' Huy took Mago's arm and led him away. 'A bowl of wine,' he suggested. 'Watching and waiting is almost as thirsty work as swinging the axe.'

Mago smiled. 'Speaking of wine, Holiness. I have a few amphorae of wine that I am sure will give no offence even to a palate as knowledgeable as yours. Will you dine with me this night?'

'I look forward to it with the keenest anticipation,' Huy assured him.

The wine was drinkable, and after the meal Huy and Tanith sang together for the guests. It was a fanciful piece of pornography of Huy's composition, a love duet between Baal and Astarte. Tanith sang the part of the goddess in a sweet and true voice, rendering the more suggestive and ambiguous lines with modestly downcast eyes, that had the guests shouting with laughter and pounding the board with their wine bowls. Huy ignored the pleas for an encore, and setting his lute aside, he became serious. He spoke of the impending battle, warning Mago and his officers not to judge the enemy too lightly.

'I nearly paid dearly for that mistake,' he told them. 'I was tempted to probe their centre in strength, and I found it as soft as freshly kneaded dough. I sensed a quick rout, a chance of victory at a single stroke. With their centre collapsing I would drive through them and split them.' Huy paused, and made the sun sign. 'Praise unto Baal, but a moment before I gave the order to commit and change the probe to a full frontal attack I was warned by an impulse from the gods.' The company assumed expressions of suitable religious solemnity, and a few of them made the sun sign as Huy went on. 'I looked to the enemy's flanks which, naturally, overlapped mine, and I saw how firmly they stood. It seemed to me that the enemy's steadiest and best troops were posted there, and suddenly I remember Cannae. I remembered how Hannibal had enmeshed the Roman Consul.' Huy broke off suddenly, and an expression of revelation dawned upon his face.

'Cannae! Hannibal!' Clearly he remembered the clay box with the battle counters of Cannae set out upon it. He remembered his own voice lecturing, and a black face intent and listening. 'Timon!' he whispered. 'It's Timon! It must be!'

Around him lay his army, a vast agglomeration of black humanity, hungry and afraid and restless in the night. The fires blossomed like a flower garden upon the southern bank of the great river, and the night sky glowed orange. The fires were for warmth alone, there was no food. There had been no food for two days now, not since they had burned his baggage.

Timon moved silently amongst them, and saw how they huddled about the fires. Hunger had made them cold, and they whispered and moaned, so the sound of his camp was murmurous, a sibilance like the hive sound of wild bees.

He hated them. They were slaves, weaklings. One in fifty of them was a man, one in a hundred was a warrior. When he had longed for a war spear in his hands, they had been a rotten twig. They were slow and clumsy in response to the lightning sallies of the enemy. Fifty of them were no match for one of the splendid warriors that opposed him. He longed for the men of his own tribe, longed to teach them what he had learned, to imbue them with his own sense of purpose, his own dreams of destiny and retribution.

On the bank of the river he stood and looked across the slick black flow of water. The reflection of the stars danced upon the surface, and at the shallow place of the ford there were whorls and eddies, a disturbance, as though some monster swam deep.

Three hundred paces out, half-way across the river, was a small islet. The flood waters would cover it, and it was thick with driftwood and mats of stranded papyrus. This was the first stage of the ford. It was here that he would anchor his lines of twisted bark that his men were plaiting now. He would rig the lines at dawn, and attempt to make the crossing in a single day. He knew how heavy his losses must be. They were weak with hunger and wounds and exhaustion, the bark ropes were unreliable, the current was swift and treacherous, and the enemy was as swift and unrelenting.

Timon moved away downstream, passing amongst his sentries, talking quietly with them, stopping to examine the huge coils of bark rope that were laid ready upon the bank, and at last he came to the perimeter of his camp.

Downstream was the garrison of Sett, 1,000 paces away, a Roman mile as Timon now thought of it. There were torches burning upon the walls and Timon could see the sentries moving vigilantly in the light.

Out on the river, anchored in a deep placid pool were the galleys of the river patrol. With oars shipped and sails furled they were saurian in shape, and Timon watched them uneasily. He had never seen warships in action and he did not know what to expect of them. When Huy Ben-Amon had spoken of the great sea battles of the Romans and Greeks and Carthaginians, he had paid scant attention. He regretted it now. He wished he could form some estimate of the threat that these strange craft afforded his crossing.

The sound of voices came faintly to him across the water, and though he could not recognize the words, yet the familiar modulations of the Punic language fanned his hatred. He listened to them and he felt it come up out of the pit of his belly. He wanted to hurl himself upon them, and destroy them. He wanted to destroy every trace, every memory of this grotesque light-skinned people with their skills and strength and strange gods and monstrous cruelties.

Standing in the darkness and staring at the distant fortress, hearing their voices in the night, he remembered the body of his woman sliding and bouncing

over the rough ground, he remembered the slaves wailing in the compounds of
Hulya, he remembered the slave smell, the sound and kiss of the lash, the
jangling weight of the chains, the searing heat of the rock, the voices of the
slave-masters, the thousand other memories burned and branded into his brain.
He massaged the thickened chain callouses at his wrist, and stared at his enemies,
and from the core of his soul his hatred bubbled and boiled, threatening to flood
his reason like the red-hot lava of an active volcano.

He wanted to swing his army about and fall upon them. He wanted to destroy
them, destroy every last trace of them.

He found with surprise that he was shaking, his whole body shuddering with
the force of his hatred, and with an immense effort of his will, he controlled
himself. Sweat poured down his face and chest in the night cool, the rank-
smelling sweat of hatred.

'My time is not now,' he thought. 'But it will come.'

There was a presence beside him in the darkness and he turned to it.

'Zama?' he asked, and his lieutenant answered softly.

'The dawn is coming.'

'Yes,' Timon nodded. 'It is time to begin.'

With loving attention Tanith braided his beard, and then twisted it up under
his chin and clubbed it out of the way where it would not catch in Huy's
breastplate nor afford a grip for a desperate enemy.

She whispered endearments as she worked, the endearments of a childless
woman, speaking to him as though he were her infant. Huy sat quietly on his
couch, delighting in the deft and gentle touch of her hands, the soft words and
the loving tone of her voice; all this contrasted so violently with what the day
would bring, and when Tanith rose from the couch and went to fetch his heavy
breastplate, he felt a sharp sense of loss.

She helped him to arm, kneeling to buckle the straps of his greaves, fussing
with the folds of his cloak, and although she smiled, he could hear the fear in
her voice.

He kissed her awkwardly, and the iron crushed her breast as he held her. She
made a small movement of protest, half pulling away, then she surrendered to
his embrace and, ignoring the pain, pressed herself to him.

'Oh Huy,' she whispered, 'my lord, my love.'

The old priestess pulled aside the hanging reed mat and stepped into the
chamber. She saw the two of them clinging to each other, oblivious of all else.
Aina stared at them through rheumy old eyes, then her mouth sagged open into
a toothless grin and she drew back silently and let the reed mat fall into place.

Tanith drew away at last. She went to the wall against which the vulture axe
leaned beside Huy's couch, and she took it up and untied the soft leather sheath
from the blade. She came to Huy, standing before him, and she lifted the blade
to her lips and kissed it.

'Fail him not!' she whispered to the axe and handed it to Huy.

In the pre-dawn darkness there was an eager group of officers on the ramparts
of the fort staring upstream to where the slave army was encamped. They were
all armed and were eating the morning meal as they stood. They greeted Huy
and Tanith with boisterous high spirits, and Tanith watched and listened as
they discussed the day. She found it difficult to understand how they could face
the possibility of dealing or receiving death with the enthusiasm of small boys
for a piece of mischief.

Tanith felt herself excluded from this mysterious male camaraderie, and she
was startled by the change which had come over Huy. Her gentle poet, her

solemn scholar and shy lover was as inflamed as any of them. She recognized all the signs of his excitement in his fluttering hand gestures, the hectic spots of colour in his cheeks and the high-pitched giggle with which he greeted one of Bakmor's sallies.

'This is the day. Enough waiting,' Huy declared, as he stared upstream into the dawn gloom. There was a heavy mist upon the river, and the smoke from 10,000 camp fires obscured the field. He paced restlessly. 'A curse upon this mist! I cannot see if they have strung their lines across the ford yet.'

'Shall I order one of the galleys upstream to investigate?' Mago asked.

'No,' Huy waved the suggestion aside. 'We will know soon enough, and I don't want to draw attention to the galleys yet.' Huy crossed to the parapet on which the food was spread. He poured a bowl of hot wine sweetened with honey and raised it to the company. 'A bright edge to your swords!'

Huy sang the greeting to Baal as the sun came up over a red and smoky horizon, and then standing bare-headed he drew the attention of the gods to the fact that he intended fighting a battle this day. In strong but respectful terms he pointed out that though the men he commanded were the finest, yet the odds were high, and he would need assistance if the day was to be carried. He relied on them for their co-operation. He made the sun sign, and then turned briskly to his staff.

'Very well, you know your stations and duties.' As they dispersed, Huy led Bakmor aside. 'You have a man to attend the priestess?'

Bakmor beckoned to a grizzled old infantry man who stood a short way off, and the man came forward.

'You know your duties?' Huy demanded, and the soldier nodded.

'I will remain with the priestess through the day.'

'Never letting her out of your sight,' Huy cautioned him.

'Should the enemy triumph, and it seem that she will fall into their hands, I will—'

'Good,' Huy interrupted him gruffly. 'If it is necessary, make the stroke swift and sure.'

Huy could not look at Tanith, he turned away quickly and went down to where a small boat waited to row him out to the largest of the two galleys.

Huy stood on the castle of the galley and waited. The sun was well up now, and the mist was dispersed. The galley was singled up to a bow anchor, and she faced into the current. The rowers were at their benches, their shields and weapons laid at their feet, the oars feathered and ready.

The slave army was committed to its crossing. Twenty lines had been strung from the south bank to the mid-stream island, and now they were laying the lines from there to the north bank.

The ford was congested with a great struggling mass of humanity. Clinging to the bark ropes, they were wading steadily across towards the island. Only their heads showed, long lines of black dots around which the water swirled and creamed. Already there were fifteen or twenty thousand slaves in the water, and the number increased steadily as the horde on the south side filed down the bank and took to the ropes.

It was happening just the way that Huy had known it would. The party on the south bank would dwindle to a size which would be a fair match for Bakmor's impatient warriors. Huy smiled as he imagined how Bakmor must be chafing at this delay. He had longer to wait, Huy decided, as he watched the first slaves emerge from the green waters and scramble thankfully out on to the island with their black skins shining wetly in the morning sunlight.

Their thankfulness was premature, Huy thought. There was still the north channel of the river between them and safety. They began filing off the island,

while behind them the bark ropes bowed downstream with the weight of human
bodies and the island itself swarmed with naked black flesh. It was an awesome
spectacle, such a multitude strung across the river, and still a dense mass of
black men upon the south bank.

If it is Timon, he will know enough to hold his best men in the rearguard.
Huy peered at the men waiting to take their turns upon the ropes, and it seemed
that they were steadier and better armed than those in the van. He must let their
number reduce further before he could risk Bakmor's tiny force against them.

Huy turned his attention back to the ford, from the island the lines of heads
were creeping slowly across towards the far bank. He could see now that he
would have a difficult choice to make. If he delayed his attack much longer, then
many of the fugitives would escape into the dense forests of the north, beyond
the reach of his arm for ever. However, if he struck before they escaped it would
mean committing Bakmor to battle with vastly superior numbers. The choice
was a delicate one, and Huy pondered it carefully. His decision was made when
he thought suddenly of the day in the future when he would report to his king.

'Not one of them escaped, Majesty.' And he could almost hear the reply, 'I
did not doubt it, my bird of the sun.'

Huy turned to the captain of the galley who stood beside him.

'Hoist the standard!' he said quietly, and immediately the order was shouted
to the foredeck. The golden battle standard soared to the masthead.

As a hoarse cheer rose from the rowing decks of the galley, Huy saw the
battle signal repeated in the other galley anchored on his starboard beam.

In the bows a sailor swung a battle-axe, severing the anchor cable and the
galleys spread their wide wings of oars. They dipped and swung and rose, wet
and gleaming golden and silver in the sunlight. Under Huy's feet the ship dashed
forward against the current, so swiftly that he staggered before he caught his
balance. The galleys flew in formation, their great wings beating, arrowing
upstream on a diverging course that would carry one through each channel of
the river.

'Steer for the centre of their line,' Huy ordered the galley captain, and the
order was shouted to the helm.

They raced down on the crowded ropes, strung like black pearls with the
heads of struggling men. Above the rush of water, and the creak and dip of oars,
Huy heard a mounting hubbub of terror from the men who looked up at the
deadly bows that towered above them.

He moved to the bulwark and looked down. He saw their faces turned up
towards him, and their eyes showed white in the dark faces. He crushed down
the stirrings of his pity, for these were not men. They were the enemy.

The archers in the bows were loosing their arrows into them now. Huy saw
an arrow strike one of them squarely in the face and stand there as the man
threw his arms high and was swept away by the current.

The galley cut into the heavily laden ropes, slowing slightly and lurching as
the weight of them checked the forward dash, then they snapped and burst
asunder beneath the iron-shod bows, and the current swept the lines of men
away into deep water, washing them close under the walls of the garrison where
Huy's archers waited to pick them like windfallen fruit.

The galleys drove through the shallows, scraping their keels against the rock
bottom of the ford and then they were into the deep water beyond, and Huy ran
to the stern and looked back. The river was filled from bank to bank with
screaming, drowning men. Some of them clung to the branches of overhanging
trees, others to slippery outcrops of rock, or to floating pieces of driftwood and
mats of papyrus. The island was completely hidden by a solid blanket of wet

and shivering humanity, and still others were trying to find a foothold upon it, floundering and struggling in the shallows.

There were so many of them that they reminded Huy of a migration of insects, rather than human beings. They were like ants, tens of thousands of ants. He held that thought as he steeled himself to give the next order.

The galley captain was watching him expectantly, he could see the sailors in the bows at the tubes. They were looking up at the castle, waiting for the order.

'Very well, Captain,' Huy said, remembering that they were ants and not men. Instantly the galley captain was shouting his orders, and the ship swung broadside to the current. The other galley conformed to this manoeuvre and from the bows of both of them the deadly jets of Opet's secret weapon, 'Baal's fire', were squirted.

It sprayed upon the surface of the river, spreading smoothly, the sunlight broke into rainbows of colour upon the floating liquid, and the stink of it was oily and rank.

Then magically it burst into flame, the entire surface of the river became a solid sheet of roaring orange flame from which banks of sooty black smoke billowed, and the heat of it was so intense that Huy drew back quickly as he felt his beard singe.

'In Baal's holy name,' Huy whispered, as he watched the fire, named for the great god Baal, sweep majestically downstream, filling the great river from bank to bank, filling the sky with dark clouds. It flowed over the crowded island, and when it had passed, the blackened bodies lay in high smouldering heaps, while the driftwood and dried papyrus burned like a funeral pyre.

The wall of fire marched downstream, past the fortress walls, searing the vegetation along each bank, sweeping the river clear of life. In ten short minutes 20,000 souls had perished, and their charred bodies floated down towards the sea or washed up as flotsam along the sand banks and back eddies of the river.

After the flames passed, Timon stood appalled and stared at the devastation. He could not believe the dreadful destructive force he had just witnessed, he could not believe that more than half of his army had vanished so swiftly. He was left with a small portion of his original command.

Those left were his best men, but in truth he knew them to be no match for the cohorts that opposed him. Although he realized that he must make his dispositions for the attack which would now surely follow, yet he wasted a few seconds staring longingly across the river to the north where his own land lay. He was cut off from it now, perhaps for ever.

The galleys lay a hundred paces off the bank, with their bows pointed towards him. They were as menacing as two great reptilian monsters, and now he had seen them in action Timon felt fear's chilly breath on his neck when he looked at them.

Behind him rose the roar of challenge and counter-challenge and the clash of shields and weapons. Timon swung about. The second attack had come, as he feared. It had come with the precision and timing he had expected. It had come crashing into his rear at the exact moment when his men's stomachs were cold with the dreadful destruction they had witnessed in the van.

Timon felt his anger swell and buoy him upwards, his hatred rose with it. Anger and hatred, the forces upon which his whole existence depended. Anger that he must fight against men like these with such fragile weapons. Even as he turned to join the conflict he swore an oath that he had sworn a hundred times before. *I will build an army from my own people which will match these pale-skinned devils.*

Timon fought his way towards the rear through the press of his own men. The attack was driving them back steadily, jamming them against the river, packing them so densely that they could neither manoeuvre nor wield their weapons.

It was a nightmare sensation, attempting to find a way through this swaying, surging sea of black bodies. Desperately Timon bellowed his orders, trying to force them forward, trying to make them deploy outwards, but his voice was lost in the battle roar and even his great strength was helpless in this jam of black humanity.

Over the heads of his men he could see the enemy helmets and plumes ringing them. The sword and axe rose and fell to a solemn rhythm, and before them his men dropped their weapons, turned their backs and tried to burrow their way into the massed bodies of their companions. The pressure increased steadily, smothering the ranks behind and driving them steadily back towards the river.

Over the heads of the attackers the archers and javelin men hurled a rain of missiles into Timon's centre, and so densely was it packed that the dead men could not fall but were held upright by their neighbours' striving bodies.

Now the galleys stole in quietly towards the bank and from the high castles the archers loosed their arrows into the van of Timon's army. The bank began to crumble away beneath the desperate feet, and living and dead slid and fell into the swift waters.

Soon the colour of the water changed from green to brown, and then to the bright scarlet of life blood.

'A river of blood, Holiness,' the galley commander remarked in conversational tones. 'I have heard it sung by the poets before, but this is the first time I have ever seen it.'

Huy nodded without answering. He could see that the battle had reached a point of equilibrium. The pressure that Bakmor's cohorts, even strengthened with those of Mago, could exert was insufficient to drive the enemy back another yard. Soon that pressure must relax, for already the axemen were tiring. When that happened the slave army would explode outwards, like a released bowstring. It needed but an ounce more pressure to topple the slaves into the river, but that pressure must come within the next few minutes.

Huy muttered impatiently, 'Come, Bakmor, are you blinded by blood? Has battle-lust drowned your reason? Now is your moment, but it is passing!' And Huy began to pace the wooden deck anxiously. It was so clear to him what should be done, that it amazed him that others could not see it.

'Come, Bakmor, come!' he pleaded, and then he grunted his relief.

'Not a moment too soon!'

Bakmor had charged his war elephants into the massed remnant of Timon's army. Trumpeting and squealing, the huge animals waded through living bodies, crushing them underfoot, lifting men in their trunks and flinging them towards the sky. A terrified screeching of despair went up from 10,000 throats, and Timon's army turned to water.

'Now!' shouted Huy, and the galleys shot in towards the bank of the river. They ran aground together, and from them poured 400 heavy axemen, led by Huy Ben-Amon.

His men tried to keep with him. For in the sixth legion the place of honour in battle was at the side of the High Priest. But the vulture axe clave forward so swiftly that it took a good man to pace it.

'For Baal!' And they reaped the bloody harvest so the ground beneath their feet turned to red mud, and the river flowed brightly.

In the midst of it Huy saw Timon. The shock of it slowed his arm for a second, and a spear jabbed at him, scoring his ribs. Huy killed the spearman with a casual back-handed stroke, then cut his way through the press towards Timon. It was slow work, and Timon retreated ahead of him towards the river bank.

'Timon!' Huy shouted in desperation, and those terrible smoky yellow eyes turned to him and held his gaze. They were the eyes of a leopard in the trap, cruel and merciless.

'A challenge!' Huy called. 'Fight me!'

In reply Timon reared to his full height and hurled his spear at Huy. Huy ducked and the point glanced off his helmet and buried itself in the neck of the man beside Huy. The man cried out and fell.

Timon turned and with three strides he had reached the bank of the river. He leapt out into the red waters, and then struck out powerfully in the over-arm stroke that Huy had taught him.

Huy reached the edge of the bank and tore off his helmet and breastplate, he snapped the leather straps of his greaves and kicked off his sandals.

Naked, except for the belt which held his axe, Huy looked out across the river. Timon was out of range of the archers on the bank, he was half-way across to the island in the time which it had taken Huy to strip.

Huy dived cleanly from the bank, and struck the water flat on his belly. Then he was swimming, dragging himself through the bloody water with those long thick arms and churning the surface white with his powerful legs.

On the island Timon had found weapons. The throwing spears of the charred bodies that lay thick upon the ground.

As Huy found his footing and waded ashore, Timon hurled the first of them. Huy deflected the spear with a swing of his axe, catching the spear blade full on the great butterfly-shaped head, swatting the spear out of the air as though it were an insect.

Again Timon threw, and again – but now Huy was charging him across the rocky, corpse-strewn ground, and each thrown spear was caught neatly upon the head of the axe and sent spinning aside to fall harmlessly on the rocky earth.

In desperation Timon stooped and picked up one of the round river boulders as large as a man's head. He lifted it over his head with both hands, and stepped forward as he threw it. The rock caught Huy a glancing blow on his shoulder, and knocked him down on his back with the axe skidding away from his hand.

Timon charged at him, careless in his anger and hatred. Huy bounced off the earth, flipping himself forward like a thrown javelin.

The top of Huy's head crashed into Timon's body just below the rib-cage and the air of his lungs rushed out of his throat in a gasp of agony. Timon doubled up and dropped to his knees, clutching at his chest with both hands.

Huy stood over him, and bunched his hand in the manner of the gladiators. He struck Timon with the bony hammer of his fist just below the ear, and Timon toppled forward senseless to the rocks.

'I cannot kill you, Timon,' Huy's voice came to him through grey mist, and from a great distance. 'Though you deserve death as no one else has done before you. You have betrayed my trust. You have carried the sword against me and my king – you deserve to die.'

Huy's face came into focus, and Timon found himself lying on his back with arms out-stretched. He tried to move and found himself bound. Leather thongs were knotted tightly about his fingers and pegged down to the earth, holding him captive. He rolled his head and found himself on the north side of the island, hidden from watchers on the south bank and alone with Huy.

On the rocks beside him a small fire of driftwood burned. Huy had lit it from a smouldering remnant, and in it was heating a broad spearhead with its shaft snapped off short.

'There is little time. Soon my men will come to find me, and then it will be out of my hands,' Huy explained reasonably. 'I have made an oath to my gods, so I cannot give you the punishment which you have earned. Yet I have a duty to my king and my people. I cannot let you carry the sword against us again.

'The Romans had an answer for this, and though I hate all things of Rome, I must use their methods now.'

Huy stood up, and leaned over Timon.

'I made a mistake with you. No man can ever tame the wild leopard.' Huy held the vulture axe in his right hand. 'You were never Timon, you were always Manatassi. You are as different from me as the colour of my skin is different from yours. There was never a bond between us, it was illusion, for though our mouths speak the same language, our ears hear the sounds differently.

'Your destiny is to seek the destruction of all that I hold dear, all that my people have built and tended. My destiny is to protect it, with my very life's blood.' Huy paused, and there was true regret in his heart as he went on. 'I cannot kill you, but I must make sure that you never carry the sword again.'

The vulture axe sang, and Timon screamed once, and then whimpered softly as his severed right hand twitched and trembled like a dying animal on the scorched earth of the island.

Huy fetched the heated spear blade from the fire and sealed off the pumping blood vessels of the stump in a hissing puff of stinking smoke. Then he cut the thongs that still bound Timon.

'Go,' he said. 'You must trust yourself to the river now. My men will come to search the island soon.'

Timon dragged himself down the beach, and at the water's edge he looked back at Huy. His huge black body was scarred and ravaged, and his eyes were terrible.

Slowly he lowered himself into the water, holding the raw stump of his arm across his chest. The current took him, and his head dwindled to a speck upon the wide river, until it was swept beyond the bend below the fort. Huy watched it out of sight, then he stooped and picked up the severed hand from the ground and dropped it on to the fire and piled dry driftwood upon it.

Bakmor had dug his cremation pits along the bank of the river, and he and Huy passed along the ranks of fallen warriors laid upon their last couch of wood. It was the ceremony of farewell, and Huy paused and looked down at old Mago. In death the garrison commander had a dignity which he had lacked in life.

'How sweet is the taste of glory now, Mago?' Huy asked him softly, and it seemed that Mago smiled in his sleep.

Huy sang the praise of Baal, and then he lit the funeral fires with his own hand.

Tanith was not upon the walls to welcome him when they marched back to the fortress of Sett, but Huy found her in her own chamber. She had been weeping and her face was pale, with dark blue smears beneath her eyes.

'I feared for you, my lord. My heart burned within me, but I did not weep. I was very brave through it all. Through all the horror of it. It was only when they told me that you were safe that I cried. Isn't that silly?'

Holding her close, Huy asked. 'Was it like the poets sang it? Was it glorious and heroic?'

'It was horrible,' Tanith whispered. 'Horrible beyond my dreams of horror. It was ugly, my lord, ugly enough to make me despair of beauty.' She was silent then, remembering it all again. 'You poets never tell of the blood, and the wounded screaming and – all the other things.'

'No,' Huy agreed. 'We never do.'

In the night Huy woke and found that Tanith was sitting beside him on the couch. The night lamp was trimmed low and her eyes were dark pools in her face.

'What troubles you?' Huy asked, and she was quiet a few seconds before she spoke.

'Holy Father, you are so gentle, so kind. How could you do what was done today?'

Huy pondered the reply a moment.

'It was my duty,' he explained at last.

'Your duty to slaughter those wretches?' Tanith asked incredulously.

'The law is death to rebel slaves.'

'The law is wrong then,' Tanith declared hotly.

'No.' Huy shook his head. 'The law is never wrong.'

'It is!' Tanith was close to tears again. 'It is!'

'The law is all we have that saves us from the void, Tanith. Obey the laws and the gods and you need never fear.'

'The laws should be changed.'

'Ah!' Huy smiled. 'Change them, by all means, but until they are changed, obey them.'

In the dawn of the next morning Lannon Hycanus arrived at Sett. He arrived at the head of two full legions in battle array, and fifty elephants of war.

'I fear I have been greedy, sire,' Huy told him at the gates. 'I left you not a single one.' And Lannon shouted with laughter and embraced Huy, turning to his staff with an arm still about Huy's shoulders.

'Which of you was it said that Ben-Amon would not fight?'

That night while he was still sober Huy sang the ballad he had composed to commemorate the Battle of the River of Blood, and Lannon wept at the telling of it, and when it was done he cried out to his own staff.

'Three against 30,000 – it will always be our shame that we did not fight with Huy Ben-Amon that day at Sett.'

Lannon stood. 'I give you the new Commander-in-Chief of all the legions of Opet. I give you Huy Ben-Amon, Axeman of the Gods.'

Then king and priest got very drunk together.

Gondweni was one of the 200 tributary chiefs of the Vendi, and his territory bounded on the broken land of the Kal Gorge, the land of the outcasts. He was fat and prosperous, and because he was a prudent man he regularly left small gifts of salt and meat at a place in the hills where the outcasts came for it. Also because he was a prudent man he gave food and shelter to solitary travellers journeying to the hills or returning from them, and when they left his town the memory of their passing went with them.

Thus a tall gaunt stranger sat one night at his hearth and ate his food and drank his beer. Gondweni sensed power and purpose behind the impassive scarred visage with the fierce yellow eyes. He felt an unusual affinity for this man and he talked more freely than was his wont. Although he spoke the language of Vendi, the traveller seemed to know nothing of the politics and affairs of the tribe, not even the name of the paramount king who had succeeded Manatassi when he was carried off by the white devils from across the river.

'Of Manatassi's six brothers, five died swiftly and mysteriously after drinking of a special brewing of beer, prepared by the middle brother, Khani. Khani alone survived the feast.' And Gondweni chuckled and nodded and winked knowingly at the stranger.

'He is now our king, the Great Black Bull, the collector of the tribute, the Thunder of Heaven, the fat lecher of Vendi with his 500 wives and his 50 young boys.' Gondweni spat forcefully into the fire, and then drank from the beer pot before passing it to the stranger. When he took it Gondweni saw that the stranger's right hand was missing and he steadied the pot with the stump.

'What of Manatassi's councillors, his war captains, his blood brothers?' the stranger asked. 'Where are they now?'

'Most of them are in the bellies of the birds.' And Gondweni drew a forefinger across his throat expressively.

'Most of them?'

'Some went over to Khani and ate his salt – other spread their wings and flew.' Gondweni pointed out into the hills which showed like the black teeth of an ancient shark against the moon sky. 'Some are my neighbours, chiefs of the outcasts, paying tribute to none, and waiting in the hills for they know not what.'

'Who are they?'

'Zingala.'

'Zingala, the ironsmith?' the stranger demanded eagerly, and Gondweni's expression changed. He turned on the stranger a hard stare.

'It seems to me you know more than is safe,' he said softly. 'Perhaps we should sleep now.' He stood up and pointed out a hut. 'There is a sleeping mat laid out for you, and I will send a young girl for your comfort.'

The stranger's need was like a raging storm on the girl's unresisting body, battering and driving, and Gondweni heard her crying out in pain and fear. He lay awake, troubled and restless, but in the dawn when he went to the stranger's hut the girl lay crumpled in exhausted sleep and the man was gone.

A deep gorge split the mountains, so deep that the path was dark and moss-covered and slippery underfoot. At the head of the gorge a fall of silver spray plunged down from the cliffs above, and the wind drove it in a fine cold mist into Manatassi's face as he climbed upwards.

At a level place he paused to rest, and the stump of his right arm ached cruelly in the cold. He ignored the pain, pushing it below the surface of his conscious mind, and he looked up the deep dark gut of the gorge.

High above him on the cliff top, outlined against the pale blue of the noon sky was the foreshortened figure of a man. The figure stood very still, and the stillness was in itself menacing.

Manatassi ate a little cold millet cake, and drank from the stream of icy clear water, before beginning the climb again. Now there were other figures. They appeared silently and unexpectedly at steep or easily defended places on the trail and they watched him.

One of them stood atop a giant boulder, fully forty feet high, which all but blocked the gorge. He was a tall man, well muscled and heavily armed. Manatassi recognized him, the man had been a captain of one of his old regiments.

Manatassi stopped below the boulder, and let the cloak fall back from his head, exposing his face, but the man did not recognise him, could not see his king in this ravaged face from which pain and hatred had stripped the flesh and which the whip and the club had remoulded.

'Am I so altered?' Manatassi thought grimly. 'Will no man recognize me again?'

He and the man stared at each other for many seconds until Manatassi spoke.

'I seek Zingala, the ironsmith.'

He knew that even though Zingala had joined the outcasts, such a famous craftsman must still have many clients seek him out. He knew that alone and unarmed he would be allowed to pass on such business.

The sentry upon the boulder turned his head slightly and pointed with his chin up the gorge, and Manatassi went on.

There were narrow steps that climbed the black rock cliff beside the waterfall, and when Manatassi came out upon the summit there were armed and silent men waiting. They fell in behind and on each side of him as he strode out along the only path, through the thick forest which covered the crest of the mountain.

The smoke of the furnaces guided Manatassi, and he came at last to a natural amphitheatre of rock, a bowl one hundred paces across, where Zingala worked his art with iron.

The old master was at one of his furnaces, packing the ore into the belly of it, each lump carefully hand selected. His apprentices were gathered around respectfully, ready to add the layers of limestone and charcoal upon the ore.

Zingala straightened up from his task and held aching back muscles as he watched the tall stranger and his escort come down into the bowl. There was something familiar in the man's walk, in the way he carried his shoulders, the tilt of his head, and Zingala frowned. He dropped his hands to his sides, and shuffled uncertainly as the man's features touched a deep memory. The stranger stopped before him and stared into Zingala's face – those eyes, yellow and fierce and compelling. Quickly he looked down at the stranger's feet and he saw the deep cleft between the toes. Zingala wailed and dropped on to his face upon the earth. He took one of Manatassi's deformed feet and placed it upon his own grey-frosted pate.

'Command me,' he cried. 'Command me, Manatassi, the great black beast, the Thunder of the Heavens.'

The others heard the name and they fell as though lightning had struck them down.

'Command us,' they cried. 'Command us, black bull of a thousand cows.'

Manatassi looked upon his band of outlaws as they grovelled about him, and he spoke softly but in a voice that cut to the heart of each of them.

'There is but one command I give you, and that is – OBEY!'

The furnace was shaped like the belly of a pregnant woman, and the entrance was slitted like her pudenda between spread thighs of moulded clay.

To fertilize the smelting of ore, Zingala introduced the buck-horn nozzle of the bellows into the opening. The nozzle was shaped like a priapus, and the work was done in a strict ritualistic sequence while the apprentices sang the birth chant, and Zingala sweated and laboured like a midwife in his leather apron, pumping away at the leather bellows.

When at last the plug of clay was drawn and the molten metal ran in a fiery stream into the sand moulds there was a murmur of relief and congratulation from the watchers.

Using an anvil of ironstone and a set of special hammers Zingala forged the lion's paw with its five massive iron claws and its pad of solid metal. He filed and dressed and polished it, then he reheated it and tempered it in the blood of a leopard and the fat of a hippopotamus.

One of the skilled leather-workers built a socket of green elephant hide and shaped it to fit the stump of Manatassi's right arm. The iron claw was fixed securely into the leather socket and when it was strapped to Manatassi's stump it made a fearsome artificial limb.

Khani, the paramount ruler of Vendi and foppish half-brother of Manatassi, was with his women when the iron claw tore the top off his skull. The girl beneath him screamed and fainted with the shock of it.

Sondala, the king of Buthelezi, had many subjects, a multitude of cattle, a little grazing land and even less water to carry his people and his kine through a season of drought.

He was a small wiry man, with quick nervous eyes and a ready smile. Of all the tribes along the great river his was the latest to come out of the north, and he was crushed between the powerful Vendi tribe on the one hand and those white-robed, long-bearded, brown-skinned Dravs on the other. He was a desperate man, ready to listen with both ears to any proposition.

He sat in the firelight and grinned and darted quick eyes at the gaunt godlike figure across the hut from him – this king with the ruined face, and bird's feet and clawed hand of iron.

'You have 12 regiments, each of 2,000 men,' Manatassi told him. 'You have five flowerings of maidens each of 5,000. You have, at the latest count, 127,000 cattle, bulls, cows, calves and oxen.'

Sondala grinned and wriggled uneasily, amazed at the accuracy of the Vendi king's intelligence.

'Where will you find food and grass and drink for such a multitude?' Manatassi asked, and Sondala smiled and listened.

'I will give you grazing, and land. I will give you a land rich with fruit and lush with grass, a land over which your people will march for ten generations without finding the limits of it.'

'What do you want of me?' Sondala whispered at last, still grinning and blinking his eyes quickly.

'I want your regiments to command. I want your spear in my hand, I want your shield to march beside me.'

'If I refuse?' Sondala asked.

'Then I will kill you,' said Manatassi. 'And take your regiments, and all five flowerings of your maidens, and all your 127,000 cattle, except for ten which I will sacrifice upon your grave as a mark of respect to your ghost.' Manatassi grinned then also, and it was such a terrible baring of teeth in that battered face that Sondala's own smile froze.

'I am your dog,' he said hoarsely, and he knelt before Manatassi. 'Command me.'

'There is but one command,' said Manatassi softly. 'And that command is, OBEY!'

In the first year Manatassi made treaties with the Vingo, the Satassa and the Bey. He fought the Xhota in a single devastating battle, employing tactics so revolutionary and relentless that the Xhota king and his wives and courtiers and princes were taken twenty minutes after battle was joined. Instead of massacring the menfolk, and taking the women and cattle as was the custom, Manatassi had only the king and royal family strangled then he assembled the defeated regiments, still intact and under their own commanders, and he made them swear their allegiance to him. They thundered it in massed voice that seemed to shake the leaves in the trees and rock the hills upon their foundations.

In the second year, after the rains had passed, Manatassi marched westwards as far as that desert coast on which a cold green surf raged eternally. He fought four great battles, strangled four kings – treated with two others, and added almost a hundred thousand warriors to his regiments.

Those close to the great black beast knew that he seldom slept. It seemed there was some driving force within him that denied him rest or pleasure. He ate food without tasting it, in the perfunctory manner in which a man might throw a log upon the fire merely to keep it burning. He never laughed, and smiled only when a task was performed to his satisfaction. He used women with a swift brutality that left them trembling and weeping, and he shared companionship with no man.

Only once did his lieutenants see him show the emotions of a man. They stood upon the tall yellow dunes at the western limit of the land. Manatassi was apart from them draped in the leopard-skin of royalty and with the blue heron feathers of his head-dress fluttering in the cold breeze that came off the sea.

Suddenly one of the war captains exclaimed aloud and pointed out across the green waters. From out of the banks of silver sea fret, looming like a ghost ship through the mist, sped one of the galleys of Opet. With her single square sail bellied by the trade winds, and her banks of oars beating rhythmically, she sped in silence towards the north on her long voyage of trade to Cadiz.

Again a captain exclaimed, and they all looked towards the king. His face shone and dripped with sweat, and his jaws clenched and ground his teeth together with a sound like rock on rock. His eyes were burning mad as he watched the passage of the galley, and his body shook and shuddered with the strength of his hatred.

The captain ran to aid him, thinking him stricken with sudden fever. He touched the king's arm.

'High-born,' he started, and Manatassi turned upon him in raging madness and struck him down with the iron claw, ripping half his face away.

'There,' he screamed, pointing with the claw at the disappearing galley. 'There is your enemy. Mark him well.'

Each day brought its own excitements, its secret delights and ventures – and its happiness. It did not seem five years since she and Huy had become lovers, so swiftly had the years sped. Yet it was so, for the Festival of the Fruitful Earth was almost come around once more.

Tanith laughed aloud at the memory of her seduction of Huy, and she made her plans to repeat the performance during the coming Festival. Beside her Aina mumbled a question, peering at her quizzically from the depths of her hood.

'Why do you laugh, child?'

'I laugh because I am happy, old mother.'

'Oh, to be young once again. You do not know what it is like to grow old.' Aina began one of her monologues, and Tanith led her through the bustle of the harbour area, past the low taverns and the taunting street girls to where steps were cut into the stone jetty. She danced down the steps and leapt lightly to the deck of the small sailing craft moored to one of the iron rings in the jetty.

Coming out of the tiny cabin, dressed in rough fisherman's clothes and with a scarf tied about his head, Huy was too late to help her aboard.

'You are late.'

'For your impertinence I shall punish you, just as soon as it is safe,' Tanith warned him.

'I look forward to it,' Huy grinned, and helped old Aina over the gunwale, while Tanith ran forward to cast off the head lines.

Huy was perched in the stern with the steering oar tucked under his arm, and Tanith sitting as close beside him as she could without touching. She had thrown off her cloak, and wore now a light cotton tunic edged with cloth thread and belted with a solid gold chain, a name-day gift from Huy.

Her hair billowed out behind her like black smoke, and her cheeks were flushed. Huy kept glancing at her, and each time she looked at him and laughed for no reason.

The wind was fine on their beam, and as they ran close-hauled for the islands the wind whipped droplets from the bow wave into their faces, and the water was cold in the warmth of the sun. Huy ran the vessel neatly through an almost invisible channel in the reeds, and they emerged into a quiet and sheltered lagoon whose surface was covered with the dark green pads of the water lilies and starred with the blue and gold of their blossoms. Water fowl paddled and dabbled and flighted over and upon the quiet waters.

They were out of the wind here and Huy took up a long pole from the deck and, standing in the stern, he poled them across the lagoon to the beach of dazzling white sand. Jumping out into knee-deep water he hauled the vessel up on to the beach.

Amongst the polished black boulders above the beach Huy rigged a sun shelter with a strip of sail, and he helped Aina across the sand and installed her beneath the shelter.

'A bowl of wine, old mother,' he suggested solicitously.

'You are too kind, Holiness.'

They left her there, snoring quietly in the shade, and they walked hand in hand along the ribbon of beach, beyond the curve of the bay. Under the ivory palms Huy spread a cloak on the firm clean sand, and they ridded themselves of their clothing and lay together talking and laughing and making love.

Then they bathed together in the clear warm lake water, and, as they lay in the shallows with the wavelets flopping lazily over them, shoals of silvery finger-long fish came to nibble at their naked skin. Tanith laughed and kicked at the tickle of their toothless mouths.

They went to lie in the sun and dry themselves, and Huy looked up at Tanith standing over him. Her hair was sodden and dangled in heavy black ropes down her back and breast. The sun had brought a glow to her shoulders, and there were water drops clinging in her eye-lashes. She stood proudly under his scrutiny, and she cupped her breasts, one in each hand.

'Do you see ought different about me, Holy Father?' She asked in her teasing voice, so that Huy smiled and shook his head.

'Look closer,' she invited him, and it seemed then that her breasts were fatter and more pointed, he noticed also that they were marbled with bluish veins beneath the white skin.

'Yes?' Tanith asked, and ran her hands down her body to cradle her belly.

'And here?' she asked. 'Anything different here?' And she puffed out her stomach, laughing at him.

'You are getting fat,' Huy reprimanded her, giving her back her laughter. 'You eat too much.'

Tanith shook her head. 'What I have in here, Holy Father, certainly never went in through my mouth.'

Slowly the laughter dried up in the back of Huy's throat, and he gawked at her.

Huy lay in the darkness and he was still stunned and bemused. It still seemed impossible that some of the seed which he had sown so carelessly should have taken root; were not the priestesses of Astarte instructed in the secret ways of preventing just such an occurrence? This was really an event to rank with earthquake and storm and defeat in battle. Something would have to be done about it, something radical.

Lightly Huy's mind touched upon the thought of the grisly old hags who lived along the harbour front, whose job it was to rectify such blunders. Instantly he rejected the idea.

'No.' He spoke aloud, and then listened to the sound of Tanith's breathing, hoping he had not woken her. He began to moderate his plans, perhaps it was not necessary for such radical action, perhaps he could arrange for another shrine to be consecrated in a remote area of the kingdom, and there, away from prying eyes and busy tongues, she could bear his son. It would be simple enough to find a foster mother, someone he could trust. There were many of the veterans of his legion, men maimed in battle, now living the simple life on one of Huy's estates. Men who would lie and steal and cheat and die for him. Men with fruitful wives, whose breasts were fat and full enough to feed another little lodger.

There they could go as often as the opportunity arose to be with their son. He could imagine it already, the happiness and the laughter, and his son kicking and gurgling, fat-bellied in the sunlight.

Stealthily Huy reached beneath the bed covers, lightly his hand settled on Tanith's naked belly and he began to explore it.

'You cannot feel anything yet,' Tanith whispered, and turned to embrace him. Into his beard she whispered, 'I didn't do the things the priestesses taught me. That was very wicked of me, wasn't it? Are you angry with me, my lord?'

'No,' said Huy. 'I am very pleased with you.'

'I thought you would be,' chuckled Tanith contentedly, and snuggled against him, and then she added drowsily. 'I mean, once you got used to the idea.'

The knocking and shouting woke them both and Huy bounded from the couch and snatched up the vulture axe before he was properly awake. Once the initial confusion had quieted, and the house slaves had satisfied themselves by shouted challenge and loud reply that the midnight callers were a contingent of the royal guard, Huy put aside the axe and lit another lamp.

'Holy Father.' One of the body slaves pounded on the door of the bedchamber.

'What is it?'

'The king's guard. The Gry-Lion cannot sleep. He bids you take your lute and attend him.'

Huy sat on the edge of the couch and cursed softly but meaningfully, running his fingers through his beard and curls, trying to knuckle the sleep from his eyes.

'Did you hear me, Holiness?'

'I heard you,' growled Huy.

'The Gry-Lion said that they were to accept no excuse, and to wait while you dressed, and to escort you to the palace.'

Huy stood up and reached for his tunic, but held his hand as he saw Tanith watching him. Her eyes were enormous in the lamp light, and with her hair in cloudy disorder she looked like a child. Huy lifted the bed clothes and slipped in beside her.

'Tell the king that my picking finger is sore, my throat is raw, my lute strings are broken—and I am drunk,' he shouted, and took Tanith in his arms.

Sheikh Hassan rinsed his fingers in the silver bowl and dried them on a square of silk.

'He seeks to impress us with this show of strength,' Omar, his younger brother, murmured. Hassan glanced at him. His brother was a famous dandy. His beard was washed and perfumed and combed until it glistened, his robes were of the finest silk and his slippers and vest were heavy with embroidery of silk and gold thread. On his finger he wore a pigeon's-blood ruby the size of the top joint of a man's thumb. He was misty-eyed from the bhang pipe beside him on the cushions. A dandy perhaps, and a pederast certainly, but nevertheless the possessor of a fine mind and an intuitive perception upon which Hassan relied heavily.

They sat together beneath the ancient fig tree with its widespread branches and its deep dark shade. The dhow that had brought them to this meeting was beached on the white sand of the island below them, and from their vantage point they could look across the channels and sandbanks and slow pools of the great river to the north bank.

There were troops of sea-cow lying on the sandbanks or half submerged in the shallows. Huge grey shapes, like river boulders upon which the white egrets perched unconcernedly.

On the north bank a thin ribbon of dark green vegetation grew along the river, but gave way immediately to the bare brown hills beyond. The country here had a blasted and desolate look to it. The hills were bleak and barren with rounded crests. The earth showed through the sparse dry grass, and the dead trees writhed and held their naked branches to the sky, trees drought-stricken and long dead.

However, as the sheikhs watched so the scene changed. Over the hills spread a dark shadow as though a storm cloud had blotted out the sun.

'Yes,' said Omar. 'This show is to open our ears to his words.'

Hassan spat a stream of bright red juice into the dust, and wiped his beard with silk as he watched the bare hills come to life, watched the dark shadow spread. He had never before seen such a vast concourse of humanity. The regiments and squadrons moved into orderly ranks until they covered the hills. Hassan was nervous, but his face was calm, his eyes grave and only the long brown fingers that fidgeted on the jewelled hilt of his dagger betrayed his disquiet. He had not expected anything like this. He had come to this place expecting to discuss trade and mutual boundaries with the new black emperor who had emerged out of that mysterious and little-known land beyond the river. Instead he had found himself confronted with one of the largest armies the world had ever seen assembled. He wondered if Alexander himself had ever commanded such a multitude.

Omar drew on his bhang pipe, held the smoke and then let it trickle thinly from his nostrils.

'He seeks to impress us,' he repeated, and Hassan's reply was brusque.

'If that is his intention, then he succeeds. I am impressed.'

Still the regiments came pouring over the sky-line in thick but orderly columns. They wheeled and fell into the pattern of the whole as though a single mind directed them, the way shoals of fish or flights of migrating birds react to unspoken commands. Indeed, this seemed to be not a gathering of individuals but a single organism, sprawling but well co-ordinated. Hassan watched it and shivered in the noon heat of the valley.

Upon the north bank all movement ceased, and a massive stillness settled over the serried ranks of black warriors. The stillness seemed more menacing than the preceding movement, and an expectant hush filled the valley, a sense of mounting tension which became unbearable, until Hassan swore and made a gesture as though to rise.

'I will not pander to the whims of a savage. This is an insult. We will go. He must come to us if he wishes to talk.' But the gesture never matured, and he sank back upon the cushions and fretted in silence until his brother spoke.

'It seems,' said Omar, 'that the world we know has changed, brother. What was true yesterday, is true no longer.'

'What is your advice?'

'Let us find the new truths, and examine them. It is possible that we shall still find something to our advantage in all of this.'

On the hills opposite them there was a disturbance, a stirring of the ranks, the way the tops of tall reeds move when a lion passes through. The sheikhs strained their eyes, calling out to their guards for advice of what was happening, but any reply was lost in an ocean of sound. The earth shook beneath the stamp of hundreds of thousands of feet, the air quivered with the drumming of spears on shield, and from the densely packed hills a single voice from the throats of that black multitude roared the royal salute to a king.

The storm of sound rolled across the valley, and died in echoes against the sky and the southern hills. Again the stillness and silence, then a large war canoe with fifty rowers a side was launched from the sandbank and shot across the green waters towards the island.

A man stepped out onto the white beach, and walked alone up the bank to where the sheikhs waited beneath the fig-tree. The very fact that he came without an escort was a mark of contempt, a sign of his strength and invulnerability.

He wore a cloak of leopard-skin and sandals upon his feet but he carried no ornament nor weapon. He stood tall and gaunt over the sheikhs, and they seemed to shrink in significance beside his bulk.

He looked at them with the fierce yellow eyes of a bird of prey, eyes that seemed to rake their souls.

'I am Manatassi,' he said in a soft deep rumble. 'I am the Black Beast.' They had known enough not to be surprised that he spoke their language fluently.

'I am Hassan, Sheikh of Sofala, Prince of Monomatapa and Viceroy of the Chan Emperor.'

'You love the yellow metal,' Manatassi said it like an accusation, and Hassan was taken off balance. He blinked and glanced at Omar.

'Yes,' said Omar. 'We love it.'

'I will give you enough to glut you,' said Manatassi.

Omar licked his lips, an unconscious expression of greed, and he smiled.

'You must have much of the precious stuff?' Hassan asked, this direct approach to trade was distasteful. This man was a savage, he did not understand the niceties of diplomacy. Yet gold was worth a little gaucherie, especially in the quantities this self-styled black beast hinted at. 'Where does it come from?'

'From the treasure house of Lannon Hycanus, Gry-Lion of Opet and king of the four kingdoms,' said Manatassi, and Hassan frowned quickly.

'I do not understand you?'

'Then you are stupid,' said Manatassi, and Hassan flushed dusky rose beneath his brown skin and a retort rose swiftly to his lips, but he felt his brother's cautionary fingers press his wrist.

'Explain it to me,' said Omar. 'Do you intend to war with Opet?'

'I will destroy them – destroy their people, their cities and their gods. I will leave not a trace of them, not a single living one.' The giant Negro began to tremble, a little white spittle wet his full purple lips and a light sheen of sweat greased his battered features.

Omar smiled delicately. 'We heard of a battle at a place named Sett.'

Manatassi roared, a sound of pain. He leaped towards the sheikh and from under his cloak he drew the clawed iron hand and held it in Omar's face. Omar scrambled backwards, and clung to his brother.

'Do not mock me, little brown man, do not mock me, or I will tear out your liver.'

Omar moaned with terror and sweat ran down into his beard.

'Peace,' Hassan intervened hurriedly. 'My brother meant only to remark that the legions of Opet will be difficult to destroy.'

Manatassi gulped for air, still shaking with his rage. He turned away and walked to the edge of the island and stared down into the water. His shoulders heaved, and his chest panted for air, but slowly he calmed himself and came back to them.

'Do you see them?' He pointed to his army that still darkened the hills.

'Numbers alone – will they be sufficient?' Hassan asked. 'You challenge a mighty foe.'

'I will show you,' said Manatassi, and he lifted the iron claw. Instantly one of his war captains ran from the canoe and knelt before him.

Manatassi spoke a few words in the Vendi language and pointed out at the river. The captain sprang to his feet with an expression of joy lighting his dark face. He saluted, went bounding away down the bank, leapt into the bows of the canoe and was sped swiftly across to the north bank.

The sheikhs watched with puzzled interest as a new movement began amongst the massed warriors on the far bank. They moved forward in two thick columns, swarming into the water, and Hassan exclaimed mildly. 'They carry no weapons.'

'They are naked,' added Omar, and his terror ebbed and was replaced by an erotic interest as he watched the black columns move out into the shallows. Like the horns of a buffalo they circled one of the sandbanks, and though the chest-deep water hampered them, yet the manoeuvre was completed before the old bull hippopotamus woke from his gargantuan slumber to find himself surrounded.

He lumbered to his feet and glared about him with his piggy pink eyes. Five tons of solid flesh, clad in a thick grey hide, splotched with pink upon the belly. His legs were short and thick and powerful, and when he opened his jaws to bellow he exposed great yellow fangs of ivory which could bite a war canoe in half.

He broke into a cumbersome gallop, leaving deep hoof-prints in the soft white sandbank, and he charged at the wall of black bodies that cut him off from the deep pool of the river. He entered the shallows, churning up a wake of foaming white water, while ahead of him the wall of black men solidified and thickened as the line bunched up to receive and absorb his charge.

The bull went into them at full gallop, and human bodies were flung about like chaff in the whirlwind. His jaws clashed as he chopped at them, and when he drove forward it seemed that nothing could stay such devastating power. He must burst through them and find safety in the deeps of the river. Yet they swarmed about him, from the sides and rear, and his charge slowed perceptively, although his bellows seemed louder and the champing of ivory tusks cutting through living flesh carried clearly to the watchers on the island.

Manatassi stood quietly, leaning forward slightly, with a small frown upon his scar-riven brow, and his eyes were yellow and watchful.

In the river the water creamed and flashed and sparkled. The bull's bellows took on a new note, a hint of panic, and he was no longer visible beneath the swarming naked bodies. It was like a scorpion attacked by army ants, creatures only a small fraction of his size smothering him with their numbers. The sunlight glittered on the wet bodies, and the bull's forward progress was arrested. He was transformed into a struggling ball of human bodies, while around him the water turned dark brown with blood, and the mauled bodies fell away like poisoned black ticks from the body of an ox. They floated down on the sluggish current, while others swarmed forward eagerly to replace them.

Now, miraculously, the striving knot of men and beast began to move towards the island; leaving the debris of death behind them, they moved slowly through the shallows.

They reached the island, and came from the water – 1,000, perhaps 2,000 men, carrying the exhausted but still struggling hippopotamus bodily from the river and up the bank. The bull slashed viciously from side to side, and all within reach of his jaws died, while the bull's head and the inside of his mouth was clotted with the bright blood of his victims.

Leaving a thick trail of dead and terribly maimed men behind them, they carried the bull to where Manatassi stood waiting. The war captain came forward unsteadily. He was weak from loss of blood for he had lost one arm above the elbow, taken away by a single bite of those terrible jaws.

He handed a stabbing spear to his king. Manatassi walked forward, and while his men held down the terrified monster, he stabbed it in the throat. Finding the jugular vein with the first thrust, the bull died in a burst of dark blood and a cry that rang against the hills.

Manatassi stepped back and watched impassively as his men despatched their wounded with swift mercy, and when the war captain came and knelt before him clutching the severed stump of an arm to his chest and begged for the honour at the hand of his king, a bright pride burned briefly in Manatassi's eyes. He made the mercy stroke, crushing the man's skull with a single blow of the iron claw, then he walked back, and smiled bleakly as he saw the sheikhs' amazement.

'That is my answer,' he said, and after a while Hassan asked,

'What do you want of us?'

'Two things,' Manatassi replied. 'An undefended passage of the river through your territory for my armies. You must forsake your pact of mutual defence with Opet – and I want iron weapons. My smiths will take another ten years to arm so many men. I want weapons from you.'

'In return you will deliver to us the gold of Opet, and the mines of the middle kingdom?'

'No!' Manatassi snarled angrily. 'You may take the gold. I have no use for it. It is a cursed metal, soft and useless. You may take all that Opet has, but,' and he paused, 'the mines of the middle kingdom will never be worked again. No more will men go down to die unnaturally in the earth.'

Hassan wanted to protest. Without the gold of the middle kingdom his own reason for existing would vanish. He could imagine the rage of the Chan Emperor denied his trade routes with the land of gold. Omar's fingers warned him gently, their soft insinuating touch speaking clearly.

'There will be another time to argue.' And Hassan heeded the warning, he choked back the protest and instead he smiled at Manatassi.

'You will have your weapons. I will see to it.'

'When?' demanded Manatassi.

'Soon,' promised Hassan, 'as soon as my ships can return from the land across the eastern seas.'

Lannon had aged these last few years, Huy thought. Yet the change was flattering, the new lines that care had chiselled dispelled the prettiness from his features and had given him dignity. Around the mouth there was the same petulance, the pout of the spoiled child, but one had to look closely to find it.

His body was as young and hard as it ever had been, however, and as he stood now, stark naked in the bows, in the attitude of the harpooner, every muscle in his back and shoulders stood out clearly beneath the oiled skin. The sun had gilded his body to a dark honey gold and only his buttocks were a creamed ivory where his breech clout had protected them. He was a beautiful creature, favoured beyond all others by the gods, and Huy compared this body to his own and felt a despair within him.

Words began to form in his mind, a song to Lannon, an ode to his beauty. As he poled the skiff silently and smoothly over the still waters of the lake the words tumbled about in his mind, like wind-blown leaves, then they began to fall into patterns and the song was born.

In the bows Lannon signalled with his free hand without looking around, still poised, staring down into the waters and Huy turned the skiff with an expert thrust of the pole. Suddenly Lannon's body unleashed its pent-up energy in a fluid explosive thrust, an uncoiling of tensed muscles as he hurled the long harpoon down through the surface. The water bulged and swirled, and the line coiled in the bottom of the skiff began tearing out over the side, hissing away into the water.

'Ha!' shouted Lannon. 'A fair thrust! Help me, Huy!' And together they jumped to the line, laughing with excitement and then swearing at the pain of scorched fingers as the line ran through them. Together they slowed the heavy run of the fish. The skiff was moving out into the lake as the fish sought the deep water, dragging them with it.

'In Baal's holy name, stop him, Huy,' Lannon panted 'Don't let him get out there and sound on us, we'll lose him for a certainty.' And they threw their combined weight on the line. The muscles in Huy's arms and shoulders bunched and corded like a sack of pythons, and the fish turned.

They brought him up swirling and kicking in circles under the skiff and when his huge whiskered head broke the surface Lannon shouted, 'Hold him!' and Huy took a turn of the line about his wrist and braced his body against the weight, the skiff heeling dangerously as Lannon snatched up the killing club and aimed a blow at the glistening black head.

The surface exploded as the fish went into its death-throes, and water cascaded over them drenching them both.

'Hit him!' yelled Huy. 'Kill him!' And half blinded with spray, Lannon hammered at the enormous snout. Some of the blows were wild, crunching against the side of the skiff and splintering the planking.

'Not the boat, you fool. Hit the fish!' shouted Huy, and at last the fish was dead, hanging in the water beside the boat.

Laughing and panting and cursing, they got a heavy line through its gills and dragged it aboard, slithering in over the gunwale, slimy and black with a belly of bright silver, and bulging eyes. The whiskers above its gaping mouth still twitched and quivered as it filled the bottom of the boat, twice as long as Huy and with a body too thick to encompass within the circle of his arms.

'It's a monster,' panted Huy. 'The biggest I have ever seen.'

'You called me a fool,' said Lannon.

'Nay, Majesty, I was talking to myself,' grinned Huy, and he unstoppered the amphora and poured wine for them.

Lannon lifted his bowl to Huy, and grinned at him over the rim.

'Fly for me, Bird of the Sun.'

'Roar for me, Gry-Lion.' And they drained the bowls at the same time, then laughed together like children.

'It has been too long, Huy,' Lannon told him. 'We must do this more often. We grow old too swiftly, you and I, our cares and duties envelop us and we are caught in a web of our own making.' A shadow passed across Lannon's eyes, and he sighed. 'I have been happy these last few days, truly happy for the first time in many years.' He looked up at Huy almost shyly. 'You are good for me, old friend.'

He reached out and clasped Huy's shoulder awkwardly. 'I do not know what I would do without you. Don't ever desert me, Huy.'

Huy flushed, clumsy in his embarrassment, this was a mood of Lannon's to which he was unaccustomed. 'Nay, Majesty,' he answered huskily, 'I will be with you always.' And Lannon dropped his hand and laughed, echoing Huy's embarrassment.

'Sweet Baal, but we grow sentimental as girls – is it old age do you think, Huy?' He rinsed his wine bowl over the side, making a great show of it, and avoiding Huy's eyes. 'There are still fish in the lake, and an hour or two of the day left, let us use it.'

In the dusk they returned to where their old shack stood, neglected and forlorn beneath the graceful ivory palms above the beach. As Huy poled the skiff around the point of the island, and they cleared the reed banks, they saw the galley lying at anchor in the bay. The royal standard of house Barca stood at her masthead, and there were lamps burning at stem and stern. The reflections of the lamps danced on the dark waters, and the sound of voices carried clearly to them.

Huy stopped the skiff and leaned on the pole, and in silence they stared at the long ship. Then Lannon spoke.

'The world has found us out, Huy.' And his voice was tired and resigned. 'Hail them for me.'

The lamp hanging in its chain from the roof of the stern cabin lit their faces unnaturally, highlighting cheeks and noses but leaving the eyes in shadow. Their faces were grim as they gathered about the table, and listened to the messenger from the north. Although he was young, an ensign in his first year of military service, yet he had the poise of high birth and he gave his report lucidly.

He described the ripples of unrest that had lapped along the northern borders in the last few weeks, small incidents, movements of large bodies of men seen at a distance, the smoke and fires of vast encampments. Spies reported rumours of strange occurrences, of a new god with the talons of an eagle and the claws of a lion, who would lead the tribes to a land of grass and water. Scouts had watched the sailing of many Drav vessels along the eastern reaches of the great river, an unusual coming and going, talk of secret meetings between nobody knew whom.

There was a restlessness, a vast stirring and muttering, a sense of pressures and tensions building, of secret affairs afoot. The itching of storm clouds gathering and lightning brewing. Things felt but not understood, signs pointing into the unknown.

Lannon listened quietly, frowning a little, his chin propped on his fist and his eyes in shadow.

'My commander bids me tell you of his fears that you might find all this fancy and starting at the hooting of owls.'

'No.' Lannon brushed aside the boy's plea for his report to be taken seriously. 'I know old Marmon better than that. He does not call out snake for an earthworm.'

'There is more,' said the boy, and he laid a leather bag upon the table. He loosed the draw-string and shook out a number of metal objects.

'Ong of the river patrols surprised a party of pagans attempting to cross in the night. They carried these, all of them.'

Lannon picked up one of the heavy spearheads, and examined it curiously. The shape and workmanship were distinctive and he glanced up at Huy.

'Well?' he asked and had his own opinions confirmed when Huy answered, 'Drav. No doubt of it.'

'Carried by the pagans?'

'Perhaps they were taken from dead Dravs, or stolen.'

'Perhaps,' Lannon nodded. He was silent a while longer then he looked up at the young officer. 'You have done well,' he said and the lad flushed with pleasure. Lannon turned next to Habbakuk Lal. 'Can you take us on another night run to Opet?' And the admiral smiled and nodded.

Lannon and Huy stood together at the stern rail and watched their island merge into the darkness as the galley drew swiftly away, leaving its wake shimmering in the light of the moon.

'I wonder when we will next return here, Huy,' Lannon asked softly, and Huy moved restlessly beside him but did not answer. 'I feel as though I am leaving something behind here. Something valuable which I will never find again,' Lannon went on. 'Do you feel it also, Huy?'

'Perhaps it is our youth, Lannon. Perhaps these last few days were the end of it.' They were silent then, swaying to the easy motion of the galley under oars. When the island was gone Lannon spoke again.

'I am sending you to the border, Huy. Be my eyes and ears, old friend.'

'It is not for long, my heart,' Huy apologized, although Tanith had said nothing, and was fully engaged in daintily devouring a bunch of purple grapes. 'I will be back before you know I have gone.'

Tanith pulled a face as though one of the grapes were sour, and Huy studied her face with exasperation. It was serene and lovely and as unyielding as that of the goddess herself.

Huy had come to know all of Tanith's moods, every expression or tilt of the head that heralded them. He had watched with fascination as she changed from child to full woman, from bud to ripe bloom, and he had studied her with the patience and dedication of love, but this was one mood he had not learned how to distract.

Tanith licked her long tapered thumb and forefinger with the tip of a pink tongue, then examined her hand with interest, twisting it from side to side to catch the light.

'There is nobody else that the king can trust to send on this mission. It is a matter of grave importance.'

'I am sure,' Tanith murmured, still examining her hand. 'Just as there was no other who could go with him to stick fish.'

'Now, Tanith,' Huy explained reasonably. 'Lannon and I have been companions since our childhood. We used to go out to the islands often in the old days. It was like a pilgrimage to revisit our youths.'

'While I sit here with a bellyful of your child, alone.'

'It was but five days,' Huy pointed out.

'But five days!' Tanith mimicked him with her cheeks flushing, signalling the change of her mood from ice to fire. 'I swear on my love of the goddess, that I do not understand you! You profess your love for me, yet when Lannon Hycanus crooks a finger you run to him, panting like a puppy dog and roll on your back that he may tickle your belly!'

'Tanith!' Huy began to grin. 'I swear you are jealous!'

'Jealous, is it!' Tanith cried, and snatched up the fruit bowl. 'I'll give you jealous!' She hurled the bowl, and while it was still in flight she was reaching for fresh missiles.

Old Aina, nodding in the sunlight at the end of the terrace, awoke in the midst of the storm and joined Huy in flight. They found shelter behind an angle of the wall, and from there Huy cautiously reconnoitred the field and found it deserted, but he could hear Tanith weeping somewhere in the house.

'Where is she?' quavered Aina.

'In the house,' answered Huy, combing fruit from his beard and mopping at wine stains on his tunic.

'What is she doing?'

'Weeping,' Huy said.

'Go to her,' commanded Aina.

'And if she attacks me again?' Huy asked nervously.

'Spank her,' instructed Aina. 'Then kiss her.' And she gave him a toothless but utterly knowing grin.

'Forgive me, Holy Father,' whispered Tanith and her tears were warm and wet upon Huy's neck. 'It was childish of me, I know, but every moment I spend away from you is a piece of my life wasted.'

Huy held her, stroking her hair, gentling her, and his chest felt congested and swollen with the strength of his love for her. He was close to tears himself as he listened to her voice.

'Is it not possible for me to go with you this time?' She made one last appeal. 'Please, Holy Father. Please, my love.'

Huy's response was regretful but firm. 'No. I go fast and hard, and you are already in your third month.'

She accepted it at last. She sat up on the couch and dried her eyes. Her smile was only a little lopsided as she asked, 'Won't you tell me again of the arrangements you have made for the baby?'

She sat beside him, soft and warm, with her pale skin glowing over the faint bulge of her belly and the new heaviness of her breasts in the lamplight. Her eyes were intent as she listened, and she nodded and smiled and exclaimed as Huy told her how it would be – of the foster mother he had selected in the cool and healthy air of the hills, on the estate at Zeng. He told her how the child would grow healthy and strong, and how they would visit it there.

'It?' Tanith demanded playfully. 'Never *it*, my lord – her!'

'*Him!*' Huy corrected and they laughed. But beneath Tanith's laughter the sadness persisted. This was not the way it would be. She could not see this, she could not catch the happiness of it, could not hear the laughter of a child nor feel the warmth of its little body against her.

For a moment the dark curtains of time opened, and, as sometimes happened, she glimpsed the future, saw dark shapes and men and things that terrified her.

She clung to Huy and listened to his voice. It gave her comfort and strength, and at last she asked softly, 'If I fetch your lute, will you sing for me?'

And he sang the poem to Tanith, but there were new verses now. Every time he sang it, there were new verses.

Marmon was the captain of the north, governor of the northern kingdom and commander of the legions and forts that guarded the northern border.

He was an old friend of Huy's, thirty years his senior but with the bond of scholarship between them. Marmon was a keen military historian, and Huy was helping him with a manuscript history of the third war with Rome. He was a tall bony man with a fine mane of silver hair of which he was inordinately proud. He kept it shampooed and neatly clubbed. His skin was smooth as a girl's and firmly drawn over the prominent bones of his skull, but the shivering sickness had yellowed the tone of his complexion and yellowed the whites of his eyes also.

He was one of the empire's most trusted generals, and for two days he and Huy discussed the situation along the border, poring over a clay-box map of the territory so that Marmon could show Huy exactly where each piece of the puzzle fitted in. Marmon's fine-boned hands touched each of the counters, or drew out the lines and areas of disturbance and dispute, while Huy listened and asked his questions.

At the end of the second day they ate the evening meal together, sitting up on the ramparts of the fortress for the sake of the cool evening breeze. A slave girl anointed their limbs with perfumed oil to discourage the mosquitoes and Marmon filled Huy's wine bowl with his own hands, but did not drink himself. The shivering sickness damages a man's liver, and for him wine turns to poison.

Huy thanked Baal for the immunity that the gods had given him against the ravages of this disease which flourished in the hot lowlands of swamp and river. Huy's mind chased after the thought: Why did the disease kill some, cripple others and leave others untouched? Why did it strike only in the lowlands, and leave the cool uplands untainted? He must think about it more, try and find answers to these questions.

However, Marmon was talking again now and Huy stopped his mind from wandering, brought it back to the problem in hand.

'I am at last building up a system of spies upon which I can rely,' Marmon was saying. 'I have men with the tribes who report to me regularly.'

'I should like to meet some of them,' Huy intervened.

'I would rather that you did not, Holiness,' Marmon began, then noticed Huy's expression and went on smoothly. 'I expect one of them to report within the next few days. He is my most reliable informant. A man named Storch, a Vendi, an ex-slave. Through him I am recruiting a body of spies across the river.'

'I will speak with him,' said Huy, and the conversation changed, Marmon asking advice of Huy about his manuscript. As old friends they talked on, until darkness had fallen and the servants lit torches for them. At last Marmon asked deferentially,

'My lord, I have been petitioned by my officers. Some of them have never heard you sing, and those who have wish to hear it again. They are importunate, Holiness, but I trust you will bear with them.'

'Send to my quarters for my lute.' Huy shrugged with resignation, and one of the young officers stepped forward with the lute.

'We have already presumed, Holy Father.'

Huy sang the songs of the legions, the drinking and marching songs, the bawdy songs and the songs of glory. They loved it. The officers crowded silently about Huy on the ramparts, and in the courtyard below the common soldiers gathered with their faces upturned, ready to come crashing in with the chorus.

It was late when an aide pressed through the throng and spoke quietly to Marmon. He nodded and dismissed the aide before whispering to Huy, 'Holiness, the man I spoke of has come.'

Huy set aside the lute. 'Where is he?'

'In my quarters.'

'Let us go to him,' suggested Huy.

Storch was a tall man, with the distinctive willowy grace displayed by so many of the Vendi, but the smooth velvety black skin of his shoulders was marred by the thickened scars of the slave lash.

He noticed Huy's glance and adjusted his cloak to cover the ugly cicatrice, and it seemed to Huy there was a flash of defiance in his eyes although his face was handsome and impassive.

'He speaks no Punic,' Marmon explained. 'But I know you speak the dialect.'

Huy nodded, and the spy looked at him a moment longer before he addressed Marmon. His voice was quiet, without either anger or accusation.

'It was our agreement that no other should see my face,' he said.

'This is different,' Marmon explained quickly. 'This is no ordinary man, but the High Priest of Opet and the General of all the armies of the king.' Marmon paused. 'This is Huy Ben-Amon.'

The spy nodded, his face still showed no expression, not even when Huy spoke in Vendi.

They talked for an hour, and at the end of it Huy turned to Marmon, speaking in Punic.

'This disagrees with much else you have told me.' Huy frowned and knockled his knuckles irritably against the table top. 'This man has heard nothing of a god with lion claws, nor of regiments of trained warriors armed with the weapons of the Drav.'

'No,' Marmon agreed. 'This section of the river is quiet. Our reports come from further east.'

'You have spies there?' Huy asked.

'Some,' Marmon nodded, and Huy thought a moment.

'I will move eastward then,' Huy made up his mind. 'I will march at dawn.'

'The patrol galley will arrive in five days.'

'I will see nothing from the deck of a galley. I will go on foot.'

'I will have an escort waiting for you before the rise of the sun,' Marmon offered.

'No,' Huy rejected the offer. 'I will move faster, and draw less attention to myself if I travel alone.' He glanced again at Storch. 'This man can serve as a guide, if he is as reliable as you say.'

Marmon relayed Huy's order to the spy and ended, 'You may go now. Eat and rest, and be ready before the sun.'

When he was gone Huy looked after Storch for a long moment then asked. 'How much do you pay such a one?'

'Very little,' Marmon admitted. 'Salt, beads, a few copper ornaments.'

'I wonder why he does it,' said Huy softly. 'Why he works for us when the scars of the lash are fresh upon his body.'

'I am no longer amazed by the acts of men,' said Marmon. 'I have seen too much strange behaviour ever to question a man's motives.'

'I never cease to do so,' murmured Huy, still looking after the spy, troubled by the man's treachery which jarred so harshly on Huy's own sense of honour.

Huy's efforts to find out more about the spy over the next four days met with but small success. Storch was a silent man, speaking only when he was questioned directly, and then answering with words barely sufficient for the occasion. He never looked directly at Huy; his eyes focused to one side of Huy's face and he looked beyond.

Huy found him a disconcerting companion, though he clearly knew every bend of the river and every fold of the ground over which they travelled.

They called at two of the forts upon the south bank, and from the men who garrisoned them Huy gleaned much first-hand intelligence. Twice they found the sign where large parties of men had crossed the river on mysterious business, and there were other small indications of secret activity which heightened Huy's feelings of unrest.

It disturbed him that these signs were in contradiction of Storch's assurances of quiet and stable conditions beyond the river.

They travelled swiftly and silently, slipping like a pair of forest spirits through the dense valley bush. They travelled much in the cool of evening and night and rested in the hissing heat of noon. They ate little, husbanding the contents of the corn bag and not wasting time upon the hunt.

On the fourth day they reached the summit of a small granite hillock from which they could survey a huge area of the valley floor, a panorama that stretched from escarpment to escarpment and only shaded away into the blue haze of distance. Before them the river made a mighty bight towards the south, a wide glittering loop of many miles that twisted back upon itself.

Although the loop was some twenty or twenty-five miles around, yet across the neck was less than five and beyond it stood the squat solid block of another garrison. The smoke from the cooking fires rose in a pale blue feather into the still, hot air.

Huy looked at the twist of the river for a long time, the choice as between a full day's hard slogging or a quick cut across the neck of the loop with its attendant risk.

'Storch,' he said, 'can we cross the river? Are there men of the tribes here?'

The spy looked away from Huy's scrutiny, hiding any expression. He sat very still, squatting upon the granite dome beside Huy – and Huy thought he had not understood the question.

'It would be shorter to cut across the bend. Is it safe?' he asked again, and Storch replied,

'I will find out. Wait here for me.'

He returned an hour after dark and led Huy down to the river bank. Hidden in the reeds was a narrow dug-out canoe. The woodwork was rotten with worm, and it stank of old fish. Huy's suspicion flared.

'Where did you find this?'

'There is a family of fishermen camped down stream.'

'How many?'

'Four of them,' Storch replied.

'Vendi?'

'No, men of Sofia.'

'Warriors?'

'Fishermen. Old men with grey heads.'

'You told them about me?'

'No.'

Huy hesitated, peering into the blank stare of Storch's eyes, trying to find a hint of treachery there.

'No,' said Huy, 'we will not cross. We will go around the long way.' It was a test. He waited for Storch's reaction, waited for him to argue, to attempt to persuade Huy to make the crossing.

'It is for you to say,' Storch nodded, and began to cover the canoe with reeds.

'Very well,' Huy agreed, 'take me across.'

Storch used the current to angle the frail little craft across the river. Ahead of them the cormorants beat the water with their wings in their frenzied efforts to launch into flight, while the chocolate and white jacanas scurried across the lily pads and the sinister log-like shapes of the crocodiles slid down the bank into deep water.

They landed on a muddy beach heavily trodden by the hooves of the game that drank here, and Storch hid the canoe. He led Huy up the bank, and into a glade of bright poisonous green swamp grass. They waded waist-deep through the thick clutching stems, and the ground was soggy and yielding underfoot.

In the centre of the glade Storch stopped abruptly and motioned Huy to stand still. He cocked his head in a listening attitude. They stood frozen for a long time, then Storch cautioned Huy to remain where he was and he moved forward.

A hundred paces from Huy, Storch stopped again, but now he turned and looked back at Huy.

For the first time his face showed expression, a wild exultation, a bright burst of triumph.

He lifted his right arm and pointed at Huy, a gesture of denunciation, and he shouted out in Vendi, 'There he is! Take him!'

The grass of the glade rustled and shook as though a high wind blew across it, and from their places of concealment rose rank upon rank of Vendi warriors. Their shields overlapped, their lines formed concentric circles about Huy, ringing him in completely, and the plumes of their head-dresses were the foaming crest of a menacing wave about him.

Like the tightening of a strangler's fist upon the throat, the rings of warriors closed in on Huy. Wildly he glared about him, seeking an avenue of escape. There was none, and he stripped the leather guard from the blade of the vulture axe and flew like a terrier at the throat of a black bull.

'For Baal!' he shouted his defiance as he charged into the solid mass of warriors.

'The air in here is foul,' Lannon complained, sniffing at it. 'Is there no way in which we can drive ventilation shafts to the surface?'

'Majesty!' Rib-Addi could not hide his horror. 'Think what that would mean. Workmen in here.' He made a wide gesture that took in the entire length of the treasury. 'Can you imagine what tales they would take with them to inflame the greed of every brigand in the four kingdoms.'

It was for this reason that the location and contents of the royal storehouse was such a closely guarded secret. The best-kept secret in the empire, known only to the king, the High Priest and Priestess, Rib-Addi and four other officials of the treasury.

'I would have them sent to the gods immediately they had completed the task,' Lannon explained reasonably.

Rib-Addi blinked with surprise. He had not envisaged such a sweeping solution to the problem. It took him a moment's beard-scratching and deep thought to unearth his next objection.

'A ventilation shaft would provide entry for thieves and rodents and damp. All these would damage and destroy.'

'Oh, very well.' Lannon dismissed the subject, knowing well that Rib-Addi resisted change merely because it was change. What had been good for the past two hundred years, must be good for the next two hundred.

Lannon watched as the latest shipment of finger ingots from the mines of the middle kingdom was reverently added to the piles of gold already laid down in the recess of the treasury. Rib-Addi noted the quantities meticulously in his scroll, and Lannon affirmed the entry by scrawling his personal sign beside the entry.

The four trusted officials filed out of the long chamber with its piles of treasure. While they climbed the flagged stairs, Rib-Addi sealed the iron gate. He pressed the Gry-Lion's mark into the clay tablet, then he and Lannon climbed the stairs and passed through the sun-door into the state archives. Lannon closed the door, and the massive slab swung into its seating with a solid clunk.

Lannon made the sun sign at the god's image upon the door, then with

Rib-Addi beside him discoursing as ever on wealth in its many manifestations, he passed down the length of the archives. The shelves were loaded with the records of the kingdom, and was little space left. Soon he must turn his mind to an extension of these catacombs, how to enlarge them without destroying or damaging the existing structure.

They went out through the main portals, with their heavy leather curtains, into the guards' ante-chamber where officers of the Sixth Legion guarded the entrance. At all times of the day and night two officers were here, and at their call a century of picked troopers of Legion Ben-Amon waited. The Sixth Legion had originally been formed as a guard to the temples and treasuries of the kingdom, and these still formed an important part of its duties.

Within the maze of the temple of Astarte, Rib-Addi took obsequious leave of Lannon and with his four underlings backed away bowing until he disappeared around the bend of the corridor.

Assisted by four priestesses, Lannon, naked and magnificent, took the ritual bath in the pool of Astarte and while they dressed him in the tunic of the supplicant, Lannon managed to insert a playful hand into the skirts of one of the novices without the others noticing. The novice's expression did not change, but she pressed eagerly onto Lannon's fingers for a moment before drawing away, and while Lannon strode down the passage to the audience chamber of the oracle he made the gesture of stroking his moustache to inhale the girl odour that lingered on his fingers.

They were all as hot as corn cakes sizzling on the griddle, these brides of the gods, having to rely as they did on the embraces of their own kind, or the furtive attentions of a priest or temple guard. Lannon grinned as he wondered how many of them took advantage of the licence of the Festival of the Fruitful Earth. How often had he committed the mortal sin of sacrilege with some heavy-cloaked and disguised priestess. The Festival was imminent, in two weeks it would begin, and as always he looked forward to it. Then with regret he remembered that Huy was unlikely to return from the north in time to join in the celebrations. It would detract from his own enjoyment. Lannon's moods were always mercurial and now within a dozen paces his good spirits evaporated. As he entered the audience chamber he was scowling heavily.

He looked up at the oracle on her throne, sitting like an ivory statue with her hands folded on her lap and her face painted with cosmetics to resemble a mask, forehead white with antimony powder, eyelids metallic shiny blue and the mouth a vivid slash of scarlet in the pale face. He found a focus for his bad temper.

As he made a perfunctory obeisance, he remembered how often this witch had thwarted and unsettled him. He detested these sessions of divination, and yet found that they exerted a weird fascination. He realized that much of her oracle was dross, probably inspired by the politically active priesthood. Yet there was also much shrewd comment and excellent counsel amongst it, and occasionally there were nuggets of purest gold to be gleaned from the witch's lips. During his regular visits he had tuned his ear to catch the nuances of the oracle's voice. As with Rib-Addi, the witch had shades of conviction or hesitation in the manner in which she delivered the oracle. Lannon was sensitive to these, but more particularly so to a rarer tone, a monotonous low-pitched voice which the witch used when she spoke the miraculous god-given truths of real prophecy.

Now he took up his stance before her, legs planted firmly astride and clenched fists on his hips. With the arrogance of royalty heightened by his temper he asked the question.

Tanith hated these sessions with the Gry-Lion. He awed and frightened her. It was like being caged with some beautiful but savage predator, with its restless energy and unpredictable moods. The pale steely blue of his eyes had a predator's cold killing lust, his features were chiselled perfect but cold also with the same relentless passion.

Usually she had the comfort of Huy's presence behind the curtains to carry her through, but this morning she was alone – and sick.

The night had been hot and airless, and the child in her womb as heavy as a stone. She had risen listless and pale from her couch, her skin damp with night sweat and she had forced down the light morning meal Aina had prepared for her, only to vomit it up again in a dizzy attack of nausea.

The taste of acid-bitter bile was in the back of her throat now, and sweat poured down beneath her cloak, tickling as it slid over her flanks and fruitful belly. She felt herself stifling, her breathing hunting raggedly for air, her body limp and weak, while the king growled his questions.

She was unprepared, her answers were empty words given without conviction, and she struggled to concentrate, to remember what Huy had told her.

The king was becoming restless, he strode back and forth before her, wearying her with his energy. She felt sweat break out beneath her mask of cosmetics. Her skin felt itchy and swollen, the pores blocked with paints and she longed to wipe it away. She had a sudden wondrous image of cool water falling over moss-covered rocks, of plunging her naked body into the green water, of sinking into it with her hair spreading on the surface, like the tendrils of a water plant.

'Come, witch! Come, oh seer of the future. It is a simple question. Answer it!'

The king was stopped before her, one foot on the throne steps, shoulders drawn back and hips thrust forward in masculine hauteur, a sneer on his handsome face and mockery in his voice.

Tanith had not heard the question, she floundered for words, and another wave of nausea washed over her. She felt sweat break through the film of paint on her upper lip, and the nausea changed to dizziness.

Lannon's face receded, and blackness closed about her. Her vision narrowed, and she looked down a long shaft of darkness at the end of which Lannon's face burned like a golden star. There was a roaring in her ears, the sound of the storm wind through the trees of the forest. Then the sound of the wind died away into silence, and a voice spoke. The voice was husky and low-pitched, even and monotonous, the voice of a deaf woman or one drugged by the smoke of the bhang pipe. With mild surprise Tanith realized that the voice issued from her own throat, and the words shocked her.

'Lannon Hycanus, last Gry-Lion of Opet, question not the future. The future for you is darkness and death.'

She saw her own shock repeated upon Lannon's face, saw the colour fly from his cheeks, and his lips turn to lines of pale marble.

'Lannon Hycanus, prisoner of time, pacing behind the bars of your cage. Blackness waits for you.'

Lannon was shaking his head trying to deny the words. The golden locks of his hair, still damp from the ritual bath, danced upon his shoulders, and he held up both hands in the sun sign, trying to avert the words which struck his soul like war arrows flighted from the bow.

'Lannon Hycanus, your gods are passing, they fly upwards, and leave you to blackness.'

Lannon retreated from the throne, hands raised to shield his face, but the words sought him out relentlessly.

'Lannon Hycanus, you who seek to know the future, know then that it lies in wait for you as the lion awaits the unwary traveller.'

Lannon cried out, and his terror exploded into violence.

'Evil!' he screamed, and rushed at the oracle, bounding up the steps of the throne. 'Witchcraft!' He struck Tanith in the face with his open hands, knocking her head across and back with heavy blows. The hood of her cloak fell back and her dark hair tumbled loose. The blows rang loudly against her flesh, but Tanith made no sound. Her silence drove Lannon on to further violence.

He caught the front of her cloak and dragged her from the throne.

'Sorceress!' he screamed, and flung her down the steps. She fell heavily and rolled, trying to come to her feet, but Lannon's first kick caught her in the belly and she doubled up, clutching at her middle and groaning as his sandalled feet smashed into her.

Lannon was bellowing as he pursued her about the chamber, between kicks he was looking wildly about for a weapon, something to destroy the woman and the words she had spoken.

Then suddenly the chamber was filled with priestesses, and Lannon drew back panting heavily, the pale eyes bright with madness.

'Majesty!' The Reverend Mother came forward, and Lannon's madness faded, but he was still shaking and his lips were white and quivering.

He turned and strode from the chamber, leaving Tanith whimpering upon the flagged floor.

The Divine Council of Astarte met in the Reverend Mother's chamber, and when she read the Gry-Lion's demand to them they listened quietly thinking their own thoughts. The Council consisted of the High Priestess and two advisers, both of them senior priestesses who stood in the direct line of succession to the Reverend Mother.

'How can we deliver one of the sisterhood to the temporal body of the Gry-Lion. What precedent would we set by doing so?' Sister Alma asked. She was small and wrinkled with a face like an inquisitive monkey. 'What crime is the child accused of? If she has erred, then it is for us to judge and punish. We must protect our own, even if it means defying the king.'

'Can the sisterhood afford such a grand gesture?' asked Sister Haka; dark-skinned and pock-marked, with long raven hair streaked with iron grey, her face was strong-jawed and her voice deep as a man's. She was not yet forty years of age, and certain to outlive the Reverend Mother. Until recently it seemed she must succeed to the head of the sisterhood, a position for which she longed. However, since an oracle had emerged in Opet, her position was less secure. History had proved that every oracle, in time, became Reverend Mother over the claims of all others. In addition, this one had the unquestioned favour of the High Priest, an important consideration when it came to the filling of a vacant position at the head of the Divine Council. In Tanith she had a strong rival, but apart from the political considerations, Sister Haka had a more intimate score to reckon.

Even now as she remembered how her advances had been rejected, she felt hot anger flood her cheeks. She still longed for the girl, dreams of her still troubled her sleep, and often when she was with a young novice in the dark she would pretend that it was Tanith.

'Are we strong enough to resist the demands of the king?' She let the question hang, and looked at their faces. All of them knew what an impetuous, irresistible force ruled in Opet. All of them knew that no one, noble or priest, friend or enemy, had ever denied him his way.

The silence persisted, until Sister Alma coughed gusts of tortured sound, that crescendoed until she spluttered up a lump of bloody phlegm and wiped her lips with a damp cloth, her face strained and her eyes tired and dull.

'Not long for you, old woman,' thought Sister Haka with her grim satisfaction hidden behind a mask of concern.

Again they were silent, until the Reverend Mother spoke hesitantly. 'Perhaps, if it could be shown that the girl has sinned, committed some crime.'

It was all that Sister Haka needed, ruthlessly she took charge. 'Send for the girl,' she instructed. 'Let us question her.'

Aina helped Tanith into the chamber, both of them hobbling and doubled over, one with age and the other with pain. They clung to each other, and the ancient priestess was mumbling encouragement to the injured girl, but her face screwed up with anger when she saw the Council, and she screeched at them.

'The child is hurt. Have you no care? Why do you summon her thus?'

'Silence, old hag,' Sister Haka spoke without passion. She was looking at Tanith. Tanith's face was swollen and the bruises were purplish and livid. Her one eye was closed, the lid puffed and blue, and her lip was cut through and scabbed.

'Let her sit,' Aina demanded. 'She is weak, and sick.'

'Nobody sits before the Council,' said Sister Haka.

'In the name of the goddess.'

'Do not blaspheme here, old crow.'

'I speak not of blasphemy, but of ordinary mercy.'

'You talk too much,' Sister Haka warned her. 'Go! Leave the girl here.'

It seemed Aina might argue still, but Sister Haka rose to her feet and her face was furious and her voice harsh with anger.

'Go!' she repeated, and Aina shuffled out grumbling and whining, leaving Tanith swaying weakly on her feet before the Council. Sister Haka sank down onto her stool and looked at Tanith. She would take her time now, there was all day if she needed it, and besides she was enjoying herself.

Tanith stayed upright by an effort of her will alone, for her senses swam and floated on waves and washes of pain. The leaden feeling in her legs and lower belly anchored her, but she could make little of the questions with which they pelted her. Sister Haka was leading her onto what it was that she had told the king to infuriate him, she was showing how Tanith had endangered the sisterhood by antagonizing him. She kept coming back to the question, 'What was it you told him?'

'I cannot remember, Sister. I cannot remember,' Tanith whispered.

'You want us to believe that words of such dire consequence can be so easily forgotten. Come, child, what were they?'

'They were not my words.'

'Whose then?' Sister Haka leaned forward attentively, her face blotched with brown speckles of the pox and the wings of grey glowing in her dark hair. 'Whose words were they if not your own? The goddess's?'

'I do not know,' breathed Tanith, and then she gasped as a fist of agony squeezed something within her lower belly.

'Do you speak with the voice of the goddess?' Sister Haka demanded in her hoarse voice, dark and cruel as a bird of prey. The hawk stooping on the sparrow.

'Oh please!' whispered Tanith, bowing slowly forward with both hands pressed to her stomach. 'Oh please, it hurts. Oh, how it hurts!'

The three priestesses watching her saw the quick flood of liquid which drenched the front of Tanith's tunic skirts, and splattered in dark red drops upon the flag stones between her feet. With slow grace Tanith folded and fell forward. She lay on her side with her knees drawn up and she moaned softly.

Sister Haka went quickly to her and stooped over her, drawing up Tanith's skirts and peering with tense lesbian interest as she pulled Tanith's knees roughly apart.

She was smiling as she straightened, and looked at the other two. 'There is your sin, Holy Mother. There is your proof of crime.' She looked down at the huddled body at her feet. 'Sacrilege!' she accused harshly. 'Sacrilege! A crime against the goddess.'

'I will not answer,' said Tanith gently. The bruises had faded and the swelling abated a little, but there was still a plum-coloured smear under one eye and her lip was distorted and scarred. She had been bed-ridden for ten days and she was still weak. 'I will not tarnish something so dear to me with words. I will not tell you his name.'

'Child, you know this is a matter of mortal sin. Your life is at stake here,' said the Reverend Mother.

'You have taken life from me already. Have done then. Take it all.' Tanith looked directly at Sister Haka, and from her to Lannon Hycanus who stood by the casement of the chamber. 'It is your intention to kill me. Nothing I say will alter that. Very well then, I will cherish the name of my child's father. I shall not let you use this against him also.'

'You are being stupid and stubborn,' said Sister Haka. 'We will find out in the end.'

'Why is it important?' Tanith asked. 'All that matters is that I stand between you and your ambitions.' Tanith looked directly at Sister Haka, and saw her words had struck by the swarthy rose flushing of the priestess's scarred cheeks. Tanith smiled and turned to Lannon. 'All that matters is that I am the source of the prophecy. You seek to destroy that. You seek to have the gods revoke their sentence upon you. It is vain, Lannon Hycanus. The winds of destiny are blowing, the hounds of fate are already hunting.'

'Enough,' snapped Lannon, striding to the centre of the chamber. 'I have no more time to waste. No longer can I listen to your idiot chatter.' He looked at Sister Haka. 'Bring the old priestess, the witch's chaperone.'

When Aina stood blinking and bewildered before the king he looked at her without passion or anger. 'You had duties. You did not discharge them. Name the bull who mounted the goddess's heifer.'

Aina wailed protest, disclaimer, pleading her ignorance. She went down on creaking knees before Lannon, crawling to him, kissing the hem of his tunic, drooling with terror. Lannon pushed her away irritably with one foot and looked at Sister Haka.

'Unless I misjudge your worth, you will not shirk man's work. Have you the belly for it?' he asked, and Sister Haka nodded, licking her lips, her eyes lighting with cruel anticipation.

'Break her arms first,' commanded Lannon. 'And let the witch stand close by to watch it.'

Sister Haka pulled Aina to her feet, holding her easily with her strong brown hands on the back of which grew long silky black hairs. Aina flapped and squawked with terror, and Sister Haka turned and pinned her, twisting one arm backwards against the elbow joint. The arm was thin and white with thick blue cords of vein showing through the skin.

'Wait!' cried Tanith. 'Let her go!'

'Release her,' ordered Lannon.

Tanith went to the old priestess and kissed her gently on the forehead and cheek. Aina was sobbing.

'Forgive me, child. I am sorry. I would have told them. Forgive me.'

'Gently, old mother. Gently now.' Tanith led her to the doorway and pushed her tenderly out of the chamber. She went back to them and spoke to the king.

'I will tell you his name – but you alone.'

'Leave us,' commanded Lannon, and the Divine Council rose and filed from the chamber.

When they were alone Tanith said the name, proudly and defiantly, and she saw Lannon reel as though it had been a physical blow.

'How long has he been your lover?' he asked at last.

'Five years,' she answered.

'So,' he said, seeing the answer to many questions. 'It seems we shared his love then.'

'Nay, Majesty.' Tanith shook her head. 'I had all of it.'

'You are wise to speak of it as past,' Lannon told her. He turned away to stand by the casement, and looked out across the lake. Nothing must come between us, he thought, I need him. I need him.

'What will it be, Majesty? Poison or the secret dagger? How will you kill a priestess of Astarte? Have you forgotten that I belong to the goddess?'

'No,' said Lannon. 'I have not forgotten, and I will send you to her, on the tenth day of the Festival of the Fruitful Earth. You will go as the messenger of Opet to the Gods.'

'Huy will not allow it,' whispered Tanith in horror.

'Huy is in the north – a long way from the pool of Astarte.'

'He will hate you for it, always. You will lose him for ever,' Tanith warned him, but he shook his head.

'He will never know that I ordered it so. He will never know that you betrayed him, and told me his name.' He smiled then, a cold and golden smile. 'No, it is you that will lose him, and I that will have him. You see, I need him, and my need is more important than yours.'

He had been borne in a litter at first, while he was unconscious and then later when he was still too weak to march, so he did not know for how long and in what direction they had travelled.

Even later when he was forced to walk, they bound and blind-folded him, so that he was aware only of the press of their bodies about him and the stench of sweat and the rancid fat with which they smeared their skin. There was no answer when he spoke, and rough hands urged him forward, and a spear blade pricked him when he baulked.

He had been badly beaten and bruised, there were still lumps and gashes in his scalp, and his body was grazed and painfully wrenched, but he had taken no serious wounds, no deep spear-thrust nor broken bones. It was as though they had carefully avoided dealing him a killing or crippling injury despite the fact that he had piled the corpses of their comrades in wind-rows about him, the vulture axe taking cruel toll before they overwhelmed him.

On the first night when they camped he began a tentative investigation of his position with escape in mind, but then when he tried to shift his blindfold enough to see out, a heavy blow in the face dissuaded him. They fed him a handful of boiled corn and a strip of badly cured meat, gamey and rank with bacon beetle. Huy ate it hungrily.

In the morning they were marching before the dawn, and when Huy felt the sun's warmth on his cheek and saw the light through his blindfold, he repeated the praise of Baal silently and asked the god for his help.

Later that day he was aware of the ground levelling beneath his feet as though they journeyed across an open plain, and there was the smell of cow dung and smoke and humanity. Over the thudding rhythm of his escorts' bare feet and the swish of their war-kilts he heard a vast susurration of voices and movement. Blending with this was the lowing of many cattle, the air quivered with sound and movement, a hive murmur which warned him of the presence of a great multitude.

At last they stopped him. He stood weary and thirsty in the hot sun with the raw-hide rope cutting into his wrists and his bruises and grazes aching. Time passed slowly in the silence of waiting men.

At last a voice called out loudly, and Huy's nerves jumped. The voice was in Vendi demanding, 'Who seeks the lion-clawed, who seeks the bird-footed?'

Huy remained silent, waiting for some indication of how to behave, and to his surprise he felt the cool touch of iron at his wrists and a blade sawed through his bonds. He rubbed his fingers, wincing at the flow of blood. Then he lifted his hands to the blindfold, expecting another blow, but none came and he loosed the cloth and blinked uncertainly in the bright sunlight.

His eyes adjusted quickly, and he felt his heart lurch with shock at what he saw. Huy stood at the centre of a wide plain, a slightly concave bowl of land rimmed in with low hills.

Except for a circular open area a hundred paces across, at the centre of which Huy now stood, the land was black with warriors. Huy gazed in awe at this multitude, and he could not begin to reckon their numbers. He would never have believed that the land could support such numbers, it was unreal, completely nightmarish – and the quality of unreality was heightened by the menacing stillness of the black hordes. Only the feathers of their head-dresses stirred in the sluggish wash of heated noonday air.

The heat and the press of humanity threatened to suffocate him, and he looked about him desperately as though seeking an avenue of escape. Storch stood near him, and he carried the vulture axe on his shoulder. Huy felt a weak flutter of anger for the man's treachery, but somehow it seemed unimportant in the enormity of this fresh experience.

Storch was not looking at him, instead he was watching a group of Vendi war captains who stood about a low mound of earth at the end of the clearing. The mound was bare, but compelled the attention of them all, like an empty stage before the principals appear.

Again the voice demanded. 'Who seeks the Great Black Beast, who hunts the lion?'

The heated silence and stillness persisted, then suddenly the multitude stirred and sighed as a man stepped up onto the mound.

The tall crown of heron feathers on his head and the height of the mound upon which he stood made him god-like. His robes of leopard skin hung to the ground about him, and he stood as still as a tall tree in a rustling plain of grass as the royal salute shook the foundations of earth and sky.

Storch carried the vulture axe to the mound and laid it at the king's feet, then he backed away, and the king looked across the open ground at Huy.

Huy drew himself up, trying to ignore the aches of his body, trying not to limp as he approached the mound and looked up at Manatassi.

'I should have guessed,' he said in Punic.

'You should have killed me,' said Manatassi, and from the folds of his robes he lifted the iron claw. 'Instead of arming me with this.'

'You do not understand,' Huy said. 'Your life was not mine to take. I made an oath.'

'Still a man who lives on his word,' Manatassi said, yet Huy looked in vain for the traces of mockery in his voice.

'There is no other way to live.' Huy felt tired now, he faced his certain death with resignation. He did not really have the energy to debate it.

Manatassi made a gesture with the claw, indicating the massed ranks of his army.

'You see what a spear I have forged?'

'Yes,' Huy nodded.

'Who can stand against me?' Manatassi asked.

'Many will try,' said Huy.

'You amongst them?'

And Huy smiled. 'I do not think I will have the chance to do so.'

Manatassi looked down at the little hunchback in his tattered tunic, his beard matted and the bruises on his face and arms, soiled and beaten, but not humble as he discussed his own fate.

'Not one of my men understands us,' Manatassi told Huy. 'We can speak freely.'

Huy nodded, puzzled, but interested in this change of mood.

'I offer you life, Huy Ben-Amon. Come to me, give me the love and duty you have given to the Gry-Lion of Opet and you will live to be an old man.'

'Why do you choose me?' Huy asked.

'I have waited for you. I knew you would come. My spies have watched for you, but it was fate that delivered you so neatly into my hands.'

'Why me?' Huy repeated.

'I need you,' Manatassi said simply. 'I need your learning, I need your understanding, and your humanity.'

'You forgive me the taking of your hand?' Huy asked.

'You could have taken my life,' Manatassi answered.

'You forgive the slave lash and the mines of Hulya?'

'Those I will never forgive,' Manatassi snarled, his face twitching and the eyes glaring smoky yellow. 'But they were not your doing.'

'You forgive the massacre at Sett?' Huy persisted.

'You are a soldier, you could do nothing else.'

Manatassi was still trembling, and Huy sensed how narrowly he skirted the abyss, but he felt compelled to explore this man's strength – and weakness.

'What would you have of me, then?' Huy asked.

'March beside me,' said Manatassi.

'Against?'

'Against Opet and its monstrous cruelties and terrible gods,' Manatassi urged him. 'With you beside me and this army at my back I will rule the world.'

'I cannot do that,' Huy shook his head.

'Why not? Tell me why. It is evil, it must be destroyed.'

'It is mine,' said Huy. 'My land, my people, my gods – therefore they cannot be evil.'

'I thought you were a man of reason,' Manatassi snarled.

'Reason can carry a man just so far, and then he must trust to his heart,' said Huy.

'You refuse me, then?'

'Yes.'

'You know that you choose death?'

'Yes.'

Manatassi raised his hand, the iron claw glowing in the sunlight, and Huy knew that when the hand fell he would die. He steeled himself to meet it as calmly as he had dealt it.

Manatassi turned away. Then after a moment he sighed, and his shoulders beneath the thick scars heaved.

'You spared me,' said Manatassi. 'I shall spare you.'

Huy felt weak with relief. He had not wanted to die, and he allowed himself at last to think of Tanith and the child. Now he would still see his son, and his heart soared.

'Go back to Opet. Go back to your king. Tell him that Manatassi, the Great Black Beast, marches out of the north to destroy him.'

'Should you warn an enemy?' Huy asked. 'Did I teach you that?'

Manatassi smiled. 'A warning will not help him,' he said. 'Tell him what you saw here. Tell him of this army – and let it chill his guts. Tell him I come for him, and I will spare none nor leave a memory of him to taint this land. Tell him I come, and I come swiftly.'

Manatassi picked up the vulture axe and handed it to Huy.

'Go!' he said. 'All debts between us have been paid. You have no call on me, and I have no call upon you. When I meet you again I shall kill you.'

They stared at each other, standing close enough to touch, but separated by a distance wider than the span of the oceans or the vastness of the land.

Huy turned and limped away down the corridor of warriors that opened for him, and no man barred his way.

'Old mother, you must not distress yourself so,' Tanith whispered. 'It was not your fault.'

'I would have told them,' Aina mumbled. 'I know I would have told them. That Sister Haka, she terrifies me.'

'You did not tell,' Tanith comforted her. 'You kept our secret well – even we ourselves did not know you had found out.'

Aina set down the food bowl beside Tanith's bed, and she smiled reflectively. 'You were so happy, the two of you. It made me feel good just to see you. He is a good person, despite his poor crooked back, he is gentle and kind.'

Tanith moved across on the couch, making room for Aina to sit. 'Sit by me for a while, old mother. I am so lonely here, it makes the waiting so much harder.'

Aina glanced fearfully across the narrow chamber at the barred doorway.

'They do not like me to stay too long.'

'Please,' Tanith entreated. 'There is so little time left.' And Aina nodded and gathered up her skirts to sit, creaking at her knee-joints, upon the coach. Tanith leaned close to her, and she whispered eagerly, 'Did you send messengers, did you find someone to go?'

'I sent two young ensigns from Legion Ben-Amon. They worship the Holy Father as though he were himself a god. I told them that you were in mortal danger, and that the Holy Father must return with all speed.'

'Do you think they will find him?'

'There are a hundred roads that he might take, and the land is wide. I would not lie to you, my child. The chance is not good.'

'I know,' said Tanith. 'And if they find him, can he return in time, and if he does, is there aught he can do to dissuade the Gry-Lion?'

'If he returns in time, then you are safe. I know the man.'

'Wait for him, Aina. If he returns, go to him secretly and tell him that the king knows about us. You must warn him of that, for he is also in danger.'

'I will warn him,' promised Aina.

'Oh, I pray to all the gods that he returns swiftly to Opet. I do not want to die, old mother. There is so much I would yet have from life, but the days run out now. It is already the sixth day of the Festival. Unless Huy comes there are but four days of my life left.'

'Gently, child,' Aina crooned and put an arm about Tanith to pat and cuddle her. 'Be brave,' she crooned, 'be brave, child.'

'It is not so easy,' Tanith told her, 'but I will try.' And she pulled away from Aina's embrace and sat up straight. 'You must go now, old mother – or Haka will beat you again.'

On the walls of the fortress at Zanat, south of the great river, a sentry held a javelin lightly in his right hand, concealing it below the level of the parapet, and he looked down on the strange wild figure below him. The man's hair was filthy and matted, he wore no armour, his tunic hung in tatters, and his face was bruised and badly swollen. He seemed to be wounded for he was doubled up painfully in an unnatural posture, bowed beneath the weight of the huge battle-axe he carried.

'What is your name, and what your business?' the sentry hailed, and the traveller looked up at him.

'I am Ben-Amon, High Priest of Baal and warrior of Opet. My business is the king's.'

The sentry started, and thrust the javelin back into its rack. He realized how close he had come to making a fool of himself. The crooked back and the axe were famous throughout the four kingdoms, he should have recognized them immediately, and he berated himself as he ran down into the courtyard shouting for the officer of the guard, warning him of their distinguished caller.

Huy came in through the side gate the moment it swung open, and he cut short the military salutes with a curt, 'Enough of that nonsense.'

The officer of the guard was startled at having the legion's beloved ceremonial dismissed in such a cavalier fashion, and he smothered a grin. Coupled with his appearance and his beggar's garb this story would go to swell the body of legend that already existed about this remarkable little man.

Huy was striding past the hastily assembled guard, demanding of the officer as he passed, 'Where is the general? Is he here?'

'Yes, my lord – Holiness. He is in his quarters.'

'Praise to Baal!' Huy grunted with relief.

Huy wolfed a thick cut of cold meat folded between two corn cakes, and he washed it down with a bowl of red wine, speaking through and around each mouthful of food as he issued his orders.

Marmon's scribe dashed off each article, racing to keep up with the flow of Huy's words. Marmon sat on his stool in the corner, his head of silver hair shining like a summer thunder cloud and his handsome face anxious and worried.

He could hardly believe what he was hearing, yet he knew better than to doubt the word of Huy Ben-Amon. He realized that he was culpable, that he should have been the one to discover this deadly threat that had grown up so swiftly on their borders. Perhaps he had spent too much of his time dreaming over his ancient histories, perhaps he had grown old and feeble without realizing it. He wondered what retribution there would be from Huy Ben-Amon and the Gry-Lion of Opet. Neither of them were men who let failure pass unnoticed.

He listened as Huy issued the orders which would place every garrison and every unit on the alert, would mobilize every disbanded legion, would send messengers racing across the land carrying the scrolls that would place the entire empire on a war footing. Marmon wondered at the courage of a man who could make this battle decision alone, a decision for which he would have to answer to the king and the council of nobles. He might be held responsible for all the losses and damages that would arise when the entire industry and commerce of the nation were suspended. It was a decision upon which his own life might hang, as well as that of Opet.

As he watched Huy signing the orders he doubted that he would have had that much certainty of the rightness of his own actions. He knew he would have sent to Opet for orders, and probably have jeopardized whatever chance there was of survival. For, from what Huy had told him, it was a matter of survival. They were confronted by an enemy so vastly superior in numbers that success lay with the gods.

Huy was finished. He signed the last scroll and the fire went out in him. It was only then that Marmon realized that the man was exhausted. He staggered slightly, his whole body slumping and he seemed to shrivel in size under the burden of his weariness.

Marmon jumped up from his stool and went to him. Huy brushed off the helping arm and tried to gather his strength in hand again.

'I must leave for Opet,' he said, slurring like a drunkard and steadying himself against a corner of the table. 'What day is it, Marmon? I seem to have lost count of the days.'

'It is the seventh day of the Festival, Holiness.'

'The Festival?' Huy looked at him stupidly.

'The Fruitful Earth,' Marmon reminded him.

'Ah!' Huy nodded. 'I did not think it was that late. Have you a war-elephant to carry me to Opet?'

'Nay, Holiness,' Marmon told him regretfully. 'There are no elephant here.'

'Then I must march.' Huy resigned himself.

'You must rest first.'

'Yes,' Huy agreed. 'I must rest.' And he let Marmon lead him to the bed-chamber. As he fell across the coach he asked, 'How long will it take to reach Opet from here, Marmon?'

'If you move fast, six days. Five, if you fly.'

'I shall fly,' said Huy. 'Wake me at dusk.' And he fell asleep.

Looking down on the sleeping figure, Marmon felt the familiar stirring of his affections. He felt his admiration for the great heart of this little fighting man, felt envy for the thrust and drive which always carried him ahead of the pack, and he was glad that Huy Ben-Amon led them at a time of such crisis.

It was then he remembered the messenger from Opet, the young ensign of Legion Ben-Amon who had passed through the garrison the previous day carrying an urgent message for the High Priest. He debated with himself for a moment, then decided not to disturb Huy's rest. He would tell him when he woke at dusk.

At dusk Huy woke, ate a light meal and oiled his body. Twenty minutes later he ran out into the cool of evening through the garrison gate with fifteen legionaries as escort, and it was only after they had disappeared into the dark and silent forests of the south that Marmon again remembered the message that the young ensign had given him.

He thought to send a messenger after Huy, but he knew that no runner of his could hope to catch the priest after he had such a head start. The speed of Huy's long legs were part of the legend.

Marmon thought comfortably, 'He will be in Opet soon enough.' And he paced along the parapet until he reached the far side of the fortress. He stayed there until after darkness had fallen, staring into the turbulent north and wondering how soon they would come.

The Divine Council came to Tanith's cell on the morning of the ninth day of the Festival of the Fruitful Earth. They were led by the Reverend Mother, frail and uncertain, shifty-eyed with guilt.

'We have joyous news for you, my child,' she told Tanith, and Tanith sat up quickly on her couch – her heart leaping within her. The Gry-Lion had changed his mind perhaps.

'Oh, Reverend Mother!' she whispered, feeling the tears of relief at the back of her eyelids. She was still shaky and weak from the loss of the child, and it took little to make her weep now.

The Reverend Mother was gabbling on, not looking at Tanith, unable to meet her eyes, and for a while Tanith was puzzled. She could not understand this talk of precedent and ecclesiastical law, until she glanced at Sister Haka's face and saw how gloating and lustful were the dark features and how brightly the cruel eyes shone.

Then suddenly she realized that this was no reprieve.

'And so in his wisdom the king has chosen you, has given to you the great honour of carrying the message of Opet to the goddess.'

They had not come to release her, but to seal her fate. Sister Haka was smiling.

'You must give thanks, my child. The king has given you life eternal. You will live in glory at the side of the goddess, hers for ever,' said the Reverend Mother, and the priestesses chorused, 'Praise to Astarte. Praise to Baal.'

The Reverend Mother went on, 'You must prepare yourself. I will send Aina to help you. She knows the path of the messenger well, for she attended many of the chosen ones. Remember to pray, my child. Pray that the goddess will find you acceptable.'

Tanith stared at them, white-faced and afraid. She did not want to die. She wanted to cry out, 'Spare me. I am too young. I want just a little more happiness, just a little more love before I die.'

The Divine Council filed from the chamber, leaving her alone. Now at last the tears flooded her eyes, and she cried out aloud.

'Huy, come to me! Please, come to me.'

Huy struggled up through the glutinous dark swamp of exhausted sleep with the nightmare cry still echoing in his ears. It took him a while to remember where he was and to realize that he had dreamed the horror that had woken him.

He lay in the sparse shade of the wild fig, and through the branches he saw the altitude of the sun and knew that they had slept for only an hour. His legs still felt leaden, his body torpid and completely enervated by two days of hard travel.

He should sleep again for another three or four hours at the least, but the nighmare stayed with him, denying him rest.

He pulled himself up on an elbow, surprised at the effort it required, but then remembering that he had run over two hundred Roman miles in two days. He looked at the remains of his escort, three of them, haggard-faced and finely drawn from their exertions, sleeping like dead men in the attitudes in which they had fallen. The other twelve had dropped along the way, unable to match the blistering pace which Huy had set.

Huy heaved himself to his feet. He could not sleep, could not rest, while dread haunted him and the safety of his king and his land was in jeopardy.

He limped stiffly down to the bed of the small stream, and knelt in the sugary white sand. He splashed his face and body with the clear water, soaking his tunic and beard, then he climbed the bank and looked at his sleeping men. He felt pity for them, pity that did not prevent him calling out, 'Up! On your feet! We march for Opet.'

One of them could not wake, though Huy kicked his ribs and slapped his cheeks with an open hand. They left him lying, whimpering in his sleep.

The other two dragged themselves up, groaning, moving with stiff sore legs, and the glazed expressions of fatigue.

Huy walked the first half mile to loosen aching muscles, with the escort staggering after him.

Then he went up onto his toes, changed the vulture axe from one shoulder to the other, and went away at a run, bouncing long-legged on a springy stride that covered the ground like the trot of an eland bull.

One of the legionaries cried out as his leg collapsed under him and he went down sprawling in the dust. He was finished, and he lay there groaning with mortification and the pain of cramped and torn muscles.

The other followed Huy, his steps firming as his legs loosened and charged with new blood.

They ran the sun to its zenith, spurning the pitiless heat of the noonday, and they ran on into the afternoon.

Ahead of them, low on the horizon, stood the perpetual bank of cloud which marked the Lake of Opet, a beacon of hope, and Huy ran with his face lifted to it, instinct guiding his feet and his will feeding his exhausted body, allowing him to run on when all physical strength was burned up.

In the last low rays of the sun the walls and towers of Opet glowed with a warm rose colour and the surface of the lake was flaming gold that pained the eye.

Huy plunged on down the caravan road, racing past other dusty travellers who pulled to the side of the track, calling after him as they recognized him.

'Pray for us, Holy Father.'

'Baal's blessing on you, Holiness.'

Half-way down the pass of the cliffs that led to the lake shore and the city, the legionary who followed Huy shouted in a clear strong voice, 'Forgive me, Holy Father, I can go no further.' And his knees buckled under him, he lost direction, blundering to the side of the track; his face contorted at the agony of his bursting heart, he went down face first and lay without movement, dead before he struck the ground.

Huy Ben-Amon ran on alone, and the guard upon the palace gate of Opet saw him afar off, and they swung the gates open to welcome him.

Tanith woke with gentle hands shaking her. There was a lamp burning beside her couch, and Aina leaned over her. Tanith saw that the old face was screwed up into a toothless grin, the monkey eyes twinkling in their web of ancient wrinkles.

'Child, are you awake?'

'What is it, Aina?' Tanith sat up quickly, her spirits leaping upwards like sparks from the bonfire of hope when she saw Aina's smile.

'He has come!' Aina told her jubilantly.

'Huy?'

'Yes, the Holy Father has come.'

'Are you sure?' Tanith demanded.

'I have heard it shouted in the streets. The whole city is agog. They say he ran from Zanat to Opet in three days, they say he killed fifteen men who tried to run with him. He broke their hearts and left them lying on the road.'

'Oh, Aina.' Tanith embraced the old priestess, hugging her to her breast. 'If he came so fast, it must be because he knows.'

'Yes, child. Of course he knows. Why else would he come with such speed? One of the ensigns would have reached him with my message. He knows all right.' Aina drooled and nodded her convictions. 'He knows!'

'Where is he now?' Tanith was laughing with her excitement. 'Do you know where he is?'

'With the king. He went straight to the palace.'

'Oh, praise the goddess and all the gods,' breathed Tanith. 'He has gone to use his influence with the Gry-Lion. Do you think he will succeed, Aina? Will the king change his mind?'

'Of course, child. Do you doubt it? If Huy Ben-Amon set his mind to it, he would make Baal himself change his mind.'

'Oh, I am so happy, old mother.' Tanith clung to Aina, and they comforted each other in the night. Until at last Tanith drew away.

'Go to him, Aina. Wait for him outside the palace. Tell him everything, and come back to me with his message.'

As Aina was about to leave the chamber Tanith called after her, 'Tell him I love him. Tell him I love him better than life – and all the gods.'

'Hush,' said Aina, 'hush, child. Someone may hear you.'

Alone, Tanith lay back on her couch and smiled.

'I don't care,' she whispered. 'Huy is here, and nothing else matters.'

Lannon listened to Huy in rising consternation. His first thought when Huy had arrived unheralded and unexpected in the night was that he had somehow learned of the sacrifice at tomorrow's ceremony. He had considered refusing Huy an audience, considered all manner of evasion, but while he was considering it Huy had barged his way into Lannon's bed-chamber past the startled and protesting guards.

Lannon had risen naked from the side of his youngest wife, angry words shrivelled on his lips when he saw the state to which Huy was reduced.

'Forgive me, Majesty. I carry dreadful tidings.'

Lannon stared at him, saw the filthy and dusty tunic, the unkempt hair and beard, the skull-like face from which the flesh had wasted, and the wild eyes in their bruised and sunken sockets.

'What is it, Huy?' He went quickly to the priest, and steadied him with a brotherly arm.

The Council of Nine, all the noble families of Opet, met in night session and they heard the report of Huy Ben-Amon in horrified silence. Only when he had croaked out the last of it and slumped wearily on his stool did the babble of fault-finding, and blame-laying, and self-pity and doubt begin.

'We were told he was destroyed at Sett!'

Huy said, 'You were told only that I slew 30,000 at Sett. I did not name them.'

'How could such an army be recruited without our knowledge? Who is to blame?'

Huy answered, 'It was recruited beyond our borders. No one is to blame.'

'What of the mines – we must protect them.'

Huy smiled wearily. 'That is what we intend.'

'Why is there only one legion on the border?'

Huy answered them grimly, 'Because you refused to vote the money for more.'

They turned on him then, their words hammering through the fog of weariness.

'How did you pass unscathed through the enemy lines?'

'Was not this Timon once your protégé?'

'You know him well, you taught him, did you not?' And Huy looked at Lannon.

'Enough!' Lannon's voice cut through the tirade. 'His Holiness has called the nation to war. He has shown me copies of the scrolls, and I am about to sign them in ratification.'

'Should we not wait a while?' That was Philo, naturally, 'Are we not being too hasty?'

'What will you wait for?' Huy demanded. 'Until they open your bowels with a spear blade and cut off your testicles?'

Lannon signed the war orders a little before dawn, and he dismissed the Council of Nine with the words:

'We will meet again at noon, after the final ceremony of the Fruitful Earth. See to your arms and take leave of your families.'

To Huy he spoke kindly when they were alone. 'Sleep here. There is nothing more you can do now.'

He was too late. Huy was already asleep, slumped forward on the table with his head on his arms. Lannon picked him up from his stool, and carried him like a sleeping child to a guest chamber.

He placed a sentry at the door.

'No one must wake the Holy Father,' he instructed. 'No one! Do you understand.'

It was almost dawn. The sacrifice would take place in a very few hours, and he knew that Huy was in a kind of death sleep that might last for many days. He left him, and went to bathe and dress for the procession.

Aina lifted the hood of her cloak over her head, covering her face. She thrust her bony old hands into the wide sleeves, and leaned forward to blow out the lamp.

She stood in the darkness, considering what she must do. She would not wait for the High Priest to leave the palace. Aina had access to the palace kitchens. The major domo there was the grandson of her youngest sister, and she often went to eat there as a change from the temple fare. All the palace slaves knew her. It would be a simple matter to find out from one of them whereabouts in the rambling mud-walled building the High Priest was, and even simpler matter to get word to him.

Quietly she drew the curtains of her cell aside, and peered out. There was a single torch guttering in its bracket at the end of the passage, but it threw only a feeble light and Aina did not see the dark figure waiting for her in a shadowy angle of the corridor until it came gliding towards her.

'Not yet asleep, old woman?' a deep, almost masculine voice asked softly, and a strong hand closed on Aina's wrist.

'Are you going visiting so late at night? Is it that you have heard of Huy Ben-Amon's return to Opet?'

'No,' whimpered Aina. 'I swear it.' And she struggled feebly. With her free hand Sister Haka pushed the old priestess's hood back from her face and peered into her eyes.

'You were going to Ben-Amon, were you not?'

'No. I swear it.' Aina saw death in Sister Haka's expression, and she began to scream. It was a thin passionless sound like the sound of the wind, and it was cut off abruptly as Sister Haka's powerful hand whipped over her mouth.

From a doorway opposite a frightened face peered out, and Sister Haka snapped, 'Go back to your couch.' And the young novice obeyed quickly.

Sister Haka forced Aina's frail body back through the curtains and onto her couch. She held her hand over mouth and nostrils, holding Aina down with an arm across her chest.

Aina's struggles exploded feverishly, her heels drummed and kicked against the wall and her arms flapped and clawed at Sister Haka's face. Then swiftly it was over and she subsided and lay still. Sister Haka held her mouth and nostrils closed for a long time after she was quiet, then with one hand she felt the scrawny old chest with its empty pendulant dugs for a heart beat.

Finding none she nodded with satisfaction, arranged the careless limbs tidily, and left the cell. Through the single window slit the first light of dawn lit Aina's face. Her mouth hung open, her eyes were startled and a wisp of silky silver hair floated on her forehead.

Lannon was conscious of the need to carry through the final ritual of the Festival meticulously. It was apparent that he faced a national emergency of vast proportions, that Opet was opposed by an enemy more powerful and relentless than any in her long history. The oracle had spoken against him, perhaps he or his kingdom had incurred the wrath of the gods.

Lannon knew that the fate of nations hangs not entirely on the actions of men, battles are not won by swords alone. He knew there were influences beyond, sometimes malignant and sometimes benign, which dictated the outcome of earthly affairs. He knew it was possible to placate an angry god, and to enlist the goodwill of one that was kindly disposed.

As the Reverend Mother led him through the catechism beside the pool of Astarte, he paid special concern to the correctness of his responses, and there was no mistaking the sincerity of his voice as he made his pledge to the goddess.

The priestesses closed in about him and light hands helped him shed his robes of purple silk. Currents of cool air stroked his naked body as he strode forward to the edge of the pool, went down the stone steps and lowered himself into the clear green waters.

His body shone white below the surface, and his long golden tresses and beard glistened with water as the priestesses beside him scooped up water in the conch shells and poured it over his head.

They emerged from the pool, and Lannon felt a sense of spiritual cleansing, as though the sacred waters had washed away his cares and armed him against the dangers that lay ahead. He was not a man of deep religious faith, and yet in this moment he felt uplifted. He was happy then that he had chosen such an important messenger for the goddess.

His own petty and personal motives no longer counted. He was sending a priestess of the blood, a god-touched oracle, a person of value and weight. Surely the goddess must find her acceptable, surely Astarte would now turn her countenance upon the children of Opet, spread her wings across the nation in this time of trial and danger.

They dried off his skin, and the muscle was firm and beautifully shaped in leg and arm and wide shoulders. Two priestesses came forward and lifted a white silk robe over his head, and the colour of joy and rejoicing. The Reverend Mother placed a garland of flowers about his neck, crimson cave lilies whose scent was sweet and heavy in the hushed cavern.

It was the moment when the praise of the goddess must be sung, and then the offertory. The silence persisted a moment longer and then a voice rang through the cavern.

The voice startled Lannon, and he turned his head searching for the singer. There was no mistaking that voice, the sweet shimmering power of it, the depth and timbre that made the hair on Lannon's forearms come erect and set the echoes flying about the temple, seeming almost to ruffle the quiet surface of the green pool.

Lannon gaped at Huy. He had stepped out of the ranks of nobles and officers and as he sang he paced slowly towards Lannon. His arms spread in the sun sign, his mouth wide open showing the strong white teeth and that achingly beautiful voice pouring from his throat. The praise song ended, and Huy stood close beside the king looking up at him. His face was still raddled with fatigue, the dark eyes still under-scored by bluish purple smears, the skin pale and drawn, but he was smiling at Lannon with an expression of loyal affection.

'Huy!' Lannon whispered in horror. 'Why are you here? I left you resting with orders not to disturb you.'

'At this time my place was with you.'

'You should not have come,' Lannon protested. This was beyond his planning. It was not part of it that Huy should witness the death of the witch. He had not intended torturing him with the deed. Wildly Lannon considered halting the ritual, withdrawing the sacrifice, ordering Huy to leave the temple.

Yet Lannon realized that the safety of the empire might be resolved in these next few moments. Could he halt the sacrifice, dare he risk antagonizing the goddess, was his duty to Huy greater than his duty to Opet, was it not already too late, had he not committed himself long ago to this path? Were the gods and demons mocking him now, could he not hear their hellish laughter echoing in the deserts of his soul?

Bewildered and appalled he stared at Huy, he took a step towards him, reaching out one hand in entreaty as though asking for understanding and forgiveness.

'I need you,' he said hoarsely, and Huy, not understanding, took the hand, thinking it the hand of friendship; proudly he smiled at his king and friend as he began to sing the offertory to the goddess.

His voice rose on eagle's wings, flying up to the sacrificial platform in the roof of the cavern high above them. All the eyes in the temple turned upwards also and a tense expectant hush gripped the throng of worshippers.

Tanith could not believe it was happening to her. When they had come to her cell in the dawn she thought it must be Huy come to fetch her away. She had leapt from her couch and run to meet him.

It was not Huy but Sister Haka. They had taken her from the temple up the secret steps to the top of the cliffs above Opet. There is a stone building with a roof of thatched beside the sacrificial platform over the gaping hole above the pool of Astarte, they had dressed her in the rich embroidered robes of the sacrifice and put flowers in her hair.

Then they had draped her with the heavy gold chains, and bracelets, and leg bangles until Tanith felt she must collapse beneath the weight of them. She knew that this treasure formed part of the sacrifice, and that it was also intended to weigh her down swiftly into the green depths of the pool. The pool which had no bottom to it, the pool which would carry her to the bosom of the goddess.

Solemnly and in silence she was seated at the small banquet table and her sister priestesses waited upon her, pressing her with choice foods and wines. It was the feast of farewell, the feast to someone who goes upon a journey. Tanith sipped a little of the wine, hoping that it might warm her icy spirit.

'Huy' she thought. 'Where are you, my love?'

At last a priestess came to the door and nodded to the others. There were fifteen of them, all strong young women, more than enough of them to overwhelm any resistance.

They closed in about where Tanith sat, not yet menacing but utterly determined. They looked down on her expressionlessly, their faces closed against pity or regret.

'Come,' said one of them, and Tanith stood up. They led her through the doorway into the sunlight, and ahead of her she saw the carved stone platform jutting out over the dark and gaping hole in the earth.

The path to the sacrificial platform was strewn with blossoms of the yellow mimosa tree, a flower sacred to the goddess. The scent was light and nostalgic on the warm still air, and the blossoms crushed beneath Tanith's bare feet as she passed over them weighted down by her chains of gold, and the heaviness of her dread.

Suddenly she stopped, frozen at the sound of the voice issuing from the pit before her, a voice faint with distance and echoing strangely from the cavern walls; but the voice of such purity and beauty that she could not help but recognize it.

'Huy!' she whispered. 'My lord!' But the upwards flight of her spirits was short-lived, for the voice of Huy Ben-Amon was uplifted in the offertory of the sacrifice.

It was Huy who was sending her to the goddess, and in that moment a vision of hell and desolation opened before her. She found herself caught in the web of some monstrous conspiracy, not understanding it clearly, knowing only that Huy had deserted her. He was against her also. He was the one offering her to the goddess.

There was nothing to live for now. It was easy to take those last few steps up onto the platform.

As she paused on the brink she spread her arms in the sun sign and looked down into the gloom of the cavern. The waters of the pool were still and dark, and beside them stood the king and the priest.

They were looking up at her, but it was too far for her to judge their expressions. All she knew was that Huy's voice was still raised in prayer, offering her to the goddess.

She felt hatred and anger replacing desolation, and she did not want to die with those emotions in her heart. To forestall them she swayed forward over the drop, over the deep green pool, and as she felt her balance go Huy's voice stopped abruptly, cut off in the middle of a word.

Slowly she leaned out over the drop, and then suddenly she was in air, plunging downwards, hurtling towards the pool by the weight of gold she carried. As her stomach swooped within her she heard Huy's voice again, raised in a shriek of despair as he called her name.

'Tanith!'

She struck the surface of the pool with such force that all life was crushed from her, and the heavy ornaments plucked her beneath the limpid waters so swiftly that Huy saw only the brief gleam of gold deep down as though a great fish had turned upon its side to feed.

Manatassi crossed the great river in the winter of the Opet year 543. He used the cooler weather to carry his armies through the valley where the water was at its lowest levels. He crossed with three armies of varying sizes. The smallest, a mere 70,000 warriors, crossed in the west and overwhelmed the garrisons there. They drove swiftly for the western shores of the lake of Opet where the narrow waterway drained the lake and gave access to the ocean for the galleys of Opet. It was called the River of Life, the artery that fed the heart of Opet.

Manatassi's impis severed the artery, freed the slaves employed at dredging the channel and slaughtered the garrison and slave-masters. Most of Habbakuk Lal's fleet was drawn up on the beach, careened for cleansing of the hulls. The galleys were burned where they lay and the sailors thrown alive on the fires.

Then Manatassi's war captain blocked the channel. His warriors, and the tens of thousands of freed slaves tore down a small granite hill which stood beside the River of Life, and dumped it into the narrowest stretch of the river, rendering it impassable to any vessel larger than a canoe. This was a labour comparable with the construction of the great pyramid of Cheops, and it effectively sealed off the city and population of Opet from the outside world.

At the same time a second larger army crossed in the east, swept unhindered through the territory of the Dravs and burst like a black storm on the hills of Zeng.

The third and largest army, nearly three quarters of a million strong, surged across the river at Sett. Manatassi commanded them in person and he chose the crossing place as a gesture.

Marmon hurried to oppose him with his single legion of 6,000 men and was crushed in a swift and bloody battle. Marmon fled the field and died on his own sword amidst the burning ruins of Zanat.

Manatassi placed his centre across the road to Opet and rolled along it. His front was three miles wide and twenty deep, a multitude whose own bulk reduced the march to a stately progress.

Manatassi swept the land. He took no prisoner, neither man nor woman nor child. He took no loot, burning cloth and book and leather, smashing pot and cup, throwing it all upon the funeral pyre of a nation. The buildings he burned, and then threw down and scattered the hot stone slabs.

As his hatred fed upon this destruction so it seemed to grow, like the very flames he lit, it burned higher the more was heaped upon it.

The total fighting strength of Opet was nine legions. Of these one had died with Marmon in the north, and two others were hacked to pieces upon the terraces of Zeng, the survivors holding out in a dozen besieged fortresses upon the crest of the hills.

With the remaining six legions Lannon Hycanus marched from Opet to meet Manatassi. They came together 150 miles north-east of Opet, and Lannon won a victory which gained him two miles of territory and one day's respite – but which cost him 4,000 dead and wounded.

Bakmor, who commanded Legion Ben-Amon in the absence of the High Priest, came to Lannon's tent upon the battlefield when the sky still glowed like a furnace from the cremation fires, and the stench of scorching flesh spoiled what little appetite for food that battle fatigue had left.

'The enemy left 48,000 dead upon the field,' Bakmor reported exultantly, and Lannon saw he was a young man no longer. How the years had sped away. 'We took twelve for each of ours,' Bakmor went on.

Lannon looked up at him, sitting on his couch while a physician dressed a minor wound in his arm, and he saw that dried sweat and blood had stiffened Bakmor's hair and beard and that there were new lines and shadows in the handsome face.

'How soon can you fight again?' Lannon asked, and the shadows around Bakmor's eyes deepened.

'It was a hard day,' he said. Legion Ben-Amon had held the centre firm during those desperate hours when it seemed the line must sunder at the pressure of black bodies and darting steel.

'How soon?' Lannon repeated.

'In four or five days,' Bakmor told him. 'My men are weary.'

'It will be sooner than that,' Lannon warned him.

They fought again the following day, a battle as desperate and as costly as the other. Again Lannon won a heavy victory, but he could not hold the field and he must leave over a thousand of his wounded to the hyena and jackal while he fell back to a new defensive line of hills.

They fought again five days later, and five times more in the next seventy days. At the end of that time they were encamped twenty Roman miles from Opet, and Lannon's six fine legions had shrunk to three.

It mattered not that they had won eight great battles, and that they had slain almost 200,000 of the enemy. For Zeng had fallen, only a handful of warriors winning through to describe its fate. The towns were burned and razed to the ground, the gardens cut down and burned also. The mines of the middle kingdom were destroyed, the slaves freed to join Manatassi's horde and the shafts blocked with earth and rock.

The channel of the River of Life was chocked with rock, there was no escape upon Habbakuk Lal's galleys now, and from east and west new armies marched to reinforce Manatassi's drive on Opet.

Despite the toll that Lannon had taken from the armies of Manatassi, they seemed unaffected in number or determination. Each time Lannon planted his standards and stood to dispute Manatassi's advance, fresh hordes poured forward to attack him. Though he cut them down by the tens of thousands, they bled his own legions and left them each time more exhausted and with despair more deeply corroding their fighting spirit.

On the seventy-first day one full legion, 6,000 men, stabbed their officers in the night and scattered away into the darkness in small groups. Stopping only to pick up their women from the villages around Opet, they disappeared into the south.

Bakmor pursued them a short distance and dragged a hundred of them back in chains to face Lannon's wrath. They were all men of mixed Yuye blood, one class above that of freed slave, the lowest type of citizen allowed the privilege of bearing arms for the king. It seemed they did not count the privilege dear. Made bold by the certainty of execution, their spokesman told the king:

'If you had given us something to fight for, some station above that of dog, we might have stayed with you.'

Lannon had the man scalded to death with boiling water for his insolence, and retired his two remaining legions on the city.

They camped upon the lake shore without the city wall and Lannon looked to the north in the night and saw the bivouac fires of Manatassi's army spread like a field of yellow Namaqua daisies upon the hills. Manatassi was pressing him hard.

Bakmor found the king on the outskirts of the camp, watching the enemy positions. He approached Lannon eagerly bearing the first good news they had received in many long days.

'There is word of Huy Ben-Amon, Majesty.' And Lannon felt a lift of his spirits.

'Where is he? Is he alive? Has he returned?' Lannon demanded. It was only now he admitted to himself how he had missed the little priest. He had not seen him since Huy had run out of the cavern of Astarte in the midst of the ceremony of the Fruitful Earth.

Although Lannon had conducted a diligent search, even offering a reward of 100 gold fingers for information about him, Huy had disappeared.

'Has he returned?' How many times in the long nights since then had Lannon longed for his companionship, his counsel and his comfort.

How often in the din of battle had he listened for Huy's cry 'For Baal!' and the song of the great axe.

How often had he wished that he could stiffen a crumbling centre or check a pivoting flank with the priest's presence.

'Where is he?' demanded Lannon.

'A fisherman saw him. He is out on the island,' said Bakmor.

The days had drifted past in a haze of grief. Huy had lost count of them, one slid so easily into the next. Most of the time he spent working on the scrolls. He had brought all five of the golden books with him and when he was not in the hut he kept them buried beneath his sleeping mat.

He wrote exclusively of Tanith, of his love for her and her death. In the beginning he worked through the nights as well as the days, but then he used up the last of the oil for the lamp and he spent his nights wandering along the beach and listening to the low surf hiss and growl upon the sands, and the wind across the lake rattle the palm fronds.

He lived on the fresh-water clams and a few fish that he took in the shallows, and he grew lean and unkempt; his beard and hair tangled and uncared for.

His grief showed in his eyes, making them wild and haunted, half mad and uncaring for anything but his own loss. Many of these hopeless days passed before anger and resentment began to work within him. From deep within him rose thoughts dark and dangerous as the shapes of killer sharks rising to the smell of blood.

Brooding over a smoky cooking fire he thought about his land and his gods. It seemed to him that both of them were cruel and greedy. A land devoted to the accumulation of wealth, counting not the toll in human suffering. Frivolous gods demanding the sacrifice, both of them greedy and devouring.

Huy left the fire and went down to the lake shore. He sat in the sand and the water ran up and tugged at his ankles before sliding back. The dark thoughts persisted, and mingled with them were the memories of Tanith.

He pondered the gods who would choose for the sacrifice the beloved of their faithful servant. What more did they demand of him, he wondered. He had given them everything he held dear, and still they wanted more.

How cruel that they should choose Lannon as the instrument to strip him of his love. He wished now that he could have told Lannon about Tanith. If Lannon had known of their love he would have protected her, Huy was sure of this. In the beginning he had hated Lannon, for it was he who had named Tanith as the sacrifice. Then reason had prevailed with Huy. He realized now that Lannon had acted in good faith. He had known nothing of Huy's and Tanith's relationship. He had known only that the nation was in dire danger and a valuable messenger was needed. Tanith was a natural choice then, reluctantly Huy saw that this was so, and knew that he would have done the same.

He no longer hated Lannon, but suddenly he found himself hating those who had forced him to it. The gods – the merciless gods.

Out of the lake great Baal rose in all his splendour of glittering gold and red, and across the waters he could see the rosy cliffs and towers of Opet glowing on the horizon.

From life-long habit Huy rose to his feet and spread his arms in the sun sign, and he opened his mouth to sing the praise of Baal.

Suddenly he was shaking with anger. He felt fiery gusts of it rising through his soul, setting his hatred alight, the funeral fire on which his faith perished.

'Damn you!' he shouted. 'What more do you want of me, you eater of flesh? How much longer must I be your plaything?'

Now his fists were clenched as he shook them in defiance at the rising sun, his face contorted and his tears streaming down into the wild bush of his beard. He walked forward into the lake.

'How much longer must I feed your cruel appetite, man-killer? How many more innocents before you quench your monstrous lust for blood?'

He dropped to his knees in the wet sand, and the running waters surged about his waist.

'I reject you!' he shouted. 'You and your bloodless mate. I want no more of you – I hate you. Do you hear me, I hate you!'

Then he fell silent, and bowed his head. The water surged softly about him and after a while he scooped handfuls of it and washed his face. Then he rose and walked back to the hut above the beach. He felt a sense of fateful release, the peace which follows an irrevocable decision. He was priest no longer.

He ate a piece of smoked fish and drank a bowl of lake water, before he began work on the scrolls.

Again he wrote of Tanith, trying to recall every tone of her voice, every smile and frown, the way she laughed, and the way she held her head – as though he could give her immortality in words, as though he could give her life for the next 1,000 years in words cut into a sheet of imperishable gold.

Once he looked up from the scroll with peering short-sighted eyes and saw that the day was passing, and the long shadows of the palms cast tiger-stripes upon the yellow sands of the beach. He stooped again to the scroll and worked on.

There was the crunch of a footstep in the sand outside the hut, and a dark shape blocked out the light.

Again Huy looked up, and Lannon Hycanus stood in the doorway.

'I need you,' he said.

Huy did not reply. He sat hunched over the scroll blinking up at Lannon.

'It was on this island that you promised me you would never desert me,' Lannon went on softly. 'Do you remember?'

Huy stared at him. He saw the deep lines of care and suffering cut into Lannon's flesh, the dark shadowed eye sockets in the gaunt face. He saw the greyish tone of the skin and the silver glint of old man's hair in the beard and at the temples.

He saw the wounds half healed, and freshly weeping through the linen bindings. He saw a man who was extended to the limits of his strength and determination, and in whose throat was the bitter taste of defeat.

'Yes,' said Huy. 'I remember.' He stood up and went to Lannon.

They came back to Opet in the early morning. All night they had sat together beside the fire in Huy's hut and they had talked.

Lannon told him of the course of the campaign, and the state of the nation. He told him of each battle, every strategy the enemy had employed.

'I had placed much reliance upon the war elephants. That trust was ill-founded. We lost most of them in the very first encounter. They used spears dipped in the poison taken from countless bees. I learned from a prisoner how they had smoked out hundreds of hives and laboriously squeezed out the poison sack from each sting. The burning pain of the wounds drove my elephants insane. They raged through our lines, and we had to use spikes on them.

'Also they had trained athletes who could vault on to the elephants' backs. They half leapt and were half thrown by their companions, flipped through the air like professional tumblers to kill the drivers and then stab the beast in the back of the neck.'

'I was to blame for that,' said Huy. 'I told him of those tactics that the Romans used against Hannibal's elephants. He has not forgotten a single word of my teaching.'

Lannon went on to tell Huy of each battle which, though victorious, left Opet weakened, of the slow retreat before the black hordes, of the mounting despair amongst the legions, of the desertions and mutinies, of the destruction of the greater part of the fleet upon the beaches and the blocking of the channel.

'How many ships remain?'

'Nine galleys,' Lannon replied, 'and an assortment of fishing craft.'

'Enough to carry all of us across the lake, to the southern shores?'

'No,' Lannon shook his head. 'Not nearly enough.'

They talked on through the night, and in the dark hour before the first glimmer of dawn Lannon asked the question that had hovered on his lips all evening. He knew Huy would expect it.

'Why did you desert me, Huy?' Lannon asked softly. If Huy were to believe that Lannon knew nothing of his relationship with the witch, if he were to believe that Lannon's choice of sacrifice was accidental, then Lannon must pretend ignorance.

Huy looked up at the question and the firelight lit his face from below, leaving his eyes as dark pits.

'You do not know?' he asked, watching Lannon intently.

'I know only that you called out the witch's name, and then you were gone.'

Huy went on studying Lannon's face in the firelight, searching for some sign of guilt, some flicker of deceit. There was none. Lannon's face was tired and strained, but the pale blue eyes were direct and steadfast.

'What was it, Huy?' he insisted. 'I have puzzled over it so often now. What drove you from the temple?'

'Tanith. I loved her,' said Huy, and Lannon's expression changed. He stared at Huy for long seconds, appalled and stricken.

'Oh, my friend, what have I done to you? I did not know, Huy, I did not know.'

Huy dropped his gaze to the fire, and he sighed.

'I believe you,' he said.

'Pray Baal's forgiveness for me, Huy,' whispered Lannon and leaned across to grip Huy's shoulder, 'that I should ever have given you grief.'

'No, Lannon,' Huy answered. 'I shall never pray again. I have lost my love, and denied my gods. Now I have nothing.'

'You still have me, old friend,' said Lannon, and Huy smiled shyly at him.

'Yes,' he agreed, 'I still have you.'

They carried the golden scrolls and the vulture axe down to the beach where Bakmor and the crew of the fishing-boat waited patiently, and they came to Opet in the early morning.

The legions cheered them, king and priest, as they moved through the encampment and Huy felt tears scalding his eyelids.

'I do not deserve it,' he whispered. 'I deserted them. I should have been with them.'

Although the two legions were reconstituted from the shattered remnants of the original nine, yet it seemed to Huy they were built around the foundation of Legion Ben-Amon. Everywhere he saw the familiar faces, grinning affectionately at him out of the ranks. He stopped to talk with them, trying to keep his tone cheerful as he noted the dented armour and the roughly bound wounds, half healing or suppurating.

He saw how exhausted they were, an exhaustion of the soul as well as the body. The smiles were short-blooming and the cheers were forced from reluctant throats – yet they were in hand, and there was fight left in them. They were lucky that none of the fevers that so often attended an encamped army had not yet weakened them further. It was strange how when they moved regularly, not staying at any one place long enough to foul the water supply or to allow their dung heaps to fester, then the fevers often did not appear.

There were 26,000 men encamped upon the lake shore, and they made a brave show. Huy felt small flames of confidence and hope warming his belly as he passed amongst them. Perhaps there was still something that could be done with this force.

Lannon and Huy ate the noon meal with their officers. There was no shortage of corn or meat or wine so close to the granaries of Opet, and they feasted and toasted each other while their men enjoyed the double wine ration that Lannon had ordered. In the afternoon Lannon allowed the wives into the camp. This was a privilege usually granted only after a great victory, not before a battle. They came streaming out of the city in their thousands, many of them wives for a day – to more than one husband.

'Let them enjoy it,' Lannon remarked with a little regret in his voice, as they strode through the camp with an escort of officers and picked legionaries. 'The gods know well that it may be the last time any of them do so.' Then his voice hardened. 'But see to it that none of the women remain after sundown.'

There was a desperate quality to the mass matings, as though life was trying to ensure its survival on the eve of extinction. As though in the motions of love the morrow's slaughter might be discounted.

Lannon left them to their frenzy and led his party out of the camp at a trot, the easy ground-devouring gait of a legion in forced march. Lannon led them to a spur of high ground which jutted out from the cliffs to overlook the lake shore for twenty miles in each direction. They stayed for many hours, watching Manatassi's hordes debauch from the passes of the cliffs on to the gently sloping lake shore. They watched mainly in silence, for it was a sight to strike ice into the souls of the bravest men.

It was as though a nest of black pythons was uncoiling, flowing outwards in long thick columns. It seemed endless, this massing of men; this stretching and bunching of primeval forces. It seemed as inevitable and undeviating as the tides of the sea, or the march of black storm clouds across a summer sky, and in the face of it they were silent and subdued.

Manatassi went into camp upon the lake shore with his vanguard only five miles from Lannon's own camp. However, the rear of his army had not yet emerged from the hills, and the plain between was thick with his regiments. There was no end to his numbers, no chance of counting them, for they knew not where his columns ended.

Lannon and Huy went down from the high ground in the dusk. The star of Astarte was a bright prick of light in the indigo sky above Opet. Huy averted his eyes from it.

They went to the harbour and watched the embarkation of the women and children upon the remaining galleys of Habbakuk Lal. They would lie off-shore during the night, and the following day until the battle was decided. If the day went against Opet, as Huy knew it must, then they would be taken across the lake and would strike southwards in an attempt to stay ahead of Manatassi. The men who survived would follow as best they might.

There was not room for all of them aboard the galleys, so the royal and noble women went first, followed by the priestesses and the merchant families. At one stage there was an ugly and fierce moment when a mob of the Yuye women and classless ones tried to rush the harbour and find seats aboard the ferries. They were clubbed down and driven back by Habbakuk Lal's sailors. Huy felt a deep pity for them as they screamed and covered their heads with their hands against the spear butts. One of them, a young Yuye girl, sat dazed upon the flags of the wharf with her head bowed over the baby in her lap and the blood flowing down the ropes of her long black hair to form a dark shadow on the stone.

Lannon took leave of his wives and the children on the deck of Habbakuk Lal's flagship. He was remote and dignified as each woman came to kneel briefly before him. The children followed their mothers, and Lannon barely glanced down at them.

The twins had grown into marriageable young women now. Pretty and vital with long blonde hair plaited and roped. They came to kiss Huy for the last time, and his voice was husky as he said his farewells. The younger children were unaware of the gravity of the moment, and they were tired and petulant, squabbling amongst themselves or squalling in their nurses' arms.

Lannon and Huy were rowed back across the black waters on which the reflected fire-flies of torch-light danced. The crowds upon the wharf were massed and silent, opening reluctantly to give them passage through, and Huy detected a sullenness close to open hostility. The escort closed in about them and they hurried through the streets of the city towards the encampment.

There were bonfires burning in the streets and about them drunkenness and revelry as the lowly citizens of Opet snatched a few last hours of pleasure before the dreaded morrow. The revels were more wild and grotesque than even those of the religious festivals. Men and women danced naked in the leaping firelight, or lay in puddles of their own vomit besotted with drink, while others rutted unashamedly in open view.

Huy saw a woman reeling drunkenly past them with her tunic torn and stained with red wine hanging in tatters from pale shoulders, and one breast protruding, round and fat with a big copper-coloured nipple. She tripped and fell into one of the fires, her hair exploding in a flare of orange flame.

In the shadows and dark lanes scurried other shapes, bowed under heavy burdens, and Huy knew that the looters were already at work, plundering the empty homes of the rich. Huy knew that his own slaves would still be protecting his house, but none the less he felt a pang of alarm as he remembered the golden books.

'Majesty, grant me an hour,' he said as they came abreast of the turning that led down to his house beside the lake.

'What is it, Huy? Lannon demanded irritably. 'There is still much to do, and we must rest. What is it that demands your time?'

'I must take leave of my household. My slaves must be released from their duties and my valuables hidden, especially the scrolls – the golden scrolls.'

'As you will,' Lannon conceded bad-temperedly. 'But do not waste time. Return as soon as you can.'

The old slaves could not understand Huy's dismissal.

'This is our home,' they pleaded. 'Do not drive us out.' And Huy could not explain. He left them there sitting huddled together in the kitchens, bewildered and afraid.

With one of the younger slaves to help him, both of them bowed under the immense weight of the scrolls, Huy crossed the temple of Baal and went through the cleft into the cavern of Astarte. It was silent and deserted. The priestesses were all aboard the galleys in the harbour. Huy paused beside the pool and looked down into its depths.

'Wait for me, my love,' he said. 'I will follow close behind you. Keep a place for me at your side.'

He crossed the audience hall of the oracle and found the officers of the temple guards in the chamber beyond. They greeted him joyfully.

'We had heard you were dead, Holiness.'

'Is our duty still at this post, Holy Father?'

'Release us from the temple, Holiness. Let us fight at your side.'

They helped him place the scrolls in the pottery jars and seal them with the golden tablets. Then they carried them through into the archives and placed them upon the stone shelves, hidden by a row of the larger jars.

Huy led the four officers and one hundred men of Legion Ben-Amon back through the city to the camp of the army, leaving the temple unguarded, and Lannon greeted him with relief.

'I doubted you would return, Huy. I thought the fates might keep us apart once more.'

'I gave you a promise, Majesty,' Huy reassured him. 'See what I have for you.' And he led him from the tent to show him the temple guard. One hundred of the finest warriors of Opet, worth as much as a cohort of Yuye troops. Lannon laughed.

'Huy, my worker of miracles.' Then he turned to the men and looked at them. They were fresh, their armour burnished and bright, and there was a fierce wolfish quality about them which contrasted with the battle weariness of the rest of Lannon's army.

Lannon spoke to their officers. 'You are mine own guard. When the battle begins, stay with me, close with me and Huy Ben-Amon.' Then he dismissed them to eat and rest.

In the big leather tent Lannon and Huy planned the battle, deciding what formations to employ, working out the evolutions for every eventuality, while scribes wrote out the orders.

They were interrupted continually by officers and aides asking for orders, or reporting the movements of the enemy.

Rib-Addi came into the tent begging audience, dry-washing his hands, tugging nervously at his beard and whispering in his scretive book-keeper's voice.

'The treasury, Majesty. Should we not move it to a place of safety?'

'Tell me what place is safe,' Lannon snarled at him, looking up from the clay box in which he and Huy were studying the dispositions. 'Nobody out there knows about the sun door. Leave the treasure where it is, it will remain there until we come for it.'

'The guards have been withdrawn,' Rib-Addi persisted. 'It is not right—'

'Listen to me, old man. It would require 1,000 men and ten days to remove that treasure. I have neither the men nor the time to spare. Go, leave us alone. We have more important matters to employ us now.'

Rib-Addi went, looking very distressed. What more important matters were there than gold and treasure?'

Before midnight Lannon straightened up and ran his hands through his thick golden curls, now laced with silver. He sighed, and he looked ill and tired.

'That is all we can do now, Huy. The rest is in the hands of the gods.' He placed an arm about Huy's shoulders and led him to the flap of the tent. 'A bowl of wine, a breath of lake air – then sleep.'

They stood outside the tent, drinking together and a cool breeze came off the lake, fluttering the tassels upon the golden battle standards.

Something which Huy thought for a moment was a big brown dog sleeping curled against the side of the tent stirred at their voices. Then Huy saw it was the little bushman hunt-master, Xhai, faithful as ever, sleeping at the opening of his master's tent. He shook himself awake, grinned when he saw Lannon and Huy, and came to squat beside Lannon.

'I have tried to send him away,' said Lannon. 'He does not understand. He will not leave.' Lannon sighed. 'It seems unnecessary that he should die also, but how can I force him to go.'

'Send him on an errand,' suggest Huy and Lannon glanced at him thoughtfully.

'What errand?'

'Send him to search for sign of the gry-lion upon the southern shores. He will believe that.

'Yes, he will believe that,' Lannon agreed. 'Tell him, Huy.'

In his own language Huy explained to the little yellow man that the king wanted to hunt the gry-lion once more. Xhai's slanted yellow eyes crinkled and he grinned and nodded with delight, pleased to be of service to the man he considered a god.

'You must go at once,' Huy told him. 'It is an urgent matter.'

Xhai clasped Lannon's knees, bobbing his head, and then he rolled up his sleeping mat and vanished amongst the shadows of the camp. Once he had gone they were silent for a while until Lannon said, 'Do you recall the prophecy, Huy?'

And Huy nodded, remembering it upon Tanith's lips.

'Who shall reign in Opet after me?'

'He who slays the gry-lion.'

He remembered also the prophecy that followed.

'What must I fear?'

'Blackness.'

Huy turned and looked to the north where the great black beast crouched, ready to spring. Lannon's thoughts paralleled his own.

'Yes, Huy,' he murmured. 'Blackness!' And then he drained his wine bowl and hurled it upon the watch fire. A spout of sparks flew upwards.

'At the hand of a friend,' he said, remembering the final prophecy. 'We shall see,' he said. 'We shall see.' Then he glanced at Huy and saw his face.

'Oh, forgive me, old friend. I did not mean to add fuel to the fires of your sorrow. I should not have reminded you of the girl.'

Huy drank the last of his wine and threw the bowl upon the fire. He did not need to be reminded of Tanith, she was ever in his thoughts.

'Let us rest now,' Huy said, but his face was ravished with grief.

The shouting and the trumpets woke Huy, and his first thought was of a night attack upon the camp. He threw on his armour and snatched up the vulture axe, stumbling out of the tent still fumbling with the straps of his breastplate.

The night sky was aglow with a light like that of the dawn, but it was rising from the wrong direction, coming up out of the lake, lighting the towers and walls of Opet.

Lannon joined him, still half-asleep, cursing as he struggled with his armour and helmet.

'What is it, Huy?' he demanded.

'I do not know,' Huy admitted, and they stood staring at the strange light which grew brighter, until they could clearly see each other's features.

'The harbour,' said Huy, understanding at last. 'The fleet. The women.'

'Merciful Baal,' gasped Lannon. 'Come!' And they ran together.

Manatassi had taken the tubes from the beached galleys before he burned them. A little experimentation had shown him how they worked. It was a simple procedure, dependent mostly upon current and wind direction. He had carried the tubes overland, and installed them in the bows of a pair of captured fishing-boats, whose slave crew were skilled seamen and eager to join Manatassi.

The on-shore wind had suited his purpose ideally and carried the boats silently into the mouth of the harbour of Opet. He had personally gone aboard one of the boats and he stood now in the stern, wrapped in a leopard-skin robe, watching with fierce and hungry eyes as the jets squirted upon the surface of the wind-chopped water and burst into flame.

Carried on the wind the flame swept into the harbour in a solid wall, roaring like a waterfall and lighting the sky with a false dawn.

Huy stood beside Lannon upon the wharf. The entire basin of the harbour was filled with tall yellow flame, roaring hungrily, the black smoke clouds blocking out the starry sky and rolling in thick evil-smelling billows across the city.

The galleys of Habbakuk Lal stood like islands in a sea of fire. The decks were crowded with the women and the children of all the noble families of Opet, and their screams carried over the dull furnace roar of flame.

The watchers upon the shore were unable to offer any escape to them, they looked on helplessly while from the alleyways the lowly ones who had been denied passage hooted and screeched with laughter.

The flames caught upon the wooden hulls and the mooring lines, racing upwards to the crowded decks.

Like ants upon a piece of rotten firewood, they scrambled and milled aimlessly, until the circle of flame tightened about them and shrivelled them.

One of the galleys began drifting in towards the shore. Its anchor lines were burned through, and the wind pushed it so it turned and swung gently, its mast and rigging traced in outlines of yellow fire. Upon the high castle at the stern, clinging together with their blonde hair shining in the firelight, stood Helanca and Imilce, the twin daughters of Lannon Hycanus.

Before the galley touched the stone wall of the quayside, the flames had smothered it, and the girls were gone.

Manatassi watched intently, the firelight glinting on those fierce yellow eyes. When the last flames had died and only the burnt-out hulks of the galleys still smouldered, he lifted his iron hand in command. The two fishing-boats hoisted sail and bore out, close on the wind, northwards to where Manatassi's army was stirring like an awakening monster in the dawn.

This was the mood in which to fight the last battle, this fine blend of sadness and anger, Huy thought as he strode with Lannon along the ranks.

The sun was up, throwing long shadows on the pale brown grass of the plain. On their left stretched the cheerful azure of the lake, flecked with crests of white by the morning breeze. The water fowl flew low in loose V-formations, white against the cloudless blue of the high heavens. On their left rose the rugged rampart of the cliffs, touched with subtle shades of rose and pink and capped with dark green vegetation.

Huy, looking at lake and cliff, saw them only as points on which to anchor his flanks.

Ahead, in front of the walls, the land was open, with low scrub and a very few big shady trees; it sloped gently from cliff to lake shore, a Roman mile wide. It was a clear front from which no surprise could spring, although it undulated in a series of low rises like the swell of a sleepy ocean.

In their rear were the buildings and streets of the lower city, a maze of low clay walls and flat roofs, while further back rose the massive stone walls of the temple, and above them showed the tops of the sun towers.

This then was a good place in which to fight the last battle, this attenuated front with firm flanks and an open line of retreat.

Lannon strode along the ranks. There was a spring and purpose in his step that belied his tired eyes and grief-sick face; the face of a man who had seen his family burn to death while he stood by. Huy followed a pace behind him, walking with the long-legged crabbing gait which was so familiar to them all. The axe was on his shoulder, and the armour shaped to his bowed back was highly polished and sparkled in the sunlight. Bakmor and a group of officers followed him.

The legions were drawn up into their battle formations, and Huy could find no fault with the placing. The light infantry thrown out in a screen, each man armed with a bundle of javelins as well as his side arms. Behind them were placed the heavy infantry, big men armed with axe and war-spear, carrying a great weight of armour, these men were the backbone of the legions. When hard-pressed, the light infantry could retire through their ranks, and let the enemy spend themselves upon this solid reef of armour.

In the rear were the archers. Drawn up in neat blocks from which they could deliver massed flights of arrows over the heads of the infantry.

Behind them again were the baggage boys, ready with the bundles of fresh javelins and arrows, bags of cold meat and corn cakes, amphorae of water and wine, spare helmets, swords and axes, and those other items which the battle would expend or destroy.

At first Lannon's procession along the ranks was in silence. The men at ease, resting on their weapons, many with their helmets removed, some of them munching a last mouthful of food, all of them with that surface calm of the veteran who has walked many times with old Dame Death, who knows well her whore's face and the smell of her breath. Many of them still showed the recent marks of her claws upon their bodies, but there was no sign of fear on their faces, no shadows in their eyes.

Huy felt a humbleness when he met their steady gaze, a pride when one of them grinned and called out, 'We've missed you, Holiness.'

'It's good to be back,' Huy told him, and there was a growl of assent from those who heard him. Huy passed on, a ripple of animation followed him now.

Quick banter, in which Lannon and the officers joined.

'Leave a few for us, Sunbird,' a grizzled old centurion shouted.

'I think there will be enough for all of us,' Huy grinned at him.

'Too many?' another voice called out.

'Not enough,' Lannon answered. 'For none of those who oppose us is named Ben-Amon.'

They cheered then lustily, and it was taken up all along the line from cliff to lake. New waves of sound and shouting followed them as they went to take their place at the centre of the line upon a rise of higher ground where they could see over the whole field.

Above their heads the standards stood, gaudy with gleaming gold and silken multi-coloured tassels, and at their backs the hundred men of the temple guard. Huy looked over the precisely laid-out cohorts with the sun sparkling on their helmets and weapons, and thought that these were good men with which to fight the last battle, good men in whose company to die.

He loosened his helmet and lifted it from his head, holding it in the crook of his arm.

'Wine here!' he called, and baggage boys came scampering to them with bowls and amphorae. It was the best of Huy's own stocks, rich and red as the blood which would soon soak this field.

Huy saluted his officers with a raised bowl, then turned to Lannon. They looked at each other for a long moment.

'Fly for me, Bird of the Sun,' said Lannon softly.

'Roar for me today, Lion of Opet,' Huy answered him and they drank and broke the bowls and laughed together for the last time. The men about them heard them laugh, and taking courage from it they looked to the north.

Manatassi came in the middle of the bright hot morning. He came on a front that filled the plain from lake shore to cliff foot. He came singing with 500,000 throats, and the rhythmic slapping of bare feet and war rattles which rolled across the sky like the thunder of the heavens. He came in orderly ranks, spaced to give each man fighting space, but the rank behind pressed hard upon that ahead, ready to close any gap in the line, to show a solid unbroken front.

He came in rank upon countless rank, so there was no end to his advance, and the singing was deep and murmurous.

He came like the shadow of storm clouds moving stately and slow across the land, he came dark as night and numerous as the grass of the fields, and the singing took on a harsher more menacing sound.

Huy settled his helmet and tightened the strap. He untied the leather sheath from the vulture axe and watched Manatassi advance on a million moving legs like a single vast black animal topped with a froth of feather head-dresses, and the spear blades sparkled like multiple insect eyes in the blackness.

He had never in all his life seen a sight to compare with Manatassi in his full power. This is a worthy foe with whom to fight the last battle, he thought, for there will be no dishonour in defeat by such a one.

Manatassi rolled on deliberately past the markers which Huy had placed on his front to measure the range; 200 paces, 150 – and the dust from a million stamping feet rose as a bank of fire-golden smoke over the horde, blanketing them so that they seemed to appear endlessly out of the moving shifting loom of it.

Huy felt his mouth drying out, and the tingle of his blood as it sped through his tensed body. He lifted the vulture axe high, and glanced left and right to make certain that each commander of the archery had seen the signal.

One hundred and fifty paces, the black tide washed towards him and the singing changed again, rising, shrilling into the blood trill, the high ululation as chilling as any sound Huy had ever heard. He felt the hair on his forearms and at the back of his neck come erect, and his bowels seemed to drop out of his body.

They came on still, trilling, stamping, drumming with spear on shields, head-dresses dipping and tossing, and Huy stood with his axe held aloft.

One hundred paces, and Huy brought down the axe and instantly the air was filled with the soft fluting, the whistle of the wings of wild duck at dusk.

The arrows rose and arched over and fell into them in thick dark flights like that of the locust, and a growl came out of the blackness, the growl of the beast, but it came on steadily into the javelins, seeming to pass through them unscathed for the gaps in the front were instantly filled and the fallen were hidden by the dense mass of bodies passing over them.

Huy's light infantry melted away before this massive advance, falling back through the heavies behind them, and Manatassi rolled weightily into Huy's front.

It seemed as though nothing could check it, it was too heavy, too wide and deep and strong. It must burst through this line of bright helmets.

Then unbelievably the blackness was no longer moving forward, but piling up on itself like a log jam in a river. The ranks pressing forward violated the fighting space of those in the van, catching them in a struggling mass, throwing them onto the prickly metal hedge that was Huy's front line.

Suddenly it was drawing back, sucked away like the wave of the sea from a steep beach.

Immediately the javelin men advanced through the heavies to harass the retreat, while the cry of the centurions carried clearly to Huy as they repaired their line.

'Close up here!'
'Javelins here!'

'Fill that gap!'

'Men here! Men here!'

Manatassi drew back, and bunched, gathered himself like a humping wave and surged forward again, struck and pressed hard, gained a yard of ground and drew back again, gathered himself, started forward gaining momentum and crashing into Huy's front once more.

At noon Lannon and Huy were forced from their vantage point, as the fighting surged about their feet. The standards moved back.

An hour after noon, Huy ordered the last of his reserves into the line, holding only the temple guard under his own hand in a bunch around the battle standards. Still the black waves burst upon the line with a terrible unvarying rhythm, like the ground swell of the ocean.

Huy gave them ground slowly, drawing back each time just enough to reaffirm his line. It was stretched so finely now, that it seemed each new rush of blackness must rip through it, but still it held.

Then they were into the lower city, fighting back along the streets, and Huy was cut off from visual contact with the battle as a whole. It was merely a narrow street plugged with a knot of legionaries, holding back a steady rush of black warriors.

For the first time that day Huy was drawn into the fighting. A small group of wild-eyed black men burst through the rank ahead of him, they were shiny with sweat and grease, their faces painted with stripes of white ochre, making them appear monstrous and unreal.

Huy cut them down quickly, and ordered a squad of the temple guard into the gap they had opened.

He knew then that the battle was out of his control. He and Lannon were isolated in a cell of fighting men, able only to direct those of their men within sound of their voices.

From some distant part of the field came an animal roar of triumph, and Lannon caught Huy's shoulder and shouted into his ear, 'I think they have broken through.' And Huy nodded.

The set battle was over now, Huy knew that through many gaps in his shattered line the enemy was pouring. It would become a rout now. The miracle had not taken place – the last battle was lost.

'Fall back on the temple?' Lannon shouted the question, and again Huy nodded. The army of Opet was no more, it was reduced to hundreds of isolated groups of desperate men locked shoulder to shoulder and back to back in their last fight, a fight from which there would be no surrender, from which death was the only surcease.

They gathered the temple guard about them, and moved back along the street, keeping a steady pace, closed up and in hand, offering a solid carapace of shields to the enemy.

Manatassi's hordes were in their rear now, between them and the temple. They had put fire into the lower city, and the flames were taking a swift grip. The streets through which Huy marched were choked with terrified citizens and groups of wild blood-spattered warriors. Huy drove through all of them, his shields locked in the testudo formation, immune to the press of black men at the rear and the greasy billows of black smoke which spread over him.

The main temple gate was open and undefended. The guards had fled, the temple enclosure was empty and silent. Huy and ten men held the steps, while Lannon had the gates swung closed, and at the last instant Huy raced back with his men through the closing gap.

They were resting on their bloody weapons, loosening helmets, wiping the sweat out of their eyes.

'The east gate?' Huy demanded of Lannon. 'It is held? Did you send men to close it?'

Lannon stared at him with dismay, his silence answering Huy's question eloquently.

'You men!' Huy picked a group with a quick wave of his arm. 'Follow me.' But it was too late. Across the temple enclosure black warriors were streaming through the smaller gate.

'Testudo!' shouted Huy. 'Back to the cavern.' They formed the tortoise again, and moved like an armadillo with metal scales across the enclosure while the warriors swarmed about them, unable to pierce the shell. Smoke from the burning city eddied about them, choking them, blinding them.

Suddenly the man beside Huy cried out and grabbed at his groin. Blood spurted out between his fingers and he dropped to his knees. The ground over which they were advancing was strewn with dead warriors cut down by the head of the tortoise. They had to step over them. Dozens of these bodies who had been feigning death came suddenly to life, rolling quickly on to their backs and stabbing up under the skirts of the men above them.

Huy shouted a warning, but it was in vain. The enemy were inside the body of the tortoise, leaping to their feet, thrusting and hacking about them, forcing Huy's men to turn and defend themselves, exposing their backs to the warriors on the outside.

The tortoise disintegrated into a mob of individuals, and the black swarm poured over them as hiving bees.

'With me!' Huy gathered Lannon, Bakmor and a few others about him and they broke out of the mob in a tight bunch and raced for the cleft of the cavern. The smoke was thick and oily, choking them so they coughed as they ran. Huy swung the axe, cutting a path for them and five of them reached the entrance to the cavern but Bakmor had taken a thrust through the ribs. He pressed one fist to it, trying to staunch the flow of life blood. Huy changed the axe to his other hand, and helped Bakmor up the steps into the mouth of the cleft. His blood ran down Huy's side, it felt hot and gelatinous. On the top step Bakmor stumbled to his knees.

'It is finished, Huy,' he choked, but Huy picked him up bodily and carried him into the entrance. He propped him against the wall of the cavern.

'Bakmor,' he panted, and pushed his head back to look into his face. Bakmor's eyes looked back at him without seeing, dead and glazed. Huy let the handsome head drop forward, and stood up.

'Here they come,' shouted Lannon, and Huy hefted the axe and leapt to Lannon's side to meet the first dark rush of bodies into the passage. The four of them – Lannon, Huy and two legionaries – held the entrance long enough to clog it with piles of dead warriors.

Then the archers came up and the first volley of arrows swept the passage. One of them struck a legionary in the throat, and he fell with a dark gush of blood from the mouth.

'No cover in here,' Huy shouted. 'Back to the temple.' They raced back along the passage, and the next volley whistled amongst them. One struck Huy's helmet and glanced away to light sparks off the wall beside him, another found the seam in the last legionary's breastplate and lodged in the bone of his spinal column. His legs collapsed under him. Desperately he clawed his way after Huy, dragging his crippled body by the sheer strength of his arms alone.

'Your favour, my lord,' he screamed, in terror of the castrating blade, the ripping of his bowels while he still lived. 'Don't leave me for them, Holiness.'

Huy checked his run, and shouted, 'Go on, Lannon. I'll follow you.' He went back, and the legionary saw him coming.

'Baal's blessing on you, Holiness,' he cried, and tore his helmet loose, bowing his head forward to expose the neck.

'Find peace!' Huy told him, and cut his head from the trunk with a single stroke of the axe, turning to run again as he did so. An arrow hit Huy in the face below the eye, glanced off the bone and sliced him open to the ear, dangling there by the barb in the fleshy skin.

Huy tore it loose as he ran after Lannon.

Together they crossed the cavern of Astarte, their footsteps echoing from the domed walls; skirting the still green pool, they reached the door of the temple as the next flight of arrows hummed around them. Lannon stumbled slightly, and then they were into the temple.

'Can we hold them here?' Lannon gasped.

'No.' Huy stopped to catch his breath. 'The archives!' Then he looked at Lannon. 'What is it, Majesty?'

'I also am hit, Huy.' The arrow stood out of the joint of his armour near the left armpit. The angle of penetration was such that Huy felt a cold gust of despair. The arrow-head must lie close to the heart. It was mortal, no man could ever recover from a wound of that nature.

'How is it?' Lannon demanded. 'There is no pain, Huy. It cannot be too bad.'

'You're lucky,' said Huy, and snapped off the shaft, leaving a short stub protruding from the wound.

'Come,' he said, and with a gentle hand on Lannon's arm led him back through the temple into the archives.

'The sun door?' Lannon asked.

'Only at the very end,' said Huy. 'Only when all else fails.' And he steered Lannon into one of the stone recesses.

'Your face.' Lannon stared at Huy in the uncertain light of the torches, as though he had noticed the gaping slash across his cheek for the first time.

'No doubt it's an improvement,' Huy grunted as he tore a strip from his tunic and knotted it into a crude sling for Lannon's left arm.

'Can you use it?' he asked and Lannon worked his fingers, opening and closing them.

'Good,' Huy nodded, and placed the tang of Lannon's shield in his left hand. The sling would help support the weight of it.

Huy cocked his head, listening to the stealthy footsteps, the whispered voices and the clink of weapons within the temple of Astarte.

'They are coming,' he said. 'It will not take them long to find the passage.'

As he spoke the first of them stepped through the entrance from the guard room, and peered into the archives. The wavering light of the smoky torches in their wall brackets emphasized the man's size. He was huge and black, shiny with grease and paint, and Huy smelled him, a warm musky smell like that of a predatory cat.

Huy stepped out of the recess into the light, and in Vendi shouted a challenge at him. The warrior came bounding down the passage at Huy, and their shields came together with a clash that echoed through the temple.

Huy felt the spear blade sting his side, but the lance on the tip of the vulture axe bit in deep, touching bone, and the warrior slid down off the steel.

Lannon limped out of the recess and took his place on Huy's left hand, they stepped over the shivering twitching corpse and went down the passage side by side to meet the rush of dark bodies that came at them.

Manatassi stood in the temple of Astarte. It was after midnight but there were many torches burning and the halls were crowded with warriors, so many that

Manatassi had ordered the interior walls torn out of the building to give them access to the mouth of the tunnel.

The dark, evil-looking stone mouth which had already swallowed up so many of his men, was where the two fighting devils of Opet still held out, defying all his efforts to dislodge them. Even now they were dragging dead and badly wounded from the entrance. One of them had his right arm lopped off above the elbow. He made no sound as he clutched at the stump, but his eyes were huge and white in the torch-light.

Manatassi knew what weapon had inflicted that wound, and his anger and his hatred smouldered hotly, warring with the superstitious dread that gripped him.

He had learned enough about the gods of Opet while he was a slave to know their vast powers, their strengths and cruelties. He feared them, and he knew that he stood now in the stronghold of these terrible gods, in their holy place.

He remembered now hearing of this underground place beyond the temple of Astarte, he knew that a death curse guarded it.

Clearly this was the reason why they had taken sanctuary here, in this dark hole.

His anger cooled, chilled by religious awe. He knew the white gods were watching him. He wanted to end it now, destroy this place and go – however, two doomed but stubborn men defied him.

'Fire!' he said. 'Smoke them from their den like wild dogs.'

They built the fire in the entrance of the tunnel, and fed it with green branches, and dense acrid smoke filled the temple and the tunnel. They ringed the tunnel entrance, coughing and choking in the smoke, and they held their weapons ready, knowing that no man could live in there. This must bring them out, surely – but an hour passed with no movement through the smoke.

The fire burned down into a smouldering pile of logs, and the smoke cleared gradually. Manatassi ordered it quenched with water from the pool, and once again they stared into the dark passage from which wisps and streamers of smoke still drifted.

The floor of the passage was still carpeted with the dead, but there was no sign of life.

Manatassi subdued his religious awe, and abruptly snatched a torch from the hand of one of his warriors. Holding it high above his head, he stepped over the hot and sizzling logs and into the passage.

He picked his way amongst the dead, and the floor was puddled and sticky with blood that clung to his bare feet. The torch threw yellow light into each of the stone recesses with their burdened shelves. Manatassi knew what the earthenware pots contained. He had assisted Huy often enough with the scrolls.

He looked for sign of him now, but there was none. Only the black bodies, and the empty recesses.

He reached the end of the passage and the torch lit the engraved image. Manatassi recognized it as the symbol of the sun god, and his courage melted at this tangible evidence of divine influence.

On the floor below the image something caught his eye, sparkling in the torch light.

He suppressed a gasp. It was the vulture axe, laid like an offering before the god image – and the place was empty.

They had gone to their gods. They had cheated him of his revenge, and led him into deadly peril, into a direct confrontation with supernatural forces.

Manatassi backed away, until the god image merged into the darkness and he turned and ran from the place into the hall of the temple of Astarte. There he looked back at the mouth of the tunnel.

'Bring me masons from amongst the freed slaves. Seal off that entrance. It is evil. Seal it.'

They ran to obey, and Manatassi's courage – his anger and his hatred – returned to him.

'I will destroy this evil. I place a curse upon this place, upon these cliffs. A curse that will last for ever.' His voice rose into a scream. 'Burn it. Burn it all. Destroy it. It is an evil to be cleaned from the earth and from the minds of men, for ever.'

So the masons sealed off the entrance to the tomb of the kings. They worked with all the skill that the men of Opet had taught them, and when they were finished the entrance had vanished.

Then Manatassi destroyed the city. He slew every single living thing and threw them on the fires which raged through the lower city for many days. Then he looked at the walls and the towers, and he pointed with his iron claw. They tore it down block by massive block. The walls and the sun towers and the beautiful temple of Astarte. They went down to the very foundations. They lifted the flagged pavings. They tore out the stone wharves of the harbour. Working like a million ants they razed the city until no trace of it remained. They carried each block of masonry up to the cavern and dropped it into the bottomless green pool. They took the entire city and gave it to the goddess, and the pool was so deep – or the goddess so eternally greedy – that it was swallowed without trace and the level of the green clear waters rose not a finger's width.

When Manatassi marched from Opet, eastwards to complete the destruction of the empire, he left nothing behind him but piles of loose ash which the wind was already scattering in pale runs of dust.

Manatassi spread his regiments like a net across the four kingdoms, with the command to destroy all trace of the cities and the mines and the gardens built by the men of Opet. But his hatred had burned low now, like a forest fire when the trees are gone. The hatred had left him hollow and blackened and dying, his huge battered frame a husk, even the smoky yellow eyes dull and uncaring.

He came to Zimbao, the great walled city of the middle kingdom, and the men of Opet were dead. The city like his own body was untenanted, empty and deserted.

Manatassi wrapped himself in a fur kaross and lay down beside the watch fire, and in the morning his body was stiff and cold.

They buried him outside the walls, and then they quarrelled and fought, for Manatassi had named no successor. Each war captain named himself, and the army of Manatassi split into a hundred tribes.

In time Manatassi and the city of Opet faded from the memory of men.

When Xhai the bushman was an old man and knew he was dying, he came back to Opet.

The lake had dwindled, its shores were twenty miles from the red cliffs and the waters were brackish and shallow and sunwarmed.

Xhai walked over the spot on which the temple of Baal had stood without recognizing it, until he saw the cleft in the red rock leading to the cavern of Astarte.

He camped beside the pool, building a small fire and sitting over it mumbling to himself in the manner of old men. When his memories paraded before him they were magnified and magnificent, and he sought to capture and fix them.

He picked up his belt on which were strung the little horn pots of pigment, each plugged with a piece of wood, and he went to the wall at the rear of the cavern.

He made the outline of the figure in charcoal upon the smoothest place of the wall. He worked slowly and carefully, with great love.

Then he mixed his pigment and began to paint the proud god-like figure with its white face, red-gold beard and majestic vaunting manhood, and as he worked it seemed as though ghost voices whispered deep in the rock, down in the vault of the kings.

'Huy, I am cold. Favour me, old friend. Give me the hand of friendship that the oracle foresaw.'

'I cannot, Lannon. I cannot do it.'

'I am cold and in pain, Huy. If you love me, you will do it.'

'I love you.'

'Fly for me, Bird of the Sun.'

As the old man worked, the wind whispered and sighed along the cliffs, and the sigh was that which a man might make when he has lost his love and his land, has denied his gods and has given mercy to his friend. He might sigh like that as he takes the sword still dulled with his friend's blood and sets the hilt firmly in a niche of the stone floor and places the point up under his ribs, and falls forward upon it.

THE RAND DAILY MAIL
27th May

Death of Multi-Millionaire Financier Louren Sturvesant Dies of Mystery Disease

BOTSWANA, SATURDAY. The well-known millionaire financier and sportsman, Mr. Louren Sturvesant of Kleine Schuur, Sandown, Johannesburg, died here yesterday after a brief illness.

Mr. Sturvesant was visiting the site of the recently discovered ancient Carthaginian city in Botswana. The leader of the expedition, Dr. Benjamin Kazin, has also contracted the disease which is believed to be infectious.

Dr. Kazin has been flown to Johannesburg where a hospital spokesman stated that his condition was critical.

THE FINANCIAL GAZETTE
28th May

Stop Press

Anglo-Sturvesant Crashes 97 Points
Panic on Exchange

HOLLARD STR. MONDAY. Following reports of the death of Mr. Louren Sturvesant, Chairman of Anglo-Sturvesant, quoted prices of the Sturvesant Group of Companies fell sharply on the Johannesburg Stock Exchange today.

THE STAR
3rd June

Famous Archaeologist Regains
Consciousness

JOHANNESBURG. FRIDAY. After ten days in coma, Dr. Benjamin Kazin today regained consciousness, according to a hospital spokesman.

Dr. Kazin is the Director of the Institute of Anthropology and African Prehistory, and the discoverer of the ancient Carthaginian city of Opet. He was suffering from a rare fungus infection contracted while working on the site of his recent find.

Today Dr. Kazin was visited by his assistant, Dr. Sally Benator, who said afterwards that Dr. Kazin was 'very much better but still terribly upset by the death of Mr. Sturvesant.'

THE STAR
6th Sept.

Well-known Archaeologists Marry

CAPE TOWN. FRIDAY. The discoverer of the city of Opet, Dr. Benjamin Kazin, was married to his long-time assistant, Dr. Sally Benator, in a brief civil ceremony here today. The bride said that she planned a working honeymoon at the site of the ancient city of Opet.

THE TIMES
20th April

Archaeologist Honoured

LONDON. SATURDAY. At the Royal Geographical Society, an Extraordinary General Meeting of the Society was held today during which Dr. Benjamin Kazin was awarded the Society's much-prized Founder's and Patron's Medal.

After the meeting there was a short ceremony at which a portrait of Dr. Kazin by the well-known artist Pietro Annigoni was hung in the Society.

Dr. Kazin was accompanied by his wife, Dr. Sally Kazin, formerly Benator, who is also a well-known figure in archaeological circles. The couple will spend two weeks holidaying in Britain and on the continent before returning to Africa.

TITLES IN THIS SERIES

Eric Ambler
The Mask of Dimitrios
Passage of Arms
The Schirmer Inheritance
Journey into Fear
The Light of Day
Judgement on Deltchev

John le Carré
The Spy Who Came in from the Cold
Call for the Dead
A Murder of Quality
The Looking-Glass War
A Small Town in Germany

Raymond Chandler*
Farewell My Lovely
The Lady in the Lake
Playback
The Long Goodbye
The High Window
The Big Sleep

Agatha Christie
The Murder of Roger Ackroyd
The Mystery of the Blue Train
Dumb Witness
Death on the Nile

Joseph Conrad
Lord Jim
The Nigger of the 'Narcissus'
Typhoon
Nostromo
The Secret Agent

Catherine Cookson
The Round Tower
The Fifteen Streets
Feathers in the Fire
A Grand Man
The Blind Miller

Catherine Cookson
The Mallen Streak
The Girl
The Gambling Man
The Cinder Path
The Invisible Cord

Catherine Cookson
The Mallen Girl
The Mallen Litter
The Tide of Life
The Man Who Cried

Monica Dickens
One Pair of Hands
The Happy Prisoner
Mariana
Kate and Emma
One Pair of Feet

Daphne du Maurier
Rebecca
Jamaica Inn
Frenchman's Creek
My Cousin Rachel

Gerald Durrell
My Family and Other Animals
The Bafut Beagles
The Drunken Forest
Encounters with Animals
The Whispering Land
Menagerie Manor
A Zoo in My Luggage

F. Scott Fitzgerald*
The Great Gatsby
Tender is the Night
This Side of Paradise
The Beautiful and Damned
The Last Tycoon

Ian Fleming
Dr. No
Thunderball
Goldfinger
On Her Majesty's Secret Service
Moonraker
From Russia, With Love

C. S. Forester
The Ship
Mr Midshipman Hornblower
The Captain from Connecticut
The General
The Earthly Paradise
The African Queen

E. M. Forester
Where Angels Fear to Tread
The Longest Journey
A Room with a View
Howards End
A Passage to India

Fourteen Great Plays*

Dick Francis
For Kicks
Odds Against
Flying Against
Bonecrack
In the Frame

Dick Francis
Whip Hand
Rat Race
Forfeit
High Stakes
Twice Shy

John Galsworthy
The Forsyte Saga
The Man of Property
In Chancery
To Let
A Modern Comedy
The White Monkey
The Silver Spoon
Swan Song

Erle Stanley Gardner
Perry Mason in the Case of:
The Gilded Lady
The Daring Decoy
The Fiery Players
The Lucky Loser
The Calendar Girl
The Deadly Toy
The Mischievous Doll
The Amorous Aunt

Catherine Gaskin
Fiona
A Falcon for a Queen
Blake's Reach

Richard Gordon
Doctor in the House
Doctor at Sea
Doctor at Large
Doctor in Love
Doctor in Clover
The Facemaker
The Medical Witness

Winston Graham
Ross Poldark
Demelza
Jeremy Poldark

Graham Greene
Brighton Rock
The End of the Affair
It's a Battlefield
England Made Me
The Ministry of Fear
Our Man in Havana

Graham Greene
The Heart of the Matter
Stamboul Train
A Burnt-out Case
The Third Man
Loser Takes All
The Quiet American
The Power and the Glory

Ernest Hemingway*
For Whom the Bell Tolls
The Snows of Kilimanjaro
Fiesta
The Short Happy Life of Francis
    Macomber
Across the River and into the Trees
The Old Man and the Sea

James Herriot
If Only They Could Talk
It Shouldn't Happen to a Vet
Let Sleeping Vets Lie
Vet in Harness
Vets Might Fly
Vet in a Spin

Georgette Heyer
These Old Shades
Sprig Muslin
Sylvester
The Corinthian
The Convenient Marriage

Hammond Innes
Wreckers Must Breathe
The Mary Deare
Atlantic Fury
The Strode Venturer

Henry James
The Europeans
Daisy Miller
Washington Square
The Aspern Papers
The Turn of the Screw
The Portrait of a Lady

Franz Kafka*
The Trial
America
In the Penal Settlement
Metamorphosis
The Castle
The Great Wall of China
Investigations of a Dog
Letter to his Father
The Diaries 1910-1923

Rudyard Kipling
The Jungle Book
The Second Jungle Book
Just So Stories
Puck of Pook's Hill
Stalky and Co.
Kim

D. H. Lawrence
Sons and Lovers
St. Mawr
The Fox
The White Peacock
Love among the Haystacks
The Virgin and the Gipsy
Lady Chatterley's Lover

D. H. Lawrence
Women in Love
The Ladybird
The Man Who Died
The Captain's Doll
The Rainbow

Norah Lofts
Jassy
Bless This House
Scent of Cloves
How Far to Bethlehem?

Robert Ludlum*
The Scarlatti Inheritance
The Osterman Weekend
The Matlock Paper
The Gemini Contenders

Alistair MacLean
H.M.S. Ulysses
The Guns of Navarone
Where Eagles Dare
Force Ten from Navarone

Thomas Mann*
Death in Venice
Tristan
Tonio Kröger
Doctor Faustus
Mario and the Magician
A Man and His Dog
The Black Swan
Confessions of Felix Krull, Confidence
    Man

W. Somerset Maugham
Cakes and Ale
The Painted Veil
Liza of Lambeth
The Razor's Edge
Theatre
The Moon and Sixpence

W. Somerset Maugham
Sixty-five Short Stories

Ed McBain*
Cop Hater
Give the Boys a Great Big Hand
Doll
Eighty Million Eyes
Hail, Hail, the Gang's All Here!
Sadie When She Died
Let's Hear it for the Deaf Man

James A. Michener*
The Source
The Bridges at Toko-Ri
Caravans
Sayonara

George Orwell
Animal Farm
Burmese Days
A Clergyman's Daughter
Coming up for Air
Keep the Aspidistra Flying
Nineteen Eighty-four

George Orwell
Down and Out in Paris & London
Homage to Catalonia
Selections from Essays and Journalism:
    1931-1949
The Road to Wigan Pier

Jean Plaidy
St. Thomas's Eve
Royal Road to Fotheringay
The Goldsmith's Wife
Perdita's Prince

Nevil Shute
A Town Like Alice
Pied Piper
The Far Country
The Chequer Board
No Highway

Georges Simenon
Ten Maigret Stories

Wilbur Smith
When the Lion Feeds
The Diamond Hunters
Eagle in the Sky
Gold Mine
Shout at the Devil

Wilbur Smith
Hungry as the Sea
The Sound of Thunder
The Eye of the Tiger

Wilbur Smith
A Falcon Flies
The Dark of the Sun
The Sun Bird

John Steinbeck*
The Grapes of Wrath
The Moon is Down
Cannery Row
East of Eden
Of Mice and Men

Mary Stewart
The Crystal Cave
The Hollow Hills
Wildfire at Midnight
Airs Above the Ground

Mary Stewart
Touch Not The Cat
The Gabriel Hounds
Nine Coaches Waiting
Madam, Will You Talk?

Evelyn Waugh
Decline and Fall
Black Mischief
A Handful of Dust
Scoop
Put Out More Flags
Brideshead Revisited

H. G. Wells
The Time Machine
The Island of Dr. Moreau
The Invisible Man
The First Men in the Moon
The Food of the Gods
In the Days of the Comet
The War of the Worlds

Morris West
The Devil's Advocate
The Second Victory
Daughter of Silence
The Salamander
The Shoes of the Fisherman

Dennis Wheatley
The Devil Rides Out
The Haunting of Toby Jugg
Gateway to Hell
To the Devil – A Daughter

John Wyndham
The Day of the Triffids
The Kraken Wakes
The Chrysalids
The Seeds of Time
Trouble With Lichen
The Midwich Cuckoos

*** Not currently available in Canada
for copyright reasons**